THE REALITY DYSFUNCTION

Peter F. Hamilton was born in Rutland in 1960 and still lives nearby. He began writing in 1987 and sold his first short story to *Fear* magazine in 1988. He has written many bestselling novels, including the Greg Mandel series, the Night's Dawn trilogy, the Commonwealth novels, the Void trilogy, The Chronicle of the Fallers, two short story collections and several standalone novels.

Find out more about Peter F. Hamilton at

www.peterfhamilton.co.uk

or discover more Pan Macmillan and Tor UK books at

www.torbooks.co.uk

By Peter F. Hamilton

The Greg Mandel series

Mindstar Rising

A Quantum Murder

The Nano Flower

The Night's Dawn trilogy

The Reality Dysfunction

The Neutronium Alchemist

The Naked God

The Commonwealth Saga

Pandora's Star

Judas Unchained

Chronicle of the Fallers

The Abyss Beyond Dreams

The Void trilogy

The Dreaming Void

The Temporal Void

The Evolutionary Void

Short story collections

A Second Chance at Eden

Manhattan in Reverse

Fallen Dragon

Misspent Youth

The Confederation Handbook
(a vital guide to the Night's Dawn trilogy)

Great North Road

Praise for Peter F. Hamilton

'*The Reality Dysfunction* is an astonishing read crammed full of Golden Age wonders . . . In the accomplished manner in which Hamilton bridges the scales between the star-crossed voids of space and the hollowness of the human heart, I can only compare this work with Dan Simmons' Hyperion Cantos or Iain Banks' *Consider Phlebas*. This book is super-intelligent space opera, wrought by an author who knows his stuff . . . And it's a rattling page-turner too' **Stephen Baxter**

'Literate, intelligent and highly readable. A gripping, riveting banquet for the imagination. Peter Hamilton writes vividly and elegantly. *The Reality Dysfunction* is a tour de force that reaches the farthest boundaries of outer space and the innermost recesses of the human mind' **Peter James**

'Painted on the vast canvas of classic space opera . . . the story builds to an explosive climax. Its mix of star-spanning intrigue and men with big guns will give the remaining American space operas a run for their money, and the climactic cross-genre slide into horror is a brave move that succeeds spectacularly well' ***SFX***

'A space opera with a difference . . . all the disparate plot strands converge to knot together in an exhilarating climax' ***Starburst***

'Hamilton blows open our perception of the book with a colossal eruption of supernatural horror into the space opera we thought we were reading. This is a nervy, risky, audacious book which compels a certain respect for Hamilton's preparedness to go further in his chosen direction of genre-bending than anyone has ever quite done before . . .' ***Good Book Guide***

'An epic in the traditional sense of the word – big, brash, sweeping, hyperbolic, exuberant, thoroughly enjoyable' ***Interzone***

'The book has literally everything plus the kitchen sink . . . That he can pull this off puts Hamilton amongst a rare breed of writers. If you've gotta do it big, do it well. Do it like this' ***sfreviews.net***

Peter F. Hamilton

THE REALITY DYSFUNCTION

Book One of the Night's Dawn trilogy

PAN BOOKS

First published 1996 by Macmillan

This edition published 2012 by Pan Books
an imprint of Pan Macmillan
20 New Wharf Road, London N1 9RR
Associated companies throughout the world
www.panmacmillan.com

ISBN 978-1-4472-0857-0

9

A CIP catalogue record for this book is available from
the British Library.

Typeset by SetSystems Ltd, Saffron Walden, Essex
Printed and bound by CPI Group (UK) Ltd, Croydon, CR0 4YY

1

Space outside the attack cruiser *Beezling* tore open in five places. For a moment anyone looking into the expanding rents would have received a true glimpse into empty infinity. The pseudofabric structure of the wormholes was a photonic dead zone, a darkness so profound it seemed to be spilling out to contaminate the real universe. Then ships were suddenly streaking up out of the gaping termini, accelerating away at six gees, twisting round on interception trajectories. They were different from the spherical Garissan naval craft which they had tracked between the stars, graceful, streamlined teardrop shapes. Larger and dangerously powerful. Alive.

Nestled snugly in the armoured and sealed command capsule at the heart of the *Beezling*, Captain Kyle Prager was shocked out of a simple astrogration review by a datavised proximity alert from the flight computer. His neural nanonics relayed information from the ship's external sensor clusters directly into his brain. Out here in the great emptiness of interstellar space starlight wasn't powerful enough to provide an optical-band return. He was relying on the infrared signature alone, arching smears of pinkness which the discrimination programs struggled to resolve. Radar pulses were fuzzed and hashed by the ships' electronic-warfare pods.

The combat programs stored in the memory clusters of his neural nanonics went into primary mode. He datavised a quick sequence of instructions into the flight computer, desperate for more information. Trajectories from the five newcomers were computed, appearing as scarlet vector lines curving through space to line up ominously on the *Beezling* and her two escort frigates. They were still accelerating, yet there was no reaction-drive exhaust plume. Kyle Prager's heart sank. 'Voidhawks,' he said.

On the couch next to him, Tane Ogilie, the *Beezling*'s patterning-node officer, groaned in dismay. 'How did they know?'

'Confederation Navy Intelligence is good,' Kyle Prager retorted. 'They knew we'd try a direct retaliation. They must have monitored our naval traffic and followed us.' In his mind a black pressure was building. He could almost sense the antimatter-confinement chambers inside the *Beezling*, twinkling like devilish red stars all around him.

Antimatter was the one anathema which was universal throughout the Confederation. No matter what planet or asteroid settlement you were brought up on, they all condemned it.

The penalty if a Confederation Navy ship caught them was an immediate death sentence for the captain, and a one-way ticket on a drop capsule to a penal planet for everyone else on board.

There was no choice, of course, the *Beezling* needed the fantastic delta-V reserve which only antimatter provided, far superior to the usual fusion drives of Adamist starships. The Omutan Defence Force ships would be equipped with antimatter drives. They have it because we have it; we have it because they have it. One of the oldest, and feeblest, arguments history had produced.

Kyle Prager's shoulder muscles relaxed, an involuntary submission. He'd known and accepted the risk, or at least told himself and the admirals he did.

It would be quick and painless, and under ordinary circumstances the crew would survive. But he had orders from the Garissan Admiralty. Nobody was to be allowed access to the Alchemist which the *Beezling* was carrying; and certainly not the Edenists crewing the voidhawks: their bitek science was powerful enough already.

'A distortion field has locked onto us,' Tane Ogilie reported. His voice was strained, high. 'We can't jump clear.'

For a brief moment Kyle Prager wondered what it would be like to command a voidhawk, the effortless power and total superiority. It was almost a feeling of envy.

Three of the intercepting ships were curving round to chase the *Beezling*, while the frigates, *Chengho* and *Gombari*, only rated one pursuer each.

Mother Mary, with that formation they must know what we're carrying.

He formed the scuttle code in his mind, reviewing the procedure before datavising it into the flight computer. It was simple enough, shutting down the safeguards in the main drive's antimatter-confinement chambers, engulfing nearby space with a nova blast of light and hard radiation.

I could wait until the voidhawks rendezvoused, take them with us. But the crews are only doing their job.

The flimsy infrared image of the three pursuit craft suddenly increased dramatically, brightening, expanding. Eight wavering petals of energy opened outwards from each of them, the sharp, glaring tips moving swiftly away from the centre. Analysis programs cut in; flight vector projections materialized, linking all twenty-four projectiles to the *Beezling* with looped laserlike threads of light. The exhaust plumes were hugely radioactive. Acceleration was hitting forty gees. Antimatter propulsion.

'Combat wasp launch,' Tane Ogilie shouted hoarsely.

'They're not voidhawks,' Kyle Prager said with grim fury. 'They're fucking blackhawks. Omuta's hired blackhawks!' He datavised an evasion manoeuvre order into the flight computer, frantically activating the *Beezling*'s defence procedures. He'd been almost criminally negligent in not identifying the hostiles as soon as they emerged. He checked his neural nanonics; elapsed time since their emergence was seven seconds. Was that really all? Even so, his response had been woefully sloppy in an arena where milliseconds was the most precious currency. They would pay for that, maybe with their lives.

An acceleration warning blared through the *Beezling* – audio, optical, and datavise. His crew would be strapped in, but Mother Mary alone knew what the civilians they carried were doing.

The ship's acceleration built smoothly, and he felt the nanonic membrane supplements in his body hardening, supporting his internal organs against the gee force, preventing them from being pushed through his spine, ensuring an undiminished blood supply to his brain, forestalling blackout. *Beezling* shuddered violently as its own volley of combat wasps launched. Acceleration reached eight gees, and carried on building.

In the *Beezling*'s forward crew module, Dr Alkad Mzu had been reviewing the ship's status as it flew towards their next jump coordinate at one and a half gees. Neural nanonics processed the raw data to provide a composite of the starship's external sensor images, along with flight vector projections. The picture unfurled behind her retinas, scintillating ghost shadows until she closed her eyelids. *Chengho* and *Gombari* showed as intense streaks of blue-white light, the glare from their drive exhausts overwhelming the background starfield.

It was a tight formation. *Chengho* was two thousand kilometres away, *Gombari* just over three thousand. Alkad knew it took superb astrogation for ships to emerge within five thousand kilometres of each other after a jump of ten light-years. Garissa had spent a lot of money on equipping its navy with the best hardware available.

Money which could have been better spent at the university, or on supporting the national medical service. Garissa wasn't a particularly rich world. And as to where the Department of Defence had acquired such large amounts of antimatter, Alkad had studiously avoided asking.

'It will be about thirty minutes before the next jump,' Peter Adul said.

Alkad cancelled the datavise. The sensor visualization of the ships faded from her perception, replaced by the spartan grey-green composite of the cabin walls. Peter was standing in the open oval hatch, wearing a dark turquoise ship-suit, padded on all the joints to protect him from bruising knocks in free fall. He smiled invitingly at her. She could see the worry behind the bright, lively eyes.

Peter was thirty-five, a metre eighty tall, with skin actually darker than her own deep ebony. He worked in the university mathematics department, and they had been engaged for eighteen months. Never the outgoing boisterous type, but quietly supportive. One person who genuinely didn't seem to mind the fact that she was brighter than him – and they were rare enough. Even the prospect of her being for ever damned as the Alchemist's creator left him unperturbed. He had actually accompanied her to the ultra-secure navy asteroid base to help with the device's mathematics.

'I thought we could spend them together,' he said.

She grinned back up at him and slipped out of the restraint net as he sat on the edge of her acceleration cushioning beside her. 'Thanks. Navy types don't mind being cooped up by themselves during realignment. But it certainly gets to me.' Various hums and buzzes from the ship's environmental systems invaded the cabin, crew-members talking softly at their stations, vague words echoing along the cramped companionways. *Beezling* had been assembled specifically to deploy the Alchemist device, its design concentrating on durability and performance; crew comforts had come a long way down the navy's priority list.

Alkad swung her legs over the side of the cushioning ledge,

feet *pulled* down to the decking by the strong gravity, and leaned against him, thankful for the warmth of the contact, his just being there.

His arm went round her shoulders. 'What is it about the prospect of incipient mortality which gets the hormones flowing?'

She smiled and pressed harder into his side. 'What is it in the male make-up that simply being awake gets your hormones going?'

'That's a no?'

'That's a no,' she said firmly. 'There's no door, and we'd do ourselves an injury in this gravity. Besides, there will be plenty of time once we get back.'

'Yes.' If we do. But he didn't say that out loud.

That was when the acceleration warning sounded. Even then it took them a second to react, breaking through the initial moment of shock.

'Get back on the cushioning,' Peter yelled as the gee force leapt upwards. Alkad attempted to swing her legs back up on the ledge. They were made of uranium, impossibly heavy. Muscles and tendons grated horribly as she strained against the weight.

Come on. It's easy. It's only your legs. Dear Mother, how many times have you lifted your legs? Come on!

Neural-nanonic nerve-impulse overrides bullied her thigh muscles. She got one leg back on the cushioning. By that time the acceleration had reached seven gees. She was stuck with her left leg on the floor, foot slipping along the decking as the enormous weight of her thigh pushed down, forcing her knee joint open.

The two opposing swarms of combat wasps engaged; attacking and defending drones splitting open, each releasing a barrage of submunitions. Space seethed with directed energy beams. Electronic warfare pulses popped and burned up and down the electromagnetic spectrum, trying to deflect, goad, confuse, harass. A second later it was the turn of the missiles. Solid kinetic bullets bloomed like antique shotgun blasts. All it took was the slightest graze, at those closing velocities both projectile and target alike detonated into billowing plumes of plasma. Fusion explosions followed, intense flares of blue-white starfire flinging off violet coronae. Antimatter added its vehemence to the fray, producing even larger explosions amid the ionic maelstrom.

The nebula which blazed between the *Beezling* and her attackers was roughly lenticular, and over three hundred kilometres broad, choked with dense cyclonic concentrations, spewing tremendous cataracts of fire from its edges. No sensor in existence could penetrate such chaos.

Beezling lurched round violently, drive deflector coils working at maximum pitch, taking advantage of the momentary blind spot to change course. A second volley of combat wasps shot out of their bays around the attack cruiser's lower hull, just in time to meet a new salvo fired from the blackhawks.

Peter had barely managed to roll off the acceleration couch where he was sitting, landing hard on the floor of Alkad's cabin, when the terrible acceleration began. He watched helplessly as Alkad's left leg slowly gave way under the crushing gee force; her whimpering filling him with futile guilt. The composite deck was trying to ram its way up through his back. His neck was agony. Half of the stars he could see were pain spots, the rest were a datavised nonsense. The flight computer had reduced the external combat arena to neat ordered graphics which buffeted against priority metabolic warnings. He couldn't even focus his thoughts on them. There were more important things to worry about, like how the hell was he going to force his chest up so he could breathe again?

Suddenly the gravity field shifted. He left the decking behind, and slammed into the cabin wall. His teeth were punched clean through his lip; he heard his nose break with an ugly *crunch*. Hot blood squirted into his mouth, frightening him. No wound could possibly heal in this environment. He would very probably bleed to death if this went on much longer.

Then gravity righted again, squeezing him back against the decking. He screamed in shock and pain. The datavised visualization from the flight computer had collapsed into an eerily calm moiré pattern of red, green, and blue lines. Darkness was encroaching around the edges.

The second clash of combat wasps took place over a wider front. Sensors and processors on both sides were overloaded and confused by the vivid nebula and its wild energy efflux. New explosions were splattered against the background of destruction. Some of the attacking combat wasps pierced the defensive cordon. A third volley of defenders left the *Beezling*.

Six thousand kilometres away, another nuclear-fuelled nebula burst into existence as the *Chengho* fought off its solitary hunter's swarm of combat wasps. The *Gombari* wasn't so fortunate. Its antimatter-confinement chambers were shattered by the incoming weapons. *Beezling*'s sensor filters engaged instantly as an ephemeral star ignited. Kyle Prager lost his datavised visualization across half of the universe. He never saw the blackhawk which attacked the frigate wrenching open a wormhole interstice and vanish within, fleeing the lethal sleet of radiation its attack had liberated.

The combat wasp closing on *Beezling* at forty-six gees analysed the formation of the robot defenders approaching it. Missiles and ECM pods raced away, fighting a fluid battle of evasion and deception for over a tenth of a second. Then the attacker was through, a single defender left between it and the starship, moving to intercept, but slowly, the defender had only just left its launch cradle, accelerating at barely twenty gees.

Situation displays flipped into Kyle Prager's mind. The blackhawks' positions, their trajectories. Combat wasp performance. Likely reserves. He reviewed them, mind augmented by the tactics program, and made his decision, committing half of his remaining combat wasps to offensive duties.

Beezling rang like a bell as they launched.

At a hundred and fifty kilometres from its prey, the incoming combat wasp's guidance processors computed it wouldn't quite reach the starship before it was intercepted. It ran through the available options, making its choice.

At a hundred and twenty kilometres away it loaded a deactivation sequence into the hardware of the seven antimatter-confine chambers it was carrying.

At ninety-five kilometres away the magnetic field of the first confinement chamber snapped off. Forty-six gravities took over. The frozen pellet of antimatter was smashed into the rear wall. Long before contact was actually made the magnetic field of the second confinement chamber was switched off. All seven shut down over a period of a hundred picoseconds, producing a specifically shaped blast wave.

At eighty-eight kilometres away, the antimatter pellets had annihilated an equal mass of matter, resulting in a titanic energy release. The spear of plasma which formed was a thousand times hotter than the core of a star, hurtling towards the *Beezling* at relativistic velocities.

Sensor clusters and thermo-dump panels vaporized immediately as the stream of disassociated ions slammed into the *Beezling*. Molecular-binding force generators laboured to maintain the silicon hull's integrity, a struggle they were always destined to lose against such ferocity. Breakthrough occurred in a dozen different places at once. Plasma surged in, playing over the complex, delicate systems like a blowtorch over snow crystals.

The luckless *Beezling* suffered a further blow from fate. One of the plasma streams hit a deuterium tank, searing its way through the foam insulation and titanium shell. The cryogenic liquid reverted to its natural gaseous state under immense pressure, ripping the tank open, and blasting fragments in every direction. An eight-metre section of the hull buckled upwards, and a volcanic geyser of deuterium haemorrhaged out towards the stars past shredded fingers of silicon.

Combat wasp explosions were still flooding surrounding space with torrents of light and elementary particles. But the *Beezling* was an inert hulk at the centre of a dissipating halo, her hull fissured, reaction drive off, spinning like a broken bird.

The three attacking blackhawk captains observed the last volley of *Beezling*'s combat wasps lock on to their own ships and race vengefully across the gulf. Thousands of kilometres away, their colleague scored a debilitating strike on the *Chengho*. And the *Beezling*'s combat wasps had halved the separation distance.

Energy patterning cells applied a terrible stress against the fabric of space, and the blackhawks slipped into the gaping wormholes which opened, contracting the interstices behind them. The *Beezling*'s combat wasps lost track of their targets; on-board processors began to scan round and round in an increasingly futile attempt to re-acquire the missing signatures as the drones rushed further and further away from the disabled warship.

*

The return of consciousness wasn't quite as welcome as it should have been, even though it meant that Dr Alkad Mzu was still alive. Her left leg was a source of nauseous pain. She could remember hearing the bones snapping as her knee hinged fully open. Then came the twists of a shifting gravity field, far more effective than any torturer. Her neural nanonics had damped down the worst of the pain, but the *Beezling*'s final convulsion had brought a blessed oblivion.

How in Mother Mary's name did we survive that?

She thought she had been prepared for the inherent risk of the mission failing, for death to claim her. Her work at the university back on Garissa made her all too aware of the energy levels required to push a starship through a ZTT jump, and what would happen should an instability occur in the patterning nodes. It never seemed to bother the navy crew, or rather they were better at hiding it. She knew also that there was a small chance they would be intercepted by Omutan naval craft once the *Beezling* emerged above their target star. But even that wouldn't be so bad, the end should a combat wasp break through *Beezling*'s defensive shield would probably be instantaneous. She even acknowledged that the Alchemist might malfunction. But this . . . Hunted down out here, unprepared physically or mentally, and then to survive, however tenuously. How could the good Mother Mary be so callous? Unless perhaps even She feared the Alchemist?

Residual graphics seemed to swirl obstinately among the ailing thoughts of her consciousness. Vector lines intersected their original jump coordinate thirty-seven thousand kilometres ahead. Omuta was a small, unremarkable star directly in front of the coordinate. Two more jumps, and they would have been in the system's Oort cloud, the sparse halo of ice-dust clouds and slumbering comets which marked the boundary of interstellar space. They were approaching from galactic north, well outside the plane of the ecliptic, trying to avoid detection.

She had helped plan the mission profile, offering her comments to a room full of senior navy staff who were visibly nervous in her presence. It was a syndrome which had affected more and more people in the secret military station as her work progressed.

Alkad had given the Confederation something new to fear, something which surpassed even the destructive power of antimatter. A star slayer. And that prospect was as humbling as it was terrifying. She had resigned herself that after the war billions of planet dwellers would look up at the naked stars, waiting for the twinkling light which had been Omuta to vanish from the night sky. Then they would remember her name, and curse her to hell.

All because I was too stupid to learn from past mistakes. Just like all the other dreaming fools throughout history, wrapped up with seductive, clean equations, their simplistic, isolated elegance, giving no thought to the messy, bloody, *physical* application that was their ultimate reality. As if we didn't have enough weapons already. But that's human nature, we've always got to go one better, to increase the terror another notch. And for what?

Three hundred and eighty-seven Dorados: large asteroids with a nearly pure metal content. They were orbiting a red-dwarf sun twenty light-years away from Garissa, twenty-nine light-years from Omuta. Scoutships from both inhabited systems had stumbled across them virtually simultaneously. Who had actually been first would never now be known. Both governments had claimed them: the wealth contained in the lonely metal chunks would be a heady boost for the planet whose companies could mine and refine such plentiful ore.

At first it had been a squabble, a collection of *incidents*. Prospecting and survey ships dispatched to the Dorados had been attacked by 'pirates'. And, as always, the conflict had escalated. It ceased to be the ships, and started to become their home asteroid ports. Then nearby industrial stations had proved tempting targets. The Confederation Assembly's attempt to mediate had come to nothing.

Both sides had called in their registered naval reserves, and started to hire the independent traders, with their fast, well-equipped ships capable of deploying combat wasps. Finally, last month, Omuta had used an antimatter bomb against an industrial asteroid settlement in the Garissa system. Fifty-six thousand people had been killed when the biosphere chamber ruptured, spewing them out into space. Those who survived, another eighteen thousand with their mashed fluid-clogged lungs, decompressed capillaries, and dissevered skin, had strained the planet's medical facilities close to breaking point. Over seven hundred had been sent to the university's medical school, which had beds for three hundred. Alkad had witnessed the chaos and pain first hand, heard the gurgling screams that never ended.

So now it was retaliation time. Because, as everybody knew, the next stage would be planetary bombardment. And Alkad Mzu had been surprised to find her nationalistic jingoism supplanting the academic aloofness which had ruled her life to date. Her *world* was being threatened.

The only credible defence was to hit Omuta first, and hit it hard. Her precious hypothetical equations had been grasped at by the navy, which rushed to turn them into functional hardware.

'I wish I could stop you from feeling so much guilt,' Peter had said. That was the day they had left the planet, the two of them waiting in the officers' mess of a navy spaceport while their shuttle was prepared.

'Wouldn't you feel guilty?' she asked irritably. She didn't want to talk, but she didn't want to be silent either.

'Yes. But not as much as you. You're taking the blame for the entire conflict. You shouldn't do that. Both of us, all of us, everyone on the planet, we're all being propelled by fate.'

'How many despots and warlords have said that down the centuries, I wonder?' she retorted.

His face managed to be sad and sympathetic at the same time.

Alkad relented, and took his hand. 'But thank you for coming with me, anyway. I don't think I could stand the navy people by myself.'

'It will be all right, you know,' he said softly. 'The government isn't going to release any details, least of all the name of the inventor.'

'I'll be able to walk straight back into the job, you mean?' she asked. There was too much bitterness in her voice. 'As if nothing had happened?' She knew it wouldn't happen that way. Intelligence agencies from half the governments in the

Confederation would find out who she was, if they hadn't already. Her fate wouldn't be decided by any cabinet minister on politically insignificant Garissa.

'Maybe not nothing,' he said. 'But the university will still be there. The students. That's what you and I live for, isn't it? The real reason we're here, protecting all that.'

'Yes,' she said, as if uttering the word made it fact. She looked out of the window. They were close to the equator here, Garissa's sun bleaching the sky to a featureless white glare. 'It's October back there now. The campus will be knee deep in featherseeds. I always used to think that stuff was a bloody great nuisance. Whoever had the idea of founding an African-ethnic colony on a world that's three-quarters temperate zones?'

'Now that's a tired old myth, that we have to be limited to tropical hellholes. It's our society which counts. In any case, I like the winters. And you'd bitch if it was as hot as this place the whole year round.'

'You're right.' She gave a brittle laugh.

He sighed, studying her face. 'It's their star we're aiming for, Alkad, not Omuta itself. They'll have a chance. A good chance.'

'There are seventy-five million people on that planet. There will be no light, no warmth.'

'The Confederation will help. Hell, when the Great Dispersal was at its peak, Earth was deporting over ten million people a week.'

'Those old colony-transport ships have gone now.'

'Earth's Govcentral is still kicking out a good million a week even now; and there are thousands of military transports. It can be done.'

She nodded mutely, knowing it was all hopeless. The Confederation couldn't even get two minor governments to agree to a peace formula when we both wanted it. What chance has the Assembly got trying to coordinate grudgingly donated resources from eight hundred and sixty disparate inhabited star systems?

The sunlight pouring through the mess window deepened to a sickly red and started to fade. Alkad wondered woozily if the Alchemist was already at work on it. But then the stimulant programs steadied her thoughts, and she realized she was in free fall, her cabin illuminated by a weak pink-tinged emergency light. People were floating around her. *Beezling*'s crew, murmuring in quiet worried tones. Something warm and damp brushed against her cheek, sticking. She brought her hand up instinctively. A swarm of dark motes swam across her field of view, glistening in the light. Blood!

'Peter?' She thought she was shouting his name, but her voice seemed very faint. 'Peter!'

'Easy, easy.' That was a crew-member. Menzul? He was holding her arms, preventing her from bouncing around the confined space.

She caught sight of Peter. Two more crew were hovering over him. His entire face was encased by a medical nanonic package which looked like a sheet of thick green polythene.

'Oh, merciful Mary!'

'He's OK,' Menzul said quickly. 'He'll be all right. The nanonic package can cope.'

'What happened?'

'A squadron of blackhawks caught us. An antimatter blast breached the hull. Screwed us pretty good.'

'What about the Alchemist?'

Menzul shrugged loosely. 'In one piece. Not that it matters much now.'

'Why?' Even as she asked she didn't want to know.

'The hull breach wrecked thirty per cent of our jump nodes. We're a navy ship, we can jump with ten per cent knocked out. But thirty . . . Looks like we're stuck out here; seven light-years from the nearest inhabited star system.'

*

At that moment they were precisely thirty-six and a half light-years from their G3 home star, Garissa. If they had trained the *Beezling*'s remaining optical sensors on the faint diamond of light far behind, and if those sensors possessed sufficient resolution, then in thirty-six years, six months, and two days they would have seen a brief surge in the apparent magnitude as Omuta's mercenary ships dropped fifteen antimatter planet-buster bombs on their home world. Each one had a megatonnage blast equivalent to the asteroid impact which wiped out the dinosaurs on Earth. Garissa's atmosphere was ruined beyond redemption. Superstorms arose which would rage for millennia to come. By themselves, they weren't fatal. On Earth, the shielded arcologies had sheltered people from their heat-wrecked climate for five and a half centuries. But unlike an asteroid impact, where the energy release was purely thermal, the planet-busters each emitted the same amount of radiation as a small solar flare. Within eight hours, the rampaging storms had spread the nuclear fallout right across the planet, rendering it completely uninhabitable. Total sterilization took a further two months.

2

The Ly-cilph home planet was located in a galaxy far removed from the one which would ultimately host the human Confederation. Strictly speaking it wasn't a planet at all, but a moon, one of twenty-nine orbiting a gas supergiant, a formidable orb two hundred thousand kilometres in diameter, itself a failed brown-dwarf star. After its accretion had finished it lacked enough mass for fusion ignition; but none the less its inexorable gravitational contraction generated a massive thermal output. What was ostensibly its nightside fluoresced near the bottom end of the visible spectrum, producing a weary emberlike glow which fluctuated in continental-sized patterns as the dense turbulent clouds raged in never ending cyclones. Across the dayside, where lemon-shaded rays from the K4 primary sun fell, the storm bands shone a lambent salmon-pink.

There were five major moons, with the Ly-cilph planet the fourth out from the cloud tops, and the only one with an atmosphere. The remaining twenty-four satellites were all barren rocks: captured asteroids, junk left over from the solar system's formation, all of them less than seven hundred kilometres in diameter. They ranged from a baked rock ball skimming one thousand kilometres above the clouds, from which the metal ores had boiled away like a comet's volatiles, up to a glaciated planetoid in a retrograde orbit five and a half million kilometres out.

Local space was hazardous in the extreme. A vast magnetosphere confined and channelled the supergiant's prodigious outpouring of charged particles, producing a lethal radiation belt. Radio emission was a ceaseless white-noise howl. The three large moons orbiting below the Ly-cilph homeworld were all inside the radiation belt, and completely sterile. The innermost of the three was chained to the ionosphere with a colossal flux tube, along which titanic energies sizzled. It also trailed a plasma torus around its orbital path, the densest ring of particles inside the magnetosphere's comprehensive embrace. Instant death to living tissue.

The tidal-locked Ly-cilph world coasted along seventy thousand kilometres above the tenuous outer fringes of the magnetosphere, beyond the reach of the worst radiation. Occasional palpitations within the flux lines would bombard the upper atmosphere with protons and electrons, sending squalls of solar-bright borealis lights slithering and twisting silently across the rusty sky.

Atmospheric composition was an oxygen-nitrogen mix, with various sulphurous compounds, and an inordinately high water-vapour level. Mist, fog, and stacked cloud layers were the norm. Proximity to the infrared glow of the supergiant gave it a perpetual tropical climate, with the warm, wet air of the nearside constantly on the move, rushing around to the farside where it cooled, radiating its thermal load away into space, and then returning via storms which traversed the poles. Weather was a drab constant, always blowing, always raining, the strength of the gusts and downpours dictated by the orbital location. Night fell in one place, at one time. On the farside, when supergiant and planet were in an inferior conjunction, and the hellish red cloudscape eclipsed the nearside's brief glimpse of the sun.

It was a cycle which was broken only once every nine years, when a new force was applied to the timeless equation. A four-moon conjunction, which brought chaos and devastation to the surface with storms of biblical ferocity.

The warmth and the light had incubated life on this world, as they had on countless billions throughout the universe. There had been no seas, no oceans when the first migratory interstellar germ fell onto the pristine planet, rooting its way into the mucky stain of chemicals infecting the bubbling muddy waters. Tidal forces had left a smooth surface, breaking down mountains, grinding away at the steppes left over from the time of formation. Lakes, rivers, and flood plains covered the land, steaming and being rained on. There was no free oxygen back then, it was all combined with carbon. A solid stratum of white cloud ensured the infrared radiation found it hard to escape, even in the centre of the farside. Temperatures were intolerably high.

The first life, as always, was algae, a tough slime which spread through the water, seeping down rivers and streams to contaminate the lakes, hurried through the air by the tireless convection currents. It altered and adapted over geological eras, slowly learning to utilize the two contrasting light sources as an additional energy supply. Success, when it came, was swift, mere millennia. Oxygen poured forth. Carbon was digested. The temperature fell. The rain quickened, thinning the clouds, clearing the sky. Evolution began once more.

For millions of years, the planet's governing nine year cycle was of no importance. Storms and hurricanes were an irrelevance to single-cell amoebas floating sluggishly through the lakes and rivers, nor did they matter to the primitive lichens which were creeping over the rocks. But the cells adrift in the water gradually began to form cooperative colonies, and specialization occurred. Jelly-like worms appeared in the lakes, brainless, instinct-driven and metabolically inefficient, little more than mobile lichen. But it was a start. Birth and death began to replace fission as the premier method of reproduction. Mutations crept in, sometimes producing improvements, more often resulting in inviability. Failed strains were rapidly culled by merciless nature. Divergence appeared, the dawn of a million species; DNA strands lengthened, a chemical record of progress and blind alleys. Crawling creatures emerged onto the lakesides, only to be scalded by the harsh chemicals making up the atmosphere. Yet they persisted.

Life was a steady progression, following a pattern which was as standard as circumstances would allow. There were no such things as ice ages to alter the direction which this world's creatures were taking, no instabilities causing profound climate changes. Only the nine-yearly storms, appearing without fail, which became the dominant influence. The new animals' breeding cycles were structured around it, plant growth was restricted by it.

The planet matured into a jungle world, a landscape of swamps and lush verdancy, where giant ferns covered the surface from pole to pole, and were themselves webbed and choked with tenacious creepers reaching for the clear sky. Floating weeds turned the smaller lakes into vast marshlands. Elaborate ruff flowers vied for the attention of insects and birds, seed pods with skirts of hardened petals flew like kites through the air. Wood was non-existent, of course, wood required decades of uninterrupted growth to form.

Two wildly different flora genealogies sprang up, with the terminator as an unbreachable dividing line, and battleground. Farside plants adapted to the sun's yellow light: they were capable of tolerating the long nights accompanying conjunction, the cooler temperatures. Nearside was the province of red light, falling without end: its black-leafed plants were taller, stronger, more vigorous, yet they were unable to conquer farside. Night killed them, yellow light alone was insufficient to drive their demanding photosynthesis, and the scattered refraction of red light by the thick atmosphere never carried far enough, haunting the land for a couple of hundred kilometres beyond the terminator.

The animals were more adaptive, ranging freely across far-side and nearside. Dinosaur-analogues never appeared, they were too big, requiring too much time to grow. Apart from bird-analogues, lizard creatures with membranous wings, most animals were smallish, reflecting their aquatic heritage. All were cold-blooded, at home in the muddy streams and weed-clogged pools. They retained that ancestral trait out of pure necessity. For that was where their eggs were laid, buried deep and safe in the mud of the lakebeds, hidden away from the worst ravages of the storm. That was how all life survived while the winds scoured the world, as seeds and eggs and spores, ready to surge forth when stability returned in a few short weeks.

On such an inimical world life can evolve in one of two ways. There are the defeated, littered on countless planets across the cosmos, weak, anaemic creatures huddled in their dead-end sanctuaries, a little protective niche in the local ecology, never rising above a rudimentary level, their very lack of sophistication providing them with the means of continuation. Or there are the triumphant, the creatures which refuse to be beaten, which fight tooth and nail and claw and tentacle against their adversity; those for which circumstances act as an evolutionary spur. The dividing line is thin; it might even be that a devastating storm every eight years could bring genetic ruination. But nine years . . . nine proved enough time to ensure survival, allowing the denizens to rise to the challenge rather than sink back into their ubiquitous mires.

The Ly-cilph claimed such a victory. A mere eight hundred million years after life had begun on their world they had reached their pinnacle of evolution. They became transcendent entities.

Their nine-year cycle starts in a fish form, hatching from the black egg-clusters concealed below the mud. Billions of free-floating slugs emerge, two centimetres long, and are eaten by faster, meaner predators as they gorge themselves on the abundant sludge of decayed vegetation putrefying in the water.

They grow and change over three years, losing their tails, developing a snail-like skirt. They cling to the bottom of their lakes, an ovoid body ninety centimetres high, with ten tentacles rising up from the crown. The tentacles are smooth, sixty centimetres long, devoid of suckers, but with a sharp curved horn on the tip; and they're fast, exploding like a nest of enraged pythons to snatch their ignorant prey swimming overhead.

When their full size has been reached they slide up out of the water to range through the planetwide jungle. Gills adapt to breathe the harsh musky air, tentacle muscles strengthen to support the drooping limbs away from the water's cosy buoyancy. And they eat, rummaging through the matted undergrowth with insistent horns to find the black, wizened nutlike nodes that have been lying there neglected since the storm. The nodes are made up of cells saturated with chemical memory tracers, memories containing information, the knowledge accumulated by the Ly-cilph race throughout time. They bring understanding, an instant leap to sentience, and trigger the telepathic centre of their brains. Now they have risen above a simple animal level of existence they have much to converse about.

The knowledge is mainly of a philosophical nature, although mathematics is highly developed; what they know is what they have observed and speculated upon, and added to with each generation. Farside night acts as a magnet as they gather to observe the stars. Eyes and minds linked by telepathy, acting as a gigantic multi-segment telescope. There is no technology, no economy. Their culture is not orientated towards the mechanical or materialistic; their knowledge is their wealth. The data-processing capacity of their linked minds far exceeds that of any electronic computer system, and their perception is not limited to the meagre electromagnetic wavelengths of the optical bands.

Once awoken, they learn. It is their purpose. They have so

little time in their corporeal form, and the universe they find themselves in, the splendour of the gas supergiant and its multifarious satellites, is large. Nature has ordained them as gatherers of knowledge. If life has a purpose, they speculate, then it must be a journey to complete understanding. In that respect intellect and nature have come to a smooth concordance.

In the ninth year after their hatching, the four large innermost moons line up once more. The distortion they cause in the supergiant's magnetosphere acts like an extension to the flux tube. The agitated particles of the ionosphere which use it as a conduit up to the first moon's plasma torus now find themselves rising higher, up to the second moon, then the third, higher still, fountaining out of the magnetosphere altogether. The Ly-cilph world swings round into their path.

It is not a tight directed beam; up at the mushrooming crown the protons and electrons and neutrons have none of the energy they possessed when the roiling flux lines flung them past the first moon. But as always it is the sheer scale of events within the gas supergiant's domain which proves so overwhelming.

The Ly-cilph world takes ten hours to traverse through the invisible cloud of ions loitering outside the flux lines. In that time, the energy which floods into the atmosphere is more than sufficient to destroy the equilibrium of the slowly circulating convection currents.

The deluge arrives at the end of the planet's one and only mating season. The Ly-cilph and their non-sentient cousins have produced their eggs and secreted them into the lakebeds. Plants have flowered and scattered their seeds across the landscape. Now there is only the prospect of death.

When the first titanic bursts of azure lightning break overhead, the Ly-cilph stop their analysing and deliberations, and begin to impart all they know into the empty cells of the nodes which have grown out of their skin like warts around the base of their tentacles.

The winds howl, voicing the planet's torment. Gusts are strong enough to break the metre-thick stems of the fern trees. Once one goes it starts a domino effect in the jungle. Destruction spreads out in vast ripples, looking like bomb blasts from above. Clouds are torn apart by the violence, reduced to cotton tufts spinning frantically in the grip of small, ferocious whirlwinds. Micro-typhoons plunge back and forth, accelerating the obliteration of the jungle.

All the while the Ly-cilph remain steadfast, their adhesive skirts anchoring them to the ground as the air around them fills with broken fronds and shredded leaves. The nodes, now saturated with their precious heritage, drop off like ripe fruit. They will lie hidden amongst the grass and roots for another three years.

Nearside is ablaze with potent lightstorms. High above the tattered clouds, the aurora borealis forms a veil across the sky, a garish mother-of-pearl haze riddled with thousands of long, lurid scintillations, like giant shooting stars. Beyond that, the conjunction is joined, three moons sliding into alignment, bathed in an eerie trillion-amp phosphorescence. An epicentre to one of the gas supergiant's planet-swallowing cyclones.

The particle jet has reached its zenith. The flux tube's rain of energy penetrates the tormented lower atmosphere. It is embraced by the Ly-cilph. Their minds consume the power, using it to metamorphose once again. The nodes brought them sentience, the supergiant's surplus energy brings them transcendence. They leave the chrysalis of the flesh behind, shooting up the stream of particles at lightspeed, spacefree and eternal.

The liberated minds swarm above their abandoned world for several days, watching the storms abate, the clouds re-form, the old convection currents return to their familiar courses. The Ly-cilph have achieved incorporeality, but their perspective, shaped by the formative material existence, remains unchanged. As before, they deem the purpose of their life is experience, perhaps eventually to be followed by understanding. The difference is that they are no longer restricted to a single world and brief glimpses of the stars; now the entire universe is laid out before them, they wish to know it all.

They begin to drift away from the odd planet which birthed them, tentatively at first, then with greater boldness, dispersing like an expanding wave of eager ghosts. One day they will return to this point, all the generations of Ly-cilph that ever lived. It will not happen while the primary star still burns; they will travel until they meet the boundary of the universe as it contracts once more, following the galactic superclusters as they fall into the reborn dark mass at the centre, the cosmic egg regathering all it has lost. Then they will be back, congregating around the black star husk, sharing the knowledge they have brought, searching through it for that elusive ultimate understanding. And after understanding they will know what lies beyond, and with that a hope of a further switch to yet another level of existence. Possibly the Ly-cilph will be the only entities to survive the present universe's final reconfiguration.

But until then they are content to observe and learn. Their very nature precludes them from taking part in the myriad dramas of life and matter unfolding before their ethereal senses.

Or so they believe.

3

Iasius had come back to Saturn to die.

Three hundred and fifty thousand kilometres above the gas giant's wan beige cloudscape the wormhole terminus expanded, and the voidhawk slipped out into real space. Sensors mounted on the strategic-defence satellites patrolling the gas giant's designated starship emergence zone found the infrared glow straight away, as radar waves tickled the hull. *Iasius* hailed the nearest habitat with its affinity, and identified itself. The satellite sensors slid their focus away, resuming their vigil.

Captain and crew borrowed the bitek starship's paramount senses to observe the glorious ringed planet outside, whilst all the time their minds wept with the knowledge of what was to come. They were flying above the gas giant's sunlit hemisphere, a nearly full crescent showing. The rings were spread out ahead and two degrees below them, seemingly solid, yet stirring, as if a gritty gas had been trapped between two panes of glass. Starlight twinkled through. Such majestic beauty seemed to deny their terrible reason for returning.

Iasius's affinity touched their minds. **Feel no sorrow**, the bitek starship said silently. **I do not. What is, is. You have helped to fill my life. For that I thank you.**

Alone in her cabin, Captain Athene felt her mental tears become real. She was as tall as any woman of the hundred families, whose geneticists had concentrated on enhancing sturdiness so their descendants could comfortably spend a lifetime coping with the arduous conditions of spaceflight. Her carefully formatted evolution had given her a long, handsome face, now heavily wrinkled, and rich auburn hair which had lost its youthful sheen to a lustrous silver. In her immaculate ocean-blue ship-tunic she projected a regal quality of assurance, which always elicited total confidence from her crews. But now her composure had vanished, expressive violet eyes reflecting the utter anguish welling up inside.

No, Athene, please don't.

I can't help it, her mind cried back. **It's so unfair. We should go together, we should be allowed.**

There was an eldritch caress down her spine, more tender than any human lover could ever bestow. She had felt that same touch on every day of all her hundred and eight years. Her only true love. None of her three husbands received as much emotional devotion as *Iasius*, nor, she admitted with something approaching sacrilege, had her eight children, and three of them she had carried in her own womb. But other Edenists understood and sympathized; with their communal affinity there was no hiding emotions or truth. The birthbond between the voidhawks and their captains was strong enough to survive anything the universe could possibly throw at them. *Except death*, the most private section of her mind whispered.

It is my time, *Iasius* said simply. There was an overtone of contentment within the silent voice. If the voidhawk had had lungs, Athene thought it would have sighed at that moment.

I know, she said wistfully. It had been increasingly obvious during the last few weeks. The once omnipotent energy patterning cells were now struggling to open a wormhole interstice. Where over half a century ago there had been a feeling that a single swallow manoeuvre could span the galaxy, the pair of them now experienced a muted sense of relief if a planned fifteen light-year swallow was accomplished only a light-month short of the required coordinate. **Damn the geneticists. Is parity so much to ask for?** she demanded.

One day perhaps they will make ship and captain live as long as each other. But this which we have now, I feel a rightness to it. Someone has to mother our children. You will be as good a mother as you have been a captain. I know this.

The sudden burst of self-satisfied conviction in the mental voice made her grin. Sticky lashes batted some of the moisture away. **Raising ten children at my age. Goodness!**

You will do well. They will prosper. I am happy.

I love you, *Iasius*. If I was allowed to have my life again, I would never change a second of it.

I would.

You would? she asked, startled.

Yes. I would spend one day as a human. To see what it was like.

Believe me, both the pleasures and the pain are greatly exaggerated.

Iasius chuckled. Optically sensitive cells protruding like blisters from its hull located the Romulus habitat, and the starship felt for its mass with a tiny ripple in the spacial distortion field its energy patterning cells were generating. The habitat's solidity registered in its consciousness, a substantial mote orbiting the outside edge of the F-ring. Substantial but hollow, a bitek polyp cylinder forty-five kilometres long, ten wide; it was one of the two original voidhawk bases germinated by the hundred families back in 2225. There were two hundred and sixty-eight similar habitats orbiting Saturn now, along with their subsidiary industrial stations, their numbers tangible evidence of just how important the bitek starships had become to the whole Edenist economy.

The starship sent power flashing through its patterning cells, focusing energy towards infinity, the loci distorting space outside the hull, but never enough to open a wormhole interstice. They rode the distortion wave towards the habitat like a surfer racing for the beach, quickly accelerating to three gees.

A secondary manipulation of the distortion field generated a counter-acceleration force for the benefit of the crew, providing them an apparent acceleration of one gee. A smooth and comfortable ride, unmatched by Adamist starships with their fusion drives.

Athene knew she would never be quite so comfortable if she ever took a trip in a voidhawk again. With *Iasius* she could always feel the nothingness of the vacuum flowing by; a sensation she equated with being in a rowing-boat on some country river, and letting her hand trail through the calm water. Passengers never received that feeling. Passengers were meat.

Go on, she told the starship. **Call for them.**

All right.

She smiled for both of them at the eagerness in the tone.

Iasius called. Opening its affinity full, projecting a wordless shout of joy and sorrow over a spherical zone thirty astronomical units in radius. Calling for mates.

Like all voidhawks, *Iasius* was a creature of deep space, unable to operate close to the confines of a strong gravity field. It had a lenticular shape, measuring one hundred and ten metres in diameter, thirty metres deep at the centre. The hull was a tough polyp, midnight blue in colour, its outer layer gradually boiling away in the vacuum, replaced by new cells growing up from the mitosis layer. Internally, twenty per cent of its mass was given over to specialist organs – nutrient reserve bladders, heart pumps supplying the vast capillary network, and neuron cells – all packaged together neatly within a cylindrical chamber at the centre of the body. The remaining eighty per cent of its bulk was made up from a solid honeycomb of energy patterning cells which generated the spatial distortion field it used for both propulsion modes. It was those cells which were decaying in ever larger quantities. Like human neurons they were unable to regenerate effectively, which dictated the starship's life expectancy. Voidhawks rarely saw out more than a hundred and ten years.

Both the upper and lower hull surfaces had a wide circular groove halfway out from the middle, which the mechanical systems were slotted into. The lower hull groove was fitted mainly with cradles for cargo-pods, the circle of folded titanium struts interrupted only by a few sealed ancillary systems modules. Crew quarters nestled in the upper hull groove, a chrome-silver toroid equipped with lounges, cabins, a small hangar for the atmospheric flyer, fusion generators, fuel, life-support units. Human essentials.

Athene walked around the toroid's central corridor one last time. Her current husband, Sinon, accompanied her as she performed her final sacrosanct duty: initiating the children who would grow up to be the captains of the next generation. There were ten of them, zygotes, Athene's ova fertilized with sperm from her three husbands and two dear lovers. They had been waiting in zero-tau from the moment of conception, protected from entropy, ready for this day.

Sinon had provided the sperm for only one child. But walking beside her, he found he held no resentment. He was from the original hundred families; several of his ancestors had been captains, as well as two of his half-siblings; for just one of his own children to be given the privilege was honour enough.

The corridor had a hexagonal cross-section, its surface made out of a smooth pale-green composite that glowed from within. Athene and Sinon walked at the head of the silent procession of the seven-strong crew, air whirring softly from overhead grilles the only sound. They came to a section of the corridor where the composite strip of the lower wall angle merged seamlessly with the hull, revealing an oval patch of the dark blue polyp. Athene stopped before it.

This egg I name *Oenone*, *Iasius* said.

The polyp bulged up at the centre, its apex thinning as it rose, becoming translucent. Red rawness showed beneath it, the crest of a stem as thick as a human leg which stretched right down into the core of the starship's body. The tumescent apex split open, dribbling a thick gelatinous goo onto the corridor floor. Inside, the sphincter muscle at the top of the red stem dilated, looking remarkably similar to a waiting toothless mouth. The dark tube inside palpitated slowly.

Athene held up the bitek sustentator, a sphere five centimetres in diameter, flesh-purple, maintained at body temperature. According to the data core on the zero-tau pod it had been kept in, the zygote inside was female; it was also the one Sinon had fathered. She bent down and pushed it gently into the waiting orifice.

This child I name Syrinx.

The little sustentator globe was ingested with a quiet wet *slurp*. The sphincter lips closed, and the stem sank back down out of sight. Sinon patted her shoulder, and they gave each other a proud smile.

They will flourish together, *Iasius* said proudly.

Yes.

Athene walked on. There were another four zygotes left to initiate, and Romulus was growing larger outside.

The Saturn habitats were keening their regret at *Iasius*'s call. Voidhawks throughout the solar system answered with pride and camaraderie; those that weren't outbound with cargo abandoned their flights to flock around Romulus in anticipation.

Iasius curved gently round the non-rotational dock at the northern endcap. With her eyes closed, Athene let the affinity bond image from the voidhawk's sensor blisters expand into her mind with superhuman clarity. Her visual reference of the habitat altered as the endcap loomed large beyond the rim of the starship's hull. She saw the vast expanse of finely textured red-brown polyp as an approaching cliff face; one with four concentrically arrayed ledges, as if ripples had raced out from the axis in some distant time, only to be frozen as they peaked.

The voidhawk chased after the second ledge, two kilometres out from the axis, swooping round to match the habitat's rotation. Adamist reaction-drive spaceships didn't have anything like the manoeuvrability necessary to land on the ledges, and they were reserved for voidhawks alone.

Iasius shot in over the edge, seeming to hover above the long rank of mushroomlike docking pedestals which protruded from the floor, before choosing a vacant one. For all its bulk, it alighted with the delicate grace of a hummingbird.

Athene and Sinon felt the gravity fade down to half a gee as the distortion field dissipated. She watched the big flat-tyred crew bus rolling slowly towards the bitek starship, elephant-snout airlock tube held upwards.

Come along, Sinon urged, his mind dark with emotion. He touched her elbow, seeing all too plainly the wish to remain during the last flight.

She nodded her head reluctantly. 'You're right,' she said out loud.

I'm sorry that doesn't make it any easier.

She gave him a tired smile and allowed him to lead her out of the lounge. The bus had arrived at the rim of the voidhawk. Its airlock tube lengthened, sliding over the upper hull surface to reach the crew toroid.

Sinon diverted his attention away from his wife to the flock of voidhawks matching pace with the ledge. There were over seventy waiting, latecomers rising into view as they left their crews behind on the other ledges. The emotional backwash from the waiting bitek starships was impossible to filter out, and he could feel his own blood singing in response.

It wasn't until he and Athene reached the passage to the airlock that he noticed an irregularity in the flock. *Iasius* obligingly focused on the starship in question.

That's a blackhawk! Sinon exclaimed.

Amidst the classic lens shapes it seemed oddly asymmetric, drawing the eye. A flattened teardrop, slightly asymmetric, with the upper hull's dorsal bulge fatter than that on the lower hull; from what he supposed was prow to stern it measured an easy hundred and thirty metres; the blue polyp hull was mottled with a tattered purple web pattern.

The larger size and various unorthodox configurations which set the blackhawks apart, their divergence from the voidhawk norm (some called it evolution), came about because of their captains' requirement for greater power. Actually, improved combat performance was what they were after, Sinon thought acrimoniously. The price for that agility usually came in the form of a shorter lifespan.

That is the *Udat*, *Iasius* said equably. **It is fast and powerful. A worthy aspirant.**

There's your answer, then, Athene said, using affinity's singular-engagement mode so the rest of the crew were excluded from the exchange. She had a gleam in her eye as they paused by the airlock's inner hatch.

Sinon pulled a sour face, then shrugged and walked off down the tube to the bus, giving her the final moment alone with her ship.

There was a hum in the corridor she had never heard before, a resonance coming from *Iasius*'s excitement. When she put her fingers to the sleek composite wall there was nothing, no tremor or vibration. Perhaps it was only in her mind. She turned and looked back into the toroid, the familiar confined corridors and lounges. Their whole world.

'Goodbye,' she whispered.

I will love you always.

*

The crew bus trundled back over the ledge towards the cliff of polyp, nuzzling up to a metal airlock set into the base. *Iasius* laughed uproariously across the communal affinity band; it could feel the ten eggs inside its body, glowing with vitality, their urgency to be born. Without warning it streaked away from the pedestal, straight towards the waiting flock of its cousins. They scattered in delighted alarm.

This time there was no counter-acceleration force required for the crew toroid, no protection for fragile humans. No artificial safety limits. *Iasius* curved sharply, pulling an easy nine gees, then flattened its trajectory to fly between the endcap and the giant metal arm of the counter-rotating dock. Weak pearl-white sunlight fell on the hull as it moved out of the ledge's shadow. Saturn lay ahead, the razor-sharp line of the rings bisecting it cleanly. The bitek starship headed in for the planet-swathing streamers of ice crystals and primitive molecules at twelve gees, stray dust-motes and particles brushed smoothly aside by the distortion field's bow wave. Enthusiastic voidhawks raced after it, looking more and more like a stippled comet's tail as they emerged into the light.

In the crew quarters, metal was buckling under its new and enormous weight. Empty lounges and corridors were filled with drawn-out creaking sounds, composite furniture was splintering, collapsing onto the floor, each fresh fragment hitting with the force of a hammer blow, leaving a deep indentation. The cabins and galley were awash with water that squirted from broken pipes, strange ripples quivered across the surface as *Iasius* performed minute course adjustments.

Iasius entered the rings, optical-band perception degrading rapidly as the blizzard raging outside the hull thickened. It curved round again, bending its path in the direction which the ring particles orbited, but always at an angle, always heading inwards towards the massive presence of the gas giant. It was a glorious game, dodging the larger chunks, the dagger fragments of ice which glittered so coldly, the frosted boulders, sable-black chunks of near-pure carbon. The bitek starship soared around them all, spiralling, diving, swooping in huge loops, heedless of the stress, of the toll its frenzy extracted from the precious patterning cells. Energy was free, coursing through the ring. Cosmic radiation, the planet's undulating magnetic flux, the doughty gusts of solar wind; *Iasius* swept it all in with the distortion field, concentrating it into an abundant coherent stream which the patterning cells absorbed and redirected.

By the time it reached the Encke division the power surplus was enough to energize the first egg. *Iasius* let out a shrill cry of triumph. The other voidhawks responded. They had followed tenaciously, striving to match the giddy helter-skelter route *Iasius* had flown, boring down the passage it had broken through the ring mass, desperately deflecting the whirling particles tossed about by its wake. The leader of the flock kept changing, none could equal the speed, nor match the carefree audacity; often they were caught out by the savage turns, overshooting, blundering about in a squall of undisturbed particles. It was a test of skill as well as power. Even luck played a part. Luck was a trait worth inheriting.

When *Iasius* called the first time, *Hyale* was the closest, a mere two hundred kilometres behind. It surged forward, and *Iasius* relented, slowing fractionally, holding a straight course. They rendezvoused, *Hyale* sliding in to hold position ten metres away, their hulls overlapping perfectly. Ring particles skidded round them like snow from a ski blade.

Hyale began to impart its compositional pattern through their affinity bond, a software DNA flowing into *Iasius* with a sense of near orgasmic glory. *Iasius* incorporated the *Hyale*'s structural format into the vast energy squirt it discharged into the first egg.

The egg, *Acetes*, awoke in a blaze of wonder and exhilaration. Alive with racing currents of power, every cell charged with rapture and purpose and the urge to burst into immediate growth.

Iasius filled space with its glee.

Acetes found itself propelled out into the naked vacuum. Shattered fragments of *Iasius*'s hull were spinning away, a dark red hole set in midnight blue receding at a bewildering speed.

Free! the egg sang. **I'm free!**

A huge dark bulk hung above it. Forces it could sense

but couldn't understand were slowing its wild tumbling. The universe seemed to be composed entirely of tiny splinters of matter pervaded by glowing energy bands. Voidhawks flashed past at frightening velocities.

Yes, you are free. I bid you welcome to life.

What is this place? What am I? Why can't I move like you? *Acetes* struggled to make sense of the scraps of knowledge fluttering around its racing mind, *Iasius*'s final gift.

Patience, *Hyale* counselled. **You will grow, you will learn. The data you possess will be integrated in time.**

Acetes cautiously opened its affinity sensitivity to cover the whole of Saturn's environment, and received a chorus of greetings from the habitats, an even greater wave of acknowledgement from individual adult Edenists, excited trills from children; and then its own kind offered encouragement, infant voidhawks nesting within the rings.

Its tumbling halted, it hung below *Hyale*'s lower hull, looking round with raw senses. *Hyale* began to alter their trajectory, moving the egg into a stable circular orbit around the gas giant where it would spend the next eighteen years growing to full size.

Iasius plunged on towards the cloudscape, ploughing a dark telltale furrow through the rings for any entity watching with the right kind of senses. Its flight produced enough power to energize two more eggs, *Briseis* and *Epopeus*, while it was still in the A-ring. *Hesperus* emerged while it was passing through the Cassini division. *Graeae*, *Ixion*, *Laocoön* and *Merope* all awoke in the B-ring, to be borne away by the voidhawks whose compositional patterns they had been given.

Udat caught up with *Iasius* near the inner edge of the B-ring. It had been a long, arduous flight, straining even the blackhawk's power reserves, testing manoeuvrability as seldom before. But now *Iasius* was calling for a mate again, and *Udat* glided across the gap until their distortion fields merged and the hulls almost touched. It sent *Iasius* its own compositional pattern through the affinity bond, swept away by a fervent gratification.

I thank you, *Iasius* said at the end. **I feel this one will be something special. There is a greatness to it.**

The egg cannoned up from its ovary, sending out a cascade of polyp flakes, and *Udat* was left to exert its distortion field to brake the intrigued, eager infant as *Iasius* departed. The puzzled blackhawk had no chance to ask what it had meant by that last enigmatic statement.

I welcome you to life, *Udat* said formally, when it had finally stopped the seven-metre globe from spinning.

Thank you, *Oenone* replied. **Where are we going now?**

To a higher orbit. This one is too close to the planet.

Oh! A pause as it probed round with immature senses, its giddy thoughts quietening down. **What is a planet?**

The last egg was *Priam*, ejected well below the meagre lip of the B-ring. Those voidhawks remaining in the flight, now down to some thirty strong, peeled away from *Iasius*. They were already dangerously close to the cloudscape which dominated a third of the sky; gravity was exerting its malign influence on local space, gnawing at the fringes of their distortion fields, impairing the propulsive efficiency.

Iasius continued to descend, its lower, faster orbit carrying it ahead of the others. Its distortion field began to falter, finally overwhelmed by the intensity of the gravitational effect five hundred kilometres above the gas giant.

The terminator rose ahead, a black occlusion devouring the silently meandering clouds. Faint phosphene speckles swam through the eddies and peaks, weaving in and out of the thicker ammonia-laden braids, their light ebbing and kindling in hesitant patterns. *Iasius* shot into the penumbra, darkness expanding around it like an elemental force. Saturn had ceased to be a planet, an astronomical object, it was becoming hugely solid. The bitek starship curved down at an ever increasing angle. Ahead of it was a single fiery streak, growing brighter in its optical sensors. The darkside equator, that frozen remote wasteland, was redolent with sublime grandeur.

Ring particles were falling alongside *Iasius*, a thick, dark rain, captured by the gossamer fingers of the ionosphere, a treacherously insistent caress which robbed them of speed, of altitude. And, ultimately, existence.

When they had been lured down to the fringes of the ionosphere, icy gusts of hydrogen molecules burnt around them, emitting banners of spectral flame. They dipped rapidly as atmospheric resistance built, first glowing like embers, then crowned by incandescent light; sunsparks, stretching a hundred-kilometre contrail behind them. Their billion-year flight ended swiftly in a violent spectacle: a dazzling concussion which flung out a shower of twinkling debris, quickly extinguished. All that remained was a tenuous trail of black soot which was swept up by the howling cyclones.

Iasius reached the extremity of the ionosphere. The light of the dying ring particles was hot on its lower hull. A tremulous glow appeared around its rim. Polyp began to char and flake away, orange flecks bulleting off into the distance. The bitek starship began to lose peripheral senses as its specialist receptor cells grew warm. Denser layers of hydrogen pummelled the hull. The decent curve began to get bumpy, vexatious supersonic winds were beginning to bite. *Iasius* flipped over. The abrupt turn had disastrous consequences on its avian glide; with the hull's blunt underside smashing head on into the hydrogen, the starship was suddenly subjected to a huge deceleration force. Dangerous quantities of flame blossomed right across the hull as broad swaths of polyp ablated. *Iasius* started to tumble helplessly down towards the scorching river of light.

The retinue of voidhawks watched solemnly from their safe orbit a thousand kilometres above, singing their silent hymn of mourning. After they had honoured *Iasius*'s passing with a single orbit they extended their distortion fields, and launched themselves back towards Romulus.

*

The human captains of the voidhawks involved with the mating flight and the *Iasius*'s crew had passed the time of the flight in a circular hall reserved for that one purpose. It reminded Athene of some of the medieval churches she had visited during her rare trips to Earth, the same vaulted ceiling and elaborate pillars, the intimidating air of reverence, though here the polyp walls were a clean snow-white, and instead of an altar there was a fountain bubbling out of an antique marble Venus.

She stood at the head of her crew, the image of Saturn's searing equator lingering in her mind. A last gentle emanation of peacefulness as the plasma sheath wrapped *Iasius* in its terminal embrace.

It was over.

The captains stopped by one at a time to extend their congratulations, their minds touching hers, bestowing a fragile compassion and understanding. Never, ever a commiseration; these gatherings were supposed to be a reaffirmation of life, celebrating the birth of the eggs. And *Iasius* had energized all ten; some voidhawks went to meet the equator with several eggs remaining.

Yes, they were right to toast *Iasius*.

He's coming over, look, Sinon said. There was a mild tone of resentment in the thought.

Athene raised her eyes from the captain of the *Pelion*, and observed Meyer making his way through the crowd towards her. The *Udat*'s captain was a broad-shouldered man in his late thirties, black hair cut back close to his skull. In contrast to the silky blue ceremonial ship-tunics of the voidhawk captains he wore a functional grey-green ship's one-piece and matching boots. He nodded curtly in response to the formal greetings he received.

If you can't say anything nice, Athene told Sinon, using singular-engagement mode, **don't say anything at all.** She didn't want anything to spoil the wake; besides she felt a certain sympathy for someone so obviously out of place as Meyer was. Nor would it do the hundred families any harm to introduce some diversity into their stock. She kept that thought tightly locked at the core of her mind, knowing full well how this bunch of traditionalists would react to such heresy.

Meyer stood before her, and inclined his head in a swift bow. He was a good five centimetres shorter than her, and she was one of the smaller Edenists in the hall.

Captain– she began. She cleared her throat. No fool like an old one; his affinity bond was with *Udat* alone. A unique neuron symbiont meshed with his medulla, providing him with a secure link to its clone-analogue in the *Udat*, nothing like the hereditary Edenist communal affinity. 'Captain Meyer, my compliments to your ship. It was an excellent flight.'

'Thank you for saying so, Captain. It was an honour to take part. You must be proud all the eggs were energized.'

'Yes.' She lifted her glass of white wine in salute. 'So what brings you to Saturn?'

'Trade.' He glanced round stiffly at the other Edenists. 'I was delivering a cargo of electronics from Kulu.'

Athene felt like laughing out loud, his freshness was just the tonic she needed. She put her arm through his, ignoring the startled looks it caused, and drew him away from the rest of the crew. 'Come on, you're not comfortable with them. And I'm too old to be bothered by how many navy flight code violation warrants are hanging over your head. *Iasius* and I left all that behind us a long time ago.'

'You used to be in the Confederation Navy?'

'Yes. Most of us put in a shift. We Edenists have a strong sense of duty sequenced into us.'

He grinned into his glass. 'You must have been a formidable team, that was some mating flight.'

'History now. What about you? I want to hear all about life on the knife edge. The gung-ho adventures of an independent trader, the shady deals, the wild flights. Are you fabulously wealthy? I have several granddaughters I wouldn't mind getting rid of.'

Meyer laughed. 'You have no grandchildren. You're too young.'

'Nonsense. Stop being so gallant. Some of the girls are older than you.' She enjoyed drawing him out, listening to his stories, his difficulties in making the repayments to the bank for the loan he'd taken to buy *Udat*, his anger at the shipping cartels. He provided a welcome anodyne to the black fissure of emptiness which had opened in her heart, the one that would never close.

And when he left, when the wake was over, the thanks given, she lay on her new bed in her new house and found ten young stars burning brightly at the back of her mind. *Iasius* had been right after all, hope was eternal.

*

For the next eighteen years *Oenone* floated passively within the B-ring where *Udat* had left it. The particles flowing around it were occasionally deluged with bursts of static, interacting with the gas giant's magnetosphere to stir the dust grains into aberrant patterns, looking like the spokes of a massive wheel. But for most of the time they obeyed the simpler laws of orbital mechanics, and whirled obediently around their gravitonic master without deviation. *Oenone* didn't care, both states were equally nourishing.

As soon as the blackhawk departed, the egg began to ingest the tides of mass and energy which washed over its shell. Elongating at first, then slowly bloating into two bulbs over the course of the first five months. One of these flattened out into the familiar voidhawk lens shape, the other remained globular, squatting at the centre of what would ultimately evolve into the bitek starship's lower hull. It extruded fine strands of organic conductor, which acted as an induction mechanism, picking up a strong electrical current from the magnetosphere to power the digestive organs inside. Ice grains and carbon dust, along with a host of other minerals, were sucked into pores dotting the shell and converted into thick protein-rich fluids to supply the multiplying cells within the main hull.

At the core of the nutrient-production globe, the zygote called Syrinx began to gestate inside a womb-analogue organ, supported by a cluster of haematopoiesis organs.

Human and voidhawk grew in union for a year, developing the bond that was unique even among Edenists. The memory fragments which had come from *Iasius*, the navigation and flight instincts it had imparted at the birth, became a common heritage. Throughout their lives they would always know exactly where the other was; flight trajectories and swallow manoeuvres were a joint intuitive choice.

Volscen arrived a year to the day after *Iasius*'s last flight, rendezvousing with the fledgeling voidhawk egg as it orbited contentedly amid the ring. *Oenone*'s nutrient-production globe disgorged the womb-analogue and its related organs in a neat package, which the *Volscen*'s crew retrieved.

Athene was waiting just inside the airlock as they brought the organ package on board. It was about the size of a human torso, a dark crinkled shell sprayed with rays of frost where liquids had frozen during its brief exposure to space. They started to melt as soon as it came into contact with the *Volscen*'s atmosphere, leaving little viscous puddles on the green composite decking.

Athene could sense the infant's mind inside, quietly cheerful, with a hint of expectancy. She searched through the background whispers of the affinity band for the insect-sentience of the package's controlling bitek processor, and ordered it to open.

It split apart into five segments like a fruit; fluids and mucus spilled out. At the centre was a milk-coloured sac connected to the organs with thick ropy cords, pulsing rhythmically. The infant was a dark shadow, stirring in agitation as the unaccustomed light shone on her. There was a gurgling sound as the package voided its amniotic fluid across the floor, and the sac began to deflate. The membrane peeled back.

Is she all right? *Oenone* asked anxiously. The mental tone reminded Athene of a wide-eyed ten-year-old.

She's just perfect, Sinon said gently.

Syrinx smiled up at the expectant adults peering down at her, and kicked her feet in the air.

Athene couldn't help but smile back down at the placid infant. It's all so much easier this way, she thought, at a year old they are much better able to cope with the transition; and there's no blood, no pain, almost as though we weren't meant to have them ourselves.

Breathe, Athene told the baby girl.

Syrinx spluttered on the gummy mass in her mouth and spat it out. With her affinity sensitivity opened to the full, Athene could feel the passage of the coolish air down into the baby's lungs. It was strange and uncomfortable, and the lights and colours were frightening after the pastel dream images of the rings which she was used to. Syrinx began to cry.

Crooning sympathy both mentally and verbally Athene unplugged the bitek umbilical from her navel, and lifted the baby out of the sac's slippery folds. Sinon hovered around her with a towel to wipe the girl down, radiating pride and concern. *Volscen*'s crew began to clear up the pulpy mess of the package, ready to dump it out of the airlock. Bouncing Syrinx on her arm, Athene moved down the corridor towards the lounge that was serving as a temporary nursery.

She's hungry, *Oenone* said. A thought which was vigorously echoed by Syrinx.

Stop fussing, Athene said. **She'll be fed once we've dressed her. And we've got another six to pick up yet. She's going to have to learn to take her turn.**

Syrinx let out a plaintive mental wail of protest.

'Oh, you are going to be a bonny handful, aren't you?'

*

She was, but then so were all of her nine siblings as well. The house Athene had taken was a circular one, consisting of a single-storey ring of rooms surrounding a central courtyard. Its walls were polyp, and its curved roof was a single sheet of transparent composite which could be opaqued as required. It had been grown to order by a retired captain two hundred years previously when arches and curves were the fashion, and there wasn't a flat surface anywhere.

The valley it sat in was typical of Romulus's interior, with low, rolling sides, lush tropical vegetation, a stream feeding a series of lakes. Small, colourful birds glided through the branches of the old vine-webbed trees, and the air was rich with the scent of the flower cascades. It resembled a wilderness paradise, conjuring up images of the pre-industrial Amazon forests, but like all the Edenist habitats every square centimetre was meticulously planned and maintained.

Syrinx and her brothers and sisters had the run of it as soon as they learnt to toddle. Nothing harmful could happen to children (or anybody else) with the habitat personality watching the entire interior the whole of the time. Athene and Sinon had help, of course, both human nursery workers and the housechimps, monkey-derived bitek servitors. But even so, it was exhausting work.

As she grew up it was obvious that Syrinx had inherited her mother's auburn hair and slightly oriental jade eyes; from her father she got her height and reach. Neither parent claimed responsibility for her impetuosity. Sinon was terribly careful not to display any public favouritism, though the whole brood soon learnt to their creative advantage that he could never say no or stay cross with his daughter for long.

When she was five years old the whispers in her sleep began.

It was Romulus who was responsible for her education, not *Oenone.* The habitat personality acted as her teacher, directing a steady stream of information into her sleeping brain; the process was interactive, allowing the habitat to quiz her silently and repeat anything which hadn't been fully assimilated the first time. She learnt about the difference between Edenists and Adamists, those humans who had the affinity gene and those who didn't, the 'originals', whose DNA was geneered but not expanded. The flood of knowledge sparked an equally impressive curiosity. Romulus didn't mind, it had infinite patience with all its half-million-strong population.

This difference seems silly to me, she confided to *Oenone* one night as she lay in her bed. **The Adamists could all have affinity if they wanted to. It must be horrible to be so alone in your head. I couldn't live without you.**

If people don't want to do something, you shouldn't force them, *Oenone* replied.

For a moment they shared the vista of the rings. That night *Oenone* was orbiting high above the dayside of the saffron gas giant planet; it loomed through the misty particle drifts, a two-thirds crescent which always held her entranced. Sometimes she seemed to spend the whole night watching the colossal cloud armies at war.

It's still silly of them, she insisted.

One day we will visit Adamist worlds, then we'll understand.

I wish we could go now. I wish you were big enough.

Soon, Syrinx.

For ever.

I'm thirty-five metres broad now. The particles have been thick this month. Just another thirteen years.

Double for ever, the six-year-old replied brokenly.

Edenism was supposed to be a completely egalitarian society. Everybody had a share in its financial, technical, and industrial resources, everybody (thanks to affinity) had a voice in the consensus which was their government. But in all the Saturn habitats the voidhawk captains formed a distinct stratum of their own, fortune's favourites. There was no animosity from the other children, neither the habitat personality nor the adults would tolerate that, and animosity couldn't be hidden with communal affinity. But there was a certain amount of manoeuvring; after all, the captains would one day choose their own crews from the people they could get on with. The inevitable childhood groups which formed did so around the cub captains.

By the time she was eight, Syrinx was the best swimmer out of all her siblings, her long spidery limbs giving her an unbeatable advantage over the others in the water. The group of children she led spent most of their time playing around the streams and lakes of the valley, either swimming or building rafts and canoes. This was around the time they discovered how to fox Romulus's constant surveillance, misusing affinity to generate loitering phantasms in the sensor cells which covered every exposed polyp surface.

When they were nine years old she challenged her brother Thetis to an evasion race as a way of testing their new-found powers. Both teams of children set off on their precarious rafts, gliding down the stream out of the valley. Syrinx and her juvenile cohorts made it all the way down to the big salt-water reservoir which ringed the base of the southern endcap. That was where their punts became useless in the hundred-metre depth; and so there they drifted in happy conspiracy until the axial light-tube dimmed before responding to the increasingly frantic affinity calls from their parents.

You shouldn't have done it, *Oenone* chided solemnly that evening. **You didn't have any life jackets.**

But it was fun. And we had a real zing of a ride back in the Hydro Department officer's boat. It was so fast, there was spray and wind and everything.

I'm going to speak to Romulus about your moral responsibility

traits. I don't think they integrated properly. Athene and Sinon were very worried, you know.

You knew I was all right; so Mother must have known as well.

There is such a thing as propriety.

I know. I'm sorry, really. I'll be nice to Mother and Father tomorrow, promise. She rolled over onto her back, pulling the duvet a little tighter. The ceiling was transparent, and she could just make out the dim silverish moon-glow of the habitat's light-tube through the clouds. **I imagined it was you I was riding on, not just a stupid raft.**

Did you?

Yes. There was that unique flash of oneness as their thoughts kissed at every level of consciousness.

You're just trying to gain my sympathy, *Oenone* accused.

Course I am. That's what makes me me. Am I really horrible, do you think?

I think I will be glad when you're older, and more responsible.

I'm sorry. No more raft rides. Honest. She giggled. **It was still heaps of fun, though.**

Sinon died when the children were eleven; he was a hundred and sixty-eight. Syrinx cried for days, even though he had done his best to prepare the children. 'I'll always remain with you,' he told the dejected group when they gathered round his bed. Syrinx and Pomona had picked fresh angel-trumpets from the garden to be put into vases beside the bed. 'We have continuity, us Edenists. I'll be a part of the habitat personality, I'll see what you're all up to, and we can talk whenever you want. So don't be sad, and don't be frightened. Death isn't something to be afraid of, not for us.' **And I want to watch you grow up and start your captaincy,** he told Syrinx privately. **You're going to be the best captain ever, Sly-minx, you see.** She gave him a tentative smile, and then hugged his frail form, feeling the hot, sweaty skin, and hearing in her mind his inner wince as he shifted his position.

That night she and *Oenone* listened to his memories as they fled his decaying brain, a bewildering discharge of images and smells and emotional triggers. That was when she first found out about the nagging worry he held about *Oenone*, the tiny shred of doubt which persisted about the voidhawk's unusual co-parent. His concern hanging in the darkened bedroom like one of the phantasms she bamboozled the habitat receptor cells with.

See, Sly-minx, I told you I'd never desert you. Not you.

She smiled into the empty air as his distinctive mental tone sounded in her head. Nobody else ever called her that, only Daddy. There was a curious background burble, as if a thousand people were all holding whispered conversations somewhere far behind him.

But the next morning, the sight of his body wrapped in a white shroud being carried out of the house to be buried in the habitat's arbour was too much for her, and the tears began.

'How long will he live for in the habitat multiplicity?' she asked Athene after the short burial ceremony.

'As long as he wants,' Athene said slowly. She never lied to any of the children, but there were times when she wished she wasn't so damn noble. 'Most people retain their integrity for about a couple of centuries within the multiplicity, then they just gradually blend in to the overall habitat personality. So even then they don't vanish completely. But at that, it's a lot better than any heavenly salvation which Adamist religions offer their followers.'

Tell me about religion, Syrinx asked the habitat personality later that day. She was sitting at the bottom of the garden, watching fast bronze-coloured fish sliding through the big stone-lined lily pond.

It is an organized form of deity worship, usually originating in primitive cultures. Most religions perceive God as male, because they all have their roots in a time prior to female emancipation – which serves to illustrate how contrived they are.

But people still follow them today?

A majority of Adamists retain their faith, yes. There are several religions current in their culture, notably the Christian and Muslim sects. Both convey the belief that holy prophets walked the Earth at some time in the past, and both promise a form of eternal salvation for those who adhere to the teachings of said prophets.

Oh. Why don't Edenists believe, then?

Our culture proscribes nothing providing it doesn't harm the majority. You may, if you wish, practise the worship of any god. The major reason no Edenist chooses this action is that we have extremely stable personalities. We can look at the whole concept of God and spirituality from a vantage point built on logic and physics. Under such an intensive scientific scrutiny, religion always fails. Our knowledge of quantum cosmology is now sufficiently advanced to eliminate the notion of God altogether. The universe is an entirely natural phenomenon, if extraordinarily complex. It was not created by an external act of will.

So we don't have souls?

The concept of soul is as flawed as that of religion. Pagan priests preyed on people's fear of death by promising them there was an afterlife in which they would be rewarded if they lived a good life. Therefore belief in your soul is also an individual choice. However, as Edenists have continuation through becoming part of a habitat personality, no Edenists have required this particular aspect of faith. Edenists know their existence does not end with physical death. We have, to some extent, superseded religion thanks to the mechanics of our culture.

But what about you? Do you have a soul?

No. My mentality is, after all, the summation of individual Edenists. Nor was I ever one of God's creatures. I am entirely artificial.

But you're alive.

Yes.

So if there were souls, you'd have one.

I concede your argument. Do you think there are souls?

Not really. It seems a bit silly. But I can see how Adamists believe

in it so easily. If I didn't have the option of transferring my memories into a habitat, I'd want to believe I had a soul, too.

An excellent observation. It was the memory transfer ability which resulted in the mass excommunication of Christian Edenists by Pope Eleanor in 2090. When our founder Wing-Tsit Chong became the first human to transfer his memories into a habitat neural stratum, the Pope denounced his action as sacrilegious, an attempt to avoid divine judgement. Subsequently the affinity gene was declared to be a violation of divine heritage; the Vatican was afraid it placed too great a temptation before the devout. An Islamic proclamation was issued along similar lines a year later, proscribing the faithful from having the gene sequenced into their children. It was the start of the divergence between Edenist and Adamist culture, and also effectively ended Adamist use of bitek. Without affinity control, bitek organisms have little practical use.

But you said there are lots of different religions; how can there be many gods? There can't be more than one Creator, surely? That's a contradiction.

A good point. Several of the largest wars Earth has known have been fought over this issue. All religions claim theirs is the true faith. In actuality, any religion is dependent solely on the strength of conviction in its followers.

Syrinx gave up, and rested her head in her hands as she watched the fish scuttle under the big pink water lilies. It all sounded highly unlikely to her.

What about you? she asked *Oenone.* **Are you religious?**

I don't see the need to pray to an unseen deity for anything. I know what I am. I know why I am. You humans seem to delight in building your own complications.

Syrinx stood up, smoothing down her black mourning dress. The fish dived for deep cover at the sudden movement. **Thanks a bunch.**

I love you, *Oenone* said. **I'm sorry you're upset over Sinon. He made you happy. That's good.**

I won't cry any more, she told herself, Daddy's there whenever I want to talk to him. There, that must mean I've got a properly integrated personality. So that's all right.

If only it didn't hurt so much deep inside her chest, about where her heart was.

*

By the time she reached fifteen, her education was concentrating on subjects necessary for captaining a ship. Engineering and power systems, Confederation space law, astrogration, bitek life-support organs, mechanics, fluid behaviours, superconductivity, thermodynamics, fusion physics. She and *Oenone* listened to long lectures on the abilities and limits of voidhawks. There were practical lessons too, how to use spacesuits, practising fidgety repairs in low gravity, and acclimatization trips to the voidhawk ledges outside. Running through shipboard routines.

She was perfectly at home in free fall. Floating balance was geneered into all Edenists, and the hundred families went further with their manipulation, toughening and thickening internal membranes to withstand high-gee acceleration. Edenists were loath to use nanonic-supplement boosting unless there was no alternative.

By her mid-teens she was losing her puppy fat (not that she'd ever had much to start with) and beginning to acquire her definitive adult features. The carefully modified genes of her ancestors had bestowed her with a long face that had slightly sunken cheeks, emphasizing strong bones, and a wide mouth which could deliver a dazzling smile whenever she chose. She was as tall as most of her brothers, and her figure was filling out to her complete satisfaction. At this time she had grown her hair halfway down her back, knowing she would never have the opportunity again: when she started operational flying it would have to be cut short. Long hair was at best a nuisance and at worst a hazard in a starship.

When she was seventeen she had a month-long affaire with Aulie, who was forty-four, which made it doomed from the start, which made it *so* romantic. She enjoyed her time with Aulie unashamedly, as much for the mild censure and gossip it generated among her friends and family as the new styles of euphoria she experienced under his knowledgeable tuition. Now he was someone who *really* knew how to exploit free fall.

Teenage Edenist sexuality was one of the most talked about and envied legends among their Adamist counterparts. Edenists didn't need to worry about disease, not with their immunology systems; and affinity ensured that there were no problems of jealousy, or even possessive domination. Honest lust was nothing to be ashamed of, it was a natural aspect of teenage hormones on the boil, and there was also ample room for genuine one-to-one attraction. So given that even trainee captains only had five hours of practical engineering and technology lessons each day, and by their mid-teens Edenists needed at most six hours' sleep per night, the rest of the time was spent pursuing orgasmic release in a manner which would have impressed even the Romans.

*

Then her eighteenth birthday came around. Syrinx almost couldn't bring herself to leave the house that morning. Athene had worn her usual cheerful face, emotions hidden beyond even the most sensitive prying. But Syrinx knew exactly how much the sight of all ten children preparing to go hurt her. She had hung back after the formal breakfast, but Athene had shooed her out of the kitchen with a brief kiss. 'It's the price we all pay,' she said. 'And believe me, it's worth it.'

Syrinx and her siblings suited up and walked out onto the innermost ledge of the northern endcap, progressing with long lopes in the quarter gravity. There were a lot of people milling around outside the airlocks, service personnel, the crews of voidhawks currently perched on pedestals, All of them were eagerly awaiting the arrival of the newest voidhawks. The swirl of expectancy from them and other Edenists in the habitat caught her by surprise, but at least it helped quell her own nerves.

I'm the one that should be nervous, *Oenone* protested.

Why? All this comes naturally to you.

Ha!

Are you ready?

We could wait a little longer, see if I grow some more.

You haven't grown for two months. And you're quite big enough already.

Yes, Syrinx, the starship said, so meekly that she had to smile.

Come on, remember I was apprehensive with Hazat. That turned out to be fantastic.

I hardly think you can compare sex with spaceflight. And I wouldn't call that apprehension, more like impatience. There was a tone of pique in the mental voice.

Syrinx put her hands on her hips. **Get on with it.**

Oenone had been steadily absorbing electricity from the nutrient-production globe for the last month; with its growth phase finally complete the demand on the induction pick-off cables by the globe's organs had fallen off sharply, allowing the starship to begin the long powering-up process of its patterning cells. Now the energy levels were high enough to initiate a distortion field, which would enable it to suck power directly out of space. If it didn't get the distortion field right the cells would power down, and a rescue mission would have to be launched. In the past such missions hadn't always been a hundred per cent successful.

With Syrinx's pride and encouragement bolstering its mind, *Oenone* started to separate from the nutrient-producing globe. Fibrous tubes tore along their stress lines. Warm fluids squirted into space, acting like crude rocket engines, adding to the pressure on the remaining tubes. Organic conductors snapped and sealed, their ends whipping back and forth in the expanding cloud of vaporized fluid. The final tube broke, and the globe lurched away like a punctured balloon.

See? Easy, Syrinx said. The two of them were remembering together, reviewing the miragelike memories of a voidhawk called *Iasius.* To generate a distortion field you just had to trigger the initial energy flash through the patterning cells like *so.* Energy began to flow inside the labyrinthine honeycomb of patterning cells, compressing, the density building towards infinity in mere nanoseconds.

The distortion field flared outwards, billowing wildly.

Steady, Syrinx instructed gently. The field's fluctuations began to damp down. It changed shape, becoming more stable, twisting the radiation of local space into a viable stream. The patterning cells began to absorb it. There was a heavenly sensation of satisfaction gusting out to the stars.

Yes! We did it. They embraced mentally. Congratulations were flung at them from Edenists and voidhawks alike. Syrinx searched round to see that all her siblings and their craft had generated stable distortion fields. As if Athene's children would fail!

Together *Oenone* and Syrinx began to experiment, changing the shape of the field, altering its strength. The voidhawk began to move, rising up out of the rings, into clear space, seeing the stars unencumbered for the first time. Syrinx thought she could feel the wind blowing in her face, ruffling her hair. She was some ancient mariner standing on the wooden deck of her sailing ship, speeding across an endless ocean.

Three hours later *Oenone* slipped into the gap between Romulus's northern endcap and the counter-rotating dock. It began to curve round, racing after the ledge.

Syrinx saw it expand from nowhere out of the spinning starfield. **I can see you!** It had been *so* long.

And I you, *Oenone* replied lovingly.

She jumped for joy, legs sending her flying three metres above the ledge.

Careful, *Oenone* said.

Syrinx just laughed.

It slid in over the edge, and hovered above the pedestal closest to her. When it settled she began to glide-run towards it, whooping exuberantly, arms windmilling for balance. *Oenone*'s smooth midnight-blue hull was marbled by a fine purple web.

4

The Ruin Ring formed a slim dense halo three kilometres thick, seventy kilometres broad, orbiting five hundred and eighty thousand kilometres above the gas giant Mirchusko. Its albedo was dismayingly low; most of the constituent particles were a dowdy grey. A haze of small particles could be found up to a hundred kilometres outside the main band in the ecliptic plane; dust mainly, flung out from collisions between larger particles. Such meagre dimensions made the Ruin Ring totally insignificant on a purely astronomical scale. However, the effect it had on the course of human events was profound. Its existence alone managed to bring the richest kingdom in history to the verge of political chaos, as well as posing the Confederation's scientific community the greatest mystery it had ever known, one which remained unsolved a hundred and ninety years after its discovery.

It could so easily have gone unnoticed by the Royal Kulu Navy scoutship *Ethlyn*, which investigated the system in 2420. But system survey missions are too expensive to mount for the crew to skimp on detail even though it is obvious there is no terracompatible planet orbiting the star, and naval captains are chosen for their conscientious nature.

The robot probe which *Ethlyn* fired into orbit around Mirchusko performed standard reconnaissance fly-bys of the seven moons above a hundred and fifty kilometres in diameter (anything smaller was classed as an asteroid), then moved on to analyse the two rings encircling the gas giant. There was nothing extraordinary or even interesting about the innermost: twenty thousand kilometres broad, orbiting three hundred and seventy thousand kilometres out, the usual conglomeration of ice and carbon and rocky dust. But the outer ring had some strange spectrographic lines, and it occupied an unusually high orbit. *Ethlyn*'s planetary science officer raised the probe's orbit for a closer look.

When the achromatic pictures relayed from the probe's optical sensors began to resolve, all activity on board the *Ethlyn* came to an abrupt halt as the crew abandoned their routine to assess the scene. The ring which had the mass of a modestly sized moon was composed entirely of shattered xenoc habitats. *Ethlyn* immediately deployed every robot probe in its inventory to search the rest of the system, with depressingly negative results. There were no other habitats, no survivors. Subsequent searches by the small fleet of Kulu research ships which followed also produced a resounding blank. Neither could any trace of the xenoc race's homeworld be found. They hadn't originated on any planet in the Ruin Ring's system, nor had they come from any of the surrounding stars. Their origin and death were a complete enigma.

The builders of the wrecked habitats were called the Laymil, though even the name wasn't discovered for another sixty-seven years. It might seem that the sheer quantity of remnants would provide archaeologists and xenoc investigators with a superabundance of research material. But the destruction of the estimated seventy thousand plus habitats had been ferocious, and it had happened two thousand four hundred years previously. After the initial near-simultaneous detonation a cascade of secondary collisions had begun, a chain reaction lasting for decades, with gravel and boulders pulverizing large shell sections, setting off another round of collisions. Explosive decompression tore apart the living cells of plants and animals, leaving already badly eviscerated corpses to be decimated still further by the punishing sleet of jagged fragments. And even after a relative calm fell a century later, there was the relentless chafing of the vacuum, boiling surface molecules away one by one until only phantom-thin outlines of the original shape were left.

In another thousand years the decay would have precluded almost any investigation into the Laymil. As it was, the retrieval of useful artefacts was a dangerous, frustrating, and generally poorly rewarded task. The Laymil research project, based in Tranquillity, a custom-grown bitek habitat orbiting seven thousand kilometres above the Ruin Ring, depended on scavengers to do the dirty work.

The scavengers who ventured into the Ruin Ring were driven by a variety of reasons; some (mostly the younger ones) thought it was adventurous, some did it because they had no choice, for some it was a last resort gamble. But all of them kept going in the hope of that one elusive Big Find. Intact Laymil artefacts raised huge prices on the collector's market: there was a limited and diminishing source of unique alien *objets*, and museums and private collectors were desperate to obtain them.

There existed no prospecting technology which could sift through the Ruin Ring particles and identify the gems amid the dross; scavengers had to don their spacesuits and get out there amid the hurtling shell splinters and go through it all one piece at a time, using hands and eyeballs. Most of them earned enough from what they found to keep going. Some were better at it than others. Luck, they called it. They were the ones who found a couple of the more intriguing pieces each year, items which would tide them over in high style for months at a time. Some were exceptionally lucky, returning time and again with pieces the collectors and research project simply had to have. And some were suspiciously lucky.

*

If pressed, Joshua Calvert would have to admit membership of the second category, though it would be a self-deprecating acknowledgement. He had pulled six decent pieces out of the Ring in the last eight months; a pair of reasonably intact plants, a couple of circuit boards (fragile but OK), half of a rodentlike animal, and the big one, an intact egg, seven centimetres high. Altogether they had brought in three-quarters of a million fuseodollars (the Edenist currency, used as a base currency by the Confederation as a whole). For most scavengers that would have been enough to retire on. Back in Tranquillity people were shaking their heads and wondering why he kept returning to the Ring. Joshua was twenty-one, and that much money could keep him in a satisfactorily high-rolling style for life.

They wondered because they couldn't feel the intense need burning in him, surging down every vein like a living current, animating each cell. If they had known about that tidal-force drive they might have had an inkling of the unquiet nature lurking predator-fashion behind his endearing grin and boyish looks. He wanted one hell of a lot more than three-quarters of a million. In fact it was going to take nearer five million before he was anywhere near satisfied.

Living in a high-rolling style wasn't even an option as far as he was concerned. A life spent doing nothing but keeping a careful eye on your monthly budget, everything you did limited by the dividends of prudent investments? That sounded like living death to him, suspended inanimation, strictly loser's territory.

Joshua knew just how much more to life there could be. His body was perfectly adapted to handle free fall, a combination of useful physiological traits geneered into his family by wanderlust ancestors long distant. But it was just a consort to his mind, which was hardwired into the most riotous human trait, the hunger for new frontiers. He had spent his early childhood listening to his father telling and retelling stories of his own captaincy: the smuggling flights, outsmarting Confederation

Navy squadrons, the fights, hiring out as mercenary warriors to governments and corporations with a grudge, of travelling the universe at will, strange planets, fanciful xenocs, willing women in ports scattered across the colonized galaxy. There wasn't a planet or moon or asteroid settlement in the Confederation they hadn't explored and populated with fanciful societies before the old man finally found the combination of drugs and alcohol which could penetrate the beleaguered defences of his enhanced organs. Every night since he was four years old Joshua had dreamed that life for himself. The life Marcus Calvert had blown, condemning his son to sit out his own existence in a habitat on the edge of nowhere. Unless . . .

Five million Edenist fuseodollars, the price of repairing his father's starship – although admittedly it might even cost more, the shape old *Lady Mac* was in after so many years of neglect. Of leaving bloody boring backward Tranquillity. Of having a real life, free and independent.

Scavenging offered him a realistic way, an alternative to indenturing his soul to the banks. That money was out here in the Ruin Ring, waiting for him to pick it up. He could feel the Laymil artefacts calling to him, a gentle insistent prickling at the back of his conscious mind.

Some called it luck.

Joshua didn't call it anything. But he knew nine times out of ten when he was going to strike. And this time was it. He had been in the Ring for nine days now, nudging cautiously through the unending grey blizzard gusting outside the spaceplane's windscreen, looking at shell fragments and discarding them. Moving on. The Laymil habitats were remarkably similar to Tranquillity and the Edenist habitats, biologically engineered polyp cylinders, although at fifty kilometres long and twenty in diameter they were fatter than the human designs. Proof that technological solutions were the same the universe over. Proof that the Laymil were, at that level at least, a perfectly ordinary spacefaring race. And giving absolutely no hint of the reason behind their abrupt end. All their wondrous habitats had been destroyed within the period of a few hours. There were only two possible explanations for that: mass suicide, or a weapon. Neither option sat comfortably in the mind; they opened up too many dark speculations, especially among the scavengers who immersed themselves in the Ruin Ring, constantly surrounding themselves with the physical reality of that terrifying unknowable day over two and a half thousand years ago. A third option was the favourite speculation of scavengers. Joshua had never thought of one.

Eighty metres ahead of him was a habitat shell section, one of the larger ones; roughly oval, two hundred and fifty metres at its widest. It was spinning slowly about its long axis, taking seventeen hours to complete each revolution. One side was the biscuit-coloured outer crust, a tough envelope of silicon similar to Adamist starship hulls. The xenoc researchers back in Tranquillity couldn't work out whether or not it was secreted by the habitat's internal polyp layers; if so then Laymil biological engineering was even more advanced than Edenism's bitek. Stacked above the silicon were various strata of polyp, forty-five metres thick, dulled and darkened by vacuum exposure. Sitting on top of the polyp was a seam of soil six metres deep, frozen and fused into a concrete-hard clay. Whatever vegetation had once grown here had been ripped away when the habitat split open, grass and trees torn out by the roots as typhoons spun and roared for a few brief seconds on their way to oblivion. Every square centimetre of surface was pockmarked by tiny impact craters from the millennia-long bombardment of Ring gravel and dust.

Joshua studied it thoughtfully through the gritty mist of particles blurring its outlines. In the three years he had been scavenging he'd seen hundreds of shell fragments just like it, barren and inert. But this one had something, he knew it.

He switched his retinal implants to their highest resolution, narrowed the focus, and scanned the soil surface back and forth. His neural nanonics built up a cartographic image pixel by pixel.

There were foundations sticking up out of the soil. The Laymil used a rigidly geometric architecture for their buildings, all flat planes and right angles, No one had ever found a curving wall. This outline was no different, but if the floorplan was anything to go by it was larger than any of the domestic residences he had explored.

Joshua cancelled the cartographic image, and datavised an instruction into the spaceplane's flight computer. Reaction-control-thruster clusters in the tail squeezed out hot streams of ions, and the sleek craft began to nose in towards the foundations. He slipped out of the pilot's seat where he'd been strapped for the last five hours, and stretched elaborately before making his way out of the cockpit into the main cabin.

When the spaceplane was being employed in its designed role of a starship's ground to orbit shuttle the cabin was fitted with fifteen seats. Now he was using it purely to ferry himself between Tranquillity and the Ruin Ring, he had stripped them out, utilizing the space for a jury-rigged free-fall shower, a galley, and an anti-atrophy gym unit. Even with a geneered physique he needed some form of exercise; muscles wouldn't waste away in free fall, but they would weaken.

He started to take off his ship's one-piece. His body was slim and well muscled, the chest slightly broader than average, pointers to the thickened internal membranes, and a metabolism which refused to let him bloat no matter how much he ate or drank. His family's geneering had concentrated purely on the practicalities of free-fall adaptation, so he was left with a face that was rather too angular, the jaw too prominent, to be classically handsome, and mouse-brown hair which he kept longer than he ought to for flying. His retinal implants were the same colour as the original irises: blue-grey.

Once he was naked he used the tube to pee in before putting on his spacesuit, managing to avoid any painful knocks while he pulled the suit equipment from various lockers. The cabin was only six metres long, and there were too many awkward corners in too little space. Every movement seemed to set something moving, food wrappers he'd misplaced flapping about like giant silver butterflies and crumbs imitating bee swarms. When he got back to port he would have to have a serious cleaning session, the spaceplane's life-support filters really weren't designed to cope with so much crap.

In its inactive state the Lunar State Industrial Institute (SII) programmable amorphous silicon spacesuit consisted of a thick collar seven centimetres high with an integral respirator tube, and a black football-sized globe attached to the bottom. Joshua slipped the collar round his neck, and bit the end of the tube, chewing his lips round until it was comfortable. When he was ready he let go of the handhold, making sure he wasn't touching anything, and datavised an activation code into the suit's control processor.

The SII spacesuit had been the astronautics industry standard since before Joshua was born. Developed by the Confederation's only pure Communist nation, it was produced in the Lunar city factories and under licence by nearly every industrialized star system. It insulated human skin perfectly against the hostile vacuum, permitted sweat transpiration, and protected the wearer from reasonably high radiation levels. It also gave complete freedom of motion.

The globe began to change shape, turning to oil and flowing over him, clinging to his skin like a tacky rubber glove. He closed his eyes as it slithered over his head. Optical sensors studding the collar section datavised an image directly into his neural nanonics.

The armour which went on top of his new shiny-black skin was a dull monobonded-carbon exoskeleton with a built-in cold-gas manoeuvring pack, capable of withstanding virtually any kinetic impact the Ruin Ring would shoot at him. The SII suit wouldn't puncture, no matter what struck him, but it would transmit any physical knock. He ran both suit and armour checklists again while he clipped tools to his belt. Both fully functional.

When he emerged into the Ruin Ring the first thing he did was datavise a codelock order to the outer hatch. The airlock chamber was unprotected against particle bombardment, and there were some relatively delicate systems inside. It was a thousand to one chance, but five or six scavengers disappeared in the Ring each year. He knew some scavengers and even starship crews who had grown blasé about procedures, always moaning at Confederation Astronautics Board operational safety requirements. More losers, probably with a deep death-wish.

He didn't have to worry about the rest of the spaceplane. With its wings retracted, it was a streamlined fifteen-metre needle, designed to take up as little room in a starship's hangar as possible. Its carbotanium fuselage was tough, but for working the Ruin Ring he had coated it with a thick layer of cream-coloured foam. There were several dozen long score lines etched into it, as well as some small blackened craters.

Joshua orientated himself to face the shell section, and fired the manoeuvring pack's gas jets. The spaceplane began to shrink behind him. Out here in deep space the sleek shape seemed completely incongruous, but it had been the only craft he could use. Seven additional reaction-mass tanks and five high-capacity electron-matrix cells were strapped around the tail, also covered in foam, looking like some kind of bizarre cancerous growths.

The detritus of the Ruin Ring drifted unhurriedly around him, a slow-tempo snowstorm, averaging two or three particles per cubic metre. Most of it was soil and polyp, brittle, petrified chips. They brushed against the armour, some bouncing off, some fragmenting.

There were other objects too, twisted scraps of metal, ice crystals, smooth rounded pebbles, lengths of cabling gradually flexing. None of them had any colour; the F3 star was one-point-seven-billion kilometres away, too distant to produce anything other than a pallid monochrome even with the sensors' amplification. Mirchusko was just visible, a bleached, weary, green bulk, misted over like a dawn sun behind a band of cloud.

Whenever Joshua went EVA it was always the absolute quiet which got to him. In the spaceplane there was never any silence; the hums and whines of the life support, sudden *snaps* from the thruster-nozzle linings as they expanded and contracted, gurgles from the makeshift water lines. They were constant reassuring companions. But out here there was nothing. The suit skin clogged his ears, muffling even the sound of his own breathing. If he concentrated he could just make out his heartbeat, waves breaking on a very distant shore. He had to battle against the sense of smothering, the universe contracting.

There was something drifting in amongst the particles, a long feather-shape. He shifted the suit sensors' focus, glad of the diversion. It was a complete bough from a tree, about five metres away on his left. The forked branches were the palest grey, tapering down to small twigs laden with long triangular leaves; the end which had broken away from the trunk was barbed with narrow blades of wood.

Joshua datavised an order into the manoeuvring pack, and curved round to catch the bough. When he reached it he closed his gauntleted hand around the middle. It was like trying to grasp a sculpture of sun-baked sand. The wood crumbled below his fingers, dissociating into minute flakes. Tremors ran along the branches, shaking the origami leaves as if they were in a breeze. He caught himself listening for the dry rustle, then he was suddenly in the heart of an expanding cloud of ash. He watched it for a long regretful moment before unclipping the slim sampler box from his belt in a reflex action, and swatting a few of the flakes.

The gas jets fired, agitating the cloud, and he emerged into a clearer section of space. The shell section was twenty metres away. For a disconcerting moment it looked like solid ground, and he was falling towards it. He shut down the collar sensor input for half a second, redefining his visual orientation in his mind. When the image came back, the shell section was a vertical cliff face, and he was flying towards it horizontally. Much better.

The soil was in shadow, although no part of the shell section was truly black, there was too much scattered light from Mirchusko for that. He could clearly see the foundations now, walls of black glass, snapped off a metre above the frozen quagmire of lustreless soil. The largest room had some kind of mosaic flooring, and a quarter of the small tiles were still in place. He halted seven metres from the darkened shell surface, and slid sideways. When he switched on the armour suit's lights, white spot beams picked out an elaborate pattern of green, scarlet, and mauve tiles. From where he was it looked almost like a giant eight-taloned claw. Rivulets of water had solidified over it. They sparkled in the twin beams.

Joshua assigned the image a file code, storing it in an empty neural nanonic memory cell. The mosaic would bring in about thirty thousand fuseodollars, he guessed, if he could chip the hundreds of tiles out without breaking them. Unlikely. And the water, or whatever, would have to be scraped or evaporated away first. Risky. Even if he did work out a suitable method, it would probably take at least a week. That couldn't have been the siren call he'd heard with his mind.

The gas jets burped again.

He began to build up a picture of the edifice as he glided over the stumpy walls: it was definitely a public building of some description. The room with the tile floor was probably a reception hall; there were five equally spaced gaps in one wall which suggested entrance doors. Corridors led off from the other three walls, each with ten small rooms on either side. There was a T-junction at the end of each of them, more corridors, more side rooms. Offices? There was no way of telling, nothing had been left when the building took flight, whirling off into space. But if it were a human building, he would call them offices.

Like most scavengers, Joshua thought he knew the Laymil well enough to build up a working image. In his mind they weren't so much different from humans. Weird shape, trisymmetric: three arms, three legs, three stumpy serpentlike sensor heads, standing slightly shorter than a man. Strange biochemistry: there were three sexes, one female egg-carrier, two male sperm-carriers. But essentially human in basic motivation; they ate and shitted, and had kids, and built machines, and put together a technological civilization, probably even cursed their boss and went for a drink after work. All perfectly normal until that one day when they encountered something they couldn't handle. Something which either had the power to destroy them in a couple of hours, or make them destroy themselves.

Joshua shivered inside the perfectly regulated environment of the SII suit. Too much time in the Ruin Ring could do that, set a man to brooding. So call the cramped square rooms offices, and think what happens in human offices. Over-paid intransigent bureaucrats endlessly shuffling data.

Central data-storage system!

Joshua halted his aimless meander around the serrated foundations and flew in close to the nearest office. Low, craggy black walls marked out a square five metres to a side. He got to within two metres of the floor and stopped, hanging parallel to it. Gas from the manoeuvring jets coaxed little twisters of dust from the network of fine fissures lacing the rumpled polyp surface.

He started at a corner, switching the sensors to cover an area of half a square metre, then fired the jets to carry him sideways. His neural nanonics monitored the inertial guidance module in a peripheral mode, allowing him to give his full attention to the ancient polyp as the search navigation program carried him backwards and forwards across the floor, each sweep overlapping the last by five centimetres.

He had to keep reminding himself of scale, otherwise he might have been flying an atmosphere craft over a desert of leaden sand. Deep dry valleys were actually impact scratches, sludgy oases marked where mud particles had hit, kinetic energy melting them, only to re-freeze immediately.

A circular hole one centimetre in diameter. Expanded to fill half his vision. Metal glinted within, a spiral ramp leading down. Bolt hole. He found another one; this time the bolt was still inside, sheered off. Two more, both with snapped bolts. Then he found it. A hole four centimetres across. Frayed cable ends inside waved at him like seaweed fronds. The optical fibres were unmistakable, different tolerances to the Kulu Corporation standard he was used to but apart from that they could have been human made. A buried communication net, which must logically be linked with the central data-storage system. But where?

Joshua smiled around the respirator tube. The entrance hall gave access to every other part of the building, why not the maintenance ducts? It fell into place without even having to think. So obvious. Destiny, or something close. Laughter and excitement were vibrating his nerves. This was it, the Big Strike. His ticket out into the real universe. Back in Tranquillity, in the clubs and scavenger pubs, they would talk in envious respectful tones about Joshua and his strike for decades. He'd made it!

The datavised order he shot into the manoeuvring pack sent him backing away from the office's floor. His suit sensors clicked down the magnification scale, jumping his vision field back to normal in a lurching sequence of snapshots. The pack rotated him ninety degrees, pointing him at the mosaic, and he raced towards it, pale white ribbons of gas gushing from the jet nozzles.

That was when he saw it. An infrared blob swelling out of

the Ruin Ring. Impossible, but there it was. Another scavenger. And there was no way it could be a coincidence.

His initial surprise was replaced by a burst of dangerous anger. They must have tracked him here. It wouldn't have been particularly difficult, now he thought about it. All you needed was an orbit twenty kilometres above the Ring plane, where you could watch for the infrared signature of reaction drives as scavenger craft matched orbits with their chosen shell sections. You would need military-grade sensors, though, to see through all the gunk in the Ring. Which implied some pretty cold-blooded planning on someone's part. Someone determined in a way Joshua had never been. Someone who wouldn't shrink from eliminating the scavenger whose craft they intercepted.

The anger was beginning to give way to something colder.

Just how many scavengers had failed to return in the last few years?

He focused the collar sensors on the still-growing craft, and upped the magnification. Pink smear enveloped by brighter pink mist of the reaction-drive exhaust. But there was a rough outline. The standard twenty-metre-long hexagonal grid of an inter-orbit cargo tug, with a spherical life-support module on one end, tanks and power cells filling the rear cargo cradles, nesting round the reaction drive.

No two scavenger craft were the same. They were put together from whatever was available at the time, whatever components were cheapest. It helped with identification. Everyone knew their friends' ships, and Joshua recognized this one. The *Madeeir*, owned by Sam Neeves and Octal Sipika. Both of them were a lot older than him; they'd been scavengers for decades, one of the few two-man teams working the Ruin Ring.

Sam Neeves: a ruddy-faced jovial man, sixty-five years old now, with fluid retention adding considerable bulk to his torso due to the time he spent in free fall. His body wasn't geneered for long-term zero-gee exposure like Joshua's, he had to go in for a lot of internal nanonic supplements to compensate for the creeping atrophy. Joshua could remember pleasant evenings spent with Sam, back around the time he started out scavenging, eagerly listening to the older man's tips and tall stories. And more recently the admiration, being treated almost like a protégé made good. The not quite polite questions of how come he came up trumps so often. So many finds in such a short time. Exactly how much were they worth? If anyone else had tried prying like that he would have told them to piss off. But not Sam. You couldn't treat good old Sam like that.

Good old fucking Sam.

The *Madeeir* had matched velocities with the shell section. Its main reaction drive shut down, shimmering vapour veil dissipating. The image began to clarify, details filling in. There were small bursts of topaz flame from its thruster clusters, edging it in closer. It was already three hundred metres behind the spaceplane.

Joshua's manoeuvring pack fired, halting him above the mosaic, still in the shell's umbra.

His neural nanonics reported a localized communication-frequency carrier wave switching on, and he just managed to datavise a response prohibition order into his suit transponder beacon as the interrogation code was transmitted. They obviously couldn't see him just yet, but it wouldn't take long for their sensors to pinpoint his suit's infrared signature, not now they had shut down their reaction drive. He rotated so that his manoeuvring pack's thermo-dump fins were pointing at the shell, away from the *Madeeir*, then considered his options. A dash for the spaceplane? That would be heading towards them, making it even easier for their sensors. Hide round the back of the shell section? It would be putting off the inevitable, the suit's regenerator gills could scrub carbon dioxide from his breath for another ten days before its power cells needed recharging, but Sam and Octal would hunt him down eventually, they knew he couldn't afford to stray far from the spaceplane. Thank Christ the airlock was shut and codelocked; it would take time for them to break in however powerful their cutting equipment was.

'Joshua, old son, is that you?' Sam's datavise was muzzy with interference, ghostly whines and crackling caused by the static which crawled through the particles. 'Your transponder doesn't respond. Are you in trouble? Joshua? It's Sam. Are you OK?'

They wanted a location fix, they still hadn't seen him. But it wouldn't be long. He had to hide, get out of their sensor range, then he could decide what to do. He switched the suit sensors back to the mosaic floor behind him. The dendrite tendrils of ice cast occasional pinpoint sparkles as they reflected the *Madeeir*'s reaction-control-thruster flames. A coherent-microwave emission washed over him; radar wasn't much use in the Ruin Ring, the particles acted like old-fashioned chaff. To use a scanner which only had the remotest chance of spotting him showed just how serious they were. And for the first time in his life he felt real fear. It concentrated the mind to a fantastic degree.

'Joshua? Come on, Joshua, this is Sam. Where are you?'

The ribbons of frozen water spread across the tiles resembled a river tributary network. Joshua hurriedly accessed the visual file of his approach from his neural nanonics, studying the exact pattern. The grubby ice was thickest in one of the corners, a zone of peaks and clefts interspaced by valleys of impenetrable shadow. He cautiously ordered the manoeuvring pack to push him towards that corner, using the smallest gas release possible, always keeping the thermo-dump fins away from the *Madeeir*.

'Joshua, you're worrying us. Are you OK? Can we assist?'

The *Madeeir* was only a hundred metres away from the spaceplane now. Flames speared out from its thruster clusters, stabilizing its position. Joshua reached the rugged crystalline stalagmites rearing up a couple of metres from the floor. He was convinced he was right; the water had surged up here, escaping its pipes or tubing or whatever had carried it through subterranean depths. He grabbed one of the stalagmites, the armour's gauntlet slipping round alarmingly on the iron-hard ice until he killed his momentum.

Crawling around the tapering cones hunting for some kind of break in the shell was hard work, and slow. He had to brace himself firmly each time he moved a hand or leg. Even with the sensors' photonic reception increased to full sensitivity the floor obstinately refused to resolve. He was having to feel his way round, metre by metre, using the inertial guidance display to navigate to the centre, logically where the break should be. If there was one. If it led somewhere. If, if, if . . .

It took three agonizing minutes, expecting Sam's exuberant mocking laughter and the unbearable searing heat of a laser to lash out at any second, before he found a crevice deeper than his arm could reach. He explored the rim with his hands, letting his neural nanonics assemble a comprehensible picture from the tactile impressions. The visualization that materialized in his mind showed him a gash which was barely three metres long, forty centimetres wide, but definitely extending below the floor level. A way in, but too small for him to use.

His imagination was gibbering with images of the pursuit Sam and Octal were putting together behind him. Bubbling up from that strange core of conviction was the knowledge that he didn't have time to wriggle about looking for a wider gap. This was it, his one chance.

He levered himself back down to the widest part of the gash, and wedged himself securely between the puckered furrows of ice, then took the thermal inducer from his belt. It was a dark orange cylinder, twenty centimetres long, sculpted to fit neatly into his gauntleted hand. All scavengers used one: with its adjustable induction field it was a perfect tool for liberating items frozen into ice, or vacuum-welded to shell sections.

Joshua could feel his heart racing as he datavised the field profile he wanted into the inducer's processor, and ordered his neural nanonics to override his pacemaker, nulling the adrenalin's effect. He lined the thermal inducer up on the centre of the gap, took a deep breath, tensed his muscles, and initiated the program he'd loaded in his neural nanonics.

His armour suit's lights flooded the little glaciated valley with an intense white glare. He could see dark formless phantoms lurking within the murky ice. Pressure ridges that formed sheer planes refracted rainbow fans of light back at the collar sensors. A gash that sank deep into the shell section's interior, a depth hidden beyond even that intrusive light's ability to expose.

The thermal inducer switched on simultaneously with the lights, fluorescing a metre-wide shaft of ice into a hazy red tube. At the power level he used it turned from solid to liquid to gas in less than two seconds. A thick pillar of steam howled past him, blasting lumps of solid matter out into the Ruin Ring. He fought to keep his hold on the ice as the edge of the stream grazed the armour suit.

'See you, Joshua,' Sam's datavise echoed round his brain, laughing derisively.

The thermal inducer snapped off. A second later the rush of steam had abated enough to show him the tunnel it had cut, slick walls reflecting the suit's light like rippled chrome. It ended ten metres down in a polyp cave. Joshua spun round his centre of gravity, fists hammering into the still bubbling ice, clawing desperately for traction on the slippery surface as he dived head-first down the tunnel.

Madeir's laser struck the ice as his boots disappeared below the floor. Stalagmites blew apart instantly under the violent energy input, ice vaporized across an area three metres wide. A mushroom cloud of livid steam boiled up into space, carrying with it a wavefront of semi-solid debris. The laser shone like a shaft of red sunlight at its centre.

'Got the little shit!' Sam Neeves' triumphant exclamation rang in the ether.

The laser blinked out. Slush splattered against the spaceplane's foam-encased fuselage. A second later it reached the *Madeeir*, pattering weakly against the alithium struts. Reaction-control thrusters flamed momentarily, holding its position steady.

Once the storm of vapour had dwindled away, *Madeeir* refocused its sensor suite on the vibrating shell section. There was no ice left among the building's foundations, the scouring had plucked the tiles free as well, even some of the low-lying walls had been razed by the blast-wave of steam. A roughly circular patch of the polyp floor glowed a dull vermilion.

The sheer power of the laser saved Joshua. The soles of his armour suit had been caught in the initial blaze of photons, melting the mono-bonded-carbon boots, boring into the tough black membrane of the SII suit underneath. Even the miraculous Lunar technology couldn't withstand that assault. His skin had charred, broiling the meat, singeing bone.

But the steam which had erupted so violently absorbed a great deal of the laser's power. The seething gas also distorted the beam, and it didn't just surge outwards, it also slammed down through the tunnel, punching at any blockage.

Joshua hurtled out of the gash in the polyp cave's roof, cannoning into the floor, bouncing, arms flailing helplessly. He was almost unconscious from the pain in his feet, the analgesic block his neural nanonics had erected in his cortex was faltering under the nerve impulse overload. Blood was spraying out of his soles from the arteries which hadn't been cauterized by the heat. The SII suit redistributed its molecules, flowing around the roasted feet, sealing the broken blood vessels. He hit the cave roof, recoiling. His neural nanonic circuits were visualizing a physiological schematic of his body, an *écorché* figure with feet flashing urgent red. Neatly tabulated information that was neither sound nor vision was pulsing into his consciousness, telling him the extent of the wounds. He really didn't want to know, the gruesome details were acting like an emetic.

Steam was still gushing into the cave, building in pressure.

He could actually hear the gale screeching its affliction. Caustic probes of red light stabbed down through the gash in the ceiling, fluctuating erratically. He hit the polyp again, jarring his arm. The knocks and spinning and pain were too much; he vomited. The SII suit immediately vented the acidic fluid as his stomach spasmed. He cried out in anguish as the sour juices sloshed round in his mouth, rationality fading away. His neural nanonics recognized what was happening and damped down all external nerve inputs, ordered the suit processor to feed him a draught of cool, clear oxygen, then fired the manoeuvring pack jets at full power to stop his madcap oscillations.

The suspension couldn't have lasted more than ten seconds. When he took notice of the sensor visualization again the red light illuminating the cave had been extinguished, and the steam was rushing back out of the gap, currents tugging him gently back up towards it again. He reached out an arm to steady himself against the ceiling. His fingers closed automatically around a metal conduit pinned to the polyp.

Joshua did a fast double take, then began to scan the suit collar sensors round the cave. There were no ends in sight. It wasn't a cave, it was a passage, slightly curved. The conduit was one of twenty running along the ceiling. They had all broken open below the gash, a familiar feathery fan of ragged photonic cables protruded.

His neural nanonics were clamouring for attention, medical data insistent against his synapses. He reviewed it quickly, quashing the return of the nausea. His soles had burnt down to the bone. There were several options stored in the neural nanonics' medical program. He chose the simplest: shut-off for nerves below the knees, infusing a dose of antibiotics from the armour's emergency pack, and shunting a mild tranquillizer program into primary mode to calm his inflamed thoughts.

While he waited for the drugs to start working he took a more measured assessment of the passage. The polyp had ruptured in several places, water and a syrupy fluid had spouted in, freezing over the walls in long streaks, turning the passage into a winterland grotto. They were boiling now, crusty surface temporarily turned back to a liquid by the retreating steam, frothing like bad beer. When he shone the suit's lights into the rents he could see tubes running parallel to the passage; water ducts, nutrient arteries, sewage ducts – whatever, they were the habitat's utilities. Edenist habitats were riddled with similar channels.

He summoned up the inertial guidance display, and integrated the passage into the data construct of the shell section. If the curve was reasonably constant, one end would emerge from the section's edge after thirty metres. He started to move up the other way, watching the conduits. He didn't have anywhere else to go.

The passage branched, then branched again. One junction had five passages. Ice clogged a lot of the walls, bulging outward in smooth mounds. In several places it was virtually impassable. Once he had to use the thermal inducer again. The conduits were often buried under frosted waves. The destruction had been as great down here as it had everywhere else in the habitat. That should have warned him.

The hemispherical chamber might have held the central storage system for the offices above; there was no way of telling now. The conduits which had led him loyally this far all snaked in through an open archway, then split at the apex three metres over his head, running down the curving walls like silver ribs. There had been a great deal of electronic equipment in here at one time: slate-grey columns, a metre or so high, with radiator fins running down the outside, the equivalent of human processor-module stacks. Some of them were visible, badly vacuum eroded now, their fragile complex innards mashed beyond salvation, battered ends sticking out of the rubble. Nearly half of the ceiling had collapsed, and the resulting pile of polyp slivers had agglutinated in an alarmingly concave wall, as though the avalanche had halted half-way through. If gravity was ever reapplied here, the whole lot would come crashing down. Whatever force had rampaged through the chamber when the habitat broke apart had left total devastation in its wake.

Maybe it was deliberate, he mused, because it's certainly very thorough. Maybe they didn't want any records to survive?

The manoeuvring pack rotated him, allowing him to perform a complete survey. Over by the archway, a tongue of that viscous brownish fluid had crept in, stealing along the wall until the temperature drop congealed it into a translucent solid. A regular outline was just visible below the gritty surface.

He sailed over, trying to ignore the debilitating effect his maimed feet were having on the rest of his body. He had developed a splitting headache despite the tranquillizer program, and he'd caught his limbs trembling several times as he drifted along the passage. The neural nanonics had reported his core temperature dropping one degree. He suspected a form of mild shock was tightening its malicious grip. When he got back to the spaceplane he was going to have to use the medical nanonic packages to stabilize himself straight away. That brought a grin. When! He'd almost forgotten about Sam and Octal.

He was right about the frozen liquid, though. Up close, with the suit lights on full, he could make out the definite shape of one of the grey electronics pillars. It was in there waiting for him; waiting patiently for over two and a half thousand years, since the time Jesus was nailed to the cross on a primitive, ignorant Earth, immaculately preserved in grubby ice against the insidious decay so prevalent in the Ruin Ring. Every circuit chip, every memory crystal, just waiting for that first current of electrons to reawaken them. His Strike!

Now all he had to do was get it back to Tranquillity.

*

The communication band was devoid of human data traffic as he perched on the lip of the passage, and all his suit communication block could pick up was the usual background pop and fizz of Mirchusko's emissions. He'd experienced a strange kind of joy just seeing the Ruin Ring again after retracing his course down the passage. Hope had dwindled to that extent. But now he felt a stubborn determination rising up against the tranquillizer program muffling his mind.

It was impossible to see his spaceplane or the *Madeeir* from where he was, the passage lip was fourteen metres below the soil seam, a maggot hole in a sheer cliff face. Looking down he could see the ochre silicon envelope thirty-five metres below. And he still didn't like to think of the force it would take to snap something that thick the way he snapped biscuits.

This part of the shell surface was exposed to the sunlight, a pale lemon radiance, alive with flickering ever-changing shadows cast by the unceasing swarm of Ring particles. His inertial-guidance unit was projecting a course vector into his mind, a warm orange tube stretching out to vanishing point somewhere in the Ring ahead of him. He datavised the trajectory into the manoeuvring pack, and its jets pulsed, pushing him gently away from the passage, slipping silently down the imaginary tube.

He waited until he was a kilometre and a half from the cover of the shell section before changing direction, then headed out at a steep angle to his previous course, facing into the sun, nozzles firing continually, building velocity. What he was actually doing was raising his orbital altitude in respect to Mirchusko. A higher altitude would give him a longer orbital period. When he halted he was still in the same inclination as the *Madeeir* and the shell section, but five kilometres higher. In their lower, faster orbit, the ship and shell section began to overhaul him.

He couldn't even see them any more. Five kilometres of particles was as effective a shield as the output from a military electronic-warfare pod. The neural nanonics kept flashing up a graphic overlay for him, a small red circle around the shell section, his one tenuous link with salvation. He had never been so far from the spaceplane before, never been so achingly alone.

His armour suit's communication block began to pick up first scraps of datavised exchanges between Sam and Octal, unintelligible bursts of digital code with a curious echo effect. He was glad of the diversion, using his neural nanonics to try and decrypt the signals. His universe seemed to fill with numbers, galactic constellations of colourless digits, all twisting elusively as he loaded tracer program after tracer program, searching for a pattern.

'. . . no chance. It's built for landing security, no telling what'll . . . on a planet. A thermal inducer would just anneal the . . .' That was Octal's datavise, emitted from a suit block. It made sense, he was the younger, fifty-two; Sam would be sitting comfortably back in the *Madeeir* directing his junior to recover what they could from the spaceplane.

Joshua felt a shiver run down his ribcage. The cold of the gas giant's environment was reaching in through the SII suit to close around him.

Sam's datavise: '. . . the tail where the tanks . . . anything large would have to be . . .'

Octal's datavise: '. . . there now. I can see some kind of cradle he's . . . can't be for . . .'

They faded in and out, chattering, snarling at each other. Sam seemed certain that Joshua had picked something up. He listened to it in a waking daze as the *Madeeir* drifted past. Slowly, it was all happening in time stretched thin.

A lump of clear ice coasted past, as broad as his hand. There was a turquoise and orange fish inside, three eyes around a triangular beaklike mouth, staring ahead, as if it was somehow aware of its surroundings, swimming along its eternal migration path. He watched it dwindle away, too numb to try and collect it – gone for ever now.

He had virtually fallen asleep when the inertial-guidance program warned him he was now falling behind the *Madeeir.*

The manoeuvring-pack jets began to fire in a long, elaborate pattern, reducing his velocity and altitude again, sending him curving down behind the *Madeeir.*

Sam's datavise: '. . . response from the flight computer . . . photonic interface point . . .'

Octal's datavise: '. . . fission blade won't work, the fucking hatch is monobonded carbon, I'm telling you . . . Why don't you listen, arsehole . . .'

Sam's datavise: '. . . little shit . . . find his body . . . chew on his bones . . .'

The manoeuvring pack took Joshua behind the *Madeeir*, the ship a fuzzed pink outline a kilometre ahead of him. He could catch an intermittent view of it through the swirl of particles. Then he lowered his orbit again, a few hundred metres this time, and orbital mechanics reeled him in towards it with painful slowness.

His approach was conducted solely within its blind spot, a cone extending backwards from its reaction drive. All he had to do was keep the bulk of the engine bay between himself and the sensors protruding from the life-support module, and he would remain undetected, especially in the clutter of the Ruin Ring. He also had the advantage that they thought he was dead. They wouldn't be looking, not for anything as small as a suit.

The last hundred metres were the worst. A quick burst of speed, rushing headlong into the twin pits of the reaction-drive nozzles. If they started up now . . .

Joshua slid between the two fat bell-shapes, and anchored himself on the maze of thrust-distribution struts. The rockets were similar in principle to the engines in his spaceplane, though he didn't know the marque. A working fluid (usually a hydrocarbon) was pumped into an energizer chamber where it was heated to about seventy-five thousand degrees Kelvin by a colossal discharge from the power cells. It was a simple system, with few moving parts, little to go wrong, and cheap to maintain. Scavengers didn't need anything more, the delta-V you needed to travel between Tranquillity and the Ruin Ring was small. Joshua couldn't think of anyone who used a fusion drive.

He began to move around the gimbals, going hand over hand, careful not to jar his feet against anything. The power leads were easy to find, superconductor cables as thick as his arm. He fished round his belt for the fission knife. The ten-centimetre blade glowed a spectral yellow, unusually bright in the shade-soaked engine bay. It made short work of the cables.

Another quick climb brought him up against the hulking tanks. They were covered by a quilt of nultherm insulation blanket. He settled himself at the bottom of one tank, and stripped a patch of the insulation away. The tank itself was a smooth dull silver, merging seamlessly into the turbopump casing at its base. He jammed the thermal inducer into a support-strut joint, squirted on some epoxy to make sure it wouldn't slip, and datavised a series of orders into its processor.

*

Ten minutes later, the processor switched on the thermal-induction field. Joshua had programmed it to produce a narrow beam, ten centimetres wide, three metres long. Three-quarters of it was actually projected inside the tank, where it started to vaporize the hydrocarbon liquid. Frenzied currents churned, carrying more fluid into the field. Pressure built swiftly, rising to dangerous levels.

The metal shell of the tank wasn't quite so susceptible to the field. Its molecular structure retained cohesion for almost twenty seconds before the sheer quantity of heat concentrated into such a small area disrupted the valency bonds. The metal turned malleable and began to bulge outwards, impelled by the irresistible pressure mounting inside the tank.

In the *Madeeir*'s cramped cabin, Sam Neeves widened his eyes in horror as datavised alarms shrilled in his brain. Complex ship schematics unfurled across his consciousness, fuel sections a frantic red. Emergency safety programs sent a torrent of binary pulses into the engine bay. None of it made any difference to the rising pressure.

They were contingencies for malfunctions, he realized. This was something else, the tank was being subjected to a tremendous energy input. The trouble was external. Deliberate.

'Joshua!' he roared in helpless fury.

After operating for twenty-five seconds at maximum expenditure the thermal inducer's electron matrix was exhausted. The field shut down. But the damage had been done.

The protuberance swelling from the tank was glowing a brilliant coral-pink. Its apex burst open. A fountain of boiling gas streaked out, playing across the engine bay. Thermal blankets took flight, whirling away; composite structures and delicate electronics modules melted, sending out spumes of incendiary droplets. *Madeeir* lurched forward, slewing slowly around its long axis as the rocketlike thrust of the erupting tank shoved against the hull.

'Holy shit,' Sam Neeves spat. 'Octal! Octal, for Christ's sake get back here!'

'What's happening?'

'It's Joshua, he's fucked us. Get back here. The reaction control can't keep her stable.'

Even as he said it the guidance data pouring into his mind showed the thruster clusters losing the battle to hold the ship level. He tried to activate the main drive, the only engines with the strength to compensate for the rogue impulse of the ruptured fuel tank. Dead.

A neural nanonic medical monitor program overrode his pacemaker, calming his frightened heart. Adrenalin buzzed in his head.

Sensors and control linkages from the engine bay were failing at an unbelievable rate. Large areas of the schematic in his mind were an ominous black. The shell section loomed large in the forward sensors.

Joshua watched from behind the relative safety of a boulder

three hundred metres away. The *Madeeir* was starting to tumble like the universe's largest drumstick. Sparkly gas spewed out of one end, tracing a wavering arc through space.

'We're going to hit!' Sam Neeves datavised.

The *Madeeir* had already wobbled past the spaceplane, giving Joshua a nasty moment. Now it was careering towards the shell section. He held his breath.

It should have hit, he thought, it really should. But the rotation it had picked up saved it. *Madeeir* flipped over the edge of the polyp cliff as if it was on pivots, its life-support module no more than five metres from the surface. At that speed it would have been split open as though it was made of glass.

Joshua sighed as the gritty tension contracting every tendon drained away. They deserved death, but it would just have to wait now. He had other priorities. Like making sure he lived. At the back of his mind there was a phantom throbbing from his feet. His neural nanonics were reporting his blood was laced with toxins, probably some contamination from the burned flesh, too.

Madeeir raced onwards, deeper into the Ruin Ring. Already two hundred metres beyond the shell section. The plume of gas was visibly weaker.

A small pearl-white mote curved over the edge of the shell section, chasing after the ship. Octal, desperate not to be stranded alone with a spaceplane he couldn't open. If he'd stopped to think, he might have sabotaged Joshua's craft.

Be thankful for small mercies, Joshua told himself.

The manoeuvring pack lifted him from his hiding place behind the boulder. Its gas reserve was down to five per cent. Just enough to get back to the spaceplane. Although he would have found a way even if it was empty. Somehow. Today he was fortune's child.

5

Like a fool Quinn Dexter had been waiting for the jolt, a blink of cold emptiness which would tell him the voyage had actually taken place. It hadn't happened, of course. The crewman had tugged him into the coffin-sized zero-tau pod, one of thousands arranged in a three-dimensional lattice within the colonist-carrier starship's vast life-support capsule. Unfamiliar with free fall, and hating the disorientating giddiness every motion brought, Quinn had meekly allowed himself to be shoved about like he was so much cargo. The cortical-suppressor collar pinching his neck made any thoughts of escape a pitiful fantasy.

Right up until the moment the pod cover had hinged smoothly over him he refused to believe it was happening, clinging to the notion that Banneth would pull strings and get him off. Banneth was plugged into Govcentral's State of Canada administration as deep as a high magus in a virgin. One word, one nod of her head, and he would be free once more. But no. It hadn't happened. Quinn, it seemed, wasn't important enough. There were hundreds of eager waster boys and girls in the Edmonton arcology who even now would be vying to replace him, hungry for Banneth's attention, her bed and her smile, a place in the Light Bringer sect's hierarchy. Youths with verve, with more style than Quinn. Youths who would strut rather than sweat when they were carrying Banneth's cargo of weird persona-sequestrator nanonics into Edmonton. Who wouldn't be dumb enough to try and run when the police stopped them at the vac train station.

Even the police had thought Quinn was crazy for doing that, laughing as they hauled his twitching stunned body back to Edmonton's Justice Hall. The carton had self-destructed, of course, an internecine energy flare reducing the nanonics to indecipherable clusters of crumbling molecules. The police couldn't prove he was carrying anything illegal. But the charge of resisting arrest was good enough for the magistrate to slap an Involuntary Transport order on him.

Quinn had even tried giving the sect's sign to the crewman, the inverted cross, fingers squeezing so tight his knuckles had whitened. *Help me!* But the man hadn't noticed, or understood. Did they even have Light Brother sects out amongst the stars?

The pod cover closed.

Banneth didn't care about him, Quinn realized bitterly. God's Brother, after the loyalty he'd shown her! The atrocious sex she had demanded from him. 'My little Sunchild,' she had crooned as he penetrated and was penetrated. The pain he had pridefully endured at his initiation to become a sergeant acolyte. The weary hours spent on the most trivial sect business. Helping to recruit his own friends, betraying them to Banneth. Even his silence after he was arrested; the beating the police had given him. None of it meant shit to Banneth. *He* didn't mean shit to Banneth. That was wrong.

After years bumming round as an ordinary waster kid, it had taken the sect to show him what he really was, an animal, pure and simple. What they'd done to him, what they'd made him do to others, it was liberation, freeing the serpent beast which lurked in the soul of every man. Knowing his true self was glorious. Knowing that he had the power to do what he wanted to others, simply because he chose to. It was a magnificent way to live.

It made the lower ranks obey, out of fear, out of respect,

out of adoration. He was more than their chapter leader, he was their saviour. As Banneth was his.

But now Banneth had abandoned him, because Banneth thought him weak. Or perhaps because Banneth knew his true strength, the conviction he had in himself. There were few in the sect who were as committed to worshipping the Night as Quinn. Had she come to see him as a threat?

Yes. That was more likely. The true reason. Everyone feared him, his purity. And by God's Brother they were right to do so.

The pod cover opened.

'I'll get you,' Quinn Dexter whispered through clenched teeth. 'Whatever it takes, I'm coming after you.' He could see it then: Banneth violated with her own persona-sequestrator nanonics, the glittery black filaments worming their way through her cortex, infiltrating naked synapses with obscene eagerness. And Quinn would have the command codes, reducing mighty Banneth to a puppet made of flesh. But aware. Always aware of what she was being made to do. Yes!

'Oh, yeah?' a coarse voice sneered. 'Well, cop this, pal.'

Quinn felt a red-hot needle jab up his spine pressing in hard. He yelped more with shock than pain, his back convulsing frantically, pushing him out of the pod.

The laughing crewman grabbed him before he hit the mesh bulkhead three metres in front of the pod. It wasn't the same man that had put Quinn into the pod seconds before. Days before. Weeks . . .

God's Brother, Quinn thought, how long has it been? He gripped the mesh with sweaty fingers, pressing his forehead against the cool metal. They were still in free fall. His stomach oscillating like jelly.

'You going to put up a fight, Ivet?' the crewman asked.

Quinn shook his head weakly. 'No.' His arms were trembling at the memory of the pain. God's Brother, but it had hurt. He was frightened the neural blitz had damaged his implants. That would have been the final irony, to have got this far only for them to be broken. The two nanonic clusters the sect had given him were the best, high quality and very expensive. Both of them had passed undetected in the standard body scan the police had given him back on Earth. They had to, possessing the biolectric pattern-mimic cluster would have qualified him for immediate passage to a penal planet.

Being entrusted with it was another token of the sect's faith in him, in his abilities. Copying someone's biolectric pattern so he could use their credit disk inevitably meant having to dispose of them afterwards. Weaker members might shirk from the task. Not Quinn. He'd used it on over seventeen victims in the last five months.

A quick status check revealed both the nanonic clusters were still functional. God's Brother hadn't deserted him, not entirely.

'Smart boy. Come on, then.' The crewman grabbed Quinn's shoulder, and began to swim along the mesh with nonchalant flips of his free hand.

Most of the pods they passed were empty. Quinn could see the outlines of more pods on the other side of the mesh. The light was dim, casting long grey shadows. Looking round him he knew how a fly must feel crawling about inside an air-conditioning duct.

After the life-support module, there were a couple of long tubular corridors. Crewmen and colonists floated past. One family was clustered around a wailing four-year-old girl who clung to a grab hoop with a death-grip. Nothing her parents could say would make her let go.

They went through an airlock into a long cylindrical compartment with several hundred seats, nearly all of them occupied. Spaceplane, Quinn realized. He had left Earth on the Brazilian orbital tower, a ten-hour journey crammed into a lift capsule with twenty-five other Involuntary Transportees. It suddenly struck him he didn't even know where he was now, nothing had been said about his destination during his fifty-second hearing in front of the magistrate.

'Where are we?' he asked the crewman. 'What planet?'

The crewman gave him a funny look. 'Lalonde. Why, didn't they tell you?'

'No.'

'Oh. Well, you could have copped a worse one, believe me. Lalonde is EuroChristian-ethnic, opened up about thirty years ago. I think there's a Tyrathca settlement, but it's mainly humans. You'll do all right. But take my advice, don't get the Ivet supervisor pissed at you.'

'Right.' He was afraid to ask what a Tyrathca was. Some kind of xenoc, presumably. He shuddered at that, he who had never ventured out of the arcologies or vac-train stations back on Earth. Now they were expecting him to live under open skies with talking animals. God's Brother!

The crewman hauled Quinn down to the rear of the spaceplane, then took his collar off and told him to find a spare seat. There was a group of about twenty people sitting in the last section, most of them lads barely out of their teens, all with the same slate-grey one-piece jump suit he'd been issued with. IVT was printed in bright scarlet letters on their sleeves. Waster kids. Quinn could recognize them, it was like looking into a mirror which reflected the past. Him a year ago, before he joined the Light Brothers, before his life meant something.

Quinn approached them, fingers arranged casually in the inverted cross sign. Nobody responded. Ah well. He strapped himself in next to a man with a pale face and short-cropped ginger hair.

'Jackson Gael,' his neighbour said.

Quinn nodded numbly and muttered his own name. Jackson Gael looked about nineteen or twenty, with the kind of lean body and contemptuous air that marked him down as a street soldier, tough and uncomplicated. Quinn wondered idly what he had done to be transported.

The PA came on, and the pilot announced they would be undocking in three minutes. A chorus of whoops and cheers came from the colonists in the front seats. Someone started playing a mini-synth, the jolly tune grating on Quinn's nerves.

'Balls,' Jackson Gael said. 'Look at 'em, they want to go down there. They actually believe in that New Frontier crap the development company has peddled them. And we've got to spend the rest of our lives with these dickheads.'

'Not me,' Quinn said automatically.

'Yeah?' Jackson grinned. 'If you're rich how come you didn't bribe the captain, have him drop you off at Kulu or New California?'

'I'm not rich. But I'm not staying.'

'Yeah, right. After you finish your work-time you're gonna make it as some hotshot merchant. I believe you. Me, I'm gonna keep my head down. See if I can't get assigned to a farm for my work-time.' He winked. 'Some good-looking daughters in this batch. Lonely for them out there in their little wilderness homesteads. People like you and me, they start looking at us in a better light after a while. And if you ain't noticed yet, there ain't many Ivet fems.'

Quinn stared at him blankly. 'Work-time?'

'Yeah, work-time. Your sentence, man. Why, you think they were going to turn us loose once we hit the planet?'

'They didn't tell me anything,' Quinn said. He could feel the despair opening up inside him, a black gulf. Only now was he beginning to realize how ignorant of the universe outside the arcology he truly was.

'Man, you must've pissed someone off bad,' Jackson said. 'You get dumped on by a politico?'

'No.' Not a politician, somebody far worse, and infinitely subtler. He watched the last colonist family emerge from the airlock, it was the one with the terrified four-year-old girl. Her arms were wrapped tightly round her father's neck and she was still crying. 'So what do we do for work-time?'

'Well, once we get down there, you, me, and the other Ivets start doing ten years' hard labour. See, the Lalonde

Development Company paid for our passage from Earth, and now they want a return on that investment. So we spend the prime of our life shovelling shit for these colonists. Community maintenance, they call it. But basically we're a convict gang, Quinn, that's what we are; we build roads, clear trees, dig latrines. You name it, every crappy job the colonists need doing, we do it for them. Work where we're told, eat what we're given, wear what we're given, all for fifteen Lalonde francs a month, which is about five fuseodollars' worth. Welcome to pioneer paradise, Quinn.'

*

The McBoeing BDA-9008 spaceplane was a no-frills machine designed for operations on stage one agrarian planets; remote basic colonies where spare parts were limited, and maintenance crews were made up of wash-outs and inexperienced youngsters working their first contract. It was a sturdy delta shape built in a New Californian asteroid settlement, seventy-five metres long, with a wingspan of sixty metres; there were no ports for the passengers, just a single curving transparent strip for the pilot. A fuselage of thermal-resistant boron-beryllium alloy glinted a dull oyster in the sharp light of the F-type star a hundred and thirty-two million kilometres away.

Faint jets of dusty gas spurted out of the airlock chamber as the seal disengaged. Docking latches withdrew into the bulk of the starship, leaving the spaceplane floating free.

The pilot fired the reaction-control thrusters, moving away from the seamless curve of the huge starship's hull. From a distance the McBoeing resembled a moth retreating from a football. When they were five hundred metres apart, a second, longer, burn from the thrusters sent the spaceplane curving down towards the waiting planet.

Lalonde was a world which barely qualified as terracompatible. With a small axial tilt and uncomfortable proximity to its bright primary, the planet's climate was predominantly hot and humid, a perennial tropical summer. Out of its six continents only Amarisk in the southern hemisphere had been opened for settlement by the development company. Humans couldn't venture into the equatorial zone without temperature-regulated suits. The one, northern, polar continent, Wyman, was subject to severe storms as the hot and cool air fronts clashed around its edges all year long. Shrivelled ice-caps covered less than a fifth of the area normal for terracompatible planets.

The spaceplane sliced cleanly down through the atmosphere, its leading edges glowing a dull cerise. Ocean rolled past below it, a placid azure expanse dotted with volcanic island chains and tiny coral atolls. Pristine clouds boiled across nearly half of the visible surface, generated by the relentless heat. Barely a day went by anywhere on Lalonde without some form of rain. It was one of the reasons the development company had managed to attract funding; the regular heat and moisture was an ideal climate for certain types of plants, rewarding the farmer colonists with vigorous growth and high yields.

By the time the McBoeing dropped to subsonic velocity it had fallen below the vast cloudband sweeping in towards Amarisk's western coast. The continent ahead covered over eight million square kilometres, stretching from the flood plains of the western coast to a long range of fold mountains in the east. Under the midday sun it glared a brilliant emerald, jungle country, broken by huge steppes in the south where the temperature dropped towards subtropical.

Beneath the spaceplane the sea was stained with mud, a grubby brown blemish extending for seventy to eighty kilometres out from the boggy shore. It marked the mouth of the Juliffe, a river whose main course stretched just under two thousand kilometres inland, way into the foothills guarding the eastern coast. The river's tributary network was extensive enough to rival Earth's Amazon. For that reason alone, the development company had chosen its southern bank as the site of the planet's capital (and sole) city, Durringham.

The McBoeing passed low over the coastal swamps, lowering its undercarriage, bullet-shaped nose lining up on the runway thirty kilometres ahead. Lalonde's only spaceport was situated five kilometres outside Durringham, a clearing hacked out of the jungle containing a single prefabricated metal grid runway, a flight-control centre, and ten hangars made from sun-bleached ezystak panels.

The spaceplane touched down with tyres squealing, greasy smoke shooting up as the flight computer applied the brakes. The nose lowered, and it rolled to a halt, then started to taxi back towards the hangars.

*

An alien world. A new beginning. Gerald Skibbow emerged from the stuffy atmosphere of the spaceplane's cabin, looking about with reverence. Just seeing the solid picket of raw jungle bubbling around the spaceport's perimeter he knew he'd done the right thing coming here. He hugged his wife, Loren, as they started down the stairs.

'Damn, will you look at that! Trees, real bloody trees. Millions of them. Trillions of them! A whole bloody world of them.' He breathed in deep. It wasn't quite what he'd expected. The air here was solid enough to cut with a knife, and sweat was erupting all over his olive-green jump suit. There was a smell, vaguely sulphurous, of something rotting. But by damn it was natural air; air that wasn't laced with seven centuries of industrial pollutants. And that's what really counted. Lalonde was dreamland made real, unspoilt, a world on which the kids could make anything come true just by working at it.

Marie was following him down the stairs, her pretty face registering a slight sulk, nose all crinkled up at the scent of the jungle. Even that didn't bother him; she was seventeen, nothing in life was right when you were seventeen. Give her two years, she'd grow out of it.

His eldest daughter, Paula, who was nineteen, was staring

round appreciatively. Her new husband, Frank Kava, stood beside her with his arm protectively round her shoulder, smiling at the vista. The two of them sharing the moment of realization, making it special. Now Frank had what it took, a perfect son-in-law. He wasn't afraid of hard work. Any homestead with Frank as a partner was bound to prosper.

The apron in front of the hangar was made from compacted rock chips, with puddles everywhere. Six harried Lalonde Development Company officers were collecting the passengers' registration cards at the bottom of the steps, running them through processor blocks. Once the data was verified, each immigrant was handed a Lalonde citizenship card and an LDC credit disk with their Govcentral funds converted to Lalonde francs, a closed currency, no good anywhere else in the Confederation. Gerald had known that would happen; he had a Jovian Bank credit disk stashed in an inner pocket, carrying three and a half thousand fuseodollars. He nodded thanks as he received his new card and disk, and the officer directed him towards the cavernous hangar.

'You'd think they'd be a bit better organized,' Loren muttered, cheeks puffed against the heat. It had taken fifteen minutes' queueing before they got their new cards.

'Want to go back already?' Gerald teased. He was holding up his citizenship card, grinning at it.

'No, you wouldn't come with me.' The eyes smiled, but the tone lacked conviction.

Gerald didn't notice.

In the hangar they joined the waiting passengers from an earlier spaceplane flight, where the LDC officer collectively labelled them Transient Group Seven. A manager from the Land Allocation Office told them there was a boat scheduled to take them upriver to their allocated settlement land in two days. They would be sleeping in a transients' dormitory in Durringham until it departed. And they'd have to walk into town, though she promised a bus for the smaller children.

'Dad!' Marie hissed through her teeth as the groans rose from the crowd.

'What? You haven't got legs? You spent half the time at your day club in the gym.'

'That was muscle toning,' she said. 'Not forced labour in a sauna.'

'Get used to it.'

Marie almost started to answer back, but caught the look in his eye. She exchanged a slightly worried glance with her mother, then shrugged acceptance. 'OK.'

'What about our gear?' someone asked the manager.

'The Ivets will unload it from the spaceplane,' she said. 'We've got a lorry ready to take it into town, it'll go straight onto the boat with you.'

After the colonists started their march into town a couple of the spaceport ground crew marshalled Quinn and the other Involuntary Transportees into a work party. So his first experience of Lalonde was spending two hours lugging sealed composite containers out of a spaceplane's cargo hold, and stacking them on lorries. It was heavy work, and the Ivets stripped down to their shorts; it didn't seem to make a lot of difference to Quinn, sweat appeared to have consolidated into a permanent layer on his skin. One of the ground crew told them that Lalonde's gravity was fractionally less than Earth standard; he couldn't feel that, either.

About quarter of an hour into the job he noticed the ground crew had all slunk back into the shade of the hangar. Nobody was bothering with the Ivets.

Two more McBoeing BDA-9008s landed, bringing another batch of colonists down from the orbiting starship. One spaceplane took off, ferrying LDC personnel up to the empty berths; they were going home, their contract time expired. He stopped to watch the big dark delta-shape soar into the sky, dwindling away to the east. The sight laced his thoughts with vicious envy. And still nobody was paying him any attention. He could run, here and now, away into that awesome expanse of untamed land beyond the perimeter. But the spaceport was the place where he wanted to run *to*, and he could well imagine how the homesteaders would treat fugitive Ivets. He might have been stupid enough to be Transported, but he wasn't that naïve. Cursing softly under his breath, he hauled another composite box full of carpentry tools out of the McBoeing's hold and carried it over to the lorry.

By the time the Ivets finished the unloading and began their long trudge into Durringham the clouds from the west had arrived bringing a warm, persistent rain. Quinn wasn't surprised to find his grey jump suit turned out not to be waterproof.

*

The Lalonde Immigration Registration Department manager's office was in an administration block grafted onto the spaceport's flight-control centre. A long rectangular flat roof structure of ezystak panels clipped onto a metal frame. It had been assembled twenty-five years previously when the first colonists arrived, and its austere fittings were showing their age.

Lalonde didn't even rate programmed-silicon constructs for its administration buildings, Darcy thought bleakly; at least the Lunar-built structures had some concessions to comfortable living. If ever a colony project was funded on the cheap, it was Lalonde. But the office did have air-conditioning, powered from solar cells. The temperature was appreciably lower than outside, though the humidity remained constant.

He sat on the settee working his way through the registration cards which the latest batch of arrivals had handed over in exchange for their citizenship and LDC credit disks. The starship had brought five and a half thousand people from Earth; five and a half thousand losers, dreamers, and criminals let loose to wreck another planet in the name of noble destiny. After sixty years in the Edenist Intelligence agency, Darcy couldn't think of Adamists in any other terms. And they claim they're the normal ones, he thought wryly, give me ungodly freakishness every time.

He entered another card's memory into his processor block, glancing briefly at the hologram. A fairly handsome twenty-year-old man, face composed, eyes haunted with fear and hatred. Quinn Dexter, an Involuntary Transportee. The processor block balanced on his lap didn't respond to the name.

The card was tossed onto the growing pile. Darcy picked up another.

'Something you never told me,' Nico Frihagen said from behind his desk. 'Who are you people looking for?'

Darcy looked up. Nico Frihagen was Lalonde's Immigration Registrar, a grand title for what was essentially a clerk working in the Governor's Civil Administration Division. He was in his late fifties, dourly Slavic in appearance, with rolling jowls and limp receding hair. Darcy suspected his ancestors had had very little to do with geneering. The slobbish civil servant was drinking beer from a tube, an offworld brand, no doubt pilfered from some unsuspecting arrival's farmsteading gear. Spaceport staff had a nice racket going ripping off the new colonists. Nico Frihagen was an essential segment of the scam; a list of belongings was included on the colonists' registration cards.

That readiness to jam his nose in the trough made the registrar an ideal contact for the Edenist operatives. For a straight five hundred fuseodollars a month, Darcy and his partner, Lori, ran through the new immigrants' identification without having to access the colony's civic data store.

Details on the immigrants were sparse, the Lalonde Development Company didn't really care who settled the planet as long as they paid their passage and land registration fee. The company wouldn't declare a dividend for another century yet, when the population had grown above a hundred million and an industrial economy was rising to replace the agrarian beginnings. Planets were always very long term investments. But

Darcy and Lori kept ploughing through the data. Routine procedure. Besides, someone might get careless.

'Why do you want to know? Has somebody been showing an interest?' Lori asked, sitting at the other end of the settee from Darcy. A seventy-three-year-old woman with plain auburn hair and a round face, she looked about half of Nico Frihagen's age. Like Darcy she lacked the distinctive height of most Edenists, which made both of them ideal for deep cover work.

'No.' Nico Frihagen gestured with the beer tube. 'But you've been doing this for three years now, hell probably for three years before that for all I know. It's not just the money, that doesn't mean much to you people. No, it's the time you spend. That's got to mean you're searching for someone important.'

'Not really,' Lori said. 'It's a type of person we're after, not a specific individual.'

Good enough, Darcy told her silently.

Let's hope he's satisfied with it, she replied.

Nico Frihagen took a swig of beer. 'What type?'

Darcy held up his personal processor block. 'The profile is loaded in here, available on a need to know basis. Do you think you need to know, Nico?'

'No. I just wondered. There have been rumours, that's all.'

'What sort of rumours, Nico?'

Nico Frihagen gazed out of the office's window, watching an Ivet team unloading a McBoeing BDA-9008. 'Upriver. Some settlers vanished, a couple of homesteads up in Schuster County. The sheriffs couldn't find any trace of them, no sign of a struggle, no bodies; just empty houses.'

Where the heck is Schuster County? Lori asked.

Darcy queried the bitek processor in his block; a map of the Juliffe's tributary basin bloomed in his mind. Schuster County glowed a soft amber, a sprawling area, roughly rectangular, clinging to the side of the Quallheim River, one of the hundreds of tributaries. **Like Nico said, way upriver. Over a thousand kilometres; it's an area they're just opening up for settlement.**

It could be some kind of big animal. A kroclion, or even something the ecological analysis crew didn't find.

Maybe. Darcy couldn't bring himself to believe that. 'So what was the rumour about it, Nico? What are people saying?'

'Not much, not many people know. The Governor wanted it kept quiet, he was worried about stirring up trouble with the Tyrathca farmers, there's a group of them on the other side of the savannah which borders Schuster County. He thought they'd get the blame, so the county sheriff hasn't made an official report. The homesteads have been listed as abandoned.'

'When did this happen?' Lori asked.

'Couple of weeks back.'

Not much to go on, Lori said.

It's remote enough. The kind of area he'd go to.

I concede that. But what would he want with some hick farmers?

Insufficient data.

Are we going to go and check?

Check what? That the homesteads are empty? We can't go gallivanting off into the jungle over a couple of families who have broken their settlement contract. Goodness, if you stuck me out there in the middle of nowhere, I'd want to run away.

I still say it's odd. If they had been ordinary malcontents, the local sheriff would have known about it.

Yes. But even if we did go, it would take us two or three weeks to reach Schuster County. That means the trail would be well over a month old and cold. How good are you at tracking trails like that through a jungle?

We could take Abraham and Catlin out of zero-tau, use them to scout the area.

Darcy weighed up the options. Abraham and Catlin, their eagles, had enhanced senses, but even so sending them off without even a reasonable idea of where their quarry might be was pointless. They could spend half a year covering Schuster County alone. If they had more operatives he might have sanctioned it, but not with just the two of them. Covering

Lalonde's immigrants was a long shot, acting on one piece of dubious information nearly forty years old: that Laton had bought a copy of the original ecological assessment team's report. Chasing off into the hinterlands was completely out of the question.

No, he said reluctantly. **We'll keep them for when we have a definite scent. But there's a voidhawk due from Jospool in a month, I'll ask the captain for a complete survey of Schuster County.**

OK, you're the boss.

He sent the mental image of a grin. They had worked together for too long for rank to be anything other than nominal between them.

'Thanks for mentioning this,' Darcy told Nico Frihagen.

'It was useful?'

'Could be. We'll certainly show our appreciation.'

'Thank you.' Nico Frihagen smiled thinly and took another gulp of beer.

He is a disgusting oaf, Lori said.

'We'd be even more grateful if you let us know of any more disappearances,' Darcy said.

Nico Frihagen cocked his beer tube in his direction. 'Do my best.'

Darcy picked up another registration card. The name Marie Skibbow was printed along the top; an attractive teenage girl smiled rebelliously at him from her hologram. Her parents were in for a few years of hell, he decided. Outside the grimy window, thick grey clouds were massing on the western horizon.

*

The road linking Durringham to the spaceport was a broad strip of pinkish rock chippings slicing straight through the thick jungle. Father Horst Elwes marched towards the capital as best he could with his swelling feet rubbing what felt suspiciously like blisters on both heels. He kept a cautionary eye on the clouds accumulating above the gently waving treetops, hoping the rain would hold off until he made it to the transients' dormitory.

Thin spires of steam drifted out of the chippings around his feet. The narrow gorge between the trees seemed to act as a lens for the sun, and the heat was awesome. A carpet of bushy grass was besieging the edge of the road. Vegetation on Lalonde certainly was vigorous. Birdsong filled the air, a resonant chittering. That would be the chikrows, he thought, reviewing the didactic memory of local conditions which the Church had given him before he left Earth. About the size of a terran pheasant, with bright scarlet plumage. Eatable, but not recommended, the artificial memory informed him.

There wasn't much traffic on the road. Battered lorries rumbling to and from the spaceport, carrying wooden crates and ancient-looking composite cargo-pods, some loaded up with homesteading gear. The spaceport crews riding power bikes with broad, deep-tread tyres, tooting their horns as they sped past, the men shouting at the girls. Several horse-drawn carts trundled by. Horst stared with unashamed delight at the big creatures. He'd never visited his arcology's zoo back on Earth. How strange that the first time he should meet them was on a planet over three hundred light-years from their birthworld. And how could they stand the heat with such thick coats?

There were five hundred members in Group Seven, of which he was included. They had all started off down the road in a tightly packed group following the LDC officer, chattering brightly. Now, after a couple of kilometres, they had become well spread out, and subdued. Horst was close to the rear. His joints were already creaking in protest, and the need for a drink was rising sharply. Yet the air was so moist. Most of the men had shrugged out of their jump suit tops and T-shirts, tying the arms around their waist. So too had several of the women. He noticed that all the locals on power bikes were in shorts and thin shirts; so was the LDC officer leading them, come to that.

He stopped, surprised by the amount of blood pounding away in his cheeks, and gave the seal catch at his neck a full ninety-degree twist. The front of his jump suit split open to reveal his thin powder-blue T-shirt, stained a shade deeper by sweat. The lightweight silk-smooth garment might be ideal for shipboard use, and even in an arcology, but for dealing with raw nature it was ridiculous. Somebody must have got their communication channels fouled up. Surely colonists hadn't been arriving dressed like this for twenty-five years?

A little girl, about ten or eleven years old, was looking up at him. She had that miniature angel's face of all young children, with straight shoulder-length white-blonde hair, gathered into two pony-tails by small red cords. He was surprised to see she was wearing sturdy ankle-length hiker boots, along with baggy yellow shorts and a small white cotton top. A wide-brimmed green felt hat was tilted back sharply. Horst found himself smiling down at her automatically.

'Hello, there. Shouldn't you have got on the bus back at the spaceport?' he asked.

Her face screwed up in indignation. 'I'm not a baby!'

'I never said you were. But you could have fooled the development company officer into giving you that lift. I would have done it, if I had the chance.'

Her eyes darted to the white crucifix on his T-shirt sleeve. 'But you're a priest.'

'Father Horst Elwes, *your* priest, if you are in Group Seven.'

'Yes, I am. But claiming a lift would have been dishonest,' she persisted.

'It would have been sensible. And I'm sure Jesus would understand.'

She grinned at that, which made the day seem even brighter to Horst.

'You're nothing like Father Varhoos back home.'

'Is that good?'

'Oh, yes.' She nodded vigorously.

'Where's your family?'

'There's only me and Mother.' The girl pointed to a woman who was walking towards them. She was in her mid-thirties, a strong face with the same fair hair as her daughter. Her robust figure made Horst sigh for what could never be. Not that the Unified Christian Church forbade its priests from marrying, far from it, but even in his prime, twenty years ago, he had been curved in most directions. Now he was what his kinder colleagues described as cuddly, and that was after treating every calorie like an invading virus.

Her name was Ruth Hilton, she told him briskly, and her daughter was Jay. There was no mention of a husband or boyfriend. The three of them started walking down the road together.

'It's nice to see someone was thinking along practical lines,' Horst said. 'A fine band of pioneers we turned out to be.' Ruth was also dressed for the heat, with shorts, cloth hat, and a sleeveless vest; her boots were larger versions of Jay's. She was carrying a well-loaded rucksack; and her broad leather belt had several devices clipped on to it. Horst didn't recognize any of them.

'This is a tropical planet, Father. Didn't the Church give you a generalist didactic memory of Lalonde before you left?' Ruth asked.

'Yes. But I hardly expected to be undertaking a route march the minute we arrived. By my personal timetable, it's only been fifteen hours since I left the arcology abbey.'

'This is a stage one colony,' Ruth said, without any sympathy. 'You think they're going to have the time or the inclination to wet-nurse five thousand arcology dwellers who have never seen the open sky before? Do me a favour!'

'I still think we might have been given some warning. Perhaps a chance to change into more appropriate clothing.'

'You should have carried it with you in the zero-tau pod. That's what I did. There's an allowance for up to twenty kilos of personal luggage in the passage contract.'

'The Church paid for my passage,' Horst answered carefully. He could see Ruth had what it took to survive in this new, demanding world; but she would have to learn to soften her somewhat mercenary attitude or he could imagine himself trying to calm a lynch mob. He forbade a grin. Now that would be a true test of my ability.

'Know what your problem is, Father?' Ruth asked. 'Too much faith.'

Quite the contrary, Horst thought, I have nowhere near enough. Which is why I'm here in the remotest part of the human dominion, where I can do little or no harm. Though the bishop was far too kind to put it like that.

'What do you intend doing when we reach our destination?' he asked. 'Farming? Fishing in the Juliffe, perhaps?'

'Not likely! We'll be self-sufficient, of course, I brought enough seeds for that. But I'm a qualified didactic assessor.' She grinned roguishly. 'I'm going to be the village schoolmarm. Probably the county schoolmarm, seeing the scraploose way this place is put together. I've got a laser imprinter and every educational course you can think of stored in here.' She patted the rucksack. 'Jay and I are going to be able to write our own ticket with that. You wouldn't believe the things you're going to need to know once we're dumped in the middle of nowhere.'

'I expect you're right,' he said without much enthusiasm. Were all the other colonists experiencing the subtle feeling of doubt now they were facing the daunting physical reality of Lalonde? He looked round at the people nearest to him. They were all plodding along lethargically. A gorgeous teenage girl trudged past, face down, lips set in grim misery. Her jump suit top was tied round her waist; she was wearing a tangerine scoop-neck T-shirt underneath, revealing plenty of smooth skin that was coated in sweat and dust. A silent martyr, Horst decided; he had seen the type often enough when he put in a stint at his arcology's refuge. None of the males nearby paid her the slightest attention.

'You bet I am,' Ruth boomed irrepressibly. 'Take shoes, now. You probably brought two or three pairs, right?'

'Two pairs of boots, yes.'

'Smart. But they're not going to last five years in the jungle, no matter what fancy composite they're made out of. After that you make your own. And for that you come to me for a course in cobbling.'

'I see. You have thought this out, haven't you?'

'Wouldn't be here if I hadn't.'

Jay smiled up at her mother with complete adoration.

'Isn't an imprinter rather heavy to be lugging about?' Horst asked curiously.

Ruth guffawed loudly, and ran the back of her hand across her brow in a theatrical motion. 'Sure is. But it's valuable, especially the newest technical courses, stuff this planet's never heard of. I'm not about to leave that in the hands of the spaceport crew. No way, no how.'

A chill of alarm slithered through Horst. 'You don't think . . .'

'I'm bloody sure they are. It's what I'd do.'

'Why didn't you say something back there?' he demanded in exasperation. 'I have reading primer books in my container, medicines, communion wine. Some of us could have remained with it for security.'

'Listen, Father, I'm not aiming to be mayor of this group, I'll leave that to some hulking macho male, thank you. And I can't see myself being applauded for standing up in front of that manager woman and saying we should stay behind to stop her friends from stealing our gear. Would you have done that, you with your goodwill to all men?'

'Not publicly, no,' Horst said. 'But there are ways.'

'Well, start thinking of them, because those precious containers of ours are going to be left piled up in a warehouse in town for the next couple of days before we set sail. And we're going to need what's inside them, and I really do mean *need*; because anyone who thinks that all it takes to survive out there is determination and honest toil is in for the shock of their pampered lives.'

'Do you always have to be right about absolutely everything?'

'Listen, you're here to look after our souls, Father. You'll be good at that, I can see, you're the caring type. Deep down, anyway. But keeping my soul connected to my body, that's all down to me. And I intend to do the best job I can.'

'All right,' he said. 'It might be a good idea for me to speak with some of our group this evening. Perhaps we could organize some kind of watch at the warehouse.'

'Wouldn't be a bad idea to see if we can acquire replacements for anything that's gone walkabout, as well. There's bound to be other groups' gear stored with ours, it shouldn't be too difficult.'

'Alternatively, we could go to the Sheriff's office, and ask them to find anything that's been stolen from us,' Horst said forcibly.

Ruth laughed out loud.

They walked on in silence for several minutes.

'Ruth?' he asked eventually. 'Why have you come here?'

She exchanged a mournful glance with Jay, the two of them suddenly vulnerable. 'I'm running away,' she said. 'Aren't you?'

*

Durringham had been founded in 2582, a couple of (Earth) years after the Confederation inspection team had confirmed the results of the land venture company's ecological analysis crew, agreeing that Lalonde had no biota exceptionally hazardous to humans – a certificate which was vital for any planet seeking to attract colonists. The hiatus was due to the venture company (which had bought the settlement rights from the scoutship which discovered the planet) attracting partners, and turning itself into the Lalonde Development Company. With enough financial backing to establish a working spaceport and provide a minimal level of civil administration, as well as securing an agreement with the Edenists to germinate a bitek habitat above Murora, the system's largest gas giant, the task of attracting colonists began in earnest.

After reviewing the predominantly South-East Asian catchment profiles and intended culture-base of other stage one colony planets in the same sector as Lalonde, the LDC board decided to concentrate on EuroChristian-ethnic stock to give themselves an adequate immigrant pool. They wrote a broadly democratic constitution which would come into effect over a century, with the LDC turning over local civil administration functions to elected councils, and ultimately the governorship to a congress and president at the end of the first hundred years. Theory had it that when the process was complete Lalonde would have developed a burgeoning industrial/technological society, with the LDC as the largest across-the-board shareholder in the planet's commercial enterprises. That was when the real profits would start to roll in.

At the start of the preliminary stage, cargo starships delivered thirty-five dumpers into low orbit: squat, conical, atmospheric-entry craft, packed full of heavy machinery, supplies, fuel, ground vehicles, and the prefabricated sections of runway. The dumpers were aerobraked below orbital velocity, and one by one began their long fiery descent curve towards the jungle below. They rode the beacon signals down to land beside the Juliffe's southern bank, spread out in a line fifteen kilometres long.

Each dumper was thirty metres high, fifteen metres across its base, weighing three hundred and fifty tonnes fully loaded. Small fins around the base steered them with reasonable accuracy through the atmosphere until they were seven hundred metres above the ground, by which time they had slowed to subsonic speed. A cluster of eight giant parachutes lowered them for the final few hundred metres, bringing them to a landing which resembled a controlled crash to the small flight-control team watching from a safe distance. They were designed for a one-way trip; where they landed, they stayed.

Construction crews followed them down in small VTOL spaceplanes, and began unloading. When the dumpers had been emptied they formed environment-proof accommodation for the crews' families and offices for the governor's civil administration staff.

The jungle surrounding the dumpers was levelled first, a chop and burn policy producing a wide swath of desolated foliage and charred animals; the spaceport clearing followed. After the runway grids were assembled, a second wave of workers arrived in the McBoeings, along with more equipment. This time they had to build their own accommodation, using the profusion of logs the earlier crews had left scattered across the ground. Rings of crude wooden cabins sprang up around all of the dumpers, looking as if they were rafts floating on a sea of mud. Stripped of its scrub cover, subject to continual heavy plant traffic and Lalonde's daily rains, the rich black loam was reduced to a fetid-smelling sludge which was over half a metre thick in places. The rock crushers worked continuously throughout the planet's twenty-six-hour day, but they could never supply enough chippings to stabilize the expanding city's quagmire roads.

The view from the scuffed and algae-splattered window of Ralph Hiltch's office, on the third floor of the dumper which housed the Kulu Embassy, showed him the sun-soaked timber-plank roofs of Durringham spread out across the gently undulating land next to the river. The conglomeration was devoid of any methodical street pattern. Durringham hadn't been laid down with logical forethought, it had erupted like a tumour. He was sure even Earth's eighteenth-century cities had more charm than this. Lalonde was his fourth offworld assignment, and he had never seen anything more primitive. The weather-stained hulls of the dumpers rose above the shanty-town precincts like arcane temples, linked to the ramshackle buildings with a monstrous spider web of sable-black power cables slung between tall poles. The dumpers' integral fusion generators provided ninety per cent of the planet's electrical power, and Durringham was completely dependent on their output.

By virtue of the Royal Kulu Bank taking a two per cent stake in the LDC, Kulu's Foreign Office had acquired the dumper for its staff as soon as the start-up phase of colonization was over, ousting the Governor's Aboriginal Fruit Classification Division in the process. Ralph Hiltch was grateful for the political arm-twisting manoeuvre of twenty years ago; it allowed him to claim an air-conditioned office, and a tiny two-room apartment next door. As the Commercial Attaché he was entitled to a bigger apartment in the embassy's residential block outside, but his actual position as Head of Station for the Kulu External Security Agency operation on Lalonde meant he needed the kind of secure quarters which the old dumper with its carbotanium structure could provide. Besides, like everything else in Durringham, the residential block was made of wood, and leaked something rotten.

He watched the near-solid cliff of silver-grey rain sweeping in from the ocean, obscuring the narrow verdant line peeping above the rooftops to the south which marked the boundary of the jungle. It was the third downpour of the day. One of the five screens on the wall opposite his desk showed a real-time weather-satellite image of Amarisk and the ocean to the west, both covered by spiral arms of cloud. To his wearily experienced eye the rain would last for a good hour and a half.

Ralph eased himself back in his chair and regarded the man sitting nervously on the other side of his desk. Maki Gruter tried not to shift about under the stare. He was a twenty-eight-year-old grade three manager working for the Governor's Transport Office, dressed in fawn shorts and a jade shirt, his lemon-yellow cagoule hanging off the back of his chair. Like almost everyone else in Lalonde's civil administration he was for sale; they universally regarded this backwoods posting as an opportunity to rip off both the LDC and the colonists. Ralph had recruited Maki Gruter two and a half years ago, a month after he himself had arrived. It wasn't so much an entrapment exercise as simply making a selection from a host of eager volunteers. There were times, Ralph reflected sagely, when he would like to see an official who wouldn't sell out for just a sniff of the ubiquitous Edenist fuseodollar. Once his duty tour on Lalonde was finished in another three years he would have to go through innumerable refresher courses. Subversion was so *easy* here.

In fact there were times when he questioned the whole point of the ESA mounting an operation on what was basically a jungle populated by psychological Neanderthals. But Lalonde was only twenty-two light-years from the Principality of Ombey, the Kulu Kingdom's newest dominion star system, itself only just out of stage two development. The ruling Saldana dynasty wanted to make sure that Lalonde didn't mature along hostile lines. Ralph and his colleagues were assigned to watch the colony's political evolution, occasionally offering covert assistance to aspirants with coincident policies; money, or black data on opposing candidates, it didn't make any difference in the end. The formative years of a colony's independence set the political agenda for centuries to come, so the ESA did its best to make sure the first elected leaders were ideologically benign as regards the Kingdom. Placemen, basically.

It made sense if you took the long-term consequences into account; a few million pounds spent now as opposed to the billions any form of naval action would cost once Lalonde had a technoeconomy capable of building military starships. And God knows, Ralph thought, the Saldanas approached every problem from that angle – with their life-expectancy long term was the only term they understood.

Ralph smiled pleasantly at Maki Gruter. 'Anyone of any interest in this batch?'

'Not that I can see,' the civil servant said. 'All Earth nationals. Usual Ivet types, waster kids dumb enough to get caught. No political exiles, or at least, none listed.' Behind his head, the screen displaying the vectors of Lalonde's miserly orbital traffic showed another spaceplane docking with the vast colonist-carrier starship.

'Fine. I'll have it checked, of course,' Ralph said expectantly.

'Oh, right.' Maki Gruter's mouth twitched in a half-embarrassed grin. He pulled out a processor block and datavised the files over.

Ralph observed the information flood into his neural nanonics, assigning it to spare storage cells. Tracer programs ran through the fifty-five hundred names, comparing them to his primary list, the most troublesome of Earth's political agitators known to the ESA. There was no match-up. Later he would datavise the files into a processor block, running a comparison with the huge catalogue of recidivist names, facial images, and in some cases DNA prints which the ESA had trawled from right across the Confederation.

He glanced out through the window again to see a group of the new arrivals slogging along the mushy road which led down the side of the square of grass and straggly roses which passed for the embassy gardens. The rain had arrived, drenching them in seconds. Women, children, and men with their hair beaten down, jump suits clinging to their bodies like a dark, crinkled, lizard hide, all looking thoroughly wretched. There might have been tears on their faces, but he couldn't tell with the rain. And they still had another three kilometres to go before they reached the transients' dormitories down by the river.

'Christ, look at them,' he murmured. 'And they're supposed to be this planet's hope for the future. They can't even organize a walk from the spaceport properly, none of them thought to take waterproofs.'

'Have you ever been to Earth?' Maki Gruter asked.

Ralph turned away from the window, surprised by the younger man's question. Maki was normally keen to simply collect the money and run. 'No.'

'I have. That planet is one giant hive queen for misbegottens. Our noble past. Compared to that, what this planet offers in the way of a future doesn't look so bad.'

'Yeah, maybe.' Ralph opened a drawer and took out his Jovian Bank credit disk.

'There's someone else going upriver with this batch of colonists,' Maki said. 'My office had to arrange a berth for him, that's how I know.'

Ralph stopped in the act of authorizing the usual three-hundred-fuseodollar payment. 'Who's that?'

'A marshal from the Sheriff's Office. Don't know his name, but he's being sent up to Schuster County to scout round.'

Ralph listened to Maki Gruter explain about the missing homestead families, his mind running over the implications. Somebody in the Governor's Office must consider it important, he thought, there were only five marshals on the planet: combat specialists with nanonic-boosted metabolisms, and well armed. Colony Governors deployed them to sort out severe problems, like bandits and potential revolts, problems that had to be eliminated fast.

Another of Ralph's briefs was to watch for pirate activity in the Lalonde system. Prosperous Kulu with its large merchant fleet was engaged in a constant battle with mercenary vessels. Undisciplined, under-policed colony planets with woefully deficient communications were an ideal market for stolen cargoes, and most of the immigrants were at least bright enough to bring a credit disk primed with fuseodollars. The contraband was invariably sold deep in the hinterlands, where dreams soured within weeks when it became clear just how tough it was to survive outside the enclosed comfort of an arcology, and nobody was going to question where sophisticated power hardware and medical packages came from.

Perhaps those families had questioned the source of their windfall?

'Thanks for telling me,' he said, and upped the payment to five hundred fuseodollars.

Maki Gruter smiled in gratitude as his credit disk registered the financial bonus. 'My pleasure.'

Jenny Harris came in a minute after the transport manager left. A thirty-year-old ESA lieutenant, on her second offworld mission. She had a flat face, her nose slightly crooked, with short dark ginger hair, and a slim figure which belied her strength. Ralph had found her a competent officer in the two years she'd been on Lalonde, if a little bit too rigorous in applying agency procedure to every situation.

She listened attentively as Ralph repeated what Maki Gruter had told him.

'I haven't heard any word on unexplained hardware appearing upriver,' she said. 'Just the usual black-market activity, selling off the gear which the spaceport crews lift from new colonists.'

'What assets have we got up in the Schuster area?'

'Few,' she said reluctantly. 'We mainly rely on our contacts in the Sheriff's Office for reports on contraband, and the boat crews fill in a bit more of the picture. Communication is the problem, naturally. We can give our upriver assets communication blocks, but the Confederation Navy satellites would spot any transmissions even if they were prime encrypted.'

'OK,' Ralph nodded. It was an old argument, urgency against exposure risk. At this stage of its development nothing on Lalonde was considered urgent. 'Do we have anyone going upriver?'

Jenny Harris paused as her neural nanonics reviewed schedules. 'Yes. Captain Lambourne is due to take a new colonist group upriver in a couple of days, they're settling land just past Schuster itself. She's a good courier, I use her to collect reports from our *in situ* assets.'

'Right, ask her to find out what she can, about the missing families and whether or not there's been any unexplained equipment appearing up there. In the meantime I'll contact Solanki, see if he's heard anything about it.' Kelven Solanki worked at the small Confederation Navy office in Durringham. Confederation Navy policy was that even the humblest of colony worlds was entitled to the same degree of protection as any of the developed planets, and the office was supposed to be visible proof of that. To underline the fact, Lalonde received a twice-yearly visit by a frigate from the 7th Fleet, based at Roherheim, forty-two light-years away. Between visits, a flock of ELINT sensor satellites watched over the star system, reporting their observations directly to the navy office.

Like Ralph and the ESA, their secondary role was to keep an eye out for pirate activity.

Ralph had introduced himself to Lieutenant-Commander Solanki soon after he arrived. The Saldanas were strong supporters of the Confederation, so cooperation as far as locating pirate activity was concerned was a sensible arrangement. He got on reasonably well with the commander, partly due to the navy's mess, which served arguably the best meals in the city, and neither of them made any mention of Ralph's other duties.

'Good idea,' Jenny Harris said. 'I'll meet with Lambourne tonight, and brief her on what we want. She'll want paying,' she added in a cautionary tone.

Ralph requested Lambourne's file from his neural nanonics, shaking his head ruefully when he saw how much the woman cost them. He could guess how much she would ask for this fact-finding mission upriver. 'OK, I'll authorize it. Try and keep her under a thousand, please.'

'Do my best.'

'Once you've dealt with her, I want you to activate an asset in the Governor's office, find out why the Honourable Colin Rexrew thinks it's necessary to send a marshal to investigate some missing farmers no one has ever heard of before.'

After Jenny Harris left he datavised the list of new arrivals into his processor block for analysis, then sat back and thought about how much to tell Commander Solanki. With a bit of luck he could drag out the meeting and get himself invited to dinner at the mess.

Twenty-two thousand kilometres ahead of *Oenone*, the tiny blue ion-manoeuvring jets of the Adamist starship *Dymasio* were consumed by the interstellar night. Syrinx watched through the voidhawk's optical senses as the intense pinprick of light dwindled away to nothing. Directional vectors swirled away at the back of her mind, an unconscious calculation performed in conjunction with *Oenone*'s spacial instinct. The *Dymasio* had lined up on the Honeck star system eight light-years away, the alignment checked out perfectly.

I think this is it, she told Thetis. *Graeae*, her brother's voidhawk, was drifting a thousand kilometres to one side of *Oenone*; the two voidhawks had their distortion fields reduced to a minimum. They were operating in full stealth mode, with minimal energy expenditure. There wasn't even any gravity in the crew toroid. The crew hadn't eaten any hot meals, there had been no waste dumps, all of them peeing and crapping into sanitary bags, and there was definitely no hot water. Blanket webs of heat-duct cables had been laid over *Oenone*'s hull and crew toroid alike, then smothered by a thick light-absorbent insulation foam. All the starship's waste heat was siphoned off by the blankets and radiated away through a single dump panel, always orientated away from their prey. Holes had been left for *Oenone*'s sensor blisters, but that was all. *Oenone* kept complaining that the covering itched, which was ridiculous, but Syrinx held her peace – for now.

I agree, Thetis replied.

Syrinx felt a shiver of trepidation mingling with a release of pent-up tension. They had been following the *Dymasio* for seventeen days, keeping twenty to thirty thousand kilometres behind as it zigzagged between uninhabited star systems on a totally random course designed to spot and shake off any possible pursuer. A chase of that nature was demanding and difficult, putting a strain on even Edenist psyches, let alone the twenty-strong Adamist naval marine squad they were carrying. Seeing the way their hard-pressed captain, Larry Kouritz, had maintained discipline throughout the mission had sparked a rare respect. And there weren't many Adamists who rated that.

With the final coordinate insertion manoeuvres complete, she could imagine the *Dymasio* retracting its sensors and thermo-dump panels, configuring itself for the jump, charging its patterning nodes with energy. **Ready?** she asked *Oenone*.

I'm always ready, the voidhawk replied tartly.

Yes, she would be very glad when this mission was over.

It had been Thetis who persuaded her to sign on with the Confederation Navy for a seven-year tour, Thetis with his strong sense of duty and commitment, goaded by a wilful zest. Syrinx had always intended to put in a naval stint, Athene had often told her rumbustious children of her service days, painting an enticing picture of gallantry and camaraderie. She just hadn't anticipated it to be quite so soon, three years after she and *Oenone* started flying.

With their power and agility, voidhawks were an essential component of the Confederation Navy, employed by Fleet admirals as ideal interception craft. After being fitted out with both offensive and defensive combat systems and an extensive array of electronic sensors, then undergoing a three-month procedural-training course, *Oenone* and *Graeae* had been assigned to the 4th Fleet, operating from the Japanese Imperium capital Oshanko.

Although the Confederation Navy was a dedicated supranational organization, voidhawks always had Edenist crews. Syrinx had kept her original crew: Cacus, the life-support engineer; Edwin, in charge of the toroid's mechanical and electrical systems; Oxley, who piloted both the multifunction service vehicle and the atmospheric ion-field flyer; Tula, the ship's generalist and medical officer. And Ruben, the fusion-generator technician, who had become Syrinx's lover a month after he came aboard, and at a hundred and twenty-five was exactly a century older than her.

It was like Aulie all over again, an aspect which made her feel incredibly girlish and carefree, almost an antithesis of her responsibilities as captain. They slept together when ship's schedules permitted, and spent all their shore leave ranging across whichever planet, habitat, or asteroid settlement they were visiting. Although well into middle age, Ruben, like all Edenists, was still more than capable physically, so their sex life was pretty reasonable; and they both shared a delight in exploring the different cultures flourishing within the Confederation, marvelling in their sheer variety. Through Ruben, and his seemingly inexhaustible patience, she had learned to be far more tolerant of Adamists and their idiosyncrasies. Which was another reason for accepting the Confederation Navy commission.

Then there was also that familiar miscreant thrill to be had from the way everyone regarded their relationship as mildly scandalous. Given their life expectancy, large age gaps were common among Edenist partners, but a hundred years was pushing the limits of propriety. Only Athene didn't make the mistake of objecting, she knew Syrinx far too well for that. In any case, the relationship wasn't *that* serious; Ruben was convenient, uncomplicated, and fun.

The final crew-member was Chi, who had been posted to

Oenone by the navy to be their weapons officer. He was a career Confederation Navy man, as far as any Edenist could be in an organization which demanded staff officers renounce their national citizenship (hardly practical for Edenists).

Oenone and *Graeae* had spent four years of patrolling uninhabited star systems, providing occasional random escorts for merchant ships in the hope of engaging pirates, exercised with the Fleet on full-system defence attacks, taken part in a marine assault on an industrial station suspected of building antimatter combat wasps, and making innumerable goodwill calls at ports throughout the 4th Fleet's sector. For the last eight months the Admiralty had assigned them to an independent interception duty, under the command of the Confederation Naval Intelligence Service. This was the third chase flight the CNIS had sent them on: the first ship had been empty when they reached it; the second, a blackhawk, managed to elude them with its longer swallow range, much to Syrinx's extreme chagrin. But the *Dymasio* was undeniably guilty; the CNIS had suspected it of carrying antimatter for some time, and this flight proved it. Now the ship was preparing to enter an inhabited system to make contact with an asteroid separatist group. This time they would make their arrest. This time! *Oenone*'s cabin atmosphere seemed compressed by the prospect.

Even Eileen Carouch, the CNIS lieutenant who was liaising with them, had picked up on the Edenists' expectancy. She was strapped into the couch next to Syrinx, a middle-aged woman with a bland, unmemorable face, the kind Syrinx supposed was ideal for an active agent. But the personality behind it was resolute and resourceful; discovering the *Dymasio*'s hoarded cache was proof of that.

Right now she had her eyes tight closed, accessing the datavised information *Oenone* was providing through bitek processors interfaced with their hardware equivalents, allowing all the Adamists to see what was going on.

'*Dymasio*'s ready to jump,' Syrinx said.

'Thank heavens for that. My nerves can't stand much more of this.'

Syrinx felt a grin on her lips. She always found a slight edge of tension in her dealings with Adamists on an individual basis; them and their emotions locked inside impenetrable bone, you never knew quite what they felt, which was difficult for the empathic Edenists to handle. But Eileen had turned out to be amazingly blunt with her opinions. Syrinx quite enjoyed her company.

The *Dymasio* vanished. Syrinx felt the sharp kink in space as the ship's patterning nodes warped the fabric of reality around her hull; to *Oenone* the distortion was like a flare. One that was totally quantifiable. The voidhawk instinctively knew the emergence-point coordinate.

Let's go! Syrinx broadcast loudly.

Power flooded through the voidhawk's patterning cells. An interstice was torn open. They plunged into the expanding wormhole. Syrinx could feel *Gracac* generating its own worm hole away to one side, then the interstice closed behind them, sealing them in timeless oblivion. Imagination, twinned with genuine voidhawk sensorium input, provided a giddy rushing sensation for the couple of heartbeats it took to traverse the wormhole. A terminus opened at some indeterminable distance, a different texture of negation, seemingly curving round them. Starlight began to pour in, bending into a filigree of slender blue-white lines around the hull. *Oenone* shot out into space. Stars became hard diamond points again.

The event horizon had evaporated from the *Dymasio*'s hull, depositing the starship five light-days out from Honeck's sun. Its sensor clusters and thermo-dump panels emerged from the hull with the timidity of a hibernating creature venturing out into a spring day. As with all Adamist starships, it took time to check its location, and scan local space for stray comets or rock fragments. That crucial time lapse allowed the tremendous spacial flaws accompanying the opening of the voidhawks' terminuses to remain undetected.

Ignorant of his invisible followers, the *Dymasio*'s captain activated the starship's main fusion drive, heading towards the next jump coordinate.

'It's moving again,' Syrinx said. 'Preparing to go insystem. Do you want to interdict?' The thought of antimatter being carried into an inhabited system disturbed her.

'What's the new destination?' Eileen Carouch asked.

Syrinx consulted the system's almanac stored in *Oenone*'s memory cells. 'It looks like Kirchol, the outer gas giant.'

'Any settlements in orbit?' She hadn't quite grasped how to pull information from *Oenone* the way she could from hardware memory cores.

'None listed.'

'It has to be heading for a rendezvous, then. Don't interdict it, follow it in.'

'Let it into an inhabited system?'

'Sure. Look, if it was just the antimatter we wanted, we could have boarded any time in the last three months. That's how long we've known the stuff was on board. *Dymasio* has visited seven inhabited star systems since we started monitoring it, without threatening any of them. Now my agent confirms the captain has found a buyer with these separatist hotheads, and I want them. This way we can wrap up both supplier and destination. We could even come out of it with the location of the antimatter-production station. Commendations all round, so just be patient.'

'OK.' **Did you catch all that?** Syrinx asked Thetis.

Certainly did. And she's quite right.

I know, but . . . She broadcast a complex emotional harmonic of eagerness and frustration.

Bear with it, little sister. Mental laughter. Thetis always knew how to tweak her. *Graeae* had been born before *Oenone*, but there was a marked comparison in size; with a hull diameter of a hundred and fifteen metres *Oenone* was the largest of all *Iasius*'s children. And it wasn't until puberty's growth hormones came into effect that Thetis outmatched her in physical tussles. But they had always been the closest, always competing against each other.

I've never met anyone more unsuitable for a captaincy, Ruben chided. **No composure, all teenage recklessness, that's your fault, young lady. I'm jumping ship when this is over, bugger what the contract says.**

She laughed out loud, quickly turning it into a cough for Eileen's benefit. Even though she was used to the degree of honesty which affinity fostered, Ruben always astounded her with his intimate knowledge of her emotional composition. **You don't complain about my other teenage attributes,** she shot back, complete with a very graphic image.

Oh, lady, you just wait till we're off duty.

I'll hold you to that.

The prospect almost made the tense waiting worthwhile.

Because of the need for a more precise trajectory when jumping towards a planet than for an interstellar jump, *Dymasio* spent a good fifty minutes re-aligning its course with considerable accuracy. Once its new orbital vector intersected Kirchol, the starship reconfigured itself for a jump.

Weapons status check, please, Syrinx demanded when the light from *Dymasio*'s dive flame began to fade.

Combat wasps and proximity defence systems on-line, Chi replied.

OK, everybody, alert status one. We don't know how many hostiles there are going to be around Kirchol, so we'll proceed with extreme caution. The admiral wants this ship interdicted, not destroyed, but if we're outnumbered we let loose the combat wasps and retreat. Let's just hope this is the nest.

She caught an indistinct mental grumble: **It can't possibly be another decoy jump. Please.** From the tiredness of the tone she guessed it was Oxley, who was actually older than Ruben, a hundred and fifty. Sinon had recommended him when she was assembling her first crew. He had stayed on mostly out of loyalty to her when she signed on with the navy. More cause for guilt.

Dymasio jumped.

Kirchol was a muddy brown globe three hundred and seventy thousand kilometres below *Oenone*'s hull, attendant moons glimmering dimly in the exhausted sunlight. The gas giant had nothing like the majesty of Saturn, it was too drab, too listless. Even the stormbands lacked ferocity.

Dymasio and the two voidhawks had emerged above the south pole; insignificant on such a scale, one dull speck, and two coal-black motes, falling with imperceptible slowness as the gravity field tugged at them.

Syrinx opened her mind to Chi, combining *Oenone*'s perceptual awareness with the weapons officer's knowledge of their combat wasps' performance capabilities. Her nerves stretching over a huge volume of space, making a far-off body tremble in reaction.

The *Dymasio* started to transmit a simple radio code, beaming it down towards the gas giant. Given their position, there would be no overspill falling on the populated inner system, Syrinx realized, no chance of being detected even in a few hours when the radio waves finally bridged the gulf.

An answering pulse flashed out from something in orbit around Kirchol, well outside *Oenone*'s mass-detection range. The source point began to move, vaulting out of its orbit at five gees. *Oenone* couldn't detect any infrared trace, and there was no reaction-drive exhaust. The radio signal cut out.

A blackhawk. The thought leapt between the Edenists on both voidhawks, a shared frisson of glee.

It's mine, Syrinx told Thetis on singular-engagement mode. She hadn't forgotten how the last blackhawk had given them the slip. It rankled still.

Oh, come on, he protested.

Mine, she repeated coolly. **You get all the glory nabbing that actual antimatter. What more do you want?**

The next blackhawk we come across is mine.

Of course, she cooed.

Thetis retreated, his subconscious grousing away. But he knew better than try and argue with his sister when she was in that mood.

We're going after it? *Oenone* demanded.

We certainly are, she reassured it.

Good, I didn't like losing that last one. I could have matched its swallow.

No, you couldn't. That was nineteen light-years. You'd damage your patterning cells trying to emulate that. Fifteen light-years is our limit.

Oenone didn't answer, but she could sense the resentment in its mind. She had almost been tempted to try the larger than usual swallow, but fear of injuring the voidhawk held her back. That and the prospect of stranding the rest of the crew in deep space.

I would never harm you or the crew, *Oenone* said gently.

I know. But it was annoying, wasn't it?

Very!

*

The blackhawk rose up out of the ecliptic plane in a long, graceful curve. Even when it slowed to rendezvous with the *Dymasio* the two waiting voidhawks couldn't discern its shape or size. They were thirty thousand kilometres away, too far for optical resolution, and the slightest use of the distortion effect to probe it would have given them away.

Both target craft used their radios when they were five thousand kilometres apart, a steady stream of encrypted data. It made tracking absurdly easy, *Oenone*'s passive electronic sensor array triangulating them to half a metre. Syrinx waited until they were only two thousand kilometres apart, then issued the order to interdict.

HOLD YOUR LOCATION, *Oenone* bellowed across the affinity band. It detected a mental flinch from the blackhawk. **CANCEL YOUR ACCELERATION, DO NOT ATTEMPT TO INITIATE A SWALLOW. STAND BY FOR RENDEZVOUS AND BOARDING.**

Gravity surged back into the crew toroid, building with uncomfortable speed. *Oenone* and *Graeae* streaked in towards their prey at eight gees. *Oenone* was capable of generating a counter-acceleration force of three gees around the crew toroid, which still left Syrinx subject to a harsh five gees. Her toughened internal membranes could just about take the strain, but she worried that the blackhawk would try to run. Their crews nearly always used nanonic supplements, enabling them to withstand much higher acceleration. If it developed into a straight chase, *Oenone*'s crew were going to suffer, especially Ruben and Oxley.

She needn't have worried. After *Oenone*'s affinity shout, the blackhawk folded in its distortion field. But she was keenly aware of the sullen anger colouring its thoughts, presumably echoing those of its captain. There was a name, too, or rather an insistence of identity: *Vermuden.*

Graeae was broadcasting a radio message at the *Dymasio,* the same demand to maintain position. In the Adamist starship's case, enforcement was a more practical option. The voidhawk reached out with its distortion field, disrupting the quantum state of space around the *Dymasio*'s hull; if it tried to jump away now, the interference would produce instabilities in its patterning nodes, with spectacularly lethal results as the desynchronized energy loci imploded.

Oenone and *Graeae* drew apart as they closed on their respective targets. The *Vermuden* was a sharp profile in Syrinx's mind now, a flattish onion shape one hundred and five metres in diameter, its central spire tapering to a needle-sharp point sixty metres above the hull rim. There was no crew toroid, instead three silvery mechanical capsules were fixed equidistantly around the upper hull; one was a life-support cabin large enough for about five or six people, another was a hangar for a small spaceplane, the third was its cargo hold. Energy currents simmered below its hull, spectral iridescent whirls that suggested extreme agitation.

'Captain Kouritz, you and your squad to the airlock, please,' Syrinx said when they began to slow for rendezvous. 'Be advised, the blackhawk's cabin space is approximately four hundred cubic metres.'

Vermuden hung in space three hundred kilometres away, a dusky crescent, slightly ginger in colour. She could feel Chi locking the proximity defence lasers onto the blackhawk, a mix of electronic and bitek senses providing the focus.

'I'll go with them,' Eileen Carouch said. She tapped her restraint-strap release catch.

'Make sure the *Vermuden*'s captain is brought straight back here,' Syrinx said. 'I'll send one of my people with you to fly *Vermuden* back to Fleet headquarters.' Without its captain, the blackhawk would have to obey an Edenist.

Oenone flipped over as it approached *Vermuden*, inverting itself so that it seemed to be descending vertically towards the blackhawk's upper hull. An airlock tube extended out from the crew toroid. The marine squad waited in the chamber behind it, fully armoured, weapons powered up. Gravity throughout the toroid had returned to a welcome Earth standard.

Syrinx ordered the *Vermuden*'s captain to extend the blackhawk's airlock.

The *Dymasio* exploded.

Its captain, faced with the total certainty of a personality debrief followed by a Confederation Navy firing squad, decided his crew and ship were a worthwhile price to pay for taking *Graeae* with him. He waited until the voidhawk was a scant kilometre away, beginning its docking manoeuvres, then turned off the antimatter-confinement chambers.

Five hundred grams of antimatter rushed to embrace an equal mass of ordinary matter.

From *Oenone*'s position, two thousand kilometres away, the elemental energy wavefront split the universe in two. On one side the stars burnt with their usual untroubled tranquillity; opposite that infinity vanished, replaced by a solid flat plane of raging photons.

Syrinx felt the light searing into *Oenone*, scorching optical-receptor cells into crisps. Affinity acted like a conductor for purple-white light, allowing it to shine straight into her own mind, a torrent of photons that threatened to engulf her sanity. In amongst the glare were fissures of darkness, fluttering around like tiny birds caught by a gale. They called out to her as they passed, mental cries, sometimes words, sometimes visions of people and places, sometimes smells – phantasm tastes, a touch, the laughter, music, heat, chill, wetness. Minds transferring into *Oenone*'s neural cells. But broken, incomplete. Flawed.

Thetis! Syrinx cried.

She couldn't find him, not amid such turmoil. And the light had become a pervasive pain. She howled in anguish and hatred.

Vermuden's distortion field distended, strengthened, applying stress against the perpetual structure of reality. An interstice yawned wide.

Chi fired the gamma lasers. But the beams raked emptiness. The interstice was already closing.

Less than two seconds after the *Dymasio* exploded, a blast wave of particles arrived to assault *Oenone*'s hull, supplementing the corrosive electromagnetic radiation already striking against the foam. The voidhawk looked past the immediate chaos, observing *Vermuden*'s wormhole forming, a tunnel through empty dimensions. Size and determinant length defined by the blackhawk's energy input. *Oenone* knew the terminus coordinate exactly, twenty-one light-years away, the blackhawk's utter limit.

This time! *Oenone* thought tempestuously. Energy blazed through its own patterning cells.

No! Syrinx shouted, shocked out of her grief.

There is a way, I know how. Trust me.

She waited helplessly as the interstice engulfed them, some treacherous aspect of her subconscious granting the voidhawk permission, urging them on towards retribution. Worry faded when she saw the wormhole was only thirteen light-years long. As its terminus began to open, she felt the patterning cells activate again. Realization was instantaneous, and she laughed with vengeful fury.

Told you so, *Oenone* said smugly.

The desperate twenty-one light-year swallow had stretched *Vermuden*'s energy loading capacity virtually to breaking point. It could sense its captain prone on his acceleration couch, muscles locked solid, back arched, the exertion twinned. The wormhole's pseudofabric slithered round the hull, not a physical pressure, but tangible none the less. Finally, up ahead, the terminus manifested. Starlight traced strange shapes as it filtered through.

Vermuden popped out into the clean vacuum of normal space, mind radiating vivid relief.

Well done, its captain said. *Vermuden* felt arm and chest muscles slacken, an indrawn breath.

Powerful laserlight illuminated its hull, washing out its optical receptor cells in a pink dazzle. A lens-shaped mass a hundred and fifteen metres in diameter hung eighty metres off its central spire in the direction of Betelgeuse's demonic red gleam.

'What the fuck . . . How?' the captain yelped.

This is just the targeting laser, *Oenone* said. **If I sense any flux change in your patterning cells I'll switch to the gamma lasers and**

slice you in half. Now extend your airlock. I have some people on board keen to meet you.

*

'I didn't know voidhawks could do that,' Eileen Carouch said a couple of hours later. *Vermuden*'s captain, Henry Siclari, and the blackhawk's other two crewmen, were in *Oenone*'s brig; and the navy prize crew, headed by Cacus, were familiarizing themselves with the blackhawk's systems. Cacus reckoned they would be able to take the ship back to Oshanko in a day.

'Sequential swallows?' Syrinx said. 'Nothing to stop them, you just need a voidhawk with an acute spacial sense.' **Like you.**

I love you, *Oenone* replied, unabashed by the alternate praise and admonitions the Edenists had been bombarding it with since the manoeuvre.

Got an answer to everything, haven't you? she said. But the humour wasn't there.

Thetis. His broad, smiling face covered in boyish freckles, the uncombed sandy hair, the lanky, slightly awkward body. All the hours together spent roving around Romulus.

He was a part of her identity in the same way as *Oenone*. Soulsibling, so much had been shared. And now he was gone. Torn away from her, torn *out* of her, the voyages together, frustrations and achievements.

I mourn for him too, *Oenone* whispered into her mind, its thoughts drenched with regret.

Thank you. And *Graeae*'s eggs have been lost as well. What a terrible, filthy thing to do. I hate Adamists.

No, That is beneath us. See, Eileen and the marines share our loss. It is not Adamists. Only individuals. Always individuals. Even Edenists have our failures, do we not?

Yes. We do, she said, because it was true enough. But there was still that fraction of her mind which remained vacant, the vanished smile.

*

Athene knew something was shockingly wrong as soon as *Oenone* emerged above Saturn. She was in the garden lounge, feeding two-month-old Clymene from a bitek mammary orb when the cold premonition closed about her. It made her clutch at her second great-great-grandchild for fear of the future and what it held. The infant wailed in protest at the loss of the nipple and the tightness of her grip. She hurriedly handed Clymene back to her great-grandson, who tried to calm the baby girl with mental coos of reassurance. Then Syrinx's alarmingly dulled mind touched Athene, and the awful knowledge was revealed in full.

Is there nothing of him left? she asked softly.

Some, Syrinx said. **But so little, I'm sorry, Mother.**

A single thought would be enough for me.

As *Oenone* neared Romulus it gave up the thought fragments it had stored to the habitat personality. A precious intangible residue of life, the sole legacy of Thetis and his crew.

Athene's past friends, lovers, and husbands emerged from the multiplicity of Romulus's personality to offer support and encouragement, cushioning the blow as best they could. **We will do what we can**, they assured her. She could feel the tremulous remnants of her son being slowly woven into a more cohesive whole, and drew a brief measure of comfort from that.

Although no stranger to death, Athene found this bereavement particularly difficult. Always at the back of her mind was the belief that the voidhawks and their captains were somehow immortal, or at least immune to such wasteful calamity. A foolish, almost childish belief, because they were the children she prized the most. Her last link with *Iasius*, their offspring.

Half an hour later, dressed in a plain jet-black ship-tunic, Athene stood in the spaceport reception lounge, a proud, solitary figure, the lines on her face betraying every one of her hundred and thirty-five years as they never had before. She looked out over the ledge as *Oenone* and its anxious escort of two voidhawks from the Saturn defence squadron crept out of the darkness. *Oenone* sank onto a vacant pedestal with a very human mindsigh of relief. Feed tubes in the pedestal stirred like blind stumpy tentacles, searching for the female orifices on the voidhawk's underside; various sphincter muscles expanded and gripped, producing tight seals. *Oenone* gulped down the nutrient fluid which Romulus synthesized, filling its internal bladders, quenching the thirst which leached vitality from every cell. They hadn't stayed at Oshanko any longer than it took to hand Henry Siclari and his crew over to the Fleet port authorities, and allow Edenist bonding-adjustment specialists to assume command of *Vermuden.* After that Syrinx had insisted on coming direct to Saturn.

Athene looked out at the big voidhawk with real concern rising.

Oenone was in a sorry state: hull foam scorched and flaking, toroid thermo-dump panels melted, electronic sensor systems reduced to rivulets of congealed slag, the sensor blisters that had faced the *Dymasio* roasted, their cells dead.

I'm all right, *Oenone* told her. **It's mostly the mechanical systems that were damaged. And the biotechnicians can graft new sensor blisters into me. I'm never going to complain about being covered in foam again,** it added humbly.

When Syrinx came through the airlock her cheeks had become almost hollow, her hair was hanging limp over her skull, and she walked as though she had been condemned. Athene felt the tears come at last, and put her arms round her woebegone daughter, soothing the drained thoughts with an empathic compassion, the maternal balm.

It's not your fault.

If I hadn't . . .

Don't, Athene ordered sternly. **You owe Thetis and *Graeae* this much, not to sink into pointless remorse. You're stronger than that, much stronger.**

Yes, Mother.

He did what he wanted to. He did what was right. Tell me how

many millions of lives would have been lost if that antimatter had been used against a naked planetary surface?

A lot, Syrinx said numbly.

And he saved them. My son. Because of him, they will live, and have children, and laugh.

But it hurts!

That's because we're human, more so than Adamists can ever be. Our empathy means we can never hide from what we feel, and that's good. But you must always walk the balance, Syrinx; the balance is the penalty of being human: the danger of allowing yourself to feel. For this we walk a narrow path high above rocky ground. On one side we have the descent into animalism, on the other a godhead delusion. Both pulling at us, both tempting. But without these forces tugging at your psyche, stirring it into conflict, you can never love. They awaken us, you see, these warring sides, they arouse our passion. So learn from this wretched episode, learn to be proud of Thetis and what he accomplished, use it to counter the grief. It is hard, I know; for captains more than anyone. We are the ones who truly open our souls to another entity, we feel the deepest, and suffer the most. And knowing that, knowing what you would endure in life, I still chose to bring you into existence, because there is so much joy to be had from the living.

*

The circular house snug in arms of its gentle valley hadn't changed, still a frantic noisy vortex of excited children, slightly weary adults, and harassed bitek housechimps. Syrinx might never have been away. With eighteen children, and, so far, forty-two grandchildren, eleven great-grandchildren, and the two newest fourth-generation additions, Athene headed a family that never gave her a moment's rest. Ninety per cent of the adults were involved with spaceflight in one field or another, which meant long absences were the norm. But when they came back, it was the house and Athene they always visited first, staying or passing through as the fancy took them.

'Athene's boarding-house, bordello, and playpen,' the old ex-captain had called it on more than one occasion.

The younger children were delighted to see Syrinx, whooping as they gathered round her, demanding kisses and stories of the planets she'd visited, while the adults offered subdued condolences. Being with them, knowing and feeling the heart-ache being shared, lifted the load. Slightly.

After the evening meal Syrinx went back to her old room, asking to be left alone for a few hours. Ruben and Athene acceded, retreating to the white iron chairs on the patio and conversing on the singular-engagement mode, sober faces betraying their worry.

She lay back on the bed, staring through the transparent roof at the lazy winding valleys beyond the dimming axial light-tube. In the seven years since *Oenone* reached maturity the trees had grown and bushes fattened, expanding the green-on-green patterns of her childhood.

She could feel *Oenone* out on the ledge, hull being cleaned of foam, mobile gantry arms in position, giving technicians full access to the battered crew toroid. Now it had completed its nutrient digestion its mindtone was returning to normal. It was enjoying being the centre of attention, busy conversing with the ledge crews over aspects of the repairs. Two biotechnicians were squatting over a ruined sensor blister with portable probes, taking samples.

Daddy?

I'm here, Sly-minx. I told you I always would be.

Thank you. I never doubted. How is he?

Happy.

A little of the dread lifted from her heart. **Is he ready?**

Yes. But there was so much missing from recent years. We have integrated what we can. The core of identity is viable but it lacks substance. He remains a child, perhaps the part of him you loved the most.

Can I talk to him yet?

You may.

She was standing barefoot on thick, cool grass beside a broad stream, the axial light-tube shining like a thread of captured sunlight overhead. There were tall trees around her, bowing under the weight of vines hanging between their branches, and long cascades of flowers fell to the floor, some of them trailing in the clear water. Butterflies flapped lazily through the still air, contending with bees for perches on the flowers, birds cheeped all around.

It was the clearing where she had spent so many days as a girl, just past the bottom of the lawn. Looking down she saw she was wearing a simple cotton summer dress with a tiny blue and white check. Long loose hair swirled around skinny hips. Her body was thirteen years old; and she knew why even as she heard the children shouting and laughing. Young enough to be regarded as part of childhood's conspiracy, old enough to be revered, to hold herself aloof and not be resented for it.

They burst into the clearing, six ten-year-old boys, in shorts and T-shirts, bare chested and in swimming trunks, smiling and laughing, strong limbs flashing in the warm light.

'Syrinx!' He was in their middle, sandy hair askew, grinning up at her.

'Hello, Thetis,' she said.

'Are you coming with us?' he asked breathlessly.

A raft of rough silicon sheets, foamed aluminium I-beams, and empty plastic drink tanks – familiar enough to bring tears to her eyes – was lying on the bank, half in the water.

'I can't, Thetis. I just came to make sure you're all right.'

'Course I'm all right!' He tried to do a cartwheel on the grass, but toppled over and fell into a laughing heap. 'We're going all the way down to the salt-water reservoir. It'll be fun, we've not told anyone, and the personality won't see us. We could meet anything down there, pirates or monsters. And we might find some treasure. I'll bring it back, and I'll be the most famous captain in all of the habitat.' He scrambled to his feet again, eyes shining. '*Please* come, Syrinx. Please?'

'Another time, I promise.'

There were shouts from the other boys as the raft was pushed into the fast-flowing stream. It bobbed about at alarming angles for a few seconds before gradually righting itself. The boys started to pile on.

Thetis's head swivelled between Syrinx and the raft, desperately torn. 'Promise? Really promise?'

'I do.' She reached out and held his head between her hands, and kissed him lightly on his brow.

'Syrinx!' He squirmed in agitation, colouring as the other boys launched into a flurry of catcalls.

'Here,' she said, and took off a slim silver necklace with an intricately carved pale jade stone the size of a grape. 'Wear this, it'll be like I'm there with you. And next time I visit, you can tell me all about it.'

'Right!' And he ran for the raft, splashing through the shallows as he fumbled to fasten the chain round his neck. 'Don't forget, come back. You promised.'

How far will he go? she asked Sinon as a soaking Thetis was hauled over the edge of the raft by a couple of his friends.

As far as he wishes.

And how long will it last?

As long as he wants.

Daddy!

I'm sorry, I didn't mean to be flippant. Probably about ten or fifteen years. You see, even childhood will ultimately pale. Games that defy adults and friends that mean the whole world are all very well, but a major part of what a ten-year-old is, is the wish to be old; his actions are a shadow of what he sees as adult behaviour. There is an old saying, that the boy is the father of the man. So when he has had his fill of adventure and realizes he will never be that man, that he is a sterile child, his identity will fade out of the

multiplicity into the overall personality. Like all of us will eventually, Sly-minx, even you.

You mean he will lose hope.

No. Death is the loss of hope, everything else is merely despair.

The children were paddling now, getting the hang of the raft. Thetis was sitting at the front shouting orders, in his element. He looked round, smiled and waved. Syrinx raised a hand.

Adamists lose hope, she said. **The *Dymasio*'s captain lost all hope. That's why he did what he did.**

Adamists are incomplete. We know we will continue after the body dies; in some way, some fraction of us will linger for hundreds of millennia. For myself, I cannot even contemplate abandoning the multiplicity segment of the personality, not with you and my other children and grandchildren to watch over. Perhaps in ten or fifteen generations, when I can conjure up no sense of attachment, then I may seek full unity with the habitat personality, and transfer my allegiance to all Edenists. But it will be a very long time.

Adamists have their religions. I thought their gods gave them hope.

They do, to the very devout. But consider the disadvantage under which the ordinary Adamist labours. The mythical kingdom, that is all their heaven can ever be, beyond ever knowing. In the end, such belief is very hard for poor sinful mortals to retain. Our afterlife, however, is tangible, real. For us it is not a question of faith, we have fact.

Unless you are Thetis.

Even he survives.

Some of him, a stunted existence. Floating down a river that will never end.

Loved, treasured, welcomed, eternal.

The raft disappeared round a bend, a clump of willows blocking it from sight. High-pitched voices drifted through the air. Syrinx let her hand drop. 'I will visit you again, big brother,' she told the empty gurgling stream. 'Again and again, every time I come back. I will make you look forward to my visits and the stories I bring, I will give you something to hope for. Promise.'

In her room she looked up at the darkened indistinct landscape far above. The axial light-tube had been reduced to a lunar presence masked by the evening's first rain-clouds.

Syrinx closed her mind to the other Edenists, closed it to the voidhawks flying outside, closed it to the habitat personality. Only *Oenone* remained. Beloved who would understand, because they were one.

Emerging from the jumble of doubt and misery was the tenuous wish that the Adamists were right after all, and there was such a thing as God, and an afterlife, and souls. That way Thetis wouldn't be lost. Not for ever.

It was such a tiny sliver of hope.

Oenone's thoughts rubbed against hers, soothing and sympathetic.

If there is a God, and if somewhere my brother's soul is intact, please look after him. He will be so alone.

7

Over a thousand tributaries contributed towards the Juliffe's rapacious flow, a wrinkled network of rivers and streams gathering in the rainfall over an area of one and a half million square kilometres. They emptied themselves into the main course at full volume throughout the whole two hundred and ninety-five days of Lalonde's year, bringing with them immense amounts of silt, rotting vegetation, and broken trees. The turbulence and power of the huge flow was such that the water along the last five hundred kilometres turned the same colour and thickness as milky coffee. By the time it reached the coast the river's width had swollen to over seventeen kilometres; and the sheer weight of water backed up for two thousand kilometres behind it was awesome. At the mouth it looked as though one sea was bleeding into another.

For the final hundred-kilometre stretch, the banks on the northern side were non-existent; marshland extended up to a hundred and fifty kilometres into the countryside. Named the Hultain Marsh after the first reckless ecological assessment team member to venture a few brief kilometres inside its fringes, it proved an inhospitable zone of reeds and algae and sharp-toothed lizard-analogue animals of varying sizes. No human explorer ever managed to traverse it; the ecological evaluators contented themselves with Hultain's sketchy report and the satellite survey pictures. When the wind blew from the north, it carried a powerful smell of corruption over the river into Durringham. To the city's residents the Hultain Marsh had virtually assumed the quality of myth, a repository of bad luck and ghoulish creatures.

The land on the Juliffe's southern side, however, rose up to twelve metres above the surging brown waters. Sprawling aloof along the bank, Durringham was relatively safe from the most potent of the Juliffe's spring floods. Poised between spaceport and water, the city was the key to colonizing the entire river basin.

The Juliffe provided the Lalonde Development Company with the greatest conceivable natural roadway into Amarisk's interior. With its tributaries extending into every valley in the centre of the landmass, there was no need to hack out and maintain expensive tracks in the jungle. Abundant wood provided the raw material for boat hulls, the simplest and cheapest form of travel possible. So shipbuilding swiftly became the capital's principal industry, with nearly a quarter of its population dependent on the success of the shipyards.

Captains under contract to the LDC would take newly arrived colonist groups upriver, and bring down the surplus produce from the established farms to be sold in the city. There were several hundred boats docking and sailing every day. The port with its jetties and warehouses and fishmarkets and shipyards grew until it stretched the entire length of the city. It was also the logical place to site the transients' dormitories.

*

Jay Hilton thought the dormitory was tremendously exciting. It was so different from anything in her life to date. A simple angled roof of ezystak panels eighty metres long, supported by a framework of metal girders. There were no walls, the LDC officer said they would have made it too hot inside. There was a concrete floor, and row after row of hard wooden cots. She had slept in a sleeping-bag the first night, right at the centre of the dormitory with the rest of Group Seven's kids. It had taken her an age to fall asleep, people kept talking, and the river made great swooshing noises as it flowed past the embankment. And she didn't think she would ever get used to the humidity, her clothes hadn't been completely dry since she got off the spaceplane.

During the day the dormitory thronged with people, and the alleyways between the cots were great for chases and other games. Life underneath its rattling roof was very easygoing; nothing was organized for the kids, so they were free to please themselves how they chose. She had spent the second day getting to know the other kids in Group Seven. In the morning they ran riot among the adults, then after lunch they had all made their way down to the riverside to watch the boats. Jay had loved it. The whole port area looked like something out of a historical AV programme, a slice of the Earth's Middle Ages preserved on a far planet. Everything was made of wood, and the boats were so beautiful, with their big paddles on each side, and tall iron stacks that sent out long plumes of grey-white smoke.

Twice during the day the sky had clouded over, and rain had fallen like a solid sheet. The kids had all retreated under the dormitory roof, watching spellbound as the grey veil obscured the Juliffe, and huge lightning bolts crashed overhead.

She had never imagined the wild was *so* wild. But her mother wasn't worried, so she wasn't. Sitting down and just watching had never been such fun before. She couldn't think how wonderful it was going to be actually travelling on a river-boat. From a starship one day to a paddle-steamer the next! Life was glorious.

The food they had been served was strange, the aboriginal fruit was all odd shapes with a mildly spicy flavouring, but at least there wasn't any vat meat like they had at the arcology. After the high tea the staff served for the kids in the big canteen at one end of the dormitory, she went back to the riverside to see if she could spot any aboriginal animals. She remembered the vennal, something like a cross between a lizard and a monkey. It featured prominently in the didactic memory which the LDC immigration advisory team at the orbital-tower base-station had imprinted before she left Earth. In the mirage floating round inside her skull it looked kind of cute. She was secretly hoping she'd be able to have one as a pet once they reached their allotted land upriver.

The embankment was a solid wall of bitek polyp, a dull apricot in colour, preventing any more of the rich black soil from being chewed away by the frighteningly large river. It was thrilling to see so much bitek being used; Jay had never met an Edenist, although back at the arcology Father Varhoos had warned the congregation about them and their soulless technology of perverted life. But using the polyp here was a good idea, the kernels were cheap, and the coral didn't need constant repairs the way concrete would. She couldn't see the harm. The whole universe was being turned upside-down this week.

She slid right down the sloping wall to the water itself, and started walking, hoping to see a xenoc fish. The water here was almost clear. Wavelets lapping on the polyp sent up sprays that showered her bare legs; she was still wearing the shorts and blouse that her mother had made her carry in the zero-tau pod. A lot of the other colonists in Group Seven had spent the morning chasing after their gear in one of the warehouses, trying to find more practical clothes.

Everyone had been envious and admiring of her and mother yesterday. That felt good. So much better than the way people back in the arcology regarded them. She pushed that thought away hurriedly.

Her boots splashed through the shallows, the water droplets slithering off the shiny coating. There were a lot of big pipe outlets venting into the river, along with the drainage gullies which were like medium-sized streams, so she had to be careful as she dodged under the pipes not to get splattered by the discharges. Up ahead was one of the circular harbours, six hundred metres in diameter, also made out of polyp; a refuge where the larger boats could dock in calmer waters. The harbours were spaced every kilometre or so along the embankment, with clusters of warehouses and timber mills springing up on the ground behind them. In between the harbours were rows of wooden jetties sticking out into the river, which the smaller traders and fishing boats used.

The sky was growing darker again. But it wasn't rain, the sun was low in the west. And she was getting very tired, the day here was awfully long.

She ducked under a jetty, hand stroking the black timber pillars. Mayope wood, her eidetic memory said, one of the hardest woods found in the Confederation. The tree had big scarlet flowers. She rapped her knuckles against it experimentally. It really was hard, like a metal, or stone.

Out on the river one of the big paddle-boats was sailing past, churning up a big wake of frothy water as its bows drove against the current. Colonists were lined up along the rails, and they all seemed to be looking at her. She grinned and waved at them.

Group Seven was sailing tomorrow. The *real* adventure. She stared wistfully after the boat as it slipped away upriver.

That was when she saw the thing caught around a support pillar of the next jetty. A dirty yellow-pink lump, about a metre long. There was more of it underwater, she could tell from the way it bobbed about. With a whoop, she raced forwards, feet kicking up fans of water. It was a xenoc fish, or amphibian, or something. Trapped and waiting for her to inspect it. Names and shapes whirled through her mind, the didactic memory on full recall, trying to match up with what she was seeing.

Maybe it's something new, she thought. Maybe they'll name it after me. I'll be famous!

She was five metres away, and still running as hard as she could, when she saw the head. It was someone in the water, someone without any clothes on. Face down! The shock threw her rhythm, and her feet skidded from under her. She yelled as her knee hit the rough, unyielding polyp. She felt a hot pain as she grazed the side of her leg. She finished up flat against the embankment, legs half in the water, feeling numb all over and sick inside. Blood started to well up in the graze. She bit her lip, eyes watering as she watched it, fighting not to cry.

A wave lifted the corpse in the river, knocking it against the support pillar again. Through sticky tears Jay saw that it was a man, all swollen up. His head turned towards her. There was a long purple weal along one cheek. He had no eyes, only empty holes where they should be. His flesh was rippling. Jay blinked. Long white worms with a million legs were feeding on the battered flesh. One oozed out of his half-open mouth like a slender anaemic tongue, its tip waving around slowly as though it was tasting the air.

She threw her head back and screamed.

*

The rain which came after the sun sank from the sky an hour later that evening was a big help to Quinn Dexter. Between them, Lalonde's three moons conspired to cast a bright spectral phosphorescence on the night-time city: people could see their way quite clearly down the slushy streets, but with the thick clouds scudding overhead the light level was drastically reduced. Durringham didn't have street lighting; individual pubs would floodlight the street outside their entrance, and the bigger cabins had porch lights, but outside their pools of radiance there was only a faint backscatter of photons. In amongst the large industrial buildings of the port where Quinn lurked there wasn't even that, only gloom and impenetrable shadows.

He had slipped away from the transients' dormitory after the evening meal, finding himself a concealing gap between a couple of single-storey outbuildings tacked on to the end of a long warehouse. Jackson Gael was crouched down behind some barrels on the other side of the path. Behind him was the high blank wall of a mill, slatted wooden planks rearing up like a cliff face.

There wouldn't be many people wandering around this part of the port at night, and those that did would probably be colonists waiting for a boat upriver. There was another transients' dormitory two hundred metres to the north. Quinn had decided that colonists would make the best targets.

The sheriffs would pay more attention to a city resident being mugged than some new arrival who nobody cared about. Colonists were human cattle to the LDC; and if the dopey bastards hadn't worked that out for themselves, then more fool them. But Jackson had been right about one thing, the colonists were better off than him. Ivets were the lowest of the low.

They had discovered that yesterday evening. When they finally arrived at the dormitory they were immediately detailed to unload the lorries they had just loaded at the spaceport. After they finished stacking Group Seven's gear in a harbourside warehouse a group of them had wandered off into town. They didn't have any money, but that didn't matter, they deserved a break. That was when they found the grey Ivet jump-suit with its scarlet letters acted like a flashing beacon: *Shit on me.* They hadn't got more than a few hundred metres out of the port before they turned tail and hurried back to the dormitory. They'd been spat on, shouted at, jeered by children, had stones flung at them, and finally someone had let a xenoc animal charge at them. That had frightened Quinn the most, though he didn't show it to the others. The creature was like a cat scaled up to dog size; it had jet-black scales and a wedge-shaped head, with a lot of sharp needle teeth in its gaping mouth. The mud didn't slow it down appreciably as it ran at them, and several Ivets had skidded onto their knees as the group panicked and ran away.

Worst of all were the sounds the thing made, like a drawn-out whine; but there were words in the cry, strangely twisted by the xenoc gullet, human words. 'City scum,' and 'Kid fuckers,' and others that were distorted beyond recognition, yet all carrying the same message. The *thing* hated them, echoing its master who had laughed as its huge jaws snapped at their running legs.

Back in the dormitory, Quinn had sat down and started to think for the first time since the police stunned him back on Earth. He had to get off this planet which even God's Brother would reject. To do that he needed information. He needed to know how the local set-up worked, how to get himself an edge. All the other Ivets would dream about leaving, some must have made attempts to escape in the past. The biggest mistake he could make would be rushing it. And dressed in his signpost jump-suit, he wouldn't even be able to scout around.

He had caught Jackson Gael's eye, and flicked his head at the velvet walls of night encircling the dormitory. The two of them slipped out unnoticed, and didn't return till dawn.

Now he waited crouched against the warehouse wall, stripped down to his shorts, nerves burning with excitement at the prospect of repeating last night's spree. Rain was drumming on the rooftops and splashing into the puddles and mud of the path, kicking up a loud din. More water was gurgling down the drainage gully at the side of the warehouse. His skin and hair were soaked. At least the drops were warm.

The man in the canary-yellow cagoule was almost level with the little gap between the outhouses before Quinn heard him. He was squelching through the mud, muttering and humming under his breath. Quinn peered out round the corner. His left eye had been boosted by a nanonic cluster, giving him infrared vision. It was his first implant, and he'd used it for exactly the same purpose back at the arcology: to give him an edge in the dark. One thing Banneth had taught him was never fight until you've already won.

The retinal implant showed him a ghostly red figure weaving

unsteadily from side to side. Rain showed as a gritty pale pink mist, the buildings were claret-coloured crags.

Quinn waited until the man had passed the gap before he moved. He slid out onto the path, the length of wood gripped tightly in his hand. And still the man was unaware of him, rain and blackness providing perfect cover. He took three paces, raised the improvised club, then slammed it down at the base of the man's neck. The cagoule's fabric tore under the impact. Quinn felt the blow reverberate all the way back up to his elbows, jarring his joints. God's Brother! He didn't want the man dead, not yet.

His victim gave a single grunt of pain, and collapsed forwards into the mud.

'Jackson!' Quinn called. 'God's Brother, where are you? I can't shift him by myself. Get a move on.'

'Quinn? Christ, I can't see a bloody thing.'

He looked round, seeing Jackson emerge from behind the barrels. His skin shone a strong burgundy in the infrared spectrum, arteries and veins near the surface showing up as brighter scarlet lines.

'Over here. Walk forward three steps, then turn left.' He guided Jackson up to the body, enjoying the sense of power. Jackson would follow his leadership, and the others would fall into line.

Together they dragged their victim into the outhouse – Quinn guessed it had been some kind of office, abandoned years ago now. Four bare wooden slat walls and a roof that leaked. Tapers of slime ran down the walls, fungal growths blooming from the cracks. There was a strong citric scent in the air. Overhead the clouds were drifting away inland. Beriana, the second moon, came out, shining a wan lemon light onto the city, and a few meagre beams filtered through the skylight. They were enough for Jackson to see by.

Both of them went over to the pile of clothes they had left heaped on a broken composite cargo-pod. Quinn watched

Jackson towelling himself dry. The lad had a strong body, broad shoulders.

'Forget it, Quinn,' Jackson said in a neutral voice, but one that carried in the silence following the rain. 'I don't turn on to that. Strictly het, OK?' It came out like a challenge.

'Hey, don't lose cool,' Quinn said. 'I got my eye on someone, and it ain't you.' He wasn't entirely sure he could whip the lanky lad from a straight start. Besides he needed Jackson. For now.

He started to pull on the clothes which belonged to one of last night's victims, a green short-sleeved shirt and baggy blue shorts, waterproof boots which were only fractionally too large. Three pairs of socks stopped them from rubbing blisters. He was strongly tempted to take those boots upriver, he didn't like to think what would happen to his feet in the lightweight Ivet-issue shoes.

'Right, let's see what we've got,' he said. They stripped the cagoule from the unconscious man. He groaned weakly. His shorts were soiled, and a ribbon of piss ran out of the cagoule.

Definitely a new colonist, Quinn decided, as he wrinkled his nose up at the smell. The clothes were new, the boots were new, he was clean shaven; and he had the slightly overweight appearance of an arcology dweller. Locals were nearly always lean, and most sported longish hair and thick beards.

His belt carried a fission-blade knife, a miniature thermal inducer, and a personal MF flek-player block.

Quinn unclipped the knife and the inducer. 'We'll take those with us upriver. They'll come in useful.'

'We'll be searched,' Jackson said. 'Anything you like, we'll be searched.'

'So? We stash them in the colonists' gear. We'll be the ones that load it onto the boat, we'll be the ones that unload it at the other end.'

'Right.'

Quinn thought he heard a grudging respect in the lad's voice.

He started frisking the man's pockets, hoping the dampness in the fabric wasn't piss. There was a citizenship card naming their victim as Jerry Baker, a credit disk of Lalonde francs, then he hit the jackpot. 'God's Brother!' He held up a Jovian Bank credit disk, holographic silver on one side, royal purple on the other. 'Will you look at this. Mr Pioneer here wasn't going to take any chances in the hinterlands. He must have been planning on buying his way out of any trouble he hit upriver. Not so dumb after all. Just his bad luck he ran into us.'

'Can you use it?' Jackson asked urgently.

Quinn turned Jerry Baker's head over. A soft liquid moan emerged from his lips at the motion. His eyelids were fluttering, a bead of blood ran out of his mouth; his breathing was erratic. 'Shut up,' Quinn said absently. 'Shit, I hit him too hard. Let's see.' He pressed his right thumb against Jerry Baker's, and engaged his second implant. The danger was that with Jerry Baker's nervous system fucked up from the blow, the biolectric pattern of his cells which activated the credit disk might be scrambled.

When the nanonic signalled the pattern had been recorded, he held up the Jovian Bank credit disk and touched his thumb to the centre. Green figures lit up on the silver side.

Jackson Gael let out a fast triumphant hoot, and slapped Quinn on the back. Quinn had been right: Jerry Baker had come to Lalonde prepared to buy himself out of fifteen hundred fuseodollars' worth of trouble.

They both stood up.

'Hell, we don't even have to go upriver now,' Jackson said. 'We can set up in town. Christ, we can live like kings.'

'Don't be bloody stupid. This is only going to be good until he's reported missing, which will be tomorrow morning.' His toe nudged the inert form on the wet floor.

'So change it into something; gold, diamonds, bales of cloth.'

Quinn gave the grinning lad a sharp look, wondering if he'd misjudged him after all. 'This isn't our town, we don't know who's safe, who to grease. Whoever changed that much money would know it was bent, they'd give our descriptions to the sheriffs first chance they got. They probably wouldn't want us upsetting their own operations.'

'So what do we do with it, then?'

'We change some of it. These local francs have a cash issue as well as disks. So we spend heavily, and the locals will love giving a pair of dumb-arse colonists their toy francs as change instead of real money. Then we buy a few goodies we can take upriver that will make life a lot easier, like a decent weapon or two. After that . . .' He brought the disk up to his face. 'It goes into the mud. We don't leave any evidence, OK?'

Jackson pulled a face, but nodded regretfully. 'OK, Quinn. I guess I hadn't thought it through.'

Baker moaned again, the wavery sound of a man trapped in a bad dream.

Quinn kicked him absently. 'Don't worry about it. Now first help me put Jerry Baker into the drainage gully outside where he'll wash down into the river. Then we'll find somewhere where we can spend his fuseodollars in style.' He started looking round for the wooden club to silence Baker and his moaning once and for all.

*

After visiting a couple of pubs, the place they wound up at was called Donovan's. It was several kilometres away from the port district, safely distant from any Group Seven members who might be having a last night in the big city. In any case, it wasn't the sort of place that the staunchly family types of Group Seven sought out.

Like most of Durringham's buildings, it was single storey, with walls of thick black wood. Stone piles raised it a metre above the ground, and there was a veranda right along the front, with drinkers slouched over the railing, glass tankards of beer in their hands, watching the newcomers with hazed eyes.

The road outside had a thick layer of stone chippings spread over it. For once Quinn's boots didn't sink in up to his ankles.

Their clothes marked them down as colonists, machine-made synthetic fabric; locals were dressed in loom-woven cloth, shirts and shorts hand sewn, solid boots that came up to the top of their calves, caked in mud. But nobody shouted a challenge as they walked up the steps. Quinn felt almost home for the first time since he'd stepped off the spaceplane. These were people he understood, hard workers who pleased themselves any damn way they chose after dark. They heard the xenoc animals even before they went through the open doors. It was that same eerie whine of the thing which had chased them yesterday evening, only this time there were five or six of them all doing it at the same time. He exchanged a fast glance with Jackson, then they were inside.

The bar was a single plank of wood running along one side of the main bar, a metre wide, fifteen metres long. People were lined up along it, two deep, the six barmaids hard pushed to cope.

Quinn waited until he reached the bar, and held up the Jovian Bank disk. 'You take this?'

The girl barely glanced at it. 'Yeah.'

'Great, two beers.'

She started pulling them from the cask.

'It's my last night here before I sail upriver. Do you know where I can maybe get a bit of sport? Don't want to waste it.'

'In the back.' She didn't look up.

'Gee, thanks. Have one yourself.'

'A brightlime, thanks.' She put his half-litre tankards down in the puddles on the bar. 'Six fuseodollars.'

Which Quinn reckoned was three times what the drinks should cost, unless a brightlime was more expensive than Norfolk Tears. Yes, the locals knew how to treat transient colonists. He activated the credit disk, shunting the money to her bar account block.

The vicious black catlike animals were called sayce, the local dog-analogue, with a degree more intelligence than Earth's canines. Quinn and Jackson saw them as soon as they pushed aside the rug hanging across the doorway and elbowed their way into Donovan's rear room. It was a baiting arena; three tiers of benches ringing a single pit dug into the floor and lined with cut stone, five metres in diameter, three deep. Bright spotlights were strung up on the rafters, casting a white glare on the proceedings. Every centimetre of bench space was taken. Men and women with flushed red faces, cheering and shouting, soaked in sweat. It was hot in the room, hotter than the spaceport clearing at midday. Big cages were lined up along the back wall, sayce prowling about inside, highly agitated, some of them butting the bars of that ubiquitous black wood, emitting their anguished whine.

Quinn felt a grin rising. Now this was more like it!

They found a bench and squirmed on. Quinn asked the man he was next to who was taking the money.

It turned out the bookie was called Baxter, a thin oriental with a nasty scar leading from the corner of his left eye down below his grubby red T-shirt neck.

'Pay out only in Lalonde francs,' he said gruffly.

A man mountain with a black beard stood at Baxter's side, and gave Quinn a cannibal look.

'Fine by me,' Quinn said amicably. He put a hundred fuseodollars on the favourite.

The fights were impressive, fast, violent, gory, and short. The owners would stand on opposite sides of the pit, holding back their animals, shouting orders into the flat triangular ears. When the sayce had reached a fever pitch of anger they were shoved into the pit. Streamlined black bodies clashed in a snarl of six-clawed paws and snapping jaws, muscle bands like steel pistons bunching and stretching the shiny skin. Losing a leg didn't even slow them down. Quinn saw them tear off legs, jaws, rip out eyes, rake underbellies. The pit floor became slippery with blood, fluid, and sausage-string entrails. A crushed skull usually ended it, the losing sayce being repeatedly smashed against the stone wall until bone splintered and the brain was torn. Their blood was surprisingly red.

Quinn lost money on the first three fights, then picked up a wad of six hundred francs on the fourth, equivalent to a hundred and fifty fuseodollars. He handed a third of the plastic notes to Jackson, and put another two hundred fuseodollars on the next fight.

After seven fights he was eight hundred fuseodollars down, with two and a half thousand Lalonde francs in his pocket.

'I know her,' Jackson said as the next two sayce were being goaded on the side of the pit by their owners. One of them was an old bull, his skin a cross web of scars. That was the one Quinn had put his money on. Always trust in proven survivors.

'Who?'

'Girl over there. She's from Group Seven.'

Quinn followed his gaze. The girl was a teenager, very attractive, with longish dark hair falling down over her shoulders. She was wearing a sleeveless singlet with a scoop neck; it looked new, the fabric was shiny, definitely synthetic. Her face was burning with astonishment and excitement, the taste of forbidden fruit, sweetest of all. She was sitting between two brothers, twins, about thirty years old, with sandy blond hair, just beginning to thin. They were dressed in shirts of checked cotton, crudely cut. Both of them had the kind of thick brown skin that came from working outdoors.

'Are you sure?' With the glare of the lights it was difficult for him to tell.

'I'm sure. I couldn't forget those tits. I think she's called Mary, Mandy, something like that.'

The sayce were shoved into the pit, and the crowd roared. The two powerful vulpine bodies locked together, spinning madly, teeth and claws slicing through the air.

'I suppose she's entitled to be here,' Quinn said. He was

annoyed, he didn't need complications like the girl. 'I'm going to have a word with Baxter. Make sure she doesn't see you, we don't want her to know we were here.'

Jackson gave him a thumbs up and took another gulp from his tankard.

Baxter was standing on the ramp leading from the pit to the cages, head flicking from side to side as he followed the battling beasts. He acknowledged Quinn with a terse nod.

A spume of blood flew out of the pit, splattering the people on the lowest benches. One of the sayce was screeching. Quinn thought it was calling, 'Help.'

'You done all right tonight,' Baxter said. 'Break even, beginner's luck. I let you place bigger bets, you want.'

'No, I need the money. I'm going upriver soon.'

'You build nice home for family, good luck.'

'I need more than luck up there. Suppose I bump into one of those?' He flicked a finger at the pit. The old bull had its jaws around the younger sayce's throat, it was slamming its head against the side of the pit, oblivious to the deep gouges the other's claws were raking down its flanks.

'Sayce not like living near river,' Baxter said. 'Air too wet. You be all right.'

'A sayce or one of its cousins. I could do with something with a bit of punch, something that'll stop it dead.'

'You bring plenty gear from Earth.'

'Can't bring everything we need, the company doesn't let us. And I want some recreational items as well. I thought maybe I could pick it all up in town. I thought maybe you might know who I needed to see.'

'You think too much.'

'I also pay a lot.'

Down in the pit a sayce's head virtually exploded as it was slammed against the wall for the last time. Pulpy gobs of brain sleeted down.

Quinn smiled when he saw the old bull raise its head to

its cheering owner and let out a gurgling high-pitched bleat: 'Yessss!'

'You owe me another thousand francs,' he told Baxter. 'You can keep half of it as a finder's fee.'

Baxter's voice dropped an octave. 'Come back here, ten minutes; I show you man who can help.'

'Gotcha.'

The old bull sayce was sniffling round the floor of the pit when Quinn got back to Jackson. A blue tongue started to lick up the rich gore sloshing about on the stone.

Jackson watched the spectacle glumly. 'She's gone. She left with the twins after the fight. Christ, putting out like that, and she's only been here a day.'

'Yeah? Well, just remember she's going to be trapped on a river cruise with you for a fortnight. You can work your angle then.'

He brightened. 'Right.'

'I think I got us what we need. Although God's Brother knows what kind of weapons they sell in this dump. Crossbows, I should think.'

Jackson turned to face him. 'I still think we should stay here. What do you hope to do upriver, take over the settlement?'

'If I have to. Jerry Baker isn't going to be the only one who brought a Jovian Bank disk with him. If we get enough of them, we can buy ourselves off this shit heap.'

'Christ, you really think so? We can get off? All the way off?'

'Yeah. But it's going to take a big pile of hard cash, that means we've got to separate a lot of colonists from their disks.' He fixed the lad with the kind of stare Banneth used when she interviewed new recruits. 'Are you up to that, Jackson? I've got to have people who are going to back me the whole way. I ain't got space for anyone who farts out at the first sign of trouble.'

'I'm with you. All the way. Christ, Quinn, you know that, I proved that last night and tonight.'

There was a note of desperation creeping into the voice.

Jackson was insisting on having a part of what Quinn offered. The ground rules were laid out.

So let the game start, Quinn thought. The greatest game of all, the one God's Brother plays for all eternity. The vengeance game. 'Come on,' he said. 'Let's go see what Baxter's got for us.'

*

Horst Elwes checked the metabolic function read-out on his medical block's display screen, then glanced down at the sleeping figure of Jay Hilton. The girl was curled up inside a sleeping-bag, her facial features relaxed into serenity. He had cleaned the nasty graze on her leg, given her an antibiotic, and wrapped the leg in a sheath of epithelium membrane. The tough protective tissue would help accelerate natural dermal regeneration.

It was a pity the membrane could only be used once. Horst was beginning to wonder if he had stocked enough in his medical case. According to his didactic medical course, damaged human skin could rot away if it was constantly exposed to high humidity. And humidity didn't come any higher than around the Juliffe.

He plucked the sensor pad from Jay's neck, and put it back in the medical block's slot.

Ruth Hilton gave him an expectant stare. 'Well?'

'I've given her a sedative. She'll sleep for a solid ten hours now. It might be a good idea for you to be at her side when she wakes up.'

'Of course I'll be here,' she snapped.

Horst nodded. Ruth had shown nothing but concern and sympathy when the sobbing girl had stumbled back into the dormitory, never letting a hint of weakness show. She had held Jay's hand all the time while Horst disinfected the graze, and the sheriff asked his questions. Only now did the worry spill out.

'Sorry,' Ruth said.

Horst gave her a reassuring smile, and picked up the medical block. It was larger than a standard processor block, a rectangle thirty-five centimetres long, twenty-five wide and three thick, with several ancillary sensor units, and a memory loaded with the symptoms and treatment of every known human illness. And that was as much a worry as the epithelium membrane; Group Seven was going to be completely dependent on him and the block for their general health for years to come. The responsibility was already starting to gnaw at his thoughts. His brief spell in the arcology refuge had shown him how little use theoretical medicine was in the face of real injuries. He had swiftly picked up enough about first aid to be of some practical use to the hard-pressed medics, but anything more serious than cuts and fractures could well prove fatal upriver.

At least the block had been left in his pod; several other items had gone missing between the spaceport and the warehouse. Damn, but why did Ruth have to be right about that? And the sheriffs hadn't shown any interest when he reported the missing drugs. Again, just like she said.

He sighed and rested his hand on her shoulder as she sat on the edge of the cot, stroking Jay's hair.

'She's a lot tougher than me,' he said. 'She'll be all right. At that age, horror fades very quickly. And we'll be going upriver straight away. Getting out of the area where it happened is going to help a lot.'

'Thank you, Horst.'

'Do you have any geneering in your heritage?'

'Yes, some. We're not Saldanas, but one of my ancestors was comfortably off, God bless him, we had a few basic enhancements about six or seven generations ago. Why?'

'I was thinking of infection. There is a kind of fungal spore here which can live in human blood. But if your family had even a modest improvement to your immune system there won't be any problem.'

He stood and straightened his back, wincing at the twinges along his spine. It was quiet in the dormitory; the lights were off in the centre where the rest of Group Seven's children had been settled down for the night. Bee-sized insects with large grey wings were swarming round the long light panels that had been left on. He and Ruth had been left alone by the other colonists after the sheriff departed to examine the body in the river. He could see some kind of meeting underway in the canteen, most of the adults were there. The Ivets formed a close-knit huddle in a corner at the other end, all of them looking sullen. And frightened, Horst could tell. Waster kids who had probably never even seen an open sky before, never mind primeval jungle. They had stayed in the dormitory all day. Horst knew he should make an effort to get to know them, help build a bridge between them and the genuine colonists, unite the community. After all, they were going to spend the rest of their lives together. Somehow he couldn't find the energy.

Tomorrow, he promised himself. We'll all be on the ship for a fortnight, that'll give me ample opportunity.

'I ought to be at the meeting,' he said. From where he was he could see two people standing up for a shouting match.

'Let 'em talk,' Ruth grunted. 'It keeps them out of mischief. They won't get anything sorted until after the settlement supervisor shows up.'

'He should have been here this morning. We need advice on how to establish our homes. We don't even know the location we've been assigned.'

'We'll find out soon enough; and the supervisor will have the whole river trip to lecture us. I expect he's out prowling the town tonight. I can't blame him, stuck with us for the next eighteen months. Poor sod.'

'Must you always think the worst of people?'

'It's what I'd do. But that isn't what worries me right now.'

Horst sneaked another look at the meeting. They were taking

a vote, hands raised in the air. He sat down on the cot facing Ruth. 'What does worry you?'

'The murder.'

'We don't know it was a murder.'

'Get real. The body was stripped. What else could it be?'

'He could have been drunk.' Because God knows a drink is what I need just looking at that river.

'Drunk and taking a swim? In the Juliffe? Come on, Horst!'

'The autopsy should tell us if . . .' He trailed off under Ruth's gaze. 'No, I don't suppose there will be one, will there?'

'No. He must have been dumped in the river. The sheriff told me that two colonists from Group Three were reported missing by their wives this morning. Pete Cox and Alun Reuther. I'll give you ten to one that body is one of them.'

'Probably,' Horst admitted. 'I suppose it's shocking that urban crime is rife here. Somehow you don't imagine such a thing on a stage one colony world. Then again, Lalonde isn't quite what I imagined. But we'll be leaving it all behind shortly. Our own community will be too small for such things, we will all know each other.'

Ruth rubbed at her eyes, her expression haunted. 'Horst, you're not thinking. Why was the body stripped?'

'I don't know. For the clothes, I suppose, and the boots.'

'Right. Now what sort of mugger is going to kill for a pair of boots? Actually kill two people in cold blood. God, the people here are poor, I'm not denying it, but they're not that desperate.'

'Who then?'

She looked pointedly over his shoulder. Horst turned round. 'The Ivets? That's rather prejudiced, isn't it?' he asked reproachfully.

'You've seen the way they're treated in the town, and we don't treat them any better. They can't move outside the port district without getting beaten up. Not with their jump suits on, and they don't have anything else to wear. So who is more likely to want ordinary clothes? Who isn't going to care what they have to do to get them? And whoever did murder that man did it inside the port, uncomfortably close to this dormitory.'

'You don't think it was one of ours?' he exclaimed.

'Let's say, I'm praying it wasn't. But with the way our luck is turning out, I wouldn't count on it.'

*

Diranol, Lalonde's smallest, outermost moon, was the only one of the planet's three natural satellites left in the night sky, a nine-hundred-kilometre globe of rock with a red ochre regolith, half a million kilometres distant. It hovered above the eastern horizon, painting Durringham in a timid rose-pink fluorescence when the power bike skidded to a halt just outside the skirt of light leaking from the big transients' dormitory. Marie Skibbow loosened her grip on Furgus. The ride through the darkened city had been sensational, drawing out every second, filling it with glee and excitement. The walls slashing past, sensed rather than seen, the headlight beam revealing ruts and mud patches on the road almost as soon as they hit them, wind whipping her hair about, eyes stung by the slipstream. Taunting danger with every turn of the wheel, and beating it, *living*.

'Here we go, your stop,' Furgus said.

'Right.' She swung her leg over the saddle, and stood beside him. Now the weariness swept through her, a frozen wave of depression that hung poised high above, waiting to crash down at the prospect of the future and what it held.

'You're the best, Marie.' He kissed her, one hand fondling her right breast through the singlet's fabric. Then he was gone, red tail light sinking into the blackness.

Her shoulders drooped as she made her way into the dormitory. Most of the cots were full, people were snoring, coughing, tossing about. She wanted to turn and run, back to Furgus and Hamish, back to the dark fulfilment of the last few hours. Her brain was still fizzing from the experiences, the naked savagery of the sayce-baiting, and the jubilant crowd in Donovan's, blood heat inflaming her senses. Then the delicious indecency of the twins' quiet cabin on the other side of town, with their straining bodies pounding against her first singly then both at once. That crazy bike ride in the vermilion moonlight. Marie wanted every night to be the same, without end.

'Where the hell have you been?'

Her father was standing in front of her, mouth all squeezed up that way it did when he was really angry. And for once she didn't care.

'Out,' she said.

'Out where?'

'Enjoying myself. Exactly what you think I shouldn't do.'

He slapped her on the cheek, the sound echoing from the high roof. 'Don't you be so bloody impudent, girl. I asked you a question. What have you been doing?'

Marie glared at him, feeling the heat grow in her stinging cheek, refusing to rub it. 'What's next, *Daddy*? Will you take your belt to me? Or are you just going to use your fists?'

Gerald Skibbow's jaw dropped. People on the nearby cots were turning over, peering at them blearily.

'Do you know how late it is? What have you been up to?' he hissed.

'Are you quite sure you want a truthful answer to that, Daddy? *Quite* sure?'

'You despicable little vixen. Your mother's been fretting over you all night. Doesn't that even bother you?'

Marie curled her lip up. 'What tragedy could possibly happen to me in this paradise you've brought us to?'

For a moment she thought he was going to strike her again.

'There have been two murders in the port this week,' he said.

'Yeah? That doesn't surprise me.'

'Get into bed,' Gerald said through clenched teeth. 'We'll discuss this in the morning.'

'Discuss it?' she asked archly. 'You mean I get an equal say?'

'For fuck's sake, can it, Skibbow,' someone shouted. 'We want to get some sleep here.'

Under the impotent stare of her father, Marie pulled her shoes off and sauntered over to her cot.

*

Quinn was still dozing in his sleeping-bag, struggling against the effects of the rough beer he had drunk in Donovan's, when someone gripped the side of his cot and yanked it through ninety degrees. His arms and legs thrashed about in the sleeping-bag as he tumbled onto the floor, but there was no way he could prevent the fall. His hip smacked into the concrete first, jarring his pelvis badly, then his jaw landed. Quinn yelled out in surprise and pain.

'Get up, Ivet,' a voice shouted.

A man was standing over him, grinning down evilly. He was in his early forties, tall and well built, with a stock of black hair and a full beard. The brown leather skin of his face and arms was scarred with a lunar relief of pocks and the tiny red lines of broken capillaries. His clothes were all natural fabric, a thick red and black check cotton shirt with the arms torn off, green denim trousers, lace-up boots that came up to his knees, and a belt which carried various powered gadgets and a vicious-looking ninety-centimetre steel machete. A silver crucifix on a slim chain glinted at the base of his neck.

He laughed in a bass roar as Quinn groaned at the hot pain in his throbbing hip. Which was too much. Quinn grappled with the seal catch at the top of the bag. He was going to make the bastard *pay.* The seal opened. His hands came out, and he kicked his legs, trying to shake off the constricting fabric. Somewhere around the edges of his perception the other Ivets were shouting in alarm and jumping over the cots. A huge damp jaw closed around his right hand, *completely* around, sharp teeth pinching the thin skin of his wrist, their tips grating between his tendons. Shock froze him for a horrific second. It was a dog, a hound, a fucking hellhound. Even a sayce would have thought twice before taking it on. The thing must have stood a metre high. It had short grizzled grey fur, a blunt hammerhead muzzle, jowls of black rubber, wet with gooey saliva. Big liquid eyes were fixed on him. It was growling softly. Quinn could feel the vibration all the way along his arm. He waited numbly, expecting the jaws to close, the mauling to begin. But the eyes just kept staring at him.

'My name is Powel Manani,' said the bearded man. 'And our glorious leader, Governor Colin Rexrew, has appointed me as Group Seven's settlement supervisor. That means, Ivets, I own you: body, and soul. And just to make my position absolutely clear from the start: I don't like Ivets. I think this world would be a better place without putrid pieces of crap like you screwing it up. But the LDC board has decided to lumber us with you, so I am going to make bloody sure every franc's worth of your passage fee is squeezed out of you before your work-time is up. So when I say lick shit, you lick; you eat what I give you to eat; and you wear what I give you to wear. And because you are lazy bastards by nature, there is going to be no such thing as a day off for the next ten years.'

He squatted down beside Quinn and beamed broadly. 'What's your name, dickhead?'

'Quinn Dexter . . . sir.'

Powel's eyebrows lifted in appreciation. 'Well done. You're a smart one, Quinn. You learn quick.'

'Thank you, sir.' The dog's tongue was pressing against his fingers, sliding up and down his knuckles. It felt utterly disgusting. He had never heard of an animal being trained so perfectly before.

'Smartarses are troublemakers, Quinn. Are you going to be a troublemaker for me?'

'No, sir.'

'Are you going to get up in the mornings in future, Quinn?'

'Yes, sir.'

'Fine. We understand each other, then.' Powel stood up. The dog released Quinn's hand, and backed off a pace.

Quinn held his hand up: it glistened from all the saliva; there were red marks like a tattooed bracelet around his wrist, and two drops of blood welled up.

Powel patted the dog's head fondly. 'This is my friend, Vorix. He and I are affinity bonded, which means I can quite literally smell out any scams you dickheads cook up. So don't even try to pull any fast ones, because I know them all. If I find you doing anything I don't like, it will be Vorix who deals with you. And it won't be your hand he bites off next time, he'll be dining on your balls. Do I make myself clear?'

The Ivets mumbled their answer, heads bowed, avoiding Powel's eye.

'I'm glad none of us are suffering any illusions about the other. Now then, your instructions for the day. I will not repeat them. Group Seven is going upriver on three ships: the *Swithland*, the *Nassier*, and the *Hycel*. They are currently docked in harbour three, and they're sailing in four hours. So that is the time you have to get the colonists' gear loaded. Any pods that aren't loaded, I will have you carry on your backs the whole way to the landing site upriver. Do not expect me to act as your permanent nursemaid, get yourselves organized and get on with it. You will be travelling with me and Vorix on the *Swithland*. Now move!'

Vorix barked, jowls peeled back from his teeth. Powel watched Quinn skitter backwards like a crab, then pick himself up and chase off after the other Ivets. He knew Quinn was going to be trouble, after helping to start five settlements he could read the Ivets' thoughts like a personality debrief. The youth was highly resentful, and smart with it. He was more than a waster kid, probably got tied in with some underground organization before he was transported. Powel toyed with the idea of simply leaving him behind when the *Swithland* sailed, let the Durringham sheriffs deal with him. But the Land Allocation Office would know what he'd done, and it would be entered in his file, which had too many incidents already. 'Bugger,' he muttered under his breath. The Ivets were all outside the dormitory, heading along the path to the warehouse. And it looked like they were gathering round Quinn, waiting for him to start directing them. Oh well, if it came to it, Quinn would just have to have an accident in the jungle.

Horst Elwes had been watching the episode with a number of Group Seven's members, and now he stepped up to Powel. The supervisor's dog turned its neck to look at him. Lord, but it was a brute. Lalonde was becoming a sore test for him indeed. 'Was it necessary to be quite so unpleasant to those boys?' he asked Powel Manani.

Powel looked him up and down, eyes catching on the white crucifix. 'Yes. If you want the blunt truth, Father. That's the way I always deal with them. They have to know who's in charge from the word go. Believe me, they respect toughness.'

'They would also respond to kindness.'

'Fine, well you show them plenty of it, Father. And just to prove there's no ill feeling, I'll give them time off to attend mass.'

Horst had to quicken his pace to keep up. 'Your dog,' he said cautiously.

'What about him?'

'You say you are bonded with affinity?'

'That's right.'

'Are you an Edenist, then?'

Vorix made a noise that sounded suspiciously like a snicker.

'No, Father,' Powel said. 'I'm simply practical. And if I had a fuseodollar for every new-landed priest who asked me that I would be a millionaire. I need Vorix upriver; I need him to hunt, to scout, to keep the Ivets in line. Neuron symbionts give me control over him. I use them because they are cheap and they work. The same as all the other settlement supervisors, and half of the county sheriffs as well. It's only the major Earth-based religions which maintain people's prejudice against bitek. But on worlds like Lalonde we can't afford your prissy theological debates. We use what we have to, when we have to. And if you want to survive long enough to fill Group Seven's second generation with your noble bigotry over a single chromosome which makes people a blasphemy, then you'll do the same. Now if you'll excuse me, I have a settlement expedition to sort out.' He brushed past, heading for the harbour.

Gerald Skibbow and the other members of Group Seven followed after him, several of them giving shamefaced glances to the startled priest. Gerald watched Rai Molvi gathering up his nerve to speak. Molvi had made a lot of noise at the meeting last night, he seemed to fancy himself as a leader of men. There had been plenty of suggestions that they form an official committee, elect a spokesperson. It would help the group interface with the authorities, Rai Molvi said. Gerald privately gave him six months before he was running back to Durringham with his tail between his legs. The man was an obvious lawyer type, didn't have what it took to be a farmer.

'You were supposed to be here yesterday to brief us,' Rai Molvi said.

'Quite right,' Powel said without breaking stride. 'I apologize. If you would like to make an official complaint about me, the Land Allocation Office which issues my contract is in a dumper down on the western edge of town. It's only six kilometres.'

'No, we weren't going to complain,' Rai Molvi said quickly. 'But we do need to establish certain facts to prepare ourselves. It would have been helpful had you attended.'

'Attended what?'

'Last night's council meeting.'

'What council?'

'Group Seven's council.'

Powel took a breath. He never did understand why half of the colonists came to Lalonde in the first place. The LDC must employ some pretty amazing advertising techniques back on Earth, he thought. 'What was it the *council* wanted to know?'

'Well . . . where are we going, for a start?'

'Upriver.' Powel stretched out the pause long enough to make the other man uncomfortable. 'A place called Schuster County, on the Quallheim tributary. Although I'm sure that if you have somewhere else in mind the river-boat captain will be happy to take you there instead.'

Rai Molvi reddened.

Gerald pushed his way to the front as they all moved out from under the dormitory's creaking roof. Powel had turned, making for the circular harbour two hundred metres away, Vorix padding along eagerly behind him. There were several paddle-boats pulled up at the wooden quays inside the artificial lagoon. The bright red specks of scavenging chikrows swirled overhead. The sight with its sense of purpose and adventure was unbeatable, quickening his blood.

'Is there anything we need to know about the paddle-boats?' he asked.

'Not really,' Powel said. 'They carry about a hundred and fifty people each, and it'll take us about a fortnight to reach the Quallheim. Your meals are provided as part of your transit fee, and I'll be giving talks on the more practical aspects of jungle lore and setting up your home. So just find yourself a bunk, and enjoy the trip, for you won't ever have another like it. After we make landfall the real work begins.'

Gerald nodded his thanks and turned back to the dormitory. Let the others pester the man with irrelevant questions, he would get the family packed and onto the *Swithland* straight away. A long river trip would be just what Marie needed to calm her down.

*

The *Swithland* followed a standard design for the larger paddle-boats operating on the Juliffe. She had a broad, shallow hull made of mayope planks, measuring sixty metres from prow to stern and twenty metres broad. With the water flowing by a mere metre and a half below the deck she could almost have been mistaken for a well-crafted raft had it not been for her superstructure, which resembled a large rectangular barn. Her odd blend of ancient and modern technologies was yet another indicator of Lalonde's development status. Two paddles midway down the hull because they were far simpler to manufacture and maintain than the more efficient screws. Electric motors because the industrial machinery to assemble them was cheaper than the equivalent necessary to produce a steam generator and turbine unit. But then electric motors required a power source, which was a solid-state thermal-exchange furnace imported from Oshanko. Such costly imports would only be tolerated while the number of paddle-boats made the generator and turbine factory uneconomical. When their numbers increased the governing economic equations would change in tandem, quite probably sweeping them away entirely to be replaced with another equally improbable mismatch craft. Such was the way of progress on Lalonde.

The *Swithland* herself was only seventeen years old, and good for another fifty or sixty at least. Her captain, Rosemary Lambourne, had taken out a mortgage with the LDC that her grandchildren would be paying off. As far as she was concerned, that was a bargain. Seventeen years of watching hapless colonists sailing upriver to their dream's ruin convinced her she had done the right thing. Her colonist shipment contract with the Governor's Transport Office was a solid income, guaranteed for the next twenty years, and everything she brought downriver for Durringham's growing merchant community was pure profit, earning hard fuseodollars.

Life on the river was the best, she could hardly remember her existence back on Earth, working in a Govcentral design bureau to improve vac-train carriages. That was somebody else's existence.

A quarter of an hour before they were due to cast off, Rosemary stood on the open bridge, which took up the forward quarter of the superstructure's top deck. Powel Manani had joined her after he had led his horse up the gangplank, tethering it on the aft deck; now the two of them watched the colonists embarking. Children and adults alike shuffled round. The children were mostly gathered round the horse, patting and stroking it gently. Shoulder-bags and larger cases were strewn about over the dark planking. The sound of several heated arguments drifted up to the top deck. Nobody had thought to count how many people were coming on board. Now the boat was overladen, and latecomers were reluctant to find another berth on one of the other ships.

'You got your Ivets organized well,' she told the supervisor. 'I don't think I've ever seen the gear stowed so professionally before. They finished over an hour ago. The harbour-master ought to nab them from you and put them to work as stevedores.'

'Humm,' Powel said. Vorix, who was lying on the deck behind them, gave an uneasy growl.

Rosemary grinned at that. Sometimes she wasn't sure who was bonded to who.

'Something wrong?' she asked.

'Someone, actually. They've got themselves a leader. He's going to be trouble, Rosemary. I know he is.'

'You'll keep them in line. Hell, you've supered five settlements, and all of them wound up viable. If you can't do it nobody can.'

'Thanks. You run a pretty tight ship yourself.'

'Keep an eye out for yourself this time, Powel. There's people gone missing up in Schuster County recently. Rumour has it the Governor's none too happy.'

'Yeah?'

'The *Hycel* is carrying a marshal upriver. Going to have a scout round.'

'I wonder if there's a bounty for finding them? The Governor doesn't like homesteaders ducking out of their settlement contract, it sets a bad example. Everyone would come and live in Durringham otherwise.'

'From what I hear, they want to find out what happened to them, not where they are.'

'Oh?'

'They just vanished. No sign of a fight. Left all their gear and animals behind.'

'Fine, well, I'll keep alert.' He took a broad-rimmed hat out of the pack at his feet. It was yellow-green in colour, much stained. 'Are we sharing a bunk this trip, Rose?'

'No chance.' She leant further over the rail to scan the foredeck for her four children, who along with two stokers were her only other crew. 'I've got me a brand-new Ivet as my second stoker. Barry MacArple, he's nineteen, real talented mechanic on both sides of the sheets. I think it shocks my eldest boy. That is, when he actually stops boffing the colonists' daughters himself.'

'Fine.'

Vorix let out a plaintive whine, and dropped his head onto his forepaws.

'When are you back in Schuster County next?' Powel asked.

'A couple of months, maybe three. I'm taking a group up to Colane County on the Dibowa tributary next time out. After that I'll be up in your area. Want me to visit?'

He settled the hat on his head, working out agendas and timescales in his mind. 'No, it's too soon. This bunch won't have exhausted their gear by then. Make it nine or ten months, let them feel a little deprivation, we'll be able to flog them a bar of soap for fifty fuseodollars by then.'

'That's a date.'

They shook on it, and turned back to watch the quarrelling colonists below.

*

Swithland cast off more or less on time. Rosemary's eldest boy, Karl, a strapping fifteen-year-old, ran along the deck shouting orders to the colonists who were helping with the cables. A cheer went up from the passengers as the paddles started turning and they moved away from the quay.

Rosemary was in the bridge herself. The harbour didn't have much spare water anyway, and *Swithland* was sluggish with a hold full of logs for the furnace, the colonists, their gear, and enough food to last them three weeks. She steered past the end of the quay and out into the centre of the artificial lagoon. The furnace was burning furiously, twin stacks sending out a high plume of grey-blue smoke. Standing on the prow, Karl gave her a smiling thumbs-up. He's going to break a lot of female hearts, that one, she thought proudly.

For once there wasn't a rain-cloud to be seen, and the forward-sweep mass-detector showed her a clean channel. Rosemary gave the horn a single toot, and pushed both paddle-control levers forward, moving out of the harbour and onto her beloved untamed river that stretched away into the unknown. How could life possibly be better than this?

For the first hundred kilometres the colonists of Group Seven could only agree with her. This was the oldest inhabited section of Amarisk outside Durringham, settled almost twenty-five years previously. The jungle had been cleared in great swaths, making way for fields, groves, and grazing land. As they stood on the side of the deck they could see herds of animals roaming free over the broad pastures, picking teams working the groves and plantations, their piles of wicker baskets full of fruit or nuts. Villages formed a continual chain along the southern bank, the rural idyll; sturdy, brightly painted wooden cottages set in the centre of large gardens that were alive with flowers, lines of tall, verdant trees providing a leafy shade. The lanes between the trunks were planted with thick grasses, shining a brilliant emerald in the intense sunlight. Out here, where people could spread without constraint, there wasn't the foot and wheel traffic to pound the damp soil into the kind of permanent repellent mud which made up Durringham's roads. Horses plodded along, pulling wains loaded with bounties of hay and barley. Windmills formed a row of regular pinnacles along the skyline, their sails turning lazily in the persistent wind. Long jetties struck out into the choppy ochre water of the Juliffe, two or three to each village. They had constant visitors in the form of small paddle-driven barges eager for the farms' produce. Children sat on the end of the jetties dangling rods and lines into the water, waving at the eternal procession of boats speeding by. In the morning small sailing boats cast off to fish the river, and the *Swithland* would cruise sedately through the flotilla of canvas triangles thrumming in the fresh breeze.

In the evening, when the sky flared into deep orange around the western horizon, and the stars came out overhead, bonfires would be lit in the village greens. Leaning on the deck rail that first night as the fires appeared, Gerald Skibbow was reduced to an inarticulate longing. The black water reflected long tapers of orange light from the bonfires, and he could hear gusty snatches of songs as the villagers gathered round for their communal meal.

'I never thought it could be this perfect,' he told Loren.

She smiled as his arm circled her. 'It does look pretty, doesn't it. Something out of a fairy story.'

'It can be ours, this sort of life. It's waiting up there at the end of the river. In ten years' time we'll be dancing round a bonfire while the boats go by.'

'And the new colonists will look at us and dream!'

'We'll have our house built, like a palace made from wood. That's what you'll live in, Loren, a miniature palace that the King of Kulu himself will envy. And you'll have a garden full of vegetables and flowers; and I'll be out in the grove, or tending the herds. Paula and Marie will live nearby, and the grandchildren will run both of us off our feet.'

Loren hugged him tightly. He lifted his head and let out a bellow of joy. 'God, how could we have wasted so many years on Earth? This is where we all belong, all of us Loren. We should throw away our arcologies and our starships, and live like the Lord intended. We really should.'

Ruth and Jay stood together beside the taffrail and watched the sun sink below the horizon, crowning the vast river with an aura of purple-gold light for one sublime magical minute.

'Listen, Mummy, they're singing,' Jay said. Her face was a picture of serenity. The horrid corpse of yesterday was long forgotten; she had found utter contentment with the big beige-coloured horse hitched up to the port railing. Those huge black eyes were so soft and loving, and the feel of its wet nose on her palm when she fed it a sweet was ticklish and wonderful. She couldn't believe something so huge was so gentle. Mr Manani had already said he would let her walk it round the deck each morning for exercise and teach her how to groom it. The *Swithland* was paradise come early. 'What are they singing?'

'It sounds like a hymn,' Ruth said. For the first time since they had landed she was beginning to feel as though she'd made the right decision. The villages certainly looked attractive, and well organized. Knowing that it was possible to succeed was half the battle. It would be tougher further from the capital, but not impossible. 'I can't say I blame them.'

The wind had died down, sending flames from the bonfires shooting straight up into the starry night, but the aroma of cooking food stole over the water to the *Swithland* and her two sister craft. The scent of freshly baked bread and thick spicy stews played hell with Quinn's stomach. The Ivets had been given cold meat and a fruit that looked like an orange, except it had a purple-bluish coloured skin and tasted salty. All the colonists had eaten a hot meal. Bastards. But the Ivets were starting to turn to him, that was something. He sat on the deck at the front of the superstructure, looking out to the north, away from all those fucking medieval hovels the colonists were wetting themselves over. The north was dark, he liked that. Darkness had many forms, physical and mental, and it conquered all in the end. The sect had taught him that, darkness was strength, and those that embrace the dark will always triumph.

Quinn's lips moved soundlessly. 'After darkness comes the Bringer of Light. And He shall reward those that followed His path into the void of Night. For they are true unto themselves and the nature of man, which is beast. They shall sit upon His hand, and cast down those who dress in the falsehood of Our Lord and His brother.'

A hand touched Quinn's shoulder, and the fat priest smiled down at him. 'I'm holding a service on the aft deck in a few minutes. We are going to bless our venture. You would be very welcome to attend.'

'No, thank you, Father,' Quinn said levelly.

Horst gave him a sad smile. 'I understand. But the Lord's door is always open for you.' He walked on towards the aft deck.

'Your Lord,' Quinn whispered to his departing back. 'Not mine.'

Jackson Gael saw the girl from Donovan's slouched against the port rail just aft of the paddle, head resting on her hands. She was wearing a crumpled Oxford-blue shirt tucked into black rugby shorts, white pumps on her feet, no socks. At first he thought she was gazing out over the river, then he caught sight of the personal MF block clipped to her belt, the silver lenses in her eyes. Her foot was tapping out a rhythm on the decking.

He shrugged out of the top of his grey jump suit, tying the arms round his waist so she wouldn't see the damning scarlet letters. There was no appreciable drop in temperature as the humid air flowed over his skin. Had there ever been a single molecule of cool air on this planet?

He tapped her on the shoulder. 'Hi.'

A spasm of annoyance crossed her face. Blind mirror irises turned in his direction as her hand fumbled with the little block's controls. The silver vanished to show dark, expressive eyes. 'Yeah?'

'Was that a local broadcast?'

'Here? You've got to be kidding. The reason we're on a boat is because this planet hasn't invented the wheel yet.'

Jackson laughed. 'You're right there. So what were you 'vising?'

'*Life Kinetic*. That's Jezzibella's latest album.'

'Hey, I rate Jezzibella.'

Her sulk lifted for a moment. 'Course you do. She turns males to jelly. Shows us fems what we can all do if we want. She makes herself succeed.'

'I saw her live, once.'

'God. You did? When?'

'She played my arcology a year ago. Five nights in the stadium, sold out.'

'Any good?'

'Supreme.' He spread his arms exuberantly. 'Nothing like an ordinary Mood Fantasy band, it's almost straight sex, but she went on for hours. She just sets your whole body on fire, what she does with the dancers. They reckoned her AV broadcast pillars were using illegal sense-activant codes. Who gives a shit? You would have loved it.'

Marie Skibbow's pout returned. 'I'll never know now, will I? Not on this bloody retarded planet.'

'Didn't you want to come here?'

'No.'

The hot resentment in her voice surprised him. The colonists had seemed such a dopey bunch, every one of them wrapped up in the prospect of all that rustic charm crap spread out along the riverbank. It hadn't occurred to him that they were anything other than unified in their goal. Marie might be a valuable ally.

He saw the captain's son, Karl, making his way down the side of the superstructure. The boy was wearing a pair of white canvas shorts, and rubber-soled plimsolls. *Swithland* was riding some choppy water, but Karl's balance was uncanny, he could anticipate the slightest degree of pitch.

'There you are,' he said to Marie. 'I've been looking everywhere for you, I thought you'd be at the service the priest's giving.'

'I'm not helping to bless this trip,' she said smartly.

Karl grinned broadly, his teeth showing a gleam in the deepening twilight. He was a head shorter than Jackson, which put him a few centimetres below Marie's height, and his torso was muscled like a medical text illustration. His family must have had plenty of geneering, he was too perfect. Jackson watched in growing bewilderment as he held his hand out expectantly to the girl.

'Are you ready to go?' Karl asked. 'My cabin's up forward, just below the bridge.'

Marie accepted the boy's hand. 'Sure.'

Jackson was given a lurid wink from Karl as he led Marie down the deck. They disappeared into the superstructure, and Jackson was sure he heard Marie giggle. He couldn't believe it. She preferred Karl? The boy was five years younger than him! His fists clenched in anger. It was being an Ivet, he *knew* it was. The little bitch!

Karl's cabin was a compact compartment overlooking the prow, definitely a teenager's room. A couple of processor blocks lay on the desk, along with some micro-tool units and a half-dismantled electronics stack from one of the bridge systems. There were holograms on the wall showing starfields and planets; clothes, shoes, and towels were scattered about on the deck planks. It had about ten times as much space as the cabin the Skibbows and Kavas were forced to share.

The door shut behind Marie, muting the sound of the congregation gathered on the aft deck. Karl immediately kicked off his plimsolls, and unlatched a broad bunk which had been folded flat against the wall.

He's only fifteen years old, Marie thought, but he has got a tremendous body, and that smile . . . God, I shouldn't have allowed him to smooth talk me in here, never mind be thinking of bedding him. Which only made her feel even randier.

The congregation started to sing a hymn, their voices bringing a rich enthusiasm to the slow melody. She thought of her father out there, his eager-to-make-amends expression this morning, telling her how the river trip would show her the wholesome satisfaction to be earned from the quieter side of life and honest labours. So please, darling, try to understand Lalonde is our future now, and a fine future at that.

Marie unbuttoned her shirt under Karl's triumphant gaze, then started on her shorts.

*

The settlements along the Juliffe changed subtly after the third day. The *Swithland* passed the end of the Hultain Marsh, and villages began to appear on the distant northern bank. They lacked the trimness of the earlier buildings, there were fewer animals and cultivated fields; less jungle had been cleared, and the trees standing so close to the cabins looked far more imposing.

The river branched, but the *Swithland* sailed on purposefully down the main channel. The water traffic began to fall off. These villages were still hard at work to tame the land, they couldn't afford the time it took to make sailing boats. Big barges were chugging down the river, loaded mainly with mayope timber cut by new settlements to sell to the shipyards in the city. But by the end of the first week even the barges were left behind. It simply wasn't economical to carry timber to the capital over such a distance.

There were tributary forks every hour now. The Juliffe was narrower, down to a couple of kilometres, its fast waters almost clear. Sometimes they would sail for five or six hours without seeing a village.

Horst felt the mood on board turning, and prayed that the despondency would end once they made landfall. The devil makes work for idle hands, and it had never been truer than out here. Once they were busy building their village and preparing the land Group Seven would have no time for brooding. But the second week seemed to last for ever, and the daily rains had returned with a vengeance. People were muttering about why they had to travel quite this far from the city for their allocated land.

The jungle had become an oppressive presence on either side, hemming them in, trees and undergrowth packed so tightly that the riverbanks created a solid barricade of leaves extending right down to the water. Foltwine, a tenacious freshwater aquatic plant, was a progressive nuisance. Its long, brown ribbonlike fronds grew just below the surface right across the width of the river. Rosemary avoided the larger clumps with ease, but strands would inevitably wrap themselves around the paddles. The *Swithland* made frequent stops while Karl and his younger sister clambered over them, cutting the tough slippery fronds free with the radiant yellow blades of fission knives.

Thirteen days after they departed from Durringham they had left the Juliffe itself behind and started to sail along the Quallheim tributary. It was three hundred metres wide, fast flowing, with vine-swamped trees thirty metres high forming a stockade on both banks. Away to the south, the colonists could just make out the purple and grey peaks of a distant mountain range. They stared in wonder at the snowcaps shining brightly in the sun; ice seemed to belong to an alien planet, not native to Lalonde.

In the early morning of the fourteenth day after leaving Durringham, a village crept into view as they edged their way up the river, the first they had seen for thirty-six hours. It was set in a semicircular clearing, a bite into the jungle nearly a kilometre deep. Felled trees lay everywhere. Thin towers of smoke rose from a few fire pits. The shacks were crude parodies of the cottages belonging to villages downriver; lashed-up frames with walls and roofs made from panels of woven palm fronds. There was a single jetty that looked terribly unsafe, with three hollowed-out log canoes tied up to it. A small stream trickling through the middle of the clearing into the river was an open sewer. Goats were tied to stakes, foraging in the short grass. Emaciated chickens scratched around in the mud and sawdust. The inhabitants stood about listlessly and watched the *Swithland* go past with numb, hooded eyes. Most of them were wearing shorts and boots, their skin a deep brown, whether from the sun or dirt it was hard to say. Even the apparently eternal chittering of the jungle creatures was hushed.

'Welcome to the town of Schuster,' Rosemary said with some irony. She was standing on the bridge, one eye permanently on the forward-sweep mass-detector, watching out for foltwine and submerged snags.

Group Seven's council and Powel Manani were ranged around the bridge behind her, grateful to be in the shade.

'This is it?' Rai Molvi asked, aghast.

'The county capital, yeah,' Powel said. 'They've been going for about a year now.'

'Don't worry,' Rosemary said. 'The land you've been allocated is another twelve kilometres upriver. You won't have to have much contact with them. No bad thing, too, if you ask me. I've seen communities like this before, they infect their neighbours. Better you have a fresh start.'

Rai Molvi nodded briefly, not trusting himself to speak.

The three rivercraft sailed on slowly, leaving behind the shanty town and its torpid inhabitants. The colonists gathered on *Swithland*'s aft deck watched them disappear as the boat rounded a bend in the river, silent and contemplative.

Horst made the sign of the cross, muttering an invocation. Perhaps a requiem would be more appropriate, he thought.

Jay Hilton turned to her mother. 'Will we have to live like that, Mummy?'

'No,' she said firmly. 'Never.'

Two hours later, with the river down to a hundred and fifty metre width, Rosemary watched the digits on the inertial-guidance block flick round to match the coordinates the Land Allocation Office had given her. Karl stood on the prow as the *Swithland* crept along at a walking pace, his keen eyes searching the impenetrable green barrier of vegetation along the southern bank. The jungle was steaming softly from the rain of an hour earlier, white tendrils wafting out of the treetops, then spiralling away into the burning azure sky. Small, colourful birds darted about between the branches, shrieking brazenly.

Karl suddenly jumped up and waved to his mother, pointing at the bank. Rosemary saw the tarnished silver pillar with its hexagonal sign on top. It was stuck in the soil five metres above the water. Vines with big purple flowers had already climbed halfway up it.

She gave the horn a triumphant hoot. 'End of the line,' she sang out. 'This is Aberdale. Last stop.'

'All right,' Powel said, holding up his hands for silence. He was standing on a barrel to address the assembled colonists on the foredeck. 'You've seen what can be done with a little bit of determination and hard work, and you've also seen how easy it is to fail. Which road you go down is entirely up to you. I'm here to help you for eighteen months, which is the period your future will be settled in. That's the make or break time. Now, tell me, are you going to make a go of it?'

He received a throaty cheer, and smiled round. 'Fine. Our first job is going to be building a jetty so that Captain Lambourne and the other two river-boats can dock. That way we can unload your gear properly, without getting it wet. Now a jetty is an important part of any village on this river. It tells a visitor straight away what sort of community you want to carve out for yourselves. You'll notice our good captain wasn't too eager to stop at Schuster. Not surprising, is it? A good jetty is one that the boats are always going to stop at, even out here. It's a statement that you want to take part in what the planet has to offer. It says you want to trade and grow rich. It says that there are opportunities here for clever captains. It makes you a part of civilization. So I think it would be a good idea if we start off as we mean to go on, and build ourselves a solid decent jetty that's going to last out your grandchildren. That's what I think. Am I right?'

The chorus of 'Yes!' was deafening.

He clapped his hands together, and hopped down off the barrel. 'Quinn?' He beckoned to the lad, who was in the group of quiet Ivets standing in the shade of the superstructure.

Quinn trotted forward. 'Yes, sir?'

The respectful tone didn't fool Powel for a second. 'The captain is holding station against the current for now. But it's costing her power, so we have to secure the *Swithland* if we want her to stay for any length of time. I want you to ferry a cable out to the shore, and tie it onto a tree large enough to take the strain. Think you can manage that?'

Quinn looked from Powel to the mass of dark green vegetation on the bank then back to Powel. 'How do I get over there?'

'Swim, boy! And don't try telling me you can't. It's only thirty-five metres.'

Karl came over, uncoiling a rope. 'Once you've secured it, we'll haul the *Swithland* into the shallows, and rig a proper mooring,' the boy said. 'Everyone else can wade ashore from there.'

'Great,' Quinn said sourly. He took his shoes off, then started to shrug out of his jump suit. Vorix nosed around the two shoes, sniffing eagerly.

Quinn left his shorts on, and sat on the decking to put his shoes back on. 'Can Vorix come with me, please?' he asked.

The dog looked round, long tongue hanging out of the side of its big jaw.

'What the hell do you want him with you for?' Powel asked.

Quinn gestured to the jungle with its barrage of animal sounds. 'To take care of any wild sayce.'

'Get in the water, Quinn, and stop whingeing. There aren't any wild sayce around here.' Powel watched as the lad eased himself over the side of the deck and into the river. Jackson Gael lay flat on the deck, and handed the rope down.

Quinn started swimming for the shore with a powerful sidestroke, dragging the rope behind him.

'The kroclions ate all the sayce,' Powel yelled after him; then, laughing heartily, went aft to get the jetty-building team organized.

8

Tranquillity: a polyp cylinder with hemispherical endcaps, its shell the colour of fired unglazed clay, sixty-five kilometres long, seventeen kilometres in diameter, the largest of all bitek habitats ever to be germinated within the Confederation. It was drab and uninviting in appearance, and difficult to see from a distance; what little sunlight eventually reached it from the F3 primary one-point seven billion kilometres away seemed to be repulsed, preferring to flow around the curving shell rather than strike the surface. It was the only human settlement in the star system, orbiting seven thousand kilometres above the Ruin Ring. The shattered remnants of those very remote xenoc cousins were its sole companions. A permanent reminder that for all its size and power, it was terribly mortal. Lonely, isolated, and politically impotent, there should be few people who would choose to live in such a place.

And yet . . .

Starships and scavenger vessels on an approach trajectory could discern a stippled haze of light hovering around the endcap orientated to galactic north. A cluster of industrial stations floated in attendance. Owned by some of the largest astroengineering companies in the Confederation, they were permanently busy serving the constant stream of starships arriving and departing. Cargo tugs, fuel tankers, personnel carriers, and multipurpose service vehicles shuttled around them, their reaction drives pulsing out a smog of hot blue ions.

A three-kilometre spindle connected Tranquillity's northern endcap to a non-rotating spaceport: a disc of metal girders, four and a half kilometres in diameter, with a confusing jumble of support facilities, tanks, and docking bays arrayed across its surface, resembling a gigantic metal cobweb that had snagged a swarm of fantastic cybernetic insects. It was as busy as any Edenist habitat, with Adamist starships loading and unloading their cargoes, taking on fuel, embarking passengers.

Behind the tarnished silver-white disc, three circular ledges stood out proud from the endcap: havens for the bitek starships which came and went with quick, graceful agility. Their geometrical diversity fascinated the entire spaceport, and most of the habitat's population; observation lounges overlooking the ledges were popular among the young and not-so-young. Mirchusko was where the blackhawks mated and died and gestated. Tranquillity offered itself as one of their few legitimate home bases. Their eggs could be bought here, changing hands for upwards of twenty million fuseodollars and absolutely no questions.

Around the rim of the endcap hundreds of organic conductor cables stretched out into space; subject to constant dust abrasion and particle impact, they were extruded on a permanent basis by specialist glands to compensate for the near-daily breakages. The habitat's rotation kept the cables perfectly straight, radiating away from the shell like the leaden-grey spokes of some cosmic bicycle wheel. They sliced through the flux lines of Mirchusko's prodigious magnetosphere, generating a gigantic electrical current which powered the biological processes of Tranquillity's mitosis layer as well as the axial light-tube and the domestic demands of its inhabitants. Tranquillity ingested thousands of tonnes of asteroidal minerals each year to regenerate its own polyp structure and invigorate the biosphere, but chemical reactions alone could never produce a fraction of the energy it needed to nurture its human occupants.

Beyond the endcap and the induction cables, exactly halfway down the cylinder, there was a city, home to over three million people: a band of starscrapers wrapped around the median equator, five-hundred-metre-long towers projecting out of the shell, studded with long, curving transparencies that radiated warm yellow light out into space. The view from the luxurious apartments inside was breathtaking; stars alternated with the storm-wracked gas giant and its little empire of rings and moons, eternal yet ever-changing as the cylinder rotated to provide an Earth-standard gravity at the base of the towers. Here, Adamists were granted the sight which was every Edenist's birthright.

Small wonder, then, that Tranquillity, with its liberal banking laws, low income tax, the availability of blackhawks to charter, and an impartial habitat-personality which policed the interior to ensure a crime-free environment (essential for the peace of mind of the millionaires and billionaires who resided within), had prospered, becoming one of the Confederation's premier independent trading and finance centres.

But it hadn't been designed as a tax haven, not at first; that came later, born out of desperate necessity. Tranquillity was germinated in 2428, on the order of the then Crown Prince of Kulu, Michael Saldana, as a modified version of an Edenist habitat, with a number of unique attributes the Prince himself requested. He intended it to act as a base from which the cream of Kulu's xenoc specialists could study the Laymil, and determine what fate had befallen them. It was an action which brought down the considerable wrath of his entire family.

Kulu was a Christian-ethnic culture, and very devout. The King of Kulu was the principal guardian of that faith throughout the kingdom; and because of bitek's synonymous association with Edenists, Adamists (especially good Christian ones) had virtually abandoned that particular branch of technology.

Possibly Prince Michael could have got away with bringing Tranquillity into existence; a self-sustaining bitek habitat was a logical solution for an isolated academic research project, and astute propaganda could have smoothed over the scandal. Royalty is no stranger to controversy, if anything it adds to its mystique, especially when relatively harmless.

But the whitewash option never arose; having germinated the habitat, Prince Michael went and compounded his original 'crime' (in the eyes of the Church, and more importantly the Privy Council) by having neuron symbionts implanted enabling him to establish an affinity bond with the young Tranquillity.

His final act of defiance, condemned as heretical by Kulu's conclave of bishops, came in 2432, the year his father, King James, died. Michael had a modified affinity gene spliced into his first son, Maurice, so that he too might commune with the kingdom's newest, and most unusual, subject.

Both were excommunicated (Maurice was a three-month-old embryo residing in an exowomb at the time). Michael abdicated before his coronation in favour of his brother, Prince Lukas. And father and son were unceremoniously exiled to Tranquillity, which was granted to them in perpetuity as a duchy.

One of the most ambitious xenoc research projects ever mounted, the unravelling of an entire species from its chromosomes to whatever pinnacles of culture it achieved, virtually collapsed overnight as its royal treasury funds were withdrawn and staff recalled.

And as for Michael: from being the rightful monarch of the seven wealthiest star systems in the Confederation, he became the de facto owner of a half-grown bitek habitat. From commanding a navy of seven hundred warships, the third most powerful military force in existence, he had at his disposal five ex-navy transports, all over twenty-five years old. From having the absolute power of life and death over a population of one and three-quarter billion loyal human subjects, he became an administrator of seventeen thousand abandoned, shit-listed technicians and their families, resentful at their circumstances. From being First Lord of the Treasury dealing in trillion-pound budgets, he was left to write a tax-haven constitution in the hope of attracting the idle rich so he could live off their surplus.

For time evermore, Michael Saldana was known as the Lord of Ruin.

*

'I am bid three hundred thousand fuseodollars for this excellent plant. Really, ladies and gentlemen, this is a remarkable specimen. There are over five intact leaves, and it is of a type never seen before, completely unclassified.' The plant sat in a glass vacuum bubble on the auctioneer's table: a dusty grey stalk, sprouting five long drooping fern-like leaves with frayed edges. The audience gazed at it in unappreciative silence. 'Come along now, that protuberance at the top may well be a flower bud. Its cloning will be such a simple matter, and the genome patent will remain exclusively in your hands, an incalculable font of wealth.'

Someone datavised another ten thousand fuseodollars.

Joshua Calvert didn't try to see who. This crowd were experts, facial expressions like poker players running downer programs. And they were all here today, packing the room, there wasn't a spare chair to be had. People stood four deep around the walls, spilling down the aisles; the casuals, billionaires looking for a spark of excitement, the serious collectors, consortium bidders, even some industrial company reps hoping for technological templates.

Here because of me.

Barrington Grier's outfit wasn't the largest auction house in Tranquillity, and it dealt in art as much as Laymil artefacts, but it was a tight, polished operation. And Barrington Grier had treated a nineteen-year-old Joshua Calvert who had just returned from his first scavenging flight as an equal, as a professional. With respect. He had used the house ever since.

The bidding room was on the fiftieth floor of the StMary's starscraper, its polyp walls overlaid by dark oak panelling, with velvet burgundy curtains on either side of the entrance arches and thick royal-blue carpets. Elaborate crystal lights cast a bright glow on the proceedings. Joshua could almost imagine himself in some Victorian London establishment. Barrington Grier had told him once that was the effect he wanted, quiet and dignified, fostering an atmosphere of confidence. The broad window behind the auctioneer spoilt the period effect somewhat; stars spun lazily outside, while Falsia, Mirchusko's sixth moon, slowly traversed the panorama, a sliver of aquamarine.

'Three hundred and fifty thousand, once.'

Falsia was eclipsed by the auctioneer's chest.

'Three hundred and fifty thousand, twice.'

The antique wooden gavel was raised. Falsia reappeared, peeping out over the man's shoulder.

'Final time.'

There was a smack as the gavel came down. 'Sold to Ms Melissa Strandberg.'

The room buzzed with voices as the glass bubble was carried away, excitement and nervousness throttling the air. In his second-row seat, with his nerves alight, Joshua felt it build around him, and shifted round uncomfortably, careful not to knock his legs against those of his neighbours. His feet were still painful if he applied pressure too quickly. Medical nanonic packages had swallowed both legs up to his knees, looking like strange green-leather boots, five sizes too large. The packages had a spongy texture, and he felt as though he was bouncing as he walked.

Three auctioneer's assistants carried a new bubble over to the table, it was a metre and a half high, with a dull gold crown of thermo-dump fins on top, keeping the internal temperature below freezing. A faint patina of condensation misted the glass. The voices in the room chopped off dead.

Joshua caught sight of Barrington Grier standing at the side of the stage, a middle-aged man with chubby red cheeks and a ginger moustache. He wore a sober navy-blue suit with baggy trousers and neck-sealed jacket with flared arms, the faintest of orange lines glowing on the satin material in a spiral pattern. He caught Joshua's eye, and gave him a wink.

'Now, ladies and gentlemen, we come to the final item of the day, lot 127. I think I can safely say that it is unique in my experience; a module stack of Laymil circuitry which has been preserved in ice since the cataclysm. We have identified both processor chips, and a considerable number of solid-state crystal memories inside. All of them in pristine condition. In this one cylinder there are more than five times the number of crystals we have recovered since the discovery of the Ruin Ring itself. I will leave it to you to imagine the sheer wealth of information stored within. This is undoubtedly the greatest find since the first intact Laymil body, over a century ago. And it is my great privilege to open the bidding at the reserve price of two million Edenist fuseodollars.'

Joshua had been bracing himself, but there wasn't even a murmur of protest from the crowd.

The bids came in fast and furious, rising in units of fifty thousand fuseodollars. The background level of conversation crept up again. Heads were swivelling around, bidders trying to make eye contact with their opponents, gauge the level of determination.

Joshua gritted his teeth together as the bids rose through four million. Come on, keep going. Four million three hundred thousand. The answer could be stored in there, why the Laymil did it. Four and a half. You'll solve the biggest problem facing science since we cracked the lightspeed barrier. Four million eight hundred thousand. You'll be famous, they'll name the discovery after you, not me. Come on, you bastards. Bid!

'Five million,' the auctioneer announced calmly.

Joshua sank back into the chair, a little whimper of relief leaking from his throat. Looking down he saw his fists were clenched, palms sweating.

I've done it. I can start repairing *Lady Mac*, get a crew together. The replacement patterning nodes will have to come from the Sol system. Say a month if I charter a blackhawk to collect them. She could be spaceworthy within ten weeks. Jesus!

He brought his attention back to the auctioneer just as the bidding went through six million. For a second he thought he'd misheard, but no, there was Barrington Grier grinning at him as if he was running wacko stimulant programs through his neural nanonics.

Seven million.

Joshua listened in a waking trance. He could afford more than a simple node replacement and repair job now. *Lady Mac* could have a complete refit, the best systems, no expense spared, new fusion generators, maybe a new spaceplane, no, better than that, an ion-field flyer from Kulu or New California. Yes!

'Seven million, four hundred and fifty thousand for the first time.' The auctioneer looked round expectantly, gavel engulfed by his meaty fist.

Rich. I'm fucking rich!

'Twice.'

Joshua closed his eyes.

'For the last time, seven million, four hundred and fifty thousand. Anybody?'

The smack the gavel made was as loud as the big bang. The start of a whole new existence for Joshua Calvert. Independent starship owner captain.

A deep chime sounded. Joshua's eyes snapped open. Everyone had gone silent, staring at the small omnidirectional AV projector on the desk in front of the auctioneer, a slim crystal pillar one metre high. Curlicues of abstract colour swam below the surface. If anything, Barrington Grier's grin had become even wider.

'Tranquillity reserves the right of last bid on lot 127.' A mellow male voice sounded throughout the auction room.

'Oh, for fuck's sake—' An angry voice to Joshua's left. The winning bidder? He hadn't caught the name.

The auction room descended into a bedlam of shouting.

Barrington Grier was giving him a manic thumbs-up. The three assistants started to carry the bubble and its precious – seven and a half million! – contents out into the wings.

Joshua waited as the room cleared; a noisy crush of people jostling and gossiping, Tranquillity's right to reserve the last bid their only topic for discussion.

He didn't care, last bid meant the agreed price plus an extra five per cent. The pillar of electronics would go to the Laymil research team now, analysed by the most experienced xenoc experts in the Confederation. He felt quite good about that, virtuous, maybe it was right they should have it.

Michael Saldana had reassembled as much of the team as he could after those first few traumatic years of exile, building it up in tandem with Tranquillity's new economy and rapidly increasing financial strength. There were currently around seven thousand specialists working on the problem, including several xenoc members of the Confederation, providing a welcome alternative viewpoint when it came to interpreting the more baroque artefacts.

Michael had died in 2513, and Maurice had assumed the title of Lord of Ruin with pride, continuing his father's labours. As far as he was concerned, uncovering the reason behind the Laymil cataclysm was Tranquillity's sole reason for existence. And he pursued it vigorously until his own death nine years ago in 2601.

Since then, the project had gone on apparently unabated. Tranquillity said Maurice's heir, the third Lord of Ruin, was running things as before, but chose not to seek a high public profile. There had been a flurry of rumours at the time, saying that the habitat personality had taken over completely, that the Kulu Kingdom was trying to reclaim the habitat, that the Edenists were going to incorporate it into their culture (earlier rumour said Michael stole the habitat seed from Edenists), throwing out the Adamists. They had all come to nothing. Right from the start the habitat personality had acted as both the civil service and police force, using its servitors to preserve order, so nothing changed, taxes were still two per cent, the blackhawks continued their mating flights, commercial enterprise was encouraged, creative finance tolerated. As long as the status quo was maintained, who cared exactly which kind of neurones were running the show, human or bitek?

Joshua felt a hand come down hard on his shoulder as he shuffled towards the exit, the weight pressed through his left leg. 'Ouch.'

'Joshua, my friend, my very rich friend. This is the day, hey? The day you made it.' Barrington Grier beamed rapturously at him. 'So what are you going to do with it all? Women? Fancy living?' His eyes lacked focus, he was definitely running a stimulant program. And he was entitled, the auction house was in line for a three per cent cut of the sale price.

Joshua smiled back, almost sheepish. 'No, I'm going back into space. See a bit of the Confederation for myself, that kind of thing, the old wanderlust.'

'Ah, if I had my youth back I would do the same thing. The good life, it ties you down, and it's a waste, especially for someone your age. Party till you puke every night, I mean what's the point of it all in the end? You should use the money to get out there and accomplish something. Glad to see you've got some sense. So, are you going to buy a blackhawk egg?'

'No, I'm taking the *Lady Mac* back out.'

Barrington Grier pursed his lips in rueful admiration. 'I remember when your father arrived here. You take after him, some. Same effect on the women, from what I hear.'

Joshua raised a wicked smile.

'Come on,' Barrington Grier said. 'I'll buy you a drink, in fact I'll buy you a whole meal.'

'Tomorrow maybe, Barrington, tonight I'm going to party till I puke.'

*

The lakehouse belonged to Dominique's father, who said it used to belong to Michael Saldana, that it was his home in the days before the starscrapers had matured to their full size. It was a series of looping chambers sunk into the side of a cliff above a lake up near the northern endcap. The walls looked as though they had been wind-carved. Inside the decor was simplistic and expensive, a holiday and entertainment *pied-à-terre*, not a home; artwork of various eras had been blended perfectly, and big plants from several planets flourished in the corners, chosen for their striking contrasts.

Outside the broad glass window-doors overlooking the huge lake, Tranquillity's axial light-tube was dimming towards its usual iridescent twilight. Inside, the party was just beginning to warm up. The eight-piece band was playing twenty-third-century ragas, processor blocks were loaded with *outré* stimulant programs, and the caterers were assembling a seafood buffet of freshly imported Atlantis delicacies.

Joshua lay back on a long couch to one side of the main lounge, dressed in a pair of baggy grey-blue trousers and a green Chinese jacket, receiving and dispensing greetings to strangers and acquaintances alike. Dominique's set were all young, and carefree, and very rich even by Tranquillity's standards. And they certainly knew how to party. He thought he could see the solid raw polyp walls vibrating from the sound they kicked up on the temporary dance-floor.

He took another sip of Norfolk Tears; the clear, light liquid ran down his throat like the lightest chilled wine, punching his gut like boiling whisky. It was glorious. Five hundred fuseodollars a bottle. Jesus!

'Joshua! I just heard. Congratulations.' It was Dominique's father, Parris Vasilkovsky, pumping his hand. He had a round face, with a curly beret of glossy silver-grey hair. There were very few lines on his skin, a sure sign of a geneering heritage; he must have been at least ninety. 'One of us idle rich now, eh? God, I can hardly remember what it was like right back at the beginning. Let me tell you, the first ten million is always the most difficult. After that . . . no problem.'

'Thanks.' People had been congratulating him all evening. He was the party's star attraction. The day's novelty. Since his mother had remarried a vice-president of the Brandstad Bank he had dwelt on the fringes of the plutocrat set which occupied the heart of Tranquillity. They were free enough with their hospitality, especially the daughters who liked to think of themselves as bohemian; and his scavenging flights made him notorious enough to enjoy both their patronage and bodies. But he had always been an observer. Until now.

'Dominique tells me you're going into the cargo business,' Parris Vasilkovsky said.

'That's right. I'm going to refit *Lady Mac*, Dad's old ship, take her out again.'

'Going to undercut me?' Parris Vasilkovsky owned over two hundred and fifty starships, ranging from small clippers up to ten-thousand-tonne bulk freighters, even some colonist-carrier ships. It was the seventh largest private merchant fleet in the Confederation.

Joshua looked him straight in the eye without smiling. 'Yes.'

Parris nodded, suddenly serious. He had started with nothing seventy years ago. 'You'll do all right, Joshua. Come down to the apartment one night before you go, have dinner as my guest. I mean it.'

'I'll do that.'

'Great.' A thick white eyebrow was raised knowingly. 'Dominique will be there. You could do a lot worse, she's one hell of a girl. A little fancy free, but tough underneath.'

'Er, yes.' Joshua managed a weak smile. Parris Vasilkovsky: matchmaker! And I'm considered suitable for that family? Jesus!

I wonder what he'd think if he knew what his little darling daughter was doing last night? Although knowing this lot, he'd probably want to join in.

Joshua caught sight of Zoe, another sometimes girlfriend, who was on the other side of the room, her sleeveless white gown creating a sharp contrast with her midnight-black skin. She met his eye and smiled, wiggling her glass. He recognized one of the other teenage girls in the group she was with, smaller than her, with short blonde hair, wearing a sea-blue sarong skirt and loose matching blouse. Pretty freckled face, a thinnish nose with a slight downward curve at the end, and deep blue eyes. He had met her once or twice before, a quick hello, friend of a friend. His neural nanonics located her visual image in a file and produced the name: Ione.

Dominique was striding through the throng towards him. He took another gulp of Norfolk Tears in reflex. People seemed to teleport out of her way for fear of heavy bruising should her swaying hips catch them a glancing blow. Dominique was twenty-six, almost as tall as him; sports mad, she had cultivated a splendidly athletic figure, straight blonde hair falling halfway down her back. She was wearing a small purple bikini halter and a split skirt of some shimmering silver fabric.

'Hi, Josh.' She plonked herself down on the edge of the couch, and plucked his glass from unresisting fingers, taking a swift sip for herself. 'Look what I ran up for us.' She held up a processor block. 'Twenty-five possibles, all we can manage, taking your poor feet into account. Should be fun. We'll start working through them tonight.'

Shadowy images flickered over the surface of the block.

'Fine,' Joshua said automatically. He hadn't got a clue what she was talking about.

She patted his thigh, and bounced to her feet. 'Don't go away, I'm going to do my rounds here, then I'll be back to collect you later.'

'Er, yes.' What else was there to say? He still wasn't sure who had seduced who the day after he returned from the Ruin Ring, but he'd spent every night since then in Dominique's big bed, and a lot of the daytime, too. She had the same kind of sexual stamina as Jezzibella, boisterous and frighteningly energetic.

He glanced down at the processor block, datavising a file-title request. It was a program that analysed all the possible free-fall sexual positions where bounceback didn't use the male's feet. The block's screen was showing two humanoid simulacrums running through contortional permutations.

'Hello.'

Joshua tipped the processor block screen side down with an incredibly guilty start, datavising a shutdown instruction, and codelocked the file.

Ione was standing next to the couch, head cocked to one side, smiling innocently.

'Er, hello, Ione.'

The smile widened. 'You remembered my name.'

'Hard to forget a girl like you.'

She sat in the imprint Dominique had left in the cushions. There was something quirky about her, a suggestion of hidden depth. He experienced that same uncanny thrill he had when he was on the trail of a Laymil artefact, not quite arousal, but close.

'I'm afraid I forgot what you do, though,' he said.

'Same as everyone else in here, a rich heiress.'

'Not quite everybody.'

'No?' Her mouth flickered in an uncertain smile.

'No, there's me, you see. I didn't inherit anything.' Joshua let his eyes linger on the outline of her figure below the light blouse. She was nicely proportioned, skin silk-smooth and sun kissed. He wondered what she would look like naked. Very nice, he decided.

'Apart from your ship, the *Lady Macbeth*.'

'Now it's my turn to say: you remembered.'

She laughed. 'No. It's what everyone is talking about. That and your find. Do you know what's in those Laymil memory crystals?'

'No idea. I just find them, I don't understand them.'

'Do you ever wonder why they did it? Kill themselves like that? There must have been millions of them, children, babies. I can't believe it was suicide the way everyone says.'

'You try not to think about it when you're out in the Ruin Ring. There are just too many ghosts out there. Have you ever been in it?'

She shook her head.

'It's spooky, Ione. Really, people laugh, but sometimes they'll creep in on you out of the shadows if you don't keep your guard up. And there are a lot of shadows out there; sometimes I think it isn't made of anything else.'

'Is that why you're leaving?'

'Not really. The Ruin Ring was a means to me, a way to get the money for *Lady Mac*. I've always planned on leaving.'

'Is Tranquillity that bad?'

'No. It's more of a pride thing. I want to see *Lady Mac* spaceworthy again. She got damaged quite badly in the rescue attempt. My father barely made it back to Tranquillity alive. The old girl deserves another chance. I could never bring myself to sell her. That's why I started scavenging, despite the risks. I just wish my father could have stayed around to see me succeed.'

'A rescue mission?' She sucked in her lower lip, intrigued. It was an endearing action, making her look even younger.

Dominique was nowhere to be seen, and the music was almost painfully loud now, the band just hitting their stride. Ione was clearly hooked on the story, on him. They could find a bedroom and spend a couple of hours screwing each other's brains out. And it was only early evening, this party wouldn't wind down for another five or six hours yet, he could still be back in time for his night with Dominique.

Jesus! What a way to celebrate.

'It's a long story,' he said, gesturing round. 'Let's find somewhere quieter.'

She nodded eagerly. 'I know a place.'

*

The trip on the tube carriage wasn't quite what Joshua had in mind. There were plenty of spare bedrooms at the lakehouse which he could codelock. But Ione had been surprisingly adamant, that elusive hint of steel in her personality surfacing as she said: 'My apartment is the quietest in Tranquillity, you can tell me everything there, and we'll never be overheard.' She paused, eyes teasing. 'Or interrupted.'

That settled it.

They took the carriage from the little underground station which served all the residences around the lake. The tube trains were a mechanical system, like the lifts in the starscrapers, which were all installed after Tranquillity reached its full size. Bitek was a powerful technology, but even it had limits on the services it could provide; internal transport lay outside the geneticists' ability. The tubes formed a grid network throughout the cylinder, providing access to all sections of the interior. Carriages were independent, taking passengers to whichever station they wanted, a system orchestrated by the habitat personality, which was spliced into processor blocks in every station. There was no private transport in Tranquillity, and everyone from billionaires to the lowest-paid spaceport handler used the tubes to get around.

Joshua and Ione got into a waiting ten-seater carriage, sitting opposite each other. It started off straight away under Ione's command, accelerating smoothly. Joshua offered her a sip from the fresh bottle of Norfolk Tears he'd liberated from Parris

Vasilkovsky's bar, and started to tell her about the rescue mission, eyes tracing the line of her legs under the flimsy sarong.

There had been a research starship in orbit around a gas giant, he said, it had suffered a life-support blow-out. His father had got the twenty-five-strong crew out, straining the *Lady Macbeth*'s own life support dangerously close to capacity. And because several of the injured research crew needed treatment urgently they jumped while they were still inside the gas giant's gravity field, which wrecked some of *Lady Macbeth*'s energy-patterning nodes, which in turn put a massive strain on the remaining nodes when the next jump was made. The starship managed the jump into Tranquillity's system, a distance of eight light-years, ruining forty per cent of her remaining nodes in the process.

'He was lucky to make it,' Joshua said. 'The nodes have a built-in compensation factor in case a few fail, but that distance was really tempting fate.'

'I can see why you're so proud of him.'

'Yes, well . . .' He shrugged.

The carriage slowed its madcap dash down the length of the habitat, and pulled to a halt. The door slid open. Joshua didn't recognize the station: it was small, barely large enough to hold the length of the carriage, a featureless white bubble of polyp. Broad strips of electrophorescent cells in the ceiling gave off a strong light; a semicircular muscle membrane door was set in the wall at the back of the narrow platform. Certainly not a starscraper lobby.

The carriage door closed, and the grey cylinder slipped noiselessly into the tunnel on its magnetic track. Currents of dry air flapped Ione's sarong as it vanished from sight.

Joshua felt unaccountably chilly. 'Where are we?' he asked.

Ione gave him a bright smile. 'Home.'

Hidden depths. The chill persisted obstinately.

The muscle membrane door opened like a pair of stone

curtains being drawn apart, and Joshua gaped at the apartment inside, bad vibes forgotten.

Starscraper apartments were luxurious even without money for elaborate furnishings; given time the polyp would grow into the shapes of any furniture you wanted, but this . . .

It was split level, a wide oblong reception area with an iron rail running along one side opposite the door, overlooking a lounge four metres below. A staircase set in the middle of the railings extended out for three metres, then split into two symmetrically opposed loops that wound down to the lower floor. Every wall was marbled. Up in the reception area it was green and cream; on both sides of the lounge it was purple and ruby; at the back of the lounge it was hazel and sapphire; the stairs were snow white. Recessed alcoves were spaced equidistantly around the whole reception area, bordered in fluted sable-black columns. One of them framed an ancient orange spacesuit, the lettering Russian Cyrillic. The furniture was heavy and ornate, rosewood and teak, polished to a gleam, carved with beautiful intaglio designs, rich with age, the work of master craftsmen from centuries past. A thick living apricot-coloured moss absorbed every footfall.

Joshua walked over to the top of the stairs without a word, trying to take it all in. The wall ahead of him, some thirty metres long and ten high, was a single window. It showed him a seabed.

Tranquillity had a circumfluous salt-water reservoir at its southern end, like all Edenist habitats. In keeping with the size of the habitat, it was some eight kilometres wide, and two hundred metres deep at the centre; more sea than lake. Both coastlines were a mix of sandy coves and high cliffs. An archipelago of islands and atolls ran all the way around it.

Joshua realized the apartment must be at the foot of one of the coastal cliffs. He could see sand stretching into dark blue distance, half-buried boulders smothered beneath crustaceans, long ribbons of red and green fronds waving idly. Shoals of small colourful fish were darting about; caught in the vast spill of light from the window they looked like jewelled ornaments. He thought he saw something large and dark swimming around the boundary of light.

The breath came out of him in an amazed rush. 'How did you get this place?'

There was no immediate answer.

He turned to see Ione standing behind him, eyes closed, head tilted back slightly, as if in deep contemplation. She took a deep breath, and slowly opened her eyes to show the deepest ocean-blue irises, an enigmatic smile on her lips. 'It's the one Tranquillity assigned me,' she said simply.

'I never knew there were any here that you could ask for. And these furnishings—'

Her smile turned mischievous. And she was suddenly all little girlish again. It was her hair, he thought, all the girls he knew in Tranquillity had long, perfectly arranged hair. With her short, shaggy style she looked almost elfin, and supremely sexy.

'I told you I was an heiress,' she said.

'Yes, but *this* . . .'

'You like it?'

'I'm afraid of it. I think I've been scavenging in the wrong place.'

'Come on.' She held out her hand.

He took her proffered fingers in a light grip. 'Where are we going?'

'To get what you came for.'

'What's that?'

She grinned, pulling him away from the stairs, along the reception area to the wall at the end. Another muscle membrane in one of the alcoves parted.

'Me,' she said.

It was a bedroom, circular, with a curving window band looking into the sea, its polyp ceiling hidden by drapes of dark red fabric. In the middle of the floor was a crater filled with perfectly clear jelly and covered by a thin rubbery sheet, silk pillows lining the rim. And Ione was standing very close. They kissed. He could feel her shiver slightly as his arms went round her. Heat began to seep into his body.

'Do you know why I wanted you?' she said.

'No.' He was kissing her throat, hands sliding across her blouse to cup her breasts.

'I've watched you,' Ione whispered.

'Er—' Joshua broke off fondling her breasts, and stared at her, the dreamy expression.

'You and all those beautiful rich girls. You're an excellent lover, Joshua. Did you know that?'

'Yeah. Thanks.' Jesus. She's watched me? When? The night before last had been pretty wild, but he didn't remember anyone else joining them. Although knowing Dominique it was highly possible. Hell, but I must have been smashed out of my skull.

Ione tugged at his jacket's sash, opening the front. 'You wait for the girls to climax, you want them to enjoy it. You make them enjoy it.' She kissed his sternum, tongue licking the ridges of his pectoral muscles. 'That's very rare, very bold.'

Her words and deeds were acting like the devil's own stimulant program, sending a sparkling phantom fire shooting down his nerves to invade his groin and send his heart racing. He felt his cock growing incredibly hard as his breathing turned harsh.

Ione's blouse came open easily under his impatient hands, and he pushed it off her shoulders. Her breasts were high and nicely rounded, with large areolae only a shade darker than her tan. He sucked on a nipple, fingers tracing the sleek muscle tone of her abdomen, eliciting indrawn hisses. Hands clutched and clawed at the back of his neck. He heard his name being called, the delight in her voice.

They fell onto the bed together, the jelly-substance under

the sheet undulating wildly. The two of them rode the turbulent waves which their own threshing limbs whipped up.

Entering her was sheer perfection. She was delectably responsive, and strong, sinuous. He had to use his neural nanonics to restrain his body, making sure he remained in control. His secret glee. That way he could wait despite her furious pleading shouts. Wait as she strained and twisted sensually against him. Wait, and provoke, and prolong . . . Until the orgasm convulsed her, and a jubilant screech burst out of her mouth. Then he cancelled the artificial prohibitions, allowing his body to spend itself in frenzied bliss, gloating at her wide-eyed incredulity as his semen surged into her in a long exultant consummation.

They watched each other in silence as the bed slowly calmed. There was a moment's silent contemplation, then they were both grinning lazily.

'Was I as good as all the others, Joshua?'

He nodded fervently.

'Good enough to make you stay in Tranquillity, knowing I'm available whenever you want?'

'Er—' He rolled onto his side, disquieted by the gleam in her eye. 'That's unfair, and you know it.'

She giggled. 'Yes.'

Looking at her, sprawled out on her back, with her arms flung above her head, perspiration slowly drying, he wondered why it should be that girls were always so much more alluring just after they'd had sex. So blatantly rampant, probably. 'Are you going to ask me to stay, slap down an ultimatum? You or the *Lady Mac*?'

'Not stay, no.' She rolled over onto her side. 'But I have other demands.'

The second time, Ione insisted on straddling him. It was easier on his feet, and that way he was able to play with her breasts for the whole time she rode him to their twinned climax. For their third encounter, he arranged the cushions into a pile to support her as she went down on all fours, then mounted her from behind.

After the fifth time Joshua really didn't care that he'd missed the party. Dominique would probably have found herself someone else for the night, too.

'When will you leave?' Ione asked.

'It'll take a couple of months to make *Lady Mac* spaceworthy again, maybe three. I placed an order for the patterning nodes right after the auction. A lot depends on how long it takes to deliver them.'

'You know Sam Neeves and Octal Sipika haven't returned yet?'

'I know,' he said grimly. He had told his story a dozen times a day since he docked, especially among the other scavengers and spaceport crews. The word was out now. He knew they would deny it, maybe even say he attacked them. And he had no proof, it was their word against his. But it was his version which had been told first, his version which was accepted, which carried all the weight. Ultimately, he had money on his side as well now. Tranquillity didn't have a death penalty, but he had filed a charge of attempted murder with the personality as soon as he'd docked; they ought to get twenty years. The personality certainly hadn't challenged his story, which gave his confidence a healthy boost.

'Well, make sure you don't do anything stupid when they do turn up,' Ione said. 'Leave it to the serjeants.'

Tranquillity's serjeants were an addition to the usual habitat servitor genealogy, hulking exoskeleton-clad humanoids that served as a police force.

'Yes,' he groused. An unpleasant thought intruded. 'You do believe it was them who attacked me, don't you?'

Her cheeks dimpled as she smiled. 'Oh, yes, we checked as best we could. There have been eight scavengers lost in the past five years. In six cases, Neeves and Sipika were out in the Ring at the same time, and in each instance they auctioned a larger than usual number of Laymil artefacts after they docked.'

Despite the warm weight of her pressing down on him, that eerie chill returned. It was the casual way she said it, the supreme confidence in her tone. 'Who checked, Ione? Who's we?'

She giggled again. 'Oh, Joshua! Haven't you worked it out yet? Perhaps I was wrong about you, although I admit you have been distracted with other matters since we arrived.'

'Worked what out?'

'Me. Who I am, of course.'

The intimation of disaster rose through him like a tidal wave. 'No,' he said hoarsely. 'I don't know.'

She smiled, and raised herself on her elbows, head held ten centimetres above his, taunting. 'I'm the Lord of Ruin.'

He laughed, a sort of nervous choke which trailed off. 'Jesus, you mean it.'

'Absolutely.' She rubbed her nose against his. 'Look at my nose, Joshua.'

He did. It was a thin nose, with a down-turned end. The Saldana nose, that famous trademark which the Kulu royal family had kept through every genetic modification for the last ten generations. Some said the characteristic had deliberately been turned into a dominant gene by the geneticists.

What she said was true, he knew it was. Intuition yammered in his mind, as strong as the day he found the Laymil electronics. 'Oh shit.'

She kissed him, and sat back, arms folded in her lap, looking smug.

'But why?' he asked.

'Why what?'

'Jesus!' His arms waved about in exasperated agitation. 'Why not let people know you're running things? Show them who you are. Why . . . why carry on with this charade of the research project? And your father's dead; who's been looking after you for the last eight years? And why *me*? What did you mean, being wrong about me?'

'Which order do you want them in? Actually, they're all connected, but I'll start at the beginning for you. I'm an eighteen-year-old girl, Joshua. I'm also a Saldana, or at least I have their genetic super-heritage, which means I'll live for damn near two centuries, my IQ is way above normal, and I've got the same kind of internal strengthening you have, among other improvements. Oh, we're a breed above, us Saldanas. Just right to rule you common mortals.'

'So why don't you? Why spend your time skulking around parties picking up people like me to screw?'

'It's an image thing which makes me a shrinking violet for the moment. Maybe you don't realize just how much authority the habitat personality has in Tranquillity. It is omnipotent, Joshua, it runs the whole shebang, there is no need for a court, for civil servants, it enforces the constitution with perfect impartiality. It provides the most stable political environment in the Confederation outside Edenism and the Kulu Kingdom. That's why it is such a successful haven; not just a tax haven either, but economically and financially. You'll always be safe living in Tranquillity. You can't corrupt it, you can't bribe it, you can't get it to change its laws even through logical argument. *You* can't. I can. It takes orders from me, and only me, the Lord of Ruin. That's the way grandfather Michael wanted it, one ruler, dedicated to one job: government. My father had a lot of children by quite a number of women, and they all had the affinity gene, but they all left to become Edenists. All but me, because I was gestated in a womb-analogue set-up similar to the voidhawks and their captains. We're bonded, you see, little me and a sixty-five-kilometre-long coral-armoured beastie, mind-mated for life.'

'Then come forward publicly, let people know you exist. We've been living on rumours for eight years.'

'And that was the best thing for you. Like I said, I'm eighteen.

Would you trust me to run a nation of three million people? To make alterations to the constitution, tinker with the investment laws, put up the price of the He_3 the starships use, which *Lady Macbeth* uses? That's what I can do, change anything I want. You see, unlike Kulu with its court politics, and the Edenists with their communal consensus, I have no one to guide me, or more importantly, to restrain me. What I say goes, and anyone who argues is flung out of an airlock. That's the law, my law.'

'Trust,' he said, realizing. 'Nobody would trust you. Everything works smoothly because we thought the habitat personality was carrying on your father's policies.'

'That's right. No billionaire like Parris Vasilkovsky, who has spent seventy years building up his commercial empire, is going to deposit his entire fortune in a nation which has a dizzy teenage girl as absolute ruler. I mean, he's only got to look at the way his daughter behaves, and she's a lot older than I am.'

Joshua grinned. 'Point taken.' He remembered the crack about watching; of course Ione would be able to receive Tranquillity's sensory images through her affinity bond, she could watch anything and anybody she wanted. A slight flush warmed his face. 'So that's why you keep on wasting money on the Laymil research project, so people will think it's business as usual. Not that I'm complaining. Jesus! That last bid right you've got, seven and a half million fuseodollars.' His smile faded at the expression of disapproval registering on her face.

'You couldn't be further from the truth, Joshua. I consider research into the Laymil to be the single most important issue in my life.'

'Oh, come on! I've spent years grubbing round in the Ruin Ring. Sure, it's a mystery. Why did they do it? But don't you see, it doesn't matter. Not to the degree which the research team pursue it. The Laymil are xenocs, for Christ's sake, who cares how weird their psychology was, or that they found some fruitcake death-cult religion.'

Ione exhaled, shaking her head in consternation. 'Some people refuse to see the problem, I accept that, but I never thought you'd be one of them.'

'Refuse to see what problem?'

'It's like that sometimes, something so big, so frightening, staring you right in the face, and you just block it out. Planet dwellers live in earthquake zones and on the side of volcanoes, yet they can't see anything crazy about it, how stupid they're being. The reason is all important, Joshua, vitally important. Why do you think my grandfather did what he did?'

'I haven't got a clue. I thought that was supposed to be the universe's second greatest mystery.'

'No, Joshua, no mystery. Michael Saldana established the Laymil research project because he thought it was his duty, not just to the kingdom but to all humanity. He could see just how long a project it would be. That's why he alienated his family and endured the wrath of the Christian Church to grow Tranquillity. So that there would always be someone who shared the need, and had the resources to continue the research. He could have ordered Kulu's xenoc-research institutions to perform the investigation. But how long would that have lasted? His reign, certainly. Maurice's reign, too. Possibly even for that of Maurice's eldest son. But he was worried sick that wouldn't be long enough. It's such a colossal task; you know that more than most. Even the Kings of Kulu couldn't keep a project like this going on a priority budget for more than two or three centuries. He had to be free of his heritage and obligations in order to ensure the most important undertaking in human history wasn't allowed to waste away and die.'

Joshua gazed at her levelly, remembering the didactic course he had taken on affinity and Edenist culture. 'You talk to him, don't you? Your grandfather. He transferred his memories into the habitat personality, and they leaked into you when you were in the womb-analogue. That's why you spout all this crap. He's contaminated you, Ione.'

For a moment Ione looked hurt, then she summoned up a rueful smile. 'Wrong again, Joshua. Neither Michael nor Maurice transferred their memories during death. The Saldanas are pretty devout Christians; my Kulu cousins are supposed to rule by divine right, remember?'

'Michael Saldana was excommunicated.'

'By the Bishop of Nova Kong, never by the Pope in Rome. It was politics, that's all. His punishment, dished out by the Kulu court. He shocked the family to its odiously complacent core by growing Tranquillity. The whole basis of their sovereignty is that they simply cannot be bribed or corrupted, their wealth and privileges make it totally impossible. They are the ultimate straight arrows, dedicated to service, because they have every physical and material whim catered for. There isn't anything else for them to do but rule. And I have to admit they make quite a good job of it; Kulu is wealthy, strong, independent, with the highest socioeconomic index outside Edenism. The Saldanas and their century-long development projects did that for the Kingdom, a leadership which genuinely considers that its nation's interests are paramount. That's remarkable, bordering on unique. And they are revered for it, there are *gods* who receive less adulation than the Saldanas. Yet Michael considered an intellectual problem sufficient grounds to lay all that aside. Small wonder the family were terrified, not to mention furious with him. He showed it was possible to suborn a mighty Saldana, to turn their attention from parochial matters. That's why the bishop did what he was ordered to do. But my grandfather remained a Christian until the day he died. And I am too.'

'Sorry.' Joshua leant over and rummaged round in his pile of clothes until he found the small pear-shaped bottle of Norfolk Tears. He took a swig. 'You take some getting used to, Ione.'

'I know. Now imagine your reaction magnified three million times. There'd be riots.'

Joshua passed her the bottle. It was tipped up daintily, a few drops of the precious imported liquor sliding down past her lips. He admired the way the skin pulled taut over her abdomen as her head went back, the breasts pushed forward. He let a hand slide up the side of her ribs, questing innocently. The initial shock of her identity was fading like a stolen daydream, he wanted the reassurance she was still the same rutty teenager who had turned him on so badly back at the party.

'So if it's not prenatal ideological indoctrination, what convinces you that the research project is worthwhile?' he asked.

Ione lowered the bottle, marshalling her thoughts. Joshua, among his many other faults, could be depressingly cynical. 'Proximity. Like I said, Tranquillity and I are bonded. I see what it sees. And the Ruin Ring is always there, just below us. Seventy thousand habitats, not so different from Tranquillity, pulverized into gravel. And it was suicide, Joshua. The research team believes that the living cells in the Laymil habitats underwent some kind of spasm, cracking the outer silicon shell. They would have to be ordered to do it, compelled, probably. I doubt I could get Tranquillity to do it just by asking nicely.'

I might, Tranquillity said silently in her mind. **But you would have to give me a very good reason.**

To save me from a fate worse than death?

That would do it.

Name one.

That is something only you can decide.

She grinned and had another nip from the bottle. It was an amazing drink. She could feel its warmth seeping through her. And Joshua's lower torso was cradled between her thighs. The insidious combination was becoming highly arousing.

He was giving her a curious look.

'Tranquillity says it's not very likely,' she told him.

'Oh.' He took the bottle back. 'But this constant awareness of the Ruin Ring is still a kind of unnatural motivation. Tranquillity worries about it, so you do.'

'It's more of a gentle reminder, like a crucifix reminds us of what Christ suffered, and why. It means I don't suffer a lack of faith in the work the research team does. I know we have to find the reason.'

'Why, though? Why do you and your father, and your grandfather, all consider it so important?'

'Because the Laymil were ordinary.' That got through to him, she saw. A frown crinkled his brow below the sticky strands of tawny hair. 'Oh, they have a substantially different body chemistry, and three sexes, and monster bodies, but their minds worked along reasonably similar lines to ours. That makes them understandable. It also makes us dangerously similar. And because they were at least equal to us, if not more advanced, technologically. Whatever it was they came up against is something that one day we are also going to encounter. If we know what it is, we can prepare ourselves, maybe even defend ourselves. Provided we have some warning. That's what Michael realized, his revelation. So you see, he never really did abandon his duty and commitment to Kulu. It's just that this was the only possible way he could hope to safeguard the Kingdom in the ultra-long-term. However unconventional, it had to be done.'

'And is it being done? Is your precious team any closer to finding out what happened?'

'Not really. Sometimes I get afraid that we are too late, that too much has been lost. We know so much about the Laymil physically, but so little about their culture. That's why we nabbed your electronics. That much stored data might be the breakthrough we need. We wouldn't need much, just a pointer. There's only two real options.'

'Which are?'

'They discovered something that made them do it. Their scientists uncovered some fundamental physical truth or law; or a priest group stumbled across an unbearable theological revelation, that death cult you mentioned. The second option is even worse: that something discovered them, something so fearsome that they felt racial death was a preferable alternative to submission. If it was the second, then that menace is still out there, and it's only a matter of time until we encounter it.'

'Which do you think it was?'

She squeezed her legs just that fraction tighter against him, welcoming the comfort his physical presence bestowed. As always when she thought about it, the brooding seemed to sap a portion of her will. Racial pride aside, the Laymil were very advanced, and strong . . . 'I tend to think it was the second, an external threat. Mainly because of the question over the Laymil's origin. They didn't evolve on any planet in this star system. Nor did they come from any local star. And from the spacecraft fragments we've found we're pretty sure they didn't have our ZTT technology, which leaves a multi-generation interstellar ark as the most likely option. But that's the kind of ship you only use to colonize nearby stars, within fifteen or twenty light-years. And in any case, why travel across interstellar space just to build habitats to live in? There's no need to leave your original star system if that's all you're going to do. No, I think they came a very long way through ordinary space, for a very real reason. They were fleeing. Like the Tyrathca abandoned their homeworld when its star blew up into a red supergiant.'

'But this nemesis still found them.'

'Yes.'

'Has anyone found remnants of an ark ship?'

'No. If the Laymil did travel to Mirchusko in a slower-than-light ship then they must have arrived around seven to eight thousand years ago. To build up a population base of seventy thousand habitats from one, or even ten ships, would take at least three thousand years. Apparently the Laymil didn't have quite our fecundity when it comes to reproduction. Such an ark ship would have been very old by the time it reached Mirchusko. It was probably abandoned. If it was in the same orbit as the habitats when they were destroyed, then the secondary collisions would have broken it apart.'

'Pity.'

She bent over to kiss him, enjoying the way his hands tightened around her waist. The hazy blue-shadow images she had poached from Tranquillity's sensitive cells, the private cries she had eavesdropped through the affinity bond, had been borne out. Joshua was the most dynamic lover she had ever known. Gentle and domineering; it was a lethal combination. If only he wasn't quite so ruthlessly mechanical about it. A little too much of his pleasure had come from seeing her lose all control. But then that was Joshua, unwilling to share; the life he led – the endless casual sex offered by Dominique and her set, and the false sense of independence incurred from scavenging – left him too hardened for that. Joshua didn't trust people.

'That just leaves me,' he said. His breath was hot on her face. 'Why me, Ione?'

'Because you're not quite normal.'

'What?'

The intimacy shattered.

Ione tried not to laugh. 'How many big strikes have you had this year, Joshua?'

'It's been a reasonable year,' he said evasively.

'It's been a stupendous year, Joshua. Counting the electronics stack, you found nine artefacts, which netted you a total of over eight million fuseodollars. No other scavenger has ever earned that much in one year in the hundred and eighty years since Tranquillity was germinated. In fact, no other scavenger has ever earned that much, period. I checked. Someone earned six hundred thousand fuseodollars in 2532 for finding an intact Laymil corpse, and she retired straight away. You are either *amazingly* lucky, Joshua, or . . .' She trailed off, leaving the suggestion hanging tantalizingly in the air.

'Or what?' There was no humour in his tone.

'I think you are psychic.'

It was the flash of guilt which convinced her she was right. Later, she made Tranquillity replay the moment countless times, the image from its optically sensitive cells in the mock-marble walls providing her a perfectly focused close up of the flattish planes which made up his face. For a brief second after she said it, Joshua looked fearful and frightened. He rallied beautifully, of course, sneering, laughing.

'Bollocks!' he cried.

'How do you explain it, then? Because believe me, it hasn't gone unnoticed amongst your fellow scavengers, and I don't just mean Messrs Neeves and Sipika.'

'You said it: amazingly lucky. It's sheer probability. If I went out into the Ruin Ring again, I wouldn't find a single strike for the next fifty years.'

She stroked a single finger along the smooth skin of his chin. He didn't have any stubble, facial hair was another free fall irritant geneering had disposed of. 'Bet you would.'

He folded his arms behind his head and grinned up at her. 'We'll never know now, will we?'

'No.'

'And that's what made me irresistible to you? My X-ray sight?'

'Sort of. It would be useful.'

'Just: useful?'

'Yes.'

'Why, what did you expect me to do for you?'

'Make me pregnant.'

This time the fright took longer to fade. '*What?*' He looked almost panic stricken.

'Make me pregnant. Psychic intuition would be a very useful trait for the next Lord of Ruin to have.'

'I'm not psychic,' he said petulantly.

'So you say. But even if you're not, you would still make a

more than satisfactory genetic donor to any child. And I do have a paramount duty to provide the habitat with an heir.'

'Careful, you're almost getting romantic.'

'You wouldn't be tied down by any parental responsibilities, if that's what bothers you. The zygote would be placed in zero-tau until I'm reaching the end of my life. Tranquillity and the servitor housechimps will bring it up.'

'Fine way to treat a kid.'

She sat up straight, stretching, and ran her hands up her belly, toying with her breasts. You couldn't be any more unfair to a male, especially when he was naked and trapped below you. 'Why? Do you think I turned out badly? Point to the flaw, Joshua.'

Joshua reddened. 'Jesus.'

'Will you do it?' Ione picked up the nearly empty liquor bottle. 'If I don't turn you on, there is a clinic in the StAnne starscraper which can perform an in-vitro fertilization.' She carefully let a single drop of Norfolk Tears fall onto her erect nipple. It stayed there, glistening softly, and she moved the bottle to her other breast. 'You just have to say no, Joshua. Can you do that? Say no. Tell me you've had your fill of me. Go on.'

His mouth closed around her left breast, teeth biting almost painfully, and he started sucking.

*

What do you think? Ione asked Tranquillity hours later, when Joshua had finally sated himself with her. He was sleeping on the bed, ripples of aquamarine light played across him, filtering in through the window. High above the water, the axial light-tube was bringing a bright dawn to the habitat's parkland.

I think the blood supply to your brain got cut off when you were in the womb-analogue organ. The damage is obviously irreparable.

What's wrong with him?

He lies continually, he sponges off his friends, he steals whenever he thinks it won't be noticed, he has used stimulant programs illegal on most Confederation worlds, he shows no respect to the girls he has sexual relations with, he even tried to avoid paying his income tax last year, claiming repairs to his spacecraft were legitimate expenses.

But he found all those artefacts.

I admit that is somewhat puzzling.

Do you think he attacked Neeves and Sipika?

No. Joshua was not in the Ruin Ring when those other scavengers disappeared.

So he must be psychic.

I cannot logically refute the hypothesis. But I don't believe it.

You, acting on a hunch!

Where you are concerned, I act on my feelings. Ione, you grew inside me, I nurtured you. How could I not feel for you?

She smiled dreamily at the ceiling. Well, I do think he's psychic. There's certainly something different about him. He has this sort of radiance, it animates him more than any other person I know.

I haven't seen it.

It's not something you can see.

Even assuming you are correct about him being psychic, why would your child retain the trait? It's not exactly something sequenced into any known gene.

Magic passes down through families the same way as red hair and green eyes.

This isn't an argument I'm going to win, is it?

No. Sorry.

Very well. Would you like me to book you an appointment in the StAnne clinic's administration processor?

What for?

An in-vitro fertilization.

No, the child will be conceived naturally. But I will need the clinic later to take the zygote out and prepare it for storage.

Is there a specific reason for doing it this way? In vitro would be much simpler.

Maybe, but Joshua really is superb in bed. It'll be a lot more fun this way.

Humans!

9

The hot rain falling on Durringham had started shortly after daybreak on Wednesday; it was now noon on Thursday and there had been no let-up. The satellite pictures showed there was at least another five hours' worth of cloud waiting over the ocean. Even the inhabitants, normally unperturbed by mere thunderstorms, had deserted the streets. Scummy water swirled round the stone supports of raised wooden buildings, seeping up through the floorboards. More worryingly, there had been several mudslides on the north-east side of the city. Durringham's civic engineers (all eight of them) were alarmed that an avalanche effect would sweep whole districts into the Juliffe.

Lalonde's Governor, Colin Rexrew, received their datavised report phlegmatically. He couldn't honestly say the prospect of losing half of the capital was an idea which roused any great regret. Pity it wasn't more.

At sixty years old he had reached the penultimate position in his chosen profession. Born in Earth's O'Neill Halo, he had started working for the astroengineering giant Miconia Industrial straight after university, qualifying with a degree in business finance, then diversified into subsidiary management, a highly specialized profession, making sure semi-independent divisions retained their corporate identity even though they were hundreds of light-years from Earth. The company's widespread offices meant he was shunted around the Confederation's inhabited systems in three-year shifts, slowly building an impressive portfolio of experience and qualifications, always putting his personal life second to the company.

Miconia Industrial had taken a ten per cent stake in the Lalonde Development Company, the third largest single investor. And Colin Rexrew had been appointed Governor two years ago. He had another eight years of office to run, after which he'd be in line for a seat on Miconia's board. He would be sixty-eight by then, but some geneering in his heritage gave him a life expectancy of around a hundred and twenty. At sixty-eight he would be just hitting his peak. With a successful governorship under his belt, his chances of nabbing the board seat were good verging on excellent.

Although, as he now knew to his cost, success on Lalonde was a slippery concept to define. After twenty-five years of investment by the LDC, Lalonde wasn't even twenty per cent self-financing. He was beginning to think that if the planet was still here in eight years' time he would have accomplished the impossible.

His office took up the entire third storey of a dumper on the eastern edge of the city. The furniture itself was all made by local carpenters from mayope wood, Lalonde's one really useful resource. He had inherited it from his predecessor, and it was a trifle sturdy for his taste. The thick bright jade carpet of kilian hair had come from Mulbekh, and the computer systems were from Kulu. A glass-fronted drinks cabinet was well stocked, with a good third of the bottles in the chiller containing local wines, which he was acquiring a palate for. Curving windows gave him a view out over the cultivated rural areas beyond the suburb, a sight far more pleasing than the backward mundane city itself. But today even the neat white clapboard houses were afflicted by the downpour, appearing dowdy and beleaguered, the usually green fields covered by vast pools of water. Distressed animals crowded onto the island mounds, bleating pathetically.

Colin sat behind his desk, ignoring the datawork flashing urgently on his screens to watch the deluge through the window. Like everyone on Lalonde he wore shorts, although his were tailored in the London arcology; his pale blue jacket was slung over one of the conference chairs, and the conditioner failed to stop sweat stains from appearing under the arms of his pale lemon silk shirt.

There was no such thing as a gym on the whole planet, and he could never bring himself to jog from his official residence to the office in the morning, so he was starting to put on weight at a disappointing rate. His already round face now had accentuated jowls, and a third chin was developing; a smattering of freckles had expanded under Lalonde's sunlight to cover both cheeks and his forehead. Once hale ginger hair was thinning and fading towards silver. Whatever ancestor had paid for the geneered metabolic improvements which increased his life expectancy had obviously stinted on the cosmetic side.

More lightning bolts stabbed down out of the smothering cloud blanket. He counted to four before he heard the thunder. If this goes on much longer even the puddles will develop puddles, he thought bleakly.

There was a bleep from the door, and it slid open. His neural nanonics told him it was his executive aide, Terrance Smith.

Colin swivelled his chair back round to the desk. Terrance Smith was thirty-five, a tall, elegant man with thick black hair and a firm jaw; today he was dressed in knee-length grey shorts and a green short-sleeved shirt. His weight was never anything less than optimum. The rumour around Colin's staff said Smith had bedded half of the women in the administration office.

'Meteorology say we're due for a dry week after this passes over,' Terrance said as he sat in the chair in front of Colin's desk.

Colin grunted. 'Meteorology didn't say this lot was expected.'

‘True.’ Terrance consulted a file in his neural nanonics. ‘The geological engineers up at Kenyon have finished their preliminary survey. They are ready to move on to more extensive drilling for the biosphere cavern.’ He datavised the report over to Colin.

Kenyon was the twelve-kilometre-diameter stony iron asteroid that had been knocked into orbit a hundred and twelve thousand kilometres above Lalonde by a series of nuclear explosions. When Lalonde’s first stage of development was complete, and the planetary economy was up and functioning without requiring any additional investment, the LDC wanted to progress to developing a space industry station cluster. That was where the real money lay, fully industrial worlds. And the first essential for any zero-gee industrial stations was an abundant supply of cheap raw material, which the asteroid would provide. The mining crews would tunnel out the ores, literally carving themselves a habitable biosphere in the process.

Unfortunately, now Kenyon was finally in place after its fifteen-year journey from the system’s asteroid belt, Colin doubted he had the budget even to maintain the geological engineering team, let alone pay for exploratory drilling. Transporting new colonists into the continental interior was absorbing funds at a frightening rate, and the first thing an asteroid settlement needed was a reliable home market as a financial foundation before it could start competing on the interstellar market.

‘I’ll look into it later,’ he told Terrance. ‘But I’m not making any promises. Somebody jumped the gun on that one by about twenty years. The asteroid industry project looks good on our yearly reports. Moving it into orbit is something you can point to and show the board how progressive you’re being. They know it doesn’t make a dollar while it’s underway. But as soon as it’s here in orbit they expect it to be instantly profitable. So I’m lumbered with the bloody thing while my cretinous predecessor is drawing his standard pension plus a nice fat bonus for being so dynamic while he was in office. The auditors should have caught this, you know. It's going to be another fifty years before these mud farmers can scrape together enough capital to support high-technology industries. There's no demand here.'

Terrance nodded, handsome features composed into a grave expression. 'We've authorized start-up loans for another eight engineering companies in the last two months. Power bike sales are healthy in the city, and we should have an indigenous four-wheel-drive jeep within another five years. But I agree, large-scale consumer manufacturing is still a long way off.'

'Ah, never mind,' Colin sighed. 'You weren't the one who authorized Kenyon. If they'd just stop sending us colonists for six months, allow us to catch our breath. A ship every twenty days is too much, and the passage fees the colonists pay don't cover half of the cost of sending them upriver. Once the starship's been paid for the board doesn't care. But what I wouldn't give for some extra funds to spend on basic infrastructure, instead of subsidizing the river-boats. It's not as if the captains don't make enough.'

'That was something else I wanted to bring up. I've just finished accessing the latest schedules flek from the board; they're going to send us five colonist-carrier starships over the next seventy days.'

'Typical.' Colin couldn't even be bothered with a token protest.

'I was thinking we might ask the river-boat captains to take more passengers each trip. They could easily cram another fifty on board if they rigged up some awnings over the open decks. It wouldn't be any different from the transients' dormitories, really.'

'You think they'd go for that?'

'Why not? We pay their livelihood, after all. And it's only temporary. If they don't want to take them, then they can sit in harbour and lose money. The paddle-boats can hardly be used for bulk cargo. Once we've repossessed the boats, we'll give them to captains who are more flexible.'

'Unless they all band together; those captains are a clannish lot. Remember that fuss over Crompton's accident? He rams a log, and blames us for sending him off into an uncharted tributary. We had to pay for the repairs. The last thing we need right now is an outbreak of trade unionism.'

'What shall I do, then? The transients' dormitories can't hold more than seven thousand at once.'

'Ah, to hell with it. Tell the captains they're taking more heads per trip and that's final. I don't want the transients in Durringham a moment longer than necessary.' He tried not to think what would ever happen if one of the paddle-boats capsized in the Juliffe. Lalonde had no organized emergency services; there were five or six ambulances working out of the church hospital for casualties in the city, but a disaster a thousand kilometres upriver . . . And the colonists were nearly all arcology dwellers, half of them couldn't swim. 'But after this we'll have to see about increasing the number of boats. Because as sure as pigs shit, we won't ever get a reduction in the number of colonists they send us. I heard on the grapevine Earth's population is creeping up again, the number of illegal births rose three per cent last year. And that's just the official illegals.'

'If you want more boats, that will mean more mortgage loans,' Terrance observed.

'I can do basic arithmetic, thank you. Tell the comptroller to shrink some other budgets to compensate.'

Terrance wanted to ask which divisions, every administration department was chronically underfunded. The look on Colin Rexrew's face stopped him. 'Right, I'll get onto it.' He loaded a note in his neural nanonics general business file.

'It wouldn't be a bad idea to look into safety on those paddle-boats some time. Make them carry lifebelts.'

'Nobody in Durringham makes lifebelts.'

'So that's a fresh business opportunity for some smart

entrepreneur. And yes I know it would need another loan to establish. Hell, do we have a cork-analogue tree here? They could carve them, everything else on this bloody planet is made out of wood.'

'Or mud.'

'God, don't remind me.' Colin glanced out of the window again. The clouds had descended until they were only about four hundred metres above the ground. Dante got it all wrong, he thought, hell isn't about searing heat, it's about being permanently wet. 'Anything else?'

'Yes. The marshal you sent up to Schuster County has filed his report. I didn't want to load it into the office datanet.'

'Good thinking.' Colin knew the CNIS team monitored their satellite communications. There was also Ralph Hiltch sitting snugly over in the Kulu Embassy, like a landbound octopus with its tentacles plugged into damn near every administration office, siphoning out information. Although God alone knew why Kulu bothered, maybe paranoia was a trait the Saldanas had geneered into their super genes. He had also heard a strictly unofficial whisper that the Edenists had an active intelligence team on the planet, which was pushing credulity beyond any sane limits.

'What was the summary?' he asked Terrance.

'He drew a complete blank.'

'Nothing?'

'Four families have definitely gone missing, just like the sheriff said. All of them lived out on the savannah a fair distance away from Schuster town itself. He visited their homesteads, and said it was like they walked out one morning and never came back. All their gear had been looted by the time he arrived, of course, but he asked around, apparently there was even food laid out ready for a meal in one home. No sign of a struggle, no sayce or kroclion attack. Nothing. It really spooked the other colonists.'

'Strange. Have we had any reports of bandit gangs operating up there?'

'No. In any case, bandits wouldn't stop after just a few families. They'd keep going until they were caught. Those families disappeared nine weeks ago now, and there have been no reports of any repetition. Whatever did happen, it looks like a one off.'

'And bandits would have stripped the homesteads of every remotely useful piece of gear, anyway,' Colin mused out loud. 'What about the Tyrathca farmers? Do they know anything?'

'The marshal rode out to their territory. They claim they've had no contact with humans since they left Durringham. He's pretty sure they're telling the truth. There was certainly no sign of any humans ever being in their houses. His affinity-bonded dog had a good scout round.'

Colin stopped himself from making the sign of the cross; his Halo asteroid upbringing had been pretty formal. Supervisors and sheriffs using affinity was something he could never get used to.

'The families all had daughters; some teenagers, a couple in their early twenties,' Terrance said. 'I checked their registration files.'

'So?'

'Several of the girls were quite pretty. They could have moved downriver to one of the larger towns, set up a brothel. It wouldn't be the first time. And from what we know, conditions in Schuster are fairly dire.'

'Then why not take their gear with them?'

'I don't know. That was the only explanation I could think of.'

'Ah, forget it. If there aren't any more disappearances, and the situation isn't developing into an insurrection, I'm not interested. Write it down to an animal carrying them off for nest food, and call the marshal back. Those colonists know the risks of alien frontiers before they start out. If they're mad enough to go and live out in the jungle and play at being cavemen, let them. I've got enough real problems to deal with at this end of the river.'

*

Quinn Dexter had heard of the disappearances, it was all round the Aberdale village camp the day a party from Schuster made their official welcome visit to Group Seven. Four complete families, seventeen people flying off into thin air. It interested him, especially the rumours. Bandits, xenocs (especially the Tyrathca farmers over in the foothills), secret metamorph aborigines, they had all been advanced as theories, and all found wanting. But the metamorph stories fascinated Quinn. One of Schuster's Ivets told him there had been several sightings when they had first arrived a year ago.

'I saw one myself,' Sean Pallas told him. Sean was a couple of years older than Quinn, and could have passed for thirty. His face was gaunt, his ribs were starkly outlined. Fingers and arms were covered in red weals, and pocked sores where insects had bitten him. 'Out in the jungle. It was just like a man, only completely black. It was horrible.'

'Hey,' Scott Williams complained. He was the only Afro-Caribbean among Aberdale's eighteen Ivets. 'Ain't nothing wrong with that.'

'No, man, you don't understand. It didn't have any face, just black skin, there was no mouth or eyes; nothing like that.'

'You sure?' Jackson Gael asked.

'Yeah. I was twenty metres from it. I know what I saw. I shouted out and pointed, and it just vanished, ducked down behind a bush or something. And when we got there—'

'The cupboard was bare,' Quinn said.

The others laughed.

'It's not funny, man,' Sean said hotly. 'It was there, I swear. There was no way it could have got away without us seeing. It changed shape, turned into a tree or something. And there's more just like it. They are out there in the jungle, man, and they're angry with us for stealing their planet.'

'If they're that primitive, how do they know we've stolen their planet?' Scott Williams asked. 'How do they know we're not the true aboriginals?'

'It's no joke, man. You won't be laughing when one of them morphs out of the trees and grabs you. They'll drag you underground where they live in big cave cities. Then you'll be sorry.'

Quinn and the others had talked about Sean and what he said that night. They agreed that he was badly undernourished, probably hysterical, certainly suffering from sun dreams. The visitors from Schuster had cast a tangible gloom on the mood of all Aberdale's residents, an all too physical reminder of how close failure lurked. There hadn't been much contact between the two groups since the *Swithland* departed.

But Quinn had thought a lot about what Sean said, and the talk he picked up around the village. A black humanoid, without a face, who could disappear into the jungle without a trace (more than one, judging by the number of sightings). Quinn was pretty sure he knew what that was: someone wearing a chameleon camouflage suit. Nobody else in Aberdale had guessed, their minds just weren't thinking along those lines, because it would be totally ridiculous to expect someone to be hiding out in the hinterlands of the greatest shit-hole planet in the Confederation. Which, when Quinn considered it, was the really interesting part. To hide away on Lalonde, where *nobody* would ever look, you must be the most desperate wanted criminal in the universe. Group of criminals, he corrected himself; well organized, well equipped. Conceivably, with their own spacecraft.

Later he discovered all the families who had disappeared had been living in savannah homesteads to the south-east of Schuster. Aberdale was east of Schuster.

Could a retinal implant operating in the infrared spectrum spot a chameleon suit?

The options opening up were amazing.

*

A fortnight after the *Swithland* left Group Seven at their new home on the Quallheim, the voidhawk *Niobe* emerged above Lalonde. With the Edenists having a five per cent stake in the LDC a visit from Jovian Bank officials was a regular occurrence. The visiting voidhawks also brought supplies and fresh personnel to the station in orbit around Murora, the largest of the system's five gas giants. They were there to supervise Aethra, a bitek habitat that had been germinated in 2602 as part of the Edenist contribution to developing the Lalonde system.

Darcy requested the *Niobe*'s captain perform a detailed scan of Schuster County as soon as the voidhawk slipped into equatorial orbit. *Niobe* altered its orbital track to take it over Schuster at an altitude of two hundred kilometres. The verdant, undulating quilt of jungle rolled past below the voidhawk's sensor blisters, and it concentrated every spare neural cell on analysing the images. Resolution was ten centimetres, enough to distinguish individual humans.

After five daylight passes *Niobe* reported that there were no unauthorized human buildings within a one-hundred-kilometre radius of Schuster town, and all humans observed within that area were listed in the immigrant file Lori and Darcy had built up. Aboriginal-animal density was within expected parameters, which suggested than even if a group had concealed themselves in caves or stealth-cloaked structures, they weren't hunting for food. It found no trace of the missing seventeen people.

*

After six months Aberdale was looking more like a village and less like a lumberyard with each passing day. Group Seven had waded ashore that first day, armed with fission saws from their gear, and single-minded resolution. They had felled the mayope trees nearest the water, trimmed the trunks to form sturdy pillars which they had driven deep into the shingly riverbed, then sliced out thick planks from the boughs to make a solid walkway. Fission blades made easy work of the timber, ripping through the compacted cellulose like a laser through ice. They sawed like mechanoids, and sweated the cuts into place, and hammered away until an hour before the sun set. By then they had a jetty three metres wide that extended twenty-five metres out into the river, with piles that could moor a half-dozen paddle-craft securely against the current.

The next day they had formed a human chain to unload their cargo-pods and cases as the paddle-boats docked one by one. Will-power and camaraderie made light of the task. And when the paddle-boats had set off back down the river the next day, they stood on the sloping bank and sang their hymn: 'Onward, Christian Soldiers'. Loud, proud voices carrying a long way down the twisting Quallheim.

The clearing which formed over the next fortnight was a broad semicircle, stretching a kilometre along the waterfront with the jetty at its centre. But unlike Schuster, Aberdale trimmed each tree as it came down, carrying the trunks and usable boughs to a neat stack, and flinging the smaller leftover branches into a firewood pile.

They built a community hall first, a smaller wooden version of the transients' dormitory with a wooden slat roof and woven palm walls a metre high. Everyone helped, and everyone learnt the more practical aspects of gussets and joists and tenons and rabbet grooves that a didactic carpentry course could never impart. Food came from frequent hunting trips into the jungle where lasers and electromagnetic rifles would bring down a variety of game. Then there were wild cherry-oak trees with their edible nutty-tasting fruit and acillus vines with small clusters of apple-analogue fruit. The children would be sent on foraging expeditions each day, scouring the fringes of the clearing for the succulent globes. And there was also the river with its shoals of brownspines that tasted similar to trout, and bottom-clinging mousecrabs. It was a bland diet to start with, often supplemented with chocolate and freeze-dried stocks taken from the cargo-pods, but they never fell anywhere near Schuster's iron regimen.

They had to learn how to cook for batches of a hundred on open fires, mastering the technique of building clay ovens which didn't collapse, and binding up carcasses of sayce and danderil (a gazelle-analogue) to be spit-roasted. How to boil water in twenty-five-litre containers.

There were stinging insects to recognize, and thorny plants, and poisonous berries, nearly all of which somehow managed to look different from their didactic memory images. There were ways of lashing wood together; and firing clay so that it didn't crack. Some fronds were good for weaving and some shredded immediately; vines could be dried and used for string and nets. How to dig latrines that nobody fell into (the Ivets were given that task). A long, long list of practicalities which had to be grasped, the essential and the merely convenient. And, by and large, they managed.

After the hall came the houses, springing up in a crescent just inside the perimeter of the clearing. Two-room shacks with overhanging veranda roofs, standing half a metre off the ground thanks to astute management of the tree stumps. They were designed to be added to, a room at a time extending out of the gable walls.

Out of the two hundred and eighteen family groups, forty-two elected to live away from the village, out on the savannah which began south of the river where the jungle eventually faded away to scrub then finally grassland, a sea of rippling green stalks stretching away to the foothills of the distant mountain range, its uniformity broken only by occasional lonely trees and the far-off silver glimmer of narrow watercourses. They were the families who had brought calves and lambs and goat kids and foals, geneered to withstand months of hibernation; pumped full of drugs, and transported in marsupium shells. All the animals were female, so that they could be inseminated from the stock of frozen sperm that had accompanied them across three hundred light-years from Earth.

The Skibbows and the Kavas were among the families who had visions of filling the vast, empty savannah with huge herds of meat-laden beasts. They slept in a tent on the edge of the jungle for five weeks while Gerald and Frank assembled their new home, a four-room log cabin with a stone fireplace, and solar panels nailed on the roof to power lights and a fridge. Outside, they built a small lean-to barn and a stockade; then dammed the little nearby stream with grey stones to form a pool they could wash and bathe in.

Four months and three days after the *Swithland* departed, they split open their seventeen marsupium shells (three had been stolen at the spaceport). The animals were curled up in a form-fitting sponge, almost as though they were in wombs, with tubes and cables inserted in every orifice. Fifteen made it through the revival process: three shire-horse foals, three calves, one bison, three goats, four lambs, and an Alsatian pup. It was a healthy percentage, but Gerald found himself wishing he could have afforded zero-tau pods for them.

All five family members spent the day helping the groggy animals stand and walk, feeding them a special vitamin-rich milk to speed recovery. Marie, who had never even patted a living animal before let alone nursed one, was bitten, peed on, butted, and had the yellowy milk spewed up over her dungarees. At nightfall she rolled into bed and cried herself to sleep; it was her eighteenth birthday, and no one had remembered.

*

Rai Molvi made his way across the clearing towards the jetty where the tramp trader boat was waiting, exchanging greetings with several adults. He felt a surge of pride at what he saw, the sturdy buildings, neat stacks of timber, fish smoking over open fires, danderil hides pegged out on frames to dry in the sun. A well-ordered community chasing a common goal. The LDC could use Aberdale in its promotional campaign without any falsehood, it was exemplary.

A second wave of tree felling had been underway for a month now, cutting rectangular gashes deep into the jungle around the perimeter of the clearing. From the air the village resembled a gear cog with exceptionally long teeth. The colonists were starting to cultivate the new fields, digging out the tree stumps, ploughing the soil with rotovators that charged from solar cells, planting their vegetable plots and fruit groves. Lines of small green shoots were already visible, pushing up through the rich black soil, and the farmers had to organize a bird patrol to scare off the hungry flocks perched waiting in the surrounding trees.

Not all of the Earth seeds had germinated successfully, which was surprising because they were geneered for Lalonde's environment. But Rai had every confidence the village would triumph. Today's fields would become tomorrow's estates. In six months they had accomplished more than Schuster had in eighteen. It was down to effective organization, he felt. His council was acknowledged as a stroke of salutary foresight, organizing them into an effective interactive work unit even back in the transients' dormitory.

He passed the community hall and stood to one side to let a group of children march by, carrying braces of fat polot birds they had caught in their traps. Their skin was scratched from thorns, and their legs were coated in mud, but they were smiling and laughing. Yes, Rai Molvi felt very good indeed.

He reached the jetty and walked its length. A couple of Ivets were in the river, Irley and Scott, hauling up their creels full of mousecrabs. The creels were adaptations of lobster-pots, one of Quinn's ideas.

Rai waved at the two lads, receiving a grinning thumbs-up. The Ivets were undoubtedly his greatest success. A month after they had arrived, Quinn Dexter had asked to talk to him. 'Anything we say to Powel Manani just gets automatically ignored, but we know you'll give us a fair hearing, Mr Molvi.'

Which was so true. It was his job to arbitrate, and like it or not, the Ivets were part of Aberdale. He must appear strictly impartial.

'We want to organize ourselves,' Quinn had said earnestly. 'Right now you have all eighteen of us working for you each day, but you have to feed us and let us live in the hall. It's not the best arrangement, because we just sweat our arses off for you and don't get anything out of it for ourselves, so we don't give a hundred per cent, that's only human nature. None of us asked to come to Aberdale, but we're here now, and we want to make the most of it. We thought that if we had a rota so that thirteen of us are available as a general work team each day, then the remaining five could use the time to build something for ourselves, something to give us a bit of pride. We want to have our own cabin; and we could trap and grow our own food. That way you don't have to support us, and you get a far more enthusiastic work team to help put up your cabins and fell the trees.'

'I don't know,' Rai had said, although he could see the logic behind the idea. It was just Quinn he was unsettled over; he had encountered waster kids back in the arcology often enough, and Quinn's sinewy frame and assertive mannerisms brought the memories back. But he didn't want to appear prejudicial, and the lad was making an honest appeal which might well be beneficial to the whole community.

'We could try it for three weeks,' Quinn suggested. 'What have you got to lose? It's only Powel Manani who could say no to you.'

'Mr Manani is here to help us,' Rai answered stiffly. 'If this arrangement is what the town council wants, then he must see that it is implemented.'

Powel Manani had indeed objected, which Rai thought was a challenge to his authority and that of the council. In a session to which Powel Manani was not invited, the council decided that they would give the Ivets a trial period to see if they could become self-sufficient.

Now the Ivets had built themselves a long (and very well constructed, Rai grudgingly conceded) A-frame building on the eastern side of the clearing where they all lived. They caught a huge number of mousecrabs in their creels, which they traded for other types of food among the other villagers. They had their own chicken run and vegetable allotments (villagers had chipped in with three chicks and a few seeds from their own stocks). They joined the hunting parties, even being trusted to carry power weapons, although those did have to be handed back at the end of the day. And the daily work team were enthusiastic in the tasks they were given. There was also some kind of still producing a rough drink, which Rai didn't strictly approve of, but could hardly object to now.

It all added up to a lot of credit in Rai Molvi's favour for pushing the idea so hard. And it wouldn't be long before the time was right for Aberdale to think about formally electing a mayor. After that, there was the county itself to consider. Schuster town was hardly flourishing; several of its inhabitants had already asked if they could move to Aberdale. Who knew what a positive, forthright man could aspire to out here where this world's history was being carved?

Rai Molvi came to the end of the jetty flushed with a strong sense of contentment. Which was why he was only slightly put out by a close-up view of the *Coogan.* The boat was twenty metres long, a bizarre combination of raft and catamaran. Flotation came from a pair of big hollowed-out trunks of some fibrous red wood, and a deck of badly planed planks had been laid out above them, supporting a palm-thatched cabin which ran virtually the whole length. The aft section was an engine house, with a small ancient thermal-exchange furnace, and a couple of time-expired electric motors used by the McBoeings in their flap actuators which the captain had salvaged from the spaceport. Forward of that was a raised wheel-house, with a roof made entirely of solar panels, then came the galley and bunk cabin. The rest of the cabin was given over to cargo.

The *Coogan*'s captain was Len Buchannan, a wire-thin man in his mid-fifties, dressed in a pair of worn, faded shorts and a tight-fitting blue cap. Rai suspected he had little geneering; the hair peeking out from his cap was tightly curled and pale grey, dark brown skin showed stringy muscles stretched taut and slightly swollen joints, several teeth had rotted away.

He stood in front of the wheel-house and welcomed Rai on board.

'I need a few supplies,' Rai said.

'I ain't interested in barter,' he said straight away, cheeks puffing out for emphasis. 'Not unless it's powered equipment you're offering. I've had my fill of pickled vegetables and fruit preserves and cured hides. And don't even think about saying fish. They're coming out my ears. I can't sell anything like that downriver. Nobody's interested.'

Rai fished a roll of plastic Lalonde francs out of his pocket. Buchannan was the third trader captain to appear at Aberdale recently. All of them wanted cash for their goods, and none had bought much of Aberdale's produce in return. 'I understand. I'm looking for cloth. Cotton mainly, but I'll take denim or canvas.'

'Cost you a lot of francs. You got anything harder?'

'I might have,' Rai said, with a grey inevitability. Didn't anybody use Lalonde francs? 'Let's see what you've got first.'

Gail Buchannan was sitting in the wheel-house, wearing a coolie hat and a shapeless khaki dress. An obese fifty-year-old with long, straggly dark hair, her legs were like water-filled sacks of skin; when she walked it was with a painful waddle.

Most of her life was spent sitting on the *Coogan*'s deck watching the world go by. She looked up from the clothes she was sewing to give Rai a friendly nod. 'Cloth you wanted, is it, lovie?'

'That's right.'

'Plenty of cloth, we've got. All woven in Durringham. Dyed, too. Won't find better anywhere.'

'I'm sure.'

'No patterns yet. But that'll come.'

'Yes.'

'Does your wife know how to sew, then?'

'I . . . Yes, I suppose so.' Rai hadn't thought about it. Arcology synthetics came perfectly tailored; load your size into the commercial circuit and they arrived within six hours. If they started to wear, throw them into the recycler. Waster kids dressed in patched and frayed garments, but not decent people.

'If she doesn't, you send her to me.'

'Thank you.'

'Knitting too. None of the women that come here know how to knit. I give lessons. Best lessons east of Durringham. Know why, lovie?'

'No,' Rai said helplessly.

'Because they're the only ones.' Gail Buchannan slapped her leg and laughed, rolls of flesh quivering.

Rai gave her a sickly smile and fled into the cargo hold, wondering how many times that joke had been cracked over the years.

Len Buchannan had everything a farmstead could ever possibly want stacked up on his long shelves. Rai Molvi shuffled down the tiny aisle, staring round in awe and envy. There were power tools still in their boxes, solar cells (half of Rai's had been stolen back in Durringham), fridges, microwaves, cryostats full of frozen animal sperm, MF album flek-players, laser rifles, nanonic medical packages, drugs, and bottle after bottle of liquor. The Lalonde-made products were equally impressive: nails, pots, pans, glass (Rai saw the panes and groaned, what he wouldn't give for a window of glass), drinking glasses, boots, nets, seeds, cakes of dried meat, flour, rice, saws, hammers, and bale after bale of cloth.

'What kind of things would you take downriver?' Rai asked as Len unrolled some of the cotton for him.

Len pulled his cap off, and scratched his largely bald head. 'Truth to tell, not much. What you produce up here, food and the like. People need it. But it's the transport costs, see? I couldn't take fruit more than a hundred kilometres and make a profit.'

'Small and valuable then?'

'Yes, that's your best bet.'

'Meat?'

'Could do. There's some villages not doing as well as you. They want the food, but how are they going to pay for it? If they spend all their money buying food, it's going to run out fast, then they won't be able to buy in new stocks of what they really need like seed and animals. I seen that happen before. Bad business.'

'Oh?'

'The Arklow Counties, a tributary over in the northern territory. All the villages failed about six or seven years back. No food, no money left to buy any in. They started marching downriver towards villages that did have food.'

'What happened?'

'Governor sent in the marshals, plus a few boosted mercenaries from offplanet if you believe what people say. Them starving villagers took a right pounding. Some escaped into the jungle, still there by all accounts, lot of bandit reports in the north. Most got themselves killed. The rest got a twenty-year work-time sentence; the Governor parcelled them out to other villages to work, just like Ivets. Families broken up, children never see their parents.' He sucked his cheeks in, scowling. 'Yes, bad business.'

Rai sorted out the cloth he wanted, and on impulse bought

a packet of sweetcorn seed for Skyba, his wife. He offered the Lalonde notes again.

'Cost you double, that way,' Len Buchannan said. 'The LDC people at the spaceport, they don't give you anything like the proper exchange rate.'

Rai made one last attempt. 'How about chickens?'

Len pointed to a shelf given over to cryostats, their tiny green LEDs twinkling brightly in the gloomy cabin. 'See that? Two of those chambers are crammed full of eggs. There's chickens, ducks, geese, pheasants, emus, and turkeys stored in there; I've even got three swans. I don't need live chickens crapping on my deck.'

'OK.' Rai gave up; he dug into his inside pocket and offered his Jovian Bank disk, feeling a little bit shabby. People should believe in their own planet's currency. If – when – Schuster County became an important commercial region, he would make damn sure every transaction was made in Lalonde francs. Patriotism like that would be very popular with the voters.

Len stood beside his wife as Rai walked back down the jetty. 'Ten thousand born every second,' he murmured.

Gail chuckled. 'Aye, and all of them come to live here.'

From their vantage point in the river shallows, Irley and Scott gave Rai a cheery wave as he carried his cloth ashore. Another who had a Jovian Bank credit disk, that made seventy-eight known residents now. Quinn would be pleased with them.

Rai reached the end of the jetty just as Marie Skibbow arrived carrying a bulky shoulder-bag. She gave him an uninterested glance and hurried on towards the *Coogan.*

What's she come to pick up? Rai wondered. Gerald's place was one of the prime savannah homesteads. Although the man himself was a complete self-righteous pain in the arse.

*

Horst Elwes stood at the base of the church's wooden corner stanchion, holding the cloth bag full of nails, and still managing to feel completely useless. Leslie didn't need anyone to hold the nails ready. But Horst could hardly let the Ivet work team assemble the church without being there, without at least the pretence of being involved.

The church was one of the last of Aberdale's buildings to be put up. He didn't mind that at all. These people had toiled hard to build their village and clear their fields. They couldn't spare the time on a structure that would only be used once or twice a week (though he liked to think there would be more services eventually). Nor was it right they should do so. Horst could never forget how the cathedrals of medieval Europe had risen like stone palaces out of the mouldering, stinking wooden slums. How the Church demanded the people of that time give and give and give. How fear was rooted in every soul and carefully nurtured. And because we were so arrogant, as aloof as God Himself, we suffered a terrible price in later centuries. Which again was right. Such a crime deserved a penance that lasted for so long.

So he held his services in the hall, and never complained when only thirty or forty people turned up. The church must be a focal point for unity, a place where people could come together and share their faith, not a baron demanding tribute.

And now the fields had been rotovated, the first batch of crops planted, and the animals brought out of hibernation, Aberdale had a moment of time to spare. Three Ivets had been assigned to him for a fortnight. They had built a long raftlike floor supported half a metre off the ground by old tree stumps, then put up four-metre-high stanchions to hold up the sloping roof.

At the moment it looked like a skeleton of some boxy dinosaur. Leslie Atcliffe was busy hammering the trusses into place, while Daniel held them steady. Ann was busy cutting slates from the sheets of qualtook bark they had stripped off the felled trunks. The church itself would occupy a third of the structure, with a small infirmary at the rear, and Horst's room sandwiched between the two.

It was all going very well, and would probably go better if Horst wasn't there asking what he could do to help the whole time.

The church was going to be a fine building, second only to the Ivets' own A-frame. And how that structure had shown up the hall and the other houses. Horst had joined Rai Molvi in urging the council to allow the Ivets some independence and dignity. Now Quinn was the one who had really worked miracles in Aberdale. Since the long bark-slate covered A-frame had gone up the other residents had taken to quietly improving the structure of their own homes, adding corner braces, putting up shutters.

And none of us will use an A-frame design, Horst thought. Oh, foolish pride! Everyone was captured by the quaint white-painted cottages we saw on the first days of the voyage upriver, we thought if we could emulate the look we would have the life that went with it. Now the most practical method of construction is a monopoly. Because using it would mean the Ivets knew best. And I can't even build the church that way, the sensible way, because people would be offended. Not out loud, but they would see and in their hearts they would object. But at least I can use the bark slates rather than slats that will warp and let in the rain like the houses which were built first.

Leslie climbed down the ladder, a rangy twenty-two-year-old wearing shorts sewn together from an old jump suit. A specially made belt had loops to hold all his carpentry tools. To start with Powel Manani had issued the tools on a daily basis, and demanded their return at night; now the Ivets kept them permanently. Several of them had developed into highly skilled carpenters; Leslie was one of them.

'We'll fetch the last two transverse frames now, Father,' Leslie said. 'They'll be up by lunch, then we can start with the lathing and the slates. You know, I think we will be finished by the end of the fortnight after all. It's just those pew benches I'm worried about, cutting that many dovetail joints in time is going to be tricky, even with fission blades.'

'Don't pay it a second thought,' Horst said. 'I don't get enough of a congregation to fill every pew. A roof over our heads is more than enough. The rest can wait. The Lord understands that the farms must come first.' He smiled, keenly aware of how shabby he was in his stained ochre shirt and oversize knee-length shorts. So much at variance from these uniformly trim young men.

'Yes, Father.'

Horst felt a pang of regret. The Ivets were so insular, yet they did more work than most. Aberdale's success was in no small part due to their efforts. And Powel Manani still grumbled about the liberties they were shown. It didn't happen in other settlements, he complained. But then other settlements didn't have Quinn Dexter. It was a thought Horst couldn't be quite as grateful for as he should be. Quinn was a very cold fish. Horst knew waster kids, their motivations, their shallow wishes. But what went on behind those chilling bright eyes was an utter mystery, one he was afraid to probe.

'I shall be holding a consecration service once the roof's on,' he said to the two Ivets. 'I hope you'll all come to it.'

'We'll think about it,' Leslie said with smooth politeness. 'Thank you for asking, Father.'

'I notice that not many of you come to my services. Everybody is welcome. Even Mr Manani, although I don't think he's particularly impressed with me.' He tried to make it sound jovial, but their expressions never flickered.

'We're not very religious,' Leslie said.

'I'd be happy to explain the broader ramifications of Christianity to anybody. Ignorance isn't a crime, only a misfortune. If nothing else we could have a good argument about it, you needn't worry about shocking me there. Why, I remember some debates from my novice years, we really gave the bishop a roasting.' Now he knew he'd lost them. Their earlier magnanimity had turned to stiff-backed formality, faces hard, sparks of resentment agleam in their eyes. And once more he was aware of how ominous these young men could appear.

'We have the Light Brother—' Daniel began. He broke off at a furious look from Leslie.

'Light Brother?' Horst asked mildly. He was sure he'd heard that phrase before.

'Was there anything else, Father?' Leslie said. 'We'd like to collect the transverse frames now.'

Horst knew when to push, and this wasn't the time. 'Yes, of course. What would you like me to do? Help you fetch them?'

Leslie looked around the church impatiently. 'We could do with the slates stacking round the floor ready for when we get the lathing up,' he said grudgingly. 'Piles of twenty by each stanchion.'

'Jolly good, I'll start doing that then.'

He walked over to where Ann was standing beside a workbench, slicing up the bark with a fission jigsaw. She was wearing a pair of hand-stitched shorts and a halter top, both made from grey jump suit fabric. There was a huge pile of the slates on the ground around her. Her long face was crunched up in an expression of furious concentration, dark auburn hair hanging in damp tassels.

'We don't need the slates that urgently,' Horst said lightly. 'And I'm certainly not going to complain to Mr Manani if you slacken off a bit.'

Ann's hand moved with mechanical precision, guiding the slender blade in a rectangular pattern through the big sheet of glossy ginger-coloured qualtook bark. She never bothered to mark out the shape, but each one came out more or less identical.

'Stops me thinking,' she said.

Horst started to pick up some of the slates. 'I was sent here to encourage people to think. It's good for you.'

'Not me. I've got Irley tonight. I don't want to think about it.'

Irley was one of the Ivets; Horst knew him as a thin-faced lad, who was quiet even by their standards.

'What do you mean, you've got him?'

'It's his turn.'

'Turn?'

Ann suddenly looked up, her face a mask of cold rage, most of it directed at Horst. 'He's going to fuck me. It's his turn tonight. Do you want it in writing, Father?'

'I . . .' Horst knew his face was reddening. 'I didn't know.'

'What the hell do you think we do in that big hut at night? Basket weaving? There are three girls, and fifteen boys. And the boys all need it pretty bad, banging their fists each night isn't enough, so they take it in turns with us, those that aren't AC/DC. Quinn draws up a nice little impartial list, and we stick to it. He makes sure it's dished out fairly, and he makes sure nobody spoils the merchandise. But Irley knows how to make it hurt without making it painful, without it showing. Do you want to know how, Father? You want the details? The tricks he's got.'

'Oh, my child. This must stop, at once. I'll speak to Powel and the council.'

Ann surprised him. She burst into shrill contemptuous laughter. 'God's Brother. I can see why they dumped you out here, Father. You'd be bloody useless back on Earth. You're going to stop the boys from screwing me and Jemima and Kay, are you? Then where are they going to go for it? Huh? Lotsa your good parishioners got daughters. You think they want Ivets prowling round at night? And how about you, Father, do you want Leslie and Douglas giving your sweet little friend Jay the eye? Do you? Because they will if they can't get it from me. Get real, Father.' She turned back to the sheet of bark. A dismissal that was frightening in its finality. Nothing Horst could offer was of the remotest use. Nothing.

*

It was there, right at the bottom of his pack where it had lain for six and a half months. Untouched, *unneeded*, because the world was full of worthy challenges, and the sun shone, and the village grew, and the plants blossomed, and the children danced and laughed.

Horst took out the bottle, and poured a long measure. Scotch, though this thick amber liquid had never rested in oak barrels in the Highlands. It had come straight out of a molecular filter programmed with the taste of a long-lost ideal. But it burnt as it went down, and slowly lit up his belly and his skull, which was all he wanted from it.

How stupid. How blind to think the serpent hadn't come with them to this fresh world. How obtuse that he, a priest, hadn't thought to look below the shining surface of achievement, to see the sewer beneath.

He poured another measure of Scotch. Breath coming in hot bursts between gulps. God, but it felt good, to abandon mortal failings for a few brief hours. To hide in this warm, silent, forgiving place of sanctuary.

God's Brother, she had said. And she was right. Satan is here amongst us, piercing our very heart.

Horst filled his glass to the very top, staring at it in abject dread. Satan: Lucifer, the light bringer. The Light Brother.

'Oh no,' he whispered. Tears filled his eyes. 'Not that, not that here. Not the sects spreading over this world's purity. I can't, dear Lord. I can't fight that. *Look at me.* I'm here because I can't.' He trailed off into sobs.

Now as always, the Lord answered only with silence. Faith alone wasn't enough for Horst Elwes. But then he'd always known that.

*

The bird was back again, thirty centimetres long, its plumage a tawny brown flecked with gold. It hovered twenty metres above Quinn, half hidden by the jungle's curving branches, its wings blurring in an intricate pattern as it maintained position.

He watched it out of the corner of his eye. It wasn't like any other bird he'd seen on Lalonde; their feathers were almost like membrane scales. When he scanned it with his retinal implant on high magnification he could see it had real feathers, Earth genealogy feathers.

He gave the hand signal, and they advanced steadily through the bush, Jackson Gael on one side of him, Lawrence Dillon on the other. Lawrence was the youngest Ivet, seventeen, with a slim figure, skinny limbs, and sandy blond hair. Lawrence was a gift from God's Brother. It had taken Quinn a month to break him. There had been the favouritism, the extra food, the smiles and making sure he wasn't bullied by the others. Then there had been the drugs Quinn had bought from Baxter, the gentle lifts which removed Aberdale and all its squalor and endless toil, blurring away the edges until life was easier again. The midnight rape performed in the middle of the A-frame with everybody watching; Lawrence tied to the floor with a pentagon drawn around him in danderil blood, his mind blown out of his skull by the drugs. Now Lawrence belonged to him, his sweet arse, the golden length of his dick, and his mind. Lawrence's devotion to Quinn had evolved to a form of worship.

Sex showed the others the power Quinn had. It showed them how in touch with God's Brother he was. It showed them the glory of freeing the serpent beast that was trapped in every man's heart. It showed them what would happen if they failed him.

He had given them hope and power. All he demanded in return was obedience.

Demanded and received.

The big spongy leaves of the vines which shrouded the trees brushed lightly against Quinn's damp skin as he advanced on his prey. After months of working under the brilliant sun he was a rich all-over brown, wearing just a pair of shorts cut from his jump suit, and the boots he'd stolen in Durringham. He'd eaten well since the Ivets started fending for themselves, and put on muscle weight from the work he'd done around the homesteads.

Creepers were hung between the trunks like a net the jungle had woven to catch its smaller denizens. They crackled annoyingly as he waded through them, booted feet crunching on the spindly mosslike grass that grew deep in the jungle. Birds clucked and squawked as they arrowed through the latticework of branches. He could see the distant movement of vennals high overhead, spiralling round trunks and branches like three-dimensional shadows.

The light filtering down through the leaf canopy was growing darker. He spotted an increasing number of young giganteas interspaced with the usual trees. They resembled elongated cones, with an outer coating of mauve-brown fibrous hair rather than a true bark. Their boughs emerged in rings from the trunk, spaced regularly up the entire length; they all sloped downwards at a fifty-degree angle, supporting fanlike arrangements of twigs, densely packed as birds' nests. Leaves grew on the upper surface like a dark green fur.

The first time Quinn had seen a mature gigantea he thought he must have been tripping. It stood two hundred and thirty metres high, with a base forty-five metres in diameter, rearing out of the jungle like a misplaced mountain. Creepers and vines had wrapped themselves around its lower branches, adding a colourful speckle of multicoloured flowers to its uninspiring leaden-green leaves. But even the vigorous vines couldn't hope to challenge a gigantea.

Jackson clicked his fingers, and pointed ahead. Quinn risked raising his head above the shoulder-high rall bushes and spindly light-starved saplings.

The sayce they had been tracking was padding through the skimpy undergrowth ten metres away. It was a big specimen, a buck, its black hide scarred and flecked with blue spots, ears chewed down to stubs. It had been in a lot of fights, and won them.

Quinn smiled happily, and signalled Lawrence forwards. Jackson stayed where he was, sighting the laser rifle on the sayce's head. Back-up, in case their attack went wrong.

The hunt had taken a while to set up. There were thirty of Aberdale's residents spread out through the jungle today, but they were all nearer to the river. Quinn, Jackson, and Lawrence had made off south-west into the deeper jungle as soon as they could, away from the river and its humidity, into the country where the sayce lurked. Powel Manani had ridden off at dawn to help one of the savannah homesteads track down the sheep that had wandered off after their stockade had failed. Most importantly, he'd taken Vorix with him to find the scent. Irley had arranged for the stockade fence to fail last night.

Quinn put down the pump-action shotgun he'd bought from Baxter, and took the bolas from his belt. He started spinning it above his head, letting out a fearsome yell. To his right Lawrence was running towards the sayce, his bolas whirling frantically. Nobody knew the Ivets used bolas. The weapon was simple enough to build, all they needed was the dried vine to link the three stones with. They could carry the vine lengths about quite openly, using them as belts.

The sayce turned, its jaws hinging wide to let out its peculiar keening cry. It charged straight at Lawrence. The boy let the bolas fly, yelling with adrenalin intoxication, and it caught the sayce on its forelegs, stones twisting in ever-shorter arcs with incredible speed. Quinn's whirled around the animal's right flank a second later, tangling one of the hind legs. The sayce fell, skidding through the grass and loam, its body bucking in epileptic frenzy.

Quinn ran forward, tugging the lasso off his shoulder. The sayce was thrashing about, howling, trying to get its razor-sharp teeth into the infuriating vine strands binding its legs.

He twisted the lasso, working up a good speed, studying the sayce's movements, then threw.

The sayce's jaws shut between cries, and the lasso's loop slipped over the muzzle. He jerked back with all his strength. The jaws strained to open, but the loop held; it was silicon fibre, stolen from one of the homesteads. All three Ivets could hear the furious and increasingly frantic cries, muted to a harsh sneezing sound.

Lawrence landed heavily on the writhing sayce, struggling to shove its kicking hind legs into his own loop of rope. Quinn joined him, hugging the sayce's thick gnarled hide as he fought to coil another length of rope round the forelegs.

It took another three minutes to subdue and bind the sayce completely. Quinn and Lawrence wrestled with it on the ground, getting covered in scratches and mud. But eventually they stood, bruised and shaking from the effort, looking down at their trussed victim lying helplessly on its side. Its green-tinted eye glared back up at them.

'Stage two,' said Quinn.

*

It was Jay who found Horst late in the afternoon. He was sitting slumped against a qualtook tree in the light drizzle, virtually comatose. She giggled at how silly he was being and shook him by the shoulder. Horst mumbled incoherently then told her to piss off.

Jay stared at him for a mortified second, her lower lip trembling, then rushed to get her mother.

'Ho boy, look at you,' Ruth said when she arrived.

Horst burped.

'Come on, get up. I'll help you get home.'

The weight of him nearly cracked her spine as he leant against her. With a solemn-faced Jay following a couple of paces behind they staggered across the clearing to the little cabin Horst used.

Ruth let him fall onto his cot, and watched impassively as he tried to vomit onto the duckboard floor. All that came out of his mouth was a few beads of sour yellow stomach juices.

Jay stood in a corner and clutched at Drusilla, her white rabbit. The doe squirmed around in agitation. 'Is he going to be all right?'

'Yes,' Ruth said.

'I thought it was a heart attack.'

'No. He's been drinking.'

'But he's a priest,' the girl insisted.

Ruth stroked her daughter's hair. 'I know, darling. But that doesn't mean they're saints.'

Jay nodded wisely. 'I see. I won't tell anyone.'

Ruth turned and stared at Horst. 'Why did you do it, Horst? Why now? You'd been doing so well.'

Bloodshot eyes blinked at her. 'Evil,' he groaned. 'They're evil.'

'Who are?'

'Ivets. All of them. Devil's children. Burn down the church. Can't consecrate it now. They built it. Evil built it. Herit— here— heretical. Burn it to cinders.'

'Horst, you're not setting fire to anything.'

'Evil!' he slurred.

'See if there's enough charge in his electron matrix cells to power the microwave,' Ruth told Jay. 'We'll boil some water.' She started to rummage through Horst's gear looking for his silver-foil sachets of coffee.

*

Right up until the moment the electric motors began to thrum, Marie Skibbow hadn't believed it was actually happening. But here it was, bubbles rising from the *Coogan*'s propeller, the gap between the boat and the jetty growing.

'I've done it,' she said under her breath.

The ramshackle boat began to chug its way out into the

middle of the Quallheim, the prow pointing downriver, gradually picking up speed. She stopped dropping logs into the thermal-exchange furnace's square hopper-funnel and started to laugh. 'Screw you,' she told the village as it began to slide astern. 'Screw all of you. And good fucking riddance. You won't ever see me again.' She shook her fist at them. Nobody was looking, not even the Ivet lads in the water. 'Never ever.'

Aberdale disappeared from sight as they steered round a curve. Her laughter became suspiciously similar to weeping. She heard someone making their way aft from the wheel-house, and started lobbing logs into the hopper again.

It was Gail Buchannan, who barely fitted on the narrow strip of decking between the cabin and the half-metre-high gunwale. She wheezed heavily for a moment, leaning against the cabin wall, her face red and sweating below her coolie hat. 'Happier now, lovie?'

'Much!' Marie beamed a sunlight smile.

'It's not the kind of place a girlie like you should be living in. You'll be much better off downriver.'

'You don't have to tell me. God, it was awful. I hated it. I hate animals, I hate vegetables, I hate fruit trees, I hate the jungle. I hate wood!'

'You're not going to be trouble for us are you, lovie?'

'Oh no, I promise. I never signed a settlement contract with the LDC, I was still legally a minor when we left Earth. But I'm over eighteen now, so I can leave home any time I want to.'

A nonplussed frown creased the folds of spare flesh on Gail's gibbous face for a second. 'Aye, well you can stop loading the hopper now, there's enough logs in there to last the rest of today. We're only sailing for a couple of hours. Lennie'll moor somewhere below Schuster for the night.'

'Right.' Marie stood up straight, hands pressed against her side. Her heart was racing, pounding away against her ribs. *I did it!*

'You can start preparing supper in a while,' Gail said.

'Yes, of course.'

'I expect you'd like a shower first, lovie. Get cleaned up a bit.'

'A shower?' Marie thought she'd misheard.

She hadn't. It was in the cabin between the galley and the bunks, an alcove with a curtain across the front, broad enough to fit Gail. When she looked down, Marie could see the river through the gaps between the deck boards. The pump and the heater ran off electricity from the thermal-exchange furnace, producing a weak warm spray from the copper nozzle. To Marie it was more luxurious than a sybarite's jacuzzi. She hadn't had a shower since her last day on Earth. Dirt was something you lived with in Aberdale and the savannah homesteads. It got into the pores, under nails, scaled your hair. And it never came out, not completely. Not in cold stream water, not without decent soap and gels.

The first sluice of water from the nozzle disgusted her as it drained away. It was *filthy*. But Gail had given her a bar of unperfumed green soap, and a bottle of liquid soap for her hair. Marie started scrubbing with a vengeance, singing at the top of her voice.

*

Gwyn Lawes never even knew the Ivets were there until the club smashed into the small of his back. He blacked out for a while from the pain. Certainly he didn't remember falling. One minute he was lining up his electromagnetic rifle on a danderil, anticipating the praise he would earn from the rest of the hunting party. And the next thing he knew was that there was loam in his mouth, he could barely breathe, and his spine was sheer agony. All he could do was retch weakly.

Hands grabbed his shoulders, and he was turned over. Another blast of fire shot up his spine. The world shuddered nauseously.

Quinn, Lawrence, and Jackson were standing above him,

grinning broadly. They were smothered in mud, hair hanging in soiled dreadlocks, spittle saturating their tufty beards, scratches bleeding, dribbles of red blood curdling with the mud. They were savages reincarnated out of Earth's dawn times. He whimpered in fright.

Jackson bent down, teeth bared with venomous joy. A ball of cloth was thrust into Gwyn's mouth, tied into place with a gag. Breathing became even harder, his nose flaring, sucking down precious oxygen. Then he was turned again, face pressed into the wet ground. All he could see was muddy grass. He could feel thin, hard cord binding his wrists and ankles. Hands began to search him, sliding into every pocket, patting the fabric. There was a hesitant fumble when fingers found the inside leg pouch on his dungarees trousers, tracing the shape of his precious Jovian Bank credit disk.

'Got it, Quinn,' Lawrence's voice called triumphantly.

Fingers gripped Gwyn's right thumb, bending it back.

'Pattern copied,' Quinn said. 'Let's see what he's got.' There was a short pause, then a whistle. 'Four thousand three hundred fuseodollars. Hey, Gwyn, where's your faith in your new planet?'

Cruel laughter followed.

'OK, it's transferred. Lawrence, put it back where you found it. They can't activate it once he's dead, they'll never know it's been emptied.'

Dead. The word cut through Gwyn's sluggish thoughts. He groaned, trying to lift himself. A boot slammed into his ribs. He screamed, or tried to. The gag was virtually suffocating him.

'He's got some handy gear here, Quinn,' Lawrence said. 'Fission knife, firelighter, and that's a personal guido block. Spare power mags for the rifle, too.'

'Leave it,' Quinn ordered. 'If anything's missing when they find him, they might get suspicious. We can't afford that, not yet. It will all belong to us in the end.'

They lifted Gwyn, carrying him on their shoulders like some

kind of trophy. He kept drifting in and out of consciousness as he jounced about, twigs and vines slapping against him.

The light was darker when they finally slung him down. Gwyn looked about, and saw the smooth ebony trunk of an old deirar tree twenty metres away, its single giant umbrella-leaf casting a wide circular shadow. A sayce had been tethered to it, straining at the unbreakable silicon-fibre rope, forelegs scrabbling at the loam as it tried to reach its captors, its snapping jaws dripping long chains of saliva. Gwyn suddenly knew what was going to happen next. His bladder gave out.

'Get it riled good and proper,' Quinn ordered.

Jackson and Lawrence started throwing stones at the sayce. It keened in torment, its body jacking about as though an electric current was being run through it.

Gwyn saw a pair of boots appear twenty centimetres from his nose. Quinn squatted down. 'Know what's going to happen afterwards, Gwyn? We're going to be assigned to help out your widow. Everyone else is busy with their own little plots of heaven. So it'll be the Ivets who get dumped on. Once again. I'm going to be one of them, Gwyn. I'm going to be a regular visitor to poor, grieving Rachel. She'll like me, I'll make sure of that. Just like you and all the others, you want to believe that everything's so perfect on this planet. You convinced yourselves we're just a bunch of regular lads who got a bad break in life. Anything else would have cracked your dream open and made you face reality. Illusion is easy. Illusion is the loser's way out. Your way. You and all the others grubbing round in the dirt and the rain. In a couple of months I'll be in the bed you made, under the roof you sweated over, and I'll have my dick rammed up inside Rachel making her squeal like a pig in heat. I hope you hate that idea, Gwyn. I hope it makes you sick inside. Because that's not the worst. Oh, no. Once I'm through with her, I'll have Jason. Your shiny-eyed beautiful son. I'll be his new father. I'll be his lover. I'll be his owner. He'll be joining us, Gwyn, me and the Ivets. I'll bind him to the Night, I'll show him where his serpent beast is hidden within. He's not going to be a dickhead loser like his old man. You're only the first, Gwyn. One by one I will come to you all, and very few will be given the chance to follow me into darkness. Inside of six months this whole village, the only hope for a future you ever had, will belong to God's Brother.

'Do you despise me, Gwyn? I want you to. I want you to hate me as much as I hate you and all you stand for. Then you will understand that I'm speaking the truth. You will go to your pitiful Lord Jesus weeping in terror. And you will find no comfort there, because the Light Bringer will be the ultimate victor. You will lose in death, as you have lost in life. You made the wrong choice in life, Gwyn. My path is the one you should have walked. And now it's too late.'

Gwyn strained and wheezed against the gag until he thought his lungs would burst from the effort. It made no difference, the shriek of hatred and all the threats, the curses condemning Quinn to an eternity of damnation, were left jailed inside his skull.

Quinn's hands curled round the lapels of Gwyn's shirt, hauling him upright. Jackson took his feet, and the two of them swung him back and forth, building momentum. They let go, and Gwyn's tumbling body flew in a shallow trajectory right over the top of the berserk sayce. He hit the loam with a dull thud, face contorted with insane dread. The sayce leapt.

Quinn put his arms round the shoulders of Lawrence and Jackson as the three of them watched the sayce mauling the man, its teeth tearing out great strips of flesh. The power to bring death was equal to that of bringing about life. He felt enraptured as the hot scarlet blood flowed into the soil.

'After life, death,' he chanted. 'After darkness, light.'

He looked up, and stared round until he found the brown bird. It was perched up in a cherry oak's branches, head cocked on one side, observing the carnage.

'You've seen what we are,' Quinn called out. 'You've seen us naked. You've seen we're not afraid. We should talk. I think we have a lot to offer each other. What have you got to lose?'

The bird blinked as if in surprise, and launched itself into the air.

*

Laton let the kestrel's wonderfully clear sensorium fade from his mind. The sensation of air flowing over wings remained for several minutes. Flying the predator via affinity was always an experience he enjoyed, the freedom granted to creatures of the air was unsurpassed.

The ordinary world rushed back in on him.

He was in his study, sitting in the lotus position on a black velvet cushion. It was an unusual room, an ovoid, five metres high, its curving walls a smooth polished wood. A cluster of electrophorescent cells were fitted flush with the apex, supplying a glimmer of jade light. The single cushion on the cup of the floor was the only thing to break the symmetry; even the door was hard to see, its lines blending with the grain.

The study possessed a unifying simplicity, freeing his mind of distractions. In here, his body motionless, his affinity expanding his consciousness through bitek processors and incorporated brains, his mentality was raised by an order of magnitude. It was a hint of what could be. A pale shadow of the goal he chased before his exile.

Laton remained sitting, thinking about Quinn Dexter and the atrocity he had perpetrated. There had been a lurid flash of gratification in Dexter's eyes as that helpless colonist had been thrown to the sayce. Yet he must be more than a brainless sadistic brute. The fact that he had recognized the kestrel for what it was, and worked out what it represented, was proof of that.

Who is God's Brother? Laton asked the house's sub-sentient bitek processor network.

Satan. The Christian devil.

Is this a term in wide use?

The term is common among Earth's waster population. Most arcologies have sects built up around the worship of this deity. Their priest/acolyte hierarchy is a simple variant on that of the more standard officer/soldier criminal organization. Those at the top control those at the bottom through a quasi-religious doctrine, and status is enforced by initiation rituals. Their theology states that after Armageddon has been fought, and the universe abandoned to lost souls, Satan will return bringing light. The sects are unusual only in the degree of violence involved to maintain discipline among the ranks. Because of the level of devotion involved, the authorities have been generally unsuccessful in eradicating the sects.

That explains Quinn, then, Laton thought to himself. But why did he want the money in the colonist's Jovian Bank credit disk? If he was successful in taking over Aberdale no trading boat would ever stop there; he couldn't buy anything. In fact, the Governor would be more than likely to send in a posse of sheriffs and deputies to stamp out any Ivet rebellion as soon as word leaked out. Quinn must know that, he wasn't stupid.

The last thing Laton wanted was for the outside world to show an interest in Schuster County. One marshal digging around was an acceptable risk, he'd known that when he took the colonists from their homesteads. But a whole team of them scouting through the jungle in search of renegade Devil worshippers was totally out of the question.

He had to know more of Quinn Dexter's plans. They would have to meet, just like Quinn had suggested. Somehow the idea of agreeing to his proposition was vaguely disturbing.

*

The *Coogan* was moored against a small sandy spit an hour's sailing downriver from Schuster town. Two silicon-fibre ropes had been fastened to trees on the shore, holding the tramp trader secure against the current.

Marie Skibbow sat on the prow, letting the warm evening

air dry the last traces of water from her hair. Even the humidity had fallen off. Rennison, Lalonde's largest moon, was rising slowly above the dusky-grey treetops, adding a glimmering oyster light to the gloaming. She sat back against the flimsy cabin wall and watched it contentedly.

Water lapped gently against the *Coogan*'s twin hulls. Fish made occasional ripples on the glass-smooth surface.

They've probably realized I've gone by now. Mother will cry, and Father will explode; Frank won't care, and Paula will be sad. They'll all worry about how it will affect them and the animals not having an extra hand at their beck and call all day long. Not one of them will think about what I want, what's good for me.

She heard Gail Buchannan calling, and made her way back to the wheel-house.

'We thought you'd fallen overboard, lovie,' Gail said. A splash of light from the galley shone out, showing the sweat beading on her blubbery arms. At supper she had eaten more than half of all the food Marie prepared for the three of them.

'No. I was watching the moon come up.'

Gail gave her a lopsided wink. 'Very romantic. Get you in the mood.'

Marie felt the hairs on the nape of her neck rising. She was cold despite the jungle's breath.

'I've got your night clothes ready,' Gail said.

'Night clothes?'

'Very pretty. I did the lacework myself. Len likes his brides to have frills. You won't find better this side of Durringham,' she said generously. 'That T-shirt's nice and tight. But it hardly flatters your figure, now does it?'

'I paid you,' Marie said in a frail voice. 'All the way to Durringham.'

'That won't cover our costs, lovie. We told you, it's expensive travelling this river. You have to work your passage.'

'No.'

There was nothing left of the bumptious nature left in the huge woman. 'We can put you off. Right here.'

Marie shook her head. 'I can't.'

'Course you can. Pretty girl like you.' Gail wrapped a weighty hand around Marie's forearm. 'Come on, lovie,' she coaxed. 'Old Lennie, he knows how to treat his brides right.'

Marie put one foot forward.

'That's it, lovie. Down you come. It's all laid out here, look.'

There was a white cotton negligée on the galley table. Gail led her over to it. 'You just slip this on. And don't let's hear any more silly talk about can't.' She held it up against Marie. 'Oh, you're going to look a picture in this, aren't you?'

She glanced down numbly at it.

'Aren't you?' Gail Buchannan repeated.

'Yes.'

'Good girl. Now put it on.'

'Where?'

'Here, lovie. Right here.'

Marie turned her back to the gross woman, and began to pull her T-shirt off over her head.

Gail chortled thickly. 'Oh, you're a one, lovie, you really are. This is going to be a chuckle.'

The negligée's hem barely came below Marie's buttocks, but if she tried to pull it down any further her breasts would fall out of the top. She had felt cleaner when she was covered in dirt from the jungle.

Still chortling, and giving her little nudges in her back, Gail followed her into the cabin where Len was waiting dressed in an amber towelling robe. A single electric lamp hanging on the ceiling cast a halo of yellow light. Len's mouth split in a jagged smile as he took in the sight of her.

Gail sank down onto a sturdy stool by the door, puffing in relief. 'There now, don't you worry about me, lovie, I only ever watch.'

Marie thought that perhaps with the sound of the lapping

water and the close wooden walls she could pretend it was Karl and the *Swithland* again.

She couldn't.

*

The Ly-cilph had been travelling for over five billion years when it arrived at the galaxy which was home to the Confederation, although at that time it was the dinosaurs which were Earth's premier life-form. Half of its existence had been spent traversing intergalactic space. It knew how to slip through the wormhole interstices; a creature of energy, the physical structure of the cosmos was no mystery to it. But its nature was to observe and record, so it sped along at a velocity just short of lightspeed, extending its perceptive field around the outcast hydrogen atoms on their aeons-long fall towards the bright, distant star whorls. Each one was unique, an existence to be treasured, extending the knowledge base, its history placed in the transdimensional storage lattice which provided the Ly-cilph with its identity focus. The Ly-cilph was the section of space through which it passed with less disturbance than a neutrino. Like a quantum black hole, it had almost no physical size, yet within was an entire universe. A carefully patterned universe of pure data.

After it arrived at the rim stars it spent millions of years drifting among them, categorizing the life-forms which rose and fell on their planets, indexing the physical parameters of the multitudinous solar systems. It witnessed interstellar empires that bloomed and failed, and planet-bound civilizations that were lost to the final night as their stars cooled to frozen iron. Saint-like cultures and the most bestial savagery; all clicking neatly into place within its infinite interior.

It progressed inwards on a loose line towards the scintillating glow of the galactic core. And in doing so, arrived at the volume of space populated by the Confederation. Lalonde, freshly discovered, and on the edge of the territory, was the first human world it encountered.

The Ly-cilph arrived at the star's Oort cloud in 2610. After it passed through the band of circling, sleeping comets, occasional laser and microwave emissions impinged on its perception field boundary. They were weak, random fragments of overspill from the communication beams of starships entering orbit above Lalonde.

A preliminary survey showed the Ly-cilph two centres of sentient life in the solar system: Lalonde itself with the human and Tyrathca settlers, and Aethra, the young Edenist habitat in its solitary orbit above Murora.

As always in cases of life discovery, it first performed analytical sweeps of the barren planets. The four inner worlds: sunblasted Calcott and the colossal Gatley with its immense lethal atmosphere, then skipping past Lalonde to review airless Plewis and the icy Mars-like Coum. The five gas giants followed, Murora, Bullus, Achillea, Tol, and distant Puschk with its strange cryochemistry. All of them had their own moon systems and individual milieux requiring examination. The Ly-cilph took fifteen months to classify their composition and environment, then swooped in towards Lalonde.

*

The search through the jungle took eight hours. Three-quarters of Aberdale's adult population turned out to help. They found Gwyn Lawes fifteen minutes after Rennison had set below the horizon. Most of him.

Because it was a sayce which had killed him; because the ropes had been taken off his wrists and ankles, and the gag removed from his mouth; because his electromagnetic rifle and all his other possessions were accounted for, everyone accepted it was a natural, if horrible, death.

It was the Ivets who were assigned to dig the grave.

10

The *Udat* slid over the surface of Tranquillity's non-rotating spaceport as though it was running on an invisible wire. A honeycomb of deep docking-bays flashed past below the blue and purple hull; the spherical fuselages of Adamist starships nested inside, glinting dully under the rim floodlights. Meyer watched through the blackhawk's sensors as a fifty-five-metre-diameter clipper-class starship manoeuvred itself onto a cradle that had risen out of a bay, orange balls of chemical flame spitting out of its vernier nozzles. He could see the ubiquitous intersecting violet and green loops of the Vasilkovsky Line bold across the forward quarter. It touched the cradle, and pistonlike latches engaged, slipping into sockets around the hull. Umbilical gantries swung round, plugging it into the spaceport's coolant and environmental circuits. The starship's thermo-dump panels retracted, and the cradle started to descend into the bay.

So much effort just to arrive, *Udat* observed.

Quiet down, you'll hurt people's feelings, Meyer told it fondly.

I wish there were more ships like me. Your race should stop clinging to the past. These mechanical ships belong in a museum.

My race, is it? There are human chromosomes in you, don't forget.

Are you sure?

I think I accessed it in a memory core somewhere. There are in voidhawks.

Oh. Them.

Meyer grinned at the overtone of disparagement. **I thought you liked voidhawks.**

Some of them are all right. But they think like their captains.

And how do voidhawk captains think?

They don't like blackhawks. They think we're trouble.

We have been known.

Only when money is short, *Udat* said, gently reproachful.

And if there were more blackhawks and fewer Adamist starships, money would be even tighter. I have wages to pay.

At least we've paid off the mortgage you took out to buy me.

Yes. And there's money to save to buy another when you're gone. But he didn't let that thought filter out of his mind. *Udat* was fifty-seven now; seventy-five to eighty was the usual blackhawk lifespan. Meyer wasn't at all convinced he would want another ship after *Udat.* But there was a quarter of a century of togetherness to look forward to yet, and money wasn't such a problem these days. There was only life-support-section maintenance and the four crew members to pay for. He could afford to pick and choose his charters now. Not like the first twenty years. Now those had been wild days. Fortunately the power compressed into the big asymmetric teardrop shape of *Udat*'s hull gave them a terrific speed and agility. They had needed it on occasion. Some of the more covert missions had been hazardous in the extreme. Not all their colleagues had returned.

I'd still like more of my own kind to talk to, *Udat* said.

Do you talk to Tranquillity?

Oh, yes, all the time. We're good friends.

What do you talk about?

I show it places we visit. And it shows me its interior, what humans get up to.

Really?

Yes, it's interesting. This Joshua Calvert who chartered us, Tranquillity says he's a recidivist of the worst kind.

Tranquillity is absolutely right. That's why I like Joshua so much. He reminds me of me at that age.

No. You were never that bad.

Udat's nose turned slightly, gliding delicately between two designated traffic streams congested with He_3 tankers and personnel commuters. The bays in this section of the mammoth spaceport disk were larger, it was where the repairs and maintenance work was carried out. Only half of them were occupied.

The big blackhawk came to a halt directly over bay MB 0–330, then slowly rotated around its long axis so that its upper hull was pointing down over the rim. Unlike voidhawks, with their separate lower hull cargo hold and upper hull crew toroid, *Udat* had all its mechanical sections contained in a horseshoe which embraced its dorsal bulge. The bridge and individual crew cabins were at the front, with the two cargo holds occupying the wings, and an ion-field flyer stored in a small hangar on the port side.

Cherri Barnes walked into the bridge compartment. She was *Udat*'s cargo officer, doubling as a systems generalist: forty-five years old, with light coffee skin and a wide face prone to contemplative pouts. She had been with Meyer for three years.

She datavised a series of orders into her console processors, receiving images fed from the electronic sensors mounted on the hull. The three-dimensional picture which built up in her mind showed her *Udat* hanging poised thirty metres over the repair bay, holding its position steady.

'Over to you,' Meyer said.

'Thanks.' She opened a channel to the bay's datanet. 'MB 0–330, this is *Udat*. We have your cargo paid for and waiting. Ready for your unload instructions. How do you want to handle it, Joshua? Time is money.'

'Cherri, is that you?' Joshua datavised back.

'No one else on board will lower themselves to talk to you.'

'I wasn't expecting you for another week, you've made good time.'

Meyer datavised an access order into his console. 'You hire the best ship, you get the best time.'

'I'll remember that,' Joshua told him. 'Next time I have some money I'll make sure I go for a decent ship.'

'We can always take our nodes elsewhere, Mr Hotshot Starship Captain who's never been outside the Ruin Ring.'

'*My* nodes, genetic throwback who's too scared to go in the Ruin Ring and earn a living.'

'It's not the Ruin Ring which worries me, it's what the Lord of Ruin does to people who skip outsystem before they register their finds in Tranquillity.'

There was an unusually long pause. Meyer and Cherri shared a bemused glance.

'I'll send Ashly out with the *Lady Mac*'s MSV to pick up the nodes,' Joshua said. 'And you're all invited to the party tonight.'

*

'So this is the famous *Lady Macbeth*?' Meyer asked a couple of hours later. He was in bay 0–330's cramped control centre with Joshua, his left foot anchored by a stikpad, looking out through the glass bubble wall into the bay itself. The fifty-seven-metre ship resting on the cradle in the middle of the floor was naked to space. Its hull plates had been stripped off, exposing the systems and tanks and engines, fantastically complex silver and white entrails. They were all contained inside a hexagonal-lattice stress structure. Jump nodes were positioned over each junction. Red and green striped superconductor cabling wormed inwards from each node, plugged directly into the ship's fusion generators. Meyer hadn't thought about it before, but the lenticular nodes were almost identical to the voidhawk profile.

Engineers wearing black SII suits and manoeuvring packs were propelling themselves over the open stress structure, running tests and replacing components. Others rode platforms on the end of multi-segment arms which were fitted out with heavy tools to handle the larger systems. Yellow strobes flashed on all the bay's mobile equipment, sending sharp-edged amber circles slicing over every surface in crazy gyrating patterns.

Hundreds of data cables were stretched between the ship and the five interface couplings around the base of the cradle. It was almost as though *Lady Macbeth* was being tethered down by a net of optical fibres. A two-metre-diameter airlock tube had concertinaed out from the bay wall, just below the control centre, giving the maintenance team access to the life-support capsules buried at the core of the ship. Brackets on the bay walls held various systems waiting to be installed. Meyer couldn't see where they could possibly fit. *Lady Macbeth*'s spaceplane clung to one wall like a giant supersonic moth, wings in their forward-sweep position. The additional tanks and power cells Joshua had strapped on for flights to the Ruin Ring were gone; a couple of suited figures and a cyberdrone were trying to remove the thick foam from the fuselage with a solvent spray. Crumbling grey flakes were flying off in all directions.

'What were you expecting?' Joshua asked. 'A Saturn V?' He was strapped into a restraint web behind a cyberdrone operations console. The boxy drones ran along the rails which spiralled up the bay walls, giving them access to any part of the docked ship. Three of them were currently clustered round an auxiliary fusion generator, which was being eased into its mountings at the end of long white waldo arms. Engineers floated around it, supervising the cyberdrones which were performing the installation, mating cables, coolant lines, and fuel hoses. Joshua monitored their progress through the omnidirectional AV projectors arrayed around his console.

'More like a battle cruiser,' Meyer said. 'I saw the power ratings on those nodes, Joshua. You could jump fifteen light-years with those brutes fully charged.'

'Something like that,' he said absently.

Meyer grunted, and turned back to the starship. The MSV was returning from another trip to *Udat*, a pale green oblong box three metres long with small spherical tanks bunched together on the base, and three segmented waldo arms ending in complex manipulators sprouting from the mid-fuselage section. It was carrying a packaged node, coasting down towards one of the engineering shop airlocks.

Cherri Barnes frowned, peering forwards into the bay. 'How many reaction drives has she got?' she asked. There seemed an inordinate number of umbilicals jacked into the *Lady Macbeth*'s rear quarter. She could see a pair of fusion tubes resting in the wall brackets, fat ten-metre cylinders swathed with magnetic coils, ion-beam injectors, and molecular-binding initiators.

Joshua turned his head fractionally, switching AV projectors. The new pillar shot a barrage of photons along his optical nerves, giving him a different angle on the auxiliary fusion generator. He studied it for a while, then datavised an instruction into one of the cyberdrones. 'Four main drives.'

'Four?' Adamist ships usually had one fusion drive, with a couple of induction engines running off the generator as an emergency back-up.

'Yeah. Three fusion tubes, and an antimatter drive.'

'You can't be serious,' Cherri Barnes exclaimed. 'That's a capital offence!'

'Wrong!'

Joshua and Meyer both grinned at her, infuriatingly superior. There were smiles from the other five console operators in the control centre.

'It's a capital offence to *possess* antimatter,' Joshua said. 'But there's nothing in the Confederation space law about possessing an engine which uses antimatter. As long as you don't fill up the confinement chambers and use it, you're fine.'

'Bloody hell.'

'It makes you very popular when there's a war on. You can write your own ticket. Or so I'm told.'

'I bet you've got a real powerful communication maser as

well. One that can punch a message clean through another starship's hull.'

'No, actually. *Lady Mac* has eight. Dad was a real stickler for multiple redundancy.'

*

Harkey's Bar was on the thirty-first floor of the StMartha starscraper. There was a real band on the tiny stage, churning out scarr jazz, fractured melodies with wailing trumpets. A fifteen-metre bar made from real oak that Harkey swore blind came from a twenty-second-century Paris brothel, serving thirty-eight kinds of beer, and three times that number of spirits, including Norfolk Tears for those who could afford it. It had wall booths that could be screened from casual observation, a dance floor, long party tables, lighting globes emitting photons right down at the bottom of the yellow spectrum. And Harkey prided himself on its food, prepared by a chef who claimed he had worked in the royal kitchens of Kulu's Jerez Principality. The waitresses were young, pretty, and wore revealing black dresses.

With its ritzy atmosphere, and not too expensive drinks, it attracted a lot of the crews from ships docked at Tranquillity's port. Most nights saw a good crowd. Joshua had always used it. First when he was a cocky teenager looking for his nightly fix of spaceflight tales, then when he was scavenging, lying about how much he made and the unbelievable find that had just slipped from his fingers, and now as one of the super-élite, a starship owner-captain, one of the youngest ever.

'I don't know what kind of crap that foam is which you sprayed on the spaceplane, Joshua, but the bloody stuff just won't come off,' Warlow complained bitterly.

When Warlow spoke everybody listened. You couldn't avoid it, not within an eight-metre radius. He was a cosmonik, born on an industrial asteroid settlement. He had spent over sixty-five per cent of his seventy-two years in free fall, and he didn't have the kind of geneering bequeathed to Joshua and the Edenists by their ancestors. After a while his organs had begun to degenerate, depleted calcium levels had reduced his bones to brittle porcelain sticks, muscles had atrophied, and fluid bloated his tissues, impairing his lungs, degrading his lymphatic system. He had used drugs and nanonic supplements to compensate at first, then supplements became replacements, with bones exchanged for carbon-fibre struts. Electrical consumption supplanted food intake. The final transition was his skin, replacing the eczema-ridden epidermis with a smooth ochre silicon membrane. Warlow didn't need a spacesuit to work in the vacuum, he could survive for over three weeks without a power and oxygen recharge. His facial features had become purely cosmetic, a crude mannequin-like caricature of human physiognomy, although there was an inlet valve at the back of his throat for fluid intake. There was no hair, and he certainly didn't bother with clothes. Sex was something he lost in his fifties.

Although some cosmoniks had metamorphosed into little more than free-flying maintenance craft with a brain at the centre, Warlow had kept his humanoid shape. The only noticeable adaptation was his arms; they forked at each elbow, giving him two pairs of forearms. One set retained the basic hand and finger layout, the other set ended in titanium sockets, capable of accepting a variety of rigger tools.

Joshua grinned and raised his champagne glass at the sleek-skinned two-metre-tall gargoyle dominating the table. 'That's why I put you on it. If anybody can scrape it off, you can.' He counted himself lucky to get Warlow on his crew. Some captains rejected him for his age, Joshua welcomed him for his experience.

'You should get Ashly to fly it on a bypass trajectory that grazes Mirchusko's atmosphere. Burn it off like an ablative. One *zip* and it's all gone.' Warlow's primary left forearm came down, palm slapping the table. Glasses and bottles juddered.

'Alternatively, you could plug a pump in your belly, and use your arse as a vacuum cleaner,' Ashly Hanson said. 'Suck it off.' His cheeks caved in as he made a slurping sound.

The pilot was a tall sixty-seven-year-old, whom geneering had given a compact frame, floppy brown hair, and a ten-year-old's wonderstruck smile. The whole universe was a constant delight for him. He lived for his skill, moving tonnes of metal through any atmosphere with avian grace. His Confederation Astronautics Board licence said he was qualified for both air and space operations, but it was three hundred and twenty years out of date. Ashly Hanson was temporally displaced; born into reasonable wealth, he had signed over his trust fund to the Jovian Bank in 2229 in exchange for a secure zero-tau pod maintenance contract (even then the Edenists had been the obvious choice as custodians). He alternated fifty years in entropy-free stasis, and five years 'bumming round' the Confederation.

'I'm a futurologist,' he told Joshua the first time they met. 'On a one-way ride to eternity. I just get out of my time machine for a look round every now and then.'

Joshua had signed him on as much for the tales he could tell as his piloting ability.

'We'll just remove the foam according to the manual, thanks,' he told the bickering pair.

The vocal synthesizer diaphragm protruding from Warlow's chest, just above his air-inlet gills, let out a metallic sigh. He shoved his squeezy bulb into his mouth and squirted some champagne into the valve. Drink was one thing he wasn't giving up, although with his blood filters he could sober up with astonishing speed if he had to.

Meyer leant across the table. 'Any word on Neeves and Sipika yet?' he asked Joshua quietly.

'Yeah. I forgot, you wouldn't know. They arrived back in port a couple of days after you left for Earth. They bloody nearly got lynched. The serjeants had to rescue them. They're in jail, waiting judicial pronouncement.'

Meyer frowned. 'Why the wait? I thought Tranquillity processed the charges right away?'

'There's a lot of bereaved relatives of scavengers who never came back who are claiming Neeves and Sipika are responsible. Then there's the question of compensation. The *Madeeir* is still worth a million and a half fuseodollars even after my axe work. I waived my claim, but I suppose the families are entitled.'

Meyer took another sip. 'Nasty business.'

'There's talk about fitting emergency beacons to all the scavenger craft, making it an official requirement.'

'They'll never go for that, they're too independent.'

'Yeah, well, I'm out of it now.'

'Too true,' Kelly Tirrel said. She was sitting pressed up next to Joshua, one leg hooked over his, arm draped around his shoulders.

It was a position he found extremely comfortable. Kelly was wearing an amethyst dress with a broad square-cut neckline which showed off her figure, especially from his angle. She was twenty-four, slightly shorter than medium build, with red-brown hair and a delicate face. For the last couple of years she had been a rover correspondent for Tranquillity's office of the Collins news group.

They had met eighteen months earlier when she was doing a piece on scavengers for distribution across the Confederation. He liked her for her independence, and the fact that she wasn't born rich.

'Nice to know you worry about me,' he said.

'I don't, it's the dataloss when you detonate your brain across the cosmos in that relic you're flying, that's what I'm concerned over.' She turned to Meyer. 'Do you know he won't give me the coordinates for this castle he found?'

'What castle?' Meyer asked.

'Where he found the Laymil electronics stack.'

A smile spread across Meyer's whole face. 'A castle. You didn't tell me that, Joshua. Did it have knights and wizards in it?'

'No,' Joshua said firmly. 'It was a big cube structure. I called it a castle because of the weapons systems. It was tough work getting in, one wrong move and . . .' Grave lines scored his face.

Kelly squirmed a fraction closer.

'It was operational?' Meyer was enjoying himself.

'No.'

'So why was it dangerous?'

'Some of the systems still had power in their storage cells. So given how much molecular decay they've suffered out there in the Ring, just brushing against them could have triggered off a short circuit. They would have blown like a chain reaction.'

'Electronic stacks, *and* functional power cells. That really was a terrific find, Joshua.'

Joshua glared at him.

'And he won't tell me where it is,' Kelly complained. 'Just think, something that big which survived the suicide could well hold the key to the whole Laymil secret. If I could capture that on a sensevise, I'd be made. I could pick my own office with Collins, then. Hell, I'd be in charge of my own office.'

'I'll sell you where it is,' Joshua said, 'it's all up here.' He tapped his head. 'My neural nanonics have got its orbital parameters down to a metre. I can locate it any time in the next ten years for you.'

'How much are you asking?' Meyer asked.

'Ten million fuseodollars.'

'Thanks, I'll pass.'

'Doesn't it bother you, standing in the way of progress?' Kelly asked.

'No. Besides, what happens if the answer turns out to be something we don't particularly like?'

'Good point.' Meyer raised his glass.

'Joshua! People have a right to know. They are quite capable of making up their own minds, they don't need to be protected from facts by people like you. Secrets seed oppression.'

Joshua rolled his eyes. 'Jesus. You just like to think reporters have a God-given right to stuff their noses in anywhere they want.'

Kelly tipped a glass to his lips, encouraging him to sip the champagne. 'But we do.'

'You'll get it bitten off one day, you see. In any case, we will know what happened to the Laymil. With the size of the research team Tranquillity employs, results are inevitable.'

'That's you, Joshua, the eternal optimist. Only an optimist would even think about going anywhere in that ship of yours.'

'There's nothing wrong with the *Lady Mac*,' Joshua bridled. 'You ask Meyer, those systems are the finest money can buy.'

Kelly fluttered long dark lashes enquiringly at Meyer.

'Oh, absolutely,' he said.

'I still don't want you to go,' she said quietly. She kissed Joshua's cheek. 'They were good systems when your father was flying her, and they were newer then. Look what happened to him.'

'That's different. Those orphans on the hospital station would never have made it back here without the *Lady Mac*. Dad had to jump while he was too close to that neutron star.'

Meyer let out a distressed groan, and drained his glass.

*

Joshua was up at the bar when the woman approached him. He didn't even see her until she spoke, his attention was elsewhere. The barmaid's name was Helen Vanham, she was nineteen, with a dress cut lower than Harkey's normal, and she seemed eager to serve Joshua Calvert, the starship captain. She said she finished work at two in the morning.

'Captain Calvert?'

He turned from the pleasing display of cleavage and thigh. Jesus, but that title felt good. 'You got me.'

The woman was black, very black. There couldn't have been much geneering in her family, he decided, although he was suspicious about that deep pigmentation; she was fifty centimetres shorter than him, and her short beret of hair was frosted with strands of silver. He reckoned she was about sixty years old, and ageing naturally.

'I'm Dr Alkad Mzu,' she said.

'Good evening, Doctor.'

'I understand you have a ship you're fitting out?'

'That's right, the *Lady Macbeth.* Finest independent trader this side of the Kulu Kingdom. Are you interested in chartering her?'

'I may be.'

Joshua skipped a beat. He took another look at the small woman. Alkad Mzu was dressed in a suit of grey fabric, a slim collar turned up around her neck. She seemed very serious, her features composed in a permanent expression of resignation. And right at the back of his mind there was a faint tingle of warning.

You're being oversensitive, he told himself, just because she doesn't smile doesn't mean she's a threat. Nothing is a threat in Tranquillity, that's the beauty of this place.

'Medicine must pay very well these days,' he said.

'It's a physics doctorate.'

'Oh, sorry. Physics must pay very well.'

'Not really. I'm a member of the team researching Laymil artefacts.'

'Yeah? You must have heard of me, then, I found the electronics stack.'

'Yes, I heard, although memory crystals aren't my field. I mainly study their fusion drives.'

'Really? Can I get you a drink?'

Alkad Mzu blinked, then slowly looked about. 'Yes, this is a bar, isn't it. I'll just have a white wine, then, thank you.'

Joshua signalled to Helen Vanham for a wine. Receiving a *very* friendly smile in return.

'What exactly was the charter?' he asked.

'I need to visit a star system.'

Definitely weird, Joshua thought. 'That's what *Lady Mac* does best. Which star system?'

'Garissa.'

Joshua frowned, he thought he knew most star systems. He consulted his neural nanonics cosmology file. That was when his humour really started to deflate. 'Garissa was abandoned thirty years ago.'

Alkad Mzu received her slim glass from the barmaid, and tasted the wine. 'It wasn't abandoned, Captain. It was annihilated. Ninety-five million people were slaughtered by the Omutan government. The Confederation Navy managed to get some off after the planet-buster strike, about seven hundred thousand. They used marine transports and colonist-carrier ships.' Her eyes clouded over. 'They abandoned the rescue effort after a month. There wasn't a lot of point. The radiation fallout had reached everyone who survived the blasts and tsunamis and earthquakes and superstorms. Seven hundred thousand out of ninety-five million.'

'I'm sorry, I didn't know.'

Her lips twitched around the rim of the glass. 'Why should you? An obscure little planet that died before you were born; for politics that never made any sense even then. Why should anybody remember?'

Joshua shot the fuseodollars from his Jovian Bank credit card into the bar's accounts block as the barmaid delivered his tray of champagne bottles. There was an oriental man at the far end of the bar who was keeping an unobtrusive watch on himself and Dr Mzu over his beer mug. Joshua forced himself not to stare in return. He smiled at Helen Vanham and added a generous tip. 'Dr Mzu, I have to be honest. I can take you to the Garissan system, but a landing given those circumstances is out of the question.'

'I understand, Captain. And I appreciate your honesty. I don't wish to land, simply to visit.'

'Ah, er, good. Garissa was your homeworld?'

'Yes.'

'I'm sorry.'

'That's the third time you've said that to me.'

'One of those evenings, I guess.'

'How much would it cost me?'

'For a single passenger, there and back; you're looking at about five hundred thousand fuseodollars. I know it's a lot, but the fuel expenditure will be the same for one person as a full cargo hold. And the crew time is the same as well, they all need paying.'

'I doubt I can raise your full charter fee in advance. My research position is a comfortable one, but not that comfortable. However, I can assure you that once we reach our destination adequate funds will be available. Does that interest you?'

Joshua gripped the tray tighter, interested despite himself. 'It may be possible to come to an arrangement, subject to a suitable deposit. And my rates are quite reasonable, you won't find any cheaper.'

'Thank you, Captain. Can I have a copy of your ship's handling parameters and cargo capacity? I need to know whether the *Lady Macbeth* can fulfil my requirements, they are rather specialized.'

Jesus, if she needs to know how big the cargo hold is, just what is she planning on bringing back? Whatever it is, it must have been hidden for thirty years.

His neural nanonics reported she had opened a channel. 'Sure.' He datavised over the *Lady Mac*'s performance tables.

'I'll be in touch, Captain. Thank you for the drink.'

'My pleasure.'

At the other end of the bar, Onku Noi, First Lieutenant

serving in the Oshanko Imperial Navy, and assigned to the C5 Intelligence arm (Foreign Observation Division), finished his beer and paid the bill. The audio discrimination program in his neural nanonics had filtered out the bar's chatter and background music, allowing him to record the conversation between Alkad Mzu and the handsome young starship captain. He stood up and opened a channel into Tranquillity's communication net, requesting access to the spaceport's standard commercial reference memory core. The file on the *Lady Macbeth* and Joshua Calvert was datavised into his neural nanonics. What he accessed caused an involuntary twitch in his jaw muscle. *Lady Macbeth* was a combat-capable starship, complete with antimatter drive and combat-wasp launch–rails, and she was being capaciously refurbished. Pausing only to confirm Joshua Calvert's visual profile was filed correctly in his neural nanonics memory cell, he followed Dr Mzu out of Harkey's Bar, keeping an unobtrusive thirty seconds behind her.

Joshua, interested before, was now outright fascinated as he surreptitiously watched the three men trailing after the diminutive Dr Mzu almost collide in the doorway. His intuition had been right again.

Jesus, who is she?

Tranquillity would know. But then Tranquillity would know she was being tailed as well, and who the tails were. Which meant that Ione would know.

He still hadn't resolved his feelings about Ione. There couldn't be anyone in the universe who was better at sex, but knowing that Tranquillity was looking at him out of those enchanting sea-blue eyes, that all those fluffy girlish mannerisms were wrapped around thought processes cooler than solid helium, was more than a little disconcerting. Though never inhibiting. She had been quite right about that, he simply couldn't say no. Not to her.

He returned to her every day, as instinctively as a migrating bird to an equatorial continent. It was exciting screwing the

Lord of Ruin, a Saldana. And the feel of her body pressed against his was supremely erotic.

The male ego, he often reflected these days, was a puppet master with a very black sense of humour.

Joshua didn't have any time to ponder the puzzle of Dr Mzu before someone else hailed him. He turned with a slightly pained expression on his face.

A thirty-year-old man in a slightly worn navy-blue ship's one-piece was pushing through the throng, waving hopefully. He was just a few centimetres shorter than Joshua with the kind of regular features below short black hair that suggested a good deal of geneering. There was a smile on his face, apprehensive and keen at the same time.

'Yes?' Joshua asked wearily, he was only halfway back to his table.

'Captain Calvert? I'm Erick Thakrar, a ship's general systems engineer, grade five.'

'Ah,' Joshua said.

Warlow's thousand-decibel laugh blasted out, silencing the bar for an instant.

'Grade ratings are mostly down to logged flight hours,' Erick said. 'I did a lot of time in port maintenance. I'm up to grade three level in practice, if not more.'

'And you're looking for a berth?'

'That's right.'

Joshua hesitated, He still had a couple of berths to fill, and one of them was for a systems generalist. But that itchy sensation of discomfort had returned, much stronger than it had been with Dr Mzu.

Jesus, what's this one, a serial killer?

'I see,' he said.

'I would be a bargain, I'm only asking grade five pay.'

'I prefer to make flight pay a percentage of the charter fee, or a percentage of profits if we trade our own cargo.'

'Sounds pretty good to me.'

Joshua couldn't fault his attitude. Youthful, enthusiastic, no doubt a good worker, obviously willing to accept the rule bending necessary to keep independent ships flying. Ordinarily, a man you'd want at your back. But that intimation of *wrongness* wouldn't leave.

'OK, let me have your CV file, and I'll look it over,' he said. 'But not tonight, I'm in no fit state to make command judgements tonight.'

In the end he invited Erick Thakrar back to the table to see how he got on with the other three crew members. He shared their sense of humour, had some good stories of his own, drank a lot, but not excessively.

Joshua watched it happen through the increasingly rosy glow fostered by the champagne, occasionally having to push Kelly to one side for a proper view of the table. Warlow liked him, Ashly Hanson liked him, Melvyn Ducharme, the *Lady Mac's* fusion specialist, liked him, even Meyer and the *Udat* crew liked him. He was one of them.

And that, Joshua decided, was the problem. Erick fitted into his role a little too perfectly.

At quarter past two in the morning, feeling very smug, Joshua managed to give Kelly the slip, and sneaked out of Harkey's Bar with Helen Vanham. She lived by herself in an apartment a couple of floors below Harkey's. It was sparsely furnished, the walls of the lounge were bare white polyp; big brightly coloured cushions had been scattered around on a topaz moss floor, several aluminium cargo-pods served as tables with bottles and glasses, a giant AV projector pillar occupied one corner. The archways into different rooms all had folding silk screens for doors. Someone had been painting outlines of animals on them, there were paint pots and brushes lying on one of the pods. Joshua saw new tumours of polyp pushing up through the moss like rock mushrooms: furniture buds starting the slow growth into the form Helen wanted.

There was a food secretion panel on the wall opposite the

window; a row of teats, like small yellow-brown rubber sacks, were standing proud, indicating regular use. It had been a long time since Joshua had used a panel for food, though a few years ago when money was tight they had been a godsend.

Every apartment in Tranquillity had one. The teats secreted edible pastes and fruit juices synthesized by a series of glands in the wall behind. There was nothing wrong with the taste, the pastes were indistinguishable from real chicken, and beef, and pork, and lamb, even the colours were reasonable. It was the constituency, like viscid grease, which always put Joshua off.

The glands ingested a nutrient fluid from a habitatwide network of veins which were fed from Tranquillity's mineral digestion organs in the southern endcap. There was also a degree of recycling, human wastes and organic scraps being broken down in specialist organs at the bottom of each star-scraper. Porous sections of the shell vented toxic chemicals, preventing any dangerous build-up in the habitat's closed biosphere.

There was no such thing as starvation in bitek habitats, though both Edenists and Tranquillity's residents imported vast quantities of delicacies and wines from across the Confederation. They could afford it. But Helen obviously couldn't. Despite its size, the full teats and absence of materialism marked the apartment down as student digs.

'Help yourself to a drink,' Helen said. 'I'm getting out of this customer-friendly dress.' She walked through an archway into the bedroom, leaving the screen folded back.

'What else do you do apart from serve bar at Harkey's?' he asked.

'I'm studying art,' she called back. 'Harkey's is just for fun-time money.'

Joshua broke off from examining the bottles and gave the screens with their animals a more appraising look. 'Are you any good?'

'I might be eventually. My tutor says I have a good feel for form. But it's a five-year course, we're still on basic sketching and painting. We don't even get to AV technology until next year, and mood synthesis is another year after that. It's a drag, but you need to know the fundamentals.'

'So how long have you been at Harkey's?'

'A couple of months. It's not bad work, you space industry people tip well, and you're not a pain like the finance mob. I worked at a bar over in the StPelham for a week. Crapoodle!'

'Have you ever seen Erick Thakrar before? He was sitting at my table, thirtyish, in a blue ship-suit.'

'Yes. He's been in most nights for a fortnight or so. He's another good tipper.'

'Do you know where he's been working?'

'Out in the dock; the Lowndes company, I think. He started a couple of days after he arrived.'

'Which ship did he arrive on?'

'The *Shah of Kai*.'

Joshua opened a channel into Tranquillity's communication net, and datavised a search request into the Lloyd's office. The *Shah of Kai* was a cargo vessel registered to a holding company in the New Californian system. It was an ex-navy transport ship, with a six-gee fusion drive; one hold was equipped with zero-tau pods for a company of marines, and it had proximity-range defence lasers. An asteroid assault craft.

Gotcha, Joshua thought.

'Did you ever meet any of the crew?' he asked.

Helen reappeared in the bedroom archway. She was wearing a long-sleeved net body-stocking, and white suede boots which came halfway up her thighs.

'Tell you later,' she said.

Joshua gave his lips an involuntary lick. 'I've got a great location file to match that costume, if you want to try it.'

She took a step into the room. 'Sure.'

He accessed the sensenviron file, and ordered his neural nanonics to open a channel to Helen. A subliminal flicker crossed his optic nerves. Her sparse apartment gave way to the silk walls of a magnificent desert pavilion. There were tall ferns in brass urns around the entrance, a banquet table along one side was laid out with golden plates and jewelled goblets, and exotic, intricate drapes swung slowly in the warm, dry breeze that blew in from the crimson desert outside. Behind Helen was a curtained-off section, with the silk drawn apart just enough to show them a huge bed with purple sheets and a satin canopy which rose behind the scarlet-tasselled pillows like a sunrise sculpted from fabric.

'Nice,' she said, glancing round.

'It's where Lawrence of Arabia pleasured his harem back in the eighteenth century. He was some sort of sheik king who fought the Roman Empire. Absolutely guaranteed genuine sensevise recording from old Earth. I got it from a starship captain friend of mine who visited the museum.'

'Really?'

'Yeah. Old Lawrence had about a hundred and fifty wives, so they say.'

'Wow. And he pleasured all of them himself?'

'Oh, yeah, he had to, there was an army of eunuchs to protect them. No other men could get in.'

'Does the magic linger?'

'Wanna find out?'

*

Ione's mind encompassed the entirety of Helen Vanham's bedroom, the photosensitive cells in the bare polyp walls, floor, and ceiling giving her a complete visualization. It was a thousand times more detailed than an AV projection. She could move through the bedroom as if she was there, which in a way she was.

The bed was simply a plump mattress on the floor. Helen lay across it, with a naked Joshua straddling her. He was slowly and deliberately tearing the body-stocking off her.

Interesting, Ione observed.

If you say so, Tranquillity replied coolly.

Helen's long booted legs kicked the air behind his back. She was giggling and squealing as more and more strips of her stocking were ripped away.

I don't mean the sex, though judging by the way he's turned on I'll have to try wearing something like that for him myself one day. I was thinking of the way he latched on to Erick Thakrar.

His alleged psychic ability again?

He has had twelve applicants for the post of ship's general systems engineer so far. All of them legitimate. Yet the minute Erick asked for the berth, he was suspicious. Are you going to maintain it was nothing but luck?

I acknowledge Joshua's actions do indicate a degree of prescience on his part.

At last! Thank you.

This means you will be going ahead with the zygote extraction, then?

Yes. Unless you have an objection.

I would never object to receiving your child into me, no matter who was the father. It will be our child, too.

And I'll never know him, she said sadly, **not really, just for a few years of his childhood, like I saw Daddy. Sometimes I think our way is too harsh.**

I will love him. I will tell him of you when he asks.

Thank you. I shall have other children, though. And I'll know them.

With Joshua?

Possibly.

What are you going to do about him and Dr Mzu?

Ione sighed in exasperation. The image of Helen's bedroom rippled away. She glanced round her own study; it was cluttered with dark wooden furniture, centuries old, brought from Kulu by her grandfather. Her whole environment was steeped in history, reminding her who she was, her responsibilities. It was a depressing burden, one which she'd managed to avoid for a long time. But even that would have to end soon.

I'm not going to say anything to him, not now, anyway. Joshua is the seventh captain Mzu has approached in the last five months, she's just testing the water, seeing what sort of reaction she generates.

She is giving all the Intelligence operatives a bad case of the jitters.

I know. That's partly my fault. They don't know what will happen if she tries to leave. There isn't a Lord of Ruin they can ask, all they have is Daddy's promise.

And that holds true?

Yes, of course it does. She cannot be allowed to leave. The serjeants must be used to restrain her if she ever attempts it. And if she does get into a ship, you're going to have to use the strategic defence weapons.

Even if that ship is the *Lady Macbeth*?

Joshua wouldn't try to take her out, especially if I asked him not to.

But if he does?

Ione's fingers curled about the small silver crucifix round her neck. **Then you shoot her out of space.**

I'm sorry. I can feel the pain in you.

It's a null situation. He won't do it. I trust Joshua. Money isn't his prime motivation. He could have told people I exist. That reporter woman, Kelly Tirrel, she would have paid him a fortune for a scoop like that.

I don't think he will accept Dr Mzu's charter, either.

Good. All this is making me think. People do need some kind of reassurance that there is an authority figure behind you. Do you think I'm old enough to start making public appearances yet?

Mentally, you have been mature enough for years. Physically, possibly; you are old enough to face motherhood, after all. Although I think a more suitable mode of attire would help. Image is the paramount issue in your case.

Ione glanced down. She was wearing a pink bikini and a

small green beach jacket, ideal for the swim in the cove she took each evening.

I think you may have a point there.

*

Tranquillity had no blackhawk docking-ledges on its southern endcap. The polyp which made up that hemisphere was twice the usual thickness of the shell so that it could incorporate the massive mineral-digestion organs, as well as several lake-sized hydrocarbon reservoirs. These were the organs which produced the various nutrient fluids circulating in the shell's vast network of ducts, sustaining the mitosis layer which regenerated the polyp, the starscraper apartment food-secretion glands, the ledge pedestals which fed the visiting blackhawks and voidhawks, as well as various specialist organs responsible for environmental maintenance. Access passages to the outer shell would have been difficult to route through such a tightly packed grouping of titanic viscera.

There was no non-rotational spaceport either. The external hub was taken up by a craterlike maw, fifteen hundred metres in diameter. Its inner surface was lined with tubular cilia, hundred-metre spikes that impaled the asteroidal rubble which ships boosted out of Mirchusko's inner ring. Once in the maw, the rocks were coated by enzymes ejected from the cilia and broken down into dust and gravel, more manageable chunks which could be ingested and consumed with ease.

The lack of any spaceport outside the endcap, plus the circumfluous salt-water sea lapping around the base on the inside, meant that there was little activity on its curving slopes. The first two kilometres above the coves were terraced like an ancient hill farm, planted with flowering bushes and orchards tended by agronomy servitors. Above the terraces a claggy soil clung to the ever-steepening polyp wall, a vast annular meadow land of thick grasses, whose roots strove to counteract gravity and keep the soil in place. Both grass and soil stopped short three kilometres from the hub, where the polyp was virtually a vertical cliff. Right at the axis, the light-tube emerged, running the entire length of the massive habitat: a cylindrical mesh of organic conductors, their powerful magnetic field containing the fluorescent plasma which brought light and heat to the interior.

Michael Saldana had decided that the quiet, semi-secluded southern endcap would be an ideal site for the research project into the Laymil. Its offices and laboratories now sprawled over two square kilometres of the lower terraces, the largest cluster of buildings inside the habitat, resembling the campus of some wealthy private university.

The project director's office was on the top floor of the five-storey administration building, a squat, circular pillar of copper-mirror glass ringed with grey stone colonnaded balconies. It sat on the terrace at the back of the campus, five hundred metres above the circumfluous sea, giving it an unsurpassed view of the cycloramic sub-tropical parkland stretching away into misty distance.

The view was something Parker Higgens was immensely proud of, easily the finest in Tranquillity, another fitting perk due to the research project's eighth director – along with the scrumptious office itself, with its deep-burgundy coloured ossalwood furniture that had come from Kulu in the days before the abdication crisis. Parker Higgens was eighty-five. His appointment had come nine years ago, almost the last act of the Lord of Ruin, and by the grace of God (plus an ancestor wealthy enough to afford some decent geneering) he would keep the post for another nine. He had left actual research behind twenty years ago to concentrate on administration. It was a field he excelled in; building the right teams, massaging mercurial egos, knowing when to push, when to ease off. Genuinely effective scientific administrators were rare, and under his leadership the project had functioned reasonably smoothly, everyone acknowledged that. Parker Higgens liked to keep his world neat and tidy, it was one of his formulas for success, which was why he was particularly shocked to come into work one morning and find a young blonde-haired girl lounging in the deep cushioning of *his* straight-backed chair behind *his* desk.

'Who the bloody hell are you?' he shouted. Then he saw the five serjeants standing to attention around the room.

Tranquillity's serjeants were the habitat's sole police force, sub-sentient bitek servitors controlled via affinity by the personality, enforcing the law with scrupulous impartiality. They were (intentionally) intimidating humanoids, two metres tall, with a reddish-brown exoskeleton, limb joints encased by segmented rings permitting full articulation. The heads had a sculpted appearance, with eyes concealed in a deep horizontal crease. Their hands were their most human characteristic, with leathery skin replacing the exoskeleton. It meant they could use any artefact built for a human, with emphasis on weapons. Each of them carried a laser pistol and a cortical jammer on their belts, along with restraint cuffs. The belt was their sole article of clothing.

Parker Higgens glanced round dumbly at the serjeants, then back at the girl. She was wearing a very expensive pale blue suit, and her ice-blue eyes conveyed an unnerving impression of depth. Her nose . . . Parker Higgens might have been a bureaucrat, but he wasn't stupid. 'You?' he whispered incredulously.

Ione gave him a faint smile and stood up, extending her hand. 'Yes, Mr Director. Me, I'm afraid. Ione Saldana.'

He shook the hand weakly, it was very small and cool in his. There was a signet ring on her finger, a red ruby carved with the Saldana crest: the crowned phoenix. It was the Kulu Crown Prince's ring, Michael hadn't bothered to return it to the keeper of the crown jewellery when he was sent into exile. Parker Higgens had last seen it on Maurice Saldana's finger.

'I'm honoured, ma'am,' Parker Higgens said; he had come

very close to blurting: *but you're a girl.* 'I knew your father, he was an inspiring man.'

'Thank you.' There was no trace of humour on Ione's face. 'I appreciate you're busy, Mr Director, but I'd like to inspect the project's major facilities this morning. Then I shall require each division's senior staff to assemble summaries of their work for a presentation in two days' time. I have tried to keep abreast of the findings, but remote viewing through Tranquillity's senses and having them explained in person are two different things.'

Parker Higgens's whole universe trembled. A review, and like it or not this slip of a girl held the purse strings, the *life* strings of the research project. What if . . . 'Of course, ma'am, I'll show you round myself.'

Ione started to walk round the desk.

'Ma'am? May I ask what your policy towards the Laymil research project is? Previous Lords of Ruin have been very—'

'Relax, Mr Director. My ancestors were quite right: unravelling the Laymil mystery should be given the highest priority.'

The prospect of imminent disaster retreated from his view, like rain-clouds rolling away to reveal the sun. It was going to be all right after all. Almost. A girl! Saldana heirs were always male. 'Yes, ma'am!'

The serjeants lined up into an escort squad around Ione. 'Come along,' she said, and swept out of the office.

Parker Higgens found his legs racing in an undignified manner to catch up. He wished he could make people jump obediently like that.

*

There *is* a third Lord of Ruin.

The news broke thirty-seven seconds after Ione and Parker Higgens walked into the laboratory block housing the Laymil Plant Genetics Division. Everybody who worked for the project was fitted with neural nanonics. So once the instinctive flash of guilt and the accompanying shock of having the director and five serjeants walk in unannounced ten minutes into the working day had worn off, and the introductions began, professors and technicians alike opened channels into the habitat's communication net. Nearly every datavise began: *You're not going to believe this—*

Ione was shown AV projections of Laymil plant genes, sealed propagators with seed shoots worming their way up through the soil, and large fern-analogue plants with scarlet fronds growing in pots, and given small shrivelled black fruits to taste.

After friends, relatives, and colleagues were brought up to speed, it took another fifteen seconds before anyone thought of contacting the news company offices.

Ione and Parker Higgens walked on from the plant genetics laboratory to the Laymil Habitat Structure Analysis office. People were lining the stone path, trampling on the shrubs. Applause and cheers followed her like a wave effect, wolf-whistles were flung boisterously. The serjeants had to gently push aside the more enthusiastic spectators. Ione started to shake hands and wave.

There were five major Confederationwide news companies who maintained offices in Tranquillity, and all of them had been told about Ione's arrival at the research project campus within ninety seconds of her tour beginning. The disbelieving assistant editor at Collins immediately asked the habitat personality if it was true.

'Yes,' Tranquillity said simply.

The scheduled morning programmes were immediately interrupted to carry the news. Reporters sprinted for tube carriages. Editors frantically opened channels to their contacts in the Laymil project staff, seeking immediate on-the-ground coverage. Datavises became sensevises, relaying optical and auditory nerve inputs directly to the studio. After twelve minutes, eighty per cent of Tranquillity's residents were hooked in, either watching Ione's impromptu walkabout on the AV broadcasts, or receiving the sensevise direct through neural nanonics.

It's a girl, the Lord of Ruin is a girl. God, the Royal Saldanas will go mad over that, there's not a chance of reconciliation with the Kingdom now.

There were two Kiint working in the physiology laboratory; one of them came into the glass-walled lobby to greet Ione. It was an impressive and moving sight, the slight human girl standing in front of the huge xenoc.

The Kiint was an adult female, icy-white hide glimmering softly in the bright morning light, almost as if she was wearing a halo. She had an oval cross-section body nine metres long, three wide, standing on eight fat elephantlike legs. Her head was as long as Ione was tall, which was slightly intimidating as it reminded her of a primitive shield; a bony, slightly convex, downward pointing triangle with a central vertical ridge which gave it two distinct planes. There were a pair of limpid eyes halfway up, just above a series of six breathing vents, each of which had a furry fringe that undulated with every breath. The pointed base of the head served as her beak, with two smaller hinged sections behind.

Two arm-appendages emerged from the base of her neck, curving round the lower half of her head. They looked almost like featureless tentacles. Then tractamorphic muscles rippled below the skin, and the end of the right arm shaped itself into a human hand.

You are much welcome here, Ione Saldana, the Kiint spoke into her mind.

Kiint could always use the human affinity band, but Edenists had found it almost impossible to sense any form of private Kiint communication. Perhaps they had a true telepathic ability? It was one of the lesser mysteries about the enigmatic xenocs.

Your interest in this research venture does you credit, the Kiint continued.

My thanks to you for assisting us, Ione replied. **I'm told the analysis instruments you have made available here have been an immeasurable help.**

How could we refuse your grandfather's invitation? Foresight such as his is a rare quality among your race.

I would like to speak with you about that sometime.

Of course. But now you must complete your grand progress. There was a note of lofty amusement behind the thought.

The Kiint extended her new-formed hand, and they touched palms briefly. She inclined her massive head in a bow. Murmurs of surprise rippled round the others in the lobby.

Hell, look at that, even the Kiint's bowled over by her.

After the tour Ione stood alone in one of the orchards outside the campus, surrounded by trees rigorously pruned into mushroom shapes, their branches congested with a fleece of blossom. Petals swirled slowly through the air about her, sprinkling the ankle-length grass with a snowy mantle. She had her back to the habitat, so that the entire interior appeared to curve around her like a pair of emerald waves, their peaks clashing in a long, straight flame of scintillating white light far overhead.

'I want to tell you of the faith I have in everybody who lives in Tranquillity,' she began. 'Out of nothing a hundred and seventy-five years ago we have built a society that is respected throughout the Confederation. We are independent, we are virtually crime free, and we are wealthy, both collectively and individually. We can be justifiably proud in that achievement. It was not given to us, it was bought with hard work and sacrifices. And it will continue only by encouraging the industry and enterprise that has generated this wealth. My father and grandfather gave their wholehearted support to the business community, in creating an environment where trade and industry enrich our lives, and allow us to aspire for our children. In Tranquillity, dreams are given a greater than average chance to become real. That you will continue to pursue your dreams is the faith I have in you. To this end I pledge that my reign will be devoted to maintaining the economic, legal, and political environs which have brought us to the enviable position we find ourselves in today and enable us to look forward to the future with courage.'

The image and voice faded from the news studios, along with the aromatic scent of blossom. But not the shy half-smile, that lingered for a long time.

Christ: young, pretty, rich, and smart. How about that!

By the end of the day, Tranquillity had received eighty-four thousand invitations for Ione. She was wanted at parties and dinners, she was asked to give speeches and present prizes, her name was wanted on the board of interstellar companies, designers offered their entire portfolio for her to wear, charities begged her to become their patron. Old friends treated her as though she was a reincarnated messiah. Everyone wanted to be her new friend. And Joshua – Joshua got very grumpy when she spent the first evening reviewing Tranquillity's summaries of the incredible public reaction rather than spending it in bed with him.

He was also none too happy that *Lady Macbeth*'s refit was still a fortnight short of completion. Over the next twenty hours, seventy-five charter flights were organized to carry recordings of Ione around the Confederation. The news company offices were engaged in a ferocious ratings war; they were desperate to break the scoop on as many worlds as possible, as soon as possible. Starship captains cursed their earlier binding contracts to deliver mundane cargoes, and some even broke them. Those that didn't have immediate contracts named wholly unreasonable prices to the news companies, which were paid without question.

Right across the Confederation, the sensation-hungry devoured Ione, rekindling an avid interest in the black sheep branch of the Saldana family; and even briefly pushing the old Laymil enigma into the limelight again.

Merchants became extremely wealthy on Ione fashions and Ione accessories. Bluesense directors remodelled their female meat to look and feel like her. Mood Fantasy bands composed tracks about her. Even Jezzibella announced she looked cute, and said she'd like to fuck her one day.

The news agencies on Kulu and its Principality worlds treated her appearance as a minor footnote. The royal family didn't believe in censoring the press, but the court certainly didn't see her appearance as anything to celebrate. Black-market sensevise recordings of her sold for an absolute fortune right across the Kingdom.

*

It was one of the abandoned cargo contracts which brought Joshua his first charter two days later.

Roland Frampton was a merchant friend of Barrington Grier, which was how he heard of the *Lady Macbeth* and how she would be ready to depart in fourteen days.

'When I get my hands on that bastard Captain McDonald I'll have him broken up for transplant meat,' Roland said angrily. 'The *Corum Sister* won't get another cargo contract this side of Jupiter, that I do promise.'

Joshua sipped his mineral water and nodded sympathetically. Harkey's Bar didn't have the same appeal by day, although the term was ambiguous in a starscraper. But people's biorhythms were in tune with the habitat light-tube; his body knew this was midmorning.

'I paid good rates, you know, not like I was ripping him off. It was a regular run. Now this bloody girl comes along, and everyone goes berserk.'

'Hey, I'm glad we've got a Saldana back running things,' Barrington Grier protested. 'If she's half as good as the last two Lords, this place is going to be swinging.'

'Yeah, well, I haven't got no quarrel with her,' Roland Frampton said hurriedly. 'But the way people react.' He shook his head in bemusement. 'Did you hear what the news companies were offering captains for the Avon run?'

'Yeah. Meyer and the *Udat* got the Time Universe charter to Avon,' Joshua said with a grin.

'The point is, Joshua, I'm up shit creek,' Roland Frampton said. 'I've got my clients screaming for those nanonic medical supplements. There are a lot of wealthy old people in Tranquillity, the medical industry here is big business.'

'I'm sure we can come to an arrangement.'

'Cards on the table, Joshua, I'll pay you three hundred and fifty thousand fuseodollars for the flight, with an extra seventy thousand bonus if you can get them back here in five weeks from today. After that, I can offer you a regular contract, a flight to Rosenheim every six months. Not to be sneered at, Joshua.'

Joshua glanced at Melvyn Ducharme, who was stirring his coffee idly. He had come to rely a lot on his fusion engineer during *Lady Mac*'s refit; he was forty-eight, with over twenty years' solid starflight experience behind him. The dark-skinned little man gave a small nod.

'OK,' Joshua said. 'But you know the score, Roland, the *Lady Mac* doesn't leave that bay until I'm happy she's integrated properly. I'm not rushing it and botching it just for the sake of a seventy-thousand-dollar bonus.'

Roland Frampton gave him an unhappy look. 'Sure, Joshua, I appreciate that.'

They shook on it and started to work out details.

Kelly Tirrel arrived twenty minutes later, dropped her bag on the carpet, and sat down with an exaggerated sigh. She called a waitress over and ordered a coffee, then gave Joshua a perfunctory kiss.

'Have you got your contract?' she asked.

'We're working on it.' He gave the bar a quick scan. Helen Vanham wasn't anywhere to be seen.

'Good for you. God what a day! My editor's been having kittens.'

'Ione caught you all on the hop, did she?' Barrington Grier asked.

'And then some,' Kelly admitted. 'I've been researching for the last fifteen hours without a break, going through the Saldana family history. We're putting together an hour-long documentary for tonight. Those royals are one bunch of weird people.'

'Are you going to present it?' Joshua asked.

'No chance. Kirstie McShane got it. Bitch. She's sleeping with the current affairs editor, you know, that's why. I'll probably wind up as fashion correspondent or something. If only we'd had some advance warning, I could have prepared, found an angle.'

'Ione wasn't sure about the timing herself,' he said. 'She's only been thinking about public appearances for the last fortnight.'

There was a murderous silence as Kelly's head slowly turned to focus on Joshua. 'What?'

'Er . . .' He felt as though he'd suddenly been dumped into free fall.

'You know her? You've known who she is?'

'Well, sort of, in a way, I suppose, yes. She did mention it.'

Kelly stood up fast, the motion nearly toppling her chair. 'Mention it! You SHIT, Joshua Calvert! Ione Saldana is the biggest story to hit the whole Confederation for three years, and you KNEW about it, and you didn't tell me! You selfish, egotistical, mean-minded, xenoc-buggering bastard! I was sleeping with you, I cared . . .' She clamped her mouth shut and snatched her bag up. 'Didn't that mean anything to you?'

'Of course. It was . . .' He accessed his neural nanonics' thesaurus file. 'Stupendous?'

'Bastard!' She took two paces towards the door then turned round. 'And you're shit-useless in bed, too,' she shouted.

Everyone in Harkey's Bar was staring at him. He could see

a lot of grins forming. He closed his eyes for a moment and let out a resigned sigh. 'Women.' He swivelled round in his chair to face Roland Frampton. 'About the insurance rates . . .'

*

The cavern wasn't like anything Joshua had seen in Tranquillity before. It was roughly hemispherical, about twenty metres across, with the usual level white polyp floor. But the walls' regularity was broken up by organic protuberances, great cauliflower growths that quivered occasionally as he watched; there were also the tight doughnuts of sphincter muscles. Equipment cabinets, with a medical look, were fused into the polyp; as though they were being extruded, or osmotically absorbed. He couldn't tell which.

The whole place was so *biological.* It made him want to squirm.

'What is it?' he asked Ione.

'A clone womb centre.' She pointed to one of the sphincters. 'We gestate the servitor housechimps in these ones. All of the habitat's servitors are sexless, you see, they don't mate. So Tranquillity has to grow them. We've got several varieties of chimps, and the serjeants, of course, then there are some specialist constructs for things like tract repair and light-tube maintenance. There are forty-three separate species in all.'

'Ah. Good.'

'The wombs are plumbed directly into the nutrient ducts, there's very little hardware needed.'

'Right.'

'I was gestated in here.'

Joshua's nose wrinkled up. He didn't like to think about it.

Ione walked over to a waist-high, steel-grey equipment stack standing on the floor. Green and amber LEDs winked at her. There was a cylindrical zero-tau pod recessed into the top, twenty centimetres long, ten wide; its surface resembled a badly tarnished mirror. She used her affinity to load an order into the stack's bitek processors, and the pod hinged open.

Joshua watched silently as she placed the little sustentator globe inside. His son. Part of him wanted to put a stop to this right now, to have the child born properly, to know him, watch him grow up.

'It is customary to name the child now,' Ione said. 'If you want to.'

'Marcus.' His father's name. He didn't even have to think about that.

Her sapphire eyes were damp, reflecting the soft pearl light from the electrophorescent strips in the ceiling. 'Of course. Marcus Saldana it is, then.'

Joshua's mouth opened to protest. 'Thank you,' he said meekly.

The pod closed and the surface turned black. It didn't look solid, more like a fissure which had opened into space.

He stared at it for a long time. You just can't say no to Ione.

She slipped her arm through his and steered him out of the clone womb centre into the corridor outside. 'How's the *Lady Macbeth* coming along?'

'Not so bad. The Confederation Astronautics Board inspectors have cleared our systems integration. We're starting to reassemble the hull now, it should be finished in another three days. One final inspection for the spaceworthiness certificate, and we're away. I've got a contract with Roland Frampton to collect some cargo from Rosenheim.'

'That's good news. So I've got you to myself for another four nights.'

He pulled her a bit closer. 'Yeah, if you can fit me in between engagements.'

'Oh, I think I might manage to grant you a couple of hours. I've got a charity dinner tonight, but I'll be finished before eleven. Promise.'

'Great. You've done beautifully, Ione, really, you just blew them away. They love you out there.'

'And nobody's packed up and left yet, none of the major companies, nor the plutocrats. That's my real success.'

'It was that speech you made. Jesus, if there were elections tomorrow you'd be president.'

They reached the tube carriage waiting in the little station. Two serjeants stood aside as the door opened.

Joshua looked at them, then looked into the ten-seater carriage. 'Can they wait out here?' he asked innocently.

'Why?'

He leered.

*

She clung to him tightly afterwards, trembling slightly, their bodies hot and sweaty. He was sitting right on the edge of one of the seats, with her as the clinging vine, legs bent up behind his back. The carriage's air-conditioning fans made a loud whirring sound as they recycled the unusually humid air.

'Joshua?'

'Uh huh.' He kissed her neck, hands stroking her buttocks.

'I can't protect you once you leave.'

'I know.'

'Don't do anything stupid. Don't try to beat anything your father did.'

His nose nuzzled the base of her chin. 'I won't. I'm no death wisher.'

'Joshua?'

'What?'

She pulled her head back and looked straight into his eyes, trying to make him believe. 'Trust your instincts.'

'Hey, I do.'

'Please, Joshua. Not just about objects, people too. Be careful of people.'

'Yes.'

'Promise me.'

'I promise.'

He rose up, with Ione still wrapped round his torso. She could feel him getting hard again.

'See those hand hoops?' he asked.

She glanced up. 'Yes.'

'Catch hold, and don't let go.'

She reached up with both hands and gripped a pair of the steel loops on the ceiling. Joshua let go of her, and she yelped. Her toes didn't quite reach the floor. He stood in front of her, grinning, and gave her a small shove, starting her swinging.

'Joshua!' Ione forked her legs at the top of the arc.

He moved forward, laughing.

*

Erick Thakrar floated into bay MB 0-330's control centre towing his bag. He stopped himself with an expert nudge against a grab loop. There was an unusually large number of people grouped round the observation bubble. He recognized all of them, engineers who had worked on the *Lady Macbeth*'s refit. All of them had been working long shifts together for the last couple of weeks.

Erick didn't mind the work, it meant he had won his place on the *Lady Macbeth*'s crew. A stiff back and perpetual tiredness was a price worth paying for that. And in another two hours he would be on his way.

The buzz of voices faded away as people became aware of him. A vacant slot around the observation bubble materialized. He steadied himself and looked out.

The cradle had telescoped up out of the bay, taking the *Lady Macbeth* with it. As he watched, the starship's thermo-dump panels unfolded from their recesses in the lustreless grey hull. Cradle umbilical couplings withdrew from the rear quarter.

'You are cleared for disconnection,' the bay supervisor datavised. '*Bon voyage*, Joshua. Take care.'

Orange candle-flames ignited around the *Lady Macbeth*'s equator, and the chemical verniers lifted her clear of the cradle with a dexterity only a master pilot could ever achieve.

The engineering team whooped and cheered.

'Erick?'

He looked round at the supervisor.

'Joshua says to say sorry, but the Lord of Ruin thinks you're an arsehole.'

Erick turned back to the empty bay. The cradle was sinking slowly back towards the floor. Blue light washed down as the *Lady Macbeth*'s ion thrusters took over from the verniers.

'Son of a bitch,' he muttered numbly.

*

There were four separate life-support capsules in the *Lady Macbeth*, twelve-metre spheres grouped together in a pyramid shape at the very heart of the ship. With the expense of fitting them out coming to a minute fraction of the starship's overall cost, they were well appointed.

Capsules B, C, and D, the lower spheres, were split into four decks apiece, with the two middle levels following a basic layout of cabins, a lounge, galley, and bathroom. The other decks were variously storage compartments, maintenance shops, equipment bays, and airlock chambers for the spaceplane and MSV hangars.

Capsule A housed the bridge, taking up half of the upper middle deck, with consoles and acceleration couches for all six crew-members. Because neural nanonics could interface with the flight computer from anywhere in the ship, it was more of a management office than the traditional command centre, with console screens and AV projectors providing specialist systems displays to back up datavised information.

Lady Macbeth was licensed to carry up to thirty active passengers, or if the cabin bunks were removed and zero-tau pods installed, eighty people travelling in stasis. With only Joshua and five crew on board, there was a luxurious amount of space available. Joshua's cabin was the largest, taking up a quarter of the bridge deck. He refused to change it from the layout Marcus Calvert had chosen. The chairs were from some luxury passenger ship decommissioned over half a century ago, hinged black-foam sculptures which looked like giant seashells in their folded positions. A bookcase held acceleration-reinforced leather-bound volumes of ancient star charts. An Apollo command module guidance computer (of dubious provenance) was displayed in a transparent bubble. But the major feature, from his point of view, was the free-fall-sex cage, a mesh globe of rubberized struts which deployed from the ceiling. You could bounce around happily inside that without any danger of crashing into inconvenient (and sharp) pieces of furniture or decking. He intended to get into full practice with Sarha Mitcham, the twenty-four-year-old general systems engineer who had taken Erick Thakrar's place.

Everyone was strapped in their bridge couch when Joshua lifted the *Lady Macbeth* off bay 0–330's cradle. He did it with instinctive ease, he did it like a chrysalis opening its wings to the sun, he did it knowing *this* was what his spiralling DNA had been reconfigured to do.

Flight vectors from the spaceport traffic control centre insinuated their way into his mind, and ion thrusters rolled the ship lazily. He took them out over the edge of the giant disk of girders using the secondary reaction drive, then powered up the three primary fusion drives. The gee-force built rapidly, and they headed up out of Mirchusko's gravity well towards the green crescent of Falsia, seven hundred thousand kilometres away.

The shakedown flight lasted for fifteen hours. Test programs ran systems checks; the fusion drives were pushed up to producing a brief period of seven-gee thrust, and their plasma was scanned for instabilities; life-support capacity was tested in each capsule. The guidance systems, the sensors, fuel tank slosh baffles, thermal insulation, power circuits, generators . . . the million components that went into making up the starship structure.

Joshua inserted *Lady Mac* into orbit two hundred kilometres above the craterous lifeless moon while they took a rest for ninety minutes. After a final, formal report confirming overall performance efficiency matched the Confederation Astronautics Board's requirements, he powered up the fusion drives again, and accelerated back in towards the hazy ochre gas giant.

Adamist starships lacked the flexibility of voidhawks not only in manoeuvrability, but also in their respective methods of faster than light translation. While the bitek craft could tailor their wormholes to produce a terminus at the required location irrespective of their orbit and acceleration vector, ships like the *Lady Macbeth* jumped along their orbital track without any leeway at all. It was that limitation which cost captains a great deal of time between jumps. The starship had to align itself directly on its target star. In interstellar space it wasn't so difficult, simply a question of adjusting for natural error. But the initial jump out of a star system had to be as accurate as humanly possible to prevent emergence point inaccuracies from growing out of hand. If a starship was departing an asteroid that was heading away from its next port of call, the captain could spend days reversing his orbit, and the cost in delta-V reserve was horrendous. Most captains simply employed the nearest available planet, giving them the choice of jumping towards any star in the galaxy once every orbit.

Lady Macbeth fell into a circular orbit a hundred and eighty-five thousand kilometres above Mirchusko, a ten-thousand-kilometre safety margin. Gravity distortion prohibited Adamist starships from jumping within a hundred and seventy-five thousand kilometres of gas giants.

The flight computer datavised the vector lines into Joshua's mind. He saw the vast curved bulk of quarrelling storm bands below, the black cave-lip of the terminator creeping towards him. *Lady Mac*'s trajectory was a tube of green neon rings stretching out ahead until they merged into a single thread which looped round behind Mirchusko's darkside. The green rings swept past the hull at a dizzying velocity.

Rosenheim showed as an insignificant point of white light, bracketed by red graphics, rising above the gas giant.

'Generators on line,' Melvyn Ducharme reported.

'Dahybi?' Joshua asked.

'Patterning circuits are stable,' Dahybi Yadev, their node specialist, said in a calm voice.

'OK, looks like we're go for a jump.' He ordered the nodes to power up, feeding the generators' full output into the patterning circuits. Rosenheim was rising higher and higher above the gas giant as *Lady Mac* raced round her orbit.

Jesus, an actual jump.

According to his neural nanonics physiological monitor program his heart rate was up to a hundred beats a minute and rising. It had been known for some first-time crew-members to panic when the actual moment came, terrified by the thought of the energy loci being desynchronized. All it took was one glitch, one failed monitor program.

Not me! Not this ship.

He datavised the flight computer to pull in the thermo-dump panels and the sensor clusters.

'Nodes fully charged,' Dahybi Yadev said. 'She's all yours, Joshua.'

He had to grin at that. She always had been.

Ion thrusters flickered briefly, fine tuning their trajectory. Rosenheim slid across the vector of green rings, right into the centre. Decimals spun down to zero, tens of seconds, hundredths, thousandths.

Joshua's command flashed through the patterning nodes at lightspeed. Energy flowed, its density racing to achieve infinity.

An event horizon rose from nowhere to cloak the *Lady*

Macbeth's hull. Within five milliseconds it had shrunk to nothing, taking the starship with it.

*

Erick Thakrar took the StMichelle starscraper's lift down to the forty-third floor, then got out and walked down two flights of stairs. There was nobody about on the forty-fifth floor vestibule. This was office country, half of them unoccupied; and it was nineteen hundred hours local time.

He walked into the Confederation Navy bureau.

Commander Olsen Neale looked up in surprise when Erick entered his office. 'What the hell are you doing here? I thought the *Lady Macbeth* had departed.'

Erick sat down heavily in the chair in front of Neale's desk. 'She has.' He explained what happened.

Commander Neale rested his head in his hands, frowning. Erick Thakrar was one of half a dozen agents the CNIS was operating in Tranquillity, trying to insert them on independent traders (especially those with antimatter drives) and blackhawks in the hope of getting a lead on pirate activity and antimatter production stations.

'The Lord of Ruin warned Calvert?' Commander Neale asked in a puzzled tone.

'That's what the maintenance bay supervisor said.'

'Good God, that's all we need, this Ione girl turning Tranquillity into some kind of anarchistic pirate nation. It might be a blackhawk base, but the Lords of Ruin have always supported the Confederation before.' Commander Neale glanced round the polyp walls, then stared at the AV pillar sticking out of his desk's processor block, half expecting the personality to contact him and deny the accusation. 'Do you think your cover's blown?'

'I don't know. The refit team thought it was all a big joke. Apparently Joshua Calvert signed on some girl to replace me. They said she was rather attractive.'

'Well, it certainly fits what we know about him; he could very easily have dumped you for a doxy and a quick leg-over.'

'Then why the reference to the Lord of Ruin?'

'God knows.' He let out a long breath. 'I want you to keep trying for a berth on a ship; you'll find out soon enough if you have been blown. I'm going to put all this on the diplomatic report flek, and let Admiral Aleksandrovich worry about it.'

'Yes, sir.' Erick Thakrar saluted and left.

Commander Neale sat in his chair for a long time, watching the starfield rotate past the window. The prospect of Tranquillity going renegade was horrifying, especially given the one particular status quo it had maintained for twenty-seven years. Eventually he accessed his neural nanonics file on Dr Mzu, and started to check through the circumstances under which he was authorized to have her assassinated.

11

Some of the more superstitious amongst Aberdale's population were heard to say that Marie Skibbow had taken the village's luck with her when she departed. There was no change in their physical circumstances, but they seemed to suffer a veritable plague of depressing and unfortunate incidents.

Marie had been right about her family's reaction. After the truth was finally established (Rai Molvi confirmed she boarded the *Coogan*, Scott Williams confirmed she was loading the thermal furnace when it cast off) Gerald Skibbow's reaction to what he thought of as his daughter's betrayal was pure fury. He demanded Powel Manani either chase after the tramp trader on his horse, or use his communication block to have the county sheriff arrest her when the *Coogan* sailed past Schuster.

Powel politely explained that Marie was now legally an adult, and didn't have a settlement contract with the LDC, and was therefore free to do as she pleased. Gerald, with Loren weeping quietly at his side, raged at the injustice, then went on to complain bitterly of the incompetence of the LDC's local representatives. At which point the Ivet supervisor, exhausted from leading the search for Gwyn Lawes after a full day spent in the saddle rounding up stray animals on the savannah, came very close to punching Gerald Skibbow's lights out. Rai Molvi, Horst Elwes, and Leslie Atcliffe had to pull them apart.

Marie Skibbow's name was never mentioned again.

The fields and plantations carved out of the jungle at the rear of Aberdale's clearing were now so large that the vigorous ground creepers which invaded the rotovated soil were growing back almost as fast as they could be chopped up. It was a wearisome task, taxing even the disciplined Ivets. Any further expansion was clearly out of the question until the first batch of crops was firmly established. The more delicate varieties of terrestrial vegetables were struggling laboriously under the never-ending assault from the rain. Even with their geneering, tomatoes, courgettes, lettuce, kale, celeriac, and aubergines laboured upwards, their leaves bent and drooping, yellowing round the edges. One violent storm which left the jungle shrouded in mist for days afterwards scattered half of the village's chickens, few of which were ever found.

A fortnight after the *Coogan* departed, another tramp trader, the *Louis Leonid*, arrived. There was almost a riot at the prices the captain charged; he cast off hurriedly, swearing to warn every boat in the Juliffe basin to avoid the Quallheim tributary in future.

And there were the deaths as well. After Gwyn Lawes there was Roger Chadwick, drowned in the Quallheim, his body discovered a kilometre downriver. Then the terrible tragedy of the Hoffman family: Donnie and Judy, along with their two young teenage children, Angie and Thomas, burnt to death in their savannah homestead one night. It wasn't until morning when Frank Kava saw the thin pyre of smoke rising from the ashes that the alarm was raised. The bodies were charred beyond recognition. Even a well-equipped pathology lab would have been hard pressed to realize that they had all died from having a hunting laser fired through their eyes at a five-centimetre range.

*

Horst Elwes pushed the sharpened bottom of the cross thirty centimetres into the sodden black loam, and started to press it in with his boot. He had made the cross himself from mayope wood, not as good as anything Leslie could make, of course, but untainted. He felt that was important for little Angie.

'There's no proof,' he said as he looked down at the pathetically small oblong mound of earth.

'Ha!' Ruth Hilton said as she handed him Thomas's cross.

They went over to the boy's grave. Horst found it very hard to visualize Thomas's face now. The boy had been thirteen, all smiles, always running everywhere. The cross went in the ground with a sucking sound.

'You said yourself they are Satanists,' Ruth insisted. 'And we damn well know those three colonists were murdered back in Durringham.'

'Mugged,' Horst said. 'They were mugged.'

'They were murdered.'

The cross had Thomas's name burnt in crudely with a fission blade. I could have done better than that, Horst thought, it wouldn't have been much to ask for the poor boy, staying sober while I carved his headmarker.

'Murdered, mugged, it happened in a different world, Ruth. Was there ever really such a place as Earth? They say the past is only a memory. I find it very hard to remember Earth now. Does that mean it's gone, do you think?'

She looked at him with real concern. He was unshaven, and probably hadn't been eating properly. The vegetable garden he kept was choked with weeds and vine tendrils. His beefy figure had thinned down considerably. Most people in Aberdale had lost weight since they'd arrived, but they'd built muscle to compensate. Horst's flesh was starting to hang in folds below his chin. She suspected he'd found another supply of drink since she stood on the end of the jetty and emptied his last three bottles of Scotch into the Quallheim. 'Where was Jesus born, Horst? Where did he die for our mortal sins?'

'Oh, very good. Yes, very good indeed. I could train you up as a lay preacher in no time if you'd let me.'

'I have a field to tend. I have chickens and a goat to feed. I have Jay to look after. What are we going to do about the Ivets?'

'Let he who has not sinned cast the first stone.'

'Horst!'

'I'm sorry.' He looked mournfully at the cross she was holding.

Ruth thrust it into his hand. 'I don't want them living here. Hell, have you seen the way that little Jason Lawes trots around after Quinn Dexter? He's like a puppy on a leash.'

'How many of us stop by to look after Rachel and Jason? Oh, we were all such fine neighbours to her for the first week after Gwyn died, ten days even. But now . . . To keep on and on for weeks without end when you have your own family to nurture. People can't do it, they lack the tenacity. Of course they designate the Ivets to help Rachel. Something is done, and conscience is saved. But I attach no blame for that. This place drains us, Ruth. It turns us inwards, we only have time for ourselves.'

Ruth bit back on what she had heard about Rachel and Quinn Dexter. Hell, poor Gwyn had only been gone five weeks, couldn't the damn woman wait a little longer? 'Where is it going to stop, Horst? Who's next? Do you know what I dream about? I dream of Jay running round after that super-macho Jackson Gael, or Lawrence Dillon with his pretty face and his dead smile. That's what I dream. Are you going to tell me I have nothing to worry about, that I'm just paranoid? Six deaths in five weeks. Six *accidents* in five weeks. We have to do something.'

'I know!' Horst jabbed Judy Hoffman's cross into the ground. Water oozed up around the edge of the wood. Like blood, he thought, filthy blood.

*

The jungle steamed softly. It had rained less than an hour ago, and every trunk and leaf was still slick with water. One thick stratum of swan-white mist had formed at waist height. It meant the four Ivets tramping down the animal track could barely see their feet. Fingers of sunlight probing down through the screen of overhead leaves shone out like solid strands of gold in the ultra-humid air. Away in the distance was the tremulous gobbling and cooing of the birds, the chorus they had long since learnt to filter out.

The ground here was rough, distorted by meandering hummocks twice the height of a man. Trees grew out of their sides at slapdash angles, curving upwards, supported by vast buttress roots. Their ash-grey trunks were slender in relation to their height, seldom more than thirty centimetres wide, yet they were all over twenty metres high, crowned by interlaced umbrellas of emerald foliage. Nothing grew on the trunks below. Even the vines and scrub plants around the triangular roots lacked their usual vigour.

'There's no game here,' Scott Williams said after half an hour of scrambling over interminable hummocks and splashing through the water that pooled around them. 'It's the wrong sort of country.'

'That's right,' Quinn Dexter said. 'No reason for anyone to come this way.' They had started out early that morning, marching down the well-worn path towards the savannah homesteads to the south of Aberdale, a legitimate hunting party, with four borrowed laser rifles and one electromagnetic rifle. Quinn had led them straight down the path for five kilometres, then broke off into the jungle towards the west. He made one sweep each week, the guido block he'd taken from the Hoffmans' homestead making sure a different area was searched each time.

They had done well from the Hoffmans that night a fortnight ago. Donnie had come to Lalonde well prepared for the rigours of pioneering life. There had been freeze-dried food, tools, medical supplies, several rifles, and two Jovian Bank credit disks. The six Ivets he had led on the night-time mission to the homestead had feasted well before he turned them loose on Judy and the two children.

That had been the first time Quinn had conducted the full ceremony, the dark mass of dedication to God's Brother. Binding the others to him with the shared corruption. Before that it had been fear which made them obey. Now he owned their souls.

Two of them had been the weakest of the Ivet group, Irley and Scott, disbelievers until lovely Angie was offered to them. The serpent beast had awoken in each of them, as it always did, inflamed by the heat, and chanting, and orange torchlight shining on naked skin. God's Brother had whispered into their hearts, and shown them the true way of the flesh, the animal way. Temptation had triumphed yet again, and Angie's cries had carried far across the savannah in the still night air. Since the ceremony they had become Quinn's most trusted comrades.

It was something Banneth had shown him; the ceremonies were more than simple worship, they had a purpose. If you lived through them, if you committed the rituals, you became part of the sect for ever. There was nobody else after that. You were a pariah, irredeemable; loathed, hated, and rejected by decent society, by the followers of Jesus and Allah.

Soon there would be more ceremonies, and all the Ivets would undergo their initiation.

The ground began to flatten out. The trees were growing closer together now, with thicker undergrowth. Quinn plodded through another stream, boots crunching on the pebbles. He was wearing knee-length green denim shorts and a sleeveless vest of the same material, just right to protect his skin from thorns and twigs. They used to belong to Gwyn Lawes; Rachel had given all his clothes to the Ivets as a thank you for keeping her field free of weeds and creepers. Poor Rachel Lawes was not a well woman these days, she had become very brittle since her husband's death. She talked to herself and heard the voices of saints. But at night she listened to what Quinn wanted, and did it. Rachel hated Lalonde as much as he did, and she wasn't alone in the village. Quinn took note of the names she confessed, and ordered the Ivets to ingratiate themselves with the disaffected.

Lawrence Dillon let out an exuberant whoop, and fired off his borrowed laser rifle. Quinn looked up in time to see a vennal shooting through the tops of the trees, the little lizardlike animal flowing like liquid along the high branches, its paws barely touching the bark.

Lawrence fired again. A puff of smoke squirted from a branch where the vennal had been an instant before. 'Sheech, but it's fast.'

'Leave it,' Quinn said. 'You'll only have to carry it the rest of the day. We'll bag some meat on the way back.'

'OK, Quinn,' Lawrence Dillon said doubtfully. His head was cranked back, shifting from side to side as he squinted upwards. 'I've lost it, anyway.'

Quinn looked up at where the vennal had been. The nimble tree-dwelling creatures had a blue-green hide which was nearly impossible to distinguish from more than fifteen metres. He switched to infrared, and scanned the treetops of the shadowless red and pink world his retinal implant revealed. The vennal was a bright salmon-pink corona, lying prone along the top of a thick bough, triangular head peering down nervously at them. Quinn turned a complete circle.

'I want you to put your weapons down,' he said.

The others gave him puzzled glances. 'Quinn—'

'Now.' He unslung his laser rifle, and laid it on the wet grass. It was a tribute to his authority that the others did as they were told without any further protest.

Quinn spread his hands, palms open. 'Satisfied?' he demanded.

The chameleon suit lost its bark pattern, reverting to a dark grey.

Lawrence Dillon took a pace backwards in surprise. 'Shit. I never saw him.'

Quinn only laughed.

The man was standing with his back pressed against a qualtook tree eight metres away. He pulled the hood back revealing a round forty-year-old face with a steep chin and light grey eyes.

'Morning,' Quinn said in a jaunty tone. He had been expecting someone different, someone with Banneth's brand of lashed-up mania; this man seemed to have no presence at all. 'You've taken my advice, then? Very wise.'

'Tell me why you should not be eliminated,' the man said.

Quinn thought his voice sounded as though it had been synthesized by a processor block, completely neutral. 'Because you don't know who I've told, or what I've told them. That makes me safe. If you could go around snuffing out entire villages whenever your security had been compromised, you wouldn't be stashed away here. Now would you?'

'What do you want to talk about?'

'I won't know that until I see what you've got. For a start, who are you?'

'This body's name is Clive Jenson.'

'What have you done to him, put in a persona sequestrator nanonic?'

'Not quite, but the situation is similar.'

'So, are you ready to talk now?'

'I will listen.' The man beckoned. 'You will come with me, the others will remain here.'

'Hey, no way,' Jackson Gael said.

Quinn held his hands up. 'It's OK, it's cool. Stay here for three hours, then go back to Aberdale whether I'm back or not.' He checked the coordinate on the guido block, and started walking after the man in the chameleon suit whose name used to be Clive Jenson.

*

After six weeks' travelling and trading the *Coogan* was approaching the end of its voyage. Marie Skibbow knew they were within days of Durringham even though Len Buchannan had said nothing. She recognized the lying villages again; the white-painted slat walls of the trim houses, neat gardens, the pastoral fantasy. The Juliffe was coffee brown again, running eagerly towards the freedom of the ocean that couldn't be far away now. She could see the Hultain Marsh squatting on the north shore when the wavelets weren't riding too high, a dismal snarl of mouldy vegetation sending out eye-smarting streamers of brimstone gases. Big paddle-craft similar to the *Swithland* were churning their way upriver, leaving a foamy wake behind them. Fresh colonists gazed out at the shoreline with wonder and desire animating their faces, and children raced round the decks laughing and giggling.

Fools. All of them, utter fools.

The *Coogan* was stopping at fewer and fewer jetties now. Their original stocks were almost depleted, the tramp trader riding half a metre higher in the water. The balance in Len Buchannan's Jovian Bank credit disk had grown in proportion. Now he was buying cured meat to sell in the city.

'Stop loading,' Len shouted at her from the wheel-house. 'We're putting ashore here.'

The *Coogan*'s blunt prow turned a couple of degrees, aiming for a jetty below a row of large wooden warehouses. There were several cylindrical grain silos to one side. Power bikes bumped along the dirt tracks winding round the houses. The village was a wealthy one. The kind Marie thought Group Seven was heading for, the kind that had tricked her.

She abandoned the logs she was loading into the hopper, and straightened her back. Weeks spent cutting up timber with a fission saw then feeding the hopper in all weathers had given her the kind of muscles she'd never got from the gym at the arcology's day centre. She had lost almost two centimetres from her waist, her old shorts didn't cling anything like the way they used to.

Thin smoke from the furnace's leaky iron stack made her eyes water. She blinked furiously, staring at the village they were approaching, then ahead to the west. She made up her mind, and walked forward.

Gail Buchannan was sitting at the side of the wheel-house, her scraggly hair tied back, coolie hat casting a shadow over her knitting needles. She had knitted and sewed her way down the whole length of the river from Aberdale.

'Where do you think you're going, lovie?' the huge woman asked.

'My cabin.'

'Well, you make sure you get back out here in time to help my Lennie with the mooring. I'm not having you slacking off while he has work to do. I've never known anyone as lazy as you. My poor husband works like a mechanoid to keep us afloat.'

Marie ignored the obloquy and brushed past her, ducking down into the cabin. She had turned a corner of the cargo hold into a little nest of her own, sleeping on a length of shelving at nights after Len had finished with her. The wood was hard, and she'd repeatedly knocked her head on the frame during the first week until she got used to the confined space; but there was no way she was going to spend the night lying in his embrace.

She stripped off the colourless dungarees she used on deck, and pulled a clean bra and a T-shirt from her bag where they had lain throughout the voyage. Feeling the smooth synthetic fabric snug against her skin brought back memories of Earth and the arcology. Her world, where there was life and a future, where Govcentral gave away didactic courses, and people had proper jobs, and went to clubs, and had a thousand sensevise entertainment channels to choose from, and the vac trains could take you to the other side of the planet in six hours.

Black tropical-weave jeans with a leathery look finished the change. It was like wearing civilization. She picked up the shoulder-bag, and went forwards.

Gail Buchannan was hollering for her as she slid the bolt on the toilet door. The toilet itself was just a wooden box (built from mayope so it could take Gail's weight) with a hole in the top; there was a stack of big vine leaves to wipe with. Marie knelt down and prised the bottom plank off the front of the box. The river gurgled by a metre below. Her two packets were hanging below the decking, tied into place with silicon-fibre fishing-line. She cut the fibre with a pocket fission blade and stuffed the two polythene-wrapped bundles into her shoulder-bag. They were mostly medical nanonic packages, the highest value-for-weight-ratio items the *Coogan* carried; she'd also included some personal MF players, a couple of processor blocks, small power tools. A hoard that had been steadily built up over the voyage. The shoulder-bag's seal barely closed around them.

Gail's voice was reaching hysteria pitch by the time Marie got back to the galley and gave a last look round the wooden cell where she had spent an eternity cooking and cleaning. She took down the big brown clay pot of mixed herbs, and tugged out a thick wad of Lalonde francs. It was only one of the various bundles Gail had secreted around the tramp trader. She stuffed the crisp plastic notes into a rear pocket, then, on impulse, picked up a match before she went out on deck.

The *Coogan* had already pulled up next to the jetty and Len Buchannan was busy tying one of the cables to a bollard. Gail's face had turned a thunderous purple below her coolie hat.

She took in Marie's appearance with one flabbergasted look. 'What the hell do you think you're doing dressed like that, you little strumpet? You've got to give Lennie a hand loading the meat. My poor Lennie can't shift all those heavy carcasses by himself. And where the hell do you think you're going with that bag? And what have you got in it?'

Marie smiled her lazy smile, the one her father always called intolerably indolent. She struck the match on the cabin wall.

Both of them watched the phosphorus tip splutter into life, the yellow flame biting into the splinter of wood, eating its way along towards her fingers. Gail's mouth dropped open as realization dawned.

'Goodbye,' she said brightly. 'It's been so nice knowing you.' She dropped the match into the sewing box at Gail's feet.

Gail screeched in panic as the match disappeared under her scraps of cotton and lace. Bright orange flames licked upwards.

Marie marched off down the jetty. Len was standing by the bollard ahead of her, a length of silicon-fibre rope coiled in his hands.

'You're leaving,' he said.

Gail was shouting a tirade of obscenities and threats after her. There was a loud splash as the precious sewing box hit the water.

Marie couldn't manage the blasé expression she wanted. Not in front of him. There was a curious look of dismay on the skinny old man's face.

'Don't go,' he said. It was a plea, she'd never heard his voice so whiny before.

'Why? Was there something you didn't have? Something you forgot to try out?' Her voice came close to breaking.

'I'll get rid of her,' he said desperately.

'For me?'

'You're beautiful, Marie.'

'Is that it? All you've got to say to me?'

'Yes. I thought . . . I never hurt you. Never once.'

'And you want it to go on? Is that what you want, Len? The two of us sailing up and down the Juliffe for the rest of our days?'

'Please, Marie. I hate her. I want you, not her.'

She stood ten centimetres away from him, smelling the fruit he'd eaten that morning on his breath. 'Is that so?'

'I have money. You would live like a princess, I promise.'

'Money is nothing. I would have to be loved. I could give everything of myself to a man who loved me. Do you love me, Len? Do you really love me?'

'I do, Marie. God, I do. *Please.* Come with me!'

She ran a finger along his chin. Tears were welling up in his eyes.

'Then kill yourself, Len,' she whispered thickly. 'For she is all you have. She is all you'll ever have. For the rest of your life, Len, you're going to live with the knowledge that I am always beyond you.'

She waited until his tragi-hopeful face crumpled in utter mortification, then laughed. It was so much more satisfactory than kneeing him in the balls.

There was a wagon loaded with silage trundling along the main dirt track, heading west. A fourteen-year-old boy in dungarees was driving it, giving occasional flicks on the big shire-horse's reins. Marie stuck out her thumb, and he nodded eagerly, overawed eyes goggling at her. She clambered aboard while it was still moving.

'How far to Durringham?' she asked.

'Fifty kilometres. But I'm not going that far, just to Mepal.'

'That'll do for a start.' She sat back on the hard wooden plank seat, the jolting wheels rocking her gently from side to side. The sun was boiling, the swaying was uncomfortable, the horse stank. She felt wonderful.

*

The gigantea was over seven thousand years old when Laton and his small band of followers arrived on Lalonde. It was set on a small rise in the land, which pushed its three-hundred-metre-plus length even further above the surrounding jungle. Storms had frayed and broken the tip, resulting in a bulbous knot of snarled twigs with tufts of leaves sticking out at odd angles. Birds had turned this malformed pinnacle into a voluminous eyrie, pecking away at it over the centuries until it was riddled with a warren of holes.

When it rained, water would clog in the gigantea's thick fuzzy leaves, their weight pushing the downward-sloping boughs even closer towards the fat bole. Then for hours afterwards droplets would sprinkle down, drying the gigantea out from the top, the boughs slowly rising again. Standing on the ground below was like standing under a small, powerful waterfall. The last traces of soil had been washed away from under the boughs several millennia ago. All that remained was a solid undulating tangle of roots, extending outwards for a hundred metres, slimed like seaside rocks at low tide.

Laton's blackhawk had brought him to Lalonde in 2575. At that time there were less than a hundred people on the planet, a caretaker squad looking after the landing site camp. The ecological assessment team had completed their analysis and left; the Confederation inspection team wasn't due for another year. He had obtained a classified copy of the company report; the planet was habitable, it would gain the Confederation's certification. There would be colonists eventually; dirt poor, ignorant, without any advanced technology. Given his own particular designs on the future, it would be a perfect culture to infiltrate.

They had landed in the mountains on Amarisk's eastern side, twenty humans and seven landcruisers loaded with enough luxuries to make exile bearable, along with more essential stocks: small cybernetic manufacturing systems, and his genetics equipment. He also had the blackhawk's nine eggs, removed from its ovaries and stored in zero-tau. The blackhawk was sent to oblivion in the fierce blue-white star; and the little convoy started to batter its way through the jungle. It took them two days to reach the tributary river which would one day be called the Quallheim. Three days' sailing (the landcruisers had amphibious fuselages) brought them to Schuster County, a territory where the soil was deep enough to support the giganteas. Jungle again, and half a day later he found what must surely be the largest gigantea specimen on the continent.

'This will do,' he told his fellowship. 'In fact, I think it is rather appropriate.'

*

The branches were still shedding their weight of water from the earlier rain when Clive Jenson led Quinn Dexter onto the slippery coils of the gigantea's roots. There was a perpetual twilight under the huge shaggy boughs. Water pattered down, forming runnels that gurgled and sucked their way around the intestinal tangle below his feet.

Quinn resisted the impulse to hunch his shoulders against the big drops splashing on his head. Spores or sap – something organic – had curdled with the water, making it tacky. It was cool in the shade, the coolest he'd ever been on Lalonde.

They neared the colossal bole. The roots began to curve up to the vertical, wooden waves crashing against a wooden cliff. Between the thick cords were dark anfractuous clefts five times his height, tapering away to knife-thin fissures. Clive Jenson stepped into one. Quinn watched him disappear round a curve, then shrugged and followed him in.

After five metres the floor became level and the walls widened out to a couple of metres, the coarse mat of fibre which passed for the gigantea's bark giving way to smooth bare wood. Carved, he realized. God's Brother, he's cut his home into the tree. How much effort has gone into this?

There was a glimmer of light up ahead. He walked round an S-bend, and into a brightly lit room. It was fifteen metres long, ten wide, perfectly ordinary except for the lack of windows. Pegs on one wall held a row of dark green cagoules. Gigantea wood was a pale walnut colour, with a widely spaced grain, making it look as though the walls were built from exceptionally broad planks. There was a desk, like a long bar, running down one side, that had been carved from a single block. A woman stood at the far end of it, watching him impassively.

Quinn broke into a slow grin. She looked about twenty-five, taller than him, with black skin and long chestnut hair, a petite button nose. Her sleeveless amber blouse and white culottes showed off a full figure.

A flicker of distaste crossed her face. 'Don't be disgusting, Dexter.'

'What? I never said a word.'

'You didn't have to. I'd sooner screw a servitor housechimp.'

'Do I get to watch?'

Her expression intensified. 'Stand still, don't move, or I'll have Clive dissect you.' She picked a sensor wand off the desk.

Still grinning, Quinn lifted his arms out, and let her run the wand around him. Clive stood to attention a couple of metres away, perfectly still, as if he was a mechanoid construct that had been switched off. Quinn tried not to let it show how much that bothered him.

'So how long have you been here?' he asked.

'Long enough.'

'What do I call you?'

'Camilla.'

'OK, Camilla, that's cool. So what's the story here?'

'I'll let Laton tell you.' Her tongue was pushed into her cheek. 'That's if he doesn't just decide to incorporate you like Clive here.'

Quinn threw a glance at the stationary man. 'One of the colonists from the Schuster homesteads?'

'That's right.'

'Ah.'

'Your heart rate is high, Dexter. Worried about something?'

'No. Are you?'

She put the wand back on the desk. 'You can see Laton now. You're no danger; two implants and a whole load of attitude.'

He flinched at the mention of implants. There went his last advantage, tiny though it had been. 'Got me this far, hasn't it?'

Camilla started to walk towards the door. 'Getting in is the easy part.'

There was a broad spiral staircase leading up through the bole. Quinn caught glimpses of corridors and rooms. A whole level was given over to a large pool-cum-spa. Steam was thick in the air, men and women were lounging about in the water or on various ledges; one was lying flat on a slab being given a massage by a middle-aged woman with an empty expression he was beginning to recognize. He realized what was missing: some people were laughing, but nobody was talking. Servitor housechimps scurried down corridors on mysterious errands; they were about a metre and a half tall, walking with an almost human gait, their golden fur well groomed. When he looked closely he saw they had proper feet rather than the paws of their Earth-jungle ancestors.

God's Brother, those are Edenist constructs. What the fuck is this?

Camilla took him down a corridor that looked no different to any other. A door opened soundlessly, a thick wooden rectangle with some kind of synthetic muscle as a hinge.

'Lion's den, Dexter; in you go.'

The door closed as silently as it had opened. Inside was a large circular space with a vaulted ceiling. The furniture was a severe minimalist style: a glass-topped desk with metal legs, a dining table, also glass topped, two settees facing each other; every piece arranged to put a maximum amount of distance between them. One section of the wall was a vast holographic screen with a view of the jungle outside. The camera was well above the treetops, showing an unbroken expanse of leaves; steamy scraps of cloud drifted in meandering patterns. An iron perch, three metres high, stood in the centre of the room. On it was the kestrel, watching him intently. Two people were waiting, a man seated behind the desk and a young girl standing beside the settees.

Laton rose from behind the desk. He was one of the tallest men Quinn had ever seen; well muscled, with cinnamon-coloured skin, looking like a tan rather than natural pigmentation, a handsome, vaguely Asian face with deep-set grey-green eyes and a neat beard, ebony hair tied back in a small pony-tail. He wore a simple green silk robe, belted at the waist. His age was indeterminable, over thirty, less than a hundred. That he was the product of geneering was in no doubt.

This was the presence Quinn had looked for when Clive Jenson had pulled off his chameleon-suit hood. The invincible self-assurance, a man who inspired devotion.

'Quinn Dexter, you've caused quite a stir among my colleagues. We have very few visitors, as you can imagine. Do sit down.' Laton gestured to a royal-purple settee where the girl was waiting. 'Can we get you anything while you're here? A decent drink? A proper meal, perhaps? Dear old Aberdale isn't exactly flowing with milk and honey yet.'

Quinn's instinct was to refuse, but the offer was too tempting. So bollocks if it made him look grasping and inferior. 'A steak, medium rare, with chips and a side salad, no mustard. And a glass of milk. Never thought I'd miss milk.' He gave Laton what he hoped was a phlegmatic smile as the big man sat down on the settee opposite. Out-cooling him was going to be a major problem.

'Certainly, I think we can manage that. We use starscraper food-secretion glands, modified to work from the gigantea's sap. The taste is quite passable.' Laton raised his voice a degree. 'Anname, see to that, would you, please.'

The girl gave a slight, uncertain bow. She must have been about twelve or thirteen, Quinn thought, with thick blonde hair coming down below her shoulders and pale Nordic skin; her lashes were almost invisible. Her light blue eyes put Quinn in mind of Gwyn Lawes in the moments before his death. Anname was one very badly frightened little girl.

'Another member of the missing homestead families?' Quinn guessed.

'Indeed.'

'And you haven't incorporated her?'

'She's given me no reason to. The adult males are useful for various labour-intensive tasks, which is why I kept them on; but the young boys I had no requirement for at all, so they were stored for transplant material.'

'And what were your requirements?'

'Ovaries, basically. I didn't have a sufficient quantity for the next stage of my project. It was a situation which the homestead females were fortunately able to rectify for me. We have enough suspension tanks here to maintain their Fallopian tubes in a fully functional state, thus ensuring they keep dropping their precious little gifts into my palm each month. Anname hasn't quite matured enough for that yet. And seeing as how organs never really prosper in tanks, we allow her to run around the place until she's ready. Some of my companions have become quite fond of her. I even confess to finding her moderately tolerable myself.'

Anname flashed him a glance of pure terror before the door opened and let her out.

'There's a lot of bitek at work here,' Quinn said. 'If I didn't know better, I'd say you were an Edenist.'

Laton frowned. 'Oh dear. My name doesn't register amongst your memories, then?'

'No. Should it?'

'Alas, such is fame. Fleeting at best. Of course, I did achieve my notoriety a considerable number of years before you were born, so I suppose it's to be expected.'

'What did you do?'

'There was an irregularity concerning a quantity of anti-matter, and a proteanic virus which damaged my habitat's personality rather badly. I'm afraid I released it before the replicant code RNA transfer was perfected.'

'Your habitat? Then you are an Edenist?'

'Wrong tense. I was an Edenist, yes.'

'But you're all affinity bonded. None of you breaks the law. You can't.'

'Ah, there, I'm afraid, my young friend, you are a victim of popular prejudice, not to mention some rather sickly propaganda on Jupiter's behalf. There aren't many of us; but believe me, not everybody born an Edenist dies an Edenist. Some of us rebel, we shut off that cacophony of nobility and unity that vomits into our minds every living second. We regain our individuality, and our mental freedom. And more often than not, we choose to pursue our independent course through life. Our ex-peers refer to us as Serpents.' He gave an ironic smile. 'Naturally they don't like to admit we exist. In fact they go to rather tedious lengths to track us down. Hence my current position.'

'Serpents,' Quinn whispered. 'That's what all men are. That's what God's Brother teaches us. Everyone is a beast in their heart, it is the strongest part of us, and so we fear it the most. But if you find the courage to let it rule, you can never be beaten. I just never thought an Edenist could free his beast.'

'Interesting linguistic coincidence,' Laton murmured.

Quinn leaned forwards. 'Don't you see, we're the same, you and me. We both walk the same path. We are brothers.'

'Quinn Dexter, you and I share certain qualities; but understand this, you became a waster kid, and from that a Light Brother sect member, because of social conditions. That sect was your only route away from mediocrity. I chose to be what I am only after a careful review of the alternatives. And the one thing I retain from my Edenist past is complete atheism.'

'That's it! You said it. Shit, both of us told ordinary life to go fuck itself. We follow God's Brother in our own way, but we both follow him.'

Laton raised an exasperated eyebrow. 'I can see this is a pointless argument. What did you want to talk to me about?'

'I want your help to subdue Aberdale.'

'Why should I want to do that?'

'Because I'll turn it over to you afterwards.'

Laton looked blank for a second, then inclined his head in understanding. 'Of course, the money. I wondered what you wanted the money for. You don't want to be Aberdale's feudal lord, you intend to leave Lalonde altogether.'

'Yeah, on the first starship I can buy passage on. If I can get down to Durringham before any alarm gets out, then I can use one of the villagers' Jovian Bank credit disks without any trouble. And with you in charge back here there wouldn't be no alarm.'

'What about your Ivet friends, the ones you seem to be busy baptizing in blood?'

'Fuck 'em. I want out. I got business back on Earth, serious business.'

'I'm sure you have.'

'How about it? We could work it together. Me and the Ivets could round up the women and children during the day when the men are out hunting and farming, use 'em as hostages. Get 'em all into the hall and take their guns away. Once the men are disarmed, it'll be no problem for you to incorporate 'em all. Then you just make 'em live like they do now. Anyone turns up later, Aberdale is just another crappy colonist village full of arse scratchers. I get what I want, which is *out of here*, and you get plenty of warm bods; plus there's no more security risk of someone stumbling on this wood palace and shouting to Durringham about it.'

'I think you're overestimating my ability.'

'No way. Not now I've seen what you've got. This incorporation gimmick has got to be like persona sequestration. You could run a whole arcology with that technology.'

'Yes, but the bitek regulators we implant would have to be

grown first. I don't have them in store, certainly not five hundred and fifty of them. It all takes time.'

'So? I ain't going anywhere.'

'No, indeed. And of course, were I to agree, you would make no mention of me once you returned to Earth?'

'I'm no squeal. One of the reasons I'm here.'

Laton eased back onto his settee and gave Quinn a long thoughtful look. 'Very well. Now let me make you an offer. Leave Aberdale and join me. I can always use someone with your nerve.'

Quinn let his gaze wander round the big vacuous room. 'How long have you been here?'

'In the region of thirty-five years.'

'I figured something like that; you couldn't have landed after the colonists arrived, not if you're as well known as you say you are. Thirty-five years living in a tree without any windows, I gotta tell you, it ain't me. In any case, I ain't no Edenist, I don't have this affinity trick to control the bitek.'

'That can be rectified, you can use neuron symbionts just like your friend Powel Manani. More than a third of my colleagues are Adamists, the rest are my children. You'd fit in. You see, I can give you what you want most.'

'I want Banneth, and she's three hundred light-years away. You ain't got her to give.'

'I meant, Quinn Dexter, what you really want. What all of us want.'

'Oh, yeah? What?'

'A form of immortality.'

'Bullshit. Even I know that ain't on. The best the Saldanas can do is a couple of centuries, and that's with all their money and genetic research teams.'

'That's because they are going about it the wrong way. The Adamist way.'

Quinn hated the way he was being drawn into this conversation. It wasn't what he wanted, he'd seen himself making his pitch on how to subdue Aberdale, and the boss-man seeing the sense of it. Now he was having to think about freaky ideas like living for ever, and trying to make up an excuse why he didn't want to. Which was stupid because he did. But Laton couldn't possibly have it to offer anyway. Except this was a very high-technology operation, and he was using the girls for some kind of biological experiment. God's Brother, but Laton was a smooth one. 'So what's your way?' he asked reluctantly.

'A combination of affinity and parallel thought-processes. You know Edenists transfer their memories into their habitat's neural cells when they die?'

'I'd heard about it, yeah.'

'That's a form of immortality, although I consider it somewhat unsatisfactory. Identity fades after a few centuries. The will to live, if you like, is lost. Understandable, really, there are no human activities to maintain the spark of vitality which goads us on, all that's left is observation, living your life through your descendants' achievements. Hardly inspiring. So I began to explore the option of simply transferring my memories into a fresh body. There are several immediate problems which prevent a direct transfer. Firstly you require an empty brain capable of storing an adult's memories. An infant brain would be empty, but the capacity to retain an adult personality, the century and a half of accumulated memories that go towards making us who we are, that simply isn't there. So I began looking at the neuron structure to see if it could be improved. It's not an area that's been well researched. Brain size has been increased to provide a memory capacity capable of seeing you through a century and a half, and IQ has been raised a few points, but the actual structure is something the geneticists have left alone. I started to examine the idea of human parallel thought-processing, just like the Edenist habitats. They can hold a million conversations at once, as well as regulating their environment, acting as an administrative executive, and a thousand other functions, although they have only the one consciousness. Yet we poor mortal humans can only ever think about or do one thing at a time. I sought to reprofile a neural network so that it could conduct several operations simultaneously. That was the key. I realized that as there was no limit to the number of operations which could be conducted, you could even have multiple independent units, bonded by affinity, and sharing a single identity. That way, when one dies, there is no identity loss, the consciousness remains intact and a new unit is grown to replace it.'

'Unit?' Quinn said heavily. 'You mean a person?'

'I mean a human body with a modified brain, bonded to any number of cloned replicas via affinity. That is the project to which I have devoted my energies here in this exile. With some considerable degree of success, I might add, despite the difficulties of isolation. A parallel-processing brain has been designed, and my colleagues are currently sequencing it into my germ plasm's DNA. After that, my clones will be grown in exowombs. Our thoughts will be linked right from the moment of conception, they will feel what I feel, see what I see. My personality will reside in each of us equally, a homogenized presence. Ultimately, this original body will wither away to nothing, but I shall remain. Death shall become a thing of the past for me. Death will die. I intend to spread out through this world until its resources belong to me, its industries and its population. Then a new form of human society will take shape, one which is not governed by the blind overwhelming biological imperative to reproduce. We shall be more ordered, more deliberate. Ultimately I envisage incorporating bitek constructs into myself; as well as human bodies I will be starships and habitats. Life without temporal limit nor physical restriction. I shall transcend, Quinn; isn't that a dream worth chasing? And now I offer it to you. The homestead girls can provide enough ova for all of us to be cloned. Modifying your DNA is a simple matter, and each of your clones will breed true. You can join us, Quinn, you can live for ever. You can even deal with this

Banneth person; ten of you, twenty, an army of your mirror-selves can descend on her arcology to effect your revenge. Now doesn't that appeal, Quinn? Hasn't that got more style than rushing round a jungle at night carving people's guts out for a few thousand fuseodollars?'

Sheer willpower kept Quinn's face composed into an indifferent mask. He wished he had never come, wished he had never figured out the kestrel. God's Brother, how he wished. Banneth was nothing compared to this crazo, Banneth was pure reasoned sanity. Yet all the shit Laton spouted had a terrible logic, drawing him in like the dance of the black widow. Telling him he could be immortal was the same trick he had used against the Ivets, but with such demonic panache, blooding him in conspiracy, making sure there was no turning back. He knew Laton would never let him get to Durringham's spaceport, let alone reach an orbiting starship. Not now, not with him knowing. The only way out of this tree – this room! – with his brain still his own was by agreeing. And it was going to have to be the most convincing agreement he had ever made in his life.

'This spreading your mind around gimmick, would I have to give up my belief?' he asked.

Laton gave him a thin smile. 'Your belief would be amplified, safeguarded against loss in your multiple units, and carried down the centuries. You could even step out of the shadows to exhort your belief. What difference would it make if individual units were flung in jail or executed? The you that is you would remain.'

'And sex, I'd still have sex, wouldn't I?'

'Yes, with one small difference, every gene would be dominant. Every child you sired would be another of your units.'

'How far along are you with this parallel-processor brain? Have you actually grown one to see if it works?'

'A numerical simulacrum has been run through a bitek processor array. The analysis program proved its validity. It's a standard technique; the one Edenist geneticists used to design the voidhawks. They work, don't they?'

'Sure. Look, I'm interested. I can hardly deny that. God's Brother, living for ever, who wouldn't want it? Tell you what, I won't make any move to get back to Earth until after these clones of yours have popped out the exowombs. If they check out as good as you say, I'll be with you like a shot. If not, we'll review where we stand. Fuck, I don't mind waiting around a few years if that's what it takes to perfect it.'

'Commendable prudence,' Laton purred.

'Meantime, it'd be a good idea to bugger up Supervisor Manani's communicator block. For both our sakes. However it turns out, neither of us wants the villagers shouting to the capital for help. Can you let me have a flek loaded with some kind of processor-buster virus? If I just smash it, he's gonna know it's me.'

Anname walked in carrying a tray with Quinn's steak, and a half-litre glass of milk. She put it down on Quinn's lap, and glanced hesitantly at Laton.

'No, my dear,' Laton told her. 'This is definitely not St George come to spirit you away from my fire-breathing self.'

She sniffed hard, cheeks reddening.

Quinn grinned wolfishly at her round a mouthful of steak.

'I think I can live with that arrangement,' Laton said. 'I'll have one of my people prepare a flek for you before you go.'

Quinn slurped some of his milk, and wiped his mouth with the back of his hand. 'Great.'

*

There was something wrong with Aberdale's church. Only half of the pews had ever been built and installed, though Horst Elwes occasionally worked on the planks of planed wood the Ivets had cut ready for the remainder. He doubted the three pews he had already assembled in the occasional bouts of shame-induced activity would take the weight of more than four people. But the roof didn't leak, there was the familiarity of hymn books and vestments, the paraphernalia of worship, and he had a vast collection of devotional music on fleks which the audio-player block projected across the building. For all its deviant inception, it still symbolized a form of hope. Of late, it had become his refuge. Hallowed ground or not, and Horst wasn't stupid enough to think that was any form of protection, the Ivets never came inside.

But something had.

Horst stood in front of the bench which served as an altar, hair on his arms pricked up as though he was standing in some kind of massive static stream. There was a presence in the church, ethereal yet with an almost brutal strength. He could feel it watching him. He could feel age almost beyond comprehension. The first time Horst had seen a gigantea he had spent over an hour just looking up at it in stupefaction, a living thing that had been old when Christ walked the Earth. But the gigantea was nothing compared to this, the tree was a mere infant. Age, real age, was a fearful thing.

Horst didn't believe in ghosts. Besides, the presence was too real for that. It enervated the church, absorbing what scant ration of divinity had once existed.

'What are you?' he whispered to the gentle breeze. Night was falling outside, waving treetops cast a jagged sable-black silhouette against the gold-pink sky. The men were returning from the fields, sweaty and tired, but smiling. Voices carried through the clearing. Aberdale was so peaceful, it looked like everything he had wanted when he left Earth.

'What are you?' Horst demanded. 'This is a church, a house of God. I will have no sacrilege committed here. Only those who truly repent are welcome.'

For a giddy moment his thoughts were rushing headlong through empty space. The velocity was terrifying. He yelled in shock, there was nothing around him, no body, no stars. This was what he imagined the null-dimension that existed outside a starship would look like while it jumped.

Abruptly, he was back in the church. A small ruby star burnt in the air a couple of metres in front of him.

He stared at it in shock, then giggled. 'Twinkle twinkle, little star. How I wonder what you are.'

The star vanished.

His laughter turned to a strangled pule. He fled out into the dusky clearing, stumbling through the soft loam of his vegetable garden, heedless of the shabby plants he trampled.

It was his singing which drew the villagers a few hours later. He was sitting on the jetty with a bottle of home-brew vodka. The group that had gathered looked down at him with contempt.

'Demons!' Horst shouted when Powel Manani and a couple of the others pulled him to his feet. 'They've only gone and summoned bloody demons here.'

Ruth gave him one disgusted glance, and stalked off back to her cabin.

Horst was dragged back to his cot, where they administered one of his own tranquillizers. He fell asleep still mumbling warnings.

*

The Ly-cilph was interested in humans. Out of the hundred and seventy million sentient species it had encountered, only three hundred thousand had been able to perceive it, either by technology or their own mentalities.

The priest had clearly been aware of its identity focus, although not understanding the nature. Humans obviously had a rudimentary attunement to their energistic environment. It searched through the records it had compiled by accessing the few processor blocks and memory fleks available in Aberdale, which mostly comprised the educational texts owned by Ruth Hilton. The so-called psychic ability was largely dismissed as hallucinatory or fraud committed for financial gain. However the race had a vast history of incidents and myths in its past. And its strong continuing religious beliefs were an indication of how widespread the faculty was, granting the 'supernatural' events a respectable orthodoxy. There was obviously a great deal of potential for energistic perception development, which was inhibited by the rational mentality. The conflict was a familiar one to the Ly-cilph, although it had no record of a race in which the two opposing natures were quite so antagonistic.

*

What do you think? Laton asked his colleagues when the door closed behind Quinn Dexter.

He's a psychopathic little shit, with a nasty steak of sadism thrown in, said Waldsey, the group's chief viral technologist.

Dexter is certainly unstable, Camilla said. **I don't think you can trust him to keep any agreement. His revenge obsession with this Banneth person is the dominant motivator. Our immortality scheme is unlikely to replace it; too cerebral.**

I say we should eliminate him, Salkid said.

I'm inclined to agree, Laton said. **Pity. It's rather like watching a miniature version of one's self.**

You were never that gratuitous, Father, Camilla said.

Given the circumstances, I might have been. However, that is an irrelevant speculation. Our immediate problem is our own security. One can reasonably assume Quinn Dexter has informed most, if not all, of his fellow Ivets that something wicked lurks in the woods. That is going to make life difficult.

So? We just take out all of them, Salkid said. Out of all the exiles, the ex-blackhawk captain found the decades of inactivity hardest to handle. **I'll lead the incorporated. It'll be a pleasure.**

Salkid, stop acting the oaf, Laton said. **We can't possibly eliminate all the Ivets ourselves. The attention such an overt action would generate would be quite intolerable coming so soon after the homesteads.**

What, then?

Firstly we shall wait until Quinn Dexter incapacitates Supervisor Manani's communicator, then we shall have to get the villagers to eliminate the Ivets for us.

How? Waldsey asked.

The priest already knows the Ivets are Devil worshippers. We shall simply make the knowledge available to everyone else in a fashion they cannot possibly ignore.

12

Idria traced a slightly elliptical orbit through the Lyll asteroid belt in the New Californian system, with a median distance of a hundred and seventy million kilometres from the G5 primary star. It was a stony-iron rock, which looked like a bruised, flaking swede, measuring seventeen kilometres across at its broadest and eleven down the short spin axis. A ring formation of thirty-two industrial stations hung over the crinkled black rock, insatiable recipients of a never-ending flow of raw material ferried out from Idria's non-rotating spaceport.

It was the variety of those compounds which justified the considerable investment made in the rock. Idria's combination of resources was rare, and rarity always attracts money.

In 2402 a survey craft found long veins of minerals smeared like a diseased rainbow through the ordinary metal ores, their chemistry a curious mixture of sulphurs, alumina, and silicas. A planetside board meeting deemed that the particular concentration of crystalline strata was valuable enough to warrant an extraction operation; and the miners and their heavy digging machinery began chewing shafts into the interior in 2408. Industrial stations followed, refining and processing the ores on site. Population began to creep upwards, caverns were expanded, biospheres started. By 2450 the central cavern was five kilometres long and four wide, Idria's rotation was increased to give it a half-standard gravity on the floor. There were ninety thousand people living in it by then, forming a community which was self-sufficient in most areas. It was declared independent, and earned a seat in the system assembly. But it was a company town, the company being Lassen Interstellar.

Lassen was into mining, and shipping, and finance, and starship components, and military systems, amongst other endeavours. It was a typical New Californian outfit, a product of innumerable mergers and takeovers; a linear extension of its old Earth predecessors which had thrived on America's western seaboard. Its management worshipped the super-capitalist ethic, expanding aggressively, milking governments for development contracts, pressuring the assembly for ever more convenient tax breaks, spreading subsidiaries across the Confederation, shafting the opposition at every opportunity.

There were thousands of companies like it based on New California. Corporate tigers whose spoils elevated the standard of living right across the system. The nature of their competition was fierce and confrontational. The Confederation assembly had passed several censure motions on their dubious exports, and held inquiries into individual supply contracts. New California's level of technology was high, its military products were in great demand. Companies were indifferent to the use they would ultimately be put to: once the buyer was identified, the pitch made, the finance organized, nothing would be allowed to stop the sale. Not the Government Export Licence office, and certainly not the meddlesome Confederation inspectors. With this in mind, shipping could be a problem, especially the trickier contracts to star systems operating unreasonable embargoes. Captains who took on those contracts could expect high rewards. And the challenge always attracted a certain type of individual.

*

The *Lady Macbeth* was resting on a docking cradle in one of the thirty-odd industrial stations coasting in a loose orbit around Idria. Both of her circular cargo hold doors on the forward hull were open, each showing a metallic cave of bracing struts coiled by power and data cables, load clamps, and environmental regulation interface sockets; all of it wrapped in tarnished gold foil and badly illuminated to boot.

The docking bay was a seventy-five-metre crater of carbotanium and composite, ribbed by various conduits and pipes. Spotlights around the curving walls shone stark white beams on the starship's leaden hull, compensating for the pallid slivers of sunlight falling on the station while it was in Idria's penumbra. Several storage frames stood around the rim of the bay, looking much like scaffold towers left over from the station's construction. Each of them was equipped with a long quadruple-jointed waldo arm to load and unload cargo from ships. The arms were operated from a console inside small transparent bubbles protruding from the carbotanium surface like polished barnacles.

Joshua Calvert hung on a grab hoop inside the cargo supervisor's compartment, his face centimetres from the curving radiation-shielded glass, watching the waldo arm raising another cargo-pod out of its storage frame. The pods were two metres long, pressurized cylinders with slightly domed ends; a thick white silicon-composite shell protected them from the wider temperature shifts encountered in space. They were stamped with Lassen's geometric eagle logo, and line after line of red stencil lettering. According to the code they were high-density magnetic-compression coils for tokamaks. And ninety per cent of the pods did indeed contain what they said; the other ten per cent held smaller, more compact coils which produced an even stronger magnetic field, suitable for antimatter confinement.

The waldo arm lowered the pod into *Lady Mac*'s hold, and a set of load clamps closed around it. Joshua felt a considerable twinge of apprehension. Inside the New Californian system the coils were a legitimate cargo, no matter the misleading coding. In interstellar space their legality was extremely ambiguous, although a decent lawyer should be able to quash any charges. And in the Puerto de Santa Maria system where he was going they spelt deep shit in capital letters ten metres high.

Sarha Mitcham's hand tightened around his. 'Do we really need this?' she asked in a murmur. She had left her padded skullcap off in the transparent hemisphere, letting her short hazel hair wave around lethargically in free fall. Her lips were drawn together in concern.

' 'Fraid so.' He tickled her palm with a finger, a private signal they often used on board *Lady Mac.* Sarha was a spirited lover, they had spent long hours experimenting in his cabin's cage; but this time it didn't break her mood.

It wasn't that the *Lady Macbeth* didn't make money: in the eight months since Roland Frampton's first charter they had landed seven cargoes and one passenger group, some bacteriology specialists on their way to join an ecology review team on Northway. But *Lady Macbeth* also consumed money at a colossal rate: there was fuel and consumables each time they docked; an endless list of component spares, there wasn't a flight which went by without some kind of burn-out or a mandatory time-expiry replacement; the crew's wages had to be met; and then there were spaceport charges and customs and immigration fees. Joshua hadn't quite realized the sheer expense involved in operating the *Lady Macbeth.* Somehow Marcus Calvert had glossed over that part. Profits were slim verging on non-existent, and he couldn't afford to bump his rates up any higher, he wouldn't land a single charter. He'd made more money while he was scavenging.

So now he knew the truth behind the captains' talk in Harkey's Bar, and its countless equivalents across the Confederation. Like him they all said how well they were doing, how they only kept flying for the life it offered rather than financial necessity. Lies, all of it a magnificent, artistic construct of lies. Banks sat back and made money, everyone else worked for a living.

'There's no shame in it,' Hasan Rawand had told him a fortnight ago. 'Everyone's in the same grind. Hell, Joshua, you're a lot better off than most of us. You haven't got a mortgage to pay off.'

Hasan Rawand was the captain of the *Dechal*, an independent trader smaller than the *Lady Mac*. He was in his mid-seventies, and he'd been flying for fifty years, the last fifteen as an owner-captain.

'The real money isn't in cargo charters,' he explained. 'Not for people like us. That's just makework to tide us over. The big lines have got all the really profitable routes tied up. They operate vacuum-sealed cartels the likes of you and I aren't going to break in.'

They were drinking in a club in the dormitory section of an industrial station orbiting Baydon, a two-kilometre alithium wheel spinning to produce a two-thirds standard gravity around the rim. Joshua leant against the bar, and watched the planet's nightside sliding past the huge window. Sparkles of light from cities and towns sketched strange curves across the darkness.

'Where is the money, then?' Joshua asked. He'd been drinking for three solid hours, long enough to sluice enough alcohol past his enhanced organs and into his brain, giving the universe a snug aura.

'Flights which use that fancy fourth drive tube the *Lady Mac*'s fitted out with.'

'Forget it, I'm not that anxious to make money.'

'All right, OK,' Hasan Rawand gestured extravagantly, beer slopping over his glass, drops falling in a slight curve. 'I'm just saying that's the nature of it: combat and sanctions busting. That kind of thing is what the independents like you and me were put in this galaxy for. Everybody makes one of those trips every now and then. Some of us, like me, more often than most. That's what keeps the hull intact, and the radiation outside the baffles.'

'You make a lot of runs?' Joshua asked, staring into his glass morosely.

'Some. Not a lot. That's where us owner-captains' bad-boy reputation comes from. People think we do it all the time. We don't. But they don't hear about that, about the mundane flights we make for fifty weeks a year. They only hear about us when we get caught, and the news agencies blitz the networks with the arrest. We're the perpetual victims of bad publicity. We should sue.'

'But you don't get caught?'

'Haven't yet. There's a method I use, virtually foolproof, but it needs two ships.'

'Ah.' Joshua must have been drunker than he realized, because the next thing he heard himself saying was: 'Tell me more.'

And now two weeks later he was starting to regret listening. Although, he had to admit, it damn near was foolproof. Those two weeks had been spent in furious preparation. In a way, he supposed having Hasan Rawand consider him for any kind of partner was an oblique compliment, since only the very best captains could hope to pull it off. And the ultimate risk wasn't his, not this run. He was the junior partner. But still, twenty per cent wasn't to be sneered at, not when it came to a straight eight hundred thousand fuseodollars, half in advance.

The last pod of magnetic coils was secured in the *Lady Mac*'s cargo hold. Sarha Mitcham let out a soft, rueful sigh as the waldo arm folded down on its cradle. This flight worried her, but she had agreed, along with the rest of the crew when Joshua explained what it entailed. And their money situation was becoming uncomfortably shaky. Even the fleks of MF-band albums the crew always hawked around ports to the bootleg distributors were fetching minimal prices. A lot of her private stock was getting obsolete, official company distribution was catching up on her. Here on Idria she had actually bought more albums than she'd sold. At least New California was a hot system for MF culture, she ought to be able to sell the fresh recordings for another six months yet, especially on the kind of backworld ports *Lady Macbeth* flew to.

The money would go into the crew's pooled account so they could finance their own cargo in a couple of months' time. It was their one bright dream, which made the mundane tolerable. Norfolk was reaching conjunction soon, a cargo of Tears would make some real profit for them if they owned it rather than simply carried it for someone else. And then just maybe they wouldn't have to do this kind of flight again for a long time.

'All loaded, and not a scratch on your hull,' the woman operating the waldo arm said cheerfully.

Joshua looked back over his shoulder and smiled at her. She was slender, and a bit tall for his taste, but her one-piece uniform showed a nice collection of curves below its emerald fabric. 'Yeah, good work, thanks.' He datavised her console, loading in his personal code to confirm the cargo had been transferred on board the *Lady Mac.*

She checked the data, and handed him his manifest flek. '*Bon voyage*, Captain.'

Joshua and Sarha glided out of the compartment, negotiating the maze of narrow corridors down to the telescoping airlock tube that linked the *Lady Mac's* life support capsules to the station.

The waldo operator waited for a minute after they left, then closed her eyes. **The cargo pods are all loaded. *Lady Macbeth* is scheduled to disengage from the station in eighteen minutes.**

Thank you, *Oenone* replied.

*

Tranquillity's senses perceived the gravitational disturbance caused by the wormhole terminus opening in a designated emergence zone a hundred and fifteen thousand kilometres away from the habitat itself. Against Mirchusko's mud-yellow immensity the terminus was a neutral two-dimensional disk. Yet observing it through an optical sensor on one of the strategic-defence platforms ringing the zone, Tranquillity received an inordinately powerful intimation of *depth.*

Ilex flew out of the wormhole. A voidhawk with a hull that was more grey than the usual blue. It slipped smoothly away from the rapidly shrinking terminus, yawing gracefully as it orientated itself.

***Ilex*, Confederation Navy ship ALV-90100, requesting approach and docking permission**, it said formally.

Granted, Tranquillity replied.

The voidhawk accelerated in towards the habitat, building up to three gees almost immediately.

You're very welcome, Tranquillity said. **I don't get many voidhawks visiting me.**

Thank you. Though this is not a privilege I was expecting. Up until three days ago we were assigned to fleet patrol duties in the Ellas sector. Now we've been switched to diplomatic courier duty. My captain, Auster, is experiencing a mild notion of displeasure, he says we didn't sign on to be used as a taxi service.

Oh, this sounds interesting.

I believe the circumstances are exceptional. And in connection with this, my captain has another request. He asks that Ione Saldana receive a special envoy from First Admiral Samual Aleksandrovich: one Captain Maynard Khanna.

You have come directly from Avon to bring this captain?

Yes.

The Lord of Ruin is honoured to accept the Admiral's envoy, and she invites Captain Auster and his crew to dinner this evening.

My captain accepts. He is curious about Ione Saldana, the news agencies have been most effusive on her behalf.

I could tell you a tale or two about her.

Really?

And I'd be interested to hear about the Ellas sector. Are there many pirates there?

*

The tube carriage slid to a halt and Captain Khanna stepped out onto the small station's platform. He was thirty-eight years old, with crew-cut sandy red hair, pale skin given to freckles if he was caught by the sun, regular features, and dark brown eyes. His body was kept in trim by a stiff forty-minute navy-approved workout each morning without fail. Out of his academy class of one hundred and fifteen officer cadets he had finished third; it would have been first but the computer psychological assessment said his flexibility wasn't all that it could be, he was 'doctrine orientated'.

He had been on the First Admiral's executive staff for eighteen months, and in that time hadn't made a single mistake. This was his first independent assignment, and he was frankly terrified. Tactics and command decisions he could handle, even Admiralty office politics; but a semi-reclusive universally revered black sheep Saldana teenage girl affinity-bonded to a non-Edenist bitek habitat was another matter. How the hell did you prepare motivation-analysis profiles on such a creature?

'You'll do all right,' Admiral Aleksandrovich had said in his final briefing. 'Young enough not to alienate her, smart enough not to insult her intelligence. And all the girls love a uniform.' The old man had winked and given him a companionable pat on the back.

Maynard Khanna pulled the jacket of his immaculate deep-blue dress uniform straight, placed his peaked cap firmly on his head, squared his shoulders, and marched up the stairs out of the station. He came out onto a courtyard of flagstones, lined with troughs full of colourful begonias and fuchsias. Paths led off from all sides into the surrounding sub-tropical parkland. He could see some sort of building a hundred metres away; but it was given only a fleeting glance as he stared round in astonishment. After coming through the airlock from the docking-ledge he had climbed straight into the waiting tube carriage, he hadn't seen anything of the interior until now. The sheer size of Tranquillity was awesome, big enough to put a couple of standard Edenist habitats inside and shake them around like dice in a cup. A blinding light-tube glared hotly overhead, white candyfloss clouds trailed slowly through the air. A panorama of forests and meadows flecked with silver lakes and long watercourses rose up on either side of him like the walls of God's own valley. And there was a sea about eight kilometres away – it couldn't be called anything else with its sparkling wavelets and picturesque islands. He followed the arch of it rising up and up, his neck tilting back until his cap threatened to fall off. Millions of tonnes of water were poised above him ready to crash down in a flood which would have defeated Noah.

He brought his head down hurriedly, trying to remember how he had got rid of the giddiness when he visited the Edenist habitats orbiting Jupiter.

'Don't look outside the horizontal, and always remember the poor sod above you thinks you're going to fall on him,' his crusty old guide had said.

Knowing he had been defeated before he even started, Maynard Khanna walked along the yellow-brown stone path towards the building that resembled a Hellenic temple. It was a long basilica which had one end opening out into a circular area with a domed roof of some jet-black material supported by white pillars, the gaps between them filled by sheets of blue-mirror glass.

The path took him to the opposite end of the basilica, where a pair of serjeants stood guard duty like nightmare goblin statues on either side of the entrance arch.

'Captain Khanna?' one asked. The voice was mild and friendly, completely at odds with its appearance.

'Yes.'

'The Lord of Ruin is expecting you, please follow my servitor.' The serjeant turned and led him into the building. They walked down a central nave with large gilt-framed pictures hanging on the brown and white marble walls.

Maynard Khanna assumed they were holograms at first, then he realized they were two-dimensional, and a more detailed look revealed that they were oil paintings. There were a lot of countryside scenes where people wore elaborate, if baroque, costumes, riding on horses or gathered in ostentatious groups. Scenes from old Earth, pre-industrial age. And a Saldana would never make do with copies. They must be genuine. His mind balked at how much they must be worth; you could buy a battle cruiser with the money just one of them would fetch.

At the far end of the nave a Vostok capsule was resting on a cradle under a protective glass dome. Maynard stopped and looked at the battered old sphere with a mixture of trepidation and admiration. It was so small, so *crude*, yet for a few brief years it had represented the pinnacle of human technology. What ever would the cosmonaut who rode it into space think of Tranquillity?

'Which one is it?' he asked the serjeant in a hushed tone.

'Vostok 6, it carried Valentina Tereshkova into orbit in 1963. She was the first woman in space.'

Ione Saldana was waiting for him in the large circular audience chamber at the end of the nave. She sat behind a crescent-shaped wooden desk positioned in the centre; thick planes of light streamed in through the giant sheets of glass set between the pillars, turning the air into a platinum haze.

The white polyp floor was etched with a giant crowned phoenix emblem in scarlet and blue. It took an eternity for him to cover the distance from the door to the desk; the sound of his boot heels clicking against the polished surface echoed drily in the huge empty space.

Intended to intimidate, he thought. You know how alone you are when you confront her.

He snapped a perfect salute when he reached the desk. She was a head of state, after all; the Admiral's protocol office had been most insistent about that, and how he should treat her.

Ione was wearing a simple sea-green summer dress with long sleeves. The intense lighting made her short gold-blonde hair glimmer softly.

She was just as lovely as all the AV recordings he'd studied.

'Do take a seat, Captain Khanna,' she said, smiling. 'You look most uncomfortable standing up like that.'

'Thank you, ma'am.' There were two high-backed chairs on his side of the desk; he sat in one, still keeping his poise rigid.

'I understand you've come all the way from the First Fleet headquarters at Avon just to see me?'

'Yes, ma'am.'

'In a voidhawk?'

'Yes, ma'am.'

'Owing to the somewhat unusual nature of this worldlet, we don't have a diplomatic corps, nor a civil service,' she said airily. A delicate hand waved around at the audience chamber. 'The habitat personality handles all the administrative functions quite effectively. But the Lords of Ruin employ a legal firm on Avon to represent Tranquillity's interests in the Confederation Assembly chamber. If there's a matter of urgency arising, you only have to consult them. I have met the senior partners, and I have a lot of confidence in them.'

'Yes, ma'am—'

'Maynard, please. Stop calling me ma'am. This is a private meeting, and you're making me sound like a day-club governess for junior aristocrats.'

'Yes, Ione.'

She smiled brightly. The effect was devastating. Her eyes were an enchanting shade of blue, he noticed.

'That's better,' she said. 'Now what have you come to talk about?'

'Dr Alkad Mzu.'

'Ah.'

'Are you familiar with the name?'

'The name and most of the circumstances.'

'Admiral Aleksandrovich felt this was not a matter to take to your legal representatives on Avon. It is his opinion that the fewer people who are aware of the situation, the better.'

Her smile turned speculative. 'Fewer people? Maynard, there are eight different Intelligence agencies who have set up shop in Tranquillity; and all of them run surveillance operations on poor Dr Mzu. There are times when their pursuit becomes dangerously close to a slapstick routine. Even the Kulu ESA have posted a team here. I imagine that must be a real thorn in my cousin Alastair's regal pride.'

'I think what the Admiral meant was: fewer people outside high government office.'

'Yes, of course, the people *most* able to deal with the situation.'

The irony in her tone made Maynard Khanna give an inward flinch. 'In view of the fact that Dr Mzu is now contacting a number of starship captains, and the Omutan sanctions are about to expire, the Admiral would be extremely grateful if we could be told of your policy regarding Dr Mzu,' he said formally.

'Are you recording this for the Admiral?'

'Yes, a full sensevise.'

Ione stared straight into his eyes, speaking in a clear precise diction. 'My father promised Admiral Aleksandrovich's predecessor that Dr Alkad Mzu would never be allowed to leave Tranquillity, and I repeat that promise to the Admiral. She will not be permitted to leave, nor will I countenance any attempt to sell or hand over the information she presumably holds to anybody, including the Confederation Navy. Upon her death, she will be cremated in order to destroy her neural nanonics. And I hope to God that sees the end of the threat.'

'Thank you,' Maynard Khanna said.

Ione relaxed a little. 'I hadn't even been gestated when she arrived here twenty-six years ago, so tell me, I'm curious. Has Fleet Intelligence discovered yet how she survived Garissa's destruction?'

'No. She can't have been on the planet. The Confederation Navy was in charge of the evacuation, and we have no record of carrying her on any of our ships. Nor was she listed as being in any of the asteroid settlements. The only logical conclusion is that she was outsystem on some kind of clandestine military mission when Omuta bombed Garissa.'

'Deploying the Alchemist?'

'Who knows. The device certainly wasn't used; so either it didn't work or they were intercepted. The general staff favours the interception scenario.'

'And if she survived, so did the Alchemist,' Ione concluded.

'If it was ever built.'

She raised an eyebrow. 'After all this time, I thought that was taken for granted.'

'The thinking goes that after all this time, we should have heard something other than rumours. If it does exist, why haven't the Garissan survivors tried to use it against Omuta?'

'When it comes to Doomsday machines, rumours are all I want to hear.'

'Yes.'

'You know, I've watched her sometimes while she's been working over in the Laymil project's physics centre. She's a good physicist, her colleagues respect her. But she's nothing exceptional, not mentally.'

'One idea in a lifetime is all it takes.'

'You're right. Clever of her to come here, really. The one place where her security is guaranteed, and at the same time the one mini-nation which everybody knows is no military threat to other Confederation members.'

'So may I say you have no objection to our maintaining our observation team?'

'You can, providing you don't flaunt the privilege. But please reassure yourselves. I don't think she's received much geneering, if any. She can't last more than another thirty years, forty at the outside. Then it will all be over.'

'Excellent.' He leant forward a few millimetres, lips moving upwards into a slight awkward smile. 'There was one other matter.'

Ione's eyes widened with innocent anticipation. 'Yes?'

'An independent trader captain called Joshua Calvert mentioned your name in connection with one of our agents.'

She squinted up at the ceiling as if lost in a particularly difficult feat of recall. 'Oh, yes, Joshua. I remember him, he caused quite a stir at the start of the year. Found a big chunk of Laymil electronics in the Ruin Ring. I met him at a party once. A nice young man.'

'Yes,' Maynard Khanna said gingerly. 'So you didn't warn him about Erick Thakrar being one of our deep-cover operatives?'

'Erick Thakrar's name never passed my lips. Actually, Thakrar has just been accepted by Captain André Duchamp for a berth on the *Villeneuve's Revenge*, that's an Adamist ship with an antimatter drive fitted. I'm sure Commander Olsen Neale will confirm that for you. Erick Thakrar's cover is completely intact, I can assure you that André Duchamp doesn't suspect a thing.'

'Well, that's a great relief, the Admiral will be pleased.'

'I'm glad to hear it. And please don't concern yourself over Joshua Calvert, I'm sure he'd never do anything illegal, he's really an exemplary citizen.'

*

The *Lady Macbeth* is preparing to jump insystem, *Oenone* warned the crew. They were two light-weeks from Puerto de Santa Maria's star, which cast a barely perceptible shadow on the voidhawk's foam-encased hull. The *Nephele* was drifting eight hundred kilometres over the upper hull, yet *Oenone*'s optical sensors were unable to see it.

Twenty-eight thousand kilometres further in towards the faint star, the *Lady Macbeth*'s sensor clusters and thermo-dump panels were folding with the neatness of an alighting eagle.

If only everything about the Adamist starship's flight was that neat, Syrinx wished. This Captain Calvert was a born incompetent. It had taken them six days to get here from New California, a distance of fifty-three light-years. The manoeuvres which *Lady Macbeth* performed every time she reached a jump coordinate were appallingly sloppy, they went on for hours at a time. Time was money in the cargo business. And if this was the way Calvert navigated on every voyage it was no wonder he needed the money so desperately.

'Stand by,' Syrinx told Larry Kouritz. 'He's lined up on the Ciudad asteroid.'

'Roger,' the marine captain acknowledged.

'The Ciudad,' Eileen Carouch muttered as she accessed the Puerto de Santa Maria file in her neural nanonics. 'There are several insurrectionist cells based there, according to the planetary government's Intelligence agency. They are pushing hard for independence.'

Attention everybody, Syrinx broadcast, **I want us out of stealth mode the moment we emerge. This *Lady Macbeth* is fitted with maser cannons, so let's not have any mistakes. Chi, you have fire-control authority as of now. If they make one smartarse move, slice them in two. *Nephele*, you keep a sharp watch for approaching ships. If these insurrectionists are desperate enough to try and obtain antimatter-confinement technology they may be dumb enough to try and assist their courier.**

We'll cover you, Targard, the *Nephele*'s captain, replied.

Syrinx returned her attention to *Oenone*'s sensor inputs. The *Lady Macbeth* had reverted to a perfect sphere. Blue ion flames shrank away to nothing. There was a sharp twist in space's uniformity.

Go, she commanded.

Oenone erupted out of the wormhole terminus seventeen hundred kilometres distant from the *Lady Macbeth.* A blizzard of foam flakes swirled away as electronic sensors and thermo-dump panels were uncovered around the crew toroid. Fusion generators in the lower hull combat systems toroid powered up. X-ray lasers deployed. Gravity returned to the crew toroid. The distortion field swelled outwards, accelerating the voidhawk up to seven gees. It chased a sharp curve round to align on the *Lady Macbeth.* Two hundred kilometres away the *Nephele* was shaking off its stealth cloak.

Ciudad was a distant lacklustre speck, with a small constellation of industrial stations wrapped around it. Strategic defence sensor radiation raked across the *Oenone.*

Syrinx was aware of a curious secondary oscillation in the distortion field. Foam was streaming away from all across the hull.

That's better, *Oenone* sighed almost subliminally.

Syrinx didn't have time to form a rebuke. A transmitter dish unfolded from the lower hull toroid, swinging round to focus on the *Lady Macbeth.*

'Starship *Lady Macbeth*,' she relayed through the transmitter's bitek processors. 'This is Confederation Navy ship *Oenone.* You are ordered to hold your position. Do not activate your reaction drive, do not attempt to jump away. Stand by for rendezvous and boarding.'

Oenone's distortion field reached out to engulf the Adamist starship.

Syrinx could hear Tula communicating with Ciudad's defence control centre, informing them of the interception.

'Hi there, *Oenone*,' Joshua Calvert's voice came cheerfully out of the bridge's AV pillars. 'Are you in some kind of trouble? How can we assist?'

Lying prone on her couch, her teeth gritted against the four-gee acceleration, Syrinx could only glance at the offending pillar in disconcerted amazement.

*

Oenone covered the last five kilometres cautiously, every sensor and weapon trained on the *Lady Macbeth*, alert for the slightest hint of treachery. At a hundred and fifty metres' distance, the voidhawk rotated slowly, presenting its upper hull towards the Adamist starship. The two extended airlock tubes, then touched and sealed. Larry Kouritz led his squad into the *Lady Macbeth*'s life-support capsules, executing the penetration and securement procedures with textbook precision.

Syrinx watched through *Oenone*'s sensor blisters as the crew toroid's clamshell hangar doors hinged apart. Oxley piloted their small boxy multifunction service vehicle out into space, yellow-orange chemical flames propelling it round towards *Lady Macbeth*'s open cargo hatch.

Joshua Calvert was marched into the bridge by two marines in dark carbotanium armour suits. He grinned round affably at the members of Syrinx's crew, with an even wider display of teeth when his eyes found her.

She shifted uncomfortably under the handsome young man's attention. This was not how the interception was supposed to be going.

We've been had, Ruben told her abruptly.

Syrinx flicked a glance at her lover. He was sitting behind his console, an expression of glum resignation settling on his features. He combed his fingers back through his beret of curly white hair.

What do you mean? she asked.

Oh, just look at him, Syrinx. Does that look like a man facing a forty-year sentence for smuggling?

We were on the *Lady Macbeth* for the whole flight, she never rendezvoused with anybody.

Ruben simply raised an ironic eyebrow.

She returned her attention to the tall captain. She was annoyed at the way his gaze seemed to be fastened on her breasts.

'Captain Syrinx,' he said warmly. 'I must congratulate you and your ship. That was a superb piece of flying, really quite superb. Jesus, you scared the crap out of some of my crew the way you jumped us like that. We thought you were a pair of blackhawks.' He stuck his hand out. 'It's a pleasure to meet a captain who is so obviously talented. And I hope you don't take offence, but an extremely attractive captain as well.'

Yes, we've definitely been had.

Syrinx ignored the offered hand. 'Captain Calvert, we have reason to suspect you are involved with importing proscribed technology into this star system. I am therefore cautioning you that your ship will be searched under the powers invested in me by the Confederation Assembly. Any refusal to permit our search is a violation of Confederation space regulatory code which permits lawful officers full access to all systems and records once a request has been made by said officers. I am now making that request. Do you understand?'

'Well, gosh, yes,' Joshua said earnestly. A note of doubt crept in. 'I hate to ask, but are you quite sure you've got the right ship?'

'Perfectly sure,' Syrinx said icily.

'Oh, well of course I'll cooperate in any way I can. I think you navy people do a great job. It's always reassuring for us commercial vessels to know we can always rely on you to maintain interstellar order.'

'Please. Don't spoil the effect now, son,' Ruben said wearily. 'You've been doing so well.'

'I'm just a citizen happy to oblige,' Joshua said.

'A citizen who owns a ship that has an antimatter drive,' Syrinx said sharply.

Joshua's gaze refocused on the front of her pale blue ship-tunic. 'I didn't design it. That's the way it was built. Actually it was built by the Ferring Astronautics company in Earth's O'Neill Halo. I understand Earth is the greatest Edenist ally in the Confederation? That's what my didactic history courses say, anyway.'

'We have a common viewpoint,' Syrinx said reluctantly, anything else would have sounded like an admission of guilt.

'Couldn't you have the drive taken out?' Ruben asked.

Joshua managed an appropriately concerned expression. 'I wish I could afford to. But there was a lot of damage when my father saved those Edenists from the pirates. The refit took all the money I had.'

'Saved which Edenists?' Cacus blurted.

Idiot, Syrinx and Ruben told him together. The life-support engineer spread his hands helplessly.

'It was an aid convoy to Anglade,' Joshua said. 'There was a bacteriological plague there several years ago. My father joined the relief effort, of course; what are commercial needs compared to saving human life? They were taking viral-processing equipment to the planet to manufacture an antidote. Unfortunately they were attacked by blackhawks who wanted to steal the cargo, that kind of equipment is expensive. Jesus, I mean some people are really low, you know? There was a fight, and one of the escort voidhawks was wounded. The blackhawks were closing in for the kill, but my father waited until the crew got out. He jumped with a blackhawk's distortion field locked on. It was the only chance they had, they were badly damaged, but the old *Lady Mac*, she got them out alive.' Joshua closed his eyes, remembering old pain. 'Father didn't like to mention it much.'

No kidding? Ruben asked heavily.

Was there ever a plague on Anglade? Tula asked.

Yes, *Oenone* said. **Twenty-three years ago. I don't have any record of an attack on an aid convoy, though.**

You do surprise me, Syrinx said.

This captain seems to be a nice young man, *Oenone* said. **He's obviously very taken with you.**

I'd sooner join an Adamist nunnery. And just leave the psychological analysis to us humans, please.

The silence in her mind was reproachful.

'Yes, well, that was the past,' Syrinx said awkwardly to Joshua Calvert. 'Your problem is here in the present.'

Syrinx? Oxley called.

The cautious mental tone warned her. **Yes?**

We've opened two of their cargo-pods. They both contain the tokamak coils listed in the manifest. No antimatter-confinement technology in sight.

What? They can't have tokamak coils. She looked through Oxley's eyes into the MSV's tiny cabin. Eileen Carouch was strapped in a web next to him; several screens were covered in complicated multi-coloured graphics. The liaison officer wore a worried frown as she studied the displays. Outside the port, Syrinx could see one of the *Lady Macbeth*'s cargo-pods gripped in the MSV's heavy-duty waldo arm. It had been opened, and the tokamak coils had been removed by some of the mandible-like manipulator waldos.

Eileen Carouch turned to face Oxley. 'It doesn't look good. According to our information both of these pods should contain the confinement coils.'

We've been had, Ruben said.

Will you stop saying that, Syrinx demanded.

What do you want us to do? Oxley asked.

Examine every pod supposed to hold the antimatter-confinement coils.

OK.

'Everything all right?' Joshua asked.

Syrinx opened her eyes, and manufactured a killer-sweet smile. 'Just fine, thank you.'

Eileen Carouch and Oxley opened all eighteen cargo-pods supposed to contain the illegal coils. In every one they found neatly packaged tokamak coils.

Syrinx ordered them to open another five pods at random. They contained tokamak coils.

Syrinx gave up. Ruben was right, they'd been had.

*

That night she lay on her bunk, unable to sleep even though the body tensions due to ten days of enforced stealth routine had almost abated. Ruben was asleep beside her. There had been no prospect of sex when they came off duty, her mood was too black. He seemed to accept their defeat with a phlegmatism which she found annoying.

Where did we go wrong? she asked *Oenone*. **That ratty old ship was never out of your sight. You followed them superbly. I was more worried about the *Nephele* keeping up. Its spacial orientation isn't a patch on yours.**

Perhaps it was the operatives at Idria who lost track of the coils?

They were very certain the coils had been put on board. I could accept Calvert hiding one set in the ship, there's a lot of cubic volume there, but not eighteen.

There must have been a switch.

But how?

I don't know. I'm sorry.

Hey, it's not your fault. You did everything you were asked to, even when you were coated in foam.

I hate that stuff.

I know. Well, we've only got another two months to go. We'll be civilians after that.

Great!

Syrinx smiled in the cabin's half light. **I thought you liked military duty.**

I do.

But?

But it's lonely, all those patrols. When we're on commercial runs we'll meet lots of other voidhawks and habitats. It'll be fun.

Yes, I suppose it will. It's just that I would have liked to finish on a high note.

Joshua Calvert?

Yes! He was laughing at us.

I thought he was nice. Young and carefree, roaming the universe. Very romantic.

Please! He won't be roaming it for much longer. Not with an ego like that. He'll make a mistake soon enough, that sheer arrogance of his will force him into it. I'm only sorry we won't be there when he does. She put an arm over Ruben so that he would know she wasn't angry with him when he woke. But when she closed her eyes the normal vista of starfields that accompanied her into sleep had been replaced by a roguish smile and a rugged face that was all angles.

13

His name was Carter McBride, and he was ten years old; an only child, the pride of his parents Dimitri and Victoria, who spoilt him as best their circumstances would allow. Like most of Aberdale's younger generation he enjoyed the jungle and the river; Lalonde was much more fun than the cheerless dry concrete, steel, and composite caves of Earth's arcologies. The opportunities for games in his new land were limitless. He had his own little garden in the corner of his father's field, which he kept chock-full of strawberry plants, geneered so that the big scarlet fruits didn't rot in the rain and humidity. He had a copper spaniel called Chomper that was always getting underfoot and making off with clothes from the McBride cabin. He was receiving didactic courses from Ruth Hilton, who said he was absorbing the agronomy data at a satisfactory rate, and would make a promising farmer one day. And because he was almost eleven his parents trusted him to play unsupervised, saying he was responsible enough not to wander too far into the jungle.

The morning after Horst Elwes encountered the Ly-cilph in the church, Carter was down by the river where he and the other kids were building a raft from scraps of timber left over from one of the adults' construction projects. He realized that he hadn't seen Chomper for about fifteen minutes, and looked around the clearing. A flash of ginger fur in the trees behind the community hall made him shout in exasperation at the silly animal. There was no immediate response, so he set off in vigorous pursuit, boots kicking up a splash in the thin layer of mud. By the time he reached the boundary of the jungle he could hear Chomper barking excitedly somewhere inside the crush of trees and creepers. He waved at Mr Travis, who was hoeing the soil around his baby pineapple plants, and plunged into the jungle after his dog.

Chomper seemed intent on leading him directly away from the village. Carter called and called until his throat felt raw. He was hot and sticky and his fraying T-shirt was smeared in long streaks of green-yellow sap from the broken creepers. He was also very angry with Chomper, who was going to be put on a choker lead as soon as they got home. And after that there would be the proper obedience-training classes that Mr Manani had promised him.

The chase finally came to an end in a small glade of tall qualtook trees, whose thick canopy of foliage didn't let much sunlight through. Spindly blades of grass grew up to Carter's knees, vines with a mass of lemon-coloured berries foamed up around the glossy trunks. Chomper was standing in the middle of the glade, his hackles raised, growling at a tree.

Carter grabbed hold of his neck, yelling out exactly what he thought of dogs at that moment. The spaniel resisted the pulling and urging, yapping frantically.

'What's the matter with you?' he demanded in exasperation.

Then the tall black lady appeared. One second there was only a qualtook tree in front of him, the next she was standing five metres away, dressed in a grey jump suit, and pulling her hood off. Long chestnut hair tumbled down.

Chomper had fallen silent. Carter clung to him, gazing at the lady with his mouth open, too surprised to say anything. She winked and beckoned. Carter smiled up at her trustingly, and trotted over.

*

Got him, Camilla said. **He's very sweet.**

So is my neck, Laton replied curtly. **Just make sure you leave him where they can find him without too much trouble.**

*

'Horst, this can't go on,' Ruth said.

The priest just groaned with immense self-pity. He was lying on the cot where he'd been dumped the night before, crumpled olive-green blankets wound tightly round his legs. Sometime during the night he'd been sick again. A congealing puddle of waxy vomit lay on the floorboards below his pillow.

'Go away,' he mumbled.

'Stop feeling so bloody sorry for yourself, and get up.'

He rolled over slowly. She could see he'd been crying, his eyes were red rimmed, the lashes sticky. 'I mean it, Ruth. Go away, right away. Take Jay with you, and leave. Find a boat, pay whatever it costs, get yourself back to Durringham, then get off this planet. Just *leave*.'

'Stop talking like an idiot. Aberdale isn't that bad. We'll find a way to deal with the Ivets. I'm going to have Rai Molvi call a town meeting tonight, I'm going to tell people what I think is going on.' She took a breath. 'I want you to back me up, Horst.'

'No. You mustn't. Don't antagonize the Ivets. Please, for your own safety, Ruth. Don't do it. There's still time for you to get away.'

'For God's sake, Horst—'

'Ha! God is dead,' he said bitterly. 'Or at least He's banished this planet from His kingdom long ago.' He beckoned her down with an agitated hand signal, glancing furtively at the open door.

Ruth took a reluctant step closer to the cot, wrinkling her nose up at the smell.

'I saw it,' Horst said in a throaty whisper. 'Last night. It was there in the church.'

'What was there?'

'It. The demon they've summoned. I saw it, Ruth. Red, gleaming red, blinding red. The light of hell. Satan's eye opened and stared right at me. This is his world, Ruth. Not our lord Christ's. We should never have come here. Never.'

'Oh, shit,' she murmured under her breath. A whole host of practical problems ran through her mind: how to get him back to Durringham, whether there was even a psychiatrist on the planet, who could take over the little clinic he ran for the village. She scratched at the back of her sweaty hair, looking down at him as if he was some kind of elaborate riddle she was supposed to solve.

Rai Molvi ran up the wooden steps to the door and barged in. 'Ruth,' he said breathlessly. 'I thought I'd find you here. Carter McBride is missing; kid's been gone a couple of hours now. Someone said they saw him chasing that damn nuisance dog of his into the jungle. I'm organizing a search party. Are you in?' Rai Molvi didn't even seem to have noticed Horst.

'Yes,' she said. 'I'll get someone to watch Jay.'

'Mrs Cranthorp is taking care of that, she'll get the kids into a group and give them some lunch. We're assembling by the hall in ten minutes.' He turned to go.

'I'll help,' Horst said.

'As you like,' Rai said, and hurried out.

'Well, you made a big impression on him,' Ruth said.

'Please, Ruth, you must leave this place.'

'We'll see after tonight. Right now I've got a child to help find.' She paused. 'Damn, Carter's about the same age as Jay.'

*

The drawn-out whistle brought them all running. Arnold Travis was sitting slumped against the foot of a mayope tree. He just stared brokenly at the ground, silver whistle hanging from a corner of his mouth.

The villagers arrived in pairs, crashing through the vines and scrub bushes, sending hordes of birds screeching into the baking sky. When they did stumble into the little glade the sight which greeted them seemed to suck the strength from their limbs. A semicircle formed round the big cherry oak tree, stricken faces staring at its grisly burden.

Powel Manani was one of the last to arrive. Vorix was with him, loping easily through the lush undergrowth. Canine senses bubbled into Powel's mind, the monochrome images, the sharp sounds, and the vast range of smells. There was an overpowering scent of blood in the air.

He pushed and elbowed his way to the front of the shocked crowd, caught sight of the cherry oak tree – 'Jesus!' His hand came up to cover his mouth. Something deep inside wanted to let loose a primaeval wail, just to shout and shout until all the pain was disgorged.

Carter McBride was hanging upside-down against the tree. His feet had been bound to the trunk with dried vine cords, making it look as though he was standing on his head. Both arms were spread wide, held parallel to the ground by a pair of stakes at each wrist. The long wounds were no longer bleeding. Tiny insects wriggled through the saturated grass below his head, gorging on the bounty.

Dimitri McBride took two tottering steps towards his son, then sank down to his knees as though in prayer. He looked round at the circle of ashen faces with a faintly bewildered expression. 'I don't understand. Carter was ten years old. Who did this? I don't understand. Please tell me.' He saw his own pain reflected in the weeping eyes surrounding him. 'Why this? Why do this?'

'The Ivets,' Horst said. Little Carter's scarlet eyeballs were staring right into him, urging him to speak. 'This is the inverted cross,' he said pedantically. It was important to be right in a matter like this, he felt, important that they should all fully comprehend. 'The opposite of the crucifix. They worship the Light Brother, you see. The Light Brother is diametrically opposed to our lord Jesus, so the sects perform this sacrifice as a mockery. It's very logical, really.' Horst found his breath was hard to come by, as if he'd been running a long distance.

Dimitri McBride crashed into him with the force of a jack-hammer. He was flung backwards, Dimitri riding him down. 'You knew! You knew!' he cried. Metal fingers closed round Horst's throat, clawing. 'That was my son. And you knew!' Horst's head was yanked up, then slammed down into the spongy loam. 'He'd still be alive if you'd told us. You killed him! You killed him! You!'

Horst's world was turning black around the edges. He tried to speak, to explain. That was what he had been trained for, to make people accept the world the way it was. But all he could see was Dimitri McBride's open screaming mouth.

'Get him off,' Ruth told Powel Manani.

The supervisor gave her a dark look, then nodded reluctantly. He signalled to a couple of the villagers, and between them they prised Dimitri's fingers from Horst's throat. The priest lay as he was left, sucking air down like a cardiac victim.

Dimitri McBride collapsed into a limp, sobbing bundle.

Three of the villagers cut little Carter down, wrapping him in a coat.

'What do I tell Victoria?' Dimitri McBride asked vacantly. 'What do I tell her?' The reassuring hands found his shoulders again, patting, offering their pathetically inadequate sympathy. A hip-flask was pressed to his lips. He spluttered as the acidic brew went down his gullet.

Powel Manani stood over Horst Elwes. I'm as guilty as the priest, he thought. I knew that little ratprick Quinn was trouble. But dear God, *this*. The Ivets, they're not human. Somebody who could do this could do anything.

Anything. The thought struck him like a twister of gelid wind. It cleared away even the remotest feeling of pity for the wretched drunken priest. He nudged Horst with the toe of his boot. 'You? Can you hear me?'

Horst gurgled, his eyes rolling around.

Powel let his full fury vent into Vorix's mind. The dog lurched towards Horst, snarling in rage.

Horst saw it coming, and scrabbled feebly on all fours, cringing from the hound's ferocity. Vorix barked loudly, his muzzle centimetres away from his face.

'Hey!' Ruth protested.

'Shut up,' Powel said, not even looking at her. 'You. Priest. Are you listening to me?'

Vorix growled.

Everybody was watching the tableau now, even Dimitri McBride.

'It's what they are,' Horst said. 'The balance of nature. Black and white, good and evil. God's kingdom of heaven, and hell. Earth and Lalonde. Do you see?' He smiled up at Powel.

'The Ivets didn't all come from the same arcology,' Powel said with a dangerously level voice. 'They'd never even met each other before they came here. That means Quinn did this since we arrived, turned them into what they are now. You know about this doctrine of theirs. You know all about it. How long have they been a part of this sect movement? Before Gwyn Lawes? Were they, priest? Were they all involved before his odd, unseen, bloody death out here in the jungle? *Were they?*'

Several of the watchers gasped. Powel heard someone moaning: 'Oh, God, please no.'

Horst's mad smile was still directed up at the supervisor.

'Is that when it started, priest?' Powel asked. 'Quinn had months to turn them, to break them, to control them. Didn't he? That's what he was doing all the time inside that fancy A-frame hut of theirs. Then when he'd got them all whipped into line, they started to come after us.' His finger lined up on Horst. He wanted it to be a hunting rifle, to blow this failed wreckage of a man to pieces. 'Those muggings back in Durringham, Gwyn Lawes, Roger Chadwick, the Hoffmans. My God, what did they do to the Hoffmans that they had to incinerate them afterwards so we wouldn't see? And all because you didn't tell us. How are you going to explain that to your God when you face him, priest? Tell me that.'

'I wasn't sure,' Horst wailed. 'You're as bad as them. You're a savage, you love it out here. The only difference between you and an Ivet is that you get paid for what you do. You would have gone berserk if I even hinted that they had turned to the sect instead of me.'

'*When did you know?*' Powel screamed at him.

Horst's shoulders quaked, he hugged his chest, curling up. 'The day Gwyn died.'

Powel threw his head back, fists thrust into the sky. 'QUINN!' he bellowed. 'I'll have you. I'll have every fucking one of you. Do you hear me, Quinn? You're dead.' Vorix was howling defiance into the heavens.

He looked round at the numb expressions centred on him, seeing the cracks opening into their fear, and the anger that was beginning to spark inside. He knew people, and these were with him now. At long last, every one of them. There would be no rest now until the Ivets had been tracked down and exterminated.

'We can't just assume the Ivets are guilty like this,' Rai Molvi said. 'Not on his word.' He glanced scathingly down at Horst. That was how Vorix took him unawares. The hound landed on his chest, bowling him over. Rai Molvi yelped in terror as Vorix barked, long fangs snapping centimetres from his nose.

'You,' Powel Manani said. It was spat out like an allegation. 'You, lawyer man! You are the one who wanted me to ease off them. You let them have their A-frame. You wanted them walking round free. If we had done this by the book, kept those dickheads in the filth where they belong, none of this would have happened.' He called Vorix off from the panting, badly scared man. 'But you're right. We don't *know* the Ivets had anything to do with Gwyn or Roger or the Hoffmans. We can't prove that, can we, counsel for the defence? So all we've got is Carter. Do you know anyone else out here that is going to rip apart a ten-year-old child? Do you? Because if you do, I think we'd all like to hear who.'

Rai Molvi shook his head, teeth clamped together in anguish.

'Right then,' Powel said. 'So what do you say, Dimitri? Carter was your boy. What do you think we should do to the people who did this to your son?'

'Kill them,' Dimitri said from the centre of the little knot of people who were trying to comfort him. 'Kill every last one of them.'

*

High above the treetops, the kestrel wheeled and turned in an agile aerial dance, using the fast streams of hot, moist air to stay aloft with minimum effort. Laton always allowed the bird's natural instincts to take over on such occasions, contenting himself simply to direct. Down below, under the almost impenetrable barrier of leaves, people were moving. Little flecks of colour were visible through the minute gaps, the distinctive pattern of a particular shirt, grubby, sweaty skin. The kestrel's predator instincts amplified each motion, building up a comprehensive picture.

Four men carried the body of the boy on a makeshift stretcher. They moved slowly, picking their way over roots and small gullies, all of them labouring under an air of reluctance.

Ahead of them was the main body of men, led by Supervisor Manani. They walked with a bold stride. Men who had a purpose. Laton could see it in the stern, hate-filled faces, the grim determination. Those that didn't have laser rifles had acquired clubs or stout sticks.

Trailing way behind everyone else the kestrel saw Ruth Hilton and Rai Molvi. Weak, dejected figures who never said a word. Both lost in their own private guilt.

Horst Elwes was left by himself in the small clearing. He was still curled up on the ground, shivering quite violently. Every now and then he would let out a loud cry, as if something had bitten him. Laton suspected his mind had gone completely. It didn't matter, he had fulfilled his role beautifully.

*

Leslie Atcliffe broke surface ten metres away from the end of Aberdale's jetty, a creel full of mousecrabs clamped between his hands. He rolled onto his back, and began to kick towards the shore, towing the creel. Rifts of gun-metal cloud were starting to slash the western horizon. It would rain in another thirty minutes, he reckoned.

Kay was sitting on the shore just above the water, opening a creel and tipping the still wriggling mousecrabs into a box ready for filleting. She was wearing a pair of faded shorts, halter made out of a cut-up T-shirt, boots with blue socks rolled down, and a scrappy dried-grass hat she had woven herself. Leslie enjoyed the look of her lean body, a rich nut-brown after all these months in the sun. It was another three days until they would have a night together. And he liked to think Kay enjoyed screwing with him more than the others. She certainly talked to him the rest of the time, like a friend.

His feet found the shingle and he stood up. 'Another lot for you,' he called. The mousecrabs slithered and squirmed round each other in the creel, ten at least; narrow flat bodies with twelve spindly legs apiece, brown scales that did resemble wet fur, and a pointed head ending in a black tip like a rodent nose.

Kay grinned, and waved at him, her filleting knife gripped in her hand, steel blade glinting in the sun. That grin made his whole day worthwhile.

The search party emerged from the jungle forty metres away from the quay. Leslie knew something was wrong straight away. They were walking too fast, the way angry men walk. And they were heading towards the jetty, all of them, fifty or more. Leslie stared uncertainly. It wasn't the jetty, they were heading for him!

'God's Brother,' he murmured. They looked like a lynch mob. Quinn! It had be something Quinn had done. Quinn who was always so smart he never got caught.

Kay twisted round at the sound of the low rumble of voices, shielding her eyes from the sun. Tony had just surfaced with a full creel; he was watching the approaching crowd in confusion.

Leslie looked behind him, over the river. The far shore with its muddy bank and wall of creeper-bound trees was a hundred and forty metres away. It suddenly looked very tempting, he had become a strong swimmer over the last few months. They wouldn't catch him if he started straight away.

The first members of the crowd reached Kay where she was sitting. She was punched full in the face without the slightest warning. Leslie saw who did it, Mr Garlworth, a forty-five-year-old oenophile who was determined to establish his own vineyard. A quiet, peaceable man who was fairly reclusive. Now his face was flushed, berserker exhilaration lighting his features. He grunted in triumph as his knuckles connected with Kay's jaw.

She cried out in pain and toppled over, a bead of blood spurting from her mouth. Men clustered round, kicking at her with a fierceness that rivalled a sayce's blood-lust.

'Fuck you!' Leslie yelled. He slung the creel away and drove his legs through the knee-high water towards the shore, sending up long tails of spray. Kay was screaming, lost behind the flurry of kicking legs. Leslie saw the filleting knife slash once. One of the men fell, clutching at his shin. Then a club was raised high.

Leslie never heard nor saw if it fell on the battered girl. He cannoned into the band of villagers who were racing down the slope at him. Powel Manani was one of them, a big fist cocked back. Leslie's world disintegrated into a chaos where instinct ruled. Fists slammed into him from all directions. He lashed out with blind violence. Men shouted and roared. His hair was gripped by a meaty hand, strands making a terrible ripping sound as they were torn slowly out of his scalp. A torrent of foam raged around him, almost as though he was fighting under a waterfall. Fangs clamped around his wrist, dragging his arm down. There was snarling, the snap of splintering bone that went on interminably. Pain was everything now, flooding down every nerve. Somehow it didn't bother him nearly as much as it should. He couldn't strike back the way he wanted to now. His arms didn't respond. He found he was on his knees, vision fading away into pink-grey streaks. The muddy river water was boiling scarlet.

There was a moment when nothing happened. He was being held prone by invincible hands. Powel Manani towered in front of him, his thick black beard soaked and straggly, grinning savagely as he lined himself up. In the silent pause, Leslie could hear a child wailing frantically somewhere off in the distance. Then Powel's heavy boot smashed into his balls with all the force the brawny supervisor could summon.

The pulse of agony knocked out every other thread of awareness. Leslie was cut off from life at the centre of a dense red neon mist, feeling or hearing nothing from outside. There was only the sickening pain.

Red turned to black. Twinges of sensation oozed back in on him. His face was being crushed into cold gravel. That was important, but he couldn't think why. His lungs ached abominably. With his jaw shattered and useless, Leslie tried to suck air through his mashed nose. The Quallheim's grubby, blood stained water rushed into his lungs.

*

Lawrence Dillon was running for his life, running away from the insanity that had claimed the inhabitants of Aberdale. He and Douglas had been working in the allotments behind the A-frame when the villagers arrived back from the search. The tall bean canes and flourishing sweetcorn plants had partially hidden them from view as the men attacked Kay and Leslie and Tony down by the river. Lawrence had never seen such a display of wanton violence before. Even Quinn wasn't that rabid, Quinn's violence was directed and purposeful.

Both he and Douglas stood mesmerized as their fellow Ivets disappeared beneath the blows. Only when Powel Manani came wading out of the river did they think to flee.

'Split up,' Lawrence Dillon yelled at Douglas as they crashed into the jungle. 'We'll stand more chance that way.' He heard that monster hound, Vorix, barking loudly behind them, caught a glimpse of it racing across the village clearing in pursuit. 'Get to Quinn. Warn him.' Then they peeled apart, tearing through the undergrowth as if it was made from tissue paper.

Lawrence found a small animal path a minute later. It was becoming overgrown, deserted by the danderil ever since the village had been built. But it was good enough to give him an extra burst of speed. His tatty shoes were falling apart, and he only had shorts on. Creepers and branches tore at him with needle-sharp claws. Irrelevant. Living was all that mattered, building distance from the village.

Then Vorix went after Douglas. Lawrence threw a wordless cry of thanks to the Light Brother for sparing him, and slackened off his pace a fraction, scanning the ground for suitable stones. The hound would find him as soon as it had dispatched Douglas. The hound could pick up scents even in the damp jungle. The hound would lead the villagers to any hidden Ivet. He must do something about it if any of them were to have the slightest chance of surviving this day. And that bastard supervisor didn't know just how big a menace those who followed the Light Brother could be to any who stood in their way. The thought lifted his spirit, enabling him to throw off some of the panic. He had Quinn to thank for that. Quinn had shown him there was no fear in true release. Quinn had helped him find his own inner strength, showing him how to embrace the serpent beast. Quinn who featured so powerfully in his dreams, a dark fantasy figure crowned in searing orange flames.

Grimacing at the multitude of scratches he had picked up

during his mad flight, Lawrence looked around with a determined gaze.

*

Powel Manani was used to seeing the world through Vorix's eyes. It was a prospect of blues and greys, as if every structure was bonded together from layers of shadow. Trees stretched far overhead until they vanished into an almost hazy veil of sky and the bushes and undergrowth of the jungle loomed in oppressively, black leaves flicking aside like cards snapped down by an expert dealer.

The robust dog was chasing down an old animal track after Lawrence Dillon. The young Ivet's scent was everywhere. It lay like an oily mist in the footprints left behind in the soft loam, it wafted down from the leaves he had brushed against. Occasional spots of blood from lacerated feet were soaking into the spongy loam. Vorix didn't even have to press his nose to the ground.

Sensations flowed into Powel's mind, the tireless bands of muscle pumping in his haunches, tongue lolling over his jaw, hot breath flaring in his nostrils. They were a duality, Vorix's body, Powel's mind, working in perfect fusion. Just like they had when the dog caught up with Douglas. Animal attack reflexes and human skill combined into a synergistic engine of destruction, knowing exactly where to strike to cause the maximum damage. Powel could still feel the soft flesh giving beneath hardened paws, the taste of blood lingered long after fangs had punctured the lad's throat, severing the carotid. Sometimes the rustling breeze seemed to carry Douglas's gurgling cries.

But that was just a foretaste. Soon it would be Quinn who faced the dog. Quinn who would scream in fright. Just like little Carter must have done. The thought spurred both of them on, Vorix's heart thudding gleefully.

The scent trail petered out. Vorix lumbered on for a few

paces then stopped and raised his blunt head, sniffing intently. Powel knew a frown would be crinkling his own face. There was a touch of rain in the air, but not nearly enough to wash away such a strong trace. He had almost caught up with Lawrence, the Ivet couldn't be far away.

There was a soft thud behind the dog. Vorix whipped round with electric speed. Lawrence Dillon stood on the track seven metres away, crouched on bloody feet as though he was about to spring at the dog, a fission blade in one hand, some kind of vine loop in the other.

The lad must have backtracked and scampered up one of the trees. Cunning little shit. But it wouldn't do him any good, not against Vorix. His only chance had been to drop on the dog and plunge the knife in before either of them realized what was happening. And he'd blown it.

Powel laughed as the dog started its run. Lawrence twirled the length of vine around. Too late Powel realized it was weighted with oval stones. Vorix was already leaping as the supervisor's mind bawled its warning. Lawrence let go of the bolas.

Insidious coils of vine snagged Vorix's forelegs with a barely audible *whirr*, the spinning cord biting sharply into his fur. One of the stones knocked heavily against his cranium, sending a shower of pain stars down the affinity link to daze Powel. Vorix crashed into the ground, slightly groggy. He flexed round trying to reach the vine with his teeth. An incredibly heavy mass landed hard on his back, nearly snapping his spine. His breath was knocked out of his lungs, winding him. Several ribs cracked. Hind legs scrabbled frantically for purchase to try and buck the Ivet off.

An excruciating lance of pain fired into Powel Manani's brain. He yelled out loud, stumbling around. He felt one knee give out, and pitched over. For a moment the affinity link wavered, and he saw a ring of villagers gazing down in dismay. Hands reached out to steady him.

Vorix had frozen in pain and shock. There was no feeling at all from one of his hind legs. The dog squirmed round on the rucked loam. His leg was lying on the bloody grass, twitching and jerking.

Lawrence cut the second hind leg off with his fission knife. Blood hissed and steamed as it bubbled over the radiant yellow blade.

Both of Powel's legs were being squeezed by tourniquets made from bands of ice. He fell leadenly to sit on his rump, breath wheezing out of parched lips. His thigh muscles were spasming uncontrollably.

The fission blade penetrated Vorix's left mandible joint, skewering through muscle, bone, and gristle. Its tip emerged into the back of his mouth, severing a large portion of the tongue.

Powel started to gag, fighting for breath. His whole body was shaking wildly. He vomited weakly down his beard.

Vorix was emitting a harrowing whining from his ruined jaw. Sallow eyes rolled round, glazed with pain, trying to find his tormentor. Lawrence aimed a blow at each of his forelegs, slicing clean through the knees, leaving the dog with stumps.

At the far end of a murky whorled tunnel, Powel saw the sandy-haired teenager walk round in front of the dog. He spat on Vorix's squat muzzle. 'Not so fucking smart now, are you?' Lawrence shouted. Powel could barely hear him, his voice sounded as though it was coming from the bottom of a deep rocky shaft. 'Want to play chase again, doggy?' Lawrence did a little jig, laughing. Vorix's stumps knocked feebly against the soil in a parody of walking. The sight sent him off into another bout of laughter. 'Walkies! Come on, walkies!'

Powel groaned with helpless fury. The affinity bond was weakening, stretching the dog's pain-lashed thoughts to a tenuous thread. He coughed some of the bile out of his mouth.

'I know you can hear me, Manani, you superfuck,' Lawrence called. 'And I hope your heart's bleeding out through these cuts. I'm not going to kill your hound, not all quick and clean and neat. No, I'm going to leave him here rolling round in his own shit and piss and blood. That way you'll feel him dying the whole time, however long it takes. I like that idea, cos you really loved this dog. God's Brother always takes his retribution on those who displease him. Vorix is kind of like an omen, see? I did this to a dog, think what Quinn's gonna do to you.'

*

It was raining steadily when Jay led Sango, Powel Manani's beige horse, from the lean-to at the back of the supervisor's cabin which served as a stable. Mr Manani had been true to his word back on the *Swithland*, he had let her groom Sango, and help feed him, and take him for exercise. Two months ago, when the frantic urgency which governed Aberdale while the cabins were going up and the fields were being levelled had abated, he had taught her how to ride.

Aberdale wasn't quite the dreamy rural existence she had expected, but it was pretty nice in its own fashion. And Sango played a huge part in making it right. Jay knew one thing, she didn't want to go back to any arcology.

Or at least she hadn't before today.

Something had happened out in the jungle this morning that none of the adults would talk about. She and all the other kids knew that Carter was dead, they'd been told that much. But there had been the awful fight down by the jetty, and a lot of the women had cried, the men too though they tried to hide it. Then twenty minutes ago Mr Manani had some kind of dreadful drawn-out fit, howling and panting as he keeled about.

Things had quietened down after that. There had been a meeting in the hall, and afterwards people had gone back to their cabins. Now though she could see them congregating in the centre of the village again; they were all dressed like they did when they went hunting. Everyone seemed to be carrying a weapon.

She knocked on the front stanchion of Mr Manani's cabin. He came out dressed in navy-blue jeans, a green and blue check shirt, and a fawn waistcoat that held a lot of cylindrical power magazines for laser rifles. He carried a couple of slate-grey tubes fifty centimetres long, with pistol grips at one end. She had never seen them before, but she knew they were weapons.

Their eyes met for a moment, then Jay looked at the muddy ground.

'Jay?'

She glanced up.

'Listen, honey. The Ivets have been bad, very bad. They're all funny in their heads.'

'Like waster kids in the arcologies, you mean?'

A sad smile flickered on his lips at the bright curiosity in her voice. 'Something like that. They killed Carter McBride.'

'We thought so,' she admitted.

'So we're going to have to catch them and stop them from doing anything like it again.'

'I understand.'

He slotted the maser carbines into their saddle holsters. 'It's for the best, honey, really it is. Listen, Aberdale's not going to be very nice for a couple of weeks, but afterwards it'll get better. I promise. Before you know it, we'll be the best village on the whole tributary. I've seen it happen before.'

She nodded. 'Be careful, Mr Manani. Please.'

He kissed the top of her head. Her hair was sprinkled with tiny drops of water.

'I will be,' he said. 'And thank you for saddling up Sango. Now go and find your mum, she's a bit upset about what happened this morning.'

'I haven't seen Father Elwes for hours. Will he be coming back?'

He stiffened his back, unable to look at the girl. 'Only to pick up his things. He won't be staying in Aberdale any longer. His work's done here.'

Powel rode Sango over to the waiting hunters, hoofs splattering in the mud. Most of them were wearing waterproof ponchos, slick with rain. They looked more worried than angry now. The initial heat of Carter's death had abated, and the shock of killing the three Ivets was percolating through their minds. They were more scared for their families and their own skin than they were bothered about vengeance. But the end product was the same. Their fear of Quinn would compel them until the job was done.

He saw Rai Molvi standing among them, clutching a laser rifle beneath his poncho. It wasn't worth making an issue over. He leaned forward from the saddle to address them. 'First thing you should know is that my communication block is out. I haven't been able to tell Schuster's sheriff what's been happening here, or the Governor's office in Durringham. Now those communication blocks are more or less solid chunks of circuitry with all kinds of redundancy built in, I've never heard of one failing before. The LED lights up, so it's not a simple power loss. It was working when I made my routine report three days ago. I'll leave it to you to work out the significance of it failing today.'

'Christ, just what are we up against?' someone asked.

'We're up against waster kids,' Powel said. 'Vicious and frightened. That's all they are. This sect crap is just an excuse for Quinn to order them about.'

'They've got guns.'

'They have eight laser rifles, and no spare power magazines. Now I can see about a hundred and twenty rifles just from here. They aren't going to be any problem. Shoot to kill, and don't give any warning. That's all we have to do. We don't have courts, we don't have time for courts, not out here. I sure as hell know they're guilty. And I want to make damn sure that the rest of your kids can walk about this village without looking over their shoulders for the rest of their lives. That's what you came here for, isn't it? To get away from all this shit Earth kept flinging at you. Well, a little bit got carried here with you. But today we finish it. After today there won't be any more Carter McBrides.'

Determination returned to the gathering; men nodded and exchanged bolstering glances with their neighbours, rifles were gripped just that fraction harder at the mention of Carter's name. It was a collective building up of nerve, absolving them of any guilt in advance.

Powel Manani watched it accumulate with satisfaction. They were his again, just like the day they came off the *Swithland*, before that dickhead Molvi started interfering. 'OK, the Ivets got split into three work parties this morning. There's two out helping the savannah homesteads, and one lot with the hunting party to the east. We'll split into two groups. Arnold Travis, you know the eastern jungle pretty well, you take fifty men with you and try and find the hunting party. I'm going to ride out to the homesteads to try and warn them. I expect that's where Lawrence Dillon is headed, because that's where Quinn is. The rest of you follow after me as fast as you can, and for Christ's sake don't get spread out. Once you get to the homesteads, we'll decide what to do next. OK, let's go.'

Enlarging the Skibbow homestead's stockade was hard work; the wood for the fence had to be pre-cut in the jungle, a kilometre away, then hauled all the way back. The ground was difficult to prepare for the posts, with a vast accumulation of dead matted grass to scrape away before the hard, sandy soil was uncovered. Loren Skibbow's lunch had been cold chikrow meat and some kind of flaccid tasteless stewed vegetable which most of the Ivets had left. And on top of all that, Gerald Skibbow was off on the savannah somewhere looking for a lost sheep, which left Frank Kava in charge, who was a bossy little shit.

By midafternoon Quinn had already decided that the

Skibbows and Kavas were going to be playing a very prominent role in his next black mass ceremony.

The lengths of wood they had cut that morning were laid out across the grass, marking out a square of land thirty-five metres a side next to the existing stockade. Quinn and Jackson Gael were working together, taking it in turns to hammer the upright posts into the ground. The other four Ivets in the work party were busy nailing the horizontal beams into place behind them. They had already completed one side, and were three posts along the next. It had rained earlier, but Frank hadn't let them stop work.

'Bastard,' Jackson Gael muttered as he took another swing with the sledgehammer. The post shook as it thudded another three centimetres into the soil. 'He wants to have this finished by tonight so he can show Gerald what a good keen little boy he's been. Means we're gonna be walking back in the dark.'

'Don't worry about it,' Quinn said. He was kneeling down, holding the black post upright. The mayope wood was wet, difficult to grip.

'This rain makes everything slippery,' Jackson grumbled. 'Accidents come easy, and on this planet you get damaged, you stay damaged. That drunken old fart of a priest don't know shit about proper doctoring.' The sledgehammer hit the post again.

'Relax. I been thinking, this place would be a good target for us.'

'Yeah. You know what really pisses me off? Frank climbs into bed with that Paula every bloody night. I mean, she's not got tits like Marie had, but God's Brother, every night!'

'Will you stop thinking with your dick for one fucking minute. I let you have Rachel, don't I? That's as well as our girls.'

'Yeah. Thanks, Quinn. Sorry.'

'Right, we'll start working out who we want to bring, and when we're going to do it.'

Jackson tightened the scraps of cloth he had wrapped round his palms to give a tighter grip on the sledgehammer's handle. 'Tony, maybe. He's pretty easy around the village; talks to the residents. Think he could do with reminding where his loyalties lie.'

'Could be.'

Jackson swung the sledgehammer again.

Quinn caught a flash of motion out on the vast plain of rippling grass back towards the thin dark green line which marked the start of the jungle. 'Hold it.' He upped his retinal implant to full magnification. The running figure resolved. 'It's Lawrence. God's Brother, he looks about dead.' He scanned the land behind the youth, looking for a sayce or a kroclion. Something must be making him run like that. 'Come on.' He started trotting towards the floundering teenager.

Jackson dropped the sledgehammer and followed Quinn.

Frank Kava was measuring out the distance between the posts, setting them up correctly for the Ivets. Not that those idle buggers would appreciate the effort, he thought. You had to watch them the whole time, and they had no initiative, everything had to be explained. He strongly believed most of them were retarded, their sullen silence certainly indicated it.

He leaned in on the spade, tearing out the knobby roots of grass. This stockade was going to be a mighty useful addition to the homestead. The original one was far too cramped now the animals were reaching adult size. They'd need the extra room for the second generation soon. Certainly the sheep would be mature enough to be inseminated in a few more months.

Frank had been faintly dubious about coming to Lalonde. But now he had to admit it was the greatest decision he'd ever made. A man could sit back every evening and see what he'd achieved. It was a tremendous feeling.

And there was Paula, too. She hadn't said anything yet. But Frank had his suspicions. She looked so *vital* of late.

The sounds made him look up – something wrong. Four of

the Ivets were still hammering away at the horizontal bars, but there was no one using the sledgehammer. He cursed under his breath. Quinn Dexter and the stalwart Jackson Gael were a hundred metres away, running through the grass. Unbelievable. He cupped his hands to his mouth and shouted, but they either didn't hear him, or they just ignored him. Probably the latter, knowing them. Then he saw the figure running in from the jungle, the erratic stumbling gait of a desperate man on his last legs. As he watched, the figure fell, arms windmilling; Quinn and Jackson increased their pace. Frowning, Frank started towards them.

The voices led Frank for the last twenty metres. All three of them were crouched below the wispy grass.

It was another Ivet, the young one. He was lying on his back, sucking down air in huge gulps, trying to talk in a high-pitched choking voice. His feet were reduced to bloody meat. Quinn and Jackson were kneeling beside him.

'What's going on here?' Frank asked.

Quinn glanced back over his shoulder. 'Take him out,' he said calmly.

Frank took a pace backwards as Jackson rose. 'Wait—'

*

Paula and Loren were in the homestead's living-room, waiting for their freshly prepared elwisie jam to boil. The elwisie was one of the local edible fruits, a dark purple sphere ten centimetres in diameter. A whole cluster of the small, wizened trees grew on the fringe of the jungle; they'd had a long picking session yesterday. Sugar was going to be the main problem; several people grew cane in the village, but the few kilos they'd traded weren't particularly high quality.

It would get better though, Loren thought. Everything about Aberdale was slowly getting better. That was part of the joy of living here.

Paula took the clay jars from the oven where they'd been warming.

'Could do with a minute longer,' Loren said. She was stirring the mixture that was bubbling away inside the big pan.

Paula put the tray of jars down, and looked out through the open door. A party of people were coming round the corner of the stockade. Jackson Gael was carrying someone in his arms, a teenage boy whose feet were dripping blood. Another two Ivets were carrying the unmistakable figure of Frank.

'Mother!' Paula charged out of the door.

Frank's face was terribly battered, his nose squashed almost flat, lips torn, eyes and cheeks swollen and bruised. He groaned weakly.

'Oh my God!' Paula's hands came up to press against her face. 'What happened to him?'

'We did,' said Quinn.

Loren Skibbow almost made it. There was something about Quinn Dexter which had always made her uncomfortable, and the sight of Frank had set every mental alarm ringing. Without hesitating she turned and raced back into the house. The laser hunting rifles were hung up on the living-room wall. Five of them, one each. Gerald had taken his with him this morning. She reached for the next one, the one that used to be Marie's.

Quinn punched her in the kidneys. The blow slammed her into the wall. She rebounded, and Quinn kicked her on the back of the knee. She collapsed onto the floorboards, moaning at the pain. The rifle clattered down beside her.

'I'll take that, thank you,' Quinn said.

Loren's vision was blurred by tears. She heard Paula screaming, and managed to turn her head. Jackson Gael had dragged her inside, holding her under one arm while her legs kicked wildly.

'Irley, Malcolm; I want the guns and every spare power magazine, any medical gear, and all their freeze-dried food. Get to it,' Quinn ordered as the other Ivets piled in. 'Ann, take watch outside. Manani will be coming out here on his horse, and keep an eye out for Gerald as well.' He threw the rifle to her. She caught it and nodded crisply.

Irley and Malcolm started to ransack the shelves.

'Shut up,' Quinn yelled at Paula.

She broke off screaming, staring at him with huge, terrified eyes. Jackson Gael shoved her into a corner, and she shrank down, hugging herself.

'That's better,' Quinn said. 'Imran, put Lawrence down in the chair, then search out the boots in this house, as many pairs as you can find. We're gonna need 'em. Got a long way to go.'

Loren saw the young Ivet with the ruined feet being lowered into one of the chairs around the square kitchen table. His face was grey, sweating profusely.

'You just find me some bandages and some boots, I'll be all right,' Lawrence said. 'Really, Quinn, I'll be fine.'

Quinn caressed his forehead, fingers teasing back the damp strands of blond hair. 'I know. That was a hell of a run out here. You did great, Lawrence. Really. You're the best.'

Loren saw Lawrence look up at Quinn, reverence in the lad's eyes. She saw Quinn slide a fission blade from his shorts. She tried to say something as the blade came alive in a burst of yellow light, but only a gurgle emerged from her throat.

Quinn sank the blade into the nape of Lawrence's neck, angling it upwards so it penetrated the brain. 'The very best,' he whispered. 'God's Brother will welcome you into the Night.'

Paula opened her mouth in a silent wail as Lawrence's body slid down onto the floor. Loren started to sob quietly.

'Shit, Quinn!' Irley protested.

'What? We've got to get out of here, yesterday. You saw his feet; he would have held us up. That way we all get caught. That what you want?'

'No,' Irley mumbled lamely.

'It was quicker than what they would have done to him,' Quinn said half to himself.

'You did the right thing,' Jackson Gael said. He turned back to Paula and grinned broadly. She whimpered, trying to push herself further back into the corner. He grabbed her hair and pulled her up.

'We don't have time,' Quinn said mildly.

'Sure we do. I won't be long.'

Loren tried to pick herself off the floor as Paula's screams began again.

'Naughty,' Quinn said. His boot caught her on the side of the temple. She flopped onto her back like a broken mechanoid, incapable of movement. Her vision was fuzzy, shapes were obscured behind blotches of grey. But she saw Quinn take Paula's rifle off the wall, calmly check the power level, and shoot Frank. He turned round, and aimed the barrel at her.

*

The recall whistle sounded sharply through the jungle. Scott Williams sighed and picked himself off the ground, brushing dead leaves from his threadbare jump suit.

The arseholes! He was sure that had been a danderil rustling through the undergrowth up ahead. Well, he'd never know now.

'Wonder what's happened?' Alex Fitton said.

'Dunno,' Scott replied. He didn't mind Alex too much. The man was twenty-eight, and he was happy enough to talk to an Ivet. He knew some good filthy jokes too. Scott had hunted with him regularly.

The whistle sounded again.

Alex grunted. 'Come on.'

They trudged towards the sound. Several other pairs of hunters appeared out of the trees, all of them walking towards the insistent whistle. Queries were shouted to and fro. Nobody knew why they were being called in. The whistle was supposed to be for injuries and the end of the day.

Scott was surprised to see a big group of people lined up waiting at the top of a steepish earth mound, there were about forty or fifty of them. They must have come out from the village. He saw Rai Molvi standing in front of them, blowing the whistle for all he was worth. He was very conscious of all those eyes on him as he and Alex Fitton made their way up the incline.

There was a large qualtook tree straddling the brow of the mound. One of its thick lower branches overhung the slope on the other side. Three silicon-fibre ropes had been slung over it.

The group of villagers parted silently, forming an alley towards the tree. Definitely worried now, Scott walked through them and saw what was hanging from the ropes. Jemima had been the last, she was still choking and kicking. Her face was purple, eyes bulging.

He tried to run, but they shot him in the thigh with a laser pulse, and dragged him back. It was Alex Fitton who pulled the noose tight around his neck. Tears ran down his cheeks as he did it, but then Alex had been Roger Chadwick's brother-in-law.

*

The run back to his homestead had nearly killed Gerald Skibbow. He had been returning anyway when he saw the smoke, tugging the errant sheep along on a leash. Orlando, the Skibbow family's Alsatian, bounded about through the long grass in high spirits. He knew he'd done well following the sheep's scent. Gerald smiled indulgently at his antics. He was almost fully grown now. Oddly enough it was Loren who was the best at training him.

Gerald had traipsed across what had seemed like half of the savannah that morning. He couldn't believe how far the damn sheep had strayed in just a few hours. They had eventually found it bleating at the end of a steep-walled gully about three kilometres from the homestead. He was just grateful that sayce kept to the jungle. They had never had any trouble from the kroclions which were supposed to roam the grassland, a few distant glimpses of sleek bodies in the grass, some night-time roars.

Then when he was a couple of kilometres from home that terrible blue-white streamer of smoke twisted idly into the sky ahead of him, its root hidden beyond the horizon. He stared at it in cold fear. All the other homesteads were kilometres away, and there was only one possible source. It was like watching his own life's blood pouring up into the cloudless azure heavens. The homestead was everything, he'd invested his life in it, there was no other future.

'Loren!' he called. He let go of the sheep's leash and started to run. 'Paula!' The laser rifle banged against his side. He slung it away. Orlando barked urgently, picking up on his master's agitation.

It was the grass, the bloody grass. It clung to his pounding legs, hindering him. Rucks and folds in the ground kept tripping him. He fell headlong, grazing his hands, knocking his knee. It didn't matter. He picked himself up and kept on running. Again and again.

The savannah sucked sounds away from him. The slashing of the grass on his dungarees trousers, his laboured panting, the grunts each time he fell. All of them soaked away into the hot, still air as though it fed on them, hungry for the slightest noise.

The last two hundred yards were the worst. He topped a small rise, and the homestead was revealed to him. Only the skeleton remained upright, sturdy black timbers swathed by shooting flames. The slats and roof planks had already burnt through, peeling off like putrid skin to lie in crumbling strips around the base.

The animals had scattered. Panicked by the heat and roaring

flames they had butted their way through the stockade fence. They had run for a hundred metres or so until their immediate fear slackened, then wandered about aimlessly. He could see the horse and a couple of pigs over by the pool, drinking unconcernedly. Others were dotted about among the grass.

There was no other movement. No people. He gaped numbly. Where were Frank and Loren and Paula? And the Ivet work team; they should all be trying to put out the fire.

With legs like weights of dead meat, and breath burning in his lungs, he ran the last length in a daze. A bright golden rain of sparks swirled high into the sky. The homestead's frame gave one harrowed creak, and buckled in on itself with a series of jerks.

Gerald let out a single wretched wail as the last timbers crashed down. He slowed to a halt fifteen metres from the wreckage. 'Loren? Paula? Frank? Where are you?' The cry was snatched up with the sparks. Nobody answered. He was too frightened to go over to the remnants of the homestead. Then he heard Orlando whine softly. He walked up to the dog.

It was Paula. Darling Paula, the little girl who would sit on his lap in their apartment back in the arcology and try to pull his nose, giggling wildly. Who grew up into a lovely young woman possessed of a quiet dignified strength. Who had bloomed out here in this venturesome land.

Paula. Eyes staring blindly at the swarm of sparks. A two-centimetre hole in the centre of her forehead, cauterized by the hunting laser.

Gerald Skibbow looked down at his daughter, knuckles jammed into his gaping mouth. His legs gave way, and he slowly folded up onto the trampled grass beside her.

*

That was how Powel Manani found him when he rode up forty minutes later. The supervisor took in the scene with a single glance. All the anger and hatred that had been building up during the day crystallized into a lethal Zen-like calmness.

He inspected the smouldering ruin of the homestead. There were three scorched bodies inside, which puzzled him for a while until he realized the second male was probably Lawrence Dillon.

Quinn would want to move swiftly, of course. And Lawrence's feet had been in poor shape even back when he killed Vorix. Christ, but Quinn was a cold bastard.

The question was, where would he go?

There were just six Ivets left now. Powel had arrived at the Nicholls' homestead where the second Ivet work team was busy assembling a barn. His maser carbine had picked them off one at a time under the horrified eyes of the Nicholls family. He had explained why afterwards. But they had still looked at him as though he was some kind of monster. He didn't much care. The rest of the villagers would put them right tomorrow.

Powel stared at the band of jungle a kilometre away. Quinn was in there, that much was obvious. But finding him was going to be difficult. Unless . . . Quinn might just head back to the village. He was a true bandit now, he'd need food and weapons, enough supplies to get well clear of Schuster County. A small roving band could elude the sheriffs and even a marshal (assuming the Governor sent one) for a long time out here.

Orlando nosed around his legs and Powel stroked him absently. He missed Vorix more than ever now. Vorix would have tracked Quinn down within an hour.

'Right,' he said to the Alsatian. 'Back to Aberdale it is.' It was his duty to warn the villagers what had happened in any case. Quinn would have taken the homestead's weapons. Thank Christ the colonists were only allowed hunting rifles, no heavy-calibre stuff.

Gerald Skibbow said nothing when Powel covered Paula with a canvas tarpaulin used to keep the pile of hay dry. But he allowed Powel to lead him away, and mounted Sango when he was told.

The two of them rode off across the savannah back to the Nicholls homestead, Orlando racing alongside through the thick grass. Behind them, the abandoned animals began to wander over to the pool to drink, nervous with their new-found freedom.

*

Jay Hilton was bored. The village felt most peculiar with no one working in the fields and allotments. By late afternoon all the children had been called to their cabins. The whole place looked deserted, although she could see people glancing out of their cabin windows as she wandered aimlessly along the familiar paths.

Her mother didn't want to talk, which was unusual. After she had come back from the search for Carter McBride she had rolled onto her bunk and just stared at the ceiling. She hadn't joined the party which left with Mr Manani to hunt down the Ivets.

Jay walked past the church. Father Elwes wasn't back yet. She knew he'd done something terribly wrong from the way Mr Manani had reacted when she mentioned his name earlier, more than just his drinking. But it still wasn't right for him to be out in the jungle alone with the evening coming in. The sun was already invisible, skulking below the tops of the trees.

Her enthusiastic and imaginative mind filled the blank jungle with all sorts of images. The priest had fallen over and broken an ankle. He was blundering about lost. He was hiding up a tree from a wild sayce.

Jay knew the jungle immediately around the village as though a didactic map had been laser imprinted in her brain. If she was the one who found Father Elwes she'd be a real heroine. She threw a quick glance at her cabin. There was no light on inside, Mother wouldn't notice her missing for half an hour or so. She hurried towards the sombre fence of trees.

It was quiet in the jungle. Even the chikrows had departed. And the shadows were deeper than she was used to. Spires of orange and pink light pierced the rustling leaves, unnaturally bright in the gathering gloom.

After ten minutes she thought that maybe this wasn't such a good idea after all. The well-worn track leading to the savannah homesteads wasn't far off. She cut quickly through the undergrowth, coming out on the path a couple of minutes later.

This was much better, she could see for about seventy metres in each direction. Some of her anxiety evaporated.

'Father?' she called experimentally. Her voice was loud in the hushed ranks of dusky trees looming all around. 'Father, it's me, Jay.' She turned a complete circle. Nothing moved, nothing made a sound. She wanted the hunting parties to come marching into view so she could walk home with them. Some company would be very welcome.

There was a crackling noise behind her, like someone treading on a twig.

'Father?' Jay turned round, and let out a squeak. At first she thought the black woman's head was hovering in the air all by itself, but when Jay squinted hard she could just make out the silhouette of her body. It was as though light bent round it, leaving a tiny blue and purple ripple effect around the edges.

The woman raised a hand. Leaves and twigs flowed fluidly over her palm, an exact pattern of what was behind her. She put a finger to her lips, then beckoned.

*

Sango cantered down the track back to Aberdale, keeping to a steady rhythm as darkness began to pool around the base of the trees. Powel Manani ducked occasionally to avoid low hanging branches. The route was one he knew by heart now. He rode automatically as his mind reviewed possibilities.

Everyone would have to stay in the village tomorrow, they could post guards so that work in the fields could continue. Any major interruption to their lives would be a victory for Quinn, and he mustn't allow that to happen. People were already badly shaken up by what had happened, their confidence in themselves had to be built up from scratch again.

He had passed Arnold Travis's group a quarter of an hour ago on their way home. They'd hanged all their Ivets. And the group that had gone out to the homesteads was burying the Ivets he'd shot at the Nicholls place. Tomorrow a gang would trek out to the Skibbow homestead and do what they could.

Which wasn't going to be much, he admitted bitterly. But it could have been worse. Then again, it could have been a whole lot better.

Powel sucked air in through his teeth at the thought of Quinn on the loose. At first light he would ride downriver to Schuster. The sheriff there would contact Durringham, and a proper manhunt could be organized. He knew Schuster's supervisor, Gregor O'Keefe, who had an affinity-bonded Dobermann. They could go after Quinn straight away, before the trail went cold. Gregor would understand the need.

None of this was going to look good on his record. Families murdered and Ivets in open revolt. The Land Allocation Office probably wouldn't give him another supervisor contract after this. Well, screw them. Quinn was all that mattered now.

Sango shrieked, rearing up violently, He grabbed the reins hard in reflex. The horse came down, and he realized its legs were collapsing. Momentum carried him forward, his head meeting Sango's neck as it snaked back. Mane hair lashed across his face, and his nose squashed into the bristly beige coat. He tasted blood.

Sango hit the ground, inertia skidding him forwards a couple of metres before he finally rolled onto his side. Powel heard his right leg break with a shockingly loud snap as the horse's full weight came down on it. He blanked out for a moment. When he came to he promptly threw up. His right leg was completely numb below the hip. He felt dangerously light headed. Cold sweat prickled his skin.

The horse's flank had his leg pinned to the ground. He hunched himself up on his elbow, and tried to pull it out. Red-hot pain flared along his nerve paths. He groaned, and slumped back down onto the mossy grass, panting heavily.

The undergrowth swished behind him. There was the sound of footfalls on the loam.

'Hey!' he cried. 'Christ, help me. The bloody horse keeled over on me. I can't feel my leg.' He craned round. Six figures were walking out of the murky shadows which lined the track.

Quinn Dexter laughed.

Powel made a frantic lunge for the maser carbine in the saddle holster. His fingers curled round the grip.

Ann had been waiting for the move. She fired her laser rifle. The infrared pulse struck the back of Powel's hand, slicing clean through. Skin and muscle vaporized in a five-centimetre crater, veins instantly cauterized, his straining tendons roasted and snapped. Around the edge of the wound skin blackened and flaked away, a huge ring of blisters erupted. Powel let out a guttural snarl, jerking his hand back.

'Bring him,' Quinn ordered.

*

The demon sprite had come back to the church. It was the first thing Horst Elwes discovered when he returned.

Most of the day was lost to him. He must have lain in the little clearing for hours. His shirt and trousers were damp from the rain, and smeared with mud. And Carter McBride's blood-filmed eyes still stared at him.

'Your fault!' Supervisor Manani had shouted in rage. He was right, too.

A sin by omission. The belief that human dignity would

triumph. That all he had to do was wait and the Ivets would grow tired of their foolish rituals and genuflecting. That they would realize the Light Brother sect was a charade designed to make them do Quinn's bidding. Then he would be there for them, waiting to forgive and welcome them into the Lord's fold.

Well, now that arrogance had cost a child his life, perhaps others too if the suspicions of Ruth and Manani were correct. Horst wasn't at all sure he wanted to go on living.

He walked back into the village clearing as the penumbra arose from the east and the brighter stars started to shine above the black treetops. A few cabins had yellow lights glimmering inside, but the village was deathly quiet. The life had gone out of it.

The spirit, Horst thought, that is what's missing. Even afterwards, even after they've had their revenge and slaughtered the Ivets, this place will be tainted. They have bitten their apple now, and the knowledge of truth has corrupted their souls. They know what beasts lie in their hearts. Even though they dress it up as honour and civilized justice. They know.

He walked heavily out of the shadows towards the church. That simple little church which symbolized all that was wrong with the village. Built on a lie, home to a fool, laughed at by all. Even here, the most God-forsaken planet in the Confederation, where nothing really matters, I can't get it right. I can't do the one thing I vowed before God that my life was for, I can't give them faith in themselves.

He pushed through the swing door at the rear of the church. Carter McBride was laid out on a pew at the front, draped in a blanket. Someone had lit one of the altar candles.

A dainty red star flickered a metre over the body.

All Horst's anguish returned in a deluge that threatened to extinguish his sanity. He bit his trembling lower lip.

If God the Holy Trinity exists, said the waster sect Satanists, then, *ipso facto*, the Dark One is also real. For Jesus was tempted by Satan, both have touched the Earth, both will return.

Now Horst Elwes looked at the speck of red light and felt the dry weight of aeons press in on his mind again. To have the existence of supernatural divinity proven like this was a hideous travesty. Men were supposed to come to faith, not have it forced upon them.

He dropped to one knee as if pushed down by a giant irresistible hand. 'O my Lord, forgive me. Forgive me my weakness. I beg Thee.'

The star slid through the air towards him. It didn't seem to cast any light on the pews or floor.

'What are you? What have you come here for? The boy's soul? Did Quinn Dexter summon you for that? How I pity you. That boy was pure in mind no matter what they did to him, no matter what they made him say. Our Lord would not reject him because of your acolytes' inhumanity. Carter will be welcomed into heaven by Gabriel himself.'

The star stopped two metres short of Horst.

'Out,' Horst said. He stood, the strength of recklessness infusing his limbs. 'Get ye gone from this place. You have failed. Doubly you have failed.' His face split in a slow grin, a drop of spittle running down his beard. 'This old sinner has taken heart again from your presence. And this place you desecrate is holy ground. Now out!' He thrust a rigid forefinger at the gloaming-soaked jungle beyond the door. '*Out!*'

Footsteps thudded on the steps outside the church, the swing door banged open. 'Father!' Jay yelled at the top of her voice.

Small, thin arms hugged his waist with a strength a full-grown man would be hard put to match. He instinctively cradled her, hands smoothing her knotted white-blonde hair.

'Oh, Father,' she sobbed. 'It was horrible, they killed Sango. They shot him. He's dead. Sango's dead.'

'Who did? Who shot him?'

'Quinn. The Ivets.' Her face tilted up to look at him. The

skin was blotchy from crying. 'She made me hide. They were very close.'

'You've seen Quinn Dexter?'

'Yes. He shot Sango. I *hate* him!'

'When was this?'

'Just now.'

'Here? In the village?'

'No. We were on the track to the homesteads, about half a kilometre.'

'Who was with you?'

Jay sniffled, screwing a fist into her eye. 'I don't know her name. She was a black lady. She just came out of the jungle in a funny suit. She said I must be careful because the Ivets were very near. I was frightened. We hid from them behind some bushes. And then Sango came down the track.' Her chin began to tremble. 'He's dead, Father.'

'Where is this woman now?'

'Gone. She walked back to the village with me, then left.'

More puzzled than worried, Horst tried to calm his whirling thoughts. 'What was funny about her suit?'

'It was like a piece of jungle, you couldn't see her.'

'A marshal?' he said under his breath. That didn't make any sense at all. Then he abruptly realized something missing from her story. He took hold of her shoulders, staring down at her intently. 'Was Mr Manani riding Sango when Quinn shot him?'

'Yes.'

'Is he dead?'

'No. He was shouting cos he was hurt. Then the Ivets carried him away.'

'Oh, dear Lord. Was that where the woman was going, back to help Mr Manani?'

Jay's face radiated misery. 'Don't think so. She didn't say anything, she just vanished as soon as we reached the fields around the village.'

Horst turned to the demon sprite. But it had gone. He

started to hustle Jay out of the church. 'You are to go straight home to your mother, and I mean *straight* home. Tell her what you told me, and tell her to get the other villagers organized. They must be warned that the Ivets are near.'

Jay nodded, her eyes round and immensely serious.

Horst glanced about the clearing. Night had almost fallen, the trees seemed much nearer, much larger in the dark. He shivered.

'What are you going to do, Father?'

'Just have a look, that's all. Now go on with you.' He gave her a gentle push in the direction of Ruth's cabin. 'Home.'

She scampered off between the rows of cabins, long, slender legs flying in a shaky gait that looked as though she was perpetually about to lose her balance. Then Horst was all by himself. He gave the jungle a grim glance, and set off towards the gap in the trees where the track to the savannah homesteads started.

*

Sentimental fool, Laton said.

Listen, Father, after what I did today I'm entitled to show some sentiment, Camilla retorted. **Quinn would have ripped her apart. There's no need for that kind of bloodshed any more. We have achieved what we set out to do.**

Well, now this idiot priest is heading out to be a hero. Do you intend to save him as well?

No. He's an adult. He makes his own choices.

Very well. The loss of Supervisor Manani is vexing, though. I was relying on him to eradicate the rest of the Ivets.

Do you want me to shoot them?

No, the hunting party is returning, they will find the horse soon enough, and the trail Quinn Dexter has left. They would wonder what killed them. There must be no hint of our existence. Though Jay—

Nobody will believe her.

Possibly.

So what are you going to do about Dexter? Our original scenario didn't envisage him surviving this long.

Quinn Dexter will come to me now, there is nowhere else he can go. The sheriffs will assume he has run off into the wilderness, never to be seen again. Not quite the perfect solution, but no battle plan survives the opening shot. And Ann's ova will be a welcome addition to our genetic resources.

Is my provocateur duty over now?

Yes, I don't believe the situation requires further intervention on our part. We can monitor events through the servitor scouts.

Good. I'm on my way home; have a bath and a tall drink waiting, it's been a long day.

*

Quinn looked down at Powel Manani. The naked supervisor had regained consciousness again now they had finished lashing his badly crushed legs to the mayope's trunk. His head hung a few centimetres from the ground; cheeks puffed out from all the fluid that was building up in the facial tissue. They had spread his arms wide, tying his hands to small stakes in the ground. The inverted cross.

Powel Manani moaned dazedly.

Quinn held out his hands for silence. 'The Night grows strong. Welcome to our world, Powel.'

'Dickhead,' Powel grunted.

Quinn flicked on a pocket-sized thermal inducer, and pressed it against Powel's broken shin. He groaned, and jerked about feebly.

'Why did you do it, Powel? Why did you drown Leslie and Tony? Why did you kill Kay? Why did you send Vorix after Douglas?'

'And the others,' Powel wheezed. 'Don't forget them.'

Quinn stiffened. 'Others?'

'You're all that's left, Quinn. And tomorrow there won't even be you.'

The thermal inducer was applied to his leg again.

'Why?' Quinn asked.

'Carter McBride. Why do you think? You're fucking animals, all of you. Just *animals.* No human could do that to another. He was ten years old!'

Quinn frowned, turning off the thermal inducer. 'What happened to Carter McBride?'

'This! You dickhead. You strung him up, you and your Light Brother bastards. You split him in half!'

'Quinn?' Jackson Gael asked uncertainly.

Quinn gestured him quiet with a wave. 'We never touched Carter. How could we? We were out at the Skibbow homestead.'

Powel pulled at the vines holding his hands. 'And Gwyn Lawes, and Roger Chadwick, and the Hoffmans? What about them? You got alibis for them, too?'

'Ah, well now I have to admit, you have a point there. But how did you know we followed the Light Brother?'

'Elwes, he told us.'

'Yes, I should have realized a priest would know what was going down. Not that it matters now.' He took his fission blade from his dungarees pocket.

'Quinn,' Jackson said hotly. 'This is weird, man. Who snuffed out Carter if we didn't?'

Quinn held the blade up in front of his face, regarding it in a virtual trance. 'What happened after Carter was found?'

'What do you mean?' Jackson yelled. 'What are you talking about? Shit, Quinn, snap out of it, man. We're gonna die if we don't move.'

'That's right. We're gonna die. We've been set up.' The blade came alive, radiating a spectral yellow light that gave his face a phosphene hue. He smiled.

Jackson Gael felt a deadly frost settle around his heart. He hadn't realized how insane Quinn was before this; nutty, sure, a psycho streak thrown in. But this – God's Brother, Quinn was actually enjoying himself, he *believed* he was the Night's disciple.

The other Ivets were giving each other very edgy glances.

Quinn didn't notice. He leaned closer to Powel Manani. The supervisor sagged, giving up the struggle.

'We are the princes of the Night,' Quinn intoned.

'We are the princes of the Night,' the Ivets chanted with numb obedience.

*

Camilla, get back there now. Eliminate all of them immediately. I'm dispatching the incorporated to help you clear away the bodies. If the hunting party arrive first, use a thermal grenade to obliterate the scene. It's hardly elegant, but it will have to suffice. Quinn Dexter must not be allowed to divulge our existence.

I'm on my way, Father.

*

The Ly-cilph moved its identity focus between Quinn Dexter and Powel Manani, extending its perception field around all the people in the cramped jungle clearing. It couldn't quite read individual thoughts, not yet, the complexity of human synaptic discharges would take some time to unravel and catalogue, but their brains' emotional content was plain enough.

The emotional polarity between Quinn Dexter and Powel Manani was enormous; one triumphant and elated, life loving; the other defeated and withdrawn, willing death to come quickly. It mirrored their religious traits, the diametric opposition.

Right out on the fringe of awareness, the Ly-cilph could detect a minute transmission of energy from Powel Manani into Quinn Dexter. It came from the basic energistic force which pervaded every living cell. This kind of transference was extraordinarily rare in corporeal entities. And Quinn Dexter seemed to be aware of it at some fundamental level, he possessed an energistic sense far superior to that of the priest. To Quinn Dexter the black mass sacrifices were a lot more than an empty ritual of worship, they generated a weighty expectation in his mind, confirming his belief. The Ly-cilph watched the sensation growing inside him, and waited with every perceptive faculty extended eagerly to record the phenomenon.

'When the false lord leads his legions away into oblivion, we will be here,' Quinn said.

'We will be here,' the Ivets repeated.

'When You bring light into the darkness, we will be here.'

'We will be here.'

'When time ends, and space collapses into itself, we will be here.'

'We will be here.'

Quinn reached out with the fission blade. He pushed the tip into Powel Manani's groin, just above the root of his penis. Skin sizzled as the blade sank in, pubic hair singed and shrivelled. Powel clenched his teeth, neck muscles bulging out like ropes as he struggled against the scream. Quinn began to saw the blade down through the supervisor's abdomen.

'This is our sacrament to You, Lord,' Quinn said. 'We have freed our serpents, we are the beast we were made. We are real. Accept this life as a token of our love and devotion.' The knife reached Powel's navel, ribbons of blood were pouring out of the wound. Quinn watched the scarlet liquid mat the man's thick body hair, experiencing a fierce delight. 'Give us Your strength, Lord, help us defeat Your enemies.' The dark joy of the serpent beast had never been so good before; he felt intoxicated. Every cell in his body vibrated with euphoria. 'Show us, Lord!' he cried. 'Speak to us!'

Powel Manani was dying. The Ly-cilph observed the swirl of energistic patterns raging throughout his body. A small discharge crackled into Quinn, where it was hungrily absorbed, raising the Ivet's mental rapture to greater heights. The remainder of Powel's life energy dwindled, but its dissipation wasn't entirely entropic, a minute fraction flowed away through some kind of arcane dimensional twist. The Ly-cilph was fascinated, this ceremony was releasing an incredible wealth of knowledge; it had never attuned itself to an entity's death so pervasively before in all its terrible length of being.

It inserted itself into the energy flow from Manani's cells, tracing it between the neat folds of quantum reality, and finding itself emerging in a continuum it had no prior conception of: an energistic vacuum. A void as daunting to it as space was to a naked human. Retaining cohesion in such an environment was inordinately difficult, it had to contract its density to prevent flares of self-energy from streaming away like cometary volatiles. Once it had stabilized its internal structure, the Ly-cilph opened its perception field wide. It wasn't alone.

Ill-focused swirls of information raced through this foreign void, similar in nature to the Ly-cilph's own memory facility. They were separate entities, it was sure, though they continually mingled themselves, interpenetrating then diverging. The Ly-cilph observed the alien mentalities cluster around the boundary zone of its identity focus. Delicate wisps of radiation stroked it, bringing a multitude of impossibly jumbled images. It assembled a standardized identity and interpretation message and broadcast it on the same radiation bands they were using. Horrifyingly, instead of responding, the aliens penetrated its boundary.

The Ly-cilph fought to retain its fundamental integrity as its thought routines were violated and subsumed by the incursive alien mentalities. But there were too many of them to block. It started to lose control of its functions; the perception field contracted, access to the vast repository of stored knowledge began to falter, it was unable to move. They began to alter its internal energy structure, opening a wide channel between their empty continuum and space-time. Patterns started to surge back through the dimensional twist, strands of raw memory using the Ly-cilph as a conduit, seeking a specific physical matrix in which they could operate.

It was a monstrous usurpation, one which contravened the Ly-cilph's most intrinsic nature. The alien mentalities were forcing it to participate in the flux of events which ordered the universe, to interfere. There was only one option left. It stored itself. Thought processes and immediate memory were loaded into the macro-data lattice. The active functions ceased to exist.

The Ly-cilph would hang in stasis between the two variant continua until it was discovered and re-animated by one of its own kind. The chance of that discovery before the universe ended was infinitesimal, but time was of no consequence to a Ly-cilph. It had done all it could.

Thirty metres away from the Ivets and Powel Manani, Horst Elwes crept through the undergrowth, drawn by the low chanting voices. The trail of broken vines and torn leaves leading away from the dead horse had been absurdly easy to follow even in the last flickers of fading sunlight. It was as though Quinn didn't care who found them.

Night had fallen with bewildering suddenness after Horst left the track, and the jungle had constricted ominously around him. Blackness assumed the quality of a thin liquid. He was drowning in it.

Then he heard the grating voices, the truculent incantation. The voices of frightened people.

A spark of yellow light bobbed between the trees ahead of him. He pressed himself against a big qualtook trunk, and peered round. Quinn sank the fission blade into Powel Manani's prostrate body.

Horst gasped, and crossed himself. 'Lord, receive Your son—'

The demon sprite flared like a miniature nova between Quinn and Powel, turning the jungle to a lurid crimson all around. It was pulsing in a mockery of organic life.

Incandescent webs of vermilion light crawled over Quinn like icy flames.

Horst clung to the tree, beyond both terror and hope. None of the Ivets had even noticed the manifestation. Except for Quinn. Quinn was smiling with orgasmic joy.

When the rapture reached an almost unbearable peak, Quinn heard the voices. They came from inside his head, similar to the fractured whispers which dream chimeras uttered. But these grew louder, entire words rising out of the clamorous babble. He saw light arise before him, a scarlet aureole that cloaked Powel's body. Right at the heart there was a crevice of absolute darkness.

Quinn stretched out his arms towards the empty tear in space. 'My Lord! You are come!'

The multitude of voices came together. 'Is the darkness what you crave, Quinn?' they asked in unison.

'Yes, oh yes.'

'We are of the dark, Quinn. Aeons we have spent here, seeking one such as you.'

'I am yours, Lord.'

'Welcome us, Quinn.'

'I do. Bring me the Night, Lord.'

Seething tendrils of spectral two-dimensional lightning burst out of Powel Manani's corpse with an ear-puncturing screech. They reached directly for Quinn like an avaricious succubus. Jackson Gael staggered backwards yelling in shock, shielding his eyes from the blinding purple-white light. Beside him, Ann clung to a slender tree trunk as though caught in the blast of a hurricane, her hair whipping about, eyes squeezed shut. The flat lightning strands were coiling relentlessly around Quinn. His limbs danced about in spastic reflex. Mad shadows flickered across the little clearing. The stench of burning meat filled the air. Powel's body was smouldering.

'You are the chosen one, Quinn,' the unified voices called inside his skull.

He felt them emerging out of the shadows, out of Night so profound it was perpetual torment. His heart filled with glory at their presence, they were kindred, serpent beasts. He offered himself to them and they rushed into his mind like a psychic gale. Darkness engulfed him, the world of light and colour falling away at tremendous speed.

Alone in his cherished Night, Quinn Dexter waited for the coming of the Light Brother.

Horst Elwes saw the red demon light wink out. The ungodly lightning blazed in its place, arcing through the air, stray ribbons raking around the clearing. Things seemed to be swimming down the incandescent strands, slender, turbid shadows, like the negative image of a shooting star. Leaves and vine creepers flapped and shook as air rushed by.

The Ivets were screaming, flailing about in panic. Horst saw Irley being struck by a wild quivering lightning bolt; the lad was flung two metres through the air to land stunned and twitching.

Quinn stood fast at the centre of the storm, his body shaking, yet always remaining upright. An incredulous smile on his face.

The lightning cut off.

He turned slowly, uncertainly, as though he was unacquainted with his own body, testing his musculature. Horst realized he could see him perfectly even though it was now pitch black. The other Ivets were near-invisible shadows. Quinn's beatific gaze swept round them all.

'You as well,' he said gently.

Lightning streamed out of him, slender bucking threads that flashed unerringly at his five companions. Screams laced the air.

'Our Father, Who art in Heaven—' Horst said. He was waiting for the lightning to seek him out. 'Hallowed be Thy name—' The Ivets' cries were fading. 'Forgive us our trespass—'

The terrible surging light vanished. Silence descended.

Horst peeked round the tree. All six Ivets were standing in the clearing. Each had their own nimbus of light.

Like angels, he thought, so handsome with their youthfully splendid bodies. What a cruel deceiver nature is.

As he watched they began to dim. Jackson Gael turned and looked straight at him. Horst's heart froze.

'A priest,' Jackson laughed. 'How wonderful. Well, we don't require your services, padre. But we do need your body.' He took a step forwards.

'Up there,' Ann cried. She pointed deeper into the jungle.

Camilla had arrived right at the end of the sacrifice ceremony, just in time to see the lightning writhe around the clearing. She used the chameleon suit's takpads to climb up a big tree, and crouched in the fork of a bough, looking down on them.

I don't know what the hell that lightning is, Laton said. **It can't be electrical, they'd be dead.**

Does it matter? she demanded. Adrenalin was tingling inside her veins. **Whatever is causing it isn't working for us.**

True. But look how they are staying visible. It's like a holographic effect.

Where's it coming from?

I have no idea. Somebody must be projecting it.

But the scouts haven't seen anything.

Ann called out and pointed. The other Ivets swiveled round.

Camilla knew what fear was for the first time in her life. **Shit, they can see me!** She brought her maser rifle up.

Don't! Laton called.

The chameleon suit ignited. Bright white flame engulfed her completely. She felt her skin burning and screamed. The plastic fabric melted rapidly, flaming droplets raining down out of the tree. She squirmed about, beating at herself frantically with her arms. She fell from her perch, a tumbling fireball, flames streaming out behind her. By then she had no air left in her lungs to scream with. She hit the ground with a dull *whoomp*, flinging out a wreath of flame. The temperature of the internecine fire increased, burning like a magnesium flare, consuming muscles, organs, and bone alike.

The Ivets gathered round as the last flames sputtered and died. All that remained was a blackened outline of scorched earth scattered with glowing clinker-like ashes. They crackled sharply as they cooled.

'What a waste,' Jackson Gael said.

They turned as one to look for Horst Elwes. But he had fled long ago.

*

Ruth Hilton and the other remaining adult villagers were grouped around the community hall in a defensive ring. The children were all inside it. Nobody knew quite what to make of Jay's story, but there was no disputing she had seen Quinn Dexter.

Torchlight sliced round the empty cabins and muddy paths. The wooden slat walls shone a pale grey in the beams. Those whose rifles were equipped with nightsights were scanning the surrounding jungle.

'Christ, how much longer before the hunting party gets back?' Skyba Molvi complained. 'They've got enough fire-power to blow out an army of Ivets.'

'Won't be long,' Ruth muttered tightly.

'I see him!' someone bellowed.

'What?' Ruth spun round, every nerve hotwired.

Targeting lasers stabbed out, forming bright ruby and emerald zigzag patterns in the air. A magnetic rifle trilled. A patch of ground forty metres away bucked as the slugs hit, forming deep narrow craters, and surrounding vegetation caught light.

The firing stopped.

'Bugger; it's a dog.'

The breath rushed out of Ruth. Her arms were trembling.

Children were shouting from the hall, demanding to know what was happening.

I should be in there with Jay, Ruth thought. Fine mother I am, letting her wander off into the jungle while I'm busy moping. And what the hell did happen out there anyway?

Horst came ploughing out of the jungle, arms spinning madly for balance. His clothes were torn, face and hands scratched and grazed. He saw the beams of light sweeping out from the hall, and shouted at the top of his voice.

Ruth heard someone say: 'It's that idiot priest.'

'Drunk again.'

'That bastard could have saved Carter.'

Ruth wanted to shrink up into a little ball that no one could see. She was sure everybody could smell her own guilt.

'Demons,' Horst cried as he ran towards the hall. 'They've unleashed demons. Lord save us. Flee! Flee!'

'He *is* drunk.'

'It should have been him, not Carter.'

Horst staggered to a halt in front of them, his body aching so badly from the exertion he could hardly stand. He saw the disgust and contempt in their faces, and wanted to weep. 'For pity's sake. I promise you. Quinn is out there, he killed Powel Manani. Something happened, something *came*.'

There were angry murmurs from the crowd. One of them spat in Horst's direction.

Ruth noticed her torch was dimming. She slapped it.

'Why didn't you help Powel, priest?' someone asked.

'Ruth?' Horst begged. 'Please, tell them how evil Quinn is.'

'We know.'

'Shut up, priest. We don't need a worthless piss-artist telling us about the Ivets. If Quinn shows his face here, he's dead.'

Ruth's torch went out.

Alarmed gasps went up from the others as all the torches began to flicker and fade.

'Demons are coming!' Horst yelled.

Fierce orange flames shot out of one of the cabins fifty metres away from the hall; they licked along its base then raced up the stanchions to the roof. Within thirty seconds the whole structure was ablaze. The twisting flames were ten metres high.

'Holy shit,' Ruth whispered. Nothing should burn that quickly.

'Mummy!' a child called from the hall.

'Horst, what *happened* out there?' Ruth cried.

Horst shook his head, a bubbling giggle coming from his lips. 'Too late, too late. Satan's beasts walk among us now. I told you.'

A second cabin began to blaze.

'Get the children out of the hall,' Skyba Molvi shouted. There was a general rush for the door. Ruth hesitated, looking at Horst imploringly. Most of the village clearing was now illuminated by erratic amber light. Shadows possessed a life of their own, leaping about at random. A black silhouette fluttered between the cabins in the distance behind the priest.

'They're here,' she said. Nobody was listening. 'They're here, the Ivets!' She tugged her laser rifle up. The green targeting beam pierced the air, sending relief flooding through her. At least something bloody worked. She pulled the trigger, sending a barrage of infrared pulses after the elusive figure.

The children swept out of the hall like a wave, some of the older ones scaling the flimsy metre-high side walls. Cries and shouts broke out as they tried to run to their parents.

'Jay!' Ruth called.

A line of flame streaked along the roof. It was an unerringly straight line, Ruth could see the wood turning black an instant before the actual flame shot up. Maser!

She worked out roughly where it must be firing from, and brought the laser rifle to bear. Her finger punched down on the trigger stud.

'Mummy,' Jay called.

'Here.'

The laser rifle bleeped. Ruth ejected the drained power magazine and slammed in a fresh one.

Several other people were firing into the jungle. The neon threads of targeting lasers lashed out, chasing elusive phantoms.

There was a concerted movement away from the hall, everyone crouching low. It was pandemonium, children wailing, adults shouting. The woven palm wall of the hall caught fire.

They could kill every one of us if they wanted to, she realized.

Jay rushed up and flung her arms round her waist. Ruth grabbed her arm. 'Come on, this way.' She started towards the jetty. Another three cabins were on fire.

She saw Horst a couple of metres away, and jerked her head in a determined gesture. He began to lumber along after them.

A scream sounded across Aberdale, a gruesome drawn-out warbling that could never have come from a human throat. It shocked even the distraught children into silence. Targeting lasers jabbed out in reflex, spearing the gaps between the cabins.

The scream faded to a poignant desperate whimper.

'Jesus God, they're everywhere, all around.'

'Where are the hunters? The hunters!'

There seemed to be fewer targeting lasers active now. The first burning cabin suddenly crumpled up, blowing out ephemeral spires of brilliant sparks.

'Horst, we've got to get Jay away,' Ruth said urgently.

'No escape,' he mumbled. 'Not for the damned. And were we ever anything but?'

'Oh, yeah? Don't you believe it.' She began to pull Jay across the stream of people, heading towards the nearest row of cabins. Horst lowered his head and followed.

They reached the cabins just as some kind of commotion started down by the jetty: shouting, the splash of something heavy falling into the river. It meant nobody was paying her much attention.

'Thank Christ for that,' Ruth said. She led Jay down the gap between two cabins.

'Where are we going, Mummy?' Jay asked.

'We'll hide out for a couple of hours until that bloody hunting party gets back. God damn Powel for stripping the village.'

'He's beyond damnation now,' Horst said.

'Look, Horst, just what—'

Jackson Gael stepped around the end of the cabin and planted himself firmly in front of them. 'Ruth. Little Jay. Father Horst. Come to me. You are so welcome.'

'Bollocks,' Ruth snarled. She swung the laser rifle round. There was no targeting beam, even the power-level LEDs were dead. 'Shit!'

Jackson Gael took a step towards them. 'There is no death any more, Ruth,' he said. 'There will never be death again.'

Ruth thrust Jay towards Horst. It was one of the hardest things she had ever done. 'Get her out of here, Horst, get her away.'

'Trust me, Ruth, you will not die.' Jackson Gael held out his hand. 'Come.'

'Screw you.' She dropped the useless laser rifle, standing between him and Jay.

'There is no sanctuary,' Horst mumbled. 'Not on this cursed planet.'

'Mummy!' Jay wailed.

'Horst, just for once in your fucking pitiful life do something right; take my daughter and get her out of here. This bastard isn't getting past me.'

'I—'

'Do it!'

'God bless you, Ruth.' He started to pull a struggling Jay back the way they had come.

'Mummy, please!' she shrieked.

'Go with Horst. I love you.' She drew her Bowie knife from its belt scabbard. Good solid dependable steel.

Jackson Gael grinned. Ruth could have sworn she saw fangs.

14

Ione Saldana stood in front of the tube carriage's door, urging it to open.

I can't make it go any faster, Tranquillity grumbled as the backwash of emotion dissipated through the affinity bond.

I know. I'm not blaming you. She clenched her fists, shifting her weight from one foot to the other. The carriage started to slow, and she reached up to hold one of the hand hoops. The memory of Joshua flashed into her mind – she'd never be able to use the carriages without thinking of him again. She smiled.

There was a frisson of disparagement from Tranquillity sounding in her mind.

Jealous, she teased.

Hardly, came the piqued reply.

The carriage door slid open. Ione stepped out on the deserted platform and raced up the stairs, her serjeant bodyguard clumping along behind.

It was a southern endcap cove station, a couple of kilometres away from the Laymil research project campus. The cove was six hundred metres long, a gentle crescent with fine gold-white sands and several outcrops of granite boulders. A rank of ageing coconut trees followed the beach's curve; several had keeled over, pulling up large clods of sand and roots, and three had snapped off halfway up the trunk, adding to the vaguely wild look of the place. At the centre of the cove, sixty metres out from the shore, there was a tiny island with a few tall palm trees, providing an appealing nook for the more enthusiastic swimmers. A shingly bluff planted with coarse reeds rose up from the rear of the sands, blending into the first and widest of the endcap's terraces.

Six low polyp domes, forty metres in diameter, broke the expanse of grass and silk oak trees behind the bluff, giving the impression of being partially buried. They were the Kiint residences, grown specifically for the eight big xenocs who participated in the Laymil project.

Their involvement had been quite a coup for Michael Saldana. Even though they didn't build ZTT starships (they claimed their psychology meant they had no real interest in space travel), the Kiint remained the most technologically advanced race in the Confederation. Up until Michael's invitation was accepted they had refrained from any joint scientific enterprise with other Confederation members. However, Michael succeeded where countless others had failed, in presenting them with a peaceful challenge which would tax even their capabilities. Their intellect, along with the instrumentation they provided, would inevitably speed up the research. And of course their presence had helped to bolster Tranquillity's kudos in the difficult early days.

Eight was the largest number of Kiint resident on a human world or habitat outside the Confederation capital, Avon. Something else which had given Michael a considerable degree of underhand satisfaction – Kulu only rated the customary pair as ambassadors.

Inside Tranquillity the Kiint were as insular as they were in the Confederation at large. Although cordial with their fellow project staff members, they did not socialize with any of the habitat's population, and Tranquillity guarded their physical privacy quite rigorously. Even Ione had only had a few formal meetings with them, where both sides stuck to small-talk pleasantries. It was just as bad as having to 'receive' all those national ambassadors. The hours she'd spent with those semi-senile bores . . .

Ione had never been out to the Kiint buildings before, and probably never would have. But this occasion justified it, she felt, even if they were upset with her breach of etiquette.

She stood on the top of the bluff, and looked down at the bulky white xenocs bathing in the shallows. From her vantage point she could see a lot of splashing going on.

Thirty metres away, there was a wide path of crumbling soil leading to the sands. She started down.

How do they get to the project campus every day? she asked, suddenly curious.

They walk. Only humans demand mechanized transport to move from one room to another.

My, but we are touchy this morning.

I would point out that guaranteed seclusion was part of the original agreement between the Kiint and your grandfather.

Yes, yes, she said impatiently. She reached the bottom of the path, and took her sandals off to walk across the sand. The towelling robe she wore over her bikini flapped loosely.

There were three Kiint in the water, Nang and Lieria, a pair who worked in the Laymil project Physiology Division, and a baby. Tranquillity had reported its appearance as soon as Ione woke up that morning, although the personality refused to show her its own memory of the birth, which had come some time in the night. **Would you like recordings of your labour pains shown to xenocs simply because they were morbidly curious?** it asked sternly.

She had acquiesced with bad grace.

The baby Kiint was about two metres long, its body more rounded than the adults' and slightly whiter. The legs were a metre high, which brought the top of the head level with Ione's. It was clearly having a rare old time in the water. The tractamorphic arms were formshifting at a frantic rate, first scoops, then paddles slapped about to raise sheets of spray, now bulblike pods which squirted out jets of water. Its beak was flapping open and shut.

The parents were patting and stroking it with their arms as it charged about in circles. Then it caught sight of Ione.

Panic. Alarm. Incredulity. *Thing* has not enough legs. Topple walk. Fall over not. Why why why? What *is* it?

Ione blinked against the sudden wash of jumbled emotions and frantic questions that seemed to be shouted into her mind.

That'll teach you to creep up on entities, Tranquillity said drily.

The baby Kiint butted up against Lieria's flank, hiding itself from Ione.

What is it? What is it? Fear strangeness.

Ione caught the briefest exchange of mental images that the adult Kiints directed at the baby, an information stream more complex than anything she'd known before. The speed was bewildering, over almost as it began.

She stopped with her feet in the warm, clear water and gave the adults a small bow. **Nang, Lieria, I came to offer my congratulations on the birth, and to see if your child has any special requirements. My apologies if I intrude.**

Thank you, Ione Saldana, Lieria said. There was a suggestion of lofty amusement behind the mental voice. **Your interest and concern is gratifying, no apology is required. This is Haile, our daughter.**

Welcome to Tranquillity, Haile, Ione told the baby, projecting as much warmth and delight as she could muster. It came easily, the little Kiint was so cute. Very different from the solemn adults.

Haile pushed her head comically round Lieria's neck, huge violet-tinged eyes looked steadily at Ione. **It communicates! Alive think.**

There was another fast mental communiqué from one of the adults. The baby turned to look at Nang, then back at Ione. The tumult of emotions leaking into the affinity band began to slow.

Formal address wrongness. Much sorriness. Greetings ritual observance. The thoughts stopped abruptly, almost like a mental gathering of breath. **Hello Ione Saldana. Rightness?**

Very much.

Human you are?

I am.

I Haile am.

Hello, Haile, I'm pleased to meet you.

Haile squirmed round excitedly, water frothed around her eight feet. **It likes me! Happiness feel much.**

I'm glad.

Human identity query: Part of the all-around?

She means me, Tranquillity said.

No, I'm not part of the all-around. We're just good friends.

Haile surged forward, ploughing the water aside. She still hadn't quite got the hang of walking, and her rear pair of legs almost tripped her up.

This time Ione could understand the adults' warning perfectly. **Careful!**

Haile stopped a metre short of her. Warm breath exhaled from the facial vents smelt slightly spicy, and the tractamorphic arms waved about. She held her hand out, palm facing the baby, fingers spread. Haile tried to imitate the hand; her attempt looked like a melted wax model.

Fail! Sorrowness. Show me how, Ione Saldana.

I can't, mine's always like this.

Haile emitted a burst of shock.

Ione giggled. **It's all right. I'm very happy with the way I am.**

It is rightness?

It is rightness.

There is so much strangeness to life, Haile said wistfully.

You're right there.

Haile bent her neck almost double to look back round at her parents. The fast affinity exchange which followed made Ione feel woefully inadequate.

Are you my friend, Ione Saldana? Haile asked tentatively.

I think I could be, yes.

Will you show me the all-around? It has a vastness. I don't want to go alone. Loneliness fear.

It would be a pleasure, she said, surprised.

Haile's arms hit the water sending up a giant plume of spray. Ione was instantly drenched. She pulled the wet hair from her eyes, sighing ruefully.

You have no liking of water? Haile asked anxiously.

I'll have you know I'm a better swimmer than you.

Much gleeful!

Ione, Tranquillity said. **The *Lady Macbeth* has just emerged from a ZTT jump. Joshua has requested docking permission.**

'Joshua!' Ione shouted. Too late she remembered Kiint did have auditory senses.

Haile's arms writhed in alarm. **Panic. Fright. Joy shared.** She shied back from Ione and promptly fell down.

'Oh, I'm sorry,' Ione splashed towards her.

Nang and Lieria came up and slipped their arms under Haile's belly, while the baby Kiint coiled an arm tip around Ione's hand. She tugged.

Query Joshua identity? Haile asked as she regained her feet and stood swaying unsteadily.

He's another friend of mine.

More friends? My friend? I meet him?

Ione opened her mouth – then thought about it. Away at the back of her mind Tranquillity was registering a serene hauteur.

Ione closed her mouth. **I think we'll wait until you understand humans a little better.**

*

It was almost an infallible rule that to be an Edenist a human must have affinity and live in a habitat; certainly every Edenist returned to a habitat for their death, or had their thoughts transferred to one after death. Physically, the bitek systems integral to their society were capable of sustaining a very high standard of living at little financial cost: the price of steering asteroidal rubble into a habitat maw, the internal mechanical systems like starscraper lifts and the tube carriage network. Culturally though the symbiosis was much more subtle. With the exception of Serpents, there were no psychological problems among the Edenist population; although they displayed a full emotional range, as individuals there were all extremely well adjusted. The knowledge that they would continue as part of the habitat personality after bodily death acted as a tremendous stabilizing influence, banishing a great many common human psychoses. It was a liberation which bestowed them with a universal confidence and poise that Adamists nearly always considered to be unbridled arrogance. The disparity in wealth between the two cultures also contributed to the image of Edenists being humanity's aristocrats.

Edenism, then, was dependent on habitats. And bitek habitats were only to be found orbiting gas giants. They were totally reliant on the vast magnetospheres of such worlds for power. Photosynthesis was a wholly impractical method of supplying a habitat's energy demands; it necessitated the deployment of vast leaf-analogue membranes, and the numerous difficulties inherent in doing so from a rotating structure, as well as being unacceptably susceptible to damage from both particle impact and cosmic radiation. So the Edenists were confined to colonizing the Confederation's gas giants.

However there was one exception, one terracompatible planet which they settled successfully: Atlantis; so named because it was a single giant ocean of salt water. Its sole exports were the seafood delicacies for which it was renowned across the Confederation. The variety of marine life below its waves was so great that even two hundred and forty years after its discovery barely one-third had been classified. A vast number of traders, both independent and corporate, were attracted to it; which was why Syrinx flew *Oenone* there right after their navy duty tour finished.

Syrinx had decided to go straight into the independent trading business once her discharge order came through. The prospect of years spent on He_3 deliveries depressed her. A lot of voidhawk captains took on the tanker contracts for the stability they offered, it was exactly what she'd done when *Oenone* started flying, but the last thing she wanted was to wind up in a rigid flight routine again; the navy had given her quite enough of that already, a feeling the rest of the crew heartily shared (apart from Chi, who left along with all the weapons hardware in the lower hull). Although some doubts lingered obstinately in her mind, it was a big step from the precisely ordered navy life she was used to.

On seeing her daughter dithering, Athene pointed out that Norfolk was approaching conjunction, and spent an evening reminiscing on her own flights to collect the planet's fabled Tears. Three days later *Oenone* left the maintenance station dock at Romulus; new cargo cradles fitted, a new civilian registration filed, licensed by the Confederation Astronautics Board to carry freight and up to twenty passengers, crew toroid refurbished, and crew-members in a tigerish frame of mind.

It emerged from its wormhole terminus a hundred and fifteen thousand kilometres above Atlantis, almost directly over the dawn terminator. Syrinx felt the rest of the crew observing the planet through the voidhawk's sensor blisters. There was a collective emission of admiration.

Atlantis was a seamless blue, overlaid with rucked spirals of pure white cloud. There were fewer storms than an ordinary world, where continental and sea winds whipped up high and low air fronts in unceasing turmoil. Most of the storms below were concentrated in the tropical zones, stirred by the Coriolis effect. Both the polar icecaps were nearly identical circles, their edges amazingly regular.

Ruben, who was sitting in Syrinx's day cabin in the shape-moulding couch beside her, gripped her hand a fraction tighter. **This was an excellent choice, darling. A true fresh start to our civilian life. You know, in all my years I've never been here before.**

Syrinx knew she was still too tense after every swallow manoeuvre, alert for hostile ships. True navy paranoia. She let the external image bathe her mind, soothing away the old stress habits. The ocean had a delightful sapphire radiance to it. **Thank you. I think I can smell the salt already.**

As long as you don't try and drink this ocean like you did on Uighur.

She laughed at the memory of the time he had taught her how to wind surf in that beautiful deserted cove on a resort island. Four – no five years ago. Where did the time go?

Oenone descended into a five-hundred-kilometre orbit, complaining all the while. The planet's gravity was exerting its inexorable influence over local space, tugging at the stability of the voidhawk's distortion field, requiring extra power to compensate, a degradation which increased steadily as it approached the surface. When *Oenone* reached the injection point, it could barely generate half a gee acceleration.

There were over six hundred voidhawks (and thirty-eight blackhawks, Syrinx noted with vague disapproval), and close to a thousand Adamist starships, sharing the same standard equatorial orbit. *Oenone*'s mass-sensitivity revealed them to Syrinx's mind like muddy footprints across snow. Every now and then sunlight would flash off a silvered surface betraying their position to the optical sensors. Ground to orbit craft were shuttling constantly between them and the buoyant islands floating far below. She saw that most of them were spaceplanes rather than the newer ion-field craft. There was a quiet background hum in the affinity band as the voidhawks conversed and exchanged astrogation updates.

Can you find Eysk for me? she asked.

Of course, *Oenone* replied. **Pernik Island is just over the horizon,**

it is midday for them. It would be easier to reach from a higher orbit, it added with apparent innocence.

No chance. We're only here for a week.

She sensed the affinity link to Eysk opening. They exchanged identity traits. He was fifty-eight years old, a senior in a family business that trawled for fish and harvested various seaweeds then packaged them for transit.

My sister Pomona said I should contact you, Syrinx said.

I'm not sure if that's good or bad, Eysk replied. **We haven't quite recovered from her last visit.**

That's my sister, all right. But I'll let you decide. I'm sitting up here with a tragically empty cargo hold which needs filling. Four hundred tonnes of the classiest, tastiest products you have.

Mental laughter followed. **Heading for Norfolk by any chance?**

How did you guess?

Take a look around you, Syrinx, half the ships in orbit are loading up ready for that flight. And they place contracts a year in advance.

I couldn't do that.

Why not?

We just finished a Confederation Navy duty tour three weeks ago. *Oenone* has spent the time since then in dock having the combat-wasp launchers removed and standard cargo systems fitted. She felt his mind close up slightly as he considered her request.

Ruben crossed his fingers and pulled a face.

We might have some surplus, he declared eventually.

Great!

It's not cheap, and it's nowhere near four hundred tonnes.

Money's no problem. She could sense the dismay tweak of the crew at that blasé statement. They had all pooled their navy severance pay, and taken out a big loan option from the Jovian Bank, in the hope of putting together a cargo deal with a Norfolk roseyard-association merchant. Contrary to the firmly seated Adamist belief, the Jovian Bank did not hand out money to any Edenist on request. Between them, *Oenone*'s crew had only just scraped together enough fuseodollars for a cash collateral.

I should be so lucky, Eysk said. **Still, anything to help out an old naval hand. Do you know what you're looking for?**

I had some unlin crab once, they were gorgeous. Orangesole, too, if you have some.

Futchi, Cacus chipped in.

And silvereel, Edwin said eagerly.

I think you'd better come down and have a tasting session, Eysk said. **Give you a better idea of what we have available.**

Right away. And do you know any other families who might have a surplus we can buy up?

I'll ask round. See you for supper.

The affinity link faded.

Syrinx clapped her hands together. Ruben kissed her lightly. 'You're a marvel,' he told her.

She kissed him back. 'This is only half the battle. I'm still relying on your contact once we get to Norfolk.'

'Relax, he's a sucker for seafood.'

Oxley, she called. **Break out the flyer, it looks like we're in business.**

*

Joshua hadn't expected to feel like this. He lived for space, for alien worlds, the hard edge of cargo deals, an unlimited supply of adventurous girls in port cities. But now Tranquillity's drab matt-russet exterior was filling half of the *Lady Mac*'s sensor array visualization, and it looked just *wonderful*. I'm coming home.

A break from Ashly moaning about how much better life was two centuries ago, no more of Warlow's grumpiness, an end to Dahybi's fastidious and perfidious attention to detail. Even Sarha was getting stale, free fall didn't provide an infinite variety of positions after all – and once you'd discounted the sex, there wasn't much else between them.

Yes, a rest was most definitely what he needed. And he could certainly afford one after that Puerto de Santa Maria run. Harkey's Bar was going to resemble a pressure blow-out after he hit it this evening.

The rest of the crew were hooked into the flight computer via their neural nanonics, sharing the view. Joshua guided the ship along the vector spaceport traffic control had datavised to him, keeping the ion-thruster burns to a strict minimum. *Lady Mac*'s mass distribution held no mysteries now, he knew how she would respond to the impact of a single photon.

She settled without a bounce on the cradle, and the hold-down latches clicked home. Joshua joined the rest of them in cheering.

Two serjeants were waiting for him when they came through the rotating pressure seal connecting the spaceport disk with the habitat. He just shrugged lamely at his open-mouthed crew as the bitek servitors hauled him towards a waiting tube carriage, all three of them skip gliding in the ten per cent gravity field, his shoulder-bag with its precious contents trailing in the air like a half-inflated balloon.

'I'll catch up with you tonight,' he called over his shoulder as the door slid shut.

Ione was standing on the platform when it opened again. It was the little station outside her cliff-base apartment.

She was wearing a black dress with cut-away sides and a fabulously tight skirt. Her hair was frizzed elaborately.

When he stopped looking at her legs and breasts in anticipation he saw there was a daunting expression on her face.

'Well?' she said.

'Er . . .'

'Where is it?'

'What exactly?'

A black shoe with a sharply pointed toe tapped impatiently on the polyp. 'Joshua Calvert, you have spent over eleven months gallivanting around the universe, without, I might point out, sending me a single memory flek to say how you were getting on.'

'Yes. Sorry. Busy, you see.' Jesus, but he wanted to rip that dress off. She looked ten times more sexy than she did when he replayed the neural nanonic memories. And everywhere he went people were talking about the new young Lord of Ruin. Their fantasy figure was his girl. It just made her all the more desirable.

'So where's my present?'

He almost did it, he almost said: 'I'm your present.' But even as he started grinning he felt that little spike of anxiety inside. He didn't want anything to foul up this reunion. Besides, she was only a kid, she needed him. So best to leave off the crappy jokes. 'Oh, that,' he murmured.

Sea-blue eyes hardened. 'Joshua!'

He twisted the catch on his shoulder-bag. She pulled it open eagerly. The sailu blinked at the light, looking up at her with eyes that were completely black and stupendously appealing.

They were described as living gnomes by the first people to see them, thirty centimetres fully grown, with black and white fur remarkably similar to a terrestrial panda. On their home world, Oshanko, they were so rare they were kept exclusively in an imperial reserve. Only the Emperor's children were allowed to have them as pets. Cloning and breeding programmes were an anathema to the imperial court, they lived by natural selection alone. No official numbers of their population were given, but strong rumour suggested there were less than two thousand of them left.

Despite the bipedal shape, they had a very different skeleton and musculature to terrestrial anthropoids. There were no elbows or knees, their limbs bent along their whole length, making their movements incredibly ponderous. They were herbivores, and, if official AV recordings of the Emperor's family were to be believed, clingingly affectionate.

Ione covered her mouth with one hand, eyes alight with

incredulity. The creature was about twenty centimetres high. 'It's a sailu,' she said dumbly.

'Yes.'

She put a hand into the bag, extending one finger. The sailu reached for it in a graceful slow motion, deliciously silky fur stroked against her knuckle. 'But only the Emperor's children are supposed to have these.'

'Emperor, Lord – what's the difference? I got it because I thought you'd like it.'

The sailu had clambered upright, still holding itself against her finger. Its flat wet nose sniffed her. 'How?' she asked.

Joshua gave her a precocious smile.

'No. I don't want to know.' She heard a soft crooning, and looked down, only to lose herself in the adoring gaze. 'It's very wicked of you, Joshua. But he's quite lovely. Thank you.'

'Not sure about the "him". I think there are three or four sexes. There's not much on them in any reference library. But it does eat lettuce and strawberries.'

'I'll remember.' She eased her finger from the sailu's grip.

'So what about my present?' Joshua asked.

Ione struck a pose, tongue licking her lips. 'I'm your present.'

They didn't make it to the bedroom. Joshua got her dress off just inside the door, and in return Ione tugged at his ship-suit seal so hard it broke. The first time was on one of the alcove tables, after that they used the ornate iron stair railings for support, then it was rolling around on the apricot moss carpet.

The bed did get used eventually, after a shower and a bottle of champagne. Hours later, Joshua knew he'd missed the party in Harkey's Bar, and didn't much care. Outside the window the light filtering through the water had faded to a dusky green, small orange and yellow fish were looking in at him.

Ione was sitting cross-legged on the rubbery transparent sheet with her back resting against some of the silk cushions. The sailu was snuggled up in her hand as she fed it with the crinkled red and green leaves of a lollo lettuce. It munched them daintily, gazing up at her.

Isn't he adorable? she said happily.

The sailu genus exhibit a great many anthropomorphic traits which endear them to humans.

I bet you'd be nicer if it wasn't Joshua who brought him.

Removing the sailu from its home planet is not only in complete contravention of the planetary statutes, it is also a direct personal insult to the Emperor himself. Joshua has put you in an invidious position. A typically thoughtless action on his part.

I won't tell the Emperor if you won't.

I was not proposing to tell the Emperor, nor even the Japanese Imperium's ambassador.

That old fart.

Ione, please, Ambassador Ng is a very senior diplomat. His appointment here is a mark of the Emperor's respect towards you.

I know. She tickled the sailu under its tiny chin. Face and body were both flattish ovals, joined by a short neck. Its legs curved slowly, pressing the torso against her finger.

'I'm going to call him Augustine,' she announced. 'That's a noble name.'

'Great,' Joshua said. He leant over to the side of the bed and pulled the champagne bottle out of its ice bucket. 'Flat,' he said, after he tipped some into his glass.

'Proves you have staying power,' she said coyly.

He reached for her left breast, smiling.

'No, don't,' she moved out of the way. 'Augustine's still feeding. You'll upset him.'

He lay back, disgruntled.

'Joshua, how long are you staying this time?'

'Couple of weeks. I need to get a contract with Roland Frampton sorted out. Distribution, not a charter. We're going for a Norfolk run, Ione. We raised a lot of capital on some of our contracts; put that together with what I had left over from scavenging, and we'll have enough for a cargo of Norfolk Tears. Imagine that! A hold full of the stuff.'

'Really? That's wonderful, Joshua.'

'Yeah, if I can swing it. Distribution isn't the problem. Acquisition is. I've been talking to some of the other captains. Those Norfolk roseyard-association merchants are tough nuts to crack. They won't allow a futures market, which is pretty smart of them actually. It would be dominated by offworld finance houses. You have to show up with a ship and the cash, and even then it's not a certainty you'll get any bottles. You need a pretty reliable contact in the trade.'

'But you've never been there, you don't have any contacts.'

'I know. First-time captains need a cargo to sell, a part-exchange deal. You've got to have something the merchants can't do without, that way you can get a foot in the door.'

'What sort of cargo?'

'Ah, now that's the real problem. Norfolk is constitutionally a pastoral world, there's hardly any high technology they'll allow you to import. Most captains take cordon bleu food, or works of antique art, fancy fabrics, stuff like that.'

Ione put Augustine down carefully on the other side of the silk pillows, and rolled onto her side facing him. 'But you've got something else, haven't you? I know that tone, Joshua Calvert. You're feeling smug.'

He smiled up at the ceiling. 'I was thinking about it: something essential, and new, but not synthetic. Something all those Stone Age towns and farms are going to want.'

'Which is?'

'Wood.'

'You're kidding? Wood as in timber?'

'Yeah.'

'But they have wood on Norfolk. It's heavily forested.'

'I know. That's the beauty of it, they use it for everything. I've studied some sensevise recordings of the place; they make their buildings with it, their bridges, their boats, Jesus they even make carts out of it. Carpentry is a major industry there. But what I'm going to take them is a hard wood, and I mean really hard, like metal. They can use it in their furniture, or for their tool handles, their windmill cogs even, anything that's used every day, or rots or wears out. It's not high technology, yet it'll be a real cost-effective upgrade. That ought to get me in with the merchants.'

'Hauling wood across interstellar space!' She shook her head in amazement. Only Joshua could come up with an idea so wonderfully crazy.

'Yep, *Lady Mac* should be able to carry almost a thousand tonnes if we really pack the stuff in.'

'What sort of wood?'

'I checked in a botanical reference library file when I was in the New California system. The hardest known wood in the Confederation is mayope, it comes from a new colony planet called Lalonde.'

*

Oenone's flyer was a flattened egg-shape, eleven metres long, with a fuselage that gleamed like purple chrome. It was built by the Brasov Dynamics company on Kulu, who had been heavily involved with the Kulu Corporation (owned by the Crown) in pioneering the ion-field technology which had sent panic waves through the rest of the Confederation's astro-engineering companies. Spaceplanes were on their way out, and Kulu was using its technological prowess to devastating political effect, granting preferential licence production to the companies of allied star systems.

Standard ion thrusters lifted it out of *Oenone*'s little hangar and pushed it into an elliptical orbit that grazed Atlantis's upper atmosphere. When the first wisps of molecular fog began to thicken outside the fuselage, Oxley activated the coherent magnetic field. The flyer was immediately surrounded by a bubble of golden haze, moderating the flow of gas streaking around the fuselage. Oxley used the flux lines to grab at the mesosphere, braking the flyer's velocity, and they dropped in a steep curve towards the ocean far below.

Syrinx settled back in her deeply cushioned seat in the cabin along with Ruben, Tula, and the newest member of the crew, Serina, a crew toroid generalist who had replaced Chi. All of them were gazing keenly out of the single curving transparency around the front of the cabin. The flyer had been customized by an industrial station at Jupiter, replacing Brasov's original silicon flight-control circuits with a bitek processor array; but the image from the sensors had a poor resolution compared to *Oenone*'s sensor blisters. Eyes were almost as good.

There was absolutely no way of judging scale, no reference points. Unless she consulted the flyer's processors, Syrinx didn't know what their altitude was. The ocean rolled past below, seemingly without end.

After forty minutes Pernik Island appeared on the horizon. It was a circle of verdant green that was so obviously vegetation. The islands which Edenists had used to colonize Atlantis were a variant of habitat bitek. They were circular disks, two kilometres in diameter when they matured, made from polyp that was foamed like a sponge for buoyancy. A kilometre-wide park straddled the centre, with five accommodation towers spaced equidistantly around it, along with a host of civic buildings and light industry domes. The outer edge bristled with floating quays for the boats.

Like habitat starscrapers, the tower apartments had basic food-synthesis glands, though they were primarily for fruit juices and milk – there simply wasn't any need to supply food when you were floating on what was virtually a protein-packed soup. An island had two sources of energy to power its biological functions. There was photosynthesis, from the thick moss which grew over every outside surface including the tower walls, and triplicated digestive tracts which were fed from the tonnes of krill-analogues captured by baleen scoops around the rim.

The krill also provided the raw material for the polyp, as well as nutrient fluids. Electricity for industry came from thermal potential cables; complex organic conductors trailing kilometres below the island, exploiting the difference in temperature between the cool deep waters and the sun-heated surface layer to generate a current.

There was no propulsion system. Islands drifted where they would, carried by sluggish currents. So far six hundred and fifty had been germinated. The chances of collision were minute; for two to approach within visible range of each other was an event.

Oxley circled Pernik once. The water in the immediate vicinity was host to a flotilla of boats. Pernik Island's trawlers and harvesters produced a crisscross of large V-shaped wakes as they departed for their fishing fields. Pleasure craft bobbed about behind them, small dinghies and yachts with their verdant green membrane sails fully extended.

The flyer darted in towards one of the landing pads between the towers and the rim. Eysk himself and three members of his family walked over as soon as the haze of ionized air around the flyer dissolved, grounding out through the metal grid.

Syrinx came down the stairs that had folded out of the airlock, breathing in a humid, salty, and strangely silent air. She greeted the reception party, exchanging identity traits: Alto and Kilda, a married couple in their thirties who supervised the preparation of the family's catches, and Mosul, who was Eysk's son, a broad-shouldered twenty-four-year-old with dark hair curling gypsy-style below his shoulders, wearing a pair of blue canvas shorts. He skippered one of the fishing boats.

A fellow captain, Syrinx said appreciatively.

It's not quite the same, he replied courteously as they all started to walk towards the nearest tower. **Our boats have a few bitek items grafted in, but they are basically mechanical. I sail across waves, you sail across light-years.**

To each their own, she replied playfully. There was an almost audible buzz as their thoughts meshed at a deeper, more intense, level. For a moment she felt the sun on his bare torso, the strength in his figure, a sense of balance which was the equal to her spacial orientation. And the physical admiration, which was mutual.

Do you mind if I go to bed with him? she asked Ruben on singular engagement. **He is rather gorgeous.**

I never stand in the way of the inevitable, he replied, and winked.

Eysk had an apartment on the tower's fifteenth floor, a large one which doubled as an entertainment suite for visiting traders. He had chosen a rich style, combining modernist crystal furniture with a multi-ethnic, multi-era blend of artwork from across the Confederation.

The reception room had a transparent wall with archways leading out onto a broad balcony. A long table of sculpted blue crystals flecked with firefly sparks sat in the middle of the room, laid with a scrumptious buffet of Atlantean seafood.

Ruben glanced round at the collection of ornaments and pictures, pulling his lower lip thoughtfully. **The seafood trade must be pretty good.**

Don't let Eysk's dragon hoard fool you, Kilda said, bringing him a goblet of pale rose wine. **His grandfather, Gadra, started it a hundred and eighty years ago. Pernik is one of the older islands. Our family could have its own island by now if we didn't suffer from these 'investments'. Pieces lose their relevance so fast these days.**

Ignore the woman, Ruben, Gadra spoke out of the island's multiplicity. **A lot of this stuff is worth double what it was bought for. And all of it retains its beauty providing you view it in context. That's the trouble with young people, they take no time to appreciate life's finer qualities.**

Syrinx allowed Eysk to lead her along the table. There was an enormous range of dishes arrayed, white meats arranged on leaves, fish steaks in sauces, some wild-looking things that were all legs and antenna and didn't even seem to have been cooked. He handed her a silver fork and a goblet of carbonated water.

The art is to taste then flush the mouth with a sip, he told her.

Like a wine tasting?

Yes, but with so much more to savour. Wines are simply variants on a theme. Here we have diversity that defies even the island personalities to catalogue. We'll start with unlin crab, you said you remembered it.

She pushed her fork into the pâté-like slab he indicated. It melted like fudge in her mouth. **Oh! This is just as good as I remember. How much do you have?**

They started to discuss details as they moved round the table. Everybody joined in good-naturedly, advising and arguing over individual dishes, but the final agreements were always between Syrinx and Eysk. The Jovian Bank segment of the island's personality was brought in to record the transactions as they were finalized.

They wound up with a complicated arrangement whereby Syrinx agreed to sell ten per cent of any cargo of Norfolk Tears back to Eysk's family in return for preferential treatment to obtain the seafood she wanted. The ten per cent would be sold at just three per cent above the transport cost, to allow Eysk to make a decent profit distributing it to the rest of the island. Syrinx wasn't entirely happy, but she had come into the Norfolk run too late to make heavy demands to her only supplier. Besides, ninety per cent was still a lot of drink, and *Oenone* could transport it right across the Confederation. The price was always set in relation to the distance from Norfolk it had travelled, and a voidhawk's costs were minimal compared to an Adamist starship's.

After two hours negotiating Syrinx stepped out onto the balcony with Serina and Mosul. Ruben, Tula, and Alto had gathered on one of the reception room's low settees to polish off some of the wine.

They were on a corner of the tower which gave them a view

over both the park and the ocean. A gentle moist breeze ruffled Syrinx's hair as she leaned on the railing, a glass of honey wine held loosely in her hand.

I'm not going to eat for days after that, she told the other two, giving away a sense of rumbling pressure inside her belly. **I'm bloated.**

I often think we named this planet wrong, Mosul said. **It should have been Bounty.**

You're right, Serina said. **No Norfolk merchant is going to be able to resist this cargo.** She was twenty-two, the only crew-member younger than Syrinx, slightly shorter than the Edenist norm, with black skin and a delicate face. She was watching Syrinx and Mosul with quiet amusement, enjoying the vaguely erotic overspill of their growing rapport.

Syrinx was delighted with her company, it was nice to have someone so unashamedly girlish on board. She'd chosen her original crew for their experience, and they were highly professional, but it was nice to have someone she could really let her hair down with. Serina added a sparkle to shipboard life which had been absent before.

We're a pretty common choice, Mosul said. **But none the less successful for that. Nearly every first-time captain takes some of our produce. That's if they've got any sense. You know, even the Saldanas send a ship here every couple of months to supply the palace kitchens.**

Does Ione Saldana send one as well? Serina asked interestedly.

I don't think so.

Tranquillity doesn't own any starships, Syrinx said.

Have you been there? Mosul asked.

Certainly not, it's a blackhawk base.

Ah.

Serina looked up suddenly, her head swivelling round. **At last! I've just worked out what's missing.**

What? Syrinx asked.

Birds. There are always birds by the shore on normal terracompatible worlds. That's why it's so quiet here.

One of the larger cargo spaceplanes chose that moment to lift from its pad. The vertical-lift engines produced a strident metallic whine until it was a hundred metres in the air. It banked to starboard and slid off over the ocean, picking up speed rapidly.

Serina started laughing. **Almost quiet!**

Be a friend, Syrinx said in singular engagement. **Vanish!**

She pulled a wry face, and drained her wineglass. 'Refill time. I'll leave you two alone for a moment.' She sauntered off into the reception room with a suspicious wiggle.

Syrinx grinned. **My loyal crew**, she told Mosul in singular engagement.

Your attractive crew, he replied on the same mode.

I'll tell her you said that. Once we're safely outsystem.

He came over and put his arm round her shoulder.

I have a small confession, she said. **This isn't all pleasure.**

It looks that way to me.

I want to hire a boat and visit the whales. I'd also need someone who can navigate properly to take me. Is that possible?

Alone on a boat with you? That's not merely possible, that's a guaranteed certainty.

Are there any schools near here, or do we have to go from a different island? I've only got a week.

There was a school of blues a hundred kilometres south of here a day ago. Hang on, I'll ask the dolphins if they're still there.

Dolphins?

Yes. We use dolphins to help with the fishing.

I didn't know you had servitor dolphins.

We don't. They're just plain ordinary dolphins with an affinity gene spliced in.

She followed his mind as he called. The answer was strange, more of a tune than phrases or emotions. A gentle harmony that quietened the soul. Accompanying senses flooded in. She was barrelling through solid greyness, seeing little, receiving sharp outlines of sound. Shapes moved around her like a galaxy of dark stars. She reached the surface and flashed through the ephemeral mirror into the dazzle and the emptiness where she hung with tingling skin stretched taut.

She felt her own body stretch luxuriously in tandem. The affinity link faded away, and she sighed in regret.

Dolphins are fun, *Oenone* said. **They make you feel good. And they rejoice in their freedom.**

Like voidhawks in water, you mean?

No! Well, yes. A bit.

Happy with being able to tease *Oenone* successfully, Syrinx turned to Mosul. **It was very beautiful, but I didn't understand any of it.**

Roughly translated from the scherzo, it means the whales are still within range. It'll take a day's sailing if we use my boat. Good enough?

Excellent. Can your family spare you?

Yes. This is a slow month coming up. We've been working our arses off for the last nine weeks preparing for the Norfolk trade, I'm entitled to a rest.

So you think you're going to get some rest on that boat, do you?

I sincerely hope not. Although you didn't strike me as someone who'd do the tourist routine. Not that the whales aren't worth a look.

Syrinx turned to face the ocean again, squinting at the white cloud stripe where the sky merged with the water. **It's a memory for someone else.** 'My brother.'

Mosul sensed the pain integral with the thought, and didn't pry.

*

Alkad Mzu walked up the stairs from her first-floor apartment in the StPelham starscraper, coming out into the circular foyer with its high, wave-curved ceiling and tall transparent walls looking out across the habitat parkland. A dozen or so other early risers were moving around the foyer, waiting for the lifts in the central pillar, or heading for the broad stairs around the rim which led down to the starscraper's tube stations. It was an hour after the axial light-tube had brought a timid rosy dawn to Tranquillity's interior; patches of fine mist were still lurking amid the deeper tracts of undergrowth. The parkland around each of the starscraper foyers was maintained as open meadow dotted with small copses of ornate trees and clumps of flowering bushes. She stepped out through the sliding doors into damp air flush with the perfume of midnight-blooming nicotiana. Colourful birds arrowed through the air, trilling loudly.

She set off down the raked sand path towards a lake two hundred metres away, with only the slightest hint of a limp in her walk. Flamingos were wading through the shallows between the thick clusters of white and blue lilies. Scarlet avian lizards floated among them; the xenoc creatures were smaller than the terrestrial birds, with brilliant turquoise eyes, holding themselves very still before suddenly diving below the glass-smooth surface. Both species began to move towards the shore as she walked past. Alkad reached into her jacket pocket and pulled out some stale biscuits, throwing the crumbs. The birds and lizard-things (she never had bothered to learn their name) gobbled them up hungrily. They were old friends, she had fed them every morning for the last twenty-six years.

Alkad found Tranquillity's interior tremendously relaxing, its sheer size went a long way to suggesting invulnerability. She wished she could find an apartment which was above the surface. Naked space outside the starscraper apartment window still made her shiver even after all this time. But repeated requests to be re-allocated inside were always politely refused by the habitat personality who said there were none. So she made do with the first-floor apartment which was close to the security of the shell, and spent long hours hiking or horse riding through the parkland during her spare time. Partly for her own frame of mind, and partly because it made life very difficult for the Intelligence agency watchers.

A couple of metres from the path a gardener servitor was ambling round an old tree stump which was now hidden beneath the shaggy coat of a stephanotis creeper. It was a heavily geneered tortoise, with a shell diameter of a metre. As well as enlarging the body, geneticists had added a secondary digestive system that turned dead vegetation into small pellets of nitrogen-rich compost which it excreted. It had also been given a pair of stumpy scaled arms which emerged from holes on either side of its neck, ending in pincerlike claws. As she watched it started to clip off the shrivelled tubular flowers and put them into its mouth.

'Happy eating,' she told it as she walked on.

Her destination was Glover's, a restaurant right on the edge of the lake. It was built out of bare wood, and the architect had given it a distinct Caribbean ancestry. The roof was a steep thatch, and there was a veranda on stilts actually over the water, wide enough for ten tables. Inside it had the same raw-cut appearance, with thirty tables, and a long counter running along the back where the chefs prepared the food over glow-stone grills. During the evening it took three chefs to keep up with the orders; Glover's was popular with tourists and middle-management corporate executives.

When Alkad Mzu walked in there were ten people sitting eating. The usual breakfast crowd, bachelor types who couldn't be bothered to cook for themselves. An AV projection pillar stood on the counter between the tea urn and the coffee percolator, throwing off a weak moiré glow. Vincent raised a hand in acknowledgement from behind the counter where he was whisking some eggs. He had been the morning cook for the last fifteen years. Alkad waved back, nodded to a regular couple she knew, then pointedly ignored the Edenist Intelligence operative, a ninety-seven-year-old called Samuel, who in turn pretended she didn't exist. Her table was in the corner, giving her a prime view out over the lake. It was set for one.

Sharleene, the waitress, came over with her iced orange juice and a bowl of bran. 'Eggs or pancakes today?'

Alkad poured some milk onto the bran. 'Pancakes, thanks.'

'New face this morning,' Sharleene said in a quiet voice. 'Right nob-case.' She gave Alkad a secret little smile and went back to the bar.

Alkad ate a few spoonfuls of the bran, then sipped her orange, which gave her a chance to look round.

Lady Tessa Moncrieff was sitting by herself at a table near the bar where the smell of frying bacon and bubbling coffee was strongest. She was forty-six, a major in the Kulu ESA, and head of station in Tranquillity. She had a thin, tired face, and fading blonde hair cut into a not very stylish bob; her white blouse and grey skirt gave the impression of an office worker stuck in the promotion groove. Which was almost true. The Tranquillity assignment was one she had accepted with relish two years ago when she'd been briefed on the nature of the observation duty and the underlying reason. It was a hellish responsibility, which meant she'd finally been accepted in her rank. Reverse snobbery was a fact of life in all branches of the Kulu services, and anyone with a hereditary title had to work twice as hard as normal to prove themselves.

Tranquillity had turned out to be a quiet duty, which meant maintaining discipline was difficult. Dr Alkad Mzu was very much a creature of habit, and very boring habit at that. If it hadn't been for her frequent rambles over the parkland, which presented a challenge to the observation team, morale might have gone to pot long ago.

In fact the biggest upset since Lady Moncrieff arrived hadn't been Dr Mzu at all, but rather the sudden appearance of Ione Saldana almost a year ago. Lady Moncrieff had to compile a huge flek report on the girl for Alastair II himself. Interesting to think the royal family shared the same intense thirst for details as the general public.

Lady Moncrieff made sure she was munching her toast

impassively as Dr Mzu's glance took her in. This was only the third time she had seen Mzu in the flesh. But this morning wasn't something she could entrust to the team, she wanted to observe the doctor's reactions first hand. Today could well be the beginning of the end of the ESA's twenty-three-year observation duty.

Alkad Mzu ran a visual identity search through her neural nanonics, but drew a blank. The woman could be a new operative, or even a genuine customer. Somehow Alkad didn't think it was the latter; Sharleene was right, there was a refined air about her. She loaded the visual image in the already large neural nanonics file labelled *adversary*.

When she finished her bran and orange, Alkad sat back and looked straight at the AV pillar on the bar. It was relaying the Collins morning news programme. A sparkle of monochrome green light shot down her optic nerve, and the news studio materialized in front of her. Kelly Tirrel was introducing the items, dressed in a green suit and lace tie, hair fastened up in a tight turban. Her rigidly professional appearance added ten years to her age.

She had done local items on finance and trade, a charity dinner Ione had attended the previous evening. Regional items followed, the politics of nearby star systems. An update on Confederation Assembly debates. Military stories:

'This report comes from Omuta, filed nine days ago by Tim Beard.' The image changed from the studio to a terracompatible planet seen from space. 'The Confederation imposed a thirty-year sanction against Omuta for its part in the Garissan holocaust of 2581, prohibiting both trade and travel to the star system. Since then, the 7th Fleet has been responsible for enforcing this sanction. Nine days ago, that duty officially ended.'

Alkad opened a channel into Tranquillity's communication net, and accessed the Collins sensevise programme directly. She looked out of Tim Beard's eyes, listening through his ears. And finally her feet were pressed against the ground of Omuta as she filled her lungs with the world's mild pine-scented air.

What a wretched irony, she thought.

Tim Beard was standing on the concrete desert apron of some vast spaceport. Away to one side were the grey and blue walls of composite hangars, faded with age, stained by streaks of rust from the panel pins. Five large swept-delta Sukhoi SuAS-686 spaceplanes were lined up ahead of him, pearl-grey fuselages gleaming in the warm mid-morning sunlight. A military band stood to rigid attention just in front of their bullet-shaped noses. On one side a temporary seating stand had been erected, holding a couple of hundred people. Omuta's twenty-strong cabinet were standing on the red carpet at the front, fourteen men, six women, dressed in smart formal grey-blue suits.

'You join me in the last minutes of Omuta's isolation,' Tim Beard said. 'We are now awaiting the arrival of Rear-Admiral Meredith Saldana, who commands a squadron of the 7th Fleet on detachment here in the Omutan system.'

In the western sky a glowing golden speck appeared, expanding rapidly. Tim Beard's retinal implant zoomed in to reveal a navy ion-field flyer. It was a neutral-grey wedge-shape forty metres long, which hovered lightly over the concrete for a moment while the landing struts deployed. The scintillating cloud of ionized air molecules popped like a soap bubble after it touched down.

'This is actually the first ion-field flyer to be seen on Omuta,' Tim Beard said, filling in as the Foreign Minister greeted the Rear-Admiral. Meredith Saldana was as tall and imposing as his royal cousins, with that same distinctive nose. 'Although the press cadre received special dispensation to come down last night, we had to use Omuta's own spaceplanes, some of which are now fifty years old with spare parts hard to come by. That's an indication of just how hard the sanctions have hit this world; it has fallen behind both industrially and economically. But most of all, it lacks investment. It's a situation the cabinet is keen to remedy; we've been briefed that establishing trade missions will be a priority.'

The Rear-Admiral and his retinue were escorted over to the President of Omuta, a smiling, silver-haired man a hundred and ten years old. The two shook hands.

'There's some irony in this situation,' Tim Beard said. Alkad could feel his facial muscles shifting into a small smile. 'The last time a squadron commander of the Confederation Navy's 7th Fleet met the Omutan planetary president was thirty years ago, when the entire cabinet were executed for their part in the Garissan holocaust. Today things are a little different.' His retinal implants provided a close-up of the Rear-Admiral handing a scroll to the President. 'That is the official invitation from the President of the Confederation Assembly for Omuta to take up its seat again. And now you can see the President handing over the acceptance.'

Alkad Mzu cancelled the channel to Collins, and looked away from the counter. She poured some thick lemon syrup over her pancakes, and used a fork to cut them up, chewing thoughtfully. The AV pillar next to the tea urn buzzed softly as Kelly Tirrel nattered away.

The date was seared into Alkad's brain, of course, she'd known it was coming. But even so her neural nanonics had to send a deluge of overrides through her nervous system to prevent her tears from falling and her jaw from quaking.

Knowing and seeing were two very different things, she discovered painfully. And that ridiculous ceremony, almost designed to reopen the wound in her soul. A handshake and an exchange of symbolic letters, and all was forgiven. Ninety-five million people. Dear Mother Mary!

A single tear leaked out of her left eye despite the best efforts of her neural nanonics. She wiped it away with a paper tissue, then paid for her breakfast leaving the usual tip. She walked slowly back to the StPelham foyer to catch a tube carriage to work.

Lady Moncrieff and Samuel watched her go, her left leg trailing slightly on the gravel path. They exchanged a mildly embarrassed glance.

The tableau hung in Ione's mind as she stirred her morning tea. **That poor, poor woman.**

I think her reaction was admirably restrained, Tranquillity said.

Only on the outside, Ione said glumly. She had a hangover from the charity dinner party of the previous night. It was a mistake to sit next to Dominique Vasilkovsky all evening; Dominique was a good friend, and hadn't exploited that friendship either, which was refreshing – but heavens how the girl drank.

Ione watched as Lady Moncrieff paid her bill and left Glover's. **I wish those agency operatives would leave Mzu alone, that kind of perpetual reminder can't make her life any easier.**

You can always expel them.

She sipped her tea, pondering the option as the housechimp cleared away her breakfast dishes. Augustine was sitting on top of the oranges in the silver fruit bowl, trying to pull a grape from the cluster. He didn't have the strength.

Better the devil we know, she said in resignation. **Sometimes I wish she'd never come here. Then again, I'd hate anyone else to have her expertise at their disposal.**

I imagine there are several governments who feel the same with respect to you and me. Human nature.

Maybe, maybe not. None of them has volunteered for the job.

They are probably worried about instigating a conflict over possessing her. If one made an approach to you, they would all have to. Such a wrangle would be impossible to keep under wraps. In that respect, the First Admiral is quite correct, the fewer people who know about her the better. Public reaction to super-doomsday weapons would not be favourable.

Yes, I suppose so. That Rear-Admiral Meredith Saldana, I take it he's a relative of mine?

Indeed. He is the son of the last Prince of Nesko, which makes him an earl in his own right. But he chose to become a Confederation fleet career officer, which couldn't be easy, with his name acting against him.

Did he turn his back on Kulu like my grandfather?

No, the fifth son of a principality ruler is not naturally destined for high office. Meredith Saldana decided to achieve what he could on his own merit; had he remained on Nesko such an action could well have brought him into conflict with the new prince. So he left to pursue an independent course; given his position, it was the act of a loyal subject. The family are proud of his accomplishment.

He'll never make First Admiral, then?

No, given his heritage it would be politically impossible, but he might manage 7th Fleet commander. He is a highly competent and popular officer.

Nice to know we're not totally decadent yet. She picked Augustine off the oranges, putting him down beside her side plate, then cut a grape open for him. He hummed contentedly and lifted a segment to his mouth in the dawdling fashion that so bewitched her. As always, her mind wandered to Joshua. He must be halfway to Lalonde by now.

I have two messages for you.

You're trying to distract me, she accused.

Yes. You know I don't like it when you are upset. It is my failure as well.

No, it isn't. I'm a big girl now, I knew exactly what I was getting into with Joshua. So what are the messages?

Haile wants to know when you are coming for a swim.

Ione brightened. **Tell her I'll see her in an hour.**

Very well. Secondly, Parker Higgens requests you visit him today, as soon as possible, in fact. He was rather insistent.

Why?

I believe the team analysing Joshua's Laymil electronics stack have made a breakthrough.

*

Pernik's fishing boats were halfway to the horizon by the time Syrinx emerged from the base of the tower on the morning she was due to visit the whales. The cool dawn sun had coloured the island's covering of moss a matt black. She breathed in the salty air, relishing the cleanliness.

I never really thought of our air as anything exceptional, Mosul said. He was walking beside her, holding a big box full of supplies for the voyage.

It isn't once the humidity gets up. But don't forget, over ninety per cent of my life is spent in a perfectly regulated environment. This is an exhilarating change.

Oh, thank you! *Oenone* said tartly.

Syrinx grinned.

We're in luck, Mosul said. **I've checked with the dolphins, and the whales are actually closer today. We should be there by late afternoon.**

Great.

Mosul led her along the broad avenue down to the rim quays. Water slapped lazily against the polyp. Pernik could have been a genuine island rooted in the planet's crust for all the motion it made.

Sometimes a real storm rocks us a degree or so.

Ah, right. Her grin faded. **I'm sorry, I didn't realize I was leaking so much. It's very rude of me. Preoccupied, I guess.**

No problem. Do you want Ruben to come with us? Perhaps he would make you feel easier.

Syrinx thought of him curled up in the bed where she'd left him half an hour ago. There was no response to her half-hearted query. He had gone back to sleep. **No. I'm never alone, I have *Oenone*.**

She watched a frown form on Mosul's handsome sea-browned face. **How old is Ruben?** the semi-apologetic thought came.

She told him and had to stifle a laugh as the surprise and faint disapproval spilled out of his mind despite a frantic effort to cover them up. Gets them every time.

You shouldn't tease people so, *Oenone* said. **He's a nice young man, I like him.**

You always say that.

I only voice what you feel.

The quay was balanced on big cylindrical flotation drums which rode the swell in long undulations. Thick purple-red tubes ran along the edge, carrying nutrient fluid out to the boats. Leaky couplings dribbled the dark syrupy fluid into the water.

Syrinx stood to one side as a couple of servitor chimps carrying boxes passed by. They were wildly different from the standard habitat housechimps, with a scaled reptilian skin a mild blue-green in colour. Their feet were broad, with long webbed toes.

The boat that waited for them was called the *Spiros*, a seventeen-metre sailing craft with a white composite hull. Bitek units were blended into the structure with a skill that went far beyond mechanical practicality, it was almost artistry. The digestive organs and nutrient-reserve bladders were in the bilges, supporting the sub-sentient processor array and the mainsail membrane, as well as various ancillary systems. Her cabin fittings were all wooden, the timber coming from trees grown in the island's central park. She was used by Mosul's whole family for recreation. Which explained why the cabin was in a bit of a mess when they came on board.

Mosul stood in the galley clutching his box of supplies and looking round darkly at the discarded wrappers, unwashed pans, and crusty stains on the work surface. He muttered under his breath. **My younger cousins had her out a couple of days ago,** he apologized.

Well, don't be too hard on them, youth is a time to be treasured.

They're not that young. And it's not as though they couldn't have detailed a housechimp to clean up afterwards. No damn thought for others. There were more curses when he went forward and found the bunks in the same state.

Syrinx overheard a furious affinity conversation with the juvenile offenders. Smiling to herself she started stowing supplies.

Mosul unplugged the quay's nutrient-feed veins from their couplings on the *Spiros*'s aft deck, then cast off. Leaning over the taffrail Syrinx watched the five-metre-long silver-grey eel-derived tail wriggling energetically just below the surface, nudging the boat away from the quay. The tightly whorled sail membrane began to unfurl from its twenty-metre-high mast. When it was fully open it was a triangle the colour of spring-fresh beech leaves, reinforced with a rubbery hexagonal web of muscle cells.

It caught the morning breeze, filling out. A small white wake arose, curling around the bow. The tail straightened out, giving just the occasional tempestuous flick to maintain the course Mosul had loaded into the processor array.

Syrinx made her way forward carefully. The decking was damp below her rubber-soled plimsolls, and they had already picked up a surprising turn of speed. She leaned contentedly on the rail, letting the wind bathe her face. Mosul came up and put his arm round her shoulder.

You know, I think I'm finding this ocean more daunting than space, Syrinx said as Pernik fell astern rapidly. **I know space is infinite, and that doesn't bother me in the slightest, but Atlantis *looks* infinite. Thousands of kilometres of empty ocean conjures up a more readily accessible concept for the human mind than all those light-years.**

To your mind, Mosul said. **I was born here, to me it doesn't seem infinite at all, I could never be lost. But space, that's something else.**

In space you can set out in a straight line and never return. That's scary.

They spent the morning talking, exchanging the memories of particularly intense or moving or treasured incidents from their respective lives. Syrinx found herself feeling slightly envious of his simplistic life of fishing and sailing, realizing that was the instinctive attraction she had felt at their first meeting. Mosul was so wonderfully uncomplicated. In turn he was almost in awe of her sophistication, the worlds she'd seen, people she'd met, the arduous naval duty.

Once the sun had risen high enough to be felt on her skin, Syrinx stripped off and rubbed on a healthy dose of screening cream.

That's another difference, she said as Mosul ran his hands over her back, between her shoulder blades where she couldn't reach. **Look at the contrast, I'm like an albino compared to you.**

I like it, he told her. **All the girls here are coffee coloured or darker, how are we supposed to tell if we're African-ethnic or not?**

She sighed and stretched out on a towel on the cabin's roof, forward of the sail membrane. **It doesn't matter. All our ethnic ancestors disowned us long ago.**

There's a lot of resentment in that thought. I don't know why. The Adamists we get here are pleasant enough.

Of course they are, they want your foodstuffs.

And we want their money.

The sail creaked and fluttered gently as the day wore on. Syrinx found the rhythm of the boat lulling her, and coupled with the warmth of the sun she almost went to sleep.

I can see you, *Oenone* whispered on that unique section of affinity which was theirs alone.

Without conscious thought she knew its orbit was taking it over the *Spiros*. She opened her eyes and looked into boundless azure sky. **My eyes aren't as good as your sensor blisters. Sorry.**

I like seeing you. It doesn't happen often.

She waved inanely. And behind the velvet blueness she saw

herself prone on the little ship, waving. The boat dropped away, becoming a speck, then vanishing. Both universes were solid blue.

Hurry back, *Oenone* said. **I'm crippled this close to a planet.**

I will. Soon, I promise.

They sighted the whales that afternoon.

Black mountains were leaping out of the water. Syrinx saw them in the distance. Huge curved bodies sliding out of the waves in defiance of gravity, crashing down amid breakers of boiling surf. Fountain plumes of vapour rocketing into the sky from their blow-holes.

Syrinx couldn't help it, she jumped up and down on the deck, pointing. 'Look, look!'

I see them, Mosul said, amusement and a strange pride mingling in his thoughts. **They are blue whales, a big school, I reckon there's about a hundred or more.**

Can you see? Syrinx demanded.

I can see, *Oenone* reassured her. **I can feel too. You are happy. I am happy. The whales look happy too, they are smiling.**

Yes! Syrinx laughed. Their mouths were upturned, smiling. A perpetual smile. And why not? Such creatures' existing was cause to smile.

Mosul angled *Spiros* in closer, ordering the edges of the sail to furl. The noise of the school rolled over the boat. The smack of those huge bodies as they jumped and splashed, a deep gullet-shaking whistle from the blow-holes. She tried to work out how big they were as the *Spiros* approached the school's fringes. Some, the big adult bulls, must have been thirty metres long.

A calf came swimming over to the *Spiros*; over ten metres long, spurting from his blow-hole. His mother followed him closely, the two of them bumping together and sliding against each other. Huge forked tails churned up and down, flukes slapping the water, while flippers beat like shrunken wings. Syrinx watched in utter fascination as the two passed within fifty metres of the boat, rocking it alarmingly in their pounding wake. But she hardly noticed the pitching, the calf was feeding, suckling from its mother as she rolled onto her side.

'That is the most stupendous, miraculous sight,' she said, spellbound. Her hands were gripping the rail, knuckles whitening. 'And they're not even xenocs. They're ours. Earth's.'

'Not any more.' Mosul was at her side, as mesmerized as she.

Thank Providence we had the sense to preserve the genes. Although I'm still staggered the Confederation Assembly allowed you to bring them here.

The whales don't interfere with the food chain, they stand outside it. This ocean can easily spare a million tonnes of krill a day. And nothing analogous could ever possibly evolve on Atlantis, so they're not competing with anything. The whales are mammals, after all, they need land for part of their development. No, the largest thing Atlantis has produced is the redshark, and that's only six metres long.

Syrinx curled her arm round his, and pressed against him. **I meant, it's pretty staggering for the Assembly to show this much common sense. It would have been a monumental crime to allow these creatures to die out.**

What a cynical old soul you are.

She kissed him lightly. **A foretaste of what's to come.** Then rested her head against him, and returned her entire attention to the whales, gathering up every nuance and committing it lovingly to memory.

They followed the school for the rest of the afternoon as the giant animals played and wallowed in the ocean. Then when dusk fell, Mosul turned the *Spiros*'s bow away. The last she saw of the school was their massive dark bodies arching gracefully against the golden red skyline, whilst the roar of the blow-holes faded away into the ocean's swell.

That night twisters of phosphenic radiance wriggled through the water around the hull, casting a wan diamond-blue light over the half-reefed sail membrane. Syrinx and Mosul brought cushions out onto the deck, and made love under the stars. Several times *Oenone* gazed down on their entwined bodies, its presence contributing to the wondrous sense of fulfilment in Syrinx's mind. She didn't tell Mosul.

*

The Laymil project's Electronics Division was housed in a three-storey octagonal building near the middle of the campus. The walls were a soft white polyp with large oval windows, and climbing hydrangeas had reached the bottom of the second-storey windows. Chuantawa trees from Raouil were planted around the outside, forty-metre-high specimens, their rubbery bark and long tongue-shaped leaves a bright purple, clusters of bronze berries dangling from every branch.

Ione walked towards it down the amaranthus-lined path from the nearest of the campus's five tube stations, three serjeant bodyguards in tow. Her hair was still slightly damp from her swim with Haile, and the ends brushed against the collar of her formal green-silk suit jacket. She drew wide-eyed stares and cautious smiles from the few project staff wandering around the campus.

Parker Higgens was waiting just outside the main entrance, dressed as ever in his hazel-coloured suit with red spirals on the flared arms. The trousers were fashionably baggy, but he was filling out the jacket quite comfortably. His mop of white hair hung down over his forehead in some disarray.

Ione forbade a smile as they shook hands. The director was always so nervous around her. He was good at his job, but they certainly didn't share the same sense of humour. He would think teasing was a personal insult.

She greeted Oski Katsura, the head of the Electronics Division. She had taken over from the former head six months ago; her appointment had been the first Ione had confirmed. A seventy-year-old, taller than Ione, with a distinguished willowy beauty, wearing an ordinary white lab smock.

'You have some good news for me, then?' Ione asked as they went inside and started walking down the central corridor.

'Yes, ma'am,' Parker Higgens said.

'Most of the stack's circuitry was composed of memory crystals,' Oski Katsura said. 'The processors were subsidiary elements to facilitate access and recording. Basically it was a memory core.'

'I see. And had the ice preserved it like we hoped?' Ione asked. 'It looked intact when I saw it.'

'Oh, yes. It was almost completely intact, the chips and crystals encased in ice functioned perfectly after they had been removed and cleaned. The reason it has taken us so long to decrypt the data stored in the crystals is that it is non-standard.' They came to a set of wide double doors, and Oski Katsura datavised a security code to open them, gesturing Ione through.

The Electronics Division always reminded her of a cyber-factory: rows of identical clean rooms illuminated by harsh white lighting, all of them filled with enigmatic blocks of equipment trailing wires and cables everywhere. This room was no different, broad benches ran round the walls, with another down the centre, cluttered with customized electronics cabinets and test rigs. The far end was a glass wall partitioning off six workshop cubicles. Several researchers were inside, using robot precision-assembly cells to fabricate various units. At the opposite end of the room to the cubicles a stainless steel pedestal sat on the floor, supporting a big sphere made up of tough transparent composite. Thick environmental-support hoses snaked away from the lower quarter of the sphere, plugging into bulky conditioning units. Ione saw the Laymil electronics stack in the middle of the sphere, with power leads and fibre-optic cables radiating out of its base. More surprisingly, Lieria was standing in front of the long bench in the middle of the room, her tractamorphic arms branching into five or six tentacles apiece, all of which were wound through an electronics cabinet.

Ione was quite proud she could recognize the Kiint immediately. **Good morning, Lieria, I thought you worked in the Physiology Division.**

The tentacle appendages uncoiled from the cabinet, flowing back into one solid pillar of flesh again. Lieria turned ponderously, careful not to knock into anything. **Welcome, Ione Saldana. I am here because Oski Katsura requested my input in this program. I have been able to contribute to the analysis of data stored in the Laymil crystals; there is some crossover into my primary field of study.**

Excellent.

I note your cranial hair carries a residue of salt water; have you been swimming?

Yes, I gave Haile a scrub down. She's getting impatient to look around Tranquillity. You'll have to let me know when you think she's ready.

Your kindness is most welcome. We judge her mature enough to be allowed outside parental restriction providing she is accompanied. But do not permit her to impose upon your own time.

She's no bother.

One of Lieria's arms lengthened to pick up a slender white wafer ten centimetres square from the bench. The unit emitted a single whistle, then spoke. 'Greetings, Director Parker Higgens.'

He gave the xenoc a small bow.

Oski Katsura tapped the environment bubble with a fingernail. 'We cleaned and tested all the components before we reassembled it,' she told Ione. 'That ice wasn't pure water, there were some peculiar hydrocarbons mixed in.'

'Laymil faecal matter,' Lieria said through the wafer.

'Quite. But the real challenge came from the data itself, it was like nothing we have found so far. It seemed almost totally randomized. At first we thought it might be some kind of artform, then we began to notice irregular trait repetition.'

The same patterns repeated in different combinations, Tranquillity translated.

The science staff always go through this rigmarole, don't they? she asked, half amused.

It is their chance to demonstrate to you, their paymaster, the effort they put in. Don't disillusion them, it is impolite.

Ione kept her face neutral during the second-long exchange. 'Which was enough to formulate a recognition program,' she said smoothly.

'Quite,' said Oski Katsura. 'Ninety per cent of the data was garbage to us, but these patterns kept appearing.'

'Once we had enough of them clearly identified we held an interdisciplinary conference and asked for best guesses,' Parker Higgens said. 'Bit of a long shot, but it paid off handsomely. I'm pleased to say Lieria said they resembled Laymil optical impulses.'

'Correct,' Lieria said through the wafer. 'Similarity approaching eighty-five per cent. The data packages represented colours to a Laymil eye.'

'Once we'd established that, we ran a comparison on the rest of the data, trying to match it with other Laymil nerve impulses,' Oski Katsura said. 'Jackpot. Well, more or less. It took four months to write interpretation programs and build suitable interface units, but we got there in the end.' A wave of her hand took in the benches and all their elaborate equipment. 'We unravelled the first full sequence last night.'

Dawning realization at what Oski Katsura was actually saying brought a sense of real excitement to Ione. Her eyes were drawn to the stack in its protective bubble. She touched the transparent surface reverently, it was warmer than the ambient temperature. 'This is a recording of a Laymil sensorium?' she asked.

Parker Higgens and Oski Katsura grinned like ten-year-olds. 'Yes, ma'am,' Parker Higgens said.

She turned to him sharply. 'How much is there? How long does it go on for?'

Oski Katsura gave a modest shrug. 'We don't quite understand the file sequences yet. The one which we have translated so far lasts a little over three minutes.'

'How long?' Ione let a waspish note creep into her voice.

'If the bit rate holds constant for the other sequences . . . approximately eight thousand hours.'

Did she say eight *thousand*?

Yes, said Tranquillity.

'Bloody hell!' An oafish smile appeared on Ione's face. 'When you said translated, what did you mean?'

'The sequence has been adapted for human sensevise reception,' Oski Katsura said.

'Have you reviewed it?'

'Yes. The quality is below normal commercial standards, but that ought to improve once we refine our programs and equipment.'

'Can Tranquillity access your equipment through the communication net?' Ione asked urgently.

'It should be simple enough. One moment, I'll datavise the entry code,' Oski Katsura said. 'That's it.'

Show me!

Senses which were fundamentally *wrong* engulfed her conscious thoughts, leaving her as a passive, faintly protesting, observer. The Laymil body was trisymmetric, standing one metre seventy-five high, possessing a tough, heavily crinkled slate grey skin. There were three legs, with a double-jointed knee, and feet which ended in a hoof. Three arms with a bulbous shoulder which permitted a great deal of articulation, a single elbow, and hands with four triple-jointed fingers as thick as a human thumb and twice as long, bestowing considerable strength and dexterity. Most disturbing of all were the three sensor heads, emerging like truncated serpents between the shoulders. Each one had an eye at the front, with a triangular bat-ear above it, and a toothless breathing mouth below. All the mouths could vocalize, but one was larger and more sophisticated than the other two, which made up for their deficiency with a more acute sense of smell. The feeding mouth was on the top of the torso, in the cleft between the necks, a circular orifice equipped with sharp needle teeth.

The body Ione now wore constricted her own figure severely, pulping it below circular bands of muscle that flexed and twisted sinuously, squeezing protesting flesh and bone into a new shape, forcing her to conform to the resurgent identity suspended in the crystal matrix. She felt as though her limbs were being systematically twisted in every direction apart from the ones nature intended. But there was no pain inherent in the metamorphosis. Feverish thoughts, electrified by instinctive revulsion, began to calm. She started to look around, accepting the trinocular viewpoint input as best she could.

She was wearing clothes. The first surprise; born of prejudice, the foreign physique was *animal*, unhuman, no anthropomorphism could possibly exist here to build a bridge. But the trousers were easily recognizable, tubes of midnight-purple fabric, sleek as silk against the coarse skin. They came halfway down the lower leg, there was even a recognizable belt. The shirt was a stretchy cylinder of light green, with hoops that hung over the necks.

And she was walking, a three-legged walk that was so easy, so natural that she didn't even have to think how to move the limbs to avoid tripping. The sensor head with the speaking mouth was always at the front, swinging slowly from side to side. Her other two heads scanned the surrounding countryside.

Sights and sounds besieged her. There were few half-tones in her visual world, bright primary colours dominated; but the image was flecked with minute black fissures, like an AV projection running heavy interference; the myriad sounds sliced with half-second breaks of silence.

Ione glossed over the flaws. She was walking through a Laymil habitat. If Tranquillity was manicured perfection, this was manicured anarchy. The trees were at war, thrusting and clashing against each other. Nothing grew upright. It was like a jungle hit by a hurricane, but with the trunks packed so closely they couldn't fall, only topple onto their neighbours. She saw trees with their kinked trunks cupped together, trunks that spiralled round each other wrestling for height and light, young shoots piercing old flaking boles. Roots the size of a man's torso emerged from the trunks well above her head, stabbing down like fleshy beige fork prongs into the sandy soil, producing a buttress cone. The leaves were long ribbons, curled into spirals, a deep olive-green in colour. And down where she walked, where shadows and sunbeams alternated like incorporeal pillars, every nook and crevice was crammed with tiny cobalt-blue flowering mushrooms, their pilei fringed with vermilion stamens, swaying like sea anemones in a weak current.

Pleasure and peace soaked into her like sunlight through amber. The forest was in harmony, its life spirit resonating with the spaceholm mother essence, singing their madrigal in unison. She listened with her heart, thankful for the privilege of living.

Hoofs trod evenly along the meandering trail carrying her towards the fourth marriage community. Her husbands/mates awaited her, the eagerness inside her was woven into the forest song and rejoiced over by the mother essence.

She reached the borders of the jungle, saddened by the smaller trees, the end of song, jubilant that she had passed through cleanly, that she was worthy of a fourth reproduction cycle. The trees gave way to open land, a gentle valley swathed in high, lush grasses and speckled with vivid reds and yellows and blues of bell-shaped flowers. Spaceholm reared around her, a landscape of tangled greens, rampant vegetation choking the silver veins of streams and rivers, smeared with fragile tufts of cloud. Sunspires stabbed out along the axis from the centre of each endcap, thin sabres stretching for twenty kilometres, furiously radiant.

'**Tree spirit song unity**,' she called with voice and mind. Her two clarion heads bugled gleefully. '**I await**.'

'Richness reward embryo growth daughter,' the spaceholm mother entity replied.

'Male selection?'

'Concord.'

'Unison awaits.'

'Life urge rapture.'

She started to walk down the slope. Ahead of her on the floor of the valley was the fourth marriage community. Blue polyp cuboidal structures, rigidly symmetrical, arrayed in concentric rings. On the paths between the featureless walls she could see other Laymil moving about. All her heads craned forward.

The memory ended.

The lurch back into the conformity of the electronics lab was as abrupt as it was shocking. Ione put a hand on the bench to steady herself. Oski Katsura and Parker Higgens were giving her an anxious look, even Lieria's dark violet eyes were focused on her.

'That was . . . astonishing,' she managed to say. The hot Laymil jungle lurked around the fringes of sight like a vengeful daydream. 'Those trees, she seemed to think of them as alive.'

'Yes,' Parker Higgens said. 'It was obviously some kind of mating selection test or ritual. We know Laymil females are capable of five reproductive cycles, it never occurred to anybody that they might be subject to artificial restraints. In fact I find it amazing that a culture so sophisticated should still indulge in what was almost a pagan rite.'

'I'm not sure it was pagan,' Oski Katsura said. 'We have already identified a gene sequence similar to the Edenist affinity gene in the Laymil genome. However they are obviously far more Gaiaistic than Edenist humans; their habitat, the spaceholm, was virtually a part of the reproductive process. It certainly seemed to possess some kind of veto power.'

'Like me and Tranquillity,' Ione said under her breath.

Hardly.

Give us another five thousand years, and the birth of a new Lord of Ruin could easily become ritualized.

You are entirely correct, Ione Saldana, Lieria said. The Kiint continued speaking through her white wafer. 'I note considerable evidence to indicate the Laymil mate-selection process is based on scientific eugenics rather than primitive spiritualism. Suitability is considerably more than possession of desirable physical characteristics, mental strength is obviously a prime requirement.'

'Whatever, it opens up a fantastic window into their culture,' Parker Higgens said. 'We knew so little before this. To think that a mere three minutes could show us so much. The possibilities it reveals . . .' He looked at the electronics stack almost in worship.

'Will there be any problem in translating the rest of it?' Ione asked Oski Katsura.

'I don't see any. What you accessed was still pretty crude, the emotional analogues were only rough approximates. We'll tweak the program, of course, but I doubt we could have direct parallels with a race that alien.'

Ione stared at the electronics stack. An oracle for a whole race. And possibly, just possibly, the secret was inside it: why they did it. The more she thought about it, the more puzzling it became. The Laymil were so vibrantly alive. What in God's name could ever make an entity like that commit suicide?

She shivered slightly, then turned to Parker Higgens. 'Set up a priority budget for the Electronics Division,' she said decisively. 'I want all eight thousand hours translated as soon as possible. And the Cultural Analysis Division is going to have to be expanded considerably. We've concentrated far too much on the technological and physical side of the Laymil to date, that's going to have to change now.'

Parker Higgens opened his mouth to protest.

'That wasn't a criticism, Parker,' she said quickly. 'The physical is all we've had to go on so far. But now we have these sensory and emotional memories we're entering a new phase. Extend invitations to whichever xenoc psychology experts you think will be of help, offer endowment sabbaticals from their current tenures. I'll add a personal message to the invitations if you think my name will carry any weight with them.'

'Yes, ma'am.' Parker Higgens appeared bemused by her speed.

'Lieria, I'd like you or one of your colleagues to assist with the cultural interpretation, I can see your viewpoints will be invaluable.'

Lieria's arms rippled from root to tip (a Kiint laugh?). 'It will be my pleasure to assist, Ione Saldana.'

'One final thing. I want Tranquillity to be the first to review the memories as and when they are translated.'

'Yes,' Oski Katsura said uncertainly.

'Sorry,' Ione said with an earnest smile. 'But as Lord of Ruin I retain the right to embargo weapons technology. The cultural experts might argue over the finer nuances of what we see for months at a time, but a weapon is pretty easy to spot. I don't want any particularly unsavoury armaments released to the Confederation at large.' And if it was an enemy's weapon that destroyed the Laymil habitats I want to know before I decide what to tell everybody.

15

Night had come to Durringham. It brought with it a thick grey mist which flowed down the slushy streets and over the mouldering roof slats, depositing an unctuous coating of droplets in its wake. The water filmed every exterior wall until the whole city was glistening darkly, droplets running together and dribbling off the eaves and overhangs. Doors and shutters were no protection, the mist penetrated buildings with ease, soaking into fabrics and condensing over furniture. It was worse than the rain.

The Governor's office was faring little better than the rest of the city. Colin Rexrew had turned up the conditioning until it made an aggravated rattling sound, but the atmosphere inside remained obstinately muggy. He was reviewing satellite images with Terrance Smith and Candace Elford, Lalonde's Chief Sheriff. The three big wall-screens opposite the curving window were displaying pictures of a riverside settlement village. They showed the usual collection of shambolic huts and small fields, large piles of felled trunks, and stumps which played host to ears of orange fungi. Chickens scratched around in the dirt between the huts, while dogs roamed free. The few people captured by the camera were dressed in dirty, ragged clothes. One child, about two years old, was completely naked.

'These are very poor images,' Colin Rexrew complained. Most of the edges were blurred, even the colours appeared wan.

'Yes,' Candace Elford agreed. 'We ran a diagnostic check on the observation satellite, but there was no malfunction. The images from any other area it views are flawless. The satellite only has trouble when it's passing over the Quallheim.'

'Oh, come on,' Terrance Smith said. 'You can't mean that the people in the Quallheim Counties can distort our observation, surely?'

Candace Elford considered her answer. She was fifty-seven, and Lalonde was her second appointment as chief sheriff. Both senior appointments had been won because of her thoroughness; she had worked her way up through various colony planet police services, and harboured a kind of bewildered contempt for colonists, who, she had discovered, were capable of damn near anything out in the frontier lands. 'It's unlikely,' she admitted. 'The Confederation Navy ELINT satellites haven't detected any unusual emissions from Schuster County. It's probably a glitch, that satellite is fifteen years old, and it hasn't been serviced for the last eleven years.'

'All right,' Colin Rexrew said. 'Point noted. We don't have the money for regular services, as you well know.'

'When it breaks down, a replacement will cost the LDC a lot more than the expense of proper triennial maintenance,' Candace Elford countered.

'Please! Can we stick with the topic in hand,' Colin Rexrew said. He eyed the drinks cabinet longingly. It would have been nice to break open one of the chilled white wines and have a more relaxed session, but Candace Elford would have refused, which would make it awkward. She was such an uncompromising officer; one of his best though, someone the sheriffs respected and obeyed. He needed her, so he put up with her rigid adherence to protocol, counting his blessings.

'Very well,' she said crisply. 'As you can see, Aberdale has twelve burnt-out buildings. According to the sheriff in Schuster town, Matthew Skinner, there was some kind of Ivet disturbance four days ago, which is when the buildings were razed. The

Ivets allegedly murdered a ten-year-old boy, and the villagers set about hunting them down. Supervisor Manani's communication block wasn't working, so an Aberdale villager visited Schuster the day after this murder, and Matthew Skinner reported it to my office. That was three days ago. He said he was riding to Aberdale to investigate; apparently most of the Ivets had been killed by that time. We heard nothing until this morning, when Matthew Skinner said the disturbance was over, and the Aberdale Ivets were all dead.'

'I disapprove of vigilante action,' Colin Rexrew said. 'Officially, that is. But given the circumstances I can't say I blame the Aberdale villagers, those Ivets have always been a mixed blessing. Half of them should never be sent here, ten years' work-time isn't going to rehabilitate the real recidivists.'

'Yes, sir,' Candace Elford said. 'But that's not the problem.'

Colin Rexrew brushed back tufts of his thinning hair with clammy hands. 'I didn't think it would be that simple. Go on.'

She datavised an order into the office's computer. The screens started to display another village; it looked even more impecunious than Aberdale. 'This is Schuster town itself,' she said. 'The image was recorded this morning. As you can see, there are three burnt-out buildings.'

Colin Rexrew sat up a little straighter behind his desk. 'They had Ivet trouble, too?'

'That is the curious thing,' Candace Elford said. 'Matthew Skinner never mentioned the fires, and he should have done, fires like that are dangerous in those kinds of communities. The last routine satellite images we have of Schuster are two weeks old, the buildings were intact then.'

'It's pushing coincidence a long way,' Colin Rexrew said, half to himself.

'That's what my office thought,' Candace Elford said. 'So we started checking a little closer. The Land Allocation Office divided the Quallheim territory up into three counties, Schuster, Medellin, and Rossan, which between them now have ten villages. We spotted burnt-out buildings in six of those villages: Aberdale, Schuster, Qayen, Pamiers, Kilkee, and Medellin.' She datavised more instructions. The screens started to run through the images of the villages her office had recorded that morning.

'Oh, Jesus,' Colin Rexrew muttered. Some of the blackened timbers were still smoking. 'What's been happening up there?'

'First thing we asked. So we called up each of the village supervisors,' Candace Elford said. 'Qayen's didn't answer, the other three said everything was fine. So we called up the villages that didn't show any damage. Salkhad, Guer, and Suttal didn't answer; Rossan's supervisor said they were all OK, and nothing out of the ordinary was happening. They hadn't heard or seen anything from any of the other villages.'

'What's your opinion?' Colin Rexrew asked.

The chief sheriff turned back to the screens. 'One final piece of information. The satellite made seven passes over the Quallheim Counties today. Despite the shoddy images, at no time did we see anybody working in any of those fields; not in any of the ten villages.'

Terrance Smith whistled as he sucked air through his teeth. 'Not good. There's no way you'd keep a colonist from his field, not on a day with weather like it has been up there. They are utterly dependent on those crops. The supervisors make it quite plain from the start, once they're settled, they don't get any help from Durringham. They can't afford to leave the fields untended. Remember what happened in Arklow County?'

Colin Rexrew gave his aide an irritable look. 'Don't remind me, I accessed the files when I arrived.' He transferred his gaze to the screens, and the image of Qayen village. A black premonition was rising in his mind. 'So what are you telling me, Candace?'

'I know what it looks like,' she said. 'I just can't believe it, that's all. An Ivet revolt which has successfully taken control of the Quallheim Counties, and in just four days, too.'

'There are over six thousand colonists spread out in those

counties,' Terrance Smith said. 'Most of them have weapons and aren't afraid to use them. Against that, there are a hundred and eighty-six Ivets, unarmed and unorganized, and without any form of reliable communication. They're Earth's junk, waster kids; if they could organize something like this they would never be here in the first place.'

'I know,' she said. 'That's why I said I don't believe it. But what else could it be? Someone from outside? Who?'

Colin Rexrew frowned. 'Schuster's been a problem before. What . . .' He trailed off, requesting a search through the files stored in his neural nanonics. 'Ah, yes; the disappearing homestead families. Do you remember, Terrance, I sent a marshal up to investigate last year. Bloody great waste of money that was.'

'It was a waste of money from our point of view because the marshal didn't find anything,' Terrance Smith said. 'That in itself was unusual. Those marshals are good. Which means either it was a genuine case of some animal carrying the families away, or some unknown group was responsible, and managed to cover their tracks to such an extent it fooled both the local supervisor and the marshal. If it was an organized raid, then the perpetrators were at least the equal of our marshal.'

'So?' Colin Rexrew asked.

'So now we have another event, originating in the same county, that would be hard to explain away in terms of an Ivet revolt. Certainly the scale of the trouble argues against it being the Ivets by themselves. But an external group taking over the Quallheim Counties would fit the facts we have.'

'We only have a secondhand report that it was Ivets anyway,' Colin Rexrew said, pondering the unwelcome idea.

'It still doesn't make any sense,' Candace Elford said. 'I concede that the facts indicate the Ivets are getting help. But what external group? And why the Quallheim Counties, for God's sake? There's no wealth out there; the colonists are barely self-sufficient. There's no wealth anywhere on Lalonde, come to that.'

'This isn't getting us anywhere,' Colin Rexrew said. 'Look, I've got three river-boats scheduled to leave in two days, they're taking six hundred fresh settlers up to Schuster County so they can start another village. You're my security adviser, Candace, are you telling me not to send them?'

'I think my advice would have to be, yes; certainly at this stage. It's not as if you're short of destinations. Sending unsuspecting raw colonists into the middle of a potential revolt wouldn't look good on any of our records. Is there a nearby alternative to Schuster where you can settle them?'

'Willow West County on the Frenshaw tributary,' Terrance Smith suggested. 'It's only a hundred kilometres north-west of Schuster; plenty of room for them there. It's on our current territory development list anyway.'

'OK,' Colin Rexrew said. 'Get it organized with the Land Allocation Office. In the meantime, what do you intend to do about the Quallheim situation, Candace?'

'I want your permission to send a posse up there on the boats with the colonists. Once the colonists have been dropped off at Willow West, the boats can take them on to the Quallheim. As soon as I've got reliable people on the ground we can establish what's really going on and restore some order.'

'How many do you want to send?'

'A hundred ought to be enough. Twenty full-time sheriffs, and the rest we can deputize. God knows, there's enough men in Durringham who'll jump at the chance of five weeks cruising the river on full pay. I'd like three marshals, as well, just to be on the safe side.'

'Yes, all right,' Colin Rexrew said. 'But just remember it comes out of your budget.'

'It'll be nearly three weeks before you can get your people up there,' Terrance Smith said thoughtfully.

'So?' the chief sheriff asked. 'I can't make the boats go any faster.'

'No, but a lot can happen in that time. If we believe what we've seen so far, this revolt spread down the Quallheim in four days. Taking a worst case scenario, the revolt could carry on growing at the same rate, leaving your initial hundred-strong posse heavily outgunned. What I suggest is that we get the posse out there as fast as physically possible, and stop any further expansion before it gets totally out of hand. We have three VTOL aircraft at the spaceport, BK133s that our ecology research team use for survey missions. They're subsonic, and they only seat ten, but they could run a relay out to the mouth of the Quallheim. That way we'd have your posse there in two days.'

Colin Rexrew let his head rest on the back of the chair, and ran a cost comparison through his neural nanonics. 'Bloody expensive,' he said. 'And one of those VTOLs is out of service anyway after last year's cuts reduced the Aboriginal Fruit Classification budget. We'll compromise, as always. Candace sends her sheriffs and deputies up to the Quallheim on the river-boats, and her office here in town continues to monitor the situation with the observation satellite. If this revolt, or whatever it is, looks like it's spreading down out of the Quallheim Counties, we'll use the VTOLs to reinforce the posse before they get there.'

*

The electrophoresecent cells at the apex of Laton's singular study were darkened, eradicating external stimuli so he could focus himself on the inner self. Senses crept in on his glacial mind, impressions garnered via affinity from the servitor scouts spread throughout the jungle. The results displeased him enormously. In fact they were edging him towards worry. He hadn't felt like this since the Edenist Intelligence operatives had closed in, forcing him to flee his original habitat nearly seventy years previously. At that time he had felt fury, fear, and dismay the intensity of which he had never known as an Edenist; it had made him realize how worthless that culture truly was. His rejection had been total after that.

And now something was closing in on him again. Something he neither knew nor understood; something which acted like sequestration nanonics, usurping a human's original personality and replacing it with mechanoid warrior traits. He had watched the drastically modified behaviour of Quinn Dexter and the Ivets after the incident with the lightning in the jungle, They acted like fully trained mercenary troops, and others they came into contact with soon exhibited similar traits, though a minority of those usurped acted almost normally – most puzzling. Nor did they need weapons, they acquired an ability to throw sprays of photons like a holographic projector, light which could act like a thermal-induction field, but with tremendous power and reach. Yet there was no visible physical mechanism.

Laton had felt the first overspill of pain from Camilla when the Ivets cremated her, mercifully shortened as she lost consciousness. He mourned his daughter as was proper, away in some subsidiary section of his mind, her absence from his life a sting of regret. But the important thing now was the threat he himself faced. In order to confront your enemy without fear, for fear is a bolt in the enemy's quiver, you must understand your enemy. And understanding was the one thing which had not come in four solid days of supreme cerebral effort.

Some of the glimpses he had snatched through the scouts defied physics. Either that or physics had advanced beyond all reasonable expectations during his exile. That was conceivable, he reasoned, weapons science was always kept very close to the government's chest, receiving the most funds and the least publicity.

Memory: of a man looking up at the sky and seeing the affinity bonded kestrel. The man laughed and raised his hand, snapping his fingers. Air around the kestrel solidified, entombing it in a matrix of frozen molecules, and sending it tumbling from the sky to dash its body against the rocks two hundred metres below. A snap of the fingers . . .

Memory: of a frantic terrified villager from Kilkee firing his laser hunting rifle at one of the usurped. The range had been fifteen metres, and the beam had no effect whatsoever. After the first few shots the rifle had died completely. Then the vennal Laton was using to scout with had curled up and sunk into some kind of coma.

The villages throughout the Quallheim Counties had been conquered with bewildering swiftness. That more than anything convinced Laton he was up against some kind of military force. There was a directing intelligence behind the usurped, expanding their numerical strength at an exponential rate. But what really baffled him was why. He had chosen Lalonde because it fitted his long-range goals; other than that it was a worthless planet. Why take control of people out here?

A test was the only explanation he could think of. Which begged the question what was it a preliminary to? The potential was awesome.

Laton? Waldsey's mental tone was fearful and uncertain, not like him at all.

Yes, Laton replied equitably. He could guess what was coming next. After sixty years he knew the way his colleagues' minds worked better than they did. He was only mildly surprised that it had taken them so long to confront him.

Do you know what it is yet?

No. I have been considering some kind of viral nanonic, but the number of demonstrated functions it possesses would be orders of magnitude above anything we even have theories for. And some of those functions are difficult to explain in terms of the physics we know and understand. In short, if you have a technology that powerful, why bother using it in this fashion? It is most puzzling.

Puzzling! Tao said angrily. **Father, it is bloody lethal, and it's right outside the tree. To hell with *puzzling*, we have to do something.**

Laton let the glimmer image of a smile penetrate their shared affinity. Only his children ever dared to contradict him, which pleased him after a fashion; obsequiousness was something he disapproved of almost as much as disloyalty. Which gave everybody a narrow, and perilous, balance to maintain. No doubt you have an idea as to what we should do.

Yeah. Load up the landcruisers, and head for the hills. Call it a strategic withdrawal, call it prudence, but just let's get *out* of this tree. Now. While we still can. I don't mind admitting I'm frightened, if nobody else will.

I would imagine that even this planet's chief sheriff will know that something odd is happening in Aberdale and the other Quallheim villages by now, Laton said. He sensed the others coming into the conversation, their minds carefully shielded from leaking too many emotions. The LDC's surveillance satellite may be in a deplorable condition, but I assure you it would be quite capable of spotting the landcruisers. And it will be focused on the Quallheim Counties with considerable diligence.

So? We just zap it. The old blackhawk masers you brought down can reach it. It'll be weeks before the LDC replace it. By that time we'll be long gone. They'll see the track we made breaking through the jungle, but once we reach the savannah they'll lose us.

I would remind you just how close to success our immortality project is. Are you willing to sacrifice that?

Father, unless we get out of here, we aren't going to have a project left, or a life to immortalize. We can't defend ourselves against these usurped villagers. I've watched what happens when anyone shoots them. They don't even notice it! And even if somebody does manage to beat them, the Quallheim Counties are going to be searched a centimetre at a time afterwards. Either way, we can't stay here.

The lad's got a point there, Laton, Salkid said. We can't cling on here simply out of sentiment.

You always told me knowledge can't be destroyed, Tao said. We know how to splice a parallel-processing brain together. What we

need is a secure location in which to do it. The tree certainly isn't it, not any more.

Well argued, Laton said. **Except I'm not sure anywhere on Lalonde can be classed as safe any more. This technology is fearsome.** He deliberately allowed his emotional shield to slip, and felt the shocked recoil of their thoughts that he who never demonstrated weakness was so deeply perturbed.

We can hardly walk into Durringham's spaceport and ask for a lift outsystem, Waldsey said.

The children can, Laton said. **They have been born here, the intelligence agencies have no record of them. Once in orbit they can secure a starship for us.**

Bloody hell, you mean it.

Indeed. It is the logical course. At the ultimate extreme, I am prepared to contact the Intelligence agencies in Durringham and report the situation to them. They will take me seriously, and that way a warning will get out.

Is it that bad, Father? Salsett asked anxiously.

Laton projected a burst of reassuring warmth at the fifteen-year-old girl. **I don't think it will come to that, darling.**

Leaving the tree, she said wonderingly.

Yes, he said. **Tao, that was a good suggestion of yours; you and Salkid take a blackhawk maser out of storage, and be ready to eliminate that observation satellite. The rest of you have ten hours to pack. We start for Durringham tonight.**

He couldn't detect a single whiff of dissension. Minds retreated from the affinity contact.

In the hours which followed, the gigantea tree was subject to the kind of coordinated activity it hadn't seen since their arrival. Orders were flung frantically at the incorporated and the housechimps as the residents attempted to dismantle the work of thirty years in the short hours they had left. Heartbreaking decisions were made over what could go and what must stay, several couples arguing. The landcruisers had to be checked over and prepared after thirty years' unemployment.

Laton's younger children scampered about getting in the way, nervous and elated at the prospect of leaving; the older members of the fellowship started thinking about the Confederation worlds again. Thermal charges were set throughout the rooms and corridors, ready to obliterate all trace of the gigantea's secrets.

The hectic activity registered as a background burble amid Laton's steely thoughts. Occasionally someone would intrude into his contemplation to ask for instructions.

After designating the few personal items he wanted to accompany them, he spent his time reviewing the memory of what happened in the clearing when Quinn Dexter killed Supervisor Manani. That strange lightning was the start of it. He ran and re-ran Camilla's memory images, which were stored in the tree's sub-sentient bitek processor array. The lightning seemed to be flat, almost compressed, some sections darker than others. As he ran the memory again the dark areas moved, sliding down the glaring streamers of rampaging electrons. The lightning bolts were acting as conduits to some kind of energy pattern, one which behaved outside the accepted norm.

A draught of air stroked his face. He opened his eyes to darkness. The study was as it always had been. He switched his retinal implants to infrared. Jackson Gael and Ruth Hilton stood on the curving wood before him.

'Clever,' Laton said. His contact with the processors faded away. Affinity was reduced to a whisper rattling round the closed confines of his skull. 'It's energy, isn't it? A self-determining viral program that can store itself in a non-physical lattice.'

Ruth bent down, and put her hand under his chin, tilting his face up so she could examine him. 'Edenists. Always so rational.'

'But where did it come from, I wonder?' Laton asked.

'What will it take to break his beliefs?' Jackson Gael asked.

'It's not of human origin,' Laton said. 'I'm sure of that; nor any of the xenoc races we know.'

'We'll find out tonight,' Ruth said. She let go of Laton's chin, and held out her hand. 'Come along.'

*

The morning after Governor Rexrew's briefing with Candace Elford, Ralph Hiltch was sitting behind his own desk in the Kulu Embassy dumper receiving a condensed version of events from Jenny Harris. One of the ESA assets she ran in the sheriff's office had asked for a meeting and told her about the trouble brewing in the Quallheim Counties.

All well and good, it was nice to see the Governor couldn't fart without the ESA knowing, but like Rexrew before him, Ralph was having a lot of trouble with the concept of an Ivet uprising.

'An open revolt?' he asked the lieutenant sceptically.

'It looks that way,' she said apologetically. 'Here, my contact gave me a flek of the surveillance satellite images.' She loaded it into the processor block on Ralph's desk, and the screens on the wall began to show the Quallheim's motley collection of villages.

Ralph stood in front of them, hands on his hips as the semicircular clearings cut into solid jungle appeared. The tree-tops looked like green foam, broken by occasional glades, and virtually sealing over streams and the smaller rivers. 'There's been a lot of fires,' he agreed unhappily. 'And recently, too. Can't you manage a better resolution than this?'

'Apparently not, and that's the second cause for alarm. Something is affecting the satellite every time it passes over the Quallheim tributary. No other section of Amarisk is affected.'

He gave her a long look.

'I know,' she said. 'It sounds ridiculous.'

Ralph gave his neural nanonics a search request and returned his attention to the screens while it was running. 'There's certainly been some kind of fight down there. And this isn't the first time Schuster County has come to our attention.' The neural nanonics reported a blank; so he opened a channel to access his processor block's classified military systems file, extending the search.

'Captain Lambourne reported that nothing ever came out of the marshal's visit last year,' Jenny Harris said. 'We still don't know what happened to those homestead families.'

Ralph's neural nanonics told him that the processor block file couldn't find a match for his request. 'Interesting. According to our files, there is no known electronic warfare system which can distort a satellite image like this.'

'How up to date are the files?'

'Last year's.' He walked back to his seat. 'But you're missing the point. Firstly it's a wholly ineffective system, all it does is fuzz the image slightly. Secondly, if you've gone to all the trouble to tamper with the satellite why not knock it out altogether? Given the age of Lalonde's satellite, everyone would assume it was a natural malfunction. This method actually draws attention to the Quallheim.'

'Or draws attention away from somewhere else,' she said.

'I'm paranoid, but am I paranoid enough?' he muttered. Outside the window the dark rooftops of Durringham were steaming softly in the bright morning sun. It was all so cheerfully primitive, the residents walking through the tacky streets, power bikes throwing up fans of mud, a teenage couple lost in each other, the tail end of a new colonist group making their way down to the transients' dormitories. Every morning for the last four years he'd seen variants on the same scene. Lalonde's inhabitants got on with their basic, modestly corrupt lives, and never bothered anyone. They couldn't, they didn't have the means. 'The thing which disturbs me most is Rexrew's idea that it could be an external group attempting some kind of coup. I almost agree with him, it's certainly more logical than an Ivet revolt.' He rapped his knuckles on the desktop, trying to think. 'When is this posse of Candace Elford's setting off?'

'Tomorrow; she's going to start recruiting her deputies this morning. And incidentally, the *Swithland* is one of the boats that will be carrying them. Captain Lambourne can keep us updated if you allow her to use a communication block.'

'OK, but I want at least five of our assets in that group of deputies, more if you can manage. We need to know what's going on up in the Quallheim Counties. Equip them with communication blocks as well, but make sure they understand they must only use them if the situation is urgent. I'll speak to Kelven Solanki about the issue, he's probably as keen as we are to know what's going on.'

'I'll get onto it,' she said. 'One of the sheriffs Elford is sending belongs to me anyway, that'll make placing assets among the deputies a lot easier.'

'Good, well done.'

Jenny Harris saluted professionally, but before she got to the door she turned back and said, 'I don't understand. Why would anyone want to stage a coup out in the middle of the hinterlands?'

'Someone with an eye to the future, maybe. If it is, our duty is very clear cut.'

'Yes, sir; but if that is the case, they'd need help from outsystem.'

'True. Well, at least that's easy enough to watch for.'

Ralph occupied himself with genuine embassy attaché work for the next two hours. Lalonde imported very little, but from the list of what it did require he tried to secure a reasonable portion for Kulu companies. He was trying to find a supplier for the high-temperature moulds a new glassworks factory wanted when his neural nanonics alerted him to an unscheduled starship that had just jumped into Lalonde's designated emergence zone, fifty thousand kilometres above the planet's surface. The dumper's electronics tapped the downlink from Lalonde's two civil spaceflight monitor satellites, giving him access to the raw data. What it didn't provide was system command authority, he was a passive observer.

Lalonde's traffic control took a long time to respond to the monitor satellite's discovery. There were three starships in an equatorial parking orbit, two colonist transports from Earth, and a freighter from New California, nothing else was due for a week. The staff probably hadn't even been in the control centre, he thought impatiently as he waited for them to get off their arses and provide him with more information.

Starship visits outside the regular LDC contracted vessels, and the voidhawk supply run for Aethra, were rare events, there were never more than five or six a year. That this one should appear at this time was a coincidence he couldn't put out of his mind.

The starship was already under power and heading for a standard equatorial parking orbit when traffic control eventually triggered its transponder and established a communication channel. Data flooded into Ralph's mind, the standard Confederation Astronautics Board registration and certification. It was an independent trader vessel called *Lady Macbeth.*

His suspicion deepened.

*

Rumour hit Durringham and spread with a speed that a news company's distribution division would have envied. It started when Candace Elford's staff went out for a drink after a hard day assessing the scrambled information they were getting from the Quallheim Counties. Durringham's strong beer, sweet wines from nearby estates, and running mild mood-stimulant programs through their neural nanonics liberated a quantity of almost accurate information about exactly what had been going on all day in the chief sheriff's office.

It took half of Lalonde's long night to filter out of the pubs the sheriffs used and down into the more basic taverns the agricultural workers, port labourers, and river crews favoured. Distance, time, alcohol, and weak hallucinogens distorted and amplified the story in creative surges. The end results which were shouted and argued over loudly through the riverside drinking dens would have impressed any student of social dynamics. The following day, it proliferated through every workplace and home.

The main exchanges of conversations went thus.

The colonists in the Quallheim Counties had been ritually massacred by the Ivets, who had taken up Devil worship. A Satanic theocracy had been declared to the Governor and demanded recognition as an independent state, and all the Ivets were to be sent there.

An army of radical anarchistic Ivets was marching downriver, razing villages as they went, looting and raping. They were kamikazes, sworn to destroy Lalonde.

Kulu Royal Marines had landed upriver and established a beachhead for a full invasion force: all the locals who resisted had been executed. The Ivets had welcomed the marines, betraying colonists who resisted. Supplementary: Lalonde was going to be incorporated into the Kulu Kingdom by force. (Pure crap, people said, why would Alastair II want this God-awful shit-tip of a planet?)

The Tyrathca farmers had suffered a famine and they were eating humans, starting with Aberdale. (No, not possible. Weren't the Tyrathca herbivores?)

Waster kids from Earth had stolen a starship, and after zapping the sheriff's surveillance satellite they'd landed to help their old gang mates, the Ivets.

Blackhawks and mercenary starships had banded together; they were invading Lalonde, and they were planning on turning it into a rebel world which would be a base for raiding the Confederation. Colonists were being used for slave labour to build fortifications and secret landing sites out in the jungle. Ivets were captaining the work parties.

Two things remained reasonably constant amid all the wild theorizing. One: colonists had been killed by Ivets. Two: Ivets were heading/helping the revolt.

Durringham was a frontier town, the vast majority of its population scraping their living with long hours of hard labour. They were poor and proud, and the only group which stood between them and the bottom rung were those evil, workshy, criminal, daughter-raping Ivets; and by God that's where the Ivets were going to stay: underfoot.

When Candace Elford's sheriffs started to recruit deputies for the posse, tension and nervousness was already gripping the town. Seeing the posse actually assembling down at the port, confirming there really was something going on upriver, tipped unrest into physical aggression.

*

Darcy and Lori were lucky to miss the worst of the mayhem. On Lalonde they acted as the local representatives for Ward Molecular, a Kulu company that imported various solid-state units as well as a lot of the electron-matrix power cells which the capital's embryonic industries were incorporating into an increasing number of products. The Kulu connection was an ironic added touch to their cover; the deeply religious Kulu and the Edenists were not closely allied in the Confederation. Edenists were not permitted to germinate their habitats in any of the Kingdom's star systems, which made it unlikely that anyone would think of them as anything other than loyal subjects of King Alastair II.

They handled their business from a long wooden warehouse structure, a standard industrial building with an overhanging roof, and a floor which was supported on raised stone pillars a metre above the muddy gravel. Built entirely from mayope, it was strong enough to resist any casual break-in attempt by the capital's slowly increasing population of petty criminals. The single-storey cabin which they lived in sat in the middle of a half-acre plot of land at the back, which like most of Durringham's residents they used to grow vegetables and fruit bushes.

Warehouse and cabin were situated on the western edge of the port, five hundred metres from the water. The majority of nearby buildings were commercial premises – sawmills, lumber-yards, a few forges, and some relatively new cloth factories, their bleak ranks broken by streets of cabins to accommodate their workers. This end of town had stayed the same for years. It was the eastern end and long southern side which were expanding, and no one seemed keen to develop out towards the coastal swamps ten kilometres down the Juliffe. Nor were there any farms to the west; the raw jungle was less than two kilometres away.

But their proximity to the port did put them on the fringe of the trouble. They were in the office at the side of the warehouse when Stewart Danielsson, one of the three men who worked for them, came barging in.

'People outside,' he said.

Lori and Darcy swapped a glance at the agitation in his tone, and went to see.

There was a loose progression of men from the nearby factories and mills heading towards the port. Darcy stood on the ramp outside the big open doorway at the front of the warehouse; there was a work area just inside, where they would pack orders and even perform repairs on Ward Molecular's simpler units. Cole Este and Gaven Hough, the company's other two employees, had both left their benches to join him.

'Where are they all going?' Lori asked. **And why do they look so angry?** she addressed Darcy on singular engagement.

'Going down to the port,' Gaven Hough said.

'Why?'

He hunched his shoulders up, embarrassed. 'Sort the Ivets out.'

'Bloody right,' Cole Este mumbled sullenly. 'Wouldn't mind going on that posse myself. The sheriffs've been recruiting deputies all morning.'

Damnation, trust this town to think with its arse, Darcy said.

He and Lori had only been told about the Quallheim Counties revolt by one of their contacts in the Land Allocation Office the previous evening. **Those bloody sheriffs must have been shouting the news about Schuster.** 'Gaven, Stewart, let's get these doors shut. We're closing for the day.'

They started to slide the big doors shut, while Cole Este stood on the ramp, grinning and exchanging a few shouted comments with the odd person he knew. He was nineteen, the youngest of the three workers, and it was obvious he wanted to join the crowd.

Just look at the little idiot, Lori said.

Easy. We don't involve ourselves, nor criticize. Prime rule.

Tell me about it. They'll kill the Ivets down in the transients' dormitories. You know that, don't you?

Darcy slammed the bolt home on the door, and locked it with a padlock keyed to his finger pattern. **I know.**

'You want us to stay?' Stewart Danielsson asked dubiously.

'No, that's all right, Stewart, you three get off home. We'll take care of things here.'

Darcy and Lori sat in the office with all but one of the windows shuttered on the inside. A partition with a line of tall glass panes in wooden frames looked out over the darkened warehouse. The furniture was basic, a couple of tables and five chairs Darcy had made himself. A conditioner whirred almost silently in one corner, keeping the atmosphere cool and dry. The office was one of the few rooms on the planet that was actually dusty.

Once is acceptable, Lori said. **Twice is not. Something strange is happening in Schuster County.**

Possibly. Darcy put his maser carbine on the table between them. The solitary shaft of sunlight shining through the window made the smooth grey composite casing glimmer softly. Protection, just in case the riot spread back through the town.

They could both hear the distant growl of the crowd down in the port; the newly arrived Ivets being hunted down and killed. Beaten into the mud with makeshift clubs, or gored by baying sayce to the sound of cheers. If they looked through the window at an angle they would be able to see boats of all sizes sailing hurriedly out of the circular polyp harbours for the safety of the water.

I hate Adamists, Lori said. **Only Adamists could do this to one another. They do it because they don't know one another. They don't love, they can only lust and fear.**

Darcy smiled, and reached out to touch her, because her mind was leaking a longing for the reassurance of physical contact. His hand never bridged the gap. An affinity voice with the power of a thunderstorm roared into their minds.

ATTENTION INTELLIGENCE OPERATIVES ON LALONDE, I AM LATON. THERE IS A XENOC ENERGY VIRUS LOOSE IN THE QUALLHEIM COUNTIES. HOSTILE AND EXTREMELY DANGEROUS. LEAVE LALONDE IMMEDIATELY. THE CONFEDERATION NAVY MUST BE INFORMED. THIS IS YOUR ONLY PRIORITY NOW. I CANNOT LAST LONG.

Lori was whimpering, her hands clutching at her ears, mouth frozen open in a horrified wail. Darcy saw her dissolve under a discharge of chaotic mental images, each of them bright enough to dazzle.

Jungle. A village seen from the air. More jungle. A little boy hanging upside-down from a tree, his stomach sliced open. A bearded man hanging upside-down from a different tree, light ning flaring wildly.

Heat, excruciating heat.

Darcy grunted at the pain, he was on fire. Skin blackening, hair singeing, his throat shrivelling.

It stopped.

He was prone on the floor. Flames in the background. Always flames. A man and a woman were leaning over him, naked. Their skin was changing, darkening to green, becoming scaled. Eyes and mouth were scarlet red. The woman parted her lips and a serpent's forked tongue slipped out.

His children were crying all around.

Sorry, so sorry I failed you at the last.

Father shame: ignominy that extended down to a cellular level.

Leathery green hands began to run across his chest, a parody of sensuality. Where the fingers touched he could feel the ruptures begin deep below his skin.

NOW DO YOU BELIEVE?

And voices, audible above his agony. Coming from within, from a deeper part of his brain than affinity originated. Whisperers in chorus: 'We can help, we can make it stop. Let us in, let us free you. Give yourself.'

WARN THEM, CURSE YOU.

Then nothing.

Darcy found himself curled up on the mayope planks of the office floor. He had bitten his lip; a trickle of blood wept down his chin.

He touched himself gingerly, fingers probing his ribs, terrified of what he would find. But there was no pain, no open wounds, no internal damage.

'It was him,' Lori croaked. She was in her chair, head bowed, hugging her chest, hands clenched into tight fists. 'Laton. He's here, he really is here.'

Darcy managed to right himself into a kneeling position, it was enough for now, if he tried to stand he was sure he'd faint. 'Those images . . .' **Did you see them?**

The reptile people? Yes. But the power in that affinity. It . . . it damn near overwhelmed me.

The Quallheim Counties, that's where he said it was. That's over a thousand kilometres away upriver. Human affinity can only reach a hundred at most.

He's had thirty years to perfect his diabolical genetic schemes. Her thoughts were contaminated with fright and revulsion.

'A xenoc energy virus,' Darcy muttered, nonplussed. **What did he mean? And he was being tortured, along with his children. Why? What is going on upriver?**

I don't know. All I know is I wouldn't trust him, not ever. We saw images, fantasy figures. He's had thirty years to construct them, after all.

But they were so real. And why reveal himself? He knows we will eliminate him whatever the cost.

Yes, he knows we will come in force. But with that affinity power he could probably compel even a voidhawk. It would allow himself and his cronies to spread through the Confederation.

It was so real, Darcy repeated numbly. **And now we know he is so powerful we can guard against him. It makes no sense, unless he really has run into something he can't handle. Something more powerful than he.**

Lori gave him a sad, almost defeated look. **We need to know, don't we?**

Yes.

They let their thoughts flow and entwine like the bodies of amorous lovers, reinforcing their strengths, eliminating weaknesses. Gathering courage.

Darcy used a chair as support, and pulled himself up. Every joint felt ponderously stiff. He sat heavily and dabbed at his bitten lip.

Lori smiled fondly, and handed him a handkerchief.

Duty first, he said. **We have to inform Jupiter that Laton is here. That takes precedence over everything. We're not due a voidhawk visit for another couple of months. I'll see Kelven Solanki and request he sends a message to Aethra and the support station out at Murora immediately, his office has the equipment to do that direct. The Confederation Navy would have to be told anyway, so it might as well be now. He can also include a report in the diplomatic flek on a colonist-carrier ship that's heading back to Earth. That ought to cover us.**

And after that we go upriver, Lori said.

Yes.

*

'Next!' the sheriff called.

Yuri Wilkin stepped up to the table, keeping the leash tight on his sayce, Randolf. Rain pattered on the empty warehouse's roof high above his head. Outside the open end, behind the sheriff, the yellow-brown polyp crater of harbour five was returning to a semblance of normality. Most of the boats had returned after their night on the river. A work crew from one of the shipyards were surveying the fire-ravaged hull that was bobbing low in the water. Some captain who hadn't been fast enough to cast off when the rioters came boiling along the polyp in search of Ivets.

The smell of burnt wood mingled with more exotic smells from the stored goods that had caught fire in several warehouses. The flames shooting out of the doomed buildings had been tremendous, even Lalonde's rain had taken hours to extinguish them.

Yuri had milled around watching along with the rest of the rioters last night, mesmerized with the destruction. The flames had lit something inside him, something that felt joyful at the sight of a young terrified Ivet reduced to a bloody chunk of unrecognizable meat beneath the crowd's clubs. He had yelled encouragement until his throat was hoarse.

'Age?' the sheriff asked.

'Twenty,' Yuri lied. He was seventeen, but he already had a reasonable beard. He crossed his fingers, hoping it would be enough. There were over two hundred people waiting behind him, all wanting their chance now the sheriffs had started recruiting again.

The sheriff glanced up from his processor block. 'Sure you are. You ever used a weapon, son?'

'I eat chikrows every week, shoot them myself. I know how to move around in the jungle OK. And I got Randolf, trained him all by myself, he's an ace baiter, knows how to fight, knows how to hunt. He'll be a big help upriver, you get two of us for the price of one.'

The sheriff leant forwards slightly, peering over the edge of the table.

Randolf bared his stained fangs. 'Killl Ivezss,' the beast snarled.

'OK,' the sheriff grunted. 'You willing to take orders? We don't need people who aren't prepared to work in a team.'

'Yes, sir.'

'Reckon you might, at that. You got a change of clothes?'

Grinning, Yuri twisted round to show him the canvas duffle bag slung over his shoulder; his laser rifle was strapped to it.

The sheriff picked a vermilion-coloured deputy's badge from the pile beside his processor block. 'There you go. Get yourself down to the *Swithland* and find a bunk. We'll swear you in officially once we're underway. And muzzle that bloody sayce, I don't want him chewing up colonists before we get there.'

Yuri rubbed the black scales between Randolf's battered ears. 'Don't you worry about old Randolf, he ain't going to hurt no one, not till I tell him to.'

'Next!' the sheriff called.

Yuri Wilkin settled his hat firmly on his head, and headed for the sun-drenched harbour outside, a song in his heart and mayhem in mind.

*

'Gods, I've seen some rough planets in my time, Joshua,' Ashly Hanson said. 'But this one takes the biscuit. There isn't even anyone at the spaceport who wanted to buy copies of Jezzibella's MF album, let alone a black-market distribution net.' He took a drink of juice from his long glass, it was a purplish liquid with plenty of ice bobbing around, some aboriginal fruit. The pilot never touched alcohol while the *Lady Macbeth* was docked to a station or in a parking orbit.

Joshua sipped his glass of bitter, which was warm and carried a punch almost as strong as some spirits he'd tasted. At least it had a decent head.

The pub they were drinking in was called the Crashed Dumper, a wooden barnlike structure at the end of the road that linked the spaceport with Durringham. Various time-expired spaceplane components were fastened up against the walls, the most prominent a compressor fan from one of the McBoeings that took up most of the end wall, with a couple of the fat blades buckled from a bird impact. The pub was used by spaceport staff along with the pilots and starship crews. It was, allegedly, one of the classier pubs in Durringham.

If this was refinement, Joshua didn't like to think what the rest of the city's hostelries must be like.

'I've been on worse,' Warlow growled. The bass harmonics set up vibrations on the surface of the brightlime in his bulbous brandy glass.

'Where?' Ashly demanded.

Joshua ignored them. This was their second day in Durringham, and he was starting to worry. The day Ashly had flown them down there had been some sort of riot next to the river. Everything had shut down, shops, warehouses, government offices. Spaceport procedures had been minimal, but then he suspected they were always like that on Lalonde. Ashly was right, this was one massively primitive colony. Today had been little better; the Governor's industrial secretary had put him in touch with a Durringham timber merchant. The address turned out to be a small office down near the waterfront. Closed, naturally. Enquiries had eventually traced the owner, Mr Purcell, to a nearby pub. He assured Joshua a thousand tonnes of mayope was no problem. 'You can't give it away down here, we've got stocks backlogged halfway up the Juliffe.' He quoted a price of thirty-five thousand fuseodollars inclusive, and promised deliveries could start to the spaceport tomorrow. The wood was a ridiculous price, but Joshua didn't argue. He even paid a two thousand fuseodollar deposit.

Joshua, Ashly, and Warlow had gone back to the spaceport on their hired power bikes (and the rental charge on those was bloody legalized robbery) to try to arrange for a McBoeing charter to ship the wood up to *Lady Mac.* That had taken the rest of the day, and another three thousand fuseodollars in bribe money.

It wasn't the money which bothered him particularly; even taking Lalonde's necessary lubrication into account the mayope was only a small percentage of the cost of a Norfolk flight. Joshua was used to datavised deals, and instant access to anybody he wanted via the local communication net. On Lalonde, where there was no net, and few people with neural nanonics, he was beginning to feel out of his depth.

When he had ridden back into town in the late afternoon to find Mr Purcell and confirm they had a McBoeing lined up, the timber merchant was nowhere to be found. Joshua retreated to the Crashed Dumper in a dark mood. He wasn't at all sure the mayope would even turn up tomorrow; and they had to leave in six days to stand any chance of securing a cargo of Norfolk Tears from a roseyard merchant. Six days, and he didn't have any alternative to mayope. It had seemed such a good idea.

He took another gulp of his bitter. The pub was filling up as the spaceport staff came off shift. Over in one corner an audio block was playing a ballad which some of the customers were singing along to. Large fans spun listlessly overhead, trying to circulate some of the humid air.

'Captain Calvert?'

Joshua looked up.

Marie Skibbow was dressed in a tight-fitting sleeveless green stretch blouse, and a short pleated black skirt. Her thick hair was neatly plaited. She was carrying a circular tray loaded with empty glasses.

'Now this is what I call improved service,' Ashly said brightly.

'That's me,' Joshua said. Jesus, but she had tremendous legs. Nice face too, ever so slightly wiser than her age.

'I understand you're looking for a cargo of mayope, is that right?' Marie asked.

'Does everybody in town know?' Joshua asked.

'Just about. A visit from an independent trader starship isn't exactly common around here. If we weren't having all this trouble with the Quallheim Counties and the anti-Ivet riots you'd be the most gossiped over item in Durringham.'

'I see.'

'Can I join you?'

'Sure.' He pushed out one of the vacant chairs. People had tended to avoid their table, it was one of the reasons he'd brought Warlow down. Only someone who was stoned out of his brain would try and tangle with the amount of boosted muscle the old cosmonik packed into his giant frame.

Marie sat down and fixed Joshua with an uncompromising gaze. 'Would you be interested in taking on an extra crew-member?'

'You?' Joshua asked.

'Yes.'

'Do you have neural nanonics?'

'No.'

'Then, I'm sorry, but the answer's no. I have a full complement anyway.'

'How much do you charge for a trip?'

'Where to?'

'Wherever you're going next.'

'If we can acquire a cargo of mayope, I'm going to Norfolk. I'd charge you thirty thousand fuseodollars for passage in zero-tau, more if you wanted a cabin. Starflight isn't cheap.'

Marie's air of sophisticated confidence faltered slightly. 'Yes, I know.'

'You want to leave pretty badly?' Ashly asked sympathetically.

She dropped her gaze and nodded. 'Wouldn't you? I lived on Earth until last year. I hate it here, I'm not staying no matter what it costs. I want civilization.'

'Earth,' Ashly mused whimsically. 'Lord, I haven't been there for a couple of centuries. Wouldn't call it particularly civilized even back then.'

'He's a time hopper,' Joshua explained as Marie gave the pilot a confused look. 'And if you hate this place as much as you say, then Norfolk isn't where you want to go either. It's strictly a pastoral planet. They have a policy of minimal technological usage, and the government enforces it pretty rigorously from what I hear. Sorry.'

She gave a small shrug. 'I never thought it would be that easy.'

'The idea of signing on with a ship is a good one,' Ashly said. 'But you really need neural nanonics before a captain will consider you.'

'Yes, I know, I'm saving up for a set.'

Joshua put on a neutral expression. 'Good.'

Marie actually laughed, he was being so careful not to hurt her feelings. 'You think I waitress for a living? That I'm a dumb waster girl saving up tips and dreaming of better days?'

'Er . . . no.'

'I waitress here in the evenings because it's the place the starship crews come. This way I get to hear of any openings before the rest of Durringham. And yes there are the tips, too, every little helps. But for real money I bought myself a secretarial job at the Kulu Embassy, in their Commercial Office.'

'Bought a job?' Warlow rumbled. His sculpted dark-yellow face was incapable of expression, but the voice booming from his chest diaphragm carried a heavy query. People turned to look as he drowned out the ballad.

'Of course. You think they give away a gig like that? The embassy pays its staff in Kulu pounds.' It was the second hardest currency in the Confederation after fuseodollars. 'That's where I'm going to get the money to pay for my neural nanonics.'

'Ah, now I see.' Joshua raised his glass in salute. He admired the girl's toughness – almost as much as he admired her figure.

'That, or the deputy ambassador's son might get me off,' Marie said quietly. 'He's twenty-two, and he likes me a lot. If we married then obviously I'd go back to Kulu with him once his father's tour was over.'

Ashly grinned and knocked back some of his fruit juice. A suspect grumble emerged from Warlow's chest.

Marie gave Joshua a questioning glance. 'So. Do you still want your mayope, Captain?'

'You think you can get me some?'

'Like I said, I work in the Commercial Office. And I'm good at it, too,' she said fiercely. 'I know more about this town's economic structure than my boss. You're buying your cargo from Dodd Purcell, right?'

'Yes,' Joshua said cautiously.

'Thought so; he's the nephew of the governor's industrial secretary. Dodd Purcell is a complete screwup, but he's a good partner for his uncle. All official tenders for timber go through the company he owns, except it's actually his uncle's, and all it consists of is an office down at the port. They don't actually own a yard, or even any timber. The LDC pays through the nose, but nobody queries it because no lower quotes ever make it past the industrial secretary's office. All that happens is Purcell contracts a real lumber-yard to supply whatever project the LDC is paying for; they do all the work while he and uncle cream off thirty per cent. No effort, and all profit.'

Warlow's chair creaked alarmed protests as his bulk shifted round. He tilted the brandy glass to his mouth aperture, the brightlime surged out, almost sucked down into his inlet nozzle. 'Smart bastards.'

'Jesus,' Joshua said. 'And I'll bet the price goes up tomorrow.'

'I expect so,' Marie said. 'And then again the day after, then it will become a rush order to meet your deadline, so you'll have to pay a surcharge.'

Joshua put his empty glass down on the stained table. 'All right, you win. What's your counter-offer?'

'You are paying Purcell thirty-five thousand fuseodollars, which is about thirty per cent over the odds. I'm offering to put you in touch with a lumber-yard direct, they'll supply the wood at the market rate, and you pay me five per cent of the difference.'

'Suppose we just go to a lumber-yard direct now you've told us what's happening?' Ashly asked.

Marie smiled sweetly. 'Which one? Are you going back to the Governor's industrial secretary for a list? Once you've picked one, do you know if it was burnt down in the riots? Where is it, and how do you get to it? Parts of this town are very unhealthy for visitors, especially after the riots. Does it have that much mayope in stock or is the owner stringing you along? What are you going to use to transport it out to the spaceport? And how much time can you spend sorting all that out? Even a relatively honest lumber-yard owner is going to catch on that you've got a deadline once you start fretting because you haven't got permits and procedures smoothed out in advance. I mean, God, it took you almost a day to hire a McBoeing. Bet you didn't buy energy for it either, they'll hit you for that tomorrow. And when they scent blood it'll be Purcell all over again.'

Joshua held up a warning hand to Ashly. Nobody at the spaceport had mentioned energy for the McBoeing. Jesus! On a normal planet it would be part of the charter; and of course he couldn't use his neural nanonics to access the contract and run a legal program check because his copy of the fucking thing was printed out on paper. *Paper*, for Christ's sake. 'I'll deal with you,' he told Marie. 'But I only pay on delivery to orbit, and that includes your fee. So you're going to have to clear all those obstacles you mentioned out of our way, because I don't pay a single fuseodollar once those six days are up.'

She stuck out her hand, and after a moment's hesitation Joshua shook.

'We're sleeping in my spaceplane, seeing as how it has the only functional air-conditioner on the entire planet,' he told her. 'I want you there at seven o'clock tomorrow morning ready to take us to this lumber-yard of yours.'

'Aye, aye, Captain.' She stood and picked up her tray.

Joshua pulled a wad of Lalonde francs from his jacket pocket and peeled a few off. 'We'll have the same again, and have a large one yourself. I think you've just earned it.'

Marie plucked the notes from him and stuffed them in a side pocket on her skirt. She gave them all a ludicrously sassy twitch with her backside as she walked off to the bar.

Ashly watched her go with a lugubrious expression, then drained his juice in one gulp. 'God help that ambassador's son.'

*

Darcy and Lori spent the day after the riots preparing for their trip. There was Kelven Solanki to brief on the situation, and their eagles Abraham and Catlin to take out of zero-tau, equipment to make ready. Above all, they had to find transport. The harbour-master's office had been damaged in the riot, so there was no list available of the boats in dock. In the afternoon they sent the eagles skimming over the polyp rings searching for something they could use.

What do you think? Darcy asked. Abraham was turning lazy circles over harbour seven, his enhanced retinas providing an uncluttered image of the boats moored up against the quays.

Them? Lori exclaimed in dismay.

Have you found someone else?

No.

At least we know we can bully them with money.

The port still hadn't recovered from the riot when they made their way down to harbour seven first thing the next morning. Huge piles of ashes which used to be buildings were still radiating heat from their smouldering cores, giving off thin streamers of acrid smoke. Long runnels of mushed ashes meandered away from their bases, sluiced out by the rain; they had coagulated under the morning sunlight, looking like damp lava flows.

Gangs of workers were raking through the piles with long mayope poles, searching for anything salvageable. They passed one ruined transients' warehouse where a stack of cargo-pods had been pulled from the gutted remains, the warped composite resembling surrealistic sculptures. Darcy watched a forlorn family prise open a badly contorted marsupium shell with deep scorch marks on the oyster-coloured casing. The infant quadruped had been roasted in its chemical sleep, reduced to a shrivelled black mummy. Darcy couldn't even tell what species it was.

Lori had to turn away from the empty-faced colonists scrabbling at the pods' distorted lids, shiny new ship-suits smeared with dirt and sweat. They had come to Lalonde with such high hopes, and now they were faced with utter ruin before they'd even been given a chance at a life.

This is awful, she said.

This is dangerous, Darcy replied. **They are numbed and shocked now, but that will soon give way to anger. Without their farmsteading gear they can't be sent upriver, and Rexrew will be hard pushed to replace it.**

It wasn't all burnt, she said sorrowfully. The afternoon and evening of the riot there had been a steady stream of people walking past the Ward Molecular warehouse carrying pods and cartons of equipment they had looted.

They walked round harbour seven until they came to the quay where the *Coogan* was moored. The ageing tramp trader was in a dilapidated state, with holes in its cabin roof and a long gash in the wood up at the prow where it had struck some snag. Len Buchannan had only just managed to get out of the harbour ahead of the rioters, flinging planks from the cabin walls into the furnace hopper in his desperation.

Gail Buchannan was sitting in her usual place outside the galley doorway, coolie hat shading her sweating face, a kitchen knife almost engulfed by her huge hand. She was chopping some long vegetable root, slices falling into a pewter-coloured pan at her feet. Her eyes fastened shrewdly on Darcy and Lori as they stepped onto the decking. 'You again. Len! Len, get yourself out here, we've got visitors. Now, Len!'

Darcy waited impassively. They had used the Buchannans as an information source in the past, occasionally asking them to pick up fleks from assets upriver. But they had proved so unreliable and cranky, Darcy hadn't bothered with them for the last twenty months.

Len Buchannan walked forward from the little engine-room, where he'd been patching the cabin walls. He was wearing jeans and his cap, a carpenter's suede utility belt hanging loosely round his skinny hips, with only a few tools in its hoops.

Darcy thought he looked hungover, which fitted the talk he'd heard around the port. The *Coogan* had hit hard times of late.

'Have you got a cargo to take upriver?' Darcy asked.

'No,' Len said sullenly.

'It's been a difficult season for us,' Gail said. 'Things aren't like they used to be. Nobody shows any loyalty these days. Why, if it wasn't for us virtually giving our goods away half of the settlements upriver would have starved to death. But do they show any gratitude? Ha!'

'Is the *Coogan* fit to be taken out?' Darcy asked, cutting through the woman's screed. 'Now? Today?'

Len pulled his cap off and scratched his head. 'Suppose so. Engines are OK. I always service them regular.'

'Of course it's in tiptop shape,' Gail told him loudly. 'There's nothing wrong with the *Coogan*'s hull. It's only because this drunken buffoon spends all his time pining away over that little bitch-brat that the cabin's in the state it is.'

Len sighed irksomely, and leant against the galley doorframe. 'Don't start,' he said.

'I knew she was trouble,' Gail said. 'I told you not to let her on board. I warned you. And after all we did for her.'

'Shut up!'

She glared at him and resumed slicing up the cream-white vegetable.

'What do you want the *Coogan* for?' Len asked.

'We have to get upriver, today,' Darcy said. 'There's no cargo, only us.'

Len made a play of putting his cap back on. 'There's trouble upriver.'

'I know. That's where we want to go, the Quallheim Counties.'

'No,' Len Buchannan said. 'Sorry, anywhere else in the tributary basin, but not there.'

'That's where *she* came from,' Gail hissed venomously. 'That's what you're afraid of.'

'There's a bloody war going on up there, woman. You saw the boats with the posse leaving.'

'Ten thousand fuseodollars,' Gail said. 'And don't you two try haggling with me, that's the only offer you'll get, I'm starving myself as it is. I'll take you up on my own if Lennie's too frightened.'

If that's starvation, I'd like to see gluttony, Darcy said.

'This is my boat,' Len said. 'Made with my own hands.'

'Half yours,' Gail shouted back, waving the knife at him. 'Half! I have a say too, and I say *Coogan* is going back to the Quallheim. If you don't like it, go and cry in her skirts if she'll have you. Drunken old fool.'

If this is the way they carry on, they'll kill each other before we get out of the harbour, Lori said. She watched Len staring at the burnt-out sections of the port, his brown weathered face lost with longing.

'All right,' he said eventually. 'I'll take you to the mouth of the Quallheim, or as near as we can get. But I'm not going anywhere near the trouble.'

'Fair enough,' Darcy said. 'How long will it take us at full speed?'

'Going upriver?' Len closed his eyes, lips moving around figures. 'Without stopping to trade, ten or twelve days. Mind, we'll have to moor in the evenings, and cut logs. You'll have to work your passage.'

'Forget that,' Darcy said. 'I'll have some firewood delivered this afternoon, enough to get us there in one go; we can store it in the forward hold instead of a cargo. And I'll spell you at night, I don't need much sleep. How long travelling like that?'

'A week, maybe,' Len Buchannan said. He didn't seem terribly happy with the idea.

'That's fine. We'll start this afternoon.'

'We'll take half of the money now, as a deposit,' Gail said. A Jovian Bank disk appeared from nowhere in her hand.

'You'll get a thousand now as a deposit, plus five hundred to buy enough food and water for three weeks,' Lori said. 'I'll pay another two thousand once we leave the harbour this afternoon, two more when we get to Schuster, and the sum when we get back here.'

Gail Buchannan made a lot of indignant noise, but the sight of actual cash piling up in her disk silenced her.

'Make sure it's decent food,' Lori told her. 'Freeze dried, I'm sure you know where to get stocks of that from.'

They left the Buchannans bickering and went on to a lumber-yard to arrange for the logs to be delivered. It took an hour longer than it should have done to get their order sorted out; the only reason they got it at all was because they were regular customers. The yard was frantically busy with an order for a thousand tonnes of mayope. The laughing foreman told them a lunatic starship captain was planning to carry it to another star.

*

They were going to make Joshua Calvert's deadline. Marie Skibbow couldn't keep the thought out of her mind. It was mid-afternoon, and she was sitting up at the bar in the nearly deserted Crashed Dumper having a celebratory drink. What she really felt like doing was singing and dancing, it was a wonderful experience. All the contacts she'd meticulously built up over the last few months had finally paid off. The deals she put together had clicked into place all the way down the line, smoothing the way for the wood to get from the lumber-yard into orbit with minimum fuss and maximum speed. In fact it had turned out they were being limited by how fast Ashly Hanson could load the foam-covered bundles into the *Lady Macbeth*'s cargo holds. The starship only carried one MSV, which imposed a two hundred and fifty tonne per day restriction. The pilot simply couldn't work any faster; and not even Marie could obtain a MSV from Kenyon, which was the only other place they were in use within the Lalonde star system. But even so, they should have the last bundle loaded tomorrow, a day before the deadline.

Her Jovian Bank disk was burning like a small thermal-induction field in her sawn-off jeans pocket. Joshua had paid her on the nose, every McBoeing flight that lifted off the spaceport's metal grid runway saw another batch of fuseodollars added to her account. And he'd given her a bonus for arranging the lorries. The drivers were taking colonists' farmsteading gear from the spaceport down to the harbour and returning half-empty; it didn't take much organization or money to fix it so they brought the mayope with them when they came back. That way Joshua saved money on an official contract with the haulage company that owned them.

Her first major-league deal. She sipped her iced brightlime, enjoying the bitter taste as it went down her throat. Was this how millionaires felt every day? The total satisfaction which came from tangible accomplishment. And all the famous merchant names in history must have started with a first deal like this, even Richard Saldana, who founded Kulu. Now there was a thought.

But there weren't many opportunities for deals this big on Lalonde. She simply had to leave, that goal had never changed. The money from the deal would be a hefty slice towards the eighteen thousand fuseodollars she needed for a basic set of neural nanonics. Joshua would probably pay her an overall bonus as well. He was honest enough.

Which brought her to the real question of the day: whether or not she was going to go to bed with him. He had certainly asked her often enough over the last four days. He was handsome, if a trifle gaunt, with a good-looking body; and he must be talented after all the girls he'd been with. An owner–captain under twenty-five years old, it would surely run into hundreds. Especially with that grin. He must practise it; *so* sexy. She rather liked the notion of what they'd be capable of doing to each other if they flung off every inhibition. There had been rumours back at the arcology about the prowess of people geneered for spaceflight, something to do with enhanced flexibility.

And if she did – which she probably would – he might just take her with him when he left. It really wasn't a possibility she could afford to ignore. After Norfolk he said he was planning on returning to Tranquillity. That habitat was premier real estate, superior even to Earth and Kulu. I've already whored my way down the river; whoring to Tranquillity would hardly be a hardship after that.

The Crashed Dumper's door creaked open. A young man in a blue and red checked shirt and long khaki shorts walked in, and sat down at the other end of the bar. He never even glanced at Marie, which was odd. She was wearing her sawn-off jeans and a dark-orange singlet, long limbs on show. His face looked familiar, early twenties, ruggedly attractive with a neatly trimmed beard. His clothes were new, and clean, made locally. Was he one of Durringham's new generation of merchants? She'd met a lot of them since she got the job at the embassy, and they were always keen to talk while they waited for Ralph Hiltch, her boss.

She pouted slightly. There, if she had neural nanonics she'd have no trouble placing the name.

'Beer, please,' he told the barkeeper.

The voice fixed him, it just took a moment for her incredulity to die down. No wonder she hadn't recognized him to start with. She went over to him.

'Quinn Dexter, what the bloody hell are you doing here?'

He turned slowly, blinking at her uncertainly in the pub's filtered light. She held back on a laugh, because it was obvious he didn't recognize her either.

His fingers clicked, and he smiled. 'Marie Skibbow. Glad to see you made it to the big city. Everybody wondered if you would. They didn't stop talking about you for a month.'

'Yeah, well . . .' She sat on the stool next to him as he paid for his beer from a thick wad of Lalonde francs. That wasn't right, Ivets didn't have hard cash. She waited until the barkeeper went away then dropped her voice. 'Quinn, don't tell people who you are. They're killing Ivets in this town right now. It's pretty nasty.'

'No problem. I'm not an Ivet any more. I bought myself out of my work time contract.'

'Bought yourself out?' Marie had never known you could do that.

'Sure,' he winked. 'Everything on this planet is financially orientated.'

'Ah, right. How did you buy it? Don't tell me dear old Aberdale started being successful.'

'No, not a chance, it never changed. I found some gold in the river.'

'Gold?'

'Yes, a nugget you wouldn't believe.' He held up his hand, making a fist. 'This big, Marie, and that's the honest truth. So I kept going back, there was nothing ever as big as that first one, but I built up quite a little hoard. They thought it must have washed down from the mountains on the other side of the savannah, remember them?'

'God, don't remind me. I don't want to remember anything about that village.'

'Can't say I blame you. First thing I did was get out. Sailed straight down the Juliffe on a trader boat; took me a week and I got ripped off by the captain, but here I am. Arrived today.'

'Yeah, I got ripped off too.' Marie studied her glass of brightlime. 'So what's happening upriver, Quinn? Have the Ivets really taken over the Quallheim Counties?'

'It was all news to me when we docked this morning. There was nothing like that in the offing when I left. Maybe they're fighting over the gold. Whoever owns the motherlode is going to be seriously rich.'

'They've sent a load of sheriffs and deputies up there, armed to the teeth.'

'Oh, dear. That doesn't sound good. Guess I'm lucky I got out when I did.'

Marie realized how hot she had become in the last couple of minutes. When she glanced up she saw the fans had stopped spinning. Bloody typical, right when the sun was at its zenith. 'Quinn? How are my family?'

'Well . . .' He pulled a sardonic face. 'Your father's not changed much.'

She lifted her glass level with her face. 'Amen.'

'Let's see; your mother's OK', your brother-in-law is OK. Oh yes, Paula's pregnant.'

'Really? God, I'll be an aunt.'

'Looks like it.' He took a swig of his beer.

'So what are you going to do now?'

'Leave. Get on a starship and go, some planet where I can start over.'

'There was that much gold?' she asked.

'Yeah, that much, and then some.'

Marie thought fast, weighing up her options. 'I can get you off Lalonde by tomorrow afternoon, and not back to Earth either, this is a fresh planet the captain is heading for. Clean air, open spaces, and a rock-solid economy.'

'Yeah?' Quinn brightened considerably. The overhead fans began to turn again.

'Yes. I have a contact in the ship, but I charge commission for introducing you.'

'You really landed on your feet, didn't you?'

'I do OK.'

'Marie, there weren't any girls on the boat down the river.'

She wasn't sure how he had suddenly got so close. He was pressed up beside her, and his presence was sending fissures of doubt straight through her self-confidence. Something about Quinn was monstrously intimidating, verging on menacing. 'I can help there, I think. I know a place, the girls are clean.'

'I don't want a *place*, Marie. Dear God, seeing you sitting there triggered all those memories I thought I'd put behind me.'

'Quinn,' she said laconically.

'You think I can help it? You were every Ivet's wet dream back at Aberdale, we'd spend hours talking about you. There'd be fights over who got on the work detail to your homestead. I did, I got it every time, I made bloody sure I did.'

'Quinn!'

'You were everything I could never have, Marie. Damn Christ, I worshipped you, you were perfection, everything that was right and good in the world.'

'Don't, Quinn.' Her head was spinning, making her dizzy. What he was saying was crazy, he'd never even noticed her when he walked in the Crashed Dumper. It was so hot, the sweat was running down her back. His arm went round her, making her look into fevered eyes.

'And now here you are again. My very own idol. Like God gave me a second chance. And I'm not giving up this chance,

Marie. Whatever it takes, I want you. I want you, Marie.' Then his lips were on hers.

She was shaking against him when he finished the kiss. 'Quinn no,' she mumbled. He tightened his grip, squashing her against him. His chest felt as though it was carved from rock, every muscle a steel band. She couldn't understand why she wasn't pushing him away. But she wasn't, the thought was inconceivable.

'I'm going to make it so good you're never going to leave me,' he said in a frantic whisper. 'I'm going to make you see I'm the one for you, that there is no one else in the whole galaxy who can replace me. I'm going to take you from this atrocity of a planet when I go; and we're going to live somewhere sweet and beautiful, where there isn't any jungle, and people are happy. And I'm going to buy us a big house, and I'm going to make you pregnant, and our children are going to be so lovely it hurts to look at them. You'll see, Marie. You'll see what true love can bring when you give yourself up to me.'

There were tears in her eyes at the terrible wonderful words. Words that spoke out every dream she owned. And how could he possibly know? Yet there was only desire and yearning in his face. So maybe – please God – just maybe it was true. Because nobody could be so cruel as to lie about such things.

They leant together as they stumbled out of the Crashed Dumper, the pair of them drunk with their own brand of desire.

*

The Confederation Navy office on Lalonde was a two-storey structure, an oblong box sixty-five metres broad, twenty deep. The outer walls were blue-silver mirrors, broken by a single black band halfway up, which ran round the entire circumference. The flat roof had seven satellite uplinks covered by geodesic weather casings that resembled particularly virile bright orange toadstools. Only five of them actually housed communication equipment, the other two covered maser cannon which provided a short-range defence capability. The building was situated in the eastern sector of Durringham, five hundred metres from the dumper which housed the Governor's office.

It was a class 050-6B office, suitable for phase one colonies and non-capital missions (tropical); a programmed silicon structure made by the Lunar SII. It had arrived on Lalonde in a cubic container five metres to a side. The Fleet marine engineers who activated it had to sink corner foundations fifteen metres deep into the loam in order to secure it against the wind. The silicon walls might have been as strong as mayope, but they were only as thick as paper; it was terribly vulnerable to even mild gusts. And given Lalonde's temperature there was some speculation that warm air accumulating inside might actually provide sufficient lift to get it airborne.

There were fifty Confederation Navy staff assigned to Lalonde: officers, NCOs, and ratings, who ate, worked, and slept inside. The most active department was the recruitment centre, where fifteen permanent staff dealt with youngsters who shared Marie Skibbow's opinion of their world, but lacked her individual resourcefulness. Enlistment offered a golden ticket offplanet, away from the rain, the heat, and the remorseless physical labour of the farms.

Every time Ralph Hiltch walked through the wide automated entrance doors and breathed in clean, dry, conditioned air he felt just that fraction closer to home. Back in a world of right angles, synthetic materials, uniforms, humming machinery, and government-issue furniture.

A pretty rating barely out of her teens was waiting to escort him from the entrance hall where all the farmboy and -girl hopefuls were queueing in their hand-stitched shirts and mud-stained denim trousers. He opened his lightweight cagoule and shook some of the rain from it as she escorted him up the stairs and into the security zone of the second floor.

Lieutenant-Commander Kelven Solanki was waiting for Ralph Hiltch in his large corner office. A career officer who had left his Polish-ethnic world of Mazowiecki twenty-nine years previously, he was forty-seven: a narrow-faced man with a lean build, several centimetres shorter than Ralph, with thick raven-black hair trimmed to a regular one centimetre. His dark-blue port uniform fitted well, although he'd left the jacket on the back of his desk chair.

Ralph was given a genuinely warm handshake when he came in, and the rating was dismissed. She saluted smartly and closed the door.

Kelven Solanki's welcoming smile faded considerably as he gestured Ralph to the imitation-leather settee. 'Who's going to start?'

He hung his cagoule on the edge of the settee and leaned back. 'We're on your home territory, so I'll tell you what I know first.'

'OK.' Kelven sat on the chair opposite.

'First, Joshua Calvert and the *Lady Macbeth*; stunning though it appears, he is actually genuine as far as we can make out. I've got an inside track: my secretary, Marie, is running a deal for him, so she's keeping a strong tab on him for me. He's bought a thousand tonnes of mayope, got himself an export licence, and he's loading the stuff into his starship as fast as the McBoeing he hired can boost it into orbit. He's made no attempt to get in touch with any known fence, he didn't bring any cargo down in his own spaceplane, legal or illegal, and he'll be gone tomorrow.'

Kelven found he was more interested in the independent trader captain than the situation really required. 'He's genuinely transporting timber to another star?'

'Yes. To Norfolk, apparently. Which, given their import restrictions, isn't quite as insane as it sounds. They may just have a use for it with their pastoral tech. I haven't decided if he's an idiot or a genius. I'd love to know how he gets on.'

'Me too. But he isn't quite the innocent you think he is. The *Lady Macbeth* has an antimatter drive unit. And my last general security file update from Avon carried a report that he was intercepted by a navy voidhawk a couple of months back; Fleet Intelligence was convinced he was trying to smuggle proscribed technology. They actually watched the units being loaded into his cargo bay. Yet when the voidhawk captain searched his ship – nothing. So it doesn't look like he's an idiot.'

'Interesting. He's not due to leave until tomorrow, so he might still try something. I'll keep him under close observation. Will you?'

'I have been keeping a quiet eye on Captain Calvert since his arrival, and I'll continue to do so. Now, the Quallheim Counties situation. I don't like it at all. We've been reviewing the images the chief sheriff's observation satellite has been downloading this morning, and the trouble is spreading into Willow West County. There are several burnt-out buildings in the villages, evidence of fighting, and the fields are being ignored.'

'Hell, I didn't know that.'

'Well, this time Candace Elford has managed to keep it quiet, at least for now. But the sheriffs and supervisors in the Quallheim Counties and Willow West still insist there's nothing wrong. Those that answer their communication blocks. I think that's the strangest aspect of this situation; I can't see the Ivets pointing a laser at their heads all day every day.'

'I find it very hard to believe the Ivets could take over a whole county in the first place, let alone four. Rexrew might be right about an external group being behind it. Were these new Willow West images fuzzed like the last batch from the Quallheim?'

Kelven gave his counterpart a significant look. 'Yes, unfortunately they were; and my technical officer can't work out how it was done. She's not the greatest electronic warfare expert in the navy, but she says there isn't even a theory which could account for it. I have to give serious consideration to the fact that Rexrew is right. And there's something else, too.'

Ralph broke out of his reverie at the tone.

'I have been *authorized*' – he emphasized the word – 'to tell you that Edenist Intelligence agents believe Laton is still alive, and may be on Lalonde, specifically in Schuster County. They say he contacted them to warn them of some kind of xenoc incursion. They left Durringham three days ago, heading upriver to investigate, but not before they made me contact Aethra to update it on the situation. And, Ralph, they looked worried.'

'Edenist Intelligence is operative here?' Ralph asked. He'd never had the slightest hint.

'Yes.'

'Laton, I think I know the name, some kind of Serpent insurrectionist; but he's not stored in my neural nanonics files. Probably got him in my processor block back in the embassy.'

'I'll save you the trouble. His file's in the computer. It's not nice reading, but be my guest.'

Ralph datavised the request into the office computer, and sat in a disturbed silence as the information ran through his brain. His training had covered Edenist Serpents, but in a remote, academic fashion. He was used to dealing with mercenaries, blackhawks, smugglers, and devious politicians, not someone like this. The datavise seemed to be pumping cryogenic liquid down his spinal cord. 'And the Edenists think he's on Lalonde?' he asked Kelven, aghast.

'That's right. They were never sure, but he showed an interest in the place decades ago, so they kept a watch. Now it's confirmed, he survived the navy assault and came here. According to the agents he called them because whatever is behind the Quallheim disturbances was breaking through his defences.'

'Jesus wept!'

'There is a remote possibility that it was some kind of bluff to attract voidhawks here so he could take them over and get himself and his associates offplanet. But I have to say it's not likely. It looks like there really is some kind of external influence at work in the Quallheim Counties.'

'The Edenists wanted me to know?'

'Yes. They thought it was important enough to override minor political constraints – their words. They want the First Admiral and your senior Saldanas warned as well as their Jupiter Consensus. Laton by himself would require a major military action, something which can defeat him would probably mean deployment at Fleet level.'

Ralph stared at Kelven Solanki. The navy officer was badly frightened. 'Have you told the Governor?'

'No. Rexrew has enough problems. There are over four thousand colonists in the transients' dormitories who have had their farmsteading gear either burnt or looted. He can't ship them upriver, and he hasn't got any replacement gear – nor is he going to get any in the near future. There are three colonist-carrier starships in orbit with their Ivets left in zero-tau; Rexrew can't bring them down because they'll be murdered as soon as they step out of the McBoeings. The starship captains aren't authorized to take them back to Earth. There are still sectors in the east of Durringham where full civil order hasn't been re-established. Frankly, given the state of the city, we're expecting widespread civil disobedience within three weeks, sooner if word about the Quallheim revolts spreading downriver reaches town. And with the way those idiot sheriffs leak confidential information, it will. We're looking at virtual anarchy breaking out. I don't consider the Governor as someone we can turn to with this information. He's between the classic rock and a hard place right now.'

'You're right,' Ralph agreed unhappily. God, why Lalonde? He'd hated the place when it was a seedy backward colony going nowhere. But right now a return to that state would have been a blessing. 'I consider it my priority to inform Kulu what's happened, and what may happen with regards to Laton and these possible xenocs in the Quallheim Counties.'

'Good. I have the legal authority to declare a system-wide emergency and commandeer any available starship. Hopefully it won't come to that, but I am sending one of my officers up to a colonist-carrier starship and diverting it to Avon. That's in hand now, the *Eurydice* finished unloading all its colonists yesterday, it only has about fifty Ivets left in zero-tau. They'll be transferred over to the *Martijn*, where they can stay until Rexrew works out what he's going to do with them. Barring anything totally unforeseen, *Eurydice* should be leaving within another twelve hours. It'll carry my report to the First Admiral on a diplomatic flek, with another flek for the Edenist Ambassador on Avon. You can include a flek to Kulu's mission at the Confederation Assembly.'

'Thank you. Although I haven't got a clue how to compile a report like that. They'll think we're crazy.'

Kelven glanced out at the rain bouncing on the dark rooftops. The simplicity of the scene made the events in the distant Quallheim Counties seem surreal. 'Maybe we are. But we have to do something.'

'The first thing our respective bosses will do is send back for confirmation and more information.'

'Yes, I thought about that. We must have that information ready for them.'

'Somebody has to go to the Quallheim Counties.'

'The Edenists are already on their way, but I'd like to send my own team. The marines are itching for the chance, of course. Do you have anyone capable of performing this kind of scout mission? I really think we need to pool resources.'

'I agree with you on that. Hell, I even agree with the Edenists.' And he had to smile cynically at that. 'A joint venture would produce the best results. I have a couple of people trained to perform a covert penetration and scout mission. In fact, if you let me have access to the communication circuits on your ELINT satellites I can activate some assets I have upriver, see if they can fill us in on what's happening.'

'I'll see you get that.'

'OK, I'll send my Lieutenant Jenny Harris over to supervise the operation. How were you planning on getting the scout teams upriver?'

Kelven datavised an instruction to the office computer and a wall-mounted screen lit up, showing a map of the Juliffe basin tributary network. The Quallheim Counties showed as a red slash clinging to the southern side of the tributary; Willow West glowed a warning amber to the north-west. The next county along was outlined in black, the name Kristo blinking in white script. 'A fast boat up to Kristo County, then horses into the trouble zone. If they left by tomorrow, they ought to arrive around only a day or so after the *Swithland* and its posse, perhaps even a little beforehand.'

'Couldn't we airlift them in? I can obtain one of the BK133s, they could be there by tonight.'

'And how would they get about? This is a scouting mission, remember. You can't take horses in a VTOL, and nothing else can get through that jungle.'

Ralph scowled at the map on the screen. 'Bugger, you're right. Hell, this planet is bloody pitiful.'

'Convenient, though. One of the few places in the Confederation where a thousand kilometres makes a mockery of our usual transportation systems. We're so used to instantaneous response, it spoils us.'

'Yes. Well, if any planet can bring us back to fundamentals, it's Lalonde.'

*

The bundle of mayope trunks on the payload-handling truck had been assembled by the ground crew in one of the spaceport's hangars. A simple enough job, even for this planet's meagre cargo-preparation facilities; the trunks were almost perfectly cylindrical, a metre wide, cut to the same fifteen-metre length. Bright yellow straps held them together; ten load pins had been spaced correctly around the outside. Yet so far, two of the bundles had fallen apart when Ashly used the MSV's waldo arm to manoeuvre them from the spaceplane into the *Lady Macbeth*'s hold. The delay had cost them eight hours, and replacement wood had to be ordered and paid for.

Since then Warlow had inspected every bundle before it was loaded into the McBoeing. He'd sent three back to the hangar to be reassembled after he found loose straps, his enhanced audio senses picking up the ground crew's grumbles when they thought they were out of earshot.

But this bundle seemed satisfactory. The grapple socket plugged into his lower left arm closed around the last loading pin. He braced himself on the truck's base, and tried to shift the pin. The metal below his feet emitted a hesitant creak as his boosted muscles exerted their carefully measured force. The pin remained perfectly steady.

'OK, load it in,' he told the waiting ground crew. His grapple socket disengaged, and he jumped down onto the rough tarmac.

The truck driver edged the vehicle back under the waiting McBoeing. Hydraulics began to slide the bundle into the lower fuselage cargo hold. Warlow stood beside the spaceplane's rear wheel bogies, in the shade. His body's thermal-distribution system had more than enough capacity to cope with Lalonde's blue-white sun, but he *felt* cooler here.

A power bike rounded the corner of the hangar and turned towards the spaceplane. Two people were riding on it, Marie Skibbow and a young man wearing a check shirt and khaki shorts. She drew to a halt in front of Warlow, giving the big cosmonik a breezy grin.

Cradles in the spaceplane's hold started to snap shut around the bundle's load pins. The truck's payload-handling mechanism slowly withdrew.

'How's it going?' Marie asked.

'One more flight after this, and we'll be finished,' Warlow said. 'Ten hours, maximum.'

'Great.' She swung her leg over the bike's saddle. The young man dismounted a moment later. 'Warlow, this is Quinn Dexter.'

Quinn smiled amicably. 'Warlow, pleasure to meet you. Marie here tells me you're heading for Norfolk.'

'That's right.' Warlow watched the truck drive off back to the hangar; the bright orange vehicle looked strangely washed out. His neural nanonics reported a small data drop-out from his optical sensors, and he ordered a diagnostics program interrogation.

'This could be fortunate for both of us, then,' Quinn Dexter said. 'I'd like to buy passage on the *Lady Macbeth*, Marie said you're licensed for passengers.'

'We are.'

'OK, fine. So how much is a berth?'

'You want to go to Norfolk?' Warlow asked. His optical sensors had come back on line, the diagnostics had been unable to pinpoint the glitch.

'Sure.' Quinn's happy smile broadened. 'I'm a sales agent for Dobson Engineering. It's a Kulu company. We produce a range of basic farm implements – ploughshares, wheel bearings for carts, that kind of thing. Suitable for low-technology worlds.'

'Well, you definitely came to the right place when you came to Lalonde,' Warlow said, upping the diaphragm's bass level, his best approximation of irony.

'Yes. But I think I need to wait another fifty years before Lalonde even gets up to low technology. I haven't been able to break into the official monopoly, not even with the embassy's help, so it's time to move on.'

'I see. One moment.' Warlow used his neural nanonics to open a channel to the spaceplane's flight computer, and requested a link to the *Lady Macbeth*.

'What is it?' Joshua datavised.

'A customer,' Warlow told him.

'Give me a visual,' he said when Warlow finished explaining.

Warlow focused his optical sensors on Quinn's face. The smile hadn't faded, if anything it had expanded.

'Must be pretty keen to leave if he's willing to buy passage on *Lady Mac* rather than wait for his berth on a company ship,' Joshua said. 'Tell him it's forty-five thousand fuseodollars for a zero-tau passage.'

There were times when Warlow regretted losing the ability to give a really plaintive sigh. 'He'll never pay that,' he retorted. If Joshua didn't always try to extort clients they might win more business.

'So?' Joshua shot back. 'We can haggle. Besides he might, and we need the money. The expenses I've shelled out on this bloody planet have just about emptied our petty cash account. We'll be breaking into our Norfolk fund if we're not careful.'

'My captain is currently charging forty-five thousand fuseodollars for a zero-tau flight to Norfolk,' Warlow said out loud.

'Zero-tau?' Quinn sounded puzzled.

'Yes.'

He glanced at Marie, who remained impassive.

Warlow waited patiently while the spaceplane's cargo hold doors began to swing shut. His neural nanonics relayed the background chitter of the pilot running through the flight-prep sequence.

'I don't want to travel in zero-tau,' Quinn said woodenly.

'Got him. Fifty-five thousand for a real-time cabin,' Joshua datavised.

'Then I'm afraid cabin passage will cost you fifty-five thousand,' Warlow recited laboriously. 'Consumables, food, environmental equipment maintenance, it all adds up.'

'Yes, so I see. Very well, fifty-five thousand it is then.' Quinn produced a Jovian Bank disk from his shorts pocket.

'Jesus,' Joshua datavised. 'This guy has an expense account a Saldana princeling would envy. Grab the money off him now, before he comes to his senses, then send him up on the McBoeing. The channel to *Lady Macbeth* closed.

Warlow took his own Jovian Bank credit disk from a small pouch in his utility belt, and proffered it to Quinn Dexter. 'Welcome aboard,' he boomed.

16

Oenone reduced and refocused its distortion field, allowing the wormhole terminus to close behind it. It looked round curiously with its many senses. Norfolk was a hundred and sixty thousand kilometres away; and the contrasting light from two different stars fell upon its hull. The upper hull was washed in a rosy glow from Duchess, the system's red-dwarf sun two hundred million kilometres away, darkening and highlighting the blue polyp's elaborate purple web pattern. Duke, the K2 primary, shone a strong yellowish light across the environmentally stabilized pods clasped in *Oenone*'s cargo bay from a hundred and seventy-three million kilometres in the opposite direction.

Norfolk was almost in direct conjunction between the binary pair. It was a planet that was forty per cent land, made up of large islands a hundred to a hundred and fifty thousand square kilometres each, and uncountable smaller archipelagos. *Oenone* hung over the only sliver of darkness which was left on the surface; for the approaching conjunction had banished night to a small crescent extending from pole to pole, measuring about a thousand kilometres wide at the equator, almost as if a slice had been taken out of the planet. Convoluted seas and winding straits sparkled blue and crimson in their respective hemispheres, and cloud swirls were divided into white and scarlet. Under Duke's glare the land was the usual blend of browns and greens, cool and welcoming, whereas the land illuminated by Duchess had turned a dark vermilion, creased with black folds, a harshly inhospitable domain in appearance.

Syrinx requested and received permission to enter a parking orbit from the civil spaceflight authority. *Oenone* swooped towards the planet in high spirits, chattering happily to the huge flock of voidhawks ahead of it. Three hundred and seventy-five kilometres above the equator a diamanté ring was shimmering delicately against the interstellar blackness as twenty-five thousand starships reflected fragments of light from the twin suns off their mirror-bright thermal panels and communication dishes.

Norfolk's star system wasn't an obvious choice for a terracompatible world. When the Govcentral scoutship *Duke of Rutland* emerged into the system in 2207 a preliminary sensor sweep revealed six planets, all of them solid. Two of them were in orbit twenty-eight million kilometres above Duchess; Westmorland and Brenock, forming their own binary as they tumbled round each other at a distance of half a million kilometres. The other four – Derby, Lincoln, Norfolk, and Kent – orbited Duke. It was soon obvious that only Norfolk with its two moons, Argyll and Fife, could support life.

The already cluttered interplanetary space played host to a pair of major asteroid belts, and five minor belts, as well as innumerable rocks which traded stars as their gravity fields duelled for adherents. There was also a considerable quantity of comets and small pebble-sized debris loose in the system. The scoutship's cosmologist was heard to say that it was almost as though it hadn't quite finished condensing out of the whirling protostar disk.

One final point against colonization was the lack of a gas giant for the Edenists to mine for He_3. Without a cheap local source of fuel for fusion, industry and spaceflight would be prohibitively expensive.

With this gloomy prognosis in mind, the *Duke of Rutland*

went into orbit around Norfolk to conduct its obligatory resources and environment survey. It was bound to be an odd planet, with its seasons governed by conjunction between the Duke and Duchess rather than its sidereal period: midwinter, which came at a distance of a hundred and seventy-three million kilometres from the coolish primary, was Siberian, while midsummer, at equipoise between two stars, was a time when night vanished completely, bringing a Mediterranean balm. There was no distinction between the usual geographical tropical and temperate zones found on ordinary worlds (although there were small polar ice-caps); instead the seasons were experienced uniformly across the whole planet. Naturally, the aboriginal life followed this cycle, although there were no wild variants from standard evolutionary patterns. Norfolk turned out to have a lower than usual variety of mammals, marine species, and insects. Hibernation was common, in avian species it replaced migration, and they all bred to give birth in the spring. Nothing unusual there. But the plants would only flower and ripen when they were bathed in both yellow and pink light throughout the twenty-three hour, forty-three minute day. That wasn't a condition which could be duplicated easily anywhere, even on Edenist habitats. It made the plants unique. And uniqueness was always valuable.

The discovery was sufficient for Govcentral's English State to fund a follow-up ecological assessment mission. After three months classifying aboriginal plants for edibility and taste, midsummer came to Norfolk, and the team hit paydirt.

Oenone slipped into orbit three hundred and seventy-five kilometres above the eccentrically coloured planet, and contracted its distortion field until it was only generating a gravity field for the crew toroid and gathering in cosmic energy. The nearby starships were mostly Adamist cargo vessels, big spheres performing slow balletic thermal rolls; with their dump panels extended they looked bizarrely like cumbersome windmills. Directly ahead of *Oenone* was a large cargo clipper with the violet and green loops of the Vasilkovsky line prominent on its hull.

The voidhawk was still conversing eagerly with its fellows when Syrinx, Ruben, Oxley, and Tula took the ion-field flyer down to Kesteven, one of the larger islands seven hundred kilometres south of the equator. Its capital was Boston, a trade centre of some hundred and twenty thousand souls, nestling in the intersection of two gentle valleys. The area was heavily forested, and the inhabitants had only thinned the trees out to make room for their houses, almost camouflaging the city from the air. Syrinx could see some parks, and several grey church spires rising up above the trees. The city's aerodrome was a broad greensward set aside a mile and a half (Norfolk refused to use metric measurements) to the north of its winding leafy boulevards.

Oxley brought the craft in from the north-west, careful not to overfly the city itself. Aircraft were banned on Norfolk, except for a small ambulance and flying doctor service, and ninety per cent of its interstellar trade was conducted at mid-summer, which was the only time the planet ever really saw spaceplanes. Consequently, Norfolk's population were a little sensitive to twenty-five-tonne objects shooting through the sky over their rooftops.

There were over three hundred spaceplanes and ion-field flyers already sitting on the grassy aerodrome when they arrived. Oxley settled three-quarters of a mile from the small cluster of buildings that housed the control tower and aerodrome administration.

The airlock stairs unfolded in front of Syrinx revealing the distant verdant wall of trees, and she saw someone pedalling a bicycle along the long rank of spaceplanes, with a dog running alongside. She breathed in, tasting dry, slightly dusty air with a distinct coppery tang of pollen.

The city's larger than I remember, Ruben said, with a mild sense of perplexity jumbled in with his thoughts.

What I saw looked very orderly, quaint almost. I love the way they've incorporated the forest rather than obliterated it.

He raised his eyebrows in dismay. **Quaint, she says. Well, don't tell the natives that.** He cleared his throat. 'And don't use affinity too much while you're around them, they consider it very impolite.'

Syrinx eyed the approaching cyclist. It was a boy no more than fourteen years old, with a satchel slung over his shoulder. **I'll remember.**

'They are fairly strict Christians, after all. And our facial expressions give us away.'

'I suppose they do. Does the religious factor affect our chances of getting a cargo?'

'Definitely not, they're English-ethnic, far too polite to be prejudiced, at least in public.' **And while we're on the subject,** he broadcast to his three shipmates, **no passes, please. They like to maintain the illusion they have high moral standards. Let them make the running, they invariably do.**

'Who, me?' Syrinx asked in mock horror.

Andrew Unwin rode his bicycle up to the group of people standing beside the gleaming purple flyer and braked to a halt, rear wheel squeaking loudly. He had gingerish hair and a sunny face swamped by freckles. His shirt was simple white cotton, with buttons down the front and the arms rolled up to his elbows; his green shorts were held up by a thick black leather belt with an ornate brass buckle. There wasn't a modern fabric seal anywhere in sight. He glanced at Syrinx's smart blue ship-tunic with its single silver epaulette star, and stiffened slightly. 'Captain, ma'am?'

'That's me.' She smiled.

Andrew Unwin couldn't quite keep his formal attitude going, and the corners of his mouth twitched up towards a grin. 'Aerodrome Manager's compliments, Captain, ma'am. He apologizes for not meeting you in person, but we're chocker busy right now.'

'Yes, I can see that. It's very kind of him to send you.'

'Oh, Dad didn't send me. I'm the Acting Passport Officer,' he said proudly, and drew himself up. 'Have you got yours, please? I've got my processor block.' He dived into his satchel, which excited the dog, who started barking and jumping about. 'Stop it, Mel!' he shouted.

Syrinx found she rather liked the idea of a boy helping out like this, walking up to utter strangers with curiosity and awe, obviously never thinking they might be dangerous. It spoke of an easy-going world which had few cares, and trust was prevalent. Perhaps the Adamists could get things right occasionally.

They handed their passport fleks over one at a time for Andrew to slot into his processor block. The unit looked terribly obsolete to Syrinx, fifty years out of date at least.

'Is Drayton's Import business in Penn Street still going strong?' Ruben asked Andrew Unwin, overdoing his wide I-want-to-be-friends smile.

Andrew gave him a blank stare, then his pixie face was alive with mirth. 'Yes, it's still there. Why, have you been to Norfolk before?'

'Yes, it was a few years ago now, though,' Ruben said.

'All right!' Andrew handed Syrinx her passport flek as his dog sniffed round her feet. 'Thank you, Captain, ma'am. Welcome to Norfolk. I hope you find a cargo.'

'That's very kind of you.' Syrinx sent a silent affinity command to the dog to desist, only to feel foolish when it ignored her.

Andrew Unwin was looking up expectantly.

'For your trouble,' Ruben murmured, and his hand passed over Andrew's.

'Thank you, sir!' There was a silver flash as he pocketed the coin.

'Where can we get a ride into town?' Ruben asked.

'Over by the tower, there's lots of taxi cabs. Don't take one that asks for more than five guineas. You can get your money changed in the Admin block after you get through Customs, as well.' A small delta spaceplane flew low overhead, compressors whistling as the nozzles started to rotate to the vertical, already deploying its undercarriage. Andrew turned to watch it. 'I think there's still some rooms at the Wheatsheaf if you're looking for lodgings.' He hopped back on his bicycle and pedalled off towards the spaceplane that was landing, the dog chasing after him.

Syrinx watched him go in amusement. Passport control was obviously a serious business on Norfolk.

'But how do we get to the tower?' Tula asked querulously. Her hand was shielding her eyes from the Duke's golden radiance.

'One guess,' Ruben said happily.

'We walk,' Syrinx said.

'That's my girl.'

Oxley went back into the spaceplane to collect the coolbox loaded with samples of food from Atlantis, and then rummaged through the lockers for their personal shoulder-bags. He sent a coded order to the flyer's bitek processor as he came out, and the stairs folded away, the airlock closing silently. Tula picked up the coolbox, and they started off towards the white control tower that was wobbling in the heat shimmer.

'What did he mean about overpaying the taxis?' Syrinx asked Ruben. 'Surely they have a standard tariff metre?'

Ruben started chuckling, He slipped Syrinx's arm through his. 'When you say taxi, I suppose you mean one of those neat little cars Adamists always use on developed planets, with magnetic suspension, and maybe air-conditioning?'

Syrinx nearly said: 'Well of course.' But the gleam in his eyes cautioned her. 'No . . . What do they use here?'

He just pulled her closer and laughed.

*

The bridge of heaven had returned to the skies. Louise Kavanagh wandered across Cricklade Manor's paddock with her sister Genevieve, the two of them craning their necks to look up at it. They had come out early every Duke-day morning for the past week to see how it had grown during Duchess-night.

The western horizon was suffused with a huge deep-red corona thrown out by the Duchess as she sank below the wolds, but in the northern quadrant orbiting starships sparkled and shone. Glint-specks of vivid ruby light that raced through the sky, strung together so tightly they formed a near-solid band, like a rainbow of red sequins. The western horizon, where the Duke was rising, had a similar arc, one of pure gold. Directly to the north, the band hung low over the rolling dales of Stoke County, lacking the brightness of the two horizon arcs where the reflection angle was most favourable, but still visible by Duke-day.

'I wish they'd stay for ever,' Genevieve said forlornly. 'Summer is a truly lovely time.' She was twelve (Earth) years old, a tall, spindly girl with an oval face and inquisitive brown eyes; she had inherited her mother's dark hair, which hung halfway down her back in the appropriate style for a member of the land-owning class. Her dress was a pale blue with tiny white dots and a broad lacework collar, complemented with long white socks, and polished navy-blue leather sandals.

'Without winter, summer would never come,' Louise said. 'Everything would be the same all year round, and we'd have nothing to look forward to. There are lots of worlds like that out there.' They looked up together at the ribbon of starships.

Louise was the elder of the two sisters, sixteen years old, the heir to the Cricklade estate which was their home, and an easy fifteen inches taller than Genevieve, with hair a shade lighter and long enough to reach her hips when it was unbound. They shared the same facial features, with small noses and narrow eyes, although Louise's cheeks were now more pronounced as her puppy fat burned away. Her skin boasted a clear complexion though to her dismay her cheeks remained obstinately rosy – just like a fieldworker.

This morning she was wearing a plain canary-yellow summer dress; and, wonder of all, this was the year Mother had *finally* allowed her to have a square-cut neck on some of her clothes, although her skirt hems had to remain well below her knees. The audacious necks allowed her to show how she was blossoming into womanhood. This summer there wasn't a young male in Stoke County who didn't look twice as she walked past.

But Louise was quite used to being the centre of attention. She had been since the day she was born. The Kavanaghs were Kesteven's premier family; one of the clanlike network of large rich land-owner families who when acting in concert exerted more influence than any of the regional island councils, simply because of their wealth. Louise and Genevieve were members of an army of relatives who ran Kesteven virtually as a private fiefdom. And the Kavanaghs also had strong blood ties with the royal Mountbattens, a family descended from the original British Windsor monarchy, whose prince undertook the role of planetary constitutional guardian. Norfolk might have been English-ethnic, but it owed its social structure to an idealized version of sixteenth-century Britain rather than the federal republic state of Govcentral which had founded the original colony four centuries ago.

Louise's uncle Roland, the senior of her grandfather's six children, owned nearly ten per cent of the island's arable land. Cricklade Manor's estate itself sprawled over a hundred and fifty thousand acres, incorporating forests and farmland and parkland, even whole villages, providing employment to thousands of labourers who toiled in its fields and woods and rosegroves, as well as tending to its herds and flocks. Another three hundred families farmed tithed crofts within its capacious boundaries. Craftsmen right across Stoke County were dependent on the industry it generated for their livelihood. And, of course, the estate owned a majority share in the county roseyard.

Louise was the most eligible heiress on Kesteven island. And she adored the position, people showed her nothing but respect, and willingly extended favours without expecting any return other than her patronage.

Cricklade Manor itself was a resplendent three-storey grey-stone building with a hundred-yard frontage. Its long stone-mullioned windows gazed out across a vast expanse of lawns and spinneys and walled orchards. An avenue of terrestrial cedars had been set out to mark out the perimeter of the grounds, geneered to endure Norfolk's long year and peculiar dual bombardment of photons. They had been planted three hundred years ago, and were now several hundred feet in height. Louise adored the stately ancient trees; their graceful layered boughs possessed a mystique which the smaller aboriginal pine-analogues could never hope to match. They were a part of her heritage that was for ever lost among the stars, alluding to a romantic past.

The paddock the sisters were walking through lay beyond the cedars on the western side of the manor, taking up most of a gentle slope that led down to a stream which fed the trout lake. Jumps for their horses were scattered around, unused for weeks in the excitement of the approaching rose crop. Midsummer was always a fraught time for Norfolk, and Cricklade seemed to be at the centre of a small cyclone of activity as the estate geared itself up for the roses when they ripened.

When they tired of the starships' grandeur, Louise and Genevieve carried on down to the water. Several horses with rust-red coats were wandering round the paddock, nuzzling amongst the tufty grass. Norfolk's grass-analogue was reasonably similar to Earth's, the blades were all tubular, and throughout the summer conjunction they produced minute white flowers at their tips. Starcrowns, Louise had called them when she was much younger.

'Father says he's thinking of inviting William Elphinstone to act as an assistant estate manager to Mr Butterworth,' Genevieve said slyly as they approached the mouldering wooden bar fence at the foot of the paddock.

'That was clever of Father,' Louise replied, straight faced.

'How so?'

'William will need to learn the practicalities of estate management if he is to take over Glassmoor Hall, and he could have nobody finer than Mr Butterworth to tutor him. That puts the Elphinstones under obligation to Father, and they have powerful connections among Kesteven's farm merchants.'

'And William will be here for two midsummers, that's the usual period of tutelage.'

'Indeed he will.'

'And you'll be here as well.'

'Genevieve Kavanagh, silence that evil tongue this instant.'

Genevieve danced across the grass. 'He's handsome, he's handsome!' she laughed. 'I've seen the way he looks at you, especially in *those* dresses you wear for the dances.' Her hands traced imaginary breasts over her chest.

Louise giggled. 'Devil child, you have a faulty brain. I'm not interested in William.'

'You're not?'

'No. Oh, I like him, and I hope we can be friends. But that's all. In any case, he's five years older than me.'

'I think he's gorgeous.'

'Then you can have him.'

Genevieve's face fell. 'I'll not be offered anyone so grand. You're the heiress, after all. Mother will make me marry some troll from a minor family, I'm sure of it.'

'Mother won't *make* us marry anyone. Honest to goodness, Genny, she won't.'

'Really truly?'

'Really truly,' Louise said, even though she couldn't quite bring herself to believe it. Truth to be told, there weren't that many eligible suitors for her on Kesteven. Hers was an invidious position: a husband should hold equal status, but someone of equal wealth would have his own estate and she would be expected to live there. Yet Cricklade was her life, it was beautiful even in midwinter's long barren months when yards of snow covered the ground, the pine trees on the surrounding wolds were denuded, and the birds buried themselves below the frost-line. She couldn't bear the thought of leaving it. So who could she marry? It was probably something her parents had discussed; her uncles and aunts too, most likely.

She didn't like to think about what the outcome would be. At the very least she hoped they would give her a list rather than an ultimatum.

One of the butterflies caught her eye, a geneered red admiral sunning itself on one of the glass blades. It was freer than she was, she realized miserably.

'Will you marry for love, then?' Genevieve asked, all dewy eyed.

'Yes, I'll marry for love.'

'That's super. I wish I were as bold.'

Louise put her hands on the top rail of the fence, looking across the gurgling stream. Forget-me-nots had run wild on the banks, their blue flowers attracting hordes of butterflies. Some time-distant master of Cricklade had released hundreds of species across the grounds. Every year they flourished, invading the orchards and gardens with their fluttering harlequin colours. 'I'm not bold, I'm a dithery dreamer. Do you know what I dream?'

'No.' Genevieve shook her head, her face rapt.

'I dream that Father lets me travel before I have to take on any of my family responsibilities.'

'To Norwich?'

'No, not the capital, that's just like Boston only bigger, and I'll be going there anyway for finishing school. I want to travel to other worlds and see how their people live.'

'Gosh! Travel on a starship, that's stupendously wonderful. Can I come too? Please!'

'If I go, then I suppose Father will have to let you go when you reach your age. Fair's fair.'

'He'll never let me go. I'm not even allowed to go to the dances.'

'But you sneak past Nanny and watch them anyway.'

'Yes!'

'Well, then.'

'He won't let me go.'

Louise grinned down at her sister's petulant tone. 'It is only a dream.'

'You always make your dreams come real. You're so clever, Louise.'

'I don't want to change this world with new ideas,' she said, half to herself. 'I just want to be allowed out, just once. Everything here is so duty-bound, so regimented. Some days I feel as though I've already lived my life.'

'William could get you away from here. He could ask for a star voyage as a honeymoon; Father could never refuse that.'

'Oh! You impudent baby ogress!' She aimed a lazy swipe at her sister's head, but Genevieve had already skipped out of range.

'Honeymoon, honeymoon,' Genevieve chanted so loudly that even the nearby horses looked up. 'Louise is going on honeymoon!' She picked up her skirts and ran, long slender legs flying over the flower-laden grass.

Louise gave chase, the two of them giggling and squealing in delight as they gallivanted about, scattering the butterflies before them.

*

Lady Macbeth emerged from her final jump insystem, and Joshua allowed himself a breath of silent relief that they were still intact. The trip from Lalonde had been an utter *bitch.*

For a start Joshua found he neither liked nor trusted Quinn Dexter. His intuition told him there was something desperately wrong about him. Wrong in a way he couldn't define, but Dexter seemed to drain life from a cabin when he entered. And his behaviour was weird, too; he had no instinct, no natural rhythm for events or conversation, as though he was working on a two-second time-delay to reality.

In fact, if Joshua had met him in the flesh back down on Lalonde's spaceport he probably wouldn't have accepted him as a passenger no matter how much money was stashed in his credit disk. Too late now. Although, thankfully, Dexter had spent most of his time alone in his cabin down in capsule C, venturing out only for meals and the bathroom.

That was one of his more rational quirks. After he'd come on board, he had given the compact bulkheads a quick suspicious look, and said: 'I'd forgotten how much mechanization there is on a starship.'

Forgotten? Joshua couldn't work that one out at all. How could you forget the way a starship looked?

Yet the oddest thing of all was how inept Dexter was at free-fall manoeuvring. Had he been asked, Joshua would have said that the man had never been in space before. Which was ridiculous, because he was a travelling sales manager. One who didn't have neural nanonics. And one who wore a frightened expression the whole time. There had even been occasions when Joshua had caught him flinching from some sudden metallic sound rattling out of the capsule systems, or the creak of the stress structure as they were under acceleration.

Of course, given *Lady Mac*'s performance during the voyage, that part of Dexter's behaviour was almost understandable. Joshua had experienced enough nasty moments on the flight himself. It seemed like there wasn't a system on board that hadn't suffered from some kind of glitch since they boosted out of Lalonde's orbit. What should have been a simple four-day trip had stretched out to nearly a week as the crew tackled power surges, data drop-outs, actuator failures, and dozens of smaller niggling malfunctions. Joshua hated to think what was going to happen when he handed over the maintenance log to the Confederation Astronautics Board's inspectors, they'd probably insist on a complete overhaul. At least the jump nodes had functioned, though he'd even begun to have his doubts about them.

He datavised the flight computer to unfold the thermo-dump panels and extend the sensor booms. Fault alerts jangled in his mind; one of the thermo-dump panels refused to open past halfway, and three booms were jammed in their recesses.

'Jesus!' he snarled.

There were mutters from the rest of the crew strapped into their bridge couches on either side of him.

'I thought you fixed that fucking panel,' Joshua shouted at Warlow.

'I did!' the answer thumped back. 'If you think you can do any better, put on a suit and get out there yourself.'

Joshua ran a hand over his brow. 'See what you can do,' he said sullenly. Warlow grunted something unintelligible, and ordered the couch's straps to release him. He pushed himself towards the open hatchway. Ashly Hanson freed himself, too, and went after the cosmonik to help.

Sensor data was coming in from the booms which were functional. The flight computer started tracking nearby stars to produce an accurate astrogration fix. Norfolk with its divergent illumination looked unusually small for a terracompatible planet. Joshua didn't have time to puzzle that, the sensors reported laser radar pulses were bouncing off the hull, and a voidhawk distortion field had locked on.

'Jesus, now what?' Joshua asked even as the astrogration fix slipped into his mind. *Lady Mac* had translated two hundred and ninety thousand kilometres above Norfolk, way outside the planet's designated emergence zone. He groaned out loud and hurriedly datavised the communication dish to transmit their identification code. The Confederation Navy ships patrolling Norfolk would start using *Lady Mac* for target practice soon.

Norfolk was almost unique among the Confederation's terra-compatible planets in that it didn't have a strategic-defence network. There was no high-technology industry, no asteroid settlements in orbit, and consequently there was nothing worth stealing. Protection from mercenaries and pirate ships wasn't needed; except for the two weeks every season when the starships came to collect their cargoes of Norfolk Tears.

As the planet moved towards midsummer a squadron from the Confederation Navy's 6th Fleet was assigned to protection duties, paid for by the planetary government. It was a popular duty with the crews; after the cargo starships departed they were allowed shore leave, where they were entertained in grand style, and all the crews were presented with a special half-sized bottle of Norfolk Tears by the grateful government.

The *Lady Macbeth*'s main communication dish servos spun round once, then packed up. Power-loss signals appeared across the schematic the flight computer was datavising into Joshua's brain. 'I don't fucking believe it. Sarha, get that bastard dish sorted out!' Out of the corner of his eye he saw her activate the console by her couch. He routed the *Lady Mac*'s identification code through her omnidirectional antenna.

An inter-ship radio channel came alive, and the communication console routed the datavise into Joshua's neural nanonics. 'Starship *Lady Macbeth*, this is Confederation Navy ship *Pestravka*. You have emerged outside this planet's designated starship emergence zones, are you in trouble?'

'Thank you, *Pestravka*,' Joshua datavised in reply. 'We've been having some system malfunctions, my apologies for causing any panic.'

'What is the nature of your malfunction?'

'Sensor error.'

'That's simple enough to sort out; you should know better than to jump insystem with inaccurate guidance information.'

'Up yours,' Melvin Ducharme grumbled from his couch.

'The error percentage has only just become apparent,' Joshua said. 'We're updating now.'

'What's wrong with your main communications dish?'

'Overloaded servo, it's scheduled for replacement.'

'Well, activate your back-up.'

Sarha let out an indignant snort. 'I'll point one of the masers at him if he likes. They'll receive that blast loud and bloody clear.'

'Complying now, *Pestravka*.' Joshua glared at Sarha.

He launched a quiet prayer as the ribbed silver pencil of the second dish slid out of *Lady Macbeth*'s dark silicon hull, and opened like a flower. It tracked round to point at the *Pestravka.*

'I'm datavising a copy of this incident to the Confederation Astronautics Board office on Norfolk,' the *Pestravka*'s officer continued. 'And I'll add a strong recommendation that they inspect your spaceworthiness certificate.'

'Thank you so much, *Pestravka.* Are we now cleared to contact civil flight control for an approach vector? I'd hate to be shot at for not asking your permission first.'

'Don't push your luck, Calvert. I can easily take a fortnight searching your cargo holds.'

'Looks like your reputation's preceding you, Joshua,' Dahybi Yadev said after the *Pestravka* cut the link.

'Let's hope it hasn't reached the planet's surface yet,' Sarha said.

Joshua aligned the secondary dish on the civil flight control's communication satellite, and received permission to enter a parking orbit. *Lady Mac*'s three fusion tubes came alive, sending out long rivers of hazy plasma, and the starship accelerated in towards the gaudy planet at a tenth of a gee.

*

Chinks of light were glinting down into Quinn Dexter's vacant world, accompanied by faint scratchy sounds. It was like intermittent squalls of luminous rain falling through fissures from an external universe. Some beams of light flickered in the far distance, others splashed across him. When they did, he saw the images they carried.

A boat. One of the grotty traders on the Quallheim, little more than a bodged-together raft. Speeding downriver.

A town of wooden buildings. Durringham in the rain.

A girl.

He knew her. Marie Skibbow, naked, tied to a bed with rope.

His heartbeat thudded in the silence.

'Yes,' said the voice he knew from before, from the clearing in the jungle, the voice which came out of Night. 'I thought you'd like this.'

Marie was tugging frantically at her bonds, her figure every bit as lush as his imagination had once conceived it.

'What would you do with her, Quinn?'

What would he do? What *couldn't* he do with such an exquisite body. How oh how she would suffer beneath him.

'You are bloody repugnant, Quinn. But so terribly useful.'

Energy twisted eagerly inside his body, and a phantasm come forth to overlay reality. Quinn's interpretation of the physical form which God's Brother might assume should He ever choose to manifest Himself in the flesh. And what flesh. Capable of the most wondrous assaults, amplifying every degradation the sect had ever taught him.

The flux of sorcerous power reached a triumphal peak, opening a rift into the terrible empty beyond, and so another emerged to take possession as Marie pleaded and wept.

'Back you go, Quinn.'

And the images shrank back to the dry wispy beams of flickering light.

'You're not the Light Brother!' Quinn shouted into the nothingness. Fury at the acknowledgement of betrayal heightened his perception, the light became brighter, sound louder.

'Of course not, Quinn. I'm worse than that, worse than any mythical devil. All of us are.'

Laughter echoed through the prison universe, tormenting him.

Time was so different in here . . .

A spaceplane.

A starship.

Uncertainty. Quinn felt it run through him like a hormonal surge. The electrical machinery upon which he was now dependent recoiled from his estranged body, which made his dependence still deeper as the delicate apparatuses broke down one by one. Uncertainty gave way to fear. His body trembled as it tried desperately to quieten the currents of exotic energy which infiltrated every cell.

It wasn't omnipotent, Quinn realized, this thing which controlled his body, it had limits. He let the dribs and drabs of light soak into what was left of his mind, concentrating on what he saw, the words he heard. Watching, waiting. Trying to understand.

*

Syrinx thought Boston was the most delightful city she had seen in fourteen years of travelling about the Confederation, and that included the sheltered enclaves of houses in the Saturn-orbiting habitats of her birth. Every house was built from stone, with thick walls to keep the heat out during the long summer, then keep it in for the equally long winter. Most of them were two storeys high, with some of the larger ones having three; they had small railed gardens at the front, and rows of stables along the back. Terrestrial honeysuckle and ivy were popular creepers for covering the stonework, while hanging baskets provided cheerful dabs of colour to most porches. Roofs were always steep to withstand the heavy snow, and grey slate tiles alternated with jet-black solar panels in pleasing geometric patterns. Wood was burnt to provide warmth and sometimes for cooking, which produced a forest of chimneys thrusting out of the gable ends, topped by red clay pots with elaborate crowns. Every building, be it private, civic, or commercial, was individual, possessing the kind of character impossible on worlds where mass-production facilities were commonplace. Wide streets were all cobbled, with tall cast-iron street lights spaced along them. It was only after a while she realized that as there were no mechanoids or servitors each of the little granite cubes must have been laid by human hand – the time and effort that must have entailed! There were trees lining each pavement, mainly Norfolk's pine-analogues, with some geneered terrestrial evergreens for variety. Traffic was comprised entirely of bicycles, trike scooters (very few, and mostly with adolescent riders), horses, and horse-drawn cabs and carts. She had seen power vans, but only on the roads around the outskirts, and those were farm vehicles.

After they had cleared Customs (altogether more rigorous than Passport Control) they'd found the horse-drawn taxi coaches waiting by the aerodrome's tower. Syrinx had grinned, and Tula had let out an exasperated groan. But the one they used was well sprung, proving a reasonably smooth trip into town. Following Andrew Unwin's advice, they had rented some rooms at the Wheatsheaf, a coaching house on the side of one of the rivers which the town was built around.

Once they had unpacked and eaten a light lunch in the courtyard, Syrinx and Ruben had taken another coach to Penn Street, the precious coolbox on the floor by their feet.

Ruben watched the traffic and pedestrians parading past with a contented feeling. Starship crews strolling about were easy to spot: their clothes of synthetic fabric were curiously bland in comparison to the locals' attire. Bostonians in summer favoured bright colours and raffish styles; this year multicoloured waistcoats were in vogue among the young men, while the girls wore crinkled cheesecloth skirts with bold circular patterns (hems always below their knees, he noted sadly). It was like stepping back into pre-spaceflight history, though he suspected no historical period on Earth was ever as clean as this.

'Penn Street, guv'nor,' the driver cried as the horse turned into a road parallel to the River Gwash. It was the commercial sector of the city, with wharves lining the river, and a lengthy rank of prodigious warehouses standing behind them. Here for the first time they encountered powered lorries. A railway marshalling yard was visible at the other end of the dusty road.

Ruben looked down the long row of warehouses and busy yards and offices, only too well aware of Syrinx's gaze hot on his neck. Mordant thoughts started pressing against his mind. Drayton's Import wasn't *in* Penn Street, it was Penn Street. The name was on signs across every building.

'Where to now, guv'nor?' the driver asked.

'Head Office,' Ruben replied. The last time he'd been here, Drayton's Import had consisted of a single office in a rented warehouse.

Head Office turned out to be a building in the middle of the street, on the waterfront side, sandwiched between two warehouses. Its arched windows were all iron rimmed, and a large, brightly polished brass plaque was set in the wall next to the double doors. The cab pulled to a halt in front of its curving stone stairs.

'Looks like old Dominic Kavanagh is doing all right for himself,' Ruben said as they climbed out. He handed the driver a guinea, with a sixpenny piece for a tip.

Syrinx's stare could have cut diamond.

'Old Dominic, one of the best. Boy, did we have some times together, he knows every pub in town.' Ruben wondered who his bravado was intended to reassure.

'Exactly how long ago was this?' Syrinx asked as they walked into reception.

'About fifteen or twenty years,' Ruben offered. He was sure that was it, although he had a horrible feeling that Dominic had been the same age as himself. That's the trouble with crewing a voidhawk, he thought, every day the same, and all of them squashed together. How am I supposed to know the exact date?

The reception hall had a black and white marble floor, and a wide staircase leading up the rear wall. A young woman sat behind a desk ten yards inside the door, a uniformed concierge standing beside her.

'I'd like to see Dominic Kavanagh,' Ruben told her blithely. 'Just tell him Ruben's back in town.'

'I'm sorry, sir,' she said. 'I don't think we have a Kavanagh of that name working here.'

'But he owns Drayton's Import,' Ruben said forlornly.

'Kenneth Kavanagh owns this establishment, sir.'

'Oh.'

'Can we see him?' Syrinx asked. 'I have flown all the way from Earth.'

The woman took in Syrinx's blue ship-tunic with its silver star. 'Your business, Captain?'

'As everyone else, I'm looking for a cargo.'

'I'll ask if Mr Kenneth is in.' The woman picked up a pearl handset.

Eight minutes later they were being ushered into Kenneth Kavanagh's office on the top floor. Half of one wall was an arched window giving a view out over the river. Broad barges were gliding over the smooth black water, as sedate as swans.

Kenneth Kavanagh was in his late thirties, a broad-shouldered man wearing a neat charcoal-grey suit, white shirt, and a red silk tie. His raven-black hair was glossed straight back from his forehead.

Syrinx almost paid him no attention at all. There was another man in the room, in his mid-twenties, with a flat, square-jawed face, and a mop of pale copper hair combed into a rough parting. He had the kind of build Syrinx associated with sportsmen, or (more likely on this world) outdoor labourers. His suit was made from some shiny grey-green material. The jacket's left arm was flat, pinned neatly to his side. Syrinx had never seen anyone with a limb missing before.

You're staring, Ruben warned her as he shook hands with Kenneth Kavanagh.

Syrinx felt the blood warm her ears. **But what's wrong with him?**

Nothing. They don't allow clone vats on this planet.

That's absurd. It forces him to go through life crippled, I wouldn't wish that on anyone.

Medical technology is where the big arguments rage about what they should and shouldn't permit. And wholesale cloning is pretty advanced.

Syrinx recovered and extended her hand to Kenneth Kavanagh. He said hello, then introduced the other man as: 'My cousin Gideon.'

They shook hands, Syrinx trying to avoid eye contact. The young man had such a defeated air it threatened to drag her down into whatever private misery he was in.

'Gideon is my aide,' Kenneth said. 'He's learning the business from the bottom upwards.'

'It seems the best thing,' Gideon Kavanagh said in a quiet voice. 'I can hardly manage the family estate now. That requires a great deal of physical involvement.'

'What happened?' Ruben asked.

'I fell from my horse. Bad luck, really. Falling is part of horse riding. This time I landed awkwardly, took a fence railing through my shoulder.'

Syrinx gave him an ineffectual grimace of sympathy, unsure what to say. *Oenone* was in her mind, its presence alone immensely supportive.

Kenneth Kavanagh indicated the chairs in front of his pale

wooden desk. 'It's certainly a pleasure to have you here, Captain.'

'I think you've said that to a few captains this week,' she told him wryly as she sat down.

'Yes, a few,' Kenneth Kavanagh admitted. 'But a first-time captain is always welcome here. Some of my fellow exporters take a blasé approach about our planet's product, and say there will always be a demand. I think a little warmth in the relationship never comes amiss, especially as it is just the one product upon which our entire economy is so dependent. I'd hate to see anyone discouraged from returning.'

'Am I going to have cause to be discouraged?'

He spread his hands. 'We can always find the odd case or two. What exactly is your starship's capacity?'

'*Oenone* can manage seven hundred tonnes.'

'Then I'm afraid that a little bit of disappointment is going to be inevitable.'

'Old Dominic always kept some cases back for a decent trade,' Ruben said. 'And we certainly have a trade in mind.'

'You knew Dominic Kavanagh?' Kenneth asked with a note of interest.

'I certainly did. Your father?'

'My late grandfather.'

Ruben's shoulders sank back into his seat. 'Hoh, boy, he was such a lovely old rogue.'

'Alas, his wisdom is sorely missed by all of us.'

'Did he go from natural causes?'

'Yes. Twenty-five years ago.'

'Twenty-five . . .' Ruben appeared to lose himself in reverie.

I'm sorry, Syrinx told him.

Twenty-five years. That means I must have been here at least thirty-five years ago, probably more. Bugger, but there's no fool like an old fool.

'You mentioned a trade,' Kenneth said.

Syrinx patted the coolbox on the floor by her chair. 'The best Atlantis has to offer.'

'Ah, a wise choice. I can always sell Atlantean delicacies; my own family alone will eat half of them. Do you have an inventory?'

She handed over a sheaf of hard copy. There was no desktop processor block, she noticed, although there was a keyboard and a small holoscreen.

Kenneth read down the list, his eyebrows raised in appreciation. 'Excellent, I see you have brought some orangesole, that's one of my personal favourites.'

'You're in luck, there are five fillets in this coolbox. You can see if they're up to standard.'

'I'm sure they are.'

'None the less, I'd like you to accept the contents as my gift for your hospitality.'

'That's really most kind, Syrinx.' He started touch-typing on the keyboard, looking directly at the holoscreen. She was sure her fingers couldn't move at such a speed.

'Happily, my family has interests in several roseyards on Kesteven,' Kenneth said. 'As you know, we can't officially sell any Norfolk Tears until midsummer when the new crop is in; however, there is an informal allocation system operating amongst ourselves which I can make use of. And I see my cousin Abel has several cases unclaimed, he owns the Eaglethorpe estate in the south of Kesteven. They produce a very reasonable bouquet in that district. Regrettably, I can't offer you a full hold, but I think possibly we can provide you with six hundred cases of bottled Tears, which works out at just under two hundred tonnes.'

'That sounds quite satisfactory,' Syrinx said.

'Jolly good. So, that just leaves us with the nitty-gritty of working out a price.'

*

Andrew Unwin loaded Quinn Dexter's passport flek into his processor block, and the unit immediately went dead. He rapped on it with his knuckles, but nothing happened. The three men from the spaceplane were watching him keenly. Andrew knew his cheeks would be bright scarlet. He didn't like to think what his father would say. Passport Officer was an important job.

'Thank you, sir.' Andrew meekly handed the unread flek back to Quinn Dexter, who took it without comment. Mel was still barking, from a distance, hiding behind the front wheel of his bike. The dog hadn't stopped since the group trotted down the spaceplane's airlock stairs.

And the day had been going so well until the spaceplane from the *Lady Macbeth* landed.

'Is that it?' Joshua asked, his voice raised above the barking.

'Yes, thank you, Captain, sir. Welcome to Norfolk. I hope you find a cargo.'

Joshua grinned, and beckoned him over. The two of them walked away from Quinn Dexter and Ashly Hanson who waited at the foot of the stairs, the dog scampering after them.

'Good of you to deal with us so promptly,' Joshua said. 'I can see the aerodrome's busy.'

'It's my job, Captain, sir.'

Joshua took a bundle of leftover Lalonde francs from his ship-suit pocket, and slipped three out. 'I appreciate it.' The plastic notes were pressed into the boy's hand. A smile returned to his face.

'Now tell me,' Joshua said in a low tone. 'Someone who can be trusted with passport duty must know what goes on around here, where the bodies are buried, am I right?'

Andrew Unwin nodded, too nervous to speak. What bodies?

'I hear there are some pretty important families on Norfolk, do you know which is the most influential here on Kesteven?'

'That would be the Kavanaghs, Captain, sir. There's dozens

and dozens of them, real gentry; they own farms and houses and businesses all over the island.'

'Do they have any roseyards?'

'Yes, there's several of their estates which bottle their own Tears.'

'Great. Now, the big question: do you know who handles their offworld sales for them?'

'Yes, Captain, sir,' he said proudly. That wad of crisp notes was still in the captain's hand, he did his best not to stare at it. 'You want Kenneth Kavanagh for that. If anyone can find you a cargo, he can.'

Ten notes were counted off. 'Where can I find him?'

'Drayton's Import company, in Penn Street.'

Joshua handed over the notes.

Andrew folded them with practised alacrity, and shoved them in his shorts pocket. After he'd ridden twenty yards from the spaceplane his processor block let out a quiet bleep. It was fully functional again. He gave it a bewildered look, then shrugged and rode off towards the spaceplane that was just landing.

*

Judging by the receptionist's initial attitude, Joshua guessed he wasn't the first starship captain to come knocking at Drayton's Import this week. But he managed to catch her eye as she held the pearl handset to her ear, and earned a demure smile.

'Mr Kavanagh will see you now, Captain Calvert,' she said.

'That's very kind of you to press my case.'

'Not at all.'

'I wonder if you could recommend a decent restaurant for tonight. My associate and I haven't eaten for hours, we're looking forward to a meal. Somewhere you use, perhaps?'

She straightened her back self-consciously, and her voice slid up a social stratum. 'I sometimes visit the Metropole,' she said airily.

'Then I'm sure it must be delightful.'

Ashly raised his eyes heavenwards in silent appeal.

It was another quarter of an hour before they were shown into Kenneth Kavanagh's office. Joshua didn't shirk from eye contact with Gideon when Kenneth introduced them. He got the distinct impression the amputee victim was suppressing extreme nervousness, his face was held too rigidly, as if he was afraid of showing emotions. Then he realized that Kenneth was watching his own reaction. Something about the situation wasn't quite right.

Kenneth offered them seats in front of the desk as Gideon explained how he'd lost his arm. The restriction on medical cloning was a stiff one, Joshua thought, although he could appreciate the reasoning. Once the line was drawn, Norfolk had to stick to it. They wanted a stable pastoral culture. If you opened the doors to one medical technology, where did you stop? He was glad he didn't have to decide.

'Is this your first visit to Norfolk, Captain?' Kenneth asked.

'Yes. I only started flying last year.'

'Is that so? Well, I always like to welcome first-time captains. I believe it's important to build up personal contacts.'

'That sounds like a good policy.'

'Exporting Norfolk Tears is our lifeblood, alienating starship captains is not a wise option.'

'I'm hoping I won't be alienated.'

'And so do I. I try not to send anyone away empty handed, although you must understand there is a high level of demand, and I do have long-established customers to whom I owe a certain loyalty. And most of them have been here a week or more already. I have to say, you have left it somewhat late. What sort of cargo size were you thinking of?'

'*Lady Mac* can boost a thousand tonnes without too much trouble.'

'Captain Calvert, there are some of my oldest customers who don't get that many cases.'

'I have a trade proposition for you, a part exchange.'

'Well, a trade is always helpful; although Norfolk's import laws are rather strict. I couldn't countenance breaking, or even bending them. I have the family reputation to consider.'

'I understand perfectly,' Joshua said.

'Jolly good. What is it you've brought?'

'Wood.'

Kenneth Kavanagh gave him a stupefied stare, then burst out laughing. Even Gideon's sombre expression perked up.

'Wood? Are you serious?' Kenneth asked. 'Your starship hold is full of wood?'

'A thousand tonnes.' Joshua turned the seal of the shoulder-bag and pulled out the black wedge of mayope he'd brought. He had chosen it specially in the lumberyard back on Lalonde. It was a standard slice, twenty-five centimetres long, but the bark was still attached, and more importantly, there was a small twig with a few shrivelled leaves. He dropped it on the middle of the desk, making a solid thud.

Kenneth stopped laughing and leaned forward. 'Good Lord.' He tapped it with a fingernail, then gave it a harder knock with his knuckles.

Without speaking, Joshua handed over a stainless steel chisel.

Kenneth applied the sharp blade to the wood. 'I can't even scratch it.'

'You normally need a fission blade to cut mayope. But it can be cut with the mechanical power saws you have on Norfolk,' Joshua said. 'Though it's a brute of a job. As you can imagine, once it's cut into shape it's incredibly hard wearing. I expect your artisans could come up with a few interesting applications if they put their minds to it.'

Kenneth picked the wedge up in one hand to test the weight, pulling thoughtfully on his lower lip with the other. 'Mayope, you call it?'

'That's right, it comes from a planet called Lalonde. Which is tropical; in other words it won't grow here on Norfolk. Not without extensive geneering, anyway.' He looked at Gideon who was standing behind Kenneth's chair. The man showed a certain admiration for the wood, but he wasn't particularly involved, not like his senior cousin. Surely an aide should at least ask one question? But then he hadn't said a word since they had been introduced. Why was he present? Joshua instinctively knew the reason was important. If the Kavanaghs were as eminent as they appeared, even an injured one wouldn't be wasting time standing about in an office doing nothing.

He thought of Ione again. 'Trust yourself when it comes to people,' she'd said.

'Have you been to any other importer with this?' Kenneth asked cautiously.

'I only arrived today. Naturally, I came to a Kavanagh first.'

'That's most courteous of you to honour my family in such a fashion, Captain. And I'd very much like to return the gesture. I'm sure we can come to some arrangement. As you know, roseyards aren't legally allowed to sell their produce before the new crop comes in, but fortunately my family does have an unofficial allocation system. Let me see what I can find for you.' He put the mayope down and began typing.

Joshua met Gideon's gaze levelly. 'Did you lead a very physically active life before your accident?'

'Yes, we of the gentry do tend to enjoy our sports. There is little to do in Kesteven during the winter months, so we have an extensive range of events to amuse us. My fall was a sorry blow.'

'So office life doesn't really suit you?'

'It's the best occupation given my circumstances, I felt.'

Kenneth had stopped typing.

'You know, you wouldn't be nearly so restricted in free fall,' Joshua said. 'There are many people with medical problems who lead very full lives on starships and industrial stations.'

'Is that so?' Gideon asked tonelessly.

'Yes. Perhaps you'd care to consider it? I have a vacancy on board *Lady Macbeth* at the moment. Nothing technical, but it's decent work. You could try it for a Norfolk year, see if it's more agreeable to you than office work. If not, I'll bring you back when I return for another cargo of Tears next summer. The pay is reasonable, and I provide insurance for all my crew.' Joshua looked straight at Kenneth. 'Which includes complete medical cover.'

'That is extraordinarily generous of you, Captain,' Gideon said. 'I'd like to accept those terms. I'll try shipboard life for a year.'

'Welcome aboard.'

Kenneth resumed typing, then studied the holoscreen display. 'You're in luck, Captain Calvert. I believe I can supply you with three thousand cases of Norfolk Tears, which comes to approximately one thousand tonnes. My cousin Grant Kavanagh has some extensive rosegroves in his Cricklade estate, and he hasn't yet placed all the cases. That district produces an absolutely first-rate bouquet.'

'Wonderful,' Joshua said.

'I'm sure cousin Grant will want to meet such an important client,' Kenneth said. 'On behalf of the family, I extend an invitation to you and Mr Hanson to stay at Cricklade for the midsummer harvest. You can see our famous Tears being collected.'

*

The light from Duchess was just making its presence felt as Joshua and Ashly walked out of the Drayton's Import office. Norfolk's short period of darkness was giving way to the light of the red dwarf. Walls and cobbles were acquiring a pinkish shading.

'You did it!' Ashly whooped.

'Yeah, I did,' Joshua said.

'A thousand tonnes, I've never heard of anyone getting that much before. You are the sneakiest, most underhand, deviously corrupt little bugger I have met in all my centuries.' He flung an arm round Joshua's neck and dragged him towards the main street. 'God damn, but we're going to be rich. Medical insurance, by God! Joshua you are beautiful!'

'We'll put Gideon in zero-tau till we reach Tranquillity. It shouldn't take a clinic more than eight months to clone a new arm for him. He can enjoy himself with Dominique's party set for the rest of the time after that. I'll have a word with her.'

'How's he going to explain away a new arm when he gets back?'

'Jesus, I don't know. Magic clockwork, I expect. This world is backward enough to believe it.'

Laughing, the two of them waved for a taxi coach.

*

When Duchess had risen well above the horizon, sending her bold scarlet rays to discolour the city, Joshua settled himself on a stool in the Wheatsheaf's wharfside bar and ordered a local brandy. The view outside the window was fascinating, casting everything in tones of red. Some colours were almost invisible. A regular train of barges sailed down the willow-lined river, helmsmen standing by the big tillers at the rear.

It was wonderful to watch, the whole city was a giant tourist fantasy pageant. But some of the inhabitants must lead incredibly dull lives, doing the same thing day after day.

'We worked out how you did it eventually,' a female voice said in his ear.

Joshua turned, putting his eyes level with a delightful swelling at the front of a blue satin ship-tunic. 'Captain Syrinx, this is a pleasure. Can I get you a drink? This brandy is more than passable, I can recommend it, or perhaps you'd like a wine?'

'Doesn't it bother you?'

'No, I'll drink anything.'

'I don't know how you can sleep at night. Antimatter kills people, you know. It's not a game, it's not funny.'

'A beer, maybe?'

'Good day, Captain Calvert.' Syrinx started to walk past.

Joshua caught her arm. 'If you don't join me for a drink, how can you brag about working *it* out? And incidentally demonstrate how superior you Edenists all are to us poor mud-chewing primitives. Or maybe you don't want to hear my counter-argument. After all, you've convinced yourself I'm guilty of something. I don't even know what that is yet. Nobody ever had the decency to tell me what you thought I was carrying. Have Edenists left justice behind as well as the rest of our poor flawed Adamist customs?'

Syrinx's mouth dropped open. The man was intolerable! How did he twist phrases like that? It was almost as if she was in the wrong. 'I never said you were a mud-chewing primitive,' she hissed. 'That's not what we think at all.'

Joshua's eyes slid pointedly to one side. Syrinx realized everyone in the bar was staring at them.

Are you all right? *Oenone* asked anxiously, picking up on the flustered thoughts in her skull.

I'm fine. It's this bloody Calvert man again.

Oh, is Joshua there?

'Joshua?' She winced. She'd been so surprised at *Oenone*'s use of his first name it had slipped out.

'You remembered,' Joshua said warmly.

'I . . .'

'Have a stool, what are you drinking?'

Furious and embarrassed, Syrinx sat on a barstool. At least it would stop everyone from looking. 'I'll try a wine.'

He signalled the barmaid for drinks. 'You're not wearing your naval stripe.'

'No. Our duty tour finished a few weeks back.'

'So you're an honest trader now?'

'Yes.'

'Have you got yourself a cargo?'

'Yes, thank you.'

'Hey, that's great news, well done. These Norfolk merchants are tough buggers to crack. I got the *Lady Mac* stocked up, too.' He collected the drinks, and touched his glass to hers. 'Have dinner with me tonight, we can celebrate together.'

'I don't think so.'

'Do you have a previous engagement?'

'Well . . .' she couldn't bring herself to lie outright, that would make her no better than him. 'I was just on my way to bed. It's been a long day with some tough negotiations. But thanks for the invitation. Another time.'

'That's a real shame,' he said. 'Looks like you've condemned me to a terminally dull evening, then. There's only my pilot down here, and he's too old for my kind of fun-seeking. I'm waiting for him now. We seem to have lost our paying passenger. Not that I'm complaining, he wasn't the party type. Apparently there's a good restaurant in town called the Metropole, we were going to check it out. It's our one night in town, we've been invited to an estate for the midsummer itself. So, tough negotiations, eh? How many cases did you get?'

'You were a decoy,' Syrinx said, jumping at the chance to get a word in.

'I'm sorry?'

'You were smuggling antimatter-confinement coils into the Puerto de Santa Maria system.'

'Not me.'

'We were trailing you all the way from Idria, we'd got you in our sensors every kilometre. That's what we couldn't understand. It was a direct flight. The confinement coils were on board when you left, and they were gone when you arrived. At the time we assumed you hadn't rendezvoused with anybody, because we never detected them. But then you didn't know we were there, did you?'

Joshua drank some of his brandy, his eyes never leaving her over the rim of the glass. 'No, you were in full stealth mode, remember?'

'So was your friend.'

'What friend?'

'You took a long time to manoeuvre into each jump coordinate. I've never seen anyone so clumsy before.'

'Nobody's perfect.'

'No, but nobody's that imperfect either.' She took a sip of the wine. Oh, he was a canny one, this Joshua Calvert; she could see why she'd been fooled before. 'What I think happened was this. You had your friend waiting a light-month outside the New California system, in full stealth mode, at a very precise coordinate. When you left Idria you jumped to within a few thousand kilometres of him. It would be difficult, but you could do that. With the nodes the *Lady Macbeth* is equipped with, and your own astrogration skill, that sort of accuracy is possible. And who would suspect? Nobody is that accurate jumping out of a system; it's when you come insystem you need precision to jump into the correct emergence zones.'

'Go on, this is riveting stuff.'

She took another sip. 'Once you jumped outsystem, you shoved the illegal coils out of the cargo hold, and jumped away again. We couldn't detect that sort of dump of inert mass, not by using passive sensors at the distance we were operating from. Then as soon as *Oenone* and *Nephele* jumped in pursuit, your friend moved in and picked them up. So while you were taking an age to get to Puerto de Santa Maria, and keeping us occupied tracking you, he was racing on ahead. The coils were already there by the time we arrived.'

'Brilliant.' Joshua tossed down the last of his brandy and called the barmaid over. 'That would work, wouldn't it?'

'It did work.'

'No, not really. You see, your hypothesis is based on one assumption. Tragically false.'

Syrinx picked up the second glass of wine. 'What's that?'

'That I'm an ace astrogrator.'

'I think you are.'

'Right, so on a normal commercial run I would use this alleged skill of mine to shave hours off the journey time, wouldn't I?'

'Yes.'

'So I would have used this skill to get here, to Norfolk, wouldn't I? I mean, I brought a cargo to trade, I'm not going to waste time, money, and fuel getting it here, now am I?'

'No.'

'Right, so first of all ask the captain on the good ship *Pestravka* when and where I emerged in the Norfolk system. Then you can go and check my departure time from Lalonde, and work out how long it took me. Tell me after that if you think I'm a good astrogrator.' He gave her an annoying toothsome smile.

Thanks to *Oenone*, she was instantly aware of Lalonde's spacial location; how long it ought to take an Adamist starship of *Lady Macbeth*'s class and performance to make the trip. 'How long did it take you?' she asked in resignation.

'Six and a half days.'

It shouldn't have taken them that long, *Oenone* said.

Syrinx said nothing. She simply couldn't bring herself to believe he was innocent. His whole attitude spelt complicity.

'Ah, here's Ashly now.' Joshua stood and waved at the pilot. 'And simply because you committed an extraordinarily rude *faux pas* don't think you have to pay for the drinks to make up for it. They're on me, I insist.' He raised his glass. 'Here's to mutual understanding and future friendship.'

17

The *Coogan*'s battered prow was riding heavily over the steep wavelets the Zamjan tributary sent rushing down its length towards the Juliffe. Lori could feel the length of the light trader boat exaggerating each pitch as they drove against the current. After four and a half days nothing about the *Coogan* bothered her any more; it creaked continually, the engines produced a vibration felt throughout every timber, it was hot, dark, airless, and cramped. But enforced routine had made it all inconsequential. Besides, she spent a lot of time lying inertly on her cot, reviewing the images the eagles Abraham and Catlin provided her.

Right now the birds were six kilometres ahead of *Coogan*, gliding five hundred metres above the water, with just the occasional indolent flick of a wing needed to maintain their flight. The jungle on either side of the swollen river was choked with mist from the rain that had just fallen, swan-white wisps clinging to the glistening green trees like some kind of animate creeper. There was no understanding the jungle's immensity, Lori thought. The sights she saw through the eagles brought home how little impression the settlers had made to the Juliffe basin in twenty-five years. The timorous villages huddled along the riverbanks were a sorry example of the human condition. Microscopic parasites upon the jungle biota rather than bold challengers out to subdue a world.

Abraham saw a ragged line of smoke staining the sky ahead. A village cooking pit, judging by the shape and colour: she'd certainly had enough practice over the last few days to recognize one. She consulted her bitek processor block, and the visualization of the Zamjan eclipsed the image from the eagles. A vast four-hundred-kilometre river in its own right, the broad tributary was the one which the Quallheim emptied into. Inertial guidance coordinates flicked round. The village was called Oconto, founded three years ago. They had an asset planted there, a man by the name of Quentin Montrose.

Lori, Darcy called, **I think there's another one, you'd better come and have a look.**

The visualization withdrew into the bitek processor. **I'm on my way.** She opened her eyes, and looked out through the nearest slit in the side of the rickety cabin wall. All she could see was the grizzled water being lashed by the squall. Warm droplets ran along the inside of the roof, defying gravity before they plopped down on the cots where she and Darcy had spread their sleeping-bags. There was more room now a third of the logs had been fed into the insatiable hopper, but she still had to squirm out through the Buchannans' cabin and the galley.

Gail was sitting at the table on one of the special stools that could take her weight. Packets of freeze-dried food were strewn across the greasy wood in front of her. 'What would you like tonight?' she asked as Lori hurried past.

'Doesn't matter.'

'That's typically thoughtless. How am I supposed to prepare an adequate meal for people who won't help? It would serve all of you right if I was to do nothing but boiled rice. Then you'd all moan and complain, I'd be given no peace at all.'

Lori gave her a grimace-smile and ducked through the hatch out onto the deck. The fat woman disgusted her, not just her size, but her manner. Gail Buchannan surely represented the antithesis of Edenism, everything her culture strove to distance themselves from in human nature.

Rain was pelting down on the little wheel-house's solar-cell roof. Darcy and Len Buchannan were inside, hunched against the drops which came streaking in through the open sides. Lori dashed the four metres round to the door, drenching her loose grey jacket in the process.

'It'll be over in a minute,' Darcy said. Up ahead, the end of the steel rainclouds was visible as a bright haze band surmounting the river and jungle.

'Where's the boat?' she asked, screwing her eyes against the stinging rain.

'There.' Len raised a hand from the wheel and pointed ahead.

It was one of the big paddle-boats used to take colonists upriver, slicing imperiously through the water towards them. It didn't pitch about like the *Coogan*, its greater mass kept it level as the wavelets broke against its side and stern. Smoke streamed almost horizontally from its twin stacks.

'Dangerous fast, that is,' Len said. 'Specially for these waters. Plenty of foltwine about; catch a bundle of that in the paddle and she'll do her bearings a ton of damage. And we're heading into the snowlily season now as well, they're as bad as foltwine when they stick together.'

Lori nodded briefly in understanding. Len had pointed out the thin grasslike leaves multiplying along the shallow waters near the shores, fist-sized pods just beginning to rise above the surface. Snowlilies bloomed twice every Lalonde year. They looked beautiful, but they caused havoc with the boats.

In fact Len Buchannan had opened up considerably once the trip started. He still didn't like the idea of Lori and Darcy steering his precious boat, but had grudgingly come to admit they could manage it almost as well as himself. He seemed to enjoy having someone to talk to other than his wife; he and Gail hadn't shared ten words since they cast off from Durringham. His conversation was mostly about river lore and the way Lalonde was developing, he had no interest in the

Confederation. Some of the information was useful to her when she took the wheel. He seemed surprised by the way she remembered it all. The only time he'd gone sullen on her was when she told him her age, he thought it was some kind of poor-taste joke; she looked about half as old as he did.

The three of them watched the paddle-boat race past. Len turned the wheel a couple of points, giving it a wide passage. Darcy switched his retinal implants up to full resolution and studied the deck. There were about thirty-five people milling about on the foredeck; farmer-types, the men with thick beards, women with sun-ripened faces, all in clothes made from local cloth. They paid very little attention to the *Coogan*, apparently intent on the river ahead.

Len shook his head, a mystified expression in place. 'That ain't right. The *Broadmoor* ought to be in a convoy, three or more. That's the way them paddlers always travel. Captain didn't call us on the radio neither.' He tapped the short-range radio block beside the forward-sweep mass-detector. 'Boats always talk out here, ain't so much traffic as you can ignore each other.'

'And those weren't colonists on the deck,' Darcy said.

The *Coogan* pitched up hard as the prow reached the first of the deep furrows of water which the wayward *Broadmoor* produced in its wake.

'Not going downriver, no,' Len said.

'Refugees?' Lori suggested.

'Possibly,' Darcy said. 'But if the situation is that bad, why weren't there more of them?' He replayed the memory of the paddle-boat. It was the third they had encountered in twenty hours; the other two had steamed past in the dark. The attitude of the people on deck bothered him. They just stood there, not talking, not clustered together the way people usually did for companionship. They even seemed immune to the rain.

Are you thinking the same as me? Lori asked. She conjured up an image of the reptile people from Laton's call, and superimposed them on the deck of the *Broadmoor* – rain running off their green skin without wetting it.

Yes, he said. **It's possible. Probable, in fact. Some kind of sequestration is obviously involved. And those people on board weren't behaving normally.**

If boats are carrying the sequestrated downriver, it would mean that the posse on the *Swithland* have been circumvented.

I never expected them to be anything other than a token, and a rather pathetic one at that. If this is a xenoc invasion, then obviously they will want to subdue the entire planet. The Juliffe tributaries are the only feasible transport routes. Naturally they would use the riverboats.

I can't believe that anyone with the technology to cross interstellar space would then be reduced to using wooden boats to get about on a planet.

Human settlers do. Darcy projected an ironic moue.

Yes, colonists who can't afford anything better, but a military conquest force?

Point taken. But there's an awful lot about this situation we don't understand. For a start, why invade Lalonde?

True. But to return to the immediate, if we've already penetrated the incursion front, do we need to go on?

I don't know. We need information.

We have an asset in the next village. I suggest we stop there and see what he knows.

Good idea. And Solanki will have to be informed about the aberrant river traffic.

Lori left Darcy to feed the furnace hopper and made her way back to the space in the cabin they shared. She pulled her backpack from under the cot and retrieved the palm-sized slate-grey communication block from among her clothes. It took a couple of seconds for the Confederation Navy's ELINT satellite to lock on to the scrambled channel. Kelven Solanki's tired-looking face appeared on the front of the slim rectangular unit.

'We may have a problem,' she said.

'One more won't make any difference.'

'This one might. We believe the presence Laton warned us of is spreading itself downriver on the boats. In other words, it can't be confined by the posse.'

'Bloody hell. Candace Elford decided last night that Kristo County has also been taken over, that's halfway down the Zamjan from the mouth of the Quallheim. And after reviewing the satellite images, I have to concur. She's reinforcing the posse by BK133. They have a new landing point, Ozark, in Mayhew County, fifty kilometres short of Kristo. The BK133s are lifting in men and weapons right now. The *Swithland* should reach them early tomorrow, they can't be far ahead of you.'

'We're approaching Oconto village right now.'

'About thirty kilometres, then. What are you going to do?'

'We haven't decided yet. We'll need to go ashore whatever the outcome.'

'Well, be careful, this is turning out to be even bigger than my worst-case scenarios.'

'We don't intend to jeopardize ourselves.'

'Good. Your message flek was dispatched to your embassy on Avon, along with mine to the First Admiral, and one from Ralph Hiltch to his embassy. Rexrew sent one to the LDC office as well.'

'Thank you. Let's hope the Confederation Navy responds swiftly.'

'Yes. I think you should know, Hiltch and I have dispatched a combined scout team upriver. If you want to wait in Oconto for them to arrive, you're more than welcome to join them. They're making good time, I estimate they should be with you in a couple of days at the most. And my marines are carrying a fair amount of fire-power.'

'We'll retain it as an option. Though Darcy and I don't believe fire-power is going to be an overwhelming factor in this case. Judging by what we gleaned from Laton, and what we've observed on the paddle-boats, it appears wide-scale sequestration is playing a major part in the invasion.'

'Dear Christ!'

She smiled at his expletive, Why did Adamists always appeal to their deities? It wasn't something she understood. If there was an omnipotent god, why did he make life so full of pain? 'You might find a prudent course of action is to review river traffic out of the affected areas over the last ten days.'

'Are you saying they've already reached Durringham?'

'It is more than likely, I'm afraid. We are almost at Kristo, and we're travelling against the current on a decidedly third-rate boat.'

'I see what you mean, if they left Aberdale right at the start they could have been here a week ago.'

'Theoretically, yes.'

'All right, thanks for the warning. I'll pull some people in and start analysing the boats that have come down out of the Zamjan. Hell, this is just what the city needs on top of everything else.'

'How are things in Durringham?'

'None too good, actually. Everyone's starting to hoard food, so prices are going through the roof. Candace Elford is deputizing young men left, right, and centre. There's a lot of unrest among the residents about what's happening upriver. She's afraid it's going to spiral out of control. Then on Wednesday the transient colonists decided to hold a peaceful rally outside the Governor's dumper demanding new gear to replace what was stolen, and extra land in compensation for the upset. I could see it from my window. Rexrew refused to talk to them. Too scared they'd lynch him, I should think. It was that sort of mood. Things got a bit rough, and they clashed with the sheriffs. Quite a lot of casualties on both sides. Some idiot let a sayce loose. The power cables from the dumper's fusion generator were torn down. So there was no electricity in the precinct for two days, and of course that includes the main hospital. Guess what happened to its back-up power supply.'

'It failed?'

'Yeah. Someone had been flogging off the electron-matrix crystals to use in power bikes. There was only about twenty per cent capacity left.'

'Sounds like there's not much to choose between your position and mine.'

Kelven Solanki gave her a measured stare. 'Oh, I think there is.'

*

Oconto was a typical Lalonde village: a roughly square clearing shorn straight into the jungle, with the official Land Allocation Office marker as its pivot; cabins with trim vegetable gardens clustered at the nucleus, while broader fields made up the periphery. The normally black mayope planks of the buildings were turning a lighter grey from years of exposure to the sun and heat and rain, hardening and cracking, like driftwood on a tropical shore. Pigs squealed in their pens, while cows munched contentedly at their silage in circular stockades. A line of over thirty goats were tethered to stakes around the border of the jungle, chomping away at the creepers which edged in towards the fields.

The village had done well for itself during the three years since its founding. The communal buildings like the hall and church were well maintained; the council had organized the construction of a low, earth-covered lodge to smoke fish in. Major paths were scattered with wood flakes to stem the mud. There was even a football pitch marked out. Three jetties stuck out of the gently sloped bank into the Zamjan's insipid water; two of them responsible for mooring the village's small number of fishing boats.

When the *Coogan* nosed up to the main central jetty Darcy and Lori were relieved to see a considerable number of people working the fields. Oconto hadn't succumbed yet. Several shouts went up as the trader boat was spotted. Men came running, all of them carrying guns.

It took a quarter of an hour to convince the nervous reception committee that they posed no threat, and for a few minutes at the start Darcy thought they were going to be shot out of hand. Len and Gail Buchannan were well known (though not terribly popular), which acted in their favour. The *Coogan* was travelling upriver, heading towards the rebel counties, not bringing people down from them. And finally, Lori and Darcy themselves, with their synthetic fabric clothes and expensive hardware units, were accepted as some kind of official team. With what mandate was never asked.

'You gotta understand, people round here are getting mighty trigger happy since last Tuesday,' Geoffrey Tunnard said. He was Oconto's acting leader, a lean fifty-year-old with curly white hair, wearing much-patched colourless dungarees. Now he was satisfied the *Coogan* wasn't bringing revolution and destruction, and his laser rifle was slung over his beefy shoulder again, he was happy to talk.

'What happened last Tuesday?' Darcy asked.

'The Ivets.' Geoffrey Tunnard spat over the side of the jetty. 'We heard there'd been trouble up Willow West way, so we shoved ours in a pen. They've been good workers since we arrived. But there's no point in taking chances, right?'

'Right,' Darcy agreed diplomatically.

'But on Monday we had some people visit, claimed they were from Waldersy village, up in Kristo County. They said the Ivets were all rebelling in the Quallheim Counties and Willow West, killing the men and raping the women. Said plenty of younger colonists had joined them, too. They was nothing but a vigilante group, you could see that, all hyped up they were, on a high. I reckoned they'd been smoking some canus; that'll send you tripping if you dry the leaves right. Trouble they were, just wanted to kill our Ivets. We wouldn't have it. A man can't kill another in cold blood, not just on someone else's say so. We sent them on downriver. Then blow me if they didn't creep back that night. And you know what?'

'They let the Ivets out,' Lori said.

Geoffrey Tunnard gave her a respectful look. 'That's right. Stole back in here right under our noses. Dogs never even noticed them. Slit old Jamie Austin's throat, him that was standing guard on the pen. Our supervisor Neil Barlow went right off after them that morning. Took a bunch of fifty men with him, armed men they were, too. And we haven't heard a damn thing since. That ain't like Neil, it's been six days. He should have sent word. Them men have families. We've got wives and kiddies left here that are worried sick.' He glanced from Darcy to Lori. 'Can you tell us anything?' His tone was laboured; Geoffrey Tunnard was a man under a great deal of strain.

'Sorry, I don't know anything,' Darcy said. 'Not yet. That's why we're here, to find out. But whatever you do, don't go after them. The larger your numbers, the safer you are.'

Geoffrey Tunnard pursed his lips and looked away, eyes raking the jungle with bitter enmity. 'Thought you'd say something like that. Course, there's those that have gone looking. Some of the women. We couldn't stop them.'

Darcy put his hand on Geoffrey Tunnard's shoulder, gripping firmly. 'If any more want to go, stop them. Have a log fall on their foot if that's what it takes, but you must stop them.'

'I'll do my best.' Geoffrey Tunnard dipped his head in defeat. 'I'd leave if I could, take the family downriver on a boat. But I built this place with my own hands, and no damn Govcentral interference. It was a good life, it was. It can be again. Bloody Ivets never were any use for anything, waster kids in dungarees, that's all.'

'We'll do what we can,' Lori said.

'Sure you will. You're doing what you tell me not to: go out in the jungle. Just the two of you. That's madness.'

Lori thought Geoffrey Tunnard had been about to say suicide. 'Can you tell us where Quentin Montrose lives?' she asked.

Geoffrey Tunnard pointed out one of the cabins, no different to any of the others; solar panels on the roof, a sagging overhang above the verandah. 'Won't do you no good, he was in Neil's group.'

Lori stood at the side of the wheel-house as the *Coogan* cast off; Darcy was aft, heaving more of the interminable logs into the furnace hopper. Len Buchannan whistled tunelessly as he steered his boat into the middle of the river. Oconto gradually shrank away to stern until it was nothing but a deeper than usual gash in the emerald cliff. Smoke from the cooking fires drifted apathetically across the choppy water.

We could send one of the eagles looking for them, Lori suggested.

You don't really mean that.

No. I'm sorry, I was just trying to save my own conscience.

Fifty armed men, and no trace. I don't know about your conscience, but my courage has almost deserted me.

We could go back, or even wait for Solanki's marines.

Yes, we could.

You're right. We'll go on.

We should have told Geoffrey Tunnard to leave, Darcy said. **I should have told him; take his family and flee back to Durringham. At least it would have been honest. None of this false hope we left him with.**

That's all right, I think he already knows.

*

Karl Lambourne woke without knowing why. It wasn't noon yet, and he hadn't got to go back on watch until two o'clock. The blinds on his cabin's port were still shut, reducing the light inside to a mysterious and enticing dusk. Booted feet thudded along the deck outside the door. Conversation was a persistent background hum, children calling out in their whiny voices.

Everything normal. So why was he awake with a vague feeling of unease?

The colonist girl – what was her name? – stirred beside him. She was a few months younger than him, with dark hair teased into ringlets around a dainty face. Despite his initial dismay with the *Swithland* carrying all those extra sheriffs and deputies it was turning out to be a good trip. The girls appreciated the space and privacy his cabin gave them; the boat was very crowded, with sleeping-bags clogging every metre of deck space.

The girl's eyelids fluttered, then opened slowly. She – Anne, no Alison; that was it, Alison! remember that – grinned at him.

'Hi,' she said.

He glanced along her body. The sheet was tangled up round her waist, affording him a splendid view of breasts, lean belly muscles, and sharply curving hips. 'Hi yourself.' He brushed some of the ringlets from her face.

Shouts and a barking laugh sounded from outside. Alison gave a timid giggle. 'God, they're only a metre away.'

'You should have thought of that before you made all that noise earlier.'

Her tongue was caught between her teeth. 'Didn't make any noise.'

'Did.'

'Didn't.'

His arms circled her, and he pulled her closer. 'You did, and I can prove it.'

'Oh yeah?'

'Yeah.' He kissed her softly, and she started to respond. His hand stole downwards, pushing the sheet off her legs.

Alison turned over when he told her to, shivering in anticipation as his arm slid under her waist, lifting her buttocks up. Her mouth parted in expectation.

'What the hell was that?'

'Karl?' She bent her head round to see him kneeling behind her, frowning up at the ceiling. 'Karl!'

'Shush. Listen, can you hear it?'

She couldn't believe this was happening. People were still clumping up and down the deck outside. There wasn't any other sound! And she'd never ever been so turned on before. Right now she hated Karl with the same intensity she'd adored him a second before.

Karl twitched his head round, trying to catch the noise again. Except it wasn't so much a noise, more a vibration, a grumble. He knew every sound, every tremble the *Swithland* made, and that wasn't in its repertoire.

He heard it again, and identified it. A hull timber quaking somewhere aft. The creak of wood under pressure, almost as if they had touched a snag. But his mother would never steer anywhere near a snag, that was crazy.

Alison was looking up at him, all anger and hurt. The magic had gone. He felt his penis softening.

The noise came again. A grinding sound that lasted for about three seconds. It was muted by the bilges, but this time it was loud enough even for Alison to hear.

She blinked in confusion. 'What . . .'

Karl jumped off the bed, snatching up his shorts. He jammed his legs into them, and was still struggling with the button when he yanked the door lock back and rushed out onto the deck.

Alison squealed behind him, trying to cover herself with her arms as vibrant midmorning sunlight flooded into the cabin. She grabbed the thin sheet to wrap herself in, and started hunting round for her clothes.

After the seductive shadows of his cabin the sunlight on deck sent glaring purple after-images chasing down Karl's optic nerves. Tear ducts released their stored liquid, which he had to wipe away annoyingly. A couple of colonists and three deputies, barely older than him, were staring at him. He leaned out over the rail and peered down at the river. There was some sediment carried by the water, and shimmering sunlight reflections skittering across the surface, but he could see a good three or four metres down. But there was nothing solid, no silt bank, no submerged tree trunk.

Up on the bridge Rosemary Lambourne hadn't been sure about the first scrape, but like her eldest son she was perfectly in tune with the *Swithland*. Something had left her with heightened senses, a suddenly hollow stomach. She automatically checked the forward-sweep mass-detector. This section of the Zamjan was twelve metres deep, giving her a good ten metres of clearance below the flat keel, even overloaded like this. There was nothing in front, nothing below, and nothing to the side.

Then it happened again. The aft hull struck something. Rosemary immediately reduced power to the paddles.

'Mother!'

She bent over the starboard side to see Karl looking up at her.

'What was that?'

He beat her to it by a fraction.

'I don't know,' she shouted down. 'The mass-detector shows clear. Can you see anything in the water?'

'No.'

The river current was slowing the *Swithland* rapidly now the paddles were stilled. Without the steady thrash of the blades, the racket the colonists made seemed to have doubled.

It came again, a long rending sound of abused wood. There was a definite crunching at the end.

'That was aft,' Rosemary yelled. 'Get back there and see what happened. Report back.' She pulled a handset from its slot below the communication console, and dropped it over the edge of the rail. Karl caught it with an easy snap of his wrist and raced off down the narrow decking, slipping through the knots of colonists with urgent fluid movements.

'*Swithland*, come in, please,' the speaker on the communication console said. 'Rosemary, can you hear me? This is Dale here. What's happening, why have you stopped?'

She picked up the microphone. 'I'm here, Dale,' she told the *Nassier*'s captain. When she glanced up she could see the *Nassier* half a kilometre upriver, pulling ahead; the *Hycel* was downriver on the starboard side, catching up fast. 'It sounds like we struck something.'

'How bad?'

'I don't know yet. I'll get back to you.'

'Rosemary, this is Callan, I think it would be best if we didn't get separated. I'll heave to until you know if you need any assistance.'

'Thanks, Callan.' She leant out over the bridge rail and waved at the *Hycel*. A small figure on its bridge waved back.

A screech loud enough to silence all the colonists erupted from the *Swithland*'s hull. Rosemary felt the boat judder, its prow shifting a degree. It was like nothing she had ever experienced before. They were almost dead in the water, it couldn't possibly be a snag. It couldn't be!

Karl reached the afterdeck just as the *Swithland* juddered. He could feel the whole boat actually lift a couple of centimetres.

The afterdeck was packed full of colonists and posse members. Several groups of men were lying down, playing cards or eating. Kids charged about. Eight or nine people were fishing over the stern. Cases of farmsteading gear were piled against the superstructure and the taffrail. Dogs ran about underfoot; there were five horses tethered to the side rail, and two of them started pulling at their harnesses as the brassy scrunching noise broke across the boat. Everybody froze in expectation.

'Out of the way!' Karl shouted. 'Out of the way.' He started elbowing people aside. The noise was coming from the keel, just aft of the furnace room which was tacked on to the back of the superstructure. 'Come on, move.'

A sayce snarled at him. 'Killl.'

'Get that fucking thing out of my way!'

Yuri Wilken dragged Randolf aside.

The whole afterdeck complement was watching Karl. He reached the hatchway over the feed mechanism that shunted logs into the furnace. It was hidden beneath a clutter of composite pods. 'Help me move these,' he yelled.

Barry MacArple emerged from the furnace room, a brawny twenty-year-old, sweaty and sooty. He had kept indoors for most of this trip, and carefully avoided any member of the posse. None of the Lambourne family had mentioned that he was an Ivet.

The noise came to an abrupt halt. Karl was very aware of the apprehensive faces focusing on him, the silent appeal for guidance. He held up his hands as Barry started to haul the pods off the hatchway. 'OK, we're riding on some sort of rock. So I want all the kids to slowly make their way forwards. Slowly mind. Then the women. Not the men. You'll upset the balance with that much weight forward. And whoever those horses belong to, calm them down now.'

Parents hustled their children towards the prow. A hushed murmur swept round the adults. Three men were helping Barry clear the hatchway. Karl lifted off a couple of the pods himself. Then he heard the noise again, but it was distant this time, not from the *Swithland*'s hull.

'What the hell—' He looked up to see the *Hycel* a hundred metres astern.

'Karl, what's happening?' Rosemary's voice demanded from the handset.

He raised the unit to his mouth. 'It's the *Hycel*, Mum. They've hit it as well.'

'Bloody hell. What about our hull?'

'Tell you in a minute.'

The last of the pods were cleared away, revealing a two-metre-square hatch. Karl bent down to unclip the latches.

That was when the second sound rang out, a water-muffled

THUNK of something heavy and immensely powerful slamming into the keel. *Swithland* gave a small jolt, riding up several centimetres. Some of the more loosely stacked cases and pods tumbled over. The colonists shouted in panic and dismay, and there was a general surge for the prow. One of the horses reared up, forelegs scraping the air.

Karl ripped the hatch open.

THUNK

Ripples rolled away from the *Swithland* as it wallowed about.

'Karl!' the handset squawked.

He looked down into the hull. The log-feed mechanism took up most of the space below the hatch, a primitive-looking clump of motors, pulley loops, and pistons. Two grab belts ran away to the port and starboard log holds. The black mayope planks of the hull itself were just visible. Water was welling out of cracks between them.

THUNK

Karl stared down in stupefaction as the planks bowed inward. That was mayope wood, nothing could dint mayope.

THUNK

Splinters appeared, long dagger fingers levering apart.

THUNK

Water poured in through the widening gaps. An area over a metre wide was being slowly hammered upwards.

THUNK

THUNK

Swithland was rocking up and down. Equipment and pods rolled about across the half-abandoned afterdeck. Men and women were clinging to the rail, others were spread-eagled on the decking, clawing for a handhold.

'It's trying to punch its way in!' Karl bellowed into the handset.

'What? What?' his mother shouted back.

'There's something below us, something alive. For Christ's

sake, get us underway, get us to the shore. The shore, Mum. Go! Go!'

THUNK

The water was foaming up now, covering the hull planks completely. 'Get this shut,' Karl called. He was terribly afraid of what would come through once the hole was big enough. Together, he and Barry MacArple slammed the hatch back down, dogging the latches.

THUNK

Swithland's hull broke. Karl could hear a long dreadful tearing sound as the iron-hard wood was wrenched apart. Water seethed in, gurgling and slurping. It ripped the log feeder from its mountings, crashing it against the decking above. The hatch quaked violently.

A gloriously welcome whine from the paddle engines sounded. The familiar slow thrashing of the paddles started up. *Swithland* turned ponderously for the unbroken rampart of jungle eighty metres away.

Karl realized people were sobbing and shouting out. A lot of them must have made it forward, the boat was riding at a downward incline.

THUNK

This time it was the afterdeck planks. Karl, lying prone next to the hatch, yelled in shock as his feet left the deck from the impact. He twisted round immediately, rolling over three times to get clear. Pods bounced and pirouetted chaotically. The horses were going berserk. One of them broke its harness, and plunged over the side. Another was kicking wildly. A blood-soaked body lay beside it.

THUNK

The planks beside the hatch lifted in unison, snapping back as if they were elastic. Water started to seep out.

Barry MacArple was scrambling on all fours along the deck, his face engorged with desperation. Karl held out his hand to the Ivet, willing him on.

THUNK

The planks directly below Barry were smashed asunder. They ruptured upwards, jagged edges puncturing the Ivet's belly and chest, then ripping his torso apart like a giant claw. A metre-wide geyser of water slammed upwards out of the gap, buffeting the corpse with it.

Karl turned to follow the water rising, fear stunned out of him by the incredible, impossible sight. The geyser roared ferociously, shaking Karl's bones and obliterating the impassioned shouts from the colonists. It rose a full thirty metres above the decking, its crown blossoming out like a flower. Water, silt, and fragments of mayope plank splattered down.

Clinging for dear life to one of the cable drums as the *Swithland* bucked about like a wounded brownspine, Karl watched the geyser chewing away at the ragged sides of the hole it had bored. It was creeping forward towards the superstructure. The bilges must be full already. Slowly and surely more and more wood was eroded by the terrific force of the water. In another minute it would reach the furnace room. He thought of what would happen when the water struck all fifteen tonnes of the searingly hot furnace, and whimpered.

Rosemary Lambourne had a hard struggle to stay upright as the *Swithland* tossed about. Only by clinging to the wheel could she even stay on her feet. It was the sheer fright in Karl's voice which had spurred her into action. He wasn't afraid of anything on the river, he had been born on the *Swithland.*

That deadly battering noise was knocking into her heart as much as the hull. The strength behind anything that could thump the boat about like this was awesome.

How much of the *Swithland* is going to be left after this? God damn Colin Rexrew, his laxness and stupidity. The Ivets would never dare to revolt with a firm, competent governor in charge.

A roar like a continual explosion made her jump, almost

sending her feet from under her. It was suddenly raining on the *Swithland* alone. The entire superstructure was trembling. What was *happening* back there?

She checked the little holoscreen which displayed the boat's engineering schematics. They were losing power rapidly from the furnace. Reserve electron-matrix crystals cut in, maintaining the full current to the engines.

'Rosemary,' the radio called.

She couldn't spare the time to answer.

Swithland's prow was pointing directly at the bank sixty-five metres away, and they were picking up speed again. Pods and cases were scattered in the boat's wake, jouncing about in the water. She saw a couple of people splashing among them. More people went falling from the foredeck; it was as tightly packed as a rugby scrum down there. And there wasn't a thing she could do, except get them to the shore.

Off on the port side, *Nassier* was floundering about, paddles spinning intermittently. Rosemary saw a giant fountain of water smash through the middle of its superstructure, debris whirling away into the sky. What the fuck could do that? Some kind of water monster skulking around the riverbed? Even as the fantasy germinated in her mind she knew that wasn't the real answer. But she did know what the roaring noise behind her was now. The knowledge sucked at the last of her strength. If it hit the furnace . . .

Nassier's prow lifted into the air, shoving the afterdeck below the water. The superstructure crumpled up, large chunks being flung aside by the tremendous jet of water. Dozens of people were swept into the river, arms and legs twirling frantically. In her mind she could hear the screams.

There were just too many people on board the paddle-boats. Rexrew had already increased the numbers of colonists they were made to carry, refusing to listen to the warning from the captains' delegation. Then he dumped this posse on them as well.

If I ever get back to Durringham, you're dead, Rexrew, she promised herself. You haven't just failed us, you've condemned us.

Then the *Nassier* began to capsize, rolling ever faster onto her starboard side. The jet of water died away as the keel flipped up. Rosemary saw a huge hole in the planks amidships as it reached the vertical. That was when the water must have rushed in on the furnace. A massive blast of white steam devoured the rear of the boat, rolling out across the surface of the river. Mercifully, it shielded the final act in the *Nassier*'s convulsive death.

Swithland's prow was fifteen metres from the trees and creepers which were strangling the bank. Rosemary could hear the sound of their own bedevilling geyser reducing. She fought the wheel to keep the boat lined up straight on the bank. The bottom was shelving up rapidly, the forward-sweep mass-detector emitting a frantic howl in warning. Five metres deep. Four. Three. They struck mud eight metres from the long flower-heavy vines trailing in the water. The big boat's awesome inertia propelled them along, slithering and sliding through the thick black alluvial muck. Bubbles of foul-smelling sulphurous gas churned around the sides of the hull. The geyser had died completely. There was a moment of pure dreamy silence before they hit the bank.

Rosemary saw a huge qualtook tree dead ahead; one of its thick boughs was the same height as the bridge. She ducked—

The impact threw Yuri Wilken back onto his belly just as he was starting to get up again. His nose slammed painfully against the deck. He tasted warm blood. The boat was making hideous crunching sounds as it ploughed into the frill of vegetation along the bank. Long vine strands lashed through the air with the brutality of bullwhips. He tried to bury himself into the hard decking as they slashed centimetres above his head.

Swithland's blunt prow rammed the low bank, jolting

upwards to ride a good ten metres across the dark-red sandy earth. The paddle-boat finally came to a bruising halt with its forward deck badly mangled, and the qualtook tree embedded in the front of the superstructure.

Screams and wailing gave way to moans and shrill cries for help. Yuri risked glancing about, seeing the way in which the jungle had shrink-wrapped itself around the forward half of the boat. The superstructure looked dangerously unstable, it was leaning over sharply, with tonnes of vegetation pressing against the front and side.

His limbs were shaking uncontrollably. He wanted to be home in Durringham, taking Randolf for walks or playing football with his mates. He didn't belong here in the jungle.

'Are you all right, son?' Mansing asked.

Sheriff Mansing was the one who had signed him on for the expedition. He was a lot more approachable than some of the sheriffs, keeping a fatherly eye out for him.

'I think so.' He dabbed at his nose experimentally, sniffing hard. There was blood on his hand.

'You'll live,' Mansing said. 'Where's Randolf?'

'I don't know.' He climbed shakily to his feet. They were standing at the front corner of the superstructure. People were lying about all around, slowly picking themselves up, asking for help, wearing a numb, frightened expression. Two bodies had been trapped between the qualtook trunk and the superstructure; one was a small girl aged about eight. Yuri could only tell because she was wearing a dress. He turned away, gagging.

'Call for him,' Mansing said. 'We're going to need all the help we can get pretty soon.'

'Sir?'

'You think this was an accident?'

Yuri hadn't thought it was anything. The notion sent a tremble down his spine. He put his lips together, and managed a feeble whistle.

'Twelve years I've been sailing up and down this river,' Mansing said grimly. 'I've never seen anything like that geyser before. What the hell can shoot water about like that? And there was more than one of them.'

Randolf came lumbering up over the gunwale, his sleek black hide covered in smelly mud. The sayce had lost all of his usual aggressive arrogance, slinking straight over to Yuri and pressing against his master's legs. 'Waaterrr baddd,' he growled.

'He's not far wrong there,' Mansing agreed cheerlessly.

It took quarter of an hour to establish any kind of order around the wrecked paddle-boat. The sheriffs organized parties to tend to the wounded and set up a makeshift camp. By general consensus they moved fifty metres inland, away from the river and whatever prowled below the water.

Several survivors from the *Nassier* managed to swim to the stern of the *Swithland* which was half submerged; the boat formed a useful bridge over the stinking quagmire which lined the bank. The *Hycel* had managed to reach the Zamjan's far bank; it had been spared the destructive geyser, but its hull had taken a dreadful pounding. Radio contact was established and both groups decided to stay where they were rather than attempt to cross the river and join forces.

Sheriff Mansing located an unbroken communication block amongst the remnants of the posse's gear, and patched a call through the LDC's single geostationary satellite to Candace Elford. The shocked chief sheriff agreed to divert the two BK133s to the *Swithland* and fly the seriously injured back to Durringham straight away. What she never mentioned was the possibility of reinforcing the forsaken boats. But Sheriff Mansing was above all a pragmatic man, he really hadn't expected any.

After making three trips to the camp, carrying pods of gear from the paddle-boat, Yuri was included into a small scout party of three sheriffs and nine deputies. He suspected they only included him because of Randolf. But that was OK, the other detail of deputies was now removing bodies from the *Swithland.* He preferred to take his chances with the jungle.

When Yuri and the scouts marched away, colonists with fission-blade saws were felling trees on one side of the camp's glade so the VTOL aircraft could land. A fire was burning in the centre.

It didn't take long for the groans of the casualties to fade away, blocked by the density of the foliage. Yuri couldn't get over how dark this jungle was, very little actual sunlight penetrated down to ground level. When he held his hand up the skin was tinted a deep green, the cinnamon-coloured jacket they had issued him with to protect him from thorns was jet black. The jungle around Durringham was nothing like this. It was tame, he realized, with its well-worn paths and tall trees spiralled with thin colourful vines. Here there were no paths, branches jutted out at all heights, and the vines were slung between boughs either at ankle height or level with his neck. A sticky kind of fungal mould slimed every leaf for three metres above the ground.

The scouts paired up, fanning out from the camp. The idea was to familiarize themselves with the immediate area out to five hundred metres, search for any more survivors from *Nassier,* and verify that no hostiles were near the camp.

'This is stupid,' Mansing said after they had gone fifty metres. He was leading, chopping at the vines and small branches and bushes with a fission-blade machete. 'I couldn't see you if you were three metres away.'

'Perhaps it thins out up ahead,' Yuri said.

Mansing slashed at another branch. 'You're giving away your age again, son. Only the very young are that hopelessly optimistic.'

They took turns to lead. Even with the fission blade hacking out every metre of path it was tiring work. Randolf loped along behind, occasionally butting against Yuri's calves.

According to Mansing's guidance block they had travelled

about three hundred metres when the sayce stood still, head held up, sniffing the humid air. The species didn't have quite the sense of smell terrestrial canines possessed, but they were still excellent hunters in their own territory: the jungle.

'Peeeople,' Randolf grunted.

'Which way?' Yuri asked.

'Here.' The sayce pushed into the severed branches that made up the walls of the path. He turned to look at them. 'Here.'

'Is this for real?' Mansing asked sceptically.

'Sure is,' Yuri answered, stung by the doubt. 'How far, boy?'

'Sooon.'

'All right,' Mansing said. He started to hack at the jungle where the sayce indicated.

It was another two minutes of sweaty labour before they heard the voices. They were high and light, female. One of them was singing.

Mansing was so intent on cutting the cloying vegetation away, swinging the heavy machete in endless rhythm, that he nearly fell head first into the stream when the creepers came to an abrupt end. Yuri grabbed his jacket collar to stop him slipping down the small grassy slope. Both of them stared ahead in astonishment.

Sunlight poured down through the overhead gap in the trees, hovering above the water like a thin golden mist. The stream widened out into a rock-lined pool fifteen metres across. Creepers with huge ruffed orange blooms hung like curtains from the trees on the far side. Tiny turquoise and yellow birds fluttered about through the air. It was a scene lifted from Greek mythology. Seven naked girls were bathing in the pool, ranging from about fifteen years up to twenty-five. All of them were slender and long limbed, sunlight glinting on their skin. White robes were strewn over the black rocks at the water's edge.

'Nooo,' Randolf moaned. 'Baddd.'

'Bollocks,' Yuri said.

The girls caught sight of them and shrieked with delight, smiling and waving.

Yuri shouldered his laser rifle, grinning deliriously at the seven pairs of wet breasts bouncing about.

'Bloody hell,' Mansing muttered.

Yuri pushed past him, and scuttled down the slope into the stream. The girls cheered.

'Nooo.'

'Yuri,' Mansing gestured ineffectually.

He turned round, face illuminated with delight. 'What? We've got to find out where their village is, haven't we? That's our assignment, scout the terrain.'

'Yes. I suppose so.' He couldn't keep his eyes from the naiads sporting about.

Yuri was plunging on, legs sending up a wave of spray.

'Nooo,' Randolf bayed urgently. 'Baddd. Peeeople baddd.'

Mansing watched the girls whooping encouragement to Yuri as the lad ploughed through the water towards them. 'Oh, to hell with dignity,' he said under his breath, and splashed down into the stream.

The first girl Yuri reached was about nineteen, with scarlet flowers tucked into her wet hair. She smiled radiantly up at him, hands holding his. 'I'm Polly,' she laughed.

'All right!' Yuri cried. The water only came halfway up her thighs; she really was completely naked. 'I'm Yuri.'

She kissed him, damp body pressing against his sleeveless shirt, leaving a dark imprint. When she broke off another girl slipped a garland of the orange vine flowers round his neck. 'And I'm Samantha,' she said.

'You gonna kiss me too?'

She twined her arms round his neck, tongue slipping hungrily into his mouth. Other girls were circling round, scooping up handfuls of spray and showering them. Yuri was in the midst of a warm silver rain with raw ecstasy pounding down his nerves. Here in the middle of nowhere, paradise had come to Lalonde. The droplets fell in slow motion, tinkling sweetly as they went. He felt hands slip the rifle strap from his shoulder, more hands pulled at his shirt buttons. His trousers were undone, and his penis stroked lovingly.

Samantha took a pace back looking at him in adoration. She cupped her breasts, lifting them up towards him. 'Now, Yuri,' she pleaded. 'Take me now.'

Yuri pulled her roughly against him, his soaking trousers tangling round his knees. He heard an alarmed shout that was cut off. Three of the girls had pushed Mansing under the water, his legs were thrashing above the surface. The girls were laughing hysterically, muscles straining with the effort of keeping him down.

'Hey—' Yuri said. He couldn't move because of his stupid trousers.

'Yuri,' Samantha called.

He turned back to her. She was opening her mouth wider than he would have believed physically possible. Long bands of muscle writhed around her chin as if fat worms were tunnelling through her veins. Her cheeks started to split, beginning at the corners of her mouth and tearing back towards her ears. Blood leapt out of the wounds in regular beats, and she was still hinging her jaw apart.

Yuri stared for one petrified second then let loose a guttural roar of fright that reverberated round the impassive sentinel trees. His bladder gave out.

Samantha's grisly head darted forward, carmine teeth clamping solidly round his throat, her blood spraying against his skin.

'Randolf—' he yelled. Then her teeth tore into his throat, and his own blood burst out of his carotid artery to flood his gullet, quashing any further sounds.

Randolf howled in rage as his master fell into the water with Samantha riding him down. But one of the other girls looked straight at him and hissed in warning, flecks of saliva spitting out between her bared teeth. The sayce turned tail and sprinted back into the jungle.

*

'Power's going. Losing height. Losing height!' The BK133 pilot's frantic voice boomed out of the command centre's AV pillars.

Every sheriff in the room stared at the tactical communication station.

'We're going down!'

The carrier wave hissed for another couple of seconds, then fell silent. 'God Almighty,' Candace Elford whispered. She was sitting at her desk at the end of the rectangular room. Like most of the capital's civic buildings, the sheriff's headquarters was made of wood. It sat in its own square fortified enclosure a couple of hundred metres from the governor's dumper, a simplistic design that any pre-twentieth-century soldier would have felt at home in. The command centre itself formed one side of the parade ground, a long single-storey building with four grey composite spheres housing the satellite uplinks spaced along the apex of the roof. Inside, plain wooden benches ran around the walls, supporting an impressive array of modern desktop processor consoles operated by sheriffs seated in composite chairs. On the wall opposite Candace Elford's desk a big projection screen displayed a street map of Durringham (as far as it was possible to map that conglomeration of erratic alleyways and private passages). Conditioners hummed unobtrusively to keep the temperature down. The atmosphere of technological efficiency was spoilt slightly by the fans of yellow-grey fungus growing out of the skirting-board underneath the benches.

'Contact lost,' Mitch Verkaik, the sheriff sitting at the tactical communication station reported, stone faced.

Candace turned to the small team she had assigned to monitor the posse's progress. 'What about the sheriffs on the ground? Did they see it come down?'

Jan Routley was operating the satellite link to the *Swithland* survivors; she loaded an order into her console. 'There is no response from any communicator on the *Swithland* or the *Hycel.* I can't even raise a transponder identity code.'

Candace studied the situation display projected by her own console's AV pillar, more out of habit than anything else. She knew they were all waiting for her to rap out orders, smooth and confident, producing instant perfect solutions like an ambulatory computer. It wasn't going to happen. The last week had been a complete nightmare. They couldn't contact anyone in the Quallheim Counties or Willow West any more, and communications with villages along the Zamjan were patchy. The reinforcement flights to Ozark were a stopgap at best; privately she had intended that the fresh men and weapons would simply safeguard an evacuation of settlers down the river. She had long since abandoned the idea of restoring order to the Quallheim Counties, confinement was her best hope. Now it looked like Ozark was inside the affected zone. Seventy men and almost a quarter of her armoury.

'Call the second BK133 back to Durringham right away,' she said shortly. 'If the invaders can bring down one, they can bring down another.' And at least ten sheriffs with their heavy-duty weapons would be saved. They might need them badly in the weeks to come. It was pretty obvious the invaders were intent on complete domination of the planet.

'Yes, ma'am.' Mitch Verkaik turned back to his console.

'How long before the observation satellite makes a pass over the paddle-boats?' Candace asked.

'Fifteen minutes,' Jan Routley answered.

'Program it for an infrared overscan fifty kilometres either side of its orbital track, see if it can locate the downed BK133. It shouldn't be too hard to spot.' She rested her chin in her hands, staring blankly at her desktop processor. Protecting Durringham was her priority now, she decided. They must hold on to the city until the LDC sent a combat force capable of regaining the countryside. She was convinced they were faced with an invasion, the hour-long briefing she'd had with Kelven Solanki that morning had put paid to any final doubts. Kelven was badly worried, which wasn't like him at all.

Candace hadn't told her staff what Kelven had said to her, about the possible use of sequestration and river-boats that might have already brought a preliminary platoon of invaders to Durringham. It didn't bear thinking about. There were three chairs conspicuously empty in the command centre today; even the sheriffs were reverting to a self-protective mentality. She couldn't blame them; most had a family in the city, and none had signed on to fight a well-organized military force. But she'd agreed to cooperate with the Confederation Navy office in reviewing satellite image records of river traffic for the last fortnight.

'We're receiving the images now,' Jan Routley called out.

Candace stirred herself, and walked over to the woman's position. Kilometre after kilometre of jungle streamed across the high-definition holoscreen; the green treetops were overlaid by transparent red shadows to indicate the temperature profile. The Zamjan leapt into view at the bottom of the screen, *Swithland*'s stern jutting out onto the water from under the bankside canopy of vegetation. Graphics flashed across the holoscreen, drawing orange circles around a glade close to the water.

'It's a fire,' Jan Routley said. She datavised an order into the desktop processor to centre on the infrared source. The clearing expanded on the screen, showing a bonfire burning in its centre. There were blankets and the unmistakable white cargo-pods of homesteading gear littered about. Several trees had been felled on one side. 'Where have all the people gone?' she asked in a small voice.

'I don't know,' Candace said. 'I really don't.'

*

It was midafternoon, and the *Coogan* was twenty-five kilometres downriver from the abandoned paddle-boats when Len Buchannan and Darcy spotted the first pieces of flotsam bobbing about in the water. Crates of farmsteading gear, lengths of planking, fruit. Five minutes later they saw the first body: a woman in a one-piece ship-suit, face down, with arms and legs spread wide.

'We're turning back now,' Len informed him.

'All the way to the mouth of the Quallheim,' Darcy reminded him.

'Shove your money and your contract.' He started turning the wheel. 'You think I'm blind to what's going on? We're already in the rebel area. It's gonna take a miracle to get us downriver if we start now, never mind from another hundred and fifty kilometres further east.'

'Wait,' Darcy put his hand on the wheel. 'How far to Ozark?'

Scowling, Len consulted an ancient guidance block sitting on a shelf in the wheel-house. 'Thirty kilometres, maybe thirty-five.'

'Put us ashore five kilometres short of the village.'

'I dunno—'

'Look, the eagles can spot any boat coming down the river ten kilometres ahead of us. If one does come, then we turn round immediately and sail for Durringham. How does that sound?'

'Why didn't the eagles spot all this, then? Hardly something you could miss.'

'They're out over the jungle. We'll call them back now. Besides, it could be a genuine accident. There might be people hurt up ahead.'

The lines around Len's mouth tightened, reflecting his indecision. No true captain would ignore another boat in distress. A broken chunk of yellow foam packaging scraped down the side of the *Coogan*. 'All right,' he said, clutching at the wheel. 'But the first sign of trouble, and I'm off downriver. It's not the money. *Coogan*'s all I've got, I built her with my own hands. I ain't risking the old girl for you.'

'I'm not asking you to. I'm just as anxious as you that nothing happens to the boat, or you. No matter what we find in the villages, we've still got to get back to Durringham. Lori and I are too old to walk.'

Len grunted dismissively, but started feeding the wheel round again, lining the prow up on the eastern horizon.

The affinity call went out, and Abraham and Catlin curved through the clear air, racing for the river. From their vantage point seven kilometres ahead of the *Coogan* they could see tiny scraps of debris floating slowly in the current. They were also high enough for the water to be almost completely transparent. Lori could see large schools of brownspines and reddish eel-analogues swimming idly.

It wasn't until the sun was a red-gold ball touching the treetops ahead of the little trader boat that the eagles found the paddle-boats jammed into opposite banks. Lori and Darcy guided them in long spirals above the surrounding jungle, searching for the colonists and crew and posse. There was nobody on the boats, or in the camps that had been set up.

There's one, Lori said. She felt Darcy come into the link with Abraham, looking through the bird's enhanced eyes. Down below, a figure was slipping through the jungle. The tightly packed leaves made observation difficult, granting them only the most fleeting of glimpses. It was a man, a new colonist they judged, because he was wearing a shirt of synthetic fabric. He was walking unhurriedly westwards, parallel to the river about a kilometre inland.

Where does he think he's going? Darcy asked. **There isn't another village on this side for fifty kilometres.**

Do you want to send Abraham down below the tree level for a better look?

No. My guess is this man's been sequestrated. They all have.

There were nearly seven hundred people on those three boats.

Yes.

And there are close to twenty million people on Lalonde. How much would it cost to sequestrate them all?

A lot, if you used nanonics.

You don't think it is nanonics?

No; Laton said it was an energy virus. Whatever that is.

And you believe him?

I hate to say it, but I'm giving what he said a great deal of credence right now. There's certainly something at work here beyond our normal experience.

Do you want to capture this man? If he is a victim of the virus we should learn all we need to know from him.

I'd hate to try chasing anyone through this jungle, especially a lone man on foot who obviously has colleagues nearby.

We go on to Ozark, then?

Yes.

The *Coogan* advanced up the river at a much slower pace, waiting for the sun to set before passing the two paddle-boats. For the first time since he arrived on the planet, Darcy actually found himself wishing it would rain. A nice thick squall would provide extra cover. As it was they had to settle for thin clouds gusting over Diranol, subduing its red lambency to a sourceless candle-glow which reduced ordinary visibility to a few hundred metres. Even so the trader's wheezing engines and clanking gearbox sounded appallingly loud on the night-time river where silence was sacrosanct.

Lori engaged her retinal implants as they crept thieflike between the two boats. Nothing moved, there were no lights. The two derelicts set up cold resonances in her heart she couldn't ignore. The ships brooded.

'There should be a small tributary around here,' Darcy said an hour later. 'You can moor the *Coogan* in it; that ought to make it invisible from anyone on the Zamjan.'

'How long for?' Len asked.

'Until tomorrow night. That should give us plenty of time,

Ozark is only another four kilometres east of here. If we're not back by 04:00 hours, then cast off and get home.'

'Right you are. And I ain't spending a minute more, mind.'

'Make sure you don't cook anything. The smell will give you away if there's any trained hunting beasts in the area.'

The little tributary stream was only twice the width of the *Coogan*, with tall cherry oak trees growing on the boggy banks. Len Buchannan backed his boat down it, cursing every centimetre of the way. Once cables had secured it in the middle of the channel, Len, Lori, and Darcy worked for an hour cutting branches to camouflage the cabin.

Len's dark mood became apprehensive when Darcy and Lori were finally set to leave. Both of them had put on their chameleon suits; matt grey, tight fitting, with a ring of broad equipment pouches around the waist. He couldn't see an empty one.

'Look out for yourselves,' he mumbled, embarrassed at what he was saying, as they walked down the plank to the jungle.

'Thank you, Len,' Darcy said. 'We will. Just make sure you're here when we get back.' He pulled the hood over his head.

Len raised a hand. The air around the Edenists turned impenetrably black, flowing like oily smoke around their bodies. Then they were gone. He could hear their feet squelching softly in the mud, slowly fading into the distance. A sudden chill breeze seemed to rise out of the cloying jungle humidity, and he hastened back into the galley. Those chameleon suits were too much like magic.

*

Four kilometres through the jungle in the dead of night.

It wasn't too bad, their retinal implants had low-light and infrared capability. Their world was a two-tone of green and red, shot through with strange white sparkles, like interference on a badly tuned holoscreen. Depth perception was the trickiest, compressing trees and bushes into a flat mantle of landscape.

Twice they came across sayces on a nocturnal prowl. The animals' hot bodies shone like a dawn star amongst the lack-lustre vegetation. Each time, Darcy killed them with a single shot from his maser carbine.

Lori's inertial guidance block navigated them towards the village, its bitek processor pumping their coordinates directly into her brain, giving her the mindless knowledge and accuracy of a migratory bird. All she had to watch out for was the lie of the land; even the most exhaustive satellite survey couldn't reveal the folds, rillets, and gullies that hid below the treetops.

Two hundred metres from the edge of Ozark's clearing, their green and red world began to grow lighter. Lori checked through Abraham high overhead, keeping the bird circling outside the clearing. There were a number of fires blazing in open pits outside the cabins.

Seems pretty normal, she told Darcy.

From here, yes. Let's see if we can get in closer and spot any of the sheriffs and their weapons.

OK. One minute, I'll bring Kelven in. We'll update him as we go. In case anything happens and we don't get back, that way they'll have some record – but she tried not to think that. She ordered her communication block to open a channel to the naval ELINT satellite. The unit had a bitek processor, so the conversation wouldn't be audible.

We're at Ozark village now, she told the navy commander.

Are you all right? Kelven Solanki asked.

Yes.

What's your situation?

Right now we're on our hands and knees about a hundred metres from the fields around the village. There are several fires burning in the village, and a lot of people moving round for this time of night. There must be three or four hundred of them outside, can't be many in the cabins. Apart from that it looks pretty ordinary. She wormed her way forward through the tangle of long grass and creepers, avoiding the bushes. Darcy was a metre to her left. It had been a long time since her last fieldcraft training session, she was moderately pleased by how little noise she was making.

Kelven, I want you to datavise a list of the sheriffs the BK133s landed at Ozark, Darcy said. **We'll see if we can identify any of them.**

Right away, here they come.

Lori pressed the twigs of a low-hanging branch to the ground, and slithered over them. There was the trunk of a large mayope four metres ahead, its roots sloping up out of the soil. Light from the fires fluoresced the bark to a lurid topaz.

The list of sheriffs streamed into her mind; facts, figures, and profiles, most importantly the holograms. Mirages of seventy men shimmered over the vapid low-light image of Ozark. Lori reached the mayope trunk and looked out over the lines of seedy cabins, trying to match the visual patterns in her mind with what she could see.

There's one, Darcy said. His mind indicated one of the men squatting in a circle of people around a fire. Some kind of animal carcass was roasting above the flames.

And another, Lori indicated.

They swiftly located a further twelve sheriffs at various fires.

None of them look particularly concerned that their communications with Candace Elford have been cut off, she said.

Have they been sequestrated? Kelven Solanki asked.

There's no way of knowing for sure, but my best guess is yes, Darcy said. **Given their current situation, their behaviour is abnormal. They should at least have posted a perimeter guard.**

The bitek processor in Lori's back-up communication block reported a power loss in the unit's electron-matrix crystal. She automatically ordered the reserve crystal to be brought on line, the thought was virtually subconscious.

I concur, Lori said. **I think our original primary goal of verifying Laton's presence is irrelevant in these circumstances.**

Seconded. We'll attempt to seize one of these people and bring them back to Durringham for examination. The mimetic governor circuitry on Darcy's chameleon suit indicated a databus glitch in his right leg; alternative channels were brought on line by the master processor.

Our best bet will be that cabin there, it's reasonably isolated, and I saw someone go in just now. Lori evinced a five-room building standing apart from the others. It was a hundred and twenty metres from the edge of the jungle, but the intervening ground was mostly allotments, providing as much cover as the trees. She took an image enhancer out of a pouch on her waist, and brought it up to her eyes. **Bloody thing's broken. Try yours, we need to know how many are inside.**

Darcy's chemical/biological agent detector shut down. **It hasn't broken**, he said in consternation. **We're in some kind of electronic warfare field!**

Damn it! Lori's back-up communicator and target-laser-acquisition warning sensors dropped out. **Kelven, did you hear that? They're using highly sophisticated electronic warfare systems.**

Your signal strength is fading, Kelven said.

Darcy felt his affinity link with his maser carbine's controlling processor vanish. When he looked at the gun its LDC display panel was dead. **Come on, move it! Back to the *Coogan*.**

Darcy!

He twisted round to see five people standing in a semicircle right-behind them. One woman, four men. All of them with strange placid smiles; dressed like settlers in denim trousers and cotton shirts, the men with thick beards. Even with shock paralysing his nerves he retained enough presence of mind to glance at his own arm. Infrared showed him a faint pink outline, but low-light simply revealed long blades of grass. The chameleon circuitry was still functional.

'Shit!' **Kelven, they can see chameleon suits. Warn your people. Kelven?** The hardware units he wore round his waist were all failing in rapid succession, affinity filling his mind with processor caution warnings. They started to wink out. There was no reply from Kelven Solanki.

'You must be the pair Laton called,' one of the men said. He looked from Lori to Darcy. 'You can get up now.'

The power supply to Lori's chameleon suit ebbed to nothing, and the fabric reverted to its natural dull grey. She rolled to one side and stood in one smooth motion. Implant glands were feeding a gutsy brew of hormones into her blood supply, hyping her muscles. She dropped both her maser carbine and the image enhancer, freeing her hands. Five wouldn't be a problem. 'Where do you come from?' she asked. 'I'm talking to you that's in charge of them. Is your origin in your memory?'

'You're an atheist,' the woman replied. 'It would be kinder to spare you the answer.'

Take them out, Darcy said.

Lori stepped forwards, turning, arms and legs moving *fast.* Left ankle swinging into the man's kneecap with her full bodyweight behind it – satisfying crackle of breaking bone; right hand chopping the woman's larynx, slamming her Adam's apple into her vertebrae. Darcy was wreaking similar mayhem on his targets. Lori spun round on one foot, left leg kicking out again, back arching supplely, and her boot's toecap caught a man just below and behind his ear, splitting his skull.

Hands gripped at her arms from behind. Lori yelped in shock. Nobody should be there. But reflexes took over, a fast back-kick which connected with a thigh, and she completed the turn with her arms locking into a defensive posture in time to see the woman staggering back. She blinked in incomprehension. The woman had blood pouring out of her mouth, her throat was severely disfigured from the first blow. As she watched, the skin inflated out, Adam's apple reappearing. The gush of blood stopped.

Sweet shit, what does it take to stop them?

The two men Darcy had knocked over were regaining their feet. One had a shattered shin bone, its jagged end protruding from the flesh just below his knee; he stood on it and walked forwards.

Electrodes, Darcy ordered. The first of the men was reaching for him, the side of his face caved in where Darcy's boot had impacted, eyeball mashed in its socket, shedding tears of syrupy yellow fluid, but still smiling. He deliberately stepped inside the groping embrace, bringing his hands up, fingers wide, and clamping his palms on either side of the man's head. The long cords of eel-derived electroplaque cells buried in his forearms discharged through organic conductors that emerged from his fingertips in the form of tiny warts. The man's head was crowned with a blinding flare of purple-white static accompanied by a gunshot *crack* as the full two-thousand-volt charge slammed into his brain.

A vicious tingling erupted across Darcy's hands as some of the current leaked through the subcutaneous insulation. But the effect on the man was like nothing Darcy had ever seen before. The discharge should have felled him instantly, nothing living could withstand that much electricity. Instead he lurched backwards clutching at his mangled head, emitting a soprano keening. His skin began to glow, shining brighter and brighter. The shirt and jeans flamed briefly, falling away from the incandescent body as blackened petals. Darcy shielded his eyes with his hand. There was no heat, he realized, with a light so bright he ought to feel a scorch wave breaking across his chameleon suit. The man had become translucent now, so powerful was the surge of photons, revealing bones and veins and organs as deep scarlet and purple shadows. Their solidity dissolved, as if they were different coloured gases caught in a hurricane. He managed one last wretched wail as his body gave a massive epileptic spasm.

The light snuffed out, and the man fell flat on his face.

The other four assailants began to howl. Lori had heard a dog lamenting the death of its master once; their voices had that same bitter resentful grieving. She realized some of her hardware units were coming back on-line, the disruption effect was abating. Her chameleon suit circuitry sent psychedelic scarlet and green fireworks zipping over the fabric.

'Kelven!' she shouted desperately.

Alone in his darkened office a thousand kilometres away Kelven Solanki jerked to attention behind his desk as her static-jarred voice crashed into his neural nanonics.

'Kelven, he was right, Laton was right, there is some kind of energy field involved. It interfaces with matter somehow, controls it. You can beat it with electricity. Sometimes. Hell, she's getting up again.'

Darcy's voice broke in. 'Run! Now!'

'Don't let them gang up on you, Kelven. They're powerful when they group together. It's got to be xenocs.'

'Shit, the whole village is swarming after us,' Darcy called.

Static roared along the satellite link like a rogue binary blitzkrieg, making Kelven wince.

'Kelven, you must quarantine . . .' Lori never finished, her signal drowning below the deluge of rampaging whines and hisses. Then the racket ended.

TRANSPONDER SIGNAL DISCONTINUED, the computer printed neatly on Kelven's desk screen.

*

'I told you we shouldn't have come up here, didn't I?' Gail Buchannan said. 'Plain as day, I said no, I said you can't trust Edenists. But you wouldn't listen. Oh no. They just waved their fancy credit disk in front of your eyes, and you rolled over like a wet puppy. It's worse than when she was on board.'

Sitting on the other side of the galley's table, Len covered his eyes with his hands. The diatribes didn't bother him much now, he had learnt to filter them out years ago. Perhaps it was one of the reasons they had stayed together so long, not from attraction, simply because they ignored each other ninety per cent of the time. He had taken to thinking about such things recently, since Marie had left.

'Is there any coffee left?' he asked.

Gail never even glanced up from her knitting needles. 'In the pot. You're as lazy as she was.'

'Marie wasn't lazy.' He got up and walked over to the electric hotplate where the coffee-pot was resting.

'Oh, it's *Marie* now, is it? I bet you can't name ten of the others we ferried downriver.'

He poured half a mug of coffee and sat back down. 'Neither can you.'

She actually stopped knitting. 'Lennie, for God's sake, none of them had this effect on you. Look at what's happened to us, to the boat. What was so special about her? There must have been over a hundred brides in that bunk of yours down the years.'

Len glanced up in surprise. With her bloated features rendering her face almost expressionless it was difficult to know what went on behind his wife's eyes, but he could tell how confused she was. He dropped his gaze to the steaming mug, and blew on it absently. 'I don't know.'

Gail grunted, and resumed her knitting.

'Why don't you go to bed?' he said. 'It's late, and we ought to stay awake in shifts.'

'If you hadn't been so eager to come here we wouldn't have to mess our routine up.'

Arguing just wasn't worth the effort. 'Well, we're here now. I'll keep watch until midmorning.'

'Those damn Ivets. I hope Rexrew has every one of them shot.'

The lighting panel screwed into the galley's ceiling began to dim. Len gave it a puzzled glance; all the boat's electrical systems ran off the big electron-matrix crystals in the engine-room, and they were always kept fully charged. If nothing else, he did keep the boat's machinery in good order. Point of honour, that was.

Someone stepped onto the *Coogan*'s deck between the wheel-house and the long cabin. It was only the slightest sound, but Len and Gail both looked up sharply, meeting each other's gaze.

A young-looking teenage lad walked into the galley. Len saw he was wearing a sheriff's beige-coloured jungle jacket, the name Yuri Wilken printed on the left breast. Darcy had told him about the invaders using sequestration techniques. At the time he'd listened cynically; now he was prepared to believe utterly. There was a vicious wound on the lad's throat, long scars of red tender skin all knotted up. A huge ribbon of dried blood ran down the front of his sleeveless shirt. He wore the kind of dazed expression belonging to the very drunk.

'Get off my boat,' Len growled.

Yuri Wilken parted his mouth in a parody of a smile. Liquid rasps emerged as he tried to speak. The lighting panel was flashing on and off at high frequency.

Len stood up and calmly walked over to the long counter fitted along the starboard wall.

'Sit,' Yuri grated. His hand closed on Gail's shoulder. There was a sizzling sound, and her dress strap ignited, sending licks of yellow flame curling round his fingers. His skin remained completely unblemished.

Gail let out an anguished groan at the pain, her mouth yawning open. Wisps of blue smoke were rising from below Yuri's hand as her skin was roasted. 'Sit or she's dead.'

Len opened the top drawer next to the fridge, and pulled out the 9mm, semi-automatic pistol he kept for emergencies. He never had trusted lasers and magnetic rifles, not exposed to the Juliffe's corrosive humidity. If anyone came aboard looking for trouble after a deal went sour, or a village got worked up about prices, he wanted something that would be guaranteed to work first time.

He flicked the safety catch off, and swung the heavy blue-black gun around to point at Yuri.

'No,' the lad's malaised voice croaked. He brought his hands up in front of his face, cowering back.

Len fired. The first bullet caught Yuri on his shoulder, spinning him round and pushing him into the wall. Yuri snarled, furious eyes glaring at him. The second was aimed at Yuri's heart. It hit his sternum and the planks behind him were splashed with crimson as two of his ribs were blown apart. He began to slide down the wall, breath hissing through feral teeth. The lighting panel jumped up to its full brightness.

Len watched with numb dismay as the shoulder wound closed up. Yuri squirmed round, trying to regain his feet with slow tenacity. He grinned evilly. The grip on the pistol was growing alarmingly warm inside Len's hand.

'Kill him, Lennie!' Gail shouted. 'Kill, kill!'

Feeling preternaturally calm, Len took aim at the lad's head and squeezed the trigger. Once. Twice. The first punched Yuri's nose into his skull, ripping through his brain. He sucked air in, warbling frantically. Blood and gore slurped out of the hole. The second shot caught the right side of his temple, driving splinters of bone into the wood behind like a flight of Stone Age darts. His feet began to drum on the deck.

Len was seeing it through a cold mist. The punished, mutilated body just refused to give up. He yelled a wordless curse, finger tugging back again and again.

The pistol was clicking uselessly, its magazine empty. He blinked, trying to pull the world back into focus. Yuri had finally fallen still, there was very little left of his head. Len turned aside, grasping the side of the basin for support as a flush of nausea travelled through him. Gail was whimpering softly, a hand stroking the terrible blisters and long blackened burn marks that mottled her shoulder.

He went over and cradled her head with a tenderness he hadn't shown in years.

'Get us out of here,' she pleaded. 'Please, Lennie.'

'Darcy and Lori . . .'

'Us, Lennie. Get *us* out of here. You don't think they're going to live through tonight, do you?'

He licked his lips, making up his mind. 'No.' He brought her the first aid kit and applied a small anaesthetic patch to her shoulder. She let out a blissful little sigh as it discharged.

'You go start the engines,' she said. 'I'll see to this. I've never held you back yet.' She started to rummage through the kit box, hunting for a medical nanonic package.

Len went out onto the deck and untied the silicon-fibre cables mooring the *Coogan*, slinging the ends over the side. They were expensive, and hard to come by, but it would take another quarter of an hour if he went stumbling round the banks coiling them all up properly.

The furnace was quite cool, but the electron-matrix crystals had enough power to take *Coogan* an easy seventy kilometres downstream before they were drained. He started the motors, shoving the trader boat out from under the lacework awning of cut branches veiling it from casual eyes. As if there were any of those left on the river, he mused.

Getting underway was a miraculous morale booster. Alone on the lively Zamjan amid the first tinges of dawn's grey light he could almost believe they were trading again. Simple times, watching the wheel-house's basic instrumentation, and enjoying the prospect of milking another batch of dumb dreamers at the next village. He even managed to keep his mind from the macabre corpse in the galley.

They had gone six kilometres almost due west, helped by the broad river's swift current, when Len saw two dark smudges on the water up ahead. *Swithland* and *Hycel* were steaming towards him. A great cleft had been made in the *Swithland*'s prow, and the superstructure was leaning over at a hellish angle; but neither seemed to be affecting her speed.

The short-range radio block beside the forward-sweep mass-detector let out a bleep, then the general contact band came on. 'Hoi there, Captain Buchannan, this is the *Hycel.* Reduce speed and prepare to come alongside.'

Len ignored it. He steered a couple of degrees to starboard. The two paddle-boats altered course to match. Blocking him.

'Come on, Buchannan, what do you hope to gain? That pitiful little boat can't out-race us. One way or the other, you're coming on board. Now heave to.'

Len thought of the burns the lad had inflicted with his bare hand, the flickering lighting panel. It was all way beyond anything he could hope to understand or resolve. There was no going back to life as it had been, not now. And in the main it had been a good life.

He increased the power to the motors, and held the course steady, aiming for the *Hycel*'s growing prow. With a bit of luck Gail would never know.

He was still standing resolutely behind the *Coogan*'s wheel when the two boats collided. The *Hycel* with its greater bulk and stalwart hull rode the impact easily, smashing the flimsy *Coogan* apart like so much kindling, and sucking the debris below its hull in a riot of bubbles.

Various chunks of wood and plastic bobbed about in the paddle-boat's wake, spinning in the turbulent water. Thick black oil patches welled up among them. The current slowly pushed the scraps of wreckage downriver, dispersing them over a wide area. Within quarter of an hour there was no evidence left to illustrate the trader boat's demise.

Swithland and *Hycel* continued on their way upriver without slowing.

18

Joshua Calvert was surprised to find himself enjoying the train journey. He had almost expected to see a nineteenth-century steam engine pumping out clouds of white smoke and clanking pistons spinning iron wheels. Reality was a sleek eight-wheel tractor unit with magnetic axle-motors powered from electron matrices, pulling six coaches.

The Kavanaghs had provided him with a first-class ticket, so he sat in a private compartment with his feet up on the opposite seat, watching the sprawling forests and picturesque hamlets go past. Dahybi Yadev sat next to him, eyelids blinking heavily as a mild stimulant program trickled through his neural nanonics. In the end they had decided that Ashly Hanson should remain behind to operate the *Lady Mac*'s MSV as the crew emptied the mayope from her cargo holds. Dahybi had volunteered to take his place quickly enough, and as the nodes had been glitch free on the trip to Norfolk, Joshua had agreed. The rest of the crew had been detailed to maintenance duty. Sarha had sulked at the prospect, she'd been looking forward to an extended leave exploring the gentle planet.

The train compartment's PA came on to announce they were pulling in to Colsterworth Station. Joshua stretched his limbs, and loaded a formal etiquette program into his neural nanonics. He had found it in *Lady Mac*'s memory cores; his father must have visited the planet at some time, though he had never mentioned it. The program might well turn out to be a saviour, country-dwelling Norfolk was supposed to be even more stuffy than swinging cosmopolitan Boston. Pursing his lips at the prospect, Joshua shook Dahybi Yadev's shoulder. 'Come on, cancel the program. We've arrived.'

Dahybi's face lost its narcotic expression, and he squinted out of the window. 'This is it?'

'This is it.'

'It looks like a field with a couple of houses in it.'

'Don't yell that kind of comment about, for God's sake. Here.' He datavised a copy of the etiquette program over. 'Keep that in primary mode. We don't want to annoy our benefactor.'

Dahybi ran through some of the social jurisprudence listed in the program. 'Bloody hell, I think *Lady Mac* fell through a time warp to get here.'

Joshua rang for the steward to carry their cases. The etiquette program said the man should be tipped five per cent of the ticket price, or a shilling, whichever was the larger sum.

Colsterworth Station consisted of two stone platforms, covered with broad wooden canopies supported by ornate wrought-iron pillars. The waiting-room and ticket office were built from red brick, and a row of metal brackets along the front wall were used to hold big hanging baskets full of bright flowering plants. Appearance was a priority to the stationmaster; the scarlet and cream paintwork was kept gleaming the whole year round, brasswork was polished, and his staff were always smartly turned out.

Such persistence had paid off handsomely today. He was standing next to the heir to Cricklade herself, Louise Kavanagh, who had remarked how nice it all looked.

The morning train from Boston pulled in slowly, and the stationmaster checked his watch. 'Thirty seconds late.'

Louise Kavanagh inclined her head graciously at the stout little man. On her other side William Elphinstone shuffled his feet impatiently. She silently prayed for him not to make a complete mess of things. He was so impetuous at times, and he looked totally out of place in his grey suit; field working clothes were much more apposite on him.

For herself, she'd carefully chosen a pale lavender dress with puff sleeves to wear. Nanny had helped to pleat her hair into an elaborate weave at the back of her head which ended in a long pony-tail. Hopefully the combination would give her a suitably dignified appearance.

The train halted, its first three coaches taking up the entire length of the platform. Doors banged open noisily, and passengers started to climb down. She straightened her back to get a better look at the people emerging from the first-class coach.

'There they are,' William Elphinstone said.

Louise wasn't entirely sure what she'd been expecting, although she was pretty sure in her own mind that starship captains were wise, serious, and mature responsible men, perhaps a bit like her father (except without the temper). Who else would be entrusted with such a fearsome responsibility? What a captain did not look like, even in her most fantastical dreams, was a young man with strong regular features, six foot tall, wearing a smart, exotically stylish uniform that emphasized his powerful build. But there was the silver star on his shoulder, plain for all the world to see.

Louise swallowed hard, tried to remember the words she was supposed to say, and stepped forwards with a polite smile in place. 'Captain Calvert, I'm Louise Kavanagh; my father apologizes for not being here to greet you in person, but the estate is very busy right now and requires his full attention. So I'd like to welcome you to Cricklade myself, and hope you enjoy your stay.' Which was almost what she'd rehearsed, but there was something about enjoying his train journey which had been missed out. Oh, well . . .

Joshua took her hand in an emphatic grip. 'That's very kind of you, Louise. And I must say I consider myself most fortunate that your father is so occupied, because there simply cannot be a nicer way of being welcomed to Cricklade than by a young lady as beautiful as yourself.'

Louise knew her cheeks would be colouring, and wanted to turn and hide. What a juvenile reaction. He was only being polite. But so utterly charming. And he sounded sincere. Could he really think that about her? Her discipline had gone all to pieces. 'Hello,' she said to Dahybi Yadev. Which was so dreadfully gauche. Her blush deepened. She realized Joshua was still holding her hand.

'My starflight engineering officer,' Joshua said, with a slight bow.

Louise recovered, and introduced William Elphinstone as an estate manager, not mentioning he was only a trainee. Which he should have been grateful for, but she got the distinct impression he wasn't terribly impressed with the starship captain.

'We have a carriage laid on to take you to the manor,' William said. He signalled to the driver to take Joshua's bags from the steward.

'That's really most thoughtful of you,' Joshua told Louise.

Dimples appeared in her cheeks. 'This way.' She gestured to the platform exit.

Joshua thought the waiting carriage looked like an oversized pram fitted with modern lightweight wheels. But the two black horses moved it along at a fair clip, and the ride over the rutted track was comfortably smooth. There hadn't been much to Colsterworth, it was a rural market town with very few industries; the countryside economy revolved around the farms. Its houses were mostly built from locally quarried stone with a bluish tinge. Doors and windows were almost always arched.

When they rode down the busy High Street, pedestrians nudged one another and glanced over as the carriage went by. At first Joshua thought they were looking at him and Dahybi, but then he realized it was Louise who drew their attention.

Outside Colsterworth the rolling countryside was a patchwork of small fields separated by immaculately layered hedges. Streams wound down through the gentle valleys, while spinneys clung to the rounded heights and deeper folds. The wheat and barley had already been harvested, he saw. Plenty of haystacks were dotted about, steeply sloping tops netted against the expected winter winds. Tractors were ploughing the stubble back into the rich red soil before drilling the second crop. There would be just enough time for the stalks to ripen before the long autumn and winter seasons began.

'You don't have any proscription against power tractors, then?' Joshua asked.

'Certainly not,' William Elphinstone replied. 'We're a stable society, Captain, not a backward one. We use whatever is appropriate to maintain the status quo, and give people a decent standard of living at the same time. Using horses to plough every field would be pure drudgery. That's not what Norfolk is about. Our founders wanted pastoral life to be enjoyable for all.' To Joshua's ears he sounded defensive, but then he had been on edge since they'd been introduced.

'Where does all the power come from?' Joshua asked.

'Solar cells are sufficient for domestic utilities, but ninety per cent of the electricity used for industry and agriculture is geothermal. We buy in thermal-potential fibres from the Confederation and drill them three or four miles down into the mantle. Most towns have five or six heat shafts; they're virtually maintenance free, and the fibres last for a couple of centuries. It's a much neater solution than building hydro dams everywhere and flooding valleys.'

Interesting how he said Confederation, Joshua thought, almost as if Norfolk wasn't a part of it.

'All this must seem terribly cumbersome to you, I expect,' Louise said.

'Not at all,' Joshua answered. 'What I've seen so far is admirable. You should visit some of the so-called advanced worlds I've been to. Technology comes with a very high price in terms of society, they have dreadful levels of crime and vice. Some urban areas have decayed into complete no-go zones.'

'Three people were murdered on Kesteven last year,' Louise said.

William Elphinstone frowned as if to object, but let it pass.

'I think your ancestors got your constitution about right,' Joshua said.

'Hard on people who are sick,' Dahybi Yadev observed.

'There aren't many illnesses,' William Elphinstone said. 'Our lifestyle means we're a very healthy people. And our hospitals can cope with most accidents.'

'Including cousin Gideon,' Louise said slyly.

Joshua pressed down on a smile as William Elphinstone gave her a curtly censorious look. The girl wasn't quite as meek as he'd first supposed. They were sitting opposite each other in the carriage, which gave him a good opportunity to study her. He had thought that she and William pain-in-the-arse Elphinstone were an item, but judging from the way she virtually ignored him it didn't seem too likely. William Elphinstone appeared none too happy with the cold-shoulder treatment, either.

'Actually, William isn't being entirely honest,' she went on. 'We don't catch diseases because most of our first-comer ancestors were recipients of geneering before they settled here. It stands to reason, on a planet which deliberately excludes the most advanced medical treatments it's wise to protect yourself in advance. So in that respect we don't quite match up to the simplistic pastoral ideal. You probably couldn't have built a society as successful as Norfolk before geneering; people would have insisted on continuing technical and medical research to better their lot.'

William Elphinstone made a show of turning his head and staring out over the fields.

'Fascinating idea,' Joshua said. 'You can only have stability once you've passed a certain technological level, and flux is the natural order until that happens. Are you going to take politics at university?'

Her lips depressed fractionally. 'I don't think I'll be going. Women don't, generally. And there aren't many universities anyway; there's no research to be done. Most of my family go to agricultural colleges, though.'

'And will you be joining your relatives there?'

'Maybe. Father hasn't said. I'd like to. Cricklade is going to be mine one day, you see. I want to be more than just a figurehead.'

'I'm sure you will be, Louise. I can't imagine you as just a figurehead for anything.' He was surprised at how earnest his voice had become.

Louise cast her eyes down to see she was knotting her fingers in her lap in a most unladylike manner. Whatever was making her babble like this?

'Is this Cricklade now?' Joshua asked. The fields had given way to larger expanses of parkland between the small woods. Sheep and cattle were grazing placidly, along with some xenoc bovine-analogue that looked similar to a very hairy deer, with fat legs and hemispherical hoofs.

'We've been riding through the Cricklade estate since we left town, actually,' William Elphinstone said snidely.

Joshua gave Louise an encouraging smile. 'As far as the eye can see, is it?'

'Yes.'

'Then I can see why you love it so much. If I ever settle down, I'd want it to be in a land like this.'

'Any chance we can see some roses?' Dahybi Yadev asked loudly.

'Yes, of course,' Louise said, suddenly brisk. 'How dreadfully remiss of me. Cousin Kenneth said this was your first time here.' She turned round and tapped the driver on his shoulder. The two of them exchanged a few words. 'There's a grove beyond the forest up ahead,' she said. 'We'll stop there.'

The grove took up ten acres on a northern-facing slope. To catch the suns, Louise explained. It was marked out by a drystone wall that was host to long patches of moss-analogue which sprouted miniature pink flowers. The flat stones themselves were often crumbling from frost erosion; little attempt had been made at repairs except in the worst sections of subsidence. In one corner of the grove there was a long barn with a thatched roof; moss had clawed its way into the reeds, loosening the age-blackened bundles. New wooden pallets stacked with what looked like thousands of conical white plant pots were just visible through the barn's open doorway.

Still, dry air magnified the grove's placid composure, adding to the impression of genteel decay. If it hadn't been for the perfectly regimented rows of plants, Joshua would have believed the grove had been neglected, simply treated as a hobby by an indulgent landowner rather than the vital industry it was.

Norfolk's weeping rose was unarguably the most famous plant in the Confederation. In its natural state it was a thornless rambling bush that favoured well-drained peaty soil. But when cultivated and planted in groves it was trained up wire trellises three metres high. The jade-green leaves were palm sized, reminiscent of terrestrial maples with their deep serrations, their tips coloured a dull red.

But it was the flowers which drew Joshua's scrutiny; they were yellow-gold blooms, twenty-five centimetres in diameter with a thick ruff of crinkled petals hugging a central onion-shaped carpel pod. Each plant in the grove had produced thirty-five to forty flowers, standing proud on fleshy green stems as thick as a man's thumb. Under Duke's unremitting glare they had acquired a spectral lemon-yellow corona.

The four of them walked a little way down the mown grass between the rows. Careful pruning of the bushes had ensured that each flower was fully exposed to the sunlight, none of them overlapped.

Joshua pressed his toe into the wiry grass, feeling the solid earth. 'It's very dry,' he said. 'Will there be enough water to fill them out?'

'It never rains at midsummer,' Louise said. 'Not on the inhabited islands, anyway. Convection takes all the clouds up to the poles; most of the ice-caps melt under the deluge, but the temperature is still only a couple of degrees above freezing. It's considered frightfully bad luck if it even drizzles here in the week before Midsummer's Day. The roses store up all the moisture they need for fruition in their roots during springtime.'

He reached up and touched one of the big flowers, surprised by how stiff the stem was. 'I had no idea they were so impressive.'

'This is an old grove,' she said. 'The roses here are fifty years old, and they're good for another twenty. We replant several groves each year from the estate's nurseries.'

'That sounds like quite an operation. I'd like to see it. Perhaps you could show me, you seem very knowledgeable about their cultivation.'

Louise blushed again. 'Yes, I do; I mean, I will,' she stammered.

'Unless you have other duties, of course. I don't wish to impose.' He smiled.

'You're not,' she assured him quickly.

'Good.'

She found herself smiling back at him for no particular reason at all.

*

Joshua and Dahybi had to wait until late afternoon before they were introduced to Grant Kavanagh and his wife, Marjorie. It was an opportunity for Joshua to be shown round the big manor house and its grounds, with Louise continuing her role of informative hostess. The manor was an impressive set-up; an unobtrusive army of servants was employed to keep the rooms in immaculate condition, and a lot of money had been spent making the decor as tasteful as possible. Naturally enough, the style was based prominently on the eighteenth-century school of design, history's miniature enclave.

Thankfully, William Elphinstone left them, claiming he had to work in the groves. They did, however, meet Genevieve Kavanagh as soon as their carriage drew up outside the entrance. Louise's young sister tagged along with them for the entire afternoon, giggling the whole time. Joshua wasn't used to children that age, in his opinion she was a spoilt brat who needed a damn good smack. If it wasn't for Louise he would have been mighty tempted to put her over his knee. Instead he suffered in silence, making the most of the way Louise's dress fabric shifted about as she moved. There was precious little else to absorb his attention. To the uninitiated eye the estate beyond the grounds was almost deserted.

Midsummer on Norfolk was a time when almost everybody living in the countryside helped out with the weeping rose crop. The travelling Romany caravans were in high demand, with estates and independent grove owners competing for their labour. Even school terms (Norfolk didn't use didactic laser imprints) were structured round the season, giving children time off to assist their parents, leaving winter as the principal time for studying. As the whole Tear crop was gathered in two days, preparation was an arduous and exacting business.

With over two hundred groves in his estate (not counting those in the crofts), Grant Kavanagh was the most industrious man in Stoke County during the days leading up to midsummer. He was fifty-six years old; modest geneering had produced a barrel-chested physique, five feet ten inches tall, with brown hair that was already greying around his mutton-chop sideboards. But a lifetime of physical activity and keeping a strict watch on what he ate meant he retained the vigour of a man in his twenties. He was able to chase up his flock of junior estate managers with unnerving doggedness. Which, as he knew from sore experience, was the only way of achieving anything in Stoke County. Not only did he have to supervise the teams which went round the groves setting up the collection cups, but he was also responsible for the county's bottling yard. Grant Kavanagh did not tolerate fools, slackers, and family sinecurists, which in his view described a good ninety-five per cent of Norfolk's population. Cricklade estate had run smoothly and profitably for the last two hundred and seventy years of its distinguished three-hundred-year existence, and by God that superb record wasn't going to end in his lifetime.

An afternoon spent in the saddle riding round some of the rosegroves closest to the manor, with the eternally enduring Mr Butterworth accompanying him, did not put him in the best frame of mind for trotting out glib niceties to dandies like visiting starship captains. He marched into the house slapping dust from his riding breeches and shouting for a drink, a bath, and a decent meal.

Having this red-faced martinet figure bearing down on him across the large airy entrance hall put Joshua in mind of a Tranquillity serjeant – only lacking the charm and good looks.

'Bit young to be skippering a starship, aren't you?' Grant Kavanagh said when Louise introduced them. 'Surprised the banks gave you the loan to fly one.'

'I inherited *Lady Mac*, and my crew made enough money in our first year of commercial flying to make the run to this planet. It's the first time we've been, and your family turned somersaults to give me three thousand cases of the best Tears on the island. What criteria would you judge my competence by?'

Louise closed her eyes and wished herself very, very small.

Grant Kavanagh stared at the utterly uncompromising expression of the young man who had answered him back in his own home, and burst out laughing. 'By Christ, now that's the sort of attitude we could do with a hell of a lot more of around here. Well done, Joshua, I approve. Don't give ground, and bite back every time.' He put a protective arm around both his daughters. 'See that, you two rapscallions? That's what you've got to have to run commercial enterprises; starships or estates, it doesn't matter which. You just have to be the boss man each and every time you open your mouth.' He kissed Louise on her forehead, and tickled a giggling Genevieve. 'Glad to meet you, Joshua. Nice to see young Kenneth hasn't lost his touch when it comes to judging people.'

'He puts together a tough deal,' Joshua said, sounding unhappy.

'So it would seem. This mayope wood, is it as good as he says? I couldn't shut him up about it when he was on the phone.'

'Yes, it's impressive. Like a tree that's grown out of steel. I brought some samples with me, of course, you can have a look for yourself.'

'I'll take you up on that later.' The manor's butler came into the hall carrying Grant's gin and tonic on a silver tray. He picked it up and took a sip. 'I suppose this damned Lalonde planet will start charging a premium once they know how valuable it is to us?' he said in a disgruntled tone.

'That depends, sir.'

'Oh?' Grant Kavanagh widened his eyes with interest at the humorously furtive tone. He let go of Genevieve, and patted her fondly. 'Run along, poppet. It looks like Captain Calvert and I have something to discuss.'

'Yes, Daddy.' Genevieve capered past Joshua, giving him a sidelong glance, and breaking into giggles again.

Louise showed him a lopsided grin as she started to walk away. She had seen the other girls at school do that when they wanted to be coquettish with their boys. 'You will be joining us for dinner, won't you, Captain Calvert?' she asked airily.

'I imagine so, yes.'

'I'll tell cook to prepare some iced chiplemon. You'll like that; it's my favourite.'

'Then I'm sure I'll like it too.'

'And don't be late, Daddy.'

'Am I ever?' Grant Kavanagh retorted, enchanted as ever by his little girl's playfulness.

She rewarded them both with a sunlight smile, then skipped off across the hall tiles after Genevieve.

*

An hour later Joshua was lying on his bed, fathoming the mysteries of the planet's communication system. His bedroom was in the west wing, a large room with *en suite* bathroom, its walls papered with a rich purple and gold pattern. The bed was a double, with a carved oak headboard and a horribly solid mattress. It required very little imagination on his part to picture Louise Kavanagh lying on it beside him.

There was a phone on the bedside table, but the impossibly antique gadget didn't have a standard processor; he couldn't use his neural nanonics to datavise the communication net control computer. It didn't even have an AV pillar, just a keyboard, a holoscreen, and a handset. He did think that Norfolk had written a wonderfully realistic Turing program into the exchange's processor array to deal patiently with requests, until he finally realized he was actually talking to a human operator. She patched him into the geostationary relay satellite circuit and opened a channel to *Lady Macbeth*. What the call must be costing Grant Kavanagh was an item he managed to put firmly at the back of his mind. Humans operating a basic computer management routine!

'We've unloaded a third of the mayope already,' Sarha said; the link was audio only, no visual. 'Your new merchant friend Kenneth Kavanagh has hired half a dozen spaceplanes from other starships to ferry it down to the surface. At this rate we'll be finished by tomorrow.'

'Great news. I don't want to sound premature, but after this run is over it looks like we'll be coming back here to finalize that arrangement we were kicking around earlier.'

'You're making progress, then?'

'Absolutely.'

'What's Cricklade like?'

'Astonishing, it's enough to make a Tranquillity plutocrat jealous. You'd love it.'

'Thanks, Joshua. That really makes me feel good.'

He grinned and took another sip of the Norfolk Tears his thoughtful host had provided. 'How are you and Warlow coping with the maintenance checks?'

'We've finished.'

'What?' He sat up abruptly, nearly spilling some of the precious drink.

'We've finished. There isn't a system on board that isn't as smooth as a baby's bum.'

'Jesus, you must have been working your arses off.'

'It took us five hours, grand total. And most of that was spent waiting for the diagnostics programs to run. There's nothing wrong with *Lady Mac*, Joshua. Her performance rating is as good as the day the CAB awarded us our spaceworthiness certificate.'

'That's ridiculous. We were so glitch prone after Lalonde we were lucky to get here at all.'

'You think I don't know how to load a diagnostics program?' she asked, her voice sounding very tetchy.

'Of course you know your job,' he said in a conciliatory tone. 'It just doesn't make a lot of sense, that's all.'

'You want me to datavise the results down to you?'

'No. You can't, anyway; this planet's net couldn't handle anything like that. What does Warlow say, is *Lady Mac* up to a CAB inspection?'

'We'll pass with flying colours.'

'OK, I'll leave it up to the pair of you what you do.'

'We'll get the inspectors up here tomorrow morning.

Norfolk's CAB office only runs stage D checks in any case. Our own diagnostics are stricter than that.'

'Fine. I'll call tomorrow for an update.'

'Sure. 'Bye, Joshua.'

*

Tehama asteroid was one of the most financially and industrially successful independent industrial settlements in the New Californian star system. A stony iron rock twenty-eight kilometres long and eighteen wide, tracing an irregular fifty-day elliptical orbit within the trailing Trojan point of Yosemite, the system's largest gas giant, it had all the elements and minerals necessary to support life, barring hydrogen and nitrogen. But that deficiency was made good from a snowball-shaped carbonaceous chondritic asteroid, one kilometre wide, which had been nudged into a fifty-kilometre orbit around Tehama in 2283. Since then its shale had been mined and refined; hydrogen was combined with oxygen to produce water, plain and simple; nitrogen underwent more complex bonding procedures to form useable nitrates; hydrocarbons were an essential. They were all introduced to the caverns being bored out of Tehama's metallic ore, producing a habitable biosphere capable of supporting the increasing population.

By 2611 there were two major caverns inside Tehama; and its small companion had been reduced to a sable lump two hundred and fifty metres wide, with a silver-white refinery station, almost as large, clinging to it barnacle-fashion.

The *Villeneuve's Revenge* jumped into an emergence zone a hundred and twenty thousand kilometres away, and began its approach manoeuvres. After months tending the starship's ageing, failure-prone systems, Erick Thakrar was grateful for any shore time. Shipboard life was one long grind, he'd lost count of how many times he'd falsified the maintenance log so they could avoid CAB penalties and keep flying. There was no doubt about it, the *Villeneuve's Revenge* was operating dangerously close to the margin, both mechanically and financially. Genuine independence was proving an elusive goal; Captain Duchamp was in debt to the banks to the tune of a million and a half fuseodollars, and charters were hard to find.

Some small part of Erick felt sorry for the old boy. Commercial starflight was a viciously tough business, a tightly woven web of large cartels and monopolies that resented the very existence of independent traders. Starships like the *Villeneuve's Revenge* forced the major carrier fleets to keep their own prices down, reducing profits. They retaliated with semi-legal syndicates in an attempt to lock out small ships.

Duchamp was an excellent captain, but his business acumen was highly questionable. His crew was loyal, though, and Erick had heard enough stories of past missions to know they had few qualms about how they earned money. If he wanted to, he could have had them arrested within a week of coming on board – neural-nanonics recorded conversation was admissible evidence in court. But he was after bigger prizes than a worn-out ship with its loser crew. The *Villeneuve's Revenge* was his access code to whole strata of illegal operations. And it looked like Tehama was going to be the start of the game.

After docking at the asteroid's non-rotating axis spaceport, four crew members from the *Villeneuve's Revenge* descended on the Catalina bar in the Los Olivos cavern, the first to be dug, a cylindrical hollow nine kilometres long and five in diameter. The Catalina was one of the spaceport crew bars, with aluminium tables and a small stage for a band. At three in the afternoon, local time, it was almost dead.

The bar was a cave drilled into the cavern's vertical cliff-face endwall, one of thousands forming an interconnected cave city, producing a band of glass windows and foliage-wrapped balconies that encircled the base of the endwall. Like an Edenist habitat, nobody lived on the cavern floor itself, it was a communal park and arable farm. But there the resemblance stopped.

Erick Thakrar sat at an alcove table near the balcony window with two of his shipmates, Bev Lennon, and Desmond Lafoe, and their captain, André Duchamp. The Catalina was near the top of the city levels, giving it a seventy-five per cent gravity field, and a good view out into the cavern. Erick wasn't impressed by what he could see. The axis was taken up by a hundred-metre diameter gantry, most of which was filled by the thick black pipes of the irrigation-sprinkler nozzles. It was ringed at two hundred and fifty metre intervals by doughnut-shaped solartubes that shone with a painful blue-white intensity. They lacked the warm incandescence of an Edenist habitat's axis light-tube, which was dramatically illustrated by the plants far below. The cavern floor's grass shaded towards the yellow, while trees and shrubs were spindly, missing their full complement of leaves. Even the fields of crops were hungry looking (one reason why imported delicacies were so popular and profitable in all asteroid settlements). It was as though an unexpected autumn had visited the tropical climate.

The whole cavern was cramped and clumsy, a poor copy of a bitek habitat's excellence. Erick found himself thinking back to Tranquillity with nostalgia.

'Here he comes,' André Duchamp muttered. 'Be nice to the *Anglo*, remember we need him.' The captain came from Carcassonne, a die-hard French nationalist, who blamed the ethnic English in the Confederation for everything from failed optical fibres in the starship's flight computer to his current overdraft. At sixty-five years old his geneered DNA maintained his physique in the lean mould which was the staple criterion of the space adapted, as well as providing him with a face that was rounded all over. When André Duchamp laughed, everyone in the room found themselves smiling along, so powerful was the appeal; he had the same emotional conviction as a painted clown.

Right now he put on his most welcoming smile for the man sidling anxiously up to the table.

Lance Coulson was a senior flight controller in Tehama's

Civil Astronautics Bureau; in his late fifties, he lacked the political contacts necessary to gain senior management ranking. It meant he was stuck in inter-system tracking and communications until retirement now; that made him resentful, and agreeable to supplying people like André Duchamp with information – for the right price.

He sat at the table and gave Erick Thakrar a long look. 'I haven't seen you before.'

Erick started recording his implant-enhanced sensorium directly into a neural nanonics memory cell, and ordered a file search. Image: of an overweight man, facial skin a red tinge of brown from exposure to the cavern solartubes; grey suit with high circular collar, pinching the neck flesh; light brown hair, colour-embellished by follicle biochemical treatments. Sound: of slightly wheezy breathing, heartbeat rate above average. Smell: sour human sweat, beads standing out on a high forehead and the back of chubby hands.

Lance Coulson was nerving himself up. A weakling ruffled by the company he kept.

'Because I haven't been here before,' Erick replied, unyielding. His CNIS file reported a blank, Lance Coulson wasn't a known criminal. Probably too petty, he thought.

'Erick Thakrar, my systems generalist,' André Duchamp said. 'Erick is an excellent engineer. Surely you don't question my judgement when it comes to my own crew?' There was just enough hint of anger to make Lance Coulson shift round in his seat.

'No, of course not.'

'Excellent!' André Duchamp was all smiles again; he clapped Lance Coulson on the back, winning a sickly smile, and pushed a glass of Montbard brandy over the scratched aluminium slab to him. 'So what have you got for me?'

'A cargo of micro-fusion generators,' he said softly.

'So? Tell me more.'

The civil servant rolled the stem of his glass between his

thumb and finger, not looking at the captain. 'A hundred thousand.' He slid his Francisco Finance credit disk across the table.

'You jest!' André Duchamp said. There was a dangerous glint to his eyes.

'There were . . . questions last time. I'm not doing this again.'

'You're not doing it this time at that price. If I had that kind of money do you think I would be here crawling to a tax-money leech like you?'

Bev Lennon put a restraining hand on Duchamp's shoulder. 'Easy,' he said smoothly. 'Look, we're all here because money is tight, right? We can certainly pay you a quarter of that figure in advance.'

Lance Coulson picked up his credit disk and stood up. 'I see I have been wasting my time.'

'Thank you for the information,' Erick said in a loud voice.

Lance Coulson gave him a frightened look. 'What?'

'That's going to be enormously useful to us. How would you like to be paid? Cash or commodities?'

'Shut up.'

'Sit down, and stop fucking about.'

He sat, checking the rest of the tables with twitchy glances.

'We want to buy, you want to sell,' Erick said. 'So let's stop the drama queen tactics, assume you've shown us what a tough negotiator you are, and we're all shitting bricks. Now what's your price? And be realistic. There are other flight controllers.'

He overcame his agitation for just long enough to shoot Erick a look of one hundred per cent hatred. 'Thirty thousand.'

'Agreed,' André Duchamp said immediately. He held out his Jovian Bank disk.

Lance Coulson gave a last furtive glance round before shoving his own disk in André's direction.

'*Merci*, Lance.' André's grin was scathing as he received the datavised flight vector.

The four crewmen watched the civil servant retreating, and

laughed. Erick was congratulated for calling the other man's bluff, Bev Lennon fetching him half a litre of imported Lübeck beer.

'You had me panicking!' the wiry fusion specialist protested as he dropped the tankards down on their table.

Erick took a sip of the icy beer. 'I had me panicking.'

It was going well, they accepted him, reservations (and he knew some still had them) were fading, breaking down. He was becoming one of the lads.

Along with Bev Lennon and Desmond Lafoe, the ship's node specialist, a brawny two-metre-tall bear of a man, Erick spent the next ten minutes talking trivia while André Duchamp sat back with a blank expression reviewing the vector he had just bought.

'I don't see any problem,' the captain announced eventually. 'If we use a Sacramento orbit to jump from we can rendezvous any time in the next six days. Fifty-five hours from now would be the ideal . . .' His voice trailed off.

Erick turned to follow his gaze. Five men wearing copper-coloured one-piece ship-suits walked into the Catalina bar.

Hasan Rawand caught sight of André Duchamp as he was about to sit at the bar. He tapped Shane Brandes, the *Dechal*'s fusion engineer, on the side of his arm and flicked a finger in the direction of the master of *Villeneuve's Revenge*. His other three crew-members, Ian O'Flaherty, Harry Levine, and Stafford Charlton, caught the gesture and turned to look.

The two crews regarded each other with mutual hostility and antagonism.

Hasan Rawand walked over to the window booth table, his crew right behind him. 'André,' he said with mock civility. 'So nice to see you. I trust you have brought my money. Eight hundred thousand, wasn't it? And that's before interest. It has been seventeen months after all.'

André Duchamp gazed straight ahead, his hands cupping his beer tankard. 'I owe you no money,' he said darkly.

'I think you do. Cast your mind back; you were carrying plutonium initiators from Sab Biyar to the Isolo system. *Dechal* waited in Sab Biyar's Oort cloud for thirty-two hours for you, André. Thirty-two hours in stealth mode, with freezing air and iced food, pissing into tubes that leaked, not even allowed a personal MF player in case the navy ships picked up its electronic emission. That's not nice, André; it's about as close as you can get to a Confederation penal colony without being shot down to the surface in a drop capsule. We waited for *thirty-two hours* in the stinking dark for you to show so we could take the initiators in, doing your dirty work for you and carrying all the risk. And when we got back to Sab Biyar what did I find?'

André Duchamp grinned round at his own crew, trying to brazen it out. 'I'm sure you'll tell me, *Anglo*.'

'You went to Nuristan and sold the initiators to one of their naval contractors, you Gallic *shithead*! I was left trying to explain to the Isolo Independence Front where their nukes had gone, and why their poxy rebellion was going to fail because they hadn't got the fire-power to back up their demands.'

'You can show me the contract?' André Duchamp asked mockingly.

Hasan Rawand glared down at him, lips compressed in rage. 'Just hand over the money. A million will see you clear.'

'To hell with you, *Anglo* filth. I, André Duchamp, owe nobody money.' He stood up and tried to barge past the *Dechal*'s captain.

It was the move Erick Thakrar was waiting for and dreading. Sure enough, Hasan Rawand shoved André Duchamp back in the booth. The back of the older captain's knee struck a seat which almost tipped him off balance. He recovered and launched himself at Hasan Rawand, fists flying.

Desmond Lafoe rose to his feet drawing a frantic gasp from Ian O'Flaherty when his size, weight, and strength became apparent. Huge hands reached forward, and Ian O'Flaherty was jerked off his feet. He kicked out wildly, toecap striking Desmond Lafoe's shin. The giant merely grunted, and then threw his victim across the room. He landed awkwardly on one of the aluminium tables, his shoulder taking the brunt of his momentum before he crashed down backwards onto a pair of chairs.

Erick felt a hand close around the neck fabric of his ship-suit. It was Shane Brandes who was hauling him out of the booth; a forty-year-old with a bald head and small gold ear-rings, smiling with ugly anticipation. The unarmed combat file in Erick's neural nanonics went into primary mode. His instinctive thought routines were superseded by logic-based patterns, calculating inertia and intent with an ease surpassing any kung fu master. Nanonic supplement boosted muscles powered up.

Shane Brandes was surprised how easy it was to pull his opponent out of the booth. Gratification became alarm when he kept on coming. Shane had to backstep to keep balance, his own neural nanonics assuming command of his mass positioning. He cocked a fist back to smash into Erick's face, only to have a nanonic warning blare in his mind as Erick's forearm swung up with incredible speed. His punch was blocked, arm chopped painfully to one side. A furious kick to Erick's groin – his knee nearly fractured from the impact of the counter-kick. He reeled to one side, banging into Harry Levine and Bev Lennon, who were locked together.

Erick slammed an elbow into Shane's ribs, hearing bone break. He let out an agonized grunt.

The unarmed combat file said that speed was essential, take out your opponent as soon as possible. His neural nanonics analysed Shane's movements, the half twist as he clutched at his ribs, bending over. The motion was projected two seconds into the future. Interception points were computed. A list materialized in his consciousness, and he selected a blow that would cause temporary incapacitation. His right leg shot out, booted foot aiming for a patch of empty air. Shane's head fell into it.

A threat assessment sub-routine shifted his peripheral senses into priority focus. André Duchamp and Hasan Rawand were still battering away at each other on the side of the booth's table. Neither was inflicting much damage in the confined space.

Harry Levine had got Bev Lennon into a head lock. The two of them were on the floor, squirming round like theatrical wrestlers, sending chairs spinning. Bev Lennon sent a flurry of elbow jabs into Harry Levine's stomach, attempting to knock his navel into his spine.

Stafford Charlton obviously had a boosted musculature. He was standing in front of Desmond Lafoe, landing blow after blow on the big man, arms moving with programmed efficiency. He had almost doubled up from the pain, his right arm hung limply, the shoulder broken. Blood ran out of his flattened nose.

Ian O'Flaherty rose behind Desmond Lafoe, berserk loathing contorting his face, a pocket fission blade in his right hand. With his enhanced retinas on full amplification, the yellow haze emitted by the activated blade dazzled Erick for an instant. The threat assessment sub-routine activated the defensive nanonic implant in his left hand. A targeting grid of fine blue lines flipped up across his vision. A rectangular section flashed red, and wrapped itself around Ian O'Flaherty, adapting to his movements like elastic thread.

'Don't!' Erick Thakrar shouted.

Ian O'Flaherty had already raised the blade high above his head when the shout came. In his wired state he probably wouldn't have obeyed even if he heard. Erick saw the muscles in his lower arm begin to contract, the knife quivered as it started on its downward slash.

The neural nanonics program reported that even with boosted muscles Erick couldn't reach Ian O'Flaherty in time.

He made his decision. A small patch of skin above the second knuckle of his left hand dilated, and the implant spat out a dart of nanonic circuitry, barely as large as a wasp stinger. It struck the bare skin of Ian O'Flaherty's neck, penetrating to a depth of six millimetres. The fission blade had already descended twenty centimetres towards Desmond Lafoe's broad back. As soon as it sensed it was buried inside the flesh, and its momentum was spent, the dart sprouted a fur of microscopic filaments. They quested round on a preprogrammed search pattern for nerve strands, tips wriggling between the close-packed honeycomb of cells. Ganglions were located, and the sharp filament tips forced their way through gossamer membranes sheathing the individual nerves. At this time the knife had descended twenty-four centimetres. Ian O'Flaherty's right eyelid gave an involuntary twitch at the small sting from the dart's entry. The dart's internal processor analysed the chemical and electrical reactions flashing along the nerves; it began to broadcast its own signal into the brain. His neural nanonics detected the signal at once, but the circuitry was powerless to help, it could only override natural impulses originating from within the brain.

Ian O'Flaherty had brought the blade thirty-eight centimetres down towards Desmond Lafoe when he felt a million lacework rivulets of fire igniting inside his body. The blade fell another four centimetres before his muscles were convulsed by the besieging deluge of impulses. His nerves were burning out, overloaded by the nanonic dart's diabolical signal, ordering the massive uncontrolled release of energy along each strand, a simultaneous chemical detonation inside every neuron cell.

Breath rasped out of his wide mouth, aghast eyes looking round the room in a final plea for life. His skin turned red, as if afflicted by instant sunburn. His muscles lost all strength, and he toppled limply onto the floor. The fission blade skittered about, shaving flakes of rock from the floor whenever it touched.

No one else was fighting any more.

Desmond Lafoe gave Erick a puzzled, pain-filled glance. 'What . . .'

'He would have killed you,' Erick said in a quiet voice; he lowered his left arm. Everyone in the bar seemed to be staring at the offending limb.

'What did you do to him?' a horrified Harry Levine asked.

Erick shrugged.

'Screw that,' André Duchamp rasped. There was blood running out of his left nostril, and his eye was swelling rapidly. 'Come on.'

'You can't just go!' Hasan Rawand shouted. 'You killed him.'

André Duchamp tugged Bev Lennon to his feet. 'It was self-defence. That *Anglo* bastard tried to kill one of my crew.'

'That's right,' Desmond Lafoe rumbled. 'It was attempted murder.' He waved Erick on towards the door.

'I'll call the cops,' Hasan Rawand said.

'Yes, you would, wouldn't you?' André Duchamp sneered. 'That's your level, *Anglo*. Lose and weep, run to the law.' He fixed the shock-frozen barkeeper with a warning stare, then jerked his head for his crew to go through the door. 'Why were we fighting, Hasan? Ask yourself that. The *gendarmes* certainly will.'

Erick stepped out into the rock tunnel which connected the Catalina with the rest of the vertical city's corridors and lifts and lobbies, helping a white-faced Desmond Lafoe to limp along.

'Run and hide then, Duchamp,' Hasan Rawand's voice echoed after them. 'And you, murderer. But this universe isn't so large. Remember that.'

*

True night, with its darkness and lordly twinkling stars, had come and gone above Cricklade. It lasted less than eight minutes before the red blaze of Duchess-night began, and even those scant minutes hadn't been particularly dim. The ring of orbiting starships had looked spectacular, dominating the cloudless northern sky with their cold sparkle. Joshua had gone out onto the manor's balcony with the Kavanagh family to see the bridge of heaven after they'd finished their five-course dinner. Louise had worn a cream dress with a tight bodice; it had come alive with a pale blue fire under the cometary light showering down. The amount of attention she had shown him during the meal verged on the embarrassing, it was almost as bad as the hostility he got from William Elphinstone. He was rather looking forward to being shown round the estate by her tomorrow. Grant Kavanagh had been enthusiastic about the idea once it was announced. Without consulting his neural nanonics he couldn't be quite sure who had brought the subject up at the dinner table.

There was a light knock on his bedroom door, and it opened before he could say anything. Hadn't he turned the key?

He rolled over on the bed where he'd been lying watching the holoscreen with its inordinately bland drama programmes. Everything was set on Norfolk, where nobody swore and nobody screwed and nobody scrapped; even the one news programme he'd caught earlier was drearily parochial, with only a couple of references to the visiting starships and nothing at all about Confederation politics.

Marjorie Kavanagh slipped into the room. She smiled and held up a duplicate key. 'Scared of things that go bump in the night, Joshua?'

He grunted in dismay, and flopped back down on the bed.

They had met for the first time just before dinner, a formal drinks session in the drawing-room. If the line hadn't been so antique and passé he would have said: 'Louise didn't tell me she had an elder sister.' Marjorie Kavanagh was a lot younger than her husband, with thick raven hair and a figure which showed that even Louise had still got quite a way to go yet. Thinking about it logically, he should have realized that someone as rich and aristocratic as Grant Kavanagh would have a beautiful young wife, especially on a planet where status ruled. But Marjorie was also a flirt, which her husband seemed to find highly amusing, especially as she delivered her teasing innuendos while clinging to his side. Joshua didn't laugh; unlike Grant he knew she was serious.

Marjorie came over to stand by the side of the bed, looking down at him. She was wearing a long blue silk robe, loosely tied around her waist. The heavy curtains were drawn against the red gleam of Duchess-night, but he could see enough of her cleavage to know she wasn't wearing anything underneath.

'Er . . .' he began.

'Not sleeping? Something on your mind, or southwards of there?' Marjorie asked archly; she looked pointedly at his groin.

'I have a lot of geneering in my heritage. I don't need much sleep.'

'Oh, goodie. Lucky me.'

'Mrs Kavanagh—'

'Knock it off, Joshua. Playing the innocent doesn't suit you.' She sat on the edge of the bed.

He raised himself up on his elbows. 'In that case, what about Grant?'

A long-fingered hand ran back through her hair, producing a dark cascade over her shoulders. 'What about him? Grant is what you might call a man's man. He excels in the more basic male pursuits of hunting, drinking, filthy jokes, gambling, and women. If you haven't yet noticed, Norfolk isn't exactly a model of social enlightenment and female emancipation. Which gives him full licence to indulge himself while I sit at home playing the good wifey. So while he's off rogering a pair of teenage Romany girls he spotted helping out in the groves this afternoon, I thought: Fuck it, I'm going to have some fun myself for once.'

'Do I get a say?'

'No, you're too perfect for me. Big, strong, young, handsome, and gone in a week. How could I possibly let that opportunity go by? Besides, I'm fiercely protective when it comes to my daughters, a proper hax bitch.'

'Er . . .'

'Ah ha!' Marjorie grinned. 'You're blushing, Joshua.' Her hand found the hem of his shirt, and slid across his abdomen. 'Grant can be so very idiotic when it comes to the girls. He had quite a chortle at the way Louise took to you at dinner. He doesn't think, that's his problem. You see, here on Norfolk they are in no danger at all from the local boys, they don't need chaperones for dances nor guardian aunts when they stay with friends. Their name protects them. But you're not a local boy, and I saw exactly what was going on inside that testosterone-fuelled mind of yours. No wonder you and Grant get on so well together, I can barely tell you apart.'

Joshua squirmed from her hand as she stroked the sensitive skin at the side of his ribs. 'I think Louise is very sweet. That's all.'

'Sweet.' Marjorie smiled softly. 'I was just eighteen when I had her. And I'll thank you not to work out how old that makes me! So you see I know exactly what she's thinking right now. Captain Romance from beyond the sky. Norfolk girls of my class are virgins in more ways than one. I'm not about to let some over-sexed stranger ruin her future, she has a slim enough chance of a happy one as it is, what with arranged marriages and minimal education, which is the lot of females on this planet, even for our class. And I'm doing you a favour into the bargain.'

'Me?'

'You. Grant would kill you if you ever laid a finger on her. And, Joshua, I don't mean metaphorically.'

'Er . . .' He couldn't believe that; not even in this society.

'So I'm going to sacrifice my virtue to save both of you.' She undid the belt, and slipped the robe from her shoulders. Sultry red light gleamed on her body, embellishing the erotic allure. 'Isn't that just so *terribly* noble of me?'

*

The emergent snowlily plants were starting to be a problem around the village jetties along the length of the Juliffe and its multitudinous tributaries. The tightly clumped red-brown fronds occupied the shallows, the banks, and the mud-banks. None of which affected the *Isakore* as it sailed its unerringly straight course along the Zamjan towards the Quallheim Counties, carrying its boisterous passenger complement of four Confederation Navy Marines, and three Kulu ESA tactical operation agents. *Isakore* hadn't put ashore once since it left Durringham. It was an eighteen-metre-long fishing boat, with a carvel hull of mayope, sturdy enough for its original owners to take it down to the mouth of the Juliffe and catch sea fish in their nets. Ralph Hiltch had ordered its thermal-conversion furnace to be taken out, and got the boatyard to install the micro-fusion generator which the Kulu Embassy used as its power reserve. With one high-pressure gas canister of He_3 and deuterium for fuel, *Isakore* now had enough power to circumnavigate the globe twice over.

Jenny Harris was lying on her sleeping-bag under the plastic awning they had rigged up over the prow, out of the light drizzle sweeping the river. The sheeting didn't make much difference, and her shorts and white T-shirt were soaking. Four days of sailing without a break from the humidity left her vainly trying to remember whether she had ever been dry.

A couple of the marines were on their sleeping-bags beside her, Louis Beith and Niels Regehr, barely out of their teens. They were both 'vising their personal MF players, eyes closed, fingers tapping out chaotic rhythms on the deck. She envied their optimism and confidence. They treated the scouting mission with an almost schoolboyish enthusiasm; although she admitted they were well trained and physically impressive with their boosted muscles. A tribute to their lieutenant, Murphy Hewlett, who had kept his small squad's morale high even on a dead-end posting like Lalonde. Niels Regehr had confided they all thought the mission upriver was a reward not a punishment.

Her communication block datavised that Ralph Hiltch was calling. She got to her feet and walked out from under the awning, giving the young marines some privacy. The dampness in the air wasn't noticeably increased. Dean Folan, her deputy, waved from the wheel-house amidships. Jenny acknowledged him, then leant on the gunwale and accepted the channel from the communication block.

'I'm updating you on the Edenist agents,' Ralph datavised.

'You've found them?' she queried. It had been twenty hours since they had gone off air.

'Chance would be a fine thing. No, and the observation satellite images show that Ozark village is being abandoned. People are just drifting away – walking into the jungle, as far as we can tell. We must assume they have been either sequestrated or eliminated. There is no trace of the boat they were using, the *Coogan*, the satellite can't see it anywhere on the river.'

'I see.'

'Unfortunately, the Edenists knew you were coming upriver behind them.'

'Hellfire!'

'Exactly, so if they have been sequestrated the invaders will be watching out for you.'

Jenny ran a hand over her head. Her ginger hair had been shaved down to a half-centimetre stubble, the same as everyone else on board. It was standard procedure for jungle missions, and her combat shell-helmet would make better contact. But it did mean anyone who saw them would immediately know what they were. 'We weren't exactly inconspicuous anyway,' she datavised.

'No, I suppose not.'

‘Does this change our mission profile?’

‘Not the directive, no. Kelven Solanki and I still want one of these sequestrated colonists brought back to Durringham. But the timing has certainly altered. Where are you now?’

She datavised the question into her inertial guidance block. ‘Twenty-five kilometres west of Oconto village.’

‘Fine, put ashore at the nearest point you can. We’re a little worried about the boats coming out of the Quallheim and Zamjan tributaries. When we reviewed the satellite images we found about twenty that have set off downriver in the last week, everything from paddle-steamers to fishing ketches. As far as we can make out they’re heading for Durringham, they certainly aren’t stopping.’

‘You mean they’re behind us as well?’ Jenny asked in dismay.

‘It looks that way. But, Jenny, I don’t leave my people behind. You know that. I’m working on a method of retrieving you that doesn’t include the river. But only ask if you really need it. There are only a limited number of seats,’ he added significantly.

She stared across the grey water at the unbroken jungle, and muttered a silent curse. She liked the marines, a lot of trust had been built up between the two groups in the last four days; there were times when the ESA seemed too duplicitous and underhand even for an Intelligence agency. ‘Yes, boss, I understand.’

‘Good. Now, remember; when you put ashore, assume everyone is hostile, and avoid all groups of locals. Solanki is convinced it was sheer numbers which overwhelmed the Edenists. And, Jenny, don’t let prejudice inflate your ego, the Edenist operatives are good.’

‘Yes, sir.’ She signed off and picked her way past the wheelhouse to the little cabin which backed onto it. A big grey-green tarpaulin had been rigged over the rear of the boat to screen the horses. She could hear them snorting softly. They were agitated and jumpy after so long cooped up in their tiny enclosure. Murphy Hewlett had kept them reasonably comfortable, but she'd be glad when they could let them loose on land again. So would the team which had to shovel their crap overboard.

Murphy Hewlett was sheltering in the lee of the tarpaulin, his black fatigue jacket open to the waist, showing a dark green shortsleeved shirt. She started to explain the change in schedule.

'They want us to go ashore right now?' he asked. He was forty-two years old, and a veteran of several combat campaigns both in space and on planets.

'That's right. Apparently people are deserting the villages in droves. Picking one of them up shouldn't be too big a problem.'

'Yeah, you're right about that.' He shook his head. 'I don't like this idea that we're already behind enemy lines.'

'I didn't ask my boss what the situation was like in Durringham right now, but to my mind this whole planet is behind the lines.'

Murphy Hewlett nodded glumly. 'There's real trouble brewing here. You get to recognize the feeling after a while, you know? Combat sharpens you, I can tell when things ain't right. And they're not.'

Jenny wondered guiltily if he could guess the essence of what Ralph Hiltch had said to her. 'I'll tell Dean to look out for a likely landing spot.'

She hadn't even reached the wheel-house before Dean Folan was shouting urgently. 'Boat coming!'

They went to the gunwale and peered ahead through the thin grey gauze of drizzle. The shape slowly resolved, and both of them watched it sail past with shocked astonishment.

It was a paddle-steamer which seemed to have ridden straight out of the nineteenth-century Mississippi River. Craft just like it were the inspiration behind Lalonde's current fleet of paddle-boats. But while the *Swithland* and her ilk were bland distaff inheritors utilizing technology instead of engineering craftsmanship, this *grande dame* could have been a true original. Her paintwork was white and glossy, black iron stacks belched out a thick, oily smoke, pistons hissed and clanked as they turned the heavy paddles. Happy people stood on the decks, the handsome men in suits with long grey jackets, white shirts, and slender lace ties, their elegant women in long frilly dresses, casually twirling parasols on their shoulders. Children ran about, sporting gaily; the boys were in sailor suits, and the girls had ribbons in their flowing hair.

'It's a dream,' Jenny whispered to herself. 'I'm living a dream.'

The stately passengers were waving invitingly. Sounds of laughter and merrymaking rang clearly across the water. Earth's mythical golden age had come back to nourish them with its supreme promise of unspoilt lands and uncomplicated times. The paddle-steamer was taking all folk of good will back to where today's cares would cease to exist.

The sight was tugging at the hearts of all on board the *Isakore*. There wasn't one of them who didn't feel the urge to jump into the river and swim across the gulf. The gulf: between them and bliss, an eternal joy of song and wine which waited beyond the cruel divide which was their own world.

'Don't,' Murphy Hewlett said.

Jenny's euphoria shattered like crystal as the discordant voice struck her ears. Murphy Hewlett's hand was on hers, pressing down painfully. She found her arms were rigid, tensed, ready to propel her over the side of the fishing boat.

'What is that?' she asked. At some deep level she was bemoaning the loss, being excluded from the journey into a different future; now she would never know if the promise was true . . .

'Don't you see?' he said. 'It's them, whatever they are. They're growing. They don't care about us seeing them unmasked any more, they don't fear us.'

The colourful solid mirage sailed on regally down the river, its wake of joyous invocation tarrying above the brown water like a dawn mist. Jenny Harris stayed at the gunwale for a long time, staring into the west.

*

The grove was a site of intense activity. Over two hundred people were working their way along the rows, positioning the collection cups around the weeping roses. It was early Duke-day; Duchess had just set, leaving a slight pink fringe splashing the western horizon. Between them, the two suns had banished all trace of moisture from the torrid air. Most of the men and women tending the big weeping roses wore light clothes. The younger children ran errands, bringing new stacks of collection cups to the teams, or supplying iced fruit juice from large jugs.

Joshua was feeling the heat despite being dressed in a burgundy sleeveless T-shirt and black jeans. He sat on the back of his horse watching the cupping teams at work. The cups that were being hung so carefully were white cardboard cones, with a waxed shiny inner surface, thirty centimetres wide at the open end, tapering down to a sealed point. Stiff hoops pasted onto the side were used to wire them onto the trellis below the weeping rose flowers. Everyone he could see carried a thick bundle of wires tucked into their belt. It didn't take more than thirty seconds for them to fix each cup.

'Is there one collection cup for every single flower?' he asked.

Louise was sitting on her horse next to him, dressed in jodhpurs and a plain white blouse, hair held by a single band at the back. She had been surprised when he accepted her invitation to take the horses rather than use a carriage to get about the estate. Where would a starship captain learn how to ride? But ride he could. Not as well as her, which gave her a little thrill, that she should be better than a man at anything. Especially Joshua. 'Yes,' she said. 'How else could you do it?'

He gave the stacks of collection cups piled up at the end of each row a puzzled frown. 'I don't know. Jesus, there must be millions of them.'

Louise had grown accustomed to his casual swearing now. It had shocked her a little at first, but people from the stars were bound to have slightly different customs. Coming from him it didn't seem profane, just exotic. Perhaps the most surprising thing was the way he could suddenly switch from being himself to using the most formal mannerisms.

'Cricklade alone has two hundred groves,' she said. 'That's why there are so many cuppers. It has to be done entirely in the week before midsummer when the roses are in bloom. Even with every able-bodied person in the county drafted in there's only just enough to get it finished in time. A team like this takes nearly a day to complete a grove.'

Joshua leant forwards in the saddle, studying the people labouring away. It all seemed so menial, yet every one of them looked intent, devoted almost. Grant Kavanagh had said that a lot of them worked through half of Duchess-night, they would never have got the work finished otherwise. 'I'm beginning to see why a bottle of Norfolk Tears costs so much. It's not just the rarity value, is it?'

'No.' She flicked the reins, and guided the horse along the end of the rows, heading for the gate in the wall. The foreman touched his wide-brimmed hat as she passed. Louise gave a reflex smile.

He rode beside her after they left the grove. Cricklade Manor's protective ring of cedars was just visible a couple of miles away across the wolds. 'Where now?' It was parkland all around, sheep clustering together under the lonely trees for shade. The grass was furry with white flowers. Everywhere he looked there seemed to be blooms of some kind – trees, bushes, ground plants.

'I thought Wardley Wood would be nice, you can see what wild Norfolk looks like.' Louise pointed at a long stretch of dark-green trees a mile away, following the bottom of a small valley. 'Genevieve and I often walk there. It's lovely.' She dropped her head. As if he would be interested in the glades with their multicoloured flowers and sweet scents.

'That sounds good. I'd like to get out of this sunlight. I don't know how you can stand it.'

'I don't notice it, really.'

He spurred his horse on, breaking into a canter. Louise rode past him easily, moving effortlessly with her horse's rhythm. They galloped across the wolds, scattering the somnolent sheep, Louise's laughter trilling through the heavy air. She beat him easily to the edge of the wood, and sat there smiling as he rode up to her, panting heavily.

'That was quite good,' she said. 'You could be a decent rider if you had a bit of practice.' She swung her leg over the saddle and dropped down.

'There are some stables on Tranquillity,' he said, dismounting. 'That's where I learnt, but I'm not there very often.'

A big mithorn tree stood just outside the main body of the wood, its coin-sized dark red flowers sprinkling the end of every twig. Louise wrapped the reins round one of its lower branches, and started off into the wood along one of the little animal tracks she knew. 'I've heard of Tranquillity. That's where the Lord of Ruin lives, Ione Saldana. She was on the news last year; she's so beautiful. I wanted to cut my hair short like hers, but Mother said no. Do you know her?'

'Now that's the trouble when you really do know someone famous; no one ever believes you when you say yes.'

She turned round, eyes wide with delight. 'You do know her!'

'Yes. I knew her before she inherited the title, we grew up together.'

'What's she like? Tell me.'

An image of a naked sweaty moaning Ione bent over a table while he was screwing her appeared in his mind. 'Fun,' he said.

The glade she led him to was on the floor of the valley; a stream ran through it, spilling down a series of five big rock-pools. Knee-high flower stems with tubular yellow and lavender blooms clotted the ground, giving off a scent similar to orange blossom. Water-monarch trees lined the stream below the pools, fifty yards tall, their long, slender branches swaying in the slight breeze, fernlike leaf fronds drooping. Birds flittered about in the upper boughs, uninspiring dun-coloured bat-analogues with long, powerful forelimbs for tunnelling into the ground. Wild weeping roses boiled over the stones along the side of two of the pools; years of dead petrified branches overlaid by a fresh growth of new living shoots to produce hemispherical bushes. Their flowers were crushed together, disfigured as they vied for light.

'You were right,' Joshua told her. 'It is lovely.'

'Thank you. Genevieve and I often bathe here in the summer.'

He perked up. 'Really?'

'It's a little place of the world that's all our own. Even the hax don't come here.'

'What's a hax? I heard someone mention the name.'

'Father calls them wolf-analogues. They're big and vicious, and they'll even attack humans. The farmers hunt them in the winter, it's good sport. But we've just about cleared them out of Cricklade now.'

'Do the hunters all get dressed up in red jackets and charge around on horses with packs of hounds?'

'Yes. How did you know?'

'Lucky guess.'

'I suppose you've seen real monsters on your travels. I've seen pictures of the Tyrathca on the holoscreen. They're horrible. I couldn't sleep for a week afterwards.'

'Yes, the Tyrathca look pretty ferocious. But I've met some breeder pairs; they don't think of themselves like that. To them we're the cruel alien ones. It's a question of perspective.'

Louise blushed and ducked her head, turning away from him. 'I'm sorry. You must think me a frightful bigot.'

'No. You're just not used to xenocs, that's all.' He stood right behind her and put his hands on her shoulders. 'But I would like to take you away from here some time and show you the rest of the Confederation. Some of it is quite spectacular. And I'd love to take you to Tranquillity.' He looked round the glade, thoughtful. 'It's a bit like this, only much much bigger. I think you'd like it a lot.'

Louise wanted to squirm away from his grip, men simply shouldn't act in such a familiar fashion. But his customs were surely different, and he was massaging her shoulder muscles gently. It felt nice. 'I always wanted to fly on a starship.'

'You will, one day. When Cricklade is yours you can do anything you want.' Joshua was enjoying the touch of her. Naïvety, a voluptuous body, and the knowledge that he should never, ever be even thinking about screwing her were combining to form a potent aphrodisiac.

'I never thought of that,' she said brightly. 'Can I charter the *Lady Macbeth*? Oh, but it will be simply ages yet. I don't want Father to die, that would be an absolutely awful thing to think. Will you still be coming to Norfolk in fifty years' time?'

'Of course I will. I have two things tying me here now. Business, and you.'

'Me?' It came out as a frightened squeak.

He turned her round to face him, and kissed her.

'Joshua!'

He put two fingers over her lips. 'Shush. No words, only us. Always us.'

Louise stood rigidly still as he unbuttoned her blouse, all kinds of strange emotions battling in her head. I ought to run. I ought to stop him.

Sunlight fell onto her bare shoulders and back. It was a peculiar sensation, a tingling warmth. And the expression on his face as he gazed at her was scary, he looked so hungry, but anxious at the same time.

'Joshua,' she murmured, half nervous, half amused. Her shoulders had hunched up of their own accord.

He pulled his T-shirt off over his head. They kissed again, his arms going around her. He seemed very strong. His skin pressing against her had started a trembling in her stomach that nothing was able to stop. Then she realized her jodhpurs were being peeled down.

'Oh God.'

His finger lifted her chin up. 'It's all right. I'll show you how.' And his smile was at least as warm as the sun.

She took her black leather riding boots off herself, then helped him with the jodhpurs. Her brassière and knickers were plain white cotton. Joshua removed them slowly, savouring the drawn-out exposure.

He spread their clothes out and lay her down. She was terribly tense to start with, her lower lip clamped between her teeth, narrow eyes peeking down fearfully at the length of her body. It took a long, pleasant time of soft caresses, kisses, stealthy whispers, and tickles before she began to respond. He coaxed a giggle from her, then another, then it was a squeal, a groan. She touched his body, curious and suddenly bold, a hand sliding down his belly to cup his balls. He shuddered and repaid her by massaging her thighs. There was another long interval while their hands and mouths explored each other. Then he slid above her, looking down at dishevelled hair, drowsy eyes, dark nipples standing proud, legs parted. He moved into her carefully, the damp warmth enveloping and squeezing his cock an erotic splendour. Louise writhed tempestuously below him, and he began a slow, provocative stroke. He used neural nanonic overrides to restrain his own body's responses, sustaining his erection as long as he wanted it, determined that she should reach a climax, that it should be as perfect for her as he could possibly make it.

After an age he was rewarded by her complete loss of control. Louise threw away every last inhibition as her orgasm built, shouting at the top of her voice, her body arching desperately below him, lifting his knees from the ground. Only then did he allow himself any release, joining her in absolute bliss.

Post-coital languor was a sweet time, one of tiny kisses, stroking individual strands of sticky hair from her face, single compassionate words. And he had been quite right all along, forbidden fruit tasted the best.

'I love you, Joshua,' she whispered into his ear.

'And I love you.'

'Don't leave.'

'That's unfair. You know I'm coming back.'

'I'm sorry.' She tightened her grip around him.

He moved his hand up to her left breast and squeezed, hearing a soft hiss of indrawn breath. 'Are you sore?'

'A bit. Not much.'

'I'm glad.'

'Me too.'

'Do you want to have that swim now? Water can be a lot of fun.'

She grinned cautiously. 'Again?'

'If you want.'

'I do.'

*

Marjorie Kavanagh came to his bedroom again that Duchess-night. The prospect of Louise sneaking through the red-shaded manor to be with him and discovering him with her mother added a spice to his lovemaking that left her exhausted and delighted.

The next day Louise, eyes possessively agleam, announced at breakfast that she would show Joshua round the county roseyard, so he could see the casks being prepared for the new Tears. Grant declared this a stupendous idea, chuckling to himself that his little cherub was having her first schoolgirl crush.

Joshua smiled neutrally, and thanked her for being so considerate. There were another three days to go until midsummer.

*

At Cricklade, and all across Norfolk, they marked the onset of Midsummer's Day with a simple ceremony. The Kavanaghs, Colsterworth's vicar, Cricklade Manor's staff, the senior estate workers, and representatives from each of the cupper teams gathered at the nearest grove to the manor towards the end of Duke-day. Joshua and Dahybi were invited, and stood at the front of the group that assembled just inside the shabby stone wall.

The rows of weeping roses stretched out ahead of them; blooms and cups alike upturned to a fading azure sky, perfectly still in the breathless evening air. Time seemed to be suspended.

Duke was falling below the western horizon, a sliver of pyrexic tangerine, pulling the world's illumination down with it. The vicar, wearing a simple cassock, held his arms up for silence. He turned to face the east. On cue, a watery pink light expanded across the horizon.

A sigh went up from the group.

Even Joshua was impressed. There had been about two minutes of darkness the previous evening. Now there would be no night for a sidereal day, Duchess-night flowing seamlessly into Duke-day. It wouldn't be until the end of the following Duchess-night that the stars would come out again for a brief minute. After that it would be the evenings when the two suns overlapped, and the morning darkness would grow longer and longer, extending back into Duchess-night until Norfolk reached inferior conjunction and only Duke was visible: mid-winter.

The vicar led his flock in a brief Harvest Thanksgiving service. Everybody knew the words to the prayers and psalms, and quiet, murmuring voices banded together to be heard right across the grove. Joshua felt quite left out. They finished by singing 'All Creatures Great and Small'. At least his neural nanonics had that in a memory file; he joined in heartily, surprised by just how good he felt.

After the service, Grant Kavanagh led his family and friends on a rambling walk along the aisles between the rows. He touched various roses, feeling their weight, rubbing petals between his thumb and forefinger, testing the texture.

'Smell that,' he told Joshua as he handed over a petal he had just picked. 'It's going to be a good crop. Not as good as five seasons ago. But well above average.'

Joshua sniffed. The scent was very weak, but recognizable, similar to the smell which clung to a cork after a bottle of Tears had been opened. 'You can tell from this?' he asked.

Grant put his arm around Louise as they sauntered along the aisle. 'I can. Mr Butterworth can. Half of the estate workers can. It just takes experience. You need to be here for a lot of summers.' He grinned broadly. 'Perhaps you will be, Joshua. I'm sure Louise will ask you back if no one else does.'

Genevieve shrieked with laughter.

Louise blushed furiously. 'Daddy!' She slapped his arm.

Joshua raised a weak smile and turned to examine one of the rose plants. He found himself facing Marjorie Kavanagh. She gave him a languid wink. His neural nanonics sent out a volley of overrides to try and stop the rush of blood to his own cheeks.

After the inspection walk the manor staff served up an outdoor buffet. Grant Kavanagh stood behind one of the trestle tables, carving from a huge joint of rare beef, playing the part of jovial host, with a word and a laugh for all his people.

As Duchess-night progressed the rose flowers began to droop. It happened so slowly that the eye could detect no motion, but hour by hour the thick stems lost their stiffness, and the weight of the large petals and their central carpel pod made gravity's triumph inevitable.

By Duke-morning most of the flowers had reached the horizontal. The petals were drying out and shrivelling.

Joshua and Louise rode out to one of the groves close to Wardley Wood, and wandered along the sagging plants. There were only a few cuppers left tending the long rows, straightening the occasional collection cup. They nodded nervously to Louise and scurried on about their business.

'Most people have gone home to sleep,' Louise said. 'The real work will begin again tomorrow.'

They stood aside as a man pulled a wooden trolley past them. A big glass ewer, webbed with rope, was resting on it. Joshua watched as he stopped the trolley at the end of a row and lifted the ewer off. About a third of the rows had a similar ewer waiting at the end.

'What's that for?' he asked.

'They empty the collection cups into those,' Louise said. 'Then the ewers are taken to the county roseyard where the Tears are casked.'

'And they stay in the cask for a year.'

'That's right.'

'Why?'

'So that they spend a winter on Norfolk. They're not proper Tears until they've felt our frost. It sharpens the taste, so they say.'

And adds to the cost, he thought.

The flowers were wilting rapidly now, the stems curving down into a U-shape. Their sunlight-fired coronal cloak had faded away as the petals darkened, and with it had gone a lot of the mystique. They were just ordinary dying flowers now.

'How do the cuppers know where to wire the cups?' he asked. 'Look at them. Every flower is bending over above a cup.' He glanced up and down the aisle. 'Every one of them.'

Louise gave him a superior smile. 'If you are born on Norfolk, you know how to place a cup.'

It wasn't just the weeping roses which were reaching fruition. As they trotted the horses over to Wardley Wood Joshua saw flowers on the trees and bushes closing up, some varieties leaning over in the same fashion as the roses.

In their peaceful glade the wild rose bushes along the rock pools seemed flaccid, as if their shape was deflating. Flowers lolled against each other, petals agglutinating into a quilt of pulp.

Louise let Joshua undress her as he always did. Then they spread a blanket down on the rocks below the weeping roses and embraced. Joshua had got to the point where Louise was shuddering in delighted anticipation as his hands roved across her lower belly and down the inside of her thighs when he felt a splash on his back. He ignored the first one and kissed Louise's navel. Another splash broke his concentration. It couldn't be raining, there wasn't a cloud in the barren blue sky. He twisted over. 'What—?'

Norfolk's roses had begun to weep. Out of the centre of the carpel pod a clear fluid was exuded in a steady monotonous drip. It was destined to last for ten to fifteen hours, well into the next Duchess-night. Only when the pod was drained would it split open and release the seeds it contained. Nature had intended the fluid to soften the soil made arid by weeks without rain, allowing the seeds to fall into mud so they would have a greater chance of germination. But then in 2209 a woman called Carys Thomas, who was a junior botanist in the ecological assessment mission, acting against all regulations (and common sense), put her finger under a weeping pod, then touched the single pearl of glistening fluid to her tongue. Norfolk's natural order came to an immediate end.

Joshua wiped up the dewy bead from his skin and licked his finger. It tasted coarser than the Norfolk Tears he'd so relished back in Tranquillity, but the ancestry was beyond doubt. A roguish light filled his eyes. 'Hey, not bad.'

A snickering Louise was moved round until she was directly underneath the lax hanging flowers. They made love under a shower of sparkling droplets prized higher than a king's ransom.

The cuppers returned to the groves as the next Duchess-night ended. They cut away the collection cups, now heavy with Tears, and poured their precious contents into the ewers.

It was a task that would take another five days of intensive round-the-clock labour to complete.

Grant Kavanagh himself drove Joshua and Dahybi down to the county roseyard in a four-wheel-drive farm ranger, a powerful boxy vehicle with tyres deep enough to plough through a shallow marsh. The yard was on the outskirts of Colsterworth, a large collection of ivy-clad stone buildings with few windows. Beneath the ground was an extensive warren of brick-lined cellars where the casks were stored throughout their year of maturation.

When he drove through the wide entrance gates the yard workers were already rolling out the casks of last year's Tears.

'A year to the day,' he said proudly as the heavy iron-bound oak cylinders rattled and skipped over the cobbles. 'This is your cargo, young Joshua. We'll have it ready for you in two days.' He braked the farm ranger to a halt outside the bottling plant where the casks were being rolled inside. The plant supervisor rushed out to meet them, sweating. 'Don't you worry about us,' Grant told him blithely. 'I'm just showing our major customer around. We won't get in the way.' And with that he marched imperiously through the broad doorway.

The bottling plant was the most sophisticated mechanical set-up Joshua had seen on the planet, even though it lacked any real cybernetic systems (the conveyor belts actually used rubber pulleys!). It was a long hall with a single-span roof, full of gleaming belts, pipes, and vats. Thousands of the ubiquitous pear-shaped bottles trundled along the narrow belts, looping overhead, winding round filling nozzles, the racket of their combined clinking making conversation difficult.

Grant walked them along the hall. The casks were all blended together in big stainless-steel vats, he explained. Stoke County's bouquet was a homogenized product. No groves had individual labels, not even his.

Joshua watched the bottles filling up below the big vats, then moving on to be corked and labelled. Each stage added to the cost. And the weight of the glass bottles reduced the amount of actual Tears each starship could carry.

Jesus, what a sweet operation. I couldn't do it better myself. And the beauty of it is we're the ones most eager to cooperate, to inflate the cost.

At the end of the line, the yard manager was waiting with the first bottle to come off the conveyor. He looked expectantly at Grant, who told him to proceed. The bottle was uncorked, and its contents poured into four cut-crystal glasses.

Grant sniffed, then took a small sip. He cocked his head to one side and looked thoughtful. 'Yes,' he said. 'This will do. Stoke can put its name to this.'

Joshua tried his own glass. It chilled every nerve in his throat, and burst into flames in his stomach.

'Good enough for you, Joshua?' Grant clapped him on the back.

Dahybi was holding his glass up to the light, staring at it with greedy enchantment.

'Yes,' Joshua declared staunchly. 'Good enough.'

*

Joshua and Dahybi took it in turns to oversee the cases the roseyard put together for them. For space travel the bottles were hermetically sealed in composite cube containers one metre square, with a thick lining of nultherm foam to protect them (more weight); the roseyard had its own loading and sealing machinery (more cost). There was a railway line leading directly from the yard to the town's station, which meant they were able to dispatch several batches to Boston every day.

All this activity severely reduced the amount of time Joshua spent at Cricklade Manor, much to Louise's chagrin. Nor was there any believable reason why she should take him riding over the estate again.

He arranged the shifts with Dahybi so that he worked most

of Duchess-night at the roseyard, which meant his tussles with Marjorie were curtailed.

The morning of the day he was leaving, however, Louise did manage to trap him in the stables. So he had to spend two hours in a dark, dusty hay loft satisfying an increasingly bold and adventurous teenager who seemed to have developed a bottomless reserve of physical stamina. She clung to him for a long time after her third climax, while he whispered assurances of how quickly he would come back.

'Just for business with Daddy?' she asked, almost as an accusation.

'No. For you. Business is an excuse, it would be difficult otherwise on this planet. Everything's so bloody formal here.'

'I don't care any more. I don't care who knows.'

He shifted round, brushing straw from his ribs. 'Well, I *do* care; because I don't want you to be treated like a pariah. So show a little discretion, Louise.'

She ran her fingertips over his cheeks, marvelling. 'You really care about me, don't you?'

'Of course I do.'

'Daddy likes you,' she said uncertainly. Now probably wasn't the best time to press him on their future after he returned. He must have a lot on his mind with the awesome responsibility of the starflight ahead of him. But it did seem as though her father's plaudit was like an omen. So few people ever met with Daddy's approval. And Joshua had said how much he adored Stoke County. The kind of land I'd like to settle in: his exact words.

'I'm rather fond of the old boy myself. But God he's got a temper.'

Louise giggled in the dark. Down below the horses were shuffling about. She straddled his abdomen, her mane of hair falling around the two of them. His hands found her breasts, fingers tightening until she moaned with desire. In a low, throaty voice he told her what he wanted her to do. She strained her body to accommodate him, trembling at her own daring. He was solid against her, wonderfully *there*, encouraging and praising.

'Tell me again,' she murmured. 'Please, Joshua.'

'I love you,' he said, breath teasingly hot on her neck. Even his neural nanonics couldn't banish the dawning guilt he felt at the words. Have I really been reduced to lying to trusting, hopelessly unsophisticated teenagers? Perhaps it's because she is so magnificent, what we all want girls to be like even though we know it's wrong. I can't help myself. 'I love you, and I'm coming back for you.'

She groaned in delirium as he entered her. Ecstasy brought its own special light, banishing the darkness of the loft.

Joshua only just managed to reach the manor's hall in time to kiss or shake hands with members of the large group of staff and family (William Elphinstone was absent) who had come to wish him and Dahybi farewell. The horse-drawn carriage carried the two of them back to Colsterworth Station, where they boarded the train back to Boston along with the last batch of their cargo.

Melvyn Ducharme met them when they arrived back in the capital, and told them that over half of the cases were already up in the *Lady Macbeth*. Kenneth Kavanagh had used his influence with captains whose spaceplanes were being under-used for their own smaller cargos. It hadn't generated much goodwill, but the loading was well ahead of schedule. Using *Lady Mac*'s small spaceplane alone would have meant taking eleven days to boost all the cases into orbit.

They returned up to the starship straight away. When Joshua floated into his cabin, Sarha was waiting with the free-fall sex cage expanded, and a hungry smile in place. 'No bloody chance,' he told her, and curled up into a ball to sleep for a solid ten hours.

Even if he had been awake he had no reason to focus the *Lady Macbeth*'s sensors on departing starships. So he would never have seen that out of the twenty-seven thousand eight hundred and forty-six starships which had come to Norfolk, twenty-two of them experienced an alarming variety of severe mechanical and electrical malfunctions as they departed for their home planets.

19

Graeme Nicholson sat on his customary stool beside the bar in the Crashed Dumper, the one furthest away from the blaring audio block, and listened to Diego Sanigra, a crewman from the *Bryant*, complain about the way the ship had been treated by Colin Rexrew. The *Bryant* was a colonist-carrier starship that had arrived at Lalonde two days ago, and so far not one of its five and a half thousand colonists had been taken out of zero-tau. It was a ruinous state of affairs, Diego Sanigra claimed, the governor had no right to refuse the colonists disembarkation. And the energy expenditure for every extra hour they spent in orbit was costing a fortune. The line company would blame the crew, as they always did. His salary would suffer, his bonus would be non-existent, his promotion prospects would be reduced if not ruined.

Graeme Nicholson nodded sympathetically as his neural nanonics carefully stored the aggrieved ramblings in a memory cell. There wasn't much which could be used, but it was good background material. How the big conflict reached down into individual lives. The kind of thing he covered so well.

Graeme had been a reporter for fifty-two of his seventy-eight years. He reckoned no journalist didactic course could teach him anything new, not now. With his experience he should have been formatting didactic courses, except there wasn't a news company editor in existence who would want junior reporters corrupted to such an extent. In every sense he was a hack reporter, with an unerring knack of turning daily misfortune into spicy epic tragedy. He went for the human underbelly every time, highlighting the suffering and misery of little people who were trampled on, the ones who couldn't fight back against the massive uncaring forces of governments, bureaucracies, and companies. It was not from any particular moral indignation, he certainly didn't see himself as championing the underdog. He simply felt emotions laid raw made for a better story, with higher audience ratings. To some degree he had even begun to look like the victims he empathized with so well; it was partly reflexive, they were less suspicious of someone whose clothes never quite fitted, who had thick ruddy skin and watery eyes.

His brand of sensationalism went down well with the tabloid broadcasts, but by concentrating on the seedy aspects he knew best, building a reputation as a specialist of dross, he found himself being squeezed out of the more prestigious assignments; he hadn't covered a half-decent story for a decade. Over the last few years his neural nanonics had been used less for sensevise recording and more for running stimulant programs. Time Universe had given him a roving assignment eight years ago, pushing him off onto all the shabby little fringe jobs that no one else with a gram of seniority would cover. Anything to keep him out of a studio, or an editorial office where his contemporaries had graduated to.

Well, no more. The joke was on the office has-beens now. Graeme Nicholson was the only man on the ground, the one with the clout, the one with the kudos. Lalonde was going to earn him the awards he'd been denied all these years; then maybe after that one of those nice cosy office seats back home on Decatur.

He had been on Lalonde for three months to do a documentary-style report on the new world frontier, and gather general sensevise impressions and locations for the company library's memory cores. Then this wonderful calamity had fallen on Lalonde. Calamitous for the planet and its people, for Rexrew and the LDC career administration staff; but for Graeme Nicholson it was manna from heaven. *It* being war, or an Ivet rebellion, or a xenoc invasion, depending on who you were talking to. He had included accounts of all three theories on the fleks *Eurydice* had taken to Avon last week. But it was strange that after two and a half weeks the Governor had still made no official announcement as to exactly what was happening up in the Quallheim and Zamjan Counties.

'That executive assistant of Rexrew's, Terrance Smith, he's talking about sending us to another phase one colony world,' Diego Sanigra grumbled. He took another gulp of bitter from his tankard. 'As if that's going to be any help. What would you say if you were a colonist who paid passage for Lalonde and came out of zero-tau to find yourself on Liao-tung Wan? That's Chinese-ethnic, you know, they wouldn't like the EuroChristian-types we've got stored on board.'

'Is that where Terrance Smith suggested you take them?' Graeme Nicholson asked.

He gave a noncommittal grunt. 'Just giving you an example.'

'What about fuel reserves? Have you got enough He_3 and deuterium to get to another colony world and then return to Earth?'

Diego Sanigra started to answer. Graeme Nicholson wasn't listening too hard, he let his eyes wander round the hot crowded room. One of the spaceport shifts had just come off duty. At the moment there were few McBoeing flights. Only the three cargo ships orbiting Lalonde were being unloaded; the six colonist-carriers were waiting for Rexrew to decide what to do with their passenger complements. Most of the spaceport crews simply turned up at the start of each shift so they could keep claiming their pay.

I wonder what they feel about the end of overtime, Graeme asked himself. Might be another story there.

The Crashed Dumper certainly wasn't suffering from the troubles afflicting the rest of the city; this outlying district didn't protest or riot over Rexrew and the Ivets, it housed too many LDC worker families. There were a lot of people in tonight, drowning their sorrows. The waitresses were harried from one end of the long room to the other. The overhead fans were spinning fast, but made little impression on the heat.

Graeme heard the audio block falter, the singer's voice slowing, deepening to a weird bass rumble. It picked up again, turning the voice to a girlish soprano. The crowd clustered round started laughing, and one of them brought his fist down on it. After a moment the loud output returned to normal.

Graeme saw a tall man and a beautiful teenage girl walk past. Something about the man's face was familiar. The girl he recognized as one of the Crashed Dumper's waitresses, although tonight she was dressed in jeans and a plain cotton blouse. But the man – he was middle-aged with a neat beard and small pony-tail, wearing a smart leather jacket and ash-grey shorts, and he was very tall, almost like an Edenist.

The glass of lager dropped from Graeme's numb fingers. It hit the mayope planks and smashed, soaking his shoes and socks. 'Holy shit,' he croaked. The fright constricting his throat prevented the exclamation being more than a whisper.

'You all right?' Diego Sanigra asked, annoyed at being interrupted in mid-complaint.

He forced himself to look away from the couple. 'Yes,' he stammered. 'Yes, I'm fine.' Thank Christ nobody was paying any attention, if *he* had looked round . . . He reddened and bent down to pick up the shards of glass. When he straightened up the couple were already at the bar. Somehow they had cut straight through the crush.

Graeme ran a priority search program through his neural nanonics. Not that he could possibly be mistaken. The public figures file produced a visual image from a memory cell, recorded forty years ago. It matched perfectly.

Laton!

*

Lieutenant Jenny Harris twitched the reins, and the dun-coloured horse gave the big qualtook tree a wide berth. Her only previous experience with the animals was her didactic course and a week in the saddle five years ago during an ESA transportation training exercise back on Kulu. Now here she was, leading an expedition through one of the toughest stretches of jungle in the Juliffe tributary network and trying to avoid the attention of a possible military invasion force at the same time. It wasn't the best reintroduction to the equestrian art. She thought the horse could sense her discomfort, he was proving awkward. A mere three hours' riding and every muscle in her lower torso was crying for relief; her arms and shoulders were stiff; her backside had gone from soreness to numbness and finally settled for a progressive hot ache.

I wonder what all this bodily offensive is doing to my implants?

Her neural nanonics were running an extended sensory analysis program, enhancing peripheral vision and threshold audio inputs, and scrutinizing them for any signs of hidden hostiles. Electronic paranoia, basically.

There had been nothing remotely threatening, except for one sayce, since they left the *Isakore*, and the sayce hadn't fancied its chances against three horses.

She could hear Dean Folan and Will Danza plodding along behind her, and wondered how they were getting on with their horses. Having the two ESA G66 Division (Tactical Combat) troops backing her up was a dose of comfort stronger than any stimulant program could provide. She had been trained in general covert fieldwork, but they had virtually been bred for it, geneering and nanonic supplements combining to make them formidable fighting machines.

Dean Folan was in his mid-thirties, a quiet ebony-skinned man with the kind of subtle good looks most of the geneered enjoyed. He was only medium height, but his limbs were long and powerful, making his torso look almost stunted by comparison. It was the boosted muscles which did that, Jenny knew; his silicon-fibre-reinforced bones had been lengthened to give him more leverage, and more room for implants.

Will Danza fitted people's conception of a modern-day soldier; twenty-five, tall, broad, with long, sleek muscles. He was an old Prussian warrior genotype, blond, courteous, and unsmiling. There was an almost psychic essence of danger emanating from him; you didn't tangle with him in any tavern brawl no matter how drunk you were. Jenny suspected he didn't have a sense of humour; but then he'd seen action in covert missions three times in the last three years. She'd accessed his file when the jungle mission was being assembled; they had been tough assignments, one had earned him eight months in hospital being rebuilt from cloned organs, and an Emerald Star presented by the Duke of Salion, Alastair II's first cousin, and chairman of the Kulu Privy Council's security commission. He had never talked about it on the journey upriver.

The nature of the jungle started to change around them. Tightly packed bushy trees gave way to tall, slender trunks with a plume of feather-fronds thirty metres overhead. A solid blanket of creepers tangled the ground, rising up to hug the lower third of the tree trunks like solid conical encrustations. It increased their visibility dramatically, but the horses had to pick their hoofs up sharply. High above their heads vennals leapt between the trees in incredible bounds, streaking up the slim trunks to hide in the foliage at the top. Jenny couldn't see how they clung to the smooth bark.

After another forty minutes they came to a small stream. She dismounted in slow tender stages, and let her horse drink.

Away in the distance she could see a herd of danderil bounding away from the trickle of softly steaming water. White clouds were rolling in from the east. It would rain in an hour, she knew.

Dean Folan dismounted behind her, leaving Will Danza sitting on his horse, keeping watch from his elevated vantage point. All three of them were dressed identically, wearing a superstrength olive-green one-piece anti-projectile suit, covered with an outer insulation layer to diffuse beam weapons. The lightweight armour fitted perfectly, with an inner sponge layer to protect the skin. Thermal-shunt fibres woven into the fabric kept body temperature to a pre-set norm, which was a real blessing on Lalonde. If they were struck by a projectile slug the micro-valency generators around her waist would activate, solidifying the fabric instantly, distributing the impact, preventing the wearer's body from being pulped by automatic fire. (Jenny's only regret was that it didn't protect her from saddle sores.) The body armour was complemented by a shell-helmet which fitted with the same tight precision as the suit. It gave them all an insect appearance, with its wide goggle lenses and a small central V-shaped air-filter vent. The collar had a ring of optical sensors which could be accessed through neural nanonics, giving them a rear-view capability. They could even survive underwater for half an hour with its oxygen-recycling capacity.

The stream was muddy, its stones slimed with algae, none of which seemed to bother the horses. Jenny watched them lapping it up, and requested a drink from her shell-helmet. She sucked ice-cold orange juice from the nipple as she reviewed their location with help from the inertial guidance block.

When Dean and Will swapped position she datavised the armour suit's communications block to open a scrambled channel to Murphy Hewlett. The ESA team had split up from the Confederation Navy Marines after leaving the *Isakore*. Acting separately they thought they stood a better chance of intercepting one of the sequestrated colonists.

'We're eight kilometres from Oconto,' she said. 'No hostiles or locals encountered so far.'

'Same with us,' the marine lieutenant answered. 'We're six kilometres south of you, and there's nobody in this jungle but us chickens. If Oconto's supervisor did lead fifty people in pursuit of the Ivets, he didn't come this way. There's a small savannah which starts about fifteen kilometres away, there are about a hundred homesteads out there. We'll try them.'

Static warbled down the channel. Jenny automatically checked her electronic warfare suite, which reported zero activity. Must be atmospherics.

'OK. We're going to keep closing on the village and hope we find someone before we reach it,' she datavised.

'Roger. I suggest we make half-hourly check-ins from now on. There isn't . . .' His signal dissolved into rowdy static.

'Hell! Dean, Will, we're being jammed.'

Dean consulted his own electronic warfare block. 'No activity detected,' he said.

Jenny steadied her horse and put her foot in the stirrup, swinging a leg over the saddle. Will was mounting hastily beside her. All three of them scanned the surrounding jungle. Dean's horse snickered nervously. Jenny tugged at the reins to keep hers from twisting about.

'They're out there,' Will said in a level tone.

'Where?' Jenny asked.

'I don't know, but they're watching us. I can feel it. They don't like us.'

Jenny bit down on the obvious retort. Soldier superstitions were hardly appropriate right now, yet Will had more direct combat experience than her. A quick hardware status check showed that only the communications block was affected so far. Her electronic warfare block remained stubbornly silent.

'All right,' she said. 'The one thing we don't want to do is run into a whole bunch of them. The Edenists said they were most powerful in groups. Let's move out, and see if we can get outside this jamming zone. We ought to be able to move faster than them.'

'Which way?' Dean asked.

'I still want to try and reach the village. But I don't think a direct route is advisable now. We'll head south-west, and curve back towards Oconto. Any questions? No. Lead off then, Dean.'

They splashed over the stream, the horses seemingly eager to be on the move again. Will Danza had pulled his thermal induction pulse carbine from its saddle holster; now it was cradled in the crook of his right arm, pointing upwards. The datavised information from its targeting processor formed a quiet buzz at the back of his mind. He didn't even notice it at a conscious level, it was as much a part of the moment as the easy rhythm of the horse or the bright sunlight, making him whole.

He made up the rear of the little procession, constantly reviewing the sensors on the back of his shell-helmet. If anyone had asked him how he knew hostiles were nearby he would just have to shrug and say he couldn't explain. But instinct was pulling at him with the same irresistible impulse that pollen exerted on bees. They were here, and they were close. Whoever, or whatever, they were.

He strained round in the saddle, upping his retinal implants' resolution to their extreme. All he could see was the long thin black trunks and their verdant cone island bases, outlines wavering in the heat and unstable magnification factor.

A movement.

The TIP carbine was discharging before he even thought about it, blue target graphics sliding across his vision field like neon cell doors as he dropped the barrel in a single smooth arc. A red circle intersected the central grid square and his neural nanonics triggered a five-hundred-shot fan pattern.

The section of jungle in the central blue square sparkled

with orange motes as the induction pulses stabbed against the wood and foliage. It lasted for two seconds.

'Down!' Will datavised. 'Hostiles four o'clock.'

He was already slithering off the horse, feet landing solidly on the broad triangular creeper leaves. Dean and Jenny obeyed automatically, rolling from their saddles to land crouched, thermal induction pulse carbines held ready. The three of them turned smoothly, each covering a different section of jungle.

'What was it?' Jenny asked.

'Two of them, I think.' Will quickly replayed the memory. It was like a dense black shadow dashing out from behind one of the trees, then it split into two. That was when he fired, and the image jolted. But the black shapes refused to clarify, no matter how many discrimination programs he ran. Definitely too big for sayce, though. And they were moving towards him, using the shaggy treebases for cover.

He felt a glow of admiration, they were good.

'What now?' he datavised. Nobody responded. 'What now?' he asked loudly.

'Reconnaissance and evaluation,' said Jenny, who had just realized even short-range datavises were being disrupted. 'We're still not out of that jamming effect.'

There was a silent orange flash above her. The top third of the tree ten metres to her left began to topple over, hinging on a section of trunk that was mostly charred splinters. Just as it reached the horizontal, the rich green plumes at the top caught on fire. They spluttered briefly, belching out a ring of blue-grey smoke, then the fire really caught. Two vennals leapt out, squeaking in pain, their hides badly scorched. Before the whole length of wood crashed down, the plumes were burning with a ferocity which matched the sun.

The horses reared up, whinnying alarm. They were pulled down by boosted muscles.

Jenny realized the animals were rapidly becoming a liability as she clung on to hers. Her neural nanonics reported the suit sensors had detected a maser beam striking the tree, which was what snapped it. But there was no detectable follow-up energy strike to account for the ignition.

Dean's sensors had also detected the maser beam. He fired a fifty-shot barrage back along the line.

The fallen tree's tip fizzled out. All that was left was a tapering core of wood and a heap of ash. Blackened ground creepers smouldered in a wide circle around it.

'What the hell did that?' Dean asked.

'No data,' Jenny answered. 'But it isn't going to be healthy.'

Globules of vivid white fire raced up the trunks of several nearby trees like some bizarre astral liquid. Bark shrivelled and peeled off in long strips behind them, the naked wood below roaring like a blast furnace as it caught alight. The flames redoubled in vehemence. Jenny, Will, and Dean were surrounded by twelve huge torches of brilliant fire.

Jenny's retinal implants struggled to cope with the vast photon flood. Her horse reared up again, fighting her, neck sweeping from side to side in an effort to make her let go, forelegs cycling dangerously close to her head. She could see the terror in its eyes. Foam sprayed out of its mouth to splatter her suit.

'Save the equipment,' she shouted. 'We can't hang on to the horses in this.'

Will heard the order as his horse began bucking, its hind legs kicking imaginary foes. He drove his fist into its head, catching it between the eyes, and it froze for a second in stunned surprise, then slowly buckled, collapsing onto the ground. One of the blazing trees gave a single creak of warning and keeled over. It slammed down on the horse's back, breaking ribs and legs, searing its way into the flesh. Oily smoke billowed up. Will darted forward, and tugged at the saddle straps. His suit datavised an amber alert to his neural nanonics as the heat impact of the flames gusted against the outer layer.

Balls of orange flame were hurtling through the air above

him, spitting greasy black liquids: vennals, fleeing and dying as their roosts were incinerated. Small withered bodies hit the ground all around, some of them moving feebly.

Dean and Jenny were still struggling with their horses, filling the air with confused curses. Will's suit sounded a preliminary caution that thermal input was reaching the limit of the handling capacity. He felt the saddle strap give, and jumped backwards, hugging the equipment packs. The suit's outer dissipator layer glowed cherry red as it radiated away the excess heat, and wisps of smoke rose from around his feet.

More trees were falling as the flame consumed the wood at a fantastic rate. For one nasty moment they were completely penned in by a rippling fence made up from solid sheets of that strange lethal white flame.

Jenny salvaged her equipment packs from her horse and let go of the bridle. It raced away blindly, only to veer to one side as another burning tree fell in its path. One of the fiery vennals landed on its back, and it charged straight into the flames, screaming piteously. She watched it tumble over. It twitched a couple of times, trying to regain its feet, then flopped down limply.

By now a ring of ground a hundred metres in diameter was burning, leaving just a small patch at the centre untouched. The three of them grouped together at the middle as the last two trees went down. Now there was only the ground creepers burning, sending up forked yellow flames and heavy blue smoke.

Jenny pulled her packs towards her and ran a systems status check. Not good. The guidance block was putting out erratic data, and the suit's laser rangefinder return was dubious. The hostiles' electronic warfare field was growing stronger. And according to her external temperature sensors, if they hadn't been wearing suits with a thermal-dispersal layer they would have been roasted alive by now.

She gripped the TIP carbine tighter. 'As soon as the flames

die down I want a sweep-scorch pattern laid down out to four hundred metres. Fight fire with fire. They've shown us what they can do, now it's our turn.'

'All right,' Will muttered happily.

Rummaging round in her packs for one of the spherical heavy duty power cells she was carrying, she plugged its coiled cable into the butt of her carbine. The other two were doing the same thing.

'Ready?' she asked. The flames were only a couple of metres high now, the air above them swarmed with ash flakes, blotting out the sun. 'Go.'

They stood, shoulders together, forming a triangle. The TIP carbines blazed, sending out two hundred and fifty invisible deadly shots every second. Targeting processors coordinated the sweep parameters, overlapping their fields of fire. Neural nanonics ordered their muscles to move in precise increments, controlling the direction of the energy blitz.

A ripple of destruction roared out across the already cremated land, then started to chew its way into the vegetation beyond. Dazzling orange stars scintillated on tree trunks and creepers, desiccating then igniting the wood and tangled cords of vine. The initial ripple became a fully-fledged hurricane firestorm, exacerbated by the relentless push of the carbines.

'Burn, you mothers,' Will yelled jubilantly. 'Burn!'

The entire jungle was on fire around them, an avalanche of flames racing outward. Once again the vennals were dying in their hundreds, plunging out of their igneous trees right into the conflagration.

Dean's neural nanonics reported that his carbine was stuttering whenever he wiped the barrel across a certain coordinate. He brought it back and held it. The shot rate declined to five a second.

'Shit. Jenny, they're locking their electronic warfare into my carbine targeting processor.'

'Let me have the section,' she said.

He datavised the coordinates over – no problem with communication any more. When she aimed her own TIP carbine along the line its output dropped off almost immediately, but her suit blocks were coming back on-line. 'Jeeze, that electronic warfare of theirs is the weirdest.'

'Want me to try?' Will asked.

'No. Finish the sweep-scorch first, we'll deal with them in a minute.' She turned back to her section. Watching the invincible rampart of flame cascade over the jungle had sent her heart racing wildly. The awe that she could command such fearsome power was soaring through her veins, taking her to a dangerous high. She had to load a suppression order into her neural nanonics, which restricted the release of natural adrenalin sharply. The sweep pattern was completed, and her flesh cooled. But she still felt supreme.

A holocaust of flame raged a hundred and twenty metres away.

'OK, they've given their position away,' she said. 'Dean, Will: gaussguns, please. Fragmentation and electron-explosive rounds, forty–sixty ratio.'

Will grinned inside his shell-helmet as he bent down to retrieve the heavy-duty weapon. The gaussgun barrel was dark grey in colour, a metre and a half long. It weighed thirty kilograms. He picked it up as if it was made from polystyrene, checked the feed tube was connected to the bulky magazine box at his feet, datavised in the ratio, and aimed it out through the shimmering flames. Dean deployed its twin beside him.

Jenny had been probing through the flames, using her TIP carbine to determine the extent and location of the dead zone simply by recording where it cut out. She datavised the coordinates over to Dean and Will: an oval area fifty metres long, roughly three hundred metres away.

'One hundred and fifty per cent coverage,' she said. 'Fire.' Even she had to marvel at how the two men handled the weapons. The gaussguns hurled ten rounds a second, leaving the muzzle at five times the speed of sound. Yet they hardly moved as the recoil hammered at them, swaying gently from side to side. She doubted her boosted muscles could cope.

Away beyond the first rank of flames, a wide island of intact jungle erupted in violent pyrotechnics. Explosions five metres above the ground slammed out hundreds of thousands of slender crystallized carbon shrapnel blades. They scythed through the air at supersonic velocity, sharp as scalpels, stronger than diamond. Those trees which had survived the firestorm disintegrated, shredded instantly by the rabid aerial swarm. Confetti fragments blew apart like a dandelion cloud in a tornado.

The rest of the shrapnel impacted on the ground, slicing through the tangled mat of creepers, blades stabbing themselves thirty to forty centimetres down into the loose moist loam. They never had a chance to settle. EE projectiles rained down, detonating in hard vicious gouts of ionic flame. Plumes of black loam jetted up high into the ash-dimmed sky. The whole area was ruptured by steep-walled two-metre craters, undulating like a sea swell.

Looking down on the desolation, it was hard to believe even an insect could have survived, let alone any large animal.

The three ESA agents stared through the ebbing flames at the dark cyclone of loam particles and wood splinters obscuring the sun.

Jenny's neural nanonics ran a series of diagnostic programs through her suit equipment blocks. 'That electronic warfare field has shut down,' she said. There was a faint quaver to her voice as she contemplated the destructive forces she had unleashed. 'Looks like we got them.'

'And everybody knows it,' Dean said flatly. 'They must be able to see this fire halfway back to Durringham. The hostiles are going to come swarming to investigate.'

'You're right,' she said.

'They're still there,' Will pronounced.

'What?!' Dean said. 'You've cracked. Nothing could survive

that kind of barrage, not even an army assault mechanoid. We blasted those bastards to hell.'

'I'm telling you; they're still out there,' Will insisted. He sounded nervous. Not like him at all.

His edginess crept in through the comfortable insulation of Jenny's suit. Listening to him she was half convinced herself. 'If someone survived, that's good,' she said. 'I still want that captive for Hiltch. Let's move out. We'd have to investigate anyway. And we can't stay here waiting for them to regroup.'

They quickly distributed the remaining ammunition and power cells from their packs, along with basic survival gear. Each of them kept their TIP carbine; Will and Dean shouldered the gaussguns without a word of protest.

Jenny led off at a fast trot across the smouldering remnants of jungle, towards the area they had bombarded with the gaussguns. She felt terribly exposed. The fire had died down, it had nothing left to burn. Away in the distance they could see a few sporadic flames licking at bushes and knots of creeper. They were in the middle of a clearing nearly a kilometre across, the only segment of colour. Everything was black, the remnants of creepers underfoot, tapering ten-metre spikes of trees devoured by natural flames (as opposed to the white stuff the hostiles threw at them), cooked vennals that lay scattered everywhere, other smaller animals, a savagely contorted corpse of one of the horses, even the air was leaden with a seam of fine dusky motes.

She datavised her communication block to open a scrambled channel to Murphy Hewlett. To her surprise, he responded straight away.

'God, Jenny, what's happened? We couldn't raise you, then we saw that bloody great fire-fight. Are you all OK?'

'We're in one piece, but we lost the horses. I think we did some damage to the hostiles.'

'*Some* damage?'

'Yeah. Murphy, watch out for a kind of white fire. So far

they've only used it to set the vegetation alight, but our sensors can't pick up how they direct the bloody stuff. It just comes at you out of nowhere. But they hit you with an electronic warfare field first. My advice is that if your electronics start to go, then lay down a scorch pattern immediately. Flush them away.'

'Christ. What the hell are we up against? First that paddle-boat illusion, now undetectable weapons.'

'I don't know. Not yet, but I'm going to find out.' She was surprised at her own determination.

'Do you need assistance? It's a long walk back to the boat.'

'Negative. I don't think we should join up. Two groups still have a better chance to achieve our objective than one, nothing has changed that.'

'OK, but we're here if it gets too tough.'

'Thanks. Listen, Murphy, I'm not aiming to stay in this jungle after dark. Hell, we can't even see them coming at us in the daytime.'

'Now that sounds like the first piece of sensible advice you've given today.'

She referred to her neural nanonics. 'There are another seven hours of daylight left. I suggest we try and rendezvous back at the *Isakore* in six hours from now. If we haven't captured a hostile, or found out what the hell is going down around here, we can review the situation then.'

'I concur.'

'Jenny,' Dean called with soft urgency.

'Call you back,' she told Murphy.

They had reached the edge of the barrage zone. Not even the tree stumps had survived here. Craters overlapped, producing a crumpled landscape of unstable cones and holes; crooked brown roots poked up into the sky from most of the denuded soil slopes. Long strands of steam, like airborne worms, wound slowly around the crumbling protrusions, sliding into the holes to pool at the bottom.

Over on the far side she watched three men emerging from

the craters, scrambling sluggishly for solid ground. They helped each other along, wriggling on their bellies when the slippery loam proved impossible to stand on.

Jenny watched their progress in the same kind of bewildered daze which had engulfed her as the fantastical paddle-steamer sailed down the river.

The men reached level ground sixty metres away from the ESA team, and stood up. Two were recognizable colonist types: dungarees, thick cotton work shirts, and woolly beards. The third was dressed in some kind of antique khaki uniform: baggy trousers, calves bound up by strips of yellowish cloth; a brown leather belt round his waist sporting a polished pistol holster; a hemispherical metal hat with a five-centimetre rim.

They couldn't possibly have survived, Jenny found herself thinking, yet here they were. For one wild second she wondered if the electronic warfare field had won, and was feeding the hallucination directly into her neural nanonics.

The two groups stared at each other for over half a minute.

Jenny's electronic warfare block reported a build-up of static in the short-range datavise band. It broke the spell. 'OK, let's go get them,' she said.

They started to circle round the edge of the barrage zone. The three men watched them silently.

'Do you want all three?' Will asked.

'No, just one. The soldier must be equipped with the most powerful systems if he can create that kind of chameleon effect. I'd like him if we can manage it.'

'I thought chameleon suits were supposed to blend in,' Dean muttered.

'I'm not even sure we're seeing men,' Will added. 'Maybe the xenocs are disguising themselves. Remember the paddle-steamer.'

Jenny ordered her suit's laser rangefinder to scan the soldier; its return should reveal the true outline to an accuracy of less than half a millimetre. The blue beam stabbed out from the side of her shell-helmet. But instead of sweeping the soldier, it broke apart a couple of metres in front of him, forming a turquoise haze. After a second the rangefinder module shut down. Her neural nanonics reported the whole unit was inoperative.

'Did you see that?' she asked. They had covered about a third of the distance round the barrage zone.

'I saw it,' Will said brusquely. 'It's a xenoc. Why else would it want to hide its shape?'

The distortion in the datavise band began to increase. Jenny saw the soldier start to unbuckle his holster.

'Stop!' she commanded, her voice booming out of the communication block's external speaker. 'The three of you are under arrest. Put your hands on your head, and don't move.'

All three men turned fractionally, focusing on her. Her neural nanonics began to report malfunctions in half of her suit's electronics.

'Screw it! We must break them up, even three of them are too powerful. Will, one round EE, five metres in front of them.'

'That's too close,' Dean said tensely as Will brought the gaussgun to bear. 'You'll kill them.'

'They survived the first barrage,' Jenny said tonelessly.

Will fired. A fountain of loam spurted up into the air, accompanied by a bright blue-white sphere of flame. The blast-wave flattened some of the nearby piles of soil.

Jenny's neural nanonics reported the electronics coming back on-line. The loam subsided, revealing the three men standing firm. A faint whistle was insinuating itself into the datavise band; her neural nanonics couldn't filter it out.

'One metre,' she snapped. 'Fire.'

The explosion sent them spinning, tottering about for balance. One fell to his knees. For the first time there was a reaction; one of the two farmer-types started snarling and shouting. His face above the beard was black, whether from loam or a flashburn she couldn't tell.

'Keep firing, keep them apart,' Jenny called to Will. 'Come on, run.'

Explosions bloomed around the three men. Will was using the gaussgun the way riot police employed a water cannon, harrying the men as they tried to come together. Blasts that would rip a human to pieces barely affected them, at the most they tumbled backwards to sprawl on the ground. He was tempted to land a round straight on one, just to see what it would do. They scared him.

Jenny's feet pounded over the scorched creepers. The packs and the TIP carbine weighed nothing as her boosted muscles powered up and took the full load. Will was doing a good job, one of the men had been separated from the other two. He was the farmer-type who had shouted earlier. She brought her TIP carbine round and aimed it at his left ankle, neural nanonics allowing her to compensate for the vigorous motion of her body. If they could disable him, they could chase off or kill the other two. A severed cauterized foot wasn't lethal.

Her neural nanonics triggered a single shot. She actually saw the induction pulse. A complete impossibility, her mind insisted. But a slender violet line materialized in the air ahead of her. It struck the farmer's ankle and splashed apart, sending luminous tendrils clawing up his leg. He yelled wildly, and tumbled headlong.

'Dean, subdue him,' she ordered. 'I want him in one piece. Will and I will fend off the other two.' Her carbine's targeting circle slithered round on the soldier as she stopped running. He was taking aim with his revolver. They both fired.

Jenny saw luminous purple tapeworms writhing across the neatly pressed khaki uniform. The soldier began to jerk about as if he was being electrocuted. Then the bullet struck her with the force of a gaussgun's kinetic round. Her suit hardened instantly, and she found herself somersaulting chaotically, grey sky and black land streaking past in a confused blur. There was an instant's silence. She landed hard, and her suit unfroze. She was rolling, arms and legs jolting the ground sharply.

The gaussgun was roaring three metres away. Will was standing his ground, feet apart to brace himself, swivelling from the hip to send EE rounds chasing after each of the men.

Jenny scrambled to her feet. The soldier and one of the farmers were fifty metres away. They were facing Will, but retreating in juddering steps from the onslaught of projectiles. Somehow she had hung on to the TIP carbine, and now she lined it up. Radiant purple lines shivered across the soldier once more. He threw up his hands, as if he was physically warding off the intense energy pulses. Then both he and the farmer looked at each other. Something must have been said, because they both turned and ran towards the rim of the jungle eighty metres behind them.

Dean Folan dropped his gaussgun and backpack, which allowed him to cover the last thirty metres in two and a half seconds. In that time he fired his TIP carbine twice. The beams tore into glaring purple streamers which knocked the farmer down into the soft loam. With his opponent out for the count, Dean took the last five metres in a flying tackle, landing straight on top of him. The weight of his own body and the suit and his equipment should have been enough to finish it. But the man started to rise straight away. Dean gave a surprised yelp as he was lifted right off the ground, and went for a stranglehold, only to find a hand clamping round each wrist pulling his arms apart. He fell onto his back as the farmer regained his feet. A booted foot kicked him in the side of his ribs. His suit hardened, and he was thrown onto his belly by the force of the blow. The farmer must be a construct made entirely out of boosted muscle! His neural nanonics combat routine programs went into primary mode. He swung the TIP carbine round, and another vicious kick actually cracked the casing. But he lashed out with his free arm, knocking the farmer's other leg out from under him. The farmer went down heavily on his backside.

Somewhere in the distance the gaussgun was thumping out a stream of EE projectiles.

Both of them struggled into a semi-crouch, then launched themselves. Once again, Dean found himself losing. The farmer's impact sent him reeling backwards, fighting to keep his feet. Arms with the strength of a hydraulic ram grappled at him. His neural nanonics reviewed tactical options, and decided his physical strength was dangerously inferior. He let himself sway backwards, taking the farmer with him. Then his leg came straight up, slamming into the man's stomach. A classic judo throw. The farmer arched through the air, snarling in rage. Dean drew his twenty-centimetre fission blade and twisted round just in time to meet the man as he charged. The blade sliced down, aiming for the meat of the right forearm. It struck, cutting through the cloth sleeve. But the yellow glow faded, and it skated across the skin, scoring a shallow gash.

Dean stared at the narrow wound, partly numbed, partly shocked. Will was right, it must be a xenoc. As he watched, the skin on the forearm rippled, closing the gash. The farmer laughed evilly, teeth showing white in his grubby face. He started to walk towards Dean, arms coming up menacingly. Dean stepped inside the embrace, and ordered his suit to solidify below his shoulders. The farmer's arms closed round him in a bear hug. Composite fibres, stiffened by the suit's integral valency generators, creaked ominously as the farmer's arms squeezed. A couple of equipment blocks snapped. Instinct made Dean switch off the fission blade's power, leaving a dull black blade with wickedly sharp edges. The hostiles seemed capable of controlling and subverting any kind of electrical circuit – maybe if the knife wasn't powered up . . . He pressed the tip up into the base of the farmer's jaw.

'You can heal wounds on your arm. But can you heal your

brain as it's sliced in half?' The blade was shoved up a fraction until a bead of blood welled out around the tip. 'Wanna try?'

The farmer hissed in animosity. He eased off his grip around Dean's chest.

'Now keep very still,' Dean said as he unlocked his suit. 'Because I'm very nervous, and an accident can happen easily and quickly.'

'You'll suffer,' the farmer said malevolently. 'You'll suffer longer than you have to. I promise.'

Dean took a pace to one side, the blade remaining poised on the man's neck. 'You speak English, do you? Where do you come from?'

'Here, I come from here, warrior man. Just like you.'

'I don't come from here.'

'We all do. And you're going to stay here. For ever, warrior man. You're never going to die, not now. Eternity in purgatory is that which awaits you. Do you like the sound of that? That's what's going to happen to you.'

Dean saw Will walk behind the farmer, and touch the muzzle of the gaussgun to the back of his skull.

'I've got him,' said Will. 'Hey, xenoc man, one bad move, one bad word, and you are countryside.' He laughed. 'You got that?'

The farmer's dirty lips curled up in a sneer.

'He's got it,' Dean said.

Jenny came over and studied the strange tableau. The farmer looked perfectly ordinary apart from his arrogance. She thought of his two comrades that had run into the jungle, the hundreds – thousands – more just like him out there. Maybe he had a right to be arrogant.

'What's your name?' she asked.

The farmer's eyes darted towards her. 'Kingsford Garrigan. What's yours?'

'Cuff him,' Jenny told Dean. 'We'll take him back to the *Isakore.* You're going for a long trip, Kingsford Garrigan. All the way to Kulu.' She thought she saw a flash of surprise in his eyes. 'And you'd better hope your friends don't try and interfere with us. I don't know what you are, but if you attempt to screw up our electronics again, or if we have to cut and run, the first thing we drop is you. And drop you we will, from a very great height.'

The farmer spat casually on her foot. Will jabbed him with the gaussgun.

Jenny opened a communication channel to the geosynchronous platform, and connected into the Kulu Embassy dumper.

'We've got you one of the hostiles,' she datavised to Ralph Hiltch. 'And when I say hostile, I'm not kidding.'

'Fantastic. Well done, Jenny. Now get back here soonest. I've got our transport to Ombey arranged. The ESA office there has the facilities for a total personality debrief.'

'I wouldn't bank on it working,' she said. 'He's immune to a TIP shot.'

'Repeat, please.'

'I said the TIP carbine doesn't hurt him, the energy pulse just breaks apart. Only physical weapons seem to have any effect. At the moment we've got him subdued with a gaussgun. He's also stronger than the G66 boys, a lot stronger.'

There was a long silence. 'Is he human?' Ralph Hiltch asked.

'He looks human. But I don't see how he can be. If you want my opinion, I'd guess at some kind of super bitek android. It's got to be a xenoc bitek, and a pretty advanced bitek at that.'

'Christ Almighty. Datavise a full-spectrum image over, please. I'll run it through some analysis programs.'

'Sure thing.'

Dean had the man's hands behind his back to slide a zipcuff over his wrists. It was a figure-of-eight band of polyminium with a latch buckle at the centre. Jenny watched Dean tighten the pewter-coloured loops; no electronic lock, thank heavens, just simple mechanics.

She ordered her neural nanonics to encode the retinal pixels, and datavised the complete image over to the embassy. Infrared followed, then a spectrographic print.

Dean ejected the power magazine from his broken TIP carbine and handed it to Jenny along with the spares, then recovered his gaussgun. With Will covering their prisoner, they started walking back towards the *Isakore* at a brisk pace. Jenny aimed them off at a slight tangent, taking them quickly back into the jungle. She still felt too exposed in the firestorm clearing.

'Jenny,' Ralph called after a minute. 'What did the hostile say his name was?'

'Kingsford Garrigan,' she replied.

'He's lying. And you're wrong about him being a xenoc android, too. I've run a search program through our records. He's a colonist from Aberdale called Gerald Skibbow.'

*

'It is a wet, humid night here in Durringham, as they always are on this poor benighted planet. The heat clogs my throat and my skin sweats as though I have caught a fever. But still I feel cold inside, a coldness that grips the very cells of my heart.' Was that a bit too purple? Oh well, the studio can always edit it out.

Graeme Nicholson was squatting on aching ankles in the deepest shadows cast by one of the spaceport's big hangars. It was drizzling hard, and his cheap synthetic suit was clinging to his flabby body. Despite the warmth of the water he really was shivering, the fat rolls of his beer belly were shaking the same way they did when he laughed.

Fifty metres away a defeated yellow light shone from an office in the spaceport's single-storey administration block. It was the only occupied office, the rest had shut long ago. With his retinal implants straining, Graeme could just make out Laton, Marie Skibbow, and two other men through the grimed glass. One of them was Emlyn Hermon, the *Yaku*'s second-in-command, who had met Marie and Laton in the Crashed Dumper. He didn't know the fourth, but he must work for the spaceport administration in some capacity.

He just wished he could listen to whatever deal they were making. But his boosted hearing was only effective inside a fifteen-metre radius. And no prize in the universe would make him creep any closer to Laton. Fifty metres was quite close enough, thank you.

'I have followed the arch-diabolist here from the city. And nothing I have seen has given me the slightest hope for the future. His interest in the spaceport can only indicate he is ready to move on. His work on Lalonde is complete. Violence and anarchy reign beyond the city. What monstrous curse he has let loose is beyond my imagination; but each new day brings darker stories down the river, sucking away the citizens' hope. Fear is his real weapon, and he possesses it in abundance.'

Marie held out a small object Graeme took to be a Jovian Bank credit disk. The spaceport administration official proffered its counterpart.

'The alliance has been formed. His plan advances another notch. And I cannot believe it will bring anything other than disaster upon us. Four decades has not reduced the fear. What has he achieved in those four decades? I ask myself this question time and again. The only answer must be: evil. He has perfected evil.'

The office light went out. Graeme emerged from his sheltered recess, and walked along the side of the hangar until he could see the administration block's main entrance. The drizzle was worsening, becoming rain. His suit felt cool, and unbearably clammy, restricting his movements. A prodigious amount of water was running off the ezystak-panel roof overhead, splattering onto the chippings round his soaking feet. Despite the physical discomfort and nagging consternation at Laton's presence, he felt an excitement that had been absent for years. This was *real* journalism: the million to one break, the hazardous follow-up, getting the story at any cost. Those shits back in the editing offices could never handle this, safe paunchy career creatures; and they would know it too. His real victory.

Laton and his cohorts had all emerged into the bleak night wearing cagoules against the weather. They had their backs to him, heading for the flight line where the indistinct outlines of the parked McBoeings formed windows into an even graver darkness. Laton (betrayed by his height) had his arm around Marie.

'The beauty and the beast, look. What can she see in him? For Marie is just a simple colony girl, proud and decent, loving her new planet, working long hours like all of this city's residents. She shares the planetary ethic of her neighbours, striving hard to achieve a better world for her children. Yet somehow she has stumbled. A warning that none of us is immune to the attraction of the dark side of human nature. I look at her, and I think: there but for the grace of God go I.'

Halfway along the McBoeings was a smaller spaceplane. It was obviously Laton's goal. Bright light shone out of its open airlock, casting a grey smear across the ground. A couple of maintenance crew personnel were tending the mobile support units under its nose.

Graeme sneaked up to the big undercarriage bogies of a McBoeing forty metres away, and crouched down below the broad tyres. The spaceplane was one of the small swing-wing VTOL marques starships carried in their hangars. He switched his retinal implants to full magnification and scanned the fuselage. Sure enough, the name *Yaku* was printed on the low angular tail.

Some kind of argument was going on at the foot of the steps leading up to the airlock. The administration official was talking heatedly to another man wearing a cagoule with the LDC emblem on the arm. Both of them were waving their arms around. Laton, Marie, and Emlyn Hermon stood to one side, watching patiently.

'The last obstacle has been reached. It is ironic to consider that all that stands between Laton and the Confederation is one immigration official. One man between us and the prospect of galactic tragedy.'

The argument ended. A Jovian Bank disk was offered.

'Can we blame him? Should we blame him? It is a foul night. He has a family which looks to him for support. And how harmless it is, a few hundred fuseodollars to avert his eyes for one swift minute. Money which can buy food for his children in these troubled times. Money which can make life that fraction easier. How many of us would do the same? How many? Would you?' Nice touch that, involve people.

Laton and Marie went up the battered aluminium stairs, followed by a furtive Emlyn Hermon. The administration official was talking to the two ground crew.

Just as he reached the airlock hatch, Laton turned, the hood of his cagoule falling back to reveal his face in full. Handsome, well proportioned, a hint of aristocracy: Edenist sophistication, but without the cultural heritage, that essential counterbalance which made the affinity gene carriers human. It looked as though he was staring straight at Graeme Nicholson. He laughed with a debonair raffishness. Mocking.

Everyone in the Confederation who accessed the sensevise in the weeks which followed experienced the old journalist's heart *thud* inside his ribs. All of a sudden breath was very hard to come by, stalling in his throat.

That pause, the derision. It wasn't an accident, chance. Laton knew he was there, and didn't care. Graeme was too far beneath him to care.

'He is going now. Free to roam the stars. Should I have tried to stop him? Put myself up against a man who can make entire worlds tremble at the mention of his name? If you think I should, then I am sorry. For I am so frightened of him. And I do not believe I would have made any difference, not against his strength. He would still be on his way.'

The airlock hatch shut. The two ground crew scuttled about, hunched against the rain, unplugging the thick dark-yellow ribbed hoses from their underbelly hatches. Compressors wound up, kicking out micro-squalls of the heavy rain. Their reedy sibilance built steadily until the spaceplane rocked on its undercarriage. It lifted into the murky sky.

'My duty now is to warn you all. I will do what I can, what I must, to ensure this sensevise reaches you. So that you know. He is coming. It is you who must fight him. I wish you luck. Those of us left here have our own battle against the calamity he has unleashed out in the hinterlands. It is not one for which we are well prepared, this is not a planet of epic heroes, just ordinary people like yourselves. As always, the burden falls upon those least able to shoulder it; for a terrible night has fallen on Lalonde, and I do not think we will see the dawn again.'

The spaceplane swooped up in a sharp climb, its wings beginning to fold back. It arrowed into the low, bulging cloud base, and disappeared from view.

*

A dozen paltry fires spluttered and hissed on the broad road outside the Governor's dumper, the flames devouring fence posts and broken carts that had been snatched for fuel. Little knots of protesters clustered round them under the watchful eyes of the sheriffs and deputies circling the carbotanium cone. An uneasy truce had broken out after the anger and violence of the day. The earlier barrages of stones and bottles had been answered each time by cortical-jamming impulses from the sheriffs. Thankfully the protesters had refrained from using any real weapons today. Now the chanting had stopped. The naked menace in a thousand throats screaming in unison wasn't something Colin Rexrew was accustomed to dealing with. He could never make out what they had been chanting for these last few days; he thought they weren't entirely sure themselves apart from wanting the turmoil to end. Well, so did he. Very badly.

Each time Colin Rexrew looked out of his window he could see some new plume of smoke rising from the vista of dark rooftops. Tonight the horizon was dotted with three or four fierce orange flares as buildings burned. If it wasn't for the rain and humidity Durringham would have been reduced to a single giant firestorm days ago.

And the deteriorating civic situation in the city wasn't even his real problem.

When Candace Elford came into the office Colin Rexrew was behind his desk as always, gazing vacantly at the window strip and the luckless city outside. Terrance Smith gave her a fast, expressive grimace, and they both sat down.

'I'm afraid I have now effectively lost control over a third of the city,' she started.

It was the nightly situation briefing. Or the nightly crisis meeting, depending on how cynical Colin felt. The intensifying pressures seemed to make it hard to concentrate at the very times he needed his full mental resources. He would have given a lot to be able to run a stimulant program through his neural nanonics, or even escape into a MF album for a few hours like he used to in his adolescence. It would have made the strain a little easier to bear.

Not even his neural nanonics with their top of the range managerial programs were much help. There were too many unaccountable – downright weird – factors cropping up to apply standard responses. Had there ever been a stage one colony governor who had lost all control of his planet? The memory cells held no record of any.

What a way to get into the history books.

'Is it the invaders?' he asked.

'No, as far as we can make out they are still some distance away. What we're dealing with here is mainly opportunist looting, and some organized grabs for power. Nothing political, but there are some strong criminal gangs who have been quick to take advantage of the unrest. I'd point out that most of the districts my sheriffs have been excluded from are on the south-eastern side of town. Those are the newest and poorest; in other words the most disaffected to begin with. The heart of the city, and more importantly the merchant and industrial sectors, remain stable. If anything, the older residents resent the lawlessness. I'm looking to recruit more deputies from them.'

'How long before you can start to regain control of the south-east districts?' Terrance Smith asked.

'At the moment I'm just looking to contain the trouble,' Candace Elford said.

'You mean you can't?'

'I didn't say that, but it isn't going to be easy. The gangs have captured two dumpers, and their fusion generators. We can't afford to damage them, and they know that. I lost a lot of good people in Ozark and on the *Swithland* fiasco. Plus we have to deal with the transient colonists. They seem to be the biggest problem right now; they're holed up in the docks and I can't shift them. There are barricades across every access route and there's a lot of wanton destruction and looting going on. So half the port is currently unusable, which has antagonized the boat captains; and I have to deploy a lot of people to keep an eye on them.'

'Starve them out,' Colin said.

She nodded reluctantly. 'That's one option. About the least expensive at the moment. But it will take time, there was a lot of food stored in those warehouses.'

'The merchants won't like that,' Terrance Smith said.

'Screw the merchants,' Colin said. 'I'm sorry about the transients' gear being looted, but that doesn't excuse this kind of behaviour. We can help them eventually, but not if they're going to hamper every effort with petty-minded belligerence.'

'Some families lost everything—'

'Tough shit! *We* are in danger of losing an entire planet of twenty million people. My priority is to the majority.'

'Yes, sir.'

There were times when Colin just felt like telling his aide: here's my seat, you take over, you with your situation summaries and cautiously formulated response suggestions. Instead, the Governor walked over to the drinks cabinet and searched through the bottles for a decent chilled white wine, and to hell with the chief sheriff's disapproval.

'Can we defend Durringham from the invaders?' he asked quietly as he flipped the neck seal and poured out a glass.

'If we had enough time to prepare, and you declared martial law, and if we had enough weapons.'

'Yes or no?'

Candace Elford watched the glass in the Governor's hand. It was shaking quite badly, the wine nearly spilling. 'I don't think so,' she said. 'Whatever it is that's out there, it's strong, well armed, and well organized. The Confederation Navy office thinks they are using some kind of sequestration technology to turn colonists into a slave army. Faced with that, I don't think we really stand much of a chance.'

'Sequestration nanonics,' Colin mumbled as he sank back into his chair. 'Dear God, who are these invaders? Xenocs? Some exiled group from another planet?'

'I'm not one hundred per cent certain,' she said. 'But my satellite image analysis people found these this morning. I think it may throw a little light on the situation.' She datavised an order into the office's computer. The wall-screens lit up, showing a blank section of jungle fifty kilometres west of Ozark.

The satellite had passed over in the middle of the afternoon, giving a clear bright image. Trees were compacted so tightly the jungle looked like an unbroken emerald plain. Five perfectly straight black lines began to probe across the green expanse, as if the talons of a huge invisible claw were being scored down the screen. The satellite cameras zoomed in on the head of one line, and Colin Rexrew saw trees being bulldozed into the ground. A big ten-wheeled vehicle rolled into view, grey metal glinting dully, a black bubble-cab protruding from a flat upper surface. It had a blunt wedge-shaped front that smashed through trunks without the slightest resistance. Viscous sprays of red-brown mud were being flung up by its rear wheels, caking the metal bodywork. There were another three identical vehicles following it along the track of shattered vegetation it was ripping through the jungle.

'We positively identified them as Dhyaan DLA404 land-cruisers; they are made on Varzquez. Or I should say, were made. The Dhyaan company stopped producing that particular model over twenty years ago.'

Colin Rexrew datavised a search order into the office computer. 'The LDC never brought any to Lalonde.'

'That's right. The invaders brought them. What you're seeing is the first definite proof that it is an external force behind all this. And they're heading straight towards Durringham.'

'Dear God.' He put his empty wineglass down on the desk, and stared at the screens. The enemy had a physical form. After weeks of helpless wrestling with an elusive, possibly imaginary, foe, it was finally real; but a reason for the invasion, logical or otherwise, was impossible to devise.

Colin Rexrew gathered up what was left of his old determination and resolve. Something tangible gave his psyche a fragment of very welcome confidence. He accessed the one neural nanonics program he had thought he would never have to use, strategic military procedure, and put it into primary mode. 'We have to stop deluding ourselves we can handle this on our own. I need combat troops backed up with real firepower. I'm going to blow these invaders right off my planet. We only need to locate the headquarters. Kill the brain and the body is irrelevant. We can see about removing the sequestration nanonics from people later.'

'The LDC board will need convincing,' Terrance Smith said. 'It won't be easy.'

'They will be told afterwards,' Colin said. 'You've seen those landcruisers. They'll be here in a week. We must move fast. After all, it's the board's interest I'm ultimately protecting; without Lalonde there will be no LDC.'

'Where can you get troops from without going through the board?' Terrance asked.

'The same place they would ultimately get them from. We buy them on a short-term contract.'

'Mercenaries?' the aide asked in surprised alarm.

'Yes. Candace, where's the nearest port we can get enough in reasonable numbers? I want armed ships, too; they can provide the fire-power back-up from low orbit. It's expensive, but cheaper than buying in strategic-defence platforms. They can also prevent any more of the invader's ships from landing.'

The chief sheriff gave him a long, testing stare. 'Tranquillity,' she said eventually. 'It's a base for blackhawks and the so called independent traders. Where you find the ships, you find the people. Ione Saldana might be young, but she's not stupid, she won't throw out the undesirables. The plutocrats who live in the habitat have too many uses for them.'

'Good,' Colin said decisively. 'Terrance, cancel all work on Kenyon as of now. We'll use the money earmarked for mining its main chamber. It always was bloody premature.'

'Yes, sir.'

'After that, you can take one of the colonist-carrier ships to Tranquillity and supervise the recruitment.'

'Me?'

'You.' Colin watched the protest form and die unvoiced on the younger man's lips. 'I want at least four thousand general troops to re-establish order in Durringham and the immediate counties. And I also want teams of combat scouts for the Quallheim Counties. They are going to have to be the best, because they are going to be assigned the search and destroy mission in the deep jungle. Once they locate the invader's home base they can zero it for the starships' weapons. We can pound it from orbit.'

'What sort of armaments are we looking for on these starships?' Terrance asked guardedly.

'Masers, X-ray lasers, particle beams, thermal inducers, kinetic harpoons, and atmospheric penetration nukes – straight fusion, I don't want any radioactives clogging the environment.' He caught the aide's eye. 'And no antimatter, not under any circumstances.'

Terrance gave a cautious grin. 'Thank you.'

'What ships have we got available in orbit right now?'

'That was something I was going to mention,' Terrance said. 'The *Yaku* left its parking orbit this evening. It jumped outsystem.'

'So?'

'Firstly, it was a cargo ship, and only fifty per cent of its cargo had been unloaded. And cargo is the one thing we are still bringing down to the spaceport. It had no reason to leave. Secondly, it had no permission to leave. There was no prior contact with our Civil Flight Control Office. The only reason I found out it had left was because Kelven Solanki got in touch with me to query it. When I checked with flight control to ask why they hadn't informed us about it, they didn't even know *Yaku* had lifted from parking orbit. It turns out someone had erased the traffic-monitor satellite data from the spaceport computer.'

'Why?' Candace asked. 'It's not as if we have anything that could prevent them from leaving.'

'No,' Colin said slowly. 'But we could have asked another ship to track it. Without the monitor satellite data we don't know its jump coordinate, we don't know where it went.'

'Solanki will have a copy,' Terrance said. 'Ralph Hiltch too, I suspect. If he was pressed.'

'That's all we need, another bloody puzzle,' Colin said. 'See what you can find out,' he told Candace.

'Yes, sir.'

'Back to the original question. What other ships are available?'

Terrance consulted his neural nanonics. 'There are eight left in orbit; three cargo ships, the rest colonist-carriers. And we're due for another two colonist-carriers this week, as well as a Tyrathca merchant ship sometime before the end of the month to check on their farmers.'

'Don't remind me,' Colin said sorely.

'I think the *Gemal* would be the best bet. That only has forty Ivets left in zero-tau. They can be transferred to the *Tachad* or the *Martijn*, both of them have spare zero-tau pods. It wouldn't take more than a few hours.'

'Get onto it tonight,' Colin said. 'And, Candace, that means the spaceport has to be defended at all costs. We have to be able get those troops down in the McBoeings. There's nowhere else for them to land. The scouts can use VTOLs to take them direct to the Quallheim Counties, but the rest will have to use the McBoeings.'

'Yes, sir, I am aware of that.'

'Good, start organizing for it, then. Terrance, I want you back here in ten days. Give me one month, and I'll have these bastards begging me for surrender terms.'

*

The gaussgun's fragmentation round hit the man full in his chest, and penetrated to a depth of ten centimetres, already starting to crater the flesh, impact shock pulverizing the entire mass of organs held within his rib cage to mucilaginous jelly. Then it exploded, silicone shrapnel reducing the entire body to a spherical cascade of scarlet cells.

Will Danza grunted in acute satisfaction. 'Try rebuilding

yourself out of that, my xenoc friend,' he told the slippery red leaves.

The hostiles were impervious to almost any major injury. The little ESA team had found that out long ago. Gaping lacerations, severed limbs – they barely slowed the hostiles down as they emerged from the thick bushes to harass the party. Wounds closed up, bones knitted in seconds. Lieutenant Jenny Harris might insist on calling the prisoner a sequestrated colonist, but Will knew what it really was. Xenoc monster. And its friends wanted it back.

Twice in the last three kilometres Jenny Harris had been forced to order a sweep-scorch pattern. The things had been throwing that eerie white fire of theirs. Once a ball had struck Dean Folan's arm, burning through the suit's energy diffusion layer as if it wasn't there. The medical nanonic package they'd put on his arm looked like a tube of translucent green exo-skeleton.

'Hey!' Dean yelled. 'Get back here!'

Jenny Harris looked round. Gerald Skibbow was running into the jungle, both arms pumping wildly. 'Shitfire,' she muttered. He had been zipcuffed a moment ago. Dean was lining up his gaussgun.

'Mine,' she called. Her blue TIP carbine targeting graphic centred on a tree five metres ahead of the running man; the shots punched straight through the slim trunk, puffs of steam and flame squirted out. Gerald Skibbow swerved frantically as the tree toppled across his path. Another volley of shots and the jungle around him caught light. One final shot on his knee knocked his legs from under him.

The three of them trotted over where he lay sprawled in the crushed muddy vines.

'What happened?' Jenny asked. She had assigned Dean to guard the prisoner. Unless a gaussgun was in his back the whole time, Gerald Skibbow felt free to cause as much trouble as possible.

Dean held up the zipcuff. It was unbroken. 'I saw a hostile,' he said. 'I only turned away for a second.'

'OK,' Jenny sighed. 'I wasn't blaming you.' She bent over Gerald Skibbow, whose grimed face was grinning up at them, and jerked his right arm up. There was a narrow red line braceleting the wrist, an old scar. 'Very clever,' she told him wearily. 'Next time, I'll order Dean to slice your legs off below the knee. We'll see how long it takes you to grow a new pair.'

Gerald Skibbow laughed. 'You don't have that much time available, Madame bitch.'

She straightened up. Her spine creaked and groaned as if she was a hundred and fifty. She felt older. The fire was crackling loudly in the surrounding bushes, flames inhibited by the green twigs.

It was another four kilometres back to the *Isakore*, and the jungle was becoming progressively thicker. Vines here wrapped the trees like major arteries, creating a solid hurdle of verdant mesh between the trunks. Visibility was down to less than twenty-five metres, and that was with enhanced senses.

We're not going to make it, she realized.

They'd been expending gaussgun ammunition at a heavy rate ever since they set off. They had to, nothing else worked against the hostiles. Even the two TIP carbines were down to forty per cent of their power reserve.

'Get him up,' she ordered curtly.

Will clamped an arm round Gerald Skibbow's shoulder and hauled him to his feet.

White fire burst out of the ground around Jenny's feet, damp loam tearing open to spit out dazzling globules which spiralled up her legs like a liquid repelled by gravity. She screamed at the pain as her skin blistered and burned inside the anti-projectile suit. Her neural nanonics isolated the nerve strands, eliminating the raw impulses with analgesic blocks.

Will and Dean started firing their gaussguns at random into the blank impassive jungle in the vain hope of hitting a hostile.

EE projectiles mashed the nearby trees. Shreds of sappy vegetation whirred through the air, forming a loose curtain behind which vivid explosions boomed.

The viscid beads of white fire evaporated as they reached Jenny's hips. She clenched her teeth against the solid ache from her legs. Frightened by the damage her neural nanonics were shielding her from. Frightened she couldn't walk. The medical program was choking up her mind with red symbols, all of them clustered around schematics of her legs like bees round honey. She felt faint.

'We can help you,' silver voices whispered in chorus.

'What?' she asked, disorientated. She sat on the lumpy ground to take the strain off her legs. Her trembling muscles had been about to dump her there anyway.

'You all right, Jenny?' Dean asked. He was standing with the gaussgun pointing threateningly into the broken trees.

'Did you say something?'

'Yes, are you OK?'

'I . . .' I'm hearing things. 'We've got to get out of here.'

'First thing you have to do is get a medical nanonic package on those legs. I think there's enough,' he said, uncertainty clouding his voice.

Jenny knew there wasn't, not to get her patched up for a hike of four kilometres under combat conditions. The neural nanonics prognosis wasn't good; the program was activating her endocrine implant, sending a potent stew of chemicals into her bloodstream. 'No,' she said forcefully. 'We're not going to get back to the boat like this.'

'We ain't going to leave you,' Will said hotly.

She grinned unseen inside her shell-helmet. 'Believe me, I wasn't going to ask you to. Even if the medical nanonics can get me walking, we don't have enough ordnance left to blast our way back to the *Isakore* from here.'

'What then?' Will demanded.

Jenny requested a channel to Murphy Hewlett. Static crashed

into her neural nanonics, that eerie whistling. 'Shitfire. I can't get the marines.' She hated the idea of abandoning them.

'I think I can see why,' Dean said. He pointed at the treetops. 'Smoke, and plenty of it. South of here. Some distance by the look of it. They must have laid down a sweep-scorch pattern. They got troubles, too.'

Jenny couldn't see any smoke. Even the leaves at the top of the trees had turned a barren grey. Her vision was tunnelling. A physiological-status request showed her endocrines were barely coping with the flayed legs. 'Sling me your medical nanonics,' she said.

'Right.' Will fired six EE rounds into the jungle then hurriedly detached his backpack and tossed it over. He was back watching the abused trees before it reached her.

She ordered her communications block to open a channel to Ralph Hiltch, then turned the backpack seal's catch and fumbled around inside. Instead of the subliminal digital bleep that signalled the block was interfacing with the geosynchronous platform, all she heard was a monotonous buzz.

'Will, Dean, open a channel to the geosync platform, maybe a combined broadcast will get through.' She picked up her TIP carbine, and pointed it at Gerald Skibbow, who was squatting sullenly beside a swath of vines four metres away. 'And you, if I think you are part of the jamming effort, I will start a little experiment to see exactly how much thermal energy you can fight off. You got me, Mr Skibbow? Is this message getting through the electronic warfare barrier?'

The communication block reported the channel to the embassy was open.

'What's happening?' Ralph Hiltch asked.

'Trouble—' Jenny broke off to hiss loudly. The medical nanonic package was contracting round her left leg, it felt as though a thousand acid-tipped needles were jabbing into the roasted gouges as the furry inner surface knitted with her flesh. She had to order the neural nanonics to block all the nerve impulses. Her legs went completely numb, lacking even the heavy vacuum feeling of chemical anaesthetics. 'Boss, I hope that fall-back scheme of yours works. Because we need it pretty badly. Now, boss.'

'OK, Jenny. I'm putting it in motion. ETA fifteen minutes, can you hang on that long?'

'No problem,' Will said. He sounded indecently cheerful.

'Are you secure where you are?' Ralph asked.

'Our security situation wouldn't change if we moved,' Jenny told him, marvelling at her own understatement.

'OK, I've got your coordinates. Use your TIP carbines to scorch a clearing at least fifty metres across. I'll need it for a landing-zone.'

'Yes, sir.'

'I'm on my way.'

Jenny swapped her TIP carbine for Dean's gaussgun. By sitting with her back to a tree she could keep it pointed at Gerald Skibbow. The two G66 troops began slashing at the jungle with their TIP carbines.

*

The captain of the *Ekwan* was a middle-aged woman in a blue ship-suit, with the kind of robust, lanky figure that suggested she was from a space-adapted geneered family. The AV projector showed her floating ten centimetres above the acceleration couch in her compact cabin. 'How did you know we were leaving orbit?' she asked. Her voice was slightly distorted by a curious whistle that was coming through the relay from the LDC's geosynchronous communication platform.

Graeme Nicholson smiled thinly at her puzzled tone. He diverted his eyes from the projection for a second. On the other side of Durringham spaceport's flight control centre Langly Bradburn rolled his eyes and turned back to his monitor console.

'I have a contact in the Kulu Embassy,' Graeme said, returning to the projection.

'This isn't a commercial flight,' the captain said, a fair amount of resentment bubbling into her voice.

'I know.' Graeme had heard of the Kulu Ambassador throwing his authority around and virtually commandeering the Kulu-registered colonist-carrier. A situation which became even more interesting when he discovered from Langly that it was Cathal Fitzgerald who was in orbit making sure the captain did as she was told. Cathal Fitzgerald was one of Ralph Hiltch's people. And now, as Graeme looked through the flight control centre's window, he could see a queue of people standing on the nearby hangar apron, shoulders angled against the rain as they embarked on a passenger McBoeing BDA-9008. The entire embassy staff and dependants. 'But it is only one memory flek,' he said winningly. 'And the Time Universe office will pay a substantial bonus when you hand it in to them, I can assure you of that.'

'I haven't been told where we're going yet.'

'We have offices in every Confederation system. And it would be a personal favour,' Graeme emphasized.

There was a pause as the captain worked out that she would receive the entire carriage fee herself. 'Very well, Mr Nicholson. Give it to the McBoeing pilot. I'll meet him when he docks.'

'Thank you, Captain, pleasure doing business with you.'

'I thought you sent a flek out with the *Gemal* this morning?' Langly observed as Graeme switched off the metre-high projection pillar.

'I did, old boy. Just covering my back.'

'Are people really going to be interested in a riot on Lalonde? Nobody even knows this planet even exists.'

'They will. Oh, indeed they will.'

*

Rain slammed against the little spaceplane's fuselage as it dived out through the bottom of the clouds. It made a fast rattling sound against the tough silicolithium-composite skin. Individual drops burst into streaks of steam, vaporized by the friction heat of the craft's Mach five velocity.

Looking over the pilot's shoulder Ralph Hiltch saw the jungle blurring past below. It was grey-green, sprinkled by flexuous strands of mist. Up ahead was a broad band of brighter grey where the clouds ended, and getting broader.

'Ninety seconds,' Kieron Syson, the pilot, shouted over the noise.

A loud metallic whirring filled the small cabin as the wings began to swing forward. The spaceplane pitched up at a sharp angle, and the noise of the rain impacts increased until talking was impossible. Deceleration hit three gees, forcing Ralph back into one of the cabin's six plastic seats.

Sunlight burst into the cabin with a fast rainbow flash. The sound of the rain vanished. They levelled out as their speed dropped to subsonic.

'We'll need a complete structure fatigue check after this,' Kieron Syson complained. 'Nobody flies supersonic through rain, half the leading edges have abraded down to their safety margins.'

'Don't worry about it,' Ralph told him. 'It'll be paid for.' He turned to check with Cathal Fitzgerald. Both of them were wearing the same model of olive green one-piece anti-projectile suits as Jenny and the two G66 troops. It had been a long time since Ralph had dressed for combat, a cool tension was compressing his body inside and out.

'Looks like your people have been having themselves a wild time,' Kieron said.

Away in the southern distance a vast column of dense soot-laden smoke was rising high into the pale blue sky, a ring of flames dancing round its base. Ten kilometres to the east a kilometre-wide ebony crater had been burned out of the trees.

The spaceplane banked sharply, variable-camber wings twisting elastically to circle it round a third, smaller, blackened clearing. This one was only a hundred metres across. Small licks of flame fluttered from the fallen trees around the perimeter, and thin blue smoke formed a mushroom dome of haze. There was a small green island of withered vegetation in the exact centre.

'That's them,' Kieron said as the spaceplane's guidance systems locked on to the signal from Jenny Harris's communication block.

Four people were standing on the crush of vine leaves and grass. As Ralph watched, one of them fired a gaussgun into the jungle.

'Down and grab them,' he told Kieron. 'And make it fast.'

Kieron whistled through closed teeth. 'Why me, Lord?' he muttered stoically.

Ralph heard the fan nozzles rotate to the vertical, and the undercarriage clunked as it unfolded. They were swinging round the black scorch zone in decreasing circles. He ordered his communication block to open a local channel to Jenny Harris.

'We're coming down in fifty seconds,' he told her. 'Get ready to run.'

The cabin airlock's outer hatch hinged open, showing him the fuselage shield sliding back. A blast of hot, moist air hurtled in, along with the howl of the compressors.

'Faster, boss,' Jenny shouted, her voice raw. 'We've only got thirty gaussgun rounds left. Once we stop this suppression fire they'll hit the spaceplane with everything they've got.'

A fine black powder was churning through the cabin like a sable sandstorm. Environment-contamination warnings sounded above the racket from the compressors, amber lights winked frantically on the forward bulkhead.

'Land us now,' Ralph ordered Kieron. 'Cathal, give them some covering fire, scorch that jungle.'

The compressor noise changed, becoming strident. Cathal Fitzgerald moved into the airlock, bracing himself against the outer hatch rim. He began to swing his TIP carbine in long arcs. A sheet of flame lashed the darkening sky around the edge of the clearing.

'Ten seconds,' Kieron said. 'I'll get as close to them as I can.'

Ash rose up in a cyclonic blizzard as the compressor nozzle efflux splashed against the ground. Visibility was reduced drastically. An orange glow from the flames fluoresced dimly on one side of the spaceplane.

Jenny Harris watched the craft touch and bounce, then settle. She could just make out the name *Ekwan* on the narrow, angled tail. Ralph Hiltch and Cathal Fitzgerald were two indistinct figures hanging on to the side of the open airlock. One of them was waving madly; she guessed it was Ralph.

Will Danza fired the last of his gaussgun rounds, and dropped the big weapon. 'Empty,' he muttered in disgust. His TIP carbine came up, and he started adding to the flames.

'Come on, move!' Ralph's datavise was tangled with discordant static.

'Get Skibbow in,' Jenny ordered Dean and Will. 'I'll cover our backs.' She brought her TIP carbine to bear on the soot-occluded jungle, putting her back to the spaceplane.

Will and Dean grabbed Gerald Skibbow and started to drag him towards the sleek little craft.

Jenny limped after them, trailing by several metres. The last heavy duty power cell banged against her side, its energy level down to seven per cent. She reduced the carbine's rate of fire, and fired off fifteen shots blindly. Grunting and shuffling sounds were coming down her headset, relayed by the suit's audio pick-ups. She flicked to her rear optical sensors for a moment and saw Gerald Skibbow putting up a struggle as four people tried to haul him through the spaceplane's airlock hatch. Ralph Hiltch slammed his carbine butt into Gerald's face. Blood poured out of the colonist's broken nose, dazing him long enough for Will to shove his legs through.

Jenny switched her attention back to her forward view. Five figures were solidifying out of the swirl of ash. They were stooped humanoids; like big apes, she thought. Blue targeting graphics closed like a noose around one. She fired, sending it flailing backwards.

A ball of white fire raced out of the gloom, too fast to duck. It splashed over her TIP carbine, intensifying. The weapon casing distorted, buckling as though it was made of soft wax. She couldn't free her fingers from the grip; it had melted round them. Her throat voiced a desolate cry as the terrible fire bit hard into her knuckles. The flaming remnants of the carbine fell to the ground. She held up her hand; there were no fingers or thumb, only the smoking stump of her palm. Her cry turned to a wail, and she tripped over a root protruding from the loam. The woody strand coiled fluidly round her ankle like a malicious serpent. Four dark figures loomed closer, a fifth lumbering up behind.

She twisted round on the ground. The spaceplane was twelve metres away. Gerald Skibbow was lying on the floor of the airlock with two suited figures on top of him pinning him down. He looked straight at Jenny, a gleeful sneer on his blooded lips. The root tightened its vicelike grip, cutting into her ankle. He was doing it, she knew that then.

'Lift,' she datavised. 'Ralph, for God's sake lift. Get him to Ombey.'

'Jenny!'

'Make it mean something.'

One of the dark figures landed on her. It was a man, strangely corpulent, bulky without being fat; thick matted hair covered his entire body. Then she couldn't see anything; his belly was pressed against her shell-helmet.

That quiet chorus spoke to her again. 'There is no need for fear,' it said. 'Let us help you.'

Another of the man-things gripped her knees, his buttocks squashing her damaged legs into the ground. The front of her anti-projectile suit was ripped open. It was difficult to breathe now.

'Jenny! Oh Christ, I can't shoot, they're on top of her.'

'Lift!' she begged. 'Just lift.'

All the neural nanonics analgesic blocks seemed to have collapsed. The pain from her legs and hand was debilitating, crushing her thoughts. More ripping sounds penetrated her dimming universe. She felt hot, damp air gust across her bared crotch.

'We can stop it,' the chorus told her. 'We can save you. Let us in.' There was a pressure against her thoughts, like a warm dry wind blowing through her skull.

'Go to hell,' she moaned. She sent one final diamond-hard thought needling into her faltering neural nanonics, a kamikaze code. The order was transferred into the high-density power cell, shorting it out. She wondered if there would be enough energy left for an explosion big enough to engulf all the man-things.

There was.

*

The *Ekwan* fell around Lalonde's equator, six hundred kilometres above the brown and ochre streaks of the deserts which littered the continent of Sarell. With its five windmill-sail thermo-dump panels extended from its central section, the colonist-carrier was rotating slowly about its drive axis, completing one revolution every twenty minutes. A passenger McBoeing BDA-9008 was docked to an airlock tube on its forward hull.

It was a tranquil scene, starship and spaceplane sliding silently over Sarell's rocky shores and out across the deepening blues of the ocean. Thousands of kilometres ahead, the terminator cast a black veil over half of Amarisk. Every few minutes a puff of smoky yellow vapour would flash out of a vernier nozzle between the starship's thermo-dump panels, gone in an eyeblink.

Such nonchalant technological prowess created an effect which totally belied the spectacle inside the airlock tube, where children cried and threw up and red-faced parents cursed as they fended off the obnoxious sticky globules. Nobody had been given time to prepare for the departure; all they had brought with them was clothes and valuable items stuffed hastily into shoulder-bags. Children hadn't even been given anti-nausea drugs. The embassy staffers shouted back and forth in angry tones, disguising both relief at leaving Lalonde and disgust at the flying vomit. But the *Ekwan*'s crew were used to the behaviour of planet dwellers; they floated around with hand-held suction sanitizers, and cajoled the reluctant children towards one of the five big zero-tau compartments.

Captain Farrah Montgomery watched the picture projected from an AV pillar on the bridge command console, indifferent to the suffering. She'd seen it all before, a thousand times over. 'Are you going to tell me where we are heading?' she asked the man strapped into her executive officer's acceleration couch. 'I can start plotting our course vector. Might save some time.'

'Ombey,' said Sir Asquith Parish, Kulu's Ambassador to Lalonde.

'You're the boss,' she said acidly.

'I don't like this any more than you.'

'We've got three thousand colonists left in zero-tau. What are you going to tell them when we get to the Principality?'

'I've no idea. Though once they hear what's actually happening down on the surface I doubt they'll complain.'

Captain Montgomery thought about the flek in her breast pocket with a glimmer of guilt. The reports they'd been receiving from Durringham over the past week were pretty garbled, too. Maybe they were better off leaving. At least she could transfer the responsibility to the ambassador when the line company started asking questions.

'How soon before we can leave orbit?' Sir Asquith asked.

'As soon as Kieron gets back. You know, you had no right to send him on a flight like that.'

'We can wait for two more orbits.'

'I'm not leaving without my pilot.'

'If they're not airborne by then, you don't have a pilot any more.'

She turned her head to look at him. 'Just what is going on down there?'

'I wish I knew, Captain. But I can tell you I'm bloody glad we're leaving.'

The McBoeing undocked as the *Ekwan* moved into the penumbra. Its pilot fired the orbital manoeuvring rockets, and it dropped away into an elliptical orbit which would intercept Lalonde's upper atmosphere. *Ekwan* started her preflight checks, testing the ion thrusters, priming the fusion tubes. The crew scurried through the life-support capsules, securing loose fittings and general rubbish.

'Got him,' the navigation officer called out.

Captain Montgomery datavised the flight computer, requesting the external sensor images.

A long contrail of blue-white plasma stretched out across Amarisk's darkened eastern side, its star-head racing over the seaboard mountains. Already fifty kilometres high and rising. Bright enough to send a backwash of lame phosphorescent light skating over the snow-capped peaks.

Ekwan's flight computer acknowledged a communication channel opening.

Ralph Hiltch watched the hyped-up Kieron Syson start to relax once he could datavise the starship again. It should have been something for Ralph to be thankful about, too, communications had been impossible in the aftermath of the landing. Instead he treated it like a non-event, he expected nothing less than the communications block to work. They were *owed* functional circuitry.

Environment-contamination warning lights were still winking amber, though the pilot had shut off the cabin's audio alarm. The air was dry and calciferous, scratching the back of Ralph's throat. Gravity was falling off as they soared ever higher above the ocean, curving up to rendezvous with the big colonist-carrier. The prolonged bass roar of the reaction rockets was reducing.

The air they breathed was bad enough, but the human atmosphere in the spaceplane's confined cabin was murderous. Gerald Skibbow sat at the rear of the cabin, shrunk down into his plastic seat, a zipcuff restraining each wrist against the armrests, his hands white knuckled as he gripped the cushioning. He had been subdued since the airlock hatch closed. But then Will and Dean were looking hard for an excuse to rip his head off. Jenny's death had been fast (thank God) but very, very messy.

Ralph knew he should be reviewing the memory of the ape-analogue creatures, gaining strategically critical information on the threat they faced, but he just couldn't bring himself to do it. Let the ESA office on Ombey study the memory sequence, they wouldn't be so emotionally involved. Jenny had been a damn good officer, and a friend.

The spaceplane's reaction drive cut off. Free fall left Ralph's stomach rising up through his chest. He accessed a nausea-suppression program and quickly activated it.

Huddled in his chair, Gerald Skibbow began to tremble as the forked strands of his filthy, blood-soaked beard waved about in front of his still-bleeding nose.

Ekwan's hangar was a cylindrical chamber ribbed by metal struts; the walls were composed of shadows and crinkled silver blankets. The spaceplane, wings fully retracted, eased its squashed-bullet nose through the open doors into the waiting clamp ring. Actuators slid catches into a circle of load sockets behind the radar dome, and the craft was drawn inside.

Three of *Ekwan*'s security personnel, experts at handling troublesome Ivets in free fall, swam into the cabin, coughing at the ash dust which filled the air.

Will took the zipcuffs off Gerald Skibbow. 'Run, why don't you,' he said silkily.

Gerald Skibbow gave him a contemptuous glance, which turned to outright alarm as he rose into the air. Hands clawed frantically for a grip on the cabin ceiling. He wound up clutching a grab loop for dear life.

The grinning security personnel closed in.

'Just tow him the whole way,' Ralph told them. 'And you, Skibbow, don't cause any trouble. We'll be right behind, and we're armed.'

'You can't use TIP carbines in the ship,' one of the security men protested.

'Oh, really? Try me.'

Gerald Skibbow reluctantly let go of the grab loop, and let the men tug him along by his arms. The eight-strong group drifted out into the tubular corridor connecting the hangar to one of the life-support capsules.

Sir Asquith Parish was waiting outside the zero-tau compartment, a stikpad holding his feet in place. He gave Gerald Skibbow a distasteful look. 'You lost Jenny Harris for him?'

'Yes, sir,' Will said through clamped teeth.

Sir Asquith recoiled.

'Whatever sequestrated him has several ancillary energy-manipulation functions,' Ralph explained. 'He is lethal; one on one, he's better than any of us.'

The ambassador gave Gerald Skibbow a fast reappraisal. Light strips circling the corridor outside the zero-tau compartment hatch flickered and dimmed.

'Stop it,' Dean growled. He jabbed his TIP carbine into the small of Skibbow's back.

The light strips came up to full strength again.

Gerald Skibbow laughed jauntily at the shaken ambassador as the security men shoved him through the hatch. Ralph Hiltch cocked an ironic eyebrow, then followed them in.

The zero-tau compartment was a big sphere, sliced into sections by mesh decking that was only three metres apart. It didn't look finished; it was poorly lit, with bare metal girders and kilometres of power cable stuck to every surface. The sarcophagus pods formed long silent ranks, their upper surface a blank void. Most of them were activated, holding the colonists who had gambled their future on conquering Lalonde.

Gerald Skibbow was manoeuvred to an open pod just inside the hatchway. He glanced around the compartment, his head turning in fractured movements to take in the compartment. The security men holding him felt his muscles tensing.

'Don't even think of it,' one said.

He was propelled firmly towards the waiting pod.

'No,' he said.

'Get in,' Ralph told him impatiently.

'No. Not that. Please. I'll be good, I'll behave.'

'Get in.'

'No.'

One of the security men anchored himself to the decking grid with a toe clip, and tugged him down.

'No!' He gripped both sides of the open pod, his features stone-carved with determination. 'I won't!' he shouted.

'In!'

'No.'

All three security men were pushing and shoving at him. Gerald Skibbow strove against them. Will tucked a leg round a nearby girder, and smacked the butt of his TIP carbine against Gerald Skibbow's left hand. There was a crunch as the bones broke.

He howled, but managed to keep hold. His fingers turned purple, the skin undulating. 'No!'

The carbine came down again. Ralph put his hands flat against the decking above, and stood on Gerald Skibbow's back, knees straining, trying to thrust him down into the pod.

Gerald Skibbow's broken hand slipped a couple of centimetres, leaving a red smear. 'Stop this, stop this.' Rivulets of white light began to shiver across his torso.

Ralph felt as though his own spine was going to snap, the force his boosted muscles were exerting against his skeleton was tremendous. The soles of his feet were tingling sharply, the worms of white light coiling round his ankles. 'Dean, switch the pod on the second he's in.'

'Sir.'

The hand slipped again. Gerald Skibbow started a high-pitched animal wailing. Will hammered away at his left elbow. Firefly sparks streaked back up the carbine every time it hit, as though he was striking flint.

'Get in, you bastard,' one of the security men shouted, nearly purple from the effort, face shrivelled like a rubber mask.

Gerald Skibbow gave way, the arm Will had hammered on finally losing hold. He crashed down into the bottom of the pod with an *oof* of air punched out through his open mouth. Ralph cried out at the shock of the jolt that was transmitted back up his cramped legs. The curving lid of the pod began to slide into place, and he bent his knees frantically, lifting his legs out of the way.

'No!' Gerald Skibbow shouted. He had begun to glow like a hologram profile, rainbow colours shining bright in the compartment's gloom. His voice was cut off by the lid sliding into place, and it locked with a satisfying mechanical *click.* There was a muffled thud of a fist striking the composite.

'Where's the bloody zero-tau?' Will said. 'Where is it?'

The lid of the pod hadn't changed, there was no sign of the slippery black field effect. Gerald Skibbow was pounding away on the inside with the fervour of a man buried alive.

'It's on,' Dean shouted hoarsely from the operator's control panel. 'Christ, it's on, it's drawing power.'

Ralph stared at the sarcophagus in desperation. Work, he pleaded silently, come on fuck you, work! Jenny died for this.

'Switch on, you shit!' Will screamed at it.

Gerald Skibbow stopped punching the side of the pod. A black emptiness irised over the lid.

Will let out a sob of exhausted breath.

Ralph realized he was clinging weakly to one of the girders, the real fear had been that Gerald Skibbow would break out. 'Tell the captain we're ready,' he said in a drained voice. 'I want to get him to Ombey as quickly as we can.'

20

The event horizon around *Villeneuve's Revenge* dissolved the instant the starship expanded out to its full forty-eight-metre size. Solar wind and emaciated light from New California's distant sun fell on the dark silicon hull which its disappearance exposed. Short-range combat sensors slid out of their jump recesses with smooth animosity, metallic black tumours inset with circular gold-mirror lenses. They scoured a volume of space five hundred kilometres across, hungry for a specific shape.

Data streams from the sensors sparkled through Erick Thakrar's mind, a rigid symbolic language written in monochromic light. Cursors chased through the vast constantly reconfiguring displays, closing in on an explicit set of values like circling photonic-sculpture vultures. Radiation, mass, and laser returns slotted neatly into their parameter definition.

The *Krystal Moon* materialized out of the fluttering binary fractals, hanging in space two hundred and sixty kilometres away. An inter-planetary cargo ship, eighty metres long; a cylindrical life-support capsule at one end, silver-foil-cloaked tanks and dull-red fusion-drive tube clustered at the other. Thermo-dump panels formed a ruff collar on the outside of the environmental-engineering deck just below the life-support capsule; communication dishes jutted out of a grid tower on the front of it. The ship's mid-section was a hexagonal gantry supporting five rings of standard cargo-pods, some of them plugged into the environmental deck via thick cables and hoses.

A slender twenty-five-metre flame of hazy blue plasma burnt steadily from the fusion tube, accelerating the *Krystal Moon* at an unvarying sixtieth of a gee. It had departed Tehama asteroid five days ago with its cargo of industrial machinery and micro-fusion generators, bound for the Ukiah asteroid settlement in the outer asteroid belt Dana, which orbited beyond the gas giant Sacramento. Of the star's three asteroid belts, Dana was the least populated; traffic this far out was thin. *Krystal Moon*'s sole link to civilization (and navy protection) was its microwave communication beam, focused on Ukiah, three hundred and twenty million kilometres ahead.

Erick's neural nanonics reported that pattern lock was complete. He commanded the X-ray lasers to fire.

Two hundred and fifty kilometres away, the *Krystal Moon*'s microwave dishes burst apart into a swirl of aluminium snowflakes. A long brown scar appeared on the forward hull of the life-support capsule.

God, I hope no one was in the cabin below.

Erick tried to push that thought right back to the bottom of his mind. Straying out of character, even for a second, could quite easily cost him his life. They'd drilled that into him enough times back at the academy. There was even a behavioural consistency program loaded into his neural nanonics to catch any wildly inaccurate reactions. But flinches and sudden gasps could be equally damning.

The *Villeneuve's Revenge* triggered its fusion drive, and accelerated in towards the stricken cargo ship at five and a half gees. Erick sent another two shots from the X-ray cannon squirting into the *Krystal Moon*'s fusion tube. Its drive flame died. Coolant fluid vented out of a tear in the casing, hidden somewhere in the deep shadows on the side away from the sun, the fountain fluorescing grey-blue as it jetted out from behind the ship.

'Nice going, Erick,' André Duchamp commented. He had

the secondary fire-control program loaded in his own neural nanonics. If the newest crew-member hadn't fired he could have taken over within milliseconds. Despite Erick's performance in the Catalina Bar, André had a single nagging doubt. After all, O'Flaherty was one of their own – after a fashion – and eliminating him didn't require many qualms no matter who you were; but firing on an unarmed civil ship . . . You have earned your place on board, André said silently. He cancelled his fire-control program.

Villeneuve's Revenge was a hundred and twenty kilometres from the *Krystal Moon* when André turned the starship and started decelerating. The hangar doors began to slide open. He started to whistle against the push of the heavy gee force.

He had a right to be pleased. Even though it had only been a tiny interplanetary jump, two hundred and sixty kilometres was an excellent separation distance. Since leaving Tehama, *Villeneuve's Revenge* had been in orbit around Sacramento. They had extended every sensor, focusing along the trajectory Lance Coulson had sold them until they had found the faint splash of the *Krystal Moon*'s exhaust. With its exact position and acceleration available in real time, it was just a question of manufacturing themselves a jump co-ordinate.

Two hundred and sixty kilometres, there were voidhawks that would be pushed to match that kind of accuracy.

Thermo-dump panels stayed inside the monobonded silicon hull as the *Villeneuve's Revenge* rendezvoused with *Krystal Moon*. The jump nodes were fully charged. André was cautious, they might need to leave in a hurry. It had happened before; stealthed voidhawks lying in wait, Confederation Navy Marines hiding in the cargo-pods. Not to him, though.

'Bev, give our target an active sensor sweep, please,' André ordered.

'Yes, Captain,' Bev Lennon said. The combat sensors sent out fingers of questing radiation to probe the *Krystal Moon*.

The brilliant lance of fusion fire at the rear of the *Villeneuve's*

Revenge sank away to a minute bubble of radiant helium clinging to the tube's nozzle. *Krystal Moon* was six kilometres away, wobbling slightly from the impulse imparted by the venting coolant fluid. Thrusters flared around the rear bays, trying to compensate and stabilize.

Ion thrusters on the *Villeneuve's Revenge* fired, nudging the bulky starship in towards its floundering prey. Brendon piloted the multifunction service vehicle up out of the hangar and set off towards the *Krystal Moon*. One of the cargo-bay doors slowly hinged upwards behind him.

'Come on, Brendon,' André murmured impatiently as the small auxiliary craft rode its bright yellow chemical rocket exhaust across the gap. Ukiah traffic control would know the communication link had been severed in another twelve minutes; it would take the bureaucrats a few minutes to react, then sensors would review the *Krystal Moon*'s track. They'd see the spaceship's fusion drive was off, coupled with the lack of an emergency distress beacon. That could only mean one thing. The navy would be alerted, and if the *Villeneuve's Revenge* was really unlucky a patrolling voidhawk would investigate. André was allowing twenty minutes maximum for the raid.

'It checks out clean,' Bev Lennon reported. 'But the crew must have survived that first X-ray laser strike, I'm picking up electronic emissions from inside the life-support capsule. The flight computers are still active.'

'And they've suppressed the distress beacon,' André said. 'That's smart, they must know we'd slice that can in half to silence any shout for help. Maybe they'll be in a co-operative mood.' He datavised the flight computer to open an inter-ship channel.

Erick heard the hiss of static fill the dimly lit bridge as the AV pillar was activated. A series of musical bleeps came with it, then the distinct sound of a child crying. He saw Madeleine Collum's head come up from her acceleration couch, turning in the direction of the communication console. Blue and red shadows flowed over her gaunt, shaven skull.

'*Krystal Moon*, acknowledge contact,' André said.

'Acknowledge?' a ragged outraged male voice shouted out of the AV pillar. 'You shithead animal, two of my crew are dead. Fried! Tina was fifteen years old!'

Erick's neural nanonics staunched the sudden damp fire in his eyes. A fifteen-year-old girl. Great God Almighty! These interplanetary ships were often family operated affairs, cousins and siblings combining into crews.

'Release the latches on pods DK-30-91 and DL-30-07,' André said as though he hadn't heard. 'That's all we're here for.'

'Screw you.'

'We'll cut them free anyway, *Anglo*, and if we cut then the capsule will be included. I'll open your hull up to space like the foil on a freeze-dried food packet.'

A visual check through the combat sensors showed Erick the MSV was two hundred metres away from the *Krystal Moon*. Desmond Lafoe had already fitted laser cutters to the craft's robot arms; the spindly white waldos were running through a preprogrammed articulation test. *Villeneuve's Revenge* was lumbering along after the smaller, more agile, auxiliary craft; three kilometres away now.

'We'll think about it,' said the voice.

'Daddy!' the girl in the background wailed. 'Daddy, make them go away.'

A woman shushed her, sounding fearful.

'Don't think about it,' André said. 'Just do it.'

The channel went silent.

'Bastards,' André muttered. 'Erick, put another blast through that capsule.'

'If we kill them, they can't release the pods.'

André scowled darkly. 'Scare them, don't kill them.'

Erick activated one of the starship's lasers; it was designed for close-range interception, the last layer of defence against incoming combat wasps. Powerful and highly accurate. He reduced the power level to five per cent, and lined it up on the front of the life-support capsule. The infrared beam sliced a forty-centimetre circle out of the foam-covered hull. Steamy gas erupted out of the breach.

André grunted at what he considered to be Erick's display of timidity, and opened the inter-ship channel again. 'Release the pods.'

There was no answer. Erick couldn't hear the girl any more.

Brendon guided the MSV around the rings of barrel-like cargo-pods circling the *Krystal Moon*'s mid-section. He found the first pod containing microfusion generators, and focused the MSV's external cameras on it. The latch clamps of the cradle it was lying in were closed solidly round the load pins. Sighing regretfully at the time and effort it would cost to cut the pod free, he engaged the MSV's attitude lock, keeping station above the pod, then datavised the waldo-control computer to extend the arm. Droplets of molten metal squirted out where the cutting laser sliced through the clamps, a micrometeorite swarm glowing as if they were grazing an atmosphere.

'Something's happening,' Bev Lennon reported. The electronic sensors were showing him power circuits coming alive inside the *Krystal Moon*'s life-support capsule. Atmosphere was still spewing out of the lasered hole, unchecked. 'Hey—'

A circular section of the hull blew out. Erick's mind automatically directed the X-ray lasers towards the hole revealed by the crumpled sheet of metal as it twirled off towards the stars. A small craft rose out of the hole, ascending on a pillar of flame. Recognition was immediate: lifeboat.

It was a cone, four metres across at the base, five metres high; with a doughnut of equipment and tanks wrapped round the nose. Tarnished-silver protective foam reflected distorted star-specks. The lifeboat could sustain six people for a month in space, or jettison the equipment doughnut and land on a terracompatible planet. Cheaper then supplying the crew with zero-tau pods, and given that the mother ship would only be operating in an inhabited star system, just as safe.

'*Merde*, now we'll have to laser every latch clamp,' André complained. He could see that Brendon had cut loose half of the first pod. By his own timetable, they had nine minutes left. It was going to be a close-run thing. 'Knock that bloody lifeboat out, Erick.'

'No,' Erick said calmly. The lifeboat had stopped accelerating. Its spent solid rocket booster was jettisoned.

'I gave you an order.'

'Piracy is one thing; I'm not being a party to slaughter. There are children on that lifeboat.'

'He's right, André,' Madeleine Collum said.

'*Merde!* All right, but once Brendon has those pods cut free I want the *Krystal Moon* vaporized. That bloody captain has put our necks on the block by defying us, I want him ruined.'

'Yes, Captain,' Erick said. How typical, he thought, we can go in with lasers blazing, but if anyone fights back, that's *unfair*. When we get back to Tranquillity, I'm going to take a great deal of unprofessional pride in having André Duchamp committed to a penal planet.

They made it with forty-five seconds to spare. Brendon cut both cargo-pods free, and manoeuvred them into the waiting cargo hold in the *Villeneuve's Revenge*. X-ray lasers started to chop at the *Krystal Moon* as the MSV docked with its own cradle to be drawn gingerly into the hangar bay. The remaining cargo-pods were split open, spilling their wrecked contents out into the void. Structural spars melted, twisting as though they were being chewed. Tanks were punctured, creating a huge vapour cloud that chased outward, its fringes swirling round the retreating lifeboat.

The starship's hangar door slid shut. Combat sensors retreated back into the funereal hull. An event horizon sprang up around the *Villeneuve's Revenge*. The starship shrank. Vanished.

Floating alone amid the fragmented debris and vacuum-chilled nebula, the lifeboat let out a passionless electromagnetic shriek for help.

*

The word was out even before the *Lady Macbeth* docked at Tranquillity's spaceport. Joshua's landed the big one. On his first Norfolk run, for Heaven's sake. How does he do it? Something about that guy is uncanny. Lucky little sod.

Joshua led his crew into a packed Harkey's Bar. The band played a martial welcome with plangent trumpets; four of the waitresses were standing on the beer-slopped bar, short black skirts letting everyone see their knickers (or not, in one case); crews and groups of spaceport workers whistled, cheered, and jeered. One long table was loaded down with bottles of wine and champagne in troughs of ice; Harkey himself stood at the end, a smile in place. Everyone quietened down.

Joshua looked round slowly, an immensely smug grin in place. This must be what Alastair II saw from his state coach every day. It was fabulous. 'Do you want a speech?'

'NO!'

His arm swept out expansively towards Harkey. He bowed low, relishing the theatre. 'Then open the bottles.'

There was a rush for the table, conversation even loud enough to drown out Warlow erupted as though someone had switched on a stack of AV pillars, the band struck up, and the waitresses struggled with the corks. Joshua pushed a bemused and slightly awestruck Gideon Kavanagh off on Ashly Hanson, and snatched some glasses from the drinks table. He was kissed a great many times on his way to the corner booth where Barrington Grier and Roland Frampton were waiting. He loaded visual images and names of three of the girls into his neural nanonics for future reference.

Roland Frampton was rising to his feet, a slightly apprehensive smile flicking on and off, obviously worried by exactly how big the cargo was – he had contracted to buy all of it. But he shook Joshua warmly by the hand. 'I thought I'd better come here,' he said in amusement. 'It would take you days to reach my office. You're the talk of Tranquillity.'

'Really?'

Barrington Grier gave him a pat on the shoulder and they all sat down.

'That Kelly girl was asking after you,' Barrington said.

'Ah.' Joshua shifted round. Kelly Tirrel, his neural nanonics file supplied, Collins news corp reporter. 'Oh, right. How is she?'

'Looked pretty good to me. She's on the broadcasts a lot these days. Presents the morning news for Collins three times a week.'

'Good. Good. Glad to hear it.' Joshua took a small bottle of Norfolk Tears from the inside pocket of the gold-yellow jacket he was wearing over his ship-suit.

Roland Frampton stared at it as he would a cobra.

'This is the Cricklade bouquet,' Joshua said smoothly. He settled the three glasses on their table, and twisted the bottle's cork slowly. 'I've tasted it. One of the finest on the planet. They bottle it in Stoke county.' The clear liquid flowed out of the pear-shaped bottle.

They all lifted a glass, Roland Frampton studying his against the yellow wall lights.

'Cheers,' Joshua said, and took a drink. A dragon breathed its diabolical fire into his belly.

Roland Frampton sipped delicately. 'Oh, Christ, it's perfect.' He glanced at Joshua. 'How much did you bring? There have been rumours . . .'

Joshua made a show of producing his inventory. It was a piece of neatly printed paper with Grant Kavanagh's stylish signature on the bottom in black ink.

'Three thousand cases!' Roland Frampton squeaked, his eyes protruded.

Barrington Grier gave Joshua a sharp glance, and plucked the inventory from Roland's hands. 'Bloody hell,' he murmured.

Roland was dabbing at his forehead with a silk handkerchief. 'This is wonderful. Yes, wonderful. But I wasn't expecting quite so much, Joshua. Nothing personal, it's just that first-time captains don't normally bring back so much. There are arrangements I have to make . . . the bank. It will take time.'

'Of course.'

'You'll wait?' Roland Frampton asked eagerly.

'You were very good to me when I started out. So I think I can wait a couple of days.'

Roland's hand sliced through the air, he ended up making a fist just above the table. Determination visibly returned his old spark. 'Right, I'll have a Jovian Bank draft for you in thirty hours. I won't forget this, Joshua. And one day I want to be told how you did it.'

'Maybe.'

Roland drained his glass in one gulp and stood up. 'Thirty hours.'

'Fine. If I'm not about, give it to one of the crew. I expect they'll still be here.'

Joshua watched the old man weave a path through the excited crowd.

'That was decent of you,' Barrington said. 'You could have made instant money going to a big commercial distribution chain.'

Joshua flashed him a smile, and they touched glasses. 'Like I said, he gave me a break when I needed it.'

'Roland Frampton doesn't need a break. He thought he was doing you a favour agreeing to buy your cargo. First-time captains on the Norfolk run are lucky if they make two hundred cases.'

'Yeah, so I heard.'

'Now you come back with a cargo worth five times as much as his business. You going to tell us how you did it?'

'Nope.'

'Didn't think so. I don't know what you've got, young Joshua. But by God, I wish I had shares in you.'

He finished his glass and treated Barrington to an iniquitous smile. He handed over the small bottle of Norfolk Tears. 'Here, with compliments.'

'Aren't you staying? It's your party.'

He looked round. Warlow was at the centre of a cluster of girls, all of them giggling as one sat on the crook of his outstretched arm, her legs swinging well off the floor. Ashly was slumped in a booth, also surrounded by girls, one of them feeding him dainty pieces of white seafood from a plate. He couldn't even spot the others. 'No,' he said. 'I have a date.'

'She must be quite something.'

'They are.'

*

The *Isakore* was still anchored where they had left it, prow wedged up on the slippery bank, hull secure against casual observation by a huge cherry oak tree which overhung the river, lower branches trailing in the water.

Lieutenant Murphy Hewlett let out what could well have been a whimper of relief when its shape registered. His retinal implants were switched to infrared now the sun had set. The fishing boat was a salmon-pink outline distorted by the darker burgundy flecks of the cherry oak leaves, as if it was hidden behind a solidified waterfall.

He hadn't really expected it to be there. Not a quantifiable end, not to this mission. His mates treated his name as a joke back in the barracks. Murphy's law: if anything can go wrong, it will. And it had, this time as no other.

They had been under attack for five hours solid now. White fireballs that came stabbing out of the trees without warning. Figures that lurked half seen in the jungle, keeping pace, never giving them a moment's rest. Figures that weren't always human. Seven times they'd fallen back to using the TIP carbines for a sweep-scorch pattern, hacking at the jungle with blades of invisible energy, then tramping on through the smouldering vine roots and cloying ash.

All four of them were wounded to some extent. Nothing seemed to extinguish the white fire once it hit flesh. Murphy was limping badly, his right knee enclosed by a medical nanonic package, his left hand was completely useless, he wasn't even sure if the package could save his fingers. But Murphy was most worried about Niels Regehr; the lad had taken a fireball straight in the face. He had no eyes nor nose left, only the armour suit sensors enabled him to see where he was going now, datavising their images directly into his neural nanonics. But even the neural nanonics pain blocks and a constant infusion of endocrines couldn't prevent him from suffering bouts of hallucination and disorientation. He kept shouting for *them* to go away and leave him alone, holding one-sided conversations, even quoting from prayers.

Murphy had detailed him to escort their prisoner; he could just about manage that. She said her name was Jacqueline Couteur, a middle-aged woman, small, overweight, with greying hair, dressed in jeans and a thick cotton shirt. She could punch harder than any of the supplement-boosted marines (Louis Beith had a broken arm to prove it), she had more stamina than them, and she could work that electronic warfare trick on their suit blocks if she wasn't being prodded with one of their heavy-calibre Bradfield chemical-projectile rifles.

They had captured her ten minutes after their last contact with Jenny Harris. That was when they'd let the horses go. The animals were panicking as balls of white fire arched down out of the sky, a deceitfully majestic display of borealis rockets.

Something made a slithering sound in the red and black jungle off to Murphy's right. Garrett Tucci fired his Bradfield, slamming explosive bullets into the vegetation. Murphy caught the swiftest glimpse of a luminous red figure scurrying away;

it was either a man with a warm cloak spread wide, or else a giant bat standing on its hind legs.

'Bloody implants are shot,' he muttered under his breath. He checked his TIP carbine's power reserve. He was down to the last heavy-duty power cell: twelve per cent. 'Niels, Garrett, take the prisoner onto the boat and get the motor going. Louis, you and I are laying down a sweep-scorch. It might give us the time we need.'

'Yes, sir,' he answered.

Murphy felt an immense pride in the tiny squad. Nobody could have done better, they were the best, the very best. And they were his.

He drew a breath, and brought the TIP carbine up again. Niels was shoving his Bradfield's muzzle into the small of Jacqueline Couteur's back, urging her towards the boat. Murphy suddenly realized she could see as well as them in the dark. It didn't matter now. One of the day's smaller mysteries.

His TIP carbine fired, nozzle aimed by his neural nanonics. Flames rose before him, leaping from tree to tree, incinerating the twigs, biting deeply into the larger branches. Vines flared and sparkled like fused electrical cables, swinging in short arcs before falling to the ground and writhing ferociously as they spat and hissed. A solid breaker of heat rolled around him, shunted into the ground by his suit's dispersal layer. Smoke rose from his feet. The medical nanonic package around his knee datavised a heat-overload warning into his neural nanonics.

'Come on, Lieutenant!' Garrett shouted.

Through the heavy crackling of the flames Murphy could hear the familiar chugging sound of the *Isakore*'s motor. The suit's rear optical sensors showed him the boat backing out from under the cherry oak, water boiling ferociously around its stern.

'Go,' Murphy told Louis Beith.

They turned and raced for the *Isakore*. Murphy could just *feel* targeting graphics circling his back.

We'll never make it, not out of this.

Flames were rising thirty metres into the night behind them. *Isakore* was completely free of the cherry oak. Niels was leaning over the gunwale, holding out a hand. The green-tinted medical nanonic package leaching to his face looked like some massive and grotesque wart.

Water splashed around his boots. Once he nearly slipped on the mud and tangled snowlily fronds. But then he was clinging to the side of the wooden boat, hauling himself up onto the deck.

'Holy shit, we made it!' He was laughing uncontrollably, tears streaming out of his eyes. 'We actually bloody made it.' He pulled his shell-helmet off, and lay on his back, looking at the fire. A stretch of jungle four hundred metres long was in flames, hurling orange sparks into the black sky far above.

The impenetrable water of the Zamjan shimmered with long orange reflections. Garrett was turning the boat, aiming the prow downriver.

'What about the Kulu team?' Louis asked. He'd taken his shell-helmet off, showing a face glinting with sweat. His breathing was heavy.

'I think that was a sonic boom we heard this afternoon,' Murphy said, raising his voice above the flames. 'Those Kulu bastards, always one move ahead of everyone else.'

'They're soft, that's all,' Garrett shouted from the wheelhouse. 'Can't take the pressure. We can. We're the fucking Confed fucking Navy fucking Marines.' He whooped.

Murphy grinned back at him; fatigue pulled at every limb. He'd been using his boosted muscles almost constantly, which meant he'd have to make sure he ate plenty of high-protein rations to regain his proper blood energy levels. He loaded a memo into his neural nanonics.

His communication block let out a bleep for the first time

in five hours; the datavise told him that there was a channel to the navy ELINT satellite open.

'Bloody hell,' Murphy said. He datavised the block: 'Sir, is that you, sir?'

'Christ, Murphy,' Kelven Solanki's datavise gushed into his mind. 'What's happening?'

'Spot of trouble, sir. Nothing we can't handle. We're back on the boat now, heading downriver.'

Louis gave an exhausted laugh, and flopped onto his back.

'The Kulu team evacuated,' Kelven Solanki reported. 'Their whole embassy contingent upped and left in the *Ekwan* this evening. Ralph Hiltch called me from orbit to say there wasn't enough room on the spaceplane to pick you up.'

Murphy could sense a great deal of anger lying behind the lieutenant-commander's smooth signal. 'Doesn't matter, sir; we got you a prisoner.'

'Fantastic. One of the sequestrated ones?'

Murphy glanced over his shoulder. Jacqueline Couteur was sitting on the deck with her back to the wheel-house. She gave him a dour stare.

'I think so, sir, she can interfere with our electronics if we give her half a chance. She's got to be watched constantly.'

'OK, when can you have her back in—' Kelven Solanki's datavise vanished under a peal of static. The communications block reported the channel was lost.

Murphy picked up his TIP carbine and pointed it at Jacqueline Couteur. 'Is that you?'

She shrugged. 'No.'

Murphy looked back at the fire on the bank. They were half a kilometre away now. People were walking along the shoreline where the *Isakore* had been anchored. The big cherry oak was still standing, intact, a black silhouette against the blanket of flame.

'Can they affect our electronics from here?'

'We don't care about your electronics,' she said. 'Such things have no place in our world.'

'Are you talking to them?'

'No.'

'Sir!' Garrett yelled.

Murphy swung round. The people on the shore were standing in a ring, holding hands. A large ball of white fire emerged from the ground in their midst and curved over their heads, soaring out across the river.

'Down!' Murphy shouted.

The fireball flashed overhead, making the air roil from its passage, bringing a false daylight to the boat. Murphy ground his teeth together, anticipating the strike, the pain as it vaporized his legs or spine. There was a clamorous *BOOM* from behind the wheel-house, the boat rocked violently, and the light went out.

'Oh shit, oh shit.' Garrett was crying.

'What is it?' Murphy demanded. He pulled himself onto his feet.

The boxy wooden structure behind the wheel-house was a smoking ruin. Fractured planks with charred edges pointed vacantly at the sky. The micro-fusion generator it had covered was a shambolic mass of heat-tarnished metal and dripping plastic.

'You will come to us in time,' Jacqueline Couteur said calmly. She hadn't moved from her sitting position. 'We have no hurry.'

The *Isakore* drifted round a bend in the river, water gurgling idly around the hull, pulling the fire from view. A duet of night and silence closed over the boat, a void surer than vacuum.

*

Ione wore a gown of rich blue-green silk gauze. A single strip of cloth which clung to her torso then flared and flowed into a long skirt, it forked around her neck, producing two ribbonlike tassels that trailed from each shoulder. Her hair had been given a damp look, it was bound up and held in place at the back by an exquisite red flower brooch, its tissue-thin petals carved from some exotic stone. A long platinum chain formed a cobweb around her neck.

The trouble with looking so elegant, Joshua thought, was that part of him just wanted to stare at her, while the other part wanted to rip the dress to shreds so he could get at the body beneath. She really did look gorgeous.

He ran a finger round the collar on his own black dinner-jacket. It was too tight. And the butterfly tie wasn't straight.

'Leave it alone,' Ione said sternly.

'But—'

'Leave it. It's fine.'

He dropped his hand and glowered at the lift's door. Two Tranquillity serjeants were in with them, making it seem crowded. The door opened on the twenty-fifth floor of the StOuen starscraper, revealing a much smaller lobby than usual. Parris Vasilkovsky's apartment took up half of the floor, his offices and staff quarters took up the other half.

'Thanks for coming with me,' Joshua said as they stood in front of the apartment door. He could feel the nerves building in the base of his stomach. This was the real big time he was bidding for now. And Ione on his arm ought to impress Parris Vasilkovsky. Precious little else would.

'I want to be with you,' Ione murmured.

He leant forward to kiss her.

The muscle membrane opened, and Dominique was standing behind it. She had chosen a sleeveless black gown with a long skirt and a deep, highly revealing V-neck. Her thick honey-blonde hair had been given a slight wave, curling around her shoulders. Broad scarlet lips lifted in appreciation as she caught the embrace.

Joshua straightened up guiltily, though his errant eyes remained fixed on Dominique's cleavage. A host of memories started to replay through his mind without any assistance from his neural nanonics. He'd forgotten how impressive she was.

'Don't mind me,' Dominique said huskily. 'I adore young love.'

Ione giggled. 'Evening, Dominique.'

The two girls kissed briefly. Then it was Joshua's turn.

'Put him down,' Ione said in amusement. 'You might catch something. Heaven only knows what he got up to on Norfolk.'

Dominique grinned as she let go. 'You think he's been bad?'

'He's Joshua; I *know* he's been bad.'

'Hey!' Joshua complained. 'That trip was strictly business.'

Both girls laughed. Dominique led the way into the apartment. Joshua saw her skirt was made up from long panels, split right up to the top of her hips. The fabric swayed apart as she walked, giving Joshua brief glimpses of her legs, and a pair of very tight white shorts.

He held back on a groan. It was going to be hard to concentrate tonight without that kind of distraction.

The dining-room had two oval windows to show Mirchusko's dusky crescent – south of the equator two huge white cyclone swirls were crashing, in a drama which had been running for six days. Slabs of warmly lit coloured glass paved the polyp walls from floor to ceiling, each with an animal engraved on its surface by fine smoky grooves. Most of them were terrestrial – lions, gazelles, elephants, hawks – though several of the more spectacular non-sentient xenoc species were included. The grooves moved at an infinitesimal speed, causing the birds to flap their wings, the animals to run; their cycles lasted for hours. The table was made from halkett wood (native to Kulu), a rich gold in colour, with bright scarlet grain. Three antique silver candelabras were spaced along the polished wood, with slender white candles tipped by tiny flames.

There were six people at the dinner. Parris himself sat at the head of the table, looking spruce in a black dinner-jacket. The formal evening attire suited him, complementing his curly silver-grey hair to give him a distinguished appearance. At the other end of the table was Symone, his current lover, a beautiful twenty-eight-year-old whose geneered chromosomes had produced a dark walnut skin and hair a shade lighter than Dominique's, a striking and delightful contrast. She was eight months pregnant with Parris's third child.

Joshua and Dominique sat together on one side of the table. And Dominique's long legs had been riding up and down his trousers all through the meal. He had done his best to ignore it, but his twitching mouth had given him away to Ione, and, he suspected, Symone as well.

Opposite them were Ione and Clement, Parris's son. He was eighteen, lacking his big sister's miscreant force, but quietly cheerful. And handsome, Ione thought, though not in the mould of Joshua's wolfish ruggedness; his younger face was softer, framed with fair curly hair that was recognizably Parris's. He had just returned from his first year at university on Kulu.

'I haven't been to Kulu yet,' Joshua said as the white-jacketed waiter cleared the dessert dishes away, assisted by a couple of housechimps.

'Wouldn't they let you in?' Dominique asked with honeyed malice.

'The Kulu merchants form a tight cartel, they're hard to crack.'

'Tell me about it,' Parris said gruffly. 'It took me eight years before I broke in with fabrics from Oshanko, until then my ships were going there empty to pick up their nanonics. That costs.'

'I'll wait until I get a charter,' Joshua said. 'I'm not going to try head-butting that kind of organization. But I'd like to play tourist sometime.'

'You did all right penetrating Norfolk,' Dominique said, eyes wide and apparently innocent over her crystal champagne glass.

'Hey, neat intro,' he said enthusiastically. 'We just slid into that subject, didn't we? I never noticed.'

She stuck her tongue out at him.

'You got off lightly, Joshua,' Parris said. 'Me, I get lumbered with her subtlety all day every day.'

'I would have thought she was old enough to have left home by now,' he said.

'Who'd have her?'

'Good point.'

Dominique lobbed a small cluster of grapes at her father.

Parris caught them awkwardly, laughing. One went bouncing off across the moss carpet. 'Make me an offer for her, Joshua, anything up to ten fuseodollars considered.'

He saw the warning gleam in Dominique's eye. 'I think I'll decline, thanks.'

'Coward.' Dominique pouted.

Parris dropped the grapes onto a side plate, and wiped his hand with a napkin. 'So how did you do it, Joshua? My captains don't get three thousand cases, and the Vasilkovsky line has been making the Norfolk run for fifty years.'

Joshua activated a neural nanonics memory cell. 'Confidentiality coverage. Agreed?' His gaze went round the table, recording everyone saying yes. They were legally bound not to repeat what they heard now. Although quite what he could do about Ione was an interesting point, since her thought processes were Tranquillity's legal system. 'I traded something they needed: wood.' He explained about the mayope.

'Very clever,' Dominique drawled when he finished, though there was a note of respect in amongst the affected languor. 'Brains as well as balls.'

'I like it,' Parris said. He studied his cut-crystal glass. 'Why tell us?'

'Supply and demand,' Joshua said. 'I've found a valuable hole in the market, and I want to fill it.'

'But the *Lady Macbeth* hasn't got the capacity to do it by herself,' Clement said. 'Right?'

Joshua had wondered how smart the lad was. Now he knew.

A real chip off the Vasilkovsky block. 'That's right. I need a partner, a big partner.'

'Why not go to a bank?' Dominique asked. 'Charter some ships for yourself.'

'There's a loose end which needs tying up.'

'Ah,' Parris, showing some real interest at last, leant forward in his seat. 'Go on.'

'The power mayope has over Norfolk lies in keeping it a monopoly, that way we can keep the price high. I have a provisional arrangement with a distributor on Norfolk who's agreed to take as much as we can ship in. What we need to do next is pin down the supply to a single source, one that only we can obtain. That is going to take upfront money, the kind which can't be explained away to bank auditors.'

'You can do that?'

'Parris, I have never been on a planet more corrupt than Lalonde. It's also very primitive and correspondingly poor. If you, with all your money, went there, you would be its king.'

'No, thank you,' Parris said sagely.

'Fine, but with money pushed into the right credit disks we can guarantee that no one else gets an export licence. OK, it won't last for ever, administration people move on, traders will offer counter-bribes when they find what we're doing; but I figure we ought to get two of Norfolk's conjunctions out of it. Two conjunctions where your ships are filled to capacity with Norfolk Tears.'

'Every ship? I do have quite a few.'

'No, not every ship. We have to walk a fine line between greed and squeeze. My Norfolk distributor will give us most favoured customer status, that's all. It'll be up to us to work out exactly how much we can squeeze them for before they start to protest. You know how jealously they guard their independence.'

'Yes.' Parris nodded thoughtfully.

'And what about Lalonde?' Ione asked quietly. Her glass was

dangling casually between thumb and forefinger, she rocked it from side to side, swirling the champagne around the bottom.

'What about Lalonde?' Joshua asked.

'Its people,' Symone said. 'It doesn't sound as though they get a very good deal out of this. The mayope is their wood.'

Joshua gave her a polite smile. Just what I need, bleeding hearts. 'What do they get at the moment?'

Symone frowned.

'He means they get nothing,' Dominique said.

'We're developing their market for them,' Joshua said. 'We'll be pumping hard cash into their economy. Not much by our standards, I admit, but to them it will buy a lot of things they need. And it will go to the people too, the colonists who are breaking their backs to tame that world, not just the administration staff. We pay the loggers upriver in the hinterlands, the barge captains, the timber-yard workers. Them, their families, the shops they buy stuff from. All of them will be better off. We'll be better off. Norfolk will be better off. It's the whole essence of trade. Sure, banks and governments make paper money from the deal, and we slant it in our favour, but the bottom line is that people benefit.' He realized he was staring hard at Symone, daring her to disagree. He dropped his eyes, almost embarrassed.

Dominique gave him a soft, and for the first time, sincere kiss on his cheek. 'You really did pick yourself the best, didn't you?' she said challengingly to Ione.

'Of course.'

'Does that answer your question?' Parris asked his lover, smiling gently at her.

'I guess it does.'

He started to use a small silver knife to peel the crisp rind from a date-sized purple fruit. Joshua recognized it as a saltplum from Atlantis.

'I think Lalonde would be in capable hands if we left it to

Joshua,' Parris said. 'What sort of partnership were you looking for?'

'Sixty–forty in your favour,' he said amicably.

'Which would cost me?'

'I was thinking of two to three million fuseodollars as an initial working fund to set up our export operation.'

'Eighty–twenty,' Dominique said.

Parris bit into the saltplum's pink flesh, watching Joshua keenly.

'Seventy–thirty,' Joshua offered.

'Seventy-five–twenty-five.'

'I get that percentage on all Norfolk Tears carried by the Vasilkovsky Line while our mayope monopoly is in operation.'

Parris winced, and gave his daughter a small nod.

'If you provide the collateral,' she said.

'You accept my share of the mayope as collateral, priced at the Norfolk sale value.'

'Done.'

Joshua sat back and let out a long breath. It could have been a lot worse.

'You see,' Dominique said wickedly. 'Brains as well as breasts.'

'And legs,' Joshua added.

She licked her lips provocatively, and took a long drink.

'We'll get the legal office to draw up a formal contract tomorrow,' Parris said. 'I can't see any problem.'

'The first stage will be to set up an office on Lalonde and secure that mayope monopoly. The *Lady Mac* has still got to be unloaded, then she needs some maintenance work, and we're due a grade-E CAB inspection as well thanks to someone I met at Norfolk. Not a problem, but it takes time. I ought to be ready to leave in ten days.'

'Good,' said Parris. 'I like that, Joshua. No beating around, you get straight to it.'

'So how did you make your fortune?'

Parris grinned and popped the last of the saltplum into his

mouth. 'Given this will hopefully develop into quite a large operation, I'll want to send my own representative with you to Lalonde to help set up our office. And keep an eye on this upfront money of mine you'll be spending.'

'Sure. Who?'

Dominique leaned over until her shoulder rubbed against Joshua's, a hand made of steel flesh closed playfully on his upper thigh. 'Guess,' she whispered salaciously into his ear.

*

Durringham had become ungovernable, a city living on spent nerves, waiting for the final crushing blow to fall.

The residents knew of the invaders marching and sailing downriver, everyone had heard the horror stories of xenoc enslavement, of torture and rape and bizarre bloodthirsty ceremonies; words distorted and swollen with every kilometre, like the river down which they travelled. They had also heard of the Kulu Embassy evacuating its personnel in one madcap night, surely the final confirmation – Sir Asquith wouldn't do that unless there was no hope left. Durringham, their homes and jobs and prosperity, was in the firing line of an unknown, unstoppable threat, and they had nowhere to run. The jungle belonged to the invaders, the seven colonist-carrier starships orbiting impotently overhead were full, they couldn't offer an escape route. There was only the river and the virgin sea beyond.

The second morning after Ralph Hiltch made his dash to the relative safety of the *Ekwan*, the twenty-eight paddle-boats remaining in the frightened city's circular harbours set off in convoy downriver. Price of a ticket was one thousand fuseodollars per person (including a child). No destination was named: some talked about crossing the ocean to Sarell; Amarisk's northern extremity was mooted. It didn't matter, leaving Durringham was the driving factor.

Given the exorbitant price the captains insisted on, and the planet's relative poverty, it was surprising just how many people turned up wanting passage. More than could be accommodated. Tempers and desperation rose with the brutal sun. Several ugly scenes flared as the gangplanks were hurriedly drawn up.

Frustrated in their last chance to escape, the crowd surged towards the colonists barricaded in the transients' dormitories at the other end of the port. Stones were flung first, then Molotovs.

Candace Elford dispatched a squad of sheriffs and newly recruited deputies, armed with cortical jammers and laser rifles, to quell this latest in a long line of disturbances. But they ran into a gang ransacking a retail district. The tactical street battle which followed left eight dead, and two dozen injured. They never got to the port.

That was when Candace finally had to call up Colin Rexrew and admit that Durringham was out of control. 'Most urban districts are forming their own defence committees,' she datavised. 'They've seen how little effect the sheriffs have against any large-scale trouble. All the riots we've had these last few weeks have shown that often enough, and everyone's heard about the *Swithland* posse. They don't trust you and me to defend them, so they're going to do it for themselves. There's been a lot of food stockpiled over the last couple of weeks. They all think they're self-sufficient, and they're not letting anyone over their district's boundary. That's going to cause trouble, because I'm getting reports of people in the outlying villages to the east abandoning their land and coming in looking for a refuge. Our residents aren't letting them through. It's a siege mentality out there. People are waiting for Terrance Smith to come back with a conquering army, and hoping they can hold out in the meantime.'

'How far away are the invaders?'

'I'm not sure. We're judging their progress by the way our communications with the villages fail. It's not constant, but I'd say their main force is no more than ten or fifteen kilometres from Durringham's eastern districts. The majority are on foot, which should give us two or three days' breathing space. Of course, you and I know there are nests of them inside the city as well. I've had some pretty weird stories about bogeymen and poltergeists coming in for days now.'

'What do you want to do?' Colin asked.

'Revert to guarding our strategic centres; the spaceport, this sector, possibly both hospitals. I'd like to say the port as well, but I don't think I've got the manpower. There have been several desertions this week, mostly among the new deputies. Besides, nearly all of the boats have left now; there's been a steady exodus of fishing craft and even some barges since the paddle-boat convoy cast off this morning, so I can't see a lot of point.'

'OK,' Colin said with his head in his hands. 'Do it.' He glanced out of the office window at the sun-lashed rooftops. There was no sign of any of the usual fires that had marked the city's torment over the last weeks. 'Can we hang on until Terrance returns?'

'I don't know. At the moment we're so busy fighting each other that I couldn't tell you what sort of resistance we can offer to the invaders.'

'Yeah. That sounds like Lalonde through and through.'

Candace sat behind her big desk, watching the situation reports paint unwelcome graphics across the console displays, and issuing orders through her staff. There were times when she wondered if anyone out there was even receiving them, let alone obeying them.

Half of her sheriffs were deployed around the spaceport, spending the afternoon digging in, and positioning some large maser cannons to cover the road. The rest took up position around the administration district in the city, covering the governor's dumper, the sheriff's headquarters, various civic buildings, and the Confederation Navy office. Five combined teams of LDC engineers and sheriffs went round all the remaining dumpers they could reach, powering down the fusion generators. If the invaders wanted Durringham's industrial base, such as it was, Rexrew was determined to thwart them. The He_3 and deuterium fuel was collected and put into storage at the spaceport. By midafternoon the city was operating on electron-matrix power reserves alone.

That more than anything else brought home the reality of the situation to the majority. Fights and squabbles between gangs and districts ended, those barricades which had been erected were strengthened, sentry details were finalized. Everyone headed home, the roads fell silent. The rain which had held off all day began to slash down. Beneath its shroud of miserable low cloud, Durringham held its breath.

Stewart Danielsson watched the rain pounding away on the office windows as the conditioner hummed away efficiently, sucking the humidity from the air. He had made the office his home over the last week; Ward Molecular had seen a busy time of it. Everybody in town was keen to have the ancillary circuits on their electron-matrix cells serviced, especially the smaller units which could double as rifle power magazines at a pinch. He'd sold a lot of interface cables as well.

The business was doing fine. Darcy and Lori would be pleased when they got back. They hadn't actually said he could sleep over when they left him in charge, but with the way things were it was only right. Twice he'd scared off would-be burglars.

His sleeping-bag with the inflatable mattress was comfy, and the office fridge was better than the one in his lodgings; he'd brought the microwave cooker over from the cabin out back of the warehouse. So now he had all the creature comforts. It was turning into a nice little sojourn. Gaven Hough stayed late most nights, keeping him company. Neither of them had seen Cole Este since the night after the first anti-Ivet riot. Stewart wasn't much bothered by that.

Gaven opened the door in the glass partition wall and stuck

his head round. 'Doesn't look like Mr Crowther is coming to pick up his unit now, it's gone four.'

Stewart stretched himself, and turned the processor block off. He'd been trying to keep their work records and payments up to date. It had always seemed so easy when Darcy was handling it. 'OK, we'll get closed up.'

'We'll be the last in the city. There's been no traffic outside for the last two hours. Everyone else has gone home, scared of these invaders.'

'Aren't you?'

'No, not really. I haven't got anything an army would want.'

'You can stay here tonight. I don't think it'll be safe walking home through this town now, not with the way people are on edge. There's enough food.'

'Thanks. I'll go and shut the doors.'

Stewart watched the younger man through the glass partition as he made his way past the workbenches to the warehouse's big doors. I ought to be worried, he thought, some of the rumours flying around town are blatantly unreal, but something is happening upriver. He gave the warehouse a more thoughtful glance. With its mayope walls it was strong enough to withstand any casual attempt at damage. But there were a lot of valuable tools and equipment inside, and everybody knew that. Maybe we should be boarding the windows up. There was no such thing as an insurance industry on Lalonde, if the warehouse went so did their jobs.

He turned back to the office windows, giving them a more objective appraisal; the frames were heavy enough to nail planks across.

Someone was walking down the muddy road outside. It was difficult to see with the way the rain was smearing the glass, but it looked like a man dressed in a suit. A very strange suit; it was grey, with a long jacket, and there was no seal up the front, only buttons. And he wore a black hat that looked like a fifty-centimetre column of brushed velvet. His right hand gripped a silver-topped cane. Rain bounced off him as though his antique clothes were coated in frictionless plastic.

'Stewart!' Gaven called from somewhere in the warehouse. 'Stewart, come back here.'

'No. Look at this.'

'There's three of them in here. Stewart!'

The native panic in Gaven's voice made him turn reluctantly from the window. He squinted through the partition wall. It was dark in the cavernous warehouse, and Gaven had shut the wide doors. Stewart couldn't see where he'd got to. Humanoid shapes were moving around down by the stacks of crates; bigger than men. And it was just too gloomy to make out quite what—

The window behind him gave a loud grating moan. He whirled round. The frames groaned again as though they had been shoved by a hurricane blast. But the rain was falling quite normally outside. It couldn't be the wind. The man in the grey suit was standing in the middle of the road, cane pressing into the mud, both hands resting on the silver pommel. He stared directly at Stewart.

'Stewart!' Gaven yelled.

The window-panes cracked, fissures multiplying and interlacing. Animal reflex made Stewart spin round, his arms coming up to protect his head. *They're going to smash!*

A two and a half metre tall yeti was standing pressed up against the glass of the partition wall. Its ochre fur was matted and greasy, red baboon lips were peeled back to show stained fangs. He gagged at it in amazement, recoiling.

All the glass in the office shattered at once. In the instant before he slammed his eyelids shut, he was engulfed by a beautiful prismatic cloud of diamonds, sparkling and shimmering in the weak light. Then the slivers of glass penetrated his skin. Blood frothed out of a thousand shallow cuts, staining every square centimetre of his clothes a bright crimson. His skin went numb as his brain rejected outright the shocking level of pain. His sight, the misty vermilion of tightly shut eyes, turned scarlet. Pain stars flared purple. Then the universe went harrowingly black. Through the numbness he could feel hot coals burning in his eye sockets.

'Blind, I'm blind!' He couldn't even tell if his voice was working.

'It doesn't have to be like that,' someone said to him. 'We can help you. We can let you see again.'

He tried to open his eyelids. There was a loathsome sensation of thin tissues ripping. And still there was only blackness. Pain began to ooze its way inwards, pain from every part of his body. He knew he was falling, plummeting to the ground.

Then the pain in his legs faded, replaced by a blissful liquid chill, as if he was bathing in a mountain tarn. He was given his sight back, a spectral girl sketched against the infinite darkness. It looked as though she was made up from translucent white membranes, folded with loving care around her svelte body, then flowing free somehow to become her fragile robes as well. She was a sublime child, in her early teens, poised between girlhood and womanhood, what he imagined an angel or fairy would be like. And she danced all the while, twirling effortlessly from foot to foot, more supple and graceful than any ballerina; her face blessed by a bountiful smile.

She held out her arms to him, ragged sleeves floating softly in the unfelt breeze. 'See?' she said. 'We can stop it hurting.' Her arms rose, palms pressing together above her head, and she spun round again, lightsome laughter echoing.

'Please,' he begged her. 'Oh, please.'

The pain returned to his legs, making him cry out. His siren vision began to retreat, skipping lightly over the emptiness.

She paused and cocked her head. 'Is this what you want?' she asked, her dainty face frowning in concern.

'No! Back, come back. Please.'

Her smile became rapturous, and her arms closed around

him in a celebratory embrace. Stewart gave himself up to her balmy caresses, drowning in a glorious tide of white light.

*

Ilex coasted out of its wormhole terminus a hundred thousand kilometres above Lalonde. The warped gateway leading out of space-time contracted behind the voidhawk as it refocused its distortion field. Sensors probed round cautiously. The bitek starship was at full combat stations alert.

Waiting tensely on his acceleration couch in the crew toroid, Captain Auster skimmed through the wealth of data which both the bitek and electronic systems gathered. His primary concern was that there were no hostile ships within a quarter of a million kilometres, and no weapon sensors were locking on to the voidhawk's hull. A resonance effect in *Ilex*'s distortion field revealed various ship-sized masses orbiting above Lalonde, then there were asteroids, satellites, moons, boulder-sized debris. Nothing large was in the starship's immediate vicinity. It took a further eight seconds for *Ilex* and Ocyroe, the weapons-systems officer, working in tandem, to confirm the absence of any valid threat.

OK, let's go for a parking orbit; seven hundred kilometres out, Auster said.

Seven hundred? *Ilex* queried.

Yes. Your distortion field won't be so badly affected at that altitude. We can still run if we have to.

Very well.

Together their unified minds arrived at a suitable flight vector. *Ilex* swooped down the imaginary line towards the bright blue and white planet.

'We're going into a parking orbit,' Auster said aloud for the benefit of the three Adamist naval officers on the bridge. 'I want combat stations maintained at all times; and please bear in mind who could be here waiting for us.' He allowed an overtone of stern anxiety to filter out to the Edenist crew to emphasize the point. 'Ocyroe, what's our local space situation?'

'Nine starships in a parking orbit, seven colonist-carriers and two cargo ships. There are three interplanetary fusion drive ships *en route* from the asteroid Kenyon, heading for Lalonde orbit. Nothing else in the system.'

'I can't get any response from Lalonde civil flight control,' said Erato, the spaceplane pilot. He looked up from the communication console he was operating. 'The geosynchronous communication platform is working, as far as I can tell. They just don't answer.'

Auster glanced over at Lieutenant Jeroen van Ewyck, the Confederation Navy Intelligence officer they had brought with them from Avon. 'What do you think?'

'This is a backward planet anyway, so their response isn't going to be instantaneous. But given the contents of those fleks I'd rather not take any chances. I'll try and contact Kelvin Solanki directly through the navy ELINT satellites. Can you see if you can get anything from your planetside agents?'

'We'll broadcast,' Auster said.

'Great. Erato, see what the other starship captains can tell us. It looks like they must have been here some time if there are this many left in orbit.'

Auster added his own voice to *Ilex*'s affinity call, spanning the colossal distance to the gas giant. Aethra answered straight away; but the immature habitat could only confirm the data which Lori and Darcy had included in their flek to the Edenist embassy on Avon. Since Kelven Solanki had transmitted the files to Murora there had only been the usual weekly status updates from Lalonde. The last one, four days ago, had contained a host of information on the colony's deteriorating civil situation.

Can you tell us what's happening? Gaura asked through the affinity link between Aethra and *Ilex*. He was the chief of the station supervising the habitat's growth out at the lonely edge of the star system.

Nobody is answering our calls, Auster said. **When we know something, *Ilex* will inform you immediately.**

If Laton is on Lalonde he may make an attempt to capture and subvert Aethra. He has had over twenty years to perfect his technique. We have no weaponry to resist him. Can you evacuate us?

That will depend on the circumstances. Our orders from the First Admiral's office are to confirm his existence and destroy him if at all possible. If he has become powerful enough to defend himself against the weapons we are carrying, then we must jump back to Fleet Headquarters and alert them. That takes priority over everything. Auster extended a burst of sympathy.

We understand. Good luck with your mission.

Thank you.

Can you sense Darcy and Lori? Auster asked *Ilex*.

No. They do not answer. But there is a melodic in the affinity band which I've never encountered before.

The voidhawk's perceptive faculty expanded into Auster's mind. He perceived a distant soprano voice, or a soft whistle; the effect was too imprecise to tell. It was an adagio, a slow harmonic which slipped in and out of mental awareness like a radio signal on a stormy night.

Where is it coming from? Auster asked.

Ahead of us, *Ilex* said. **Somewhere on the planet, but it's skipping about. I can't pin it down.**

Keep tuned in to it, and if you track down its origin let me know right away.

Of course.

Jeroen van Ewyck datavised his console processor to point one of *Ilex*'s secondary dishes at a navy ELINT satellite orbiting Lalonde, then opened a channel down to the office in Durringham. There was nothing like the usual bit rate available, the microwave beam emitted by the navy office was well below standard strength. A flustered rating answered, and switched the call straight through to Kelven Solanki.

'We're here in response to the flek you sent on the *Eurydice*,' Jeroen van Ewyck said. 'Can you advise us of the situation on the planet, please?'

'Too late,' Kelven datavised. 'You're too bloody late.'

Auster ordered the bitek processor in his command console to patch him into the channel. 'Lieutenant-Commander Solanki, this is Captain Auster. We were dispatched as soon as we were refitted for this mission. I can assure you the Admiralty took the report from you and our Intelligence operatives very seriously indeed.'

'Seriously? You call sending one ship a serious response?'

'Yes. We are primarily a reconnaissance and evaluation mission. In that respect, we are considered expendable. The Admiralty needs to know if Laton's presence has been confirmed, and what kind of force level is required to deal with the invasion.'

There was a moment's pause.

'Sorry if I shouted off,' Kelven said. 'Things are getting bad down here. The invaders have reached Durringham.'

'Are these invaders acting under Laton's orders?'

'I've no idea yet.' He started to summarize the events of the last couple of weeks.

Auster listened with growing dismay, a communal emotion distributed equally around the other Edenists on board. The Adamists too, if their facial expressions were an accurate reflection of their thoughts.

'So you still don't know if Laton is behind this invasion?' Auster asked when he finished.

'No. I'd say not; Lori and Darcy had virtually written him off by the time they got to Ozark. If it is him backing the invaders, then he's pulling a very elaborate double bluff. Why did he warn Darcy and Lori about this energy virus effect?'

'Have you managed to verify that yet?' Jeroen van Ewyck asked.

'No. Although the supporting circumstantial evidence we have so far is very strong. The invaders certainly have a powerful electronic warfare technology at their fingertips, and it's in widespread use. I suppose Kulu will be the place to ask; the ESA team managed to get their prisoner outsystem.'

Typical of the ESA, Erato said sourly.

Auster nodded silently.

'How bad are conditions in the city?' Jeroen van Ewyck asked.

'We've heard some fighting around the outlying districts this evening. The sheriffs are protecting the spaceport and the government district. But I don't think they'll hold out for more than a couple of days. You must get back to Avon and inform the First Admiral and the Confederation Assembly what's happening here. At this point we still can't discount xenocs being involved. And tell the First Admiral that Terrance Smith's mercenary army must be prevented from landing here, as well. This is far beyond the ability of a few thousand hired soldiers to sort out.'

'That goes without saying. We'll evacuate you and your staff immediately,' Auster said.

Forty-five of them? Ocyroe asked. **That's pushing our life-support capacity close to the envelope.**

We can always make a swallow direct to Jospool, That's only seven light-years away. The crew toroid can support us for that long.

'There's some of the ratings and NCOs I'd like to get off,' Kelven Solanki datavised. 'This wasn't supposed to be a front-line posting. They're only kids, really.'

'No, all of you are coming,' Auster said flatly.

'I'd like to capture one of these sequestrated invaders if possible,' Jeroen van Ewyck put in quickly.

What about the marines, Erato? Auster asked. **Do you think it's worth a try?**

I'll fly recovery if we can spot them, the pilot said. His thoughts conveyed a rising excitement.

Auster acknowledged his leaked feelings with an ironic thought. Pilots were uniformly a macho breed, unable to resist any challenge, even Edenist ones.

The Juliffe basin is proving difficult to resolve, *Ilex* said with a note of annoyance. **My optical sensors are unable to receive a clearly defined image of the river and its tributaries for about a thousand kilometres inland.**

It's night over the basin, and we're still seventy thousand kilometres away, Auster pointed out.

Even so, the optical resolution should be better than this.

'Commander Solanki, we're going to attempt to recover the marines as well,' Auster said.

'I haven't been able to contact them for over a day. God, I don't even know if they're still alive, let alone where they are.'

'None the less, they are our naval personnel. If there's any chance, we owe them the effort.'

The statement drew him a startled glance from Jeroen van Ewyck and the other two Adamists on the bridge. They quickly tried to hide their gaffe. Auster ignored it.

'Christ but— All right,' Kelven Solanki datavised. 'I'll fly the recovery myself, though. No point in risking your spaceplane. It was me who ordered them in there to start with. My responsibility.'

'As you wish. If our sensors can locate their fishing boat, do you have an aircraft available?'

'I can get one. But the invaders knocked out the last plane to fly into their territory. One thing I do know is that they've got some lethal fire-power going for them.'

'So has *Ilex*,' Auster said bluntly.

*

Joshua Calvert fell back onto the translucent sheet and let out a heartfelt breath. The bed's jelly-substance mattress was rocking him gently as the waves slowed. Sweat trickled across his chest and limbs. He gazed up at the electrophoresescent cell clusters on Ione's ceiling. Their ornate leaf pattern was becoming highly familiar.

'That's definitely one of the better ways of waking up,' he said.

'One?' Ione unwrapped her legs from his waist and sat back on his legs. She stretched provocatively, hands going behind her neck.

Joshua groaned, staring at her voraciously.

'Tell me another,' she said.

He sat up, bringing his face twenty centimetres from hers. 'Watching you,' he said in a throaty voice.

'Does that turn you on?'

'Yes.'

'Solo, or with another girl?' She felt his muscles tighten in reflex. Well, that's my answer, she thought. But then she'd always known how much he enjoyed threesomes. It wasn't Joshua's cock which was hard to satisfy, just his ego.

He grinned; the Joshua rogueish-charm grin. 'I bet this conversation is going to turn to Dominique.'

Ione gave his nose a butterfly kiss. They just couldn't fool each other; it was a togetherness similar to the one she enjoyed with the habitat personality. Comforting and eerie at the same time. 'You mentioned her name first.'

'Are you upset about her coming to Lalonde with me?'

'No. It makes sound business sense.'

'You do disapprove.' He stroked the side of her breasts tenderly. 'There's no need to be jealous. I have been to bed with Dominique, you know.'

'I know. I watched you on that big bed of hers, remember?'

He cupped her breasts and kissed each nipple in turn. 'Let's bring her to this bed.'

She looked down on the top of his head. 'Not possible, sorry. The Saldanas eradicated the gay gene from their DNA three hundred years ago. Couldn't risk the scandal, they are supposed to uphold the ten commandments throughout the kingdom, after all.'

Joshua didn't believe a word of it. 'They missed erasing the adultery gene, then.'

She smiled. 'What's your hurry to hit the mattress with her? The two of you are going to spend a week locked up in that zero-gee sex cage of yours.'

'You are jealous.'

'No. I never claimed to have an exclusive right to you. After all, I didn't complain about Norfolk.'

He pulled his head back from her breasts. 'Ione!' he complained.

'You reeked of guilt. Was she very beautiful?'

'She was . . . sweet.'

'Sweet? Why, Joshua Calvert, I do believe you're getting romantic in your old age.'

Joshua sighed and dropped back on the mattress again. He wished she'd make up her mind whether she was jealous or not. 'Do I ask about your lovers?'

Ione couldn't help the slight flush that crept up her cheeks. Hans had been fun while it lasted, but she'd never felt as free with him as she did with Joshua. 'No,' she admitted.

'Ah hah, I'm not the only one who's guilty, by the looks of it.'

She traced a forefinger down his sternum and abdomen until she was stroking his thighs. 'Quits?'

'Yes.' His hands found her hips. 'I brought you another present.'

'Joshua! What?'

'A gigantea seed. That's an aboriginal Lalonde tree. I saw a couple on the edge of Durringham, they were eighty metres tall, but Marie said they were just babies, the really big ones are further inland from the coast.'

'*Marie* said that, did she?'

'Yes.' He refused to be put off. 'It should grow all right in

Tranquillity's parkland. But you'll have to plant it where the soil is deep and there's plenty of moisture.'

'I'll remember.'

'It'll grow up to the light-tube eventually.'

She pulled a disbelieving face.

I will have to run environmental compatibility tests first, Tranquillity said. **Our biosphere is delicately balanced.**

So cynical. 'Thank you, Joshua,' she said out loud.

Joshua realized he had regained his erection. 'Why don't you just ease forward a bit?'

'I could give you a treat instead,' Ione said seductively. 'A real male fantasy come true.'

'Yes?'

'Yes. There's a girlfriend of mine I'd like you to meet. We go swimming together every morning. You'd like that, watching us get all wet and slippery. She's younger than me. And she never, ever wears a swimming costume.'

'Jesus.' Joshua's face went from greed to caution. 'This isn't on the level,' he decided.

'Yes, it is. She's also very keen to meet you. She likes it a lot when people wash her. I do it all the time, sliding my hands all over her. Don't you want to join me?'

He looked up at Ione's mock-innocent expression, and wondered what the hell he was letting himself in for. Gay gene, like bollocks. 'Lead on.'

*

They had walked fifty metres down the narrow sandy path towards the cove, Ione's escort of three serjeants an unobtrusive ten paces behind, when Joshua stopped and looked round. 'This is the southern endcap.'

'That's right,' she said slyly.

He caught up with her as she reached the top of the bluff. The long, gently curving cove below looked tremendously enticing, with a border of shaggy palm trees and a tiny island offshore. Away in the distance he could see the elaborate buildings of the Laymil project campus.

'It's all right,' she said. 'I won't have you arrested for coming here.'

He shrugged and followed her down the bluff. Ione was running on ahead as he reached the sand. Her towelling robe was flung away. 'Come on, Joshua!' Spray frothed up as her feet reached the water.

A naked girl, a tropical beach. Irresistible. He dropped his own robe and jogged down the slope. Something was moving behind him, something making dull thudding sounds as it moved, something heavy. He turned. 'Jesus!'

A Kiint was running straight at him. It was smaller than any he'd seen before, about three metres long, only just taller than him. Eight fat legs were flipping about in a rhythm which was impossible to follow.

His feet refused to budge. 'Ione!'

She was laughing hysterically. 'Morning, Haile,' she called at the top of her voice.

The Kiint lumbered to a halt in front of him. He was looking into a pair of soft violet eyes half as wide as his own face. A stream of warm damp breath poured from the breathing vents.

'Er . . .'

One of the tractamorphic arms curved up, the tip formshifting into the shape of a human hand – slightly too large.

'Well, say hello, then,' Ione said; she had walked up to stand behind him.

'I'll get you for this, Saldana.'

She giggled. 'Joshua, this is my girlfriend, Haile. Haile, this is Joshua.'

Why has he so much stiffness? Haile asked.

Ione cracked up, nearly doubling over as she laughed. Joshua gave her a furious glare.

Not want to shake hands? Not want to initiate human greetings

ritual? Not want to be friends? The Kiint sounded mournfully disappointed.

'Joshua, shake hands. Haile's upset you don't want to be friends with her.'

'How do you know?' he asked out of the corner of his mouth.

'Affinity. The Kiint can use it.'

He put his hand up. Haile's arm reached out, and he felt a dry, slightly scaly, bud of flesh flow softly around his fingers. It tickled. His neural nanonics were executing a priority search through the xenoc files he had stored in a memory cell. The Kiint could hear.

'May your thoughts always fly high, Haile,' he said, and gave a slight formal bow.

I have much likening for him!

Ione gave him a calculating stare. I might have known that charm of his would work on xenocs too, she thought.

Joshua felt the Kiint's flesh deliver a warm squeeze to his hand, then the pseudo-hand peeled back. The itchy sensation it left in his palm seemed to spread up along his spine and into his skull.

'Your new girlfriend,' he said heavily.

Ione smiled. 'Haile was born a few weeks ago. And boy, does she grow fast.'

Haile started to push Ione towards the water, flat triangular head butting the girl spiritedly, beak flapping. One of her tractamorphic arms beckoned avidly at Joshua.

He grinned. 'I'm coming.' His scalp felt as if he'd been in the sun too long, an all-over tingle.

'The water eases her skin while she's growing,' Ione said as she skipped ahead of the eager Kiint. 'She needs to bathe two or three times a day. All the Kiint houses have interior pools. But she loves the beach.'

'Well, I'll be happy to help scrub her while I'm here.'

Much gratitude.

'My pleasure,' Joshua said. He stopped. Haile was standing at the edge of the water, big eyes regarding him attentively. 'That was you.'

Yes.

'What was?' Ione asked, she looked from one to the other.

'I can hear her.'

'But you don't have an affinity gene,' she said, surprised, and maybe a little indignant.

Joshua has thoughts of strength. Much difficulty to effect interlocution, but possible. Not so with most humans. Feel hopelessness. Failure sorrow.

He swaggered. 'Strong thoughts, see?'

'Haile hasn't quite mastered our language, that's all,' Ione smiled with menace. 'She's confused strength with simplicity. You have very elementary thoughts.'

Joshua rubbed his hands together determinedly, and walked towards her. Ione backed away, then turned and ran giggling into the water. He caught her after six metres, and the two of them fell into the small clear ripples whooping and laughing. Haile plunged in after them.

Much joyness. Much joyness.

Joshua was interested by how well the young Kiint could swim. He would have considered her body too heavy to float, but she could move at a fair speed; her tractamorphic arms spread out into flippers, and angled back along her flanks. Ione wouldn't let her go out to the little island, saying it was still too far, which ruling Haile accepted with rebellious sulks.

I have seen some of the all-around's park space, she told Joshua proudly as he rubbed the dorsal ridge above her rump. **Ione has shown me. So much to absorb. Adventureness fun. Envy Joshua.**

Joshua didn't quite understand how to collect his thoughts into a voice Haile could understand, instead he simply spoke. 'You envy me? Why?'

Venture as you please. Fly to stars so distant. Welcome sights so strange. I want this, muchness!

'I don't think you'd fit in the *Lady Mac.* Besides, human ships that can carry Kiint have to be licensed by your government. I haven't got that licence.'

Sadness. Anger. Frustration. I may not venture beyond adult defined constraints. Much growth before I can.

'Bumming round the universe isn't all it's cracked up to be. Most of the Confederation planets are pretty tame, and travelling on a starship is boring; dangerous too.'

Danger? Excitement query?

Joshua moved down towards Haile's flexible neck. Ione was grinning at him over the xenoc's white back.

'No, not excitement. There's a danger of mechanical failure. That can be fatal.'

You have excitement. Achievement. Ione narrated many voyages you have undertaken. Triumph in Ruin Ring. Much gratification. Such boldness exhibited.

Ione turned her giggle into a cough. **You're a flirt, girl.**

Incorrect access mode to human males, query? Praise of character, followed by dumb admiration for feats; your instruction.

Yes, I did say that, didn't I. Perhaps not quite so literally, though.

'That was a while ago now,' Joshua said. 'Of course, life was pretty tricky in those days. One wrong move and it could have been catastrophic. The Ruin Ring is an ugly place. You've gotta have determination to be a scavenger. It's a lonely existence. Not everyone can take it.'

You achieved legend status. Most famous scavenger of all.

Don't push it, Ione warned.

'You mean the Laymil electronics stack? Yeah, it was a big find, I earned a lot of money from that one.'

Much cultural relevance.

'Oh, yeah, that too.'

Ione stopped rubbing Haile's neck and frowned. 'Joshua, haven't you accessed the records we've been decoding?'

'Er, what records?'

'Your electronics stack stored Laymil sensevise recordings. We've uncovered huge amounts of data on their culture.'

'Great. That's good news.'

She eyed him suspiciously. 'They were extremely advanced biologically. Well ahead of us on the evolutionary scale; they were almost completely in harmony with their habitat environment, so now we have to question just how artificial their habitats were. Their entire biology, the way they approached living organisms, is very different to our own perception. They revered any living entity. And their psychology is almost incomprehensible to us; they could be both highly individual, and at the same time submerge themselves into a kind of mental homogeneity. Two almost completely different states of consciousness. We think they may have been genuine telepaths. The research project geneticists are having furious arguments over the relevant gene sequence. It is similar to the Edenist affinity gene, but the Laymil psychology complements it in a way which is impossible to human Edenist culture. Edenists retain a core of identity even after they transfer their memories into the habitat personality at death, whereas the Laymil willingness to share their most private selves has to be the product of considerable mental maturity. You can't engineer behavioural instinct into DNA.'

'Have you found out what destroyed their habitats yet?' Joshua asked. Haile shuddered below his hand, a very human reflex. He felt a burst of cold alarm invading his thoughts. 'Hey, sorry.'

Fright. Scared feel. So many deaths. They had strength. Still were defeated. Query cause?

'I wish I knew,' Ione said. 'They seemed to celebrate life, much more than we do.'

*

The *Isakore* was bobbing about inertly on the Zamjan as though it was a log of elegantly carved driftwood, ripples slopping against the hull with quiet insistence. They had rigged up a couple of oarlike outriggers to steer with during the first day – the rudder alone was no good. And they'd managed to stick more or less to the centre of the river. It was eight hundred metres wide here, which gave them some leeway when the current began to shift them towards one of the banks.

According to Murphy Hewlett's inertial-guidance block they had floated about thirty kilometres downriver since the micro-fusion generator had been taken out. The current had pushed them with dogged tenacity the whole time, taking them away from the landing site and the burnt antagonistic jungle. Only another eight hundred plus kilometres to go.

Jacqueline Couteur had been no trouble, spending her time sitting up in the prow under the canvas awning. If it hadn't been for the ordeal they'd been through, the price they'd paid in their own pain and grief, to capture her, Murphy would have tied the useless micro-fusion generator round her neck and tossed her overboard. He thought she knew that. But she was their mission. And they were still alive, and still intact. Until that changed, Lieutenant Murphy Hewlett was going to obey orders and take her back to Durringham. There was nothing else left, no alternative purpose to life.

Nobody had tried to interfere with them, although their communication channels were definitely being jammed (none of the other equipment blocks were affected). Even the villages they had sailed past had shown no interest. A couple of rowing dinghies had ventured close the first morning, but they'd been warned off with shots from one of the Bradfields. After that the *Isakore* had been left alone.

It was almost a peaceful voyage. They'd eaten well, cleaned and reloaded the weapons, done what they could about their wounds. Niels Regehr swam in and out of lucidity, but the medical nanonic package clamped over his face was keeping him reasonably stable.

Murphy could just about allow himself to believe they would

return to Durringham. The placid river encouraged that kind of foolish thinking.

As night fell at the end of the second day he sat at the stern, holding on to the tiller they had fixed up, and doing his best to keep the boat in the centre of the river. At least with this job he didn't have to use his leg with its achingly stiff knee, though his left hand was incapable of gripping the tiller pole. The clammy air from the water made his fatigues uncomfortably sticky.

He saw Louis Beith making his way aft, carrying a flask. A medical nanonic package made a broad bracelet around his arm where Jacqueline Couteur had broken the bone and it glimmered dimly in the infrared spectrum.

'Brought you some juice,' Louis said. 'Straight out the cryo.'

'Thanks.' Murphy took the mug he held out. With his retinal implants switched to infrared, the liquid he poured from the flask was a blue so deep it was nearly black.

'Niels is talking to his demons again,' Louis said quietly.

'Not much we can do about it, short of loading a somnolence program into his neural nanonics.'

'Yeah, but Lieutenant; what he says, it's like it's for real, you know? I thought people hallucinating don't make any sense. He's even got me looking over my shoulder.'

Murphy took a swallow of the juice. It was freezing, numbing the back of his throat. Just perfect. 'It bothers you that bad? I could put him under, I suppose.'

'No, not *bad*. It's just kinda spooky, what with everything we saw, and all.'

'I think that electronic warfare gimmick the hostiles have affects our neural nanonics more than we like to admit.'

'Yeah?' Louis brightened. 'Maybe you're right.' He stood with his hands on his hips, staring ahead to the west. 'Man, that is some meteorite shower. I ain't never seen one that good before.'

Murphy looked up into the cloudless night sky. High above the *Isakore*'s prow the stars were tumbling down from their fixed constellations. There was a long broad slash of them scintillating and flashing. He actually smiled, they looked so picturesque. And the hazy slash was still growing as more of them hit the atmosphere, racing eastwards. It must be a prodigious swarm gliding in from interplanetary space, the remains of some burnt-out comet that had disintegrated centuries ago. The meteorites furthest away were developing huge contrails as they sizzled their way downwards. They were certainly penetrating the atmosphere a long way, tens of kilometres at least. Murphy's smile bled away. 'Oh my God,' he said in a tiny dry voice.

'What?' Louis asked happily. 'Isn't that something smooth? Wow! I could look at that all night long.'

'They're not meteorites.'

'What?'

'They're not meteorites. Shit!'

Louis looked at him in alarm.

'They're bloody kinetic harpoons!' Murphy started to run forwards as fast as his knee would allow. 'Secure yourself!' he shouted. 'Grab something and hold on. They're coming down right on top of us.'

The sky was turning to day overhead, blackness flushed away by a spreading stain of azure blue. The contrails to the west were becoming too bright to look at. They seemed to be lengthening at a terrific rate, cracks of sunlight splitting open across the wall of night.

Kinetic harpoons were the Confederation Navy's standard tactical (non-radioactive) planetary surface assault weapon. A solid splinter of toughened, heat-resistant composite, half a metre long, needle sharp, guided by a cruciform tail, steered by a processor with preprogrammed flight vector. They carried no explosives, no energy charge; they destroyed their target through speed alone.

Ilex accelerated in towards Lalonde at eight gees, following a precise hyperbolic trajectory. The apex was reached twelve hundred kilometres above Amarisk, two hundred kilometres east of Durringham. Five thousand harpoons were expelled from the voidhawk's weapons cradles, hurtling towards the night-masked continent below. *Ilex* inverted the direction of its distortion field's acceleration wave, fighting Lalonde's gravity. Stretched out on their couches, the crew raged impotently against the appalling gee force, nanonic supplement membranes turning rigid to hold soft weak human bodies together as the voidhawk dived away from the planet.

The harpoon swarm sheered down through the atmosphere, hypervelocity friction ablating away the composite's outer layer of molecules to leave a dazzling ionic tail over a hundred kilometres long. From below it resembled a rain of fierce liquid light.

Their silence was terrifying. A display of such potency should sound like the roar of an angry god. Murphy clung to one of the rails along the side of the wheel-house, squinting through squeezed-up eyelids as the solid sheet of vivid destruction plummeted towards him. He heard Jacqueline Couteur moaning in fear, and felt a cheap, malicious satisfaction. It was the first time she had shown the slightest emotion. Impact could only be seconds away now.

The harpoons were directly overhead, an atmospheric river of solar brilliance mirroring the Zamjan's course. They split down the centre, two solid planes of light diverging with immaculate symmetry, sliding down to touch the jungle away in the west then racing past the *Isakore* at a speed too fast even for enhanced human senses to follow. None of them, not one, landed in the water.

Multiple explosions obliterated the jungle. Along both sides of the Zamjan gouts of searing purple flame streaked upwards as the harpoons struck the earth, releasing their colossal kinetic energy in a single devastating burst of heat. The swath of devastation extended for a length of seven kilometres along the banks, reaching a kilometre and a half inland. A thick filthy cloud of loam and stone and wood splinters belched up high into the air, blotting out the heat flashes. The blast-wave rolled out in both directions, flattening still more of the jungle.

Then the sound broke over the boat. The roar of the explosions overlapped, merging into a single sonic battering-ram which made every plank on the *Isakore* twang as if it was an overtuned guitar string. After that came the eternal thunderclap of the air being ripped apart by the harpoons' plunge; sound waves finally catching up with the weapons.

Murphy jammed his hands across his stinging eardrums. His whole skeleton was shaking, joints resonating painfully.

Debris started to patter down, puckering the already distressed surface of the river. A sprinkling of fires burnt along the banks where shattered trees lay strewn among deep craters. Pulverized loam and wood hung in the air, an obscure black fog above the mortally wounded land.

Murphy slowly lowered his hands, staring at the awful vision of destruction. 'It was our side,' he said in dazed wonder. 'We did it.'

Garrett Tucci was at his side, jabbering away wildly. Murphy couldn't hear a thing. His ears were still ringing vociferously. 'Shout! Datavise! My ears have packed up.'

Garrett blinked, he held up his communications block. 'It's working,' he yelled.

Murphy datavised his own block, which reported the channel to the ELINT satellite was open.

A beam of bright white light slid over the *Isakore*, originating from somewhere above. Murphy watched as the beam swung out over the water, then tracked back towards the boat. He looked up, beyond surprise. It was coming from a small aircraft hovering two hundred metres overhead, outlined by the silver stars. Green, red, and white strobes flashed on the tips of its wings and canards. His neural nanonics identified the jet-black planform, a BK133.

Murphy's communication block bleeped to acknowledge a local channel opening. 'Murphy? Are you there, Murphy?'

'Sir? Is that you?' he asked incredulously.

'Expecting someone else?' Kelven Solanki datavised.

The beam found the *Isakore* again, and remained trained on the deck.

'Have you still got your prisoner?'

'Yes, sir.' Murphy glanced at Jacqueline Couteur, who was staring up at the aircraft, shielding her eyes against the spotlight.

'Good man. We'll take her back with us.'

'Sir, Niels Regehr is injured pretty badly. I don't think he can climb a rope ladder.'

'No problem.'

The BK133 was descending carefully, wings rocking in the thermal microbursts generated by the harpoons' impact. Murphy could feel the compressor jets gusting against his face, a hot dry wind, pleasant after the river's humidity. He saw a wide hatch was open on the side of the fuselage. A man in naval fatigues was slowly winching down towards the *Isakore*.

*

Floodlights on the roof of the navy office showed the grounds around the building were thick with people. All of them seemed to be looking up into the night sky.

Murphy watched them through the BK133's open mid-fuselage hatch as Kelven Solanki piloted it down onto the roof pad. A wedge-shaped spaceplane was sitting on one side of the roof, wings retracted; it only just fitted, tail and nose were overhanging the edges. It was one of the most welcome sights he had seen in a long long while.

'Who are all those people?' he asked.

'Anyone who saw *Ilex*'s spaceplane taking the staff away earlier,' Vince Burtis said. He was the nineteen-year-old navy rating who had winched the marine squad to safety. To him the invasion was exactly what he had signed on for, adventure on alien worlds; he was enjoying himself. Murphy hadn't the heart to disillusion him. The kid would realize soon enough.

'I guess they want to leave too,' Vince Burtis said soberly.

The BK133 settled on the roof. Kelven datavised the flight computer to power down the internal systems. 'Everyone out,' he said.

'Hurry, please.' Erato's appeal was relayed through his communication block. 'I'm in touch with the sheriffs outside. They say the crowd is already at the door.'

'They shouldn't be able to get in,' Kelven datavised.

'I think some of the sheriffs may be with them,' Erato said hesitantly. 'They're only human.'

Kelven released his straps and hurried back into the cabin. Vince Burtis was guiding Niels Regehr's tentative footsteps, helping him down through the hatch. Garrett Tucci and Louis Beith were already out, marching Jacqueline Couteur towards the spaceplane at gunpoint.

Murphy Hewlett gave his superior a tired smile. 'Thank you, sir.'

'Nothing to do with me. If the *Ilex* hadn't shown up you'd still be paddling home.'

'Is everyone else from the office out?'

'Yes, the spaceplane made a couple of flights earlier this evening, we're the last,' Kelven said.

They both hopped down onto the roof. The noise of the spaceplane's compressors rose, obscuring the sound of the crowd below. Kelven did his best to ignore the sensation of guilt. He had made a lot of friends among Lalonde's civil administration staff. Candace Elford had turned over the BK133 as soon as he asked, no questions. Surely some people could have been taken up to the orbiting colonist-carriers.

Who though? And who would choose?

The best – the only – way to help Lalonde now was through the Confederation Navy.

The stairwell door on the other side of the BK133 burst open. People began to spill out onto the roof, shouting frantically.

'Oh, Christ,' Kelven said under his breath. He could see three or four sheriffs among them, armed with cortical jammers, one had a laser hunting rifle. The rest were civilians. He looked round. Vince Burtis and Niels Regehr were halfway up the stairs to the airlock. One of the *Ilex*'s crew was leaning out, offering a hand to Niels. Vince was staring over his shoulder in shock.

'Get in,' Kelven datavised, waving his arms.

Two sheriffs were rounding the nose of the BK133, more people were crouched low scuttling under the fuselage. Still more were running out of the open door. There must have been thirty on the roof.

'Wait for us.'

'You can carry one more.'

'I have money, I can pay.'

Murphy aimed his Bradfield into the air and fired off two shots. The heavy-calibre weapon was startlingly loud. Several people threw themselves down, the rest froze.

'Don't even think about it,' Murphy said. The Bradfield lined up on one of the ashen-faced sheriffs. A cortical jammer fell from the man's hands.

The noise of the spaceplane's compressors was becoming strident.

'There's no room on board. Go home before anyone gets hurt.'

Kelven and Murphy started backing towards the spaceplane. A young brown-skinned woman who had crawled under the BK133 straightened up, and walked towards them defiantly. She was holding a small child in front of her, it couldn't have been more than two years old. Plump face and wide liquid eyes.

Murphy just couldn't bring himself to point the Bradfield at her. He reached the foot of the spaceplane's aluminium stairs.

'Take him with you,' the woman called. She held the child

out. 'For Jesus's sake, take my son, if you have a gram of pity in you. I'm begging you!'

Murphy's foot found the first step. Kelven had a hand on his arm, guiding him back.

'Take him!' she shrieked over the swelling compressor efflux. 'Take him, or shoot him.'

He shuddered at her fervour. She meant it, she really meant it.

'It would be a kindness. You know what will happen to him on this cursed planet.' The child was crying, squirming about in her grip.

The other people on the roof were all motionless, watching him with hard, accusing eyes. He turned to Kelven Solanki, whose face was a mask of torment.

'Get him,' Kelven blurted.

Murphy dropped the Bradfield, letting it skitter away across the silicon roof. He datavised a codelock into its controlling processor so no one could turn it on the spaceplane, then grabbed the child with his right hand.

'Shafi,' the woman shouted as he raced up the stairs. 'His name's Shafi Banaji. Remember.'

He barely had a foot in the airlock when the spaceplane lifted, its deck tilting up immediately. Hands steadied him, and the outer hatch slid shut.

Shafi's baggy cotton trousers were soiled and stinking; he let out a long fearful wail.

21

Including Tranquillity, there were only five independent (non-Edenist) bitek habitats to be found within the boundaries of the Confederation. After Tranquillity, probably the most well known, or notorious depending on your cultural outlook and degree of liberalism, was Valisk.

Although they were both, technically, dictatorships, they occupied opposite ends of the political spectrum, with the dominant ideologies of the remaining three habitats falling between them, a well-deserved mediocrity. Tranquillity was regarded as élitist, or even regal given its founder: industrious, rich, and slightly raffish, with a benevolent, chic ruler, it emphasized the grander qualities of life, somewhere you aspired to go if you made it. Valisk was older, its glory days over, or at the very least in abeyance: it played host to a more decadent population; money here (and there was still plenty) came from exploiting the darker side of human nature. And its strange governorship repelled rather than attracted.

It hadn't always been so.

Valisk was founded by an Edenist Serpent called Rubra. Unlike Laton, who terrorized the Confederation two and a half centuries later, his rebellion was of an altogether more constructive nature. He was born in Machaon, a habitat orbiting Kohistan, the largest gas giant in the Srinagar star system. After forty-four years, he abandoned his culture and his home, sold his not inconsiderable share in his family's engineering enterprise, and emigrated to a newly opened Adamist asteroid settlement in Kohistan's trailing Trojan cluster.

It was a period of substantial economic growth for the star system. Srinagar had been colonized by ethnic-Hindus in 2178 during the Great Dispersal, a hundred and sixteen years earlier. Basic industrialization had been completed, the world was tamed, and people were looking for new ways of channelling their energies. All across the Confederation emerging colony planets were exploiting space resources and increasing their wealth dramatically. Srinagar was eager to be numbered among them.

Rubra started with six leased interplanetary cargo ships. Like all Serpents he was a high achiever in his chosen field (nearly always to Edenist embarrassment, for so many of them chose crime). He made a small fortune supplying the Trojan cluster's small but wealthy population of engineers and miners with consumer goods and luxuries. He bought more ships, made a larger fortune, and named his expanding company Magellanic Itg – joking to his peers that one day he would trade with that distant star cluster. By 2306, after twelve years of steady growth, Magellanic Itg owned manufacturing stations and asteroid-mining operations, and had moved into the interstellar transport market.

At this point Rubra germinated Valisk in orbit around Opuntia, the fourth of the system's five gas giants. It was a huge gamble. He spent his company's entire financial reserves cloning the seed, mortgaging half of the starships to boot. And bitek remained technology *non grata* for the major religions, including the Hindu faith. But Srinagar was sufficiently Bolshevik about its new economic independence from its sponsoring Govcentral Indian states, and energetic enough in its approach to innovation, to cast a blind eye to proscriptions announced by fundamentalist Brahmians on a distant imperialist planet over two centuries earlier. Planet and asteroid governments saw no reason to impose embargoes against what was rapidly evolving into one of the system's premier economic assets. Valisk became, literally, a corporate state, acting as the home port for Magellanic Itg's starship fleet (already one of the largest in the sector) and dormitory town for its industrial stations.

Although Valisk was a financially advantageous location from which Rubra could run his flourishing corporate empire, he needed to attract a base population to the habitat to make it a viable pocket civilization. Industrial stations were therefore granted extremely liberal weapons and research licences and Valisk started to attract companies specializing in military hardware. Export constraints were almost non-existent.

Rubra also opened the habitat to immigration for 'people who seek cultural and religious freedom', possibly in reaction to his own formal Edenist upbringing. This invitation attracted several nonconformist religious cults, spiritual groups, and primitive lifestyle tribes, who believed that a bitek environment would fulfil the role of some benevolent Gaia and provide them free food and shelter. Over nine thousand of these people arrived over the course of the habitat's first twenty-five years, many of them drug- or stimulant-program addicts. At this time, Rubra, infuriated with their unrepentant parasitical nature, banned any more from entering.

By 2330 the population had risen to three hundred and fifty thousand. Industrial output was high, and many interstellar companies were opening regional offices inside.

Then the first blackhawks to be seen in the Confederation began to appear, all of them registered with Magellanic Itg, and captained by Rubra's plentiful offspring. Rubra had pulled off a spectacular coup against both his competitors and his former culture. Voidhawk bitek was the most sophisticated ever sequenced; copying it was a triumph of genetic retro-engineering.

With blackhawks now acting as the mainstay of his starship fleet, Rubra was unchallengeable. A large-scale cloning programme saw their numbers rising dramatically; neural symbionts were used to give captaincies to Adamists who had no qualms about using bitek, and there were many. By 2365 Magellanic Itg ceased to use anything other than blackhawks in its transport fleet.

Rubra died in 2390, one of the wealthiest men in the Confederation. He left behind an industrial conglomerate used as an example by economists ever since as the classic corporate growth model. It should have carried on. It had the potential to rival the Kulu Corporation owned by the Saldana family. Ultimately it might even have equalled the Edenist He_3 cloud-mining operation. No physical or financial restrictions existed to limit its inherent promise; banks were more than willing to advance loans, the markets existed, supplied by its own ships.

But in the end – after the end – Rubra's Serpent nature proved less than benign after all. His psychology was too different, too obsessional. Brought up knowing his personality pattern would continue to exist for centuries if not millennia, he refused to accept death as an Adamist. He transferred his personality pattern into Valisk's neural strata.

From this point onward company and habitat started to degenerate. Part of the reason was the germination of the other independent habitats, all of whom offered themselves as bases for blackhawk mating flights. The Valisk/Magellanic Itg monopoly was broken. But the company's industrial decline, and the habitat's parallel deterioration, was due principally to the inheritance problem Rubra created.

When he died he was known to have fathered over a hundred and fifty children, a hundred and twenty-two of whom were carefully conceived *in vitro* and gestated in exowombs; all had modifications made to their affinity gene, as well as general physiological improvements. Thirty of the exowomb children were appointed to Valisk's executive committee, which ran both the habitat and Magellanic Itg, while the remainder, along with the rapidly proliferating third generation, became blackhawk pilots. The naturally conceived children were virtually disinherited from the company, and many of them returned to the Edenist fold.

Even this nepotistic arrangement shouldn't have been too much trouble. There would inevitably be power struggles within such a large committee, but strong characters would rise to the top, simple human dynamics demanded it. None ever did.

The alteration Rubra had made to their affinity gene was a simple one; they were bonded to the habitat and a single family of blackhawks alone. He robbed them of the Edenist general affinity. The arrangement gave him access to their minds virtually from the moment of conception, first through the habitat personality, then after he died, as the habitat personality.

He shaped them as they lay huddled in the metal and composite exowombs, and later in their innocent childhood; a dark conscience nestled maggot-fashion at the centre of their consciousness, examining their most secret thoughts for deviations from the path he had chosen. It was a dreadfully perverted version of the love bond which existed between voidhawks and their captains. His descendants became little more than anaemic caricatures of himself at his prime. He tried to instil the qualities which had driven him, and wound up with wretched neurotic inadequates. The more he attempted to tighten his discipline, the worse their dependence upon him became. A slow change manifested in the habitat personality's psychology. In his growing frustration with his living descendants he became resentful; of their lives, of their bodily experiences, of the emotions they could feel, the humanness of glands and hormones running riot. Rubra was jealous of the living.

Edenist visits to the habitat, already few and far between, stopped altogether after 2480. They said the habitat personality had become insane.

*

Dariat was an eighth-generation descendant, born a hundred and seventy-five years after Rubra's body died. Physically he was virtually indistinguishable from his peer group; he shared the light coffee-coloured skin and raven hair that signalled the star system's ethnic origin. A majority of Valisk's population originated insystem, though few of them were practising Hindus. Only his indigo eyes marked him out as anything other than a straight Srinagar genotype.

He never knew of his calamitous inheritance until his teens, although even from his infancy he knew in his heart he was different; he was better, superior to all the other children in his day club. And when they laughed at him, or teased him, or sent him to Coventry, he laid into them with a fury that none of them could match. He didn't know where it came from himself, only that it lay within, like some slumbering lake-bottom monster. At first he felt shame at the beatings he inflicted, blood for a five-year-old is a shocking sight; but even as he ran home crying a different aspect of the alien ego would appear and soothe him, calming his pounding heart. There was nothing wrong, he was assured, no crime committed, only rightness. They shouldn't have said what they did, catcalled and sneered. You were right to assert yourself, you are strong, be proud of that.

After a while the feelings of guilt ebbed away. When he needed to hit someone he did it without remorse or regret. His leadership of the day club was undisputed, out of fear rather than respect.

He lived with his mother in a starscraper apartment; his father had left her the year he was born. He knew his father was important, that he helped to manage Magellanic Itg; but whenever he paid mother and son one of his dutiful visits he was subject to moody silences or bursts of frantic activity. Dariat didn't like him, the grown-up was weird. I can do without him, the boy thought, he's weak. The conviction was as strong as one of his didactic imprints. His father stopped visiting after he was twelve years old.

Dariat concentrated on science and finance subjects when he began receiving didactic courses at ten years old, although right at the back of his mind was the faintest notion that the arts might just have been equally appealing. But they were despicable moments of weakness, soon swallowed by the pride he felt whenever he passed another course assessment. He was headed for great things.

At fourteen the crux came. At fourteen he fell in love.

Valisk's interior did not follow the usual bitek habitat convenience of a tropical or sub-tropical environment. Rubra had decided on a scrub desert extending out from the base of the northern endcap, then blending slowly into hilly savannah plain of terrestrial and xenoc grasses before the standard circumfluous salt-water reservoir at the base of the southern endcap.

Dariat was fond of hiking round the broad grasslands with their subtle blend of species and colours. The children's day club which he used to dominate had long since broken up. Adolescents were supposed to join sports groups, or general interest clubs. He had trouble integrating, too many peers remembered his temper and violence long after he had stopped resorting to such crude methods. They shunned him, and he told himself he didn't care. Somebody told him. In dreams he would find himself walking through the habitat talking to a white-haired old man. The old man was a big comfort, the things he said, the encouragement he gave. And the habitat was slightly different, richer, with trees and flowers and happy crowds, families picnicking.

'It's going to be like this once you're in charge,' the old man told him numerous times. 'You're the best there's been for decades. Almost as good as me. You'll bring it all back to me, the power and the wealth.'

'This is the future?' Dariat asked. They were standing on a tall altar of polyp-rock, looking down on a circular starscraper entrance. People were rushing about with a vigour and purpose not usually found in Valisk. Every one of them was wearing a Magellanic Itg uniform. When he lifted his gaze it was as though the northern endcap was transparent; blackhawks flocked around their docking rings, loaded with expensive goods and rare artefacts from a hundred planets. Further out, so far away it was only a hazy ginger blob, Magellanic Itg's failed Von Neumann machine spun slowly against the gas giant's yellow-brown ring array.

'It could be the future,' the old man sighed regretfully. 'If you will only listen how.'

'I will,' Dariat said. 'I'll listen.'

The old man's schemes seemed to coincide with the pressure of conviction and certainty which was building in his own mind. Some days he seemed so full of ideas and goals he thought his skull must surely burst apart, whilst on other occasions the dream man's long rambling speeches seemed to have developed a tangible echo, lasting all day long.

That was why he enjoyed the long bouts of solitude provided by the unadventurous interior. Walking and exploring obscure areas was the only time the raging thoughts in his brain slowed and calmed.

Five days after his fourteenth birthday he saw Anastasia Rigel. She was washing in a river that ran along the floor of a deep valley. Dariat heard her singing before he saw her. The voice led him round some genuine rock boulders onto a shelf of naked polyp which the water had scoured of soil. He squatted down in the lee of the boulders, and watched her kneeling at the side of the river.

The girl was tall and much much blacker than anyone he'd seen in Valisk before. She appeared to be in her late teens (seventeen, he learned later), with legs that seemed to be all bands of muscle, and long jet-black hair that was arranged in ringlets and woven with red and yellow beads. Her face was narrow and delicate with a petite nose. There were dozens of slim silver and bronze bracelets on each arm.

She was only wearing a blue skirt of some thin cotton. A brown top of some kind lay on the polyp beside her. Dariat caught some fleeting glimpses of high pointed breasts as she rubbed water across her chest and arms. It was even better than accessing bluesense AV fleks and tossing off. For once he felt beautifully calm.

I'm going to have her, he thought, I really am. The certainty burned him.

She stood up, and pulled her brown top on. It was a sleeveless waistcoat made from thin supple leather, laced up the front. 'You can come out now,' she said in a clear voice.

Just for a moment he felt wholly inferior. Then he trotted towards her with a casualness that denied she had just caught him spying. 'I was trying not to alarm you,' he said.

She was twenty centimetres taller than him; she looked down and grinned openly. 'You couldn't.'

'Did you hear me? I thought I was being quiet.'

'I could feel you.'

'Feel me?'

'Yes. You have a very anguished spirit. It cries out.'

'And you can hear that?'

'Lin Yi was a distant ancestress.'

'Oh.'

'You have not heard of her?'

'No, sorry.'

'She was a famous spiritualist. She predicted the Big One2 quake in California back on Earth in 2058 and led her followers to safety in Oregon. A perilous pilgrimage for those times.'

'I'd like to hear that story.'

'I will tell it if you like. But I don't think you will listen. Your spirit is closed against the realm of Chi-ri.'

'You judge people very fast. We don't stand much of a chance, do we?'

'Do you know what the realm of Chi-ri is?'

'No.'

'Shall I tell you?'

'If you like.'

'Come then.'

She led him up the river, bracelets tinkling musically at every motion. They followed the tight curve of the valley; after three hundred metres the floor broadened out, and a Starbridge village was camped along the side of the river.

Starbridge was the remnants of the cults and tribes and spiritualists who had moved into Valisk during its formative years. They had slowly amalgamated down the decades, bonding together against the scorn and hostility of the other inhabitants. Now they were one big community, united spiritually with an *outré* fusion of beliefs that was often incomprehensible to any outsider. They embraced the primitive existence, living as tribes of migrants, walking round and round the interior of the habitat, tending their cattle, practising their handicraft, cultivating their opium poppies, and waiting for their nirvana.

Dariat looked out on the collection of ramshackle tepees, stringy animals with noses foraging the grass, children in rags running barefoot. He experienced a contempt so strong it verged on physical sickness. He was curious at that, he had no reason to hate the Starbridge freakos, he'd never had anything to do with them before. Even as he thought that, the loathing increased. Of course he did, slimy parasites, vermin on two legs.

Anastasia Rigel stroked his forehead in concern. 'You suffer yet you are strong,' she said. 'You spend so much time in the realm of Anstid.'

She brought him into her tepee, a cone of heavy hand-woven cloth. Wicker baskets ringed the walls. The light was dim, and the air dusty. The valley's pinkish grass was matted, dry and dying underfoot. He saw her sleeping roll bundled up against one basket, a bright orange blanket with pillows that had some kind of green and white tree motif embroidered across them, haloed by a ring of stars. He wondered if that was what he'd do it on, where he'd finally become a real man.

They sat crosslegged on a threadbare rug and drank tea, which was like coloured water, and didn't taste of much. Jasmine, she told him.

'What do you think of us?' she asked.

'Us?'

'The Starbridge tribes.'

'Never really thought about you much,' Dariat said. He was getting itchy sitting on the rug, and it was pretty obvious there weren't going to be any biscuits with the tea.

'You should. Starbridge is both our name and our dream, that which we seek to build. A bridge between stars, between all peoples. We are the final religion. They will all come to us eventually; the Christians and Muslims and Hindus and Buddhists, even the Satanists and followers of Wicca; every sect, every cult. Each and every one of them.'

'That's a pretty bold claim.'

'Not really. Just inevitable. There were so many of us, you see, when Rubra the Lost invited us here. So many beliefs, all different, yet really all the same. Then he turned on us, and confined us, and isolated us. He thought he would punish us, force us to conform to his materialistic atheism. But faith and dignity is always stronger than mortal oppression. We turned inwards for comfort, and found we had so much that we shared. We became one.'

'Starbridge being the one?'

'Yes. We burned the old scriptures and prayer books on a bonfire so high the flames reached right across the habitat. With them went all the ancient prejudices and the myths. It left us pure, in silence and darkness. Then we rebirthed ourselves, and renamed what we knew was real. There is so much that old Earth's religions have in common; so many identical beliefs and tenets and wisdoms. But their followers are forced apart by names, by priests who have grown decadent and greedy for physical reward. Whole peoples, whole planets who denounce one another so that a few evil men can wear robes of golden cloth.'

'That seems fairly logical,' Dariat said enthusiastically. 'Good idea.' He smiled. From where he was sitting he could see the whole side of her left breast through the waistcoat's lace-up front.

'I don't think you have come to faith that quickly,' she said with a trace of suspicion.

'I haven't. Because you haven't told me anything about it. But if you were telling the truth about hearing my spirit, then you've got my full attention. None of the other religions can offer tangible proof of God's existence.'

She shifted round on the rug, bracelets clinking softly. 'Neither do we offer proof. What we say is that life in this universe is only one segment of the great journey a spirit undertakes through time. We believe the journey will finish when a spirit reaches heaven, however you choose to define that existence. But don't ask how close this universe is to heaven. That depends on the individual.'

'What happens when your spirit reaches heaven?'

'Transcendence.'

'What sort?'

'That is for God to proclaim.'

'God. Not a goddess, then?' he asked teasingly.

She grinned at him. 'The word defines a concept, not an entity, not a white man with a white beard, nor even an earth mother. Physical bodies require gender. I don't think the instigator and sovereign of the multiverse is going to have physical and biological aspects, do you?'

'No.' He finished the tea, relieved the cup was empty. 'So what are these realms?'

'While the spirit is riding a body it also moves through the spiritual realms of the Lords and Ladies who govern nature. There are six realms, and five Lords and Ladies.'

'I thought you said there was only one heaven?'

'I did. The realms are not heaven, they are aspects of ourselves. The Lords and Ladies are not God, but they are of a higher order than ourselves. They affect events through the wisdoms and deceits they reveal to us. But they have no influence on the physical reality of the cosmos. They are not the instigators of miracles.'

'Like angels and demons?' he asked brightly.

'If you like. If that makes it easier to accept.'

'So they're in charge of us?'

'You are in charge of yourself. You and you alone chose where your spirit roams.'

'Then why the Lords and Ladies?'

'They grant gifts of knowledge and insight, they tempt. They test us.'

'Silly thing to do. Why don't they leave us alone?'

'Without experience there can be no growth. Existence is evolution, both on a spiritual and a personal level.'

'I see. So which is this Chi-ri I'm closed against?'

Anastasia Rigel climbed to her feet and went over to one of the wicker baskets. She pulled out a small goatskin bag. If she was aware of his hungry look following her every move she never showed it. 'These represent the Lords and Ladies,' she said as she sat back down. The bag's contents were tipped out. Six coloured pebble-sized crystals bounced on the rug. They had all been carved, he saw; cubes with their faces marked by small runes. She picked up the red one. 'This is for Thoale, Lord of destiny.' The blue crystal was held up, and she told him it was for Chi-ri, Lady of hope. Green was for Anstid, Lord of hatred. Yellow for Tarrug, Lord of mischief. Venus, Lady of love, was as clear as glass.

'You said there were six realms,' he said.

'The sixth is the emptiness.' She proffered a jet-black cube, devoid of runes. 'It has no Lord or Lady, it is where lost spirits flee.' She crossed her arms in front of herself, fingers touching her shoulders, bracelets falling to the crook of her elbows. She reminded Dariat of a statue of Shiva he'd seen in one of Valisk's four temples; Shiva as Nataraja, king of dancers. 'A terrible place,' Anastasia Rigel murmured coolly.

'You don't think I have any hope?' he asked, suddenly annoyed at this primitive paganish nonsense again.

'You resist it.'

'No, I don't. I've got lots of hope. I'm going to run this habitat one day,' he added. She ought to be impressed by that.

Her head was shaking gently, hair partly obscuring her face. 'That is Anstid deceiving you, Dariat. You spend so much time in his realm, he has an unholy grip upon your spirit.'

'How do you know?' he said scornfully.

'These are called Thoale stones. He is the Lord I am beholden to. He shows me what is to unfold.' A slight, droll smile flickered over her lips. 'Sometimes Tarrug intervenes. He shows me things I should not see, or events I cannot understand.'

'How do the stones work?'

'Each face is carved with the rune of a realm. I read the combinations, how they fall, or in the case of the emptiness where it falls in relation to the others. Would you like to know what your future contains?'

'Yeah. Go on.'

'Pick up each crystal, hold it in your hands for a moment, try to impress it with your essence, then put it in the bag.'

He picked up the clear one, naturally. Love Lady. 'How do I impress it?'

She just shrugged.

He squeezed the crystals one at a time, feeling increasingly stupid, and dropped them in the goatskin bag. Anastasia Rigel shook the bag, then tipped the crystals out.

'What does it say?' Dariat asked, a shade too eagerly for someone who was supposed to be sceptical.

She stared at them a while, eyes flicking anxiously between the runes. 'Greatness,' she said eventually. 'You will come to greatness.'

'Hey, yeah!'

Her hand came up, silencing him. 'It will not last. You shine so bright, Dariat, but for such a short time, and it is a dark flame which ignites you.'

'Then what?' he asked, disgruntled.

'Pain, death.'

'*Death?*'

'Not yours. Many people, but not yours.'

Anastasia Rigel didn't offer to sleep with him that time. Nor any of his visits during the month which followed. They walked round the savannah together, talking inanities, almost as brother and sister. She would tell him about the Starbridge philosophy, the idiosyncrasies of the realms. He listened, but became lost and impatient with a world-view which seemed to have little internal logic. In return he told her of his father, the resentment and the confusion of loss; mainly in the hope she'd feel sorry for him. He took her down into a starscraper; she said she'd never been in one before. She didn't like it, the confining walls of the apartments, although she was fascinated by the slowly spinning starfield outside.

The sexual tension died down from its initial high-voltage peak, though it was never laid to rest. It became a sort of game, jibes and smirks, played for points that neither knew how to win. Dariat enjoyed her company a lot. Someone who treated him fairly, who took time to hear what he said. Because she wanted to. He could never quite understand what she got out of the arrangement. She read his future several times, though none of the readings ever proved quite as dire as the first.

Dariat spent more and more time with her, almost divorcing himself from the culture lived out in the starscrapers and industrial stations (except for keeping up on his didactic courses). The portentous aspirations in his mind lost their grip when he was in her presence.

He learnt how to milk a goat, not that he particularly wanted to. They were smelly, bad-tempered creatures. She cooked him fish which she caught in the streams, and showed him which plants had edible roots. He found out about the tribe's way of life, how they sold a lot of their handicrafts to starship crews, chiefly the rugs and pottery, how they shunned technology. 'Except for nanonic medical packages,' she said wryly. 'Amazing how many women become technocrats around childbirth time.' He went to some of their ceremonies, which seemed little more than open air parties where everyone drank a strong distilled spirit, and sang gospel hymns late into the night.

One evening, when she was wearing just a simple white cotton poncho, she invited him into her tepee. He felt all the sexual heat return as the outline of her body was revealed through the fabric by the light of the tepee's meagre oil lamp. There was some kind of clay pot in the centre with a snakelike hose coming from the side. It was smoking docilely, filling the air with a funny sweet and sour scent.

Anastasia took a puff on the pipe, and shivered as if she'd swallowed a triple whisky. 'Try some,' she said, her voice rich with challenge.

'What is it?'

'A wide gate into Tarrug's realm. You'll like it. Anstid won't. He'll lose all control over you.'

He looked at the crimped end of the tube, still wet from her mouth. He wanted to try it. He was frightened. Her eyes were very wide.

She tipped her head back, expelling two long plumes of smoke from her nostrils. 'Don't you want to explore the realm of mischief with me?'

Dariat put the tube in his mouth and sucked. The next minute he was coughing violently.

'Not so hard,' she said. Her voice sounded all furred. 'Take it down slow. Feel it float through your bones.'

He did as he was told.

'They're hollow, you know, your bones.' Her smile was wide, shining like the light-tube against her black face.

The world spun round. He could feel the habitat moving, stars whipping round faster and faster, smearing across space. Smeared like cream. He giggled. Anastasia Rigel gave him a long, knowing grin, and took another drag on the tube.

Space was pink. Stars were black. Water smelt of cheese. 'I love you,' he told her. 'I love you, I love you.' The tepee walls were palpitating in and out. He was in the belly of some huge beast, just like Jonah.

Bloody hell.

'What did you say?'

Shit, I can't filter . . . What's green? What are you—

'My hands are green,' he explained patiently.

'Are they?' Anastasia Rigel asked. 'That's interesting.'

What has she given you?

'Tarrug?' Dariat asked. Anastasia had said that was who they were going to visit. 'Hello, Tarrug. I can hear him. He's talking to me.'

Anastasia Rigel was at right angles to him. She pulled the poncho off over her head, sitting crosslegged and naked on the rug. Now she was totally upside-down. Her nipples were black eyes following him.

'That's not Tarrug you hear,' she said. 'That's Anstid.'

'Anstid. Hi!'

What is it? What is in that bloody pipe? Wait, I'm reviewing the local memory . . . Oh, fuck, it's salfrond. I can't hold onto your thoughts when you're tripping on that, you little prick.

'I don't want you to.'

Yes, you do. Oh, believe me you do, boy. I've got the keys to every dark door in this kingdom, and you're the golden protégé. Now stop smoking that mind-rotting crap.

Dariat very deliberately stuck the tube in his mouth, and inhaled until his lungs were about to burst. His cheeks puffed out. Anastasia Rigel leant forwards and took the tube from between his lips. 'Enough.'

The tepee was spinning in the opposite direction to the habitat, and outside it was raining shoes. Black leather shoes with scarlet buckles.

Shit! I'm going to kill that little black junkie bitch for this. It's high bloody time I shoved the Starbridge tribes out of the airlock. Dariat, stand up, boy. Walk outside, get some fresh air. There's some medical nanonic packages in the village, the headman's got some. They can straighten out your blood chemistry.

Dariat's giggles returned. 'Piss off.'

GET UP!

'No.'

Weakling! Always bloody weaklings. You're no better than your bastard father.

Dariat squeezed his eyes shut. The colours were behind his eyelids too. 'I am not like him.'

Yes, you are. Weak, feeble, pathetic. All of you are. I should have cloned myself when I had the chance. Parthenogenetics would have solved all this bullshit. Two fucking centuries of weaklings I've had to endure. Two centuries, fuck it.

'Go away!' Even stoned, he could tell this wasn't part of the trip. This was more. This was much much worse.

'Is he hurting you, baby?' Anastasia Rigel asked.

'Yes.'

I'll fucking cripple you if you don't get up. Smash your legs, shred your hands to ribbons. Do you like the sound of that, boy? A life spent grubbing round like a snail. Can't walk, can't feed yourself, can't wipe your arse.

'Stop it,' Dariat screamed.

Get up!

'Don't listen to him, baby. Close your mind.'

Tell that bitch from me, she's dead.

'Please, both of you, stop it. Leave me alone.'

Get up.

Dariat tried to rise. He got up to his knees, then fell into Anastasia's lap.

'You're mine now,' she said gladly.

No, you're not. You're mine. Always mine. You can never leave. I won't allow you to.

Her hands ran over his clothes, opening seals. Kisses with the sharp cold impact of hailstones fell on his face. 'This is what you wanted, what you always wanted,' she breathed in his ear. 'Me.'

The nauseating colour stripes blitzing his sight swirled into blackness. Her hot skin sliding up and down against him. Weight pressing against every part of him. He was doing it! He was fucking! Tears poured out of his eyes.

'That's right, baby. Up inside me. Purge him. Purge him with me. Fly, fly into Venus and Chi-ri. Leave him behind. Free yourself.'

Always mine.

Dariat woke feeling awful. He was lying on the stiff tousled grass of the tepee without a stitch of clothing. The entrance flap was open, a slice of bright morning light sliding through. A heavy dew mottled his legs. Something had died and decomposed in his mouth, his tongue by the feel of it. Anastasia Rigel was lying beside him. Naked and beautiful. Arms tucked up against her chest.

Last night. I fucked her. I did it!

He tried to smother an ecstatic laugh.

Feeling better?

Dariat screamed. It was inside his head. Anstid. The realm demigod.

He jerked around, hugging himself, biting his lower lip so hard he drew blood.

Don't be an idiot. I'm not a bloody spirit bogeyman. There's no such thing. Religion is a psychological crutch for mental inadequates.

Spiritualism is for mental paraplegics. Think what that makes your girlie friend.

'What are you?'

Anastasia Rigel woke up, blinking against the light. She ran her hand through her wild hair and sat up, looking at him with a curious expression.

I'm your ancestor.

'A lost spirit from the emptiness?' he asked, wide eyed with fright.

Give me one more word of mythology and I really will have your legs broken. Now think logically. I'm your ancestor. Who can I be?

Information from his didactic history courses tumbled into his thoughts. 'Rubra?' The idea didn't make him feel any better at all.

Well done. Now stop panicking, and stop shivering. I don't normally talk direct to someone your age, I like to let you have sixteen years to yourself. But I'm not going to allow you to become a dopehead. Do not ever smoke that stuff again. Understand?

'Yes, sir.'

Stop vocalizing. Concentrate your thoughts.

'What are you saying, baby?' Anastasia Rigel asked. 'Are you still tripping?'

'No. It's Rubra, he's . . . We're talking.'

She pulled the white poncho round herself, giving him an alarmed look.

I've got plans for you, boy, Rubra said. **Big plans. You're destined for Magellanic Itg's executive committee.**

I am?

Yes. If you play your cards right. If you do as you're told.

I will.

Good. Now I've been lenient letting you sow your oats with dinky little Anastasia. I can understand that, she's got a nice body, good tits, pretty face. I had a sex drive myself, once. But you've had your fun now; so put your clothes on and say goodbye. We'll find someone a bit more suitable.

I can't leave her. Not after . . . last night.

Take a real good look at yourself, boy. Rutting with a bubblehead primitive on a filthy mat in a tepee. Some friend, she filled your brain with two kinds of shit. That's not how Valisk's future ruler is going to behave. Is it?

No, sir.

Good boy.

He started to pick up his clothes.

'Where are you going?' she asked.

'Home.'

'He told you to.'

'I . . . What is there here?'

She gave him a forlorn look over the white poncho which was still clasped to her body. 'Me. Your friend. Your lover.'

He shook his head.

'I'm human. That's more than he is.'

Come on. Leave.

Dariat pulled on his shoes. He paused by the entrance flap.

'It's Anstid,' she said in a mournful tone. 'That's who you really talk to.'

Pseudobabble. Ignore her.

Dariat walked slowly out of the village. Some of the elders gave him strange looks as he passed their steaming cooking pits. They couldn't understand. Why would anyone leave Anastasia's bed?

That's their trouble, boy. They're too backward. The real world is beyond them. I really must get round to cleaning them out one day.

*

Now Dariat knew what he was, what he was destined for, the didactic courses took on a whole new level of importance. He listened to Rubra's advice on the specializations he needed, the grades he had to achieve. He became obedient, and a shade resentful at his own compliance. But what else was there? Starbridge?

In return for acquiescence Rubra taught him how to use the affinity bond with the habitat. How to access the sensitive cells to see what was going on, how he could call on vast amounts of processing power, the tremendous amount of stored data that was available.

One of the first things Rubra did was to guide him through a list of possible replacement girls, eager to bury the lingering traces of yearning for Anastasia Rigel. Dariat felt like a voyeuristic ghost, watching the prospective candidates through the sensitive cells; seeing them at home, talking to their friends. Some of them he watched having sex with their boyfriends, two with other girls, which was exciting. Rubra didn't seem to object to these prolonged observations. At least it meant he didn't have to pay for bluesense fleks any more.

One girl he chanced on was nice, Chilone, nine months older than him. As black as Anastasia (which was what first caught his attention), but with dark auburn hair. Shy and pretty, who talked a lot about sex and boys with her girl friends.

Still he hesitated from meeting her, even though he knew her daily routine, knew her interests, what to say, which day clubs she belonged to. He could contrive a dozen encounters.

Get on with it, Rubra told him after a week of cautious scrutiny. **Screw her brains out. You don't think Anastasia's still pining over you, do you?**

What?

Try using the sensitive cells around the tepee.

That was something he'd never done, not using the habitat's perception faculty to spy on her. But the tone Rubra used had a hint of cruel amusement in it.

Anastasia had a lover, Mersin Columba, another Starbridge. A man in his forties; overweight, balding, with white pallid skin. They looked horrible locked together. Anastasia flinched silently as she lay underneath his pumping body.

The old white-hot infantile fury rose into Dariat's mind. He wanted to save her from the repellent humiliation; his beautiful girl who had loved him.

Take my advice. Go find young Chilone.

Like juvenile Edenists, it hadn't taken Dariat long to discover how to fox the habitat's sensitive cells. Unless Rubra's principal personality pattern was concentrating on him in particular, the autonomous monitoring of the sub-routines could be circumvented.

Dariat used the sensitive cells to follow Mersin Columba out of the tepee. The podgy oaf had a smug smile on his face as he made his way down to the stream. Anastasia Rigel was curled up on her rug, staring at nothing.

Mersin Columba made his way down the valley before stripping off his shirt and trousers. He splashed into a wide pool, and began to wash off the smell and stains of sex.

The first blow from Dariat's wooden cudgel caught him on the side of his head, tearing his ear. He grunted and dropped to his knees. The second blow smashed across the crown of his skull.

Stop it!

Dariat aimed another blow; laughing at the surprise on the man's face. Nobody does that to my girl. Nobody does that to me! A cascade of blows rained down on Mersin Columba's unprotected head. Rubra's furious demands were reduced to a wasp's buzz at the back of Dariat's raging mind. He was vengeance. He was omnipotent, more than any realm Lord. He struck and struck, and it felt good.

The water pushed at Mersin Columba's inert body. Long ribbons of blood wept from the battered head, turned to tattered curlicues by the current. Dariat stood over him. The bloody length of wood dropped from his fingers.

I didn't realize what I'd created with you, Rubra said. The silent voice lacked its usual conviction.

Dariat shivered suddenly. His heart was pumping hard. **Anastasia is mine.**

Well, she certainly doesn't belong to poor old Mersin Columba any more, and that's a fact.

The body had drifted five metres downstream. Dariat thought it looked repugnant, sickly white, bloated.

Now what? he asked sullenly.

I'd better get some housechimps to tidy up. And you'd better make tracks.

Is that it?

I'm not going to punish you for killing a Starbridge. But we're going to have to work on that temper of yours. It can be useful, but only if it's applied properly.

For the company.

Yes. And don't you forget it. Don't worry, you'll improve with age.

Dariat turned and walked away from the river. He hiked up out of the valley and spent the afternoon wandering aimlessly around the savannah.

His thoughts were glacial. He had killed a man, but there was no remorse, no sense of guilt. No sense of satisfaction, either. He felt nothing, as if the whole incident was an act he'd seen on an AV recording.

When the light-tube began to dim into brassy twilight he turned and made his way towards the Starbridge village.

Where do you think you're going? Rubra asked.

She's mine. I love her. I'm going to have her. Tonight, always.

No. Only I am for always.

You can't stop me. I don't care about the company. Keep it. I never wanted it. I want Anastasia.

Don't be a fool.

Dariat detected something then, a strand of emotion wound up with the mental voice: anxiety. Rubra was worried.

What's happened?

Nothing's happened. Go home. It's been a hellish day.

No. He tried to use the sensitive cells to show him the village. Nothing, Rubra was blocking his affinity.

Go home.

Dariat started running.

Don't, boy!

It was over a kilometre back to the valley. The pink and yellow grass came up to his waist in places, blades whipping his legs. He reached the brow of the slope and looked down in dismay. The village was packing up, moving on. Half of the tepees were already down, folded into bundles and put on the carts. Animals were being rounded up. All the fire pits were out.

It was a crazy time to be moving. Night was almost here. His sense of calamity redoubled.

Dariat sprinted down the steep slope, falling twice, grazing his knees and shins. He didn't care. Faces turned to watch as he dashed towards Anastasia's tepee.

He was shouting her name as he shoved the entrance flap aside.

The rope had been tied to the apex of the tepee. She must have used a stack of her wicker baskets to stand on. They were scattered all over the floor.

Her head was tilted to one side, the rope pressing into her left cheek, just behind the ear. She swayed slightly from side to side, the tepee's poles letting out quiet creaks.

Dariat stared at her for some immeasurable time. He didn't understand why. Not any of it.

Come on, boy. Come on home.

No. You did this. You made me leave her. She was mine. This would never have happened if you'd stayed out of my life. Tears were pouring down his cheeks.

I am your life.

You're not. Not not not. He closed out the voice. Refusing to hear the pleas and threats.

One of the wicker baskets had a piece of paper lying on top. It was weighted down by Anastasia's goatskin bag. Dariat picked it up, and read the message she'd written.

Dariat, I know it was you. I know you thought you did it for me. You didn't. You did it because it's what Anstid wanted, he will never allow you an alliance with Thoale. I thought I could help you. But I see I can't; I'm not strong enough to defy a realm Lord. I'm sorry.

I can't see any purpose in staying in this universe any more. I'm going to free my spirit and continue my flight towards God. The Thoale stones are my gift to you; use them please. You have so many battles to fight. Seeing the future may help you win some.

I want you to know I loved you for all the time we were together.

Anastasia Rigel

He loosened the thong at the top of the bag and spilled the six crystals onto the dusty rug. The five which were carved with runes landed with the blank face uppermost. He slowly picked them up, and threw them again. They came up blank. The empty realm, where lost spirits go.

Dariat fled the Starbridge village. He never went back. He stopped taking didactic courses, refused to acknowledge Rubra's affinity bond, argued a lot with his mother, and moved into a starscraper apartment of his own at fifteen.

There was nothing Rubra could do. His most promising protégé for decades was lost to him. The affinity window into Dariat's mind remained closed; it was the most secure block the habitat personality pattern had ever known, remaining in place even while the boy slept. After a month of steady pressure Rubra gave up, even Dariat's subconscious was sealed against subliminal suggestions. The block was more than conscious determination, it was a profound psychological inhibition. Probably trauma based.

Rubra cursed yet another failure descendant, and switched his priority to a new fledgeling. Monitoring of Dariat was assigned to an autonomic sub-routine. Occasional checks by the personality's principal consciousness revealed a total drop-out, a part-time drunk, part-time hustler picking up beer money by knowing people and where to find them, getting involved with deals which were dubious even for Valisk. Dariat never got a regular job, living off the starscraper food pap, accessing MF albums, sometimes for days on end. He never approached a girl again.

It was a stand-off which lasted for thirty years. Rubra had even stopped his intermittent checks on the wrecked man. Then the *Yaku* arrived at Valisk.

*

The *Yaku*'s emergence above Opuntia six days after it left Lalonde never raised a query. None of Graeme Nicholson's fleks had yet reached their destination when the cargo starship asked for and was granted docking permission. As far as both the habitat personality and the Avon Embassy's small Intelligence team (the only Confederation observers Rubra would allow inside) were concerned it was just another cargo starship visiting a spaceport which handled nearly thirty thousand similar visits a year.

Yaku had emerged a little further away from Valisk than was normal, and its flight vector required a more than average number of corrections – the fusion drive was fluctuating in an erratic fashion. But then a lot of the Adamist starships using Valisk operated on the borderline of CAB spaceworthiness requirements.

It docked at a resupply bay on the edge of the three-kilometre-wide disk which was the habitat's non-rotational spaceport. The captain requested a quantity of He_3 and deuterium, as well as oxygen, water, and some food. Spaceport service companies were contracted within ten minutes of its arrival.

Three people disembarked. Their passport fleks named them as Marie Skibbow, Alicia Cochrane, and Manza Balyuzi; the last two were members of *Yaku*'s crew. All three cleared Valisk's token immigration and customs carrying small bags with a single change of clothing.

The *Yaku* undocked four hours later, its cryogenic tanks full, and flew down towards Opuntia. Whatever its jump coordinate was, the gas giant was between it and Valisk when it activated its energy patterning nodes. No record of its intended destination existed.

*

Dariat was sitting up at the bar in the Tabitha Oasis when the girl caught his eye. Thirty years of little exercise, too much cheap beer, and a diet of starscraper gland synthesized pastes had brought about a detrimental effect on his once slim physique. He was fat verging on obese, his skin was flaky, his hair was dulled by a week's accumulation of oil. Appearance wasn't something he paid a lot of attention to. A togalike robe covered a multitude of laxities.

That girl, though: teenaged, long limbed, large breasted, exquisite face, bronzed, strong. Wearing a tight white T-shirt and short black skirt. He wasn't alone in watching her. The Tabitha Oasis attracted a tough crew. Girl like that was a walking gang-bang invitation. It had happened before. But she hadn't got a care in the world, there was an *élan* to her which was mesmerizing. All the more surprising, then, was her table companion.

Anders Bospoort: physically her counterpart; late twenties, slab muscles, the best swarthy face money could buy. But he didn't have her youthful exuberance, his mouth and eyes smiled (for that money they ought to) but there was no emotion powering the expression. Anders Bospoort was in almost equal proportions gigolo, pimp, pusher, and bluesense star.

Strange she couldn't see that. But he could pile on the charm when necessary, and the expensive wine bottle sitting on the table between them was nearly empty.

Dariat beckoned the barkeeper over. 'What's her name?'

'Marie. Arrived on a ship this afternoon.'

That explained a lot. Nobody had warned her. Now the wolves of the Tabitha Oasis were circling the camp-fire, enjoying her elaborate seduction. Later they would be able to share the corruption of youth, sensevising Anders Bospoort's boosted penis sliding up between her legs. Have her surprise and pleading in their ears. Feel the ripe body molested by powerful skilled hands.

Maybe Anders wasn't so stupid, Dariat thought, bringing her here was a good advert. He could ask an easy ten per cent over the odds for her flek.

The barkeeper shook his head sadly. He was three times Dariat's age, and he'd spent his every year in Valisk. He'd seen it all, so he claimed, every human foible. 'Pity, nice girl like that. Someone should tell her.'

'Yeah. Anywhere else, and someone might.' Dariat looked at her again. Surely a girl with her beauty couldn't be that naïve about men?

*

Anders Bospoort extended a gracious arm as they rose from the table. Marie smiled and accepted it. He thought she looked glad at the opportunity to stay close. The gazes she drew from the men of the Tabitha Oasis weren't exactly coy. His size and measured presence was a reassurance. She was safe with him.

They walked across the vestibule outside the bar, and Anders datavised the starscraper's mechanical systems control processor for a lift.

'Thank you for taking me there,' Marie said.

He saw the excitement in her eyes at the little taste of the illicit. 'I don't always go there. It can get a little rough. Half of the regulars have Confederation warrants hanging over them. If the navy ever comes visiting Valisk the population on penal planets would just about double overnight.'

The lift arrived. He gestured her through the open doors.

Halfway there, and it was going so smoothly. He'd been a perfect gentleman from the moment they met outside the Apartment Allocation Office (always the best place to pick up clean meat), every word clicking flawlessly into place. And she'd been drawn closer and closer, hypnotized by the old Bospoort magic.

She glanced uncertainly at the floor as the doors closed, as if she'd only just realized how far from her home and family she was. All alone with her only friend in the whole star system. No going back for her now.

He felt a tightening in his stomach as the anticipation heightened. This would all go on the flek; the prelude, the slow-burning conquest. People appreciated the build in tension. And he was an artiste supreme.

The doors opened to the eighty-third floor.

'It's a walk down two floors,' Anders told her apologetically. 'The lifts don't work below here. And the maintenance crews won't come down to fix them. Sorry.'

The vestibule hadn't been cleaned for a long time and rubbish was accumulating in the corners. There was graffiti on the walls, a smell of urine in the air. Marie looked round nervously, and stayed close to Anders' side.

He guided her to the stairwell. The light was dim, a strip of electrophorescent cells on the wall whose output had faded to an insipid yellow. Dozens of big pale moths whirred incessantly against it. Water leaked down the walls from cracks in the polyp. A cream-coloured moss grew along the edge of every step.

'It's very kind of you to let me stay with you,' Marie ventured.

'Just until you get your own apartment sorted out. There are hundreds of unused ones. It's one of life's greater mysteries why it always takes so long for the Allocation Office to assign one.'

Nobody else was using the stairs. Anders very rarely got to meet any of his neighbours. The bottom of the starscraper was perfect for him. No quick access, everyone stayed behind closed doors to conduct their chosen business in life, and no questions were ever asked. The cops Magellanic Itg contracted to maintain a kind of order in the rest of Valisk didn't come down here.

They left the stairwell on his floor, and he datavised a code at his apartment door. Nothing happened. He flashed her a strained smile, and datavised the code again. This time it opened, juddering once or twice as it slid along its rails. Marie went in first. Anders deliberately kept the inside lights low, and codelocked the door behind him – at least the processor acknowledged that. He put his arm round her shoulder and steered her into the biggest of the three bedrooms. That door was codelocked too.

Marie walked into the middle of the room, eyes straying to the double bed. There were long velvet straps fixed to each corner.

'Take your clothes off,' Anders told her. An uncompromising sternness appeared in his voice. He datavised an order to the overhead light panel, but it remained at its lowest level. Shit! And she was obediently stripping off. Nothing for it, he'd have to stay with the deep shadows and hope everyone found it erotic.

'Now take mine off,' he ordered. 'Slowly.'

He could feel her hands trembling as she pushed the shirt off his broad shoulders, which made a nice touch. Nervous ones were always more responsive.

His eyes ran over her with expert tracking as she walked ahead of him to the bed, capturing every square centimetre of flesh on display. When she was lying on the water mattress his hands traced the same route. Then his boosted cock was swelling to its full length, and he focused on her face to make sure he captured her fear. That was always a big turn on for the punters.

Marie was smiling.

The lights sprang up to full intensity.

Anders twisted round in confusion. 'Hey—'

At first he thought someone had crept up and snapped handcuffs round his wrists, but when he looked he saw it was Marie's elegant feminine hands gripping him.

'Let go.' The pain as she squeezed harder was frightening. 'Bitch! Let go. Christ—'

She laughed.

He looked back down at her, and gasped. She was sprouting hair right across her chest and stomach, thick black bristles that scratched and pricked his skin where he lay on top of her. Individual strands began to harden. It was like lying on a hedgehog hide. The long tips were puncturing his own skin, needling in through the subcutaneous layers of fat.

'Fuck me, then,' she said.

He tried to struggle, but all that did was push more needle spines into his abdomen. Marie let go of one wrist. He hit her then, on the side of her ribs, and her flesh gave way below his fist. When he brought his hand away it was covered in yellow and red slime. The spines piercing him turned to worms, slick and greasy, licking round inside the swath of puncture holes down his torso. Blood trickled out.

Anders let out an insane howl. She was rotting below him, skin melting away into a putrescent crimson film of mucus. It was acting like glue, sticking him to her. The stench was vile, stinging his eyes. He puked, the wine from the Tabitha Oasis splattering down on her deliquescing face.

'Kiss me.'

He bucked and floundered against her, weeping helplessly, praying to a God he hadn't addressed in over a decade. The worms were wriggling between his abdominal muscles, twining round tendon fibres. Blood and pus squelched and intermingled, forming a sticky glue which wedded them belly to belly like Siamese twins.

'Kiss me, Anders.'

Her free hand clamped onto the back of his skull. It felt like there was nothing left on it but bone. Sludge dripped into his coiffured hair.

'No!' he whimpered.

Her lips had dribbled away like candle wax, leaving a wide gash in the bubbling corruption that was her face. The teeth were a permanent grin. His head was being forced down towards her. He saw her teeth parting, then they were rammed against his own face.

The kiss. And hot, black, gritty liquid surged up out of her throat. Anders couldn't scream any more. It was in his own mouth, kneading its way down his air passage like a fat, eager serpent.

A voice from nowhere said: 'We can stop it.'

The liquid detonated into his lungs. He could feel it, hot and rancid inside his chest, swelling out to invade every delicate cavity. His ribcage heaved at the alien pressure from within. He had stopped struggling.

'She'll kill you unless you let us help. She's drowning you.'

He wanted to breathe. He wanted air. He would do anything to breathe. Anything.

'Then let us in.'

He did.

*

Using the sensitive cells in the polyp above Anders Bospoort's bed, Dariat watched as the injuries and manifestations reversed themselves. Marie's glutinous skin hardened, bristles retracting. The wounds down Anders Bospoort's abdomen closed up. They became what they were before: satyr and seraph.

Anders began to stroke himself, hands tracing lines of muscle across his chest. He looked down on his body with a childlike expression of awe which swiftly became a broad grin. 'I'm magnificent,' he whispered. 'Utterly magnificent.' The accent was different to Anders' usual. Dariat couldn't quite place it.

'Yes, you look pretty good,' she replied indifferently. She sat up. The sheets were stained a faint pink below her back.

'Let me have you.'

Her mouth wrinkled up with indecision.

'Please. You know I need to. Hell, it's been seven hundred years. Show a little compassion here.'

'All right then.' She lay back down. Anders started to lick her body, reminding Dariat of a feeding dog. They fucked for twenty minutes, Anders rutting with a fervour he'd never shown in any of his fleks. Electric lights and household equipment went berserk as they thrashed about. Dariat quickly checked the neighbouring apartments; a stimulant-program writer was yelling in frustration as his processors crashed at tremendous speed; a clone merchant's vats seethed and boiled as regulators fried the fragile cell clusters which they were wired up to. Doors all around the vestibule opened and shut like guillotines. He had to launch a flurry of subversive affinity orders into the floor's neural cells to prevent the local personality sub-routines from alerting Rubra's principal consciousness.

When he arrived, puffing heavily, outside the apartment, Marie and Anders Bospoort were getting dressed. He used a black-market customized processor block to break the door's codelock, and walked straight in.

Marie and Anders looked up in alarm. They ran out of the bedroom. The processor block died in Dariat's hand and the apartment was plunged into pitch darkness.

'The dark doesn't bother me,' he said loudly. The sensitive cells showed him the two of them were walking towards him menacingly.

'Nothing will bother you from now on,' Marie replied.

The belt of his toga robe began to tighten round his belly. 'Wrong. Firstly you won't be able to tyrannize me like you did poor old Anders, I'm not that weak. Secondly, if I die Rubra will see exactly what's been going on, and what you are. He might be crazy, but he'll fight like a lion to defend his precious habitat and corporation. Once he knows you exist you've lost ninety per cent of your advantage. You'll never take over Valisk without my help.'

The lights came back on. His belt loosened. Marie and Anders regarded him with expressionless faces.

'It's only thanks to me he doesn't know already. You obviously don't understand much about bitek. I can help there as well.'

'Perhaps we don't care if he knows,' Anders said.

'OK, fine. You want me to lift the limiter orders I put on this floor's sensitive cells?'

'What do you want?' Marie asked.

'Revenge. I've waited thirty years for you. It's been so long, so very tiring; I nearly broke on more than one occasion. But I knew you would come in the end.'

'You expected me?' she asked derisively.

'What you are, yes.'

'And what am I?'

'The dead.'

22

Gemal emerged from its jump six hundred and fifty thousand kilometres above Mirchusko, where the gas giant's gravity anchored it in a slightly elliptical orbit; Tranquillity, in its lower circular orbit, was trailing by two hundred thousand kilometres. Oliver Llewelyn, the colonist-carrier's captain, identified his starship to the habitat personality, and requested approach and docking permission.

'Do you require assistance?' Tranquillity asked.

'No, we're fully functional.'

'I don't get many colonist-carrier vessels visiting. I thought you might have been making an emergency maintenance call.'

'No. This flight is business.'

'Does your entire passenger complement wish to apply for residency?'

'Quite the opposite. The zero-tau pods are all empty. We've come to hire some military specialists who live here.'

'I see. Docking and approach request granted. Please datavise your projected vector to spaceport flight control.'

Terrance Smith datavised a sensor access request into the starship's flight computer, and watched the massive bitek habitat growing larger as they accelerated towards rendezvous in a complex manoeuvre at two-thirds of a gee. He opened a channel to the habitat's communication net, and asked for a list of starships currently docked. Names and classifications flowed through his mind. A collation program sorted through them, indicating possibles and probables.

'I didn't realize this was such a large port,' he said to Oliver Llewelyn.

'It has to be,' the captain replied. 'There are at least five major family-owned civil carrier fleets based here purely because of the tax situation, and most of the other line companies have offices in the habitat. Then you've got to consider the residents. They import one hell of a lot; everything you need to live the good life, from food to clothes to pretentious art. You don't think they'll eat the synthesized pulp the starscrapers grow, do you?'

'No, I suppose not.'

'A lot of ships pick up contracts for them, bringing stuff in from all over the Confederation. And of course Tranquillity is the Confederation's principal base for blackhawk mating flights now Valisk is falling from favour with the captains. The eggs gestate down in the big inner ring. It all adds together. The Lords of Ruin have built it into one of the most important commercial centres in this sector.'

Terrance looked across the bridge. Seven acceleration couches were arranged in a petal pattern on its composite decking, and only one of them was empty. The compartment had an industrial look, with cables and ducts fixed to the walls rather than being tucked neatly out of sight behind composite panels. But then that was a uniform characteristic throughout the *Gemal* and her sister ships which shuttled between Earth and stage one colony worlds. They were bulk carriers whose cargo happened to be people, and the line companies didn't waste money on cosmetic finishes.

Captain Llewelyn was lying inertly on his acceleration couch, surrounded by a horseshoe of bulky consoles; a well-built sixty-eight-year-old oriental with skin as smooth as any adolescent. His eyes were shut as he handled the datavise from the flight computer.

'Have you been here before?' Terrance asked.

'I stopped over two days, that was thirty-five years ago when I was a junior officer in a different company. Don't suppose it's changed much. Plutocrats put a lot of stock in stability.'

'I'd like you to talk to the other captains for me, the independent trader starships we want to hire. I haven't exactly done this kind of work before.'

Oliver Llewelyn snorted softly. 'You let people know what kind of flight you're putting together, then start flashing that overloaded Jovian Bank credit disk around, and you'll be beating them off with a stick.'

'What about the mercenaries and general troops?'

'The captains will put you in touch. Hell, the combat boosted will pay the captains for an introduction. You want my advice, delegate. Find yourself ten or twenty officer types with some solid experience, and let them recruit troops for you. Don't try and do it all yourself. We haven't got time, for a start. Rexrew gave us a pretty tight schedule.'

'Thanks.'

'You're paying, remember?'

'Yeah.' It had taken twenty thousand fuseodollars just to get Oliver Llewelyn to agree to take the *Gemal* to Tranquillity. 'Not part of my LDC contract,' the captain had said stubbornly. Money was easier than datavising legal requirements at him. Terrance suspected it was going to cost a lot more to take the *Gemal* back to Lalonde. 'You sound like you know what you're talking about,' he said, mildly intrigued.

'I've flown a lot of different missions in my time,' the old captain said indifferently.

'So where do I meet these starship captains?'

Oliver Llewelyn accessed a thirty-five-year-old file in his neural nanonics. 'We'll start at Harkey's Bar.'

*

Fifteen hours later Terrance Smith had to admit that Oliver Llewelyn had been perfectly correct. He didn't need to make any effort, the people he wanted came to him. Like iron to a magnet, he thought, or flies to shit. He was sitting in a wall booth, feeling like an old-style tsar holding court, receiving petitions from eager subjects. Harkey's Bar was full with starship crews hunched around tables, or concentrating in small knots at the bar. There was also a scattering of the combat boosted in the room. He had never seen them before, not in the flesh – if that's what it could be called. Several of them resembled cosmoniks, with a tough silicon outer skin, and dual – even triple – lower arms, sockets customized for weapons. But the majority had a sleeker appearance than the cosmoniks, whose technology they pilfered; they'd been sculpted for agility rather than blunt EVA endurance, although Terrance could see one combat boosted who was almost globular, his (her?) head a neckless dome, with a wrap-around retinal strip, grainy auburn below its clear lens. The lid rippled constantly, a blink moving round and round. There were four stumpy legs, and four arms, arranged symmetrically. The arms were the most human part of the modified body, since only two of them ended in burnished metal sockets. He tried not to stare at the assembled grotesqueries, not to show his inner nerves.

The bar's atmosphere was subdued, heavy with anticipation. It was long past the time the band were usually jamming on stage, but tonight they were drinking back in the kitchen, resigned to a blown gig.

'Captain André Duchamp,' Oliver Llewelyn said. 'Owner of the *Villeneuve's Revenge*.'

Terrance shook hands with the smiling round-faced captain. There was some contradiction in his mind that such a jovial-seeming man should want to join a military mission. 'I need starships capable of landing a scout team on a terracompatible planet, then backing them up with tactical ground strikes,' he said.

André put his wineglass down squarely on the table. 'The *Villeneuve's Revenge* has four X-ray lasers and two electron-beam weapons. Planetary bombardment from low orbit will not be a problem.'

'There could also be some anti-ship manoeuvres required from you. Some interdiction duties.'

'Again, monsieur, this is not a problem from my personal position; we do have combat-wasp launch-cradles. However, you would have to provide the wasps themselves. And I would require some reassurance that we will not be involved in any controversial action in a system where Confederation Navy ships are present. As a commercial vessel I have no licence to carry such items.'

'You would be operating under government licence, which allows you to carry any weapons system quite legitimately. This entire mission is completely legal.'

'So?' André Duchamp gave him a quizzical glance. 'This is excellent news. A legal combat mission is one I will welcome. As I say, I have no objection to conducting anti-ship engagements. May I ask which government you represent?'

'Lalonde.'

André Duchamp had a long blink while his neural nanonics almanac file reviewed the star system. 'A stage one colony world. Interesting.'

'I am negotiating with several astroengineering companies with stations here at Tranquillity for combat wasps,' Terrance Smith said. 'There will also be several nuclear-armed atmospheric-entry warheads to be taken on the mission. Would you be prepared to carry and deploy them?'

'*Oui*.'

'In that case, I believe we can do business, Captain Duchamp.'

'You have yet to mention money.'

'I am authorized to issue a five hundred thousand fuseodollar fee for every ship which registers for Lalonde naval duty, payable on arrival at our destination. Pay for an individual starship is three hundred thousand fuseodollars per month, with a minimum of two months' duty guaranteed. There will be bonuses for enemy starships and spaceplanes destroyed, and a completion bonus of three hundred thousand fuseodollars. We will not, however, be providing insurance cover.'

André Duchamp took a leisurely sip of wine. 'I have one further question.'

'Yes?'

'Does this *enemy* use antimatter?'

'No.'

'Very well. I would haggle the somewhat depressing price . . .' He cast a glance around the crowded room, crews not quite watching to see what the outcome would be. 'But I feel I am not in a strong bargaining position. Today it is a buyer's market.'

From his table on the other side of the bar Joshua watched André Duchamp rise from Terrance Smith's booth. The two of them shook hands again, then André went back to the table where his crew were waiting. They all went into a tight huddle. Wolfgang Kuebler, captain of the *Maranta*, was shown to Smith's booth by Oliver Llewelyn.

'That looks like five ships signed up,' Joshua said to his crew.

'Big operation,' Dahybi Yadev said. He drained his beer glass and sat it down on the table. 'Starships, combat-boosted mercs, enhanced troops; that's a long, expensive shopping list. Big money involved.'

'Lalonde can't be paying, then,' Melvyn Ducharme said. 'It doesn't have any money.'

'Yes, it does,' Ashly Hanson said quietly. 'A colony world is a massive investment, and a very solid one if you get in early enough. A healthy percentage of my zero-tau maintenance trust-fund portfolio is made up from development company shares, purely for the long-term stability they offer. I've never, ever heard of a colony failing once the go-ahead has been given. The money may not be floating around the actual colonists themselves, but the amount of financial resources required simply to initiate such a venture runs close to a trillion fuseodollars. And Lalonde has been running for over a quarter of a century, they'd even started an asteroid industrial settlement project. Remember? The development company has the money; more than enough to hire fifteen independent traders and a few thousand mercenary troops. I doubt it would even cause a ripple in their accountancy program.'

'What for, though?' Sarha Mitcham asked. 'What couldn't the sheriffs handle by themselves?'

'The Ivet riots,' Joshua said. Even he couldn't manage any conviction. He shrugged under the sceptical looks the others gave him. 'Well, there was nothing else while we were there. Marie Skibbow was worried about the scale of the civil disturbance. Nobody quite knew what was happening upriver. And the number of troops this Smith character is trying to recruit implies some kind of ground action is required.'

'Hard to believe,' Dahybi Yadev muttered. 'But the actual mission objective won't be known until after they've jumped away from Tranquillity. Simple security.'

'All right,' Joshua said. 'We all know the score. With Parris Vasilkovsky backing us on the mayope venture we have a chance to make macro money. And at the same time, with the money we made from the Norfolk run we certainly don't need to hire on with any mercenary fleet.' He looked at each of them in turn. 'Given the circumstances, we can hardly take *Lady Mac* to Lalonde ahead of the fleet. I've heard that Terrance Smith has ordered a batch of combat wasps from the McBoeing and Signal-Yakovlev industrial stations. He's clearly expecting some kind of conflict after they arrive. So the question is, do we go with him to find out what's happening, and maybe protect our interest, or do we wait here for news? We'll take a vote, and it must be unanimous.'

*

Time Universe's Tranquillity office was on the forty-third floor of the StCroix starscraper. It was the usual crush of offices, studios, editing rooms, entertainment suites, and electronic workshops; a micro-community where individual importance was graded by allocated desk space, facility size, and time allowance. Naturally, given the make-up of the habitat's population, it had a large finance and commerce bureau, but it also provided good Confederationwide news coverage.

Oliver Llewelyn walked into the wood-panelled lobby at ten thirty local time the day after the *Gemal* had docked. The receptionist palmed him off on a junior political correspondent called Matthias Rems. In the composite-walled office Matthias used to assemble his reports he produced the flek Graeme Nicholson had given him and named a carriage fee of five thousand fuseodollars. Matthias wasn't stupid, the fact that the *Gemal*'s captain had come direct from Lalonde was enough to warrant serious attention. By now the entire habitat knew about the mercenary fleet being assembled by Terrance Smith, though its purpose remained unknown. Rumour abounded. Lalonde was immediate news; plenty of Tranquillity residents would have LDC shares sleeping in their portfolios. First-hand sensevises of the planet and whatever was happening there would have strong ratings clout. Ordinarily Matthias Rems might have hesitated about the shameless rip-off fee (he guessed correctly that Llewelyn had already been paid), especially after he accessed the company personnel file on Graeme Nicholson; but given the circumstances he knuckled under and paid.

After the captain left, Matthias slotted the flek into his desktop player block. The sensevise recording was codelocked, so Graeme Nicholson had obviously considered it important. He pulled Nicholson's personal code from his file, then sat back and closed his eyes. The Crashed Dumper invaded his sensorium; its heat and noise and smell, the taste of a caustic local beer tarring his throat, unaccustomed weight of a swelling belly. Graeme Nicholson held the fragments of a broken glass in his hand, his arms and legs trembling slightly; both eyes focused unwaveringly on a tall man and lovely teenage girl over by the crude bar.

Twelve minutes later a thoroughly shaken Matthias Rems burst in on Claudia Dohan, boss of Time Universe's Tranquillity operation.

The ripple effect of Graeme Nicholson's flek was similar to the sensation Ione's appearance had caused the previous year, in every respect save one. Ione had been a feel-good item: Laton was the antithesis. He was terror and danger, history's nightmare exhumed.

'We have to show a sense of responsibility,' a twitchy Claudia Dohan said after she surfaced from the sensevise. 'Both the Confederation Navy and the Lord of Ruin must be told.'

The AV cylinder on her desktop processor block chimed. 'Thank you for your consideration,' Tranquillity said. 'I have informed Ione Saldana about Laton's reappearance. I suggest you contact Commander Olsen Neale yourself to convey the contents of the flek.'

'Right away,' Claudia Dohan said diligently.

Matthias Rems was glancing nervously round the office, disturbed by the reminder of the habitat personality's perpetual vigilance.

Claudia Dohan broke the news on the lunchtime programme. Eighteen billion fuseodollars was wiped off share values on Tranquillity's trading floor within quarter of an hour of the sensevise being broadcast. Values crept back up during the rest of the afternoon as brokers assessed possible war scenarios. By the end of the day seven billion fuseodollars had been restored to prices – mainly on astroengineering companies which would benefit from armaments sales.

The Time Universe office had done its work well, considering the short period it had in which to prepare. Its current affairs channel's usual afternoon schedule was replaced by library memories of Laton's earlier activities and earnest studio panel speculation. While Tranquillity's residents were being informed, Claudia Dohan started hiring starships to distribute copies of Graeme Nicholson's flek across the Confederation. This time she had a small lever against the captains, unlike Ione's very public appearance; she had a monopoly on Laton's advent and they were bidding against each other to deliver fleks. By the evening she had dispatched eighteen starships to various planets (Kulu, Avon, Oshanko, and Earth being the principals). Those Time Universe offices would in turn send out a second wave of fleks. Two weeks ought to see the entire Confederation brought up to speed. And warned, Claudia Dohan thought, Time Universe alone alerting the human and xenoc races to the resurgent danger. A greater boost to company fortunes simply wasn't possible.

She took the whole office out to a five-star meal that night. This coup, following so soon after Ione, should bring them all some heady bonuses, as well as boosting them way ahead of their contemporaries on the promotion scale. She was already thinking of a seat on the board for herself.

But it was a hectic afternoon. Matthias Rems (making his début as a front-line presenter) introduced forty-year-old recordings of the broken Edenist habitat Jantrit, its shell cracked like a giant egg where the antimatter had detonated. Its atmosphere jetted out of a dozen breaches in the five-hundred-metre-thick polyp, huge grey-white plumes which acted like rockets, destabilizing the cylinder's ponderous rotation. The wobble built over the period of a few hours, until it developed into an uncontrollable tumble. On the outside, induction cables lashed round in anarchic hundred-kilometre arcs, preventing even the most agile voidhawks from rendezvousing. Inside, water and soil were tossed about, acting like a permanent floating earthquake. Starscrapers, weakened by the blast, broke off like rotten icicles, whirling away at terrific velocities. And all the while their air grew thinner.

Some people were saved as the voidhawks and Adamist

starships hurtled after the spinning starscrapers. Eight thousand out of a population of one and a quarter million. Even then utter disaster might have been averted. The dying Edenists should have transferred their memories into the habitat personality. But Laton had infected Jantrit's neuron structure with his proteanic virus and its rationality was crumbling as trillions upon trillions of cells fell to the corruption every second. The other two habitats orbiting the gas giant were too far away to provide much assistance; personality transference was a complex function, distance and panic confused the issue. Twenty-seven thousand Edenists managed to bridge the gulf; three thousand patterns were later found to be incomplete, reduced to traumatized childlike entities. Voidhawks secured another two hundred and eighty personalities, but the bitek starships didn't have the capacity to store any more, and they were desperately busy anyway, chasing the starscrapers.

For Edenists it was the greatest tragedy since the founding of their culture. Even Adamists were stunned by the scale of the disaster. A living sentient creature thirty-five kilometres in length mind-raped and killed, nearly one and a quarter million people killed, over half a million stored personality patterns wiped.

And it had all been a diversion. A tactic to enable Laton and his cohorts to flee without fear of capture after their coup failed. He used the community's deaths as a cover; there was no other reason for it, no grand strategic design.

Every voidhawk, every Confederation Navy ship, every asteroid settlement, every planetary government searched for Laton and the three blackhawks he had escaped with.

He was cornered two months later in the Ragundan system: three blackhawks, armed with antimatter and refusing to surrender. Three voidhawks and five Confederation Navy frigates were lost in the ensuing battle. An asteroid settlement was badly damaged with the loss of a further eight thousand lives when the blackhawks tried to use it as a hostage, threatening to bomb it with antimatter unless the navy withdrew. The naval flotilla's commanding admiral called their bluff.

As with all space engagements there was nothing left of the vanquished but weak nebulas of radioactive molecules. There was no body to identify. But it couldn't have been anyone else.

Now it seemed there must have been four blackhawks. Nobody could mistake that tall, imperious man standing on the steps of the *Yaku*'s spaceplane, laughing at a cowering Graeme Nicholson.

The guests Matthias Rems invited into the studio, a collection of retired navy officers, political professors, and weapons engineers, observed that Laton's actual goal had never been declared. Speculation had been rife for years after the event. It obviously involved some kind of physical (biological) and mental domination, subverting the Edenists through the (fortunately) imperfect proteanic virus he had developed. *Changing* them and the habitats. But to what grandiose ideal had been thought for ever unknown. The studio debate concentrated on whether Laton was behind the current conflict on Lalonde, and if it was the first stage in his bid to impose his will on the Confederation again. Graeme Nicholson had certainly believed so.

Laton was different to the kind of planetary disputes like Omuta and Garissa; the perennial squabbling between asteroid settlements and their funding companies over autonomy. Laton wasn't a violence-tinged argument over resources or independence, he was after people, individuals. He wanted to get into your genes, your mind, and alter you, mould you to his own deviant construct. Laton was deadly personal.

One of the keenest observers of the Time Universe programmes was Terrance Smith. The Laton revelation had come as a profound shock. He, and the *Gemal*'s crew, became the objects of intense media interest. Hounded every time he left the colonist-carrier, he eventually had to appeal to Tranquillity for privacy. The habitat personality agreed (a resident's freedom from intrusion was part of the original constitution Michael Saldana had written), and the reporters were called off. They promptly switched their attention to anyone who had signed on as a member of the mercenary fleet, all of whom protested (truthfully) that they knew nothing of Laton.

'What do we do?' Terrance Smith asked in a bleak voice. He was alone with Oliver Llewelyn on the *Gemal's* bridge. Console holoscreens were showing the Time Universe evening news programme, cutting between a studio presenter and segments of Graeme Nicholson's recording. The captain was someone whose opinion Terrance valued, in fact he'd grown heavily dependent on him during the last couple of days. There weren't many other people he confided in.

'You don't have many options,' Oliver Llewelyn pointed out. 'You've already paid the registration fee to twelve ships, and you've got a third of the troops you wanted. Either you go ahead as originally planned, or you cut and run. Doing nothing isn't a valid alternative, not now.'

'Cut and run?'

'Sure. You've got enough money in the LDC's credit account to lose yourself. Life could get very comfortable for you and your family.' Oliver Llewelyn watched Terrance Smith closely, trying to anticipate his reaction. The notion obviously appealed, but he didn't think the bureaucrat would have enough backbone.

'I . . . No, we can't. There are too many people depending on me. We have to do something to help Durringham. You weren't down there, you don't know what it was like that last week. These mercenaries are the only hope they've got.'

'As you wish.' Pity, Oliver Llewelyn thought, a great pity. I'm getting too old for this kind of jaunt.

'Do you think fifteen ships is enough to go up against Laton?' Terrance Smith asked anxiously. 'I have the authority to hire another ten.'

'We're not going up against Laton,' Oliver Llewelyn said patiently.

'But—'

The captain gestured at one of the console holoscreens. 'You accessed Graeme Nicholson's sensevise. Laton has left Lalonde. All your mercenaries are faced with is a big mopping-up operation. Leave Laton to the Confederation; the navy and the voidhawks will be going after him with every weapon they've got.'

The notion of taking on Laton was something the starship captains had been discussing among themselves. Only three were sufficiently alarmed to return Terrance Smith's registration fee. He had no trouble in attracting replacements, and bringing the number of the fleet up to nineteen – six blackhawks, nine combat-capable independent traders, three cargo carriers, and the *Gemal* itself. Virtually none of the general troops or the combat-boosted mercenaries resigned. Fighting Laton's legions, being on the *right* side, gave the whole enterprise a kudos like few others; old hands and fresh youngsters queued up to sign on.

Three and a half days after he arrived, Terrance Smith had all he came for. The one request from Commander Olsen Neale to hold off and wait for a Confederation naval investigatory flight was smilingly refused. Durringham needs us now, Terrance told him.

*

Ione and Joshua walked down one of Tranquillity's winding valleys in the late afternoon, dew-heavy grass staining their sandals. She was wearing a long white cotton skirt and a matching camisole, a loose-fitting outfit which allowed the air to circulate over her warm skin. Joshua just wore some long dark mauve shorts. His skin was tanning nicely, she thought, he was almost back to his old colour. They had spent most of his stopover outside; swimming with Haile, riding, walking, having long sexual adventures. Joshua seemed to get very turned on having sex beside and in the bountiful streams meandering through the habitat.

Ione stopped at a long pool which formed the intersection of two streams. It was lined by mature rikbal trees, whose droopy branches stroked the water with their long, thin leaves. They were all in flower, bright pink blooms the size of a child's fist.

Gold and scarlet fish slithered through the water. It was tranquillity, Ione thought, small t, created by big T; name chasing form, name creating form. The lake – the whole park – was a pause from the habitat's bustle; the habitat was a pause from the Confederation's bustle. If you wanted it to be.

Joshua pushed her gently against a rikbal trunk, kissing her cheek, her neck. He opened the front of her camisole.

Hair fell down across her eyes, she was wearing it longer these days. 'Don't go,' she said quietly.

His arms dropped inertly to his sides, head slumping forwards until his brow touched hers. 'Good timing.'

'Please.'

'You said you weren't going to dump this possessive scene on me.'

'This isn't being possessive.'

'What then? It sounds like it.'

Her head came up sharply, pink spots burning on both cheeks. 'If you must know, I'm worried about you.'

'Don't be.'

'Joshua, you're flying into a war zone.'

'Not really. We're flying escort duty for a troop convoy, that's all. The soldiers and combat boosted are in at the hard edge.'

'Smith wants the starships to provide ground strikes; he's bought combat wasps for interdiction missions. That's the hard edge, Joshua, that's the dead edge. Bloody hell, you're going up against *Laton* in an antique wreck that barely rates its CAB spaceworthiness licence. And there's no reason. None. You don't need mayope, you don't need Vasilkovsky.' She held his arm, imploring. 'You're rich. You're happy. Don't try and tell me you're not. I've watched you for three years. You've never had so much fun as when you gallivanted around the galaxy in the *Lady Macbeth*. Now look at what you're doing. Paper deals, Joshua. Making paper money you can never spend. Sitting behind a desk, that's your destination. That's where you're flying to, Joshua, and it isn't you.'

'Antique, huh?'

'I didn't mean—'

'How old is Tranquillity, Ione? At least I own the *Lady Mac*, it doesn't own me.'

'I'm just trying to shock some sense into you. Joshua, it's Laton you're facing. Don't you watch the AV recordings? Didn't you access Graeme Nicholson's sensevise?'

'Yes. I did. Laton isn't on Lalonde. He left on the *Yaku*. Did you miss that bit, Ione? If I wanted to go on suicide flights I'd chase after the *Yaku*. That's where the danger is. That's where the navy heroes are going. Not me, I'm protecting my own interests.'

'But you don't need it!' she said. God, but he could be bonehead stubborn at times.

'You mean you don't.'

'What?'

'Not convenient, is it? Me having that much money. That much money would mean I make the decisions, I make the choices. It gives me control over my life. Where does that fit into your cosy scenario of us, Ione? I won't be so easy to manipulate then, will I?'

'Manipulate! One glimpse of a female nipple and your fly seal bursts apart from the pressure. That's how complicated your personality is. You don't need manipulating, Joshua, you need hormone suppressors. All I'm doing is trying to think ahead for you, because God knows you can't do it for yourself.'

'Jesus, Ione! Sometimes I can't believe you're bonded to a

cubic kilometre of neuron cells, you don't display the IQ of an ant most days. This is my *chance*, I can make it. I can be your equal.'

'I don't want an equal.' Ione jammed her mouth shut. She'd nearly done it, nearly said: 'I just want you.' But torture wouldn't bring that from her lips, not now.

'Yeah, so I noticed,' he said. 'I started with a broken-down ship. I made that work, I earned a living flying it. And now I'm moving on, moving up. That's life, Ione. Growing, evolving. You should try it sometime.' He turned and stomped off through the trees, sweeping the hanging branches aside impatiently. If she wanted to say sorry, she could damn well come after him and do it.

Ione watched him go, and fumbled with the front of her camisole. What an arsehole. He might be psychic, but only at the expense of common sense.

I'm so sorry, Tranquillity said gently.

She sniffed hard. **What about?**

Joshua.

There's no reason. If he wants to go, let him. See if I care.

You do care. He is right for you.

He doesn't think so.

Yes, he does. But he is prideful. As are you.

Thanks for nothing.

Don't cry.

Ione glanced down, seeing her hands as blobs. Her eyes were horribly warm. She wiped at them vigorously. God, how could I have been so stupid? He was just supposed to be a fun stud. Nothing more.

I love you, Tranquillity said, so full of cautious warmth that Ione had to smile. Then she winced as her stomach churned, and promptly threw up. The bile was acid and disgusting. She cupped her hands to capture some of the cool pool water so she could rinse her mouth out.

You are pregnant, Tranquillity observed.

Yes. The last time Joshua came back, before he made the Norfolk run.

Tell him.

No! That would only make it worse.

You are both fools, Tranquillity said with unaccustomed ardour.

*

Stars slid across the window behind Commander Olsen Neale. Choisya was the only one of Mirchusko's moons visible, a distant grey-brown crescent sliver peeping up over the bottom of the oval every three minutes. Erick Thakrar didn't like the sight of the starfield, it was too close, too easy to reach. He wondered, briefly, if he was developing a space-phobia. It wasn't unheard of, and there were a lot of associations involved. That horrified, distraught voice coming from the *Krystal Moon*; a fifteen-year-old girl. What had Tina looked like? It was a question he'd been asking himself a lot recently. Did she have a boyfriend? What mood fantasy bands did she cherish? Had she enjoyed her life on the old interplanetary vessel? Or did she find it intolerable?

What the fuck was she doing in the forward compartment below the communication dishes?

'The micro-fusion generators were handed directly over to the *Nolana* as soon as we docked,' Erick said. 'They never even passed through Tranquillity's cargo-storage facility. Which means there was no data work, no port manager's inspection. And of course we were all on board the *Villeneuve's Revenge* until the transfer was finished. I couldn't get a message out to you.'

'We'll track the *Nolana*, of course,' Olsen Neale said. 'See where the generators go. It should expose the distribution net. You've done well,' he added encouragingly. The young captain looked haggard, nothing like the bright eager agent who had wangled himself a berth on the *Villeneuve's Revenge* those long months ago.

It hits us all in the end, son, Olsen Neale thought soulfully to himself. We deliberately bring ourselves down to their level so we can blend in, and sometimes it costs just too much. Because nothing can go lower than human beings.

Erick remained unmoved by the compliment. 'You can have Duchamp and the rest of the crew arrested immediately,' he said. 'My neural nanonics recording of our attack on the *Krystal Moon* will be more than enough to convict them. I want you to tell the prosecutor to ask for maximum penalties. We can have them all committed to a penal planet. The whole lot of them, and that's better than they deserve.'

And it transfers your guilt, as well, Neale thought silently. 'I don't think we can do that right now, Erick,' he said.

'What? Three people have died just so that you have enough evidence against Duchamp. Two of them I killed myself.'

'I'm truly sorry, Erick, but circumstances have changed somewhat radically since your mission began. Have you accessed Time Universe's Lalonde sensevise?'

Erick gave him a demoralized stare, guessing what was coming. 'Yes.'

'Terrance Smith has signed on the *Villeneuve's Revenge* for his mercenary fleet. We've got to have somebody there, Erick. It's a legal mission for a planetary government, there's nothing I can do to prevent them from leaving. Christ, this is Laton we're talking about. I was about ten years old when he destroyed Jantrit. One and a quarter million people just so he could make a clean getaway, and the habitat itself; the Edenists had never lost a habitat before, their life expectancy is measured in millennia. And now he's had nearly forty years to perfect his megalomaniac schemes. Shit, we don't even know what they are; but what I've heard about Lalonde is enough to frighten me. I'm scared, Erick, I've got a family. I don't want him to get his hands on them. We have to know where he went on the

Yaku. Nothing is more important than that. Piracy and flogging off black-market goods are totally irrelevant by comparison. The navy has to find him and exterminate him. Properly this time. Until he's dead, we have no other goal. I've already sent a flek to Avon, a courier left on a blackhawk an hour after the Time Universe people told me about their recording.'

Erick's brow crinkled in surprise.

Olsen Neale gave a modest smile. 'Yes, a blackhawk. They're fast, they're good. And Laton will ultimately have them too if we don't stop him. Their captains are just as unnerved by him as we are.'

'All right.' Erick gave up. 'I'll go.'

'Anything. Any piece of data. What he's done out in the Lalonde hinterlands. Where the *Yaku* went. Just anything.'

'I'll get whatever I can.'

'You could try asking this journalist, Graeme Nicholson.' He shrugged at Erick's expression. 'The man's smart, resourceful. If anyone on that planet had the presence of mind to track the *Yaku*'s jump coordinate, it'll be him.'

Erick rose to his feet. 'OK.'

'Erick . . . take care.'

*

The heavy curtains in Kelly Tirrel's bedroom were drawn across the two oval windows. Ornate wall-mounted glass globes emitted a faint turquoise light. It made the white bed-sheets shimmer as if they were the surface of a moonlit lake; human skin was dark and tantalizing.

Kelly let Joshua run his hands over her, parting her legs so he could probe the damp cleft hidden below her tangle of pubic hair.

'Nice,' she purred, squirming over the rumpled sheets.

His teeth shone as he parted his lips. 'Good.'

'If you take me with you, there will be five days of this. Nonstop; and in free fall, too.'

'A powerful argument.'

'Money as well. Collins will pay triple rate for my passage.'

'I'm already rich.'

'So get richer.'

'Jesus, you're a pushy bitch.'

'Is that a complaint? Did you want to be with someone else tonight?'

'Er, no.'

'Good.' Her hand slid round his balls. 'This is the one for me, Joshua. This is my make or break chance. I blew the Ione story because of someone not a million kilometres from here.' Her fingers tightened slightly. 'Opportunities like this don't come to a place like Tranquillity three times in a life. If I pull it off I'll be made; top of the seniority table, good assignments, a decent bureau posting, a real salary. You owe me this, Joshua. You owe me very big.'

'Suppose the mercenaries don't want you with them?'

'You leave them to me. The way I'll pitch it at them, they'll eat up the offer. Heroes up against frightening odds helping to flatten Laton, rogues with a heart of gold, sensevised into every home in the Confederation. Come on!'

'Jesus.' There was still an uncomfortable pressure round his balls, long red nails touching his scrotum, a little too sharply to be described as tickling. She wouldn't. Would she? Her smart, expensive grey-blue Crusto suit was folded neatly over a chair by the dresser. It had been taken off with military regimentation as she *prepared* for sex.

She probably would. Jesus.

'Of course I'll take you.'

Thumb and forefinger nipped one ball impishly.

'Yow!' His eyes watered. 'You don't think you're getting carried away with this idea, do you? I mean, there are career moves and career moves. Landing on a hostile planet behind enemy lines is pushing company loyalty to extremes.'

'Crap.' Kelly rolled onto one elbow and glared at him. 'Did

you see who Time Universe had introducing their studio segments? Matthias bastard Rems, that's who. Just because he was in the right place at the right time. That lucky little shit. He's younger than me, barely out of his nursery pen. And they gave him three days prime scheduling time. *And* market research says he's popular because he's *boyish.* Some women like that, it turns out. Eighty-year-old virgins, I should think. The reason Time Universe won't let him record sensevises is because then we'd all know for sure he hasn't got any balls.'

'Not a problem in your case, is it?'

It came out before he could think. Kelly spent a hot violent twenty minutes making him wish it hadn't.

*

The nineteen starships under Terrance Smith's command assembled a thousand kilometres beyond Tranquillity's spaceport: the *Gemal* with five thousand general troops, three cargo clippers carrying their equipment and supplies, and fifteen combat-capable ships, six of which were blackhawks.

Tranquillity watched their drives come on, and the flotilla moved in towards Mirchusko at one gee. The Adamist starships employed a single-file formation (with *Gemal* leading) which the blackhawks encircled insolently. Strategic-defence sensor-platforms detected a vast amount of encrypted data traffic being exchanged between the ships as communication channels were tested and combat tactics exchanged.

They curved around the gas giant, heading towards its penumbra. Their drive exhausts shortened and vanished while they were still a hundred and eighty-four thousand kilometres above the unruly cloudscape, coasting towards the jump co-ordinate. Tranquillity saw the faint blue flickers of ion jets perfecting their orbital tracks; then the thermo-dump panels and sensor clusters began to withdraw. The blackhawks rushed away from the main convoy, freed of the constraints imposed by their Adamist partners, expanding in a perfectly spaced rosette. Then the bitek starships performed their swallow manoeuvre, jumping on ahead to scout for any possible trouble. Space reverberated with the gravity-wave backwash of their wormhole interstices snapping shut behind them, impinging on the habitat's sensitive mass-detection organs.

Gemal jumped. Tranquillity noted its spacial location and velocity vector. The trajectory was aligned exactly on Lalonde. One by one the remaining starships fell into the same jump coordinate and triggered their energy patterning nodes, squeezing themselves out of space-time.

23

Since the advent of its independence in 2238, Avon's government had contracted civil astroengineering teams to knock fifteen large (twenty- to twenty-five-kilometre diameter) stony iron asteroids into high orbit above the planet using precisely placed and timed nuclear explosions. Fourteen of them followed the standard formula of industrialization adopted throughout the Confederation. After their orbits were stabilized with a perigee no less than a hundred thousand kilometres, their ores had been mined out and the refined metal sent down to the planet below in the form of giant lifting bodies which coasted through the atmosphere to a splash-glide landing in the ocean. The resulting caverns were expanded, regularized into cylindrical shapes, the surface sculpted into a landscape, sealed, then turned into habitable biospheres. At the same time the original ore refineries would gradually be replaced by more sophisticated industrial stations, allowing the asteroid's economy to shift its emphasis from the bulk production of metals and minerals to finished micro-gee engineered products. The refineries moved on to a fresh asteroid in order to satisfy the demand of the planetary furnaces and steel mills, keeping the worst aspects of raw-material exploitation offplanet where the ecological pollution on the aboriginal biota was zero.

Anyone arriving at a terracompatible planet in the Confederation could tell almost at a glance how long it had been industrialized by the number of settled asteroids in orbit around it.

Avon had been opened for colonization to ethnic Canadians in 2151 during the Great Dispersal, and conformed to the usual evolutionary route out of an agrarian economy into industrialization in slightly less than a century. A satisfactory achievement, but nothing remarkable. It remained a pedestrian world until 2271 when it played host to the head of state conference called to discuss the worrying upsurge in the use of antimatter as a weapon of mass destruction. From that conference was born the Confederation, and Avon seized its chance to leapfrog an entire developmental stage by offering itself as a permanent host for the Assembly. Without any increase in exports, foreign currency poured in as governments set up diplomatic missions; and the lawyers, interstellar companies, finance institutions, influence peddlers, media conglomerates, and lobbyists followed, each with their own prestige offices and staff and dependents.

There was also the Confederation Navy, which was to police the fragile new-found unity between the inhabited stars. Avon contributed to that as well, by donating to the Assembly an orbiting asteroid named Trafalgar which was in the last phase of mining.

Trafalgar was unique within the Confederation in that it had no industrial stations after the miners moved out. It was first, foremost, and only, a naval base, developing from a basic supply and maintenance depot for the entire Confederation Navy (such as it was in the early days) up to the primary military headquarters for the eight hundred and sixty-two inhabited star systems which made up the Confederation in 2611. When First Admiral Samual Aleksandrovich took up his appointment in 2605 it was the home port for the 1st Fleet and headquarters and training centre for the Marine Corps. It housed the career Officer Academy, the Engineering School, the Navy Technical Evaluation Office, the First Admiral's Strategy Office, the Navy Budget Office, the principal research laboratories for supralight communications, and (more quietly) the headquarters of the Fleet Intelligence Arm. A black and grey peanut shape, twenty-one kilometres long, seven wide, rotating about its long axis; it contained three cylindrical biosphere caverns which housed a mixed civilian and military population of approximately three hundred thousand. There were non-rotational spaceports at each end: spheres two kilometres in diameter, the usual gridwork of girders and tanks and pipes, threaded with pressurized tubes carrying commuter cars, and docking-bays ringed by control cabins. Their surface area was just able to cope with the vast quantity of spaceship movements. The spindles were both fixed to Trafalgar's axis at the centre of deep artificial craters two kilometres wide which the voidhawks used as docking-ledges.

As well as its responsibility for defence and anti-pirate duties across the Confederation it coordinated Avon's defence in conjunction with the local navy. The strategic defence platforms protecting the planet were some of the most powerful ever built. Given the huge numbers of government diplomatic ships, as well as the above average number of commercial flights using the low-orbit docking stations, security was a paramount requirement. There hadn't been an act of piracy in the system for over two and a half centuries, but the possibility of a suicide attack against Trafalgar was uppermost in the minds of navy tacticians. Strategic sensor coverage was absolute out to a distance of two million kilometres from the planetary surface. Reaction time by the patrolling voidhawks was near instantaneous. Starships emerging outside designated areas took a formidable risk in doing so.

*

Ilex was calling for help even before the wormhole terminus closed behind it. Auster had ordered the voidhawk to fly straight to Avon, over four hundred light-years from Lalonde. Even for a voidhawk, the distance was excessive. *Ilex* needed to recharge its energy patterning cells after ten swallows, which involved a prolonged interval of ordinary flight to allow its distortion field to concentrate the meagre wisps of radiation which flittered through the interstellar medium.

The voyage had taken three and a half days. There were sixty people on board, and the bitek life-support organs were rapidly approaching their critical limit. The air smelt bad, membrane filters couldn't cope with the body gases, CO_2 was building up, oxygen reserves were almost exhausted.

Trafalgar was five thousand kilometres away when the wormhole terminus sealed. Legally, it should have been a hundred thousand. But a long sublight flight to a docking-ledge would have pushed *Ilex*'s life-support situation from critical to catastrophic.

The asteroid immediately went to defence condition C2, allowing the duty officer to engage all targets at will. Nuclear-pumped gamma-ray lasers locked onto the voidhawk's hull within three-quarters of a second of the wormhole opening.

Every Edenist officer in Trafalgar's strategic-defence command-centre heard *Ilex*'s call. They managed to load a five-second delay order into the defence platforms. Auster gave a fast résumé of the voidhawk's situation. The delay was extended for another fifteen seconds while the duty officer made her evaluation. A squadron of patrol voidhawks closed on *Ilex* at ten gees.

'Stand down,' the duty officer told the centre, and datavised a lockdown order into the fire-command computer. She looked across at the nearest Edenist. 'And tell that idiot captain from me I'll fry his arse off next time he pulls a stunt like this.'

Ilex swooped in towards Trafalgar at five gees as traffic control cleared a priority approach path ahead of it. Six patrol voidhawks spiralled round it like over-protective avian parents, all seven bitek starships exchanging fast affinity messages of anxiety, interest, and mild rebuke. The northern axial crater was a scene of frantic activity while *Ilex* chased the asteroid's rotation, looping around the globular non-rotating spaceport to fly in parallel to the spindle. It settled on a titanium pedestal with eight balloon-tyre maintenance vehicles and crew buses racing towards it, bouncing about in the low gravity.

Lalonde's navy office personnel disembarked first, hurrying along the airlock tube to the waiting bus, all of them taking deep gulps of clean, cool air. A medic team carried Niels Regehr off in a stretcher, while two paediatric nurses soothed and patted a blubbering Shafi Banaji. Environment-maintenance vehicles plugged hoses and cables into the crew toroid's umbilical sockets, sending gales of fresh air gusting through the cabins and central corridor. Resenda, *Ilex*'s life-support officer, simply vented the fouled atmosphere they'd been breathing throughout the voyage, and grey plumes jetted up out of the toroid, seeded with minute water crystals that sparkled in the powerful lights mounted on the spindle to illuminate the crater.

Once the first bus trundled away, a second nosed up to the airlock. A ten-strong marine squad in combat fatigues and armed with chemical projectile guns marched on board. Rhodri Peyton, the squad's captain, saluted an exhausted, unwashed, and unshaven Lieutenant Murphy Hewlett.

'This is her?' he asked sceptically.

Jacqueline Couteur stood in the middle of the corridor outside the airlock, with Jeroen van Ewyck and Garrett Tucci training their Bradfields on her. She was even dirtier than Murphy, the check pattern of her cotton shirt almost lost below the engrained grime picked up in the jungle.

'I'm tempted to let her show you what she can do,' Murphy said.

Kelven Solanki stepped forwards. 'All right, Murphy.' He turned to the marine captain. 'Your men are to have at least two weapons covering her at all times. She's capable of emitting an electronic warfare effect, as well as letting loose some kind of lightning bolt. Don't try to engage her in physical combat, she's quite capable of ripping you apart.'

One of the marines snickered at that. Kelven didn't have the energy left to argue.

'I'll go with her,' Jeroen van Ewyck said. 'My people need to be briefed anyway, and I'll let the science officers know what's required.'

'What is required?' Jacqueline Couteur asked.

Rhodri Peyton turned, and gave a start. In place of the dumpy middle-aged woman there was a tall, beautiful, twenty-year-old girl wearing a white cocktail gown. She gave him a silent entreating look, the maiden about to be offered to the dragon. 'Help me. Please. You're not like them. You're not an emotionless machine. They want to hurt me in their laboratories. Don't let them.'

Garrett Tucci jabbed the Bradfield into her back. 'Pack it in, bitch,' he said roughly.

She *twisted*, like an AV projection with a broken focus, and the old Jacqueline Couteur was standing there, a mocking expression on her face. Her jeans and shirt were now clean and pressed.

'My God,' Rhodri Peyton gasped.

'Now do you see?' Kelven asked.

The now nervous marine squad escorted their prisoner along the connecting tube to the bus. Jacqueline Couteur sat beside one of the windows, five guns lined up on her. She watched the bare walls of sterile rock impassively as the bus rolled back across the crater and into a downward sloping tunnel that led deep into the asteroid.

*

First Admiral Samual Aleksandrovich hadn't set foot on his native Russian-ethnic birth planet Kolomna for the last fifty-three of his seventy-three years; he hadn't been back for a holiday, nor even his parents' funeral. Regular visits might have been deemed inappropriate given that Confederation Navy career officers were supposed to renounce any national ties when they walked through the academy entrance; for a First Admiral to display any undue interest would have been a completely unacceptable breach of diplomatic etiquette. People would have understood his attending the funerals, though. So everyone assumed he was applying the same kind of steely discipline to his private affairs that ruled his professional life.

They were all wrong. Samual Aleksandrovich had never been back because there was nothing on the wretched planet with its all-over temperate climate which interested him, not family nor culture nor nostalgic scenery. The reason he left in the first place was because he couldn't stand the idea of spending a century helping his four brothers and three sisters run the family fruit-farming business. The same geneering which had produced his energetic one metre eighty frame, vivid copper hair, and enhanced metabolism, bestowed a life expectancy of at least a hundred and twenty years.

By the time he was nineteen years old he had come to realize that such a life would be a prison sentence given the vocations available on a planet just emerging from its agrarian phase. A potentially blessed life should not be faced with such finite horizons, for if it was it would turn from being a joy into a terrible burden. Variety was sanity. So on the day after his twentieth birthday he had kissed his parents and siblings goodbye, walked the seventeen kilometres into town through a heavy snowfall, and signed on at the Confederation Navy recruitment office.

Metaphorically, and otherwise, he had never looked back. He had never been anything other than an exemplary officer; he'd seen combat seven times, flown anti-pirate interdictions, commanded a flotilla raiding an illegal antimatter-production station, and gained a substantial number of distinguished service awards. But appointment to the post of First Admiral required a great deal more than an exemplary record. Much as he hated it, Samual Aleksandrovich had to play the political game; appearing before Assembly select committees, giving unofficial briefings to senior diplomats, wielding Fleet Intelligence information with as much skill as he did the rapier (he was year champion at the academy). His ability to pressure member states was admired by the Assembly President's staffers, as much for its neatness as the millions of fuseodollars saved by circumventing fleet deployment to trouble spots; and their word counted for a great deal more than the Admiralty, who advanced the names of candidates to the Assembly's Navy Committee.

In the six years he had held the office he had done a good job keeping the peace between sometimes volatile planetary governments and the even more mercurial asteroid settlements. Leaders and politicians respected his toughness and fairness.

A great deal of his renowned even-handed approach was formed when at the age of thirty-two he was serving as a lieutenant on a frigate that had been sent to Jantrit to assist the Edenists in some kind of armed rebellion (however unbelievable it sounded at the time). The frigate crew had watched helplessly while the antimatter was detonated, then spent three days in exhausting and often fruitless manoeuvres to rescue survivors of the tragedy. Samual Aleksandrovich had led one of the recovery teams after they rendezvoused with a broken starscraper. With heroic work that won him a commendation he and his crew-mates saved eighteen Edenists trapped in the tubular honeycomb of polyp. But one of the rooms they forced their way into was filled with corpses. It was a children's day club that had suffered explosive decompression. As he floated in desolated horror across the grisly chamber, he realized the Edenists were just as human as himself, and just as fallible. After that the persistent snide comments from fellow officers about the tall aloof bitek users annoyed him intensely. From then on he devoted himself body and soul to the ideal of enforcing the peace.

So when the *Eurydice* had docked at Trafalgar carrying a flek from Lieutenant-Commander Kelven Solanki about the small possibility (and he had been most unwilling to commit himself) that Laton was still alive and stirring from his self-imposed exile, First Admiral Samual Aleksandrovich had taken a highly personal interest in the Lalonde situation.

Where Laton was concerned, Samual Aleksandrovich exhibited neither his usual fairness nor a desire for justice to be done. He just wanted Laton dead. And this time there would be no error.

Even after his staff had edited down Murphy Hewlett's neural nanonics recording of the marine squad's fateful jungle mission, to provide just the salient points, there was three hours of sensorium memory to access. When he surfaced from Lalonde's savage heat and wearying humidity, Samual Aleksandrovich remained lost in thought for quarter of an hour, then took a commuter car down to the Fleet Intelligence laboratories.

Jacqueline Couteur had been isolated in a secure examin ation room. It was a cell cut into living rock with a transparent wall of metallized silicon whose structure was reinforced with molecular-binding-force generators. On one side it was furnished with a bed, wash-basin, shower, toilet, and a table, while the other side resembled a medical surgery with an adjustable couch and a quantity of analysis equipment.

She sat at the table, dressed in a green clinical robe. Five marines were in the cell with her, four of them carrying chemical-projectile guns, the fifth a TIP carbine.

Samual Aleksandrovich stood in front of the transparent wall looking at the drab woman. The monitoring room he was in resembled a warship's bridge, a white composite cube with a curved rank of consoles, all facing the transparent wall. The impersonality disturbed him slightly, an outsized vivarium.

Jacqueline Couteur returned his stare levelly. She should never have been able to do that, not a simple farmer's wife from a backwoods colony world. There were diplomats with eighty years of experienced duplicity behind them who broke into a sweat when Samual Aleksandrovich turned his gaze on them.

He likened the experience to looking into the eyes of an Edenist habitat mayor at some formal event, when the consensus intellect of every adult in the habitat looked back at him. Judging.

Whatever you are, he thought, you are not Jacqueline Couteur. This is the moment I've dreaded since I took my oath of office. A new threat, one beyond anything we know. And the burden of how to deal with it will inevitably fall heaviest on my navy.

'Do you understand the method of sequestration yet?' He asked Dr Gilmore, who was heading the research team.

The doctor made a penitent gesture. 'Not as yet. She's certainly under the control of some outside agency, but so far we haven't been able to locate the point where it interfaces with her nervous system. I'm a neural nanonics expert, and we've got several physicists on the team. But I'm not entirely sure we even have a specialization to cover this phenomenon.'

'Tell me what you can.'

'We ran a full body and neural scan on her, looking for implants. You saw what she and the other sequestrated colonists could do back on Lalonde?'

'Yes.'

'That ability to produce the white fireballs and electronic warfare impulses must logically have some kind of focusing mechanism. We found nothing. If it's there it's smaller than our nanonics, a lot smaller. Atomic sized, at least, maybe even sub-atomic.'

'Could it be biological? A virus?'

'You're thinking of Laton's proteanic virus? No, nothing like that.' He turned and beckoned to Euru.

The tall black-skinned Edenist left the monitor console he was working at and came over. 'Laton's virus attacked cells,' he explained. 'Specifically neural cells, altering their composition and DNA. This woman's brain structure remains perfectly normal, as far as we can tell.'

'If she can knock out a marine's combat electronics at over a hundred metres, how do you know your analysis equipment is giving you genuine readings?' Samual Aleksandrovich asked.

The two scientists exchanged a glance.

'Interference is a possibility we've considered,' Euru admitted. 'The next stage of our investigation will be to acquire tissue samples and subject them to analysis outside the range of her influence – if she lets us take them. It would require a great deal of effort if she refused to cooperate.'

'Has she been cooperative so far?'

'For most of the time, yes. We've witnessed two instances of visual pattern distortion,' Dr Gilmore said. 'When her jeans and shirt were removed she assumed the image of an apelike creature. It was shocking, but only because it was so unusual and unexpected. Then later on she tried to entice the marines to let her out by appearing as an adolescent girl with highly developed secondary sexual characteristics. We have AV recordings of both occasions; she can somehow change her body's photonic-emission spectrum. It's definitely not an induced hallucination, more like a chameleon suit's camouflage.'

'What we don't understand is where she gets the energy to produce these effects,' Euru said. 'The cell's environment is strictly controlled and monitored, so she can't be tapping Trafalgar's electrical power circuits. And when we ran tests on her urine and faeces we found nothing out of the ordinary. Certainly there's no unusual chemical activity going on inside her.'

'Lori and Darcy claimed Laton warned them of an energy virus,' Samual Aleksandrovich said. 'Is such a thing possible?'

'It may well be,' Euru said. His eyes darkened with emotion. 'If that *creature* was telling the truth he would probably have been attaching the nearest linguistic equivalents to a totally new phenomenon. An organized energy pattern which can sustain itself outside a physical matrix is a popular thesis with physicists. Electronics companies have been interested in the idea for a long time. It would bring about a radical transformation in our ability to store and manipulate data. But there has never been any practical demonstration of such an incorporeal matrix.'

Samual Aleksandrovich switched his glance back to the woman behind the transparent wall. 'Perhaps you are looking at the first.'

'It would be an extraordinary advance from our present knowledge base,' Dr Gilmore said.

'Have you asked the Kiint if it is possible?'

'No,' Dr Gilmore admitted.

'Then do so. They may tell us, they may not. Who understands how their minds work? But if anyone knows, they will.'

'Yes, sir.'

'What about her?' Samual Aleksandrovich asked. 'Has she said anything?'

'She is not very communicative,' Euru said.

The First Admiral grunted, and activated the intercom beside the cell's door. 'Do you know who I am?' he asked.

The marines inside the cell stiffened. Jacqueline Couteur's expression never changed; she looked him up and down slowly.

'I know,' she said.

'Who exactly am I talking to?'

'Me.'

'Are you part of Laton's schemes?'

Was there the faintest twitch of a smile on her lips? 'No.'

'What do you hope to achieve on Lalonde?'

'Achieve?'

'Yes, achieve. You have subjugated the human population, killed many people. This is not a situation I can allow to continue. Defending the Confederation from such a threat is my responsibility, even on a little planet as politically insignificant as Lalonde. I would like to know your motives so that a solution to this crisis may be found which does not involve conflict. You must have known that ultimately your action would bring about an armed response.'

'There is no "achievement" sought.'

'Then why do what you have done?'

'I do as nature binds me. As do you.'

'I do what my duty binds me to do. When you were on the *Isakore* you told the marines that they would come to you in time. If that isn't an objective I don't know what is.'

'If you believe I will aid you to comprehend what has happened, you are mistaken.'

'Then why did you allow yourself to be captured? I've seen the power you possess; Murphy Hewlett is good, but not that good. He couldn't get you here unless you wanted to come.'

'How amusing. I see governments and conspiracy theories are still inseparable. Perhaps I'm the lovechild of Elvis and Marilyn Monroe come to sue the North American Govcentral state in the Assembly court for my rightful inheritance.'

Samual Aleksandrovich gave her a nonplussed look. 'What?'

'It doesn't matter. Why did the navy want me here, Admiral?'

'To study you.'

'Precisely. And that is why I am here. To study you. Which of us will learn the most, I wonder?'

*

Kelven Solanki had never envisaged meeting the First Admiral quite so early in his career. Most commanders were introduced, certainly those serving in the 1st Fleet. But not lieutenant-commanders assigned to minor field-diplomat duties. Yet here he was being shown into the First Admiral's office by Captain Maynard Khanna. Circumstances muted the sense of excitement. He wasn't sure how the First Admiral viewed his handling of events on Lalonde, and the staff captain had given him no clues.

Samual Aleksandrovich's office was a circular chamber thirty metres across, with a slightly domed ceiling. Its curving wall had one window which looked out into Trafalgar's central biosphere cavern, and ten long holoscreens, eight slowly flicking through images from external sensors and the remaining two showing tactical displays. The ceiling was ribbed with bronze spars, with a fat AV cylinder protruding from the apex resembling a crystalline stalactite. There were two clusters of furniture; a huge teak desk with satellite chairs; and a sunken reception area lined by padded leather couches.

Maynard Khanna showed him over to the desk where the First Admiral was waiting. Auster, Dr Gilmore, Admiral Lalwani, the Fleet Intelligence chief, and Admiral Motela Kolhammer, the 1st Fleet Commander, were all sitting before the desk in the curved blue-steel chairs that had extruded out of the floor like pliable mercury.

Kelven stood to attention and gave a perfect salute, very conscious of the five sets of eyes studying him. Samual Aleksandrovich smiled thinly at the junior officer's obvious discomfort. 'At ease, Commander.' He gestured at one of the two new chairs formatting themselves out of the floor material. Kelven removed his cap, tucked it under his arm, and sat next to Maynard Khanna.

'You handled Lalonde quite well,' the First Admiral said. 'Not perfectly, but then you weren't exactly prepared for anything like this. Under the circumstances I'm satisfied with your performance.'

'Thank you, sir.'

'Bloody ESA people didn't help,' Motela Kolhammer muttered.

Samual Aleksandrovich waved him quiet. 'That is something we can take up with their ambassador later. Though I'm sure we all know what the outcome will be. Regrettable or not, you acted properly the whole time, Solanki. Capturing one of the sequestrated was exactly what we required.'

'Captain Auster made it possible, sir,' Kelven said. 'I wouldn't have got the marines out otherwise.'

The voidhawk captain nodded thankfully in acknowledgement.

'None the less, we should have given your situation a higher priority to begin with, and provided you with adequate resources,' Samual Aleksandrovich said. 'My mistake, especially given who was involved.'

'Has Jacqueline Couteur confirmed Laton's existence?' Kelven asked. Part of him was hoping that the answer was going to be a resounding no.

'She didn't have to.' Samual Aleksandrovich sighed ponderously. 'A blackhawk' – he paused, raising his bushy ginger eyebrows in emphasis – 'has just arrived from Tranquillity with a flek from Commander Olsen Neale. Under the circumstances I can quite forgive him for using the ship as a courier. If you would like to access the sensevise.'

Kelven sank deeper into the scoop of his chair as Graeme Nicholson's recording played through his brain. 'He was there all along,' he said brokenly. 'In Durringham itself, and I never knew. I thought the *Yaku*'s captain left orbit because of the deteriorating civil situation.'

'You are not in any way to blame,' Admiral Lalwani said.

Kelven glanced over at the grey-haired Edenist woman. There was an inordinate amount of sympathy and sadness in the tone.

'We should never have stopped checking, all those years ago,' she continued. 'The presence of Darcy and Lori on Lalonde was a rather miserable token to appease our paranoia. Even we were guilty of wishing Laton dead. The hope overwhelmed reason and rational thought. All of us knew how resourceful he was, and we knew he had acquired data on Lalonde. The planet should have been thoroughly searched. Our mistake. Now he has returned. I don't like to think of the price we will all have to pay before he is stopped this time.'

'Sir, Darcy and Lori seemed very uncertain that he was behind this invasion,' Kelven said. 'Laton actually warned them of this illusion-creating ability the sequestrated have.'

'And Jacqueline Couteur agrees he isn't a part of this,' Dr Gilmore said. 'That's one of the few things she will admit to.'

'I hardly think we can take her word for it,' Admiral Kolhammer said.

'Precise details are for later,' Samual Aleksandrovich said. 'What we have with Lalonde is shaping up into a major, and immediate, crisis. I'm tempted to ask the Assembly President to declare a state of emergency; that would put national navies at my disposal.'

'In theory,' Admiral Kolhammer said drily.

'Yes, and yet anything less may not suffice. This undetectable sequestration ability has me deeply worried. It has been used so freely on Lalonde, hundreds of thousands of people, if not millions. How many people does the agency behind it intend to subjugate? How many planets? It is a threat which the Assembly cannot be allowed to ignore in favour of its usual horse trading.' He considered the option of total mobilization before reluctantly dismissing it. There wasn't enough evidence to convince the president, not yet. It would come eventually, he was in no doubt of that. 'For the moment we will do what we can to contain the spread of this plague, whilst trying to find Laton. The flek from Olsen Neale also went on to report that Terrance Smith has met with some success in recruiting mercenaries and combat-capable starships for Governor Rexrew. That blackhawk made excellent time from Tranquillity; a little over two days, the captain told me. So we may just be able to put a brake on Lalonde before it gets totally out of hand. Terrance Smith's ships are scheduled to depart from Tranquillity today. Lalwani, you estimate it will take them a week to reach Lalonde?'

'Yes,' she said. 'It took the *Gemal* six days to get from Lalonde to Tranquillity. With the starships in Smith's fleet having to match formation after each jump, a single extra day is a conservative estimate. Even a navy flotilla would be hard pushed to match that. And those are not front-line ships.'

'Apart from the *Lady Macbeth*,' Maynard Khanna said in a quiet voice. 'I accessed the list of ships Smith recruited; the *Lady Macbeth* is a ship I am familiar with.' He glanced at the First Admiral.

'I know that name . . .' Kelven Solanki ran a search program through his neural nanonics. 'The *Lady Macbeth* was orbiting Lalonde when the trouble first broke out upriver.'

'That wasn't mentioned in any of your reports,' Lalwani said. Her slim forehead showed a frown.

'It was a commercial flight. Slightly odd, the captain wanted to export aboriginal wood, but as far as we could tell perfectly legitimate.'

'This name does seem to be popping up with suspicious regularity,' Maynard Khanna said.

'We should be able to look into it easily enough,' Samual Aleksandrovich said. 'Commander Solanki, the principal reason I asked you here was to inform you that you are to act as an adviser to the squadron which will blockade Lalonde.'

'Sir?'

'We're launching a dual programme to terminate this threat. The first aspect is a Confederationwide alert for Laton. We have to know where the *Yaku* went, where it is now.'

'He won't stay on board,' Lalwani said. 'Not after he reaches a port. But we'll find him. I'm organizing the search now. All the voidhawks in the Avon system will be conscripted and dispatched to alert national governments. I've already sent one to Jupiter; once the habitat consensus is informed, every void-hawk in the Sol system will be used to relay the news. I estimate it will take four to five days to blanket the Confederation.'

'Time Universe will probably beat you to it,' Admiral Kol-hammer said gruffly.

Lalwani smiled. The two of them were sparring partners from way back. 'In this case I wouldn't mind in the least.'

'Be a lot of panic. Stock markets will take a tumble.'

'If it makes people take the threat seriously, so much the better,' Samual Aleksandrovich said. 'Motela, you are to assemble a 1st Fleet squadron, a large one, to be held on fifteen-minute-departure alert. When we find Laton, eliminating him is going to be your problem.'

'What problem?'

'I admire the sentiment,' Samual Aleksandrovich said with a touch of censure. 'But kindly remember he escaped from us last time, when we were equally hungry for blood. That mistake cannot be repeated. This time I shall require proof, even though it will no doubt be expensive. I imagine Lalwani and Auster will agree.'

'We do,' Lalwani said. 'All Edenists do. If there is any risk in confirming the target is Laton, then we will bear it.'

'In the meantime, I want Lalonde to be completely isolated,' Samual Aleksandrovich said. 'The mercenary force is not to be allowed to land, nor do I want any surface bombardments from orbit. Those colonists have suffered enough already. The solution to this sequestration lies in discovering the method by which it is implemented, and devising a counter. Brute force is merely dumping plutonium in a volcano. And I suspect the mercenaries would simply be sequestrated themselves should they land. Dr Gilmore, this is your field.'

'Not really,' the doctor said expressively. 'But we shall put our female subject through an extensive series of experiments to see if we can determine the method of the sequestration and how to cancel it. However, judging by what we know so far, which is virtually nothing, I have to say an answer is going to take a considerable time to formulate. Though you are quite right to instigate a quarantine. The less contact Lalonde has with the rest of the Confederation the better, especially if it turns out Laton isn't behind the invasion.'

'The doctor has a point,' Lalwani said. 'What if the Lalonde invasion is the start of a xenoc incursion, and Laton himself has been sequestrated?'

'I'm keeping it in mind,' Samual Aleksandrovich said. 'We need to know more, either from the Couteur woman or Lalonde itself. Our principal trouble remains what it has always been: reaction time. It takes us far too long to amass any large force. Always our conflicts are larger than they would have been if we had received a warning of problems and threats earlier in their development. But just this once, we may actually be in luck. Unless there was some supreme diplomatic foul-up, Meredith Saldana's squadron was due to leave Omuta three days ago. They were in the system mainly for pomp and show, but they carried a full weapons load. A squadron of front-line ships already assembled and perfectly suited to these duties; we couldn't have planned it better. It'll take them five days to get back to Rosenheim. Captain Auster, if *Ilex* can get there before they dock at 7th Fleet headquarters and all the crews go on leave, then Meredith might just be able to get to Lalonde before Terrance Smith. And if not before, then certainly in time to prevent the bulk of the mercenary troops from landing.'

'*Ilex* will certainly try, First Admiral,' Auster said. 'I have already asked for auxiliary fusion generators to be installed in the weapons bays. The energy patterning cells can be recharged directly from them, reducing the flight time between swallows considerably. We should be ready to depart in five hours, and I believe we can make the two-day deadline.'

'My thanks to *Ilex*,' Samual Aleksandrovich said formally.

Auster inclined his head.

'Lieutenant-Commander Solanki, you'll travel with Captain Auster, and carry my orders for Rear-Admiral Saldana. And I think we can manage a promotion to full commander before you go. You've shown considerable initiative over the last few weeks, as well as personal courage.'

'Yes, sir, thank you, sir,' Kelven said. The promotion barely registered, some irreverent section of his mind was counting up the number of light-years he had flown in a week. It must be some kind of record. But he was going back to Lalonde, and bringing his old friends help. That felt good. *I've stopped running.*

'Add an extra order that the *Lady Macbeth* and her crew is to be arrested,' Samual Aleksandrovich told Maynard Khanna. 'They can try explaining themselves to Meredith's Intelligence officers.'

*

The *Santa Clara* materialized a hundred and twenty thousand kilometres above Lalonde, almost directly in line between the planet and Rennison. Dawn was racing over Amarisk, half of the Juliffe's tributary network flashing like silver veins in the low sunlight. The early hour might have accounted for the lack of response from civil traffic control. But Captain Zaretsky had been to Lalonde before, he knew the way the planet worked. Radio silence didn't particularly bother him.

Thermo-dump panels slid out of the hull, and the flight computer plotted a vector which would deliver the starship to a five hundred kilometre equatorial orbit. Zaretsky triggered the fusion drive and the ship moved in at a tenth of a gee. *Santa Clara* was a large cargo clipper, paying a twice-annual visit to the Tyrathca settlements, bringing new colonists and shipping out their rygar crop. There were over fifty Tyrathca breeders on board, all of them shuffling round the cramped life-support capsules; the dominant xenocs refused to use zero-tau pods (though their vassal castes were riding the voyage in temporal suspension). Captain Zaretsky didn't particularly like being chartered by Tyrathca merchants, but they always paid on time, which endeared them to the ship's owners.

Once the *Santa Clara* was underway, he opened channels to the nine starships in parking orbit. They told him about the riots, and rumours of invaders, and the fighting in Durringham which had lasted four days. There had been no information coming up from the city for two days now, they said, and they couldn't decide what to do.

Zaretsky didn't share their problem. *Santa Clara* had a medium-sized VTOL spaceplane in its hangar, his contract didn't call for any contact with the human settlements. Whatever rebellion the Ivets were staging, it didn't affect him.

When he opened a channel to the Tyrathca farmers on the planet they reported a few skirmishes with humans who were 'acting oddly'; but they had prepared their rygar crop, and were waiting for the equipment and new farmers the *Santa Clara* was bringing. He acknowledged the call, and continued the slow powered fall into orbit, the *Santa Clara*'s fusion exhaust drawing a slender thread of incandescence across the stars.

*

Jay Hilton sat on the rock outcrop fifty metres from the savannah homestead cabin, her legs crossed, head tipped back to watch the starship decelerating into orbit, and mournful curiosity pooling in her eyes. The weeks of living with Father Horst had brought about a considerable change in her appearance. For a start her lush silver-white hair had been cropped into a frizz barely a centimetre long, making it easier to keep clean. She had cried bucketfuls the day Father Horst took the scissors to it. Her mother had always looked after it so well, washing it with special shampoo brought from Earth, brushing it to a shine each night. Her hair was her last link with the way things used to be, her last hope that they might be that way again. When Father Horst had finished his snipping she knew in her heart that her most precious dream, that one day she'd wake up to find everything had returned to normal, was just a stupid child's imagination. She had to be tough now, had to be adult. But it was *so* hard.

I just want Mummy back, that's all.

The other children looked up to her. She was the oldest and

strongest of the group. Father Horst relied on her a great deal to keep the younger ones in order. A lot of them still cried at night. She heard them in the darkness, crying for their lost parents or siblings, crying because they wanted to go back to their arcology where none of this horrid confusion and upset happened.

Dawn's rosy crown gave way to a tide of blue which swept across the sky, erasing the stars. Rennison faded to a pale crescent, and the starship's exhaust became more difficult to see. Jay unfolded her legs and clambered down off the rocks.

The homestead on the edge of the savannah was a simple wooden structure, its solar-cell roof sheets glinting in the strong morning light. Two of the dogs, a Labrador and an Alsatian, were out and about. She patted them as she went up the creaking wooden stairs to the porch. The cows in the paddock were making plaintive calls, their udders heavy with milk.

Jay went in through the front door. The big lounge whiffed strongly – of food, and cooking, and too many people. She sniffed the air suspiciously. Someone had wet their bedding again, probably more than one.

The floor was a solid patchwork of sleeping-bags and blankets, their occupants only just beginning to stir. Grass stuffing from the makeshift mattresses of canvas sacks had leaked out again.

'Come on! Come on!' Jay clapped her hands together as she pulled the reed blinds open. Streamers of gold-tinged sunlight poured in, revealing children blinking sleep from their eyes, wincing at the brightness. Twenty-seven of them were crammed together on the mayope floorboards, ranging from a toddler about two years old up to Danny, who was nearly the same age as Jay. All of them with short haircuts and rough-tailored adult clothes which never quite fitted. 'Up you get! Danny, it's your gang's turn to do the milking. Andria, you're in charge of cooking this morning: I want tea, oatmeal, and boiled eggs for breakfast.' A groan went up, which Jay ignored; she was just as fed up with the changeless diet as they were. 'Shona, take three girls with you and collect the eggs, please.'

Shona gave a timid smile as well as she could, grateful for being included in the work assignments and not being treated any differently to the others. Jay had drilled herself not to flinch from looking at the poor girl. The six-year-old's face was covered in a bandage mask of glossy translucent epithelium membrane, with holes cut out for her eyes and mouth and nose. Her burn marks were still a livid pink below the overlapping membrane strips, and her hair was only just beginning to grow back. Father Horst said she ought to heal without any permanent scarring, but he was forever grieving over the lack of medical nanonic packages.

Coughs and grumbles and high-pitched chattering filled the room as the children struggled out of bed and into their clothes. Jay saw little Robert sitting brokenly on the side of his sleeping-bag, head in his hands, not bothering to get dressed. 'Eustice, you're to get this room tidied up, and I want all the blankets aired properly today.'

'Yes, Jay,' she answered sullenly.

The outside door was flung open as five or six children rushed out laughing, and ran for the lean-to, which they used as a toilet.

Jay picked her way over the rectangles of bedding to Robert. He was only seven, a black-skinned boy with fluffy blond hair. Sure enough, the navy blue pants he wore were damp.

'Pop down to the stream,' she said kindly. 'There will be plenty of time to wash before breakfast.'

His head was lowered even further. 'I didn't mean to,' he whispered, on the verge of tears.

'I know. Remember to wash out your sleeping-bag as well.' She caught the sound of someone giggling. 'Bo, you help him take the bag down to the stream.'

'Oh, Jay!'

'It's all right,' Robert said. 'I can manage.'

'No, you won't, not if you want to be back in time for breakfast.' The big table was already being pulled out from the kitchen corner by three of the boys, scraping loudly across the floor. They were shouting for people to get out of the way.

'Don't see why I should have to help him,' Bo said intransigently. She was an eight-year-old, meaty for her age, with chubby red cheeks. Her size was often deployed to help boss the smaller children around.

'Chocolate,' Jay said in warning.

Bo blushed, then stalked over to Robert. 'Come on then, you.'

Jay knocked once on Father Horst's door and walked in. The room had been the homestead's main bedroom when they moved in; it still had a double bed in it, but most of the floor space was taken up with packets, jars, and pots of food they'd taken from the other deserted homestead cabins. Clothes and cloth and powered tools, anything small or light enough to be carried, filled the second bedroom in piles that were taller than Jay.

Horst was getting up as the girl came in. He'd already got his trousers on, thick denim jeans with leather patches, a working man's garment, requisitioned from one of the other savannah homesteads. She picked up the faded red sweatshirt from the foot of the bed and handed it to him. He had lost a lot of weight – a lot of fat – over the last weeks; slack bands of flesh hung loosely from his torso. But even the folds were shrinking, and the muscles they covered were harder than they had ever been, though at night they felt like bands of ignescent metal. Horst spent most of every day working, hard manual work; keeping the cabin in shape, repairing and strengthening the paddock fence, building a chicken run, digging the latrines; then in the evening there would be prayers and reading lessons. At night he dropped into bed as if a giant had felled him with its fist. He had never known a human body could perform such feats of stamina, least of all one as old and decrepit as his.

Yet he never wavered, never complained. There was a fire in his eyes that had been ignited by his predicament. He was embarked on a crusade to survive, to deliver his charges to safety. The bishop would be hard pressed to recognize that dreamy well-meaning Horst Elwes who had left Earth last year. Even thinking about his earlier self with its disgusting self-pity and weaknesses repelled him.

He had been tested as few had ever been before, his faith thrown onto towering flames that had threatened to reduce him to shreds of black ash so powerful was the doubt and insecurity fuelling them: but he had emerged triumphant. Born of fire, and reforged, his conviction in self, and Christ the Saviour, was unbreakable.

And he had the children to thank. The children who were now his life and his task. The hand of God had brought them together. He would not fail them, not while there was a breath left in his body.

He smiled at Jay who was as grave faced as she always was at the break of day. The sounds of the usual morning bedlam were coming through the door as bedding was put away and the furniture brought out.

'How goes it today, Jay?'

'Same as always.' She sat on the end of the bed as he pulled on his heavy hand-tooled boots. 'I saw a starship arrive. It's coming down into low orbit.'

He glanced up from his laces. 'Just one?'

'Uh huh,' she nodded vigorously.

'Ah well, it's not to be today, then.'

'*When?*' she demanded. Her small beautiful face was screwed up in passionate rage.

'Oh, Jay.' He pulled her against him, and rocked her gently as she sniffled. 'Jay, don't give up hope. Not you.' It was the one thing he promised them, repeating it every night at prayers so they would believe. On a world far away lived a wise and powerful man called Admiral Aleksandrovich, and when he heard what terrible things had happened on Lalonde he would send a fleet of Confederation Navy starships to help its people and drive away the demons who possessed them. The soldiers and the navy crews would come down in huge spaceplanes and rescue them, and then their parents, and finally put the world to rights again. Every night Horst said it, with the door locked against the wind and rain, and the windows shuttered against the dark empty savannah. Every night he believed and they believed. Because God would not have spared them if it was not for a purpose. 'They will come,' he promised. He kissed her forehead. 'Your mother will be so proud of you when she returns to us.'

'Really?'

'Yes, really.'

She pondered this. 'Robert wet his bed again,' she said.

'Robert is a fine boy.' Horst stomped on the second boot. They were two sizes too large, which meant he had to wear three pairs of socks, which made his feet sweat, and smell.

'We should get him something,' she said.

'Should we now? And what's that?'

'A rubber mat. There might be one in another cabin. I could look,' she said, eyes all wide with innocence.

Horst laughed. 'No, Jay, I haven't forgotten. I'll take you out hunting this morning, and this time it will be Danny who stays behind.'

Jay let out a squeal of excitement and kicked her legs in the air. 'Yes! Thank you, Father.'

He finished tying his laces and stood up. 'Don't mention the starship, Jay. When the navy comes it will be in a mighty flotilla, with their exhaust plumes so strong and bright they will turn night into day. Nobody will mistake it. But in the meantime we must not pour cold water on the others' hopes.'

'I understand, Father. I'm not as dumb as them.'

He ruffled her hair, which she pretended not to like, wriggling away. 'Come along now,' he said. 'Breakfast first. Then we'll get our expedition sorted out.'

'I suppose Russ will come with us?' she asked in a martyred voice.

'Yes, he will. And stop thinking uncharitable thoughts.'

The children already had most of the bedding off the floor. Two boys were sweeping up the dried grass from the sack mattresses (Must find a better replacement, Horst thought). Eustice's voice could be heard through the open door, yelling instructions to the children airing the linen outside.

Horst helped to pull the big table into the middle of the room. Andria's team were scurrying round the kitchen corner, tending the equipment and the meal. The big urn was just starting to boil, and the three IR plates were heating up the boiling pans ready for the eggs.

Once again Horst gave a fast prayer of thanks that the solar-powered equipment functioned so well. It was easy enough for the children to use without hurting themselves, and most of them had helped their mothers with the cooking before. All they needed was some direction, as they did in every task he set them. He didn't like to think how he would have coped if the homestead hadn't been empty.

It took another fifteen minutes before Andria's cooking party were ready to serve breakfast. Several of the eggs Shona brought back were broken, so Horst himself scrambled them up in a pan on a spare IR plate. It was easier to feed Jill, the toddler, that way.

The tea was finally ready, and the eggs boiled. Everyone lined up with their mug and cutlery and eggcup, and filed past the kitchen bar which doubled as a serving counter. For a few wonderful minutes the room was actually quiet as the children drank, and cracked their eggs open, and pulled faces as they munched the dry oatmeal biscuits, dunking them in the tea to try and soften them up first. Horst looked round his extended family and tried not to feel frightened at the responsibility. He adored them in a way he had never done with his parishioners.

After breakfast it was wash time, with the extra two tanks he had installed in the rafter space struggling to provide enough hot water. Horst inspected them all to make sure they were clean and that they had jell-rinsed their teeth. That way he could have a few words with each of them, make them feel special, and wanted, and loved. It also gave him the chance to watch for any sign of illness. So far there had been remarkably little, a few colds, and one nasty outbreak of diarrhoea a fortnight ago, which he suspected was from a batch of jam that had come from another homestead.

The morning would follow its standard pattern while he and Jay were away. Clothes to be washed in the stream and hung out to dry. Hay to be taken into the cows, corn to be measured out into the chicken-run dispensers (they never did that very well), lunch to be prepared. When he went away it was always the packets of protein-balanced meals from Earth – all they had to do was put them in the microwave for ninety seconds, and nothing could go wrong. Sometimes he allowed a group to pick elwisie fruit from the trees on the edge of the jungle. But not today; he gave Danny a stern lecture that no one was to wander more than fifty metres from the cabin, and someone must be on watch the whole time in case a kroclion turned up. The plains carnivores hadn't often plagued the homesteads, but his didactic memory showed what a menace the lumbering animals could be. The boy nodded earnestly, eager to prove his worth.

Horst was still suffering from stings of doubt when he led the group's one horse from its stable. He trusted Jay to be left in charge, she acted far older than her years. But he had to hunt for meat, there were hardly any fish in the nearby stream. If they stuck to the cache of food in his bedroom it would be gone within ten days; it existed to supplement what he killed and stored in the freezer, and acted as an emergency reserve just in case he ever did get ill. And Jay deserved a break from the homestead, she hadn't been away since they arrived.

He took two other children with him as well as Jay. Mills, an energetic eight-year-old from Schuster village, and Russ, a seven-year-old who simply refused to ever leave Horst's side. The one and only time he had gone hunting without him the boy had run off into the savannah and it had taken the whole afternoon to find him.

Jay was grinning and waving and playing up to her jealous friends when they set off. The savannah grass quickly rose up around their legs; Horst had made Jay wear a pair of trousers instead of her usual shorts. A thick layer of mist started to lift from the waving stalks and blades now the sun was rising higher into the sky. Haze broke the visibility down to less than a kilometre.

'This humidity is worse than the Juliffe back in Durringham,' Jay exclaimed, waving her hand frantically in front of her face.

'Cheer up,' Horst said. 'It might rain later.'

'No, it won't.'

He glanced round to where she was walking in the track he was making through the stiff grass. Bright eyes gleamed mischievously at him from below the brim of her tatty felt sun-hat.

'How do you know?' he asked. 'It always rains on Lalonde.'

'No, it doesn't. Not any more, not during the day.'

'What do you mean?'

'Haven't you noticed? It only ever rains at night now.'

Horst gave her a perplexed stare. He was about to tell her not to be silly. But then he couldn't remember the last time he'd rushed indoors to shelter from one of Lalonde's ferocious downpours – a week, ten days? He had an uncomfortable feeling it might even have been longer. 'No, I hadn't noticed,' he said temperately.

'That's all right, you've had a lot on your mind lately.'

'I certainly have.' But the chirpy mood was broken now.

I should have noticed, he told himself. But then who regards the weather as something suspicious? He was sure it was important though, he just couldn't think how, or why. Surely *they* couldn't change the weather.

Horst made it a rule that he was never away for more than four hours. That put seven other homestead cabins within reach (eight counting the ruins of the Skibbow building) as well as allowing enough time to shoot a danderil or some vennals. Once he had shot a pig that had run wild, and they'd eaten ham and bacon for the rest of the week. It was the most delicious meat he'd ever tasted, terrestrial beasts were pure ambrosia compared to the coarse and bland aboriginal animals.

There was hardly anything of any value left in the cabins now, he had stripped them pretty thoroughly. After another couple of visits there would be little point in returning. He caught himself before brooding turned to melancholia; he wouldn't need to go back, the navy would come. And don't ever think anything different.

Jay bounded up to walk beside him, adjusting her stride to match his. She gave him a sideways smile, then returned her gaze to the front, perfectly content.

Horst felt his own tensions seeping away. Having her so close was like the time right after that dreadful night. She had screamed and fought him as he pulled her away from Ruth and Jackson Gael. He had forced her through the village towards the jungle, only once looking back. He saw it all then, in the light of the fire which pillaged their sturdy tranquil village, snuffing out their ambitions of a fair future as swiftly as rain dissolved the mud castles the children built on the riverbank. Satan's army was upon them. More figures were marching out of the dark shadows into the orange light of the flames, creatures that even Dante in his most lucid fever-dreams had never conceived, and the screams of the ensnared villagers rose in a crescendo.

Horst had never let Jay look back, not even after they reached the trees. He knew then that waiting for the hunting party to return was utter folly. Laser rifles could not harm the demon legions Lucifer in his wrath had loosed upon the land.

They had carried on far into the jungle, until a numbed, petrified Jay had finally collapsed. Dawn found them huddled together in the roots of a qualtook tree, soaked and shivering from a downpour in the night. When they eased their way cautiously back towards Aberdale and hid themselves in the vines ringing the clearing they saw a village living a dream.

Several buildings were razed to the ground. People walked by without paying them a glance. People Horst knew, his flock, who should have been overwrought by the damage. That was when he knew Satan had won, his demons had possessed the villagers. What he had seen at the Ivet ceremony had been repeated here, again and again.

'Where's Mummy?' Jay asked miserably.

'I have no idea,' he said truthfully. There were fewer people than there should have been, maybe seventy or eighty out of the population of five hundred. They acted as though devoid of purpose, walking slowly, looking round in befogged surprise, saying nothing.

The children were the exception. They ran around between the somnolent, shuffling adults, crying and shouting. But they were ignored, or sometimes cuffed for their trouble. Horst could hear their distraught voices from his sanctuary, deepening his own torment. He watched as a girl, Shona, trailed after her mother pleading for her to say something. She tugged insistently at the trousers, trying to get her to stop. For a moment it looked like she had succeeded. Her mother turned round. 'Mummy,' Shona squealed. But the woman raised a hand, and a blast of white fire streamed from her fingers to smite the girl full in the face.

Horst cringed, crossing himself instinctively as she dropped like a stone, not even uttering a cry. Then anger poured through him at his own cravenness. He stood up and strode purposefully out of the trees.

'Father,' Jay squeaked behind him. 'Father, don't.'

He paid her no heed. In a world gone mad, one more insanity would make no difference. He had sworn himself to follow Christ, a long time ago, but it meant more to him now than it ever had. And a child lay suffering before him. Father Horst Elwes was through with evasions and hiding.

Several of the adults stopped to watch as he marched into the village, Jay scuttling along behind him. Horst pitied them for the husks they were. The human state of grace had been drained from their bodies. He could tell, accepting the gift of knowledge as his right. Six or seven villagers formed a loose group standing between him and Shona, their faces known but not their souls.

One of the women, Brigitte Hearn, never a regular church-goer, laughed at him, her arm rising. A ball of white fire emerged from her open fingers and raced towards him. Jay screamed, but Horst stood perfectly still, face resolute. The fireball started to break apart a couple of metres away from him, dimming and expanding. It burst with a wet crackle as it touched him, tiny strands of static burrowing through his filthy sweatshirt. They stung like hornets across his belly, but he refused to reveal his pain to the semicircle of watchers.

'Do you know what this is?' Horst thundered. He lifted the stained and muddied silver crucifix that hung round his neck, brandishing it at Brigitte Hearn as though it was a weapon. 'I am the Lord's servant, as you are the Devil's. And I have His work to do. Now stand aside.'

A spasm of fright crossed Brigitte Hearn's face as the silver cross was shaken in front of her. 'I'm not,' she said faintly. 'I'm not the Devil's servant. None of us are.'

'Then stand aside. That girl is badly hurt.'

Brigitte Hearn glanced behind her, and took a couple of steps to one side. The other people in the group hurriedly parted, their faces apprehensive, one or two walked away. Horst gestured briefly at Jay to follow him, and went over to the fallen girl. He grimaced at the singed and blackened skin of her face. Her pulse was beating wildly. She had probably gone into shock, he decided. He scooped her up in his arms, and started for the church.

'I had to come back,' Brigitte Hearn said as Horst walked away. Her body was all hunched up, eyes brimming with tears. 'You don't know what it's like. I had to.'

'It?' Horst asked impatiently. 'What is *it*?'

'Death.'

Horst shuddered, almost breaking his stride. Jay looked round fearfully at the woman.

'Four hundred years,' Brigitte Hearn called out falteringly. 'I died four hundred years ago. Four hundred years of nothing.'

Horst barged into the small infirmary at the back of the church, and laid Shona down on the wooden table which doubled as an examination bed. He snatched the medical processor block from its shelf and applied a sensor pad to the nape of her neck. The metabolic display appeared as he described her injuries to the processor. Horst read the results and gave the girl a sedative, then started spraying a combination analgesic and cleansing fluid over the burns.

'Jay,' he said quietly. 'I want you to go into my room and fetch my rucksack from the cupboard. Put in all the packets of preprocessed food you can find, then the tent I used when we first arrived, and anything else you think will be useful to camp out in the jungle – the little fission blade, my portable heater, that kind of stuff. But leave some space for my medical supplies. Oh, and I'll need my spare boots too.'

'Are we leaving?'

'Yes.'

'Are we going to Durringham?'

'I don't know. Not straight away.'

'Can I go and fetch Drusilla?'

'I don't think it's a good idea. She'll be better off here than tramping through the jungle with us.'

'All right. I understand.'

He heard her moving about in his room as he worked on Shona. The younger girl's nose was burnt almost down to the bone, and the metabolic display said only one retina was functional. Not for the first time he despaired the lack of nanonic medical packages; a decent supply would hardly have bankrupted the Church.

He had flushed the dead skin from Shona's burns as best he could, coating them in a thin layer of corticosteroid foam to ease the inflammation, and was binding her head with a quantity of his dwindling stock of epithelium membrane when Jay came back in carrying his rucksack, It was packed professionally, and she had even rolled up his sleeping-bag.

'I got some stuff for myself,' she said, and held up a bulging shoulder-bag.

'Good girl. You didn't make the bag too heavy, did you? You might have to carry it a long way.'

'No, Father.'

Someone knocked timidly on the door post. Jay shrank into the corner of the infirmary.

'Father Horst?' Brigitte Hearn poked her head in. 'Father, they don't want you here. They say they'll kill you, that you can't defend yourself against all of them.'

'I know. We're leaving.'

'Oh.'

'Will they let us leave?'

She swallowed and looked over her shoulder. 'Yes. I think so. They don't want a fight. Not with you, not with a priest.'

Horst opened drawers in the wooden cabinet at the back of the infirmary, and started shoving his medical equipment into the rucksack. 'What are you?' he asked.

'I don't know,' she said woefully.

'You said you had died?'

'Yes.'

'What is your name?'

'Ingrid Veenkamp, I lived on Bielefeld when it was a stage one colony world, not much different to this planet.' She twitched a smile at Jay. 'I had two girls. Pretty, like you.'

'And where is Brigitte Hearn now?'

'Here, in me. I feel her. She is like a dream.'

'Possession,' Horst said.

'No.'

'Yes! I saw the red demon sprite. I witnessed the rite, the *obscenity* Quinn Dexter committed to summon you here.'

'I'm no demon,' the woman insisted. 'I lived. I am human.'

'No more. Leave this body you have stolen. Brigitte Hearn has a right to her own life.'

'I can't! I'm not going back there. Not to that.'

Horst took a grip on his trembling hands. Thomas had known this moment, he thought, when the disciple doubted his Lord's return, when in prideful arrogance he refused to believe until he had seen the print of nails in His hand. 'Believe,' he whispered. 'Jesus is the Christ, the Son of God; and that believing ye might have life through His name.'

The Brigitte/Ingrid woman bowed her head.

Horst asked the question that should never be asked: 'Where? Where, damn you!'

'Nowhere. There is nothing for us. Do you hear? Nothing!'

'You lie.'

'There is nothing, just emptiness. I'm sorry.' She took an unsteady breath, seemingly gathering up a remnant of dignity. 'You must leave now. They are coming back.'

Horst shut the flap on his rucksack and sealed it. 'Where are the rest of the villagers?'

'Gone. They hunt fresh bodies for other souls trapped in the beyond, it has become their quest. I haven't the stomach for it, nor have the others who remained in Aberdale. But you take care, Father. Your spirit is hale, but you could never withstand one of us for long.'

'They want more people to possess?'

'Yes.'

'But why?'

'Together we are strong. Together we can change what is. We can destroy death, Father. We shall bring eternity into existence here on this planet, perhaps even across the entire Confederation. I shall stay as I am for all time now; ageless, changeless. I am alive again, I won't give that up.'

'This is lunacy,' he said.

'No. This is wonder, it is our miracle.'

Horst pulled his rucksack onto his back, and picked Shona up. Several adults had started to gather around the church. He walked down the steps pointedly disregarding them, Jay pressing into his side. They stared at him, but no one made a move. He turned and headed for the jungle, mildly surprised to see Ingrid Veenkamp walking with him.

'I told you,' she said. 'They lack nerve. You will be safer if I am with you. They know I can strike back.'

'Would you?'

'Perhaps. For the girl's sake. But I don't think we will find out.'

'Please, lady,' Jay said, 'do you know where my mummy is?'

'With the others, the pernicious ones. But don't look for her, she is no longer your mother. Do you understand?'

'Yes,' she mumbled.

'We'll get her back for you, Jay,' Horst said. 'One day, somehow. I promise.'

'Such faith,' Ingrid Veenkamp said.

He thought she was mocking, but there was no trace of a smile on her face. 'What about the other children?' he asked. 'Why haven't you possessed them?'

'Because they are children. No soul would want a vessel so

small and frail, not when there are plentiful adults to be had. Millions on this planet alone.'

They had reached the fields, and the soft loam was clinging to Horst's feet in huge claggy lumps. With the weight of the rucksack and Shona conspiring to push him into the ground he wasn't even sure he could make it to the first rank of trees. Sweat was dripping from his forehead at the effort. 'Send the children after me,' he wheezed. 'They are hungry and they are frightened. I will take care of them.'

'You make a poor Pied Piper, Father. I'm not even sure you'll last until nightfall.'

'Mock and scorn as you like, but send them. They'll find me. For God knows I'll not be able to travel far or fast.'

She dipped her head briefly. 'I'll tell them.'

Horst staggered into the jungle with Jay beside him, her big shoulder-bag knocking against her legs. He managed another fifty metres through the inimical vines and undergrowth, then sank panting painfully to his knees, face perilously red and hot.

'Are you all right?' Jay asked anxiously.

'Yes. We'll just have to take it in short stages, that's all. I think we're safe for now.'

She opened the shoulder-bag's seal. 'I brought your cooler flask, I thought you might need it. I filled it with the high-vitamin orange juice you had in your room.'

'Jay, you are a twenty-four-carat angel.' He took the flask from her and drank some of the juice; she had set the thermostat so low it poured like slushy snow. They heard someone pushing their way through the undergrowth behind them, and turned. It was Russ and Andria, the first of the children.

*

Trudging across the savannah wasn't quite the holiday Jay had told herself it would be. But it was lovely being away from the homestead, even if it was only going to be for a few hours. She longed to ride the horse, too; though there was no way she was going to plead with Father Horst in front of the boys.

They arrived at the Ruttan family's old homestead after forty minutes' walking. Untended, it had suffered from Lalonde's rain and winds. The door which had been left open had swung to and fro until the hinges broke, and now it lay across the small porch. Animals (probably sayce) had used it for shelter at some time, adding to the disarray inside.

Jay waited with the two boys while Father Horst went in, carrying his laser hunting rifle, and checked over the three rooms. The abandoned cabin was eerie after the noise and bustle of their own homestead. She heard a distant rumble, and looked up, thinking it was approaching thunder. But the sky remained a perfect basin of blue. The noise grew louder, swelling out of the west.

Father Horst emerged from the homestead carrying a wooden chair. 'It sounds like a spaceplane,' he said.

The grimed window-panes were rattling in their frames. Jay searched the sky frantically as the sound began to fade into the east. But there was nothing to be seen, the spaceplane was too high. She gave the distant mountains to the south a forlorn glance. It must have been going to the Tyrathca farmers, she thought.

'Have a hunt round,' Horst said. 'See if you can find anything useful; you might try the barn as well. I'm going to the roof to cut the solar-cell sheets down.' He put the chair down under the eaves, and stood on it, squirming his way up onto the roof.

There was nothing much in the cabin; fans of grey fungus had established a foothold in the cracks between the planks, and greenish ripples of mould patterned the damp mattresses. She pulled a couple of clay mugs out from under one of the beds, and Russ found some shirts in a box below the kitchen workbench.

'They'll be all right once we wash them,' Jay declared, holding up the smelly, soiled garments.

They had more luck in the barn: two sacks of protein-concentrate cakes used to feed young animals that had just come out of hibernation, and Mills discovered a small fission-blade saw behind a pile of old cargo-pods.

'Good work!' Horst told them as he clambered down. 'And look what I got, all three sheets. We'll be able to heat the water tanks up in half the time now.'

Jay rolled up the solar-cell sheets while he lifted the sacks into the plough horse's big saddle-bags.

Horst handed round his chill flask full of icy elwisie juice, then they set off again. Jay was glad of her hat. The sunlight was scorchingly hot on her arms and back, air rippled and shimmered all around. I never thought I'd miss the rains.

There was a river to cross before they reached the Soebergs' homestead. It was less than a metre deep, but about fifteen metres wide. A fast, steady flow from the mountains, winding in broad curves along the savannah's gentle contours. The bottom was smooth rock and rounded pebbles. Snowlily plants were growing right across it, their long fronds waving in the current. Flower buds as big as her head bobbed on the surface, the first splits starting to appear in their sides.

Jay and Horst took their boots off, and waded across clinging to the side of the horse. The water was invigorating, numbing her toes. She could easily believe it must have come directly from the snow peaks themselves, she wouldn't have been surprised to see nuggets of ice bobbing about. After she sat on the bottom of the bank and dried her feet she thought she could walk for another hundred kilometres. Her skin was still tingling delightfully when they started up the bank.

They had been walking for another ten minutes when Horst held up his hand. 'Mills, Russ, come down off the horse,' he said with quiet insistence.

The tone he used set up an uncomfortable prickling along Jay's spine. 'What is it?' she asked.

'The Soebergs' homestead. I think.'

She peered over the tops of the wavering grass stems. There was something up ahead, a white silhouette against the indistinct horizon, but the sun-roiled air made it hard to tell exactly what.

Horst fished his optical intensifier from a pocket. It was a curving band of black composite that fitted over his eyes. He studied the scene ahead for a while, his right forefinger adjusting the magnification control.

'They are coming back,' he said in a soft murmur.

'Can I see?' she asked.

He handed her the band. It was large and quite heavy; the edges annealed to her skin with a pinching sensation.

She thought she was looking at some kind of AV recording, a drama play perhaps. Sitting in the middle of the savannah was a lovely old three-storey manor house, surrounded by a wide swath of tidy lawns. It was made of white stone, with a grey slate roof and large bay windows. Several people were standing under the portico.

'How do they do that?' Jay asked, more curious than alarmed.

'When you sell your soul to Satan, the material rewards are generous indeed. It is what he asks in return you should fear.'

'But Ingrid Veenkamp said—'

'I know what she said.' He removed the band from her face, and she blinked up at him. 'She is a lost soul, she knows not what she does. Lord forgive her.'

'Do they want our homestead too?' Jay asked.

'I shouldn't think so. Not if they can build that in a week.' He sighed, and took one final look at the miniature mansion. 'Come along, we'll see if we can find a nice fat danderil. If we get back early I'll have time to mince the meat, and you can have burgers tonight. What do you say?'

'Yeah!' the two boys chanted in chorus, grinning.

They turned round, and started to trek back across the heat-soaked savannah to the homestead.

*

Kelven Solanki floated through the open hatch into the *Arikara*'s bridge. The blue-grey compartment was the largest he'd ever seen in a warship before. As well as the normal flight crew it had to accommodate the admiral's twenty-strong squadron-coordination staff. Most of their couches were empty now. The flagship was orbiting Takfu, the largest gas giant in the Rosenheim star system, taking on fuel.

Commander Mircea Kroeber was stretched out along his couch, supervising the fuelling operation with three other crew-members. Kelven had seen the cryogenic tanker as *Ilex* docked with the huge flagship. A series of spherical tanks stacked on top of a reaction drive section, and sprouting thermo-dump panels like the wings of a mutant butterfly.

The squadron of twenty-five ships was in formation around the *Arikara*, holding station five hundred kilometres away from Uhewa, the Edenist habitat which was resupplying them with both fuel and consumables. It was just one of the priority operations *Ilex*'s arrival in the star system had kicked off ten hours ago. Rosenheim's planetary government had immediately placed a restriction on all starship passengers and crew wanting to visit the surface. They now had to go through a rigorous screening process to make sure Laton wasn't amongst them, creating a vast backlog in the low orbit port stations. The system's asteroid settlements had swiftly followed suit. Reserve naval officers were being called up, and the 7th Fleet elements present in the system had been put on alert status along with the national navy.

Kelven was beginning to feel like a plague carrier, infecting the Confederation with panic.

Rear-Admiral Meredith Saldana was hanging in front of a console in the C&C section of the bridge, his soles touching the decking's stikpads. He was wearing an ordinary naval ship-suit, but it seemed so much smarter on him, braid stripes shining brightly on his arm. A couple of his staff officers were in attendance behind him. One of the console's AV projection pillars was emitting a low-frequency laser sparkle. When Kelven looked straight at it he saw Jantrit breaking apart.

Meredith Saldana datavised a shutdown order at the console as Kelven let the stikpad claim his shoes. The Rear-Admiral was six centimetres taller than him, and possessed a more distinguished appearance than the First Admiral. Could the Saldanas sequence dignity into their genes?

'Commander Kelven Solanki reporting as ordered, sir.'

Meredith Saldana gave him a frank stare. 'You are my Lalonde advisory officer?'

'Yes, sir.'

'Just been promoted, Commander?'

'Yes, sir.'

'It always shows.'

'Sir, I have your orders flek from the First Admiral.' Kelven held it out.

Meredith Saldana took the black coin-sized disk with some reluctance. 'I don't know which is worse. Three months of these ridiculous ceremonial fly-bys and flag-waving exercises in the Omutan system, or a combat mission which is going to get us shot at by unknown hostiles.'

'Lalonde needs our help, sir.'

'Was it bad, Kelven?'

'Yes, sir.'

'I suppose I'd better access this flek, hadn't I? All we've received so far are the emergency deployment orders from Fleet headquarters and the news about Laton showing up again.'

'There is a full situation briefing included, sir.'

'Excellent. If we run to schedule we should be departing for Lalonde in eight hours. I've requested another three voidhawks be assigned to the squadron for liaison and interdiction duties.

Is there anything else you think I need immediately? This mission's code rating gives me the authority to requisition almost any piece of hardware the navy has in the system.'

'No, sir. But you will have a fourth extra voidhawk, *Ilex* has been assigned to the squadron as well.'

'You can never have too many voidhawks,' Meredith said lightly. There was no response from the young commander. 'Carry on, Kelven. Find yourself a berth, and get settled in. Report for duty here to me an hour before departure time, you can give me a first-hand account of what we can expect. I always feel a lot happier being brought up to date by someone with hands-on experience. Meanwhile I suggest you get some sleep, you look like you need it.'

'Yes, sir, thank you, sir.'

Kelven twisted his feet free of the stikpad, and pushed off towards the hatch.

Meredith Saldana watched him manoeuvre through the open oval without touching the rim. Commander Solanki seemed to be a very tense man. But then I'd probably be the same in his place, the admiral thought. He held up the flek with a sense of foreboding, then slotted it into his couch player to find out exactly what he was up against.

*

Horst was always glad to get back to the homestead and greet his scampish charges; after all, when all was said and done, they were only children. And profoundly shocked children at that. They should never be left on their own, and if he had his way they never would. Practicality dictated otherwise, of course, and there had never yet been any major disaster while he was roaming the savannah for meat and foraging the other homesteads. To some extent he had grown blasé about his trips. But this time, after encountering the possessed out at the Soeberg homestead, he had forced the return pace, stopping only to kill a danderil, his mind host to a whole coven of thoughts along the theme of *what if.*

When he topped a small rise six hundred metres away and saw the familiar wood cabin with the children sporting around outside he felt an eddy of relief. Thank you, Lord, he said silently.

He slowed down for the last length, giving Jay a respite. Sweat made her blue blouse cling to her skinny frame. The heat was becoming a serious problem. It seemed to have banished the hardy chikrows back into the jungle. Even the danderil he'd shot had been sheltering in the shade of one of the savannah's scarce trees.

Horst blinked up at the unforgiving sky. Surely they don't mean to burn this world to cinders? They have form now, stolen bodies; and all the physical needs, urges, and failings which go with them.

He squinted at the northern horizon. There seemed to be an effete pink haze above the jungle, dusting the sharp seam between sky and land, like the flush of dawn refracted over a deep ocean. The harder he tried to focus upon it, the more insubstantial it became.

He couldn't believe it was a natural meteorological *rara avis.* More an omen. His humour, already tainted by the Soeberg homestead, sank further.

Too much is happening at once. Whatever polluted destiny they are manufacturing, it is reaching its zenith.

They were a hundred metres from the cabin when the children spotted them. A scrum of small bodies came running over the grass, Danny in the lead. Both of the homestead's dogs chased around them, barking loudly.

'Freya's here,' the boy yelled out at the top of his voice. 'Freya's here, Father. Isn't it wonderful?'

Then they were all clinging to him, shouting jubilantly and smiling up with enthusiasm as he laughed and patted them and hugged them. For a moment he revelled in the contact, the hero returning. A knight protector and Santa Claus rolled into one. They expected so much of him.

'What did you find in the cabins, Father?'

'You were quick today.'

'Please, Father, tell Barnaby to give my reading tutor block back.'

'Was there any more chocolate?'

'Did you find any shoes for me?'

'You promised to look for some story fleks.'

With his escort swirling round and chattering happily, Horst led the horse over to the cabin. Russ and Mills had slithered off its back to talk with their friends.

'When did Freya arrive?' Horst asked Danny. He remembered the dark-haired girl from Aberdale, Freya Chester, about eight or nine, whose parents had brought a large variety of fruit trees with them. Kerry Chester's grove had always been one of the better maintained plots around the village.

'About ten minutes ago,' the boy said. 'It's great, isn't it?'

'Yes. It certainly is.' Remarkable, in fact. He was surprised she had survived this long. Most of the children had turned up during the first fortnight while they were still camping in a glade a kilometre away from Aberdale. Five of them walking from Schuster. They had said a woman was with them for most of the journey – Horst suspected it was Ingrid Veenkamp. Several others, the youngest ones, he had found himself as they wandered aimlessly through the jungle. He and Jay made a regular circuit of the area round the village in the hope of finding still more. And for every one they did save he suffered the images of ten more lost in the ferocious undergrowth, stalked by sayce and slowly starving to death.

At the end of a fortnight it was obvious that the messy, hot, damp glade was totally impractical as a permanent site. By that time he had over twenty children to look after. It was Jay who suggested they try a homestead cabin, and four days later they were safely installed. Only five more children had turned up since then, all of them in a dreadful state as they tramped down the overgrown track between Aberdale and the savannah. Dispossessed urchins, totally unable to fend for themselves, sleeping in the jungle and stealing food from the village when they could, which wasn't anything like often enough. The last had been Eustice, two weeks ago when Horst skirted the jungle on a hunting trip; a skeleton with skin, her clothes reduced to tattered grey rags. She couldn't walk, if the Alsatian hadn't scented her and raised the alarm she would have been dead inside of a day. As it was, he had nearly lost her.

'Where is Freya?' Horst asked Danny.

'Inside, Father, having a rest. I said she could use your bed.'

'Good lad. You did the right thing.'

Horst let Jay and some of the girls lead the horse over to the water trough, and detailed a group of boys to remove the danderil carcass he'd secured to its back. Inside the cabin it was degrees cooler than the air outside, the thick double layer of mayope planks which made up the walls and ceiling proving an efficient insulator. He said a cheery hello to a bunch of children sitting around the table who were using a reading tutor block, and went into his own room.

The curtains were drawn, casting a rich yellow light throughout the room. There was a small figure lying on the bed wearing a long navy-blue dress, legs tucked up. She didn't appear starved, or even hungry. Her dress was as clean as though it had just been washed.

'Hello, Freya,' Horst said softly. Then he looked at her fully, and even more of the savannah's warmth was drained from his skin.

Freya raised her head lazily, brushing her shoulder-length hair from her face. 'Father Horst, thank you so much for taking me in. It's so kind of you.'

Horst's muscles froze the welcoming smile on his face. She was one of them! A possessed. Below the healthy deeply tanned skin lay a wizened sickly child, the dark dress hid a stained adult's T-shirt. The two images overlapped each other, jumping in and out of focus. They were enormously difficult to distinguish, obscured by a covering veil which she drew over his mind as well as his eyes. Reality was repugnant, he didn't want to see, didn't want truth. A headache ignited three centimetres behind his temple.

'All are welcome here, Freya,' he said with immense effort. 'You must have had a terrible time these last weeks.'

'I did, it was horrible. Mummy and Daddy wouldn't speak to me. I hid in the jungle for ages and ages. There were berries and things to eat. But they were always cold. And I sometimes heard a sayce. It was really scary.'

'Well, there are no sayce around here, and we have plenty of hot food.' He walked along the side of the bed towards the dresser below the window, every footfall magnified to a strident thump in the still room. The noise of the children outside had perished. There was just the two of them now.

'Father?' she called.

'What do you want here?' he whispered tightly, his back towards her. He was afraid to pull the curtains open, afraid there might be nothing outside.

'It is a kindness.' Her voice was deepening, becoming a morbid atonality. 'There is no place for you on this world any more. Not as you are. You must change, become as us. The children will come to you one at a time when you call. They trust you.'

'A trust that will never be betrayed.' He turned round, Bible in hand. The leather-bound book his mother had given him when he became a novice; it even had a little inscription she had written in the cover, the black ink fading to a watery blue down the decades.

Freya gave him a slightly surprised look, then sneered. 'Oh, poor Father! Do you need your crutch so badly? Or do you hide from true life behind your belief?'

'Holy Father, Lord of Heaven and the mortal world, in

humility and obedience, I do ask Your aid in this act of sanctification, through Jesus Christ who walked among us to know our failings, grant me Your blessing in my task,' Horst incanted. It was so long ago since he had read the litany in the Unified prayer-book; and never before had he spoken the words, not in an age of science and universal knowledge, living in an arcology of crumbling concrete and gleaming composite. Even the Church questioned their need: they were a relic of the days when faith and paganism were still as one. But now they shone like the sun in his mind.

Freya's contempt descended into shock. 'What?' She flung her legs off the bed.

'My Lord God, look upon Your servant Freya Chester, fallen to this unclean spirit, and permit her cleansing; in the name of the Father, the Son, and the Holy Ghost.' Horst made the sign of the cross above the furious little girl.

'Stop it, you old fool. You think I fear that, your blind faith?' Her control over her form was slipping. The healthy clean image flickered on and off like a faulty light, exposing the frail malnourished child underneath.

'I beseech You to grant me Your strength, O Lord; so that her soul may be saved from damnation.'

The Bible burst into flames. Horst groaned as the heat gnawed at his hand. He dropped it to the floor where it sputtered close to the leg of the bed. His hand was agony, as though it was dipped in boiling oil.

Freya's face was screwed up in determination, great rubber-like folds of skin distorting her pretty features almost beyond recognition. 'Fuck you, priest.' The obscenity seemed ludicrous coming from a child. 'I'll burn your mind out of your skull. I'll cook your brain in its own blood.' Her possessed shape shimmered again. The lame Freya below was choking.

Horst clutched at his crucifix with his good hand. 'In the name of our Lord Jesus Christ, I order you, servant of Lucifer, to be gone from this girl. Return to the formless nothing where you belong.'

Freya let out a piercing shriek. 'How did you know!'

'Begone from this world. There is no place in the sight of God for those who would dwell in Evil.'

'How, priest?' Her head turned from side to side, neck muscles straining as though she was fighting some invisible force. 'Tell me . . .'

Heat was building along Horst's spine. He was sweating profusely, frightened she really would burn him. It was like the worst case of sunburn he had ever known, as though his skin was splitting open. His clothes would catch fire soon, he was sure.

He thrust the crucifix towards the girl. 'Freya Chester, come forth, come into the light and the glory of our Lord.'

And Freya Chester was solidly before him, thin sunken face racked by pain, spittle on her chin. Her mouth was working, struggling around complex words. Terror pounced from her black eyes.

'Come, Freya!' Horst shouted jubilantly. 'Come forth, there is nothing to fear. The Lord awaits.'

'Father.' Her voice was tragically frail. She coughed, spewing out a meagre spray of saliva and stomach juices. 'Father, help.'

'In God we trust, to deliver us from evil. We seek Your justice, knowing we are not worthy. We drink of Your blood, and eat of Your flesh so we may share in Your glory. Yet we are but the dust from which You made us. Guide us from our errors, Lord, for in ignorance and sin we know not what we do. And we ask for Your holy protection.'

For one last supremely lucid moment the demon possessor returned. Freya glared at him with a ferocity which withered his resolution by its sheer malice.

'I won't forget you,' she ground out between her curled lips. 'Never in all eternity will I forget you, priest.'

Unseen hands scrabbled at his throat, tiny fingers, like an

infant's. Blood emerged from the grazes sharp nails left around his Adam's apple. He held the crucifix on high, defiant that Christ's symbol would triumph.

Freya let out a last bellow of rage. Then the demon spirit was gone in a blast of noxious arctic air which blew Horst backwards. Neatly stacked piles of food packets went tumbling over, the bedlinen took flight, loose articles stampeded off the dresser and table. There was a bang like a castle door slamming in the face of an invading army.

Freya, the real Freya, all crusty sores, ragged clothes, and bony famined figure, was stretched out on the bed, emitting quiet gurgles from her chapped mouth. She started to cry.

Horst clambered to his feet, hanging on to the edge of the bed for support. He drew a gasping breath, his body aching inside and out, as though he had swum an ocean.

Jay and a troop of frantic children rushed in, shouting in a confused babble.

'It's all right,' he told them, dabbing at the scratch marks on his throat. 'Everything's all right now.'

*

When Jay awoke the next morning she was surprised to see she had overslept. She hardly ever did that, the few minutes alone to herself at the start of each morning were among the most precious of the day. But it had to be dawn. A pale tinge of hoary light was creeping into the cabin's main room around the reed blinds. The other children were all still sound asleep. She quickly pulled on her shorts, boots, and an adult-sized shirt she had altered to something approximating her own size, and slipped quietly out of the door. Thirty seconds later she ran back in shouting for Father Horst at the top of her voice.

Far above the lonely savannah cabin, the long vivid contrails of thirteen starship fusion drives formed a cosmic mandala across the black pre-dawn sky.

24

Lewis Sinclair had been born in 2059. He lived in Messopia, one of the first purpose-built industrial/accommodation/leisure complexes to be constructed on Spain's Mediterranean coast; a cheerless mathematical warren of concrete, glass, and plastic which covered five square kilometres and sheltered ninety thousand people against the ferocious armada storms which were beginning to plague Earth. It was a heavily subsidized experiment by the European Federal Parliament, by that time desperate to tackle the cancerous underclass problem thrown up by the continent's eighty-five million unemployed. Messopia was a qualified success; its medium-scale engineering industries provided only a minimal return for investors, but it provided a foretaste of the huge arcologies which in the centuries to come would house, protect, and employ Earth's dangerously expanded population.

His path through life was never going to be anything other than troublesome; born to low-income parents, who were only in the new microcosm city because of the parliamentary law requiring a socially balanced population. There was no real niche for him in an enterprise geared so resolutely towards the middle-class job/family/home ethic. He played truant from school, turned to crime, drugs, violence. A textbook delinquent, one of thousands who ran through Messopia's architecturally bankrupt corridors and malls.

It could have been different, if the education system had caught him early enough, if he had had the strength to hold out against peer pressure, if Messopia's technocrat designers had been less contemptuous of the social sciences. The opportunities existed. Lewis Sinclair lived in an age of quite profound technological and economic progress, and never really knew it, let alone shared in it. The first batches of asteroid-mined metal were starting to supplement depleted planetary reserves; biotechnology was finally living up to its initial promise; crude examples of the affinity bond were being demonstrated; more and more non-polluting fusion plants were coming on-stream as the supplies of He_3 mined from Jupiter's atmosphere increased. But none of it reached down to his level of society. He died in 2076, seventeen years old; one year after the bitek habitat Eden was germinated in orbit around Jupiter, and one year before the New Kong asteroid settlement began its FTL stardrive research project. His death was as wasteful as his life, a fight with power-blade knives in a piss-puddled subterranean warehouse, him and his opponent both high on synthetic crack. The fight was over a thirteen-year-old girl they both wanted to pimp.

He lost, the power blade chopping through his ribs to slice his stomach into two unequal portions.

*

And Lewis Sinclair made the same discovery as every human eventually made. Death was not the end of being. In the centuries that followed, spent as a virtually powerless astral entity suspended in dimensional emptiness, perceiving and envying mortals in their rich physical existence, he simply wished it were so.

*

But now Lewis Sinclair had returned. He wore a body again, weeping for joy at such simple magnificence as raindrops falling on his upturned face. He wasn't going to go back into the deprivation which lay after physical life, not ever. And he had the power to see that it was so; him and all the others, acting in combination, they were supreme badasses.

There was more to him than before, more than the strength which flesh and blood provided. Part of his soul was still back there in the terrible empty gulf; he hadn't emerged fully into life, not yet. He was trapped like a butterfly unable to complete the transformation from dirt-bound pupa to wing-free ephemeral. Often he felt as though the body he had possessed was simply a biological sensor mechanism, a mole's head peeking out from the earth, feeding sensations back to his feeling-starved soul via an incorporeal umbilical cord. Strange energistic vortices swirled around the dimensional twist where the two continua intermingled, kinking reality. The bizarre effect was usable, bending to his will. He could alter physical structures, sculpt energy, even prise open further links back into the extrinsic universe. His mastery of this power was increasing gradually, but its wild fluxes and resonances caused havoc in cybernetic machinery and electronic processor blocks around him.

So he watched through the spaceplane's narrow curving windscreen as the *Yaku* (now operating under a forged registration) dwindled against the sharp-etched stars, and felt his new muscles relaxing below the seat webbing. The spaceplane systems were an order of magnitude simpler than the *Yaku*'s, and critical malfunctions were highly unlikely now. Starflight was a disturbing business, so very *technical.* His dependency on the machines which his very presence disrupted was unnerving. With some luck he would never have to venture across the interstellar gulf again. He and his five colleagues riding down to the surface would be sufficient to conquer this unsuspecting world, turning it into a haven for other souls. Together they would make it their own.

'Retro burn in five seconds,' Walter Harman said.

'OK,' Lewis said. He concentrated hard, feeling round a

chorus of distant voices with the peculiar cell cluster in this body's brain. **We're coming down now**, he told Pernik Island.

I look forward to your arrival, the island personality replied.

The affinity voice sounded clear and loud in his mind. Bitek functioned almost flawlessly despite the energistic turmoil boiling around his cells. It was one reason for selecting this particular planet.

The manoeuvring rockets at the rear of the little spaceplane fired briefly, pushing him down into the angle of the seat. The conditioning grille above his head was emitting an annoyingly loud whine as the fan motor spun out of control. His fingers tightened their grip on the armrests.

Walter Harman claimed to have been a spaceplane pilot back in the 2280s, serving in the Kulu Navy. As only three of them had even been in space before, his right to pilot the spaceplane went unchallenged. The body he used belonged to one of *Yaku*'s crew, possessed within minutes of Lewis boarding the starship. It was equipped with neural nanonics, which unlike bitek proved almost useless in the constant exposure to the hostile energistic environment a possession generated, so Walter Harman had activated the spaceplane's manual-control system, an ergonomic joystick which deployed from the console in front of the pilot's seat. A projection pillar showed trajectory graphics and systems information, updating constantly as he muttered instructions to the flight computer.

The spaceplane rolled, and Lewis saw the mass of the planet slide round the windscreen. They were over the terminator now, heading into the penumbra.

Night was always their best time, putting mortal humans at a disadvantage, adding to their own potency. Something about the darkness embraced their nature.

The spaceplane shook gently as the upper atmosphere began to strike the heatshield belly. Walter Harman pitched them up at a slight angle, and swung the wings out a few degrees, beginning the long aerobrake glide downwards.

They were still in the darkness when they dropped below subsonic. Lewis could see a hemispherical bauble of light glinting on the horizon ahead.

'Your approach is on the beam,' the island personality informed them over the microwave channel. 'Please land on pad eighteen.' A purple and yellow flight vector diagram appeared on the console's holoscreen.

'Acknowledged, Pernik,' Walter Harman said.

A three-dimensional simulacrum of the island materialized inside Lewis's skull, an image far sharper than the porno holographs he used to peddle back in Messopia. He automatically knew which pad eighteen was. A burst of doubt and anxiety blossomed in his mind, which he did his best to prevent from leaking back down the affinity bond to the island personality. This Edenist consensual set-up was so smooth. He worried that they might be taking on more than they could reasonably expect to accomplish.

The island personality had accepted his explanation that he was representing his merchant family enterprise from Jospool. Not every Edenist used the voidhawks to carry freight, there simply weren't enough to go round.

Lewis studied the mental simulacrum. Pad eighteen was close to the rim and the floating quays, there would be machinery there. It would be easy.

Pernik's coating of moss made the two-kilometre disk a black hole in the faintly phosphorescent ocean. Pale yellow radiance shone from a few windows in the accommodation towers, and floodlights illuminated all the quays. It was 4 a.m. local time, most of the inhabitants were asleep.

Walter Harman set the spaceplane down on pad eighteen with only a minor wobble.

Welcome to Pernik, the personality said formally.

Thank you, Lewis replied.

Eysk is approaching. His family runs one of our premier fishing enterprises. He should be able to fill your requirements.

Excellent, Lewis said. **My thanks again for receiving me so promptly. I have spent weeks on that Adamist starship; it was becoming somewhat claustrophobic.**

I understand.

Lewis wasn't sure, but he thought there was a mild dose of puzzlement in the personality's tone. Too late now, though, they were down. Excitement was spilling into his blood. His part of the scheme was by far the most important.

The airlock opened with a couple of jerky motions as the actuators suffered power surges. Lewis went down the aluminium stairs.

Eysk was walking across the polyp apron towards pad eighteen. A ridge of electrophorescent cells circling the pad were casting an austere light over the spaceplane. Lewis could see very little of the island beyond; there was one accommodation tower forming a slender black rectangle against the night sky, and the sound of waves sloshing against the rim came from the other side of the spaceplane.

'Keep him busy,' Lewis ordered Walter Harman as the pilot followed him down the stairs.

'No problem, I've got a thousand dumb questions lined up. Atlantis hadn't been discovered when I was alive.'

Lewis reached the landing pad and tensed – this was it, make or break time. He had altered his facial features considerably during the starflight; that old journalist back on Lalonde had given him a nasty moment. He waited for the approaching Edenist to shout an alarm to the island.

Eysk gave a slight bow in greeting, and directed an identity trait at Lewis. He waited politely for Lewis to return the punctilio.

Lewis didn't have one. He hadn't known. His only source of data on Edenist customs was far beyond his grasp.

Deep down at the centre of his brain there was a presence, the soul which used to own the body he now possessed. A prisoner held fast by the manacle bonds of Lewis's thoughts.

All of the possessors had a similar prisoner, visualized as a tiny homunculus contained within a sphere of cephalic glass. They pleaded and they begged to be let out, to come back; annoying background voices, a gnat's buzz across consciousness. The possessed could use them, torment them with glimpses of reality in return for information, learning how to blend in with the modern, starkly alien society into which they had come forth.

But the centre of Lewis's mind contained only a heavy darkness. He hadn't told the others that, they were all so boastful of how they controlled their captives, so he just brazened it out. The soul he had usurped as he came to this body neither entreated nor threatened. Lewis knew it was there, he could sense the surface thoughts, cold and hard, formidable with resolution. Waiting. The entity frightened him, he had come to possess the body the same way he had walked Messopia's corridors, The King of Strut – thinking he could handle it. Now the first fractures of insecurity in his hyped-up confidence were multiplying. The usurped soul's personality was far stronger than him; he could never have withstood such dread isolation, not simply beyond sensation, but knowing sensation was possible. What kind of person could?

Are you all right? Eysk asked kindly.

I'm sorry. I think it may have been something I ate. And the ride down was a god-fucking bitch.

Eysk's eyebrow rose. **Indeed?**

Yeah, feel like I'm gonna puke. Be all right in a minute.

I do hope so.

'This is Walter Harman,' Lewis said out loud, knowing he was making a colossal balls-up of things. 'A pilot, so he claims. After that flight, think I'm going to ask the captain for a dekko at his licence.' He laughed at his witticism.

Walter Harman smiled broadly, and put out his hand. 'Pleasure to meet you. This is one hell of a planet. I've never been here before.'

Eysk seemed taken aback. 'Your enthusiasm is most gratifying. I hope you enjoy your stay.'

'Thanks. Say, I tasted some gollatail a year back, have you got any round here?'

I'm just going for a walk, get some air, Lewis said. Down in his memories were a thousand hangovers; he gathered together the phantom sensation of nausea and cranial malaise, then broadcast them into the affinity band. **It ought to clear my head.**

Eysk flinched at the emetic deluge. **Quite.**

'I'd like to try some again, maybe take back a stock of my own,' Walter Harman prompted. 'Old Lewis here can tell you what our ship's rations are like.'

'Yes,' Eysk said. 'I believe we have some.' His gaze never left Lewis's back.

'Great, that's just great.'

Lewis stepped over the half-metre ridge of electrophorescent cells around the pad, and headed towards the island's rim. There was one of the floating quays ahead, a twenty-metre crane to one side for lifting smaller boats out of the water.

Sorry about this, Lewis told the island personality. **A flight has never had this effect before.**

Do you require a medical nanonic package?

Let's leave it a minute and see. Sea wind always was the best cure for headaches.

As you wish.

Lewis could hear Walter Harman chattering away inanely behind him. He reached the metal railing that guarded the rim, and stood beside the crane. It was a spindly column and boom arrangement made from monobonded carbon struts, lightweight and strong. But heavy enough for his purpose. He closed his eyes, focusing his attention on the structure, feeling its texture, the rough grain of carbon crystals held together with hard plies of binding molecules. Atoms glowed scarlet and yellow, their electrons flashing in tight fast orbits.

Miscreant energistic pulses raced up and down the struts,

sparking between molecules. He felt the others in the spaceplane cabin lending their strength, concentrating on a point just below the boom pivot. The carbon's crystalline lattice began to break down. Spears of St Elmo's fire flickered around the pivot.

A tortured creaking sound washed across the rim of the island. Eysk looked round in confusion, peering against pad eighteen's glare.

Lewis, move now please, the island personality said. **Unidentified static discharge on the crane. It is weakening the structure.**

Where? He played it dumb, looking round, looking up.

Lewis, *move*.

The compulsion almost forced his legs into action. He fought it with bursts of mystification, then panic. Remembering the power blade as it descended, the sight of blood and chips of bone spewing out of the wound. It hadn't happened to him, it was some horror holo he was watching on the screen. Distant. Remote.

Lewis!

Carbon shattered with a sudden thunderclap. The boom jerked, then began to fall, curving down in that unreal slow motion he'd seen once before. And nothing had to be faked any more. Fear staked him to the ground. A yell started to emerge from his lips—

*

—Mistake. Your greatest and your last, Lewis. When this body dies my soul will be free. And then I can return to possess the living. And when that happens I will have the same power as you. After that we shall meet as equals, I promise you—

*

—as the edge of the boom smashed into his torso. There was no pain, shock saw to that. Lewis was aware of the boom finishing its work, crushing him against the polyp. Body ruined.

His head hit the ground with a brutish *smack*, and he gazed up mutely at the stars. They started to fade.

Transfer, Pernik ordered. The mental command was thick with sympathy and sorrow.

His eyes closed.

Pernik awaited. Lewis saw it through a long dark tunnel, a vast bitek construct glowing with the gentle emerald aura of life. Colourful phantom shapes slithered below its translucent surface, tens of thousands of personalities, at once separate and in concord: the multiplicity. He felt himself drifting towards it along the affinity bond, his energistic nexus abandoning the mangled body to infiltrate the naked colossus. Behind him the dark soul rose as smoothly as a shark seeking wounded prey to re-inherit the dying body. Lewis's tightly whorled thoughts quaked in fright as he reached the island's vast neural strata. He penetrated the surface, and diffused himself throughout the network, instantly surrounded by a babble of sights and sounds. The multiplicity murmuring amongst itself, autonomic sub-routines emitting pulses of strictly functional information.

His dismay and disorientation was immediately apparent. Ethereal tentacles of comfort reached out to reassure him.

Don't worry, Lewis. You are safe now . . .

–

What *are* you?

The multiplicity recoiled from him, a tide of thoughts in swift retreat, leaving him high and dry. Splendidly alone. Emergency autonomic routines to isolate him came on-line, erecting axon blockades around the swarm of neural cells in which he resided.

Lewis laughed at them. Already his thoughts were spread through more cells than the body which he'd abandoned had contained. The energistic flux resulting from such possession was tremendous. He thought of fire, and began to extend himself, burning through the multiplicity's simplistic protection, seeping through the neural strata like a wave of searing lava, obliterating anything in his path. Cell after cell fell to his domination. The multiplicity shrieked, trying to resist him. Nothing could. He was bigger than them, bigger than worlds. Omnipotent. The cries began to die away as he engulfed them, receding as though they were falling down some shaft that pierced clean to the planet's core. Squeezing. Compressing their fluttering panicked thoughts together. The polyp itself was next, contaminated by swaths of energy seething out of the transdimensional twist. Organs followed, even the thermal potential cables dangling far below the surface. He possessed every living cell of Pernik. At the heart of his triumphant mind the multiplicity lay silent, stifled.

He waited for a second, savouring the nirvana-high of absolute mastery. Then the terror began.

*

Eysk had started to run towards the rim as the crane creaked and groaned. Pernik showed him the boom starting to topple down. He knew he was too late, that there was nothing he could do to save the strangely idiosyncratic Edenist from Jospool. The boom picked up speed, slamming into the apparently dumbfounded Lewis. Eysk closed his eyes, mortified by the splash of gore.

Calm yourself, the personality said. **His head survived the impact. I have his thoughts.**

Thank goodness. Whatever caused the crane to fail like that? I've never seen such lightning on Atlantis before.

It . . . I . . .

Pernik?

The mental wail which came down the affinity link seemed capable of bursting Eysk's skull apart. He dropped to his knees, clamping his hands to his head, vision washed out by a blinding red light. Steel claws were burrowing up out of the affinity link, ripping through the delicate membranes inside his brain, shiny silver smeared with blood and viscid cranial fluid.

'Poor Eysk,' a far-off chorus spoke directly into his mind – so very different to affinity, so very insidious. 'Let us help you.' The promise of pain's alleviation hummed in the air all around.

Even numbed and bruised he recognized the gentle offer for the Trojan it was. He blinked tears from his eyes, closing his mind to affinity. And he was abruptly alone, denied even an echo of the emotional fellowship he had shared for his entire life. The grotesque mirage of the claw vanished. Eysk let out a hot breath of relief. The polyp below his trembling hands was glowing a sickly pink – that was real.

'What—'

Hairy cloven feet shuffled into view. He gasped and looked up. The hominid creature with a black-leather wolf's head howled victoriously and reached down for him.

*

Laton opened his eyes. His crushed, faltering body was suffused with pain. It wasn't relevant, so he ignored it. There wasn't going to be much time before oxygen starvation started to debilitate his reasoning. Physical shock was already making concentration difficult. He quickly loaded a sequence of localized limiter routines into the neuron cells buried beneath the polyp on which he was pinned by the twisted crane boom. Developed for his Jantrit campaign, their sophistication was orders of magnitude above the usual diversionary orders juvenile Edenists employed to avoid parental supervision. Firstly he regularized the image which the surrounding sensitive cells were supplying to the neural strata, freezing the picture of his body.

At that point his heart gave its last beat. He could sense the desperate attempts by the multiplicity to ward off Lewis's subsumption of the island. Laton was banking everything on the primitive street boy using brute force to take over. Sure enough Lewis's eerily potent, but crude, thought currents flowed through the neural strata below, flushing every other routine before him; though even his augmented power failed to root out Laton's subversive routines. They were symbiotic rather than parasitic, working within the controlling personality not against it. It would take a highly experienced Edenist bitek neuropathologist to even realize they were there, let alone expunge them.

Laton's lips gave a final quirk of contempt. He cleared a storage section in the neuron cells, and transferred his personality into it. His final act before consciousness and memory sank below the polyp was to trigger the proteanic virus infecting every cell in his body.

*

Mosul dreamed. He was lying in bed in his accommodation tower flat, with Clio beside him. Mosul woke. He looked down fondly at the sleeping girl; she was in her early twenties with long dark hair and a pretty flattish face. The sheet had slipped from her shoulders, revealing a pert rounded breast. He bent over to kiss the nipple. She stirred, smiling dreamily as his tongue traced a delicate circle. A warm overspill of gently erotic images came foaming out of her drowsy mind.

Mosul grinned in anticipation, and woke. He frowned down in puzzlement at the sleeping girl beside him. The bedroom was illuminated by a sourceless rosy glow. It shaded Clio's silky skin a dark burgundy colour. He shook the sleep from his head. They had been making love for hours last night, he was entitled to some lassitude after that.

She responded eagerly to his kisses, throwing aside the sheet so he could feast on the sight of her. Her skin hardened and wrinkled below his touch. When he looked up in alarm she had become a cackling white-haired crone.

The pink light shifted into bright scarlet, as though the room was bleeding. He could see the polyp walls palpitating. In the distance a giant heartbeat thudded.

Mosul woke. The room was illuminated by a sourceless rosy glow. He was sweating, it was intolerably hot.

Pernik, I'm having a nightmare . . . I think. Am I awake now?

Yes, Mosul.

Thank goodness. Why is it so hot?

Yes, you are having a nightmare. My nightmare.

Pernik!

Mosul woke, jerking up from the bed. The bedroom walls were glowing red; no longer safe hard polyp but a wet meat traced with a filigree of purple-black veins. They oscillated like jelly. The heartbeat sounded again, louder than before. A damp acrid smell tainted the air.

Pernik! Help me.

No, Mosul.

What are you doing?

Clio rolled over and laughed at him. Her eyes were featureless balls of jaundiced yellow. 'We're coming for you, Mosul, you and all your kind. Smug arrogant bastards that you are.'

She elbowed him in the groin. Mosul shouted at the vicious pain, and tumbled off the raised sponge cushion which formed his bed. Sour yellow vomit trickled out of his mouth as he writhed about on the slippery floor.

Mosul woke. It was real this time, he was sure of that. Everything was dangerously clear to his eyes. He was lying on the floor, all tangled up in the sheets. The bedroom glowed red, its walls raw stinking meat.

Clio was locked in her own looped nightmare, hands raking the top of the bed, staring sightlessly at the ceiling. Unformed screams stalled in her throat, as though she was choking. Mosul tried to get up, but his feet slithered all over the slimed quaking floor. He directed an order at the door muscle membrane. Too late he saw its shape had changed from a vertical oval to a horizontal slash. A giant mouth. It parted, giving him a brief glimpse of stained teeth the size of his feet, then thick yellow vomit discharged into the bedroom. The torrent of obscenely fetid liquid hit him straight on, lifting him up and throwing him against the back wall. He didn't dare cry out, it would be in his mouth. His arms thrashed about, but it was like paddling in glue. There seemed no end to the cascade, it had risen above his knees. Clio was floundering against the wall a couple of metres away, her body spinning in the hard current. He couldn't reach her. The vomit's heat was powerful enough to enervate his muscles, and the stomach acid it contained was corroding his skin. It had risen up to his chest. He struggled to stay upright. Clio had disappeared below the surface, not even waking from her nightmare. And still more poured in.

*

As far as Lewis Sinclair was aware, Laton's corpse lay perfectly still under the crumpled crane boom. Not that he bothered to check. Pernik Island was big, much larger than his imagination had ever conceived it, and for someone with his background difficult to comprehend. Every second yelled for his attention as he sent out phobic fantasies through his affinity bonds with the slumbering populace, invading their dreams, breaking their minds wide open with insane fear so more souls could come through and begin their reign of possession. He ignored the bitek's tedious minutiae – autonomic organ functions, the monitoring routines which the old multiplicity employed, enacting muscle membrane functions. All he cared about was eliminating the remaining Edenists; that task received his total devotion.

The island's cells glimmered a faint pink as a result of the energistic arrogation, even the shaggy coat of moss shone as though imbued with firefly luminescence. Pernik twinkled like a fabulous inflamed ruby in the funereal gloom of Atlantis's moonless night, sending radiant fingers probing down through the water to beckon curious fish. An observer flying overhead would have noticed flashes of blue light pulsing at random from the accommodation tower windows, as though stray lightning bolts were being flung around the interior.

Long chill screams reverberated around the borders of the park, emerging from various archways at the base of the towers. By the time they reached the rim they had blended into an almost musical madrigal, changes in pitch matching the poignant lilt of the waves washing against the polyp.

Housechimps scampered about, yammering frantically at each other. Their control routines had been wiped clean by Lewis's relentless purge of the multiplicity and all its subsidiaries, and long-suppressed simian tribal traits were surfacing. Fast, violent fights broke out among them as they instinctively fled into the thicker spinneys growing in the park.

The remaining sub-sentient servitor creatures, all eighteen separate species necessary to complement the island's static organs, either froze motionless or performed their last assigned task over and over again.

Unnoticed amid the bedlam and horror, Laton's corpse was quietly dissolving into protoplasmic soup.

Edenist biotechnicians examining the wreckage of Jantrit had called the process Laton used to doctor the habitat's neural strata a proteanic virus. In fact, it was far more complex than that. Affinity-programmable organic molecules was a term one researcher used.

Deeply disturbed by the technology and its implications, the Jovian consensus released little further information. Research continued, a classified high-priority project, which concentrated on developing methods to warn existing habitats of the sub-nanonic weapon being deployed against them, and a means of making future habitats (and people) immune. Progress over the intervening forty years was slow but satisfactory.

Of course, unknown to the Edenists, at the same time Laton was equally busy on Lalonde refining his process, and meeting with considerable success.

In its passive state, the updated proteanic virus masqueraded as inert organelles within his body cells – no matter what their nature, from liver to blood corpuscles, muscles to hair. When his last affinity command activated them, each organelle released a batch of plasmids (small, artificially synthesized DNA loops) and a considerable quantity of transcription factors, proteins capable of switching genes on or off. Once the plasmids had been inserted into the cell's DNA, mitosis began, forcing the cells to reproduce by division. Transcription factors switched off the human DNA completely, as well as an entire series of the new plasmids, leaving them to be carried passively while just one type of plasmid was activated to designate the function of the new cell. It was a drastic mutation. Hundreds of thousands of Laton's cells were already dying, millions more were killed by the induced mitosis; but over half fissioned successfully, turning into specialist diploid gametes.

They spilled out of the arms, legs, and collar of his one-piece ship-suit in a magenta sludge, draining away from stubborn clusters of dead cells that retained their original pattern – kernels of lumpy organs, slender ribs, a rubbery dendritic knot of veins. As they spread across the polyp they started to permeate the surface, slipping through microscopic gaps in the grainy texture, seeping down towards the neural stratum four metres below. Pernik's nutrient capillaries and axon conduits speeded their passage.

Four hours later, when dawn was breaking over the condemned island, the majority of the gametes had reached the neural stratum. Stage two of the proteanic virus was different. A gamete would penetrate a neural cell's membrane and release the mission-specific plasmid Laton had selected (he had four hundred to choose from). The plasmid was accompanied by a transcription factor which would activate it.

Mitosis produced a neuron cell almost identical to the original it replaced. Once begun, the reproduction cycle was unstoppable; new cells started to supplant old at an ever-increasing rate. A chain reaction of subtle modification began to ripple out from the rim of the island. It went on for a considerable time.

*

Admiral Kolhammer was almost correct about Time Universe beating the Edenists to inform the Confederation about Laton. Several dozen star systems heard the news from the company first. Governments were put in an embarrassing position of knowing less than Time Universe until the voidhawks carrying diplomatic fleks from Admiral Aleksandrovich and the Confederation Assembly President arrived, clarifying the situation.

Naturally enough, public perception was focused almost exclusively on Laton: the threat from the past risen like the devil's own phoenix. They wanted to know what was being done to track him down and exterminate him. They were quite vociferous about it.

Presidents, kings, and dictators alike had to release statements assuring their anxious citizens that every resource was being deployed to locate him.

Considerably less attention was drawn to the apparent persona sequestration of Lalonde's population. Graeme Nicholson hadn't placed much emphasis on the effect, keeping it at the rumour level. It wasn't until much later that news company science editors began to puzzle about the cost-effectiveness of sequestrating an entire backward colony world, and question exactly what had happened in the Quallheim Counties. Laton's presence blinded them much as it did everyone else. He was on Lalonde, therefore Lalonde's uprising problem was instigated by him. QED.

Privately, governments were extremely worried by the possibility of an undetectable energy virus that could strike at people without warning. Dr Gilmore's brief preliminary report on Jacqueline Couteur was not released for general public access.

Naval reserve officers were called in, warships were placed on combat alert and brought up to full flight-readiness status.

Laton gave governments the excuse to instigate rigorous screening procedures for visiting starships. Customs and Immigration officers were told to be especially vigilant for any electronic warfare nanonics.

There was also an unprecedented degree of cooperation between star systems' national groupings to ensure that the warning reached everybody and was taken seriously. Within a day of a flek courier voidhawk arriving, even the smallest, most distant asteroid settlement was informed and urged to take precautions.

Within five days of Admiral Lalwani dispatching the voidhawks, the entire Confederation had been told, with just a few notable exceptions. Most prominent of these were starships in transit.

*

Oenone raced in towards Atlantis at three gees. There were only sixty cases of Norfolk Tears left clamped into its lower hull cargo bay. Since leaving Norfolk, Syrinx had flown to Auckland, a four-hundred-light-year trip. Norfolk Tears increased in price in direct proportion to the distance from Norfolk, and Auckland was one of the richer planets in its sector of the Confederation. She had sold sixty per cent of her cargo to a planetary retailer, and another thirty per cent to a family merchant enterprise in one of the system's Edenist habitats. It was the first shipment the Auckland system had seen for fifteen months, and the price it raised had been appropriately phenomenal. They had already paid off the Jovian Bank loan and made a respectable profit. Now she was back to honour her deal with Eysk's family.

She looked through *Oenone*'s sensor blisters at the planet as they descended into equatorial orbit. Cool blues and sharp whites jumbled together in random splash patterns. Memories played below her surface thoughts, kindled by the sight of the infinite ocean. Mosul's smiling face.

We're not going to stay very long, are we? *Oenone* asked plaintively.

Why? she teased. **Don't you like talking to the islands? They make a change from habitats.**

You know why.

You stayed in Norfolk orbit for over a week.

I had lots of voidhawks to talk to. There are only fifteen here.

Don't worry. We won't stay long. Just enough time to unload the Norfolk Tears, and for me to see Mosul.

I like him.

Thank you for the vote of confidence. While we're here, would you ask the islands to see if anyone has a cargo they need shipping outsystem.

I'll start now.

Can you give me a link through to Mosul first, please.

It is midnight on Pernik. The personality says Mosul is unobtainable at the moment.

Oh dear. I wonder what her name is?

Syrinx.

Yes?

Pernik is wrong.

What do you mean? Mosul is available?

No, I mean the personality is different, altered. There is no joy in its thoughts.

Syrinx opened her eyes and stared round the contoured walls of her cabin. Familiar trinkets she had picked up on her voyages were lined up in glass-fronted alcoves. Her eyes found the fifteen-centimetre chunk of whalebone carved into a squatting Eskimo which Mosul had given her. But *Oenone*'s unease was too unsettling for the crude statue to register the way it usually did, bringing forth a warm recollection intrinsic to both of them.

Perhaps there has been an accident on one of the fishing boats, she suggested.

Then the grief should be shared, as is proper.

Yes.

Pernik hides behind a façade of correctness.

Is Eysk available?

One moment.

Syrinx felt the voidhawk's mind reach out, then Eysk was merging his thoughts with her. Still the same old kind-hearted family elder, with that deeper layer of toughness that made him such a shrewd businessman.

Syrinx, he exclaimed happily, **we were wondering where you had got to.**

Did you think I'd skipped out on you?

Me? He projected mock horror. **Not at all. The arrest warrant we had drawn up was a mere precaution.**

She laughed. **I've brought your cases of Norfolk Tears.**

How many?

Sixty.

Ah well, my family will be through that lot before the week's out. Are you coming down tonight?

Yes, if it's not too late.

Not at all. I'll have some servitors lined up to unload your flyer by the time you get down.

Fine. Is everything all right on the island?

There was a moment's hesitation, a thought-flash of bemused incomprehension. **Yes. Thank you for asking.**

Is Mosul there?

Sex, that's all you young people think of.

We learn by example. Is he there?

Yes. But I don't think Clio will welcome an interruption right now.

Is she very pretty?

Yes. He generated an image of a girl's grinning face, half hidden by long dark hair. **She's bright, too. They are on the point of formalizing the arrangement.**

I'm happy for him, for both of them.

Thank you. Don't tell Mosul I said so, but she'll make a splendid addition to the family.

That's nice. I'll see you in a couple of hours.

I'll look forward to it. Just remember, Mosul learnt everything he knows from me.

As if I could forget. She broke the contact.

Well? *Oenone* asked.

I don't know. Nothing I could put my finger on, but he was definitely stilted.

Shall I ask the other islands?

Goodness, no. I'll find out what's troubling them once I'm down. Mosul will tell me, he owes me that much.

*

Hooked into the flyer's sensors, Syrinx couldn't be sure, but Pernik appeared aged somehow. Admittedly it was darkest night, but the towers had a shabby look, almost mouldered. They put her in mind of Earth's Empire State Building, now carefully preserved in its own dome at the centre of the New York arcology. Structurally sound, but unable to throw off the greying weight of centuries.

Thirty-two years old, and you see everything in such jaded terms, she told herself wearily. Pity that Mosul had formed a permanent attachment, though. He would have made a good father.

She clucked her tongue in self-admonition. But then her mother had conceived two children by the time she was thirty.

There's always Ruben, *Oenone* suggested.

It wouldn't be fair to him, not even to ask. He'd feel obligated to say yes.

I would like you to have a child. You are feeling incomplete. It upsets you. I don't like that.

I am *not* feeling incomplete!

You haven't even prepared any zygotes for my children yet. You should think about these things.

Oh goodness. You're starting to sound like Mother.

I don't know how to lie.

Rubbish!

Not to you. And it was you who was thinking of Mosul in that light.

Yes. Syrinx stopped trying to argue, it was stupidly blinkered. **What would I do without you?**

Oenone wrapped her thoughts with a loving embrace, and for a moment Syrinx imagined the flyer's ion field had leaked inside the cabin, filling it with golden haze.

They landed on one of the pads in the commercial section. The electrophorescent-cell ridge around the metal grid shone with a strong pink radiance. Few of the accommodation tower windows were lit.

It looks like they're in mourning, Syrinx said to Oxley in singular engagement mode as she walked down the aluminium stair. They had flown down alone so that the little flyer could carry more cargo, but it was still going to take three trips to bring all sixty cases down.

Yes. He glanced about, frowning. **There aren't many fishing boats in dock, either.**

Eysk and Mosul walked out of the shadows beyond the ridge.

Syrinx forgot everything else as Mosul sent out a burst of rapturous greeting, mingled with mischievously erotic subliminals.

She put her arms around him and enjoyed a long kiss.

I'd like to meet her, she told him. **Lucky thing that she is.**

You shall.

They stood about on the pad, chatting idly, as the island's lizard-skinned housechimps unloaded the first batch of cases under Oxley's careful direction and stacked them on a processor-controlled flat-top trolley. When all eighteen cases were on, the drone trundled off towards one of the low warehouse domes ringing the park.

Do you want me to bring the rest down tonight? Oxley asked.

Please, Eysk said. **I have already organized sales with other families.**

The pilot nodded, winked at Syrinx, who was still standing with Mosul's arm around her shoulder, and went back into the flyer. Sitting in the command seat he linked his mind with the controlling processor array.

Something was affecting the coherent magnetic-field generation. It took a long time to form, and he had to bring compensator programs on-line. By the time he finally lifted from the pad the fusion generator was operating alarmingly close to maximum capacity.

He almost turned back there and then. But once he rose above a hundred metres the field stabilized rapidly. He had to cut the power levels back. Diagnostic programs reported the systems were all functioning flawlessly.

With a quick curse directed at all Kulu-produced machinery, he ordered the flight computer to design an orbital-injection trajectory that would bring him to a rendezvous with *Oenone.*

See you in three hours, Syrinx called as the sparkling artificial comet performed a tight curve around the accommodation towers before soaring up into the night sky.

Three hours! Oxley let his groan filter back down the affinity link.

You're professionals. You can handle it.

He put the flyer into a steep climb. One thing about an oceanic world, there was no worry about supersonic-boom footprints stomping all over civic areas. He was doing Mach two by the time he was fifteen kilometres away.

Pernik vanished from his affinity perception. Ordinarily a contact would simply fade with distance until it was no more. But this was different, like steel shutters slamming into place. Oxley was over a hundred and fifty years old, in his time he'd visited almost ninety per cent of the Confederation, and he had never known an Edenist habitat to react in such a manner. It was alien to the whole creed of consensual unity.

He switched in the aft sensors. A luminous red pearl haunted the horizon, sending shimmer-spears of light dancing across the black water.

'What is . . .' The words dried up at the back of his throat.

Pernik? he demanded. **Pernik, what is going on? What is that light?**

The silence was total. There wasn't the slightest trace of the personality's thoughts left anywhere in the affinity band.

Syrinx?

Nothing.

***Oenone*, something's happening on Pernik, can you reach Syrinx?**

She is there, the worried voidhawk answered. **But I cannot converse with her. Something is interfering.**

Oh, heavens. He banked the flyer round, heading back for the island.

Affinity broadened out from the single tenuous thread to the orbiting voidhawk, offering him the support of innumerable minds combining into a homogenized entity, buoying him up on a tide of intellect. He wasn't alone, and he wasn't anxious any more. Doubts and personal fears bled away, exchanged for confidence and determination, a much-needed reinforcement of his embattled psyche. For a moment, flying over the gargantuan ocean in a tiny machine, he had been horribly lonely; now his kind had joined him, from the eager honoured enthusiasms of sixteen year olds up to the glacial thoughts of the islands themselves. He felt like a child again, comforted by the loving arms of an adult, wiser and stronger. It was a reconfirmation of Edenism which left him profoundly grateful for the mere privilege of belonging.

This is Thalia Island, Oxley, we are aware of Pernik's withdrawal from affinity and we are summoning a planetary consensus to deal with the problem.

That red lighting effect has me worried, he replied. The flyer had dropped below subsonic again. Pernik gleamed a sickly vermilion eight kilometres away.

Around the planet, consensus finalized, bringing together every sentient entity in an affinity union orchestrated by the islands. Information, such as it had, was reviewed, opinions formed, discussed, discarded, or elaborated. Two seconds after considering the problem the consensus said: **We believe it to be Laton. A ship of the same class as the *Yaku* arrived last night and sent a spaceplane down to the island. From that time onward Pernik's communication has declined by sixty per cent.**

Laton? The appalled question came from *Oenone* and its crew.

Yes. The Atlantean consensus summarized the information that had been delivered by a voidhawk two days earlier. **As we have no orbital stations our checks on arriving ships were naturally less than ideal, depending solely on civil traffic control satellite-platform sensors. The ship has of course departed, but the spaceplane remained. Pernik and its population must have been sequestrated by the energy virus.**

Oh no, Oxley cried brokenly. **Not him. Not again.**

Ahead of him, Pernik issued a brilliant golden light, as though sunrise had come to the ocean. The flyer gave a violent lurch to starboard, and began to lose height.

*

Syrinx watched the little flyer disappear into the east. The night air was cooler than she remembered from her last visit, bringing up goosebumps below her ship-tunic. Mosul, who was dressed in a baggy sleeveless sweatshirt and shorts, seemed completely unaffected. She eyed him with a degree of annoyance. Macho outdoors type.

This Clio was a lucky woman.

Come along, Eysk said. **The family is dying to meet you again. You can tell the youngsters what Norfolk was like.**

I'd love to.

Mosul's arm tightened that bit extra round her shoulder as

they headed for the nearest tower. Almost proprietary, she thought.

Mosul, she asked on singular engagement, **what's wrong down here? You all seem so tense.** It was a struggle to convey the emotional weight she wanted.

Nothing is wrong. He smiled as they passed under the archway at the foot of the tower.

She stared at him, dumbfounded. He had answered on the general affinity band, an extraordinary breach of protocol.

Mosul caught her expression, and sent a wordless query.

This is . . . she began. Then her thoughts flared in alarm. *Oenone*, she couldn't perceive *Oenone*! 'Mosul! It's gone. No, wait. I can feel it, just. Mosul, something is trying to block affinity.'

'Are they?' His smile hardened into something which made her jerk away in consternation. 'Don't worry, little Syrinx. Delicate, beautiful little Syrinx, so far from home. All alone. But we treasure you for the gift you bring. We are going to welcome you into a brotherhood infinitely superior to Edenism.'

She spun round, ready to run. But there were five men standing behind her. One of them – she gasped – his head had grown until it was twice the size it should be. His features were a gross caricature, cheeks deep and lined, eyes wide and avian; his nose was huge, coming to a knife edge that hung below his black lips, both ears were pointed, rising above the top of his skull.

'What are you?' she hissed.

'Don't mind old Kincaid,' Mosul said. 'Our resident troll.'

It was getting lighter, the kind of liquid redness creeping across the island's polyp which she associated with Duchess-night on Norfolk. Her legs began to shake. It was shameful, but she was so alone. Never before had she been denied the community of thoughts that was the wonder of Edenism. ***Oenone*!** The desperate shout crashed around the confines of her own skull. ***Oenone*, my love. Help me!**

There was an answer. Not coherent, nothing she could perceive, decipher. But somewhere on the other side of the blood-veiled sky the voidhawk cried in equal anguish.

'Come, Syrinx,' Mosul said. He held out his hand. 'Come with us.'

It wasn't Mosul. She knew that now.

'Never.'

'So brave,' he said pityingly. 'So foolish.'

She was physically strong, her genes gave her that much. But there were seven of them. They half carried, half pushed her onwards.

The walls became strange. No longer polyp but stone. Big cubes hewn from some woodland granite quarry; and old, the age she thought she had seen on the approach flight. Water leaked from the lime-encrusted mortar, sliming the stone.

They descended a spiral stair which grew narrower until only one of them could march beside her. Syrinx's ship-tunic sleeve was soon streaked with water and coffee-coloured fungus. She knew it wasn't real, that it couldn't be happening. There was no 'down' in an Atlantean island. Only the sea. But her feet slipped on the worn steps, and her calves ached.

There was no red glow in the bowels of the island. Flaming torches in black iron brands lighted their way. Their acrid smoke made her eyes water.

The stairway came out onto a short corridor. A sturdy oak door was flung open, and Syrinx shoved through. Inside was a medieval torture chamber.

A wooden rack took up the centre of the room; iron chains wound round wheels at each end, manacles open and waiting. A brazier in one corner was sending out waves of heat from its radiant coals. Long slender metal instruments were plunged into it, metal sharing the furnace glow.

The torturer himself was a huge fat man in a leather jerkin. Rolls of hairy flesh spilled over his waistband. He stood beside the brazier, cursing the slender young woman who was bent over a pair of bellows.

'This is Clio,' Mosul's stolen body said. 'You did say you wanted to meet her.'

The woman turned, and laughed at Syrinx.

'What is the point?' Syrinx asked weakly. Her voice was very close to cracking.

'This is in your honour,' the torturer said. His voice was a deep bass, but soft, almost purring. 'You, we shall have to be very careful with. For you come bearing a great gift. I don't want to damage it.'

'What gift?'

'The living starship. These other mechanical devices for sailing the night gulf are difficult for us to employ. But your craft has elegance and grace. Once we have you, we have it. We can bring our crusade to new worlds with ease after that.'

FLEE! Flee, *Oenone*. Flee this dreadful world, my love. And never come back.

'Oh, Syrinx.' Mosul's handsome face wore the old sympathetic expression she remembered from such a time long ago now. 'We have taken affinity from you. We have sent Oxley away. We have taken everybody from you. You are alone but for us. And believe me, we know what being alone does to an Edenist.'

'Fool,' she sneered. 'That wasn't affinity, it is love which binds us.'

'And we shall love the *Oenone* too,' a musical chorus spoke to her.

She refused to show any hint of surprise. '*Oenone* will never love you.'

'In time all things become possible,' the witching chorus sang. 'For are we not come?'

'Never,' she said.

The corpulent paws of Kincaid the troll tightened around her arms.

Syrinx closed her eyes as she was forced towards the rack. This is not happening therefore I can feel no pain. This is not happening therefore I can feel no pain. Believe it!

Hands tore at the collar of her ship-tunic, ripping the fabric. Hot rancid air prickled her skin.

This is NOT happening therefore I can feel no pain. Not not not—

*

Ruben sat at his console station in *Oenone*'s bridge along with the rest of the crew. There were only two empty seats. Empty and accusing.

I should have gone down with her, Ruben thought. Maybe if I could have provided everything she needed from life she wouldn't have gone running to Mosul in the first place.

We all share guilt, Ruben, the Atlantean consensus said. **And ours is by far the larger failing for letting Laton come to this world. Your only crime is to love her.**

And fail her.

No. We are all responsible for ourselves. She knows that as well as you do. All individuals can ever do is share happiness wherever they can find it.

We're all ships that pass in the night?

Ultimately, yes.

Consensus was so large, so replete with wisdom, he found it easy to believe. An essential component of the quiddity.

She is in trouble down there, he said. **Frightened, alone. Edenists shouldn't be alone.**

I am with her, *Oenone* said. **She can feel me even though we cannot converse.**

We are doing what we can, the consensus said. **But this is not a world equipped for warfare.**

The part of Ruben which had joined with the consensus was suddenly aware of Pernik igniting to solar splendour – and he was sitting strapped into a metal flea that spun and tossed erratically as it fell from the sky.

SYRINX! *Oenone* cried. **Syrinx. Syrinx. Syrinx. Syrinx. Syrinx.**

The voidhawk's affinity voice was a thunderclap roar howling through the minds of its crew. Ruben thought he would surely be deafened. Serina sat with her mouth gaping wide, hands clamped over her ears, tears streaming down her face.

***Oenone*, restrain yourself**, the consensus demanded.

But the voidhawk was beyond reason. It could feel its captain's pain, her hopelessness as the white-hot metal seared into her flesh with brutal intricate skill while in her heart she thought of nothing but their love. Lost in helpless rage its distortion effect twisted and churned like a frenzied captured beast pummelling at its cage bars.

Gravity rammed Ruben down into his seat, then swung severely. His arms outside the webbing were sucked up towards the ceiling, their weight quadrupling. *Oenone* was tumbling madly, its energy patterning cells sending out vast random surges of power.

Tula was yelling at the voidhawk to stop. Loose pieces of junk were hurtling round the bridge – cups and plastic meal trays, a jacket, cutlery, several circuit wafers. Gravity was fluctuating worse than a roller-coaster ride. One moment they appeared to be hanging upside-down, the next they were at right angles, and always weighing too much. A spinning circuit wafer sliced past Edwin, nicking his cheek. Blood squirted out.

Ruben could just make out the calls of the other voidhawks in orbit above Atlantis, trying to calm their rampant cousin. They all started to alter course for a rendezvous. Together their distortion fields could probably nullify *Oenone*'s supercharged flailings.

Then the most violent convulsion of all kicked the crew toroid. Ruben actually heard the walls give a warning creak. One of the consoles buckled, big skinlike creases appearing in its composite sides as it concertinaed down towards the decking.

Coolant fluid and sparks burst out of the cracks. He must have blacked out for a second.

Gravity was at a forty-degree angle to the horizontal when he came to, and holding steady.

I'm coming. I'm coming. I'm coming, *Oenone* was braying.

Horrified, Ruben linked into the voidhawk's sensor blisters. They were heading down towards Atlantis at two and a half gees. Reaction to the berserker power thundering through the energy patterning cells made the muscles in his arms and legs bunch like hot ropes.

Fast-moving specks were rising above the hazy blue-white horizon, skimming over the atomic fog of the thermosphere like flat stones flung across a placid sea. The other voidhawks: their calls redoubled in urgency. But *Oenone* was immune to them, to the Atlantean consensus' imperious orders. Rushing to help its beloved.

They're too far away, Ruben realized in dismay, they won't reach us in time.

*

The consensus relaxed its contact with Oxley, allowing him complete independence to pilot the floundering flyer, letting his instinct and skill attempt to right the craft unencumbered. He shot order after order into the bitek processors, receiving a stream of systems information in return. The coherent magnetic generators were failing, databuses were glitched, the fusion generator was powering down, electron-matrix crystal power reserves were dropping. Whatever electronic warfare techniques Pernik had, they were the best he had ever encountered, and they were trying to kill him.

He concentrated on the few control channels which remained operational, reducing the spin and flattening out the dive. The faltering magnetic fields squeezed and pushed at glowing ion streams, countering the corkscrew trajectory. Black ocean and lustrous island chased each other round the sensor images at a decreasing rate.

There was no panic. He treated it as though it was just another simulation run. An exercise in logic and competence set by the CAB to try and trip him.

At the back of his mind he was aware of further pandemonium breaking out amid the consensus. A ghost image lying across the flyer's sensor input visualization showed him *Oenone* plummeting towards the planet.

With only a kilometre of altitude left the flyer lost its spin. The nose was dangerously low. He poured the final power reserves into raising it, using the craft's ellipsoid surface as a blunt wing, gaining a degree of lift in an attempt to glide-curve away from the island. Distance was his only chance of salvation now. Streaks of reflected starlight blurred on the sable water below, growing closer. There was no sign of the electronic warfare assault abating.

Pernik's resplendent silhouette winked out. Silence detonated into the affinity consensus, absorbing the entire planet's mental voice.

Into the emptiness came a single devastating identity trait.

Your attention, please, Laton said. **We don't have much time. *Oenone*, resume your orbit now.**

The flyer's crashed systems abruptly sprang back into zealous life. And a shock-numbed Oxley was pressed deep into his seat as it vaulted back into the sky.

*

Lewis Sinclair watched keenly as the torturer manipulated Syrinx's mangled leg with a pair of ruddy glowing tongs and a mallet. She wasn't screaming so loudly now. The fight was going out of her. But not the spirit, he suspected. She was one tough lady. He had seen the type before back in Messopia; cops mainly, the special forces mob, hard-eyed and dedicated. A pusher Lewis worked for had captured one once, and it didn't matter what was done to the man, they couldn't get him to tell them anything.

Lewis didn't think the possessed were going to gain control of the voidhawk through Syrinx. But he didn't say anything, let them sweat it. It wasn't so much his problem, possessing the island gave him a measure of security a mere human body could never offer. The range of physical sensations and experiences available to him was truly astonishing.

The sensitive cells woven through the polyp were fantastically receptive; people with their mundane eyes and ears and nose were almost insensate by comparison. His consciousness roved at random through the huge structure, tasting and sampling. He was getting the hang of splitting himself into multiples, supervising a dozen actions at once.

Syrinx groaned again as the souls from beyond sang into her mind with their strange icy promises. And Lewis saw a girl standing at the back of the dungeon. The quake her presence sent through his psyche perceptibly rocked the entire island, as though it had ridden over a tidal wave. It was *her*! The girl from Messopia, Thérèse, the one he'd fought and died over.

Thérèse was tall for thirteen, skinny, with breasts that had been pushed into maturity by a course of tailored growth hormones. Long raven hair, brown eyes, and a pretty, juvenile face with just the right amount of cuteness; everybody's girl next door. She was wearing black leather shorts to show off her tight little arse, and her breasts were almost falling out of a scarlet halter top. Her pose was indolent, chewing at her gum, one hand on her hip.

Where the hell did she come from? Lewis asked.

What? the possessed Eysk asked.

Her. Thérèse. There, behind you.

Eysk turned round, then frowned angrily at the ceiling. **Very funny. Now fuck off.**

But–

Thérèse gave a bored sigh and sauntered out of the dungeon.

Can't you see her?

None of them answered him. He knew she was real, he could hear her *clicking* walk, feel the weight of her black stilettos on his polyp, olfactory cells picked up the sugary whiff of gum on her exhaled breath. She walked away from the dungeon, down a long corridor. For some reason it was difficult to keep his perception focused on her. She was only walking, but she seemed to be moving so fast. He barely noticed as the polyp of the corridor gave way to concrete. The light became a harsh electric yellow coming from bulbs on the ceiling, each one cupped by a protective wire cage. She hurried on ahead of him, feet sending out that regular *click click click* as her stilettos rapped the ground. His filthy jeans restricted his movements, clinging to his legs as he trailed after her. The air was cooler here, he could see his breath emerging as white streamers.

Thérèse slipped through a big set of grey-painted metal doors ahead. Lewis followed her into the empty subterranean warehouse in Messopia five hundred and fifty years ago. He gagged. It was a square chamber, sixty metres to a side, twenty metres high, rough poured concrete ribbed with steel beams coated in red-oxide paint. Striplights cast a feeble moon-white glow from on high. As before, leaking sewage pipes dripped rank liquids onto the floor.

She stood in the middle of the floor, looking at him expectantly.

He glanced down, seeing his body for the first time. 'Oh no,' he said in a desperate voice. 'This isn't happening.'

Loud, positive footsteps sounded from the far end of the warehouse. Lewis didn't wait to see who was emerging from the gloom, he spun round. There was no door any more, just a concrete wall. 'Jesus Almighty. Fuck!'

'Hello, Lewis.'

His body was compelled to turn, leg muscles working like dead meat fired by a cattle prod. He bit hard on his trembling lip.

Thérèse had gone. The person walking towards him was the body he had possessed on Lalonde.

'You're dead,' Lewis whispered through a fear-knotted throat.

Laton merely smiled his superior smile. 'Of all the people resident in this universe today, Lewis, you should know there is no such thing as death.'

'I'm in charge here,' Lewis yelled. 'I am Pernik.' He tried to fling the white fire, to conjure up energistic devastation, to flay the zombie to its stinking corrupt bones and beyond.

Laton halted five metres away. 'You were Pernik. I told you once that we would meet again as equals. I lied. You cannot even begin to conceive the processes involved in your manifestation within this universe. You are a Neanderthal out of time, Lewis. You believed brute force was the key to conquest. Yet you failed to even think about the source of your energistic power. I know, I've been analysing your tiresomely sluggish thoughts ever since you possessed my body.'

'What have you done to me?'

'Done? Why, Lewis, I have made you a part of me. Possession of the possessor. It is possible given the right circumstances. In this case I simply corrupted Pernik's neural stratum with my biological weapon. The neuron cells and nerve paths only conduct my thought impulses now. You can kill the cells, but you can't subvert them. It's a question of coding, you see. I know the codes, you don't. And please don't ask me for them, Lewis, it's nothing as simple as a number. You now operate only as a subsidiary part of me, you only think because I allow you to. That is how I summoned you here.'

'I think because I am! I have been me for centuries, you bastard.'

'And were you to go back there to the beyond, you would be you again. Free and independent. Do you want to go, Lewis? That is your escape from my bondage. In this universe you require a physical, living biological matrix in which to function. You may depart now if you wish.'

A weight pulled at Lewis's belt. When he looked down he saw it was the power-blade knife hanging in its sheath. 'No.' He shook his head feebly, quailing at the prospect. 'No, I won't. That's what you want. Without me Pernik would be free again. I'm going to stop that, I'm going to beat you.'

'Don't flatter yourself, Lewis. I will never allow you to resume your barbaric act of sodomy. You think of yourself as strong, as purposeful. You are entirely incorrect. You and the other returners have a nebulous plan to re-establish yourselves permanently in this physical universe. You do so because of your own quite pathetic psychological weaknesses.'

Lewis snarled at his tall tormentor. 'So fucking smart, aren't you. Let's see what you're like after a hundred fucking years of nothing; no food, no breathing, no touch, just fucking nothing. You'll be begging to join us, shithead.'

'Really?' Laton's smile no longer contained even a vestige of humour. 'Think what you are, Lewis. Think what all the returners are. Than ask yourself, where is the rest of the human race? The hundreds of billions who have died since the day our ancestors first struck two flints together, from the time we watched the glaciers retreating as we battled with mammoths.'

'They're with me, billions of them. They're waiting for their chance. And when they get into this universe they're gonna come gunning for you, shithead.'

'But they're not with you in the beyond, Lewis, there are nothing like enough souls to account for everyone. You cannot lie to me, you are part of me. I know. They're not there. Ask yourself who and why, Lewis.'

'Fuck you.' Lewis drew the knife from its scabbard. He thumbed the switch in a smooth motion and the silver blade emitted a dangerous buzz.

'Lewis, kindly behave yourself; this is my perceptual reality, after all.'

Lewis watched the solid blade curve round towards his fingers. He dropped the knife with a yell. It vanished before it reached the floor, making as little fuss as a snowflake landing on water. 'What do you want with me?' He raised his clenched fists, knowing that it was all futile. He wanted to pound his knuckles into the concrete.

Laton took another few paces towards him. And Lewis came to realize just how imposing the big Edenist was. It was all he could do not to back away.

'I want to make amends,' Laton said. 'At least part way. I doubt I will ever be fully forgiven in this universe, not for my crime. And it was a crime, I admit that now. You see, from you I have learnt how wrong I was before. Immortality is a notion we all grasp at because we can sense that there is continuity beyond death. It is an imperfect realization due to the weakness of the fusion between this continuum and the state of emptiness which follows. So much of our misunderstanding of life is rooted in this, so many wasted opportunities, so much religious claptrap born. I was wholly wrong to try and achieve a physical life extension, when corporeal life is but the start of existence. I was no better than a monkey trying to grasp a hologram banana.'

'You're mad!' Lewis shouted recklessly. 'You're fucking mad!'

Laton became pitying. 'Not mad, but very human. Even in this hiatus state I have emotions. And I have weaknesses. One of them is the desire for revenge. But then you know all about that, don't you, Lewis? Revenge is a prime motivator; glands or no glands, chemical fury or otherwise. You burnt for it in the empty beyond, revenge on the living for the crime of living.

'Well, now I shall have my revenge for the agonies and degradations you so joyfully submitted my kind to. My kind being the Edenists. For I am one. At the end. Flawed, but proud of them, their silly pride and honour. They are a basically peaceful people, those of Pernik more than most, and you delighted in shattering their sanity. You also destroyed my children, and you revelled in it, Lewis.'

'I still do!' I hope it fucking hurt you watching! I hope the memory makes you scream at nights. I want you in pain, you shit, I want you weeping. If I'm part of your memories then you won't ever be able to forget, I won't let you.'

'Oh, Lewis, haven't you learnt anything yet?' Laton drew his own knife from a scabbard he brought into existence. Its wickedly thrumming power-blade was half a metre long. 'I'm going to free Syrinx and warn the Atlantean consensus as to the exact nature of the threat they face. However, the remaining possessed do present a slight problem. So I need you to overcome them, Lewis. I shall consume you, completely.'

'Never! I won't help.'

Laton took a pace forwards. 'It isn't a question of choice. Not on your part.'

Lewis tried to run. Even though he knew it was impossible. The concrete closed in, shrinking the warehouse to the size of a tennis court, a room, a cube five metres across.

'I require control of the energistic spillover, Lewis. The power which comes from colliding continua. For that I must have the you which is you. I must complete my possession.'

'No!' Lewis raised his arms as the blade came whistling down. Once again there was the dreadful grinding sound as bone was pierced and fragmented. A flash of intolerable pain followed by the devastating numbness. His blood spilled onto the floor in great spurts from his elbow stump.

'Goodbye, Lewis. It may be some time before we encounter one another again. But none the less I wish you luck in your search for me.'

Lewis had collapsed twitching into a corner, soles of his boots slipping on his own blood. 'Bastard,' he spat through white lips. 'Just *do* it. Get it over with and laugh, you shithead prick sucker.'

'Sorry, Lewis. But like I told you, I shall consume you in your entirety. It's almost a vampiric process, really – though I expect that particular irony is sadly lost on you. And in order for the transfer to work you must remain conscious for the entire feast.' Laton gave him a lopsided, half-apologetic smile.

The true meaning of what the Edenist was saying finally sank in. Lewis started to scream. He was still screaming when Laton picked up his severed arm and bit into it.

*

Pernik's illumination returned to normality with eye-jarring suddenness. The accommodation towers blazed with diamond-blue light from every window, winding pathways through the park were set out by orange fairy lanterns, circular landing pads glowed hotly around the entire rim, the floating quays were like fluorescent roots radiating out into the opaque glassy water.

Oxley thought it looked quite magnificent. So cruelly treacherous, that a creation of such beauty could play host to the most heinous evil.

Land immediately please, Oxley, Laton said. **I don't have much time. They are resisting me.**

Land? Oxley felt his throat snarl up as outrage vied with a shaky form of laugh. **Show me where you are, and I'll come to you, Laton. I'll be doing around Mach twenty when we embrace. Show yourself!**

Don't be a fool. I am Pernik now.

Where's Syrinx?

She lives. *Oenone* will confirm that. But you must pick her up now, she requires urgent medical attention.

***Oenone*?** He sent the querying thought lancing upwards, while at the back of his mind he was aware of Laton delivering a vast quantity of information to the Atlantean consensus.

The voidhawk registered as a subdued jumble of thoughts. It had stopped its crazed descent; now it was rising laboriously up out of the mesosphere, its distortion effect generating barely a tenth of a gee.

***Oenone*, is she alive?**

Yes.

The emotional discharge in the voidhawk's thought brought tears to his eyes.

Oxley, Ruben called, **if there's any chance . . . please.**

OK. He studied the island. Pinpricks of light were blooming and dying right across it, stars with a lifetime measurable in fractions of a second. It looked quite magical, though he didn't like to dwell too hard upon what their cause would be.

Consensus, should I go in?

Yes. No other spaceplanes can reach Pernik in time. Trust Laton.

That was it, the universe had finally gone totally insane. **Oh, shit. OK, I'm taking the flyer down.**

*

Fires had taken hold in the central park when Oxley piloted the flyer down onto one of the pads. He could see a spaceplane further along the row, wings retracted, lying on its side with its undercarriage struts sticking up in the air and its fuselage cracked open around the midsection. Bodies were sprawled on the polyp around the base of the nearest accommodation tower; most of them looked as though they had been caught in a firestorm, skin blackened, faces unrecognizable, clothes still smoking.

An explosion sounded in the distance, and a ball of orange flame rolled out of a window on the other side of the park.

They are learning, Laton said impassively. **Grouped together they can ward off my energistic assaults. It won't do them any good in the long run, of course.**

Oxley's nerves were raw edged. He still thought this was some giant trap. The steel-clad jaws would snap shut any second; conversation might just be the trigger. **Where's Syrinx?**

Coming. Open the flyer airlock.

He felt the consensus balance his insecurities with an injection of urbane courage. Somehow he was giving the order to cut the ion field and open the airlock.

Faint shouts and the drawn out screeching of metal under tremendous stress penetrated the cabin. Oxley sniffed the air. Mingled with the brine was a frowsty putrescence which furred the roof of his mouth. With his hand clamped firmly over his nose he made his way aft.

Someone was walking towards the flyer. A giant, three metres tall, hairless, naked skin a frail cream colour, virtually devoid of facial features. It was holding a figure in its outstretched arms.

'Syrinx,' he gasped. He could feel *Oenone* pushing behind his eyes, desperate to see.

Three-quarters of her body was engulfed by green medical nanonic packages. But even that thick covering couldn't disguise the terrible damage inflicted on her limbs and torso.

The nanonic packages do not function well in this environment, Laton said as the giant mounted the flyer's airstairs. **Once you are airborne their efficiency will recover.**

Who did this?

I do not know their names. But I assure you the bodies they possessed have been rendered nonfunctional.

Oxley backed into the cabin, too shaken to offer further comment. Laton must have loaded an order into the flight-control processors, because the front passenger seat hinged open to form a flat couch. It was the one designed for transporting casualty cases. Basic medical monitor and support equipment slid out from recesses in the cabin wall above it.

The giant laid Syrinx down gently, then stood, its head touching the cabin ceiling. Oxley wanted to rush over to her, but all he could do was stare dumbly at the hulking titan. Its blank face crawled as though the skin was boiling. Laton looked down at him.

'Go to the Sol system,' the simulacrum said. 'There are superior medical facilities available there in any case. But the Jovian consensus must be informed of the true nature of the threat these returning souls pose to the Confederation;

indeed to this whole section of the galaxy. That is your priority now.'

Oxley managed to jerk a nod. 'What about you?'

'I will hold the possessed off until you leave Pernik. Then I will begin the great journey.' The big lips pressed together in compassion. 'If it is of any comfort, you may tell our kind I am now truly sorry for Jantrit. I was utterly and completely wrong.'

'Yes.'

'I do not ask forgiveness, for it would not be in Edenism's power to grant. But tell them also that I came good in the end.' The face managed a small, clumsy smile. 'That ought to set the cat among the pigeons.'

The giant turned and clumped out of the cabin. When it reached the top of the airlock stairs it lost all cohesion. A huge gout of milky white liquid sloshed down onto the metal grid of the landing pad, splattering the flyer's landing gear struts.

*

The flyer was five hundred kilometres from Pernik and travelling at Mach fifteen up through the ionosphere when the end came.

Laton waited until the diminutive craft was beyond any conceivable blast range, then used his all-pervasive control to release every erg of chemical energy stored in the island's cells simultaneously. It produced an explosion to rival an antimatter planetbuster strike. Several of the tsunami which raced out from the epicentre were powerful enough to traverse the world.

25

It was a quiet evening in Harkey's Bar. Terrance Smith's bold little fleet had departed the previous day, taking with it a good many regulars. The band audibly lacked enthusiasm, and only five couples were dancing on the floor. Gideon Kavanagh sat at one table; the medical nanonic package preparing his stump for a clone graft was deftly covered by a loose-fitting purple jacket. His companion was a slim twenty-five-year-old girl in a red cocktail dress who giggled a lot. A group of bored waitresses stood at one end of the bar, talking among themselves.

Meyer didn't mind the apathetic atmosphere for once. There were some nights when he really didn't feel like maintaining the expected image of combination raconteur, *bon viveur*, ace pilot, and sex demon – the qualities that independent starship captains were supposed to possess in abundance. He was too old to be keeping up that kind of nonsense.

Leave it to the young ones like Joshua, he thought. Although with Joshua it was hardly an act.

Nor was it always an artificial pose for you, *Udat* said.

Meyer watched one of the young waitresses swish past the end of the booth, an oriental with blonde hair whose long black skirt was split up to her hips. He didn't even feel remotely randy, just appreciative of the view. **Those days seem to be long gone**, he told the blackhawk with an irony that wasn't entirely insincere.

Cherri Barnes was sitting in the booth with him; the two of them sharing a chilled bottle of imported white Valençay wine. Now there was a woman he felt perfectly comfortable with. Smart, attractive, someone who didn't feel compelled to talk into any silences, a good crew member too; and they'd been to bed on several occasions over the years. No incompatibility there.

Her company lightens you, *Udat* proclaimed. **That makes me happy.**

Oh, well, as long as you're happy . . .

We need a flight. You are growing restless. I am eager to leave.

We could have gone to Lalonde.

I think not. Such missions do not sit well with you any more.

You're right. Though Christ knows I would have liked a crack at that bastard Laton. But I suppose that's something else best left to Joshua and his ilk. Though what he wanted to go for after the money he pulled in on the Norfolk run beats me.

Perhaps he feels he has something to prove.

No. Not Joshua. There's something odd going on there. And knowing Joshua, money is at the root of it. But no doubt we'll hear about it in due course. In the meantime the Lalonde mission has left a pleasing shortage of starships docked here. Finding a charter should be relatively easy.

There were those Time Universe charters available. Claudia Dohan specifically wanted blackhawks to deliver the fleks of Graeme Nicholson's sensevise. Time was of the essence, she said.

Those charters were all rush and effort.

It would have been a challenge.

If I'd wanted my mother as a permanent companion rather than a blackhawk I would never have left home.

I am sorry. I have upset you.

No. It's this Laton business. It has me worried. Fancy him turning up again after all this time.

The navy will find him.

Yeah. Sure.

'What are you two talking about?' Cherri asked.

'Huh? Oh, sorry,' he grinned sheepishly. 'It's Laton, if you must know. Just thinking of him running round free again . . .'

'You and fifty billion others.' She picked up one of the menu sheets. 'Come on, let's order. I'm starving.'

They chose a chicken dish with side salad, along with a second bottle of wine.

'The trouble is, where can you travel to that's guaranteed safe?' Meyer said after the waitress departed. 'Until the Confederation Navy finds him, the interstellar cargo market is going to be very jumpy. Our insurance rates are going to go through the roof.'

'So shift to data-courier work. That way we don't have to physically dock with any stations. Alternatively, we just fetch and carry cargo between Edenist habitats.'

He shifted his wineglass about on the table, uncomfortable with the idea. 'That's too much like giving in, letting him win.'

'Well, make up your mind.'

He managed a desultory smile. 'I dunno.'

'Captain Meyer?'

He glanced up. A smallish black woman was standing at the end of the booth's table, dressed in a conservative grey suit; her skin was black enough to make Cherri seem white. He guessed she was in her early sixties. 'That's me.'

'You are the owner of the *Udat*?'

'Yes.' If it had been anywhere else but Tranquillity, Meyer would have pegged her as a tax inspector.

'I am Dr Alkad Mzu,' she said. 'I wonder if I could sit with you for a moment? I would like to discuss some business.'

'Be my guest.'

He signalled to a waitress for another wineglass, and poured out the last of the bottle when it arrived.

'I require some transportation outsystem,' Alkad said.

'Just for yourself? No cargo?'

'That is correct. Is it a problem?'

'Not for me. But the *Udat* doesn't come cheap. In fact, I don't think we've ever carried just one passenger before.'

We haven't, *Udat* said.

Meyer quashed a childish grin. 'Where do you want to travel? I can probably give you a quote straight away.'

'New California.' She sipped her wine, peering at him over the rim of the glass.

Out of the corner of his eye, Meyer could see Cherri frowning. There were regular commercial flights to the New Californian system from Tranquillity three or four times a week, and more non-scheduled charter flights on top of that. The Laton scare hadn't stopped any departures yet. He was suddenly very curious about Alkad Mzu.

OK, let's see how badly she wants to get there. 'That would be at least three hundred thousand fuseodollars,' he told her.

'I expected it to be about that,' she replied. 'Once we arrive, I may wish to pick up some cargo to carry on to a further destination. Could you supply me with the *Udat*'s performance and handling parameters, please?'

'Yes, of course.' He was only slightly mollified. Taking a cargo on somewhere was a viable excuse for an exclusive charter. But why not travel to New California on a regular civil flight, then hire a starship after she arrived? The only reason he could think of was that she specifically wanted a blackhawk. That wasn't good, not good at all. 'But *Udat* is only available for civil flights,' he stressed the word lightly.

'Naturally,' Alkad Mzu said.

'That's all right then.' He opened a channel to her neural nanonics and datavised the blackhawk's handling capacity over.

'What sort of cargo would we pick up?' Cherri asked. 'I'm the *Udat*'s cargo officer, I may be able to advise on suitability.'

'Medical equipment,' Alkad said. 'I have some type-definition files.' She datavised them to Meyer.

The list expanded in his mind, resembling a three-dimensional simulacrum of magnified chip circuitry, with every junction labelled. There seemed to be an awful lot of it. 'Fine,' he said, slightly at a loss. 'We'll review it later.' Have to run it through an analysis program, he thought.

'Thank you,' Alkad said. 'The journey from New California will be approximately two hundred light-years, if you'd care to work out a quote based on the cargo's mass and environmental requirements. I will be asking other captains for quotes.'

'We'll be tough to beat,' he said smoothly.

'Is there any reason why we can't know where we're going?' Cherri asked.

'My colleagues and I are still in the preliminary planning stage of the mission. I'd prefer not to say anything more at this time. But I shall certainly inform you of our destination before we leave Tranquillity.' Alkad stood up. 'Thank you for your time, Captain. I hope we see each other again. Please datavise your full quote to me at any time.'

'She hardly touched her wine,' Cherri said as the doctor departed.

'Yes,' Meyer said distantly. Five other people were leaving the bar. None of them space industry types. Merchants? But they didn't look rich enough.

'Are we putting in a formal bid?'

'Good question.'

I would like to visit New California, *Udat* said hopefully.

We've been before. You just want to fly.

I do. It is boring sitting on this ledge. *Udat* relayed an image of whirling stars as seen from Tranquillity's docking-ledge, speeded up, always tracing the same circles. The edge of the habitat's spaceport disk started to grey, then crumbled and broke apart with age.

Meyer grinned. **What an imagination you have. I'll get us a charter soon. That's a promise.**

Good!

'I think we need to know a little bit more about this Mzu woman,' he said out loud. 'No way is she on the level.'

'Oh, really?' Cherri cooed; she cocked her head on one side. 'You noticed that, did you?'

*

Ione let go of the image. Her apartment rematerialized around her. Augustine was walking determinedly across the dining-room table towards the remains of the salad she had pushed away, moving at a good fifty centimetres a minute. At the back of her mind she was aware of Alkad Mzu standing in the vestibule of the thirty-first floor of the StMartha starscraper waiting for a lift. There were seven Intelligence agency operatives hanging around in the park-level foyer above her, alerted by their colleagues in Harkey's Bar. Two of them – a female operative from New Britain, and the second-in-command of the Kulu team – resolutely refused to make eye contact. Strange really. For the last three weeks they had spent most of their off-duty hours in bed together screwing each other into delirious exhaustion.

In my history courses I recall an incident in the twentieth century when the American CIA tried to get rid of a Caribbean island's Communist president by giving him an exploding cigar, Ione said.

Yes? Tranquillity asked loyally.

Six hundred years of progress – human style.

Would you like me to inform Meyer that Alkad Mzu will not be granted an exit visa?

Informing him I'll blow him and the *Udat* out of existence if he leaves with her would be more to the point. But no, we won't do anything yet. How many captains has she contacted now?

Sixty-three in the last twenty months.

And every contact follows the same pattern, she mused. A request for a charter fee quote to carry her to a star system, then picking up a cargo to take onwards. But never the same star system; and it was Joshua who was asked to quote for Garissa. Ione tried not to consider the implications of that. It *had* to be coincidence.

I am sure it is, Tranquillity said.

I was leaking. Sorry.

There was never any follow-up to her meeting with Joshua.

No. But what is she doing, I wonder?

I have two possible explanations. First, she is aware of the agency observers – and it would be hard to believe she is not – and she is simply having fun at their expense.

Fun? You call that fun? Threatening to recover the Alchemist?

Her home planet has been annihilated. If the humour is somewhat rough, that is to be expected.

Of course. Go on.

Secondly, she is attempting to produce a range of escape options which exceed the observers' ability to keep track of. Sixty-three is an excessive number of captains to contact even for a warped game.

But she must know it isn't possible to confuse you.

Yes.

Strange woman.

A very intelligent woman.

Ione reached over to her discarded plate, and began shredding one of the lettuce leaves. Augustine crooned adoringly as he finally reached the pile of shreds, and started to munch at them.

Is it possible for her to circumvent your observation? Apparently Edenists can induce localized blindspots in their habitats' perception.

I would say it is extremely unlikely. No Edenist has ever succeeded in evading me, and there were many attempts in your grandfather's day.

Really? She perked up.

Yes, by their Intelligence agency operatives. All failed. And I acquired some valuable information on the nature of localized circumvention patterns they employed. Fortunately I do not use quite the same thought routines as Edenist habitats, so I am relatively insusceptible. And Alkad Mzu does not have affinity.

Are we sure? She was missing for some time between Garissa's

destruction and turning up here, four years. She could have had neuron symbionts implanted.

She did not. A complete medical body scan is required for health-insurance coverage for all Laymil project staff when they start work. She has neural nanonics, but no affinity symbionts. Nor any other implants, for that matter.

Oh. I'm still unhappy over these continual encounters with starship captains. Perhaps if I had a private word with her . . . explain how upsetting it is.

That might work.

Did Father ever meet her?

No.

I'll think about what to say then, I don't want to come over all heavy handed. Perhaps I could invite her for a meal, keep it informal.

Certainly. She always maintains her social propriety.

Good. In the meantime, I'd like you to double the number of serjeants we keep in her immediate vicinity. With Laton running loose in the Confederation, we really don't want to add to Admiral Aleksandrovich's troubles right now.

*

Meyer and Cherri Barnes took a lift up from Harkey's Bar to the StMartha's foyer. He walked with her down a flight of stairs to the starscraper's tube station, and datavised for a carriage.

'Are we going back to the hotel or *Udat*?' Cherri asked.

'My hotel flat has a double bed.'

She grinned, and tucked his arm round hers. 'Mine too.'

The carriage arrived, and he datavised the control processor to take them to the hotel. There was a slight surge of acceleration as it got under way. Meyer sank deeper into his cushioning; Cherri still hadn't let go of him.

His neural nanonics informed him a file stored in one of the memory cells was altering. Viral safeguard programs automatically isolated the cell. According to the menu, the file was the cargo list Alkad Mzu had datavised to him.

The viral safeguard programs reported the change had finished; tracer programs probed the file's new format. It wasn't hostile. The file had contained a time-delay code which simply re-arranged the order of the existing information into something entirely different. A hidden message.

Meyer accessed the contents.

'Holy shit,' he muttered fifteen seconds later.

Now *that* would be a real challenge, *Udat* said excitedly.

*

Ombey was the newest of Kulu's eight principality star systems. A Royal Kulu Navy scoutship discovered the one terracompatible planet in 2457, orbiting a hundred and forty-two million kilometres from its G2 star. After an ecological certification team cleared its biosphere as non-harmful, it was declared a Kulu protectorate and opened for immigration by King Lukas in 2470. Unlike other frontier worlds, such as Lalonde, which formed development companies and struggled to raise investment, Ombey was funded entirely by the Kulu Royal Treasury and the Crown-owned Kulu Corporation. Even at the beginning it couldn't be described as a stage one colony. It couldn't even be said to have gone through a purely agrarian phase. A stony iron asteroid, Guyana, was manoeuvred into orbit before the first settler arrived, and navy engineers immediately set about converting it into a base. Kulu's larger astroengineering companies brought industry stations to the system to gain a slice of the military contracts involved, and to take advantage of the huge start-up tax incentives on offer. The Kulu Corporation began a settlement on an asteroid orbiting the gas giant Nonoiut, which assembled a cloudscoop to mine He_3. As always within the Kingdom, the Edenists were excluded from germinating a habitat and building an adjunct cloudscoop, a prohibition rationalized by the Saldanas on religious grounds.

By the time the first wave of farmers arrived, the already substantial government presence produced a large ready-made consumer base for their crops. Healthcare, communications, law enforcement, and didactic education courses, although not quite up to the level of the Kingdom's more developed planets, were provided from day one. Forty hectares of land were given to each family, along with a generous low-interest loan for housing and agricultural machinery, with the promise of more land for their children. Basic planetary industrialization was given a high priority, and entire factories were imported to provide essentials for the engineering and construction business. Again, government infrastructure contracts provided a massive initial subsidy. The company and civil workers arriving during the second ten-year period was equal to the number of farmers.

In 2500 its population rose above the ten million mark, and it officially lost its protectorate status to become a principality, governed by one of the King's siblings.

Ombey was a meticulously planned endeavour, only possible to a culture as wealthy as the Kulu Kingdom. The Saldanas considered the investment costs more than worthwhile. Although the Principality didn't start to show a return for over ninety years, it allowed them to expand their family dynasty as well as their influence, both physical (economic and military) and political, inside the Confederation. It made their position even more secure, although by that time a republican revolution was virtually impossible. And it was all done without conflict or opposition with neighbouring star systems.

By 2611 there were twelve settled asteroids in orbit and two more on their way. Planetary population was a fraction under two hundred million, and the twelve settled asteroids in the system's dense inner belt were home to another two million people. Subsidies and loans from Kulu had long since ended, self-sufficiency both industrially and economically had been reached in 2545, exports were accelerating. Ombey was a thriving decent place to live, bristling with justified optimism.

*

Captain Farrah Montgomery had expected the flight from Lalonde to take four days. By the time the *Ekwan* finally jumped into the Ombey system, emerging two hundred thousand kilometres above the planet's surface, they had been in transit for eight. The big colonist-carrier had endured a multitude of irritating systems failures right from the very first minute of getting underway. Mechanical components had broken down, electrical circuits suffered a rash of surges and drop-outs. Her crew had been harried into short-tempered despair as they attempted patchwork repairs. Most worrying, the main fusion tubes produced erratic thrust levels, adding to the difficulty of reaching plotted jump coordinates, and increasing the flight duration drastically.

Fuel levels, while not yet critical, were uncomfortably low.

Sensors slid out of their jump recesses, and Captain Montgomery performed a preliminary visual orientation sweep. Ombey's solitary moon, Jethro, was rising above the horizon, a large grey-yellow globe peppered with small deep craters, and streaked with long white rays. They were above the planet's night side; the Blackdust desert continent straddling the equator was a huge ebony patch amid oceans that reflected jaundiced moonlight. On the eastern side of the planet the coastline of the Espartan continent was picked out by the purple-white lights of towns and cities; there were fewer urban sprawls in the interior, declining to zero at the central mountain range.

After Captain Montgomery had cleared their arrival with civil flight control, Ralph Hiltch contacted the navy base on Guyana, and requested docking permission along with a code four status alert. *Ekwan* closed on the asteroid at one and a quarter gravities, holding reasonably steady. The base admiral, Pascoe Farquar, after receiving Ralph's request, backed by Sir Asquith, authorized the alert. Non-essential personnel were cleared from the habitation cavern the navy used. Commercial traffic was turned away. Xenobiology, nanonic, and weapons specialists began to assemble an isolation confinement area for Gerald Skibbow.

The *Ekwan* docked at Guyana's non-rotating spaceport amid a tight security cordon. Royal Marines and port personnel worked a straight five-hour shift to bring the *Ekwan*'s three thousand grumbling, bewildered colonists out of zero-tau and assign them quarters in the navy barracks. Ralph Hiltch and Sir Asquith spent most of that time in conference with Pascoe Farquar and his staff. After he accessed sensorium recordings Dean Folan made during the jungle mission, as well as the garbled reports of Darcy and Lori claiming Laton was on Lalonde, the admiral decided to raise the alert status to code three.

Ralph Hiltch watched the last of the fifty armour-suited marines floating into the *Ekwan*'s large zero-tau compartment. They were all muscle boosted and qualified in free fall combat routines; eight of them carried medium-calibre automatic recoilless projectile carbines. The sergeants followed Cathal Fitzgerald's directions and started positioning them in three concentric circles surrounding Gerald Skibbow's zero-tau pod, with five on the decks either side in case he broke through the metal grids. Extra lights had been attached to the nearby support girders, beams focused on the one pod in the compartment which was still encased by an absorptive blackness, casting a weird jumble of multiple shadows outside the encircling ring of marines.

Ralph's neural nanonics were relaying the scene to the admiral and the waiting specialists. It made him slightly self-conscious as he anchored himself to a girder to address the marine squad.

'This might look excessive for one man,' he said to the marines, 'but don't drop your guard for an instant. We're not entirely sure he is human, certainly he has some lethal energy-projecting abilities that come outside anything we've encountered before. If it's any comfort, free fall does seem to unnerve him slightly. Your job is just to escort him down to the isolation area that's been prepared. Once he's there, the technical people will take over. They think the cell they've prepared will be able to confine him. But getting him there could get very messy.'

He backed away from the pod, noting the half-apprehensive faces of the first rank of marines.

God, they look young. I hope to hell they took my warning seriously.

He checked his own skull-helmet, and took a deep breath. 'OK, Cathal, switch it off.'

The blackness vanished from the pod revealing the smooth cylindrical composite sarcophagus. Ralph strained to hear the manic battering which Skibbow had been giving the pod before the zero-tau silenced him. The compartment was quiet apart from the occasional scuffling of the marines as they craned for a glimpse.

'Open the lid.'

It began to slide back. Ralph braced himself for Skibbow to burst out of the opening like a runaway combat wasp with a forty-gee drive. He heard a wretched whimpering sound. Cathal gave him a puzzled glance.

God, did we get the right pod?

'All right, stay back,' Ralph said. 'You two,' he indicated the marines with the carbines, 'cover me.' He pulled himself cautiously across the grid towards the pod, still expecting Skibbow to spring up. The whimpering grew louder, interspersed with low groans.

Very, *very* carefully, Ralph eased himself up the side of the pod, and peeked in. Ready to duck down fast.

Gerald Skibbow was floating listlessly inside the curving cream-white composite coffin. His whole body was trembling. He clutched his shattered hand to his chest. Both eyes were red rimmed, blood was still oozing from his mashed nose. The smell of jungle mud and urine clogged in Ralph's nose.

Gerald continued his weak gurglings, bubbles of saliva forming at the corner of his mouth. When Ralph manoeuvred himself right over the pod there was no reaction from the unfocused eyes.

'Shit.'

'What's happened?' Admiral Farquar datavised.

'I don't know, sir. It's Skibbow all right. But it looks like he's gone into some kind of shock.' He waved a hand in front of the colonist's filthy, bloody face. 'He's virtually catatonic.'

'Is he still dangerous, do you think?'

'I don't see how he could be, unless he recovers.'

'All right, Hiltch. Have the marines take him down to the isolation area as quickly as possible. I'll have an emergency medical team there by the time you arrive.'

'Yes, sir.' Ralph pushed himself away, allowing three marines to pull the still unresisting Skibbow from the zero-tau pod. His neural nanonics informed him the asteroid was being stood down to code six status.

I don't understand, he thought bleakly, we brought a walking nuke on board, and wind up with a pants-wetting vegetable. Something wiped that sequestration from him. What?

The marine squad departed the compartment noisily, joking and catcalling. Relieved they hadn't been needed after all. With one hand holding idly on a girder, Ralph hung between the two decking grids long after the last of them left, staring at the zero-tau pod.

*

Three hours after Guyana's alert status was reduced to code six, life inside had almost returned to normal. Civilians with jobs in the military-run cavern were allowed to resume their duties. Restrictions on communication and travel were lifted from the other two caverns. Spaceships were permitted to dock and depart, although the spaceport where the *Ekwan* was berthed was still off-limits to anything but navy ships.

Three and a half hours after the marines delivered a virtually comatose Gerald Skibbow to the isolation cell, Captain Farrah Montgomery walked into the small office Time Universe maintained on Guyana and handed over Graeme Nicholson's flek.

*

It was an hour after the maids had served Cricklade's breakfast, and Duke was already rising across a sky that was ribbed with slender bands of flimsy cloud. Duchess-night had seen the first sprinkling of rain since the midsummer conjunction. The fields and forests glimmered and shone under their glacé coating of water. Aboriginal flowers, reduced to wizened brown coronets after discharging their seeds, turned to a pulpy mess and started to rot away. Best of all, the dust had gone from the air. Cricklade's estate labourers had started their morning in a cheerful mood at the omen. Rain this early meant the second crop of cereals should produce a good heavy harvest.

Louise Kavanagh didn't care about the rain, nor the prospect of an impending agricultural bounty. Not even Genevieve's playful enthusiasm could summon her for their usual stroll in the paddock. Instead, she sat on the toilet in her private bathroom with her panties round her ankles and her head in her hands. Her long hair hung lankly, tasselled ends brushing her shiny blue shoes. It was stupid to have hair so long, she thought, stupid, snobbish, impractical, a waste of time, and insulting.

Why should I have to be preened and groomed like I'm a pedigree show horse? It's a wicked, filthy tradition treating women like that. Just so that I look the classic-beauty part for some ghastly clot-head young 'gentleman'. What do looks matter, and especially looks that come from a pseudo-mythical past on another planet? I already have my man.

She clenched her stomach muscles again, squeezing her guts hard as she held her breath. Her nails dug into her palms painfully with the effort. Her head started to shake, skin reddening.

It didn't make the slightest difference. She let the air out of her straining lungs in a fraught sob.

Angry now, she squeezed again. Let out her breath.

Squeezed.

Nothing.

She wanted to cry. Her shoulders were shivering, she even had the hot blotches round her eyes, but there were no tears left. She was all cried out.

Her period was at least five days overdue. And she was so regular.

She was pregnant with Joshua's baby. It was wonderful. It was horrible. It was . . . a wretched great mess.

'Please, Jesus,' she whispered. 'What we did wasn't really a sin. It wasn't. I love him so. I really do. Don't let this happen to me. Please.'

There was nothing in the world she wanted more than to have Joshua's baby. But not *now*. Joshua himself still seemed like a gorgeous fantasy she had made up to amuse herself during the long hot months of Norfolk's quiescent summer. Too perfect to be real, the kind of man who melted her inside even as he set her on fire with passion. A passion she didn't quite know she had before. Previous daydreams of romance had all sort of blurred into vague unknowns after her tall, handsome champion kissed her. But lying in bed at night the memory of Joshua's cunning hands exploring her naked body brought some most unladylike flushes below the sheets. There hadn't been a day gone by when she didn't visit their little glade in Wardley Wood, and the smell of dry hay always kindled a secret glow of arousal as she thought of their last time together in the stable.

'Please, my Lord Jesus.'

Last year one of the girls at the convent school, a year older than Louise, had moved away from the district rather abruptly. She was from one of Stoke County's more important families, her father was a landowner who had sat on the local council for over a decade. Gone to stay with a wealthy sheep-farming relative on the isle of Cumbria, the Mother Superior had told the other pupils, where she will learn the practical aspects of house management which will adequately prepare her for the role of marriage. But everyone knew the real reason. One of the Romany lads, in Stoke for the rose crop, had tumbled her in his caravan.

The girl's family had been more or less shunned by decent folk after that, and her father had to resign his council seat, saying it was due to ill health.

Not that anyone would dare do that to any branch of the Kavanagh family. But the whispers would start if she took a sudden holiday; the tarnish of shame would never be lifted from Cricklade. And Mummy would cry because her daughter had let her down frightfully badly. And Daddy would . . . Louise didn't like to think what her father would do.

No! she told herself firmly. Stop thinking like that. Nothing terrible is going to happen.

'You know I'm coming back,' Joshua had told her as they lay entwined by the side of the sun-blessed stream. And he said he loved her.

He would return. He *promised.*

Everything would be all right after that. Joshua was the one person in the galaxy who could face up to her father unafraid. Yes, everything would be fine just as soon as he arrived.

Louise brushed her – fearsomely annoying – hair from her face, and slowly stood up. When she looked in the mirror she was an utter ruin. She started to tidy herself up, pulling up her panties, splashing cold water on her face. Her light flower-pattern dress with its long skirt was badly creased. Why couldn't she wear trousers, or even shorts? She could just imagine Nanny's reaction to that innocent suggestion. Legs on public display? Good grief! But it would be so much more practical in this weather. Lots of the women working in the groves did; girls her age, too.

She started to plait her hair. That would be something else which changed after she was married.

Married. She grinned falteringly at her reflection. Joshua was going to be in for a monumental shock when he returned and she told him the stupendous news. But, ultimately, he would be happy and rejoice with her. How could he not? And they would be married at the end of summer (which was as quick as decency versus a swelling belly could allow), when the Earth flowers were at their peak and the granaries were full from the second harvest. Her bulge probably wouldn't show, not with an adequately designed dress. Genevieve would adore being chief bridesmaid. There would be huge marquees on the lawns for the reception. Family members she hadn't seen for years. It would be the biggest celebration in Stoke County for decades, everyone would be happy and they would dance under the neon-red night sky.

People might guess because of the speed. But Joshua was going to be her father's business partner in this exciting mayope venture. He was rich, of good blood (presumably – how else would he inherit a starship?), a fine manager able to take on Cricklade. An eminently suitable (if unusual) match for the Cricklade heir. Their marriage wouldn't be that extraordinary. Her reputation would remain intact. And the Kavanaghs' respectability would remain unblemished.

After the wedding they could travel Norfolk's islands for their honeymoon. Or maybe even to another planet in his starship. What was important was that she wouldn't have the baby here, with everyone noting the date of birth.

Real life could match up to her most fantastical daydreams. With a fabulous husband, and a beautiful baby.

If Joshua . . .

Always, *if Joshua . . .*

Why did it have to be like that?

*

The lone Romany caravan stood beside a tall Norfolk-aboriginal pine in a meadow which until recently had been a site for more than thirty similar caravans. Rings of flat reddish stones confined piles of ash, cold now. Grass along the bank of the little stream was trampled down where horses and goats had drunk and people had scooped water into pails. Several piles of raw earth marked the latrines, their conical sides scored with fresh runnels, evidence of last Duchess-night's rain.

The caravan, a hybrid of traditional design riding modern lightweight wheels, had seen more prosperous times. Its jaunty and elaborate paintwork was fading, but the wood was sound. Three goats were tethered to its rear axle. Two horses waited outside, one a mud-spotted piebald shire-horse with a wild shaggy mane which was used to pull the caravan, the other a black riding stallion, its coat sleek and glossy, the expensive leather saddle on its back polished to a gleam.

Grant Kavanagh stood inside the caravan, stooping so he didn't knock his head on the curving ceiling. It was dark and faintly dusty, smelling of dried herbs. He enjoyed that, it brought back sharp memories of his teenage years. Even now, the sight of the Romany caravans winding their way through Cricklade's wolds as midsummer approached always made him feel incredibly randy.

The girl pulled back the heavy curtains hanging on a cord across the middle of the caravan. Her name was Carmitha, twenty years old, with a big broad-shouldered body, which, Grant knew with depressing instinct, would be horribly overweight in another six or seven years. Rich black hair hanging below her shoulders harmonized with dark, smooth skin. She had changed into a flimsy white skirt and loose-fitting top.

'That looks fantastic,' he said.

'Why, thank you, kind sir.' She curtsied, and giggled effusively.

Grant drew her closer and started to kiss her. His hands fumbled with the buttons down the front of her blouse.

She pushed him away gently, and removed his hands, kissing the knuckles lightly. 'Let me do that for you,' she said coquettishly. Her fingers moved down to the top button in a slow, taunting caress. He looked in delight as her body was exposed. He pulled her down onto the bed, immensely gratified by her ardour.

The caravan squeaked as it started rocking. A hurricane lantern hanging from a brass chain on the ceiling clanged loudly as it swayed gently to and fro. He barely heard it above Carmitha's exuberant whoops of joy.

After a time which was nowhere near long enough, he came in drastic shudders, his spine singing raptures. Carmitha quickly squealed, claiming multiple orgasms were nearly making her swoon.

He collapsed onto the bed, prickly blankets scratching his back. Dust mingled with sweat and trickled among the curly hair on his chest.

By God but summer conjunction makes life worth living, he thought. A time when he could prove himself again and again. The Tear crop had been one of the best ever; the estate had made its usual financial killing. He had tumbled nearly a dozen young girls from the grove teams. The meteorological reports were predicting a humid month ahead, which meant a good second harvest. Young Joshua's audacious mayope proposal could only add to the family's wealth and influence.

The only blot on the horizon was the reports coming out of Boston on the disturbances. It looked like the Democratic Land Union was stirring up trouble again.

The Union was a motley collection of reformists and political agitators, a semi-subversive group who wanted to see land distributed 'fairly' among the People, the foreign earnings from the sale of Norfolk Tears invested with social relevance, and full democracy and civil rights awarded to the population. And free beer on Friday nights, too, no doubt, Grant thought caustically. The whole blessing of a Confederation of eight hundred plus planets was that it gave people a massive variety of social systems to choose from. What the Democratic Land Union activists failed to appreciate was that they were free to leave for their damned Communistic workers' paradise as soon as the workshy little buggers earned enough cash to pay their passage. But oh no, they wanted to liberate Norfolk, no matter how much damage and heartache they caused in the process of peddling their politics of envy.

A chapter of the Democratic Land Union had tried to spread its sedition in Stoke County about ten years ago. Grant had helped the county's chief constable round them up. The leaders had been deported to a Confederation penal planet. Some of the nastier elements – the ones found with home-made weapons – had been handed over to a squad of special operations constables from the capital, Norwich. The rest, the pitiful street trash who handed out leaflets and drank themselves into a coma on the Union-supplied beer, had been given fifteen years' hard labour in the polar work gangs.

There hadn't been sight or sign of them on Kesteven ever since. Some people, he thought sagely, just never learn. If it works, don't try and fix it. And Norfolk worked.

He kissed the crown of Carmitha's head. 'When do you leave?'

'Tomorrow. Most of my family has already left. There is fruit-picking work in Hurst County. It pays well.'

'And after that?'

'We'll winter over in Holbeach. There are many deep caves in the cliffs above the town. And some of us get jobs in the harbour market gutting fish.'

'Sounds like a good life. Don't you ever want to settle down?'

She shrugged, thick hair sloshing about. 'Be like you, tied to your cold stone palace? No thanks. There might not be much to see in this world, but I want to see it all.'

'Better make the most of the time we've got, then.'

She crawled on top of him, calloused hands closing round his limp penis.

There was a pathetic scratching knock on the caravan's rear door. 'Sir? Are you there, sir?' William Elphinstone asked. The voice was as quavery as the knock.

Grant chopped back on an exasperated groan. *No, I'm not in here, that's why my bloody horse is outside.* 'What do you want?'

'Sorry to bother you, sir, but there's an urgent phone call for you at the house. Mr Butterworth said it was important, it's from Boston.'

Grant frowned. Butterworth wasn't going to send anyone after him unless it was genuinely important. The estate manager knew full well what he was up to at a slack time like this. He was also wily enough not to come looking himself.

I wonder what young Elphinstone has done to annoy him, Grant thought irreverently.

'Wait there,' he shouted. 'I'll be with you in a minute.' He deliberately took his time dressing. No damn way was he going to come dashing out of the caravan tucking his shirt into his trousers and give the lad something to tell all the other junior estate managers.

He straightened his tweed riding jacket, smoothed down his muttonchops with his hands, and settled his cap. 'How do I look?'

'Masterful,' Carmitha said from the bed.

There was no detectable irony. Grant fished around in his pocket and found two silver guineas. He dropped the gratuity into a big china bowl sitting on a shelf beside the door as he went out.

*

Louise watched her father and William Elphinstone ride up to the front door. Grooms appeared, and took charge of the horses.

From the way the animals were sweating it had been a hard ride. Her father hurried into the house.

Poor old Daddy, always busy.

She strolled over to where William was talking to the grooms, both boys younger than her. He saw her coming and dismissed them. Louise stroked the black stallion's flank as the big animal was led past her.

'Whatever is all the fuss about?' she asked.

'Some call from Boston. Mr Butterworth thought it important enough to send me out looking for your father.'

'Oh.' Louise started to move away. Rather annoyingly, William walked in step with her. She wasn't in the mood for company.

'I've been asked to the Newcombes' bash on Saturday evening,' he said. 'I thought it might be rather fun. They're not quite our people, but they set a decent table. There will be dancing afterwards.'

'That's nice.' Louise always hated it when William tried to put on graces. 'Our people' indeed! She went to school with Mary Newcombe.

'I hoped you would come with me.'

She looked at him in surprise. Eagerness and anxiety squabbled over his face. 'Oh, William, that's jolly nice of you to ask. Thank you. But I really can't. Sorry.'

'Really can't?'

'Well, no. The Galfords are coming to dinner on Saturday. I simply must be there.'

'I thought that perhaps now he's left, you might find more time for my company.'

'Now who's left?' she asked sharply.

'Your friend, the gallant starship captain.'

'William, you really are talking the most appalling tosh. Now I've said I can't attend the Newcombes' party with you. Kindly leave the subject.'

He stopped and took hold of her arm. She was too surprised to say anything. People simply did not take such liberties.

'You always found plenty of time for him,' he said in a flat tone.

'William, desist this instant.'

'Every day, it was. The two of you galloping off to Wardley Wood.'

Louise felt the blood rising to her cheeks. What did he know? 'Remove your hand from me. Now!'

'You didn't mind his hands.'

'William!'

He gave her a humourless smile and let go. 'I'm not jealous. Don't get me wrong.'

'There is nothing to be jealous of. Joshua Calvert was a guest and friend of my father's. That is the end of the matter.'

'Some fiancés would think otherwise.'

'Who?' she squawked.

'Fiancés, my dearest Louise. You must be aware there is some considerable speculation upon whom you are to marry. All I'm saying is that there are some Kesteven families of good breeding, and eligible sons, who would take exception to your . . . shall we call it, indiscretion.'

She slapped him. The sound rang across the lawn as her palm struck his cheek. 'How dare you!'

He dabbed at his cheek with the fingers of his right hand, a look of distaste on his face. The imprint of her palm was clearly etched in pink. 'What an impetuous creature you are, Louise. I had no idea.'

'Get out of my sight.'

'Of course, if that's what you wish. But you might like to consider that should word get out, your currently enviable position may well become less than secure. I don't want to see that happen, Louise, I really don't. You see, I am genuinely very fond of you. Fond enough to make allowances.'

She seemed utterly incapable of movement, condemned to

stand there in front of him, gaping in astonishment. 'You . . .' It came out in a crushed gasp. For a distressing instant she thought she was going to faint.

William knelt in front of her.

No, she thought, oh no no no, this can't be happening. Joshua bloody Calvert, where are you?

'Marry me, Louise. I can obtain your father's approval, have no fear of that. Marry me, and we can have a wonderful future together here at Cricklade.' He held his hand out, face soft with expectancy.

She drew herself up into the most regal pose she could manage. And very clearly, very calmly said: 'I would sooner shovel bullock manure for a living.' One of Joshua's better expressions, though admittedly not verbatim.

William paled.

She turned on a heel and walked away. Her back held straight.

'This is not the last time we shall pursue this topic,' he called after her. 'Believe me, dearest Louise, I will not be defeated in my suit for you.'

*

Grant Kavanagh sat himself down behind the desk in his study and picked up the phone. His secretary had put a call through to Trevor Clarke, Kesteven's lord lieutenant. Grant didn't like the implications of that one jot.

'I need you to bring Stoke's militia to Boston,' Trevor Clarke said as soon as they had exchanged greetings. 'A full turnout, please, Grant.'

'That might be difficult,' Grant said. 'This is still a busy time here. The rosegroves need pruning, and there's the second grain crop to drill. We can hardly take able men from the land.'

'Can't be helped. I'm calling in all the county militias.'

'All of them?'

''Fraid so, old chap. We've blacked it from the news, you

understand, but the situation in Boston, frankly, doesn't look good.'

'What situation? You're not seriously telling me that bloody Union rabble worries you?'

'Grant . . .' Trevor Clarke's voice dropped an octave. 'Listen, this is totally confidential, but there are already five districts in Boston that have been completely taken over by this mob, rendered ungovernable. We have a state of open insurrection here. If we send the police in to re-establish order they don't come out again. The city is under martial law, insofar as we can enforce it. I'm worried, Grant.'

'Dear Christ! The Democratic Land Union has done this?'

'We're not sure. Whoever these insurrectionists are, they seem to be armed with energy weapons. That means offplanet complicity. But it's hard to believe the Union could ever organize something like that. You know what they're like, hotheads smashing up tractors and ploughs. Energy weapons break every letter in our constitution; they are everything this society was set up to avoid.'

'An outside force?' Grant Kavanagh could hardly believe what he was hearing.

'It may be. I have asked the Chancellor's office in Norwich to request the Confederation Navy squadron extends its duty tour. Fortunately the personnel are all still here having their shore leave. The squadron commander is recalling them back up to orbit now.'

'What good is that?'

'The navy starships can make damn sure nothing else is delivered to the insurrectionists from outsystem. And as a last resort they can provide our ground forces with strike power.'

Grant sat perfectly still. Ground forces. Strike power. It was unreal. Through the windows he could see Cricklade's peaceful wolds, rich and verdant. And here he was calmly talking about virtual civil war. 'But God's teeth, man, this is a city we're talking about. You can't use starship weapons against Boston. There are a hundred and twenty thousand people living there.'

'I know,' Trevor Clarke said mordantly. 'One of the militia's major assignments will be to help evacuate the civilians. You will be minimizing casualties, Grant.'

'Have you told the Chancellor what you're planning? Because if you haven't, I damn well will.'

There was a silence which lasted for several seconds. 'Grant,' Trevor Clarke said gently, 'it was the Chancellor's office that recommended this action to me. It must be done while the insurrectionists are concentrated in one place, before they have a chance to spread their damnable revolution. So many people are joining them. I . . . I never thought there was so much dissatisfaction on the planet. It has to be stopped, and stopped in a way that forbids repetition.'

'Oh, my God,' Grant Kavanagh said brokenly. 'All right, Trevor, I understand. I'll call in the militia captains this afternoon. The regiment will be ready for you by tomorrow.'

'Good man, Grant. I knew I could rely on you. There will be a train to collect you from Colsterworth Station. We'll billet you in an industrial warehouse outside town. And don't worry, man, the starships are only a last resort. I expect we'll only need one small demonstration and they'll cave in.'

'Yes. I'm sure you're right.' Grant returned the pearl-handled phone to its cradle, a morbid premonition telling him it could never be that simple.

*

The train had six passenger carriages, room enough for all of the Stoke county militia's seven hundred men. It took them twenty-five minutes to embark. The station was a scene of pure chaos; half of the town's streets were clogged with carts, carriages, buses, and farm-ranger vehicles. Families took a long time saying goodbye. Men were shifty and irritable in their grey uniforms. Complaints about ill-fitting boots rippled up and down the platform.

Louise and Marjorie were pressed against the wall of the station with a pile of kitbags on one side, and olive-green metal ammunition boxes on the other. Some of the boxes had date stamps over ten years old. Three hard-faced men were guarding the ammunition, stumpy black guns cradled in their arms. Louise was beginning to regret coming, Genevieve hadn't been allowed.

Mr Butterworth, in his sergeant-major's uniform, marched up and down the platform, ordering people about. The train was gradually filled; work teams began to load the kitbags and ammunition into the first carriage's mail compartment.

William Elphinstone came down the platform, looking very smart in his lieutenant's uniform. He stopped in front of them. 'Mrs Kavanagh,' he said crisply. 'Louise. It looks like we're off in five minutes.'

'Well, you mind you take great care, William,' Marjorie said.

'Thank you. I will.'

Louise let her gaze wander away with deliberate slowness. William looked slightly put out, but decided this wasn't the time to make an issue of it. He nodded to Marjorie and marched off.

She turned to her daughter. 'Louise, that was extremely rude.'

'Yes, Mother,' Louise said unrepentantly. How typical of William to volunteer even though it wasn't his militia, she thought. He only did it to be covered in glory, so he would seem even more acceptable to Daddy. And he would never be in the front line sharing the risk with the poor common troops, not him. Joshua would.

Marjorie gave her daughter a close look at the unexpected tone, seeing the sulky stubborn expression on her usually placid face. So Louise doesn't like William Elphinstone. Can't say I blame her. But to be so public was totally out of character.

Louise's decorum was always meticulously formal and correct, gratingly so. Suddenly, despite all the worry of Boston, she felt delighted. Her daughter wasn't the meek-minded little mouse any more. She wanted to cheer out loud. And I wonder what started this episode of independent thinking, though I've a pretty shrewd idea. Joshua Calvert, if you laid one finger on her . . .

Grant Kavanagh strode vigorously along the side of the train, making sure his troops were settled and everything was in place. His wife and daughter were waiting dutifully at the end of the platform. Both of them quite divine, Marjorie especially.

Why do I bother with those little Romany tarts?

Louise's face was all melancholic. Frightened, but trying not to show it. Trying to be brave like a good Kavanagh. What a wonderful daughter. Growing up a treat. Even though she had been a bit moody these last few days. Probably missing Joshua, he thought jovially. But that was just another reminder that he really would have to start thinking seriously about a decent bloodmatch for her. Not yet though, not this year. Cricklade Manor would still echo with her laughter over Christmas, warming his heart.

He hugged her, and her arms wrapped round his waist. 'Don't go, Daddy,' she whispered.

'I have to. It won't be for long.'

She sniffed hard, and nodded. 'I understand.'

He kissed Marjorie, ignoring the whistles and cheers which rang out from the carriages at the rear of the train.

'Now don't you try and prove anything,' she said in that weary half-censorious way which meant she was scared to the core. So he said, 'Of course I won't, I'll just sit in the command tent and let the youngsters get on with it.'

Marjorie put her arm around Louise as they waved the train out of the station. The platform was a solid mass of women with handkerchiefs flapping from frantic wrists. She wanted to laugh at how silly they must all look to the men on the train.

But she didn't because she was a Kavanagh, and must set an example. Besides, she might have started crying at the futility and stupidity of it all.

In the clear sky above, silver lights flashed and twisted as the navy squadron changed formation and orbital inclination so that Boston was always in range to one of their number.

*

Dariat was nerving himself up to commit suicide. It wasn't easy. Suicide was the culmination of failure, of despair. Since the return of the dead from the realm of emptiness, his life had become inspiring.

He watched the couple make their cautious way down the starscraper's fetid stairwell. Kiera Salter had done well seducing the boy, but then what fifteen-year-old male could possibly resist Marie Skibbow's body? Kiera didn't even have to enhance the physique she had possessed. She just put on a mauve tank top and a short sky-blue skirt and let nature wreak havoc on the boy's hormone balance – as she had done with Anders Bospoort.

The monitoring sub-routine assigned to observe Horgan flowed through the neural cells behind the stairwell's polyp walls, spreading out through the surrounding sectors to interface with the starscraper's existing routines. An invisible, all-encompassing guardian angel. It was checking for threats, the possibility of danger. Horgan was another of Rubra's myriad descendants. Cosseted, privileged, and cherished; his mind silently, stealthily guided into the correct academic spheres of interest, and bequeathed a breathtaking arrogance for one so young. He had all the hallmarks of conceit endemic to Rubra's tragic protégés. Horgan was proud and lonely and foul tempered. A lanky youth with dark Asian skin, and giveaway indigo eyes, if his chromosomes had granted him the muscle weight to back up his narcissistic personality he would have been involved in as many fights as the young Dariat.

Naturally he admitted no surprise when Kiera/Marie confided her attraction to him. A girl like that was his due.

Kiera and Horgan stepped out of the stairwell onto the eighty-fifth-floor vestibule.

Dariat felt the monitoring routine flood into the apartment's stratum of neural cells and interrogate the autonomic routines within, reviewing local memories. This was the crux. It had taken him two days to modify the apartment's routines. None of his usual evasions had ever had to withstand examination by such a large personality sub-routine before, it was virtually sentient in its own right.

There was no alarm, no bugle for help to Rubra's principal consciousness. The monitor routine saw only an empty apartment waiting for Horgan.

'They are coming,' Dariat told the others in Anders Bospoort's bedroom. All three possessed were with him. Ross Nash who rode in Bospoort's own body, a Canadian from the early twentieth century. Enid Ponter, from the Australian-ethnic planet Geraldton, dead for two centuries, who occupied Alicia Cochrane's mortal form. And Klaus Schiller, possessing Manza Balyuzi's body, a German who muttered incessantly about his Führer, and seemingly angered at having to take on an Asian appearance. The body was now markedly different to the image contained in his passport flek the day he disembarked from the *Yaku*. His skin was blanching; jet-black hair streaked with expanding tufts of fine blond strands; the gentle facial features shifting to rugged bluntness, eyes azure blue. He had even grown a couple of centimetres taller.

'And Rubra?' Enid Ponter asked. 'Does he know?'

'My disruption routines have worked. The monitor can't see us.'

Ross Nash looked slowly round the bedroom, almost as though he was sniffing a trace of some exotic scent in the air. 'I sense it. Behind the walls, there is a coldness of heart.'

'Anstid,' Dariat said. 'That's what you sense. Rubra is just an aspect of him, a servant.'

Ross Nash made no attempt to hide his disgust.

None of them really trusted him, Dariat knew. They were strong enemies who had agreed a precarious truce because of the damage they could each inflict on the other. Such a stand-off could never last long. Human doubts and insecurities gnawed at such restraints, chafing at reasonableness. And the stakes on both sides were high, accelerating the devout need to see treachery in every hesitant breath and wary footstep.

But he would prove his worthiness as few had done before. Entrusting them with not merely his life, but his death as well. It was all so absurdly logical.

He needed their awesome powers of manifestation, and at the same time retain his affinity. Their power came from death, therefore he must die and possess a body with the affinity gene. So simple when you say it quick. And completely mad. But then what he had seen these last few days defied sanity.

Horgan and Kiera entered the apartment. They were kissing even as the door closed.

Dariat concentrated hard, his affinity strumming the new neural routines alive with a delicate harmony of deceit. The image of the twined figures was incorporated into one of them. An illusive fallacy; generated by a misappropriated section of the habitat's neural cells massing ten times that of the human brain. Small in relation to the total mass of the neural strata, but enough to make the illusion perfect, giving the phantom Horgan and Kiera weight and texture and colour and smell. Even body heat. The sensitive cells registered that as they started to tug each other's clothes off with the typical impatience of teenagers in lust.

Most difficult of all for Dariat to mimic was the constant flow of emotion and feeling Horgan emitted unconsciously into the affinity band. But he managed it, by dint of careful memory and composition. The monitor routine looked on with tranquil disinterest.

There was a split in Dariat's mind, like alternative quantum-cosmology histories, two realities diverging. In one, Horgan and Kiera raced for the bedroom, laughing, clothes flying. In the other . . .

Horgan's eyes blinked open in surprise. The kiss had delivered every promise her body made. He was primed for the greatest erotic encounter of his life. But now she was sneering contemptuously. And four other people were coming into the lounge from one of the bedrooms. Two of the men were huge, in opposite directions.

Horgan barely paid them any attention. He had heard of deals like this, whispered terrors amongst the kids in the day clubs. Snuffsense. The bitch had set him up as the meat they would rape to death. He turned, his leg muscles already taut.

Something – strange, like a hard ball of liquid – hit him on the back of the head. He was falling, and in the distance a choir of infernal angels was singing.

Dariat stood aside as Ross Nash hauled the semiconscious Horgan into the bedroom. He tried not to stare at the boy's feet, they were floating ten centimetres in the air.

'Are you ready?' Kiera asked, her tone dripping with disdain.

He walked past her into the bedroom. 'Do we get to screw afterwards?'

Dariat had favoured an old-fashioned capsule you swallowed rather than a transfusion pad or medical package. It was black – naturally – two centimetres long. He had acquired it from his regular narkhal supplier. A neurotoxin, guaranteed painless, she promised. As if he could complain if it wasn't.

He grinned at that. And swallowed, almost while his conscious mind was diverted. If it did hurt she was due for some very pointed lessons on consumer rights from an unexpected direction.

'Get on with it,' he told the figures grouped round the bed.

Tall and reedy, they were now, mud-brown effigies a sculptor had captured through a blurred lens. They bent over the spread-eagled boy and sent cold fire writhing up and down his spine.

The poison was fast acting. Guaranteed. Dariat was losing all feeling in his limbs. Sight greyed out. His hearing faded, which was a relief. It meant he didn't have to listen to all that screaming. 'Anastasia,' he muttered. How easy it would be to join her now. She only had a thirty-year head start, and what was that compared to infinity? He could find her.

Death.

And beyond.

A violent jerk of both body and mind. The universe blew away in all directions at once, horrifying in its immensity. Silence shrouded him; a silence he considered only possible in the extremity of intergalactic space. Silence without heat or cold, without touch or taste. Silence singing with thoughts.

He didn't look around. There was nothing to look with, nowhere to look, not in this, the sixth realm. But he knew, was aware of, what shared this state with him, the spirits Anastasia had told him about as they sat in her tepee so long ago.

Nebulous minds wept tears of emotion, their sorrow and lamentation splashing against him. And whole spectra of hatreds; jealousy and envy, but mostly self-loathing. They were spirits, all of them, lost beyond redemption.

Outside of this was colour, all around, but never present. Untouchable and taunting. A universe he was pleased to call real. The realm of the living. A wondrous, beautiful place, a corporeality crying out for belonging.

He wanted to beat against it, to demand entry. He had no hands, and there was no wall. He wanted to call to the living to rescue him. He had no voice.

'Help me!' his mind shrieked.

The lost spirits laughed cruelly. Their numbers pressed against him, vast beyond legion. He had no single defined location, he found, no kernel with a protective shell. He was everywhere at once, conjunctive with them. Helpless against their invasion. Lust and avarice sent them prising and clawing at his memories, suckling the sweet draught of sensations he contained. A poor substitute for intrinsicality, but still fresh, still juicy with detail. The only sustenance this arcane continuum boasted.

'Anastasia, help me.'

They adored his most shameful secrets, for they carried the strongest passion – stolen glances at women through the habitat sensitive cells, masturbating, the hopeless yearning for Anastasia, impossible promises made in the depth of night, hangovers, gluttony, glee as the club smashed against Mersin Columba's head, Anastasia's vital body hot against him, limbs locking together. They drank it all, deriding him even as they idolized him for the glimpse of life he brought.

Time. Dariat could sense it going by outside. Seconds, mere seconds had elapsed. Here, though, it had little relevance. Time was the length of every memory, governed by perception. Here it was defied as his rape went on and on. A rape which wasn't going to end. Not ever. There were too many of them for it to end.

He would have to abide by it, he realized in dread. And join in. Already he craved the knowledge of warmth, of touch, of smell. Memories of such treasures were all around. He had only to reach out—

*

The bedroom was damp and cold, its furniture cheap. But he couldn't afford anything more. Not now. The dismissal papers were still in his jacket pocket. The last pay packet was in there with it, but slim now. It had been fatter this afternoon. Before he went to the bar, doing what any man would.

Debbi was rising from the bed, blinking drowsily up at him. Voice like a fucking cat, complaining complaining complaining.

Where had he been with his no-good friends? Did he know what time it was? How much had he drunk? Like she always did.

So he told the bitch to shut up, because for once he was utterly pissed off with all the grief she gave him. And when she didn't quieten down he hit her. Even that didn't do it. She was shrieking real loud now, waking up the whole goddamn neighbourhood. So he hit her again, harder this time.

*

—to devour the pitiful echoes of sensation.

'Holy Anstid, help me your eternal servant. For pity's sake. Help!'

Laughter, only laughter. So he raged back and lost himself from the mockery in—

*

The sun glinting off the Inca temple that rose unchallenged into the sky. It was greater than any cathedral he had ever seen. But its builders were now a nation quelled before Spain's might. And the wealth inside the broken city was beyond that of kings. A life of glory awaited its conquerors.

His armour acted like a furnace in the heat. And the gash on his leg was host to strange brown pustular styes, spores of accursed jungle. Already he was frightened he wouldn't live to see Spain's shores again.

*

—which wasn't an answer. Calamity and pain were thin substitutes for the explosion of experience which lay in the vaguely perceived extrinsic universe.

Ten seconds. That was all the time that had passed there since he died. And how long had some of the spirits been here? How could they stand it—

*

Centuries which ache like a lover's heart laid still. To leech and leech what is new to find only that which is stale. Yet even such an insipid taste surpasses the hell which lies further from the taunting glimmer of the lost home of our flesh. Madness and dragons lie in wait for those that venture away from what we discern. Safer to stay. Safer to suffer the known rather than the unknown.

*

—Dariat could distinguish bursts of Horgan's pain, flashing into the nothingness of the sixth realm like flames licking through black timber. They came from where the spirits were clustered thickest, as though they were dogs fighting for scraps of the rarest steak.

Colours were stronger there, oozing through cracks that curved across dimensions. And the lost spirits howled in a unison of hatred, tempting and taunting Horgan to accede, to surrender. Maidens promised oceans of pleasure while malefactors threatened eternities of torment.

The cracks from which the rich slivers of pain emerged were growing wider as Kiera, Ross, Enid, and Klaus exerted their power.

'Mine,' Dariat proclaimed in defiance. 'He is mine. Prepared for me. He belongs to me.'

'No, mine.'

'Mine.'

'Mine.'

'Mine,' rose the cry.

'Kiera, Ross, help me. Let me come back.' He knew he could not stay here. Cool quiet darkness called, away from the universe of birth. Where Anastasia had gone, where they would meet again. To linger here with only the memories of yesterday's dreams as a reason was insanity. Anastasia was brave enough to venture forth. He could follow in her wake, unworthy though he was.

'Stop it, I beg,' Horgan called. 'Rescue me.'

The uniformity in which Dariat was suspended began to warp. A tight narrow funnel resembling a cyclone vortex that led down into the fathomless unknowable heart of a gas giant. Spirits were compelled towards it, into it. Dariat was one of them, pressed ever tighter against—

*

A poorly cobbled street with cottages on either side. It was raining hard. His bare feet were numb with cold. Wood smoke hung in the air, wisps from the chimneys swirled low by the wind. Water was soaking his ragged coat and making his cough worse. His thin chest vibrated as the air bucked in his throat. Ma had taken to giving him sad smiles whenever he told her how bad it felt inside.

Beside him his little sister was sniffling. Her face was barely visible below her woollen bonnet and above her coat collar. He held her hand in his as she tottered along unquestioningly. She looked so frail, worse than him. And winter was only just beginning. There never seemed to be enough broth; and the portions they had were made mostly from vegetables. It didn't fill the belly. Yet there was meat in the butchers.

Townsfolk walked along with them as the church bell pealed incessantly, summoning them. His sister's wooden clogs made dull rapping sounds against the cobbles. They were full with water, swelling her small white feet, and making the sores worse.

Da earned a good wage labouring in the squire's fields. But there was never extra money to spend on food.

The worn penny piece with Queen Victoria's face was clutched in his free hand. Destined for the smiling, warmly dressed pastor.

It just didn't seem right.

*

'Please,' Horgan called, weaker now, thoughts bruised by the pain.

Dariat slid in towards the boy. 'I'll help, I'll help,' he lied. Light trickled through from the far end of the tunnel, flickering and shifting, glowing like sunlight shining through stained glass into a dusty church. But the other spirits were promising the boy salvation as well—

*

Cold claimed the whole world. There was no such thing as warmth, not even inside his stiff, stinking furs. In the distance the ice wall glared a dazzling silver-white as the sun beat upon it. The others of the tribe were spread out across the grassy plain, sloshing their way through ice-mushed puddles. And glimpsed up ahead through the tall, swaying spires of grass was the mammoth.

*

'Come then, Dariat,' Ross Nash called.

Dariat saw his thoughts take form, become harder, as groping fingers of energy reached for him. He was strengthened from the touch, given weight, given volume; hurtling past the other spirits, victory rapturous in his mind. They howled and cursed as he was sucked down and down. Faster – in.

Even midnight-blackness was a sight to rejoice.

Eyelids blinked away tears of joy. Pain was glorious because it was real. He moaned at the wounds scored across his thin body, and felt a strange sensation of dry fluid bathe his skin. It flowed where his mind directed. So he put forth his will and watched the lacerations close. Yes!

Oh, my darling Anastasia, you were right all along. And always I doubted, at the core, in my secret spirit. What have I done?

Kiera smiled scornfully down at him. 'Now you will forget your feeble quest for revenge against Rubra, and work with us to capture Magellanic Itg's blackhawks with your affinity so we may spread ourselves across the stars. Because to lose now will mean returning to the incarceration of the beyond. You were there for fifteen seconds, Dariat. Next time it will be for ever.'

*

Ione didn't sleep. Her body was drowsy, and her eyelids were heavy enough to remain closed. But her mind floated at random through the habitat's perception images. She re-acquainted herself with favourite slices of landscape, checking on the residents as they slumbered or partied or worked their way through the small hours. Young children were already stirring, yawning staff arrived at the restaurants which served breakfast. Starships came and (a lower number than normal) went from the spaceport outside. A couple of oddball scavenger craft were rising slowly out of the Ruin Ring along Hohmann transfer orbits which would bring them to an eventual rendezvous with the habitat. Mirchusko was ninety per cent full, its ochre-on-saffron storm-bands bold against the starfield. Five of its seven major moons were visible, various lacklustre crescents strung out across the ring plane.

Far inside the gossamer ribbon of the Ruin Ring two dozen blackhawks were rushing towards the gas giant's equator on a mating flight. Three eggs had already been ejected into Mirchusko's thick inner rings. She listened to their awed, inquisitive exchanges with the blackhawks who had helped stabilize them; whilst racing on ahead their dying parent radiated sublime gratification.

Life goes on, Ione thought, even in dire times like these.

A sub-routine pervading the lakeside house warned her Dominique was approaching the bedroom. She dismissed the habitat perception and opened her eyes. Clement was lying on the furred air mattress beside her, mouth open, eyes tight shut, snoring softly.

Ione recalled the night fondly. He was a good lover, enthusiastic, knowledgeable, slightly selfish – but that was most likely due to his age. And for all the enjoyment, he wasn't Joshua.

The muscle membrane door opened to allow Dominique in. She was dressed in a short royal-purple robe, carrying a tray. 'So how was my little brother?' She leered down at the two naked bodies.

Ione laughed. 'Growing up big and strong.'

'Really? You should abolish incest, I could find out for myself then.'

'Ask the bishop. I only do civil and financial laws. Morals are all down to him.'

'Breakfast?' Dominique asked, perching on the end of the bed. 'I've got juice, toast, coffee, and quantat slices.'

'Sounds fine.' Ione nudged Clement awake, and ordered the window to clear. The glass lost its deep hazel tint to reveal the placid lake at the foot of the cliff. Tranquillity's axial light-tube was just starting to fluoresce its way up through the orange spectrum.

'Any word in about Laton?' Dominique asked. She sat cross-legged facing Ione and Clement, pouring juice and handing round toast.

'Nothing to add to what the navy voidhawk brought yesterday,' Ione said. It was one of the reasons she had turned to Clement, for the comfort of physical contact, the need to be wanted. She had accessed the Confederation Navy's classified report on the energy virus with growing concern.

As soon as Tranquillity reported the contents of Graeme Nicholson's flek she had placed an order for another ten strategic-defence platforms from the industrial stations orbiting outside the spaceport, supplementing the thirty-five which already protected the habitat. The companies were glad of the work, starship component manufacturing was slowing along with the declining number of flights. It didn't take a military genius to work out that Laton was going to try and spread his revolution; and Tranquillity was almost on a direct line between Lalonde and Earth, the core of the Confederation. The first pair of new platforms were nearly ready to deploy, with the rest being completed over another six days. And she was already wondering if she should order more.

Within an hour of the navy voidhawk delivering the warning flek from Trafalgar, she had hired twelve blackhawks to act as close-range patrol vessels, and equipped them with nuclear-armed combat wasps from Tranquillity's reserve stocks. She was thankful there were enough of the bitek craft available to charter. But then since her grandfather opened the habitat as a base for mating flights the blackhawks and their captains had been pretty loyal to Tranquillity and the Lord of Ruin.

What with the extra defences and the patrols, the habitat was developing a siege mentality in the wake of Terrance Smith's departure.

But were her precautions enough?

'How is the alert hitting the Vasilkovsky Line?' Ione asked.

Dominique took a drink of juice. 'Hard. We've got twenty-five ships idle in Tranquillity's dock right now. No merchant is going to risk sending cargo until they know for sure Laton isn't at the destination. Three of our captains arrived yesterday, all from different star systems. They all said the same thing. Planetary governments are virtually quarantining incoming starships, asteroid governments too. Give it another week, and interstellar trade will have shut down altogether.'

'They'll find the *Yaku* by then,' Clement said, tearing a corner off his toast. 'Hell, they've probably found it already. The navy voidhawk said it was a Confederationwide alert. No ship is ever more than ten days from a star system. I bet a navy squadron is blowing it to smithereens right now.'

'That's what gets me the most,' Ione said. 'No knowing, having to wait for days for any news.'

Dominique leant forwards and squeezed her knee. 'Don't worry. The 7th Fleet squadron will stop him from becoming involved. They'll all be back here in a week with their tails between their legs complaining they didn't get a chance to play soldier.'

Ione looked up into deep, surprisingly understanding eyes. 'Yeah.'

'He'll be all right. He's the only man I know who could lie his way out of a supernova explosion. Some leftover megalomaniac isn't going to be a problem.'

'Thanks.'

'Who?' Clement asked around a full mouth, looking from one girl to another.

Ione bit into a slice of her orange-coloured quantat. It had the texture of a melon, but tasted like spicy grapefruit. Dominique was grinning roguishly at her over a coffee-cup.

'Girls' talk,' Dominique said. 'You wouldn't understand.'

Clement threw a quantat rind at her. 'It's Joshua. You've both got the hots for him.'

'He's a friend,' Ione said. 'And he's in way over his silly little head, and we're worried about him.'

'Don't be,' Clement said briskly. 'Joshua showed me round the *Lady Macbeth.* She's got more combat potential than a front-line frigate, and Smith armed her with combat wasps before they left. Anyone damn stupid enough to go up against *that* starship is dead meat.'

Ione gave him a kiss. 'Thank you, too.'

'Any time.'

They ate the rest of their breakfast in companionable peace. Ione was debating what to do for the rest of the day when Tranquillity called. That was the thing with being the absolute ruler of a bitek habitat, she reflected, you don't really have to *do* anything, thoughts were acted on instantly. But there was the human side to consider. The Chamber of Trade was nervous, the Financial and Commerce Council more so, ordinary people didn't know what was going on. Everybody wanted reassurance, and they expected her to provide it. She had done two interviews with news companies yesterday, and there were three delegations who wanted personal audiences.

Parker Higgens is requesting an immediate interview, Tranquillity told her as she was finishing her coffee. **I recommend you grant it.**

Oh, you do, do you? Well, I think there are more important things for me to attend to right now.

I believe this to be more important than the Laton crisis.

What? It was the ambiguity which made her sit up straighter on the furry bed. Tranquillity was emitting a strong impression of discomfort, as if it was unsure of a subject. Unusual enough to intrigue her.

There has been some remarkable progress with the Laymil sensorium recordings in the last seventy hours. I did not wish to trouble you with the project while you were involved with upgrading my defence and soothing the residents. That may have been my mistake. Last night some of the researchers made an extremely important find.

Which is? she asked avidly.

They believe they have located the Laymil home planet.

*

The path leading from the tube station to the octagonal Electronics Division building was littered with ripe bronze berries fallen from the tall chuantawa trees. They crunched softly as Ione's shoes helped flatten them further into the stone slabs.

Project staff emerging from the stations gave her the faintly guilty glance of all workers arriving early and finding the boss already in.

Oski Katsura greeted her at the entrance, dressed in her usual white lab smock, one of the few people in the habitat who never seemed perturbed by Ione's escort of serjeants. 'We haven't made an announcement yet,' she said as they went inside. 'Some of the implications are only just sinking in.'

The hall where the Laymil stack was kept had changed considerably since Ione's first visit. Most of the experimental electronic equipment had been cleared out. Processor blocks and AV projectors were lined up along the benches, forming individual research stations, each with a rack of fleks. Workshop cubicles behind the glass wall had been converted into offices. The impression was one of academic endeavour rather than out and out scientific pioneering.

'We use this mainly as a sorting centre now,' Oski Katsura said. 'As soon as they have been decrypted, the sensorium memories are individually reviewed by a panel of experts drawn from every discipline we have here at the project. They provide a rough initial classification, cataloguing incidents and events depicted, and decide if there is anything which will interest their profession. After that the relevant memory is datavised to an investigatory and assessment committee which each division has formed. As you can imagine, most of it has been sent to the Cultural and Psychology divisions. But even seeing their electronics used in the intended context of mundane day-to-day operation has been immensely useful to us here. And the same goes for most of the physical disciplines – engineering, fusion, structures. There's something in most memories for all of us. I'm afraid a final and exhaustive analysis is going to take a couple of decades at least. All we are doing for now is providing a preliminary interpretation.'

Ione nodded silent approval. Tranquillity's background memories were revealing how hard the review teams were working.

There were only five other people in the hall, as well as Lieria. They had all been working through the night, and now they were clustered round a tray from the canteen, drinking tea and eating croissants. Parker Higgens rose as soon as she came in. His grey suit jacket was hanging off the back of one of the chairs, revealing a crumpled blue shirt. All-night sessions were obviously something the old director was finding increasingly difficult to manage. But he proffered a tired smile as he introduced her to the other four. Malandra Sarker and Qingyn Lin were Laymil spaceship experts, she a biotechnology systems specialist, while his field was the mechanical and electrical units the xenocs employed in their craft. Ione shook hands while Tranquillity silently supplied profile summaries of the two. Malandra Sarker struck her as being young for the job at twenty-eight, but she had her doctorate from the capital university on Quang Tri, and references which were impeccable.

Ione knew Kempster Getchell, the Astronomy Division's chief; they had met during the first round of briefings, and on several formal social occasions since then. He was in his late sixties, and from a family which lacked any substantial geneering. But despite entropy's offensive, leaving him with greying, thinning hair, and a stoop to his shoulders, he projected a lively puckish attitude, the complete opposite to Parker Higgens. Astronomy was one of the smallest divisions in the Laymil project, concerned mainly with identifying stars which had Laymil-compatible spectra, and searching through radio astronomy records to see if any abnormality had ever been found to indicate a civilization. Despite frequent requests, no Lord of Ruin had ever agreed to fund the division's own radio-telescope array. They had to make do with library records from universities across the Confederation.

Kempster Getchell's assistant was Renato Vella, a swarthy thirty-five-year-old from Valencia, on a four-year sabbatical from one of its universities. He acted both excited and awed when Ione greeted him. She wasn't quite sure if it was her presence or their discovery which instigated his jitters.

'The Laymil home planet?' Ione asked Parker Higgens, permitting a note of scepticism to sound.

'Yes, ma'am,' the director said. The joy that should have been present at making the announcement was missing, he seemed more apprehensive than triumphant.

'Where is it?' she asked.

Parker Higgens traded a pleading glance with Kempster Getchell, then sighed. 'It used to be here, in this solar system.'

Ione counted to three. 'Used to be?'

'Yes.'

Tranquillity? What is going on?

Although it is an extraordinary claim, the evidence does appear to be slanted in their favour. Allow them to complete their explanation.

All right. 'Go on.'

'It was a recording that was translated two days ago,' Malandra Sarker said. 'We found we had got the memory of a Laymil spaceship crew-member. Naturally we were delighted, it would give us a definite blueprint for one of their ships, inside and out, as well as the operating procedures. Up until now all we've had is fragments of what we thought were spaceship parts. Well we found out what a Laymil ship looks like all right.' She datavised one of the nearby processor blocks; its AV pillar shone an image into Ione's eyes.

The Laymil ship had three distinct sections. At the front were four white-silver metal ovoids; the large central unit was thirty metres long, with the three twenty-metre units clustered around it – obviously life-support cabins. The midsection was drum shaped, its sides made up from interlaced stone-red pipes packed so tightly there was no chink between them, an almost intestinal configuration. Five black heat-radiation tubes protruded at right angles from its base, spaced equally around the rim. At the rear was a narrow sixty-metre-long tapering fusion tube, with slim silver rings running along its length at five-metre intervals. Right at the tip, around the plasma exhaust nozzle, was a silver foil parasol.

'Is it organic?' Ione asked.

'We think about eighty per cent,' Qingyn Lin said. 'It matches what we know of their use of biotechnology.'

Ione turned away from the projection.

'It is a passenger ship,' Malandra Sarker said. 'From what we can make out, the Laymil didn't have commercial cargo ships, although there are some tankers and specialist industrial craft.'

'This would seem to be correct,' Lieria said, speaking through the small white vocalizer block held in one of her tractamorphic arms. 'The Laymil at this cultural stage did not have economic commerce. Technical templates and DNA were exchanged between clan units, but no physical or biotechnology artefacts were traded for financial reward.'

'The thing is,' Malandra Sarker said, sinking down into a chair, 'it was leaving a parking orbit around their home planet to fly to Mirchusko's spaceholms.'

'We always wondered why the ship fuel tanks we found were so large,' Qingyn Lin said. 'There was far too much deuterium and He_3 stored for simple inter-habitat voyages, even if they made fifteen trips in a row without refuelling. Now we know. They were interplanetary spaceships.'

Ione gave Kempster Getchell a questioning look. 'A planet? Here?'

A wayward smile formed on his lips, he appeared indecently happy about the revelation. 'It does look that way. We checked the star and planet positions gathered from the spacecraft's sensor array most thoroughly. The system we saw is definitely this one. The Laymil home planet used to orbit approximately one hundred and thirty-five million kilometres from the star. That does put it rather neatly between the orbits of Jyresol and Boherol.' He pouted sadly. 'And here I've spent thirty years of my life looking at stars with spectra similar to this one. All the time it was right under my nose. God, what a waste. Still, I'm back on the cutting edge of astrophysics now, and no mistake. Trying to work out how you make a planet disappear . . . ho, boy.'

'All right,' Ione said with forced calm. 'So where is it now? Was it destroyed? There isn't an asteroid belt between Jyresol and Boherol. There isn't even a dust belt as far as I know.'

'There is no record of any extensive survey being made of this system's interplanetary medium,' Kempster said. 'I checked our library. But even assuming the planet had literally been reduced to dust, the solar wind would have blown the majority of particles beyond the Oort cloud within a few centuries.'

'Would a survey now help?' she asked.

'It might be able to confirm the dust hypothesis, if the density is still higher than is usual. But it would depend on when the planet was destroyed.'

'It was here two thousand six hundred years ago,' Renato Vella said. 'We know that from analysing the position of the other planets at the time the memory was recorded. But if we are to look for proof of the dust I believe we would be better off taking surface samples from Boherol and the gas giant moons.'

'Good idea, well done, lad,' Kempster said, patting his younger assistant on the shoulder. 'If this wave of dust was expelled outwards then it should have left traces on all the airless bodies in the system. Similar to the way sediment layers in planetary core samples show various geological epochs. If we could find it, we would get a good indication of when it actually happened as well.'

'I don't think it was reduced to dust,' Renato Vella said.

'Why not?' Ione asked.

'It was a valid idea,' he said readily. 'There aren't many other ways you can make something that mass disappear without trace. But it's a very theoretical solution. In practical terms the energy necessary to dismantle an entire planet to such an extent is orders of magnitude above anything the Confederation could muster. You have to remember that even our outlawed antimatter planetbuster bombs don't harm or ablate the mass of a terracompatible-sized planet, they just wreck and pollute the biosphere. In any case an explosion – multiple explosions even – wouldn't do the trick, they would just reduce it to asteroidal fragments. To turn it into dust or preferably vapour you would need some form of atomic disrupter weapon, probably powered by the star – I can't think what else would produce enough energy. That or a method of initiating a fission chain reaction in stable atoms.'

'Perfect mass–energy conversion,' Kempster muttered, his eyebrows beetled in concentration. 'Now there's an idea.'

'And why wasn't the same method used against the Laymil habitats?' Renato Vella said, warming to his theme. 'If you have a weapon which can destroy a planet so thoroughly as to eradicate all traces of it, why leave the remnants of the habitats for us to find?'

'Yes, yes, why indeed?' Kempster said. 'Good point, lad, well done. Good thinking.'

His assistant beamed.

'We still think the habitats destroyed themselves,' Parker Higgens said. 'It fits what we know, even now.' He looked at Ione, visibly distressed. 'I think the memory may show the start of the planet's destruction. There is clearly some kind of conflict being enacted on the surface as the ship leaves orbit.'

'Surely that was an inter-clan dispute, wasn't it?' Qingyn Lin asked dubiously. 'That's what it sounded like to me.'

'You are all mistaken in thinking of this problem purely in terms of the physical,' Lieria said. 'Consider what we now know. The planet is confirmed to have been in existence at the same time the habitats were broken. The Laymil entity whose memory we have accessed is concerned about the transformation in the life-harmony gestalt which is being propagated across an entire continent. A drastic metaphysical change which threatens nothing less than the entire Laymil racial orientation. Director Parker Higgens is correct, these events cannot be discounted as coincidence.'

Ione glanced round the group. None of them looked as though they wished to contradict the Kiint. 'I think I'd better review this memory myself.' She sat in the chair next to Malandra Sarker. **Show me.**

As before, the Laymil body hardened around her own, an exoskeleton which did not – could never – fit. The recording quality was much higher than before. Oski Katsura and her team had been working long hours on the processors and programs required to interpret the stored information. There were hardly any of the black specks which indicated fragmentary data drop-outs. Ione relaxed deeper into the chair as the sensorium buoyed her along.

The Laymil was a shipmaster, clan-bred for a life traversing the barren distance between the spaceholm constellation and Unimeron, the prime lifehost. It hung at the hub of the ship's central life-support ovoid as the drive was readied for flight. There was nothing like the human arrangement of decks and machinery, present even in voidhawks. The protective metal shell contained a biological nest-womb, a woody growth honeycombed with chambers and voyage-duration pouches for travellers, creating an exotic organic grotto. Chambers were clustered together without logic, like elongated bubbles in a dense foam; the walls had the texture of tough rubber, pocked with hundreds of small holes to restrain hoofs, and emitting a fresh green radiance. Organs to maintain the atmosphere and recycle food were encased in the thicker partitions.

The all-pervasive greenness was subtly odd to Ione's human brain. Tubular buttress struts curved through the chamber around the Laymil body, flaring out where they merged with a wall. Its three hoofs were pushed into holes, buttocks resting on a grooved mushroom-stool; its hands were closed on knobby protrusions. A teat stalactite hung centimetres from the feeding mouth. The position was rock solid and immensely comfortable, the nest-womb had grown into a flawlessly compatible layout with the shipmaster's body. All three heads slid around in slow weaving motions, observing small opaque composite instrument panels that swelled out of the wall. Ione found it hard to tell where the plastic began and the cells ended; the cellular/mechanical fusion was seamless, as though the womb-nest was actually growing machinery. Panel-mounted lenses projected strange graphics into the Laymil's eyes, in a fashion similar to human AV projectors.

As the heads moved they provided snatched glimpses into

other chambers through narrow passageways. She saw one of the Laymil passengers cocooned in its voyage-duration pouch. It was swaddled in translucent glittery membranes that held it fast against the wall, and a waxy hose supplying a nutrient fluid had been inserted into its mouth, with a similar hose inserted into its anus, maintaining the digestive cycle. A mild form of hibernation.

The Laymil shipmaster's thoughts were oddly twinned, as though the recording was of two separate thought patterns. On a subsidiary level it was aware of the ship's biological and mechanical systems. It controlled them with a processor's precision, preparing the fusion tube for ignition, maintaining attitude through small reaction thrusters, computing a course vector, surveying the four nest-wombs. There was a similarity here to the automatic functions a human's neural nanonics would perform; but as far as she could ascertain the shipmaster possessed no implants. This was the way its brain was structured to work. The ship's biotechnology was sub sentient, so, in effect, the shipmaster was the flight computer.

On an ascendant level its mind was observing the planet below through the ship's sensor faculty. Unimeron was remarkably similar to a terracompatible world, with broad blue oceans and vast white cloud swirls, the poles home to smallish icecaps. The visual difference was provided by the continents; they were a near-uniform green, even the mountain ranges had been consumed by the vegetation layer. No piece of land was wasted.

Vast blue-green cobweb structures hung in orbit, slightly below the ship's thousand-kilometre altitude. These were the skyhavens, most two hundred kilometres in diameter, some greater, rotating once every five or more hours, not for artificial gravity but simply to maintain shape. They were alive, conscious with vibrant mentalities, greater than that of a spaceholm even. A combination of spaceport and magnetosphere energy node, with manufacturing modules clumped around the hub like small bulbous tangerine barnacles. But the physical facets were just supplementary to their intellectual function. They formed an important aspect of the planet's life-harmony, smoothing and weaving the separate continental essence thoughts into a single unified planetwide gestalt. Mental communication satellites, though they contributed to the gestalt as well, and sang to distant stars. That voice was beyond Ione completely, both its message and its purpose, registering as just a vague cadence on the threshold of perception. She felt a little darker for its absence, the Laymil shipmaster considered it magnificent.

The skyhavens were packed close together, with small variants in altitude, allowing them to slide along their various orbital inclinations without ever colliding. No segment of the planet's sky was ever left open. It was an amazing display of navigational exactitude. From a distance it looked as though someone had cast a net around Unimeron. She tried to gauge the effort involved in their growth, a planet-girdling structure, and failed. Even for a species with such obvious biotechnology and engineering supremacy the skyhavens were an awesome achievement.

'**Departure initiation forthcoming**,' the shipmaster called.

'**Venture boldness reward**,' the skyhaven essence replied. '**Anticipate hope**.'

Unimeron's terminator was visible now, blackness biting into the planet. Nightside continents were studded with bright green lightpoints, smaller than human cities, and very regular. One southern continent, curving awkwardly around the planet's mass away from the ship's sensors, had delicate streamers of phosphorescent red mist meandering along its coastal zones with exploratory tendrils creeping further inland. The edges were visibly palpitating like the fringes of a terrestrial jellyfish as they curled and flowed around surface features, yet all the while retaining a remarkable degree of integrity. There was none of the braiding or churning of ordinary clouds. Ione considered the effect quite delightful, the mist looked alive, as though the air currents were infected with biofluorescent spoors.

But the Laymil shipmaster was physically repelled by the sight. '**Galheith clan essence asperity woe.**' His heads bobbed around in agitation, letting out low hoots of distress. '**Woe. Folly acknowledgement request.**'

'**No relention,**' the skyhaven essence answered sadly.

As their orbits took them over the continent, the skyhavens would hum in dismay. The life-harmony of Unimeron was being disrupted, with the skyhavens refusing to disseminate the Galheith clan essence into the gestalt. It was too radical, too antagonistic. Too different. Alien and antithetical to the harmony ethos that had gone before.

A tiny flare of sharp blue-white light sprang out of the red mist, dying down quickly.

'**Reality dysfunction,**' the shipmaster called in alarm.

'**Confirm.**'

'**Horror woe. Galheith research death essence tragedy.**'

'**Concord.**'

'**Impetuosity woe release. Reality dysfunction exponential. Prime lifehost engulfed fear.**'

'**Reality dysfunction counter. Spaceholm constellation prime essence continuation hope.**'

'**Confirm. Hope carriage.**' The shipmaster quickly reviewed the other Laymil hibernating in the nest-wombs; both mental traits converging for the evaluation. '**Essencemasters condition satisfactory. Hope reality dysfunction defeat. Hope Galheith atonement.**'

'**Hope joined. Rejoice unity commitment.**'

Where the flare of light had sprung, the jungle was now alight. Ione realized the glimmer of orange must be a firestorm easily over ten kilometres wide.

The spaceship was crossing the terminator. Skyhavens ahead glowed a fragile platinum as the Van Allen radiation belt particles gusted across their web strands.

'**Departure initiation**,' the shipmaster announced. Ionized fuel was fired into the fusion drive's magnetic pinch. A jet of plasma slowly built up. Information streamed into the Laymil's brain, equations were performed, instructions were pushed into the nest-womb's neurons and the coincident hardware's circuits. There was never any doubt, any self-questioning. The terms did not apply.

Unimeron began to shrink behind the ship. The shipmaster focused his attention on the spaceholm constellation, and the frail song of welcome it emitted, so much quieter than the prime lifehost's joyous spirit.

And the memory expired.

Ione blinked free of the stubbornly persistent, green-polluted images. Emotions and sensations were harder to discard.

'What is a reality dysfunction?' she asked. 'The shipmaster seemed frightened half to death by it.'

'We don't know,' Parker Higgens said. 'There has never been any reference to it in any of the other memories.'

'Ione Saldana, I believe the term reality dysfunction refers to a massive malevolent violation within the Laymil life-harmony essence,' Lieria said. 'The nature of the Galheith clan was being radically altered by it. However, the impression conveyed by the memory is that it is more than a mental reorientation, it also incorporated a distortion within the local physical matrix. Example: the energy flare.'

'It was a weapon?' She shot a tense glance at the two astronomers.

Kempster scratched at his shadow of stubble. 'That flare definitely started a fire, so I would have to say yes. But one forest fire is a little different from something which can cause a planet to vanish.'

'If it went on to spread through the entire planet's life essence, as seems more than likely,' Malandra Sarker said, 'then it would have Unimeron's entire technical resources at its disposal. Placed on a war footing, a race like that would have a frightening armaments-production wherewithal.'

'I disagree,' Renato Vella said. 'Granted they could build fleets of ships, and hundreds of thousands of nukes, probably antimatter too. But they are not that much further advanced than us. I still maintain the energy required to destroy a planet is beyond this level of technology.'

I was just thinking of the Alchemist, Ione said to Tranquillity. She was almost afraid to mention it in case Lieria could intercept the thought. **What was it Captain Khanna said? One idea in a lifetime is all it takes. The Laymil might not have had the initial physical resources, but what about the mental potential of a planetary mind devoted to weapons design?**

The possibility is an alarming one, Tranquillity agreed. **But why would they turn it on themselves?**

Good question. 'Even if they built a weapon, why would they turn it on themselves?'

The group regarded her with puzzled faces – a child innocently flooring adult logic with a simple question. Then Renato Vella smiled suddenly. 'We've been assuming it was destroyed, how about if they just moved it instead?'

Kempster Getchell chuckled. 'Oh my boy, what a wonderful notion.'

'I bet it would require less energy than obliteration.'

'Good point, yes.'

'And we've seen they can build massive space structures.'

'We are evading the point,' Parker Higgens said sternly. 'We believe this reality dysfunction, whatever it is, is behind both the removal of the Laymil planet and the suicide of the spaceholms. Our priority now has to be to establish what it was, and if it still exists.'

'If the planet was moved, then the reality dysfunction is still around,' Renato Vella said, refusing to be deflected. 'It is wherever the planet is.'

'Yes, but what is it?' Oski Katsura asked with some asperity.

'It seems to be many things, some kind of mental plague and a weapon system at the same time.'

'Oh shit,' Ione said out loud as she and Tranquillity made the connection simultaneously. 'Laton's energy virus.'

Tranquillity allowed the group to access the report from Dr Gilmore through the hall's communication net processors, giving the images direct to Lieria via affinity.

'My God,' Parker Higgens said. 'The similarities are startling.'

'Similarities, hell,' Kempster half-shouted. 'That fucker's come back!'

The director flinched at the astronomer's coarse anger. 'We can't be sure.'

'I'm sorry, Parker, but I cannot in all sincerity consider this to be a coincidence,' Ione told him.

'I concur,' Lieria said.

'The Confederation, specifically the First Admiral, must be informed immediately,' Ione said. 'That goes without question. The navy must understand that they are not facing Laton himself but something far more serious. Parker, you will act as my representative in this matter; you have both the authority and knowledge necessary to convey the severity of this reality dysfunction to the First Admiral.'

He looked shocked at first, then bowed. 'Yes, ma'am.'

'Oski, prepare copies of every Laymil memory we have. The rest of you put down what observations you can for the navy staff, whatever you think may help. Tranquillity is recalling one of the patrol blackhawks now, it will be ready to leave for Avon in an hour. I will ask the Confederation Navy office to provide an officer to escort you, Parker, so you had better get ready. Time is important here.'

'Yes, ma'am.'

Ione Saldana, I also request a blackhawk to convey one of my colleagues home to Jobis, Lieria said. **I judge these events to be of sufficient portent to warrant informing my race.**

Yes, of course. She was aware of Tranquillity summoning a second armed blackhawk back to the docking-ledges even as she acknowledged the Kiint's request. All the remaining resident blackhawks would have to be conscripted for patrol duties now, she thought tersely, probably the independent traders too. Then a stray thought struck. **Lieria, did the Kiint ever hear the skyhavens' starsong?**

Yes.

The finality of the tone stopped Ione from enquiring further. But only for now, she promised herself. I've had enough of this mystic superiority crap they keep peddling. 'Kempster, that red mist over Unimeron's southern continent, was that a part of the reality dysfunction, do you think? There's no mention of it being present on Lalonde.'

'Its nature would suggest so,' Kempster said. 'I can't see that it's a natural phenomenon, not even on that planet. Possibly a secondary effect, a by-product of the interaction with Unimeron's life essence, but definitely connected. Wouldn't you agree, lad?'

Renato Vella had been lost in deep contemplation ever since he accessed Dr Gilmore's report. Now he nodded briefly. 'Yes, it is likely.'

'Something on your mind?' the old astronomer asked, his cheerfulness reasserting itself.

'I was just thinking. They could build living space structures that completely encircled their world, yet this reality dysfunction still defeated them. Their spaceholms were so frightened of it they committed suicide rather than submit. What do you think is going to happen to us when we confront it?'

26

'Jesus, what's all that red gunk in the air? I don't remember that from the last time we were here. It's almost as if it's glowing. The bloody stuff's covering the whole of the Juliffe tributary network, look.' Joshua abandoned the *Lady Mac*'s sensor input and turned to Melvyn Ducharme on the acceleration couch next to his.

'Don't look at me, I'm just a simple fusion engineer. I don't know anything about meteorology. Try the mercs, they're all planet-bred.'

'Humm,' Joshua mused. Relations between the *Lady Mac*'s crew and the mercenary scout team they were carrying hadn't been exactly optimal during the voyage. Both sides kept pretty much to themselves, with Kelly Tirrel acting as diplomatic go-between – when she was out of the free-fall sex cage. That girl had certainly lived up to her side of the bargain, he thought contentedly.

'Anybody care to hazard a guess?' he called.

The rest of the crew on the bridge accessed the images, but no one volunteered an opinion.

Amarisk was slowly turning round into their line of sight as they closed on the planet. Nearly half of the continent was already in daylight. From where they were, still a hundred thousand kilometres out, the Juliffe and most of its tributaries were smothered in a nebulous red haze. At first inspection it had looked as though some unique refraction effect was making the water gleam a bright burgundy. But once the *Lady Mac*'s long-range optical sensors were focused on Lalonde, that notion had quickly been dispelled. The effect was caused by thousands of long narrow cloud bands in the air above the surface of the water, clinging to the tributary network's multiple fork pattern with startling accuracy. Although, Joshua realized, the bands were much broader than the actual rivers themselves; where the first band started, just inland from the mouth of the Juliffe, it was almost seventy kilometres across.

'I've never seen anything like it on any planet,' Ashly said flatly. 'Weird stuff; and it is glowing, Joshua. You can see it stretching beyond the terminator, all the way to the coast.'

'Blood,' Melvyn intoned solemnly. 'The river's awash with blood, and it's starting to evaporate.'

'Shut it,' Sarha snapped. The idea was too close to the thoughts bubbling round in her own mind. 'That's not funny.'

'Do you think it's hostile?' Dahybi asked. 'Something of Laton's?'

'I suppose it must be connected with him,' Joshua admitted uneasily. 'But even if it is hostile, it can't harm us at this distance. It's strictly lower atmosphere stuff. Which means it may be a hazard for the merc scouts, though. Sarha, tell them to access the image, please.' They were less likely to insult a woman.

A grumbling Sarha requested a channel to the lounge in capsule C where the seven mercenary scouts and Kelly Tirrel were lying on acceleration couches as the *Lady Mac* accelerated in towards Lalonde. There was a gruff acknowledgment from her AV pillar, and Joshua grinned in private.

The flight computer alerted him that a coded signal was being transmitted from the *Gemal*. 'We've detected an unknown atmospheric phenomenon above Amarisk,' Terrance Smith said pedantically.

'Yeah, those red clouds sticking to the tributaries,' Joshua answered. 'We see it too. What do you want us to do about it?'

'Nothing yet. As far as we can make out it is simply polluted cloud, presumably coming from the river itself. If a sensor sweep shows it to be radioactive then we will reassess the landing situation. But until then, proceed as ordered.'

'Aye, aye, Commodore,' Joshua grunted when the channel was closed.

'Polluted cloud,' Melvyn said in contempt.

'Biological warfare,' Ashly suggested in a grieved tone. 'Not nice. Typical of Laton, mark you. But definitely not nice.'

'I wonder if it's his famed proteanic virus?' Dahybi said.

'Doubt it, that was microscopic. And it didn't glow in the dark, either. I'd say it has to be radioactive dust.'

'Then why isn't the wind moving it?' Sarha asked. 'And how did it form in the first place?'

'We'll find out in due course,' Warlow said with his usual pessimism. 'Why hurry the process?'

'True enough,' Joshua agreed.

The *Lady Mac* was heading in towards the planet at a steady one gee. As soon as each ship in the little fleet had emerged from its final jump into the Lalonde system, it had accelerated away from the coordinate, the whole fleet spreading out radially at five gees to avoid presenting an easy target grouping. Now they were holding a roughly circular formation twenty thousand kilometres wide, with *Gemal* and the cargo ships at the centre.

The six blackhawks were already decelerating into low orbit above Lalonde to perform a preliminary threat assessment. Bloody show-offs, Joshua thought. *Lady Mac* could easily match their six gee manoeuvres if she wasn't encumbered with escort duties.

Even with naval tactics programs running in primary mode, Terrance Smith was ever cautious. The lack of any response from Durringham was extremely bad news, although admittedly half anticipated. What had triggered the fleet commander's paranoia was the total absence of any orbital activity. The colonist-carrier starships had gone, along with the cargo ships. The inter-orbit craft from Kenyon were circling inertly in a five-hundred-kilometre equatorial parking orbit, all systems powered down – even their navigation beacons, which was contrary to every CAB regulation in the flek. Of the sheriff's office's ageing observation satellite there was no trace. Only the geosynchronous communication platform and civil spaceflight traffic monitoring satellites remained active, their on-board processors sending out monotonously regular signals. He lacked the transponder interrogation code to see if the navy ELINT satellites were functional.

After a quick appraisal, Smith had ordered a descent into a thousand-kilometre orbit. His fleet moved in, the combat-capable starships dumping small satellites in their wake to form an extensive high-orbit gravitonic-distortion-detector network. If any starship emerged within five hundred thousand kilometres of the planet, the satellites would spot it.

The blackhawks released a quintet of military-grade communication satellites as they raced towards the planet. Ion engines pushed the comsats into geostationary orbit, positioning them to give complete coverage of the planet, with overlapping reception footprints covering Amarisk in its entirety.

Twenty thousand kilometres out from Lalonde, the blackhawks split into two groups and swept into a seven-hundred-kilometre orbit at differing inclinations. Each of them released a batch of fifteen observation satellites, football-sized globes that decelerated further, lowering themselves into a two-hundred-kilometre orbit; their parallel tracks provided a detailed coverage sweep over a thousand kilometres wide. The blackhawks themselves, with their powerful sensor blisters augmented by electronic scanner pods, were integrated into the effort to reconnoitre Durringham and the Juliffe tributary basin. The intention was to compile a comprehensive survey with a resolution below ten centimetres for the mercenary scouts to use.

'It's virtually impossible,' Idzerda, the captain of the blackhawk *Cyanea*, told Terrance Smith after the first pass. 'That red cloud is completely opaque, except for the edges where it thins out, and even there the images we're receiving of the land below are heavily distorted. I'm not even sure cloud is the word for it. It doesn't move like cloud should. It's almost as if a film of electrophorescent cells has been solidified into the air. Spectrographic analysis is useless with that light it emits. One thing we have noticed; we ran a comparison with the old cartography memory from the sheriff's observation satellite which you supplied. The cloud is brightest over towns and villages. Durringham shines like there's a star buried under there. There is no way of telling what is going on below it. The only villages we can even see are the ones furthest up the tributaries where the glow peters out. And they are wrong.'

'Wrong?' Terrance Smith asked.

'Yes. They're the most recently settled, the most primitive ones, right?'

'Yes.'

'We've seen stone houses, gardens, domelike structures, metalled roads, heck, even windmills. None of it was there on the old images you gave us, and they were only recorded a month ago.'

'That can't possibly be correct,' Terrance said.

'I know that. So either the whole lot are holograms, or it's an illusion loaded directly into the observation satellite processors by this electronic warfare gimmick you warned us about. Although we can't see how it disrupts the blackhawks' optical sensors as well. The people who put up that cloud have got some startlingly potent projection techniques. But why bother? That's what we don't understand. What's the point of these illusions?'

'What about power emission centres?' Terrance Smith asked.

'It must take a lot of energy to generate a covering layer like that red cloud.'

'We haven't found any. Even with their electronic jamming we should be able to spot the flux patterns from a medium-sized fusion generator. But we haven't.'

'Can you locate the jamming source?'

'No, sorry, it's very diffuse. But it's definitely ground based. It only affects us and the satellites when we're over Amarisk.'

'Is the red cloud radioactive?'

'No. We're fairly sure of that. No alpha, beta, or gamma emission.'

'What about biological contamination?'

'No data. We haven't attempted to sample it.'

'Make that your priority,' Terrance said. 'I have to know if it's safe to send the combat scout teams down.'

On its following pass, the *Cyanea* released two atmospheric probes. The vehicles were modified versions of the marque used by planet-survey missions, three-metre delta wing robots with the central cylindrical fuselage crammed full of biological sampling and analysis equipment.

Both of them pitched up to present their heatshield bellies to the atmosphere, curving down towards the surface as they aerobraked. Once they had fallen below subsonic velocity, airscoop intake ramps hinged back near the nose, and their compressor engines whirred into silent life. A preprogrammed flight plan sent them swooping over the first fringes of the red cloud, fifteen kilometres to the south-east of Durringham. Encrypted data pulsed up to the newly established bracelet of communication satellites.

The air was remarkably clear, with humidity thirty per cent down on Lalonde's average. Terrance Smith accessed the raw image from a camera in the nose of one probe. It looked as though it was flying over the surface of a red dwarf star. A red dwarf with an azure atmosphere. The cloud, or haze – whatever – was completely uniform, as though, finally, an electromagnetic wavefront had come to rest and achieved mass, then someone had polished it into a ruby surface. There was nothing to focus on, no perspective, no constituent particles or spores; its intensity was mechanically constant. An optically impenetrable layer floating two kilometres above the ground. Thickness unknown. Temperature unknown. Radiating entirely in the bottom end of the red spectrum.

'No real clouds anywhere above it,' Joshua murmured. Like most of the fleet's crews he had accessed the datavise from the atmospheric probes. Something had bothered him about that lack; ironically, more than the buoyant red blanket itself. 'Amarisk always had clouds.'

Sarha quickly ran a review of the images the fleet had recorded on their approach, watching the cloud formations. 'Oh my Lord, they split,' she said disbelievingly. 'About a hundred kilometres offshore the clouds split like they've hit something.' She ran the time-lapse record for them, letting the tumbling clouds sweep through their neural nanonics' visualization. Great billowing bands of cumulus and stratocumulus charged across the ocean towards Amarisk's western shoreline, only to branch and diverge, raging away to the north and south of the Juliffe's mouth.

'Jesus. What would it take to do that? Not even Kulu tries to manipulate its climate.' Joshua switched back to a real-time view from *Lady Mac*'s sensor clusters. A cyclone was being visibly sawed into two unequal sections as it pirouetted against the invisible boundary. He ordered the flight computer to open a channel to the *Gemal*.

'Yes, we've seen it,' Terrance Smith said. 'It has to be tied in with the red cloud cover. Obviously the invaders have a highly sophisticated method of energy manipulation.'

'No shit? The point is, what are you going to do about it?'

'Destroy the focal mechanism.'

'Jesus, you can't mean that. This fleet can't possibly go into orbit now. With that kind of power available they'll be able to smash us as soon as we're within range. Hell, they can probably pull us down from orbit. You'll have to abort the mission.'

'It's ground based, Calvert, we're sure of that. It can't be anywhere else. The blackhawks can sense the mass of anything larger than a tennis ball in orbit, you can't disguise mass from their distortion fields. All we have to do is send in the combat scout teams to locate the invader's bases. That's what we planned on doing all along. You knew that when you signed on. Once we find the enemy, the starships can bombard them from orbit. That's what you're here for, Calvert. Nobody promised you an easy ride. Now hold formation.'

'Oh, Jesus.' He looked round the bridge to make sure everyone shared his dismay. They did. 'What do you want to do? At five gees I can get us to a suitable jump coordinate in twelve minutes – mark.'

Melvyn looked thoroughly disgusted. 'That bloody Smith. His naval programs must have been written by the most gung-ho admiral in the galaxy. I say jump.'

'Smith has a point,' Warlow rumbled.

Joshua glanced over at the big cosmonik in surprise. Of everyone, Warlow had been the least eager to come.

'There is nothing hostile in orbit,' the bass voice proclaimed.

'It can chop up a bloody cyclone,' Ashly shouted.

'The red cloud is atmospheric. Whatever generates it affects lower atmospheric weather. It is planet based, centred on Amarisk. The blackhawks have not been destroyed. Can we really desert the fleet at this juncture? Suppose Smith and the others do liberate Lalonde? What then?'

Jesus, he's right, Joshua thought. You knew you were committed after you took the contract. But . . . Instinct. That bloody obstinate, indefinable mental itch he suffered from – and trusted. Instinct told him to run. Run now, and run fast.

'All right,' he said. 'We stay with them, for now. But at the first – and I really mean *first,* Warlow – sign of the shit hitting the fan, then we are out of orbit at ten gees. Commitment or no commitment.'

'Thank God somebody's got some sense,' Melvyn murmured.

'Sarha, I want a constant monitor of all the observation satellite data from now on. Any other shit-loopy atmospheric happenings pop up and I want to be informed immediately.'

'Yes, Captain.'

'Also, Melvyn, set up a real-time review program of the grav-detector satellite's data. I don't intend us to be dependent on the *Gemal* informing us whether we've got company.'

'Gotcha, Joshua,' Melvyn sang.

'Dahybi, nodes to be charged to maximum capacity until further notice. I want to be able to jump within thirty seconds.'

'They aren't designed for long-term readiness—'

'They'll last for five days in that state. It'll be settled one way or another by then. And I have the money for maintenance.'

Dahybi shrugged his shoulders against the couch webbing. 'Yes, sir.'

Joshua tried to relax his body, but eventually gave up and ordered his neural nanonics to send overrides into his muscles. As they began to slacken he accessed the fleet's command communication channels again, and started to format a program which would warn him if one of the ships dropped out of the network unexpectedly. It wasn't much, but it might be worth a couple of seconds.

The atmospheric probes began to lose height, sliding down towards the surface of the red cloud. 'Systems are functioning perfectly,' the flight's controlling officer reported. 'There's no sign of the electronic warfare effect.' She flew them to within five metres of the top, then levelled them out. There was no reaction from the serene red plain. 'Air analysis is negative. Whatever holds the boundary together seems to be impermeable. None of it is drifting upwards.'

'Send the probes in,' Terrance ordered.

The first probe eased its way towards the surface, observed

by cameras on the second. As it touched the top of the layer a fan of red haze jetted up behind it, arcing with slow smoothness, like powder-fine dust in low gravity.

'It is a solid!' Terrance exclaimed. 'I knew it.'

'Nothing registering, sir, no particles. Only water vapour, humidity rising sharply.'

The probe sank deeper, vanishing from its twin's view. Its data transmission began to fissure.

'High static charge building up over the fuselage,' the control officer reported. 'I'm losing it.'

The probe's datavise dissolved into garbage, then cut off. Terrance Smith ordered the second one down. They didn't learn anything new. Contact was lost twenty-five seconds after it ploughed into the cloud.

'Static-charged vapour,' Terrance said in confusion. 'Is that all?'

Oliver Llewelyn cancelled the datavise from *Gemal*'s flight computer. The bridge was dimly lit, every officer lying on an acceleration couch, eyes closed as they helped coordinate the fleet's approach. 'It reminds me of a gas giant's rings,' the captain said. 'Minute charged particles held together with a magnetic flux.'

'The blackhawks say there is no magnetic flux, only the standard planetary magnetic field,' Terrance corrected automatically. 'Was there any sign of biological activity?' he asked the flight control officer on the *Cyanea.*

'No, sir,' she said. 'No chemicals present either. Just water.'

'Then why is it glowing?'

'I don't know, sir. There must be a light-source of some kind deeper inside, where the probes can't reach.'

'What are you going to do?' Oliver Llewelyn asked.

'It's a screen, a canopy; they're covering up whatever they're doing below. It's not a weapon.'

'It might only be a screen. But it's beyond our ability to create. You can't commit your forces against a total unknown, and certainly not one of that magnitude. Standard military doctrine.'

'There are over twenty million people down there, including my friends. I can't leave without at least making one attempt to find out what's going on. Standard military doctrine is to scout first. That's what we'll do.' He drew a breath, entering the newly formatted data from the probes into his neural nanonics and letting the tactics program draw up a minimum-risk strategy for physical evaluation of the planetary situation. 'The combat scout teams go in as originally planned, although they land well clear of the red cloud. But I'm altering the search emphasis. Three teams into the Quallheim Counties to find the invader's landing site and base; that section of the mission hasn't changed. Then nine teams are to be distributed along the rest of the Juliffe tributaries to appraise the overall status of the population and engage targets of opportunity. And I want the last two teams to investigate Durringham's spaceport; they now have two objectives. One, find out if the McBoeing spaceplanes are still available to effect a landing for the general troops we're carrying in the *Gemal*. Secondly, I want them to access the records in the flight control centre and find out where the starships went. And why.'

'Suppose they didn't go anywhere?' Oliver Llewelyn said. 'Suppose Captain Calvert is right, and your invaders can just reach up and obliterate ships in orbit?'

'Then where is the wreckage? The blackhawks have catalogued every chunk of matter above the planet, there's nothing incongruous this side of Rennison's orbit.'

Oliver Llewelyn showed him a morbid grin. 'Lying in the jungle below that red cloud.'

Terrance was becoming annoyed with the captain's constant cavils. 'They were unarmed civil ships, we're not. And that makes a big difference.' He put his head back down on the couch's cushioning, closed his eyes, and began to datavise the revised landing orders through the secure combat communication channels.

*

The fleet decelerated into a one-thousand-kilometre orbit, individual ships taking up different inclinations so that Amarisk was always covered by three of them. Repeated sweeps by the swarm of observation satellites had revealed no new information on ground conditions below the red cloud. The six blackhawks rose up from their initial seven-hundred-kilometre orbit to join the rest of the starships, their crews quietly pleased at the extra distance between them and the uncanny aerial portent.

After one final orbit, alert for any attack from the invaders, the mercenary scout teams clambered into the waiting spaceplanes, and Terrance Smith gave the final go-ahead to land. As each starship crossed into the umbra its spaceplane undocked and performed a retro-burn which pushed it onto an atmosphere interception trajectory. They reached the mesosphere nine thousand kilometres west of Amarisk and aerobraked over the nightside ocean, sending a multitude of hypersonic booms crashing down over the waves.

*

Brendon couldn't keep his attention away from the red cloud. He was piloting the spaceplane from the *Villeneuve's Revenge*, taking the six-strong mercenary scout team down to their designated drop zone a hundred kilometres east of Durringham. The cloud had been visible to the forward sensors when they were still six hundred kilometres offshore. From there it hadn't been so bad, a colossal meteorological marvel. Now though, up close, the sheer size was intimidating him badly. The thought that some entity had constructed it, deliberately built a lightway of water vapour in the sky, was acutely disconcerting. It hung twenty kilometres off the starboard wing, inert and immutable.

Far ahead he could just see the first fork as it split to follow one of the tributaries. That more than anything betrayed its artificiality, the fact that it had *intent.*

As the spaceplane eased down level with it he could see the land underneath. Unbroken jungle, but dark, tinted a deep maroon.

'It's blocking a lot of light under there,' said Chas Paske, the mercenary team's leader.

'*Oui,*' Brendon agreed, without looking round. 'The computer estimates it's about eight metres thick at the edge, getting thicker deeper in, though,' he reported. 'Probably three or four hundred metres at the centre, over the river itself.'

'What about the electronic warfare field?'

'It's there all right, I'm having some trouble with the flight control processors, and the communication channel is suffering from interference, the bit rate is way down.'

'As long as we can transmit the coordinates for the starships to bombard,' Chas Paske said. 'That's all we need.'

'*Oui.* Landing in three minutes.'

The spaceplane was approaching the natural clearing they had chosen. Brendon checked with the blackhawks, which were still supervising the observation. He was assured there was no human activity within at least two kilometres of the clearing.

Qualtook and baby giganteas ringed their allocated landing site. Inside them, burnt and broken stumps were still visible through the mantle of vines, evidence of the fire which had raged decades ago. The spaceplane nosed its way cautiously over the edge of the trees, as if afraid of what it might find. Birds took to the air in dismay at the huge predator shape and the clarion squealing it emitted. A radar pulse slashed across the ground, slicing straight through the vine leaves to uncover the extent of the stumps. Landing struts unfolded from the fuselage, and after a minute of jostling to avoid the more hazardous protrusions it settled gently on the ground, compressor nozzles blasting dusty fountains of dead leaves and twigs into the air.

Even as silence stole back into the clearing the outer airlock hatch was opening. Chas Paske led his team out. Five disc-shaped aerovettes swooped into the sky, rim-mounted sensors probing the encircling jungle for motion or infrared signatures.

The mercenaries began to unload their equipment from the open belly holds. They were all boosted, their appearance way outside the human norm. Chas Paske was bigger than any cosmonik, his synthetic skin the colour of weather-worn stone. He didn't bother with clothes other than weapon belts and equipment straps.

'Hurry it up,' Brendon said. 'The jamming is getting worse, I can hardly get a signal through to the satellites.'

Pods and cases began to accumulate on the battered carpet of vines. Chas was hauling down a portable zero-tau pod containing an affinity-bonded eagle when an aerovette data-vised him that there was a movement among the trees. He picked up a gaussrifle. The aerovette was hovering a metre over the trees, providing him an image of heads bobbing about through the undergrowth. Nine of them, making no attempt to hide.

'Hey,' a woman's voice shouted.

The mercenaries were fanning out, positioning the aerovettes to provide maximum coverage.

'The blackhawks said there was no one here,' Chas Paske said. 'For Christ's sake.'

'It's the optical distortion,' Brendon replied. 'It's worse than we thought.'

The woman emerged into the clearing. She shouted again and waved. More people came out of the trees behind her, women and a couple of boys in their early teens. All of them in dirty clothes.

'Thank God you're here,' she said as she hurried over to Chas. 'We waited and waited. It's terrible back there.'

'Hold it,' Chas said.

She didn't hear him, or ignored him. Looking down to pick her way over thick tangles of vines. 'Take us away. Up to the starships, anywhere. But get us off this planet.'

'Who the hell are you? Where do you come from?' At the back of his mind Chas thought how odd it was that his appearance didn't affect her. People normally showed at least some doubt when they saw his size and shape. This woman didn't.

His neural nanonics cautioned him that the gaussrifle's targeting processor was malfunctioning. 'Stop,' he bellowed when she was six metres away. 'We can't take any chances; you may have been sequestrated. Now, where are you from?'

She jerked to a halt at the volume he poured into his voice. 'We're from the village,' she said, slightly breathless. 'There's a whole group of them devils back there.'

'Where?'

The woman took another pace forward and pointed over her shoulder. 'There.' Another step. 'Please, you must help us.' Her haggard face was imploring.

All five aerovettes fell out of the sky. The ground below Chas Paske's feet began to split open with a wet tearing sound, revealing a long fissure from which bright white light shone upwards. Neural nanonics overrode all natural human feelings of panic, enforcing a smooth threat response from his body. He jumped aside, landing beside the smiling woman. She hit him.

*

Terrance Smith had lost contact with three of the eleven spaceplanes which had landed, and the remaining three in the air were approaching the Quallheim Counties. The observation satellites were unable to provide much information on the fate of those that had been silenced, the images they produced of the drop zones were decaying by the minute. None of them had crashed, though, the blackout had come after they landed.

Encouraged by his tactics program, which estimated forty per cent losses at the first landing attempt, Terrance assumed the worst, and contacted the last three spaceplanes.

'Change your principal drop zone to one of the back-ups,' he ordered. 'I want you to land at least a hundred and fifty kilometres from the red cloud.'

'It's moving!' Oliver Llewelyn shouted as Terrance was receiving acknowledgements from the pilots.

'What is?'

'The red cloud.'

Terrance opened a channel to the processor array which was correlating the observation satellite images. Whorls and curlicues were rippling along the edges of the red bands, flat streamers, kilometres long, were shooting out horizontally, like solar prominences. The eerie symmetry of the velvet-textured clouds was rupturing, their albedo fluctuating as vast serpentine shadows skated erratically from side to side.

'It knows we're here,' Oliver Llewelyn said. 'We've agitated it.'

For one brutally nasty second Terrance Smith had the idea that the massive formation of forking cloud bands was alive, a gas-giant entity that had migrated across interplanetary space from Murora. Damn it, the thing did resemble the kind of convoluted storm braids which curled and clashed in week-long hostilities among the hydrogen and frozen ammonia crystals of gas-giant atmospheres. 'Don't be absurd,' he said. 'Something is deliberately causing those disturbances. This may be our best chance yet to discover how they shape that thing. Get onto the blackhawk captains, I want every sensor we have available focused on it. There has to be some kind of energy modulation going on down there. Something has to register on some spectrum we're covering.'

'Want to bet?' Oliver Llewelyn muttered under his breath. He was beginning to wish he had never agreed to fly the *Gemal* for Smith, and to hell with the legalities of refusing. Some things were more important than money, starting with his life. He grudgingly began datavising instructions round the blackhawks.

The communication links with another two spaceplanes dropped out. But three had landed their mercenary teams without incident and were already back in the air.

It is possible, Terrance told himself fiercely as the pearl-white specks soared to safety above the tangled tributary basin. We can find out what's happening down there.

He observed the red cloud sending huge pseudostorm streamers boiling ferociously out across the jungle. A navigational graphics overlay revealed the position of the spaceplanes still on the ground. The largest swellings were heading for the landing zones with unerring accuracy.

'Come on,' he urged them through clenched teeth. 'Get up. Get out of there.'

'Sensors report no energy perturbation of any kind,' Oliver Llewelyn said.

'Impossible. It's being directed. What about the sensors the invaders used to track our spaceplanes, have we detected those?'

'No.'

Five more spaceplanes were back in the air, streaking away from the grasping claws of red cloud. Two of them were ones they had lost contact with earlier. Terrance heard a cheer go round the *Gemal*'s bridge, and added his own whoop of exhilaration.

Now the mission was starting to come together. With the combat scout teams on the ground they would have targets soon. They could start hitting back.

The last three spaceplanes landed in the Quallheim Counties. One of them was from the *Lady Macbeth*.

*

The *Villeneuve's Revenge* had the standard pyramid structure of four life-support capsules at its core. They were spherical, divided into three decks, with enough volume to make life for the crew of six very agreeable. Fifteen passengers could be accommodated with only a modest reduction in comfort. None of the six mercenaries they had brought to Lalonde had complained. The fittings, like the rest of the ship's systems, could be classed as passable with plenty of room for improvement, upgrading, or preferably complete replacement.

Erick Thakrar and Bev Lennon sailed headfirst through the ceiling hatch of the lounge deck above the spaceplane hangar. The compartment's surfaces were coated in a thin grey-green foam with stikpads at regular intervals, though most of them had lost their cohesiveness. Furniture was all lightweight composite that had been folded back neatly into alcoves, producing a floor made up of labelled squares, hexagons, and circles like some mismatched mosaic. Walls were principally storage lockers, broken by hatchways into personal cabins, the red panels of emergency equipment cubicles, and inbuilt AV player blocks with their projector pillars. There was a watery vegetable smell in the air. Only two of the lightstrips were on. Several purple foil food wrappers were drifting through the air like lost aquatic creatures, with a couple more clamped against the roof grilles by the gentle air flow. A black flek was spinning idly. It all added up to lend the lounge a discarded appearance.

Erick slapped casually at the plastic-coated ladder stretching between floor and ceiling, angling for the floor hatch. His neural nanonics reported André Duchamp opening a direct communication channel.

'He's docking now,' the captain datavised. 'Or attempting to.'

'How is the communication link? Can you get anything from inside?'

'Nothing. It's still a three per cent bit rate, just enough to correlate docking procedures. The processors must have been bollocksed up quite badly.'

Erick glanced over his shoulder at Bev, who shrugged. The two of them were armed; Bev with a neural jammer, Erick a laser pistol he hoped to God he wouldn't have to use.

The spaceplane had emerged from the upper atmosphere and re-established contact with a weak signal from a malfunctioning reserve transmitter. Brendon claimed the craft had been subject to a ferocious electronic warfare attack which had decimated the on-board processors. They only had his word for it, the link had barely enough power to broadcast his message, a full-scale datavise to assess the internal electronic damage was impossible.

In view of the known sequestration ability of the invaders, André Duchamp wasn't taking any chances.

'That *anglo* Smith should have anticipated this,' André grumbled. 'We should have had an examination procedure set up.'

'Yes,' Erick agreed. He and Bev traded a grin.

'Typical of this bloody bodge-up mission,' André chuntered on. 'If he wants proper advice he should have experienced people like me on his general staff, not that arsehole Llewelyn. I could have told him you need to be careful when it comes to sequestration. Fifty years of experience, that's what I've got, that counts for a hell of a lot more than any neural nanonics tactics program. I've had every smartarse weapon in the Confederation thrown at me, and I'm still alive. And he goes and chooses a Celt who makes a living from flying the brain dead. *Merde!*'

Bev's legs cleared the rim of the hatch into the lounge, and he datavised a codelock at it. The carbotanium hatch slid shut, its seal engaging with a solid clunk.

'Come on, then,' Erick said. He slipped through the floor hatch into the lower deck. His neural nanonics provided him with an image from the starship's external sensor clusters. The spaceplane was floundering, just metres away from the hull. Without a full navigational datalink, Brendon was having a great deal of trouble inserting the spaceplane's nose into the hangar's docking collar. Novice pilots could do better, Erick thought, wincing as reaction-control thrusters fired hard, seconds before the radar dome tip scraped the hull. 'Ye gods. We might not have anything left to inspect at this rate.'

The lower deck was severely cramped, comprising an engineering shop for medium-sized electromechanical components, a smaller workshop for electronic repairs, two airlocks, one for the spaceplane hangar, one for EVA work, storage bins, and space armour lockers. Its walls were naked titanium, netted with conduits and pipes.

'Collar engaged,' André said. 'Madeleine is bringing him in now.'

The whine of actuators carried faintly through the starship's stress structure into the lower deck. Erick accessed a camera in the hangar, and saw the spaceplane being pulled into the cylindrical chamber. A moth crawling back inside a silver chrysalis. The retracted wings had a clearance measured in centimetres.

He datavised orders into the hangar systems processors. When the spaceplane came to rest, power lines, coolant hoses, and optical cables plugged into umbilical sockets around its fuselage.

'There's very little data coming out,' Erick said, scanning the docking operations console holoscreen to see the preliminary results of the diagnostic checks. 'I can't get any internal sensors to respond.'

'Is that the processors or the sensors themselves which are malfunctioning?' André asked.

'Difficult to tell,' Bev said, hanging from a grab hoop behind Erick to look over his shoulder. 'Only ten per cent of the internal databuses are operational, we can't access the cabin management processors to see where the fault lies. God knows how Brendon ever piloted that thing up here. He's missing half of his control systems.'

'Brendon is the best,' Madeleine Collun said.

The console's AV pillar bleeped, showing a single communication circuit was open from the spaceplane. Audio only.

'Anyone out there?' Brendon asked. 'Or have you all buggered off to lunch?'

'We're here, Brendon,' Erick said. 'What's your situation?'

'The atmosphere is really bad, total life-support failure as far as I can make out . . . I'm gulping oxygen from an emergency helmet . . . Get that airlock connected now . . . This is killing my lungs . . . I can smell some kind of plastic burning . . . Acid gas . . .'

'I can't cycle the cabin atmosphere for him,' Erick datavised to André. 'Our pumps are working and the hose seals are confirmed, but the spaceplane pressure valves won't open, there's no environmental circuit.'

'Get him into the airlock, then,' André said. 'But don't let him into the life-support cabin, not yet.'

'Aye, aye.'

'Come on!' Brendon shouted.

'On our way, Brendon.'

Bev ordered the airlock tube to extend. The spaceplane's fuselage shield panel slid back to reveal the circular airlock hatch below.

'Lucky that worked,' Erick muttered.

Bev was staring into the AV pillar's projection, watching the airlock tube seal itself to the hatch rim. 'It's a simple power circuit. Nothing delicate about that.'

'But there's still a supervising processor— Hell.' Environment sensors inside the airlock tube were picking up traces of toxic gases as the spaceplane's hatch swung open. The console holoscreen switched to a camera inside the metal tube. A curtain of thin blue smoke was wafting out of the hatch. A flickering green light shone inside the cabin. Brendon appeared, pulling himself along a line of closely spaced grab hoops. His yellow ship's one-piece was smeared with dirt and soot. The copper-mirror visor of the shell-helmet he was wearing covered his face, it was connected to a portable life-support case.

'Why didn't he put his spacesuit on?' Erick asked.

Brendon waved at the camera. 'God, thanks, I couldn't have lasted much longer. Hey, you haven't opened the hatch.'

'Brendon, we have to take precautions,' Bev said. 'We know the invaders can sequestrate people.'

'Oh, sure, yes. One moment.' He started coughing.

Erick checked the environmental readings again. Fumes were still pouring out of the spaceplane cabin; the airlock tube filters could barely cope.

Brendon opened his visor. His face was deathly white, sweating heavily. He coughed again, flinching at the pain.

'Christ,' Erick muttered. 'Brendon, datavise a physiological reading please.'

'Oh God it hurts.' Brendon coughed again, a hoarse croaking sound.

'We've got to get him out,' Bev said.

'I don't get any response from his neural nanonics,' Erick said. 'I'm trying to datavise them through the airlock tube's processor but there isn't even a carrier code acknowledgement.'

'Erick, he's in trouble!'

'We don't know that!'

'Look at him.'

'Look at Lalonde. They can build rivers of light in the sky. Faking up one injured crewman isn't going to tax them.'

'For God's sake.' Bev stared at the holoscreen. Brendon was juddering, one hand holding a grab loop as he vomited. Sallow globules of fluid burped out of his mouth, splashing and sticking to the dull-silver wall of the tube opposite.

'We don't even know if he's alone,' Erick said. 'The hatch into the spaceplane isn't shut. It won't respond to my orders. I can't even shut it, let alone codelock it.'

'Captain,' Bev datavised. 'We can't just leave him in there.'

'Erick is quite right,' André replied regretfully. 'This whole incident is highly suspicious. It is convenient for somebody who wants to get inside the ship. Too convenient.'

'He's dying!'

'You may not enter the airlock while the hatch into the spaceplane remains open.'

Bev looked round the utilitarian lower deck in desperation. 'All right. How about this? Erick goes up into the lounge and codelocks that hatch behind him, leaving me in here. That way I can take a medical nanonic in to Brendon, and I can check out the spaceplane cabin to make sure there aren't any xenoc invaders on board.'

'Erick?' André asked.

'I've no objection.'

'Very well. Do it.'

Erick swam up into the empty lounge, and poised himself on the ladder. Bev's face was framed by the floor hatch, grinning up at him. 'Good luck,' Erick said. He datavised a codelock at the hatch's seal processor, then turned the manual fail-safe handle ninety degrees.

Bev twisted round as soon as the carbotanium square closed. He pulled a medical nanonic package from a first aid case on the wall. 'Hold on, Brendon. I'm coming in.' Red environmental warning lights were flashing on the panel beside the circular airlock tube hatch. Bev datavised his override authority into the management processor, and the hatch began to swing back.

Erick opened a channel into the lounge's communication net processor, and accessed the lower deck cameras. He watched Bev screw up his face as the fumes blew out of the open hatchway. Emerald green light flared out of the spaceplane's cabin, sending a thick, blindingly intense beam searing along the airlock tube to wash the lower deck. Caught full square, Bev yelled, his hands coming up instinctively to cover his eyes. A ragged stream of raw white energy shot along the centre of the green light, smashing into him.

The camera failed.

'Bev!' Erick shouted. He sent a stream of instructions into the processor. A visualization of the lower deck's systems materialized, a ghostly reticulation of coloured lines and blinking symbols.

'Erick, what's happening?' André demanded.

'They're in! They're in the fucking ship. Codelock all the hatches now. Now, God damn it!'

The schematic's coloured lines were vanishing one by one. Erick stared wildly at the floor, as if he could see what was happening through the metal decking. Then the lounge lights went out.

*

'Five minutes until we land at our new drop zone, and the tension in the cabin is really starting to bite,' Kelly Tirrel subvocalized into a neural nanonics memory cell. 'We know something has happened to at least five other spaceplanes. What everyone is now asking themselves is, will the extra distance protect us? Do the invaders only operate below their protective covering of red cloud?'

She accessed the spaceplane's sensors to observe the magnificent, monstrous spectacle again. Thousand-kilometre-long bands of glowing red nothingness suspended in the air. Astounding. This far inland they were slim and complex, interwoven like the web of a drunken spider above the convoluted tributaries. When she had seen them from orbit, calm and regular, they had intimidated her; up close and churning like this they were just plain frightening.

Coiling belts were edge-on with the starboard wing, growing larger as they spun through the sky towards the spaceplane. It was an excellent image, a little bit too realistic for peace of mind. But then the spaceplane's sensor array was all military-grade. Long streamlined recesses on both sides of the fuselage belly were now holding tapering cylindrical weapons pods – maser cannons providing a three-hundred-and-sixty-degree cover, an electronic warfare suite, and a stealth envelope. They weren't quite an assault fighter, but neither were they a sitting duck like some of the spaceplanes.

Typical that Joshua would have a multi-role spaceplane. No! Thank God Joshua had a multi-role spaceplane.

Forty minutes into the descent, and already she missed him. You're so weak, she swore at herself.

Kelly was starting to have serious second thoughts about the whole assignment. Like all war correspondents, she supposed. Being on the ground was very different to sitting in the office anticipating being on the ground. Especially with the appearance of that red cloud.

The seven mercenaries had discussed that appearance *ad nauseam* the whole way in from the emergence point. Reza Malin, the team's leader, had seemed almost excited by the prospect of venturing below it. Such adverse circumstances were a challenge, he said. Something new.

She had taken time to get to know all of them reasonably well. So she knew what Reza said wasn't simple bravado. He had been a Confederation Navy Marine at one time. An officer, she guessed; he wasn't very forthcoming about that period of his life, nor subsequent contracts as a marshal on various stage one colony planets. But he must have been good at the second oldest profession, money in large quantities had paid for a considerable number of physical enhancements and alterations. Now he was one of the élite. Like a cosmonik, blurring the line between machine and human. The kind of hyper-boosted composite the mundane troops stored in zero-tau on the *Gemal* aspired to become.

Reza Malin retained a basic humanoid shape, although he was now two metres tall, and proportionally broad. His skin was artificial, a tough neutral grey-blue impact-resistant composite with a built-in chameleon layer. He didn't bother with clothes any more, and there were no genitalia (rather, no external genitalia, Kelly recorded faithfully). Cybernetic six-finger claws replaced his natural hands. Both forearms were wide, with integral small-calibre gaussrifles, his skeleton rigged to absorb recoil. Like Warlow, his face was incapable of expression. Black glass bubble-shields covered both eyes; the nose was now a flat circular intake which could filter chemical and biological agents. The back and sides of his bald skull were studded with a row of five sensor implants, smooth centimetre-wide ulcerlike bulges.

Despite the lack of expression, she learned a lot from his voice, which was still natural. Reza wasn't easily flustered. That and a civilized competence, the way the other six followed his orders without question, gave her more confidence than she would otherwise have had in the scouting mission. In the final analysis, she realized, she trusted him with her life.

The spaceplane banked sharply. Kelly was aware of Ashly Hanson focusing the optical sensors on a small river three kilometres below. The silvery water had a curious speckling of white dots.

'What does he think he's doing?' Pat Halahan asked. The team's second in command was sitting in the seat next to her. A ranger-scout, as he described himself, slimmer and smaller than Reza, but with the same blue-grey skin, and powerful adipose legs. Each forearm had twin wrists, onc for ordinary hands, one a power data socket for plug-ins – weapons or sensors. His senses were all enhanced, with a raised rim of flesh running from the corner of his eyes right around the back of his skull.

'Hey, what's happening, Ashly?' he called out. Electronic warfare was a thought all the mercenaries were sharing.

'I'm going to land us here,' Ashly said.

'Any particular reason?' Reza Malin asked with quiet authoritativeness. 'The surveyed back-up landing site is another seventy kilometres south-east.'

'Listen, anyone who can create that damn cloud can intercept our communications without even trying. They'll have every site Terrance Smith ever reviewed marked in a big red circle that says "hit this".'

There was a moment's silence.

'Smart man,' Pat Halahan muttered to Kelly. 'I wish we'd had him on the Camelot operation. Lost a lot of good people because the general hired too many virgins.'

'Go ahead,' Reza said.

'Thank you,' Ashly sang back. The spaceplane dived steeply, spiralling at an angle which sent Kelly's stomach pressing up against her collar bones.

'Are you quite sure you want to land?' the pilot asked. 'You ask me, we're in way over our heads. Terrance Smith couldn't organize a gang-bang in a brothel.'

'If Smith is going to beat the invaders, the starships have to know where to hit them,' Reza said. 'For that you need us. We always go in at the shit end. It's what we're good at.'

'Whatever you say.'

'Don't worry about us. Ultra-tech never works well in jungle terrain, nature is just too damn messy. And I don't think I've seen many jungles worse than this one. They can probably swat us with some energy blast, even lob a baby-nuke on us if they're feeling particularly bitchy. But they've got to find us first. And rooting us out of that forest wilderness is going to be tricky, I'll make bloody sure of that. You just make sure you and young Joshua stay intact to pick us up afterwards.'

'If I'm alive, I'll pick you up.'

'Good, I'll hold you to that.'

The spaceplane's yaw angle reversed as it performed an abrupt roll. Kelly clung to the armrests with white knuckles as the webbing shifted its hold around her body. This wasn't a clean aerodynamic dive, it was a death plummet.

'How you doing, Kell?' Sewell shouted, sounding hugely amused. Sewell was one of the team's three combat-adept types, and looked it. Standing two metres thirty, his leathery skin matt-black, and woven through with a web of energy absorption/dispersal fibres. His head was virtually globular, a glossy shell that protected his sensors, sitting on a short neck. Trunk-like upper arms supported dual elbows; he had attached heavy-calibre gaussrifles to the top joints.

Chuckles went round the cabin. Kelly realized her eyes were tight shut, and forced herself to open them. The spaceplane was shaking.

'You should eat, take your mind off it,' Sewell crowed. 'I've got some big gooey slices of strawberry creamcake in my pack. Want some?'

'When you were boosted, the doctors wired your neural nanonics to your liver,' she said. 'It was one fuck of a lot smarter than your brain, bollockhead.'

Sewell laughed.

A judder ran through the cabin as the wings began to sweep out.

'Irradiate the drop zone, Ashly, please,' Reza said.

'Affirmative.'

'There might be civilians down there,' protested Sal Yong, another of the combat-adepts.

'Doubt it,' Ashly said. 'The nearest village is fifty kilometres away.'

'We're not on a Red Cross mission, Sal,' Reza said.

'Yes, sir.'

The spaceplane twisted again.

Great swaths of maser radiation poured out of the unblemished sky around the small shallow river. Hundreds of birds dropped to the ground or splashed into the water, charred feathers smoking; vennals tumbled from the trees, limbs still twitching; sayce howled briefly as their hides wizened and cracked, then died as their brains broke apart from the intense heat; danderil nibbling at the vegetation collapsed, their long elegant legs buckling as their viscera boiled. The verdant emerald leaves of the trees and vines turned a darker, bruised shade of green. Flowers shrivelled up. Berries and fruit burst open in puffs of steam.

The spaceplane came down fast and level. It actually landed in the river, undercarriage struts crushing the stony bed, nose jutting over the grassy bank. Steam and spray erupted from the water as it was struck by the compressor jets, sending a large circular wave sloshing outwards over the bank.

Sewell and Jalal were first out, the two big combat-adept mercenaries didn't wait for the aluminium airlock stairs to extend. They jumped down into the lathery water, covering the quiet wilting trees with their gaussrifles, and sprinted ashore. The half-metre depth didn't even slow them down.

Reza released a couple of aerovettes, ordering them to scan the immediate jungle. The stealthed, disc-shaped aerial combat robots were a metre and a half wide, their central section a curving mesh-grid to protect the wide-cord contra-rotating fans in the middle. Five infrared lasers were mounted around their rim, along with a broad passive-sensor array. They hummed softly and slipped through the air, climbing up to traverse the top of the nearby trees.

Pat Halahan and Theo Connal were second to emerge, following the first two mercenaries ashore. Theo Connal had a short body, one and a half metres tall, boosted for jungle roving. His skin was the same tough chameleon envelope as Reza and Pat, but his legs and arms were disproportionately long. Both feet were equipped with fingers instead of toes. He walked with an apeish stoop. Even his bald head portrayed simian characteristics, with a tiny button nose, squashed circle mouth, and slanted eyes, heavily lidded.

He activated the chameleon circuit when he landed in the water, and scrambled up the shallow incline of the bank. Only a faint mauve optical shimmer betrayed his silhouette. As soon as he reached a tree he seemed to embrace it, then levitated, spiralling round the trunk. At which point the spaceplane sensors lost him, even the infrared.

'My God,' Kelly said. She had wondered why Reza had included someone as basically harmless-looking as Theo on the team. A small buzz of excitement began in her belly. This kind of flawless professionalism was darkly enticing; it was easy to see how combat missions became so narcotic.

Another pair of aerovettes skimmed off over the trees.

Sal Yong and Ariadne, the second ranger, came down the airlock steps. Ariadne was the only other female on the team, although her gender was obscured like all the others. There was very little difference between her and Pat, maybe lacking just a few centimetres in height, and her sensor band was broader.

'Now or never, Kelly,' Reza said.

'Oh, now,' she said, and stood up. 'Definitely.' The visor of her shell-helmet slid down. Collins had given her carte blanche on selecting her equipment back in Tranquillity, so she had asked for Reza's advice and bought what he suggested. After all, it was in his own interest not to have a liability tramping through the jungle with the scout team. 'Keep it simple, and make it the best,' he'd said. 'You're not combat trained, so all you have to do is keep up with us and stay undetected.'

'I can load combat programs into my neural nanonics,' she'd offered generously.

Reza simply laughed.

She had wound up with a one-piece suit of rubbery body-armour, produced in the New Californian system, that would protect her from a modest level of attack from both projectile and energy beam weapons. Reza had taken her to an armourer who serviced mercenary equipment, and had a chameleon layer added.

More aerovettes whirred overhead as she hurried down the airlock steps into the river. Steam hung in the air. She was glad of the shell-helmet's air filters, cremated birds bobbed around her ankles.

Pat Halahan and Jalal were unloading the gear from the forward cargo hold.

'Help them,' Reza ordered Kelly. He was wading through the shallows, carrying some composite containers. A nylon harness held a black metallic sphere about twenty centimetres in diameter to his right side, just above his equipment belt. Kelly wondered what it was, her neural nanonics couldn't identify it, there were no visible features to assist the search and comparison program. None of the other mercenaries had one. She knew this wasn't the time to ask.

The spaceplane's steps were already folding back into the fuselage. She set to, stacking the metal cases and composite containers on the muddy grass of the bank.

Reza and Pat carried a trunk-sized zero-tau pod ashore. The black negating surface evaporated to reveal a white plastic cylinder. It split open, and a mahogany-coloured geneered hound lumbered out. Kelly thought its fangs could probably cut through her armour suit.

Reza knelt down beside the big beast and ruffled its head fondly with his hand. 'Hello, Fenton. How are you, boy?'

Fenton yawned, pink tongue hanging limply between his front fangs.

'Go have a look round for me. Go on.'

Reza patted his hindquarters as he rose. Fenton swung his neolithic head round to give his master a slightly maligning look, but trotted off obediently into the undergrowth.

Kelly had been standing perfectly still. 'He's well trained,' she said vaguely.

'He's well bonded,' Reza replied. 'I have affinity neuron symbionts fitted.'

'Ah.'

Pat and Jalal were wading ashore with a second zero-tau pod.

'*Adieux*,' Ashly datavised.

The spaceplane lifted with a brassy shriek. Vigorous geysers of water sprouted under the compressor nozzles, splashing up against the carbotanium fuselage. Then it was above the trees, undercarriage folding up, and the geysers withering away to white-foam ripples.

Kelly tracked her shell-helmet sensors round the forbidding wall of water-basted jungle. Oh, crap, I'm committed now.

She watched the spaceplane pitch up nearly to the vertical and accelerate away into the eastern sky at high speed. Her neural nanonics said they had landed less than three minutes ago.

*

The explosion was large enough for the *Gemal*'s ordinary sensor clusters to pick it up as the starship fell into the planet's umbra, leaving Amarisk behind. For the vastly more sensitive observation satellites in low orbit it registered as a savage multi-spectrum glare, overloading some scanners.

Terrance Smith's neural nanonics informed him it was the spaceplane from the blackhawk *Cyanea*, which had been landing a scout team in the Quallheim Counties. It had been on the ground when the blast happened.

'What the hell did that?' he demanded.

'No idea,' Oliver Llewelyn replied.

'Shit. It was over seventy kilometres from the nearest piece of red cloud. Did the scout team get clear?'

'No response from any of their personal communicator blocks,' one of the bridge's communication officers reported.

'Bugger.' His neural nanonics' strategic display showed him the remaining four spaceplanes climbing into orbit. Seven more had already docked with their parent starships. Two were manoeuvring for a rendezvous.

'Do you want to divert a spaceplane for a rescue?' Oliver asked.

'Not without confirmation that someone is alive down there. It was a hell of an explosion. The electron matrices must have shorted out.'

'Neat trick if you can do it,' Oliver said. 'They have a lot of safeguards built in.'

'Do you suppose that electronic warfare—'

'Sir, message from the *Villeneuve's Revenge*,' the communications officer said. 'Captain Duchamp says the invaders have boarded his ship.'

'*What?*'

'That was one of the spaceplanes we lost contact with,' Oliver said.

'You mean they're up in orbit?' Terrance asked.

'Looks like it.'

'Christ.' He datavised the processor managing the command communication channels, ready to issue a general alert. But his neural nanonics informed him a couple of starships were leaving their assigned orbital slots. When he requested the strategic display it showed him *Datura* and *Gramine* under acceleration, rising out of the thousand-kilometre orbit. His fist hit the acceleration couch cushioning. 'What is happening?'

'The spaceplanes from both the *Datura* and *Gramine* experienced communication difficulties,' Oliver said in a strained voice. He glanced over at Terrance Smith. The ordinarily prim bureaucrat looked haunted.

'Cut them out of our communication net,' Terrance ordered. 'Now. I don't want them to access our observation satellite data.'

'They're running,' Oliver said. 'They must be heading for a jump coordinate.'

'Not my problem.'

'The hell it isn't. If they are xenocs, you'll be letting them loose in the Confederation.'

'If they have the technology to put together that cloud, they already have bloody starships. My concern and mission is Lalonde. I'm not sending the blackhawks to intercept them, we don't have the numbers to send ships off on wild-goose chases.'

'Their drives aren't right,' Oliver said. 'They aren't burning the fuel cleanly. Look at the spectroscopic analysis.'

'Not now, fuck it!' Terrance shouted. He glared at Oliver. 'Contribute something positive or shut up.' His neural nanonics linked him in to the communication processor, opening direct channels to the remaining starships. 'This is an emergency warning,' he datavised. Even as the painful phrase emerged, he wondered how many listeners were still under his command.

*

The *Lady Macbeth*'s bridge was completely silent as Terrance Smith's voice came out of the AV pillars.

'Oh, Jesus,' Joshua moaned. 'This is all we need.'

'It looks like *Datura* and *Gramine* are preparing to jump,' Sarha said. 'Sensor clusters and thermo-dump panels are retracting.' She frowned. 'Most of them, anyway. Their thrust is very erratic. They should be above the five-thousand-kilometre gravity-field boundary in another four minutes.'

'This invasion force is too big, isn't it,' Joshua said. 'We're not going to save Lalonde, not with what we've got.'

'Looks that way,' Dahybi said in a subdued tone.

'Right then.' Joshua's mind was immediately full of trajectory graphics. A whole range of possible jump coordinates to nearby inhabited star systems popped up.

You'll be abandoning Kelly, a voice in his head said.

It's her choice.

But she didn't know what was happening.

He instructed the flight computer to retract the thermo-dump panels. Fully extended, the panels couldn't withstand high-gee acceleration. And if he was going to run, he wanted to do it fast.

'As soon as Ashly returns we're leaving,' he announced.

'What about the merc team?' Warlow asked. 'They are dependent on us knocking out the invader's bases.'

'They knew the risks.'

'Kelly is with them.'

Joshua's mouth tightened into a hard line. The crew were looking at him with a mixture of sympathy and concern.

'I'm thinking of you, too,' he said. 'The invaders are coming up here after us. I can't order you to stay in these circumstances. Jesus, we gave it our best shot. There isn't going to be any mayope again. That's all we ever really came for.'

'We can make one attempt to pick them up,' Sarha said. 'One more orbit. A hundred minutes isn't going to make much difference.'

'And who's going to tell Ashly he has to go down there again? The invaders will know he's coming down for a pick-up.'

'I'll pilot the spaceplane down,' Melvyn said. 'If Ashly doesn't want to.'

'She's my friend,' Joshua said. 'And it's my spaceplane.'

'If there's any trouble in orbit, then we'll need you, Joshua,' Dahybi said. The slightly built node specialist was uncharacteristically firm. 'You're the best captain I've ever known.'

'This is both melodramatic and unnecessary,' Warlow said. 'You all know that Ashly will pilot it.'

'Yes,' Joshua said.

'Joshua!' Melvyn shouted.

But Joshua's neural nanonics were already feeding him an alarm. The gravitonic distortion warning satellites were recording nine large gaps in space being forcibly opened.

Thirty-five thousand kilometres above Lalonde, the voidhawks from Meredith Saldana's 7th Fleet squadron had arrived.

*

An electronic warfare technique that can knock out power circuits as well as processors? What the hell have we come up against?

A single gleam of bright pale green light shone up into the

lounge through the inspection window in the middle of the floor hatch. There was movement below.

'Erick, what's happening?' André Duchamp datavised.

The channel to the lounge's net processor was thick with interference. Erick's neural nanonics had to run a discriminator program to make any sense of the captain's signal.

'We're getting power drop-outs all over the ship!' Madeleine called.

Erick pushed off from the ladder, and grasped the floor hatch's handle to steady himself. Very gingerly he edged his face over the fifteen centimetre diameter window and directly into the beam of light. A second later he was airborne, arms and legs cycling madly as a twisted shout burst from his lips. He hit the ceiling. Bounced. Grabbed at the ladder as his body spasmed in reaction.

Erick had looked into hell. It was occupied by goblinesque figures with hideous bone faces, long, reedy limbs, large arthritis-knobbed hands. They dressed in leather harnesses sown together with gold rings. A dozen at least, boiling out of the airlock tube. Grinning with tiny pointed teeth.

Three of them had clung to Bev, yellow talon fingers slashing rents in his ship-suit. His head had been flung back, mouth open in black horror as the abdominal gashes spewed entrail strands of translucent turquoise jelly. And suicide-terror shone in his eyes.

'Did you see that?' Erick wailed.

'See what? *Merde!* The net is screwed, our databuses are glitched. I'm losing all control.'

'Dear God, they're xenocs. They're fucking xenocs!'

'Erick, *enfant*, dear child, calm down.'

'They're killing him! They love it!'

'Calm! You are an officer on my ship. Now calm. Report!'

'There's twelve – fifteen of them. Humanoid. They've got Bev. Oh, God, they're chopping him to pieces.' Erick shifted a stored sedative program into primary mode, and immediately felt his breathing regularize. It seemed heartless, callous even, wrapping Bev's suffering away behind an artificial cliff of binary digits. But he *needed* to be calm. Bev would understand.

'Are they heavily armed?' André asked.

'No. No visible weapons. But they must have something in the spaceplane, that light I saw—'

All six electronically operated bolts on the floor hatch thudded back together. The metallic bang rang clear across the lounge.

'God . . . André, they just cracked the hatch's codelock.' He stared at it, expecting the manual bolts to slide open.

'But none of the systems processors are working in that capsule!'

'I know that! But they cracked it!'

'Can you get out of the lounge?'

Erick turned to the ceiling hatch and datavised the code at it. The bolts remained stubbornly in place. 'The hatch won't respond.'

'Yet they can open it,' André said.

'We can cut through it,' Desmond Lafoe suggested.

'Our hatches and the capsule decking have a monobonded carbon layer sandwiched in,' Erick replied. 'You'd never get a fission blade through that stuff.'

'I can use a laser.'

'That will allow them into the other capsules, and the bridge,' André said. 'I cannot permit that.'

'Erick's trapped in there.'

'They will not take my ship.'

'André—' Madeleine said.

'*Non.* Madeleine, Desmond, both of you into the lifeboats. I will stay. Erick, I am so sorry. But you understand. This is my ship.'

Erick thumped the ladder, grazing his knuckles. This life-support capsule's lifeboats were accessed from the lower deck.

'Sure.' You murdering pirate bastard. What the fuck do you know about honour?

Someone started hammering on the floor hatch.

They'll be through soon, Erick thought, monobonded carbon or not. Count on it.

'Call Smith for help,' Desmond said. 'Hell, he's got five thousand troops on the *Gemal*, armed and itching to kill.'

'It will take time.'

'You got an alternative?'

Erick looked round the lounge, inventorying everything in sight – cabins, lockers filled with food and clothes, emergency equipment cubicles. All he had was a laser pistol.

Think!

Open the floor hatch and pick them off one at a time as they come through?

He aimed the laser at a cabin door, and pressed the trigger stud. A weak pink beam stabbed out, then flickered and died. Several small blisters popped and crackled where it had struck the composite.

'Bloody typical,' he said out loud.

Look round again. Come on, there must be something. Those dreary months spent on CNIS initiative courses. Adapt, improvise. *Do* something.

Erick dived across the intervening space to a wall of lockers, catching a grab loop expertly. There wasn't much in the emergency cubicle: medical nanonics, pressure patches, tools, oxygen bottles and masks, torch, processor blocks with ship's systems repair instructions, fire extinguishers, hand-held thermal sensor. No spacesuit.

'Nobody said it was going to be easy.'

'Erick?' André asked. 'What is happening?'

'Got an idea.'

'Erick, I have spoken with Smith. Several other ships have been hijacked. He is taking some of his troops out of zero-tau, but it will be at least another thirty minutes before anyone can rendezvous with us.'

The lounge was getting lighter. When Erick looked over his shoulder he saw a ring of small hemispherical blue flames chewing at a patch of the hard grey-green foam on the floor decking. Little twisters of smoke writhed out from the edge. When a circle of titanium roughly a metre in diameter had been exposed it began to glow a dull orange. 'No good, Captain. They're coming through the decking, some sort of thermal field. We haven't got five minutes.'

'Bastards.'

Erick opened the tool-box, and took out a fission-blade knife. Please, he prayed. The blade shone a cool lemon when he thumbed the actuator. 'Sweet Jesus, thank you.'

He flew cleanly through the air. A stikpad anchored him near the middle of the ceiling. He pushed the fission blade into the reinforced composite conditioning duct, and started to saw a circle about thirty centimetres wide.

'Madeleine? Desmond?' he datavised. 'Are you in spacesuits yet?'

'Yes,' Desmond replied.

'You want to do me a *real* big favour?'

'Erick, they cannot stay on board,' André warned.

'What do you want, Erick?' Desmond asked.

'Hauling out of here. Soon.'

'I forbid it,' André said.

'Stuff you,' Desmond retorted. 'I'm coming down, Erick. You may count on me, you know you can.'

'Desmond, if they break into the lounge I will scuttle the ship,' André datavised. 'I must do it before they glitch the flight computer.'

'I know. My risk,' Desmond replied.

'Wait to see if they break out of the lounge first,' Erick said. 'That'll give Desmond a chance to get clear if this doesn't work.'

There was no answer.

'You owe me that! I'm trying to save your ship, damn you.'

'*Oui, d'accord.* If they get out of the lounge.'

The yellow patch on the floor had turned white. It started to hiss, bulging up in the centre, rising into a metre-high spike of light. A ball of fire dripped off the end, gliding up to hit the ceiling where it broke into a cluster of smaller globes that darted outwards.

Erick ducked as several rushed past. He finished cutting a second circle out of the duct and moved along.

Another ball of fire dripped off the spike. Then another. The patch was spreading out over the floor decking, scorching away more of the foam.

'I'm by the hatch, Erick,' Desmond datavised.

The empty lounge was awhirl with small beads of white fire. They had stung Erick several times now, vicious skewers of pain that charred out a centimetre-wide crater of skin. He glanced at the ceiling hatch's inspection window to see the sensor-studded collar of an SII spacesuit pressed against it, and waved.

Erick had cut eight holes in the duct when he heard a shrill creaking sound rise above the hiss. When he glanced down he saw the floor decking itself had started to distend. The metal was cherry red, swelling and distorting like a cancerous volcano.

He watched, mesmerized, as the top burst open.

'Erick,' a voice called out of the rent. 'Let us out, Erick. Don't make it hard on yourself. It's not you we want.'

The triangular rips of radiant metal began to curl back like petals opening to greet the dawn. Shapes scuttled about in the gloom below.

Erick kicked away from the stikpad that was holding him to the ceiling. He landed beside the floor hatch.

'We want the ship, Erick, not you. You can go in peace. We promise.'

A big bloodshot eye with a dark green iris was looking at

him through the floor hatch's inspection window. It blinked, and the lounge lights came back on.

Erick gripped the manual lock handle, twisted it ninety degrees, and pulled up.

The possessed came up through the open hatch, cautiously at first, glancing round the sweltering smoky lounge with wide eyes. Their skin was as white as bleached bone, stretched tight over long wiry muscles. Oily black hair floated limply. They started to advance towards him, grinning and chittering.

'Erick,' they cooed and giggled. 'Erick, our friend. So kind to let us in when we knocked.'

'Yeah, that's me,' Erick said. He had positioned himself beside one of the cabin doors, a silicon-fibre strap round his waist tethering him to a grab hoop. Level with his shoulder, the environment control panel's cover swung free. Erick's right hand rested on a fat red lever inside. 'Your friend.'

'Come with us,' the one in front said as they floated sedately towards him. 'Come join us.'

'I don't think so.' Erick yanked the atmosphere-vent lever down.

The vent system on board a starship was included as a last resort to extinguish fire. It dumped the affected life-support capsule's air straight out of the hull, cutting off oxygen to the flames and killing them dead. And because of the danger a fire represented inside the confined cabin space of a starship, the vent was designed to be quick acting, evacuating an entire deck within a minute.

'NO!' The leader of the possessed screamed in fury and panic. His hands were flung forwards towards Erick in a futile belated attempt to stop the lever clicking home. Spears of white fire arced out of his fingertips.

The panel, its lever, the circuitry behind, Erick's hand, and a half metre circle of wall composite flamed into ruin. Molten metal and a fount of incendiary composite blasted outwards.

Erick cried out in agony as his entire right arm was flayed

down to the bone. His neural nanonics responded instantly, erecting an analgesic block. But the shock was too much, he lurched away from consciousness, only to have stimulant programs bully him back. Menus and medical physiological schematics appeared inside his dazed fragile mind. Options flashed in red. Demands for drugs and treatments to be administered at once. And a single constant pressure alarm.

The very air itself howled like a tormented banshee in its rush to escape from the lounge. Thin, layered sheets of smoke drifting around the ruddy cone torn in the floor condensed to form airborne whirlpools underneath the five ceiling grilles. They spun at a fantastic rate, betraying the speed of the air molecules as they were sucked into the duct.

The possessed were in turmoil, clinging desperately at grab hoops and each other, their assumed shapes withering like glitched AV projections to reveal ordinary bodies underneath. All of them were buffeted savagely by the tempest force drawing them inexorably towards the ceiling. One flew up through the hatch from the lower deck, curving helplessly through the air to slam against a ceiling grille. Suction held him there, squirming in pain.

Another lost hold of a grab hoop, to be sucked backwards up to a grille. Both of them tried to push their way off, only to find it was impossible. The strength that the external vacuum exerted was tremendous. They could feel themselves being pulled through the narrow metal bands of the grille. Sharp edges cut their clothes and began shredding the flesh underneath. Ripples of blue and red energy shimmered around their bodies for a short time, delaying the inevitable; but the exertion proved too much, and the ghostlight quickly faded. The bands of metal sawed down to their ribs. Strips of lacerated flesh were torn off. Blood burst free from a hundred broken veins and arteries, foaming away down the conduit. Organs started to swell through the gaps between the ribs.

Erick activated the Confederation Navy's emergency

vacuum-survival program stored in his neural nanonics. His heart began to slow; muscles and organs were shut down, reducing the amount of oxygen they took from his blood, extending the time which the brain could be kept alive. He hung inertly from the strap fastening him to the wall, limbs pulled towards the ceiling. The charred remnant of his right hand broke off and smacked against a grille.

Blood oozed from the blackened meat of his upper arm.

Scraps of paper, clothing, tools, miscellaneous litter, and personal items from the cabins and lower deck plunged through the lounge to crash into the grilles. There might have been enough material to block them, at least long enough for the possessed to rally and try and shut down the vent or retreat back into the spaceplane. But the extra holes Erick had cut into the duct allowed an unrestricted flow of smaller articles into space. Tattered ribbons of water from the shower and taps in the bathroom poured through the open door to streak through the nearest hole.

The uproarious torrent of air began to abate.

Through pain-hazed eyes, Erick had watched the group's leader turn from semi-naked ogre to a podgy forty-year-old man in dungarees as the micro-storm raged. He was hanging onto a grab loop two metres away, legs pointing up rigidly at the nearest grille, trousers and shirt flapping madly. His mouth worked, bellowing curses and obscenities that were snatched away. A red glow grew around his hand, bloodlight shining through the skin, illuminating the bones within. Mucus and saliva streamed from his nose, joining the flood of debris and liquids vanishing into the duct. The seepage began to turn pink, then crimson.

Now the glow from his hand was fading along with the sound and the fury of the evacuating air. He fixed Erick with a disbelieving stare as tears began to bubble and boil from the surface of his eyes. Balls of blood were spitting out of his nostrils with each beat of his heart.

The last wisp of air vanished.

Erick swung round as the force waned, rotating languidly on the end of the tether strap. The physiological medical schematic his neural nanonics were displaying appeared to be a red statue, except for the right arm which was completely black. Each turn swept the lounge into view. He saw the surviving possessed struggling through the solid cloud of junk that filled the achingly silent compartment. It was difficult to tell which of them were alive. Corpses – two badly mutilated – floated and tumbled and collided with the ones trying to reach the floor hatch. Dead or alive, everyone was weeping blood from their pores and orifices as capillaries ruptured and membranes tore from the immense pressure gradient. They were acting out a bizarre three-dimensional wrestling match in slow motion, with the hatch as their prize. It was macabre. It swam from his view.

Next time round there were fewer movements. Their faces – those he would remember without any help from his neural nanonics image-storage program. Turning.

They were slowing, running down like mechanoids suffering a power drain. The vacuum was turning foggy with fluid. He realized some of it was his own. Red. Very red.

Turning.

All purposeful movement had ceased within the lounge. There was only the gentle stirring of soggy dross.

Around and around. And the redness was fading to grey with the ponderous solemnity of a sunset.

Around.

*

Ilex and its eight cousins flew into a standard defence sphere formation two and a half thousand kilometres wide. Their distortion fields flared out to sample the masses and structure of local space. In their unique perceptive spectrum Lalonde hung below them like a deep shaft bored into the uniformity of space, radiating weak gravity streams to bind its three smaller moons and Kenyon, as it in turn was bound to the bright blue-white star. The interplanetary medium was rich with solar and electromagnetic energy; Van Allen belts encircling the planet shone like sunlight striking an angel's wings. Starships and spaceplanes were revealed in orbit, dense knots in the fabric of space-time, pulsing hotly with electrical and magnetic forces.

Electronic sensors detected a barrage of narrow-beam maser radiation flying between small high-orbit sensor satellites, communication-relay satellites, and the starships. Terrance Smith was being informed of their presence, but there was no hostile response. Satisfied there was no immediate threat, the voidhawks maintained their relative positions for another ninety seconds.

Near the centre of the formation a zone of space the size of a quark warped to an alarming degree as its mass leapt towards infinity, and the first frigate emerged. The remaining twenty warships jumped insystem over the next six minutes. It was a textbook-sharp manoeuvre, giving Admiral Meredith Saldana the widest possible number of tactical options. All he needed was the relevant data to evaluate.

The normal background murmur of voices on *Arikara*'s bridge died away into a shocked hush as the first sensor scans came in. Amarisk occupied the centre of the planet's daylight hemisphere, the red cloud bands above the Juliffe resembling a jagged thunderbolt captured in mid-discharge.

'Was there ever anything like that on this God-blighted planet before?' Meredith Saldana asked in a voice that strained for reasonableness.

'No, sir,' Kelven replied.

'Then it is part of the invasion, a new phase?'

'Yes, sir. It looks that way.'

'Captain Hinnels, do we know what it is?' the Admiral asked.

The staff science officer looked round from a discussion with two of the sensor evaluation team. 'Haven't got a clue,

Admiral. It's definitely optically radiant, but we're not picking up any energy emission. Of course, we're still a long way off. It's rearranging the local weather patterns, too.'

Meredith datavised for the sensor image again, and grunted when he saw the clouds being parted like candyfloss curtains. 'How much power would that take?'

'It would depend on the focal accuracy—' Hinnels broke off at the Admiral's gaze. 'Controlling the weather over a quarter of a continent? A hundred, two hundred gigawatts at least, sir; I can't be more specific, not until I understand how they apply it.'

'And they have that much power to spare,' Meredith mused out loud.

'More importantly, where's it coming from?' Kelven said. 'Durringham had thirty-five fusion generators in the dumpers, and three smaller units in the navy office. Their entire power output didn't add up to more than twenty megawatts.'

'Interesting point, Commander. You think there has been a massive landing operation since you left?'

'Shipping generators in would be the logical answer.'

'But?'

'I don't believe it. The amount of organization necessary to set it up would be incredible, not to mention the number of starships involved. And you saw the flek of Jacqueline Couteur, she can summon up energy from nowhere.'

The admiral gave him a dubious stare. 'There is a difference between flinging fireballs and this.' His hand waved expansively at one of the big bridge holoscreens showing the planet.

'A difference of scale, sir. There are twenty million people on Lalonde.'

Meredith didn't like either alternative. Both implied forces immeasurably superior to that available to his squadron. Probably superior to the whole damn navy, he thought in apprehension. 'Hinnels? Give me an evaluation. Is it safe to move the squadron closer?'

'Given the capability the invaders are demonstrating, I'd say it's not safe even being here, Admiral. Moving into low orbit will obviously increase the risk, but by how much I wouldn't like to say.'

'Thank you,' Meredith said acidly. He knew he shouldn't take out his anxiety on the crew. But damn, that red cloud was unnerving. The *size* of it.

'Very well, we shall attempt to accomplish the First Admiral's orders and halt any use of force by Smith's starships, with the proviso that at the first sign of aggression from the invaders we withdraw at once. I'm not committing the squadron to fight that . . . whatever it is.' He was aware of the relieved looks flashing round the bridge, and diplomatically ignored them. 'Lieutenant Kanuik, have you completed a status review of the mercenary ships?'

'Yes, sir.'

Meredith datavised the computer for a tactical situation display. The mercenary starships seemed to be in considerable disarray, with three under power, heading out of orbit. Probably running for a jump coordinate. Small VTOL spaceplanes were docked to five of the blackhawks. The Adamist craft left in orbit all had their hangar doors open. Another two spaceplanes were rising up from the planet. He cursed silently. They must have landed their scout teams already.

One of the Adamist starships was venting heavily, a grey jet of atmospheric gas shooting out of the hull. Its ion thrusters glowed bright blue to compensate the wayward thrust.

He saw a blackhawk's purple vector line begin to curl up like a corkscrew. Long-range optical sensors showed him the bitek starship tumbling and twisting hectically.

'Sir!'

He cancelled the datavise. Lieutenant Rhoecus, his staff voidhawk coordination officer, was wincing. 'One of the blackhawks, it's . . .' The Edenist puffed his cheeks out and jerked up from his acceleration couch as though someone had thumped him in the belly. 'Its captain is being attacked . . . tortured. There are voices. Singing. The blackhawk's frightened.' He closed his eyes, teeth gritted. 'They want the captain.'

'Who does?'

Rhoecus shook his head. 'I don't know. It's fading. I had the impression of thousands speaking to the captain. It was almost like a habitat multiplicity.'

'Signal from the *Gemal*, Admiral,' a communications rating said. 'Terrance Smith wants to talk to you.'

'Does he now? Put him on.'

Meredith looked into his console's AV projection pillar, seeing an exceptionally handsome man with perfectly arranged black hair. Corporate clone, the Admiral thought. Although the usual smooth flair of competence endemic to the type was in danger of crumbling. Terrance Smith looked like a man under a great deal of pressure.

'Mr Smith, I am Admiral Saldana, commander of this squadron; and under the authority invested in me by the Confederation Assembly I am now ordering you to suspend your military operation against Lalonde. Recall all your personnel from the planetary surface and do not attempt to engage the invader's forces. I also require you to hand over all combat wasps and nuclear devices to the navy. The starships currently under your command are free to leave this system once they have complied with my instructions, except for the *Lady Macbeth*, which is now under arrest. Do you understand?'

'They're up here.'

'Pardon me?'

Terrance Smith's eyes flicked to one side, glancing at someone out of pick-up range. 'Admiral, the invaders are up here. They came up in the spaceplanes that took my scout teams down. They're sequestrating my crews.'

Meredith took a second to compose himself. Four minutes into the mission, and already it was catastrophe. 'Which crews? Which starships?' He suddenly looked across the bridge at

Lieutenant Rhoecus. 'Is that what was happening to the blackhawk captain? Sequestration?'

'It could be, yes,' the startled Edenist replied.

'I want two voidhawks on that blackhawk, now. Restrain it, I don't want it to leave this system. They are authorized to engage it with combat wasps if it resists. Deploy the remaining voidhawks to prevent any of the Adamist starships from leaving. Commander Kroeber.'

'Sir?'

'Squadron to move in now. Full interception duties, I want those starships neutralized. Alert the marine squads, have them stand by for boarding and securement.'

'Aye, aye, sir.'

He turned back to the AV pillar. 'Mr Smith.'

'Yes, Admiral?'

'Which ships have been taken over?'

'I don't know for certain. The only ones which haven't sent spaceplanes down to the surface are the *Gemal*, the *Lythral*, the *Nicol*, and the *Inula*. But the *Cyanea*'s spaceplane never made it back.'

'Admiral,' Kelven interjected.

'Yes, Commander?'

'We don't know the *Gemal* didn't send a spaceplane down. There is no visible evidence of sequestration, certainly not over a communication channel.'

Gravity returned to the *Arikara*'s bridge as the fusion drive came on, building swiftly. The Admiral squirmed his shoulders, trying to get completely comfortable before the high gees squashed him. 'Point taken, Commander Solanki, thank you. Commander Kroeber, all starships are to be intercepted, no exceptions.'

'Aye, aye, sir.'

Meredith checked the tactical situation display again. There was only one spaceplane which hadn't rendezvoused with its parent starship now. 'And tell that spaceplane to remain where it is. It is not to dock. Solanki, start working out how we are going to restrain any starship crew-members that have been sequestrated.'

'Sir, if this sequestration produces the same energy-control ability in the crews that it has in Jacqueline Couteur, I recommend the marines aren't sent into the ships at all.'

'I'll bear that in mind. However, we will certainly have to make at least one attempt.'

'Admiral,' Lieutenant Rhoecus called through gritted teeth. 'Another blackhawk captain is being sequestrated.'

'Acknowledged, Lieutenant.' Meredith reviewed the tactical display again, observing the blackhawk's crazed course, a moth caught in a tornado. 'Send a voidhawk to intercept, full interdiction authority.' That was a third of his voidhawk force committed already. He needed the rest to contain the Adamist starships. If any more blackhawks were taken over he would have to order a combat wasp launch. They would probably fight back.

With his options diminishing before his eyes, Meredith let out a pained hiss of breath as the *Arikara* accelerated past six gees. Sensors reported another mercenary starship's fusion drive igniting.

*

Ashly Hanson came through the airlock tube from the spaceplane and drifted straight into the barrel of a laser rifle. Warlow was holding it, aiming it directly at his forehead.

'Sorry,' the hulking cosmonik boomed. 'But we have to be sure.'

Ashly realized there was a fission saw plugged into his spare left elbow socket, a glowing saffron blade nearly a metre long.

'Sure of what?'

Warlow rotated his principal left arm around the blade. He held a processor block in his hand. 'Datavise something into this.'

'Like what?'

'Anything, doesn't matter.'

Ashly datavised a copy of the spaceplane's maintenance record.

'Thanks. It was Joshua's idea. From the reports we've had it looks like they can't use their neural nanonics.'

'Who can't?'

'Spaceplane pilots who have been sequestrated.'

'Oh, God. I knew it, they can intercept our communications.'

'Yes.' Warlow executed a perfect mid-air roll, and headed for the airlock tube. 'I'm going to check the spaceplane's cabin, make sure you didn't bring any up. Nothing personal.'

Ashly eyed the deck's ceiling hatch. It was locked, red LEDs blinking to show the manual bolts were engaged on the other side. 'The invaders are up in orbit?'

'Yes. Busy hijacking starships.'

'What's Smith doing about it?'

'Nothing. A naval squadron has arrived, it is in their hands now. They have aborted our mission. Oh, and we're under arrest, too.' His diaphragm rattled a metallic approximation of a chuckle.

'The whole fleet? They can't do that. We're operating under *bona fide* contract to the Lalonde government.'

'No, just the *Lady Mac*.'

'Why us?' But he was talking to a pair of disappearing horned feet.

*

'Erick? Erick, are you receiving this?'

'His organs are critical, heading for all-out cellular collapse. For God's sake cancel that suspension program.'

'Got it. Physiological data coming through.'

'Program the nanonic packages for total cranial function support. We have to sustain the brain. André, where the hell's that plasma? He's lost litres of blood.'

'Here, Madeleine. Erick, you wonderful crazy *Anglo.* You got them, do you hear me? You got them!'

'Mesh the infuser with his carotid.'

'It was magnificent. Pull one little lever and all of them, *baboom*, dead.'

'Shit. Desmond, slap a nanonic package on that stump, the epithelium membrane isn't strong enough, he's leaking plasma everywhere.'

'His lungs are filling up too, they must be ruptured. Up the oxidization factor. His brain is still showing electrical activity.'

'It is? Oh, thank God.'

'Erick, don't try and datavise. We've got you. We won't let you go.'

'Do you want to put him in zero-tau?'

'Hell, yes. We're days from a decent hospital. Just let me try and get him stabilized first.'

'Erick, my dear one, don't you worry about a thing. For this I will buy you the best, the greatest, clone body in Tranquillity. I swear. Whatever the cost.'

'Shut *up*, Captain. He's in enough shock as it is. Erick, I'm going to put you back under. But don't worry, everything is going to be just fine.'

*

The last of the six aerovettes stopped transmitting. Reza Malin upped his cranial audio receptors to full sensitivity, trying to hear the noise of the little vehicle's impact. The sounds of the jungle invaded his brain – insect chirps, animal warbles, leaves crackling – filtered and reduced by discrimination programs. He counted to ten, but there was no crash.

'We're on our own now,' he said. The aerovettes had been sent off to the west at a fast walking pace as a decoy, giving the scout team time to melt away into the jungle. He had guessed the invaders could track anything electronic; as Ashly said, if they could create the cloudbands, they could do almost anything. They weren't invincible though, the fact that the team had landed was proof of that. But they were definitely going to provide a formidable challenge. Possibly the greatest Reza would ever face. He liked that idea.

His two hounds, Fenton and Ryall, were slinking through the undergrowth two hundred metres ahead of the scout team, sniffing out people. So far the jungle had been deserted. Pat Halahan's affinity-bonded harpy eagle, Octan, was skimming the treetops, retinal implants alert for the slightest motion below the fluttering leaves. The animals provided a coverage almost as good as the aerovettes.

The team was following a danderil track, heading roughly north-east towards its operational target, the Quallheim Counties. Sal Yong was leading, brushing through the dense vines with barely a sound. With his chameleon circuit activated it looked as though a heavy miniature breeze was whirling along the track. The other six followed quickly (Theo was up overhead somewhere), all of them loaded down with packs, even Kelly. He was pleased to see she was keeping up. If she didn't, it would be a maser pulse through her brain, which would upset some of the team. But he wasn't having a liability of a reporter holding them back. He wondered if she realized that, if it lent a note of urgency to her steps. Probably. She was smart enough, and her bureau chief would certainly have known the deal. So would Joshua, for all his youth, wise beyond his years.

Fenton arrived at a river, and peered out of the bushes lining the steep bank. Reza requested a chart from his inertial-guidance block, and confirmed their position.

'Pat, there's a river one eighty metres ahead, it leads into the Quallheim eventually. Send Octan along it to check for any boat traffic.'

'Right.' The voice seemed to emerge from a small qualtook tree.

'Are we going to use it?' Ariadne asked, a clump of knotted tinnus vines.

'Yes, providing Octan says nobody else is. It's narrow enough, good tree cover. We can cut a day off our time.' He called silently to his hounds, and ordered them to cut back behind the team, covering their rear.

They reached the river three minutes later, and stood at the top of the four-metre bank.

'What is that stuff?' Jalal asked.

The water was clotted with free-floating fleshy leaves, pure white discs a couple of metres in diameter, a tiny purple star in their centre. Each had an upturned rim of a few centimetres, natural coracles. They bobbed and spun and sailed calmly along with the current, undulating with the swell. Some overlapped, some collided and rebounded, but they all kept moving along. Upstream or downstream, whichever way the team looked, the river was smothered in them.

Kelly smiled inside her shell-helmet as the daylight dream of her Lalonde didactic course came slithering into her conscious thoughts. 'They're snowlilies,' she said. 'Quite something, aren't they? Apparently they all bloom at the same time then drift downstream to drop their kernel. It really screws up the Juliffe basin for boat traffic while they're in season.' She tracked her retinal implants along the river. It was all going into a neural nanonics memory cell, scenes of Lalonde. Capturing the substance of a place was always important, it gave the report that little edge, adding to reality.

'They're a bloody nuisance,' Reza said curtly. 'Sewell, Jalal, activate the hovercraft; Pat, Ariadne, point guard.'

The two combat-adepts unslung the big packs they were carrying, and took out the programmed silicon craft, cylinders sixty centimetres long, fifteen wide. They slithered down the bank to the water's edge.

Kelly focused on the sky downstream. At full magnification the northern horizon was stained a pale red. 'It's close,' she said.

'An hour away,' Reza said. 'Maybe two. This river winds a crooked course.'

Sewell shoved a couple of snowlilies aside and dropped his cylinder into the clear patch of water. The hovercraft began to take shape, its gossamer-thin silicon membrane unfolding in a strict sequence, following the pattern built into its molecules. A flat boat-shaped hull was activated first, five metres long, fifteen centimetres thick. Water was pumped into its honeycomb structure, ballast to prevent it from blowing away. The gunwales started to rise up.

Theo Connal dropped lightly to the ground beside Kelly. She gave a slight start as he turned off his chameleon circuit.

'Anything interesting?' Reza asked.

'The cloud is still shifting about. But it's slower now.'

'Figures, the spaceplanes have gone.'

'All the birds are flying away from it.'

'Don't blame 'em,' Pat said.

Kelly's communication block reported that a signal was being beamed down from the geostationary satellites, coded for their team. It was a very powerful broadcast, completely non-directional.

'Kelly, Reza, don't respond to this,' Joshua said. 'It looks like our communications are wide open to the invaders, which is why I'm transmitting on a wide footprint, a directional beam will pinpoint you for them. OK, situation update; we've got big problems up here. Several spaceplanes were taken over while they were on the ground, the invaders are now busy hijacking starships, but nobody can tell which ones. You know Ashly wasn't sequestrated, so that means you should be able to trust me. But don't take orders from anyone else, especially don't broadcast your location. Problem two, a navy squadron has just arrived and shut down the strike mission. Jesus, it's a total fucking shambles in orbit right now. Some of the hijacked ships are trying to run for a jump coordinate, I've got voidhawks blocking the *Lady Mac*'s patterning nodes, and two of my fellow combat-capable trader starships are heading up to intercept the navy squadron.

'Your best bet is to turn round from that cloud and just keep going, out into the hinterlands somewhere. There's no point in trying to locate the invader's bases any more. I'll do my best to pick you up in a day or two, if this cock-up gets sorted by then. Stay alive, that's all you have to worry about now. I'll keep you informed when I can. Out.'

The two hovercraft had finished erecting themselves. Sewell and Jalal were unpacking the energy matrices and superconductor fan motors ready to slot them into place.

'Now what?' Ariadne asked. The team had all gathered around Reza.

'Keep going,' he said.

'But you heard what Joshua said,' Kelly exclaimed. 'There's no point. We have no orbital fire-power back-up, and no mission left. If we just manage to survive for the next few days it's going to be a bloody miracle.'

'You still haven't grasped it yet, have you, Kelly?' Reza said. 'This is bigger than Lalonde; this isn't about doing a dirty job for money, not any more. These invaders are going to challenge the entire Confederation. They have the power. They can change people, their minds, their bodies; mould whole planets into something new, something that we have no part in. Some time soon those ships in orbit are going to have to try and attack, to put a stop to it all. It doesn't matter whether it is Smith or the navy squadron. If the invaders aren't stopped here, they'll keep on coming after us. Sure we can run, but they'll catch us, if not out in the hinterlands than back at Tranquillity, or even Earth if you want to run that far. But not me. Everyone has to make a stand eventually, and mine is right here. I'm going to find a base and let the ships know.'

Kelly held her tongue, she could well imagine how Reza would react to her wheedling.

'More like it!' Sal Yong proclaimed.

'OK,' Reza said. 'Finish fitting out the hovercraft, and get our gear stowed.'

It took a surprisingly short five minutes to complete their preparations and clamber in. Fully assembled the hovercraft was a simple affair, with a big fan at the rear and two cycloidal impellers filling the skirt with air. It was steered mechanically, by vanes behind the fan.

Kelly sat on a bench at the rear of her craft, riding with Sal Yong, Theo Connal, and Ariadne. Now the decision had been made, she was quite glad to be free of the pack and walking through the jungle.

Reza's lead hovercraft moved out from the bank, skimming easily over the snowlilies, and turned downstream. Fenton and Ryall sat in the prow, blunt heads thrust out into the wind as they picked up speed.

27

One thing Princess Kirsten had always insisted on after ascending to the throne of the Principality of Ombey was keeping breakfast a family affair. Crises could come and go, but giving the children quality time was sacrosanct.

Burley Palace, where she ruled from, was situated at the top of a gently sloping hill in the middle of Ombey's capital, Atherstone. Its pre eminent location gave the royal apartments at the rear of the sprawling stone edifice a grand view over the parks, gardens, and elegant residential buildings which made up the city's eastern districts. Away in the distance was the haze-blurred line of deeper blue that was the ocean.

Atherstone was only fifteen degrees south of the equator, putting it firmly in the tropical climate belt, but the early morning breeze coming in off the ocean kept the temperature bearable until about ten o'clock. So Kirsten had the servants set the table on the broad, red-tiled balcony outside her bedroom, where she could sit amid the yellow and pink flowers of the aboriginal tolla vines that choked the back of the palace, and have a leisurely hour with her husband and three natural-born children.

Zandra, Emmeline, and Benedict were aged seven, five, and three respectively, the only naturally conceived children she and Edward had produced. Their first five offspring had been gestated in exowombs after the zygotes had been carefully geneered to the latest physiological pinnacle which the Kulu geneticists had achieved. It was the Saldana family way; incorporating the freshest advances into each new generation, or at least that part of it destined to actually hold high office. Always the elder children, following the old Earth European aristocratic tradition.

Kirsten's first five children would probably live for around two hundred years, whereas she herself and the natural-born three could only hope for about a hundred and eighty years. She had been sixty-six in 2608, when she was crowned in Atherstone Cathedral, two months after her brother Alastair II had assumed the throne on Kulu. As the ninth child, she had always been destined (barring an accident among her older brothers and sister) to rule Ombey, the newest principality.

Like all her nine exowomb siblings, and the five natural-born children of her mother and father, she was tall and physically robust; geneering gave her dark red hair and an oval face with well-rounded cheeks – and of course a thin nose with a tip that curved down.

But geneering could only provide the physical stamina necessary for the stresses resulting in a century of wielding the supreme authority vested in a reigning monarch. She had been in training for the intellectual challenge from birth; first loaded up with the theory, endless politics and economics and management didactic courses, then five years at Nova Kong University learning how to apply them. After serving a twelve-year naval commission (compulsory for all senior Saldanas) she was given divisional management positions in the Kulu Corporation, the massive kingdom-wide utilities, transport, engineering, energy, and mining conglomerate founded by Richard Saldana when he settled Kulu (and still owned solely by the king), graduating up to junior cabinet posts. It was career designed with the sole intent of giving her unrivalled experience on the nature and use of power for when she came to the throne.

Only the siblings of the reigning monarch ruled the Kingdom's principalities on his behalf, keeping the family in direct command. The hierarchy was long established and extraordinarily successful in binding together nine star systems which were physically spread over hundreds of light-years. The only time it had ever come near to failure was when Crown Prince Michael germinated Tranquillity; and the Saldana family would never let anything like that happen again.

Kirsten came out onto the balcony the morning after the *Ekwan*'s arrival feeling distinctly edgy. Time Universe had been triumphantly broadcasting its Laton exclusive since yesterday evening. She had given the news programmes a quick scan after she woke, and the deluge hadn't yet abated. Speculation over the *Ekwan* and Guyana's code two alert was red hot. For the first time since her coronation she found herself considering censorship as an option for calming the mounting media hysteria. Certainly there would have to be some sort of official statement before the day was over.

She pushed up the voluminous sleeves of her rising robe and looked out over the superb lawns with their mixture of terrestrial and xenoc flower-beds, and the artificial lakes graced by black swans. The sky was a deep indigo, without any cloud. Another gorgeous, balmy day; if not in paradise, then as close as she would ever see. But the sunshine panorama left her unmoved. Laton was a name which carried too many adolescent fear-images with it. Her political instinct was telling her this wasn't a crisis that would blow over in the night. Not this one.

That same political instinct which had kept the Saldana family securely on their various thrones for four hundred years.

The children's nanny brought her excitable charges out of the nursery, and Kirsten managed to smile and kiss them all and make a fuss. Edward lifted little Benedict into his lap, while she seated Emmeline next to her own chair. Zandra sat at her place and reached eagerly for the jug of dorze juice.

'Grace first,' Kirsten admonished.

'Oh, Mummy!'

‘Grace.’

Zandra sighed woundedly, clasped her hands together and moved her lips. ‘Now can I eat?’

‘Yes, but don’t bolt it. She signalled one of the four attendant footmen to bring her own tea and toast.

Edward was feeding Benedict slim slices of bread along with his boiled egg. ‘Is the news still all Laton?’ he asked over Emmeline’s head.

‘Yes,’ Kirsten said.

He pulled a sympathetic face, and dangled another bread soldier in front of a cheerful Benedict.

They had been married forty years. A good marriage by any reasonable standards, let alone an institution as odd as a royal marriage. Edward was old money, titled as well, and an ex-navy officer who had served with some distinction. He was also geneered, which was a big plus; the court liked matches with the same range of life expectancy – it made things tidy. They hadn’t quite been pushed into it by the family, but the pressure had been there for someone like him. All the senior Saldanas displayed for public consumption the Christian monogamy ideal. Divorce was, of course, out of the question. Alastair was head of Kulu’s Church, Defender of the Faith throughout the Kingdom. Royalty didn’t break the commandments, not publicly.

However, she and Edward enjoyed a relationship of mutual respect, and trust, and even considerable fondness. Maybe love had been there too at the start of it, forty years ago. But what they had now was enough to carry them through the next century together without bitterness and regret. Which was an achievement in itself. When she thought of her brother Claude’s marriage . . .

‘Mummy’s thinking again,’ Emmeline announced loudly.

Kirsten grinned. ‘Thinking what to do with you.’

‘What?’ Emmeline squealed.

‘Depends what you’ve done wrong.’

'Nothing! Ask Nanny, I've been good. All day.'

'She pinched Rosy Oldamere's swimming towel yesterday,' Zandra said. Emmeline burst into giggles. 'You said you wouldn't tell.'

'It was so funny. Miss Eastree had to lend Rosy hers, she was shivering all over.'

'Her skin was turning blue,' Emmeline said proudly.

'Who's Laton?' Zandra asked.

'A bad man,' Edward said.

'Is he on Ombey?'

'No,' Kirsten said. 'Now eat your rice chips.'

Her neural nanonics gave a silent chime, which warned her from the start it was going to be bad news; her equerry would never allow a datavised message through unless it was serious, not at breakfast. She accessed the Defence and Security Council datapackage.

'Trouble,' she said resentfully.

Edward glanced over as she rose.

'I'll help get them ready for day club,' he said.

'Thanks.' He was a good man.

She walked through the private apartments and emerged into the wide marbled corridor which led to the cabinet offices, drawing startled looks and hurried bows from staff who were in early. She was still dressed in her turquoise and grey rising robe.

The official reception room was a decagonal chamber with a vaulting roof that dripped chandeliers. A horizontal sheet of sunlight was pouring in through a ring of azure windows halfway up the walls. Pillars were inlaid with gold and platinum under a lofriction gloss which kept the metal permanently agleam. Holoprints of impossibly violent stellar events alternated with oil paintings around the walls. There were no modern dreamphase or mood-effusion works; the Saldanas always favoured antiquity for the intimation of timeless dignity it gave.

Three people were waiting for her in the middle of the black tushkwood tile floor. Sylvester Geray was at their head; her equerry, a thirty-six-year-old captain wearing his Royal Kulu Navy dress uniform. Hopelessly formal, she always thought, but he hadn't put a foot wrong since he took up the post three months after her coronation.

The other two, both wearing civilian suits, were a less welcome sight. Roche Skark, the director of the ESA office on Ombey, smiled politely at his princess and inclined his head. Despite geneering, he was a rotund man, in his eighties, and twenty centimetres shorter than Kirsten. He had held his post for thirteen years, dealing with threats and perceived threats throughout the sector with pragmatism and a judicious application of abstruse pressure on the people who counted. Foreign governments might grumble endlessly about the ESA and its influence and meddling in local internal politics, but there was never any solid proof of involvement. Roche Skark didn't make the kind of elementary mistakes which could lead to the diplomatic embarrassment of his sovereign.

Jannike Dermot, on the other hand, was quite the opposite of the demure ESA director. The fifty-year-old woman wore a flamboyant yellow and purple cord stripe suit of some expensive silk-analogue fabric, with her blonde hair arranged in a thick, sweep-back style. It was the kind of consummate power dressing favoured by corporate executives, and she looked the part. However, her business was strictly the grubbier side of the human condition: she was the chief of the Internal Security Agency on Ombey, responsible for the discreet maintenance of civil order throughout the principality. Unlike its more covertly active sister agency, the ISA was mostly concerned with vetting politicians and mounting observations on subversives or anyone else foolish enough to question the Saldana family's right to rule. Ninety-five per cent of its work was performed by monitor programs; fieldwork by operatives was kept to a minimum. Also within its province was the removal of citizens deemed to be enemies of the state; which – contrary to popular myth – was actually a reasonably benign affair. Only people who advocated and practised violence were physically eliminated, most were simply and quietly deported to a Confederation penal planet from which there was never any return.

Quite where the boundaries of the respective agencies' operational fields were drawn tended to become a little blurred at times, especially in the asteroid settlements or the activities of foreign embassy personnel. Kirsten, who chaired Ombey's Defence and Security Council, often found herself arbitrating such disputes between the two. It always privately amused her that despite the nature of their work the agencies were both basically unrepentant empire-building bureaucracies.

'Sorry to disturb you, ma'am,' Sylvester Geray said. 'The matter was deemed urgent.'

'Naturally,' Kirsten said. She datavised a code at one set of high double doors, and gestured for them to follow. 'Let's get on with it.'

The doors opened into her private office. It was a tastefully furnished room in white and powder blue, though lacking in the ostentation of the formal State Office next door where she received diplomats and politicians. French windows looked out into a tiny walled garden where fountains played in a couple of small ornamental ponds. Glass-fronted cabinets and bookshelves stood around the walls, heavy with exquisite gifts from visitors and institutions who enjoyed her patronage. A malachite bust of Alastair II sat on a pedestal in an alcove behind her desk (Allie looking over her shoulder, as always). A classic Saldana face, broadly handsome, with a gravity the sculptor had captured perfectly. She remembered her brother practising that sombre poise in the mirror when he was a teenager.

The doors swung shut and Kirsten datavised a codelock at them. The processor in her desk confirmed the study was now physically and electronically secure.

'The datapackage said there has been a new development in

the *Ekwan* case,' she said as she sat in her high-backed chair behind the desk.

'Yes, ma'am,' Jannike Dermot said. 'Unfortunately there has.'

Kirsten waved a hand for them to sit. 'I didn't think it would be good news.'

'I'd like to bring in Admiral Farquar,' Sylvester Geray said.

'Of course.' Kirsten datavised the processor for a security level one sensenviron conference and closed her eyes.

The illusion was of a curving featureless white chamber with a central oval table; Kirsten sat at the head, with Roche Skark and Pascoe Farquar on one side, and Jannike Dermot and Sylvester Geray on the other. Interesting that the computer should be programmed to seat the two agency directors opposite each other, she thought.

'I would like to formally request a system-wide code two defence alert,' the Admiral said as his opening gambit.

Kirsten hadn't been expecting that. 'You believe Laton will attack us?' she asked mildly. Only she could issue a code two alert, which allowed the military to supersede all civil administration, and requisition whatever personnel and materials it required. Basically it was a declaration of martial law. (A code one alert was a full declaration of war, which only Alastair could proclaim.)

'It's a little more complicated than that, ma'am,' the Admiral said. 'My staff have been reviewing the whole Lalonde–Laton situation. Now this reporter Graeme Nicholson has confirmed Laton was present on the planet, we have to begin to consider other factors, specifically this energy virus which the Edenists reported.'

'I find it quite significant they wanted their findings to be known,' Roche Skark said. 'In fact they actually requested that we should be told. Which is an unusual step given the Kingdom's standard relationship with Edenism. They obviously considered the threat dangerous enough to exceed any political differences. And considering what happened to our G66 troops in Lalonde's jungle I believe they were totally justified.'

'Our analysis of both Jenny Harris's jungle mission and subsequent events on Lalonde suggests that the energy virus and this prevalent sequestration are the same thing,' said the Admiral. 'What we are dealing with is an invisible force that can take over human thought processes and bestow an extremely advanced energy manipulation ability. Sophisticated enough to act as an electronic warfare field, and construct those white fireballs out of what appears to be thin air.'

'I reviewed parts of the jungle mission,' Kirsten said. 'The physical strength those people had was phenomenal. Are you suggesting anyone who is infected will acquire similar capabilities?'

'Yes, ma'am.'

'How is the energy virus transmitted?'

'We don't know,' the Admiral admitted. 'Though we do consider the fact that Laton called it a virus to be significant. The very nature of the term virus, whether employed in the biological or software sense, implies a pattern that can reproduce itself within its host, usually at an exponential rate. But again, I'm not sure. We really are working in the dark on this one, putting together appraisals from observed data. There has to be a priority to discover its exact nature.'

'We can find out relatively easily,' Jannike Dermot said. 'The answer is in Gerald Skibbow's memory – how he was infected and sequestrated, how the energy virus behaves, what its limits are. I consider him to be the key to alleviating our lack of knowledge.'

'Has he recovered yet?' Kirsten asked.

'No. The doctors say he is suffering from a case of profound trauma; it's touch and go if he ever will recover his full intellectual faculties. I want him to undergo a personality debrief.'

'Is that wise, in his state?'

The ISA director showed no emotion. 'Medically, no, not

making him relive the events. But a debrief will provide us with the information we require.'

It was a responsibility Kirsten could have done without; Skibbow was somebody's child, probably had children of his own. For a moment she thought of Benedict sitting in Edward's lap. 'Proceed,' she said, trying to match the ISA director's impersonality.

'Thank you, ma'am.'

'The report from Lalonde said it was Laton himself who warned the Edenists of this energy virus? He claimed he was being attacked by it.'

'That's right, ma'am,' Admiral Farquar said. 'Which is what makes our current problem even more acute.'

'You think he was telling the truth, that it is a xenoc incursion?'

'Under the circumstances, I have to give it strong consideration. Which is why I want a code two alert. It will give me the resources to defend the Ombey system should they back up the virus with a physical invasion.'

Kirsten felt her palms tingle, that earlier unsettling notion that this wasn't just an ordinary crisis was abruptly resumed. 'What do you mean: back up the virus?'

The Admiral flicked a glance at Roche Skark. 'It is a possibility that the *Ekwan* brought it to Ombey,' he said.

'Oh, dear God. Do you have any proof?'

'We are ninety per cent convinced Gerald Skibbow has been purged, although none of the science team can offer an explanation as to how that happened. However, in their haste to get him here, the Lalonde Embassy's Intelligence team may have overlooked the fact that some of their own people were carrying it. After all, Graeme Nicholson's report confirms that Laton – presumably a sequestrated Laton – was in Durringham the day they left. We have to assume the virus was also present in the city's population at that time.'

'When the Admiral's staff informed me of this probability,

my Guyana operatives immediately tried to round up the *Ekwan*'s crew and all the embassy staff,' the ISA director said. 'Three embassy people were unaccounted for: Angeline Gallagher, Jacob Tremarco, and Savion Kerwin. We subsequently found that all three took a spaceplane down to Ombey as soon as the code three restrictions were lifted. We know they landed at Pasto Spaceport seven hours ago. The spaceplane which brought them down suffered from several systems failures and processor glitches during the flight.'

'*Ekwan*'s flight from Lalonde was one long list of malfunctions. But since it docked at Guyana its systems have functioned smoothly,' the Admiral said.

'And the spaceplane?' Kirsten asked, guessing.

'When my people arrived at the spaceport it was in the line company's engineering hangar,' Jannike Dermot said. 'The maintenance crews couldn't find a thing wrong with it.'

'And there was some difficulty with the zero-tau pod when Gerald Skibbow was put in it,' Roche Skark added. 'The implication is that this energy virus isn't quite under control, it interferes with nearby electronic equipment on a permanent basis.'

'So what you're telling me is that they're down here,' Kirsten said.

'Yes, ma'am,' the ISA director acknowledged. 'I'm afraid we have to assume they are. We're hunting them, of course. I've already alerted the police.'

'What about the others who were on board the *Ekwan*?'

'As far as we can tell, they have not been infected.'

'Exactly how do you tell?'

'Those that have neural nanonics can use them. We thought that if the energy virus does have an unrestrained capacity to interfere with circuitry then implants would be the first to suffer a loss of efficiency.'

'Good idea,' she said.

'The rest of *Ekwan*'s complement of colonists are being

brought into close proximity with delicate electronics. So far none of the processor arrays have been affected, but we're repeating the procedure every few hours just to be sure.'

'What about people the three from the embassy came into contact with while they were in Guyana?'

'We have reviewed the spaceport crews,' the Admiral said. 'And we're drawing up a schedule now to run the entire asteroid population through these assessments. Including myself, no exceptions.'

'I see.'

'Will you declare a code two alert, ma'am?'

'I would point out that a code two alert will allow me to quarantine the Xingun continent,' Jannike Dermot said. 'It is unlikely that Gallagher, Tremarco and Kerwin have left yet. I can shut down all air transport to and from the rest of Ombey. I can also order all road traffic to be suspended, though it may prove difficult to enforce in practice. We might get lucky and trap them in Pasto City itself.'

Kirsten summoned up the emergency statutes file from a memory cell and began to review it. Her neural nanonics started to chart a course of action, balancing necessity against the chaos that would come with an attempt to suspend all Ombey's civil and industrial activities. 'Without direct evidence of a physical threat I cannot issue a code two alert,' she said. 'However, I am declaring a code three alert, and a biohazard isolation order for the orbiting asteroids. I want them insulated from each other, from the planet, and from incoming starships. Our orbital facilities are essential to our defence, and I agree that they must be safeguarded against the carriers of this virus. Admiral Farquar, you are to order and enforce a complete quarantine as of now. All civil spacecraft in transit to return to their port of origin.

'Your primary military task is the defence of Ombey and the orbital asteroids with their associated strategic-defence systems. A code three alert will give you the authority to mobilize our resident naval reserve forces; although if it is to mean anything the quarantine order must apply equally to the fleet. Crews will have to be rearranged to ensure that personnel from different asteroid bases are not mixed together. The navy's secondary role will be guarding against further risk of infiltration within the star system as a whole. That means all incoming starships to be refused docking permission.

'As to Xingu, I agree that it should be segregated from the rest of the planet. Sylvester, you are to inform the Xingun continental parliament's speaker that there is now a state of civil emergency in existence. Shut down its air transport links now. And I do mean now, all planes in the air to return to their departure airport. Admiral, if any refuse to comply you are ordered to shoot them out of the sky. Use the low-orbit strategic-defence platforms.'

'Yes, ma'am.'

Kirsten watched Sylvester Geray's image freeze as he started to datavise her orders into the secure government communication net. 'Roche, do you believe the embassy three are going to try and spread the virus among our population?'

'Their actions so far indicate that is their main goal, yes, ma'am.'

'So it's not just them we're looking for, we're going to have to round up anyone they came into contact with?'

'Yes, ma'am. Speed in this instance is going to be essential; the faster they are caught, the fewer possible contamination cases we will have to worry about. It's an exponential problem again. If they go free for too long then it may well escalate beyond our ability to contain, as it did on Lalonde.'

'Jannike, do the police on Xingu have sufficient resources to track them down?'

'I believe so, ma'am,' the ISA director said.

'May I suggest we use someone more familiar with people who have been sequestrated by the virus?' Roche Skark said smoothly. 'I'm sure the civil authorities are capable, Jannike, but I feel hands-on experience will be of immense benefit in this instance. Someone who is perfectly aware of the urgency, and knows how to react should things turn ugly. And judging by Lalonde that may well happen.'

The ISA director stared at him levelly. 'One of your agents, you mean?'

'It is a logical appointment. I recommend Ralph Hiltch is sent to Xingu to oversee the search.'

'Him? The man who didn't even know Laton was on Lalonde, the greatest criminal psychopath the Confederation has ever known!'

'I feel that's slightly unfair, Madam Director. The Confederation and the Edenists believed Laton was dead after the navy destroyed his blackhawks. How many corpses are you currently investigating?'

'Enough,' Kirsten said. 'That will do, both of you. In this situation I think every resource has to be deployed without prejudice; I'd like to believe we can deal with this incident better than a stage one colony planet. That was a good suggestion, Roche; have Ralph Hiltch sent to Pasto immediately. He is to liaise with the civil authorities there, with a brief to advise and assist with the capture of the embassy personnel and identification of anyone else who has been sequestrated.'

'Thank you, ma'am. I'll inform him at once.'

'I just hope he can contain them,' she said, allowing her deeper worries to surface momentarily. 'If not, he could be facing a one-way trip.'

*

The cloudband which lay over the Quallheim was a muddy rouge colour when seen from the underside, streaked with long rusty gold ridges as though it was reflecting the twilight rays of a sinking sun. It grew ever broader, the frayed edges stirring and flexing in disquiet as it swam out lazily over the sweltering jungle.

Kelly, casually accustomed to the enormousness of Tranquillity, was dumbfounded by its size. To the west and east there was no visible end, the band could encircle the world for all those sitting in the hovercraft knew. Straight ahead, to the north, there might have been a hairline of blue sky above the black treetops. Amarisk was slipping gently into a deep luminous cavern.

Thunder, strident bass rumbles that echoed strangely, taking a long time to fade, had been audible for the last twenty minutes as the two hovercraft eased their way towards the Quallheim over the buoyant mass of snowlilies coating the unnamed tributary. There was no sign of any lightning.

The hovercraft slipped under the tempestuous lip of cloud, and red-tinged darkness tightened around them like a noose. With the morning sun high in the sky, the transition into shadow was abrupt, leaving none of the scout team in any doubt of the change. Kelly couldn't help a shiver inside her armour even though the suit kept her skin temperature at a comfortable constant.

Reza's communication block reported it had lost the geosynchronous communication-satellite's beacon. They were cut off from Smith, Joshua, and the navy squadron.

Trees lining the bank became dark and sullen, even the flowers which eternally sprouted from the vines lost their perky glimmer. Snowlilies were the rancid colour of drying blood. High overhead large flocks of birds were embarking on their first ever migration, flapping and gliding towards the brightness sleeting down beyond the cloud.

'The cloud stretches across the heavens like the Devil's own wedding veil. It is the coming of an immortal penumbra as Lalonde is eclipsed by a force before which nature trembles in fear. The planet is being forcibly wedded to a dark lord, and the prospect of cold alien offspring issuing forth is one which gnaws menacingly at the team's fragile spirit.'

'Please!' Sal Yong protested loudly. 'I want to eat sometime today.' The big combat-adept mercenary was sitting on the bench ahead of Kelly, shoulders slewed so the front of his rounded, dull-gloss head was aligned on her.

'Sorry,' she said. She hadn't been aware she was talking out loud. 'This is crazy, you know. We should be running the opposite way.'

'Life is crazy, Kell. Don't let that stop you from enjoying it.' He swung his doughty shoulders back.

'The problem is, I'd like to go on enjoying it, preferably for decades.'

'Then why come here?' Ariadne asked. She was sitting next to Sal Yong, steering the hovercraft with a small joystick.

'Born stupid, I guess.'

'I've been with Reza for a decade now,' the female ranger scout said. 'I've seen atrocities and violence even your scoop-happy company would never show for public consumption. We've always made it home. He's the best combat scout team leader you'll ever meet.'

'On a normal mission, yes. But this bloody thing—' Her arm rose to take in the cloud and gloomy jungle with an extravagant sweep. 'Look at it, for Christ's sake. Do you really think a couple of well-placed maser blasts from orbit are going to knock it out? We need the whole Confederation Navy armed with every gram of antimatter they've ever confiscated.'

'Still got to have somewhere to shoot that antimatter down at,' Sal Yong said. 'The navy would have to send the marines in if we weren't already here shovelling shit. Think of the money we're saving the Confederation taxpayer.'

Beside Kelly, Theo broke into a high-pitched chuckle. He even sounds like a monkey, she thought.

'Regular marines couldn't handle this,' Ariadne said cheerfully, guiding the hovercraft round a rock. 'You'd need the Trafalgar Greenjackets. Special-forces types, boosted like us.'

'Bunch of knuckle shufflers, all theory and drills,' Sal Yong said witheringly. The two of them started arguing over the merits of various regiments.

Kelly gave up. She just couldn't get through to them. Perhaps that was what made mercenaries so different, so fascinating. It wasn't just the physical supplement boosting, it was the attitude. They really didn't care about the odds, staking their life time and again. That would make a good follow-up story back at Tranquillity; interview some ex-mercs, find out why they had quit. She loaded a note in her neural nanonics. The pretence of normality. Keep the mind busy so it doesn't have time to brood.

The hovercraft arrived at the Quallheim itself after another forty minutes. It was four or five times the width of the tributary, over two hundred and fifty metres broad. Both banks were overrun with tall trees that leant over the river at sharp angles, plunging aerial roots and thick vines into the water. Snowlilies lay three deep on the surface, moving at an infinitesimal pace. Where the tributary emptied into the Quallheim they formed a mushy metre-high dune on top of the water.

Now the scout team headed upriver, keeping close to the northern bank and the paltry cover of the trees. Reza seemed more concerned about lying exposed to the cloud than proximity to possible hostiles on the land. With nothing but the lightly furrowed carpet of snowlilies opening out like an empty ten-lane motorway ahead, the hovercraft began to pick up speed.

It was dark on the river, under the centre of the cloudband, an occultation which made all the team switch to infrared vision. The trees blocked any sight of the natural sunlight beyond it. Thunder was a constant companion, booms slithering up and down the river like the backwash of some vast creature burrowing its way through the vermilion vapour above. Big insects, similar to terrestrial dragonflies but without wings, skipped across the snowlilies, only to be hurled tumbling by the wind of the hovercraft's passage. Vennals, burning with a pink-blue radiance of charcoal embers, hung in the branches of the trees, watching the small convoy rush past with wide, soft eyes.

Towards the middle of the morning, Reza stood up and signalled the second hovercraft towards the northern bank where there was a break in the trees. Ariadne rode the craft up the lush grass to a halt next to its twin. Fenton and Ryall were already bounding off into the undergrowth.

'I didn't want to datavise,' Reza said when they all gathered round. 'And from now on we'll operate a policy of minimal electronic emission. Ariadne, have you detected any broadcasts from the invaders?'

'Not yet. I've had our ELINT blocks scanning since we landed. The electromagnetic spectrum is clean. If they're communicating it's either by ultra-tight beam, or fibre optics.'

'They could be using affinity, or an analogue,' Pat said.

'In that case, you can forget homing in on them,' she said. 'Nobody can intercept that kind of transmission.'

'What about the blackhawks?' Jalal asked. 'Could they detect it?'

'No good,' Pat said. 'They can't even detect the bond between me and Octan, let alone some xenoc variant.'

'Never mind,' Reza said. 'The Quallheim Counties were the origin of the invasion. There has to be a large base station around here somewhere. We'll find it. In the meantime, there is a village called Pamiers a couple of kilometres ahead. Pat says Octan has located it.'

'That's right,' Pat Halrahan said. 'He's circling it now, at a reasonable distance. The whole place is illuminated with white light, yet there is no break in the cloud overhead. There are houses there as well, about thirty or forty proper stone buildings alongside the wood shacks the colonists build.'

'Smith said there were buildings like that in villages the observation satellites did manage to view,' Reza said.

'Yeah, but I can't see where they came from,' Pat said. 'There are no roads at all, no way to bring the stone in.'

'Air or river,' Sewell suggested.

'Invade a planet then airlift in stone houses for the population?' Pat said. 'Come on, this is weird, but not insane. Besides, there is no sign of any construction activity. The grass and paths haven't been churned up. And they should have been, the houses have only been here a fortnight at most.'

'They could be something like our programmed silicon,' Kelly said, and rapped a gloved knuckle on the hard gunwale behind her. 'Assembled in minutes, and easily airlifted in.'

'They look substantial,' Pat said with vague unease. 'I know that's not an objective opinion, but that's the way it feels. They're solid.'

'How many people?' Reza asked.

'Twenty or twenty-five walking about. There must be more inside.'

'OK, this is our first real chance to obtain serious Intelligence data as to what's going on down here,' Reza said. 'We're going to deactivate the hovercraft and cut through the jungle around the back of Pamiers. After we've reached the river again and set up a retreat option, I'll take Sewell and Ariadne with me into the village, while the rest of you provide us with some cover. Assume anyone you meet is hostile and sequestrated. Any questions?'

'I'd like to come into Pamiers with you,' Kelly said.

'Your decision,' Reza said indifferently. 'Any real questions?'

'What information are we looking for?' Ariadne asked.

'Intent and capability,' Reza said. 'Also physical disposition of their forces, if we can get it.'

Hackles raised inside her armour, Kelly let the team shove a couple of hovercraft electron matrices into her pack before they all set off again. Reza didn't want them to walk in single file, for fear of ambush; instead they fanned out through the trees with chameleon circuits on, avoiding animal paths. There was a method of trekking through the raw jungle, Kelly learnt, and for her it was always walking where Jalal walked. He seemed to instinctively find the easiest way around trees and thick undergrowth, avoiding having to force his way against the clawing branches and heavy loam. So she kept her helmet sensors focused on the low-power UV pin-point light at the nape of his neck, and bullied her legs to keep up.

It took them fifty minutes to skirt the village and wind up back at the river. Sewell and Jalal set to activating the hovercraft at the top of a short slope above the water. Kelly dumped her pack into the locker at the rear of the second craft, and felt as though she could fly without the extra weight. With equipment stowed, the team fitted their weapons, checked power and projectile magazines, and set off back towards Pamiers.

*

Reza found the first corpse two hundred metres short of the village clearing. It was Ryall who smelt it for him, a sharp tang of dead flesh which even the jungle's muggy air couldn't disguise. He sent the hound veering off towards it. Ryall promptly smelt another corpse, causing Reza to hurriedly damp down his reception of the hound's olfactory sense.

It was a child, about five or six, he guessed. Ryall had found it sitting huddled up at the foot of a mayope tree. Age was hard to determine; there wasn't a lot left, so he had to go by size. Insects and humidity had accelerated the decomposition, though it was strange no animal had disturbed it. According to his didactic memory, sayce were supposed to be fairly brutal carnivores.

He led Sewell, Kelly, and Ariadne through the trees to the body, and dispatched Ryall to the second.

'It's a girl,' Ariadne said after examining the remains. She held up a nondescript length of filthy, dripping-wet fabric. 'This is a skirt.'

Reza wasn't going to argue. 'How did she die?' he asked.

'There are no broken bones, no sign of violence. Judging by

the way she's curled up between the roots I'd say she crawled here to die. Poisoned? Starving? No way of knowing now.'

'Scared of the invaders,' Reza said thoughtfully. 'They probably didn't bother to sequestrate the children.'

'You mean the adults just ignored her?' Kelly asked in disgust.

'Ignored her, or drove her away. A child like this wouldn't walk around in the jungle by herself. The village had been established long enough for her to pick up basic jungle lore.'

Ryall trotted up to the second corpse, emitting a warm feeling of satisfaction as his muzzle touched the putrefying flesh. Reza picked up the sense of accomplishment and expanded the affinity band allowing himself to see through the hound's enhanced retinas. 'It's another kid,' he told them. 'A bit older, there's a baby in its arms.' Ryall could scent more decaying meat in the humid air, three or four blends, all subtly different. Closer to the river, Fenton had picked up a further series of traces. 'My God,' Reza growled in a dismayed whisper. 'They're everywhere, all around.'

A village like Pamiers would start off with a population of about five hundred. Say two hundred families, and they've been here a couple of years. That would mean about a hundred and fifty children.

He stood, scanning the jungle. Slender yellow target graphics slid up over the black and red image in an uncomplicated, unprogrammed reflex. He wanted to shoot something dead. His neural nanonics ordered a slight endocrine effusion, stabilizing the sudden hormonal surge.

'Come on, she can't help us any more,' he said, and began pushing briskly through the bushes and vines towards the village. He turned his chameleon circuit off, and after a few paces the others followed suit.

Pamiers followed the standard configuration of settlements along the Juliffe's tributaries. A semicircular clearing chopped out of the jungle along the side of the river. Crude single-storey houses clustered together in no particular order at the centre, along with larger barns, a church, a meeting hall, an Ivet compound. Wooden jetties ventured ten or fifteen metres into the water, with a few fishing skiffs tied up. Fields and plots ringed the outside, a surfeit of crops pushing out of rich black loam.

However, Pamiers' layout was all that remained recognizable as the four of them stepped out of the trees.

'Where is this light coming from?' Kelly asked, looking round in surprised confusion. As Pat had reported, the village bathed luxuriantly in a bright pool of sunlight, and yellow pollen was thick in the air. She scanned the cloud overhead, but there was no break. Thunder, muted while they were in the trees, rolled insistently around them once more.

Ariadne walked on a few paces, activating her full implant sensor suite as well as the specialist blocks clipped to her belt. She turned a complete circle, sampling the environment. 'It's omnidirectional. We're not even leaving shadows. See?'

'Like an AV projection,' Reza said.

'Yes and no. The spectrum matches Lalonde's sun.'

'Let's go see what those new houses are made of,' he said.

Pamiers' fields had been left untended. Terrestrial plants were fighting a fierce battle for light and height with the vines that had surged out of the jungle to reclaim their native territory. Fruit was hanging in mouldy white clusters.

Yet inside the ring of fields, the grass around the houses was short and tidy, studded with what looked suspiciously like terrestrial daisies. When he had studied the sheriff's satellite images on the flight from Tranquillity Reza had seen the way the village clearings were worn down and streaked with muddy runnels. Grass and weeds grew in patchy clumps. But this was an even, verdant carpet that matched Tranquillity's parkland for vitality.

Stranger still were the houses.

Apart from three burnt-out ruins, the original wooden

shacks had been left standing, their planks bleached a pale grey, shuttered windows open to the weather, bark slates slipping and curling, solar-cell panels flapping loosely. They were uninhabited, that was obvious at a glance. Mosses, tufts of grass, and green moulds were tucked into corners and flourishing promisingly. But jammed at random between the creaky cabins were the new structures. None of them was the same, with architectural styles ranging across centuries – a beautiful two-storey Tudor cottage, an Alpine lodge, a Californian millionaire's cinderblock ranch, a circular black landcoral turret, a marble and silverglass pyramid, a marquee which resembled a cross between a Bedouin tent and a medieval European pavilion, complete with heraldic pennants fluttering on tall poles.

'Having some trouble with my blocks,' Ariadne said. 'Several malfunctions. Guido and communications are right out.'

'If it begins to affect the weapons we'll pull back,' Reza cautioned. 'Keep running diagnostic programs.'

They cleared the fields and started to walk over the grass. Ahead of them a woman in a long blue polka-dot dress was pushing a waist-high gloss-black trolley that had a white parasol above it, and huge spindly wheels with chrome wire spokes. Whatever it was, it was impossibly primitive. Reza loaded the image's pixel pattern into his neural nanonics with an order to run a comparison search program through his encyclopaedia. Three seconds later the program reported it was a European/North American style pram *circa* 1910–50.

He walked over to the woman, who was humming softly. She had a long face that was crudely painted in so much make-up it was almost a clown's mask, with dark brown hair worn in a severe bun, encased by a net.

She smiled up happily at the four members of the team, as though their weapons and equipment and boosted form were of no consequence.

That simpleton smile was the last straw for Reza, whose

nerves were already stretched painfully thin. Either she was retarded, or this whole village was an incredibly warped trap. He activated his short-range precision sensors, and scanned her in both electromagnetic and magnetic spectrums, then linked the return into a fire-command protocol. Any change in her composition (such as an implant switching on or a neural nanonics transmission) and his forearm rifle would slam five EE rounds into her. The rest of his sensors were put into a track-while-scan mode, allowing his neural nanonics to keep tabs on the other villagers he could see walking about among the buildings behind her. He had to use four back-up units, several principal sensors had packed up altogether. The overall resolution was way down on the clarity he was used to.

'What the fucking hell's going on here?' he demanded.

'I have my baby again,' she said in a lilting tone. 'Isn't he gorgeous?'

'I asked you a question. And you will now answer.'

'Do as he says,' Kelly said hastily. 'Please.'

The woman turned to her. 'Don't worry, my dear. You can't hurt me. Not now, not any more. Would you like to see my baby? I thought I'd lost him. I lost so many back then. It was horrible, all those dead babies. The midwives tried to stop me seeing them; but I looked just the same. They were all perfect, so beautiful, my babies. An evil life it was.' She bent forwards over the pram and lifted out a squirming bundle draped in lacy white cloth. The baby cooed as she held it out.

'Where have you come from?' Reza asked. 'Are you the sequestration program?'

'I have my life back. I have my baby back. That's what I am.'

Ariadne stepped forward. 'I'm going to get a sample from one of those buildings.'

'Right,' Reza said. 'Sewell, go with her.'

The two of them walked round the woman and started off towards the nearest house, a whitewashed Spanish hacienda.

The baby let out a long gurgle, smiling blithely, feet kicking inside the wrap. 'Isn't he just adorable,' the woman said. She tickled his face with a finger.

'One more time,' Reza said. 'What are you?'

'I am me. What else could I be?'

'And that?' He pointed to the cloud.

'That is part of us. Our will.'

'Us? Who is us?'

'Those who have returned.'

'Returned from where?'

She rocked the baby against her chest, not even looking up. 'From hell.'

'She's either nuts, or she's lying,' Reza said.

'She's been sequestrated,' Kelly said. 'You won't get anything out of her.'

'So sure of yourselves,' the woman said. She gave Kelly a sly look as she cuddled the baby. 'So stupid. Your starships have been fighting among themselves. Did you know that?'

Reza's neural nanonics' optical-monitor program reported more people were appearing from the houses. 'What do you know about it?'

'We know what we feel, the pain and the iron fire. Their souls weeping in the beyond.'

'Can we check?' Kelly asked urgently.

'Not from here.'

The woman laughed, a nervous cackle. 'There aren't many left to check, my dear. You won't hear from them again. We're taking this planet away, right away. Somewhere safe, where the ships can never come to find us. It will become paradise, you know. And my baby will be with me always.'

Reza regarded her with a chill of foreboding. 'Yes, you are a part of this,' he said quietly. The yellow target graphics locked on to her torso. 'What is happening here?'

'We are come, and we are not going to leave. Soon the whole

world will be hiding from the sky. From *heaven.* And we shall live on in peace for ever.'

'There will be more of this red cloud?'

The woman slowly tilted her head back until she was staring straight up. Her mouth fell open as though in wonder. 'I see no clouds.' She started to laugh wildly.

Reza saw Ariadne had reached the hacienda. The ranger scout was bending over, scraping at the wall with some kind of tool. Sewell was standing behind her, the long gaussrifle barrels he had plugged into his lower elbow sockets swivelling from side to side in an automatic sweep pattern.

'Ariadne,' Reza bellowed. 'Get back here. We're leaving now.'

The woman's laughter chopped off. 'No, you're not.' She dropped the baby.

It was Reza's infrared sensors which caught the change. A wave of heat emerged right across her body and started to flow like a film of liquid, rushing along her arms as she brought them up, becoming denser, hotter.

His left forearm's gaussgun fired five electron explosive rounds just as a white light ignited around her hands. There was three metres between them. Impact velocity alone would have been enough to tear her body apart, with the EEs detonating as well there was nothing left for the last three rounds to hit.

Kelly's armour hardened protectively as the blast wave slammed into her. Then she screamed as a jet of spumescent gore slopped across the front of the paralysed fabric.

'Sewell, zero the area!' Reza shouted.

The twin heavy-calibre gaussrifles the big combat-adept mercenary carried began to blaze, squirting out a barrage of EE projectiles. Emerald-green laser beams emerging from Reza and Ariadne snapped on and off, traversing the clearing in a strobe waltz as their lighter weapons picked off targets.

Kelly's armour unlocked. She fell to her knees, centimetres

from the baby. Her hand went out instinctively, twitching the blood-soaked lace aside to see if it was still alive.

There was a vennal inside the wrap. The little xenoc creature had been distorted, its vulpine skull swollen and moulded into a more globular shape, scales melded together and stretched. They were losing their distinctive blue-green pigmentation, fading to pale pink. Its forepaws had become chubby, tiny human hands scrabbled feebly at the air. Squeals of terror emerged from its toothless mouth.

Her neural nanonics were unable to quell her stomach spasm in time. An emergency program triggered the shell-helmet's quick-release seal, and the visor sprang open. She vomited onto the neatly mown grass.

Sewell ran backwards across the grass, making almost as much speed as he could travelling forward. An autonomic locomotion program took care of that, guiding his feet round possible obstacles, leaving his conscious thoughts free to assist with target selection.

The first fire sequence had ripped into the houses, smashing them apart in plumes of ionic flame and smoke. Even Sewell, who was aiming for maximum destruction, was surprised by the devastating effect the rifles inflicted. As soon as the first EE projectile hit the buildings their bright colours switched off, leaving behind a neutral grey. The rifles laid down a comprehensive fire pattern. Walls and roofs buckled and collapsed, sending out billowing clouds of thick dust, support timbers splintered then seemed to crumble. Within seconds the whole area had been reduced to pulverized rubble. The old shacks bent and bowed before the pressure blasts; they were far sturdier than the new houses. Several keeled over, wood twisting and shrieking. Slate-tile roofs somersaulted, intact walls slewed through the air rippling like giant mantas.

Sewell switched to the people, concentrating on coordinates where the target-allocation program had located individuals. The feed tubes from his backpack magazine hummed smoothly as they supplied the gaussrifles with fresh ammunition. There had been eighteen people visible to his sensors before Reza's shouted order. He pumped airburst shrapnel rounds after them as they dived for cover amid the shattered houses.

Infrared sensors showed him eccentric waves of heat shimmering amid the expanding dust. White fire, like an earthbound comet, streaked towards him. Boosted muscles flung him aside. The gaussrifles swung round to the origin, compensating for his dive. EE projectiles pummelled the area.

'Up, you bitch!' Reza yelled at Kelly. 'Back to the hovercraft.'

She rolled over, seeing a fermenting red cloudscape sky lit by green lasers and white fireballs. Fear and hatred fired her limbs and she jerked to her feet. The houses were a flattened circle belching smoke and dust. White fire raged in a spiral maelstrom above them, slinging out splinters that arced overhead. Trees fell and fire bloomed where they struck the wall of jungle. Sewell and Ariadne were charging towards her, both firing back into the rubble.

Kelly took three paces towards the trees then stopped. She pulled her nine-millimetre automatic pistol from her holster in one smooth movement. The gun's familiarization and targeting program went into primary mode, and she fired two bullets into the mutated vennal. Then she sprinted after Reza, neural nanonics releasing a torrent of adrenalin and amphetamines into her bloodstream.

Pain stabbed into the back of Ariadne's left thigh as the fireball struck her. Neural nanonics erected an analgesic block straight away. Compensator programs shifted her balance, favouring her right leg, activating those left thigh muscles which remained functional. Valves in the veins and arteries of her pelvis and knee sealed, limiting the blood loss. Her speed was barely reduced. She caught up with Kelly just as a fireball hit the reporter in the side of her ribs.

Kelly's armour gleamed an all-over ruby as it tried to disperse the energy. A circle of the suit flared as it melted. The fire lingered round the rent, chewing at the exposed skin. She stumbled and fell, rolling on the damp loam of an overgrown strawberry patch, beating wildly at the flame with her gauntlets.

'Keep going,' Ariadne shouted. Her targeting program located another figure moving through the thinning dust cloud. The TIP pistol plugged into her wrist socket fired a burst of energy at it.

The entire left side of Kelly's ribs had gone numb, frightening her at a deeper level than programs or chemicals could relieve. None of the mercenaries were slowing down. *They're not going to help me!*

Kelly ordered her neural nanonics to override her trembling muscles and scrambled to her feet. Her integral medical program was signalling for attention. She ignored it and ran on. The clearing's sourceless sunlight went out, plunging her back into the stark red and black landscape of the infrared image.

It took her eight minutes to reach the hovercraft. Eight minutes of furiously punching vines out of her way and skidding on mud while the three mercenaries hurled out a barrage of fire through the jungle to cover their retreat. Eight minutes of white fireballs twisting and swerving round trunks, pursuing the team with the tenacity of smart seeker missiles. Of thunder roaring overhead and flinging down stupendous lightning bolts that rocked the ground. Sudden impossible gusts of wind rising from nowhere to slap her around like a lightweight doll. Of neural nanonic programs and endocrine implant effusions assuming more and more control of her body as its natural functions faltered under the unrelenting demands of her flight.

One hovercraft was already rushing down the slope into the snowlily-congested river when she arrived at the little glade.

'Bastards!' she yelled weakly.

Lightning struck twenty metres behind her, sending her sprawling. Reza was sitting behind the second hovercraft's control panel, hand playing over the switches. The impeller fans began to spin, forcing air into the skirt. It began to rise slowly upwards.

Sewell and Sal Yong stood on either side of it, their gauss-rifles blasting away at unseen targets.

Kelly started to crawl. The first of the white fireballs shot out of the trees, curving round to drop on the hovercraft. Lightning flashed down again. A mayope tree toppled over with a sepulchral splintering. It crashed down ten metres behind her, one of the upper boughs coming down straight on top of her legs. Her armour stiffened, and her bent knees were pushed sharply into the yielding loam.

'Wait!' Kelly begged in a rasp. 'For fuck's sake, you shit-heads. *Wait!*'

The hovercraft's skirt was fully inflated, twigs and leaves were thrown out from under the thick rubbery fabric. Sewell hopped over the gunwale.

'Jesus God, I can't move. Help me!' Her vision contracted to a tunnel with the hovercraft at the far end.

'Help me!'

Sewell was standing in the middle of the hovercraft. One of his gaussrifles turned towards her. Leaves and small branches rustled and slithered like serpents over her legs, she could feel them coiling round her calves. Then Sewell fired. The explosions sent her cartwheeling over the ground. She slammed into something hard. It grated along the side of her armour suit. Moving. Hovercraft! Her hands scrabbled with animal passion against it. And she was being lifted effortlessly into the air. Rationality ended there and she kicked and flailed against the air. 'No! No! No!'

'Easy there, Kell, I've got you.'

Her world spun round as the big mercenary dumped her unceremoniously on the floor of the hovercraft. She gagged, limbs juddering as the neural nanonics stopped sending out compulsive overrides. After a minute she began to sob, the quivering muscle motions starting deep in her belly and emerging through her mouth.

'You made it,' Sal Yong said later. How much later Kelly didn't know, her mind was furred with tranquillizers, thoughts slow. She tried to sit up, and winced at the bands of pain tightening around her ribs. A medical diagram unfolded inside her skull. Her body's decay in unwelcome detail.

'The tree!' she barked hoarsely.

'We got it,' Sewell said. 'Shitfire, but that was weird.'

'You were going to leave me!' Panic set her skin crawling. Blue lights flashed silently around the physiological display. More tranquillizers.

'You're going to have to learn to keep up, Kell,' Reza said in his normal level tones. 'We're on a combat mission. I told you when we started, I can't spare anyone for baby-sitting duties.'

'Yes.' She flopped back down. 'So you did. I'm sorry.' I simply didn't realize you were serious, that you would leave a fellow human being behind, to face . . . that.

'Hey, you did all right,' Sal Yong said. 'Lotsa people would have screwed up, they had all that shit thrown at them.'

'Oh, thanks.'

There were mechanical clunks from somewhere behind her as Sewell detached his gaussrifles. 'Let's see about getting that armour off you, Kell. You look like you could do with some field aid.' She felt him touch the suit's seal catch, and then humid sticky air was sliding over her skin. Her helmet came off, and she blinked dizzily.

Sewell was sitting on a bench above her, holding a couple of medical nanonic packages. Kelly avoided looking at her ribs; the physiological display was bad enough.

'Looks like I'm not the only one,' she said, smiling bravely. His artificial skin was pitted with small deep blackened craters where the white fire had struck, including a long score on the side of his glossy head. Blood and fluid dribbled out of the cracks each time he moved. 'Or are you going to say they're just flesh wounds?'

'Nothing critical.'

'Oh, crap, I'm drowning in macho culture.'

'You can put your gun down now, Kell.'

The nine-millimetre pistol was still in her hand, fingers solidified round its grip. She gave it a bewildered stare. 'Right. Good idea.'

He tilted her gently on her right side, then peeled the covering off the nanonic package. It moulded itself to her left side, curving round to cover her from her navel to her spine. The colours of her physiological display changed, reds diluting to amber, as it began knitting itself to her wound.

'Where are we going?' she asked. The hovercraft was moving faster than it had before. Humidity was making her sweat all over, the smell of vegetation was rank, itching her throat. Lying half-naked racing through a xenoc jungle being chased by monsters and cut off from any hope of rescue. She knew she ought to be reduced virtually to hysterics, yet really it was almost funny. You wanted a tough assignment, my girl.

'Aberdale,' Reza said. 'According to the LDC's chief sheriff, that's where the first reported trouble started.'

'Of course,' Kelly answered. There was a strange kind of strength on the far side of utter despair, she found, or maybe it was just the tranquillizers.

'Kell?'

She closed her leaden eyelids. 'Yes.'

'Why did you shoot the baby?'

'You don't want to know.'

*

The navy squadron closed on Lalonde at seven gees, crews prone on their acceleration couches with faces screwed up against the lead-weighted air which lay on top of them. When they were seventeen thousand kilometres out, the fusion flames died away and the starships rotated a hundred and eighty degrees in a virtuoso display of synchronization, ion thrusters crowning them in a triumphant blue haze. The *Arikara* and the *Shukyo* released twenty combat communication-relay satellites, streaking away at ten gees to englobe the planet. Then the warships began to decelerate.

As the merciless gee force returned to *Arikara*'s bridge Meredith Saldana accessed the tactical display. The voidhawks had performed small swallow manoeuvres, taking them to within two and a half thousand kilometres of the planet and curving into orbit ahead of the Adamist warships to which such short-range precision jumps were impossible. But the mercenary fleet was leading the bitek starships a merry dance. Three blackhawks were racing away from Lalonde, striving for the magic two thousand kilometre altitude where they would be outside the influence of the planet's gravitational field, allowing them to swallow away. Voidhawks were in pursuit. Four of the nine combat-capable independent traders were also under acceleration. Two of them, *Datura* and *Cereus*, were heading on a vector straight towards the squadron at two and a half gees. They wouldn't respond to any warning calls from the *Arikara*, nor Terrance Smith.

'*Haria*, *Gakkai*, go to defensive engagement status, please,' Meredith datavised. The situation display showed him the two frigates end their deceleration burn, flip over, and accelerate ahead of the rest of the squadron.

'What is the state of the remaining mercenary ships?' the Admiral enquired.

'Smith claims the starships remaining in orbit are obeying his orders, and therefore haven't been hijacked,' said Lieutenant Franz Grese, the squadron Intelligence officer.

'What do you think?'

'I think Commander Solanki was right, and we'd better be very careful, Admiral.'

'Agreed. Commander Kroeber, we'll send a marine squad

into the *Gemal* first. If we can verify that Smith himself hasn't been hijacked or sequestrated it may just make our job that bit easier.'

'Aye, aye, sir.'

The tactical situation warned him the *Datura* and *Cereus* were launching combat wasps. Meredith observed in astonishment as each of them released a salvo of thirty-five; according to the accompanying identification codes the starships were small vehicles, forty to forty-five metres in diameter. They couldn't have held back any reserves – what absurd tactics. The drone armaments began to accelerate from their launch craft at twenty gees.

'No antimatter, Admiral,' datavised Second Lieutenant Clark Lowie, the *Arikara*'s weapons officer. 'Fusion drives only.'

That's something, Meredith thought. 'What's their storage capacity?'

'Best estimate would be forty combat wasps maximum, Admiral.'

'So they haven't left any for their own defence?'

'Looks that way, sir.'

Haria and *Gakkai* launched a counter salvo; eighty combat wasps leaping ahead to intercept the incoming hostiles at twenty-seven gees. Purple, red, and green vector lines sprang up in Meredith's mind, as if someone was performing laser acupuncture right across his skull. The combat wasps started to squirt megawatt electronic warfare pulses at each other. Active and kinetic submunitions began to scatter. Two disc-shaped swarms formed, five hundred kilometres across, alive with deceitful impulses and infrared signatures. Electron beams flashed out, perfectly straight lightning bolts glaring against the starfield. The first explosions flared. Kiloton nuclear devices were detonated on each side. Smaller explosions followed as combat wasps blew apart under the prodigious energy impact.

A second, smaller, salvo was launched by the frigates, compensating for the loss.

'Admiral, the *Myoho* reports the blackhawk it's chasing is about to swallow outsystem,' Lieutenant Rhoecus called. 'Request permission to follow.'

'Granted. Follow and interdict; it is not to come into contact with inhabited Confederation territory.'

'Aye, aye, sir.'

A vast circle of space burst into pyrotechnic oblivion as the two antagonistic combat wasp swarms collided, as though a giant wormhole had been torn open into the heart of a nearby star. The annular plasma storm eddied violently, radiating down through the visible spectrum in seconds until only nebulous violet mists were left.

Arikara's sensor clusters struggled to burn through the conflagration and present an accurate representation of events through the tactical situation display. Some submunitions from both sides had survived. Now they were accelerating towards their intended targets. All four combatant ships began high-gee evasive manoeuvres.

Myoho and its blackhawk disappeared from the display. *Granth* and *Ilex* both fired a volley of combat wasps at their respective prey.

Haria's masers began to fire as the remaining submunitions closed on it. Small vivid explosions peppered nearby space. Rail guns thumped out a stream of steel spheres which formed a last-ditch kinetic umbrella. Eight surviving submunitions drones detected it, three of them were gamma-pulse lasers. A second before they struck the umbrella they fired.

Large oval sections of the frigate's hull turned cherry red under the radiation assault. Molecular-binding generators maxed out as they fought to keep the monobonded silicon's structure intact. The energy-dispersal web below the silicon struggled to absorb and redistribute the intense influx. All the sensor clusters either melted or had their electronics burnt out by the gamma-ray deluge. Replacement clusters rose immediately; but the starship was blind for a period of three seconds.

In that time the remaining five submunitions hit the kinetic umbrella. They disintegrated instantly, but hypervelocity fragments kept coming. With the sensors unable to see them and direct the frigate's close-range weapons they struck the hull and vaporized. The binding generators, already heavily stressed, couldn't handle the additional loading. There were half a dozen localized punctures. Fists of plasma punched inwards. Internal systems melted and fused as they were exposed. Fuel tanks ripped open sending hundred-metre fountains of vaporizing deuterium shooting out.

'*Bellah*, assist, please,' Commander Kroeber ordered. 'Rescue and recovery.' The stricken frigate's emergency beacon was howling across the distress bands. The life-support capsules should have easily withstood the strike. Even as he requested more information from the computer the sensor image showed him ion thrusters firing to slow the frigate's wayward tumble.

With all of their combat-wasp stocks exhausted in the first salvo, *Datura* and *Cereus* were left with only short-range masers to defend themselves against the assault from the frigates' drones. The electronic warfare barrage was unrelenting as the drones closed at twenty gees, defeating the starships' sensors. The two mercenary starships exploded within seconds of each other.

A cheer went round the *Arikara*'s bridge. Meredith felt like joining in.

'Admiral, another blackhawk is leaving orbit,' Lieutenant Rhoecus said.

Meredith cursed, he really couldn't spare another voidhawk. A quick check on the tactical display revealed little information, the blackhawk was on the other side of Lalonde from the squadron. 'Which is the nearest voidhawk?'

'The *Acacia*, Admiral.'

'Can they hit it with combat wasps?'

'They have a launch window, but estimate only a thirty per cent chance of success.'

'Tell them to launch, but remain in orbit.'

'Aye, aye, sir.'

'*Bellah* reports survivors from the *Haria* have been detected, Admiral,' Commander Kroeber said. 'They're matching velocities.'

'Good. Hinnels, has there been any reaction from the Juliffe cloud bands?'

'Nothing specific, sir. But they've been growing wider at a constant rate, the area they're covering has increased by one and a half per cent since we arrived. It adds up to a respectable volume.'

Another combat-wasp battle raged high above Lalonde's terminator as the drones from the *Granth* encountered defences fired by their prey. Then the blackhawk vanished down a wormhole interstice. Three seconds later *Granth* followed.

'Damn,' Meredith muttered.

But the *Ilex* was having better luck. Its combat-wasp salvo had forced the blackhawk it was chasing to flee back down towards the planet.

The Admiral requested a channel to the *Gemal*. 'We shall be boarding you first, Smith. Any resistance and the marines will shoot to kill, understood?'

'Yes, Admiral,' Terrance Smith replied.

'Have you received any updates from the teams you landed?'

'Not yet. I expect most of them were sequestrated,' he added gloomily.

'Tough. I want you to broadcast a message that their mission is over. We will pick up any survivors if at all possible. But none of them is to attempt to penetrate under the cloud, no hunting of enemy bases. This is now a Confederation Navy problem. I don't want the invaders antagonized unduly.' Not while my squadron is so close to that bloody cloud, he finished silently. It was the sheer quantity of power involved again. Frightening. And the berserk way the hijacked ships were behaving didn't help.

'I'm not sure I can guarantee that, Admiral,' Smith said.

'Why not?'

'I issued the team leaders with kiloton nukes. It would give them a fall-back in case the starships were unable to provide strike power. I was worried the captains might balk at bombarding a planetary surface.'

If it hadn't been for the fierce gee force Meredith would have put his head in his hands. 'Smith, if you get out of this with your life, it won't be on my account.'

'Well, fuck you!' Terrance Smith yelled. 'You Saldana bastard, why do you think I had to hire these people in the first place? It's because Lalonde is too poor to rate decent navy protection. Where were you when the invaders landed? You would never have come to help us put down that first insurrection, because it didn't affect your precious financial interests. Money, that's what you shits respect. What the hell would you know about ordinary people suffering? You were born with a silver spoon in your mouth that's so big it's sticking out through your arse. The only reason you're here now is because you're frightened the invasion might spread to worlds you own, that it might hit your credit balance. I'm doing what I can for *my* people.'

'And that includes nuking them, does it?' Meredith asked. He'd been subject to anti-Saldana bigotry for so long now the insults never even registered. 'They're sequestrated, you cretin, they don't even know they're your people any more. This invasion isn't going to be beaten by brute force. Now, you will broadcast that message, make the mercenary teams turn back.'

The tactical display sounded an alarm. A broad fan of curving purple vector lines were rising high over Wyman, Lalonde's small arctic continent. Someone behind the planet had launched a salvo of fifty-five combat wasps.

'My God,' Meredith muttered. 'Lowie, what are they aimed at?'

'Unclear, Admiral. There is no single target, it's a rogue

salvo. But from the vectors I'd say they were seeking to engage anything in the thousand-kilometre orbit . . . Bloody hell.'

A second salvo, of equal size, was curving round the south pole.

*

'Jesus, that's a neat pincer movement,' Joshua said. At some ridiculous private level he was delighted he didn't need any intervention from his neural nanonics to remain calm. He felt his mind function with that same cool reserve which had manifested itself back in the Ruin Ring when Neeves and Sipika appeared.

This is me, what I am: a starship captain.

The *Lady Mac*'s three fusion drives came on almost without conscious thought. 'Stand by for combat gees,' he warned.

'How many?' Sarha asked nervously.

'How high is up?'

Other starships were getting under way, retracting their thermo-dump panels. Three of them launched combat wasps in a defensive cluster formation.

'Remain in orbit,' Smith ordered over the command net. 'The navy squadron will provide us with protective cover from the salvo.'

'Like bollocks they will,' Joshua said. The squadron was still four minutes from orbital injection. A sensor scan revealed blackhawks and voidhawks alike racing up for a higher altitude; the slower Adamist starships were following, with three exceptions, *Gemal* one of them.

The gee force in *Lady Mac*'s bridge passed five gees. Ashly groaned in dismay. 'My bones can't take this.'

'You're younger than me,' Warlow countered.

'I'm more human, too.'

'Wimp.'

'Castrated mechanoid.'

Sarha suddenly noticed the trajectory Joshua had loaded

into the flight computer. 'Joshua! Where the hell are you taking us?'

Lady Mac was rising above the equatorial plane at seven gees, decreasing altitude at the same time.

'We're going under them.'

'This trajectory is going to graze the atmosphere!'

He watched more of the mercenary starships launching combat wasps. 'I know.' It had been an instinctive manoeuvre, opposing every tactic program in the flight computer's memory core; they all said altitude was the key in orbital combat situations, giving you more room to manoeuvre, more flexibility. Everyone else in the little mercenary fleet was clinging to that doctrine, escaping from Lalonde with fusion drives operating way out on the limit. 'Dad was always telling me about this one,' he said in what he hoped was a confident manner. 'He always used it in a scrape. *Lady Mac*'s still about, isn't she?'

'Your bloody father isn't!' Sarha had to datavise, she couldn't expel enough air from her lungs to talk. The acceleration had reached nine gees. She hadn't known even *Lady Mac* could produce that kind of drive level. Every internal membrane supplement had turned rock hard. An arterial implant at the base of her neck was injecting oxygen into her bloodstream, making sure her brain didn't starve. She couldn't ever remember having to use it before. Joshua Calvert, we are not a bloody combat wasp!

'Look, it's very simple,' he explained, trying to sort out the logic in his own mind. As usual, rationality was trailing well behind impetuosity. 'Combat wasps are designed for deep-space operations. They can't operate in the atmosphere.'

'We are designed for deep-space operations!'

'Yes, but we're spherical.'

Sarha couldn't snarl, she would have dislocated her jaw bone; but she managed to grate her teeth together.

Lady Macbeth flew over the Sarell continent in forty-five seconds, arching down sharply towards the brown and yellow volcanic deserts. She was three hundred kilometres in altitude when she passed over the northern coastline; the north pole was two and a half thousand kilometres ahead. Seven hundred kilometres above, and four thousand kilometres ahead, the combat wasp salvo spotted her. Six of them abruptly altered course and dived down.

'Here they come,' Joshua said. He fired eight of *Lady Mac*'s combat wasps, programming them for a tight defence-shield formation. The drones leapt upwards at twenty gees, scattering submunitions almost immediately.

Aft sensors showed the starships in orbit behind and above were releasing more and more combat wasps. Even the *Gemal* was breaking out of its thousand-kilometre orbit, the old colonist-carrier could only make one and a half gees. And there was no escort, Joshua saw sadly. Far away to the east, barely above the horizon, there was a volley of explosions followed by the unmistakable larger smeared detonation of a starship. Wonder who that was? It didn't seem to matter much, only that it wasn't him.

'Melvyn, keep monitoring the grav-detector satellite data. I want to know if any ships start jumping outsystem, and if possible where to.'

'I'm on it, Joshua.'

'Dahybi, I can't believe the voidhawks can keep jamming our nodes with all this going on, the second they slip I want to know.'

'Yes, Captain.'

The sensors showed Joshua the attacking combat wasps releasing their submunitions. Particle beams lanced out from both swarms. 'OK, everybody, here we go.' He shot an order directly into the drive deflector coils, and *Lady Mac* lurched downwards.

Meredith Saldana caught the crazy flight vector developing and datavised a request into the tactical situation computer for confirmation. The vector was recomputed and verified. Half of the squadron's frigates would be unable to produce a nine-gee thrust. 'Who's that idiot?' he asked in reflex.

'*Lady Macbeth*, sir,' Lieutenant Franz Grese said. 'None of the others have triple-fusion drives.'

'Well, if they all suicide on us I shall be a very happy man.'

It wasn't looking good. He had already changed the squadron's operational orbit from one thousand kilometres to two thousand three hundred, which would give them a superior look-down shoot-down position – but only if the mercenary ships stayed put. Injection was in ninety seconds. Combat wasps were being launched at a prodigious rate from the mercenary fleet. Intelligence and tactics programs couldn't say which were defensive and who was attacking whom. Each of his squadron's ships had launched a defence cluster salvo.

One of the voidhawks exploded with appalling savagery, and the victorious blackhawk skirted its roiling debris plume to vanish into a wormhole interstice.

'Who?' he asked Rhoecus.

'*Ericra*, but they saw the combat-wasp barrage approaching. *Ilex* has their memory patterns safe.'

Even now, after all the truths he had seen in his cosmopolitan life, Meredith felt the old twang of prejudice. Upon death, souls departed this life for ever. It was the Christian way. They were not to be ensnared in a mockery of God's living creatures.

You can leave the Kingdom, he acknowledged jadedly, but it never leaves you.

Go in peace, he prayed silently for the dead Edenists. *Wherever you roam.*

On a more pertinent level he was down to six voidhawks.

'Combat wasps have locked on to the *Gemal*, sir,' Clarke Lowie reported.

The gee force on the bridge was reducing rapidly as the *Arikara* slid into orbit.

Thank Christ for small mercies, Meredith thought. 'Commander Kroeber, squadron to engage all combat wasps launched by the mercenary fleet. We'll sort out who's friendly and who isn't when events become a little less immediate.'

'Aye, aye, sir.'

Arikara trembled as a salvo was fired.

'Issue a blanket order for all mercenary starships to cease acceleration and evasive manoeuvres as soon as the combat wasps have been cleared. Failure to comply will result in naval fire.'

'Aye, aye, sir.'

When the *Lady Mac* reached one hundred kilometres' altitude Joshua withdrew all but five sensor clusters. Wyman's fjord-etched coastline was directly below. Three hundred kilometres overhead, the two combat-wasp swarms were firing a fusillade of kinetic missiles and coherent radiation at each other. They clashed at a closing speed of over seventy kilometres per second. A patch of sky burst into pure white atomic fury, bringing a transient dawn to the arctic continent's month-long night underneath.

Eleven submunitions broke through to descend on the *Lady Macbeth* with cybernetic mayhem in their silicon brains. Two of them were one-shot gamma pulsers. They tracked the hurtling starship as it buffeted its way through the upper atmosphere, then discharged the energy in their electron matrices with one swift burst. The resulting gamma-ray beam lasted for a quarter of a second.

A sheath of ions had already built up around the *Lady Macbeth*'s hull, a tangerine florescence that radiated away from the forward fuselage in hypersonic ripples. But they were swiftly lost against the incandescent streams of energized helium emerging from the fusion tubes. The stratosphere reeled from the unrestrained tumult of the starship's passage. Her exhaust stretched out over a hundred and fifty kilometres behind her, evanescing into titanic electrical storms which lashed the sharp icy steppes seventy-five kilometres below with a vigour that threatened to split the glaciers open to the bedrock.

Insubstantial green and scarlet borealis spectres cavorted over the ice-encrusted continent in a display which rivalled the bands over the Juliffe in scale.

'Breakthrough!' Warlow cried.

Systems schematics filled Joshua's mind, laced with red symbols. The hull's molecular-binding generators, already labouring with the burden imposed by the ion sheath, had overloaded in half a dozen places as the gamma pulses drilled into the monobonded silicon.

He switched back to the flight management display. The thrust from one of the fusion tubes was reducing. 'Any physical violation?' The thought of needles of blazing atmospheric gases searing in over the delicate modules and tanks at this velocity was terrifying. Neural nanonics effused an adrenalin antidote into his bloodstream.

'Negative, it's all energy seepage. But there's some heavy component damage. Losing power from generator two, and I've got cryogenic leakages.'

'Compensate, then, just keep us functional. We'll be through the atmosphere in another twenty seconds.'

Sarha was already datavising a comprehensive list of instructions into the flight computer, closing pipes and tanks, isolating damaged sub-components, pumping vaporized coolant fluid from the malfunctioning generator into emergency dump stores. Warlow began to help her, prioritizing the power circuits.

'Three nodes are out, Joshua,' Dahybi reported.

'Irrelevant.' He took the starship down to sixty kilometres.

The nine remaining kinetic missile drones followed. They were, as Joshua said, intended for deep space operation: basically a sensor cluster riding on top of fuel tanks and a drive unit. There was no streamlining, no outer fuselage; in a vacuum there was no need for such refinements. All they had to do was collide with their victim, mass and velocity would obey Newton's equations and combine to complete the task. But now they were flying through the mesosphere, a medium implacably alien and hostile. Ionization started to accumulate around their blunt circular sensor heads as the gas thickened, turning to long tongues of violet and yellow flame which licked back along the body. Sensors burnt away in seconds, exposing the guidance electronics to the radiant incoming molecules.

Blinded, crippled, subject to intolerable heat and friction pressures, the kinetic drones detonated in garish starburst splendour twenty kilometres above the *Lady Macbeth.*

The *Arikara*'s tactical situation display showed their vectors wink out almost simultaneously. 'Very smart,' Meredith said grudgingly. It took a hell of a nerve to pilot a starship like that – nerve and egomaniacal self-confidence. I doubt I would have that much gumption.

'Stand by. Evasive manoeuvring,' Commander Kroeber said.

And Meredith had no more time to reflect on the singular antics of Joshua Calvert. Punishing gravity returned abruptly to the flagship's bridge. A third salvo of combat wasps leaped out of their launch-tubes.

Lady Macbeth soared out of the mesosphere, throwing off her dangerous cloak of glowing molecules. Behind her, Wyman's ice-fields glimmered under eerie showers of ethereal light. Combat-sensor clusters rose out of their hull recesses on short stalks, their golden-lensed optical scanners searching round.

'We're in the clear. Thank you, sweet Jesus.' Joshua reduced the thrust from the fusion drives until it was a merely uncomfortable three gees. Their trajectory was taking them straight away from the planet at a high inclination. There were no combat wasps within four thousand kilometres. I *knew* the old girl could do it. 'Told you so,' he sang at the top of his voice.

'Awesome,' Ashly said, and meant it.

On the couch next to Joshua, Melvyn shook his head in dazed admiration despite the gee force.

'Thanks, Joshua,' Sarha said gently.

'My pleasure. Now, damage assessments please. Dahybi, can we jump?'

'I'll need time to run more diagnostics. But even if we can jump it isn't going to be far. Those three nodes were physically wrecked by the gamma pulses. Our energy patterns will have to be recalculated. Ideally, we need to replace the nodes first.'

'We're only carrying two spares. I'm not made of money. Dad always jumped with nodes damaged and—'

'Don't,' Sarha pleaded. 'Just for once, Joshua. Let's deal with the present, OK?'

'Somebody's jumped outsystem,' Melvyn said. 'The grav-detector satellites registered at least two distortions while we were performing our dodo impersonation, I think there may have been a wormhole interstice opened as well. I can't tell for sure, half of the satellites have dropped out.'

'There is no jamming from the voidhawks any more,' Dahybi said.

'OK, great. Warlow, Sarha, how are our systems coping?'

'Number two generator's out,' Warlow said. 'I've shut it down. It took the main strike from the gamma rays. Lucky really, most of the energy was absorbed by its casing. We'll have to dump it when we dock, it's got a half-life longer than some geological eras now.'

'And I'd like you to stop using the number one fusion-drive tube,' Sarha said. 'The injection ionizers are damaged. Other than that, nothing serious, we've got some leaks and some component glitches. But none of the life-support capsules were breached, and our environmental-maintenance equipment is fully functional.'

'Got another jumper,' Melvyn called out.

Joshua reduced thrust to one gee, cutting drive tube one altogether, then accessed the sensors. 'Jesus, will you look at that?'

Lalonde had acquired its own ring, gloriously radiant stripes of fusion fire twining together to form a platinum amulet of immense complexity. Over five hundred combat wasps were in flight, and thousands of submunitions wove convoluted trajectories. Starships initiated high-gee evasive manoeuvres. Nuclear explosions blossomed.

The *Lady Macbeth*'s magnetic and electromagnetic sensors were recording impulses nearly off the scale. It was a radiative inferno.

'Two more wormhole interstices opening,' Melvyn said. 'Our bitek comrades are leaving in droves.'

'I think we'll join them,' Joshua said. Just for once in her life, Sarha might be right, he conceded. It was the now which counted. *Lady Mac* was already two thousand kilometres in altitude, and rising steeply from the pole; he shifted their inclination again, carrying them further north of the ecliptic and away from the conflict raging above the planet's equatorial zones. Another three thousand kilometres and they would be out of the influence of Lalonde's gravity field, and free to jump. He made a mental note to travel an additional five hundred klicks – no point in stressing the nodes, given their state. About a hundred seconds at their current acceleration. 'Dahybi, how is the patterning coming?'

'Reprogramming. Another two minutes. You really don't want to rush me with this one, Joshua.'

'Fine, the further we are from the gravity field the better.'

'What about the mercs?' Ashly said. It wasn't loud, but his level voice carried the bridge easily.

Joshua banished the display showing him possible jump coordinates. He turned his head and glared at the pilot. Why was there always one awkward bastard? 'We can't! Jesus, they're killing each other back there.'

'I promised them, Joshua. If they were alive I said I would go down and pick them up. And you said something similar in your message.'

'We'll come back.'

'Not in this ship, not in a week. If we dock at a port, it'll take a month to refit. That's without any hassle from the navy. They won't be alive in two days, not down there.'

'The navy said they'd pick up any survivors.'

'You mean that same navy which right now is shooting at our former colleagues?'

'Jesus!'

'There isn't going to be a combat wasp left in thirty minutes,' the pilot said reasonably. 'Not at the rate they're expending them. All we have to do is sit tight for a couple of hours out here.'

Instinct pushed Joshua, *repelled* him from Lalonde and the red cloud bands. 'No,' he said. 'I'm sorry, Ashly, but no. This is too big for us.' The coordinate display flipped up in his mind.

Ashly looked desperately round the bridge for an ally. His eyes found Sarha's guilty expression.

She let out an exasperated sigh. 'Joshua?'

'Now what!'

'We should jump to Murora.'

'Where?' His almanac file produced the answer, Murora was the largest gas giant in the Lalonde system. 'Oh.'

'Makes sense,' she said. 'There's even an Edenist station in orbit to supervise their new habitat's growth. We can dock there and replace the failed nodes with our spares. Then we can jump back here in a day or so and do a fast fly-by. If we get an answer from the mercs, and the navy doesn't shoot us on sight, Ashly can go down to pick them up. If not, we just head straight back to Tranquillity.'

'Dahybi, what do you think?' Joshua asked curtly. Most of his anger was directed at himself; he should have thought of Murora as an alternative destination.

'Gets my vote,' the node specialist said. 'I really don't want to try an interstellar jump unless we absolutely have to.'

'Anybody else object? No? OK, nice idea, Sarha.' For the third time, the jump coordinate display appeared in his mind.

He computed a vector to align the *Lady Mac* on the gas giant, eight hundred and fifty-seven million kilometres distant.

Ashly blew Sarha a kiss across the bridge. She grinned back.

Lady Macbeth's two remaining fusion drives powered down. Ion thrusters matched her course to the Murora jump coordinate with tiny nudges. Joshua fired a last coded message at the geostationary communications satellites, then the dish antenna and various sensor clusters started to sink down into their jump recesses.

'Dahybi?' Joshua asked.

'I've programmed in the new patterns. Look at it this way, if they don't work, we'll never know.'

'Fucking wonderful.' He ordered the flight computer to initiate the jump.

*

Two kinetic missiles hammered into the frigate *Neanthe*, almost severing it in half. When the venting deuterium and glowing debris cleared, *Arikara*'s sensors observed *Neanthe*'s four life-support capsules spinning rapidly. Still intact. Kinetic missiles found two of them while a one-shot pulser discharged eighty kilometres away, stabbing another with a beam of coherent gamma radiation.

Admiral Saldana clenched his teeth in helpless fury. The battle had rapidly escalated out of all control, or even sanity. All the mercenary ships had fired salvos of combat wasps, there was simply no way of telling which were programmed to attack ships (or which ships) and which were for defence.

The tactical situation computer estimated over six hundred had now been launched. But communications were poor even with the dedicated satellites, and sensor data was degraded by the vast amount of electronic warfare signals emitted by everybody's combat wasps. One of the bridge ratings had said they'd be better off with a periscope.

When it came, the explosion was intense enough to outshine

the combined photonic output of the six hundred-plus fusion drives whirling round above Lalonde. An unblemished radiation nimbus expanded outwards at a quarter of the speed of light, engulfing starships, combat wasps, submunitions, and observation satellites with complete dispassion; hiding their own detonation behind a shell of scintillating molecules. When it was five hundred kilometres in diameter it began to thin, swirling with secondary colours like a solar soap bubble. It was three thousand kilometres ahead of the *Arikara*, yet it was potent enough to burn out every one of the sensors which the flagship had orientated on that sector of space.

'What the hell was that?' Meredith asked. The fear was there again, as always. Antimatter.

Seven gees slammed him down in his couch as the starship accelerated away from the planet and the dwindling explosion.

Clark Lowie and Rhys Hinnels reviewed the patchy tactical situation data leading up to the explosion. 'It was one of their starships which imploded, sir,' Clarke Lowie said after a minute's consultation. 'The patterning nodes were activated.'

'But it was only three thousand kilometres above Lalonde.'

'Yes, sir. They must have known that. But they took out the *Shukyo* and the *Bellah*. I'd say it was deliberate.'

'Suicide?'

'Looks that way, sir.'

Five ships. He had lost five ships, and God knows how much damage inflicted on the rest of them. Mission elapsed time was twenty-three minutes, and most of that had been spent flying into orbit from the emergence point.

'Commander Kroeber, withdraw all squadron ships from orbit immediately. Tell them to rendezvous at the jump coordinate for Cadiz.'

'Aye, aye, sir.'

A direct repudiation of the First Admiral's orders, but there was no mission left, not any more. And he could save some crews by retreating now. He had that satisfaction, for himself.

The gravity plane shifted slightly as the *Arikara* came round onto its new vector, then reduced to five gees. Another salvo of combat wasps was fired as enemy drones curved round to intercept them.

Madness. Utter madness.

*

The river was one of the multitude of smaller unnamed tributaries that covered the south-western region of the colossal Juliffe basin. Its roots were the streams wandering round the long knolls which made up the land away to the south of Durringham, merging and splitting a dozen times until finally becoming a single steadfast river two hundred kilometres from the Juliffe itself.

At the time the spaceplanes brought down the mercenary scout teams there was still a respectable current running through it, the deflected rains hadn't yet begun to affect the flow of water. In any case, the lakes and swamps which accounted for a third of its length formed a considerable reservoir, capable of sustaining the level for months.

The snowlilies, too, were relatively unaffected. The only difference the red cloud made was to extend the period it took for the aquatic leaves to ripen and break free of their stems. But where it ran through the thickest jungle that made up the majority of the Juliffe basin, the snowlilies seemed almost as numerous as always. Certainly they managed to cover the river's thirty-metre width, even if they weren't layered two or three deep as they had been in previous seasons.

Where the tributary ran through a quiet section of deepest jungle, one of the snowlilies five metres from the bank bulged up near the centre, then tore. A fist with grey water-resistant artificial skin punched through and began to widen the tear. Chas Paske broke the surface, and looked round.

The banks on either side of him were steep walls made from the knotted roots of cherry oak trees. Tall trunks straddled the summit, their white bark stained magenta from the light filtering through the tenebrous canopy far overhead. As far as the combat-boosted mercenary could see there was nobody around. He struck out for the shore.

His left thigh had been badly damaged by the white fire flung by the women who'd ambushed them. It was one reason for diving into the river as his team fled from the spaceplane's landing zone. Nothing else seemed to extinguish the vile stuff.

Their shrill, delighted laughter had reverberated through the trees as the mercenaries crashed through the undergrowth. If he had just been granted another minute to unload their gear, establish a perimeter defence formation, the outcome would have been so very different. They had enjoyed it, those vixen women, that was the terrifying part of it, calling happily to each other as the mercenaries ran in panic. It was a game to them, exhilarating sport.

They weren't people as he understood. Chase Paske was neither a superstitious nor religious man. But he knew that whatever evil had befallen Lalonde had nothing to do with Laton, nor was it going to be solved by Terrance Smith and his rag-tag forces.

He reached the bank and started to climb. The roots were atrociously slippery, his left leg dangled uselessly, and his arms and back were badly burnt, debilitating the boosted muscles. It was a slow process, but by jamming his elbows and right knee into crannies he could lever and pull himself upwards.

The women, it appeared, hadn't understood the feats a boosted metabolism was capable of. He could survive for an easy four hours underwater without taking a breath. A useful trait when chemical and biological agents were being used.

Chas scrambled up the last couple of metres to the top of the woody bank, and rolled into the lee of a crooked trunk. Only then did he start to review the bad news his neural nanonics medical program was supplying.

The shallow flesh burns he could ignore for now – although

they would need treating eventually. Almost half of his outer thigh had been burnt away, and the dull glint of his silicolithium femur was visible through the minced and charred muscle tissue. Nothing short of a total rebuild was going to get his leg functioning again. He started picking long white worm-analogues from the lairs they were burrowing into the naked wound.

He didn't even have his pack with him when the women attacked. There was only his personal equipment belt. Which was better than nothing, he thought phlegmatically. It contained two small neural nanonic packages, which he wrapped round the top of his thigh like an old-fashioned bandage. They didn't cover half the length of the wound, but they would stop poisoned blood and aboriginal bacteria from getting into the rest of his circulatory system. The remainder of it was going to fester, he realized grimly.

Taking stock, he had a first aid kit, a laser pistol with two spare power magazines, a small fission-blade knife, a hydrocarbon analyser to tell him which vegetation contained toxins his metabolism couldn't filter, a palm-sized thermal inducer, and five EE grenades. He also had his guido block, a biological/chemical agent detector block, and an electronic warfare detector block. No communications block, though, which was a blow; he couldn't check in with Terrance Smith to request evacuation, or even find out if any other members of his team had survived.

Finally there was the kiloton fusion nuke strapped to his side in its harness. A black carbotanium sphere twenty centimetres in diameter, thoroughly innocuous looking.

Chas did nothing for five minutes while he thought about his situation; then he began to cut strips of wood from the cherry oaks to form a splint and a crutch.

*

Hidden behind its event horizon, the singularity came into being two hundred and twenty thousand kilometres above Murora, its intense mass density bending the course of nearby photons and elementary particles in tight curves. It took six milliseconds to expand from its initial subatomic size out to fifty-seven metres in diameter. As it reached its full physical dimensions the internal stresses creating the event horizon ceased to exist.

Lady Macbeth fell in towards the gas giant, ion thrusters squirting out long spokes of cold blue fire to halt the slight spin caused by venting coolant gases. Thermo-dump panels stretched wide to glow a smoky cardinal red as they disposed of the excess thermal energy acquired during the starship's frantic flight through Lalonde's polar atmosphere. Sensor clusters swept the local environment for hazards while star trackers fixed their exact position.

Joshua exhaled loudly, allowing his relief to show. 'Well done, Dahybi. That was good work under pressure.'

'I've been in worse situations.'

He refused to rise to the bait. 'Sarha, have you locked down those malfunctioning systems yet?'

'We're getting there,' she said blandly. 'Give me another five minutes.'

'Sure.' After the harsh acceleration of Lalonde orbit, free fall was superbly relaxing. Now, if she'd just give him a massage . . .

'That was one hell of a scrap back there,' Melvyn said.

'We're well out of it,' Warlow rumbled.

'Feel sorry for the scout teams, trapped on a planet full of people who behave like that.' Melvyn stopped and winced, then gave Joshua a cautious glance.

'She knew what she was going down to,' Joshua said. 'And I meant what I said about going back to check.'

'Reza Malin knew what he was about,' Ashly said. 'She'll be safe enough with him.'

'Right.' The flight computer datavised an alarm into Joshua's neural nanonics. He accessed the sensor array.

Murora's storm bands were smears of green and blue, mottled with the usual white ammonia cyclones. A thick whorl of ochre and bronze rings extended from the cloud tops out to a hundred and eighty thousand kilometres, broken by two major divisions. The gas giant boasted thirty-seven natural satellites, from a quartet of hundred-kilometre ring-shepherds up to five moons over two thousand kilometres in diameter; the largest, M-XI, named Keddie, had a thick nitrogen methane atmosphere.

Aethra had been germinated in a two hundred thousand kilometre orbit, far enough outside the fringes of the ring to mitigate any danger of collision from stray particles. The seed had been brought to the system in 2602 and attached to a suitable mineral-rich asteroid; it would take thirty years to mature into a structure capable of supporting a human population, and another twenty years to reach its full forty-five-kilometre length. After nine years of untroubled development it was already three and a half kilometres long.

In the same orbit, but trailing five hundred kilometres behind the young habitat, was the supervisory station, occupied by fifty staff (it had accommodation for a thousand). The Edenists didn't use bitek for such a small habitational environment; it was a carbotanium wheel seven hundred and fifty metres in diameter, eighty metres wide, containing three long gardens separated by blocks of richly appointed apartments. Its hub was linked to a large non-rotating cylindrical port, grossly under-used, but built in anticipation of the traffic which would start to arrive once the habitat reached its median size and He_3 cloudscoop mining began in Murora's atmosphere. During the interim there were just two inter-orbit vessels docked, which the station staff used to commute to Aethra on their inspection tours.

Lady Macbeth had emerged forty thousand kilometres away

from the solitary Edenist outpost, a jump accuracy Joshua was entirely satisfied with considering the conditions. Her sensors focused on the station in time to see it break apart. The rim had been sliced open in several places, allowing the atmosphere to jet out. Small thrusters were still firing in a useless attempt to halt the ominous wobble which had developed. Optical sensors revealed trees, bushes, and oscillating slicks of water rushing out of the long gashes.

'Like the Ruin Ring,' Joshua whispered painfully.

Small circular spots on the carbotanium shell glowed crimson. The tough metal was visibly undulating as the structure's seesaw fluctuations increased. Then one of the cryogenic fuel-storage tanks in the non-rotating port exploded, which triggered another two or three tanks. It was hard to tell the exact number, the entire station was obscured by the white vapour billowing out.

As the cloud dispersed large sections of the wheel tumbled out of the darkening centre.

A hundred kilometres away, two fusion drives burnt hotly against the icy starscape, heading for the immature habitat. One of the ships was emitting a steady beat of microwaves from its transponder.

'They're here already,' Melvyn said. 'Bloody hell. They must have jumped before we did.'

'That is the *Maranta*'s transponder code,' Warlow said without any notable inflection. 'Why would Wolfgang leave it transmitting?'

'Because he's not the captain any more,' Ashly said. 'Look at the vectors. Neither of them is maintaining a steady thrust. Their drives are unstable.'

'They're going to kill the habitat, aren't they?' Sarha said. 'Just like Laton did all those years ago. Those bastards! It can't hurt them, it can't hurt anybody. What kind of sequestration is this?'

‘A bad one,’ Warlow grumbled at an almost subliminal volume. ‘Very bad.’

‘I’m picking up lifeboat beacons,’ Melvyn said with a rush of excitement. ‘Two of them. Somebody escaped.’

Joshua, who had felt eager triumph at their successful jump to Murora and anger at the station’s violation, was left empty, leaving his mind in an almost emotion-free state. His crew was looking at him. Waiting. Dad never mentioned this part of captaining a ship.

‘Melvyn, Sarha; recalibrate the injection ionizers for the number one fusion tube. Whatever thrust we can get, please. I’m going to need it. Ashly, Warlow, get down to the airlock deck. We won’t have much time to bring them on board, make sure they come through as fast as possible.’

Warlow’s couch webbing peeled back immediately. The cosmonik and the pilot went through the floor hatch as though they were in a race.

‘Dahybi, recharge the nodes. I’ll jump outsystem as soon as we have them on board.’ *If* we get them on board.

‘Yes, Captain.’

‘Stand by for combat gees. Again!’

On the other side of hugely complex schematic diagrams, Sarha smiled knowingly at the hard-used martyred tone.

Lady Macbeth’s fusion drives ignited, driving the ship towards the twirling wreckage of the station. Thermo-dump panels hurried back into their recesses as the gee force climbed. The starship’s sensors tracked the two fusion drives forty thousand kilometres ahead. Joshua was wondering how long it would take for them to spot the rescue attempt. If they use the sensors the way they do the fusion drives they may never see us. *Maranta* was only accelerating at half a gee.

Melvyn and Sarha finished their work on fusion tube number one, and gave him control, warning it wouldn’t last for long. Joshua brought *Lady Mac* up to five gees, and held her there.

'They're launching combat wasps,' Dahybi said.

Joshua observed the flight computer plotting purple vector lines. 'That's odd.' The six combat wasps were flying around Aethra, forming a loose ring. Their drives went off when they were two hundred kilometres from the habitat, coasting past it. Submunitions burst out from two, and accelerated towards the slowly rotating cylinder.

'Kinetic missiles,' Joshua said. 'What the hell are they doing?'

Bright orange explosions rippled across the rust-red polyp surface.

'Injuring it,' Sarha said with terse determination. 'That kind of assault won't destroy it, but they'll inflict a lot of harm. Almost as if they're deliberately mutilating it.'

'Injuring it?' Dahybi asked. The normally composed node specialist was openly incredulous. 'What for? People injure. Animals injure. Not habitats. You can't hurt them like you can a mammal.'

'That's what they're doing,' Sarha insisted.

'It does look that way,' Joshua said.

The *Maranta*'s drive came on again, followed a few seconds later by the second ship.

'They've seen us,' Joshua said. It had taken eight minutes, which was appallingly sloppy detection work. *Lady Mac* was over halfway towards the lifeboats. Less than twenty thousand kilometres away now. The other ships were barely five hundred kilometres distant from the squealing beacons. 'This is where it gets interesting.' He launched eight combat wasps and upped the *Lady Mac*'s acceleration to seven gees. The drones shot ahead at twenty-five gees. An answering salvo of twelve emerged from the two starships.

'Shit,' Joshua exclaimed. 'They're running for Aethra.'

'Clever,' Melvyn said. 'We can't use the nukes when they're close to it.'

'No, but I can still use the gamma pulsers for offence.' He fired off a string of coded instructions to the combat wasps.

'And it may give us the time we need to pick up the lifeboats. None of their combat wasps are targeting them.' He thought for a moment. 'Sarha, broadcast a tight-beam warning to the lifeboats. Tell them to deactivate their beacons now. Anyone warped enough to maim a habitat won't think twice about snuffing refugees.'

The first combat-wasp conflict took place five thousand kilometres from Aethra, a ragged rosette of plasma sprawling across six hundred kilometres. Joshua watched several attackers come through unscathed and launched another salvo of five drones, programming three to form a defence-shield formation. The bridge's gravity plane shifted sharply as he initiated an evasion manoeuvre.

*

The children were crying with their voices and minds. Gaura broadcast a soothing harmonic in the general affinity band, adding to the compulsion of the other adults. What I need, he thought, is someone to calm me.

The lifeboat was a sturdy cylinder ten metres long and four wide. It had no propulsion system apart from the solid-fuel booster to fire it clear of any conceivable emergency, and reaction thrusters to hold it stable while the refugees waited for rescue. Like all the systems on the station it was spacious and well equipped. There were eight seats, lockers with enough food for a fortnight, and a month-long oxygen supply. For Edenists, even disasters would be inconvenient rather than dangerous.

Such arrogance, he cursed inside the confines of his own skull, such stupid blind faith in our technological prowess.

Right now there were fourteen adults and five children crammed inside. There hadn't been time for them to reach another lifeboat. With a hubris which hindsight revealed to be quite monstrous, the disasters which the designers anticipated had all been natural. Even a meteorite strike would leave most of the wheel intact, and evacuation would be a calm rational process.

What had never been even a theoretical contingency was insane Adamist starships slicing the station apart with lasers.

It had all happened so fast. Now little Gatje and Haykal hugged Tiya, their mother, faces distraught as she kept them anchored. The air was too hot, it stank of vomit. Aethra couldn't hide its torment over the kinetic missile attack that bit deep into its shell from the young impressionable minds. Candre's death convulsions as she went through explosive decompression was still causing wintry shivers along Gaura's spine. The combined psychological stresses of the last fifteen minutes was going to leave a trauma scar that would take a long time to heal even for the well-balanced psyche of an Edenist.

And it was all his fault. As station chief he should have taken precautions. He had known about the civil strife on Lalonde. Yet he had done nothing.

It is not your fault, Aethra said softly into his mind. **Who could have anticipated this?**

I should have.

From the information you had, this was not predictable.

I had enough data from *Ilex*. It was chaos on the planet when they left.

These starships did not come from Lalonde. They are mercenaries, recruited elsewhere.

I could still have done something. Put people into apartments closer to the lifeboats. Something! How are Candre and the others?

I have them. But now is not a good time to begin raising my consciousness to multiplicity status.

No. And you? How are you?

I was angry, frightened. Now I feel sorrow. It is a sad universe where such wanton acts can take place.

I'm sorry we brought you into existence. You have done nothing to deserve this.

I am glad I live. And I may yet continue to live. None of the

craters is more than twenty metres deep. I have lost a lot of nutrient fluid though, and my mineral-digestion organs have been damaged from the shockwaves.

Gaura's hand squeezed the grab hoop he was holding. Fury and helplessness were alien to him, but he felt them now with a daunting strength. **The physical damage can be repaired. It will be repaired, never doubt that. Not as long as one Edenist remains alive.**

Thank you, Gaura. You are a fine supervisor. I am privileged to have you and your staff attend the dawn of my intellect. And one day Gatje and Haykal shall run around in my park. I will enjoy their laughter.

A solid beam of intolerable white light stabbed into the lifeboat through its one small, heavily shielded port. Space was being devastated by another hail of fusion explosions. The children started crying again.

Through Aethra's much-degraded perception he saw the long white fusion exhaust of the third Adamist starship decelerating towards them. With its tremendous velocity it had to be a warship, but there had been no contact apart from the curt woman telling them to switch off the beacon. Who were they? Who were the other two? Why had they attacked Aethra?

Not knowing was difficult for an Edenist.

You will soon be safe, Aethra said. It widened its broadcast to include the Edenists on both lifeboats. **All of you will be safe.**

Gaura met his wife's frightened stubborn eyes. **I love you**, he said for her alone.

The blast light was fading. He looked out of the port, his mind welcoming inquisitive contacts, showing the children their solidly real rescuer approaching.

Whoever the pilot was, he was coming very close. And moving far too fast.

Space directly outside the lifeboat was filled with the brilliant fusion exhaust. Gaura flinched, jerking back from the port. **It's going to hit!**

There were screams behind him. Then the exhaust vanished, and a huge spherical starship was a hundred metres away, small sensor clusters sticking out of its dark silicon hull like metallized insect antennae. Its equatorial ion thrusters exhaled fountains of sparkling blue ions, halting its minute drift.

Bloody hell! It was a collective sentiment from the adults.

The starship rolled towards the lifeboat as though there was a solid surface below it. And its extended airlock tube was suddenly coming round to *clang* against the hatch.

Gaura took a moment to recover his poise. A voidhawk would be very hard put to match that display of precision manoeuvring.

The lifeboat's bitek processors reported the short-range inter-ship channel was picking up a transmission.

'You people in the lifeboat, as soon as the hatch opens we want you through the tube and into the lounge,' commanded the female voice they'd heard earlier. 'Make it fast! We're running out of combat wasps and we've got to pick your friends up as well.'

The hatch seal popped and it swung back. Little Gatje squealed in alarm as one of the biggest cosmoniks Gaura had ever seen floated in the airlock tube.

It's all right, he told his dismayed daughter. **He's a . . . friend. Really.**

Gatje clutched at the fabric of her mother's suit. **Promise, Daddy?**

'Shift your bastard arses through here now!' Warlow bellowed.

The children gulped into fearful silence.

Gaura couldn't help it, after all the horror they'd been through to be greeted by such utter normality, he started to laugh. **I promise.**

*

'Oh, Jesus, they've cracked it,' Joshua told the three crew-members left on the bridge when *Lady Mac* rendezvoused with the second lifeboat. Another combat wasp was curving round over Aethra's bulk, accelerating sharply. 'I knew they'd work out the numbers game eventually.' He fired a salvo of three drones in defence. It was a terrible ratio. One which the *Lady Mac* could only ever lose. Three defenders was an absolute minimum to guarantee an attacker didn't get through. If he could just have flown evasive manoeuvres, or attacked, or been able to run, the numbers would have shifted back towards something near favourable.

'Jesus!' The fourth solo combat wasp appeared from behind Aethra. He had to launch another three from *Lady Mac*'s diminishing reserves.

'Fifteen left,' Sarha said with morbid cheerfulness.

The starship's maser cannons fired at a kinetic missile that was sixty kilometres away. Five nuclear-tipped submunitions exploded perilously close to Aethra, reducing the latest attacking combat wasp to its subatomic constituents.

'Did you have to tell us that?' Melvyn said laboriously.

'You mean you didn't know?'

'Yes. But I could always hope I was wrong.'

Joshua accessed a camera on the airlock deck. Warlow had anchored himself to a stikpad beside the airlock tube. He was grabbing people as they came out and slinging them into the chamber. Ashly and one of the Edenist men were on a stikpad below the ceiling hatch, catching then shoving the human projectiles up into the lounge above.

'How many more to come, Warlow?' Joshua datavised.

'Six. That makes forty-one in total.'

'Wonderful. Stand by for combat acceleration the second the airlock seals.' He sounded the audio warning so the Edenists would know. The flight computer showed his plot of an open-ended vector heading away from Murora. At eight gees they could outrun the other starships easily, and jump outsystem.

That kind of prolonged acceleration would be tough on the Edenists (no sinecure for the crew, either), but it was one hell of a lot better than staying here.

'Joshua, Gaura has asked me to say some of the children are very young, they can't possibly survive high gees,' Warlow datavised. 'Their bones aren't strong enough.'

'Jesus shit! Kids? How old? How many gees?'

'One girl was about three. There were a couple of five-year-olds as well.'

'Fuck it!'

'What is it?' Sarha asked, real concern darkening her sea-green eyes for the first time since they'd entered the Lalonde system.

'We're not going to make it.'

The fifth solo combat wasp appeared from behind Aethra. Seven of the *Lady Mac*'s submunition drones detonated their nuclear explosives in immediate response. Joshua launched two more.

'Even if we jump without an alignment trajectory, from here, it'll take us fifteen seconds to retract the sensors and prime the nodes,' he said. 'We'll be blind for ten seconds. It's not long enough.'

'So run,' Sarha said. 'Fire every last combat wasp at them and go. *Lady Mac* can make eight gees even with tube one down. *Maranta* can't make more than four gees. We can get clear.'

'That vector's already loaded. But we've got kids on board. Shit! Shit! Shit!' He saw the last Edenist being yanked out of the airlock tube by Warlow. The flight computer was shutting the hatch before his feet were fully clear.

Do something, and do it now, Joshua Calvert, he told himself. Because you're going to be dead in twenty seconds if you don't.

His mind ordered the flight computer to start the fusion tube ignition sequence.

Another whole two seconds to think in.

There was nothing in the tactics programs, even Dad had never dug himself a hole this deep in the shit.

Can't run, can't fight, can't jump out, can't hide . . .

'Oh yes I can!' he whooped.

The fusion drives came on, and the *Lady Mac* accelerated down the vector plot that sprang from Joshua's mind even as the idea unrolled. Three gees, heading straight in towards the gas giant.

'Joshua!' Dahybi complained. 'We can't jump if you take us inward.'

'Shut up.'

Dahybi settled back and started into a recital of a scripture he remembered from his youth. 'Yes, Captain.'

'Warlow, activate the three zero-tau pods we've got in capsule C, and cram the children in. You've got four minutes maximum before we start accelerating properly.'

'Right, Joshua.'

The sensors reported that four combat wasps were pursuing them. Joshua fired an answering salvo of five. He could hear Dahybi muttering something that sounded like a prayer, it had the right dirge-like resonance.

'They're coming after us,' Melvyn said a minute later.

Maranta and its cohort were accelerating away from Aethra.

'That's the *Gramine*,' Sarha said after studying the image. 'Look at the angle its drive is deflected through. There isn't another starship that can do that. Wissler was always boasting about their combat agility.'

'Just wonderful, Sarha, thanks,' Joshua proclaimed. 'You got any other morale boosters for us?'

*

Warlow climbed the ladder into the lounge deck, boosted muscles lifting him easily against the heavy gravity. Carbon composite rungs creaked in dismay under his tripled weight.

There were Edenists packed solid across the lounge floor, none of the acceleration couches had been activated – not that there were enough anyway. They didn't have neural nanonics, the cosmonik realized. And because of it their children whimpered and snivelled in wretched distress without any cushioning below them.

He walked over to the smallest girl, who was lying wide-eyed and terribly pale beside her mother. 'I'm putting her into zero-tau,' he announced shortly, and bent down. He had plugged a pair of cargo-handling arms into his elbow sockets before coming up the ladder, they had wide metal manipulator forks which would act as a good cradle. The girl started crying again. 'There will be none of this acceleration in the pod. Explain to her. She must not squirm when I pick her up. Her spine will break.'

Be brave, Tiya told her daughter. **He will take you to a safe place where you won't hurt so.**

He's horrible, Gatje replied as the metal prongs slid underneath her.

You will be all right, Gaura said, reinforcing the pacific mental subliminal Tiya was radiating.

Warlow took care to keep Gatje's spine level, supporting her head with one set of forks while the other three arms were positioned under her torso and legs. He lifted gingerly.

'Can I help?' Gaura asked, levering himself onto his elbows. His neck felt as though it was being slowly compressed in a hydraulic vice.

'No. You are too weak.' Warlow clumped out of the lounge, an outlandish faerie-legend figure walking amongst the prone hurting bodies with a grace completely at variance with his cumbersome appearance.

There were seven children under ten years old. It took him nearly five minutes to shift them from the lounge to the zero-tau pods. His neural nanonics monitored their flight on a secondary level. The attacking starships were matching *Lady*

Mac's three-gee acceleration. Combat-wasp submunitions produced a continual astral fire of plasma between them.

Lady Mac swept over the fringes of the ring, two thousand kilometres above the ecliptic as Warlow lowered the last child into the zero-tau pod.

'Thank Christ for that,' Joshua said when the pod was enveloped by the black field. 'OK, people, stand by for high acceleration.'

Lady Mac's thrust increased to seven gees, tormenting the Edenists in the lounge still further. For all the stamina of their geneered bodies they had never been supplemented to withstand the onerous burden of combat spaceflight.

Maranta and *Gramine* began to fall behind. Sensors showed three more combat wasps eating up the distance.

'Jesus, how many of the fucking things have they got left?' Joshua asked as he launched four of the *Lady Mac*'s remaining six drones in response.

'I estimate ten,' Melvyn datavised. 'Possibly more.'

'Wonderful.' Joshua angled the *Lady Mac* down sharply towards the rings.

The slow moving pack of dusty ice chunks reflected an unaccustomed radiance as the three starships streaked past. After millennia of stasis, stirred only by the slow heartbeat of the gas giant's magnetosphere, the ring's micrometre dust was becoming aroused by the backwash of electromagnetic pulses from the fusion bombs exploding above it. Dark snowflake-crystal patterns rippled elegantly over its surface. The temperature rose by several fractions of a degree, breaking up the unique and fantastically delicate valency bonds between disparate atoms which free fall and frigidity had established. Behind the starships, the rings quivered like a choppy sea before the storm was unleashed.

Those on board the *Lady Macbeth* able to receive the sensor images watched with numbed fascination as the ring particles grew larger, changing from a grainy mist to a solid plain of drifting mud-yellow boulders. It took up half of the image; they were close enough now to make it seem like the floor of the universe.

The penultimate combat wasp darted out of the *Lady Macbeth*'s launch-tubes. Submunitions ejected almost at once, scattering like a shoal of startled fish. A hundred kilometres behind her, twenty-seven fusion bombs arrayed in an ammonite maculation detonated simultaneously, throwing up a temporary visual and electronic barrier. She turned, unseen by her pursuers, triple drive exhausts scoring vast arcs across the stars. Then the three barbs of superenergized helium were searing into the ice and rock of the ring. No physical structure was capable of withstanding that starcore temperature. The agitated surface cratered and geysered as though a depth charge had been set off far below.

Lady Macbeth dived straight into the rings, decelerating at eleven gees.

28

The watchers were there when Alkad Mzu arrived at the shoreline of Tranquillity's circumfluous salt-water sea. As always they remained several hundred metres behind, innocuous fellow hikers enjoying the balmy evening, even a couple on horses trekking along the wilder paths of the habitat. She counted eight of them as she walked along the top of the steep rocky escarpment to the path which led down to the beach. This cove was one of the remoter stretches of the northern shoreline; a broad curve of silver-white sand two kilometres long, with jutting headlands of polyp-rock cliffs. Several small islands were included within the bay's sweeping embrace, tenanted by willowy trees and a fur of colourful wild flowers. A river emptied over the escarpment two hundred metres from the path where she stood, producing a foaming waterfall which fell into a rock pool before draining away over the sands. Overhead, the giant habitat's light-tube had languished to an apricot ember strung between its endcap hubs. Vitric water caught the final rays to produce a soft-focus copper shimmer across the wavelets.

Alkad picked her way carefully along the shingle-strewn path. An accident now would be the ultimate irony, she thought. There was the familiar nagging ache in her left leg, exacerbated by the rough incline.

Her retinal implants located a pair of adolescent lovers in

the dunes at the far end of the beach. Craving solitude amid the deepening shadows, their dark entwined bodies were oblivious to the world, and nearly invisible. The girl's baby-blonde hair provided a rich contrast to her ebony skin, while the boy reminded Alkad of Peter as he stroked and caressed his willing partner. An omen, though Alkad Mzu no longer really believed in deities.

She reached the warm, dry sands and adjusted the straps of her lightweight backpack. It was the one she had brought with her to the habitat twenty-six years ago; it contained the cagoule and flask and first aid kit which she carried unfailingly on every ramble through the interior. By now the routine of her hike was scribed in stone. If she hadn't worn it, the Intelligence agencies would have been suspicious.

Alkad cut across the dunes at an angle, aiming for the middle of the beach, her feet leaving light imprints in the powdery sand. Three watchers made their way down the path behind her, the rest carried on walking along the top of the escarpment. And – a recent development, this – a couple of Tranquillity serjeants stood impassively at the foot of the escarpment beside the waterfall. She only saw them against the craggy polyp because of their infrared emission. They must have been positioned there in anticipation of her route.

It wasn't entirely unexpected. Tranquillity would have informed Ione Saldana about all those agency-teasing meetings with starship captains. The girl was erring on the side of caution, which was quite acceptable. She did have the rest of the population to think about, after all.

Alkad peered ahead, out over the huge grey valley of water to the southern shore, searching. There, to the right, twenty degrees up the curve. The Laymil project campus was a unique splash of opal light on the darkened terraces of the southern endcap. Such a shame, really, she thought with a tinge of regret. The work had been an interesting challenge, interpreting and extrapolating xenoc technology from mere fragments of clues.

She had made friends there, and progress. And now the whole campus was animated with the discovery of the Laymil sensorium memories that young scavenger had found. It was an exciting time to be a project researcher, full of promise and reward.

In another life she could easily have devoted herself to it.

Alkad reached the water's edge as the light-tube cooled to a smirched platinum. Ripples sighed contentedly against the sand. Tranquillity really was a premium place to live. She shrugged out of her backpack, then touched the seal on her boots and started to pull them off.

Samuel, the Edenist Intelligence operative, was six metres from the foot of the scarp path when he saw the lone figure by the water bend over to take her boots off. That wasn't part of the humdrum formula which governed Mzu's activities. He hurried after Pauline Webb, the CNIS second lieutenant, who had reached the beach ahead of him. She dithered in the grove of palm trees which huddled along the base of the escarpment, debating whether to break cover and walk openly on the sands.

'It looks like she's going for a swim,' he said.

Pauline gave him a cursory nod. The CNIS and the Edenists cooperated to a reasonable degree in their observation.

'At night?' she said. 'By herself?'

'The doctor is a solitary soul, but I concede this isn't the most sensible thing she's ever done.' Samuel was thinking back to that morning when the news of Omuta's sanctions being lifted had appeared in the AV projection at Glover's restaurant.

'So what do we do?'

Monica Foulkes, the ESA operative, caught up with them. She increased the magnification factor of her retinal implants just as Alkad Mzu pulled her sweatshirt off over her head. 'I don't know what you two are panicking over. Nobody as smart as Dr Mzu would choose drowning as a method of suicide. It's too prolonged.'

'Maybe she is just going for a quick swim,' Pauline suggested, without much hope. 'It's a pleasant enough evening.'

Samuel kept watching Mzu. Now her boots and clothes were off she was removing the contents of her backpack and dropping them on the sand. It was the casual way she did it which bothered him; as if she was without a care. 'I somehow doubt it.'

'We're going to look particularly stupid charging over there to rescue her if all she's doing is taking a dip to cool off,' Monica groused.

The middle-aged Edenist's lips pursed in amusement. 'You think we don't look stupid anyway?'

She scowled, and ignored him.

'Does anyone have any relevant contingency orders?' Pauline asked.

'If she wants to drown herself, then I say let her,' Monica said. 'Problem solved at long last. We can all pack up and go home then.'

'I might have known you'd take that attitude.'

'Well, I'm not swimming after her if she gets into trouble.'

'You wouldn't have to,' Samuel said, without shifting his gaze. 'Tranquillity has affinity-bonded dolphins. They'll assist any swimmers that get into difficulties.'

'Hoo-bloody-rah,' Monica said. 'Then we can have another twenty years of worrying about who the daft old biddy will talk to and what she'll say.'

Alkad datavised a code to the processor in her empty backpack. The seal around the bottom opened, and the composite curled up revealing the hidden storage space. She reached in to remove the programmable silicon spacesuit which had lain there undisturbed for twenty-six years.

Ione, Tranquillity said urgently. **We have a problem developing.**

'Excuse me,' Ione said to her cocktail party guests. They were members of the Tranquillity Banking Regulatory Council, invited to discuss the habitat's falling revenue which the massive decrease in starship movements was causing. Something needed to be done to halt the stock market's wilder fluctuations, so she had thought an informal party was the best way of handling it. She turned instinctively to face her apartment's window wall and the shoals of yellow and green fish nosing round the fan of light it threw across the dusky sand. **What?**

It's Alkad Mzu. Look.

The image fizzed up into her mind.

Samuel frowned as Mzu drew some kind of object from deep inside her backpack. It looked ridiculously like a football, but with wings attached. Even with his retinal implants on full magnification he couldn't quite make it out. 'What is that?'

Mzu fastened the collar round her neck, and bit down on the nozzle of the respirator tube. She datavised an activation code into the suit's control processor. The black ball flattened itself against her upper chest and started to flow over her skin.

Both the other Intelligence operatives turned to look at the sharpness in Samuel's voice. The two serjeants began to walk forwards over the beach.

Ione! Tranquillity's thoughts rang with surprise, turning to alarm. **I can sense a gravitonic-distortion zone building.**

So? she asked. Every starship emerging above Mirchusko registered in the habitat's mass-sensitive organs. There was no requirement for the usual network of strategic warning grav-distortion-detector satellites which guarded ordinary asteroid settlements and planets, Tranquillity's perception of local space was unrivalled, making threat response a near-instantaneous affair. **Is the starship emerging too close? Arm the strategic-defence platforms.**

No use. It's–

At first Samuel mistook it for a shadow cast by an evening cloud. There was still enough pearly radiance coming from the light-tube to give the circumfluous sea a sparse shimmer, a cloud would produce exactly that patch of darkness. But there was only one patch of darkness; and when he glanced up the air was clear. Then the noise began, a distant thunderclap which lasted for several seconds, then chopped off abruptly. A brilliant star shone at the centre of the darkness, sending long radials of frigid white light into the habitat.

Mzu was silhouetted perfectly against the white blaze reflected off the sea, encased in the black skin of the spacesuit, a consummate monochrome picture.

Shock immobilized Samuel's body for a precious second. Out of the centre of the fading star a blackhawk came skimming silently over the sea towards Mzu; a compressed ovoid one hundred and thirty metres long, with a horseshoe life-support section moulded round the rear dorsal bulge. Its blue polyp hull was marbled with an imperial-purple web.

'Jesus wept!' Pauline said in an aghast whisper. 'It jumped inside. It's come right into the fucking habitat!'

'Get her!' Monica cried. 'For Christ's sake stop the bitch!' She ran forwards.

'No, stop! Come back,' Samuel yelled. But Pauline was already charging out of the trees after the ESA agent, boosted muscles accelerating her to a phenomenal speed. 'Oh, shit.' He started to run.

Meyer saw the small spacesuited woman standing at the water's edge, and *Udat* obligingly angled round towards her. Tension had condensed his guts into a solid lump. Swallowing *inside* a habitat, it had to be the craziest stunt in the history of spaceflight. Yet they'd done it!

We are in, *Udat* observed sagely. **That's halfway.**

And don't I know it.

WHAT ARE YOU DOING? Tranquillity's outraged broadcast thundered into the blackhawk's mind.

Meyer winced. Even *Udat*'s calm thoughts fluttered.

The woman is a political dissident being persecuted by the Kulu ESA, Meyer replied with shaky bravado. **Of all people, Ione Saldana should sympathize with that. We're taking her where she will be safe.**

STOP IMMEDIATELY. I WILL NOT PERMIT THIS. *UDAT*, SWALLOW OUT *NOW*. The force of the mental compulsion which the habitat personality exerted was incredible. Meyer felt as though someone had smashed a meat hook into his skull to pull his brain out by the roots. He groaned, clutching at the cushioning of his acceleration couch, heart pounding in his ears.

STOP!

'Keep going,' he gasped. His nose started to bleed. Neural nanonics sent out a flurry of metabolic overrides.

Alkad waded through the shallows as the blackhawk descended, gliding fastidiously round one of the cove's small islands. She hadn't grasped how big the bitek creature was. To see that almighty bulk suspended so easily in the air was an uncanny marvel. Its rounded nose was streaked with long frost rays as the sea's humidity gusted over polyp which was accustomed to the radiative chill of deep space. A huge patch of water below the hull began to foam and churn as the distortion field interacted with it. She suddenly felt as though the horizontal was rolling. *Udat* turned through ninety degrees, and tilted sharply, bringing the portside wing of its life-support horseshoe down towards the water. An airlock slid open. Cherri Barnes stood inside, wearing her spacesuit. Orange silicon-fibre straps tethered her securely to the sides of the small chamber. She threw a rope-ladder down.

On the beach five figures were racing over the dunes.

Ione said: **Kill her.**

The serjeants pulled laser pistols from their holsters. Alkad Mzu already had her foot on the first rung.

Udat's maser cannon fired.

Monica Foulkes pounded hard across the sand, neural nanonics commands and boosted muscles meshing so that her body ate the distance effortlessly, a hundred and fifty metres in nine seconds. The prime order of the ESA's Tranquillity operation was to prevent Mzu from leaving, that took precedence over everything. It didn't look like Monica was going to get to the blackhawk in time, Mzu had started to claw her way up the rocking ladder. She reviewed which of her weapon implants would have the best chance; the trouble was most of them were designed for unobtrusive close-range work. And that bloody Lunar SII spacesuit didn't help. It would have to be a microdart, and hope the tip penetrated. She was aware of the serjeants off to her left pulling out their laser pistols.

A metre-wide column of air fluoresced a faint violet, drawing a line from a silver bubble on the blackhawk's lower hull to a serjeant. The bitek servitor blew apart in an explosion of steam and carbon granules. Fifteen metres behind it, where the beam struck the beach, a patch of sand became a puddle of glass, glowing a vivid rose-gold.

Over-hyped nerves sent Monica diving for cover the instant the beam appeared. She hit the loose sand, momentum ploughing a two and a half metre long furrow. There were two near-simultaneous thuds behind her as Samuel and Pauline flung themselves down. The second serjeant erupted into a black-grain mist with a loud burping sound as the maser hit it. Monica's mind gibbered as she waited, head buried in the sand. At least with that power rating it'll be quick . . .

A wind began howling over the dunes.

Samuel raised his head to see his worst expectation confirmed. A wormhole interstice was opening around the nose of the blackhawk. Alkad Mzu was halfway up the rope-ladder.

You must not take her from here, he pleaded with the starship. **You must not!**

The interstice widened, a light-devouring tunnel boring through infinity. Air streamed in.

'Hang on!' Samuel shouted to the two women agents.

COME BACK! Tranquillity commanded.

Meyer, his mind twinned with the blackhawk, quailed under the habitat's furious demand. It was too much, the storm voice had raged inside his skull for what seemed like days, bruising his neurons with its violence. Welcome surrender beckoned – to hell with Mzu, nothing was worth this. Then he felt local space twisting under the immense distortion which *Udat*'s energy patterning cells extented. A pseudoabyss leading into freedom opened before him. **Go**, he ordered. The cold physical blackness outside invaded his mind, plunging him into glorious oblivion.

A small but ferocious hurricane set Alkad spinning like a runaway propeller at the end of her precarious silicon-fibre ladder. 'Wait!' she datavised in mounting terror. 'You're supposed to wait till I'm in the airlock.' Her digitalized vehemence made no impression on *Udat.* The air buoyed her up as though she had become weightless, swinging her round until the ladder was horizontal. Oscillating gravity was doing terrible things to her inner ears. Screaming air tried to tear her from the ladder. Neural nanonics pumped muscle-lock orders into her hands and calves to reinforce her grip. She could feel ligaments ripping. Collar sensors showed her the fuzzy rim of the wormhole interstice sliding inexorably along the hull towards her. 'No. In the name of Mary, wait!' And then Dr Alkad Mzu was suddenly presented with every physicist's dream opportunity: observing the fabric of the universe from the outside.

Monica Foulkes heard Samuel's shouted warning and instinctively grabbed a tuft of reedy dune grass. The wind surged with impossible strength. Gravity shifted round until the beach was *above* her. Monica wailed fearfully as sand fell up into the sky. She felt herself following it, feet pulled into the air and sliding round to point at the interstice surrounding the blackhawk's nose. The grass clump made an awful slow tearing sound. Her hips and chest left the ground. Sand was blasting directly into her face. She couldn't see, couldn't breathe. The grass clump moved several centimetres. 'OhdearGodpreservemeee!'

A long-fingered hand clamped around her free wrist. The grass clump left the sand with a sharp sucking noise, its weight wrenching her arm out towards the blackhawk. For an eternal second Monica hung splayed in the air as the sand scudded around her. Someone groaned with pained effort.

The wormhole interstice closed behind *Udat*.

Sand, water, mangled vegetation, and demented fish cascaded down out of the sky. Monica landed flat on her belly, breath knocked out of her. 'Oh my God,' she wheezed. When she looked up, the haggard Edenist was crouched on his knees, panting heavily as he clutched his wrist. 'You' – the words were difficult to form in her throat – 'you held on to me.'

He threw her a nod. 'I think my wrist is broken.'

'I would have . . .' She shuddered, then gave a foolish jittery laugh. 'God, I don't even know your name.'

'Samuel.'

'Thank you, Samuel.'

He rolled onto his back and sighed. 'Pleasure.'

Are you all right? Tranquillity asked the Edenist.

My wrist is very painful. She's heavy.

Your colleagues are approaching. Three of them are carrying medical nanonic packages in their aid kits. They will be with you shortly.

Even after all this time spent in Tranquillity, he couldn't get used to the personality's lack of empathy. Habitats were such an essential component of Edenism. It was disconcerting to have one treat him in this cavalier fashion. **Thank you.**

'I didn't think voidhawks and blackhawks could operate in a gravity field,' Monica said.

'They can't,' he told her. 'This isn't gravity, it's centrifugal force. It's no different to the docking-ledges they use outside.'

'Ah, of course. Have you ever heard of one coming inside a habitat before?'

'Never. A swallow like that requires phenomenal accuracy. From a strictly chauvinistic point of view I hate to say this, but I think it would be beyond most voidhawks. Even most blackhawks, come to that. Mzu made an astute choice. This was a very well thought out escape.'

'Twenty-six years in the making,' Pauline said. She climbed slowly to her feet, shaking her cotton top, which had been soaked by the falling water. A fat blue fish, half a metre long, was thrashing frantically on the sand by her shoes. 'I mean that woman had us fooled for twenty-six goddamn years. Acting out the role of a flekhead physics professor with all the expected neuroses and eccentricities slotting perfectly into place. And we believed it. We patiently watched her for twenty-six years and she behaved exactly as predicted. If my home planet had been blown to shit, I'd behave like that. She never faltered, not once. But it was a twenty-six-year charade. Twenty-six goddamn years! What kind of a person can do that?'

Monica and Samuel exchanged an anxious look.

'Someone pretty obsessive,' he said.

'Obsessive!' Pauline's face darkened. She leant over to pick the big fish up, but it squirmed out of her hands. 'Keep bloody still,' she shouted at it. 'Well, God help Omuta now she's loose in the universe again.' She finally succeeded in grabbing hold of the fish. 'You do realize that thanks to our sanctions they haven't got a defensive system which can even fart loudly?'

'She won't get far,' Monica said. 'Not with this Laton scare closing down all the starship flights.'

'You hope!' Pauline staggered off towards the waterline with her wriggling burden.

Monica clambered to her feet and brushed the sand off her clothes, shaking it out of her hair. She looked down at the lanky Edenist. 'Dear me, CNIS entrance standards have really gone downhill lately.'

He grinned weakly. 'Yeah. But you know she's right about Mzu. The good doctor had us all fooled. Clever lady. And now there's going to be hell to pay.'

She put her hand under his shoulder and helped him up. 'I suppose so. One thing's for certain, there's going to be a mad scramble to catch her. Every government is going to want her tucked away on their own planet in order to safeguard democracy. And, my new friend, there are some democrats in this Confederation I don't ever want to find her.'

'Us, for instance?'

Monica hesitated, then gave her head a rueful shake. 'No. But don't tell my boss I said that.'

Samuel watched the two agents on horseback galloping across the beach toward them. Right now he couldn't even remember which services they belonged to. Not that it mattered. In a few hours they'd all be going their separate ways again. 'Damn, Tranquillity really was the only place for her, wasn't it?'

'Yes. Come on, let's see if these two have got anything for your wrist. I think that's Onku Noi on the second horse. The Imperial Oshanko mob are always loaded down with gadgets.'

*

According to his neural nanonics' timer function it was high noon. But Chas Paske wasn't sure how to tell any more. There hadn't been any fluctuation in the red cloud's lambent emission since he started walking – hobbling, rather. The black and red jungle remained mordantly uninviting. Every laboured step was accompanied by the incessant hollow rolls and booms of thunder from high above.

He had managed to splint his leg, after a fashion: five laths of cherry oak wood that stretched from his ankle to his pelvis, lashed into place by ropy vines. The thigh wound was still a real problem. He had bound it with leaves, but every time he looked it seemed to be leaking capacious amounts of ichor down his shin. And it was impossible to keep the insects out. Unlike what appeared to be every other living creature, they hadn't abandoned the jungle. And devoid of other targets, they massed around him – mosquito-analogues, maggot-analogues, things with legs and wings and pincers that had no analogue. All of them suckling at his tender flesh. Twice now he'd changed the leaves, only to find a seething mass of tiny black elytra underneath. Flies crawled round his skin burns as though they were the only oases of nourishment in a barren world.

According to his guidance block he had come two and a half

kilometres in the last three hours. It was hard going through the virgin undergrowth which lay along the side of the river. His crutch kept getting snagged by the thick cords that foamed over the loam. Slender low-hanging branches had a knack of catching the splint laths.

He picked the small wrinkled globes of abundant vine fruit as he went, chewing constantly to keep his fluid and protein levels up. But at this rate it was going to take him weeks to get anywhere.

Durringham was his ultimate goal. Whatever resources and wealth existed on this misbegotten planet, they resided in the capital. Scouting it had been his team's mission. He saw no reason to abandon that assignment. Sitting waiting to die in the jungle wasn't a serious option. Recovery and evacuation was obviously out of the question now. So, there it was, an honourable solution; one which would keep him occupied and motivated, and, should he achieve the impossible and make it, might even accomplish something worthwhile. Chas Paske was going to go down swinging.

But for all his determination he knew that he was going to have to find an easier way to travel. The medical program was releasing vast amounts of endocrines from his implants, analgesic blocks had been thrown across a good twenty per cent of his nerve fibres. Boosted metabolism or not, he couldn't keep expending energy at this rate.

He accessed his guidance block and summoned up the map. There was a village called Wryde fifteen hundred metres downstream on the other bank. According to the LDC file it had been established nine years ago.

It would have to do.

He plucked another elwisie fruit, and limped on. One advantage of the thunder was that no one would hear the racket he made ploughing through the vegetation.

The light was visible long before the first of the houses. A welcome gold-yellow nimbus shrouding the river. Snowlilies glinted and sparkled with their true opulence. Chas heard a bird again, the silly surprised warble of a chikrow. He lowered himself in tricky increments, and started to slither forward on his belly.

Wryde had become a thriving, affluent community, far beyond the norm for a stage one colony planet. The town nestled snugly in a six-square-kilometre clearing that had been turned over to dignified parkland. It was comprised of large houses built from stone or brick or landcoral, all of them the kind of elegantly sophisticated residence that a merchant or wealthy farmer would own. The main street was a handsome tree-lined boulevard, bustling with activity: people wandering in and out of the shops, sitting at the tables of pavement cafés. Horse-drawn cabs moved up and down. An impressive red-brick civic hall stood at one end, four storeys high, with an ornate central clock tower. He saw some kind of sports field just outside the main cluster of houses. People dressed all in white were playing a game he didn't know while spectators picnicked round the boundary. Close to the jungle at the back of the park, five windmills stood alongside a lake, their huge white sails turning steadily even though there was very little breeze. Grandiose houses lined the riverbank, lawns extending down to the water. They all had boat-houses or small jetties; rowing-boats and sailing dinghies were moored securely against the sluggish tide of snowlilies. Larger craft had been drawn up on wooden slipways.

It was the kind of community every sane person would want to live in; small-town cosiness, big-city stability. Even Chas, lying in muddy loam under a bush on the opposite bank, felt the subtle attraction of the place. By simply existing it offered the prospect of belonging to a perpetual golden age.

His retinal implants showed him the sunny, happy faces of the citizens as they went about their business. Scanning back and forth he couldn't see anyone labouring in the pristine gardens, or sweeping the streets; no people, no bitek servitors, no mechanoids. The nearest anyone came to work was the café proprietors, and they seemed cheerful enough, chatting and laughing with their customers. All generals and no privates, he thought to himself. It isn't real.

He accessed the guidance block again. A green reference grid slipped up over his vision and he focused on a jetty at the far end of the town's clearing. The block calculated its exact coordinate and integrated it into the map.

When he checked his physiological status, the neural nanonics reported his haemoglobin reserve was down to half an hour. His metabolism wasn't producing it with anything like its normal efficiency. He ran through the guidance block's display one last time. Half an hour ought to be enough.

Chas started to crawl forwards again, easing himself down the muddy slope and into the water like an arthritic crocodile.

Twenty minutes later he judiciously parted a pair of snowlilies and let his rigid moulded face stick up out of the water. The guidance block had functioned flawlessly, delivering him right beside the jetty. A trim blue-painted rowing-boat was pulling gently against its mooring two metres away. There was nobody anywhere near. He reached up and cut the pannier with his fission blade, grabbing the end as it fell into the water.

The boat started to drift with the snowlilies. Chas dropped below the surface.

He waited as long as he dared. The neural nanonics' physiological monitor program was flashing dire warnings of oxygen starvation into his brain before he risked surfacing.

Wryde was out of sight round a curve, although the ordinary light which clung to its rolling parkland was spilling round the trees on the bank. When he looked at his prize it had changed from the well-crafted skiff he had stolen to a dilapidated punt that was little more than a raft. Tissue-thin gunwales, which had been added in what must have been a surreal afterthought, were crumbling like rotten cork before his eyes. They left a wake of dark mushy dust on the snowlilies.

Chas waited a minute to see if any other drastic changes were going to occur. He rapped experimentally on the wood which was left. It seemed to be solid enough. So with a great deal of effort, and coming dangerously near to capsizing, he managed to half-clamber, half-roll into the shallow bottom of the boat.

He lay there inertly for a long time, then ponderously raised himself onto his elbows. The boat was drifting slowly into the bank. Long slippery ribbons of foltwine were trailing from his splint. River beetles crawled over his thigh wound. Both the medical nanonic packages were approaching overload trying to screen the blood from the lower half of his leg.

'Apart from that, fine,' he said. His grating voice provided a harsh discord to the persistent fruity rumble of thunder.

He crushed or swept away as many of the beetles and other insects as he could. Naturally there weren't any oars. He cut through the vines holding his splint together, and used one of the laths to scull away from the bank and back into the main current. It took a while, with the snowlilies resisting him, but when he was back in the middle of the river the boat began to move noticeably swifter. He made himself as comfortable as possible, and watched the tall trees go past with an increasing sense of eagerness. A keen amateur student of military history, Chas knew that back on old Earth they used to say all roads led to Rome. Here on Lalonde, all the rivers led to Durringham.

*

A bubble of bright white light squatted possessively over Aberdale. From the air it appeared as though the village was sheltering below a translucent pearl dome to ward off the perverse elements assailing the jungle. Octan circled it at a respectable distance, wings outstretched to their full metre and a half span, riding the thermals with fluid ease, contemptuous of gravity. The jungle underneath him was the same discoloured maroon as the sky. But away to the south a single narrow horizontal streak of bright green shone with compulsive intensity. Instinctively he wanted to soar towards it, to break out into the cleanliness of real light.

Tandem thoughts circulated through the bird's brain, his kindly master's wishes directing his flight away from the purity, and tilting his head so that he looked at the buildings in the middle of the illuminated clearing. Enhanced retinas zoomed in.

'It's virtually the same as Pamiers,' Pat Halahan said. 'They've got maybe fifty of those fancy houses put up. The ground is all lawns and gardens, right out to the jungle. No sign of any fields or groves.' He leaned forwards blindly. Octan casually curved a sepia wing-tip, altering his course by a degree. 'Now that is odd. Those trees along the riverbank look like terrestrial weeping willows. But they're big, twenty metres plus. Got to be thirty years old.'

'Don't count on it,' Kelly muttered in a surly undertone, covering subtler emotions. 'In any case, this is the wrong climate.'

'Yeah, right,' Pat said. 'Switching to infrared. Nope. Nothing. If there's any installation underground, Reza, then they're dug in way deep.'

'OK,' the team commander said reluctantly. 'Have Octal scout further east.'

'If you want. But it doesn't look like there are any more inhabited clearings in the jungle that way. He can see the light from Schuster quite plainly from his altitude. There's nothing like that eastwards.'

'They aren't going to advertise with hundred-kilowatt holograms, Pat.'

'Yes, sir. East it is.'

A crucial urge to explore the as-yet-unseen land beyond the village flowed through Octan's synapses, and the big eagle wheeled abruptly, reducing landscape and injured sky to chaotic smears.

The mercenary team were also marching eastwards, but they were on the Quallheim's northern shore, keeping roughly parallel to the water, a kilometre inland. They had come ashore west of Schuster where deirar trees covered the ground as thoroughly as though they were a plantation. Such regularity made the team's journey much easier than their first venture ashore when they had bypassed Pamiers.

The deirars' thick smooth boles rose straight up for twenty-five metres then opened into an umbrella of vegetation that formed a near-solid roof. Together they formed a sylvestral cathedral of enormous proportions. Everywhere the mercenaries looked they could see sturdy jet-black bark pillars supporting the dovetailing leaf domes. On this side of the river the usual deluge of vines and undergrowth was little more than a wispy clutter of straggly sun-starved weeds, long stemmed and pale, heavy with grey mould.

It was Reza who led the march, although he had sent Theo scampering across the treetop canopy on the lookout for hostiles. Few of them had escaped from Pamiers uninjured. He counted himself among the fortunate, with a burn on the rear of his skull that had scorched a couple of sensor warts down to the monobonded carbon reinforced bone; torso scores, and a spiral weal on his right leg. Of all of them, Kelly had borne the worst injury; but the medical packages had resuscitated her to mobile status. She walked with a small cylindrical shoulder-bag carrying her kit; her armour trousers protected her legs from thorns, and an olive-green T-shirt which the red light had turned a raw umber covered the bulge of medical packages on her side.

Pamiers had delivered a deft lesson, bruising their pride as well as their skin. But an important lesson, to Reza's mind. The team had learnt to give the sequestrated population a proper degree of respect. He wasn't going to risk probing a village again.

Fenton and Ryall padded tirelessly through the jungle on

the southern bank, skirting Aberdale by a wide margin. Jungle sounds filled their ears in the short gaps between the red cloud's perpetual thunder peals. The organic perfume of a hundred different flowers and ripening vine fruits trickled through the muggy air, a vital living counterpoint to the stink of dead children.

Reza nudged the hounds further south, away from the now-foreign village, from the smell of the small decaying bodies, its voodoo fence, away from the terrible price Lalonde's populace had paid under the invaders' regime. Narrow leaves, mottled with fungal furs, parted round the hounds' muzzles. Chilly distaste and shame – almost inevitably, shame – wormed its trenchant way into their minds along the affinity bond; they shared their master's susceptibilities, becoming as keen as he to leave the heartbreaker calamity behind.

New scents rode the air: sap dripping from snapped vine strands, crushed leaves, loam ruffled by footprints and wheel tracks. The hounds raced ahead, guided by primal senses. People had been this way recently. Some, but not many.

Reza saw a path through the jungle. An old animal track running north–south, enlarged some time ago – branches cut back by fission blades, bushes hacked away – only to fall into disuse again. Almost, but not quite. Somebody still used it. Someone had used it less than two hours ago.

Nerves and instinct fired now, Fenton and Ryall loped through the moist grass towards the south. After two kilometres they found a scent trail branching off into the jungle. One person, male. His clothes smearing the leaves with sweat and cotton.

'Pat, bring Octan back. I think we've got our man.'

*

Reza kept the snatch mission simple. The team activated their hovercraft again when they were back on the Quallheim east of Aberdale and started searching for a tributary fork on the south bank. According to the map stored in his guidance block there was a modest river which ran south through the jungle, coming from the mountains on the far side of the savannah. It took them five minutes to find it, and the hovercraft nosed over the clot of snowlilies guarding its mouth. Plaited tree boughs formed an arched screen overhead.

'After the snatch we'll keep going up this river and out onto the savannah,' Reza said when they had left the Quallheim behind. 'I want to get him and us out from under this bloody cloud as quickly as possible. We should be able to access the communication satellites as well once we're clear of it. That way if we can extract any useful information it can be delivered straight up to Terrance Smith.'

If Smith is still up there, Kelly thought. She couldn't forget what the woman in Pamiers had said about the starships fighting. But Joshua had promised to stay and pick them up. She gave a cynical little sniff. Oh yes, the Confederation's Mr Dependable himself.

'You all right?' Ariadne asked, raising her voice above the steady propeller whine and the rambling thunder booms.

'My analgesic blocks are holding,' Kelly said. 'It was just the size of the burn which shocked me.' She resisted the urge to scratch the medical nanonic packages.

'Adds a bit of spice to the recording, a bit of drama,' Ariadne said. 'Speaking of which, you're not going to blow us out, are you? I mean, we are the good guys.'

'Yeah. You're the good guys.'

'Great, always wanted to be a sensevise star.'

Kelly accessed her Lalonde sensevise report memory cell file and turned her head until Ariadne was in the centre of her vision field (wishing the combat-boosted could produce some halfway decent facial expressions). 'What did you learn from the sample you took from the houses?'

'Nowt. It was dust, that's all. Literally, dry loam.'

'So these ornamental buildings are just an illusion?'

'Half and half. It isn't a complete fiction; they've moulded the loam into the shape you see and cloaked it with an optical illusion. It's similar to our chameleon circuit, really.'

'How do they do that?'

'No idea. The closest human technology can come is the molecular-binding generators starships use to strengthen their hulls. But they're expensive, and use up a lot of power. Be cheaper to build a house, or use programmed silicon like you suggested. Then again' – she tilted her head back to focus her sensors on the cloudband above the trees – 'logic doesn't seem to be playing a large part in life on Lalonde right now.'

The hovercraft eased in against the crumbling loam bank. Ryall was standing among the qualtook trees above the water, waiting for them. Reza jumped ashore and ruffled the big hound's head. It pressed against his side in complete devotion.

'Jalal and Ariadne, with me,' Reza said. 'The rest of you stay here and keep the hovercraft ready. Pat, monitor us through Octan. If we blow the snatch, I suggest you keep heading south. There's a Tyrathca farming settlement on the other side of the savannah. It's as good a place as any to hide out. This snatch is our last stab at completing the mission. Don't waste yourselves trying to gather further Intelligence, and don't attempt a rescue. Got that?'

'Yes, sir,' Pat said.

Jalal and Ariadne joined Reza on the top of the bank. The big combat-adept mercenary had plugged a gaussrifle into one elbow socket and a TIP rifle into the other; power cables and feed tubes looped round into his backpack.

'Kelly?' Reza asked ingenuously. 'Not wanting to come with us this time?'

'It took eight generations of cousins marrying to produce you,' she told him.

The three mercenaries on the bank activated their chameleon circuits. Laughter floated down to the hovercraft out of unbroken jungle.

Fenton watched the little clearing from under the sloping lower branches of an infant gigantea. The light here wasn't the pure solar white of the villages, but the universal redness had veered into a pale pink shade. A log cabin had been built in the centre, not the kind of frame and plank arrangement favoured by the colonists but a rugged affair that could have come straight from some Alpine meadow. A stone chimney-stack formed almost all of one side, smoke wound drowsily upwards. A lot of trouble had been taken to transform the clearing; undergrowth had been trimmed back, animal hides were stretched drying over frames, timber had been cut and stacked, a vegetable plot planted.

The man who had done it was a well-built thirty-five-year-old with inflamed ginger hair, wearing a thick red and blue check cotton shirt and mud-caked black denim jeans. He was working at a sturdy table outside his front door, sawing up wood with old-fashioned manual tools. A half-completed rocking chair stood on the ground behind him.

Fenton moved forwards surreptitiously out of the shaggy gigantea's shade, but keeping to the cover provided by bushes and smaller trees ringing the clearing. Between thunder broadsides he could hear the regular stifled ripping sound as the man planed a piece of wood on the table. Then the sound stopped and his shoulders stiffened.

Reza wouldn't have thought it possible. The man was a good fifty metres away, with his back to the hound, and the thunder was unrelenting. Even his enhanced senses would have difficulty picking out Fenton under such circumstances. He and the other two mercenaries were still four hundred metres away. Nothing else for it . . . Fenton cantered eagerly into the clearing.

The man looked round, bushy eyebrows rising. 'What's this, then? My, you're a roguish looking brute.' He clicked his fingers, and Fenton trotted up to him. 'Ah, you'll not be on your own, then. That's a shame, a crying shame. For all of us. Your master won't be far behind, I'll warrant. Will you? Came down on the spaceplanes this morning no doubt, didn't you? That must have been a trip and a half. Aye, well, I'll not be finishing my chair this afternoon then.' He sat down on a bench beside the table, and started to change, his shirt losing colour, hair fading, thinning, stature diminishing.

By the time Reza, Jalal, and Ariadne walked into the clearing he had become an undistinguished middle-aged man with brown skin and thin features, wearing an ageing LDC one-piece jump suit. Fenton was noisily lapping up water out of a bowl at his feet, mind radiating contentment with his new friend.

Reza walked over cautiously. His retinal implants scanned the man from head to toe, and he datavised the pixel sequence into his processor block for a search and identify program. Although the earlier phantom lumberjack image had vanished, Reza saw the roots of the man's black hair were a dark ginger. 'Afternoon,' he said, not quite sure how to react to this display of passivity.

'Good afternoon to you. Not that I've seen anything like you before, mind. Not outside a kinema, and perhaps not even there.'

'My name is Reza Malin. We're part of a team employed by the LDC to find out what's going on down here.'

'Then with every ounce of sincerity I own, I wish you good luck, my boy. You're going to need it.'

An ounce was an ancient unit of measure, Reza's neural nanonics informed him (there was no reference to kinema in any file). 'Are you going to help me?'

'It doesn't look to me like I've got a lot of choice, now does it? Not with your merry gang and their big, big weapons.'

'That's true. What's your name?'

'My name? Well, now, that'd be Shaun Wallace.'

'Bad move. According to the LDC files you're Rai Molvi, a colonist who settled Aberdale.'

The man scratched his ear and gave Reza a bashful grin. 'Ah

now, you've got me there, Mr Malin. I must admit, I was indeed old Molvi. Charmless soul he is, too.'

'OK, smartarse, game over. Come on.'

Reza led the way back to the hovercraft, with Jalal walking right behind their captive, gaussrifle trained on the back of his skull. A couple of minutes after they left the clearing the pink light began to dim back into the same lustreless burgundy of the surrounding jungle. As if immediately aware of the abandonment, playful vennals slithered into the trees around the edge of the clearing. The more venturesome among them dared to scamper over the grass to the cabin itself, searching for titbits. After quarter of an hour the cabin emitted a vociferous creak. The vennals fled *en masse* back into the trees.

It was another couple of minutes before anything else happened. Then, with the tardiness of a sinking moon, its surface texture leaked away to reveal a starkly primitive mud hut. Tiny arid flakes moulted from the roof, resembling a sleet of miniature autumn leaves as they scattered over the grass below; rivulets of dust trickled down the walls. Within twenty minutes the entire edifice had dissolved like a sugar cube in soft, warm rain.

*

Forget discovering Ione Saldana existed, forget discovering Laton was still alive, *this* was the ultimate interview. For this Collins would make her their premier anchorwoman for the rest of time. For this she would be respected and lionized across the Confederation. Kelly Tirrel was the first reporter in history to interview the dead.

And as the dead went, Shaun Wallace was agreeable enough. He sat on the rear bench of the lead hovercraft, facing Kelly, and stroking Fenton the whole while. Jalal kept a heavy-calibre gaussrifle levelled at him. On the front bench beside her, Reza was listening intently, making the occasional comment.

The trees were thinning out as they raced for the end of the jungle. She could see more of the red cloudband through the black filigree of leaves overhead. It too was becoming flimsier; there were definite fast-moving serpentine currents straining its uniformity. Strangely, for there was no wind at ground level.

Shaun Wallace claimed he had lived in Northern Ireland during the early twentieth century. 'Terrible times,' he said softly. 'Especially for someone with my beliefs.' But he had just shaken his head and smiled distantly when she asked what those beliefs were. 'Nothing a lady like yourself would want to know.' He died, he said, in the mid-1920s, another martyr to the cause, another victim of English oppression. The reason the soldiers shot him was not volunteered. He claimed he hadn't died alone.

'And after?' Kelly said.

'Ah, now, Miss Kelly, afterwards is the work of the Devil.'

'You went to hell?'

'Hell is a place, so the good priests taught me. This beyond was no place. It was dry and empty, and it was cruel beyond physical pain. It was where you can see the living wasting their lives, and where you drain the substance from each other.'

'Each other? You weren't alone?'

'There was millions of us. Souls beyond the counting of a simple Ballymena lad like myself.'

'You say you can see the living from the other side?'

'From the beyond, yes. 'Tis like through a foggy window. But you strive to make out what it is that's happening in the living world. All the time you strive. And you yearn for it, you yearn for it so hard, lass, that you feel your heart should be bursting apart. I saw wonders and I saw terrors, and I could touch neither.'

'How did you come back?'

'The way was opened for us. Something came through from this side, right here on this sodden hot planet. I don't know what the creature was. Nothing Earthly, though. After that, there was no stopping us.'

'This xenoc, the creature you say let you through; is it still here, still bringing souls back from the beyond?'

'No, it was only here for the first one. It vanished after that. But it was too late, the trickle was already becoming a flood. We bring ourselves back now.'

'How?'

Shaun Wallace gave a reluctant sigh. He was quiet for so long Kelly thought he wasn't going to answer; he even stopped stroking Fenton.

'The way the devil-lovers of yesterday always tried to do it,' he said heavily. 'With their ceremonies and their pagan barbarism. And God preserve me for doing such things, I used to think what I did before was sinful. But there's no other way.'

'What is the way?'

'We break the living. We make them want to be possessed. Possession is the end of torment, you see. Even with our power we can only open a small gateway to the beyond, enough to show the lost souls the way back. But there has to be somewhere waiting for them, some host. And the host has to be willing.'

'You torture them into submission,' Reza said bluntly.

'Aye, that we do. That we do, indeed. And, mark you, there's no pride in me for saying it.'

'You mean, Rai Molvi is still there? Still alive inside you?'

'Yes. But I keep his soul locked away in a dark, safe place. I'm not sure you could call it living.'

'And this power you mentioned.' Kelly pressed the point. 'What is your power?'

'I don't know for sure. Magic of a kind. Though not a witch's magic with its spells and potions. This is a darker magic, because it's there at a thought. So easy, it is. Nothing like that should be given easily to a man. The temptations are too strong.'

'Is that where the white fire comes from?' Reza asked. 'This power you have?'

'Aye, indeed it is.'

'What's its range?'

'Ah now, Mr Malin, that's difficult to say. The more of you that fling it, the further it will go. The more impassioned you are, the stronger it will be. For a cool one such as yourself, I doubt it would be far.'

Reza grunted and shifted back on the bench.

'Could you demonstrate the power for me, please?' Kelly asked. 'Something I can record and show people. Something that will make them believe what you say is true.'

'I've never known a newspaper gal before. You did say you were from a newspaper, now didn't you?'

'What newspapers eventually became, yes.' She ran a historical search request through her neural nanonics. 'Something like the Movietone and Pathé reels at the cinema, only with colour and feeling. Now, that demonstration?'

'I normally prefer gals with longer hair, myself.'

Kelly ran her hand self-consciously over her scalp. She had shaved her hair to a blueish stubble so she could wear the armour's shell-helmet. 'I normally have longer hair,' she said resentfully.

Shaun Wallace winked broadly, then leant over the gunwale and scooped up one of the long-legged insects scampering over the snowlilies. He held it up in the palm of his hand; a long spindly tube body, dun brown, with a round bulb of a head sprouting unpleasant pincer mandibles. It was quivering, but stayed where it was as though glued to his skin. He brought his other hand down flat on top of it, making a show of pressing them together, squashing the insect. Kelly's eyes never wavered.

When he parted his hands the prince of butterflies was revealed, wings almost the size of his palms, patterned in deep turquoise and topaz and silver, colours resistant to the red light of the cloud, shining in their own right. Its wings flexed twice, then it flew off, only to be kicked about in the air by the wash of the hovercraft's powerful slipstream.

'There, you see?' Shaun Wallace said. 'We don't always destroy.'

Kelly lost sight of the delightful apparition. 'How long will it stay like that?'

'Mortality is not something you measure out like a pint of ale, Miss Kelly. It will live its life to the full, and that's all that can be said.'

'He doesn't know,' Reza muttered curtly.

Shaun Wallace practised a knowing, slightly condescending smile.

It was growing lighter around the hovercraft. Up ahead, Kelly could see the wonderfully welcome glare of pure sunlight striking emerald foliage. A colour that wasn't red! She had begun to believe that red was all there ever was, all there ever had been.

The hovercraft skimmed out from under the chafed edge of the cloudband. All of the mercenaries broke into a spontaneous cheer.

'What is that thing?' Kelly shouted above the rebel whoops, pointing up at the cloud.

'A reflection of ourselves, our fear.'

'What do you fear?'

'The emptiness of the night. It reminds us too much of the beyond. We hide from it.'

'You mean you're making that?' she asked, scepticism warring with astonishment. 'But it covers thousands of kilometres.'

'Aye, that it does. 'Tis our will that creates it; we want shelter, so shelter we have. All of us, Miss Kelly, even me who shuns the rest of them, we all pray for sanctuary with every fibre of being. And it's growing, this will of ours, spreading out to conquer. One day soon it will cover all of this planet. But even that is only the first chapter of salvation.'

'What's the second?'

'To leave. To escape the harsh gaze of this universe altogether. We'll withdraw to a place of our own making. A place where there is no emptiness hanging like a sword above the land, no death to claim us. A place where your butterfly will live for ever, Miss Kelly. Now tell me that isn't a worthy goal, tell me that isn't a dream worth having.'

Reza watched the last of the jungle's trees go past as the hovercraft reached the savannah. The lush green grassland seemed to unroll on either side of the river as though it was only just coming into existence. He wasn't really paying much attention; the strange (supposed) Irishman was a captivating performer. 'A closed universe,' he said, and the earlier scorn was lacking.

Kelly gave him a surprised glance. 'You mean it is possible?'

'It happens thousands of times a day. The blackhawks and voidhawks open interstices to travel through wormholes every time they fly between stars. Technically they're self-contained universes.'

'Yes, but taking a planet—'

'There are twenty million of us,' Shaun Wallace purred smoothly. 'We can do it, together, we can pull open the portal that leads away from mortality.'

Kelly's neural nanonics faithfully recorded the silver chill tickling her nerves at the naked conviction in his voice. 'You're really planning to generate a wormhole large enough to enclose the whole of Lalonde? And *keep* it there?'

Shaun Wallace wagged his finger at her. 'Ah, now there you go again, Miss Kelly, putting your fine, elegant words in my mouth. Plans, such a grand term. Generals and admirals and kings, now they have plans. But we don't, we have instinct. Hiding our new world from this universe God created, that comes as naturally as breathing.' He chuckled. 'It means we can go on breathing, too. I'm sure you wouldn't want to stop me from doing that, would you now? Not a sweet lass like yourself.'

'No. But what about Rai Molvi? Tell me what happens to him afterwards?'

Shaun Wallace scratched his chin, looked round at the savannah, shifted the jump-suit fabric round his shoulders, pulled a sardonic face.

'He stays, doesn't he?' Kelly said stiffly. 'You won't let him go.'

'I need the body, miss. Real bad. Perhaps there'll be a priest amongst us I can visit for absolution.'

'If what you're saying is true,' Reza said charily, focusing an optical sensor on the cloudband behind, 'then we really don't want to be staying here any longer than we have to. Wallace, when is this planetary vanishing act supposed to happen?'

'You have a few days' grace. But there are none of your starships left to sail away on. Sorry.'

'Is that why you didn't resist, because we can't escape?'

'Oh, no, Mr Malin, you've got me all wrong. You see, I don't want much to do with my fellows. That's why I live out in the woods, there. I prefer being on my own, I've had a bucketful of their company. Seven centuries of it, to be precise.'

'So you'll help us?'

He gathered himself up and threw a glance over his shoulder at the second hovercraft. 'I won't hinder you,' he announced magnanimously.

'Thank you very much.'

'Not that it will do you much good, mind.'

'How's that?'

'There's not going to be many places you can run to, I'm afraid. Quite a few of us have sailed away already.'

'Fucking hell,' Kelly gasped.

Shaun Wallace frowned in disapproval. 'To be sure, that's no word for a lady to be going and using.'

Kelly made sure he was in perfect focus. 'Are you telling me that what's happening on Lalonde is going to happen on other planets as well?'

'Indeed I am. There's a lot of very anguished souls back there in the beyond. They're all in dire need of a clean handsome body, every one of them. Something very much like the one you've got there.'

'This is occupied, to the hilt.'

His eyes flashed with black amusement. 'So was this one, Miss Kelly.'

'And all these worlds the possessed have gone to, are you going to try and imprison them in wormholes?'

'That's a funny old word you're using there: wormholes. Little muddy tunnels in the ground, with casts on top to show the fishermen where they are.'

'It means chinks in space, gaps you can fall through.'

'Does it now? Well, then, I suppose that's what I mean, yes. I like that, a gap in the air which leads you through to the other side of the rainbow.'

Surreal. The word seemed to be caught on some repeater program in Kelly's neural nanonics, flipping up in hologram violet over the image of a mad, dead Irishman sitting in front of her, grinning in delight at her discomfort. Worlds snatched out of their orbits by armies of the dead. Surreal. Surreal. Surreal.

Fenton rose growling to his feet, fangs barred, hackles sticking up like spikes. Shaun Wallace gave the hound an alarmed look, and Kelly's retinas caught the minutest white static flames twinkle over his fingertips. But Fenton swung his head round to the prow and barked.

Jalal's gaussrifle was already coming round. He saw the huge creature crouched down in the long grass at the side of the water thirty-five metres ahead of the hovercraft. The Lalonde generalist didactic memory called it a kroclion, a plains-dwelling carnivore which even the sayce ran from. He wasn't surprised, the beast must have been nearly four metres long, weighing an easy half-tonne. Its hide was a sandy yellow, well suited to the grass, making visual identification hard (infrared was, thankfully, a furnace flame). The head – like a terrestrial shark – had been grafted on, all teeth and tiny killer-bright eyes.

Blue target graphics locked on. He fired an EE round.

Everyone ducked, Kelly jamming her hands over her ears. A dazzling explosion sent a pillar of purple plasma and mashed soil spouting twenty metres into the air. Its vertex flattened out, a ring of soot-choked orange flame rolling across the river. The ululate *crack* was loud enough to drown out the tattoo of thunder chasing them from the red cloud.

Kelly lifted her head carefully.

'I think you got him,' Theo said drily, as he steered the hovercraft away from the quaking water sloshing round the new crater. A semicircle of grass on the bank was burning.

'They're vicious bastards,' Jalal protested.

'Not that one, not any more, as anyone within five kilometres will tell you,' Ariadne said.

'And you could have dealt with it better?'

'Forget it,' Reza said. 'We've got more important things to worry about.'

'You believe what this dickhead has been telling us?' Ariadne asked, jerking a thumb at Shaun Wallace.

'Some of it,' Reza said noncommittally.

'Why thank you, Mr Malin,' Shaun Wallace said. He watched the burning crater closely as the hovercraft sped past. 'Fine shooting there, Mr Jalal. Those old kroclions, they put the wind up me and no mistake. Old Lucifer was on form the day he made them.'

'Shut up,' Reza said. The one optical sensor he had left focused on the edge of the red cloud showed him a lone tendril starting to swell out, extending along the line of the narrow river behind them. Too slow to catch them, he estimated, but it was a graphically disturbing demonstration that the cloud and the possessed inhabitants were aware of the team's presence.

He opened a channel to his communication block and datavised a sequence of orders in. It began scanning the sky for communication-satellite beacons. Two of the five satellites the blackhawks had delivered into geosynchronous orbit were above the horizon and still broadcasting. The block aimed a tight beam at one, requesting contact with any of Terrance Smith's fleet. No ship was left in the command net, the satellite's computer reported, but there was a message stored in its memory. Reza datavised his personal code.

'This is a restricted access message for Reza's team,' Joshua Calvert's voice said from the communication block. 'But I have to be sure it is you and only you receiving it. The satellite is programmed to transmit it on a secure directional beam. If there is any hostile within five hundred metres of you who can intercept then do not request access. In order to access the recording, enter the name of the person who came between me and Kelly last year.'

The tip of the cloud tendril was a couple of kilometres away. Reza turned to face Shaun Wallace. 'Can any of your friends intercept a radio transmission?'

'Well, now, there's some of them living in one of the old savannah homesteads. But they're a few miles from here, yet. Is that more than five hundred metres?'

'Yes. Kelly, the name please.'

She gave him a stonefaced smile. 'Aren't you glad you didn't leave me behind at Pamiers?'

Jalal laughed. 'She got you there, Reza.'

'Yes,' Reza said heavily. 'I'm glad we didn't leave you behind. The name?'

Kelly opened a channel to his communication block and datavised: 'Ione Saldana.'

There was a moment's silence while the satellite's carrier wave emitted a few electronic bleeps.

'Well remembered, Kelly. OK, this is the bad news: the hijacked starships have started fighting us and the navy. There's a real vicious battle going on in orbit right now. *Lady Mac* got clear, but we've taken a bit of punishment in the process. Another story for you sometime. I'm about to jump us out to Murora. There's an Edenist station in orbit there, and we're hoping to dock with it to make our repairs. We estimate the damage can be patched up in a couple of days, after which we'll come back for you. Kelly, Reza, the rest of you; we're only going to make one fly-by. Hopefully you took my earlier advice and are now heading hell for leather away from that bloody cloud. Keep going, and leave your communication block scanning for my transmission. If you want to be picked up then you'll have to stay away from any hostiles. That's about it, we're battening down to jump now. Good luck, I'll see you in two, maybe three days.'

Kelly rested her head in her hands. Just hearing his voice again was a fantastic tonic. And he was alive, smart enough to elude a battle. And he was going to come back for them. Joshua, you bloody splendid marvel. She wiped tears from her cheeks.

Shaun Wallace patted her shoulder tenderly. 'Your young man, is it?'

'Yes. Sort of.' She sniffed, and brushed away the last of the tears in a businesslike manner.

'He sounds like a fine boy to me.'

'He is.'

Reza datavised a summary of events to the second hovercraft. 'I'm in complete agreement with Joshua about keeping clear of the cloud and the possessed. As of now our original mission is over. Our priority now is just to stay alive and make sure what information we have gets back to the Confederation authorities. We'll keep going up this river to the Tyrathca farmers and hope that we can hold out there until the *Lady Macbeth* comes back for us.'

*

It was the rygar bush which had brought the Tyrathca farmers to Lalonde.

When they were searching for their initial backing, the LDC sent samples of Lalonde's aboriginal flora to both of the xenoc members of the Confederation; it was standard practice to try and attract as wide a spectrum of support as possible for such ventures. The Kiint, as always, declined to participate. But the Tyrathca considered the small berries of the rygar bush a superlative delicacy. Ripe berries could be ground up to produce a cold beverage, or mixed with sugar to form a sticky fudge; LDC negotiators claimed it was the Tyrathcan equivalent of chocolate. The normally cloistered xenocs were so enamoured at the prospect of wholesale rygar cultivation they agreed to a joint colony enterprise with their merchant organization taking a four per cent stake in the LDC. It was only the third time since joining the Confederation that they had ever participated in a colony, a fact which lent the hard-pressed LDC considerable badly needed respectability. Even better for the LDC board: to a human palate the rygar berries tasted like oily grapes, so there would never be any conflict of interest arising.

Five years after the dumpers had dropped out of the sky to form the nucleus of Durringham the first batch of Tyrathcan breeder pairs arrived and settled in the foothills of the mountain range which made up the southern border of the Juliffe basin where the rygar bushes flourished. The LDC's long-range economic plans foresaw both the human and Tyrathcan settlements expanding from their respective centres until they met at the roots of the tributaries. By the time that happened both groups would have risen above their initial subsidence level and be prosperous enough to trade to their mutual enrichment. But that date was still many years in the future. The human villages furthest from Durringham were all as poor as Aberdale and Schuster, while the Tyrathcan plantations had barely cultivated enough rygar to fill the holds of the starships their merchants sent twice a year. Contact had so far been minimal.

*

It was late afternoon, and the savannah was already giving way to low humpbacked foothills when the mercenary team saw their first Tyrathcan house. There was no mistaking it, a dark cinnamon-coloured tower twenty-five metres high with slightly tapering walls, and circular windows sealed over with ebony blisters. The design had evolved on the abandoned Tyrathcan homeworld, Mastrit-PJ, over seventeen thousand years ago, and was employed on every planet their arkships had colonized right across the galaxy. They never used anything else.

This one stood like a border sentry castle overlooking the river. Octan glided round it a couple of times, seeing the vague outlines of fields and gardens reclaimed by grass and small scrub bushes. Moss and weeds were growing around the inside of the roof's turret wall where soil and dust had drifted.

'Nothing moving,' Pat reported to Reza. 'I'd say it was deserted three or four years ago.'

They had gathered together on the riverbank just downstream from the tower house, hovercraft drawn up on the grass. The river was getting narrower, little more than a stream, down to about eight metres wide, and littered with boulders which made it virtually unnavigable. For the first time since they had landed that morning there were no snowlilies in sight, only the broken tips of their stems trailing limply.

'The Tyrathca do that,' Sal Yong said. 'A house is only ever used once. When the breeders die it's sealed up as their tomb.'

Reza consulted his guidance block. 'There's a plantation village called Coastuc-RT six kilometres south-east of here. The other side of that ridge,' he pointed, datavising the map image to them. 'Ariadne, can the hovercraft take it?'

She focused her optical sensors on the rolling land which skirted the mountains. 'Shouldn't be a problem, the grass is a lot shorter here than the savannah and there isn't much stone about.' When she looked west she could see another three of the dark towers sticking out of the bleak countryside. They were all in shadow; thick black rain-clouds were surging towards them along the side of the mountains. The wind had freshened appreciably since they had left the jungle. Looking back to the north she could see the red cloud over the Quallheim forging the entire northern horizon; it was almost edge on, they had climbed steadily since leaving it behind. The sky above it was a perfect unblemished blue.

Kelly felt the first smattering of the drizzle on her bare arms as she clambered back into the hovercraft. She dug into her cylindrical kitbag for a cagoule, her burnt armour-suit jacket had been left behind in the jungle – in that state it wouldn't have been any use anyway. 'I'm sorry,' she told Shaun Wallace as he sat beside her. 'I've only got the one, and the others don't need them.'

'Ah now, don't you go worrying yourself over me, Miss Kelly,' he said. The jump suit he wore turned a rich indigo, then the fabric became stiffer. He was wearing a cagoule which was identical to the one in her hands, right down to the unobtrusive Collins logo on the left shoulder. 'There, see? Old Shaun can look after himself.'

Kelly gave him a flustered nod (thankful her memory cell was still recording), and hurriedly struggled into her own cagoule as the warm drizzle thickened. 'What about food?' she asked the Irishman as Theo goaded the hovercraft over the summit of the riverbank and started off towards the Tyrathca village.

'Don't mind if I do, thanks. Nothing too rich mind, not for me. I likes me pleasures simple.'

She dug round in the bag and found a bar of tarrit-flavoured chocolate. None of the mercenaries had brought any food, with their metabolisms they could graze off the vegetation indefinitely, potent intestinal enzymes breaking up anything with proteins and hydrocarbons.

Shaun Wallace chewed in silence for a minute. 'That's nice,' he said, 'reminds me a little of bilberries on a cold morning,' and he grinned.

Kelly found she was smiling back at him.

The hovercraft moved a lot slower over the land than on water. Cairnlike clusters of weather-smoothed stone and sudden pinched gullies made the pilots' task a demanding one. The rain, which was now a solid downpour of heavy grey water, added to the difficulty.

Pat had sent Octan northward to avoid the worst of the deluge. Back out on the savannah it was still dry and sunny, a buffer zone between nature and supernature. Reza dispatched Fenton and Ryall to survey the ground ahead. Lightning began to spear down.

'I think I preferred the river,' Jalal said glumly.

'Ah, Mr Jalal, buck up now, this is nothing for Lalonde,' Shaun Wallace said. 'A little shower, that's all. It was much worse than this before we returned from beyond.'

Jalal ignored the casual reference to the power of the possessed; Shaun Wallace, he thought, was playing a subtle war of nerves against them. Sowing the seeds of doubt and despondency.

'Hold it,' Reza datavised to Theo, and Sal Yong, who was piloting the second hovercraft. 'Deflate the skirts.'

The hovercraft sank onto their hulls with flagging whines, crushing the sturdy grass tufts, settling at awkward angles. Rain had reduced visibility to less than twenty-five metres even with enhanced sight. Kelly could just make out Ryall up ahead. The hound was shifting about uneasily in front of a big sandy-brown boulder.

Reza took off his magazine belt, and left the TIP carbine he'd been carrying with it. He hopped over the gunwale and started to trudge towards the restive animal. Kelly had to wipe a slick film of water from her face. The rain was worming its way round her cagoule hood to run down her neck. She toyed with the idea of putting on her shell-helmet again – anything to stop this insidious clammy invasion.

Reza stopped five metres short of the brown lump, and

slowly opened his arms, rain dripping from his grey-skinned fingers. He shouted something even Kelly's studio-grade audio-discrimination program couldn't catch above the wind and rain. She squinted, the rain suddenly chilling inside her T-shirt. The boulder rose up smoothly on four powerful legs. Kelly gasped. Her Confederation generalist didactic memory identified it immediately: a soldier-caste Tyrathca.

'Oh bugger,' Jalal muttered. 'They're clan creatures, it won't be alone.' He started to scan around. It was hopeless in the rain, even infrared was washed out.

The soldier-caste Tyrathca was about as big as a horse, although the legs weren't as long. Its head, too, was faintly equine, tilted back at a shallow angle at the end of a thick muscular neck. There were no visible ears, or nostrils; the mouth had a complex double-lip arrangement resembling overlapping clam shells. The sienna hide, which Kelly had thought solid like an exoskeleton, was actually scaled, with a short-cropped chestnut-brown mane running along its entire spine. Two arms extended from behind the base of its neck, ending in nine-fingered circular hands. A pair of slender antennae also protruded from its shoulder joints, swept back along the length of its body.

Although it had a strong animal appearance, it was holding a large very modern-looking rifle. A broad harnesslike belt hung round its neck, with grenades and power magazines clipped on.

It held out a processor block, and a slim AV projection pillar telescoped out. 'Turn your vehicles around,' a synthetic voice clanged through the rain. 'Humans are no longer permitted here.'

'We need somewhere to shelter for the night,' Reza replied. 'We can't go back north; you must have seen the red cloud.'

'No humans.'

'Why not? We must have somewhere to stay. Tell me, why?'

'Humans have become—' The block gave a melodic cheep. 'No direct translation available; similarity to: *elemental.*

Coastuc-RT has suffered damage, merchant spaceplane has been stolen. Breeders and other castes have been killed by amok humans. You are not permitted entry.'

'I know about the disturbances in the human villages. I have been sent by the Lalonde Development Corporation to try and restore order.'

'Then do that. Go to your own race's villages and bring order.'

'We have tried, but the situation was beyond our capability to resolve. There has been a major invasion of an unknown origin.' He just couldn't bring himself to say possession. The processor block was quiet; he guessed he was talking to a breeder, the soldier caste were only marginally sentient – not that he'd like to go up against one. 'I would like to discuss what can be done to protect you from further attack. My team are combat trained and well equipped, we should be able to augment whatever defences you have.'

'Acceptable. You may enter Coastuc-RT by yourself to view the situation. If you believe you are able to increase our defences your team will be allowed to enter and stay.'

'Reza,' Kelly datavised. 'Ask if I can come with you, please.'

'I will need to bring two others to assess the area around Coastuc-RT with any degree of accuracy before nightfall,' he said out loud, then datavised: 'That makes us quits now.'

'Absolutely,' she replied.

'Two only,' the synthetic voice agreed. 'None may carry weapons. Our soldiers will provide protection.'

'As you wish.' He turned and walked back to the first hovercraft, feet sinking up to his ankles in slimy puddles. The processor block AV projection pillar began to emit the reverberative whistles and hoots which were the Tyrathcan speech. Answering calls shrilled through the rain, causing the mercenaries to up their sensor resolution to the maximum in a vain attempt to locate the other soldier castes.

'Ariadne, you come with me and Kelly,' Reza said. 'I'll need someone who can review the area properly. The rest of you wait here. We'll try and get back before dusk. I'll leave Fenton and Ryall on picket duty for you.'

Two seemingly tireless soldiers ran alongside the hovercraft all the way to the village, antennae whipping back and forth (they were tail-analogues, helping with balance, according to Kelly's didactic memory). Kelly wasn't sure whom they were supposed to be protecting. The guns still appeared incongruous; for creatures that had evolved during the pre-technology tribal era to fight the Tyrathcan version of rough and tumble against enemy tribe soldiers bows and arrows would be more suited.

When she reviewed the entire didactic memory she found that the breeders (the only fully sentient Tyrathca) secreted what amounted to chemical control programs in specialist teats. A breeder would think out a sequence of orders – which plants were edible, how to operate a specific power tool – that would be edited into a chain of molecules by the teat gland. Once instructions were loaded in the brain of a vassal-caste species (there were six types) they could be activated by a simple verbal command whenever required. The chemicals were also used to educate young breeders, making the process a natural equivalent to Adamist didactic imprints and Edenist educational affinity lessons.

The rain was easing off when the hovercraft cleared the crest above Coastuc-RT. Kelly looked down on a broad, gentle valley with extensively cultivated terraces on both sides. An area of nearly twenty square kilometres had been cleared of scrub and grass, rebuilt into irrigated ledges, and planted with young rygar bushes. Coastuc-RT itself sat on the floor of the valley, several hundred indentical dark brown towers regimented in concentric rings around a central park space.

Reza steered the hovercraft onto a rough switchback track and set off down the slope. Numerous farmer-caste Tyrathca were out tending the emerald-green bushes – pruning, weeding, patching up the shallow drainage ditches. The farmers were slightly smaller than the soldiers but with thicker arms, endowed with the kind of plodding durability associated with oxen or shire-horses. They saw one or two hunter caste skulking among the bushes, about the same size as Reza's hounds, but with a streamlined fury that could probably give a kroclion a nasty fright. The escort soldiers whistled and hooted every time the hunters appeared, and they turned away obediently.

The first signs of damage were visible when the hovercraft reached the valley floor. Several towers in the village's outer ring were broken, five had been reduced to jagged stumps sticking up out of the rubble. Scorch marks formed barbarous black graffiti across the tower walls.

Fields on either side of the road had been churned up by fresh craters. EE explosives, Reza guessed, the village soldier caste had put up a good fight. The road itself had been repaired in several places. An earth rampart had been thrown up around the perimeter, a hundred metres from the outer turret houses. Farmers were still working around its base, using shovels which even Sewell would have been hard pressed to raise.

'Leave your vehicle now,' the synthesized voice from the processor block told them when they were twenty metres away from the barricade of raw loam.

Reza cut the fans and codelocked the power cells. The soldiers waited until they had climbed out, then walked them into the village.

Up close the tower houses were utilitarian, each with four floors, their windows arranged at precise levels. They were made by the builder caste, the largest of all the vassals, who chewed soil and mixed it with an epoxy chemical extravasated in their mouth ducts, producing a strong cement. It gave the walls a smooth, extruded feel, as though the towers had come intact from some giant kiln. There were some modern amenities, bands of solar cell panels tipped most of the turret walls; metal water pipes lay bent and tangled among the rubble. The windows were all glazed.

Arable gardens encircled every tower, trellises and stakes supporting the grasping yellow confusion of native Tyrathcan vegetation. Fruit trees lined the paved roads, huge leaves providing ample shade.

Smaller rounded silos and workshops were spaced between the towers, each with a single semicircular door. Carts and even small power trucks were parked outside.

'I don't know who is jumpier, us or them,' Kelly subvocalized into her neural nanonics memory cell. 'The Tyrathcan soldiers are clearly immensely capable, to say nothing of the hunter caste. Yet the possessed have hurt them badly. The vassal-caste bodies you can see half buried in the rubble of the outer towers have been left untended in the haste to fortify Coastuc-RT. A large breach of the Tyrathcan internment ritual, they obviously consider the threat humans present to be of more pressing importance.

'But now we are inside the village I can see very little activity apart from those vassals working on the rampart. The roads are empty. No breeder has appeared. The soldiers seem certain of their destination, leading us deeper into the village. I can now hear a great many Tyrathca away towards the park at the centre of Coastuc-RT. Yes, listen, a whistle that rises and falls in a slow regular beat. There must be hundreds of them doing it in unison to achieve that effect.'

The soldiers led them out onto one of the village's radial roads, cutting straight down past the tower houses into the central park. Right in the middle was a vast impossible dull-silver edifice. At first glimpse it looked like a hundred-metre-wide disc suspended fifty metres in the air by a central conical pillar whose tip only just touched the ground; another, identical, cone rose from the top of the disc. It was perfectly symmetrical, shining a lurid red-gold under the sinking sun. Six elaborate flying buttresses arched down from the rim of the disc, preventing the top-heavy structure from falling over.

The three humans stared in silence at the imposing artefact.

Big builder-caste Tyrathca walked ponderously along the buttresses and over the surface of the disc. The pinnacle of the upper cone wasn't quite finished, showing a geodesic grid of timber struts which a rank of builder caste clung to as they slowly covered it with their organic cement. Another team were following them up, spraying the drying cement with a gelatin mucus that shimmered with oil-slick marquetry until it hardened into the distinctive silverish hue.

Kelly took the structure in with one swift professional sweep, then focused on the park. It had been reduced to a shallow clay quarry in the haste to extract soil for the disc and its buttresses. This was where the Tyrathca breeders had gathered; several thousand of them, circling round the outside of the disc. They sat on their hindquarters in the mud, short antennae standing proud, whistling in a long slow undulation. It sounded poignant, imploring even. Entities that had been needlessly hurt questioning the reason, the same the galaxy over.

Kelly's didactic memory didn't have any reference to a Tyrathcan religion. A more comprehensive search program running through her neural nanonics said the Tyrathca didn't have a religion, and there was no explanation for the disc, either.

'If I didn't know better, I'd say they were at prayer,' Reza datavised.

'Could be the local version of the town meeting,' Ariadne suggested. 'Trying to decide what to do about us wild humans.'

'They're not talking about anything,' Kelly said. 'It's more like a song.'

'The Tyrathca don't sing,' Reza replied.

'What's that disc for? There's no way in at the bottom of the cone pillar, not from this side, but it's definitely hollow. Nothing solid like that would be able to stand up, it's almost like a mock-up. I can't find any record of them ever building anything like it before. And why build it now for Christ's sake, when they need all the builder caste to construct defences?

Something that size has taken a hell of a lot of effort to put up.'

He put his hand on her shoulder. 'Looks as if you'll be able to ask in a minute.'

The soldiers halted when they came level with the innermost ring of house towers. All of the buildings had been sealed up, black lids capping the windows, cement slabs erected over the door arches. Colourful flowering plants swamped their gardens.

A lone breeder was walking towards them from the park. Male or female, Kelly couldn't tell, not even comparing it to the images stored in a memory cell – females were supposed to be slightly larger. It was bigger than the soldiers by about half a metre, the scale hide several shades lighter, dorsal mane neatly trimmed. Apart from its stumpy black antennae, the one physiological aspect which most distinguished it from the vassal castes was a row of small chemical program teats dangling flaccidly from its throat like empty leather pouches, although the long supple fingers intimated it was a sophisticated tool user.

She saw an almost subliminal hazy film twinkling briefly on the road behind it. Superfine bronze powder, similar to the dusting on a terrestrial moth, was sprinkling down from its flanks.

The Tyrathca breeder stopped beside the soldier carrying the processor block. Its outer mouth hinged back, allowing it to whistle a long tune.

Flute music, Kelly thought.

'I am Waboto-YAU,' the processor block voice translated. 'I will mediate with you on behalf of Coastuc-RT.'

'I'm Reza Malin, combat scout team leader, under contract to the LDC.'

'Are you able to assist in our defence?'

'You'll have to tell me what happened, first, give us some idea of what we're up against.'

'Starship *Santa Clara* arrived yesterday. Spaceplane landed, bringing new Tyrathca, new equipment. Much needed. Collect rygar crop. Amok *elemental* humans attacked; stole spaceplane. No provocation. No reason. Twenty-three breeder-caste killed. One hundred and ninety vassal castes killed. Extensive damage. You can see this.'

Reza wondered how he would react if it was xenocs who had attacked a human village in a similar fashion. Allow a group of those same xenocs in afterwards to talk? Oh no, no way. The human response would be far more basic.

He felt mortally humbled as the breeder's glassy hazel eyes stared at him. 'How many humans took part in this attack?' he asked.

'Numbers not known with accuracy.'

'Roughly, how many?'

'No more than forty.'

'Forty people did all this?' Ariadne muttered.

Reza waved her quiet. 'Did they use a kind of white fire?'

'White fire. Yes. Not true fire. *Elemental* fire. Tyrathca have not been told of human *elemental* ability before. Many times witnessed delusion of form on attacking humans. *Elemental* changes of colour and shape confused soldier caste. Some amok humans stole Tyrathca hunter-caste form. Much damage before repelled.'

'On behalf of the LDC I apologize profoundly.'

'What use apology? Why not told of human *elemental* ability? Breeder ambassador family assigned to Confederation Assembly will be informed. Denouncement of humans in Assembly. Tyrathca would never have joined Confederation if had known.'

'I'm sorry. But these humans have been taken over by an invading force. We don't normally possess this ability. It's as foreign to us as it is to you.'

'Lalonde Development Company must remove all *elemental* humans from planet. Tyrathca will not inhabit same planet.'

'We'd love to. But right now it's all we can do just to stay alive. These elemental humans now control the entire Juliffe basin. We need somewhere to stay until a starship can lift us off and we can inform the Confederation what is happening.'

'Starships battle in orbit this day. Double sun in sky. No starships left.'

'One is coming back for us.'

'When?'

'In a few days.'

'Does starship have the power to kill *elemental* cloud? Tyrathca scared of cloud over rivers. We cannot defeat it.'

'No,' Reza said forlornly. 'The starship can't kill the cloud.' Especially if Shaun Wallace is telling the truth. The thought was one he had been firmly suppressing. The implications were too frightening. Just how would we actually go about fighting them?

The Tyrathca let out a clamorous hoot, almost a wail. 'Cloud will come here. Cloud will devour us; breeders, children, vassals. All.'

'You could leave,' Kelly said. 'Keep ahead of the cloud.'

'Nowhere is ahead of the cloud for long.'

'What are you doing here?' she asked, raising her arm to point at the park, the congregation of breeders. 'What is that structure you have built?'

'We are not strong. We have no *elementals* among us. Only one can now save us from *elemental* humans. We call to our Sleeping God. We show our belief by our homage. We call and call, but the Sleeping God does not yet awake.'

'I didn't know you had a God.'

'The family of Sireth-AFL is a custodian of the memory from the days of voyage on flightship Tanjuntic-RI. He shared the memory with us all after attack by *elemental* humans. Now we are united in prayer. The Sleeping God is our hope for salvation from *elemental* humans. We build its idol to show our faith.'

'This is it?' she asked. 'This is what the Sleeping God looks like?'

'Yes. This is the memory of shape. This is our Sleeping God.'

'You mean the Tyrathca on the Tanjuntic-RI actually saw a God?'

'No. Another flightship passed the Sleeping God. Not Tanjuntic-RI.'

'The Sleeping God was in space, then?'

'Why you want to know?'

'I want to know if the Sleeping God can save us from the elementals,' she said smoothly. 'Or will it only help Tyrathca?' Christ, this was beautiful, the story to end all stories; human dead and secrets the Tyrathca had kept since before Earth's ice age. How long had their arkships been in flight? Thousands of years at least.

'It will help us because we ask,' Waboto-YAU said.

'Do your legends specifically say it will return to save you?'

'Not legend!' the breeder hooted angrily. 'Truth. Humans have legends. Humans lie. Humans become *elemental*. The Sleeping God is stronger than your race. Stronger than all living things.'

'Why do you call it "Sleeping"?'

'Tyrathca say what is. Humans lie.'

'So it was Sleeping when your flightship found it?'

'Yes.'

'Then how do you know it is strong enough to ward off the *elementals*?'

'Kelly!' Reza said with edgy vexation.

Waboto-YAU hooted again. The soldiers shifted restlessly in response, eyes boring into the obsessed reporter.

'Sleeping God strong. Humans will learn. Humans must not become *elemental*. Sleeping God will awaken. Sleeping God will avenge all Tyrathca suffering.'

'Kelly, shut up, now. That's an order,' Reza datavised when

he saw her gathering herself for more questions. 'Thank you for telling us of the Sleeping God,' he said to Waboto-YAU.

Kelly fumed in moody silence.

'Sleeping God dreams of the universe,' the breeder said. 'All that happens is known to it. It will hear our call. It will answer. It will come.'

'The human elementals may attack you again,' Reza warned. 'Before the Sleeping God arrives.'

'We know. We pray hard.' Waboto-YAU twittered mournfully, head swinging round to gaze at the disk. 'Now you have heard the fate of Coastuc-RT. Are you able to assist soldier caste in defence?'

'No.' Reza heard Kelly's hissed intake of breath. 'Our weapons are not as powerful as those of your soldiers. We cannot assist in your defence.'

'Then go.'

Vast tracts of electric, electromagnetic, and magnetic energy seethed and sparked across a roughly circular section in the outermost band of Murora's rings, eight thousand kilometres in diameter. Dust, held so long in equilibrium, exploited its liberation to squall in microburst vortices around the solid imperturbable boulders and jagged icebergs which made up the bulk of the ring, their gyrations mirroring the rowdy cloudscape a hundred and seventy thousand kilometres below. The epicentre, where the *Lady Macbeth* had plunged into the drive-fomented particles, was still glowing a nervous blue as brumal waves of static washed through the thinning molecular zephyr of vaporized rock and ice.

The total energy input from the starship's fusion drives and the multiple combat-wasp explosions was taking a long time to disperse. Their full effect would take months if not years to sink back to normality. Thermally and electromagnetically, the rippling circle was the equivalent of an Arctic whiteout to any probing sensors.

It meant the *Maranta* and the *Gramine* knew little of what was going on below the surface. They kept station ten kilometres above the fuzzy boundary where boulders and ice gave way first to pebbles and then finally dust; all sensor clusters extended, focused on the disquieted strata of particles under their hulls. For the first couple of kilometres the image was sharp and reasonably clear, below that it slowly disintegrated until at seven kilometres there was nothing but a sheet of electronic slush.

The possessed who commanded the starships now had started their search right at the heart, the exact coordinate where *Lady Macbeth* had entered. Then *Maranta* had manoeuvred into an orbit five kilometres lower, while the *Gramine* had raised its altitude by a similar amount. They slowly drifted apart, *Maranta* edging ahead of the phosphorescent blue splash, *Gramine* falling behind.

There had been no sign of their prey. Nor any proof to confirm the *Lady Macbeth* had survived her impact with the rings. No wreckage had been detected. Although it was a slim chance any ever would. If she had detonated when she hit, the blowout of her drive tubes' escaping plasma would probably have vaporized most of her. And any fragments which did survive would have been flung over a huge area. The ring was eighty kilometres thick, enough volume to lose an entire squadron in.

They were further hindered by the way their energistically charged bodies interfered with on-board systems. Sensors already labouring at the limit of their resolution to try and unscramble the chaos suffered infuriating glitches and power surges, producing gaps in the overall coverage.

But the crews persevered. Debris was virtually impossible to locate, but an operating starship emitted heat, and electromagnetic impulses, and a strong magnetic flux. If she was there, they would find her eventually.

*

The soldier-caste vassals stayed with them until the hovercraft reached the top of the Coastuc-RT's valley. More tumid rain-clouds were approaching fast from the east, borne by the obdurate breeze. Reza judged they should just about reach the other hovercraft by the time they arrived. Both land and sky ahead were grey. Northwards, the red cloud cast a dispiriting corona, looking for all the world as though magma was floating, light as thistledown, through the air.

'But *why*?' Kelly demanded as soon as the soldiers were left behind. 'You saw how well armed they were, we would have been safe there.'

'Firstly, Coastuc-RT is too close to the Juliffe basin. As your friend Shaun Wallace said, the cloud is spreading. It would reach the valley long before Joshua gets back. Secondly, that valley is tactical suicide. Anyone who gets onto the high ground above the village can simply bombard it into submission, or more likely destruction. There aren't enough soldier and hunter vassals to keep the slopes clear. Right now Coastuc-RT is wide open to anything the possessed care to throw at it. And all the Tyrathca are doing to defend themselves is building giant effigies of spacegods and having a pray in. We don't need that kind of shit. By ourselves we stand a much better chance; we're mobile and well armed. So tomorrow at first light we start doing exactly what Joshua said: we run for it, through the mountains.'

*

Violent rain made a mockery of the hovercraft's blazing monochrome headlight beams, chopping them off after five or six metres. It obscured the moons, the red cloud, it damn near hid the drooping, defeated grass below the gunwale. The pilots navigated by guidance blocks alone. It took them forty minutes to retrace their route back to the first tower house above the river.

Sewell plugged a half-metre fission blade into his left elbow socket and confronted the blocked-up doorway. Water steamed and crackled as the blade came on. He placed the tip delicately against the wind-fretted cement, and pushed. The blade sank in, sending out a thick runnel of ginger sand which the rain smeared into the reeds at his feet. Relieved at how easy it was to cut, he started to slice down.

Kelly was fourth in. She stood in musty darkness shaking her arms and easing her cagoule hood back. 'God, there's as much water inside this cagoule as out. I've never known rain like this.'

''Tis a bleak night, this one,' Shaun Wallace said behind her.

Reza stepped through the oval Sewell had cut, carrying two bulky equipment packs, TIP carbines slung over his shoulder. 'Pat, Sal, check this place out.' Fenton and Ryall hurried in after their master, and immediately shook their coats, sending out a fountain of droplets.

'Great,' Kelly muttered. The blocks clipped to her broad belt were slippery with water. She wiped them ineffectually on her T-shirt. 'Can I come with you, please?'

'Sure,' Pat said.

She turned the seal catch on her bag, and searched round until she found a light stick. Shadows fled away. Collins disapproved of infrared visuals unless absolutely unavoidable.

They were in a hall that ran the diameter of the tower. Archways led off into various rooms. A ramp at the far wall started to spiral upwards. Tyrathca didn't, or couldn't, use stairs, according to her didactic memory.

Pat and Sal Yong started down the hall, Kelly followed. She realized Shaun Wallace was a pace behind. He was back in his LDC jump suit. Completely dry, she noticed enviously. Her armour-suit trousers squelched as she walked.

'You don't mind if I tag along, do you, Miss Kelly? I've never seen one of these places before.'

'No.'

'That Mr Malin there, he's a right one for doing things by the book. This place has been sealed up for years. What does he expect us to find?'

'We won't know till we look, will we?' she said coyly.

'Why, Miss Kelly, I do believe you're running me a ragged circle.'

The house was intriguing: strange furniture, and startlingly human utensils. But there was little technology, the builders had obviously been given instructions on how to utilize wood. They were excellent carpenters.

Rain drummed on the walls, adding to the sense of isolation and displacement as they mounted the ramp. Vassal castes had their own rooms; Kelly wasn't sure if they could be called stables. Some rooms, for the soldiers, she guessed, had furniture. There was only a thin layer of dust. It was as though the tower had been set aside rather than abandoned. Given her current circumstances, it wasn't the most reassuring of thoughts. The neural nanonics drank it all in.

They found the first bodies on the second floor. Three housekeeper castes (the same size as a farmer), five hunters, and four soldiers. Desiccation had turned them into creased leather mummies. She wanted to touch one, but was afraid it would crumble to dust.

'They're just sitting there, look,' Shaun Wallace said in a tamed voice. 'There's no food anywhere near them. They must have been waiting to die.'

'Without the breeders, they are nothing,' Pat said.

'Even so, 'tis a terrible thing. Like those old Pharaohs who had all their servants in their tombs with them.'

'Were there any Tyrathcan souls in the beyond?' Kelly asked.

Shaun Wallace paused at the bottom of the ramp to the

third floor, his brow crinkling. 'Now there's a thing. I don't think there were. Or at least, I never came across one.'

'Different afterworld, perhaps,' Kelly said.

'If they have one. They seem heathen creatures to me. Perhaps the Good Lord didn't see fit to give them souls.'

'But they have a god. Their own god.'

'Do they now?'

'Well, they're hardly likely to have Jesus or Allah, are they? Not human messiahs.'

'Ah, you're a smart one, Miss Kelly. I take my hat off to you. I'd never have thought of that in a million years.'

'It's a question of environment and upbringing. I'm used to thinking in these terms. I'd be lost in your century.'

'Oh, I can't see that. Not at all.'

There were more vassal-caste bodies on the third floor. The two breeders were together on the fourth.

'Do they have love, these beasties?' Shaun Wallace asked, looking down at them. 'They look like they do, to me. Dying together is romantic, I think. Like Romeo and Juliet.'

Kelly ran her tongue round her cheeks. 'You didn't strike me as the Shakespeare type.'

'Now don't you go writing me off so quickly, you with your classy education. I'm a man of hidden depths, I am, Miss Kelly.'

'Did you ever meet anyone famous in the beyond?' Pat asked.

'Meeting!' He wrung his hands together with fulsome drama. 'You're talking about the beyond as if it's some kind of social gathering. Lords and ladies spending the evening together over fine wine and a game of bridge. It's not like that, Mr Halahan, not at all.'

'But did you?' the mercenary scout persisted. 'You were there for centuries. There must have been someone important.'

'Ah now, there was that, as I recall. A gentleman by the name of Custer.'

Pat's neural nanonics ran a fast check. 'An American army general? He lost a fight with the Sioux Indians in the nineteenth century.'

'Aye, that's the one. Don't be telling me you've heard of him in this day and age?'

'He's in our history courses. How did he feel about it? Losing like that?'

Shaun Wallace's expression cooled. 'He didn't feel anything about it, Mr Halahan. He was like all of us, crying without tears to shed. You're equating death with sanity, Mr Halahan. Which is a stupid thing to do, if you don't mind me saying. You've heard of Hitler now? Surely, if you've heard of poor damned George Armstrong Custer?'

'We remember Hitler. Though he was after your time, I think.'

'Indeed he was. But do you think he changed after he died, Mr Halahan? Do you think he lost his conviction, or his righteousness? Do you think death causes you to look back on life and makes you realize what an ass you've been? Oh no, not that, Mr Halahan. You're too busy screaming, you're too busy cursing, you're too busy coveting your neighbour's memory for the bitter dregs of taste and colour it gives you. Death does not bestow wisdom, Mr Halahan. It does not make you humble before the Lord. More's the pity.'

'Hitler,' Kelly said, entranced. 'Stalin, Genghis Khan, Jack the Ripper, Helmen Nyke. The butchers and the warlords. Are they all there? Waiting in the beyond?'

Shaun Wallace gazed up at the domed ceiling partially lost amid a tapestry of shadows thrown by sparse alien architecture; for a moment his features portraying every year of his true age. 'Aye, they're all there, Miss Kelly, every one of the monsters the good earth ever spawned. All of them aching to come back, waiting for their moment to be granted. Us possessed, we might be wanting to hide from the open sky, and death; but it's not paradise we're going to be making down here on this planet. It couldn't be, there'll be humans in it, you see.'

*

It wasn't true daybreak, not yet. The sun was still half an hour from bringing any hint of grizzled light to the eastern horizon. But the rain-clouds had blown over, and night had sapped the wind's brawn. The northern sky glowed with a grievous fervour, blemishing the savannah grass a murky crimson.

Octan watched the dark speck moving along the side of the river, heading upstream towards the Tyrathcan tower house. Heavy moist air stroked the eagle's feathers as he dipped a wing, curving down in a giddy voluted dive. Pat Halahan gazed out at the lonely nocturnal wanderer through his affinity bonded friend's narrow peerless eyes.

Kelly came awake at the touch of a hand on her shoulder, and the sound of feet rapping on the hard dry floor of the second storey, where the team had rested up for the night. Neural nanonics accelerated her fatigue-soaked brain into full alertness.

The last of the combat-boosted mercenaries were disappearing down the ramp.

'Someone coming,' Shaun Wallace said.

'Your people?'

'No. I'd know if it was. Not that Mr Malin asked, mind you.' He sounded cheerful.

'Good heavens, anyone would think he doesn't trust you.' She shoved back the foil envelope she'd been sleeping in. Shaun Wallace offered his hand to help her to her feet. They made their way down the ramp to the ground-floor hall.

The seven mercenaries were clustered round the hole in the door, red light shining dully off their artificial skin. Fenton and Ryall were on their feet, growling softly as they were caught in the backwash of agitation coming from their master's mind.

Reza and Sewell slipped through the hole as Kelly reached them.

'What is it?' she asked.

'Horse coming,' Pat told her. 'Two riders.'

Kelly peered round him just as Reza and Sewell activated their chameleon circuits and flicked into the landscape. For a few seconds she tracked them thanks to the circular medical nanonic package on the big combat-adept's leg, but even that was soon lost amongst the unsavoury coloured grass.

It was one of the plough horses favoured by the colonists. A young one, but clearly on its last legs; the neck was drooping as it plodded gamely along, mouth flecked with foam. Reza worked his way unobtrusively down the slope from the tower house towards the animal, leaving Sewell to cover him. His optical sensors showed him the two people on its back; both wore stained poncho capes cut from a canvas tarpaulin. The man was showing the first signs of age, stubble shading heavy jowls, temples touched with grey; and he'd recently lost a lot of weight by the look of him. But he had a vigour animating his frame which was visible even from Reza's position across the swaying grass. The young boy behind him had been crying at some time, he had also been soaked during the ride, and now he was shivering, clinging to the man in a wearied daze.

They didn't pose any threat, Reza decided. He waited until the horse was twenty metres away, then switched off his chameleon circuit. The horse took a few more paces before the man noticed him with a start. He reined in the lethargic animal and leaned over its neck to peer at Reza in bewilderment.

'What manner of . . . You're not a possessed, you don't have their emptiness.' His fingers clicked. 'Of course! Combat boosted, that's what you are. You came down from the starships yesterday.' He smiled and whooped, then swung a leg over the horse and slithered to the ground. 'Come on, Russ, down you come, boy. They're here, the navy marines are here. I said they'd come, didn't I? I told you, never give up faith.' The boy virtually fell off the horse into his arms.

Reza went over to help. The man was none too steady on his feet, either, and one of his hands was heavily bandaged.

'Bless you, my son.' Horst Elwes embraced the surprised mercenary with tears of gratitude and supreme relief shining in his eyes. 'God bless you. These weeks have been the sorest trial my Lord has ever devised for this weak mortal servant. But now you are here after all this time spent alone in the Devil's own wilderness. Now we are saved.'

Boston had fallen to the possessed, not that the rapidly disintegrating convocation of Norfolk's martial authorities would admit it.

Edmund Rigby looked out of the hotel window, across the provincial city's steep slate rooftops. Fires were still burning in the outlying districts where the militia troops had tried to force their way in. The Devonshire market square had been struck by a navy starship's maser last Duchess-night. Its granite cobbles had transmuted to a glowing lava pool in less than a second. Even now, with its surface congealing and dimming, the heat was enough to barbecue food. Nobody had been in the square at the time; it was intended as a demonstration only. A show of naval might: you there, ant folk crawling on the filthy ground far below, we angels above have the very power of life and death over all of you. As one, the possessed had laughed at the circling starships, rendered impotent by their lack of targets. Yes, they had the physical power to destroy, but the fingers on the trigger were snared in the perpetual dilemma of the great and the good. Hostages had always struck a paralysing blow into the heart of governments. The starships wanted to pour sterilizing fire down from the sky, the officers yearning to burn the loathsome low-life crop of anarchists and revolutionaries from the pastoral idyll planet, but the city hadn't been cleaned of decent people, the women and children and frail, kindly grandparents. As far as the planetary authorities and navy officers knew this was just an uprising, a political revolt, they believed the meek were still mingled with the wolves. The lofty orbiting angels had been castrated.

Even if they suspected, believed the rumours of atrocities and massacres flittering from mouth to mouth through the nearby countryside, they could do nothing. Boston was no longer alone in its dissent, it was simply the first. Edmund Rigby had planted the germs of insurgency in every city across the planet's islands, cabals of possessed who were already annexing the populace. A captain in the Australian Marines, he had died from a landmine explosion in Vietnam in 1971; but he had studied military tactics, had even been sent to the Royal Naval College in Dartmouth for officer training. And this vast space empire of Confederated planets, for all its awesome technology, was no different to the Earth upon which he had once walked. Vietcong insurgency tactics from the past were just as applicable now, and he knew them by heart. Securing the entire planet had been his principal objective since the vast merchant fleet had left Norfolk after midsummer.

Since he arrived he had been busy indeed. Toiling in the squalor and the horror and the blood which soiled the heart of every human soul. Those living, and those dead . . . and the ones trapped between.

He closed his eyes as if to shut out the memories of recent weeks and what he had become. But there was no respite. The hotel took on substance in his mind, walls and floors woven from shadows. People, us and them, glided through it, doplered laughs and screams ricocheting through the grand corridors and sumptuous rooms. And, always, *there*, on the other side of the shadows, on the other side of everything: the beyond. Chittering souls clamouring for existence, silky insidious promises to be his lover, his slave, his acolyte. Anything, anything at all to be brought back.

Edmund Rigby shuddered in revulsion. Please, God, when

we hide Norfolk from this universe let it also be hidden from the beyond. Let me have peace, and an end to all this.

Three of his lieutenants – selected from the more stable among the newly possessed – were dragging a captive along the corridor outside to his room. He stiffened his shoulders, letting the power swell within, giving his new body grandeur and poise, as well as a Napoleonic uniform, and turned to face the door.

They burst in, cheering and jeering, young turks from the worst of the backstreets, believing swagger and noise was an easy substitute for authority. But he grinned welcomingly at them anyway.

Grant Kavanagh was flung on the floor, bleeding from cuts on his face and hands, smeared in dirt, his fine militia uniform torn. Even so, he refused to be cowed. Edmund Rigby respected that, amongst the sadness. This one, with his conviction in God and self, would be hard to break. The thought pained him. Why oh why can't they just give in?

'Present for you, Edmund,' Iqabl Geertz said. He had assumed his ghoul appearance, skin almost grey, cheeks sunken, eyeballs a uniform scarlet; thin frame dressed all in black. 'One of the nobs. Got some fight in him. Thought he might be important.'

Don Padwick, in his lion-man state, growled suggestively. Grant Kavanagh twitched as the big yellow beast dropped onto all fours and padded over to him, tail whisking about.

'We captured his troops,' Chen Tambiah informed Edmund quietly. 'They were about the last militia roaming free. Inflicted heavy casualties. Eight of us winged back to the beyond.' The dapper oriental, in ancient black and orange silks, cocked his head grudgingly towards Grant Kavanagh. 'He's a good leader.'

'Is that so?' Edmund Rigby asked.

Iqabl Geertz licked his lips with a long yellowed tongue. 'It doesn't make any difference in the end. He's ours now. To do with as we like. And we know what we like.'

Grant Kavanagh looked up at him, one eye swollen shut. 'When this is over, you mincing shit, and the rest of your friends have been shot, I will take a great deal of pleasure in ripping every one of your deviant chromosomes from your body with my own hands.'

'Now there's a man's man if ever I saw one,' Iqabl Geertz said, putting on an histrionically effeminate tone.

'Enough,' Edmund Rigby said. 'You put up a good fight,' he told Grant, 'now it's over.'

'Like hell! If you think I'm going to let you Fascist scum take over the planet my ancestors sweated blood to build you don't know me.'

'Nor shall we ever,' Edmund Rigby said. 'Not now.'

'That's right, takes bloody four of you.' Grant Kavanagh grunted in shock as Don Padwick put a paw on his ribs, talons extended.

Edmund Rigby rested his hand on Grant's head. There was so much resilience and anger in the man. It enervated him, sending the pretentious uniform shimmering back into his ordinary marine fatigues. The souls of the beyond were clamouring as he began to gather his power, flocking to the beacon of his strength.

'Don't fight me,' he said, more in hope than in expectation.

Grant snarled. 'Screw you!'

Edmund Rigby heard the vile rapturous imploring chorus of the souls beginning. Weariness engulfed him, there had been so much of this since he had returned. So much pain and torment, so wilfully inflicted. At first he had laughed, and enjoyed the fear. Now, he simply wished it over.

He hesitated, and the captive soul stirred in the prison he had forged for it within his own mind.

'There are ways,' the other soul said, and showed, obedient as always to his captor. 'Ways to make Grant Kavanagh submit quickly, ways no flesh can withstand for long.'

And the desire was there, oozing up out of the prison, corrupt and nauseous.

'But it's a part of all of us,' the other soul whispered quickly. 'We all share the shame of having the serpent beast in our secret heart of hearts. How else could you have accomplished what you have the way you have if you did not let it free?'

Trembling, Edmund Rigby let the desire rise, let it supersede the loathing and revulsion that was his own. Then it was easy. Easy to make Grant hurt. Easy to commit the profanities which quietened his lieutenants. Easy to feed the desire. And go on feeding.

It was good, because it was freedom. Complete and utter freedom. Desire ruled as it should, unrestrained. It nurtured the psyche, these heinous abominations Grant Kavanagh was forced to endure. They were sublime.

Iqabl Geertz and Chen Tambiah were yelling at him to stop. But they were nothing, less than dirt.

The souls were in retreat, fearing what was leaking from him into the beyond.

'Weak, they are all weaker than us. Together we surpass them all.'

Was that his own voice?

And still the savagery went on. It was impossible to stop. The other soul had gone too far, it had to be seen through now. To the terrible end.

Edmund Rigby rebelled in horror.

'But you did it yourself,' said the captive soul.

'No. It was you.'

'I only showed you how. You wanted it. The desire was yours, the yearning.'

'Never! Not for this.'

'Yes. You gave way to yourself for the first time. The serpent beast is in all of us. Embrace it and be at peace with yourself. Know yourself.'

'I am not that. I am not!'

'But you are. Look. Look!'

'No.' Edmund Rigby shrank from what he had done. Fleeing, *hurtling*, away, as though speed alone was proof of his innocence. Locking out the world and what he had been a party to, down in that empty vault waiting at the centre of his mind. Where it was quiet, and dark, and tasteless. Sanctuary without form. It hardened around him.

'And there you will stay; a part of me for ever.'

Quinn Dexter opened his eyes. Before him the three possessed, their exotic appearances bleached off to reveal young men with ashen faces, backed away in consternation; their confidence in their supremacy jarringly fractured. Grant Kavanagh's decimated body quivered amid the blood and piss curdling on the carpet as the soul it now hosted tried valiantly to repair the colossal tissue damage. Deep inside himself he heard Edmund Rigby's soul whimpering quietly.

Quinn smiled beatifically at his rapt audience. 'I have returned,' he said softly, and raised his hands in invocation. 'Out of the half-night; *strengthened* by the darkness as only a true believer could be. I saw the weakness in my possessor, his fright of his serpent beast. He is in me now, weeping and pleading as he denies form to his true nature. As it should be. God's Brother showed me the way, showed me the night holds no dread for those who love their real selves as He commands us to do. But so few obey. Do you obey?'

They tried then, Iqabl Geertz, Don Padwick, and Chen Tambiah, combining their energistic strength in a desperate attempt to blast the deranged usurper out of his body and into the beyond. Quinn laughed uproariously, steadfast at the calm centre of a fantastic lightning storm which filled the room. Dazzling whips of raw electricity slashed at the walls and floor and ceiling like the razor claws of a maddened gryphon. None of them could touch him, he was held inviolate in a cocoon of luminous violet silk mist.

The lightning stopped roaring, ebbing in spits and crackles

to disappear behind charred furniture and back into the bodies of the would-be thunder gods. Smoke hazed the blackened room, small flames licking greedily at the cushions and tattered curtains.

Quinn wished for justice.

Their bodies fell, cells performing the refined perversions he dreamed of, turning against themselves. He watched impassively as the terrorized, humiliated souls fled from the glistening deformities he had created, back to the beyond crying in dire warning. Then the second souls, the ones held captive, abandoned the macerated flesh.

Grant Kavanagh's body groaned at Quinn's feet, the possessing soul looking up at him in numb trepidation. The worst of the lacerations and fractures had healed, leaving a crisscross scar pattern of delicate pink skin.

'What is your name?' Quinn asked.

'Luca Comar.'

'Did you see what I performed on them, Luca?'

'Yes. Oh God, yes.' He bowed his head, bile rising in his throat.

'They were weak, you see. Unworthy fuck-ups. They had no real faith in themselves. Not like me.' Quinn took a deep breath, calming his euphoric thoughts. His marine fatigues billowed out into a flowing priest's robe, fabric turning midnight black. 'Do you have faith in yourself, Luca?'

'Yes. I do. I have faith. Really I do.'

'Would you like me to tell you of the serpent beast? Would you like me to show you your own heart and set you free?'

'Yes. Please. Please show me.'

'Good. I think that is my role now the portents walk abroad. Now the dead are risen to fight the last battle against the living and the time of the Light Bringer draws near. I have been blessed, Luca, truly blessed with His strength. My belief in Him brought me back, me alone out of all the millions who are possessed. I am the one God's Brother has chosen as His messiah.'

*

When the tributary river finally spilled into the Juliffe it was a hundred and thirty metres wide. Villages had claimed both banks, buildings gleaming inside their safe enclave bubbles of white light. By now Chas Paske was used to the striking fantasy images of halcyon hamlets dozing their life away. He had passed eight or nine of them during his slow progress down the river. All of them the same. All of them unreal.

Warned by the twin coronae ahead he had sculled his little boat back into the middle of the river, fighting the thick gunge of melding snowlilies every centimetre of the way. Now he was in a narrow channel of vermilion light which fell between the two pools of native radiance, crouched down as best he could manage.

His body was in a poor way. The nanonic medical packages had been exhausted by the demand of decontaminating his blood some time ago; now it was all they could do to stop the blood vessels they had knitted with from haemorrhaging again. His neural nanonics still maintained their analgesic blocks, delivering him from pain. But that didn't seem to be enough any more. A cold lethargy was creeping into him through his damaged leg, syphoning his remaining strength away. Any movement was a complicated business now, and muscles responded with geriatric infirmity. Several times in the last few hours he had been stricken by spasms which vibrated his arms and torso. His neural nanonics seemed incapable of preventing or halting them. So he lay on the bottom of the boat gazing up at the throbbing red cloud waiting for the ignominious spastic twitches to run their course.

At these times he thought he could see himself, a tiny shrivelled black figure, spreadeagled on the bottom of a rowing dinghy (like the one he thought he had been stealing), being borne along a sticky white river that stretched out to a terrible length. There was nothing around the river, no banks or trees, it just wound through a red sky all by itself, a silk ribbon waving in the breeze, while far, far ahead a speck of starlight twinkled with elusive, enticing coyness. Skittering voices on the brink of audibility circled round him. He was sure they talked about him even though he could never quite make out whole words. The tone was there all right, dismissive and scornful.

Not quite a dream.

He remembered, as he sailed on gently, his past missions, past colleagues, old battles, victories and routs. Half the time never knowing who he was really fighting for or what he was fighting against. For the right side or the wrong side? And how was he supposed to know which was which anyway? Him, a mercenary, a whore of violence and destruction and death. He fought for the ones with the most money, for companies and plutocrats, and sometimes maybe even governments. There was no right and wrong in his life. In that respect he had it easy, none of the big decisions.

So the river carried him on, that white band flowing through the red sky, ever onwards. The voyage was his life. He could see where he had come from, and he could see where he was going. Destination and departure were no different. And there was no way to get off. Except to jump, to drown in the vast guileful sky.

That will come anyway, he thought, no need to hurry.

The old resolve was still there, among the superficial self-pity and growing concern over his physical state, still holding together. He was glad of that. Right to the bitter end, that's where he was heading. The star glinted strongly, virtually a heliograph. It seemed nearer.

No, not quite a dream.

Chas jerked up with a start, rocking the boat hazardously. The twin villages guarding the tributary mouth were behind him now. He was out on the Juliffe itself. There was no sign of the Hultain Marsh which made up the northern side. The river could have been an ocean for all he could tell. An ocean paved with snowlilies as far as his enhanced eyes could see. This was their meridian, the end of their continental crusade. They were packed four or five deep, crumpled up against each other; decaying now, but wadded so tight they formed a serried quilt. It was a perfect reflector for the carmine light falling from the cloud, turning his world to a dimensionless red nebula.

The flimsy boat creaked and shivered as the current forced it deeper into the floating pulp. Chas gripped the gunwale in reflex. He had a nasty moment when something popped and splintered up at the prow, but the hull was so shallow it was squeezed up rather than in. He was sure it was riding on a patina of rotting leaves rather than actual water.

For all their stupendous mass, the snowlilies had no effect on the river's unflagging current. The boat began to pick up speed, moving further out from the southern bank with its near-continual chain of villages and towns.

Now he was sure he wasn't going to capsize, Chas relaxed his grip, and eased himself down again, breathing hard at the simple exertion of lifting himself. Up ahead the massive ceiling of red cloud became a bright tangerine cyclone with a concave heart, its apex hidden by distance. He could see the gravid billows of stratus being torn out of their constricted alignment, sucked over the lip to spiral upwards in a leisurely procession. It must have been twenty kilometres across at the base: an inverted whirlpool which drained away into the other side of the sky.

He realized its sharp living tangerine hue came from a fierce light shining down out of its secret pinnacle. Below it, the city of Durringham gleamed in empyrean glory.

*

Gaura floated through the floor hatch into the *Lady Macbeth*'s bridge. He took care not to move his neck suddenly, or his arms come to that; his whole body was one giant ache. He had been lucky not to break anything in that last agonizing burst of deceleration. Even watching the starships attacking the station he hadn't felt as utterly helpless as he had then, lying flat on the groaning decking of the lounge feeling his ribs bowing in, while blackness tightened its grip on his vision. Three times he had heard bone splintering, accompanied by a mental howl – it was impossible to make any sound. Together the Edenists had toughed it out, their minds embraced, sharing and mitigating the pain.

When it was over he hadn't been alone in wiping tears from his eyes. Aethra had followed their entire heart-stopping plummet into the ring, showing it to them. He had thought the end had surely come, for the second time in an hour. But the Adamist starship's exhaust had obliterated the ring particles as it crashed below the surface, eliminating any danger of collision; and the captain had matched velocities perfectly (for the second time in an hour), slotting them neatly into a circular orbit buried right in the middle of the ring. The swarm of pursuing combat wasps and their submunitions had impacted seconds behind them, kinetic explosions tossing out a ragged sheet of fire. None had penetrated more than a hundred metres below the surface.

It had been an astounding piece of flying. Gaura was very curious to meet the person who had such sublime control over a starship. It rivalled the union between a voidhawk and its captain.

There were three people standing on a stikpad around one of the consoles, two men and a woman, talking in low tones. It didn't help Gaura's composure to see that it was the youngest, a man with a flat-featured face, who had the captain's star on his ship-suit shoulder. He had been expecting someone . . . different.

Don't prejudge, Tiya admonished sternly. Most of the Edenists were using his senses to observe the scene. **Voidhawk captains are only eighteen when they start flying.**

I wasn't going to say a word, Gaura objected mildly. He swam past the ring of acceleration couches to touch his toes to a stikpad on the decking. 'Captain Calvert?'

The young man shrugged. 'It's Joshua, actually.'

Gaura felt his bottled-up emotions come close to brimming over. 'Thank you, Joshua. From all of us.'

Joshua nodded shortly, the faintest blush colouring his cheeks. The woman beside him caught his discomfort and smiled secretively.

There, Tiya said in satisfaction. **A perfectly ordinary young man, if exceptionally talented. I like him.**

Joshua introduced Sarha and Dahybi then apologized for the acceleration. 'But I had to stop us dead inside the ring,' he said. 'If we had gone through, south of the ecliptic, the other starships would have seen us, and come after us. Their drives could burn through the particles just as easily as *Lady Mac* did, then we would have been sitting ducks for their combat wasps.'

'I wasn't complaining. In fact, we're really all rather surprised that we're still alive.'

'How are your people holding out?'

'Liatri, our doctor, says none of us have acquired any fatal internal injuries. Melvyn Ducharme is helping her review my people in your surgery cabin. Metabolic scanning has revealed several broken bones and a lot of pulled muscles. She was most concerned about internal membrane damage, it could prove a problem unless treated swiftly. But Melvyn Ducharme is rigging up a processor block that can interface her with your medical nanonic packages.'

Joshua blinked, nonplussed.

'Our own medical packages all use bitek processors,' Gaura explained.

'Ah, right.'

'Liatri says we'll pull through. Mind you, it's going to take a long fortnight for the bruising to fade.'

'You're not the only one,' Sarha grimaced. 'And you should take a look at where my bruises are.'

Joshua leered. 'Promises, promises.'

'That was an awesome piece of flying you pulled off back there, Joshua,' Gaura said. 'Eluding two starships . . .'

'It's in the blood,' he said, not quite nonchalantly. 'Glad to be of help, really. We certainly haven't been much use to anybody else since we arrived in this star system.'

Go on, Tiya urged. **Ask.**

But suppose it's an illegal flight? He was carrying combat wasps, don't forget. We'd have to give evidence.

Then the law is an ass, and we'll all develop amnesia. Ask.

Gaura smiled awkwardly. 'Joshua, exactly who are you? I mean, why come to Lalonde?'

'Er . . . Good question. Technically, *Lady Mac* is part of the Lalonde government's starship fleet, helping to restore civil order. The Confederation Navy squadron has other ideas, and according to them we're under arrest.'

'Navy squadron?'

Joshua sighed theatrically, and started to explain.

The Edenists crowding the cabin in life-support capsule D, which doubled as the surgery, listened with a mixture of gloomy dismay and confusion.

'This sequestration ability sounds appalling,' Gaura said, summarizing the Edenists' unified feelings.

'You should see the red cloud,' Joshua told him. 'That really gives me the creeps. It's an instinct thing with me, I know it's *wrong*.'

Gaura gestured to the console they had been consulting; its holoscreen was alive with blue and yellow data displays. 'What is our current situation?'

'I'm playing a waiting game,' Joshua said, and datavised an order into the console processor. The holoscreen switched to an image from an external sensor cluster, showing a very dark expanse of crinkled rock. Scale was impossible to gauge. 'See that? That's the largest ring particle I could find at such short notice, near-solid stone about two hundred and fifty metres in diameter. It's twenty-five kilometres inward from the northern surface. We're keeping station directly underneath it, and I do mean directly; *Lady Mac*'s forward hull is about three metres away. Right now Warlow and Ashly are outside drilling load pins into the rock so we can tether *Lady Mac* in place with silicon fibre. That way I won't have to use the thrusters to hold our position. *Maranta* and *Gramine* would be able to spot any ion plumes easily when the rings calm down. Our on-board electronic systems are designed for minimal emission anyway, but with that rock as a shield we'll make absolutely sure we're undetectable to their sensors. It can also absorb our thermal output as well; I've deployed the thermo-dump panels so that they're radiating all our excess heat directly at the rock, it will take months to seep through. All the drive tubes and the five main fusion generators have been powered down, so our magnetic flux is negligible. We're operating on one auxiliary fusion generator which is well screened by the hull. All in all, it's a very reasonable position. As long as *Maranta* and *Gramine* stay north of the ring we'll be invisible to them.'

'And if one of them moves to a southern inclination?'

'There is fifty-five kilometres' worth of particles between us and the southern surface. It's a risk I'm prepared to take, especially with the ring so electrically and thermally active right now.'

'I see. How long do you think we'll be here?'

Joshua pulled a face. 'Hard to say. Right now we're only a hundred and seventy thousand kilometres above Murora, *Lady Mac* needs to be at least two hundred thousand out before she can jump. So if we want to leave, we either wait until *Maranta* and *Gramine* decide to call it a day and quit, or hang on until their search pattern carries them far enough away to allow us to make a dash for a jump coordinate. Whichever one it is, I think we'll be here for some time. Weeks at least.'

'I understand. Do you have enough fuel and supplies to last that long?'

'Yes, fuel's down to forty-seven per cent, those high-gee manoeuvres use up cryogenics at a hell of a rate, but what's left can supply our present consumption rate for years. So that's no problem. But we'll have to monitor our environmental systems closely given there's thirty-six of you. The limiting factor is going to be food; that'll have to be rationed pretty carefully. All of which means I really don't want you to take your children out of zero-tau just yet.'

'Of course. They will be much better off in the pods anyway. But what about your mercenary scout team?'

Joshua exchanged a significant glance with Sarha. 'Not a damn thing we can do about that. They're tough and they're mean. If anyone can survive down there, they can.'

'I see. Well if the opportunity arises to go back, then please do not hesitate on our account.'

'We'll see. It would be difficult jumping to Lalonde with *Maranta* and *Gramine* following us. Ideally I'd like to hang on until they leave Murora. Our major problem is going to be tracking them. When you came in we were discussing mounting a sensor cluster on the other side of the rock. Before we started hiding we caught a glimpse of their ion thrusters, so we know they're still out there. But we have the same problem as them, this ring is pure hell to see through. Without reliable data we're at a nasty disadvantage.'

'Ah,' Gaura smiled happily. 'I think I may be able to help there.' **Aethra? Can you see the two starships which attacked us?**

Yes, the habitat replied. **They are orbiting slightly above the ring's northern surface.**

An image formed in his mind, the dusky plain of the ring slicing across Murora, blanched of most colour. The habitat's external sensitive cells could just sense a broad zone agitated by heat and electricity. Two dull specks were poised slightly above it, ion thrusters firing intermittent tattoos to maintain their attitude.

Excellent. 'Aethra can see them.'

Joshua brightened. 'Jesus, that's great news. They're both still here, then?'

'Yes.'

'How is Aethra?' he asked belatedly.

'The shell was extensively damaged. However, there is no catastrophic internal injury, its main organs remain functional. It is going to require a considerable amount of repair work before it can resume its growth. My colleagues, the ones who were killed in the attack, their memories have been stored by the personality.'

'That's something, then.'

'Yes.'

'Can Aethra work out the exact spacial locations of the other starships for me? If we can keep updated I'll know when we can risk breaking cover and flying for a jump coordinate.'

'I can go one better than that.' Gaura slipped a processor block from his breast pocket. The slim palm-sized plastic rectangle had produced a spectacular gold and blue bruise on his pectoral muscle during the flight. 'Aethra can communicate through the bitek processor, and if you can interface this with your flight computer you'll be able to receive the images directly. And the starships hunting us will never know, affinity is undetectable.'

'Wonderful.' Joshua accepted the block. It was slightly smaller than the Kulu Corporation model he used. 'Sarha, get to work on an interface. I want Aethra tied in to our navigation processor array pronto.'

'Consider it done.' She plucked it from his fingers and datavised her systems memory core for appropriate electronic module specifications and adaptor programs.

Joshua thought the Edenist station chief still looked wrecked.

'You know, we come from Tranquillity,' he said. 'It's *Lady Mac*'s home port.'

Gaura looked at him, a surprised light showing in his worn eyes. 'Yes?'

'Yeah. I've lived there all my life, I was born there, so I know how beautiful habitats are, and I don't just mean their physical structure either. So I suppose I can empathize with what you're feeling more than most Adamists. Don't worry. We'll get out of this and bring help back for Aethra, and Lalonde too. All we need now is time, and we're home free. Fortunately time is one thing we have plenty of.'

*

'So you're not Confederation Navy marines then?' Horst asked, trying to hide his disappointment.

'No, I'm sorry, Father,' Reza said. 'The LDC hired us to scout round the Quallheim Counties and find out what was going on down here. I believe you can say we've certainly done that.'

'I see.' Horst looked round the simplicity of the Tyrathcan tower house's hall, its smooth curves illuminated by the light stick, solid shadows blending seamlessly with dark-grey arches. The red light outside was kept at bay, silhouetting the hole sliced into the doorway. In spite of the warmth he felt chilled.

'How did you know we were here?' Pat asked.

'I didn't, not that you were in this particular tower. We saw the starships arrive yesterday morning, of course. Then in the afternoon there was an explosion on the river.'

'The kroclion,' Ariadne said.

'Could be,' Reza said. 'Go on.'

'Young Russ saw it,' Horst said. 'I thought it best that we keep a watch on the savannah; that morning was the first time the red cloud appeared, and with the starships as well – it seemed sensible. By the time I got my optical intensifier band on there was only the smoke left. But it didn't look like anything the possessed do, so I rode out to see. I thought – I prayed – that it might have been the marines. Then that bedamned kroclion was skulking about in the grass. I just kept going up the river to keep ahead of it. And here we are. Delivered up to you by God's hand.' He lifted his lips in a tired victorious smile. 'Mysterious ways His wonders to perform.'

'Certainly does,' Reza said. 'That kroclion was probably the mate of the one we killed.'

'Yes. But tell me of the starships. Can they take us off this terrible planet? We saw an almighty battle in orbit before the red cloud swelled over the sky.'

'We don't know much about the events in orbit. But that was a fight between some of our starships and a Confederation Navy squadron.'

'Your starships? Why did they fight the navy?'

'Some of them. The possessed got into orbit on the spaceplanes which brought us down, they hijacked the starships and took over the crew.'

'Merciful Lord.' Horst crossed himself. 'Are there any starships left now?'

'No. Not in orbit.'

Horst's shoulders sagged. He sipped listlessly at the carton of hot coffee they had given him. This was the cruellest blow of all, he thought wretchedly, to be shown salvation shining so close and then to have it snatched away as my fingers close around it. The children cannot be made to suffer any more, merciful Lord hear me this once, they cannot.

Russ was sitting in Kelly's lap. He seemed shy of the combat-boosted mercenaries, but was content to let her spray a salve on his saddle sores. She smoothed down the damp hair on his forehead, and grinned as she offered him one of her chocolate bars. 'You must have been through a lot,' she said to Horst.

'We have.' He eyed Shaun Wallace, who had kept to the back of the hall since he had arrived. 'The Devil has cursed this planet to its very core. I have seen such evil, foul, foul deeds.

Such courage too. I'm humbled, the human spirit is capable of quite astonishing acts of munificence when confronted by fundamental tests of virtue. I have come to believe in people again.'

'I'd like to hear about it some time,' she said.

'Kell's a reporter,' Sewell said mockingly. 'Someone else who makes you sign contracts in blood.'

She glared at the big mercenary. 'Being a reporter isn't a crime. Unlike some people's occupation.'

'I shall be happy to tell you,' Horst said. 'But later.'

'Thank you.'

'You'll be safe enough now you're hooked up with us, Father,' Reza said. 'We're planning to head south, away from the cloud. And the good news is that we're expecting a starship to come back for us in a couple of days. There's plenty of room for you and Russ on our hovercraft. Your ordeal's over.'

Horst let out an incredulous snort, then put the coffee carton down ruing his slowness. 'Oh, my Lord, I haven't told you yet, have I? I'm sorry, that ride must have addled my brain. And I've had so little sleep these last days.'

'Told us what?' Reza asked edgily.

'I gathered what children I could after the possession began. We are all living together in one of the savannah homesteads. They must be terrified. I never intended to be away all night.'

There was complete silence for a second, even the red cloud's hollow thunder was hushed.

'How many children?' Reza asked.

'Counting young Russ here, twenty-nine.'

'Fucking hell.'

Horst frowned and glanced pointedly at Russ who was staring at the mercenary leader with apprehensive eyes over his half-eaten chocolate. Kelly held him a fraction tighter.

'Now what?' Sal Yong asked bluntly.

Horst looked at him in some puzzlement. 'We must go back to them in your hovercraft,' he said simply. 'I fear my poor old horse can travel no further. Why? Have you some other mission?'

The combat-adept mercenary kept still. 'No.'

'Where exactly is this homestead?' Reza asked.

'Five or six kilometres south of the jungle,' Horst replied. 'And forty minutes' walk east from the river.'

Reza datavised his guidance block for a map, and ran a search through LDC habitation records, trying to correlate. 'In other words, under the red cloud.'

'Yes, that abomination spread at a fearsome rate yesterday.'

'Reza,' Jalal said. 'The hovercraft can't possibly carry that many people. Not if we're going to keep ahead of the cloud.'

Horst looked at the hulking combat adept in growing amazement. 'What is this you are saying? Can't? Can't? They are children! The eldest is eleven years old! She is alone under that Devil's spew in the sky. Alone and frightened, holding the others to her as the sky turns to brimstone and the howling demon horde closes in. Their parents have been raped by unclean spirits. They have nothing left but a single thread of hope.' He stood abruptly, clamping down on a groan as his ride-stiffened muscles rebelled against the sharp movement, face reddening in fury. 'And you, with your guns and your mechanoid strength, you sit here thinking only of saving your own skin. You should run to embrace the possessed, they would welcome you as their own. Come along, Russ, we're going home.'

The boy started sobbing. He struggled in Kelly's grip.

She climbed to her feet, keeping her arms protectively around his thin frame. Quickly, before she lost all courage, she said: 'Russ can have my place on the hovercraft. I'll come with you, Father.' Retinas switched to high resolution, she looked at Reza. Recording.

'I knew you'd be trouble,' he datavised.

'Tough,' she said out loud.

'For a reporter you have very little understanding of people if you think I'd desert his children after all we've seen.'

Kelly pouted her lips sourly and switched her visual focus to Jalal. That exchange would have to be edited out.

'Nobody is going to leave the children behind, Father,' Reza said. 'Believe me, we have seen what happens to children driven away by the possessed. But we are not going to help them by rushing in blindly.' And he stood, rising a good thirty centimetres higher than the priest. 'Understand me, Father?'

A muscle twitched on Horst's jaw. 'Yes.'

'Good. Now they obviously can't stay at the savannah homestead. We have to take them south with us. The question is how. Are there any more horses at the homestead?'

'No. We have a few cows, that's all.'

'Pity. Ariadne, can the hovercraft carry fifteen children apiece?'

'Possibly, if we ran alongside. But it would put a hell of a strain on the skirt impellers. And it would definitely drain the electron matrices inside of six or seven hours.'

'Running like that would drain us too,' Pat said.

'I can't even recharge the matrices, not under this cloud,' Ariadne said. 'The solar-cell panels don't receive anything like enough photonic input.'

'We might be able to build some kind of cart,' Theo suggested. 'Hitch it up to the cows. It would be better than walking.'

'It would take time,' Sal Yong said. 'And there's no guarantee it would work.'

'Tow them,' Sewell said. 'Slap together a couple of rafts, and tow them back up the river. All you need is planks, we can get them from the homestead itself if need be.'

Ariadne nodded her rounded head. 'Might just work. The hovercraft could handle that. We could certainly get back here by the middle of the afternoon.'

'Then what?' Jalal said. 'Look, I'm not being a downer. But just getting them back here isn't the solution. We have to keep going. Wallace says the cloud is going to cover the whole planet, we have to find a way to outrun it, or this will all be for nothing.'

Reza turned to look at the possessed man who had kept silent and unobtrusive up until now. 'Mr Wallace, will your kind know if we return to the homestead?'

'Aye, Mr Malin,' he said sorrowfully. 'That they will. The cloud and the land are becoming one with us. We can feel you moving inside us. When you pass back under the cloud the sensation will be like treading on a nail.'

'How will they react?'

'They'll come after you, Mr Malin. But then they'll do that anyway if you stay on this world.'

'I think he's speaking the truth,' Horst said. 'One of them came to the homestead two days ago. She wanted me and the children. Our bodies, anyway.'

'What happened?' Kelly asked.

Horst forced a vapid smile. 'I exorcised her.'

'*What?*' Kelly blurted in greedy delight. 'Really?'

The priest held up his bandaged hand. The dark strips of cloth were stained with blood. 'It wasn't easy.'

'Shit Almighty. Shaun, can you be exorcised?'

Shaun Wallace had locked his gaze to that of the priest. 'If it's all the same to you, Miss Kelly, I'd be obliged if you didn't try.'

'He can,' she subvocalized into her neural nanonics memory cell, 'he really can! You can see it in his eyes. He fears the priest, this ageing worn-out man in shabby clothes. I can barely believe it. A ceremony left over from medieval times that can thwart these almost-invincible foes. Where all our fantastic technology and knowledge fails, a prayer, a simple anachronistic prayer could become our salvation. I must tell you of this, I must find a way to get a message out to the Confederation.' Damn, that sounded too much like Graeme Nicholson's recording.

For a moment she wondered what had happened to the old hack.

'Interesting,' Reza said. 'But it doesn't help our present dilemma. We have to find a way of keeping ahead of the cloud until Joshua comes back for us.'

'Christ, we don't even know when he's coming back,' Sal Yong said. 'And taking a bunch of children through these mountains isn't going to be easy, Reza, there are no roads, no detailed map image. We've got no camping equipment, no boots for them, no food supplies. It's going to be wet, slippery. I mean, God! I don't mind giving it a go if there's even a remote chance of pulling it off, but this . . .'

'Mr Wallace, would your kind consider letting the children go?' Reza asked.

'Some would, I would, but the rest . . . No, I don't think so. There are so few living human bodies left here, and so many souls trapped in the beyond. We hear them constantly, you know, they plead with us to bring them back. Giving in is so easy. I'm sorry.'

'Shit.' Reza flexed his fingers. 'OK, we'll take it in stages. First we bring the children back here, get them and us out from under that bloody cloud today. That's what is important right now. Once we've done that we can start concentrating on how to get them through the mountains. Maybe the Tyrathca will help.'

'No chance,' Ariadne said flatly.

'Yeah. But all of you keep thinking. Mr Wallace, can you tell me what sort of opposition we'll be facing? How many possessed?'

'Well now, there's a good hundred and fifty living in Aberdale. But if you race in on those fancy hover machines of yours you ought to be away again before they reach you.'

'Great.'

Shaun Wallace held up his hand. 'But there's a family of ten living in one of the other homesteads not far from the children. They can certainly cause you problems.'

'And you believe him?' Sewell asked Reza.

Shaun Wallace put on a mournfully injured expression. 'Now then, Mr Sewell, that's no way to be talking about someone who's only doing his best to help you. I didn't stick out my thumb and hitch here, you know.'

'Actually, he's right about the homestead family,' Horst said. 'I saw them a couple of days ago.'

'Thank you, Father. There now, you have the word of a man of the cloth. What more do you want?'

'Ten of them on open ground,' Reza said. 'That's nothing like as bad as Pamiers. I think we can take care of them. Are you going to add your fire-power to ours, Mr Wallace?'

'Ah now, my fire-power is a poor weak thing compared to yours, Mr Malin. But even if it were capable of shifting mountains, I would not help you in that way.'

'That makes you a liability, Mr Wallace.'

'I don't think much of a man who asks another to kill his cousins in suffering, Mr Malin. Not much at all.'

Horst took a pace forwards. 'Perhaps you could mediate for us, Mr Wallace? Nobody wants to see any more death on this world, especially as those bodies still contain their rightful souls. Could you not explain to the homestead family that attacking the mercenaries would be foolhardy in the extreme?'

Shaun Wallace stroked his chin. 'Aye, now, I could indeed do that, Father.'

Horst glanced expectantly at Reza.

'Suits me,' the mercenary leader said.

Shaun Wallace grinned his wide-boy grin. 'The priests back in Ireland were all wily old souls. I see nothing's changed in that department.'

Nobody had noticed the balmy smile growing on Kelly's face during the exchange. She let go of Russ, and slapped her hands together with surefire exultation. 'Yes! I can get Joshua back here. I think. I'm sure I can.'

They all looked at her.

'Maybe even by this afternoon. We won't have to worry about going through the mountains. All we'll have to do is get clear of the red cloud so that Ashly can land.'

'Spare us how wonderful you are, Kelly,' Reza said. 'How?'

She dived into her bag and pulled out her communication block, brandishing it as though it were a silver trophy. 'With this. The LDC's original geosynchronous communication platform had a deep-space antenna to keep in touch with the Edenist station orbiting Murora. If the platform didn't get hit in the orbital battle, we can just call him up. Send a repeating message telling him how badly we need him. Murora is about nine hundred million kilometres away, that's less than a light-hour. If he leaves as soon as he receives it, he could be here inside three or four hours. *Lady Mac* might not be able to jump outsystem, but if she can jump to Murora she can jump back again. At least we'd be safely off Lalonde.'

'Can you get the platform computer to send a message?' Reza asked. 'Terrance Smith never gave us any access codes for it.'

'Listen, I'm a bloody reporter, there's nothing I don't know about violating communication systems. And this block has quite a few less than legal chips added.'

She waited for an answer, her feet had developed a life of their own, wanting to dance.

'Well, get on with it then, Kelly,' Reza said.

She ran for the hole in the door, startling Fenton and Ryall lying on the grass outside. The sky over the savannah was split into two uneven portions of redness as the cloud band clashed with the dawn sun. She datavised an instruction into the block and it started scanning across the dissonant shades above for the platform's beacon.

*

Joshua dozed fitfully in his cabin's sleep cocoon. The envelope was a baggy lightweight spongy fabric, big enough to hold him without being restrictive. Sarha had offered to sleep with him, but he'd tactfully declined. He was still feeling the effects of that eleven-gee thrust. Even his body hadn't been geneered with that much acceleration in mind. There were long bruise crinkles on his back where the creases on his ship-suit had pressed into his skin, and when he looked into the mirror his eyes were bloodshot. He and Sarha wouldn't have had sex anyway, he really was tired. Tired and stressed out.

Everyone had been so full of praise for the way he had flown *Lady Mac.* If only they knew the emotional cold turkey that hit him once the danger was over and he stopped operating on nerve energy and arrogance. The fear from realizing what one – just *one* – mistake would have spelt.

I should have listened to Ione. What I had before was enough.

He held her image in his mind as he fell asleep, she made it a lot easier to relax, floating away on the rhythm of night. When he woke, drowsy, warm, and randy, he accessed a memory of their time back in Tranquillity. Out in the parkland, lying on the thick grass beside a stream. The two of them clinging together after sex; Ione on top, sweaty and dreamily content, light glinting an opulent gold off her hair, skin warm and soft against him, kissing him oh so slowly, lips descending along his sternum. Neither spoke, the moment was too perfect for that.

Then her head lifted and it was Louise Kavanagh, all trusting and adoring in that way only the very innocent can achieve. She smiled hesitantly as she rose up, then laughed in rapturous celebration as she was impaled once again, luscious dark hair tossed about as she rode him. Thanking him. Praising him. Promising herself for ever his.

And loving a girl hadn't been that sweet since he was her age.

Jesus! He cancelled the memory sequence. Even his neural nanonics were playing him dirty.

I *do not* need reminding. Not right now.

The flight computer datavised that Aethra was requesting a direct channel. Joshua acknowledged the distraction with guilty relief. Space warfare was easy.

Sarha had done a good job interfacing the bitek processor to *Lady Mac*'s electronics. He had talked to the habitat yesterday, which was engrossing; it came across as a mixture of child and all-knowing sage. But it had been very interested in hearing about Tranquillity. The images he received from its shell's sensitive cells were different to the *Lady Mac*'s sensor clusters. They seemed more real, somehow, bestowing a texture of depth and emptiness which space had always lacked before.

Joshua unsealed the side of the sleep cocoon and swung his legs out. He opened a locker for a fresh ship-suit. There were only three left. Sighing, he started to pull one on. 'Hello, Aethra,' he datavised.

'Good morning, Joshua. I hope you slept well.'

'Yeah, I got a few hours.'

'I am picking up a message for you.'

He was instantly alert, without any stimulus from his neural nanonics. 'Jesus. Where from?'

'It is a microwave transmission originating from the civil communication platform orbiting Lalonde.'

He was shown the starfield outside. The sun was a white glare point, nine hundred and eighty-nine million kilometres distant; to one side Lalonde shone steadily, if weakly, a sixth-magnitude star. It had now become a binary, twinned with a violet glint.

'You can see microwaves?' he asked.

'I sense, eyes see. It is part of the energy spectrum which falls upon my shell.'

'What is the message?'

'It is a voice-only transmission to you personally from a Kelly Tirrel.'

'Jesus. Let me hear it.'

' "This is Kelly Tirrel calling Captain Joshua Calvert. Joshua, I hope you're receiving this OK; and if not, could someone at Aethra's supervisory station please relay this to him immediately. It's really important. Joshua, I'm not sure if the possessed can overhear this, so I won't say anything too exact, OK? We got your message about returning. And the time-scale you mentioned is no use to us. Joshua, virtually everyone down here has been possessed. It's like the worst of the Christian Bible gospels are coming true. Dead people are coming back and taking over the living. I know that sounds crazy to you; but believe me it isn't sequestration, and it isn't a xenoc invasion. I've talked to someone who was alive at the start of the twentieth century. He's real, Joshua. So is their electronic warfare ability, only it's more like magic. They can do terrible things, Joshua, to people and animals. Truly terrible. Shit, I don't suppose you believe any of this, do you? Just think of them as an enemy, Joshua. That'll help make them real for you. And you saw the red cloud-bands over the Juliffe basin, you know how powerful that enemy is.

' "Well, the red cloud is swelling, Joshua, it's spreading over the planet. We were heading away from it. Just like you said we should, remember? But we've found someone who has been in hiding since the possession started, a priest. He's been looking after a bunch of young children. There's twenty-nine of them. And now they're trapped under that cloud. They're near the village that was our original target, so that gives you a rough idea where we are. We're going back for them, Joshua, we'll be on our way by the time this message reaches you. They're only children, for Christ's sake, we can't leave them. The trouble is that once we've got them we won't be able to run far, not with our transport. But we're pretty sure we can get the children out from under the cloud by this afternoon.

Joshua . . . you have to pick us up. Today, Joshua. We won't be able to hold out for long after sunset. I know your lady friend wasn't feeling too well when you left, but bandage her up as best you can, as soon as you can. Please. We'll be waiting for you. Our prayers are with you. Thank you, Joshua." '

'It is repeating,' Aethra said.

'Oh, Jesus.' Possession. The dead returned. Child refugees on the run. 'Jesus fucking wept. She can't do this to me! She's mad. Possession? She's fucking flipped.' He stared aghast at the ancient Apollo computer, arms half in his sleeves. 'No chance.' His arms were rammed into the ship-suit sleeves. Sealing up the front. 'She needs locking up for her own good. Her neural nanonics are looped on a glitched stimulant program.'

'You said you believed the red cloud effect was fundamentally wrong,' Aethra said.

'I said it was a little odd.'

'So is the notion of possession.'

'When you're dead, you're dead.'

'Twelve who died when the station was destroyed are stored within me. You make continual references to your deity, does this not imply a degree of belief in the nature of spirituality?'

'Je— Shit! Look, it's just a figure of speech.'

'And yet humans have believed in gods and an afterlife since the day you gained sentience.'

'Don't you fucking start! Your lot are supposed to be atheists, anyway.'

'I apologize. I can sense you are upset. What are you going to do about rescuing the children?'

Joshua pressed his fingers to his temple in the vain hope it would halt the dizzy sensation. 'Buggered if I know. How do we know there really are any children?'

'You mean it is just a bluff to trick you into returning to Lalonde?'

'Could be, yeah.'

'That would imply that Kelly Tirrel has been possessed.'

Very calmly, he datavised: 'Sequestrated. It implies she has been sequestrated.'

'Whatever has befallen her, you still have a decision to make.'

'And don't I know it.'

Melvyn was alone on the bridge when Joshua came gliding through the hatch from his cabin.

'I just heard the message,' the fusion expert said. 'She can't mean it.'

'Maybe.' Joshua touched his feet to a stikpad beside his acceleration couch. 'Call the crew in, and Gaura as well. I suppose the Edenists are entitled. It's their arses on the line as well.'

He tried to think in the short time it took for them to drift into the bridge, make some kind of sense out of Kelly's message. The trouble was she had sounded so convincing, *she* believed what she said. If it was her. Jesus. And it was a very strange sequestration. He couldn't forget the chaos in orbit.

He accessed the navigation display to see just how practical any sort of return flight was. It didn't look good. *Maranta* and *Gramine* had confined their search to the section of ring which was electrically charged, which meant one of them was always within three thousand kilometres of *Lady Mac*. The jump coordinate for Lalonde was a third of the way round the gas giant, over two hundred and seventy thousand kilometres from their present position. Out of the question. He started to hunt round for options.

'I think it's a load of balls,' Warlow said when they were all assembled. 'Possession! Kelly's cracked.'

'You said it yourself,' Ashly said. 'It's a bad form of sequestration.'

'Do you believe in the dead coming back?'

The pilot grinned at the huge ochre cosmonik clinging to a corner of an acceleration couch. 'It would make life interesting. Admit it.'

Warlow's diaphragm issued a sonic boom snort.

'It doesn't matter what name we choose to call the process,' Dahybi said. 'The sequestration ability exists. We know that. What we have to decide is whether or not Kelly has been taken over by it.' He glanced at Joshua and offered a lame shrug.

'If she hasn't then we're all in a great deal of trouble,' Sarha said.

'If she *hasn't*?' Melvyn asked.

'Yes. That will mean there are twenty-nine children we have to get off that planet by this afternoon.'

'Oh, hell,' he mumbled.

'And if she has been sequestrated then she knew we were coming back anyway. So why try and get us to come back earlier? And why include all that crap about possession, when all it would do was make us more cautious?'

'Double bluff?' Melvyn said.

'Come on!'

'Sarha's right,' Ashly said. 'We always planned to go back; as far as Kelly knew, in a couple of days. There's no logical reason to hurry us. And we know they try and hijack the spaceplanes which land. It's not as if we wouldn't have taken precautions. All this has done is make us even more cautious. My vote says she is in trouble, and they have found these stray children.'

'And me,' Dahybi said. 'But it's not our decision. Captain?'

It was the kind of oblique compliment about his status Joshua could really have done without. 'Kelly would never call unless she really was desperate,' he said slowly. 'If she has managed to avoid sequestration, or whatever, she would never have mentioned possession unless it was true. You all know what she's like: facts no matter what it costs. And if she had been possessed, she wouldn't tell us.' Oh, Jesus, be honest, I *know* she's in deep shit. 'They need to be picked up. Like she said: today.'

'Joshua, we can't,' Melvyn said. He looked desperately torn. 'I don't want to abandon a whole bunch of kids down there any more than you. Even if we don't know exactly what's going on below those bloody cloudbands, we've seen and heard enough to know it ain't good. But we're never going to get past the *Maranta* and the *Gramine.* And I'll give you good odds they've picked up Kelly's message as well. They'll be extra vigilant now. Face it, we've got to wait. They'll spot us the second we turn our drive on.'

'Maybe,' Joshua said. 'Maybe not. But first things first. Sarha, can our environmental systems cope with thirty kids and the mercenaries as well as the Edenists?'

'I dunno how big the kids are,' Sarha said, thinking out loud. 'Kelly did say young. There's probably room for four more in the zero-tau pods if we really cram them in. We can billet some in the spaceplane and the MSV, use their atmospheric filters. Carbon dioxide build-up is our main problem, the filters could never scrub the amount seventy people produce. We'd have to vent it and replace it from the cryogenic oxygen reserve.' Neural nanonics ran a best and worst case simulation. She didn't like the margins on the worst case, not one bit. 'I'll give you a provisional yes. But thirty is the absolute limit, Joshua. If the mercenaries run into any other worthy cause refugees, they're just going to have to stay down there.'

'OK. That leaves us with picking them up. Ashly?'

The pilot gave one of his engaging grins. 'I told you, Joshua, I promised them I'd go down again.'

'Fine. That just leaves you, Gaura. You've been very quiet.'

'It's your ship, Captain.'

'Yes, but your children are on board, and your friends and family. They'll be exposed to a considerable risk if *Lady Mac* attempts to go back to Lalonde. That entitles you to a say.'

'Thank you, Joshua. We say this: if it was us stranded on Lalonde right now, we would want you to come and pick us up.'

'Very well. That's settled then. We'll try and rescue the mercenaries and the children.'

'One small point, Joshua,' Melvyn said loudly. 'We're stuck

in the rings, with one combat wasp left, forty thousand kilometres from the edge of Murora's gravity field. If we stick our heads up, they'll be shot to buggery.'

'I was in a similar situation to this a year ago.'

'Joshua!' Sarha chided.

He ignored her. 'It was the Ruin Ring, when Neeves and Sipika were coming after me. Look at where the *Maranta* and the *Gramine* are right now.'

They all accessed the navigational display, neon-sharp graphics unfurling in their minds. The two searching starships extruded curved yellow orbital trajectory plots paralleling the thick gauzy green slab of the ring which filled the bottom half of the projection. *Lady Macbeth* lurked below the ring surface like some outlandish slumbering marine creature.

'*Maranta* and *Gramine* are now six thousand kilometres apart,' Joshua said. 'They've got a reasonable idea of the general area where we have to be hidden, and they've changed altitude twice in the last fifteen hours to cover different sections of the ring. If they stick to that pattern they'll change again in another four hours.' He ordered the display to extrapolate their positions. '*Gramine* will be about three hundred kilometres from us, she actually passes over us in another ninety minutes; and *Maranta* is going to be right out at the extreme, about seven and a half thousand kilometres away. After that they'll swap orbital tracks and begin a new sweep.

'So if we can break out when *Maranta* is seven and a half thousand klicks away, we'll be far enough ahead of it to escape.'

'And *Gramine*?' Melvyn asked. He didn't like Joshua's quiet tone, as if the young captain was afraid of what he was going to say.

'We know where it's going to be, we can leave one of the megaton nukes from the combat wasp waiting for it. Mine the ring where it will pass overhead, attach the nuke to a large rock particle. Between them, the emp pulse, the plasma wave, and the rock fragments should disable it.'

'How do we get it there?' Melvyn asked.

'You know bloody well how we get it there,' Sarha said. 'Someone's got to carry it using a manoeuvring pack, right Joshua? That's what you did in the Ruin Ring, isn't it?'

'Yeah. They can't detect one person fifteen kilometres deep in the ring, not using cold gas to manoeuvre.'

'Wait a minute,' Dahybi said. He had been running flight trajectory simulations in the navigation display. 'Even if you did knock out the *Gramine*, and that's a bloody long shot, we're still no better off. *Maranta* will just launch her combat wasps straight at us. There's no way we can out-run them, they'll get us before we're halfway to the edge of Murora's gravity field, let alone Lalonde's jump coordinate.'

'If we accelerate at eight gees, we'll have seven minutes fifteen seconds before the *Maranta*'s combat wasps will catch us,' Joshua said. 'Distance-wise that works out at about sixteen thousand kilometres.'

'That still won't get us outside Murora's gravity field. We couldn't even jump blind.'

'No, but there is one place we can jump from. It's only fifteen thousand kilometres away; we would have a twenty-second safety margin.'

'Where?' Melvyn demanded.

Joshua datavised an instruction into the flight computer. The navigational display drew a violet trajectory line from the *Lady Mac* towards the edge of the ring, sliding round in a retrograde curve to end at one of the four tiny ring-shepherd moonlets.

'Murora VII,' Joshua said.

A terrible realization came to Dahybi; his balls retracted as though he'd dived into an icy lake. 'Oh, Christ, *no*, Joshua. You can't be serious, not at that velocity.'

'So give me an alternative.'

'An alternative to what?' Sarha asked petulantly.

Still looking at Joshua, Dahybi said: 'The Lagrange point.

Every two-body system has them. It's where the moonlet's gravity is balanced by Murora's, which means you can activate a starship's nodes inside it without worrying about gravitonic stress desynchronization. Technically, they're points, but in practice they work out as a relatively spherical zone. A *small* zone.'

'For Murora VII, about two and a half kilometres in diameter,' Joshua said. 'Unfortunately, we'll be travelling at about twenty-seven kilometres per second when we reach it. That gives us a tenth of a second to trigger the nodes.'

'Oh, shit,' Ashly grunted.

'It won't be a problem for the flight computer,' Joshua said blandly.

'But where will the jump take us?' Melvyn asked.

'I can give us a rough alignment on Achillea, the third gas giant. It's on the other side of the system now, about seven billion kilometres away. We'll jump a billion kilometres, align *Lady Mac* properly on one of its outer moons, then jump again. No way will *Maranta* be able to follow us through those kind of manoeuvres. When we get to Achillea we slingshot round the moon onto a Lalonde trajectory and jump in. Total elapsed time eighty minutes maximum.'

'Oh, God . . . well, I suppose you know what you're talking about.'

'Him?' Sarha exclaimed. 'You must be joking.'

'It has a certain degree of style,' Dahybi said. He nodded approvingly. 'OK, Joshua, I'll have the nodes primed. But you're going to have to be staggeringly accurate when we hit that Lagrange point.'

'My middle name.'

Sarha studied the bridge decking. 'I know another one,' she muttered under her breath.

'So who's the lucky one that gets to EVA in the rings and blow up the *Gramine*?' Melvyn asked.

'Volunteers can draw lots,' Joshua said. 'Put my name in.'

'Don't be stupid,' Sarha said. 'We all know you're going to have to fly the *Lady Mac*, no one else could hit that moonlet, let alone its Lagrange point. And Ashly has to take the space-plane down, I expect that flight's going to need a professional. So the rest of us will draw for it.'

'Kindly include twenty of us,' Gaura said. 'We are all qualified in EVA work, and we have the added advantage of being able to communicate with Aethra in case the starship should alter course.'

'Nobody is volunteering, nobody is drawing lots,' Warlow said, using excessive volume to obliterate any dissent. 'This is my job. It's what I'm designed for. And I'm the oldest here. So I qualify on all counts.'

'Don't be so bloody morbid,' Joshua said, annoyance covering his real concern. 'You just plant the nuke on a rock particle and come straight back.'

Warlow laughed, making them all wince. 'Of course, so easy.'

*

Now, finally, under the slowly spinning inferno and looking up into a glaring formless void. Journey's end. Chas Paske had to turn down his optical sensors' receptivity, the light was so bright. At first he had thought some kind of miniature sun lurked up there at the centre of the flaming vortex of cloud, but now the boat had carried him faithfully under the baleful cone he could see the apex had burst open like a malignant tumour. The rent was growing larger. The cyclone was growing larger, deeper and wider.

He knew its purpose at last, that knowledge was inescapable where he was, pressed down in the bottom of the flat boat under the sheer pressure of the light. It was a mouth, jaws opening wide. One day – soon – it would devour the whole world.

He gave a wild little giggle at the notion.

That heavy, heavy light was migrating from whatever

(wherever?) lay on the other side. Weighty extrinsic photons sinking slowly downwards like snow to smother the land and river in their own special frost. Whatever they touched, gleamed, as though lit from within. Even his body, shoddy, worthless thing it was now, had acquired a dignified lustre.

Above the gashed cloud was a sheer plane of white light, a mathematical absolute. The ocean into which his white silk dream river emptied. A universal ocean into which Lalonde was destined to fall like a pearl droplet, and lose itself for evermore. He felt himself wanting to rise up towards it, to defy gravity and soar. Into the perpetual light and warmth which would cleanse him and banish sorrow. It would ripple once as he penetrated the meniscus, throwing out a polished wave crown, a single ephemeral spire rising at the centre. After that there would be no trace. To pass through was to transcend.

His remoulded face was incapable of smiling. So he lay there gladly on the boat, mind virtually divorced from his body, looking up at his future, awaiting his moment of ascension. His physical purpose long since abandoned.

Even though the red cloud's thunder had retreated to a muffled rumbling he never heard the starting gun being fired, so the first cannonball shattered his serenity with shocking abruptness.

They had known he was there, the possessed, they had been aware of him all along. From the moment he'd passed under the aegis of the red cloud he had registered in their consciousness, as an orbiting gnat might impinge upon a man's peripheral vision. His hapless journey down the river was of no consequence to them; in his miserable degenerative state he was simply not worth their attention nor a moment's effort. The river was bringing him surely to their bosom, they were content to let him come in his own time.

Now he was here, and they had assembled down by the docks to provide a maliciously frolicsome reception. It was a black-hearted jamboree suitable to celebrate the last possession before Lalonde escaped the universe for good.

The iron ball whistled low over Chas's boat with a backlash *crack* that set the insecure craft rocking, then splattered into the snowlily mush thirty metres away. Purple smoke and ten-metre magnesium flames squirted joyously into the air like a jumbo Roman candle.

Chas shunted round on his elbows, looking in disbelief at the chromatic blaze. The snowlilies started to melt away around his boat, lowering it into sparkling clear blue water. Whoops and catcalls wafted over the river from the shore. He twisted round.

Durringham with all of its white towers and onion-dome spires and lofty castles and lush hanging gardens formed a magnificent backdrop to the armada racing to collect him. There were Polynesian war canoes with flower-garlanded warriors digging their paddles into the clear water; rowing eights with lean young men sweating under the cox's bellowed orders; triremes, their massed oars flashing in immaculate unison; Viking marauders sporting resplendent scarlet and gold sun-god sails; dhows whose lateens strained ahead of the fresh breeze; junks, sampans, ketches, sloops . . . and riding fast and proud out in front was a big three-masted buccaneer, its crew in striped shirts scrambling over the rigging. A quarter of the city's population crowded the circular harbours (now ancient solid stone) cheering on their chosen team in a boisterous rollicking carnival atmosphere.

Chas gagged at the sight of it all; the nightmare dormant in every human brain *the entire world is out to get me.* The whole city was chasing him, wanted him, hated him. He was their new toy, the day's amusement.

His body spasmed in massive quakes, implants faltering. Intolerable waves of pain from his leg crashed past the crumbling analgesic blocks. 'Bastards!' he roared. 'You shit-eating bastards. You don't play with me. I am your enemy. I am not a joke. Fear me. Fear me, God damn you!'

A dainty ring of smoke puffed out of the buccaneer's forward gun. Chas screamed, fury and terror in one incoherent blast of sound.

The cannon-ball hit the water ten metres away, sending up a sheet of steaming white water. Wavelets rushed out, slapping his boat.

'Bastards.' It wasn't even a whisper. Adrenalin and nerves could do nothing more for him, he was devoid of strength. 'I'll show you. Freaks. Zoo people. I am not a joke.' Somewhere far away a soprano chorus was singing black canticles.

Chas datavised the activation code into the kiloton bomb strapped in its harness at his side. Good old faithful bomb. Stuck to him the whole time. That'll wipe the smile off their faces.

Nothing happened, his neural nanonics had shut down. Pain was burning through him, leaving only numbness in its wake. Fingers scrabbled feebly at the bomb's small manual control panel, prising open the cover. His head flopped to one side to follow the movement. He eventually managed to focus an optical sensor. The panel keyboard was dark, inert. It had failed. He had failed.

Almost forgotten natural tear glands squeezed out their very last drops as he slowly knocked a fist on the wooden planking in utter futility.

A couple of the triremes were gaining on the buccaneer. It was developing into a three-boat race, though one of the war canoes refused to give up, warriors pounding the water with their paddles, skin gleaming as though they were sweating oil. Back on the harbours the elated cheering mixed with songs and chants from across five millennia.

The buccaneer crew fired another cannon to terrorize their crushed victim.

'You won't have me!' Chas cried in defiance. He put a hand

on each gunwale and started to rock the boat as the cannon-ball's wavelets broke against the hull. 'Never. Never. I won't be a part of it, not of you.'

Pain and numbness had gorged on his torso. His arms began to fail as the swaying reached a peak. Water slopped in over the narrow gunwale. The flimsy boat turned turtle, dumping him into the Juliffe. He saw bubbles churning past. The rumpled silver foil of the surface receded. Neural nanonics told him his lungs were filling with water. Pain diminished. His implants were working again. *They* couldn't reach him under water, he was beyond them here. He focused every sensor he had on the bomb whose weight was dragging him down.

On shore the audience had stopped cheering when their prey (so unsportingly) capsized himself. A groan went up. He'd pay for that.

Boat crews stopped rowing and slumped over their oars, exhausted and angry. The buccaneer's sails calmly rolled themselves up as the sailors hung like listless spiders in the rigging. They stared morosely at the tiny half-sunken boat bobbing about ahead of them.

Together Durringham's possessed exerted their power. The river around the hull of Chas Paske's boat began to ripple energetically.

'Hey look, it's Moses!' someone yelled from the harbour wall. A laugh ran along the spectators. They clapped their hands and stomped their feet, a stadium crowd demanding their sporting hero appear. 'Moses! Moses! Moses!'

The waters of the Juliffe parted.

Chas felt it happening. His surroundings were getting lighter, pressure was reducing. Below his fingers the bomb's keyboard was a glowing ruby chessboard. He typed in the code, refusing to hurry, watching the numbered squares turn green. There was a loud gurgling sound building all around. Fast-conflicting currents sucked at him, twisting his lifeless legs about. Then the rucked surface came rushing down to seek him out. Too late.

The kiloton nuke detonated at the bottom of a twenty-metre crater in the river. Its initial blast pulse was punched straight up into the core of the transplanarity ferment raging above. A solar fireball arose from the water with splendid inevitability, and the entire river seemed to lift with it. Energy in every spectrum poured outwards, smashing solid matter apart. None of those lining the harbour wall really knew what was happening. Their stolen bodies disintegrated before the nerve impulses could reach the brain. Only after annihilation, when the possessing souls found themselves back in the bestial beyond, did the truth dawn.

Two seconds after the bomb exploded, a forty-metre wall of water moving at near-sonic speed slammed into Durringham. And the dead, ensconced in their beautiful new mansions and fanciful castles, died again in their tens of thousands beneath the usurping totem of the radiant mushroom cloud.

30

With his enhanced retinas switched to full sensitivity it appeared as though Warlow was flying through a dry iridescent mist. Ring particles still crawled with wayward spurts of energy; micrometre dust flowed in slow streams around the larger boulders and ice chunks. Despite the shimmering phosphorescence he was basically flying blind. Occasionally he could catch a glimpse of stars flickering past his feet, short-lived embers skipping from an invisible bonfire.

After leaving the *Lady Macbeth* he had moved twelve kilometres out from Murora, an orbit which saw him falling behind the sheltering starship. The big dark sphere, upper hull glinting in the livid red glow from its own thermo-dump panels, had been lost from sight in three minutes. Isolation had tightened its bewitching fingers almost immediately. Strangely enough, here, where he could barely see ten metres, a realization of the universe's vastness was all too strong.

The ten-megaton bomb was strapped to his chest, a fat ovoid seventy-five centimetres high. Weightless, yet weighing heavily in his heart – titanium and composite device though it was.

Sarha had given him one of the Edenist bitek processor blocks which she had modified with augmentation modules. The idea was to provide him with a link to Aethra in case the *Gramine* should unexpectedly alter track.

Makeshift, like this whole mission.

'Can I speak with you alone?' he datavised.

'Of course,' the habitat answered. 'I would be glad to keep you company. Yours is a fraught task.'

'But it is mine alone.'

'You are the best qualified.'

'Thank you. I wanted to ask you a question on the nature of death.'

'Yes?'

'It involves a small story.'

'Go on. I am always interested to hear of human events. I understand very little of your species so far, even though I have inherited a wealth of data.'

'Ten years ago I was a crew-member in the starship *Harper's Dragon.* It was a line cargo ship, nothing special, although the pay was comfortingly regular. We had a new cadet lieutenant join us on Woolsey, called Felix Barton. He was only twenty, but he had assimilated his didactic courses well. I found him competent, and a reasonable messmate. He was no different to any other young man starting his career. Then he fell in love with an Edenist woman.'

'Ah; this is, perhaps, a Shakespearian tragedy?'

Warlow saw thin ribbons of orange dust winding corkscrew fashion around an ice chunk straight ahead; a bird-kite's tail, he thought. They sparked pink on his carbotanium space armour as he splashed through. Then he was past them and curving round a mealy boulder, guidance and optical interpretation programs operating in tandem to steer him automatically around obstacles. 'Not at all. It is a very straightforward story. He simply became besotted. I admit she was beautiful, but then every geneered human seems to be. *Harper's Dragon* had a regular contract to supply her habitat with specialist chemicals for one of their electronics manufacturing stations. After four trips, Felix declared he could not bear to be parted from her. And he was lucky, she felt the same way about him.'

'How fortunate.'

'Yes. Felix left *Harper's Dragon* and became an Edenist. He had neuron symbionts implanted to give him general affinity, and underwent specialist counselling to help him adapt. The last time *Harper's Dragon* visited, I spoke with him, and he was extremely happy. He said he had fitted in perfectly and that she was expecting their first child.'

'That is nice. There are something like a million and a half Adamists who become Edenists every year.'

'So many? I didn't know.'

'Seventy per cent are love cases similar to your friend, the rest join because it attracts them intellectually or emotionally. Over half of the love cases are Adamists who form relationships with voidhawk crew-members, which is only to be expected given that they have the most contact with Adamists. It leads to many jokes about the voidhawk families having wild blood.'

'So tell me, is the conversion absolute, do these new-found Edenists transfer their memories into the habitat when they die?'

'Of course.'

His neural nanonics displayed a guidance plot, updating his position. Purple and yellow vectors slithered through his head, temporarily displacing his view of the irradiated dust. He was on course. His course. 'Then my question is this. Is it possible to transfer a person's memories into a habitat if that person has neural nanonics rather than affinity?'

'I have no record of it ever having been done. Although I can see no reason why not; the process would take longer, however, datavising is not as efficient as affinity.'

'I want to become an Edenist. I want you to accept my memories.'

'Warlow, why?'

'I am eighty-six, and I am not geneered. My shipmates do not know, but all that is left of my real body is the brain and a few nerve cords. The rest of me perished long ago. I spent far too much time in free fall, you see.'

'I'm sorry.'

'Don't be. It has been a full life. But now my neurons are dying at a rate which is beyond even Confederation gene therapy's ability to replace. So, understandably, I have come to think a lot about death recently. I had even considered downloading my memories into a processor array, but that would simply be an echo of myself. You on the other hand are a living entity, within you I too could continue to live.'

'I would be happy and honoured to accept your memories. But, Warlow, the transference must take place at death, only that way can continuity be achieved. Anything less would be that echo of self which you spoke of. Your personality would know it was not complete because its conclusion was missing.'

He flew along a cliff of charcoal-textured rock. A virtual mountain of a particle, worn and abraded by aeons of murmuring dust, the lethal knife blade spires unsheathed by its fractured formation now a moorland landscape of undulations, barrows of its youthful virility. 'I know.'

'Are you worried then that Captain Calvert will not be able to escape through the Lagrange point?'

'No. Joshua will be able to fly that manoeuvre with ease. My concern is that he is given the chance to fly it.'

'You mean eliminating the *Gramine*?'

'I do. This mission to mine the rings is the weakest link in Joshua's plan to escape. It assumes the *Gramine* will not deviate its orbit by more than five hundred metres in the next two hours. It assumes too much. I propose to position the warhead accurately on *Gramine*'s orbital track, and detonate it while it passes. That way I can be sure.'

'Warlow, neither *Gramine* nor *Maranta* have deviated their track by more than a hundred metres since the search began. I urge you to reconsider this action.'

'Why? I have only a few years to live at best. Most of those would be spent with my memories and rationality slipping away. Our medical science has achieved too much in that direction. My synthetic body can keep pumping blood through my comatose brain for decades yet. Would you wish that on me when you know you yourself can provide me with a worthwhile continuance?'

'That is, I believe, a loaded question.'

'Correct. My mind is made up. This way I have two chances of cheating death. There are few who can say that.'

'Two? How so?'

'Possession implies an afterlife, somewhere a soul can return from.'

'You believe that is the fate which has befallen Lalonde?'

'Do you know what a Catholic is?' A solid glacier wall of ice appeared out of the dust. The cold-gas nozzles of his manoeuvring pack fired heavily. For a moment he saw the splay of waxen vapour shiver as it was siphoned away into the blue and emerald phosphenes of dust.

'Catholicism is one of the root religions which made up the Unified Christian Church,' Aethra said.

'Almost. Officially, by decree of the Pope, Catholicism was absorbed. But it was a strong faith. You cannot modify and dilute such an intense devotion simply by compromising prayers and services to achieve unity with other Christian denominations. My home asteroid was Forli, an ethnic-Italian settlement. It kept the faith, unofficially, unobtrusively. Try as I might, I cannot throw away the teachings of my childhood. Divine justice is something I think all living things will have to face.'

'Even me?'

'Even you. And Lalonde looks to confirm my belief.'

'You think Kelly Tirrel was telling the truth?'

Warlow's manoeuvring pack was nudging him gingerly round the rimed iceberg, loyally following the ins and outs of its gentle contours. Its surface was true crystal, but eventually it sank into total blackness, as though a wormhole interstice had frozen open at its core. When his armour-suit sensors scanned round they showed him the constellations returning to their full majesty through the attenuating dust. 'I do. I am convinced of it.'

'Why?'

'Because Joshua believes her.'

'A strange rationale.'

'Joshua is more than a superlative captain. In all my years I have never come across anyone quite like him. He behaves execrably with women and money, and even his friends on occasion. But, if you will excuse my clumsy poetry, he is in tune with the universe. He knows truth. I put my faith in Joshua, I have done so ever since I signed on with the *Lady Macbeth*, and I will continue to do so.'

'Then there is an afterlife.'

'If not, I will live on as part of your multiplicity. But Kelly Tirrel has been convinced that there is. She is a tough, cynical person, she would take a lot of convincing such a thing could be. And, as now appears likely, if there is an afterlife, I have an immortal soul and death is not to be feared.'

'And do you fear death?'

He rose out of the iceberg's umbra cloak. It was similar to emerging from a dark layer of rain-cloud into clear evening sky, there was only a remote diaphanous shimmer of dust left above him. *Gramine* shone like a second-magnitude star, forty kilometres away and drifting towards him. 'Very much.'

*

The hovercraft slewed and bucked on the river, tossed about by white-water waves swelling over semi-submerged stones. Theo was concentrating hard on keeping them straight and level, but it was tough going. Kelly didn't remember yesterday's journey up this same river as being so difficult. She and Shaun

Wallace were sitting on the rear bench, clinging on grimly as they were slung about. The propeller droned behind her.

'Already I feel wearied by the journey, daunted by what we are attempting. This is not even snatching victory from the jaws of defeat, although it might be termed a last vain attempt to salvage the team's dignity. We came to this planet with such confidence and high ideals; we were going to vanquish the evil invader and restore order and stability to twenty million people, give them their lives back. Now all we dare hope for is to escape with thirty children. And even that will tax us to the limit.'

'Such a worrier, Miss Kelly.' Shaun smiled congenially.

The hovercraft swerved, pushing her against him – for the briefest second the channel to her sensorium flek recorder block dropped out – and he smiled politely as they righted themselves. 'You mean I shouldn't be worrying?'

'Now I never said that. But worry is the Devil's disciple, it rots the soul.'

'Well, you'd certainly be the one to know all about souls.'

Shaun chuckled softly.

Kelly glanced up at the red cloud. They had been under it for half an hour now. It was thicker than it had been yesterday, its constituent tresses twirling sluggishly. Somehow she was aware of its weight, a heaviness necessary to blot out not just the sight of space but the physical laws governing existence. A complex intertwining of associated emotions defeated her, as though she was sensevising some obscure xenoc ceremony. 'That cloud means a lot to you, doesn't it?' she asked.

'Not the cloud itself, Miss Kelly, that's nothing, but what it represents, yes. That's like seeing your aspirations take form. To me, to all of us damned souls, it means freedom. A precious commodity when you've been denied it for seven hundred years.'

Kelly switched her attention to the second hovercraft, with Horst Elwes and Russ sitting on the bench behind Ariadne, faces ploughed up against the biting slipstream wind. Cannonades of thunder thrashed overhead, as if the cloud was the taut skin of some gigantic drum. She saw Russ push himself closer against the priest. The simple act of trust was immensely poignant.

The privation dropped upon Shaun Wallace without the slightest warning. He experienced the dreadful exodus, the flight of souls expelled from the universe exerting a tidal force on his own precarious possession. Their lamentations and enmity spilled back from the beyond in that eerily pervasive chorus, and then came venomous anger of those who accompanied them on their expulsion, those they had possessed. All of them, preying on each other, hating each other. The conflict permeated his skull, wrenching at his thoughts. He gagged, eyes widening in shock. His face betrayed an emotion of uttermost despair, then he flung his head back and howled.

Reza never wanted to hear a cry like it again. The outpouring of anguish compressed into that one cataclysmic bawl spoke for an entire planet. Grief paralysed him, and loss, loss so profound he wanted the universe to end so he could be spared.

It finished as Shaun ran out of breath. Unsteadily, Reza twisted round on the front bench. Tears were streaming down the possessed man's cheeks. He drew breath and howled again.

Kelly's hands were clasped against her puckered lips. 'What?' she wailed. 'What is it?' Her eyes shut instinctively at the next outburst.

Reza tried to block it all out and project some comfort to Fenton and Ryall. 'Pat?' he datavised. 'Can Octan see anything happening?'

'Not a thing,' the second-in-command answered from the other hovercraft. 'What's going on? Wallace frightened the shit out of us.'

'I've no idea.'

Kelly shook Shaun's arm imploringly. 'What's wrong? What is it? Speak to me!' Panic was giving her voice a shrill edge. 'Shaun!'

Shaun gulped down a breath, his shoulders shivering. He

lowered his head until he was staring at Reza. 'You,' he hissed. 'You killed them.'

Reza looked at him through a cross-grid of yellow target graphics, his forearm gaussrifle was aimed directly at the possessed man's temple. 'Killed who?'

'The city, the whole city. I felt them go, thousands upon thousands blown back to the beyond like so much ash. Your devil bomb, it went off. No, it was set off. What kind of creatures are you to slaughter so indiscriminately?'

Reza felt a grin reflex coming on, which his restructured face portrayed as a moderate widening of his mouth slit. 'Someone got through, didn't they? Someone hit back.'

Shaun's head sagged brokenly. 'One man. That's all, one bloody man.'

'So you're not so invincible, after all. I hope it pains you, Mr Wallace, I hope it pains all your kind. That way you may begin to know something of the horror we felt when we found out what you did to this planet's children.'

The flash of guilt on the man's face proved the barb had hit home.

'Oh, yes, Mr Wallace, we know. Even if Kelly here is too tactful to mention it. We know the barbarism we are dealing with.'

'What bomb?' Kelly asked. 'What are you two talking about?'

'Ask him,' Shaun said, and sneered at Reza. 'Ask him how he was intending to help the poor people of this planet he was hired to save.'

'Reza?'

The mercenary leader swayed as the hovercraft banked around a boulder. 'Terrance Smith was concerned we might not get all the fire support we needed from the starships. He gave each team leader a nuke.'

'Oh, Christ.' Kelly looked from one man to the other. 'Do you mean you've got one as well?'

'You should know, Kelly,' Reza said. 'You're sitting on it.'

She tried to jump to her feet, only to have Shaun grab her arm and keep her sitting.

'Have you learned nothing of him yet, Miss Kelly? There's no human part left in that mockery of a body.'

'Point to your body, Mr Wallace, the one you were born with,' Reza said. 'After that I'll talk morality and ethics with you all day long.'

They stared at each other.

Darkness began to fall. Kelly looked up to see the red light bleeding from the cloud, leaving behind a swollen slate-grey mantle massing sinisterly low overhead. A blade of purple-white lightning screwed down on the savannah to the east.

'What's happening?' Kelly shouted as thunder crashed over the hovercraft.

'You are happening, Miss Kelly. They sense you. They fear and hate you now your true nature and power has been exposed. This is the last mercenary team left, you see. None of the others survived.'

'So what will they do?'

'Hunt you down, whatever the cost below the muzzles of your weapons.'

*

Two hours after Warlow had left *Lady Mac* Joshua was accessing the flight computer's memory cores, looking for records of starships jumping from inside a Lagrange point. He and Dahybi had gone through the small amount of available data on Murora VII, using it to refine their computations of the Lagrange point's size and position, locking the figures into the trajectory plot. He could pilot *Lady Mac* right into its heart – no doubt about that: now he wanted to know what would happen when the energy patterning nodes were activated. There was a lot of theory in the physics files about how it should be possible, but no actual verified ZTT jump.

Who's going to be stupid enough to take part in an

experiment like that? he asked himself. But he was lying on his acceleration couch, and Dahybi, Ashly, and Sarha were on the bridge with him, so he kept any qualms to himself. He was just wondering if there would be a reference in a history file, surely the ZTT pioneers would want to know the limits of their craft, when Aethra datavised him.

'Warlow wants to talk with you,' the habitat said.

He cancelled the link to the memory cores. 'Hello, Warlow. How's it going?'

'Superbly,' Warlow said.

'Where are you?' The cosmonik ought to be back on board in another twenty minutes if everything was running on schedule. Joshua had helped draw up the flight vector through the ring.

'Twenty kilometres from *Gramine*.'

'*What?*'

'I can see it.'

'Jesus shit, Warlow. What the fuck are you playing at? The schedule doesn't have any margin for error.'

'I know. That's why I'm here. I'm going to make certain that *Gramine* is destroyed by the blast. I shall detonate it when the ship is in an optimum position.'

'Oh, Jesus, Warlow, get your iron arse back here now!'

'Sorry, Captain. *Maranta* will only be seven thousand three hundred kilometres away when *Gramine* is eliminated. But that will still give you an eighteen-second lead on the combat wasps. That's easily enough time.'

'Warlow, stop this. We can wait until the end of the next sweep and position the bomb again. That's only another five hours. We'll still be at Lalonde before Amarisk's evening.'

'Joshua, you have six minutes before I detonate. Make sure everyone is strapped down, please.'

'Don't do it. Jesus, Warlow, I'm begging you.'

'You know this has to be done properly. And I can ensure it is.'

'Not like this. Please, come back.'

'Don't worry about me, Joshua. I've thought it out, I will be quite all right.'

'Warlow!' Joshua's face was crushed into a mask of anger and desperation. He jerked round to look at Ashly. The pilot was moving his lips silently, eyelashes sticky with tears. 'Say something,' Joshua commanded. 'Get him back.'

'Warlow, for Heaven's sake come back,' Ashly datavised. 'Just because you can't navigate properly there's no need for this. I'll do it next time, and do it right.'

'I would like you to do me a favour, Ashly.'

'What?'

'Next time you come out of zero-tau, in fifty years or so, I want you to come back here and visit me.'

'Visit you?'

'Yes. I am transferring my memories to Aethra. I'm going to become one of the multiplicity. I won't die.'

'You crazy old bastard.'

'Gaura!' Joshua shouted. 'Can he do that? He's not an Edenist.'

'The datavise has already begun,' Gaura replied. 'He is doing it.'

'Oh, Jesus wept.'

'Is everyone in their acceleration couches?' Warlow asked. 'I'm giving you the chance you really need to escape the rings. You're not going to waste that, are you, Joshua?'

'Shit.' A hot steel band was constricting Joshua's chest, far worse than any gee force. 'They're getting onto the couches, Warlow.' He datavised the flight computer for an image from the cabin cameras, watching Edenists tighten the webbing around themselves. Melvyn was swimming about, checking they had done it properly.

'And what about the thermo-dump panels, have you retrac ted them? There's only five minutes left.'

Joshua datavised the flight computer to retract the thermo-dump panels. Systems schematics appeared as he prepped the generators and drive tubes; mostly green, some amber. The old girl was in good shape. Sarha started to help him with the checklist.

'Please, Warlow?'

'Fly the bastards into the ground, Joshua. You can do it.'

'Jesus, I don't know what to say.'

'Promise me something.'

'Yes.'

'Gotcha. You should have asked me what it was first.'

Joshua coughed. Laughed painfully. It made his vision all blurred for some unfathomable reason. 'What is it?'

'Hard luck, you committed. I want you to be more considerate to your girls. You never see the effect you have on them. Some of them get hurt, Joshua.'

'Jesus, cosmonik and social worker.'

'Promise?'

'I promise.'

'You were a good captain, Joshua. *Lady Macbeth* was a great way to finish. I wouldn't have had it any other way.'

Sarha was sobbing on her acceleration couch. Ashly was clenching and unclenching his fists.

'I would,' Joshua said silently.

Aethra showed them *Gramine.* The starship was traversing the ring surface with the suavity of a maglev train, straight and sure. Three thermo-dump panels were extended to the full, shining a dull vermilion. A long, narrow flame of blue ions flickered for an instant.

'Who'd have thought it,' Warlow datavised. 'Me, an Edenist.'

Joshua had never felt so pathetically worthless as he did then. He's *my* crewman.

The bomb exploded. It sent a flat circle of sheer white light flaring out across the ring surface. *Gramine* was a tiny dark speck above its centre.

Joshua fired the restraint bolts. Taut silicon-fibre cables tethering the *Lady Macbeth* to its rock shield recoiled from the hull, writhing in serpentine coils. Lights inside the four life-support capsules dimmed and sputtered as the one active auxiliary generator powered up the four remaining primary generators. Ion thrusters fired, hosing the dark rock with unaccustomed turquoise luminosity.

A sphere of plasma inflated at the centre of the white shroud thrown across the ring, fast at first, then slowing when it was five kilometres across, diminishing slightly. Black phantoms migrated across its surface. *Gramine*'s lower hull shone brighter than a sun as it reflected the diabolical corona seething four kilometres below.

Thousands of fragmented rock splinters flew out of the heart of the fusion blast, overtaking the disbanding plasma wave. They had the same riotous glow of doomed meteorites caught by an atmosphere. Unlike the plasma they left behind, their velocity didn't fall off with distance.

'Generators on-line,' Sarha called out. 'Power output stabilizing.'

Joshua closed his eyes. Datavised displays filled his head with technicolour dragonfly wings. *Lady Mac* cleared the rock. Her radar started to fire hard microwave pulses at the loose shoal of ring particles, evaporating snowflakes and inflaming carbonaceous motes. Beams of blue-white radiance shone out of the secondary reaction-drive nozzles, rigid as lasers.

They started to rise up through the ring. Dust currents splashed over the monobonded-silicon hull, producing short-lived surf-bloom patterns. Pebbles and larger stones hit and bounced. Ice splattered and stuck, then slipped downwards to fall away in the turbulent glare of the drive exhaust.

A rock chunk crashed into the *Gramine*, shattering its hull open and decimating the internal systems. Cryogenic tanks ruptured, white gases scintillating from the dying fusion bomb's energy barrage. Four life-support capsules raced out of the destruction, charred nultherm foam flaking away, emergency beacons blaring.

Lady Mac cleared the ring surface. Fifty kilometres above her a wave of scarlet meteors streaked across the starfield.

'Stand by for high gees,' Joshua said. The fusion drives came on, tormenting the abused ring still further. *Lady Mac* tilted round, and started chasing down the inside of the tapering orange vector tube in Joshua's mind. He monitored the displays to ensure their course was aligned correctly as the gee forces built, then datavised an extra order into the flight computer.

'Joshua, what—' Ashly's startled voice faded away as the bridge trembled softly.

The last combat wasp left its launch-tube.

'Watch it coming, shitheads,' Joshua purred. Jesus, but it felt good to see the vector lines emerge as the submunitions separated. Purple threads linking *Lady Mac* with the tumbling wreckage.

It took eight seconds for the submunitions to reach the *Gramine*'s life-support capsules. A stipple of kinetic explosions boiled above the ring for a few scant seconds before the vacuum absorbed them as effortlessly as it did all human-born pollution.

*

The inside of the homestead cabin was even worse than Jay Hilton imagined hell must be like. She wouldn't let any of the other children go outside, so they had to use buckets in the small second bedroom when they wanted to go to the toilet. The smell was atrocious, and it got viler every time they opened the door. To add to their woes, the heat had reached a zenith which even Lalonde had never matched before. They had opened all the shutters as well as the door, but the air was solid, motionless. The cabin's timber creaked and popped as the frame expanded.

The physical ordeal was bad enough, but Jay felt so agonizingly lonely too. It was stupid, there were twenty-seven children crammed in around her so tight you couldn't move without nudging someone. But she didn't want other kids, she wanted Father Horst. He had *never* done this before, not leave them alone for a whole day, and certainly not at night. Jay suspected Father Horst was as scared by the night as she was.

All this wretchedness had started when the starships had appeared, and with them the red cloud. Yesterday, just yesterday. It should have been a wonderful time. Rescue was here, the navy marines would come and take them all away and make everything right again. The long dragging miserable days out here on the unchanging savannah were over.

The idea was a little bit scary, because there was always some comfort in routine, even one as difficult as the homestead. But that didn't matter, she was leaving Lalonde. And nobody was ever going to make her come back. Not even Mummy!

They had spent a happy morning outside, keeping watch over the savannah for the first sign of their rescuers. Though the growing red cloud had been a bit frightening.

Then Russ had seen what he claimed was an explosion, and Father Horst had ridden off to investigate.

'I'll be back in a couple of hours,' were his last words to her as he'd left.

They had waited and waited. And the red cloud had slid over the sky above, bringing its horrible noise with it, as though it was hiding an avalanche of boulders.

She had done what she could, organizing meals and rotas. Things to do, things to keep them busy. And still he hadn't come back.

Her watch had told her when it was night. She would never have known otherwise. They had closed the shutters and the door, but red light from the cloud seemed to slide in through every crack and cranny. There was no escape. Sleep was difficult, the boomy thunder-noise kept going the whole time, mingling with the higher pitched sounds of crying.

Even now the youngest children remained tearful, the older ones subdued. Jay leant on the window-sill, gazing off in the direction Father Horst had gone. If he didn't come back very soon, she knew she wouldn't be able to hold her own tears back. Then everything would be lost.

I must try not to.

But she had been badly shaken by the way the red light had vanished ninety minutes ago. Now ghastly black clouds swept low and silent over the savannah, turning everything to funereal greys. At first she had tried to play the shapes game, to make them less sinister, but her mind's eye could only conjure up witches and monsters.

Jay turned round from the window, registering the frightened faces. 'Danny, the fridge should have done some more ice by now. Make everyone some orange juice.'

He nodded, happy to be given some task. Usually he was a real moaner.

'Jay!' Eustice squealed. 'Jay, there's something out there.' She backed away from her window, hands pressed to her cheeks.

There was an outbreak of crying and wails behind Jay. Furniture was kicked and scraped as the children instinctively made for the rear wall.

'What was it?' Jay asked.

Eustice shook her head. 'I don't know,' she said wretchedly. 'Something!'

Jay could hear the cows mooing plaintively, sometimes the bleating of a goat. It might just be a sayce, she thought. Several had gone by yesterday, driven from the jungle by the red cloud. She gave the open door a nervous glance, she'd have to shut it. With shivers in each limb she shuffled back to the window and peeked round the frame.

Lightning was playing along the horizon. The savannah's darkling grass was perfectly still, which made the movement easy to spot. Two ebony blobs jutting up above the blade tips. They were growing steadily larger. She heard a humming noise. Mechanical.

It had been so long since she'd heard any kind of motor

that it took a moment to place the sound; and even longer for her to bring herself to believe. Nobody on this planet had ground transport.

'Father!' she shrieked. 'He's back!' Then she was out of the open door and running towards the hovercraft, heedless of the stiff, dry grass slapping and scratching her bare legs.

Horst saw her coming and jumped off the hovercraft as Ariadne slowed to a halt fifteen metres from the homestead. He had told himself all through the trip that nothing had happened to them, that they would be all right. Praying and praying that it would be so. But actually seeing Jay alive and in one piece was too much, and the repressed guilt and instituted fear burst out, overwhelming him. He fell to his knees and opened his arms.

Jay hit him as if she was giving a rugby tackle. 'I thought you were dead,' she blubbed. 'I thought you'd left us.'

'Oh, Jay, darling Jay. You know I never would.' He cradled her head and rocked her gently. Then the other children came streaming down the homestead's ramshackle steps, squealing and shouting. He smiled at them all and held out his arms once more.

'We were scared,' Eustice said.

'The sky's gone real funny.'

'It's so hot.'

'Nobody collected the eggs.'

'Or milked the cows.'

Bo narrowed her eyes as the mercenaries climbed out of the hovercraft. 'Are these the marines you promised?' she asked sceptically.

'Not quite,' Horst said. 'But they're just as good.'

Danny goggled up at Sewell. The big combat-adept had gaussrifles plugged into both elbow sockets. 'What is he?' the boy asked.

Horst grinned. 'He's a special sort of soldier. Very strong, very clever. Everything is going to be all right now. He'll look after you.'

Kelly had kept her retinas on wide-field focus, scanning the whole reunion scene. There was a big dry lump forming in her throat.

'Holy Jesus, will you look at it all,' Shaun Wallace said in a small demoralized voice. 'What kind of a God could do this to us? Not the one I was taught about, that's for sure. Look at them all, little children. Crying their bloody damn eyes out. And all for what?'

Kelly turned round at the unaccustomed savagery and bitterness in his tone. But he was already striding towards Reza, who was watching Horst and the children impassively.

'Mr Malin?'

'Yes, Mr Wallace?'

'You have to move these children away now.'

'I intend to.'

'No, I mean right now. My kind, they're over there in the edge of the jungle. There's a couple of hundred of them, if not more. They're meaning to get you, Mr Malin, to end the threat once and for all.'

Reza focused his sensors on the first rank of stunted, scrappy trees four or five kilometres away. The cloud over the jungle was still glowing a sombre red, giving the leaves a coral tinge. Heat shimmer and fluttering leaves defeated him, he couldn't tell. 'Pat, what can Octan see?'

'Nothing much. But there's definitely a few people roving round in there, and . . . Oh my God.'

The pages emerged first, young boys, ten or twelve years old, holding their heraldic banners high. Then the drums started up, and the pikemen marched out of the cover of trees. It was a long solid black line, almost as if the trees themselves were advancing. Following, and holding a tight formation at the centre, came the mounted knights. Silver armour shone by its own accord under the unbroken veil of leaden clouds.

The army assembled itself in front of the trees to the order of the drummer. Knight commanders rode up and down, organizing stragglers. Then when the ranks were neatly laid out, a single bugle note rang across the savannah. They started to tramp over the uneven grassland towards the homestead.

'OK,' Reza said equably. 'Time to go.'

Along with all the other children Jay found herself being hurriedly lifted into one of the hovercraft by a mercenary and told to hang on. Boxes and equipment were being tossed out to accommodate them. Father Horst was in the other hovercraft; Jay wanted to be with him, but she didn't think the mercenaries would listen if she asked. Shona was plonked down beside her, and Jay smiled timidly, reaching for the disfigured girl's hand. Their fingers pressed together urgently.

There was a lot of shouting going on all around. Everyone was moving at such a rush. One of the big (really big) mercenaries dashed into the homestead and came out half a minute later carrying Freya.

'Put her in my hovercraft,' Horst said. 'I'll look after her.' The limp girl was laid on the front bench, and he eased a bundle of cloth under her head.

Through all the confusion and bustle Jay saw one of the mercenaries strap a dark globe to the neck of a huge dog. A man (who she thought looked a bit like Rai Molvi) and a lady who had come with the mercenaries were arguing hotly in front of the cabin. It ended when she made a slashing motion with one arm and climbed into the pilot's seat of the second hovercraft. The other mercenaries were ransacking the ammunition boxes that lay on the ground, slotting magazines into their backpacks. Then the impellers on Jay's hovercraft began to spin and the decking wobbled as it rose up. She wondered where the mercenaries were going to fit, her hovercraft had seventeen children packed in between the pilot's seat and the fan at the rear. But when both vehicles swung round and began to pick up speed she realized they were jogging alongside.

'Where are we going?' Shona shouted above the teeth-grating buzz of the fans.

The small hairless pilot didn't seem to hear.

*

Aethra watched the *Lady Macbeth* streak across the ring. Triple fusion exhausts twining into a single braid of near-pure radiation that stretched for over two hundred kilometres behind the fleeing starship.

Murora VII was a thousand kilometres ahead of her. A battered sphere of grey-brown rock not quite a hundred and twenty kilometres in diameter. Along with the other three shepherd moonlets it brought a certain degree of order to the edge of the ring, creating a tidy boundary line. Dust, iceflakes, and pebbles extended out across the gas giant's ecliptic plane far past the immature habitat's orbit, although their density slowly dropped away until at a million kilometres it was no different to interplanetary space. But none of the larger particles, the flying mountains and icebergs, were to be found beyond the hundred and eighty thousand kilometre limit where the shepherds orbited.

Lady Macbeth's exhaust plume yawed a degree, then straightened out again, honing her trajectory. Three thousand kilometres behind her, five combat wasps, arranged in a precise diamond configuration, were accelerating at twenty gees. It had taken the *Maranta* a long time to respond to the break-out, its possessed crew wasting seven expensive seconds before launching the combat wasps – though they couldn't know that. Now the drones could never catch her.

Aethra had never known emotional tension before. Always, it had reflected the feelings of the supervisory station staff. Now though, as it watched the starship curving over the moonlet, it knew – understood – the meaning of tepidation. It *willed* the starship to succeed.

The station staff were lying on their acceleration couches,

that wicked gee force squeezing them relentlessly. Aethra could see the ceiling of the cabin through a dozen sets of pained eyes, feeling the cushioning give below overstressed back muscles.

Three seconds away from the Lagrange point. *Lady Macbeth*'s fusion drives reduced to four gees as she skimmed eight kilometres above Murora VII, tracing a slight parabola around its minuscule gravity field. A couple of ion thrusters fired. The pursuing combat wasps cleared the edge of the ring.

Aethra prepared thirty-three storage areas in its neural strata. Ready to receive the memories of the Edenists on board. Although it would be so quick . . .

An event horizon eclipsed the *Lady Macbeth*.

Her fusion plume lingered briefly like a broken-hearted wraith before melting away. Then there was no physical evidence left of her ever having existed.

Five combat wasps converged on the Lagrange point. Their courses intersected, drive exhausts a dazzling asterisk, and they sped outwards on divergent vectors, electronic brains crashing in program overload confusion.

'I told you Joshua could fly that manoeuvre,' Warlow said.

Aethra tasted smugness in the subsidiary mentality's thoughts. It wasn't used to that, but then the last twenty-four hours had contained a lot of unknowns. 'Yes, you did.'

'You should have more faith.'

'And you're the one to teach me?'

'About faith? Yes, I could try. I think we both have the time now.'

*

The hovercraft battered its way through the tall, heavy savannah grass. It had never been designed with this particular terrain in mind. The grass was too high, too resilient for the skirt to surmount; it all had to be ridden down. That took power, and they were overladen with the children as well.

Kelly datavised the vehicle's electron-matrix-management

processor for a status review. Reserves were down to thirty-five per cent; not nearly enough to make it past the end of the cloud. Impeller monitor programs were flashing amber cautions into her brain as they struggled to maintain skirt inflation. Burnout wasn't imminent, though it was something she'd have to watch for.

A long mound arose out of nowhere, and she tilted the joystick exactly right to veer round its base. The piloting program Ariadne had datavised to her was operating in primary mode, enabling her to steer with the same consummate skill the mercenary had owned. Her weight – or rather lack of it – made her the ideal choice. Theo piloted the other hovercraft, and the priest was sitting behind her, but apart from them the team ran alongside. Even Shaun Wallace, though the few times she glimpsed him he was as red faced as a marathon runner on the home straight.

The mounted knights were pushing them hard, keeping a steady three kilometres behind, just enough to put them beyond the range of the gaussrifles. One or two would occasionally break rank for a charge. Then Sewell or Jalal would fire a few EE rounds to ward them off. Thankfully the sturdy pikemen were unable to match the boosted mercenaries' physical endurance (so how come Shaun could?); they had been left nearly seven kilometres behind. So far so good, but the situation couldn't hold stable for long.

Fenton was racing ahead of the hovercraft, scouting the land, his mass and brawn making easy work of the bristling grass blades. Reza looked through the hound's eyes, leaving a locomotion program to guide his own body down the trail left by the two hovercraft. He was developing a feel for the land beneath the rhythmic pounding of the hound's paws, anticipating the folds and abrupt rises which belied the savannah's façade of interminable mellow ground.

There was a small but certain change in the texture of the grass whipping against Fenton's blunt muzzle. The dead mat of decaying blades covering the flinty soil becoming thicker, springier. Water, and close by. Fenton slowed to smell the air.

'Kelly,' Reza datavised. 'There's a small stream two hundred metres ahead, steep gully sides. Head for it. Part of the bank has collapsed, you can take the hovercraft down.'

A guidance plot filled her mind, all close-packed brown and blue contour lines, a computer image of how the earth would look stripped of vegetation. Neural nanonics integrated it with the piloting program, and she tweaked the joystick.

'Where does it lead?' she asked. So far all they had done was build distance between them and the homestead cabin, heading due south without any attempt to get back on the river which led to the mountains.

'Nowhere. It's cover for us, that's all. The knights are trying to wear us down; and the bastards are succeeding. We can't keep this pace going for ever, and the hovercraft electron matrices are being drained. Once we're immobile the pikemen will catch up, and it'll all be over. They know we can't fight off that many of them. We have to regain the initiative.'

Kelly didn't like the implications leaping round inside her skull at that statement. But she did her best to ignore them. Hunted beasts couldn't afford scruples, especially ones that knew exactly what lay in store if they were caught.

She datavised a query at her communication block. Since they left the homestead cabin it had been broadcasting a continuous signal up to the geosynchronous platform and the secure satellites Terrance Smith had brought with him. There was no need for secrecy now. But the darkened cloud was still blocking the directional beam very effectively.

Theo's hovercraft slowed as it neared the stream, then the nose fell and it went into a controlled slither down the scree of crumbling earth. The gully was three metres deep, with tall reed-grass growing along the top. Smooth grey stones filled the flat bottom, with a trickle of water running down the middle. A muddy pool had built up behind the scree.

Kelly followed the first hovercraft down, juggling the fan deflectors frantically to stop them from sliding into the opposite bank. She turned upstream keeping ten metres behind Theo. He reached the deepest part of the gully and killed the lift.

The mercenaries were jumping down from the top of the bank.

'Everybody out of the hovercraft,' Reza said. 'And sit with your backs to the gully here.' He pointed.

Northern side, Kelly thought. She stood up – don't think about it – and helped to hand the children over the gunwale. They looked round in bewilderment, young faces lost and doleful. 'It's all right,' she kept saying. 'Everything's all right.' *Don't think about it.* She kept smiling too, so they wouldn't catch her anxiety.

Octan glided down into the gully, and perched himself on Pat Halahan's broad shoulder, wings folding tightly. Fenton was already nosing round Reza's legs.

Don't think about it. Kelly sat beside Jay. The little girl obviously knew something terrible was about to happen. 'It's all right,' Kelly whispered. 'Really.' She winked, though it was more like a nervous tic. Flints in the gully wall were sharp on her back. Water gurgled round her boots.

'Joshua,' Kelly datavised into her communication block. 'Joshua, answer me, for Christ's sake. Joshua!' All she was given in reply was the oscillating ghost-wind of static.

There was a scuttling sound as the mercenaries sat down on the stones. Several children were sniffling.

'Shut your eyes, and keep them shut,' Reza said loudly. 'I shall smack anyone who I see with open eyes.'

The children hurriedly did as they were told.

Kelly closed her eyes, took a breath, and slowly folded her shaking arms over her head.

*

As soon as the event horizon collapsed, Joshua accessed the image supplied by the short-range combat sensors. *Lady Mac* had emerged from her jump six thousand kilometres above Lalonde. There was nothing within two thousand kilometres. He datavised the full sensor-suite deployment, and triggered the fusion drives. They moved in at a cautious two gees, aiming for a thousand-kilometre orbit.

No starships were left in orbit, the sensors reported, even the inter-orbit craft from Kenyon had vanished. Victim of a combat wasp, Joshua assumed. There was a lot of metallic wreckage, most of it in highly eccentric elliptical orbits, and all of it radioactive.

'Melvyn, access the communication satellites, see if there's any data traffic for us. And Sarha, see if there are any low-orbit observation satellites left, their memories might hold something useful.'

They both acknowledged their orders and datavised instructions to the flight computer. The starship's main dish found one of the secure communication satellites, and beams of microwave radiation sprang up to enmesh the planet in a loose web. *Lady Macbeth* started to receive data from the various observation systems left functional.

Everybody seemed to be working smoothly. Their flight to Achillea and the slingshot round its moon had passed off flawlessly. Jubilation at the successful jump from Murora had temporarily balanced out the loss of Warlow. Certainly Joshua experienced none of the sense of accomplishment which should have accompanied the Lagrange-point stunt. The most fantastic piece of flying in his life.

Gaura said he wasn't sure, but he thought the transference had worked, certainly a large quantity of the old cosmonik's memories had been datavised successfully into Aethra. The habitat had been integrating them when *Lady Mac* jumped.

The prospect of him living on as part of the multiplicity helped ease the grief – to a degree. Joshua felt a lot of regrets bubbling below his surface thoughts; things he'd said, things he should have said. Jesus, did Warlow have a family? *I'll have to tell them.*

'Nothing from the communication satellites, Joshua,' Melvyn said heavily.

'Thanks.' The idea that Kelly and the mercenaries had been caught was unbearable. That would mean their own flight had been for nothing, and Warlow – 'Stand by to broadcast a message from *Lady Mac*'s main dish, we'll see if we can break through the cloud with sheer power. Sarha, what have you got?'

'Not much. There are only seven low-orbit observation satellites left. They took a real pounding in the battle yesterday. But, Joshua, someone detonated a nuke down there earlier this morning.'

'Jesus. Where?'

'I think it was at Durringham. The satellite only saw the blast as it fell below the horizon.'

Joshua accessed the main sensor image. The red cloudbands over the tributaries had expanded dramatically. Individual strands had blended together producing a homogenized oval smear that covered the entire Juliffe basin. He realized the bright flame-glimmer Durringham had produced before was missing.

Then he noticed a large circular section of cloud in the south-east had lost its red nimbus altogether, becoming a malaised grey. Interest stirred at the back of his mind; it almost looked as if the red cloud was being ruined by some cancerous growth. He datavised the flight computer for a guidance grid.

'It's south of the Quallheim villages,' he said with a sense of growing confidence.

'That grey patch?' Sarha asked.

'Yeah. Exactly where Kelly said they were going.'

'Could be,' Dahybi said. 'Maybe the mercenaries have found a way of damaging the cloud.'

'Perhaps. Melvyn, focus our dish on it, and start transmitting. See if you can punch through and raise Kelly directly.' Joshua centred an optical sensor on the area and upped the magnification. The hoary amorphous cloudscape rushed out to fill his mind. It wasn't giving any clues away, there were no breaks, no glimpses of the ground below. 'Ashly, have you been following this?'

'Yes, Joshua,' the pilot answered from the spaceplane cabin.

'We'll be in orbit in another three minutes. I want you to launch as soon as we finish decelerating. Loiter above those mountains in the south, and we'll see if the mercenary team can get out from under the cloud. Under no circumstances are you to go under it.'

'No fear.'

'Good.' He datavised the flight computer to open the spaceplane hangar doors. 'Anything from Kelly, yet?'

'Sorry, Joshua, only static.'

'She said they wouldn't be out from under the cloud until the afternoon,' Sarha pointed out. 'It isn't quite noon there yet.'

'I know. But that cloud is still growing, even the grey section. If it reaches the mountains they'll be in serious trouble. The hovercraft won't be able to handle that sort of country. They'll be trapped between the two.'

'We can wait,' Dahybi said. 'For a week if we have to.'

Joshua nodded vaguely, eyes tight shut as he flipped through sensor inputs, desperate for any sort of hint. 'Come on, Kelly,' he murmured. 'Show us you're there.'

*

Ryall padded stealthily through the long grass. The scent of humans was strong in the air. Many had passed by very recently. But none were near him now.

After leaving his master he had run swiftly east, the big weight fastened round his neck jouncing about uncomfortably. After a couple of kilometres the masterlove thoughts in his brain had guided him to one side. He had traced a wide curve over the savannah, now he was heading back to his starting point.

When he reached a wide swath of grass, beaten down by many tramping feet, Ryall waited at the edge for a moment – listening, sniffing. Instinct told him he was alone. Satisfied, the masterlove thoughts urged him out. The swath led all the way back to the jungle, he turned the other way. Five hundred metres ahead of him, the homestead cabin jutted up out of the grassland. He hurried towards it, a hungering sensation racing through his blood.

The grass was beaten down all around the cabin. Fences had been broken. Cows wandered about, grazing placidly, paying no attention to him. Goats saw him coming and ran jerkily until they realized he wasn't chasing them. Chickens escaped from their smashed pen were scratching in the dirt; they scattered squawking when he trotted up to the cabin.

Height. The masterlove thoughts wanted him to have height. Ryall swung his big head from side to side, viewing the back wall of the cabin; then loped over to a pile of composite pods stacked at one corner. He jumped, bounding up the pods, then sprang for the eaves. Paws skated unsteadily on the solar-cell panels nailed to the roof, but he found his footing on the ginger qualtook-bark tiles and scampered his way up to the apex.

His master used his eyes to peer out across the savannah. The line of men carrying pikes were a kilometre away. And almost lost in the gloaming ahead of them the band of knights on horseback galloped after their prey.

Ryall felt a curious mix of excitement and sorrow. But the masterlove thoughts were full of gentle praise. He thumped his tail on the qualtook tiles in response.

Then the masterlove thoughts were guiding his left forepaw to the heavy weight hanging from his neck. He bent his head round and watched attentively as his extended nails caught the edge of a small hinged panel and eased it open. Glowing squares were revealed.

Masterlove adoration flowed through him. Very carefully his nail touched one of the squares. Once. Twice. Thrice—

*

The spaceplane stopped shaking as it dropped to subsonic velocity. It had been a fast, steep descent, Ashly had made the little craft stand almost on its tail to aerobrake. Now he levelled out and datavised the wings into their forward-sweep position. Nose-mounted sensors showed him the mountains rolling past below; the fringe of the cloud was fifty kilometres to the north. Short puffy fronds extended out from the main bulk, snaking through the air like blind searching insect antennae towards the foothills.

He datavised the flight computer for a channel up to *Lady Macbeth*. 'Any word yet?'

'Nothing,' Joshua replied. 'Sarha says the observation satellites recorded that patch of cloud turning grey immediately after the Durringham nuke. We're not too sure what that means, but then I don't think normal logic applies here.'

'Too right. I've got enough power in the electron matrices for a five-hour flight before I have to come back up and recharge. If you want that extending I could land on one of these peaks, they're fairly isolated.'

'No. You keep airborne, Ashly. Frankly, if they're not out of there in five hours I don't think we'll see them again. And I've already lost one crewman today.'

'*You* didn't lose him, Joshua. Silly old fart. Now I've got to come back and wander through Aethra's parkland talking to the trees. Hell, he'll love that. Kill himself laughing I expect.'

'Thanks, Ashly.'

The pilot loaded a course into the computer, a patrol circuit along the length of the grey cloud section, staying at eight thousand metres. Thermals shooting up off the rocky slopes rocked the wings in agitated rhythms as the spaceplane flew overhead.

*

Jay thought it was a lightning bolt. Blackness suddenly and silently turned to bright scarlet. She sucked in a breath – it must have been frightfully close. But there was no thunderclap. Not at first.

The redness faded away. She risked opening her eyes. Everything seemed normal, except it was a lot lighter than it had been before. As if the sun was finally rising behind her back. Then the noise started, a dry roar which built and built. She heard some of the children start to whimper. The ground began to tremble, the gully wall vibrating her back. And the brightness behind her kept growing. A sheet of white light sprang across the top of the gully, throwing the floor into deep shadow. It began to tilt downwards, turning the opposite bank unbearably bright. Jay could just hear the lady beside her shouting what sounded like a prayer at the top of her voice. She closed her eyes again, little squeaks of fear escaping from her throat.

*

Lady Macbeth was passing over Amarisk's western coast, a hundred kilometres north of Durringham, when Reza detonated the nuke. The sensors caught its initial flash, a concussion of photons turning the grey clouds momentarily translucent.

'Jesus Christ,' Joshua gasped. He datavised the flight computer for a secure communication channel to the spaceplane. 'Ashly, did you see that?'

'I saw it, Joshua. The spaceplane sensors registered an emp pulse equivalent to about a kiloton blast.'

'Are your electronics OK?'

'Yes. Couple of processor drop-outs, but the back-ups are on line.'

'It's them. It has to be.'

'Joshua!' Sarha called. 'Look at the cloud.'

He accessed the sensor image again. A four hundred metre circle of the cloud looked as if it was on fire below the surface. As he watched it rose up into a lofty ignescent fleuron. The tip burst open. A ragged beam of rose-gold light shone through.

Lady Mac's flight computer datavised a priority signal from one of the communication satellites direct into Joshua's neural nanonics.

'Joshua?' Kelly called. 'This is Reza's team calling *Lady Mac*. Joshua, are you up there?'

Tactical graphics immediately overlaid the optical sensor image, pinpointing her communications block to within fifteen centimetres. Close to the blast point, very close. 'I'm here, Kelly.'

'Oh, Christ, Joshua! Help us. *Now!*'

'Spaceplane's on its way. What's your situation, have you got the children?'

'Yes, damn it. They're with us, all of them. But we're being chased to hell and back by the fucking Knights of the Round Table. You've got to get us out of here.'

Vast strips of rank grey cloud were peeling back from the centre of the blast. Joshua could see down onto the savannah. It was a poor angle, but a vivid amber fireball was ascending from the centre of a calcinated wasteland.

'Go,' Joshua datavised to Ashly. 'Go go go.'

*

Reza stood on top of the gully, bracing himself against the baked wind driving out from the blast. A mushroom cloud was roiling upwards from the cemetery of the homestead, alive with gruesome internal energy surges. It had gouged a wide crater, uneven curving sides spouting runnels of capricious magma.

He brought a series of filter programs on-line, and scanned the savannah. A firestorm was raging for two kilometres around the crater. Pixels from the section of ground where the marching pikemen had been were amplified. He studied the resulting matrix of square lenses. There were no remnants, not even pyres; none of them had survived. He tracked back. Knights and horses had been hurled indiscriminately across the smouldering grass two and a half kilometres away. Encased in that metal armour human bodies should have first been triturated by the blast wave then fried by the infrared radiation.

He watched one silver figure struggle to its knees, then use a broadsword shoved into the ground to clamber to its feet.

Ye Gods, what will kill them?

A horse kicked its legs and rolled over, surging upwards. It trotted obediently over to its fallen rider. Slowly but surely the entire band was remounting.

Reza jumped back into the gully. Children were being packed back into the hovercraft.

'Joshua's here,' Kelly yelled over the trumpeting wind. Her tear-stained face framed a radiant smile. '*Lady Mac*'s in orbit. The spaceplane's on its way. We're safe, we're out of here!'

'How long?'

'Ashly says about ten minutes.'

Not enough, Reza thought. The knights will be here by then, they'll hit the spaceplane with their white fire, if they don't just switch off its circuitry with that black magic. 'Kelly, you and Theo take off south. The rest of you, with me. We're going to arrange a small delay.'

'No, Reza!' Kelly implored. 'You can't, not now. It's over. Ashly will get here.'

'That was an order, Kelly. We'll catch up with you when we've finished off these mounted pricks.'

'Oh, Christ.'

'Hey, Kell, stop fretting,' Sewell said. 'You've got the wrong attitude for this game. Win some or lose some, who cares, you've just gotta have fun playing.' He laughed and vaulted up to the top of the gully.

Horst made the sign of the cross to Reza. 'Bless you, my son. May the Lord watch over you.'

'Get in the bloody hovercraft, Father, take the kids somewhere they can have a life. Theo, blast some grass, get them clear.'

'Yes, boss.' The jungle-rover mercenary fed power into the impellers even as Horst was scrambling on board. With the skirt bouncing against the gully wall the hovercraft turned in a tight curve and sped back up the scree.

Reza joined his team on the top of the bank. Out on the savannah the knights were mustering into a V-shaped battle phalanx.

'Move out,' Reza said. There was a strange kind of glee running loose in his mind. Now we'll show you babykillers what happens when you face a real enemy, one that can fight back. See how you like that.

The six mercenaries started to march over the grass towards the waiting knights.

*

Sunlight and rain poured down on the hovercraft, surrounding them with a fantastic exhibition of rainbows. The clouds were breaking up, losing their supernatural cohesion. They were just ordinary rain-clouds again.

The rain sprayed against Kelly's face as she battled the hovercraft's inertia against the wind and damp cloying grass. Speed tossed them about like a dinghy on a storm-swollen sea.

'How big are the children?' Joshua asked.

'Small, they're mostly under ten.'

'Ashly will probably have to make two trips. He can bring the children up first then come back for you and the mercenaries.'

She tried to laugh, but all that emerged was a gullet rasping cough. 'No, Joshua, there's only going to be one flight. Reza's team won't be coming. Just the children, and me and the priest if the spaceplane can handle our mass.'

'The way you diet to keep your image, you're into negative mass, Kelly. I'll tell Ashly.'

She heard the first fusillade of EE projectiles exploding behind her.

*

Sewell and Jalal stood four metres apart, facing the apex of the charging knights. The reverberant thud of the horses galloping over the savannah rose above the hot squalls spinning off from the chthonic maelstrom of the blast's epicentre.

'I make that forty-nine,' Jalal said.

'The lead is mine, you take the right flank.'

'Sure thing.'

The knights lowered their lances, spurring on their horses. Sewell waited until his rangefinder put the lead knight a hundred and twenty metres away, and fired both heavy-calibre gaussrifles plugged into his elbow sockets. Feed tubes from his backpack hummed efficiently. He laid down three fragmentation rounds over the knight's plumed helmet, and followed it up with twenty-five EE shells into the ground ahead of the left flank.

Jalal was laying down a similar fire pattern across the right flank, his two gaussrifles traversing the line, guided by a targeting program. Pamiers had shown that the possessed were capable of defending themselves against almost anything short of a direct hit by an EE round; he was going for the horses. Kill the mounts, chop the legs out from under them, slow them down. More fragmentation bursts saturated the air. The knights were veiled by smoke, fountains of soil, and riotous static webs.

Streaks of white fire ripped out of the carnage. Sewell and Jalal leaped aside. Four knights sped towards them out of the furore. Sewell spun round as he hit the ground, white fire was gnawing into his left leg. His targeting program locked on to the first knight; one of his gaussrifles was responding sluggishly, the other fired ten EE rounds. The knight and his horse vanished inside a tangled screen of rampaging electrons. Gore spat outwards.

Sewell's optical sensors were tracking more knights riding out from the first assault point. Several bodies were scattered on the crushed grass behind them. His neural nanonics automatically fired a salvo of fragmentation rounds at the renewed charge.

He tried to get up, but there was no response from his leg. One of the gaussrifles had packed up completely. Some of his sensor inputs were wavering. Horses were charging at him from three directions. His functional gaussrifle blasted at one. Another knight aimed a lance at his head, and fire squirted out of its tip.

Sewell rolled desperately. He flung a grenade as the fire caught him on the shoulder, punching him round. The grenade went off beneath the horse, lifting it clear of the ground. It crashed down, the knight tumbling through the air before landing with a bonebreaker smash.

The horse's outline imploded into an amalgam of purple flesh and pumping organs. Eight or nine sayce had been moulded together, like living dough, into a rough sculpture of the terrestrial animal. Heads stuck out of its sides and haunches, encased in thick vein-laced membranes, jaws working silently beneath the naked protoplasm.

Neither of Sewell's gaussrifles were working. He swivelled them down, and used them as crutches to lever himself upright. His medical program was flashing red caution warnings into his mind. He cancelled it completely, and drew a TIP carbine from its holster. The fallen knight was rising to his feet, crumpled armour straightening out. Sewell flicked the TIP carbine to continuous fire with his thumb, and pulled the trigger. It was like using a battering ram. The energy pulses kept smacking into the armour with jackhammer blows, knocking him down and kicking him across the ground. A violet corona seethed around the silver metal. Sewell pulled a grenade from his belt and lobbed it at the limp figure.

A lance caught him in the middle of his back, splitting his ribs apart then puncturing his lungs and an oxygenated-blood-reserve bladder before sliding out of his chest. The blow flung him three metres across the grass. He landed awkwardly, the lance jarring round violently and causing more internal damage.

The knight who had speared him reigned his horse round and dismounted. He drew his broadsword and walked towards the crippled mercenary.

Sewell managed to achieve a precarious balance on his knees. His right hand closed on the lance, boosted fingers exerting their full power, crushing the wood. It snapped off, leaving a splintered twenty-centimetre stump sticking out of his chest. A huge quantity of blood coursed down into the grass.

'Not good enough, my friend,' the knight said. He ran his broadsword through Sewell's short neck.

Sewell reached out with his left arm and grabbed the knight's shoulder, pulling him even closer. There was a sharp grunt of surprise from the knight. Little crackles of energy skated over the surface of his armour. The broadsword penetrated up to the hilt, but Sewell opened his mouth slit wide.

The knight got out one frantic 'No!' before Sewell's silicon carbide teeth clamped round his neck, slicing cleanly through the chain-mail.

*

The northern horizon was an uncompromising clash of turquoise and red, both colours textured as fine as silk, pressing smoothly against each other. Both unyielding. Beautiful, from a distance. Directly in front of the spaceplane, filth and fire was belching from a widening fissure in the rain-clouds.

Ashly altered the camber of the wings, and sent the spaceplane on a steep dive through the dank clouds. Water slicked the pearl-white fuselage, misting the optical sensor images. Then he was through, levelling out.

It was a small confined world of darkness and squalor into which he had come. At the centre, clouds reflected the diseased irradiation of the crater, tarnishing the land with the flickers of dying atoms. Wildfire scoured the malaised savannah around its base, eating its way outwards. Twisters roamed the scorched earth, scattering soot and ash all around to form a greasy crust of embers over the flattened grass.

But further out the rain was falling, cleansing the land. Spears of sunlight wrested their way past the shredding clouds, returning cool natural colours to the fractal wilderness of greys.

Sensors locked on to Kelly's communication block. Ashly banked the spaceplane in a swift high-gee turn, riding the signal to its source. Ahead and below, two tiny hovercraft bounced and jerked their way across the uneven countryside.

*

Reza counted twenty-one knights escaping from the small holocaust Sewell and Jalal unleashed. That was good, he had expected it to be more. He and Pat Halahan were next. His sensors showed him the spaceplane sinking fast out of the sky a couple of kilometres behind him.

'Five minutes, that's all they need.'

'They've got it,' Pat said urbanely.

Reza fired his forearm gaussrifle. Targeting-program-controlled muscles shifted the barrel round as his sensors went into a track-while-scan mode. All his conscious thoughts had to do was designate.

He picked off three knights with EE rounds, and brought a further two horses down before the gaussrifle malfunctioned. Some of his processor blocks were glitched as well. Sensor resolution was falling off. He dumped the gaussrifle and switched to a ten-millimetre automatic pistol. Chemical bullets which produced a scythe of kinetic death, and nothing the possessed could do to stop it. Two more knights were down when he ran out of spare magazines. White fire hit his shoulder, blowing his left arm off. A two-metre jet of blood squirted out until his neural nanonics closed artery valves.

Pat was still sluicing bullets at a pair of knights off to Reza's left. Stimulant and suppressor programs were working hard to eliminate shock. Reza saw a mounted knight thundering towards him, whirling a mace around. A momentum prediction program went into primary mode. The horse was three metres away when Reza took one step back. His remaining hand came up inside the slashing arc of the mace. He grabbed, pulled, twisted. His carbon-fibre skeleton *twanged* at the severe loading as the inertia of the spiked iron club yanked him off his feet. Glossy armour shrieked a metallic protest as the knight was catapulted backwards out of the saddle, then clanged like a bell as he landed.

They climbed to their feet together. Reza raised the mace and started to walk forwards, a locomotion auto-balance program compensating for his lost arm.

The knight saw him coming and pointed his broadsword like a rifle. White flame raced down the blade.

'Cheat,' Reza said. He detonated the fragmentation grenades clipped to his belt. Both of them vanished inside a dense swarm of furious black silicon micro-blades.

*

A hurricane squall of rain stung Kelly's face as the spaceplane swooped fifteen metres overhead. Its compressor nozzle efflux nearly overturned the hovercraft. She engaged the fan deflector and killed the impellers. They skidded to a rumbustious halt.

The spaceplane slipped round sideways in the air then landed hard, undercarriage struts pistoning upwards. Rain pattered loosely on its extended wings, dribbling off the flaps.

Kelly turned around in her seat. The children were huddled together on the hard silicon deck, clothes soaked, hair straggly.

Terrified, crying, peeing in their shorts and pants. Wide eyes stared at her, brimming with incomprehension. There were no clever words left to accompany the scene for the recording. She simply wanted to put her arms round every one of them, pour out every scrap of comfort she owned. And that was far less than they deserved.

Three kilometres behind the hovercraft, EE explosions strobed chaotically, while antagonistic streamers of white fire curled and thrashed above the blood-soaked grass.

We did it, she thought, the knights can't reach us now. The children are going to live. Nothing else mattered, not the hardships, not the pain, not the sickening fear.

'Come on,' she said to them, and the smile came so easily. 'We're leaving now.'

'Thank you, lady,' Jay said.

Kelly glanced up as a figure hiked out of the rain. 'I thought you'd left,' she said.

Shaun Wallace grinned. His sodden LDC one-piece was shrunk round his body, mud and grass clung to his boots, but the humour in his eyes couldn't be vanquished. 'Without saying goodbye? Ah now, Miss Kelly, I wouldn't be wanting you to think the worst of me. Not you.' He lifted the first child, a seven-year-old girl, over the gunwale. 'Come along then, you rabble. You're all going on a long, beautiful trip to a place far away.'

The spaceplane's outer airlock hatch slid open, and the aluminium stairs telescoped out.

'Get a move on, Kelly, please,' Ashly datavised.

She joined Shaun at the side of the hovercraft and began lifting the exhausted, bedraggled children out.

Horst stood at the bottom of the stairs, harrying his small charges along. A word here, a smile, pat on the head. They scooted up into the cabin where Ashly cursed under his breath as he tried to work out how on earth to fit them all in.

Kelly had the last boy in her arms, a four-year-old who was

virtually asleep, when Theo started up his hovercraft. 'Oh no, Theo,' she datavised. 'Not you as well.'

'They need me,' he replied. 'I can't leave them. I'm a part of them.'

Great bands of sunlight were raking the savannah. The fighting was over. Kelly could see three or four knights on horseback milling about. None of them showed any interest in the spaceplane now. 'But they're dead, Theo.'

'You don't know that, not for sure. In any case, haven't you heard, there's no such thing, not any more.' He stuck his arm up and waved.

'Hell.' She tipped her head back, letting the sweet rain wash her face.

'Come along now, Miss Kelly.' Shaun leant over and gave her cheek a platonic kiss. 'Time you was leaving.'

'I don't suppose it would do any good asking you to come?'

'Would I ask you to stay?'

She put a foot on the bottom rung, the drowsy child heavy in her arms. 'Goodbye, Shaun. I wish it could have been different.'

'Aye, Miss Kelly. Me too.'

*

Kelly sat in the cabin with one eight-year-old boy on her lap and her arms round a pair of girls. The children squirmed round, fidgeting, excited and nervous, asking her about the waiting starship. Lalonde was already half-forgotten, yesterday's nightmare.

If only, she wished.

The compressor whine permeated the overcrowded cabin as Ashly fed power into the fans. Then they were airborne, the deck tilting up, a press of acceleration. Kelly closed her eyes and accessed the spaceplane's sensor suite. A lone figure was trudging over the savannah, a well-built man with tousled ginger hair, wearing a thick red and blue check cotton shirt, collar up against the rain as he headed for home.

A minute later a stentorian sonic boom broke across the vast grass plain. Fenton raised his great head at the sound, but there was nothing in the sky apart from rain and clouds. He lowered his gaze again, and resumed his earthbound search for his lost masterlove.

Timeline

2020 . . . Cavius base established. Mining of Lunar sub-crustal resources starts.
2037 . . . Beginning of large-scale geneering on humans; improvement to immunology system, eradication of appendix, organ efficiency increased.
2041 . . . First deuterium-fuelled fusion stations built; inefficient and expensive.
2044 . . . Christian reunification.
2047 . . . First asteroid capture mission. Beginning of Earth's O'Neill Halo.
2049 . . . Quasi-sentient bitek animals employed as servitors.
2055 . . . Jupiter mission.
2055 . . . Lunar cities granted independence from founding companies.
2057 . . . Ceres asteroid settlement founded.
2058 . . . Affinity symbiont neurons developed by Wing-Tsit Chong, providing control over animals and bitek constructs.
2064 . . . Multinational industrial consortium JSKP (Jovian Sky Power Corporation) begins mining Jupiter's atmosphere for He_3 using aerostat factories.
2064 . . . Islamic secular unification.
2067 . . . Fusion stations begin to use He_3 as fuel.
2069 . . . Affinity bond gene spliced into human DNA.

2075 . . . JSKP germinates Eden, a bitek habitat in orbit around Jupiter, with UN Protectorate status.
2077 . . . New Kong asteroid begins FTL stardrive research project.
2085 . . . Eden opened for habitation.
2086 . . . Habitat Pallas germinated in Jupiter orbit.
2090 . . . Wing-Tsit Chong dies, and transfers his memories to Eden's neural strata. Start of Edenist culture. Eden and Pallas declare independence from UN. Launch buyout of JSKP shares. Pope Eleanor excommunicates all Christians with affinity gene. Exodus of affinity capable humans to Eden. Effective end of bitek industry on Earth.
2091 . . . Lunar referendum to terraform Mars.
2094 . . . Edenists begin exowomb breeding programme coupled with extensive geneering improvement to embryos, tripling their population over a decade.
2103 . . . Earth's national governments consolidate into Govcentral.
2103 . . . Thoth base established on Mars.
2107 . . . Govcentral jurisdiction extended to cover O'Neill Halo.
2115 . . . First instantaneous translation by New Kong spaceship, Earth to Mars.
2118 . . . Mission to Proxima Centauri.
2123 . . . Terracompatible planet found at Ross 154.
2125 . . . Ross 154 planet named Felicity, first multiethnic colonists arrive.
2125–2130 . . . Four new terracompatible planets discovered. Multiethnic colonies founded.
2131 . . . Edenists germinate Perseus in orbit around Ross 154 gas giant, begin He_3 mining.
2131–2205 . . . One hundred and thirty terracompatible planets discovered. Massive starship building programme initiated in O'Neill Halo. Govcentral begins large-scale enforced outshipment of surplus population, rising to two million a

week in 2160: Great Dispersal. Civil conflict on some early multiethnic colonies. Individual Govcentral states sponsor ethnic-streaming colonies. Edenists expand their He_3 mining enterprise to every inhabited star system with a gas giant.

2139 . . . Asteroid Braun impacts on Mars.

2180 . . . First orbital tower built on Earth.

2205 . . . Antimatter production station built in orbit around sun by Govcentral in an attempt to break the Edenist energy monopoly.

2208 . . . First antimatter-drive starships operational.

2210 . . . Richard Saldana transports all of New Kong's industrial facilities from the O'Neill Halo to an asteroid orbiting Kulu. He claims independence for the Kulu star system, founds Christian-only colony, and begins to mine He_3 from the system's gas giant.

2218 . . . First voidhawk gestated, a bitek starship designed by Edenists.

2225 . . . Establishment of a hundred voidhawk families. Habitats Romulus and Remus germinated in Saturn orbit to serve as voidhawk bases.

2232 . . . Conflict at Jupiter's trailing Trojan asteroid cluster between belt alliance ships and an O'Neill Halo company hydrocarbon refinery. Antimatter used as a weapon; twenty-seven thousand people killed.

2238 . . . Treaty of Deimos; outlaws production and use of antimatter in the Sol system: signed by Govcentral, Lunar nation, asteroid alliance, and Edenists. Antimatter stations abandoned and dismantled.

2240 . . . Coronation of Gerrald Saldana as King of Kulu. Foundation of Saldana dynasty.

2267–2270 . . . Eight separate skirmishes involving use of antimatter among colony worlds. Thirteen million killed.

2271 . . . Avon summit between all planetary leaders. Treaty of Avon, banning the manufacture and use of antimatter throughout inhabited space. Formation of Human Confederation to police agreement. Construction of Confederation Navy begins.

2300 . . . Confederation expanded to include Edenists.

2301 . . . First Contact. Jiciro race discovered, a pre-technology civilization. System quarantined by Confederation to avoid cultural contamination.

2310 . . . First ice asteroid impact on Mars.

2330 . . . First blackhawks gestated at Valisk, independent habitat.

2350 . . . War between Novska and Hilversum. Novska bombed with antimatter. Confederation Navy prevents retaliatory strike against Hilversum.

2356 . . . Kiint homeworld discovered.

2357 . . . Kiint join Confederation as 'observers'.

2360 . . . A voidhawk scout discovers Atlantis.

2371 . . . Edenists colonize Atlantis.

2395 . . . Tyrathca colony world discovered.

2402 . . . Tyrathca join Confederation.

2420 . . . Kulu scoutship discovers Ruin Ring.

2428 . . . Bitek habitat Tranquillity germinated by Crown Prince Michael Saldana, orbiting above Ruin Ring.

2432 . . . Prince Michael's son, Maurice, geneered with affinity. Kulu abdication crisis. Coronation of Lukas Saldana. Prince Michael exiled.

2550 . . . Mars declared habitable by Terraforming office.

2580 . . . Dorado asteroids discovered around Tunja, claimed by both Garissa and Omuta.

2581 . . . Omuta mercenary fleet drops twelve antimatter planet-busters on Garissa, planet rendered uninhabitable. Confederation imposes thirty-year sanction against Omuta, prohibiting any interstellar trade or transport. Blockade enforced by Confederation Navy.

2582 . . . Colony established on Lalonde.